Praise for Kim Stanley Robinson's
Forty Signs of Rain, Fifty Degrees Below, and *Sixty Days and Counting*

"If I had to choose one writer whose work will set the standard for science fiction in the future, it would be Kim Stanley Robinson."
—*The New York Times*

"The *Brave New World* of global warming." —*The Guardian (UK)*

"Provides perhaps the most realistic portrayal ever created of the environmental changes that are already occurring on our planet. It should be required reading for anyone concerned about our world's future."
—*Publishers Weekly (starred review)*

"An intensely positive book, brimming with ideas and hope for the future."
—*BookPage*

"A brilliantly sustained set piece—visceral weather porn, yet rich with irony and uncommonly graceful writing." —*Los Angeles Times*

"Robinson knows how to juxtapose the quotidian details of urban life with really big, really scary environmental disasters."
—*San Francisco Chronicle*

"Robinson's vision and cleverness still radiate." —*USA Today*

"The ultimate in future history." —*Daily Mail (UK)*

"Robinson tackles global warming with incredible power and intelligence."
—*The Denver Post*

BOOKS BY KIM STANLEY ROBINSON

FICTION

SCIENCE IN THE CAPITAL

Forty Signs of Rain
Fifty Degrees Below
Sixty Days and Counting

THE MARS TRILOGY

Red Mars
Green Mars
Blue Mars

THREE CALIFORNIAS

The Wild Shore
The Gold Coast
Pacific Edge

Escape from Kathmandu
A Short, Sharp Shock
The Blind Geometer
The Memory of Whiteness
Icehenge
The Planet on the Table
Remaking History
Antarctica
The Martians
The Years of Rice and Salt
Galileo's Dream
2312
Shaman
Aurora

GREEN EARTH

GREEN EARTH

THE SCIENCE IN THE CAPITAL TRILOGY

FORTY SIGNS OF RAIN
FIFTY DEGREES BELOW
SIXTY DAYS AND COUNTING

KIM STANLEY ROBINSON

 DEL REY BOOKS NEW YORK

A Del Rey Trade Paperback Original

Forty Signs of Rain copyright © 2004, 2015 by Kim Stanley Robinson
Fifty Degrees Below copyright © 2005, 2015 by Kim Stanley Robinson
Sixty Days and Counting copyright © 2007, 2015 by Kim Stanley Robinson

Published in the United States by Del Rey, an imprint of Random House, a division of Penguin Random House LLC, New York.

DEL REY and the HOUSE colophon are registered trademarks of Penguin Random House LLC.

Forty Signs of Rain, Fifty Degrees Below, and *Sixty Days and Counting* were originally published separately in hardcover and in different form in the United States by Spectra, an imprint of Random House, a division of Penguin Random House LLC, in 2004, 2005, and 2007.

ISBN 978-1-101-96483-5
eBook ISBN 978-1-101-96486-6

Printed in the United States of America on acid-free paper

randomhousebooks.com

4   6   8   9   7   5   3

CONTENTS

PART THREE SIXTY DAYS AND COUNTING

INTRODUCTION

Peter Matthiessen, who died in 2014, was a great writer. His nonfiction is superb, and his novels are even better: *At Play In the Fields of the Lord* is an epic thing, and *Far Tortuga* is brilliant and moving, one of my favorite novels. You read those books, you've lived more lives.

His third great novel has an unusual publishing history. It first appeared as a trilogy, in volumes called *Killing Mister Watson, Lost Man's River,* and *Bone By Bone.* Then about ten years later it reappeared in a single volume, considerably compressed by Matthiessen, titled *Shadow Country.* When I picked up that book in a bookstore and read Matthiessen's foreword explaining what he had done, I immediately said to myself, "I want to do that with my climate trilogy."

This reaction surprised me. I had not been aware that I harbored any longing to revise those books. When I finish a novel I generally move on without a lot of looking back. On completion I feel a glow, as when finishing any job, but it's also a little sad, because the characters stop talking to me. It's like being Calvin and watching Hobbes turn back into a stuffed doll. Could be tragic, but in my case there is a solution, which is simply to start another novel. That's what I do, and on it goes.

But in the case of my climate trilogy, which was published between 2004 and 2007 under the titles *Forty Signs of Rain, Fifty Degrees Below,* and *Sixty Days and Counting,* it appeared that I still had the urge to tinker. After some reflection it began to make sense. Almost fifteen years have passed since I started that project, and in that time our culture's awareness of climate change has grown by magnitudes, the issue becoming one of the great problems of the age. In this changed context, I had the feeling that quite a few of my trilogy's pages now spent time telling readers things they already knew. Some of that could surely be cut, leaving the rest of the story easier to see.

Also, my original idea had been to write a realist novel as if it were science fiction. This approach struck me as funny, and also appropriate, because these days we live in a big science fiction novel we are all writing together. If you want to write a novel about our world now, you'd better write science fiction, or you will be doing some kind of inadvertent nostalgia piece; you will lack depth, miss the point, and remain confused.

So I felt then and still feel that my plan was a good one; but there was a problem in it that I didn't fully gauge while I was writing. Science fiction famously builds its fictional worlds by slipping in lots of details that help the reader to see things that don't yet exist, like bubble cities under the ice of Europa. Just as famously, novels set in the present don't have to do this. If I mention the National Mall in Washington D.C., you can conjure it up from your past exposure to it. I don't have to describe the shallowness of the reflecting pools or the height of the Washington Monument, or identify the quarries where that monument's stone came from. But the truth is I like those kinds of details, and describing Washington D.C. as if it were orbiting Aldebaran was part of my fun. So I did it, but afterward it seemed possible that occasionally I might have gone too far. Every novel is like a ship and has its own Plimsoll line, and if you load it past that line, a storm can sink it. Readers may be inclined to abandon ship, or refuse to get on in the first place.

So with those considerations in mind, I went through my text and cut various extraneous details, along with any excess verbiage I could find (and I could). Inspired by Matthiessen, who compared his middle volume to a dachsund's belly, and shortened his original 1,500 pages to 900, I compressed about 1,100 pages to about 800. Nothing important was lost in this squishing, and the new version has a better flow, as far as I can tell. Also, crucially, it now fits into one volume, and is thereby better revealed for what it was all along, which is a single novel.

If anyone wants the longer version of this story, it will always exist in the original three books. That trilogy was sometimes called The Capital Code, but more often Science In the Capital, the title I preferred. Those titles can continue to designate the original trilogy. This shorter version is called *Green Earth,* I'm happy to say. It's a chapter title in my *Blue Mars,* and I always wanted to put it on a book, as it's a very nice description of what we can achieve in the coming centuries, if we succeed in building a sustainable civilization. We haven't done that yet, but now's the time to start. This novel is one version of what that start might look like.

It's a story about many things: climate change, science administration and politics, Buddhism, biotechnology and investment capital, homelessness, sociobiology, surveillance, life in Washington D.C., life in a treehouse, life with a fractious toddler. A kitchen sink makes an appearance. With that much thrown in, it should not be surprising that the story "predicted" quite a few things that have since come to pass; near-future science fiction always does that.

Still, while working on this version I was startled pretty often by such pseudo-predictions. That the storm that wrecks the East Coast was named Sandy is strange enough to be one of J. W. Dunne's examples of precognition in *An Experiment With Time*—in other words, a coincidence, but quite a coincidence.

The other good calls, especially about climate and weather, were less accidental. As global temperatures rise, there will be more energy in the atmosphere, and more wild weather will ensue. So, Washington D.C. being so low-lying, whenever a big storm hits that area the Metro will flood, and I will get emails that are surprised or even congratulatory; it's happened two or three times already. Recently the U.S. Army Corps of Engineers began quietly building a berm across the National Mall, to limit the flooding there sure to come. That will avert the final scene of *Forty Signs of Rain*, maybe, but Hurricane Katrina's inundation of New Orleans occurred about a year after the book came out, and showed what could happen when a Corps of Engineers system is overwhelmed.

Since then some of the Sundarban islands have gone under for good, as happens to Khembalung in *Fifty Degrees Below*. And speaking of fifty below, shifts in the jet stream will keep bringing Arctic winters directly south onto the east coast of North America. It's just happened two winters in a row, and as I write this, it's colder in northern Virginia than it is in northern Alaska, hitting ten degrees below zero. Fifty below no longer seems so radical, although admittedly the numerology of my titles forced that number far down. But we'll see. For sure we'll be experiencing atmospheric rivers and polar vortexes; neither phrase existed when I wrote the book, but the phenomena did, and my story describes them both.

More disturbing, perhaps, is the way the National Security Agency's recently revealed surveillance program has confirmed and even trumped this book's spy plot. There were signs when I was writing that this kind of thing was going on, but I thought I was exaggerating it for satiric effect. Not at all. You are a person of interest, your calls are recorded, and computer programs are rating your potential danger to the system. And elections? Cross your fingers!

Anyway, with one thing or another, this book will continue to look prescient for a while longer. Already it's turned into a peculiar mix of historical fiction, contemporary fiction, and science fiction, in the sense that some of it has already happened, some is happening now, and some of it will happen soon. Some of it will never happen, which is the wild card in the mix, and one of the things that makes it fiction. But fiction doesn't have to come true to make it useful.

It's paying attention to science that helped create whatever pseudo-predictions the book may contain. Science often tells us things we couldn't see as individuals, and fiction can benefit from that infusion of artificial intelligence. Yes, science itself is the genius AI that we fear to create; it's already up and running. Attend to it and act on what you learn. It's the science fiction way.

The acknowledgments for all three volumes, now combined at the back of this book, show how much help I had along the way, and I want to thank everyone again. I also want to reiterate how much I owe to the National Science Foundation. They sent me to Antarctica as part of their Antarctic Artists and Writers Program in 1995, and that experience began this whole sequence of stories. After that they invited me to their headquarters often, first to serve on panels selecting subsequent groups of Antarctic artists, then to give talks and confer. Several NSF scientists spoke to me about their work in interesting ways, and Rita Colwell, the agency's first woman director, told me things that helped me to write Diane Chang's story. People there have been generous, and I hope it's an association that will continue.

At one point after *Forty Signs of Rain* was published, I went to the NSF building in Arlington to give a lunchtime talk. My Antarctic patron Guy Guthridge had put up flyers next to the elevators that said NSF SAVES THE WORLD! and when the time came, the lecture hall was full. I began by reading the scene where my characters go to a brown-bag lunch talk in the NSF building. As I read the passage that describes those lunches, about people attending one more talk, even after all the years and all the grant applications—just out of a sense of curiosity, that basic emotion at the heart of scientific enterprise—I looked up from the page and sure enough, there they were again. I almost got dizzy, it was so circular. We laughed a lot that day, and though I know that the people there thought and still think that the idea of NSF saving the world is ludicrous, it is nevertheless true that they have good esprit de corps, they punch above their weight, they do good work. I think of them with admiration and gratitude, and as a crucial part of government of the people, by the people, and for the people. The scientific community they help to fund and organize may indeed have a big role in saving the world, so reading a story that describes us doing it can be encouraging. At the least it can make you laugh. I was told that one senior person at NSF finished reading the trilogy and immediately sold his house and moved into a camper in a trailer park. That's taking things too far, probably, but I like the impulse, because we read novels to help create our sense of what the world means, to mentally travel in other people's lives, and to get some laughs. So whether you light out for the territory afterward or not, read on, reader, and may this story help and entertain you. And thanks.

Kim Stanley Robinson, February 2015

PART ONE

FORTY
SIGNS
OF RAIN

CHAPTER 1

THE BUDDHA ARRIVES

The Earth is bathed in a flood of sunlight. A fierce inundation of photons—on average, 342 joules per second per square meter. 4185 joules (one Calorie) will raise the temperature of one kilogram of water by one degree C. If all this energy were captured by the Earth's atmosphere, its temperature would rise by ten degrees C in one day.

Luckily much of it radiates back to space. How much depends on albedo and the chemical composition of the atmosphere, both of which vary over time.

A good portion of Earth's albedo, or reflectivity, is created by its polar ice caps. If polar ice and snow were to shrink significantly, more solar energy would stay on Earth. Sunlight would penetrate oceans previously covered by ice, and warm the water. This would add heat and melt more ice, in a positive feedback loop.

The Arctic Ocean ice pack reflects back out to space a few percent of the total annual solar energy budget. When the Arctic ice pack was first measured by nuclear submarines in the 1950s, it averaged thirty feet thick in midwinter. By the end of the century it was down to fifteen. Then one August the ice broke up into large tabular bergs, drifting on the currents, colliding and separating, leaving broad lanes of water open to the continuous polar summer sunlight. The next year the breakup started in July, and at times more than half the surface of the Arctic Ocean was open water. The third year, the breakup began in May.

That was last year.

Weekdays always begin the same. The alarm goes off and you are startled out of dreams that you immediately forget. Predawn light in a dim room. Stagger into a hot shower and try to wake up all the way. Feel the scalding hot water on the back of your neck. Fragment of a dream, you were deep in some problem set now escaping you, just as you tried to escape it in the dream. Duck down the halls of memory—gone. Dreams don't want to be remembered.

Evaluate the night's sleep: not so good. Anna Quibler was exhausted already. Joe had cried twice, and though it was Charlie who had gotten up to reassure him, as part of conveying to Joe that Mom would never again visit him at night, Anna had of course woken up too, and vaguely heard Charlie's reassurances: "Hey. Joe. What's up. Go back to sleep, buddy, nothing gets to happen until morning, this is pointless this wailing, good night damn it."

After that she had tossed and turned, trying not to think of work. In general Anna's thoughts had a tropism toward work. Last night had been no different.

Shower over, she dried and dressed in three minutes. Downstairs she filled a lunch box for her older boy, same as always, as required: peanut butter sandwich, five carrots, apple, chocolate milk, yogurt, roll of lunch meat, cheese stick, cookie. As she got the coldpack out of the freezer she saw the neat rows of plastic bottles full of her frozen milk, there for Charlie to thaw and feed to Joe during the day. That reminded her—not that she would have forgotten much longer, given how full her breasts felt—that she had to nurse the bairn before she left. She clumped back upstairs and lifted Joe out of his crib, sat on the couch beside it. "Hey love, time for some sleepy nurses."

Joe glommed on to her while still almost entirely asleep. With his eyes closed he looked like an angel. He was getting bigger but she could still cradle him in her arms and watch him curl into her like a new infant. Closer to two than one now, and a regular bruiser, a wild man who wearied her; but not now. The warm sensation of being suckled put her body back to sleep, but a part of her mind was already at work, and so she kept to the schedule, detached him and shifted him around to the other breast for four more minutes. When they were done he would go back to sleep and snooze happily until about nine, Charlie said.

She hefted him back into his crib, buttoned up and kissed all her boys lightly on the head. Charlie mumbled "Call me, be careful." Then she was down the stairs and out the door, her big work bag over her shoulder.

The cool air on her face woke her fully for the first time that day. It was May now but the mornings still had a bit of chill to them, a delicious sensation given the humid heat to come. Truck traffic roared south. Splashes of sunlight struck the blue sheen of the windows on the skyscrapers up at Bethesda Metro.

Anna passed the Metro elevator kiosk to extend her walk by fifty yards, then turned and clumped down the stairs to the bus stop. Then down the escalator into the dimness of the great tube of ribbed concrete. Card on turnstile, thwack as the triangular barriers disappeared, down the escalator to the tracks. No train there, none coming immediately, so she sat down on a concrete bench, opened her tablet, and began to study one of the jackets, as they still called them: the grant proposals that the National Science Foundation received at a rate of fifty thousand a year. "Algorithmic Analysis of Palindromic Codons as Predictors of a Gene's Protein Expression." The proposal's algorithm had shown some success in predicting which proteins any given gene sequence would express. As genes expressed a huge variety of proteins by unknown ways, this would be very useful. Anna was dubious, but genomics was not her field. It would be one to give to Frank Vanderwal. She noted it as such and queued it in a forward to him.

The arrival of a train, the getting on and finding of a seat, the change of trains at Metro Center, the getting off at the Ballston stop in Arlington, Virginia: all were actions accomplished without conscious thought, as she read proposals. The first one still struck her as the most interesting of the morning's bunch. She would be interested to hear what Frank made of it.

· · ·

Coming out of a Metro station is the same everywhere: up a long escalator, toward an oval of gray sky and the heat of the day. Emerge abruptly into a busy urban scene.

The Ballston stop's distinction was that the escalator topped out in a vestibule leading to the glass doors of a building. Anna entered this building, went to the open-walled shop selling pastries and sandwiches, and bought a lunch to eat later at her desk. Then she went back out to Starbucks.

This particular Starbucks was graced by a staff maniacally devoted to speed and precision. Anna loved to see it; she liked efficiency anywhere she found it, and more so as she grew older. That a group of young people could turn what was potentially a very boring job into a kind of strenuous athletic performance struck her as admirable. Now it cheered her again to move rapidly forward in the long queue, and see the woman at the computer spot her when she was two back in line and call out to her teammates, "Tall latte half-caf, nonfat, no foam!" and then, when Anna got to the front of the line, ask her if she wanted anything else today. It was easy to smile as she shook her head.

Then outside again and around to the NSF building. Inside she showed her badge to security, went to the elevators.

Anna liked the NSF building's interior. The structure was hollow, featuring a gigantic central atrium, an octagonal space that extended from floor to skylight, twelve stories above. This empty space, as big as some buildings, was walled by the interior windows of all the NSF offices. Its upper part was occupied by a large hanging mobile, made of curved metal bars painted in primary colors. The ground floor was occupied by various small businesses facing the atrium—pizza place, hairstylist, travel agency, bank outlet.

A disturbance caught Anna's eye. Across the atrium there was a flurry of maroon, a flash of brass, and then a resonant low chord sounded, filling the big space with a vibrating *blaaa,* as if the atrium itself were a kind of huge horn.

A bunch of Tibetans, it looked like: men and women wearing belted maroon robes and yellow winged caps. Some played long straight horns, others thumped drums or swung censers, dispensing clouds of sandalwood smoke. They crossed the atrium chanting and swirling, all in majestic slow motion.

They headed for the travel agency, and for a second Anna wondered if they had come to book a flight home. But then she saw that the travel agency's windows were empty. In the doorway the Tibetanesque performers were now massing, in a crescendo of chant and brassy brass, the incredibly low notes vibrating the air. In the midst of the celebrants stood an old man, his brown face a maze of deep wrinkles. He smiled, raised his right hand, and the music came to a ragged end in a hyperbass note that fluttered Anna's stomach.

The old man stepped free of the group and bowed to the four directions. He dipped his chin and sang, his voice splitting into two notes, with a resonant head tone distinctly audible over the clear bass, all very surprising coming out of such a slight man. Singing thus, he walked to the doorway of the travel agency and touched the doorjambs on each side, exclaiming something sharp each time.

"Rig yal ba! Chos min gon pa!"

The others all exclaimed, "Jetsun Gyatso!"

The old man bowed to them.

And then they all cried, "Om!" and filed into the little office space, the brassmen angling their long horns to make it in the door.

A young monk came back out. He took a small rectangular card from the loose sleeve of his robe, pulled some protective backing from it, and affixed it to the window next to the door. Then he retreated inside.

Anna approached the window. The little sign said

EMBASSY OF KHEMBALUNG

An embassy! And from a country she had never heard of. This was a strange place for an embassy, very far from Massachusetts Avenue's ambassadorial stretch of unlikely architecture, unfamiliar flags, and expensive landscaping; far from Georgetown, Dupont Circle, Adams Morgan, Foggy Bottom, east Capitol Hill, or any of the other likely haunts for locating a respectable embassy. Not just in Arlington, but in the NSF building no less!

Maybe it was a scientific country.

Pleased at the thought, Anna approached closer still.

The young man who had put out the sign reappeared. He had a round face, a shaved head, and a quick little mouth, like Betty Boop's.

His expressive black eyes met hers. "Can I help you?" he said, in what sounded to her almost like an Indian accent.

"Yes," Anna said. "I saw your arrival ceremony, and I was wondering where you all come from."

"Thank you for your interest," the youth said politely, ducking his head and smiling. "We are from Khembalung."

"Yes, but . . ."

"Ah. Our country is an island nation, in the Bay of Bengal, near the mouth of the Ganges."

"I see," Anna said, surprised; she had thought they would be from somewhere in the Himalayas. "I hadn't heard of it."

"It is not a big island. Nation status has been a recent development, you could say. Only now are we establishing a representation."

"Good idea. Although, to tell the truth, I'm surprised to see an embassy in here. I didn't think of this as being the right kind of space."

"We chose it very carefully," the young monk said.

They regarded each other.

"Well," Anna said, "very interesting. Good luck moving in. I'm glad you're here."

"Thank you." Again he nodded.

As Anna turned to go, something caused her to look back. The young monk still stood there in the doorway, looking across at the pizza place, his face marked by a tiny grimace of distress.

Anna recognized the expression. After her older son Nick was born she had shared the care of him with Charlie and some babysitters, and eventually they had taken him to a daycare center in Bethesda, near the Metro. At first Nick had cried furiously whenever she left, which she found excruciating; but then he had seemed to get used to it. And so did she, adjusting as everyone must to the small pains of the daily departure. It was just the way it was.

Then one day she had taken Nick down to the daycare center, and he didn't cry when she said good-bye, didn't even seem to care or to notice. But for some reason she had paused to look back in the window of the place, and there on his face she saw a look of unhappy, stoical determination—determination not to cry, determination to get through another long lonely boring day—a look that on the face of a toddler was heartbreaking. It had pierced her like an arrow. She had cried out involuntarily, even started to rush back inside to take him in her arms and comfort him. Then she reconsidered how another good-bye would affect him, and with a horrible wrenching feeling, a sort of despair at all the world, she had left.

Now here was that very same look, on the face of this young man! Anna stopped in her tracks, feeling again that stab from years before. Who knew what had caused these people to come halfway around the world? Who knew what they had left behind?

She walked back over to him.

He saw her coming, composed his features. "Yes?"

"If you want," she said, "later on, when it's convenient, I could show you some of the good lunch spots in this neighborhood."

"Why, thank you," he said. "That would be most kind."

"Is there a particular day that would be good?"

"Well—we will be getting hungry today," he said, and smiled. He had a sweet smile, not unlike Nick's.

She smiled too, feeling pleased. "I'll come back at one, if you like."

"That would be most welcome. Very kind."

She nodded. "At one, then," already recalibrating her work schedule for the day. The boxed sandwich could be stored in her office's little refrigerator.

With that Anna went to the south elevators. Waiting there she was joined by Frank Vanderwal, one of her program officers. They greeted each other, and she said, "Hey, I've got an interesting jacket for you."

He mock-rolled his eyes. "Is there any such thing for a burnt-out case like me?"

"Oh I think so." She gestured back at the atrium. "Did you see our new neighbor? We lost the travel agency but gained an embassy."

"An embassy, here?"

"I'm not sure they know much about Washington."

"Ah." Frank grinned his crooked grin, very different than the young monk's sweet smile. "Ambassadors from Shangri-La, eh?" One of the UP arrows lit, and the elevator door under it opened. "Well, we can use them."

Primates in elevators. People stood in silence looking up at the lit numbers on the display console, as per custom.

Again the experience caused Frank Vanderwal to contemplate the nature of their species, in his usual sociobiologist's mode. They were mammals, social primates: a kind of hairless chimp. Their bodies, brains, minds, and societies had grown to their current state in East Africa over a period of about two million years, while the climate was shifting and forest was giving way to savannah.

Much was explained by this. Naturally they were distressed to be trapped in a small moving box. No savannah experience could be compared to it. The closest analog might have been crawling into a cave, no doubt behind a shaman carrying a torch, everyone filled with great awe and very possibly under the influence of psychotropic drugs and religious rituals. An earthquake during such a visit to the underworld would be about all the savannah mind could contrive as an explanation for a modern trip in an elevator car. No wonder an uneasy silence reigned; they were in the presence of the sacred. And the last ten thousand years of civilization had not been anywhere near enough time for any evolutionary adaptations to alter these mental reactions. They were still only good at the things they had been good at on the savannah.

Anna Quibler broke the taboo on speech, as people would when all the fellow passengers were cohorts. She said to Frank, continuing her story, "I went over and introduced myself. They're from an island in the Bay of Bengal."

"Did they say why they rented the space here?"

"They said they had picked it very carefully."

"Using what criteria?"

"I didn't ask. On the face of it, you'd have to say proximity to NSF."

Frank snorted. "That's like the joke about the starlet and the Hollywood writer, isn't it?"

Anna wrinkled her nose at this, surprising Frank; although she was proper, she was not prudish. Then he got it: her disapproval was not at the joke, but at the idea that these new arrivals would be that hapless. She said, "I think they'll be interesting to have here."

Homo sapiens is a species that exhibits sexual dimorphism. It's more than a matter of bodies; the archeological record seemed to Frank to support the notion that the social roles of the two sexes had deviated early on. These differing roles could have led to differing thought processes, such that it would be possible to characterize plausibly the existence of unlike approaches even to ostensibly non-gender-differentiated activities, such as science. So that there could be a male practice of science and a female practice of science, in other words, and these could be substantially different activities.

These thoughts flitted through Frank's mind as their elevator ride ended and he and Anna walked down the hall to their offices. Anna was as tall as he was, with a nice figure, but the dimorphism differentiating them was in their habits of mind and their scientific practice, and that might explain why he was a bit uncomfortable with her. Not that this was a full characterization of his attitude, but she did science in a way that he found annoying. It was not a matter of her being warm and fuzzy, as you might expect from the usual characterizations of feminine thought—on the contrary, Anna's scientific work (she still often coauthored papers in statistics, despite her bureaucratic load) often displayed a finicky perfectionism that made her a very meticulous scientist, a first-rate statistician—smart, quick, competent in a range of fields and really excellent in more than one. As good a scientist as one could find for the rather odd job of running the Bioinformatics Division at NSF.

But she was so intense about it. A kind of Puritan of science, rational to an extreme. And yet of course that was all a front, as with the early Puritans; the hyperrational coexisted in her with all the emotional openness, intensity, and variability that was the American female interactional paradigm and social role. Every female scientist was therefore a kind of Mr. Spock, the rational side foregrounded and emphasized while the emotional side was denied.

On the other hand, judged on that basis, Frank had to admit that Anna seemed less split-natured than many women scientists he had known. Pretty well integrated, really. He had spent many hours of the past year working with her, engaged in interesting discussions, and he liked her. His discomfort came not from any of her irritating habits, not even the nitpicking or hairsplitting that made her so strikingly eponymous (though no one dared joke about that to her); no, it was more the way her hyperscientific attitude combined with her passionate female expressiveness to suggest a complete science, or even a complete humanity. It reminded Frank of himself!

Not of the self that he allowed others to see, of course, but rather of his internal life as he alone experienced it. He too was stuffed with extreme aspects of both rationality and emotionality. This was what made him uncomfortable: Anna was too much like him. She reminded him of things about himself he did not want to think about. But he was helpless to stop his trains of thought. That was one of his problems.

Halfway around the circumference of the sixth floor, they came to their offices. Frank's was one of a number of cubicles carving up a larger space; Anna's was a true office right across from his cubicle, a room of her own, with a foyer for her secretary, Aleesha. Both their spaces, and all the others in the maze of crannies and rooms, were filled with the computers, file cabinets, and crammed bookshelves that one found in scientific offices everywhere. The decor was standard beige for everything, indicating the purity of science.

In this case it was all rendered human, and even handsome, by the big windows on the interior sides of every room, allowing everyone to look across the central atrium and into all the other offices. This open space, and the sight of fifty to a hundred other humans, made each office a slice or echo of the savannah. The occupants were correspondingly more comfortable at the primate level. Frank did not suffer the illusion that anyone had consciously planned this effect, but he admired the architect's instinctive grasp of what would get the best work out of the building's occupants.

He sat down at his desk, gazed out across the atrium. He was near the end of his year-long stay at NSF, and the workload was becoming less and less important to him. Piles of articles lay in stacks on every horizontal surface, and his computer contained hundreds of proposals for his evaluation. He had a lot of work to do. Instead he looked out the window.

The colorful mobile filling the upper half of the atrium was a painfully simple thing, basic shapes in primary colors, very like a kindergartner's scribble. Frank's many activities included rock climbing, and often he had occupied his mind by imagining the moves he would need to climb the mobile. There were some hard sections, but it would make for a fun route.

Past the mobile, he could see into one hundred and eight other rooms (he had counted). In them people typed at screens, talked in couples or on the phone, read, or sat in seminar rooms looking at photos on screens, or talking. Mostly talking. If this place were all you had to go on, you would have to conclude that doing science consisted mostly of talking.

This was not even close to true, and it was one of the reasons Frank was bored. The real action of science took place in laboratories, or anywhere else experiments were being conducted. What happened here was different, a kind of meta-science, one might say, which coordinated scientific activities, or connected them to other human action, or funded them.

The smell of Anna's latte wafted in from her office next door, and he could hear her on the phone already. She too did a lot of talking on the phone. "I don't know, I have no idea what the other sample sizes are like . . . No, not statistically insignificant, that would mean the numbers were smaller than the margin of error. What you're talking about is just statistically meaningless."

Meanwhile Aleesha, her assistant, was on her phone as well, patiently explaining something in her rich D.C. contralto. Unraveling some misunderstanding. It was an obvious if seldom-acknowledged fact that much of NSF's daily business got done by African-American women from the area, who often seemed decidedly unconvinced of the earth-shattering importance that their mostly Caucasian employers attributed to the work. Aleesha, for instance, displayed the most skeptical politeness Frank had ever heard.

Anna appeared in the doorway, tapping on the doorjamb as she always did, to pretend that his space was an office. "Frank, I forwarded that jacket to you, the one about an algorithm."

"Let's see if it arrived." He checked, and up came a new one from aquibler@nsf.gov. He loved that address. "It's here, I'll take a look at it."

"Thanks." She hesitated. "When are you due to go back to UCSD?"

"End of July or end of August."

"Well, I'll be sorry to see you go. I know it's nice out there, but we'd love it if you'd consider putting in a second year, or even think about staying permanently, if you like it. Of course you must have a lot of irons in the fire."

"Yes," Frank said noncommittally. Staying longer than his one-year stint was completely out of the question. "That's nice of you to ask. I've enjoyed it, but I should probably get back home. I'll think about it, though."

"Thanks. It would be good to have you here."

Much of the work at NSF was done by visiting scientists, who came on leave from their home institutions to run NSF programs in their area of expertise for periods of a year or two. The grant proposals came pouring in by the thousands, and program directors like Frank read them, sorted them, convened panels of outside experts, and ran the meetings in which these experts rated batches of proposals in particular fields. This was a major manifestation of the peer-review process, a process Frank thoroughly approved of—in principle. But a year of it was enough, actually far more than enough.

Anna, watching him, said, "I suppose it's a bit of a rat race."

"Well, no more than anywhere else. At home it'd probably be worse."

They laughed.

"And you have your journal work too."

"That's right." Frank waved at the piles of typescripts: three stacks for *Review of Bioinformatics,* two for *The Journal of Sociobiology.* "Always behind. Luckily the other editors are better at keeping up."

Anna nodded. Editing a journal was an honor, though unpaid—indeed one often had to subscribe to a journal just to get copies of what one had edited. It was another of science's many noncompensated activities, part of its extensive economy of social credit.

"Okay," Anna said. "I just wanted to see if we could tempt you. That's how we do it, you know. When visitors come through who are particularly good, we try to hold on to them."

"Yes, of course." Frank nodded uncomfortably. Touched despite himself; he valued her opinion. He rolled his chair toward his screen as if to get to work, and she turned and left.

He clicked to the jacket Anna had forwarded. Immediately he recognized one of the investigators' names.

"Hey Anna?" he called out.

"Yes?"

"I know one of the guys on this jacket. The P.I. is a guy from Caltech, but the real work is by one of his students."

"Yes?" This was a typical situation, a younger scientist using the prestige of his or her advisor to advance a project.

"Well, I know the student. I was the outside member on his dissertation committee, a few years ago."

"That wouldn't be enough to be a conflict."

Frank nodded as he read on. "But he's also been working on a temporary contract at Torrey Pines Generique, which is a company in San Diego that I helped start."

"Ah. Do you still have any financial stake in it?"

"No. Well, my stocks are in a blind trust for the year I'm here, so I can't be positive, but I don't think so."

"But you're not on the board, or a consultant?"

"No. And it looks like his contract there is about over now."

"That's fine, then. Go for it."

No part of the scientific community could afford to be too picky about conflicts of interest, or they'd never find anyone to peer-review anything. Hyperspecialization made every field so small that everyone knew everyone. So as long as there were no current financial or institutional ties with a person, it was considered okay to evaluate their work in the various peer reviews.

But Frank had wanted to make sure. Yann Pierzinski was a very sharp young biomathematician, one of those doctoral students whom one watched with the certainty one would hear from them again. Now here he was, and with something Frank was particularly interested in.

"Okay," he said to Anna. "I'll put it in the hopper."

He began to read it. "Algorithmic Analysis of Palindromic Codons as Predictors of a Gene's Protein Expression." A proposal to fund continuing work on an algorithm for predicting which proteins any given gene would express.

Very interesting. This was an assault on one of the fundamental mysteries, a mystery that presented a considerable blockage to any robust biotechnology. The three billion base pairs of the human genome encoded some hundred thousand genes; most of the genes contained instructions for the assembly of one or more proteins, the basic building blocks of organic chemistry and life itself. But which genes expressed which proteins, and how exactly they did it, and why some genes created different proteins in different circumstances—all this was very poorly understood, or completely mysterious. This ignorance made most biotechnology an endless, very expensive matter of trial-and-error. A key to any part of the mystery could be very valuable. As in lucrative.

Frank scrolled down the pages of the proposal with practiced speed. Yann Pierzinski, Ph.D. biomath, Caltech. Still doing a postdoc with his advisor there, who was a real credit hog. Interesting to see that Pierzinski had gone down to Torrey Pines to work on a temporary contract, for a bioinformatics researcher whom Frank didn't know. Perhaps that had been a bid to escape the advisor.

Frank dug into the substance of the proposal. The algorithm was one Pierzinski had been working on even back in his dissertation. The chemistry of protein creation was a sort of natural algorithm, Yann was suggesting. Frank considered the idea operation by operation; this was his real expertise, this was what had interested him from childhood, when the puzzles he solved had been simple ciphers. He had always loved this work, and now perhaps more than ever, offering as it did a complete escape from consciousness of himself. Why he might want to make that escape remained moot; howsoever it might be, when he came back he felt refreshed, as if finally he had been in a good place.

He also liked to see patterns emerge from the apparent randomness of the world. This was why he had recently taken such an interest in sociobiology; he had hoped there might be algorithms to be found there which would crack the code of human behavior. So far that quest had not succeeded, as so little in human behavior was susceptible to controlled experiments, which meant that theories could not be tested. That was a shame. He badly wanted clarification in that realm.

At the level of the four chemicals of the genome, however—in the long dance of cytosine, adenine, guanine, and thymine—much more seemed to be amenable to mathematical explanation, also experiment, with results that could be conveyed to other scientists, and put to use. One could test Pierzinski's ideas, in other words, and find out if they worked.

He came out of this trance hungry. He felt quite sure there was some real potential in the work. And that was giving him ideas, strange ideas in some respects, and yet . . .

He got up stiffly. It was midafternoon already. If he left soon he would be able to hack through the traffic out to Great Falls. By then the day's heat would have subsided, and the gorge walls would be nearly empty. He could climb till sunset, and do some more thinking about this algorithm, in the only place in the D.C. area left with a touch of nature to it.

CHAPTER 2

IN THE HYPERPOWER

Mathematics sometimes seems like a universe of its own, but it comes to us as part of the brain's engagement with the world, and appears to be an aspect of the world, its structure or recipe.

Over historical time humanity has explored farther and farther into the various realms of mathematics, in a cumulative and collective process, an ongoing conversation between the species and reality. The discovery of the calculus. The invention of formal arithmetic and symbolic logic, both mathematicizing the instinctive strategies of human reason, making them as distinct and solid as geometric proofs. The attempt to make the entire system contained and self-consistent. The invention of set theory, and the finessing of the various paradoxes engendered by considering sets as members of themselves. The discovery of the incompletability of all systems. The step-by-step mechanics of programming new calculating machines. All this resulted in an amalgam of math and logic, with symbols and methods drawn from both realms, combining in the often long and complicated operations that we call algorithms.

In the time of the development of the algorithm, we also made discoveries in the real world: the double helix within our cells. Within half a century the whole genome was read, base pair by base pair. Three billion base pairs, forming the genes that serve as instruction packets for protein creation.

But despite the fully explicated genome, the details of gene expression are still very mysterious. Spiraling pairs of cytosine, guanine, adenosine, and thy-

mine: we know these are instructions for the development of life. We know the elements; we see the organisms. The code between them remains to be learned.

Mathematics continues to develop under the momentum of its own internal logic, seemingly independent of everything else. But several times in the past, purely mathematical developments have later proved to be powerfully descriptive of operations in nature that were either unknown or unexplainable at the time the math was being developed. This is a strange fact, calling into question all that we think we know about the relationship between math and reality, the mind and the cosmos.

Perhaps no explanation of this mysterious adherence of nature to mathematics of great subtlety will ever be forthcoming. Meanwhile, the operations called algorithms become ever more convoluted and interesting to those devising them. Are they making portraits, recipes, magic spells? Does reality use algorithms, do genes use algorithms? The mathematicians can't say, and many of them don't seem to care. They like the work.

Leo Mulhouse kissed his wife Roxanne and left their bedroom. The light was halfway between night and dawn. He went onto the balcony, heard the rumble of surf against the cliff. Out there lay the vast gray plate of the Pacific.

Leo had married into this clifftop house, so to speak; Roxanne had inherited it from her mother. Its view was something Leo loved, but the little grass yard below the second-story porch was only about fifteen feet wide, and beyond it was an open gulf of air and the gray foaming ocean, eighty feet below. And not that stable a cliff. He wished that the house had been placed a little farther back on its lot.

Back inside, down to the car. Down Europa, past the Pannikin in Leucadia, hang a right and head to work.

The Pacific Coast Highway in San Diego County was a beautiful drive at dawn. In any kind of weather it was handsome: in the sun with all the blues of the sea gleaming, in low clouds when shards and rays of horizontal sunlight broke through, or on rainy or foggy mornings when the narrow but rich palette of grays filled the eye. The gray dawns were the most frequent these days, as the region's climate settled into what appeared to be a permanent El Niño—the Hyperniño, as people called it. The whole idea of a Mediterranean climate was leaving the world, even in the Mediterranean. Here coastal residents were getting sunlight deficiency disorders, and taking vitamin D and antidepressants to counteract the effects, even though ten miles inland it was a cloudless baking desert all the year round. The June Gloom had come to stay.

Leo took the coast highway to work every morning, enjoying the slight roller-coaster effect of dropping down to cross the lagoons, then rising back up to Cardiff, Solana Beach, and Del Mar. These towns looked best at this hour, deserted and as if washed for the day.

Then up the big hill onto Torrey Pines, past the golf course, quick right into Torrey Pines Generique. Down into its garage, into the biotech beast.

Complete security exam, metal detector, inspection by the bored security team, hardware and software check, sniff-over by Clyde the morning dog, trained to detect signature molecules: all standard in biotech now, after some notorious incidents of industrial espionage. The stakes were too high to trust anybody.

Then Leo was inside the compound, walking down long white hallways. He turned on his desktop screen, went out to check the experiments in progress. The most important current one was reaching an endpoint, and Leo was particularly interested in the result. It was a high-throughput screening of some of the proteins in the Protein Data Bank at UCSD, trying to identify ones that would make certain cells express much more high-density lipoprotein than they would normally. Ten times as much HDL, the "good cholesterol," would be a lifesaver for people suffering from any number of ailments—atherosclerosis, obesity, diabetes, even Alzheimer's. Any one of these ailments mitigated (or cured!) would be worth billions; a therapy that helped all of them would be—well. It explained the high-alert security enclosing the compound, that was for sure.

The experiment was proceeding but not yet done, so Leo went back to his office and read *Bioworld Today* on-screen. Robotics, artificial hormones, proteomic analyses—the whole industry was looking for therapeutic proteins, and ways to get those proteins into people. They were the recalcitrant problems, standing between "biotechnology" as an idea and medicine as it actually existed. If they didn't solve these problems, the industry could go the way of nuclear power. If they did solve them, then it would be more like the computer industry in terms of financial returns—not to mention the impacts on health of course!

When Leo next checked the lab, two of his assistants, Marta and Brian, were standing at the bench, both wearing lab coats and rubber gloves, working the pipettes on a bank of flasks filling a countertop.

"Morning guys."

"Hey Leo." Marta aimed her pipette like a PowerPoint cursor at the small window on a long, low refrigerator. "Ready to check it out?"

"Sure am. Can you help?"

"In just a sec." She moved down the bench.

Brian said, "This better work, because Derek just told the press that it was the most promising self-healing therapy of the decade."

Leo was startled to hear this. "You're kidding."

"I'm not kidding."

"No, please. Not really."

"Really."

"How could he?"

"Press release. Also calls to his favorite reporters, and on his webpage. The chat room is already talking about the ramifications. They're betting one of the big pharms will buy us within the month."

"Please Bri, don't be saying these things."

"Sorry, but you know Derek." Brian gestured at one of the computer screens glowing on the bench across the way. "It's all over."

Leo squinted at a screen. "It wasn't on *Bioworld Today*."

"It will be tomorrow."

The company's website BREAKING NEWS box was blinking. Leo leaned over and jabbed it. Yep—lead story. HDL factory, potential for obesity, diabetes, Alzheimer's, heart disease . . .

"Oh my God," Leo muttered as he read. "Oh my God." His face was flushed. "Why does he *do* this?"

"He wants it to be true."

"So what? We don't know yet."

With her sly grin Marta said, "He wants you to make it happen, Leo. He's like the Road Runner and you're Wile E. Coyote. He gets you to run off the edge of a cliff, and then you have to build the bridge back to the cliff before you fall."

"But it never works! Coyote always falls!"

Marta laughed at him. She liked him, but she was tough. "Come on," she said. "This time we'll do it."

Leo nodded, tried to calm down. He appreciated Marta's spirit, and liked to be at least as positive as the most positive person in any given situation. That was getting tough these days, but he smiled the best he could and said, "Yeah, right, you're good," and started to put on rubber gloves.

"Remember the time he announced that we had hemophilia A whipped?" Brian said.

"Please."

"Remember the time he put out a press release saying he had decapitated mice at a thousand rpm to show how well our therapy worked?"

"The guillotine turntable experiment?"

"Please," Leo begged. "No more."

He picked up a pipette and tried to focus on the work. Withdraw, inject, withdraw, inject—alas, most of the work in this stage was automated, leaving people free to think, whether they wanted to or not. After a while Leo left them to it and went back to his office to check his e-mail, then helplessly to read what portion of Derek's press release he could stomach. "Why does he do this, why?"

It was a rhetorical question, but Marta and Brian were now in his doorway, Marta implacable: "I told you—he thinks he can make us do it."

"It's not us doing it," Leo protested, "it's the gene. We can't do a thing if the altered gene doesn't get into the cell we're trying to target."

"You'll just have to think of something that will work."

"You mean like, build it and they will come?"

"Yeah. Say it and they will make it. That's Derek."

Out in the lab a timer beeped, sounding uncannily like the Road Runner. *Beep-beep! Beep-beep!* They went to the incubator and read the graph paper as it rolled out of the machine, like a receipt out of an automated teller—like money out of an automated teller, in fact, if the results were good. One very big wad of twenties rolling out into the world from nowhere, if the numbers were good.

And they were. They were very good. They would have to plot it to be sure, but they had been doing this series of experiments for so long that they knew what the raw data would look like. The data were good. So now they were like Wile E. Coyote, standing in midair staring amazed at the viewers, because a bridge from the cliff had magically extended out and saved them. Saved them from the long plunge of a retraction in the press and subsequent NASDAQ free fall.

Except that Wile E. Coyote was invariably premature in his sense of relief. The Road Runner always had another devastating move to make. Leo's hand was shaking.

"Shit," he said. "I would be totally celebrating right now if it weren't for Derek. Look at this"—pointing—"it's even better than before."

"See, Derek knew it would turn out like this."

"The fuck he did."

"Pretty good numbers," Brian said with a grin. "Paper's almost written too. It's just plug these in and do a conclusion."

Marta said, "Conclusions will be simple, if we tell the truth."

Leo nodded. "Only problem is, the truth would have to admit that even though this part works, we still don't have a therapy, because we haven't got targeted delivery. We can make it but we can't get it into living bodies."

"You didn't read the whole website," Marta told him, smiling angrily.

"What do you mean?" Leo was in no mood for teasing. His stomach had already shrunk to the size of a walnut.

Marta laughed, which was her way of showing sympathy without admitting to any. "He's going to buy Urtech."

"What's Urtech?"

"They have a targeted delivery method that works."

"What do you mean, what would that be?"

"It's new. They just got awarded the patent on it."

"Oh no."

"Oh yes."

"Oh my God. It hasn't been validated?"

"Except by the patent, and Derek's offer to buy it, no."

"Oh my God. Why does he *do* this stuff?"

"Because he intends to be the CEO of the biggest pharmaceutical of all time. Like he told *People* magazine."

"Yeah right."

Torrey Pines Generique, like most biotech start-ups, was undercapitalized, and could only afford a few rolls of the dice. One of them had to look promising to attract the capital that would allow it to grow further. That was what they had been trying to accomplish for the five years of the company's existence, and the effort was just beginning to show results with these experiments. What they needed now was to be able to insert their successfully tailored gene into the patient's own cells, so that afterward it would be the patient's own body producing increased amounts of the needed proteins. If that worked, there would be no immune response from the body's immune system, and the patient would be not just helped, but cured.

Amazing.

But (and it was getting to be a big but) the problem of getting the altered DNA into living patients' cells hadn't been solved. Leo and his people were not physiologists, and they hadn't been able to do it. No one had. Immune systems existed precisely to keep these sorts of intrusions from happening. Indeed, one method of inserting the altered DNA into the body was to put it into a virus and give the patient a viral infection, benign in its ultimate effects because the altered DNA reached its target. But since the body fought viral infections, it was not a good solution. You didn't want to compromise further the immune systems of people who were already sick.

So, for a long time now they had been the same as everyone else chasing the holy grail of gene therapy, a "targeted nonviral delivery system." Any company that came up with such a system, and patented it, would immediately be able to have the method licensed for scores of procedures, and very likely one of the big pharmaceuticals would buy the company, making everyone in it rich, and often still employed. Over time the pharmaceutical might dismantle the acquisition, keeping only the method, but at that point the start-up's employees would be wealthy enough to laugh that off—retire and go surfing, or start up another start-up and try to hit the jackpot again. At that point it would be more of a philanthropic hobby than the cutthroat struggle to survive that it often seemed like before the big success arrived.

So the hunt for a targeted nonviral delivery system was most definitely on, in hundreds of labs around the world. And now Derek had bought one of these labs. Leo stared at the new announcement on the company website. Derek had to have bought it on spec, because if the method had been well proven, there was no way Derek would have been able to afford it. Some biotech firm even smaller than Torrey Pines—Urtech, based in Bethesda, Maryland (Leo had never heard of it)—had convinced Derek that they had found a way to deliver altered DNA into humans. Derek had made the purchase without consulting Leo, his chief research scientist. His scientific advice had to have come from his vice president, Dr. Sam Houston, his friend and partner. A man who had not done lab work in a decade.

So. It was true.

Leo sat at his desk, trying to relax his stomach. They would have to assimilate this new company, learn their technique, test it. It had been patented, Leo noted, which meant they had it exclusively at this point, as a kind of trade secret—a concept many working scientists had trouble accepting. A secret scientific method? Was that not a contradiction in terms? Of course a patent was a matter of public record, and eventually it would enter the public domain. So it wasn't a trade secret in literal fact. But at this stage it was secret enough. And it could not be a sure thing. There wasn't much published about it, as far as Leo could tell. Some papers in preparation, some submitted, one accepted—he would have to check that one out as soon as possible—and a patent. Sometimes they awarded them so early. Two papers were all that supported the whole approach.

Secret science. "God damn it," Leo said to his room. Derek had bought a pig in a poke. And Leo was going to have to open the poke and poke around.

There was a hesitant knock on his opened door, and he looked up.

"Oh hi, Yann, how are you?"

"I'm good Leo, thanks. I'm just coming by to say good-bye. I'm back to Pasadena now, my job here is finished."

"Too bad. I bet you could have helped us figure out this pig in a poke."

"Really?"

Yann's face brightened like a child's. He was a true mathematician, and had what Leo considered to be the standard mathematician personality: smart, spacy, enthusiastic, full of notions. All these qualities were a bit under the surface, until you really got him going. As Marta had remarked, not unkindly (for her), if it weren't for the head tilt and the speed-talking, he wouldn't have seemed like a mathematician at all. Whatever; Leo liked him, and his work on protein identification had been really interesting, and potentially very helpful.

"I don't know what we've got," Leo admitted. "It's likely to be a biology problem, but who knows? You sure have been helpful with selection protocols."

"Thanks, I appreciate that. I may be back anyway, I've got a project going with Sam's math team that might pan out. If it does they'll try to hire me on another temporary contract, he says."

"That's good to hear. Well, have fun in Pasadena in the meantime."

"Oh I will. See you soon."

And their best biomath guy slipped out the door.

Charlie Quibler had barely woken when Anna left for work. He got up an hour later to his own alarm, woke Nick with difficulty, drove him to school with the sleeping Joe in his car seat, then returned home to fall asleep again on the couch, Joe never awake during the entire process. An hour or so later Joe would rouse them both with his hungry cries, and then the day would really begin.

"Joe and Dad!" Charlie would say then. "Here we go! How about break-fast? Here—how about you get into your playpen for a second, and I'll go warm up some of Mom's milk."

"No!"

This routine had worked like a charm with Nick, but Joe refused to as-sociate with baby things, as being an affront to his dignity.

So now Charlie had Joe there with him in the kitchen, crawling under-foot or investigating the gate that blocked the stairs to the cellar. A human pinball. "Okay watch out now, don't. Don't! Your bottle will be ready in a second."

"Ba!"

"Yes, bottle."

This was satisfactory, and Joe plopped on his butt directly under Char-lie's feet. Charlie worked over him, taking some of Anna's frozen milk out of the freezer and putting it in a pot of warming water on the stove. Anna had her milk stored in precise quantities of either four or ten ounces, in tall or short permanent plastic cylinders that were filled with disposable plastic bags, and capped by brown rubber nipples topped by snap-on plastic tops to protect the nipples from contamination in the freezer. There was a lab book on the kitchen counter for Charlie to fill out the times and amounts of Joe's feedings. Anna liked to know these things, she said, to determine how much milk to pump at work, but Charlie felt that the real purpose was to fulfill Anna's pleasure in making quantified records of any kind.

He was testing the temperature of the thawed milk by taking a quick suck on the nipple when his phone rang. He whipped on a headset and answered.

"Hi Charlie, it's Roy."

"Oh hi Roy, what's up."

"Well I've got your latest draft here and I'm about to read it, and I thought I'd check to see what I should be looking for."

"Oh yeah. The new stuff that matters is all in the third section."

The bill as Charlie had drafted it for Phil would require the United States to act on certain recommendations of the Intergovernmental Panel on Climate Change.

"Did you kind of bury the part about us conforming to IPCC findings?"

"I don't think there's earth deep enough to bury that. I tried to make it look inevitable. International body we're part of, climate change clearly real, the UN the best body to work through global issues, support for them pretty much mandatory or else the world cooks, that sort of thing."

"Well, but that's never worked before, has it? Come on, Charlie, this is Phil's big pre-election bill and you're his climate guy. If he can't get this bill out of committee then we're in big trouble."

"Yeah I know. Wait just a second."

Charlie took another test pull from the bottle. Now it was at body temperature, or almost.

"A bit early to be hitting the bottle, Charlie, what you drinking there?"

"Well, I'm drinking my wife's breast milk, if you must know."

"Say what?"

"I'm testing the temperature of one of Joe's bottles. They have to be thawed to a very exact temperature or else he gets annoyed."

"So you're drinking your wife's breast milk out of a baby bottle?"

"Yes I am."

"How is it?"

"It's good. Thin but sweet. A potent mix of protein, fat, and sugar. No doubt the perfect food."

"I bet." Roy cackled. "Do you ever get it straight from the source?"

"Well I try, sure, who doesn't, but Anna doesn't like it. She says it's a mixed message and if I don't watch out she'll wean me when she weans Joe."

"Aha. So you have to take the long-term view."

"Yes. Although actually I tried it one time when Joe fell asleep nursing, so she couldn't move without waking him. She was hissing at me and I was trying to get it to work but apparently you have to suck much harder than, you know, one usually would, there's a trick to it, and I still hadn't gotten any when Joe woke up and saw me. Anna and I froze, expecting him to freak out, but he just reached out and patted me on the head."

"He understood!"

"Yeah. It was like he was saying I know how you feel, Dad, and I will share with you this amazing bounty. Didn't you Joe?" he said, handing Joe the warmed bottle. He watched with a smile as Joe took it one-handed and tilted it back, elbow thrown out like Popeye with a can of spinach. Because of all the pinpricks Charlie had made in the rubber nipples, Joe could choke down a bottle in a few minutes, and he seemed to take great satisfaction in doing so. No doubt a sugar rush.

"Okay, well, you are a kinky guy my friend and obviously deep in the world of domestic bliss, but we're still relying on you here and this may be the most important bill for Phil this session."

"Come on, it's a lot more than that, young man, it's one of the few chances we have left to avoid complete global disaster, I mean—"

"Preaching to the converted! Preaching to the converted!"

"I certainly hope so."

"Sure sure. Okay, I'll read this draft and get back to you ASAP. I want to move on with this, and the committee discussion is now scheduled for Tuesday."

"That's fine, I'll have my phone with me all day."

"Sounds good, I'll be in touch, but meanwhile be thinking about how to slip the IPCC thing in even deeper."

"Yeah okay but see what I did already."

"Sure bye."

"Bye."

Charlie pulled off the headset and turned off the stove. Joe finished his bottle, inspected it, tossed it casually aside.

"Man, you are fast," Charlie said as he always did. One of the mutual satisfactions of their days together was doing the same things over and over, and saying the same things about them. Joe was not as insistent on pattern as Nick had been, in fact he liked a kind of structured variability, as Charlie thought of it, but the pleasure in repetition was still there.

Now Joe decided he would try again to climb the baby gate and dive down the cellar stairs, but Charlie moved quickly to detach him, then shooed him out into the dining room while cleaning up the counter, ignoring the loud cries of complaint.

"Okay okay! Quiet! Hey let's go for a walk! Let's go walk!"

"No!"

"Ah come on. Oh wait, it's your day for Gymboree, and then we'll go to the park and have lunch, and then go for a walk!"

"NO!"

But that was just Joe's way of saying yes.

Charlie wrestled him into the baby backpack, which was mostly a matter of controlling his legs, not an easy thing. Joe was strong, a compact animal with bulging thigh muscles, and though not as loud a screamer as Nick had been, a tough guy to overpower. "Gymboree, Joe! You love it! Then a walk, guy, a walk to the park!"

Off they went.

First to Gymboree, located in a big building just off Wisconsin. Gymboree was a chance to get infants together when they did not have some other daycare to do it. It was an hour-long class, and always a bit depressing, Charlie felt, to be paying to get his kid into a play situation with other kids, but there it was; without Gymboree they all would have been on their own.

Joe disappeared into the tunnels of a big plastic jungle gym. It may have been a commercial replacement for real community, but Joe didn't know that; all he saw was that it had lots of stuff to play with and climb on, and so he scampered around the colorful structures, crawling through tubes and climbing up things, ignoring the other kids to the point of treating them as movable parts of the apparatus, which could cause problems. "Oops, say you're sorry, Joe. Sorry!"

Off he shot again, evading Charlie. He didn't want to waste any time. The contrast with Nick could not have been more acute. Nick had seldom moved at Gymboree. One time he had found a giant red ball and stood embracing the thing for the full hour of the class. All the moms had stared sympathetically (or not), and the instructor, Ally, had done her best to help Charlie get him interested in something else; but Nick would not budge from his mystical red ball.

Embarrassing. But Charlie was used to that. The problem was not just Nick's immobility or Joe's hyperactivity, but the fact that Charlie was always the only dad there. Without him it would have been a complete momspace, and comfortable as such. He knew that his presence wrecked that comfort. It happened in all kinds of infant-toddler contexts. As far as Charlie could tell, there was not a single other man inside the Beltway who ever spent the business hours of a weekday with preschool children. It just wasn't done. That wasn't why people moved to D.C. It wasn't why Charlie had moved there either, for that matter, but he and Anna had talked it over before Nick was born, and they had come to the realization that Charlie could do his job (on a part-time basis anyway) and their infant care at the same time, by using phone and e-mail to keep in contact with Senator Chase's office. Phil Chase himself had perfected the method of working at a distance back when he had been the World's Senator, always on the road; and being the good guy that he was, he had thoroughly approved of Charlie's plan. While on the other hand Anna's job absolutely required her to be at work at least fifty hours a week, and often more. So Charlie had happily volunteered to be the stay-at-home parent. It would be an adventure.

And an adventure it had been, there was no denying that. But first time's a charm; and now he had been doing it for over a year with kid number two, and what had been shocking and all-absorbing with kid number one was now simply routine. The repetitions were beginning to get to him. Joe was beginning to get to him.

So now Charlie sat there in Gymboree, hanging with the moms and the nannies. A nice situation in theory, but in practice a diplomatic challenge of the highest order. No one wanted to be misunderstood. No one would regard it as a coincidence if he happened to end up talking to one of the more attractive women there, or to anyone in particular on a regular basis.

That was fine with Charlie, but with Joe doing his thing, he could not completely control the situation. There was Joe now, doing it again—going after a black-haired little girl who had the perfect features of a model. Charlie was obliged to go over and make sure Joe didn't mug her, as he had a wont to do with girls he liked, and yes, the little girl had an attractive mom, or in this case a nanny—a young blonde au pair from Germany to whom Charlie had spoken before. Charlie could feel the eyes of the other women on him. Not a single adult in that room believed in his innocence.

"Hi Asta."

"Hello Charlie."

He even began to doubt it himself. Asta was one of those lively European women of twenty or so who gave the impression of being a decade ahead of their American contemporaries in terms of adult experiences—not easy, given the way American teens were these days. Charlie felt a little surge of protest: It's not me who goes after the babes, he wanted to shout, it's my son! My son the hyperactive girl-chasing mugger! But of course he couldn't do that, and now even Asta regarded him warily, perhaps because the first time they had chatted over their kids he had made some remark complimenting her on her child's nice hair. He felt himself begin to blush again, remembering the look of amused surprise she had given him as she corrected him.

Sing-along saved him from the moment. It was designed to calm the kids down a bit before the session ended and they had to be lassoed back into their car seats for the ride home. Joe took Ally's announcement as his cue to dive into the depths of the tube structure, where it was impossible to follow him or to coax him out. He would only emerge when Ally started "Ring Around the Rosie," which he enjoyed. Round in circles they all went, Charlie avoiding anyone's eye but Joe's. Ally, who was from New Jersey, belted out the lead, and so all the kids and moms joined her loudly in the final chorus:

"Eshes, eshes, we all, fall, DOWN!"

And down they all fell.

· · ·

Then it was off to the park.

Their park was a small one, located just west of Wisconsin Avenue a few blocks south of their home. A narrow grassy area held a sandpit and play structures. Tennis courts lined the south edge of the park. Out against Wisconsin stood a fire station, and to the west a field extended out to one of the many little creeks that still cut through the grid of streets.

Midday, the sandpit and the benches flanking it were almost always occupied by a few infants and toddlers, moms and nannies. Many more nannies than moms here, most of them West Indian, to judge by their appearance and voices. They sat on the benches together, resting in the steamy heat, talking. The kids wandered on their own, absorbed or bored.

Joe kept Charlie on his toes. Nick had been content to sit in one spot for long periods of time, and when playing he had been pathologically cautious; on a low wooden bouncy bridge his little fists had gone white on the chain railing. Joe however had quickly located the spot on the bridge that would launch him the highest—not at the middle, but about halfway down. He would stand right there and jump in time to the wooden oscillation until he was catching big air, his unhappy expression utterly different from Nick's, in that it was caused by his dissatisfaction that he could not get higher. This was part of his general habit of using his body as an experimental object, including walking in front of kids on swings, etc. Countless times Charlie had been forced to jerk him out of dangerous situations, and they had become less frequent only because Joe didn't like how loud Charlie yelled afterward. "Give me a break!" Charlie would shout. "What do you think, you're made of steel?"

Now Joe was flying up and down on the bouncy bridge's sweet spot. The sad little girl whose nanny talked on the phone for hours at a time wandered in slow circles around the merry-go-round. Charlie avoided meeting her eager eye, staring instead at the nanny and thinking it might be a good idea to stuff a note into the girl's clothes. "Your daughter wanders the Earth bored and lonely at age two—SHAME!"

Whereas he was virtuous. That would have been the point of such a note, and so he never wrote it. He was virtuous, but bored. No that wasn't really true. That was a disagreeable stereotype. He therefore tried to focus and play with his second-born. It was truly unfair how much less parental attention the second child got. With the first, although admittedly there was the huge Shock of Lost Adult Freedom to recover from, there was also the deep absorption of watching one's own offspring—a living human being whose genes were a fifty-fifty mix of one's own and one's partner's. It was frankly hard to believe that any such process could actually work, but there the kid was, out walking the world in the temporary guise of a kind of pet, a wordless little animal of surpassing fascination.

Whereas with the second one it was as they all said: just try to make sure they don't eat out of the cat's dish. Not always successful in Joe's case. But not to worry. They would survive. They might even prosper. Meanwhile there was the newspaper to read.

But now here they were at the park, Joe and Dad, so might as well make the best of it. And it was true that Joe was more fun to play with than Nick had been. He would chase Charlie for hours, ask to be chased, wrestle, fight, go down the slide and up the steps again like a perpetuum mobile. All this in the middle of a D.C. May day, the air going for a triple-triple, the sun smashing down through the wet air and diffusing until its light exploded out of a huge patch of the zenith. Sweaty gasping play, yes, but never a moment of coaxing. Never a dull moment.

After another such runaround they sprawled on the grass to eat lunch. Both of them liked this part. Fruit juices, various baby foods carefully spooned out and inserted into Joe's baby-bird mouth, applesauce likewise, a Cheerio or two that he could choke down by himself. He was still mostly a breast milk guy.

When they were done Joe struggled up to play again.

"Oh God Joe, can't we rest a bit."

"No!"

Ballasted by his meal, however, he staggered as if drunk. Naptime, as sudden as a blow to the head, would soon fell him.

Charlie's phone beeped. He slipped in an earplug and let the cord dangle under his face, clicked it on. "Hello."

"Hi Charlie, where are you?"

"Hey Roy. I'm at the park like always. What's up?"

"Well, I've read your latest draft, and I was wondering if you could discuss some things in it now, because we need to get it over to Senator Winston's office so they can see what's coming."

"Is that a good idea?"

"Phil thinks we have to do it."

"Okay, what do you want to discuss?"

There was a pause while Roy found a place in the draft. "Here we go. Quote, 'The Congress, being deeply concerned that the lack of speed in America's conversion from a carbon to a clean fuel economy is rapidly leading to chaotic climate changes with a profoundly negative impact on the U.S. economy,' unquote, we've been told that Ellington is only concerned, not deeply concerned. Should we change that?"

"No, we're deeply concerned. He is too, he just doesn't know it."

"Okay, then down in the third paragraph in the operative clauses, quote, 'The United States will peg carbon fuel reductions in a two-to-one ratio to such reductions by China and India, and will provide matching funds for all tidal and wind power plants built in those countries and in all countries that fall under a five in the UN's prospering countries index, these plants to be operated by a joint powers agency that will include the United States as a permanent member; four, these provisions will combine with the climate-neutral power production—'"

"Wait, call that power generation."

"Power generation, okay, 'such that any savings in environmental mitigation in participating countries as determined by IPCC ratings will be credited equally to the U.S. rating, and not less than fifty billion dollars per year in savings is to be marked specifically for the construction of more such climate-neutral power plants; and not less than fifty billion dollars per year in savings is to be marked specifically for the construction of so-called "carbon sinks," meaning any environmental engineering project designed to capture and sequester atmospheric carbon dioxide safely, in forests, peat beds, oceans, or other locations—'"

"Yeah hey you know carbon sinks are so crucial, scrubbing CO_2 out of the air may eventually turn out to be our only option, so maybe we should reverse those two clauses. Make carbon sinks come first and the climate-neutral power plants second in that paragraph."

"You think?"

"Yes. Definitely. Carbon sinks could be the only way that our kids, and about a thousand years' worth of kids actually, can save themselves from living in Swamp World. From living their whole lives on Venus."

"Or should we say Washington, D.C."

"Please."

"Okay, those are flip-flopped then. So that's that paragraph, now, hmm, that's it for text. I guess the next question is, what can we offer Winston and his gang to get them to accept this version."

"Get Winston's people to give you their list of riders, and then pick the two least offensive ones and tell them they're the most we could get Phil to accept, but only if they accept our changes first."

"But will they go for that?"

"No, but—wait—Joe?"

Charlie didn't see Joe anywhere. He ducked to be able to see under the climbing structure to the other side. No Joe.

"Hey Roy let me call you back okay? I gotta find Joe he's wandered off."

"Okay, give me a buzz."

Charlie clicked off and yanked the earplug out of his ear, jammed it in his pocket.

"JOE!"

He looked around at the West Indian nannies—none of them were watching, none of them would meet his eye. No help there. He jogged south to be able to see farther around the back of the fire station. Aha! There was Joe, trundling full speed for Wisconsin Avenue.

"JOE! STOP!"

That was as loud as Charlie could shout. He saw that Joe had indeed heard him, and had redoubled the speed of his diaper-waddle toward the busy street.

Charlie took off in a sprint after him. "JOE!" he shouted as he pelted over the grass. "STOP! JOE! STOP RIGHT THERE!" He didn't believe that Joe would stop, but possibly he would try to go even faster, and fall.

No such luck. Joe was in stride now, running like a duck trying to escape something without taking flight. He was on the sidewalk next to the fire station, and had a clear shot at Wisconsin, where trucks and cars zipped by as always.

Charlie closed in, cleared the fire station, saw big trucks bearing down; if Joe catapulted off the curb he would be right under their wheels. By the time Charlie caught up to him he was so close to the edge that Charlie had to grab him by the back of his shirt and lift him off his feet, whirling him around in a broad circle through the air, back onto Charlie as they both fell in a heap on the sidewalk.

"Ow!" Joe howled.

"WHAT ARE YOU DOING!" Charlie shouted in his face. "WHAT ARE YOU DOING? DON'T EVER DO THAT AGAIN!"

Joe, amazed, stopped howling for a moment. He stared at his father, face crimson. Then he recommenced howling.

Charlie shifted into a cross-legged position, hefted the crying boy into his lap. He was shaking, his heart was pounding; he could feel it tripping away madly in his hands and chest. In an old reflex he put his thumb to the other wrist and watched the seconds pass on his watch for fifteen seconds. Multiply by four. Impossible. One hundred and eighty beats a minute. Surely that was impossible. Sweat was pouring out of all his skin at once. He was gasping.

The parade of trucks and cars continued to roar by, inches away. Wisconsin Avenue was a major truck route from the Beltway into the city. Most of the trucks entirely filled the right lane, from curb to lane line, and most were moving at about forty miles an hour.

"Why do you do that," Charlie whispered into his boy's hair. Suddenly he was filled with fear, and some kind of dread or despair. "It's just crazy."

"Ow," Joe said.

Big shuddering sighs racked them both.

Charlie's phone rang. He clicked it on and held an earplug to his ear.

"Hi love."

"Oh hi hon!"

"What's wrong?"

"Oh nothing, nothing. I've just been chasing Joe around. We're at the park."

"Wow, you must be cooking. Isn't it the hottest part of the day?"

"Yeah it is, almost, but we've been having fun so we stayed. We're about to head back now."

"Okay, I won't keep you. I just wanted to check if we had any plans for next weekend."

"None that I know of."

"Okay, good. Because I had an interesting thing happen this morning, I met a bunch of people downstairs, new to the building. They're like Tibetans, I think, only they live on an island. They've taken the office space downstairs that the travel agency used to have."

"That's nice dear."

"Yes. I'm going to have lunch with them, and if it seems like a good idea I might ask them over for dinner sometime, if you don't mind."

"No, that's fine snooks. Whatever you like. It sounds interesting."

"Great, okay. I'm going to go meet them soon, I'll tell you about it."

"Okay good."

"Okay bye dove."

"Bye love, talk to you."

Charlie clicked off.

After ten giant breaths he stood, lifting Joe in his arms. Joe buried his face in Charlie's neck. Shakily Charlie retraced their course. It was somewhere between fifty and a hundred yards. Rivulets of sweat ran down his ribs, and off his forehead into his eyes. He wiped them against Joe's shirt. Joe was sweaty too. When he reached their stuff Charlie swung Joe around, down into his backpack. For once Joe did not resist. "Sowy Daddy," he said, and fell asleep as Charlie swung him onto his back.

Charlie took off walking. Joe's head rested against his neck, a sensation that had always pleased him before. Sometimes Joe would even suckle the tendon there. Now it was like the touch of some meaning so great that

Charlie couldn't bear it, a huge cloudy aura of danger and love. He started to cry, wiped his eyes, shook it off as if shaking away a nightmare. Hostages to fortune, he thought. You get married, have kids, you give up such hostages to fortune. No avoiding it, no help for it. It's just the price you pay for such love. His son was a complete maniac, and it only made him love him more.

He walked hard for most of an hour, through all the neighborhoods he had come to know so well in his years of lonely Mr. Momhood. The vestiges of an older way of life lay under the trees like a network of ley lines: rail beds, canal systems, Indian trails, even deer trails, all could still be discerned. Charlie walked them sightlessly. The ductile world drooped around him in the heat. Sweat lubricated his every move.

Slowly he regained his sense of normalcy. Just an ordinary day with Joe and Da.

The residential streets of Bethesda and Chevy Chase were in many ways quite beautiful. It had mostly to do with the immense trees, and the grass underfoot. Green everywhere. On a weekday afternoon like this there was almost no one to be seen. The slight hilliness was just right for walking. Tall old hardwoods gave some relief from the heat; above them the sky was an incandescent white. The trees were undoubtedly second or even third growth, there couldn't be many old-growth hardwoods anywhere east of the Mississippi. Still they were old trees, and tall. Charlie had never shifted out of his California consciousness, in which open landscapes were the norm and the desire, so that on the one hand he found the omnipresent forest claustrophobic—he pined for a pineless view—while on the other hand it remained always exotic and compelling, even slightly ominous or spooky. The dapple of leaves at every level, from the ground to the highest canopy, was a perpetual revelation to him; nothing in his home ground or his bookish sense of forests had prepared him for this vast and delicate venation of the air. On the other hand he longed for a view of distant mountains as if for oxygen itself. On this day especially he felt stifled and gasping.

His phone beeped again, and he pulled the earplugs out of his pocket and stuck them in his ears, clicked the set on.

"Hello."

"Hey Charlie I don't want to bug you, but are you and Joe okay?"

"Oh yeah, thanks Roy. Thanks for checking back in, I forgot to call you."

"So you found him."

"Yeah I found him, but I had to stop him running into traffic, and he was upset and I forgot to call back."

"Hey that's okay. It's just that I was wondering, you know, if you could finish off this draft with me."

"I guess." Charlie sighed. "To tell the truth, Roy boy, I'm not so sure how well this work-at-home thing is going for me these days."

"Oh you're doing fine. You're Phil's gold standard. But look, if now isn't a good time . . ."

"No no, Joe's asleep on my back. It's fine. I'm still just kind of freaked out."

"Sure, I can imagine. Listen we can do it later, although I must say we do need to get this thing staffed out soon or else Phil might get caught short. Dr. Strangelove"—this was their name for the President's science advisor—"has been asking to see our draft too."

"I know, okay talk to me. I can tell you what I think anyway."

So for a while as he walked he listened to Roy read sentences from his draft, and then discussed with him the whys and wherefores, and possible revisions. Roy had been Phil's chief of staff ever since Wade Norton hit the road and became an advisor in absentia, and after years of staffing for the House Resources committee (called the Environment committee until the Gingrich Congress renamed it), he was deeply knowledgeable, and sharp too; one of Charlie's favorite people. And Charlie himself was so steeped in the climate bill he could see it in his head, indeed it helped him now just to hear it, without the print before him to distract him. As if someone were telling him a bedtime story.

Eventually, however, some question of Roy's couldn't be resolved without the text before him. "Sorry. I'll call you back when I get home."

"Okay but don't forget, we need to get this finished."

"I won't."

They clicked off.

His walk home took him south, down the west edge of the Bethesda Metro district, an urban neighborhood of restaurants and apartment blocks, all ringing the hole in the ground out of which people and money fountained so prodigiously, changing everything: streets rerouted, neighborhoods redeveloped, a whole clutch of skyscrapers bursting up through the canopy and establishing another urban zone in the endless hardwood forest.

He stopped in at Second Story Books, the biggest and best of the area's several used bookstores. It was a matter of habit only; he had visited it so often with Joe asleep on his back that he had memorized the stock, and was reduced to checking the hidden books in the inner rows, or alphabetizing sections that he liked. No one in the supremely arrogant and slovenly shop cared what he did there. It was soothing in that sense.

Finally he gave up trying to pretend he felt normal, and walked past the auto dealer and home. There it was a tough call whether to take the baby backpack off and hope not to wake Joe prematurely, or just to keep him on his back and work from the bench he had put by his desk for this very purpose. The discomfort of Joe's weight was more than compensated for by the quiet, and so as usual he kept Joe snoozing on his back.

When he had his material open, and had read up on tidal power generation cost/benefit figures from the UN study on same, he called Roy back, and they got the job finished. The revised draft was ready for Phil to review, and in a pinch could be shown to Senator Winston or Dr. Strangelove.

"Thanks Charlie. That looks good."

"I like it too. It'll be interesting to see what Phil says about it. I wonder if we're hanging him too far out there."

"I think he'll be okay, but I wonder what Winston's staff will say."

"They'll have a cow."

"It's true. They're worse than Winston himself. A bunch of Sir Humphreys if I ever saw one."

"I don't know, I think they're just fundamentalist know-nothings."

"True, but we'll show them."

"I hope."

"Charles my man, you're sounding tired. I suppose the Joe is about to wake up."

"Yeah."

"Unrelenting eh?"

"Yeah."

"But you are the man, you are the greatest Mr. Mom inside the Beltway!"

Charlie laughed. "And all that competition."

Roy laughed too, pleased to be able to cheer Charlie up. "Well it's an accomplishment anyway."

"That's nice of you to say. Most people don't notice. It's just something weird that I do."

"Well that's true too. But people don't know what it entails."

"No they don't. The only ones who know are real moms, but they don't think I count."

"You'd think they'd be the ones who would."

"Well, in a way they're right. There's no reason me doing it should be anything special. It may just be me wanting some strokes. It's turned out to be harder than I thought it would be. A real psychic shock."

"Because . . ."

"Well, I was thirty-eight when Nick arrived, and I had been doing exactly what I wanted ever since I was eighteen. Twenty years of white male American freedom, just like what you have, young man, and then Nick arrived and suddenly I was at the command of a speechless mad tyrant. I mean, think about it. Tonight you can go wherever you want to, go out and have some fun, right?"

"That's right, I'm going to go to a party for some new folks at Brookings, supposed to be wild."

"All right, don't rub it in. Because I'm going to be in the same room I've been in every night for the past seven years, more or less."

"So by now you're used to it, right?"

"Well, yes. That's true. It was harder with Nick, when I could remember what freedom was."

"You have morphed into momhood."

"Yeah. But morphing hurts, baby, just like in *X-Men*. I remember the first Mother's Day after Nick was born, I was most deep into the shock of it, and Anna had to be away that day, maybe to visit her mom, I can't remember, and I was trying to get Nick to take a bottle and he was refusing it as usual. And I suddenly realized I would never be free again for the whole rest of my life, but that as a non-mom I was never going to get a day to honor *my* efforts, because Father's Day is not what this stuff is about, and Nick was whipping his head around even though he was in desperate need of a bottle—and I freaked out, Roy. I freaked out and threw that bottle down."

"You threw it?"

"Yeah. I slung it down and it hit at the wrong angle or something and just exploded. The baggie broke and the milk shot up and sprayed all over the room. I couldn't believe one bottle could hold that much. Even now when I'm cleaning the living room I come across little white dots of dried milk here and there, like on the mantelpiece or the windowsill. Another little reminder of my Mother's Day freak-out."

"Ha. The morph moment. Well Charlie you are indeed a pathetic specimen of American manhood, yearning for your own Mother's Day card, but just hang in there—only seventeen more years and you'll be free again!"

"Oh fuckyouverymuch! By then I won't want to be."

"Even now you don't wanna be. You love it, you know you do. But listen I gotta go Phil's here bye."

After talking with Charlie, Anna got absorbed in work as usual, and might well have forgotten her lunch date; but because this was a perpetual problem of hers, she had set her watch alarm, and when it beeped she saved and went downstairs. Down at the new embassy the young monk and his most elderly companion sat on the floor inspecting a box.

They noticed her and looked up curiously, then the younger one nodded, remembering her from the morning conversation after their ceremony.

"Still interested in some pizza?" Anna asked. "If pizza is okay?"

"Oh yes," the young one said. The two men got to their feet, the old man in several distinct moves; one leg was stiff. "We love pizza." The old man nodded politely, glancing at his assistant, who said something in their language.

As they crossed the atrium to Pizzeria Uno Anna said uncertainly, "Do you eat pizza where you come from?"

The younger man smiled. "No. But in Nepal I ate pizza in teahouses."

"Are you vegetarian?"

"No. Tibetan Buddhism has never been vegetarian. There were not enough vegetables."

"So you are Tibetans! But I thought you said you were an island nation?"

"We are. But originally we came from Tibet. The old ones, like Rudra Cakrin here, left when the Chinese took over. The rest of us were born in India, or on Khembalung itself."

They entered the restaurant, where big booths were walled by high wooden partitions. The three of them sat in one, Anna across from the two men.

"I am Drepung," the young man said, "and the rimpoche here, our ambassador to America, is Gyatso Sonam Rudra Cakrin."

"I'm Anna Quibler," Anna said, and shook hands with each of them. The men's hands were heavily callused.

Their waiter appeared and after a quick muttered consultation, Drepung asked Anna for suggestions, and in the end they ordered a combination pizza.

Anna sipped her water. "Tell me about Khembalung."

Drepung nodded. "I wish Rudra Cakrin himself could tell you, but he is still taking his English lessons, I'm afraid. Apparently they are going very badly. In any case, you know that China invaded Tibet in 1950, and that the Dalai Lama escaped to India in 1959?"

"Yes, that sounds familiar."

"Yes. And during those years, and ever since then too, many Tibetans moved to India to get away from the Chinese, and closer to the Dalai Lama. India took us in very hospitably, but when the Chinese and Indian governments disagreed over their border in 1960, the situation became very awkward for India. They were already in a bad way with Pakistan, and a serious controversy with China would have been too much. So, India requested that the Tibetan community in Dharamsala make itself as small and inconspicuous as possible. The Dalai Lama and his government did their best, and many Tibetans were relocated, mostly to the far south. One group took the offer of an island in the Sundarbans, and moved there. The island was ours from that point, as a kind of protectorate of India, like Sikkim, only not so formally arranged."

"Is Khembalung the island's original name?"

"No. I do not think it had a name before. Most of our group lived at one time in the valley of Khembalung. So that name was kept, and we have shifted away from the Dalai Lama's government in Dharamsala."

At the sound of the words "Dalai Lama" the old monk made a face and said something in Tibetan.

"The Dalai Lama is still number one with us," Drepung clarified. "It is a matter of some religious controversies with his associates. A matter of how best to support him."

"And your island?"

Their pizza arrived, and Drepung began talking between big bites. "Lightly populated, the Sundarbans. Ours was uninhabited."

"Did you say uninhabitable?"

"People with lots of choices might say they were uninhabitable," Drepung said. "And they may yet become so. They are best for tigers. But we have done well there. We have become like tigers. Over the years we have built a nice town. Schools, houses, hospital. All that. And seawalls. The whole island has been ringed by dikes. Lots of work. Hard labor." He nodded as if personally acquainted with this work. "Dutch advisors helped us. Very nice. Our home, you know? Khembalung has moved from age to age. But now . . ." He waggled a hand again, took another slice of pizza, bit into it.

"Global warming?" Anna ventured. "Sea level rise?"

He nodded, swallowed. "Our Dutch friends suggested that we establish an embassy here, to join their campaign to influence American policy."

Anna quickly bit into her pizza, so that she would not reveal the thought that had struck her, that the Dutch must be desperate indeed if they had been reduced to help from these people. She thought things over as she chewed. "So here you are," she said. "Have you been to America before?"

Drepung shook his head. "None of us have."

"It must be pretty overwhelming."

He frowned at this word. "I have been to Calcutta."

"Oh I see."

"This is very different, of course."

"Yes, I'm sure."

She liked him: his musical Indian English, his round face and big liquid eyes, his ready smile. The two men made quite a contrast: Drepung young and tall, round-faced, with a kind of baby-fat look; Rudra Cakrin old, small, and wizened, his face lined with a million wrinkles, his cheekbones and narrow jaw prominent in an angular, nearly fleshless face.

The wrinkles were laugh lines, however, combined with the lines of a wide-eyed expression of surprise that bunched up his forehead. He seemed cheerful, and certainly attacked his pizza with the same enthusiasm as his young assistant. With their shaved heads they shared a certain family resemblance.

She said, "I suppose going from Tibet to a tropical island must have been a bigger shock than coming from the island to here."

"I suppose. I was born in Khembalung myself, so I don't know for sure. But the old ones like Rudra here, who made that very move, seem to have adjusted well. Just to have any kind of home is a blessing."

Anna nodded. The two of them did project a certain calm. They sat in the booth as if there was no hurry to go anywhere else. Anna couldn't imagine any such state of mind. She was always in a tearing hurry. She tried to match their air of being at ease. At ease in Arlington, Virginia, after a lifetime on an island in the Ganges. Well, the climate would be familiar. But everything else had to have changed quite stupendously.

And, on closer examination, there was a certain guardedness to them. Drepung watched Anna with a slightly cautious look, reminding her of the pained expression she had seen earlier in the day.

"How is it that you came to rent a space in this particular building?"

Drepung paused to consider this question for a surprisingly long time. Rudra said something to him.

"We had some advice there," Drepung said. "The Pew Center on Global Climate Change has been helping us, and their office is located nearby."

Anna thought it over while she ate. It was good to know that they hadn't just rented the first office they found. Nevertheless, their effort in Washington looked to her to be underpowered at this point. "You should meet my husband," she said. "He works for a senator, one who is interested in climate change, and a good guy, and chair of the Foreign Relations Committee."

"Ah—Senator Chase?"

"Yes. You know about him?"

"He has visited Khembalung."

"Has he? Well, I'm not surprised, he's been every—he's been a lot of places. Anyway, my husband Charlie works for him as an environmental policy advisor. It would be good for you to talk to Charlie."

"That would be an honor."

"I don't know if I'd go that far. But useful."

"Useful, yes. Perhaps we could have you to dinner at our residence."

"Thank you, that would be nice. But we have two small boys and we've lost all our babysitters, so to tell the truth, it would be easier if you and some of your colleagues came to our place. In fact I've already talked to Charlie about this, and he's looking forward to meeting you. We live in Bethesda, just across the border from the District. It's not far."

"Red Line."

"Yes, very good. Red Line, Bethesda stop."

She got out her calendar, checked the coming weeks. Very full, as always. "How about a week from Friday? On Fridays we relax a little."

"Thank you," Drepung said, ducking his head. He and Rudra Cakrin had an exchange in Tibetan. "That would be very kind. And on the full moon, too."

"Is it? I'm afraid I don't keep track."

"We do. The tides, you see."

CHAPTER 3

INTELLECTUAL MERIT

Water flows through the oceans in steady recycling patterns, determined by the Coriolis force and the particular positions of the continents in our time. Surface currents can move in the opposite direction to bottom currents below them, and often do, forming systems like giant conveyor belts of water. The largest one is already famous, at least in part: the Gulf Stream is a segment of a warm surface current that flows north up the entire length of the Atlantic, all the way to Norway and Greenland. There the water cools and sinks, and begins a long journey south on the Atlantic Ocean floor, to the Cape of Good Hope and then east toward Australia, and even into the Pacific, where the water upwells and rejoins the surface flow, west to the Atlantic for the long haul north again. The round trip for any given water molecule takes about a thousand years.

Cooling salty water sinks more easily than fresh water. Trade winds sweep clouds generated in the Gulf of Mexico west over Central America to dump their rain in the Pacific, leaving the remaining water in the Atlantic that much saltier. So the cooling water in the North Atlantic sinks well, aiding the power of the Gulf Stream. If the surface of the North Atlantic were to become rapidly fresher, it would not sink so well when it cooled, and that could stall the conveyor belt. The Gulf Stream would have nowhere to go, and would slow down, and sink farther south. Weather everywhere would change, becoming windier and drier in the Northern Hemisphere, and colder in places, especially in Europe.

The sudden desalination of the North Atlantic might seem an unlikely oc-currence, but it has happened before. At the end of the last Ice Age, for in-stance, vast shallow lakes were created by the melting of the polar ice cap. Eventually these lakes broke through their ice dams and poured off into the oceans. North America still sports scars from three or four of these cataclys-mic floods; one flowed down the Mississippi, one the Hudson, one the St. Lawrence. These flows stalled the world ocean conveyor belt current, and the climate of the whole world changed as a result, sometimes in as little as three years.

Now, with Greenland's ice cap melting fast, and the Arctic sea ice breaking into bergs, would enough fresh water flow into the North Atlantic to stall the Gulf Stream again?

Frank Vanderwal kept track of climate news as a sort of morbid hobby. His friend Kenzo Hayakawa, an old grad school housemate, had spent time at NOAA before coming to NSF to work with the weather crowd on the ninth floor, and so Frank occasionally checked in with him, to say hi and find out the latest. Things were getting wild out there; extreme weather events were touching down all over the world, the violent short-termed ones almost daily, the chronic problems piling one on the next, so that never were they entirely clear of them. The Hyperniño, severe drought in India and Peru, lightning fires in Malaysia; then on the daily scale, a typhoon destroying most of Mindanao, a snap freeze killing crops and breaking pipes all over Texas, and so on. Something every day.

Like a lot of climatologists and other weather people Frank had met, Kenzo presented all this news with a faintly proprietary air, as if he were curating the weather. He liked the wild stuff, and enjoyed sharing news of it, especially if it supported his theory that the heat humans had added to the atmosphere had been enough to change the monsoon patterns for good, triggering global repercussions; meaning almost everything. This week for instance it was tornadoes, previously confined almost entirely to North America as a kind of freak of that continent's topography and latitude, but now appearing in East Africa and in Central Asia. Last week it had been the weakening of the Great World Ocean Current in the Indian Ocean rather than the Atlantic.

"Unbelievable," Frank would say.

"I know. Isn't it amazing?"

Before leaving for home at the end of the day, Frank often passed by another source of news, the little room filled with file cabinets and copy machines informally called "The Department of Unfortunate Statistics." Someone had started to tape onto the walls of this room extra copies of pages that held interesting statistics or other bits of recent quantitative information. No one knew who had started the tradition, but now it was clearly a communal thing.

The oldest ones were headlines, things like:

WORLD BANK PRESIDENT SAYS FOUR BILLION LIVE ON LESS THAN TWO DOLLARS A DAY.

or

AMERICA: FIVE PERCENT OF WORLD POPULATION, SEVENTY PERCENT OF CORPORATE OWNERSHIP

Later pages were charts, or tables of figures out of journal articles, or short articles out of the scientific literature.

When Frank went by on this day, Edgardo was in there at the coffee machine, as he so often was, looking at the latest. It was another headline:

352 RICHEST PEOPLE OWN AS MUCH AS THE POOREST TWO BILLION, SAYS CANADIAN FOOD PROJECT

"I don't think this can be right," Edgardo declared.

"How so?" Frank said.

"The poorest two billion have nothing, whereas the richest three hundred and fifty-two have a big percentage of the world's capital. I suspect it would take the poorest four billion at least to match the top three hundred and fifty."

Anna came in as he was saying this, and wrinkled her nose as she went to the copying machine. She didn't like this kind of conversation, Frank knew. It seemed to be a matter of distaste for belaboring the obvious. Or distrust in the data. Maybe she was the one who had taped up a brief quote: "72.8% of all statistics are made up on the spot."

Frank, wanting to bug her, said, "What do you think, Anna?"

"About what?"

Edgardo pointed to the headline and explained his objection.

Anna said, "I don't know. Seven magnitudes is a lot. Maybe if you add two billion small households up, it matches the richest three hundred."

"Not this top three hundred. Have you seen the latest Forbes 500?"

Anna shook her head impatiently, as if to say, Of course not, why would I waste my time? But Edgardo was an inveterate student of the stock market and the financial world generally. He tapped another page. "The average surplus value created by American workers is thirty-three dollars an hour."

Anna said, "I wonder how they define surplus value."

"Profit," Frank said.

Edgardo shook his head. "You can cook the books and get rid of profit, but the surplus value, the value created above and beyond the pay for the labor, is still there."

Anna said, "There was a page in here that said the average American worker puts in 1,950 hours a year. I thought that was questionable too, that's forty hours a week for about forty-nine weeks."

"Three weeks of vacation a year," Frank pointed out. "Pretty normal."

"Yeah, but average? What about all the part-time workers?"

"There must be an equivalent number of people who work overtime."

"Can that be true? I thought overtime was a thing of the past."

"You work overtime."

"Yeah but I don't get paid for it!"

The men laughed at her.

"They should have used the median," she said. "The average is a skewed measure of central tendency. Anyway, that's"—Anna could do calculations in her head—"sixty-four thousand three hundred and fifty dollars a year, generated by the average worker in surplus value. If you can believe these figures."

"What's the average income?" Edgardo asked. "Thirty thousand?"

"Maybe less," Frank said.

"We don't have any idea," Anna objected.

"Call it thirty, and what's the average taxes paid?"

"About ten? Or is it less?"

Edgardo said, "Call it ten. So let's see. You work every day of the year, except for three lousy weeks. You make around a hundred thousand dollars. Your boss takes two-thirds of that and gives you one third, then you give a third of that to the government. Your government uses what it gets to build all the roads and schools and police and pensions, and your boss takes his much larger share and buys a mansion on an island somewhere. So naturally you complain about your bloated inefficient Big Brother of a government, and you always vote for the pro-owner party." He grinned at Frank and Anna. "How stupid is that?"

Anna shook her head. "People don't see it that way."

"But here are the statistics!"

"People don't usually put them together like that. Besides, you made half of them up."

"They're close enough for people to get the idea! But they are not taught to think! In fact they're taught *not* to think. And they are stupid to begin with."

Even Frank was not willing to go this far. "It's a matter of what you can see," he suggested. "You see your boss, you see your paycheck, it's given to you. You have it. Then you're forced to give some of it to the government. You never know about the surplus value you've created, because it was disappeared in the first place. Cooked in the books."

"But the rich are all over the news! Everyone can see they have more than they have earned, because no one really earns that much."

"The only things people understand are sensory," Frank insisted. "We're hardwired to understand life on the savannah. Someone gives you meat, they're your friend. Someone takes your meat, they're your enemy. Abstract concepts like surplus value, or statistics on the value of a year's work, these just aren't as real as what you see and touch. People are only good at what they can think out in terms of their senses. That's just the way we evolved."

"That's what I'm saying," Edgardo said cheerfully. "We are stupid!"

"I've got to get back to it," Anna said, and left. It really wasn't her kind of conversation.

·   ·   ·

Frank followed her out, and finally headed home. He drove his little fuel-cell Honda out Old Dominion Parkway, already jammed; over the Beltway, and then up to a condo complex called Swink's New Mill, where he had rented a condominium for his year at NSF.

He parked in the complex's cellar garage and took the elevator up to the fourteenth floor. His apartment looked out toward the Potomac—a long view and a nice apartment, rented to Frank for the year by a young State Department guy who was doing a stint in Brasília. It was furnished in a stripped-down style that suggested the man did not live there very often. But a nice kitchen, functional spaces, everything easy, and most of the time Frank was there he was asleep, so he didn't care what it was like.

He had picked up one of the free papers back at work, and now he looked at the Personals section, a regrettable habit he had had for years, fascinated as he was by this glimpse into a subworld of radically efflorescing sexual diversity. Were people like this really out there, or were these merely the fantasies of a bunch of lonely souls like himself? The sections devoted to people looking for LTRs, meaning "long-term relationships," sometimes struck him with force. ISO LTR: *in search of long-term relationship.* The species had evolved toward monogamy, it was wired into the brain. Not a cultural imposition, but a biological instinct. They might as well be storks.

And so he read the ads, but never replied. He was only here for a year. It made no sense to take any action on this front. The ads themselves also tended to stop him.

> Husband hunting, SWF, licensed nurse, seeks a hardworking, handsome SWM for LTR. Must be a dedicated Jehovah's Witness.
> SBM, 5'5", shy, quiet, a little bit serious, seeking Woman, age open. Not good-looking or wealthy but Nice Guy. Enjoy foreign movies, opera, theater, music, books, quiet evenings.

These were not going to get a lot of responses. Frank could have written their ur-text, and one time he had, and had even sent it in, as a joke of course—it would make some of them laugh. And if any woman liked the joke well enough to call, well, that would have been a sign.

> Male *Homo sapiens* desires company of female *Homo sapiens*
> for mutual talk and grooming behaviors, possibly mating and
> reproduction. Must be happy, run fast.

But no one had replied.

He went out onto the bas-relief balcony, into the sultry late afternoon. Another two months and he would be going home, back to his real life. Thinking about that reminded him of the grant application from Yann Pierzinski. He went inside to his laptop and googled Yann to try to learn more about what he had been up to. Then he reopened the application. Recursion at the boundary limit . . . it was interesting.

Finally he called up Derek Gaspar at Torrey Pines Generique.

"What's up?" Derek said after the preliminaries.

"Well, I just got a grant proposal from one of your people, and I'm wondering if you can tell me anything about it."

"From one of mine, what do you mean?"

"A Yann Pierzinski, do you know him?"

"No, never heard of him. He works here you say?"

"He was there on a temporary contract, working with Simpson. He's a postdoc from Caltech."

"Ah yeah, here we go. Mathematician, got a paper in *Biomathematics* on algorithms."

"Yeah, that comes up first on my Google too."

"Well sure. I can't be expected to know everyone who ever worked with us here, that's hundreds of people, you know that."

"Sure sure."

"So what's his proposal about? Are you going to give him a grant?"

"Not up to me, you know that. We'll see what the panel says. But meanwhile, maybe you should check it out."

"Oh you like it then."

"I think it may be interesting, it's hard to tell. Just don't drop him."

"Well, our records show him as already gone back to Pasadena. Like you said, his gig here was temporary."

"Aha. Man, your research groups have been gutted."

"Not gutted, Frank, though we're down to the bare bones in some areas. That's one of the reasons I'll be happy when you're back out here."

"I don't work for Torrey Pines anymore."

"No, but maybe you could rejoin us when you move back."

"Maybe. If you get new financing."

"I'm trying, believe me. That's why I'd like to have you back on board."

"We'll see. I'll be out looking for a place to live in a couple of weeks, I'll come see you then."

"Good, make an appointment with Susan."

Frank clicked off his phone, sat back in his chair thinking it over. Derek was like a lot of first-generation CEOs of biotech start-ups. He had come out of the biology department at UCSD, and his business acumen had been gained on the job. Some people managed to do this successfully, others didn't, but all tended to fall behind on the science, and had to take on faith what was really possible in the labs. Certainly Derek could use some help in guiding policy.

Frank went back to studying the grant proposal. There were elements of the algorithm missing, as was typical, but he could see the potential for a very powerful method there. Earlier in the day he had thought he saw a way to plug one of the gaps that Pierzinski had left . . .

"Hmmmm," he said to the empty room.

On his return to San Diego, he could perhaps set things up quite nicely. There were some potential problems, of course. NSF's guidelines stated that NSF always kept a public right use for all grant-subsidized work. That would keep any big gains from going to any individual or company, if it was awarded a grant. Private control could only be kept if no public money had been granted.

Also, the P.I. on the proposal was Pierzinski's advisor at Caltech, battening off the work of his students in the usual way. Caltech and the P.I. would hold the rights to anything the project made, along with NSF, even if Pierzinski later moved. So, assuming Pierzinski moved back to Torrey Pines Generique soon, it would be best if this particular proposal of his failed. Then if the algorithm worked and became patentable, Torrey Pines would keep all the profit from whatever it made. A big patent was often worth billions.

This line of thought made Frank feel jumpy. In fact he was on his feet, pacing out to the mini-balcony and back in. Then he remembered he had been planning to go to Great Falls anyway. He pulled his climbing kit out of the closet, changed clothes, and went back down to his car.

The Great Falls of the Potomac was a complicated thing, a long tumble of whitewater falling down past a few islands. The spray it threw up seemed to consolidate and knock down the humidity, so that paradoxically it was less humid here than elsewhere, although wet and mossy underfoot.

Frank walked downstream along the edge of the gorge. Below the falls the river recollected itself and ran through a defile called Mather Gorge, a ravine with a south wall so steep that climbers were drawn to it. One started at the top, rappelled down to the river, and climbed back up with a top belay. Carter Rock was Frank's favorite.

There were about as many single climbers like Frank here as there were duets. Some even free-soloed the wall, dispensing with all protection. Frank liked to play it just a little safer than that.

The few routes available were all chalked from repeated use. The river and its gorge created a band of open sky that was unusual for D.C. This as much as anything gave Frank the feeling that he was in a good place: on a wall route, near water, open to the sky. Out of the claustrophobia of the great hardwood forest, one of the things about the East Coast Frank hated most. There were times he would have given a finger for the sight of open land.

Now, as he rappelled down to the small tumble of big boulders at the foot of the cliff, chalked his hands, and began to climb the fine-grained old schist of the route, he cheered up. He focused on his immediate surroundings to a degree unimaginable when he was not climbing. It was like his math work, only then he wasn't anywhere at all. Here, he was right on these very rocks.

This route was about a 5.8 or 5.9 at its crux, much easier elsewhere. It was hard to find really difficult pitches here, but that didn't matter. The constant roar and spray didn't matter. Only the climbing mattered.

His legs did most of the work. Find the footholds, fit his rock-climbing shoes into cracks or onto knobs, then look for handholds. Climbing was the bliss of perfect attention, a kind of devotion or prayer. Or simply a re- treat into the supreme competencies of the primate cerebellum. A lot was conserved there.

By now it was evening, a sultry summer evening, sunset near, the air going yellow. He topped out and sat on the rim, feeling the sweat on his face fail to evaporate.

There was a kayaker, below in the river. A woman, he thought, though she wore a helmet and was broad-shouldered and flat-chested. Paddling smoothly upstream, into the hissing water still recollecting itself as a liquid. Upstream from her began a steep rapids.

The kayaker pushed up into this wilder section, paddling hard upstream, then holding her position against the flow while she studied the falls ahead. Then she took off hard again, attacking a smooth flow, a kind of ramp through the smash, up to a terrace in the whitewater. When she reached the little flat she rested again, in another maintenance paddle, gathering her strength for the next salmonlike climb.

Abruptly leaving the refuge of the flat spot, she attacked another ramp that led up to a bigger plateau of flat black water. There she appeared to be stuck, but all of a sudden she attacked the water with a fierce flurry of pad- dle strokes, and seemingly willed her craft up the next pouring ramp. Five or seven desperate seconds later she leveled out again, on a tiny little bench of a refuge. After only a few seconds she took off and fought upstream, fists moving fast as a boxer's, the kayak at an impossible angle, looking like a miracle—until all of sudden it was swept back down, and she had to make a quick turn and then take a wild ride, bouncing down the falls by a differ- ent and steeper route than the one she had ascended, losing in a few sec- onds the height that she had worked a minute or two to gain.

"Wow," Frank said, smitten.

She was already almost down to the hissing tapestry of flat river right below him, and he felt an urge to wave to her, or stand and applaud. He restrained himself, not wanting to impose upon another athlete deep in her own space. It was sunset now, and the smooth stretches of the river had turned a pale orange. Time to go home and try to fall asleep.

"ISO kayaker gal, seen going upstream at Great Falls. Great ride, I love you, please respond."

He would not send that in to the free papers, but only spoke it as a kind of prayer to the sunset. Down below the kayaker was headed upstream again.

It could be said that science is boring, or even that science wants to be boring, in that it wants to be beyond all dispute. It wants to understand the phenomena of the world in ways that everyone can agree on; it wants to make assertions that if tested by any sentient being would cause that being to agree with the assertion. Complete agreement; the world put under a description; stated that way, it begins to sound interesting.

As indeed it is. Nevertheless, the details of the everyday grind of scientific practice can be tedious, even to the practitioners. A lot of it, as with most work in this world, involves wasted time, false leads, dead ends, faulty equipment, dubious techniques, bad data, and a huge amount of detail work. Only when it is written up in a paper does it tell a tale of things going right, in meticulous replicable detail, like a proof in Euclid. That stage is a highly artificial result of a long process of grinding.

In the case of Leo and his lab, and the matter of the new targeted nonviral delivery system from Maryland, several hundred hours of human labor and many more of computer time had been devoted to an attempted repetition of an experiment described in the crucial paper, "In Vivo Insertion of cDNA 1568rr Into CBA/H, BALB/c, and C57BL/6 Mice."

In the end, Leo had confirmed the hypothesis he had formulated the very moment he had first read the paper: "It's a goddamned artifact."

Marta and Brian sat there staring at the printouts. Marta had killed a couple hundred of the Jackson Lab's finest mice to confirm this theory of Leo's, and now she was looking more murderous than ever. You didn't want to mess with Marta on the days when she had to sacrifice some mice, nor even talk to her.

Brian sighed.

Leo said, "It only works if you pump the mice so full of the stuff they just about explode. I mean look at them, they look like guinea pigs. Their little eyes are about to pop out of their heads."

"It's no wonder," Brian said. "There's only two milliliters of blood in a mouse, and we're injecting them with one."

Leo shook his head. "How the hell did they get away with that?"

"The CBAs are kind of round and furry from the get-go."

"What are you saying, they're bred to hide artifacts?"

"No."

"It's an artifact!"

"Well, it's useless, anyway."

An artifact was an experimental result specific to the methodology of the experiment, but not illustrating anything beyond that. A kind of accident, and in a few celebrated cases, part of a deliberate hoax.

So Brian was trying to be careful about using the word. It was possible that it was no worse than a real result that happened to be useless for their purposes. Trying to turn things people have learned about biology into medicines led to that; it happened all the time, and all those findings were not necessarily artifacts. They just weren't useful facts.

Getting a useful medicinal fact was usually a matter of two to ten years of work, costing anywhere up to $500 million. In this case, however, Leo was dealing with a method Derek Gaspar had bought for $51 million on spec, a method for which there could be no stage-one human trials: "No one's gonna let themselves be blown up like a balloon! Your kidneys would get swamped, or some kind of edema would kill you."

"We're going to have to tell Derek the bad news."

"Derek is not going to like it."

"Not going to like it! Fifty-one million dollars? He's going to hate it!"

"Think about blowing that much money. What an idiot he is."

"Is it worse to have a scientist who is a bad businessman as your CEO, or a businessman who is a bad scientist?"

"What about when they're both?"

They sat around the bench looking at the mice cages and the rolls of data sheets. A Dilbert cartoon mocked them as it peeled away from the end of the counter. It was a sign of something deep that this lab had Dilberts taped to the walls rather than Far Sides.

"An in-person meeting for this particular communication is contraindicated," Brian suggested.

"No shit," Leo said.

Marta snorted. "You can't get a meeting with him anyway."

"Ha ha." But Leo was far enough out in Torrey Pine Generique's power structure that getting a meeting with Derek was indeed difficult.

"It's true," Marta insisted.

"Which is stupid," Brian pointed out. "The company is totally dependent on what happens in this lab."

"Not totally," Leo said.

"Yes it is! But that's not what the business schools teach these guys. The lab is just another place of production. Management tells production what to produce. Input from the agency of production would be wrong."

"Like the assembly line choosing what to make," Marta said.

"Right. Thus the idiocy of business management theory in our time."

"I'll send him an e-mail," Leo decided.

So Leo sent Derek an e-mail concerning what Brian and Marta persisted in calling the exploding mice problem. Derek (according to reports they heard later) swelled up like one of their experimental subjects. It appeared he had been IV'd with two liters of genetically engineered righteous indignation.

"It's in the literature!" he was reported to have shouted at Dr. Sam Houston, his vice president in charge of research and development. "It was in *The Journal of Immunology,* there were two papers that were peer-reviewed, they got a patent for it, I went out there to Maryland and checked it all out myself! It worked there, damn it. So make it work here!"

"*Make* it work?" Marta said when she heard this. "See what I mean?"

"Well, you know," Leo said grimly. "That's the tech in biotech, right?"

"Hmmm," Brian said, interested despite himself.

After all, manipulations of gene and cell were hardly ever done "just to find things out." They were done to accomplish certain things inside the cell, and later, inside a living body. Biotechnology, *bio techno logos;* the word on how to put the tool into the living organism. Genetic engineering meant putting something new inside a body's DNA, to effect something in the metabolism.

They had done the genetics; now it was time for the engineering.

So Leo and Brian and Marta, and the rest of Leo's lab, began to work on it. Sometimes at the end of a day, when the sun was breaking sideways through gaps in the clouds out to sea, shining weakly in the tinted windows, they would compare their most recent results, and try to make sense of the problem. Sometimes one of them would stand up and use the whiteboard to sketch out some diagram illustrating his or her conception of what was going on, down there forever below the level of their physical senses. The rest would comment, and drink coffee, and think it over.

"What we need is to package the inserts with a ligand that is really specific for the target cells. If we could find that specificity, out of all the possible proteins, without going through all the rigmarole of trial and error . . ."

"Too bad we don't still have Pierzinski! He could run the possibilities through his algorithm."

"Well, we could call him up and ask him to give it a try."

"Sure, but who's got time for that kind of thing?"

"He's still working on a paper with Eleanor on campus," Marta said, meaning UCSD. "I'll ask him when he comes down."

They wandered off to go home, or back to their desks and benches, thinking over plans for more experiments. Getting the mice, getting the time on the machines, sequencing genes, sequencing schedules; when you were doing scientific work the hours flew by, and the days, and the weeks. This was the main feeling: there was never enough time to do it all. Was this different from other kinds of work? Leo's things-to-do list grew and shrank, grew and shrank, grew and then refused to shrink. He spent much less time than he wanted to at home in Leucadia with Roxanne. Roxanne understood, but it bothered him, even if it didn't bother her.

He called the Jackson labs and ordered new and different strains of mice, each strain with its own number and bar code and genome. He got his lab's machines scheduled, and assigned the techs to use them, moving some things to the front burner, others to the back, all to accommodate this project's urgency.

On certain days, he went into the lab where the mouse cages were kept and opened a cage door. He took out a mouse, small and white, wriggling and sniffing the way they did, checking things out with its whiskers. Quickly he shifted it so that he was holding it at the neck with the forefingers and thumbs of both hands. A quick hard twist and the neck broke. Very soon after that the mouse was dead.

This was not unusual. During this round of experiments, he and Brian and Marta and the rest of them tourniqueted and injected about three hundred mice, drew their blood, then killed and rendered and analyzed them. That was an aspect of the process they didn't talk about, not even Brian. Marta in particular went black with disgust; it was worse than when she was premenstrual, as Brian joked (once). Her headphones stayed on her head all day long, the music turned up so loud that even the other people in the lab could hear it. Ultraprofane hip-hop. If she can't hear she can't feel, Brian joked right next to her, Marta oblivious and trembling with rage, or something like it.

But it was no joke, even though the mice existed to be killed, even though they were killed mercifully, and usually only some few months before they would have died naturally. There was no real reason to have qualms, and yet still there was no joking about it. Maybe Brian would joke about Marta (if she couldn't hear him), but he wouldn't joke about that. In fact he insisted on using the word *kill* rather than *sacrifice,* even in write-ups and papers, to keep it clear what they were doing. Usually they had to break their necks right behind the head; you couldn't inject them to "put them to sleep," because their tissue samples had to be clear of all contaminants. So it was a matter of breaking necks, as if they were tigers pouncing on prey. If done properly it paralyzed them so that it was quick and painless—or at least quick. No feeling below the head, no breathing, immediate loss of mouse consciousness, one hoped. Leaving only the killers to think it over. Usually the mice deaths occurred in the mornings, so they could get to work on the samples. By the time the scientists got home the experience was somewhat forgotten, its effects muted. But people like Marta went home and dosed themselves with drugs on those days—she said she did—and played the most hostile music they could find, 110 decibels of forgetting. Went out surfing. Didn't talk about it.

In the meantime, while they were working on this problem, their good results with the HDL "factory cells" had been plugged into the paper they had written about the process, and sent upstairs to Torrey Pines' legal department, where it had gotten hung up. Repeated queries from Leo got the same e-mailed response: still reviewing—do not publish.

"They want to see what they can patent in it," Brian said.

"They won't let us publish until we have a patent *and* a delivery method," Marta predicted.

"But that may never happen!" Leo cried. "It's good work, it's interesting! It could help make a big breakthrough!"

"That's what they don't want," Brian said.

"They don't want a big breakthrough unless it's our big breakthrough."

"Shit."

Leo had never gotten used to this. Sitting on results, doing private science, secret science—it went against the grain. It wasn't science as he understood it, which was a matter of finding out things and publishing them for all to see and test, critique, put to use.

But it was getting to be standard operating procedure. Security in the building remained intense; even e-mails out had to be checked for approval, not to mention laptops, briefcases, and boxes leaving the building. "You have to check in your brain when you leave," as Brian put it.

"Fine by me," Marta said.

"I just want to publish," Leo insisted grimly.

"You'd better find a targeted delivery method if you want to publish that particular paper, Leo."

So they continued to work on the Urtech method. The new experiments slowly yielded their results. The volumes and dosages had sharp parameters on all sides. The Maryland method stubbornly remained an artifact.

By now, however, enough time had passed that Derek could pretend that the whole Urtech purchase had never happened. It was a new financial quarter; there were other fish to fry, and for now the pretense could be plausibly maintained that it was a work in progress rather than a total bust. It wasn't as if anyone else had solved the targeted nonviral delivery problem, after all. It was a hard problem. Or so Derek could say, in all truth, and did so whenever anyone was inconsiderate enough to bring the matter up. Whiners on the company's website chat room could be ignored as always.

Analysts on Wall Street, however, and in the big pharmaceuticals, and in relevant venture capital firms, could not be ignored. And while they weren't saying anything directly, investment money started to go elsewhere. Torrey Pines' stock fell, and because it was falling it fell some more, and then more again. Biotechs were fluky, and so far Torrey Pines had not generated any potential cash cows. They remained a start-up. Fifty-one million dollars was being swept under the rug, but the big lump in the rug gave it away to anyone who remembered what it was. No—Torrey Pines Generique was in trouble.

In Leo's lab they had done what they could. Their job had been to get certain cell lines to become unnaturally prolific protein factories, and they had done that. Delivery wasn't their part of the deal, and they weren't physiologists, and now they didn't have the wherewithal to do that part of the job. Torrey Pines needed a whole different wing for that, a whole different field of science. It was not an expertise that could be bought for $51 million. Or maybe it could have been, but Derek had bought defective expertise. And because of that, a multibillion-dollar cash-cow method was stalled right on the brink, and the whole company might go under.

Nothing Leo could do about it. He couldn't even publish his results.

The Quiblers' small house was located at the end of a street of similar houses. All of them stood blankly, blinds drawn, no clues given as to who lived inside. They could have been empty for all an outsider could tell: they could have been walled compounds in Saudi Arabia, hiding their life from the desert.

Walking these streets with Joe on his back, Charlie assumed that these houses were mostly owned by people who worked in the District, people who were always either working or on vacation. Their homes were places to sleep. Charlie had been that way himself before the boys had arrived. That was how people lived in Bethesda.

So he walked to the grocery store shaking his head as he always did. "It's like a ghost town, Joe, it's like some *Twilight Zone* episode in which we're the only two people left on Earth."

Then they rounded the corner, and all thought of ghost towns was rendered ridiculous. Shopping center. They walked into a giant Giant grocery store. Joe, excited by the place as always, stood up in his baby backpack, his knees on Charlie's shoulders, and whacked Charlie on the ears as if he were directing an elephant. Charlie reached up, lifted him around and stuffed him into the baby seat of the grocery cart, then strapped him down with the cart's little red seat belt. A very useful feature.

Okay. Buddhists coming to dinner. He had no idea what to cook. He assumed they were vegetarians. It was not unusual for Anna to invite people from NSF to dinner and then be somewhat at a loss as to the meal itself. Charlie liked that; he enjoyed cooking, though he was not good at it.

Now he decided to resuscitate an old recipe from their student years, pasta with an olive and basil sauce that a friend had first cooked for them in Italy. He wandered the familiar aisles of the store, looking for the ingredients. Joe's presence disguised his tendency to talk to himself in public spaces. "Okay, whole peeled tomatoes, pitted kalamatas, olive oil extra virgin first cold press, it's the first press zat really matter," slipping into their friend's Italian accent, "but you must never keel ze pasta, my God! Oh and bread. And wine, but not more than we can carry home, huh Joe."

With groceries tucked into the backpack pocket under Joe's butt, and slung in plastic bags from both hands, Charlie walked Joe back along the empty street to their house. Their street dead-ended in a little triangle of trees next to Woodson Avenue, a feeder road that poured its load of cars onto Wisconsin south. An old four-story apartment block wrapped around their backyard like a huge brick sound barrier, its stacked windows like a hundred live webcasts streaming all at once, daily lives that were much too partial and mundane to be interesting. No *Rear Window* here, and thank God for that. Each nuclear family in its domicile was inside its own pocket universe, millions of them scattered over the surface of the planet, like the dots of light in nighttime satellite photos.

On this night, however, the bubble containing the Quiblers was breached. Visitors, aliens! When the doorbell rang they almost didn't recognize the sound.

Anna was occupied with Joe and a diaper upstairs, so Charlie left the kitchen and hurried through the house to answer the door. Four men in off-white cotton pants and shirts stood on the stoop, like visitors from Calcutta, except their vests were the maroon color Charlie associated with Tibetan monks. Joe had run to the top of the stairs, and he grabbed a banister to keep his balance, agog at the sight of them. In the living room Nick was struck shy, his nose quickly back into his book, but he was glancing over the top of it frequently as the strangers were ushered in around him. Charlie offered them drinks, and they accepted beers, and when he came back with those, Anna and Joe were downstairs and had joined the fun. Two of their visitors sat on the living room floor, laughing off Anna's offer of the little couches, and they all put their beer bottles on the coffee table.

The oldest monk and the youngest one leaned back against the radiator, down at Joe's level, and soon they were engaged with his vast collection of blocks—a heaping mound of plain or painted cubes, rhomboids, cylinders, and other polygons, which they quickly assembled into walls and towers, working with and around Joe's Godzillalike interventions.

The young one, Drepung, answered Anna's questions directly, and also

translated for the oldest one, named Rudra Cakrin. He was the official ambassador of Khembalung, but while he was without English, apparently, his
two middle-aged associates, Sucandra and Padma Sambhava, spoke it
pretty well—not as well as Drepung, but adequately.

These two followed Charlie back out into the kitchen and stood there,
beer bottles in hand, talking to him as he cooked. They stirred the unkilled
pasta to keep the pot from boiling over, checked out the spices in the spice
rack, and stuck their noses deep into the saucepot, sniffing with great interest and appreciation. Charlie found them surprisingly easy to talk to. They
were about his age. Both had been born in Tibet, and both had spent years,
they did not say how many, imprisoned by the Chinese, like so many other
Tibetan Buddhist monks. They had met in prison, and after their release
they had crossed the Himalayas and escaped Tibet together, afterward
making their way gradually to Khembalung.

"Amazing," Charlie kept saying to their stories. He could not help but
compare them to his own relatively straightforward passage through the
years. "And now after all that, you're getting flooded?"

"Many times," they said in unison. Padma, still sniffing Charlie's sauce as
if it were the perfect ambrosia, elaborated. "Used to happen only every
eighteen years or about, moon tides, you know. We could plan it happening, and be prepared. But now, whenever the monsoon hits hard."

"Also every month at moontide," Sucandra added. "Certainly three, four
times a year. No one can live that way for long. If it gets worse, then the
island will no longer be habitable. So we came here."

Charlie shook his head, tried to joke: "This place may be lower in elevation than your island."

They laughed politely. Not the funniest joke. Charlie said, "Listen, speaking of elevation, have you talked to the other low-lying countries?"

Padma said, "Oh yes, we are part of the League of Drowning Nations, of
course. Charter member."

"Headquarters in The Hague, near the World Court."

"Very appropriate," Charlie said. "And now you are establishing an embassy here . . ."

"To argue our case, yes."

Sucandra said, "We must speak to the hyperpower."

The two men smiled cheerily.

"Well. That's very interesting." Charlie tested the pasta to see if it was ready. "I've been working on climate issues myself, for Senator Chase. I'll have to get you in to talk to him. And you need to hire a good firm of lobbyists."

They regarded him with interest. Padma said, "You think it best?"

"Yes. Definitely. You're here to lobby the U.S. government, and there are pros in town to help foreign governments do that. I've got a good friend working for one of the better firms, I'll put you in touch with him."

Charlie slipped on potholders and lifted the pasta pot over to the sink, tipped it into the colander until it was overflowing. Always a problem with their little colander, which he never thought to replace except at moments like this. "I think my friend's firm already represents the Dutch on these issues—oops—so it's a perfect match. They'll be knowledgeable about your problems."

They nodded. "Thank you for that. We will enjoy that."

They took the food into the little dining room, which was a kind of corner in the passageway between kitchen and living room, and with a great deal of to-and-froing all of them just managed to fit around the dining room table. Joe consented to a booster seat to get his head up to the level of the table, where he shoveled baby food industriously into his mouth or onto the floor, as the case might be, narrating the process all the while in his own tongue. Sucandra and Rudra Cakrin had seated themselves on either side of him, and they watched his performance with pleasure. Both attended to him as if they thought he was speaking a real language. They ate in a style that was not that dissimilar to his, Charlie thought—absorbed, happy, shoveling it in. The sauce was a hit with everyone but Nick, who ate his pasta plain.

Charlie got up and followed Anna out to the kitchen when she went to get the salad. He said to her under his breath, "I bet the old man speaks English too."

"What?"

"It's like in that Ang Lee movie, remember? The old man pretends not to understand English, but really he does? It's like that I bet."

Anna shook her head. "Why would he do that? It's a hassle, all that translating. It doesn't give him any advantage."

"You don't know that! Watch his eyes, see how he's getting it all."

"He's just paying attention. Don't be silly."

"You'll see." Charlie leaned in to her conspiratorially: "Maybe he learned English in an earlier incarnation."

"Quit it," she said, laughing her low laugh. "You learn to pay attention like that."

"Oh and then you'll believe I understand English?"

"That's right yeah."

They returned to the dining room, laughing, and found Joe holding forth in a language anyone could understand, a language of imperious gesture and commanding eye, and the assumption of authority in the world. Which worked like a charm over them all, even though he was babbling.

After the salad they returned to the living room and settled around the coffee table again. Anna brought out tea and cookies. "We'll have to have Tibetan tea next time," she said.

The Khembalis nodded uncertainly.

"An acquired taste," Drepung suggested. "Not actually tea."

"Bitter," Padma said appreciatively.

"You can use as blood coagulant," Sucandra said.

Drepung added, "Also we add yak butter to it, aged until a bit rancid."

"The butter has to be rancid?" Charlie said.

"Traditional."

"Think fermentation," Sucandra explained.

"Well, let's have that for sure. Nick will love it."

A scrunch-faced pretend-scowl from Nick: Yeah right Dad.

Rudra Cakrin sat again with Joe on the floor. He stacked blocks into elaborate towers. Whenever they began to sway, Joe leaned in and chopped them to the floor. Tumbling clack of colored wood, instant catastrophe: the two of them cast their heads back and laughed in exactly the same way.

The others watched. From the couch Drepung observed the old man, smiling fondly, although Charlie thought he also saw traces of the look that Anna had tried to describe to him when explaining why she had connected with them in the first place: a kind of concern that came perhaps from an intensity of love. Charlie knew that feeling. It had been a good idea to invite them over. He had groaned when Anna told him about it, life was simply Too Busy. Or so it had seemed, though at the same time he was somewhat starved for adult company. Now he was enjoying himself, watching Rudra Cakrin and Joe play on the floor as if there were no tomorrow.

Anna was deep in conversation with Sucandra. Charlie heard Sucandra say to her, "We give patients quantities, very small, keep records, of course, and judge results. There is a personal element to all medicine, as you know. People talking about how they feel. You can average numbers, I know you do that, but the subjective feeling remains."

Anna nodded, but Charlie knew this aspect of medicine annoyed her. She kept to the quantitative as much as she could, as far as he could tell, precisely to avoid this kind of subjective residual.

Now she said, "Do you support attempts to make objective studies?"

"Of course," Sucandra replied. "Buddhist science is much like Western science in that regard."

Anna nodded, brow furrowed like a hawk. Her definition of science was extremely narrow. "Reproducible studies?"

"Yes, that is Buddhism precisely."

Now Anna's eyebrows met in a deep vertical furrow that split the horizontal ones higher on her brow. "I thought Buddhism was a kind of feeling—you know, meditation, compassion, that kind of thing?"

"This is to speak of the goal. What the investigation is for. Same for you, yes? Why do you pursue the sciences?"

"Well, to understand things better, I guess."

This was not the kind of thing Anna thought about. It was like asking her why she breathed.

"And why?" Sucandra persisted, watching her.

"Well—just because."

"A matter of curiosity."

"Yes, I suppose so."

"But what if curiosity is a luxury?"

"How so?"

"In that first you must have a full belly. Good health, a certain amount of leisure time, a certain amount of serenity. Absence of pain. Only then can one be curious."

Anna nodded, thinking it over.

Sucandra saw this and continued. "So, if curiosity is a value—a quality to be treasured—a form of contemplation, or prayer—then you must reduce suffering to reach that state. So, in Buddhism, understanding works to reduce suffering, and by reduction of suffering gains more knowledge. Just like science."

Anna frowned. Charlie watched her, fascinated. This was a basic part of her self, this stuff, but largely unconsidered. Self-definition by function. She was a scientist. And science was science, unlike anything else.

Rudra Cakrin leaned forward to say something to Sucandra, who listened to him, then asked him a question in Tibetan. Rudra answered, gesturing at Anna.

Charlie shot a quick look at her—see, he was following things! Evidence!

Rudra Cakrin insisted on something to Sucandra, who then said to Anna, "Rudra wants to say, 'What do you believe in?'"

"Me?"

"Yes. 'What do you believe in?' he says."

"I don't know," she said, surprised. "I believe in the double-blind study."

Charlie laughed, he couldn't help it. Anna blushed and beat on his arm, crying "Stop it! It's true!"

"I know it is," Charlie said, laughing harder, until she started laughing too, along with everyone else, the Khembalis looking delighted—everyone so amused that Joe got mad and stomped his foot to make them stop. But this only made them laugh more. In the end they had to stop so he would not throw a fit.

Rudra Cakrin restored Joe's mood by diving back into the blocks. Soon he and Joe sat half-buried in them, absorbed in their play. Stack them up, knock them down. They certainly spoke the same language.

The others watched them, sipping tea and offering particular blocks to them at certain moments in the construction process. Sucandra and Padma and Anna and Charlie and Nick sat on the couches, talking about Khembalung and Washington, D.C., and how much they were alike.

Then one tower of cubes and beams stood longer than the others had. Rudra Cakrin had constructed it with care, and the repetition of primary colors was pretty: blue, red, yellow, green, blue, yellow, red, green, blue, red, green, red. It was tall enough that ordinarily Joe would have already knocked it over, but he seemed to like this one. He stared at it, mouth hanging open in a less-than-brilliant expression. Rudra Cakrin looked over at Sucandra, said something. Sucandra replied quickly, sounding displeased, which surprised Charlie. Drepung and Padma suddenly paid attention. Rudra Cakrin picked out a yellow cube, showed it to Sucandra, and said something more. He put it on the top of the tower.

"Oooh," Joe said. He tilted his head to one side then the other, observing.

"He likes that one," Charlie noted.

At first no one answered. Then Drepung said, "It's an old Tibetan pattern. You see it in mandalas." He looked to Sucandra, who said something sharp in Tibetan. Rudra Cakrin replied easily, shifted so that his knee knocked into the tower, collapsing it. Joe shuddered as if startled by a noise on the street.

"Ah ga," he declared.

The Tibetans resumed the conversation. Nick was now explaining to Padma the distinction between whales and dolphins. Sucandra went out and helped Charlie a bit with the cleanup in the kitchen; finally Charlie shooed him out, feeling embarrassed that their pots were going to end up substantially cleaner than they had been before; Sucandra had been expertly scrubbing their bottoms with a wire pad found under the sink.

Around nine thirty they took their leave. Anna offered to call a cab, but they said the Metro was fine. They did not need guidance back to the station: "Very easy. And interesting. There are many fine carpets in the shop windows."

Charlie was about to explain that this was the work of Iranians who had come to Washington after the fall of the Shah, but then he thought better of it. Not a happy precedent.

Instead he said to Sucandra, "I'll give my friend Sridar a call and ask him to agree to meet with you. He'll be very helpful to you, even if you don't end up hiring his firm."

"I'm sure. Many thanks." And they were off into the balmy night.

CHAPTER 4

SCIENCE IN THE CAPITAL

What's New from the Department of Unfortunate Statistics?

Extinction Rate in Oceans Now Faster Than on Land. Coral Reef Collapses Leading to Mass Extinctions; Thirty Percent of Warm-water Species Estimated Gone. Fishing Stocks Depleted, UN Declares Scaleback Necessary or Commercial Species Will Crash.

Topsoil Loss Nears a Million Acres a Year. Deforestation now faster in temperate than tropical forests. Only 35% of tropical forests left.

The average Indian consumes 200 kilograms of grain a year; the average American, 800 kilograms; the average Italian, 400 kilograms. The Italian diet was rated best in the world for heart disease.

300 Tons of Weapons-grade Uranium and Plutonium Unaccounted For. High Mutation Rate of Microorganisms Near Radioactive Waste Treatment Sites. Antibiotics in Animal Feed Reduce Medical Effectiveness of Antibiotics for Humans. Environmental estrogens suspected in lowest ever human sperm counts.

Two Billion Tons of Carbon Added to the Atmosphere This Year. One of the five hottest years on record, again. The Fed Hopes U.S. Economy Will Grow by Four Percent in the Final Quarter.

Anna Quibler was in her office getting pumped. Her door was closed, the drapes (installed for her) were drawn. The pump was whirring in its triple sequence: low sigh, wheeze, clunk. The big suction cup made its vacuum pull during the wheeze, tugging her distended left breast outward and causing drips of white milk to fall off the end of her nipple. The milk then ran down a clear tube into the clear bag in its plastic protective tube, which she would fill to the ten-ounce mark.

It was an unconscious activity by now, and she was working on her computer while it happened. She only had to remember not to overfill the bottle, and to switch breasts. She had long since explored the biological and engineering details of this process, and had gotten not exactly bored, but as far as she could go with it, and used to the sameness of it all. There was nothing new to investigate, so she was on to other things. What Anna liked was to study new things. This was what kept her coauthoring papers with her sometime-collaborators at Duke, and working on the editorial board of *The Journal of Statistical Biology*, despite the fact that her job at NSF as director of the Bioinformatics Division might be said to be occupying her more than full-time already. But much of that job was administrative, and like the milk pumping, fully explored. It was in her other projects where she could still learn new things.

Right now her new thing was a little search investigating the NSF's ability to help Khembalung. She navigated her way through the online network of scientific institutions with an ease born of long practice, click by click.

Among NSF's array of departments was an Office of International Science and Engineering, which Anna was impressed to find had managed to garner ten percent of the total NSF budget. It ran an International Biological Program, which sponsored a project called TOGA—"Tropical Oceans, Global Atmosphere." TOGA funded study programs, many including an infrastructure-dispersion element, in which the scientific infrastructure built for the work was given to the host institution at the end of the study period.

Anna had already been tracking NSF's infrastructure dispersion programs for another project, so she added this one to that list too. Projects like these were why people joked about the mobile hanging in the atrium being meant to represent a hammer and sickle, deconstructed so that outsiders would not recognize the socialistic nature of NSF's tendency to give away capital, and to act as if everyone owned the world equally. Anna liked these tendencies and the projects that resulted, though she did not think of them in political terms. She just liked the way NSF focused on work rather than theory or talk. That was her preference too. She liked quantitative solutions to quantified problems.

In this case, the problem was the Khembalis' little island (fifty-two square kilometers, their website said), which was clearly in all-too-good a location for ongoing studies of Gangean flooding and tidal storms in the Indian Ocean. Anna tapped at her keyboard, bookmarking for an e-mail to Drepung, cc'ing also the Khembalung Institute for Higher Studies, which he had told her about. This institute's website indicated it was devoted to medicinal and religious studies (whatever those were, she didn't want to know) but that would be all right—if the Khembalis could mount a good proposal, the need for a wider range of fields among them could become part of its "broader impacts," and thus an advantage: NSF judged proposals on *intellectual merit* and *broader impacts,* the latter to count as twenty-five percent of any evaluation. So it mattered what the project might do in the world.

She searched the web further. USGCRP, the "US Global Change Research Program," two billion dollars a year; the South Asian START Regional Research Centre (SAS-RRC), based at the National Physical Laboratory in New Delhi, stations in Bangladesh, Nepal, and Mauritius . . . INDOEX, the Indian Ocean Experiment, also concerned with aerosols, as was its offspring, Project Asian Brown Cloud. These studied the ever-thickening haze covering South Asia and possibly making the monsoon irregular, with disastrous results. Certainly Khembalung was well situated to join that study. Also ALGAS, the "Asia Least Cost Greenhouse Gas

Abatement Strategy," and LOICZ, "Land Ocean Interaction In the Coastal Zones." That one had to be right on the money; Khembalung would make a perfect study site. Training, networking, biogeochemical cycle budgeting, socioeconomic modeling, impacts on the coastal systems of South Asia. Bookmark the site, add to the e-mail. A research facility in the mouth of the Ganges would be a very useful thing for all concerned.

"Ah shit."

She had overflowed the milk bottle. Not the first time. She turned off the pump, poured off some of the milk from the full bottle into a four-ounce sack. She always filled quite a few four-ouncers, for use as snacks; she had never told Charlie that most of these were the result of her inattention.

As for herself, she was starving. It was always that way after pumping sessions. Each twenty ounces of milk she gave was the result of some thousand calories burned by her in the previous day, as far as she had been able to calculate; the analyses she had found had been pretty rough. In any case, she could with a clear conscience (and great pleasure) run down to the pizza place and eat till she was stuffed. Indeed she needed to eat or she would get lightheaded.

But first she had to pump the other breast at least a little, because let-down happened in both when she pumped, and she would end up uncomfortable if she didn't. So she put the ten-ouncer in the little refrigerator, then got the other side going into the four-ouncer, while printing out a list of all the sites she had visited.

She called Drepung.

"Drepung, can you meet for lunch? I've got some ideas for how you might get some science support."

"Yes, thanks. I'll meet you at the Food Factory in twenty minutes, I'm just trying to buy some shoes for Rudra."

"What kind are you getting him?"

"Running shoes. He'll love them."

On her way out she ran into Frank, also headed for the elevator.

"What you got?" he asked, gesturing at her list.

"Some stuff for the Khembalis," she said.

"So they can study how to adapt to higher sea levels?"

She frowned. "No, it's more than that. We can get them a lot of infrastructural help."

"Good. But, you know. In the end they're going to need more. And NSF doesn't do remediation. It just serves its clients."

Frank's comment bugged Anna, and after a nice lunch with Drepung she went up to her office and called Sophie Harper, NSF's liaison to Congress.

"Sophie, is there any way that NSF can set the agenda, so to speak?"

"Well, we ask Congress for funding in very specific ways, and they designate the money for those purposes."

"So we might be able to ask for funds for certain things?"

"Yes, we do that. To an extent we set our own agenda. That's why the appropriations committees don't like us very much."

"Why?"

"Because they hold the purse strings, and they're very jealous of that power. I've had senators who believe the Earth is flat say to me, 'Are you trying to tell me that you know what's good for science better than I do?' And of course that's exactly what I'm trying to tell them, because it's true, but what can you say? That's the kind of person we sometimes have to deal with. And even with the best of committees, there's a basic dislike for science's autonomy."

"But we're only free to study things."

"I don't know what you mean."

Anna sighed. "I don't either. Listen Sophie, thanks for that. I'll get back to you when I have a better idea what I'm trying to ask."

"Always here. Check out NSF's history pages on the website, you'll learn some things you didn't know."

Anna hung up, and then did that very thing.

She had never gone to the website's history pages before; she was not much for that kind of thing. But as she read, she realized Sophie had been right; because she had worked there so long, she had felt that she knew NSF's story. But it wasn't true.

After World War Two, Vannevar Bush, head of the wartime Office of Science and Technology, had pushed for a permanent federal agency to support basic scientific research. He argued that it was basic scientific research that had won the war (radar, penicillin, the bomb), and Congress had been convinced, and had passed a bill bringing the NSF into being.

After that it was one battle after another, mostly for funding. Many administrations and Congresses had feared and hated science, as far as Anna could see. They didn't want to know things; it might get in the way of business.

For Anna there could be no greater intellectual crime. It was incomprehensible to her: they did not want to know things! And yet they did want to call the shots. To Anna this was crazy. Even Joe's logic was stronger. How could such people exist, what could they be thinking? On what basis did they build such an incoherent mix of desires, to want to stay ignorant and to be powerful as well? Were these two parts of the same insanity?

She abandoned that train of thought, and read on to the end of the brief history. Throughout the years, NSF's purposes and methods had held fast: to support basic research; to award grants; to decide things by peer review rather than bureaucratic fiat; to hire skilled scientists for permanent staff; to hire temporary staff from the expert cutting edges in every field.

Anna believed in all these, and she believed they had done demonstrable good. Fifty thousand proposals a year, eighty thousand people peer-reviewing them, ten thousand new proposals funded, twenty thousand grants continuing to be supported. All functioning to expand scientific knowledge, and the influence of science in human affairs.

She sat back in her chair, thinking it over. All that basic research, all that good work; and yet—thinking over the state of the world—somehow it had not been enough. Possibly they would have to consider doing something more. What that might be was not so clear.

Primates in the driver's seat. It looked like they should all be dead. Multicar accidents, bloody incidents of road rage. Cars should have been ramming each other in huge demolition derbies, a global auto-da-fé.

But they were social creatures. The brain had ballooned precisely to enable it to make the calculations necessary to get along in groups. These were the parts of the brain engaged when people drove in crowded traffic. Thus along with all the jockeying and frustration came the satisfactions of winning a competition, or the solidarities of cooperating to mutual advantage. Let that poor idiot merge before his on-ramp lane disappeared; it would pay off later in the overall speed of traffic. Thus the little primate buzz.

When things went well. But so often what one saw were people playing badly. It was like a giant game of prisoner's dilemma, the classic game in which two prisoners are separated and asked to tell tales on the other one, with release offered to them if they do. The standard computer model scoring system had it that if the prisoners cooperate with each other by staying silent, they each get three points; if both defect against the other, they each get one point; and if one defects and the other doesn't, the defector gets five points and the sap gets zero points. Using this scoring system to play the game time after time, there is a first iteration which says, it is best to always defect. That's the strategy that will gain the most points over the long haul, the computer simulations said—if you are only playing strangers once, and never seeing them again. And of course traffic looked as if it was that situation.

But the shadow of the future made all the difference. Day in and day out, you drove into the same traffic jam, with the same basic population of players. If you therefore played the game as if playing with the same opponent every time, which in a sense you were, with you learning them and them learning you, then more elaborate strategies would gain more points than "always defect." The first version of the more successful strategy was called "tit-for-tat," in which you did to your opponent what they last did to you. This outcompeted "always defect," which in a way was a rather encouraging finding. But tit-for-tat was not the perfect strategy, because it could spiral in either direction, good or bad, and the bad was an endless feud. Thus further trials had found successful variously revised versions of tit-for-tat, like "generous tit-for-tat," in which you gave opponents one defection before turning on them, or "always generous," which in certain limited conditions worked well. Or, the most powerful strategy Frank knew of, an irregularly generous tit-for-tat where you forgave defecting opponents once before turning on them, but only about a third of the time, and unpredictably, so you were not regularly taken advantage of by one of the less cooperative strategies, but could still pull out of a death spiral of tit-for-tat feuding if one should arise. Various versions of these "firm but fair" irregular strategies appeared to be best if you were dealing with the same opponent over and over.

In traffic, at work, in relationships of every kind—social life was nothing but a series of prisoners' dilemmas. Compete or cooperate? Be selfish or generous? It would be best if you could always trust other players to cooperate, and safely practice always generous; but in real life people did not turn out to earn that trust. That was one of the great shocks of adolescence, perhaps, that realization; which alas came to many at an even younger age. And after that you had to work things out case by case, your strategy being then a matter of your history, or your personality, who could say.

Traffic was not a good place to try to decide. Stop and go, stop and go, at a speed just faster than Frank could have walked. It had been a bad mistake to get on the Beltway in the first place. By and large Beltway drivers were defectors. In general, drivers on the East Coast were less generous than Californians, Frank found. Maybe this only meant Californians had lived through that many more traffic jams. In California cars in two merging lanes would alternate like the halves of a zipper, at considerable speed, everyone trusting everyone else to know the game and play it right. Here on the Beltway, on the other hand, it was always defect. That was what all the SUVs were about, everyone girding up for a crash. Every SUV was a defection. And so it was slow: unnecessarily, unobservantly slow. It made you want to scream.

And from time to time, Frank did scream. This was a different primate satisfaction: in traffic you could loudly curse people from ten feet away and they did not hear you. There was no way the primate brain could explain this, so it was an example of the "technological sublime." And it was indeed sublime to lose all restraint and curse someone ferociously from a few feet away, and yet suffer no ramifications from such a grave affront.

So he crept forward in traffic, cursing. The Beltway was badly over-loaded at this hour. It was so bad that Frank realized he was going to be late to work. And this was the morning when his bioinformatics panel was to begin! He needed to be there for the panel to start on time. The panel members were all in town, some would be gathering at this very moment in their third-floor conference room, ready to go, feeling that there wasn't enough time to judge all the proposals on the docket. Frank had crowded the schedule on purpose so they would not have time to properly evaluate every proposal. To arrive late in this situation would be bad form indeed. There would be looks; he would have to make excuses. It might even interfere with his plan.

So coming to Route 66, he impulsively decided to get on it going east, even though at this hour it was reserved for High Occupancy Vehicles only. Normally Frank obeyed this rule, but now he took the turn and curved onto 66, where traffic was indeed moving faster. Every vehicle was occupied by at least two people, of course, and Frank stayed in the right lane and drove as unobtrusively as possible, counting on the generally inward attention of people in vehicles to keep too many people from noticing his transgression. Of course there were highway patrol cars on the lookout for lawbreakers like Frank, so he was taking a risk that he didn't like to take, but it seemed to him a lower risk than staying on the Beltway, in terms of getting to work on time.

He drove in great suspense, therefore, until finally he could signal to get off at Fairfax. Then as he approached he saw a police car parked beside the exit, its officers walking back toward their car after dealing with another miscreant. They might easily look up and see him.

A big old pickup truck was slowing down to exit before him, and again without pausing to consider his actions, Frank floored the accelerator, swerved around the truck on its left side, using it to block the policemen's view, then cut back across in front of the truck, accelerating so as not to bother it. Room to spare and no one the wiser. He curved to the right down the exit lane, slowing for the light around the turn.

Suddenly there was loud honking from behind, and his rearview mirror was entirely filled by the front grill of the pickup truck, its headlights at about the same height as the roof of his car. Frank speeded up. Then, closing on the car in front of him, he had to slow down. Suddenly the truck was now passing him on the left, as he had passed it earlier, even though this took the truck up onto the exit lane's tilted shoulder. Frank looked and glimpsed the infuriated face of the driver, leaning over to shout down at him. Long stringy hair, mustache, red skin, furious anger.

Frank looked over again and shrugged, making a face and gesture that said, What? He slowed down so that the truck could cut in front of him, a good thing as it slammed into the lane so hard it missed Frank's left headlight by an inch. He would have struck Frank for sure if Frank hadn't slowed down. What a jerk!

Then the guy hit his brakes so hard that Frank nearly rear-ended him, which could have been a disaster given how high the truck was jacked up. Frank would have hit windshield first.

"What the fuck!" Frank said, shocked. "Fuck you! I didn't come anywhere near you!"

The truck came to a full stop, right there on the exit lane.

"Jesus, you fucking idiot!" Frank shouted.

Maybe Frank had cut closer to this guy than he thought he had. Or maybe the guy was hounding him for driving solo on 66, even though he had been doing the same thing himself. Now his door flew open and out he jumped, swaggering back toward Frank. He caught sight of Frank still shouting, stopped and pointed a quivering finger, reached into the bed of his truck, and pulled out a crowbar.

Frank reversed gear, backed up and braked, shifted into drive, and hauled on his steering wheel as he accelerated around the pickup truck's right side. People behind them were honking, but they didn't know the half of it. Frank zoomed down the now-empty exit lane, shouting triumphant abuse at the crazy guy.

Unfortunately the traffic light at the end of the exit ramp was red and there was a car stopped there, waiting for it to change. Frank had to stop. Instantly there was a thunk and he jerked forward. The pickup truck had rear-ended him, tapping him hard from behind.

"YOU FUCKER!" Frank shouted, now frightened; he had tangled with a madman! The truck was backing up, presumably to ram him again, so he put his little Honda in reverse and shot back into the truck, like hitting a wall, then shifted again and shot off into the narrow gap to the right of the car waiting at the light, turning right and accelerating into a gap between the cars zipping by, which caused more angry honks. He checked his rear-view mirror and saw that light had changed and the pickup truck was turning to follow him, and not far behind. "Shit!"

Frank accelerated, saw an opening in traffic coming the other way, and took a sharp left across all lanes onto Glebe, even though it was the wrong direction for NSF. Then he floored it and began weaving desperately through cars he was rapidly overtaking, checking the rearview mirror when he could. The pickup appeared in the distance, squealing onto Glebe after him. Frank cursed in dismay.

He decided to drive directly to a fire station he recalled seeing on Lee Highway. He took a left on Lee and accelerated as hard as the little fuel-cell car could to the fire station, squealing into its parking lot and then jumping out and hurrying toward the building, looking back down Lee toward Glebe.

But the madman never appeared. Gone. Lost the trail, or lost interest. Off to harass someone else.

Cursing still, Frank checked his car's rear. No visible damage, amazingly. He got back in and drove south to the NSF building, involuntarily reliving the experience. He had no clear idea why it had happened. He had driven around the guy but he had not really cut him off, and though it was true he had been poaching on 66, so had the guy. It was inexplicable; and it occurred to him that in the face of such behavior, modeling exercises like prisoner's dilemma were useless. People did not make rational judgments. Especially, perhaps, the people driving too-large pickup trucks, this one of the dirty-and-dinged variety rather than the factory-fresh steroidal battleships that many in the area drove. Possibly it had been some kind of class thing, the resentment of an unemployed gas-guzzler against a white-collar type in a fuel-cell car. The past attacking the future, reactionary attacking progressive, poor attacking affluent. A beta male in an alpha machine, enraged that an alpha male thought he was so alpha he could zip around in a beta machine and get away with it.

Something like that. Some kind of asshole jerk-off loser, already drunk and disorderly at 7 A.M.

Despite all that drama, Frank found himself driving into the NSF building's basement parking with just enough time to get to the elevators and up to the third floor at the last possible on-time moment. He hurried to that floor's men's room, splashed water on his face. He had to clear his mind of the ugly incident immediately, and it had been so strange and unpleasant that this was not particularly difficult. Incongruent awfulness without consequence is easily dismissed from the mind. So he pulled himself together, went out to do his job. Time to concentrate on the day's work. His plan for the panel was locked in by the people he had convened for it. The scare on the road only hardened his resolve, chilled his blood.

He entered the conference room assigned to their panel. Its big inner window gave everyone the standard view of the rest of NSF, and the panelists who hadn't been there before looked up into the beehive of offices making the usual comments about *Rear Window* and the like. "A kind of ersatz collegiality," one of them said, must have been Nigel Pritchard.

"Keeps people working, to always feel watched like this."

On the savannah a view like this would have come from a high outcrop, where the troop would be surveying everything important in their lives, secure in the realm of grooming, of chatter, of dominance conflicts. Perfect, in other words, for a grant proposal evaluation panel, which in essence was one of the most ancient of discussions: whom do we let in, whom do we kick out? A basic troop economy, of social credit, of access to food and mates—everything measured and exchanged in deeds good and bad—yes—it was another game of prisoner's dilemma. They never ended.

Frank liked this one. It was very nuanced compared to most of them, and one of the few still outside the world of money. Anonymous peer review—unpaid labor—a scandal!

But science didn't work like capitalism. That was the rub, that was one of the many rubs in the general dysfunction of the world. Capitalism ruled, but money was too simplistic and inadequate a measure of the wealth that science generated. In science, one built up over the course of a career a fund of "scientific credit," by giving work to the system in a way that could seem altruistic. People remembered what you gave, and later on there were various forms of return on the gift—jobs, labs. In that sense a good investment for the individual, but in the form of a gift to the group. It was the non-zero-sum game that prisoner's dilemma could become if everyone played by the strategies of always generous, or at the least, firm-but-fair. That was one of the things science was—a place that one entered by agreeing to hold to the strategies of cooperation, to maximize the total return of the game.

In theory that was true. It was also the usual troop of primates. There was a lot of tit-for-tat. Defections happened. Everyone was jockeying for a project of their own. As long as that was generating enough income for a comfortable physical existence for oneself and one's family, then one had reached the optimal human state. Having money beyond that was unnecessary, and usually involved a descent into the world of hassle and stupidity. That was what greed got you. So there was in science a sufficiency of means, and an achievable limited goal, that kept it tightly aligned with the brain's deepest savannah values. A scientist wanted the same things out of life as an Australopithecus; and here they were.

Thus Frank surveyed the panelists milling about the room with a rare degree of happiness. "Let's get started."

They sat down, putting laptops and coffee cups beside the computer consoles built into the tabletop. These allowed the panelists to see a spreadsheet page for each proposal in turn, displaying their grades and comments. This particular group all knew the drill. Some of them had met before, and most had read each other's work.

There were eight of them sitting around the long, cluttered conference table.

>   Dr. Frank Vanderwal, moderator, NSF (on leave from University of
>   California, San Diego, Department of Bioinformatics)
>   Dr. Nigel Pritchard, Georgia Institute of Technology,
>   Computer Sciences
>   Dr. Alice Freundlich, Harvard University,
>   Department of Biochemistry
>   Dr. Habib Ndina, University of Virginia Medical School
>   Dr. Stuart Thornton, University of Maryland,
>   College Park, Genomics Department
>   Dr. Francesca Taolini, Massachusetts Institute of Technology,
>   Center for Biocomputational Studies
>   Dr. Jerome Frenkel, University of Pennsylvania,
>   Department of Genomics
>   Dr. Yao Lee, Cambridge University (visiting George Washington
>   University's Department of Microbiology)

Frank made his usual introductory remarks and then said, "We've got a lot of them this time. I'm sorry it's so many, but that's what we've received. I'm sure we'll hack our way through them all if we keep on track. Let's start with the fifteen-minutes-per-jacket drill, and see if we can get twelve or even fourteen done before lunch. Sound good?"

Everyone nodded and tapped away, calling up the first one.

"Oh, and before we start, let's have everyone give me their conflict-of-interest forms, please. I have to remind you that as referees here, you have a conflict if you're the applying principal investigator's thesis advisor or advisee, an employee of the same institution as the P.I. or a co-P.I., a collaborator within the last four years of the P.I. or a co-P.I., an applicant for employment in any department at the submitting institution, a recipient of an honorarium or other pay from the submitting institution within the last year, someone with a close personal relationship to the P.I. or a co-P.I., a shareholder in a company participating in the proposal, or someone who would otherwise gain or lose financially if the proposal were awarded or declined.

"Everybody got that? Okay, hand those forms down to me, then. We'll have a couple of people step outside for some of the proposals today, but mostly we're clear as far as I know, is that right?"

"I'll be leaving for the Esterhaus proposal, as I told you," Stuart Thornton said.

Then they started the group evaluations. This was the heart of their task for that day and the next—also the heart of NSF's method, indeed of science more generally. Peer review; a jury of fellow experts. Frank clicked the first proposal's page onto his screen. "Seven reviewers, forty-four jackets. Let's start with EIA-02 18599, 'Electromagnetic and Informational Processes in Molecular Polymers.' Habib, you're the lead on this?"

Habib Ndina nodded and opened with a description of the proposal. "They want to immobilize cytoskeletal networks on biochips, and explore whether tubulin can be used as bits in protein logic gates. They intend to do this by measuring the electric dipole moment, and what the P.I. calls the predicted kink-solitonic electric dipole moment flip waves."

"Predicted by whom?"

"By the P.I." Habib smiled. "He also states that this will be a method to test out the theories of the so-called 'quantum brain.'"

"Hmm." People read past the abstract.

"What are you thinking?" Frank said after a while. "I see Habib has given it a Good, Stuart a Fair, and Alice a Very Good."

This represented the middle range of their scale, which ran Poor, Fair, Good, Very Good, and Excellent.

Habib replied first. "I'm not so sure that you can get these biochips to array in neural nets. I saw Inouye try something like that at MIT, and they got stuck at the level of chip viability."

"Hmm."

The others chimed in with questions and opinions. At the end of fifteen minutes, Frank stopped the discussion and asked them to mark their final judgments in the two categories they used, intellectual merit and broader impacts.

Frank summed up. "Four Goods, two Very Goods, and a Fair. Okay, let's move on. But tell you what, I'm going to start the big board right now."

He had a whiteboard in the corner next to him, and a pile of Post-it pads on the table. He drew three zones on the whiteboard with marker, and wrote at the top "Fund," "Fund If Possible," and "Don't Fund."

"I'll put this one in the Fund If Possible column for now, although naturally it may get bumped." He stuck the proposal's Post-it in the middle zone. "We'll move these around as the day progresses and we get a sense of the range."

Then they began the next one. "Okay. 'Efficient Decoherence Control Algorithms for Computing Genome Construction.'"

This jacket Frank had assigned to Stuart Thornton.

Thornton started by shaking his head. "This one's gotten two Goods and two Fairs, and it wasn't very impressive to me either. It may be a candidate for limited discussion. It doesn't really exhibit a grasp of the difficulties involved with codon tampering, and I think it replicates the work being done in Seattle. The applicant seems to have been too busy with the broader impacts component to fully acquaint himself with the literature. Besides which, it won't work."

People laughed shortly at this extra measure of disdain, which was palpable, and to those who didn't know Thornton, a little surprising. But Frank had seen Stuart Thornton on panels before. He was the kind of scientist who habitually displayed an ultrapure devotion to the scientific method, in the form of a relentless skepticism about everything. No study was designed tightly enough, no data were clean enough. To Frank it seemed obvious that it was really a kind of insecurity, part of the gestural set of a beta male convincing the group he was tough enough to be an alpha male.

The problem with these gestures was that in science, one's intellectual power was like the muscle mass of an Australopithecus, there for all to see. You couldn't fake it. No matter how much you ruffed your fur or exposed your teeth, in the end your intellectual strength was discernable in what you said and how insightful it was. Mere skepticism was like baring teeth; anyone could do it. For that reason Thornton was a bad choice for a panel, because while people could see his attitude and try to discount it, he set a tone that was hard to shake off. If there was an always-defector in the group, one had to be less generous oneself in order not to become a sap.

That was why Frank had invited him.

Thornton went on: "The basic problem is at the level of their understanding of an algorithm. An algorithm is not just a simple sequence of mathematical operations that can each be performed in turn. It's a matter of designing a grammar that will adjust the operations at each stage, depending on the results from the stage before. There's a very specific encoding math that makes that work. They don't have that here."

The others nodded and tapped in notes at their consoles. Soon enough they were on to the next proposal, with that one posted under "Don't Fund."

Now Frank could predict with some confidence how the rest of the day would go. A depressed norm had been set, and even though the third reporter, Alice Freundlich from Harvard, subtly rebuked Thornton by talking about how well designed her first jacket was, she did so in a less generous context, and was not overenthusiastic. "They think that the evolutionary processes of gene conservation can be mapped by cascade studies, and they want to model it with big computer array simulations. They claim they'll be able to identify genes prone to mutation."

Habib Ndina shook his head. He too was a habitual skeptic, although from a much deeper well of intelligence than Thornton's; he wasn't just making a display, he was thinking. "Isn't the genome's past pretty much mapped by now?" he complained. "Do we really need more about evolutionary history?"

"Well, maybe not. Broader impacts might suffer there."

And so the day proceeded, and, with some subliminal prompting from Frank ("Are you sure they have the lab space?" "Do you think that's really true though?" "How would that work?" "How could that work?") the time came when the full Shooting Gallery Syndrome had emerged. The panelists very slightly lost contact with their sense of the proposals as human efforts performed under a deadline, and started to compare them to some perfect model of scientific practice. In that light, of course, all the candidates were wanting. They all had feet of clay and so their proposals all became clay pigeons, cast into the air for the group to take potshots at. New jacket tossed up: bang! bang! bang!

"This one's toast," someone said at one point.

Of course a few people in such a situation would stay anchored, and begin to shake their heads or wrinkle their noses, or even protest the mood, humorously or otherwise. But Frank had avoided inviting any of the real stalwarts he knew, and Alice Freundlich did no more than keep things pleasant. The impulse in a group toward piling on was so strong that it often took on extraordinary momentum. On the savannah it would have meant an expulsion and a hungry night out. Or some poor guy torn limb from limb.

Frank didn't need to tip things that far. Nothing explicit, nothing heavy. He was only the facilitator. He did not express an obvious opinion on the substance of the proposals at any point. He watched the clock, ran down the list, asked if everybody had said what they wanted to say when there was three minutes left out of the fifteen; made sure everyone got their scores into the system at the end of the discussion period. "That's an Excellent and five Very Goods. Alice do you have your scores on this one?"

Meanwhile the discussions got tougher and tougher.

"I don't know what she could have been thinking with this one, it's absurd!"

"Let me start by suggesting limited discussion."

Frank began subtly to apply the brakes. He didn't want them to think he was a bad panel manager.

Nevertheless, the attack mood gained momentum. Baboons descending on wounded prey; it was almost Pavlovian, a food-rewarded joy in destruction. The pleasure taken in wrecking anything meticulous. Frank had seen it many times: a carpenter doing demolition with a sledgehammer, a vet who went duck-hunting on weekends . . . It was unfortunate, given their current overextended moment in planetary history, but nevertheless real. As a species they were therefore probably doomed. And so the only real adaptive strategy, for the individual, was to do one's best to secure one's own position. And sometimes that meant a little strategic defection.

Near the end of the day it was Thornton's turn again. Finally they had come to the proposal from Yann Pierzinski. People were getting tired.

Frank said, "Okay, almost done here. Let's finish them off, shall we? Two more to go. Stu, we're to you again, on 'Algorithmic Analysis of Palindromic Codon Sequences as Predictors of Gene/Protein Expression.' Mandel and Pierzinski, Caltech."

Thornton shook his head wearily. "I see it's got a couple of Very Goods from people, but I give it a Fair. It's a nice thought, but it seems to be promising too much. I mean, predicting the proteome from the genome would be enough in itself, but then understanding how the genome evolved, building error-tolerant biocomputers—it's like a list of the big unsolved problems."

Francesca Taolini asked him what he thought of the algorithm that the proposal hoped to develop.

"It's too sketchy to be sure! That's really what he's hoping to find, as far as I can tell. There would be a final toolbox with a software environment and language, then a gene grammar to makes sense of palindromes in particular, he seems to think those are important, but I think they're just redundancy and repair sequences, that's why the palindromic structure. They're like the reinforcement at the bottom of a zipper. To think that he could use this to predict all the proteins a gene would produce!"

"But if you could, you would see what proteins you would get without needing to do microassays," Francesca pointed out. "That would be very useful. I thought the line he was following had potential, myself. I know people working on something like this, and it would be good to have more people on it, it's a broad front. That's why I gave it a Very Good, and I'd still recommend we fund it." She kept her eyes on her screen.

"Well yeah," Thornton said crossly, "but where would he get the biosensors that would tell him if he was right or not? There's no controls."

"That would be someone else's problem. If the predictions were turning out good you wouldn't have to test all of them, that would be the point."

Frank waited a beat. "Anyone else?" he said in a neutral tone.

Pritchard and Yao Lee joined in. Lee obviously thought it was a good idea, in theory. He started describing it as a kind of cookbook with evolving recipes, and Frank ventured to say, "How would that work?"

"Well, by successive iterations of the operation, you know. It would be to get you started, suggest directions to try."

"Look," Francesca interjected, "eventually we're going to have to tackle this issue, because until we do, the mechanics of gene expression are just a black box. It's a very valid line of inquiry."

"Habib?" Frank asked.

"It would be nice, I guess, if he could make it work. It's not so easy. It would be like a roll of the dice to support it."

Before Francesca could collect herself and start again, Frank said, "Well, we could go round and round on that, but we're out of time on this one, and it's late. Those of you who haven't done it yet, write down your scores, and let's finish with one more from Alice before we go to dinner."

Hunger made them nod and tap away at their consoles, and then they were on to the last one for the day, "Ribozymes as Molecular Logic Gates." When they were done with that, Frank stuck its Post-it on the whiteboard with the rest. Each little square of paper had its proposal's averaged scores written on it. It was a tight scale; the difference between 4.63 and 4.70 could matter a great deal. They had already put three proposals in the "Fund" column, two in the "Fund If Possible," and six in the "Do Not Fund." The rest were stuck to the bottom of the board, waiting to be sorted out the following day. Pierzinski's was among those.

That evening the group went out for dinner at Tara, a good nearby Thai restaurant with a wall-sized fish tank. The conversation was animated and wide-ranging, the mood getting better as the meal wore on. Afterward a few of them went to the hotel bar; the rest retreated to their rooms. At eight the next morning they were back in the conference room doing everything over again, working their way through the proposals with an increasing efficiency. Thornton recused himself for a discussion of a proposal from someone at his university, and the mood in the room noticeably lightened; even when he returned they held to this. They were learning each other's predilections, and sometimes jetted off into discussions of theory that were very interesting even though only a few minutes long. Some of the proposals brought up interesting problems, and several strong ones in a row made them aware of just how amazing contemporary work in bioinformatics was, and what some of the potential benefits for human health might be, if all this were to come together and make a robust biotechnology. The shadow of a good future drove the group toward more generous strategies. The second day went better. The scores were, on average, higher.

"My Lord," Alice said at one point, looking at the whiteboard. "There are going to be some very good proposals that we're not going to be able to fund."

Everyone nodded. It was a common feeling at the end of a panel. Rate of funded proposals was down to around ten or twenty percent these days.

"I sometimes wonder what would happen if we could fund about ninety percent of all the applications. You know, only reject the limited-discussions. Fund everything else."

"It might speed things up."

"Might cause a revolution."

"Now back to reality," Frank suggested. "Last jacket here."

When they had all tapped in their grading of the forty-fourth jacket, Frank quickly crunched the numbers on his general spreadsheet, sorting the applicants into a hierarchy from one to forty-four, with a lot of ties.

He printed out the results, including the funding each proposal was asking for; then called the group back to order. They started moving the unsorted Post-its up into one or another of the three columns.

Pierzinski's proposal had ended up ranked fourteenth out of the forty-four. It wouldn't have been that high if it weren't for Francesca. Now she urged them to fund it; but because it was in fourteenth place, the group decided it should be put in "Fund If Possible," with a bullet.

Frank moved its Post-it on the whiteboard up into the "Fund If Possible" column, keeping his face perfectly blank. There were eight in "Fund If Possible," six in "Fund," twelve in "Do Not Fund." Eighteen to go, therefore, but the arithmetic of the situation would doom most of these to the "Do Not Fund" column, with a few stuck into the "Fund If Possible" as faint hopes, and only the best couple funded.

Later it would be Frank's job to fill out a Form Seven for every proposal, summarizing the key aspects of the discussion, acknowledging outlier reviews that were more than one full place off the average, and explaining any Excellents awarded to nonfunded reviews; this was part of keeping the process transparent to the applicants, and making sure that nothing untoward happened. The panel was advisory only, NSF had the right to overrule it, but in the great majority of cases the panels' judgments would stand—that was the whole point—that was scientific objectivity, at least in this part of the process.

In a way it was funny. Solicit seven intensely subjective and sometimes contradictory opinions; quantify them; average them; and that was objectivity. A numerical grading that you could point to on a graph. Ridiculous, of course. But it was the best they could do. Indeed, what other choice did they have? No algorithm could make these kinds of decisions. The only computer powerful enough to do it was one made up of a networked array of human brains—that is to say, a panel. Beyond that they could not reach.

So they discussed the proposals one last time, their scientific potential and also their educational and benefit-to-society aspects, the "broader impacts" rubric, usually spelled out rather vaguely in the proposals, and unpopular with research purists. But as Frank put it now, "NSF isn't here just to do science but also to promote science, and that means all these other criteria. What it will add to society." What Anna will do with it, he almost said.

And speak of the devil, Anna came in to thank the panelists for their efforts; she was slightly flushed and formal in her remarks. When she left, Frank said, "Thanks from me too. It's been exhausting as usual, but good work was done. I hope to see all of you here again at some point, but I won't bother you too soon either. I know some of you have planes to catch, so let's quit now, and if any of you have anything else you want to add, tell me individually. Okay, we're done."

Frank printed out a final copy of the spreadsheet. The money numbers

suggested they would end up funding about ten of the forty-four proposals. There were seven in the "Fund" column already, and six of those in the
"Fund If Possible" column had been ranked slightly higher than Yann Pierzinski's proposal. If Frank, as NSF's representative, did not exercise any of
his discretionary power to find a way to fund it, that proposal would be
declined.

Another day for Charlie and Joe. A late spring morning, temperatures already in the high nineties and rising, humidity likewise.

They stayed in the house for the balm of the air-conditioning, falling out of the ceiling vents like spills of clear syrup. They wrestled, they cleaned house, they ate breakfast and elevenses. Charlie read some of the *Post* while Joe devastated dinosaurs. Something in the *Post* about India's drought reminded Charlie of the Khembalis, and he put in his earphone and called his friend Sridar.

"Charlie, good to hear from you! I got your message."

"Oh good, I was hoping. How's the lobbying going?"

"We're keeping at it. We've got some interesting clients."

"As always."

Sridar worked for Branson & Ananda, a small but prestigious firm representing several foreign governments in their dealings with the American government. Some of these governments had policies and customs at home that made representing them to Congress a challenge.

"So you said something about a new country?"

"It's through Anna, like I said. Have you heard of Khembalung?"

"I think so. One of the League of Drowning Nations?"

"Yeah that's right."

"You're asking me to take on a sinking island?"

"They're not sinking, it's the ocean that's rising."

"Even worse! What are we going to do about that, stop global warming?"

"Well, yeah. That's the idea. And you know, you'd have lots of allies."

"Uh-huh."

"Anyway they could use your help, and they're good guys. Interesting. I think you'd enjoy them. You should meet them and see."

"Okay, my plate is kind of full right now, but I could do that."

"Oh good. Thanks Sridar, I appreciate that."

"No problem. Hey can I have Krakatoa too?"

After that Charlie was in the mood to talk, but he had no reason to call anybody. He and Joe played again. Bored, Charlie even resorted to turning on the TV. A pundit show came on and helplessly he watched. "They are such lapdogs," he complained to Joe. "It's disgusting."

"BOOM!" Joe concurred, catching Charlie's mood and flinging a tyrannosaurus into the radiator with a clang.

"That's right," Charlie said. "Good job."

He changed the channel to ESPN 5, which showed classic women's volleyball doubles all day along. Retired guys at home must be a big demographic. But Joe had had enough of being in the house. "Go!" he said imperiously, hammering the front door with a diplodocus. "Go! Go! Go!"

"All right all right."

Joe's point was undeniable. They couldn't stay in this house all day. "Let's go down to the Mall, we haven't done that for a while. The Mall, Joe! But you have to get in your backpack."

Joe nodded and tried to climb into his baby backpack immediately, a very tippy business. He was ready to party.

"Wait, let's change your diaper first."

"NO!"

"Ah come on Joe. Yes."

"NO!"

"But yes."

They fought like maniacs through a diaper change, each ruthless and determined, each shouting, beating, pinching. Charlie did the necessary things.

Red-faced and sweating, finally they were ready to emerge from the house into the steambath of the city. Out they went. Down to the Metro, down into that dim cool underground world.

It would have been good if the Metro pacified Joe as it once had Nick, but in fact it usually energized him. Charlie could not understand that; he himself found the dim coolness a powerful soporific. But Joe wanted to play around just above the drop to the power rail, being naturally attracted to that enormous source of energy. The hundred-thousand-watt child. Charlie ran around keeping him from the edge. Finally a train came.

Joe liked the Metro cars. He stood on the seat next to Charlie and stared at the concrete walls sliding by outside the tinted windows of the car, then at the bright orange or pink seats, the ads, the people in their car, the brief views of the underground stations they stopped in.

A young black man got on carrying a helium-filled birthday balloon. He sat down across the car from Charlie and Joe. Joe stared at the balloon, boggled by it. Clearly it was for him a kind of miraculous object. The youth pulled down on its string and let the balloon jump back up to its full extension. Joe jerked, then burst out laughing. His giggle was like his mom's, a low gorgeous burbling. People in the car grinned to hear it. The young man pulled the balloon down again, let it go again. Joe laughed so hard he had to sit down. People began to laugh with him, they couldn't help it. The young man was smiling shyly. He did the trick again and now the whole car followed Joe into paroxysms of laughter. They laughed all the way to Metro Center.

Charlie got out, grinning, and carried Joe to the Blue/Orange level. He marveled at the infectiousness of moods in a group. Strangers who would never meet again, unified suddenly by a youth and toddler playing a game. By laughter itself. Maybe the real oddity was how much one's fellow citizens were usually like furniture in one's life.

Joe bounced in Charlie's arms. He liked Metro Center's crisscrossing mysterious vastness. The incident of the balloon was already forgotten. Their next Metro car reached the Smithsonian station, and Charlie put Joe into the backpack, and they rode the escalator up into the kiln blaze of the Mall.

The sky was milky white everywhere. It felt like the inside of a sauna. Charlie fought his way through the heat to an open patch of grass in the shade of the Washington Monument. He sat them down and got out some food. The big views up to the Capitol and down to the Lincoln Memorial pleased him. Out from under the great forest. It was like escaping Mirkwood. This in Charlie's opinion accounted for the great popularity of the Mall; the monuments and the Smithsonian buildings were nice but supplementary, it was really a matter of getting out into the open. The ordinary reality of the American West was like a glimpse of heaven here in the green depths of the swamp.

Charlie cherished the old story of how the first thirteen states had needed a capital, but no particular state could be allowed to nab that honor; so they had bickered, you give up some land, no, you give it, until finally Virginia had said to Maryland, look, where the Potomac meets the Anacostia there's a big nasty swamp. It's worthless, dreadful, pestilent land. You'll never be able to make anything out of a place like that.

True, Maryland had said. Okay, we'll give that land to the nation for its capital. But not too much! Just that worst part!

And so here they were. Charlie sat on grass, drowsing. Joe gamboled about him like a bumblebee. The diffuse midday light lay on them like asthma. Big white clouds mushroomed to the west, and the scene turned glossy, bulging with internal light. The ductile world, everything bursting with light. He really had to try to remember to bring his sunglasses on these trips.

To get a good long nap from Joe, he needed to tank him up. Charlie fought his own sleep, got the food bag out of the backpack's undercarriage, waved it so Joe could see it. Joe trundled over, eyelids at half-mast; no time to lose. He settled into Charlie's lap and Charlie popped a bottle of Anna's milk into his mouth just as his head was snapping to the side.

Joe sucked himself unconscious while Charlie slumped over him, chin on chest, comatose. Snuggling an infant in mind-numbing heat, what could be cozier.

Clouds over the White House were billowing up like the spirit of the building's feisty inhabitant, round, dense, shiny white. In the other direction, over the Supreme Court's neighborhood, stood a black nine-lobed cloud, dangerously laden with incipient lightning. Yes, the powers of Washington were casting up thermals and forming clouds over themselves, clouds that expressed precisely their spirits. Charlie saw that each cumulobureaucracy transcended the individuals who temporarily performed its functions in the world. These transhuman spirits all had inborn characters and biographies, and abilities and desires and habits all their own; and in the sky over the city they contested their fates. Humans were like cells in their bodies. Probably one's cells also thought their lives were important and under their control. But the great bodies knew better.

Over the white dome of the Capitol, however, the air shimmered. Congress was a roaring thermal so hot that no cloud could form in it.

He had fallen into a slumber as deep as Joe's when his phone rang. He answered it before waking.

"Wha."

"Charlie? Charlie, where are you? We need you down here right now."

"I'm already down here."

"Really? That's great. Charlie?"

"Yes, Roy?"

"Look, Charlie, sorry to bother you, but Phil is out of town and I've got to meet with Senator Ellington in twenty minutes, and we just got a call from the White House saying that Dr. Strangelove wants to meet with us to talk about Phil's climate bill. It sounds like they're ready to listen, maybe ready to talk too, or even to deal. We need someone to get over there."

"Now?"

"Now. You've got to get over there."

"I'm already over there, but look, I can't. I've got Joe here with me. Where is Phil again?"

"San Francisco."

"Wasn't Wade supposed to get back?"

"No he's still in Antarctica. Listen Charlie, there's no one here who can do this but you."

"What about Andrea?" Andrea Palmer was Phil's legislative director, the person in charge of all his bills.

"She's in New York today. Besides you're the point man on this, it's your bill more than anyone else's, you know it inside out."

"But I've got Joe!"

"Maybe you can take Joe along."

"Yeah right."

"Hey, why not? Won't he be taking a nap soon?"

"He is right now."

Charlie could see the trees backing the White House, there on the other side of the Ellipse. He could walk over there in ten minutes. Theoretically Joe would stay asleep a couple of hours. And certainly they should seize the moment on this, because so far the President and his people had shown no interest whatsoever in dealing.

"Listen," Roy cajoled, "I've had entire lunches with you where Joe is asleep on your back, and believe me, no one can tell the difference. I mean you hold yourself upright like you've got the weight of the world on your shoulders, but you did that before you had Joe, so now he just fills up that space and makes you look more normal, I swear to God. You've voted with him on your back, you've shopped, you've showered, you sure as hell can talk to the President's science advisor. Doctor Strangelove isn't going to care."

"He's a jerk."

"So? They're all jerks over there but the President, and he is too, but he's a nice guy. And he's the family president, right? He would approve on principle, you can tell Strengloft that. You can say that if the President were there he would love it. He would autograph Joe's head like a baseball."

"Yeah right."

"Charlie, this is your bill!"

"Okay okay okay!" It was true. "I'll go give it a try."

So, by the time Charlie got Joe back on his back (the child was twice as heavy when asleep) and walked across the Mall and the Ellipse, Roy had made the calls and they were expecting him at the west entry to the White House. Joe was passed through security with a light-fingered shakedown that was especially squeamish around his diaper. Then they were through, and quickly escorted into a conference room.

The room was empty. Charlie had never been in it before, though he had visited the White House several times. Joe weighed on his shoulders.

Dr. Zacharius Strengloft, the President's science advisor, entered the room. He and Charlie had sparred by proxy before, Charlie whispering killer questions into Phil's ear while Strengloft testified before Phil's committee, but the two of them had never spoken one-on-one. Now they shook hands, Strengloft peering curiously over Charlie's shoulder. Charlie explained Joe's presence as briefly as he could, and Strengloft received the explanation with precisely the kind of frosty faux benevolence that Charlie had been expecting. Strengloft in Charlie's opinion was a pompous ex-academic of the worst kind, hauled out of the depths of a second-rate conservative think tank when the administration's first science advisor had been sent packing for saying that global warming might be real and not only that, amenable to human mitigation. That went too far for this administration. Their line was that it would be much too expensive to do anything about it, so they were going to punt and let the next generation solve the problem in their own time. In other words, the hell with them. Easier to destroy the world than to change capitalism even one little bit.

All this had become quite blatant since Strengloft's appointment. He had taken over the candidate lists for all federal science advisory panels, and now candidates were being routinely asked who they had voted for in the last election, and what they thought of stem-cell research, and abortion, and evolution. When Strengloft's views were publicized and criticized, he had commented, "You need a diversity of opinions to get good advice." Mentioning his name was enough to make Anna hiss.

Be that as it may, here he was standing before Charlie; he had to be dealt with, and in the flesh he seemed friendly.

They had just gotten through their introductory pleasantries when the President himself entered the room.

Strengloft nodded complacently, as if he were often joined in his crucial work by the happy man.

"Oh, hello, Mr. President," Charlie said helplessly.

"Hello, Charles," the President said, and came over and shook his hand.

This was bad. Not unprecedented, or even terribly surprising; the President was known for wandering into meetings apparently by accident but perhaps not. It had become part of his legendarily informal style.

Now he saw Joe sacked out on Charlie's back, and stepped around Charlie to get a better view. "What's this, Charles, you got your kid with you?"

"Yes sir, I was called in on short notice when Dr. Strengloft asked for a meeting with Phil and Wade, they're both out of town."

The President found this amusing. "Ha! Well, good for you. That's sweet. Find me a marker pen and I'll sign his little head." This was another signature move, so to speak. "Is he a boy or a girl?"

"A boy. Joe Quibler."

"Well that's great. Saving the world before bedtime, that's your story, eh Charles?" He smiled to himself and moved restlessly over to the chair at the window end of the table. One of his people was standing in the door, watching them without expression.

The President's face was smaller than it appeared on TV, Charlie found. The size of an ordinary human face, no doubt, looking small precisely because of all the TV images. On the other hand it had a tremendous solidity and three-dimensionality to it. It gleamed with reality.

His eyes were slightly close-set, as was often remarked, but apart from that he looked like an aging movie star or catalog model. A successful businessman who had retired to go into public service. His features, as many observers had observed, mixed qualities of several recent presidents into one blandly familiar and reassuring face, with a little dash of piquant antiquity and edgy charm.

Now his amused look was like that of everyone's favorite uncle. "So they reeled you in for this on the fly." Then, holding a hand up to stop all of them, he near-whispered: "Sorry—should I whisper?"

"No sir, no need for that," Charlie assured him in his ordinary speaking voice. "He's out for the duration. Pay no attention to that man behind the shoulder."

The President smiled. "Got a wizard on your back, eh?"

Charlie nodded, smiling quickly to conceal his surprise. It was a pastime in some circles to judge just how much of a dimwit the President was, but facing him in person Charlie felt instantly confirmed in his minority opinion that the man had such a huge amount of low cunning that it amounted to a kind of genius. The President was no fool. And hip to at least the most obvious of movie trivia. Charlie couldn't help feeling a bit reassured.

Now the President said, "That's nice, Charles, let's get to it then, shall we? I heard from Dr. S. here about the meeting this morning, and I wanted to check in on it in person, because I like Phil Chase. And I understand that

Phil now wants us to join in with the actions of the Intergovernmental Panel on Climate Change, to the point of introducing a bill mandating our participation in whatever action they recommend, no matter what it is. And this is a UN panel."

"Well," Charlie said, shifting gears into ultradiplomatic mode, not just for the President but for the absent Phil, who was going to be upset with him no matter what he said, since only Phil should actually be talking to the President about this stuff. "That isn't exactly how I would put it, Mr. President. You know the Senate Foreign Relations Committee held a number of hearings this year, and Phil's conclusion after all that testimony was that the global climate situation is quite real. And serious to the point of being already almost too late."

The President shot a glance at Strengloft. "Would you agree with that, Dr. S.?"

"We've agreed that there is general agreement that the observed warming is real."

The President looked to Charlie, who said, "That's good as far as it goes, certainly. It's what follows from that that matters—you know, in the sense of us trying to do something about it."

Charlie swiftly rehearsed the situation, known to all: average temperatures up by six degrees Fahrenheit already, CO_2 levels in the atmosphere topping 600 parts per million, from a start before the industrial revolution of 280, and predicted to hit 1,000 ppm within a decade, which would be higher than it had been at any time in the past seventy million years. Also the long-term persistence of greenhouse gases, on the order of thousands of years.

Charlie also spoke briefly of the death of all coral reefs, which would lead to even more severe consequences for oceanic ecosystems. "The thing is, Mr. President, the world's climate can shift very rapidly. There are scenarios in which a general warming causes parts of the Northern Hemisphere to get quite cold, especially in Europe. If that were to happen, Europe could become something like the Yukon of Asia."

"Really!" the President said. "Are we sure that would be a bad thing? Just kidding of course."

"Of course sir, ha ha."

The President fixed him with a look of mock displeasure. "Well, Charles, all that may be true, but we don't know for sure if any of that is the result of human activity. Isn't that a fact?"

"No sir," Charlie said doggedly. "The carbon we've burned is different than what was already up there, so we do know. You could say it isn't for sure that the sun will come up tomorrow morning, and in a limited sense you'd be right, but I'll bet you the sun will come up."

"Don't be tempting me to gamble now."

"Besides, Mr. President, you don't delay acting on crucial matters when you have a disaster that might happen, just because you can't be one hundred percent sure it will happen. Because you can never be one hundred percent sure of anything, and some of these matters are too important to wait on."

The President frowned at this, and Strengloft interjected, "Charlie, you know the precautionary principle is an imitation of actuarial insurance that has no real resemblance to it, because the risk and the premium paid can't be calculated. That's why we refused to hear any precautionary principle language in the discussions we attended at the UN. We said we wouldn't even attend if they talked about precautionary principles or ecological footprints, and we had very good reasons for those exclusions, because those concepts are not good science."

The President nodded his "So that is that" nod, familiar to Charlie from many a press conference. He added, "I always thought a footprint was kind of a simplistic measurement for something this complex anyway."

Charlie countered, "It's just a name for a good economic index, Mr. President, calculating use of resources in terms of how much land it would take to provide them. It's pretty educational, really," and he launched into a quick description of the way it worked. "It's a good thing to know, like balancing your checkbook, and what it shows is that America is consuming the resources of ten times the acreage it actually occupies. So that if everyone on Earth tried to live as we do, given the greater population densities in much of the world, it would take fourteen Earths to support us all."

"Come on, Charlie," Dr. Strengloft objected. "Next you'll be wanting us to use Bhutan's Gross Domestic Happiness, for goodness' sake. But we can't use little countries' indexes, they don't do the job. We're the hyperpower. And really, the anticarbon crowd is a special interest lobby in itself. You've fallen prey to their arguments, but it's not like CO_2 is some toxic pollutant. It's a gas that is natural in our air, and it's essential for plants, even good for them. The last time there was a significant rise in atmospheric carbon dioxide, human agricultural productivity boomed. The Norse settled Greenland during that period, and there were generally rising lifespans."

"The end of the Black Death might account for that," Charlie pointed out.

"Well, maybe rising CO_2 levels ended the Black Death."

Charlie felt his jaw gape.

"It's the bubbly in my club soda," the President told him gently.

"Yes." Charlie rallied. "But a greenhouse gas nevertheless. It holds in heat that would otherwise escape back into space. And we're putting more than two billion tons of it into the atmosphere every year. It's like putting a plug in your exhaust pipe, sir. The car is bound to warm up. There's general agreement from the scientific community that it causes really significant warming. Has already caused it."

"Our models show the recent temperature changes to be within the range of natural fluctuation," Dr. Strengloft replied. "In fact, temperatures in the stratosphere have gone down, and there's been eighteen years of flat air temperatures. It's complex, and we're studying it, and we're going to make the best and most cost-effective response to it. Meanwhile, we're already taking effective precautions. The President has asked American businesses to limit the growth of carbon dioxide to one-third of the economy's rate of growth."

"But that's the same ratio of emissions to growth we have already."

"Yes, but the President has gone further, by asking American businesses to try to reduce that ratio over the next decade by eighteen percent. It's a growth-based approach that will accelerate new technologies, and the partnerships that we'll need with the developing world on climate change."

As the President looked to Charlie to see what he would reply to this errant nonsense, Charlie felt Joe stir on his back. This was unfortunate, as things were already complicated enough. The President and his science advisor were not only ignoring the specifics of Phil's bill, they were actively attacking its underlying concepts. Any hope Charlie had had that the President had come to throw his weight behind some real dickering was gone.

And Joe was definitely stirring. His face was burrowed sideways into the back of Charlie's neck, as usual, and now he began doing something that he sometimes did when napping: he latched on to the right tendon at the back of Charlie's neck and began sucking it rhythmically, like a pacifier. Always before Charlie had found this a sweet thing, one of the most momlike moments of his Mr. Momhood. Now he had to steel himself to it and forge on.

The President said, "I think we have to be very careful what kind of science we use in matters like these."

Joe sucked a ticklish spot and Charlie smiled reflexively and then grimaced, not wanting to appear amused by this double-edged pronouncement.

"Naturally that's true, Mr. President. But the arguments for taking vigorous action are coming from a broad range of scientific organizations, also governments, the UN, NGOs, universities, about ninety-seven percent of all the scientists who have ever declared on the issue," everyone but the very far right end of the think tank and pundit pool, he wanted to add, everyone but hack pseudoscientists who would say anything for money, like Dr. Strengloft here—but he bit his tongue and tried to shift track. "Think of the world as a balloon, Mr. President. And the atmosphere as the skin of the balloon. Now, if you wanted the thickness of the skin of a balloon to correctly represent the thickness of our atmosphere in relation to Earth, the balloon would have to be about as big as a basketball."

At the moment this barely made sense even to Charlie, although it was a good analogy if you could enunciate it clearly. "What I mean is that the atmosphere is really, really thin, sir. It's well within our power to alter it greatly."

"No one contests that, Charles. But look, didn't you say the amount of CO_2 in the atmosphere was six hundred parts per million? So if that CO_2 were to be the skin of your balloon, and the rest of the atmosphere was the air inside it, then that balloon would have to be a lot bigger than a basketball, right? About the size of the moon or something?"

Strengloft snorted happily at this thought, and went to a computer console on a desk in the corner, no doubt to compute the exact size of the balloon in the President's analogy. Charlie suddenly understood that Strengloft would never have thought of this argument, and realized further—instantly thereby understanding several people in his past who had mystified him at the time—that sometimes people known for intelligence were actually quite dim, while people who seemed a bit dim could on the contrary be very sharp.

"Granted, sir, very good," Charlie conceded. "But think of that CO_2 skin as being a kind of glass that lets in light but traps all the heat inside. It's that kind of barrier. So the thickness isn't as important as the glassiness."

"Then maybe more of it won't make all that much of a difference," the President said kindly. "Look, Charles. Fanciful comparisons are all very well, but the truth is we have to slow these emissions' growth before we can try to stop them, much less reverse them."

This was exactly what the President had said at a recent press conference, and over at the computer Strengloft beamed and nodded to hear it, perhaps because he had authored the line. The absurdity of taking pride in writing stupid lines for a quick president suddenly struck Charlie as horribly funny. He was glad Anna wasn't there beside him, because in moments like these, the slightest shared glance could set them off guffawing like kids. Even the thought of her in such a situation almost made him laugh.

So now he banished his wife and her glorious hilarity from his mind, not without a final bizarre tactile image of the back of his neck as one of her breasts, being suckled more and more hungrily by Joe. Very soon it was going to be time for a bottle.

Charlie persevered nevertheless. "Sir, it's getting kind of urgent now. And there's no downside to taking the lead on this issue. The economic advantages of being in the forefront of climate rectification and bioinfrastructure mitigation are huge. It's a growth industry with uncharted potential. It's the future no matter which way you look at it."

Joe clamped down hard on his neck. Charlie shivered. Hungry, no doubt about it. Would be ravenous on waking. Only a bottle of milk or formula would keep him from going ballistic at that point. He could not be roused now without disaster striking. But he was beginning to inflict serious pain. Charlie lost his train of thought. He twitched. A little snort of agony combined with a giggle. He choked it back, disguised it as a smothered cough.

"What's the matter, Charles, is he waking up on you?"

"Oh no sir, still out. Maybe stirring a little—ah! The thing is, if we don't address these issues now, nothing else we're doing will matter. None of it will go well."

"That sounds like alarmist talk to me," the President said, an avuncular twinkle in his eye. "Let's calm down about this. You've got to stick to the commonsense idea that sustainable economic growth is the key to environmental progress."

"Sustainable, ah!"

"What's that?"

He clamped down on a giggle. "Sustainable's the point! Sir."

"We need to harness the power of markets," Strengloft said, and nattered on in his usual vein, apparently oblivious to Charlie's problem. The President however eyed him closely. Huge chomp. Charlie's spine went electric. He suppressed the urge to swat his son like a mosquito. His right fingers tingled. Very slowly he lifted a shoulder, trying to dislodge him. Like trying to budge a limpet. Sometimes Anna had to squeeze his nostrils shut to get him to come off. Don't think about that.

The President said, "Charles, we'd be sucking the life out of the economy if we were to go too far with this. You chew on that awhile. As it is, we're taking bites out of this problem every day. Why, I'm like a dog with a bone on this thing! Those enviro special interests are like pigs at a trough. We're weaning them from all that now, and they don't like it, but they're going to have to learn that if you can't lick them, you—"

And Charlie dissolved into gales of helpless laughter.

CHAPTER 5

ATHENA ON THE PACIFIC

California is a place apart.

Gold chasers went west until the ocean stopped them, and there in that remote and beautiful land, separated from the rest of the world by desert and mountain, prairie and ocean, they saw there could be no more moving on. They would have to stop and make a life there.

Civil society, post–Civil War. A motley of argonauts, infused with Manifest Destiny and gold fever, also with Emerson and Thoreau, Lincoln and Twain, their own John Muir. They said to each other, Here at the end of the road it had better be different, or else world history has all come to naught.

So they did many things, good and bad. In the end it turned out the same as everywhere else, maybe a little bit more so.

But among the good things, encouraged by Lincoln, was the founding of a public university. Berkeley in 1867, the farm at Davis in 1905, the other campuses after that; in the 1960s new ones sprang up like flowers in a field. The University of California. A power in this world.

An oceanographic institute near La Jolla wanted one of the new campuses of the sixties to be located nearby. Next door was a U.S. Marine Corps rifle training facility. The oceanographers asked the Marines for the land, and the Marines said yes. Donated land, just like Washington, D.C., but in this case a eucalyptus grove on a sea cliff, high over the Pacific.

The University of California, San Diego.

By then California had become a crossroads, San Francisco the great city,

Hollywood the dream machine. UCSD was the lucky child of all that, Athena leaping out of the tall forehead of the state. Prominent scientists came from everywhere to start it, caught by the siren song of a new start on a Mediterranean edge to the world.

They founded a school and helped to invent a technology: biotech, Athena's gift to humankind. University as teacher and doctor too, owned by the people, no profit skimmed off. A public project in an ever-more-privatized world, tough and determined, benign in intent, but very intent. What does it mean to give?

Frank considered adding a postscript to Yann Pierzinski's Form Seven, suggesting that he pursue internal support at Torrey Pines Generique. Then he decided it would be better to work through Derek Gaspar. He could do it in person during his trip to San Diego to prepare for his move back.

A week later he was off. Transfer at Dallas, up into the air again, back to sleep. He woke when he felt the plane tilt down. They were still over Arizona, its huge baked landforms flowing by underneath. A part of Frank that had been asleep for much longer than his nap began to wake up too: he was returning to home ground. It was amazing the way things changed in the American West. Frank put his forehead against the inner window of the plane, looked ahead to the next burnt range coming into view. Thought to himself, I'll go surfing.

The pale umber of the Mojave gave way to Southern California's big scrubby coastal mountains. Then suburbia hove into view, spilling eastward on filled valleys and shaved hilltops: greater San Diego, bigger all the time. He could see bulldozers scraping platforms for the newest neighborhood, and freeways glittering with their arterial flow.

Frank's plane drifted down. Downtown's cluster of glassy skyscrapers came into view immediately to the left of the plane, seemingly at about the same height. Those buildings had been Frank's workplace for a year of his youth, and he watched them as he would any old home. He knew exactly which buildings he had climbed; they were etched on his mind. That had been a good year. Disgusted with his advisor, he had taken a leave of absence from graduate school, and after a season of climbing in Yosemite and living at Camp Four, he had run out of money and decided to do something for a living that would require his physical skills and not his intellectual ones. A young person's mistake, although at least he had not thought he could make his living as a professional climber. But those same skills were needed for the work of skyscraper window maintenance; not just window washing, which he had also done, but repair and replacement. It had been an odd but wonderful thing, going off the roofs of those sky-scrapers and descending their sides to clean windows, repair leaking caulk and flashing, replace cracked panes, and so on. The climbing was straight-forward, usually involving platforms for convenience; the belays and T-bars and dashboards and other gear had been bombproof. His fellow workers had been a mixed bag, as was always true with climbers—everything from nearly illiterate cowboys to eccentric scholars of Nietzsche or Adam Smith. And the window work itself had been a funny thing, what the Nietzsche scholar had called the apotheosis of kindergarten skills, very satisfying to perform—slicing out old caulk, applying heated caulk, un-screwing and screwing screws and bolts, sticking giant suckers to panes, levering them out and winching them up to the roofs or onto the platforms—and all under the cool onrush of the marine layer, just under clouds all mixed together with bright sun, so that it was warm when it was sunny, cool when it was cloudy, and the whole spread of downtown San Diego there below to entertain him when he wasn't working. Often he had felt surges of happiness, filling him in moments when he stopped to look around: a rare thing in his life.

Eventually the repetition got boring, as it will, and he had moved on, first to go traveling, until the money he had saved was gone; then back into academia again, as a sort of test—in a different lab, with a different advisor, at a different university. Things had gone better there. Eventually he had ended up back at UCSD, back in San Diego—his childhood home, and still the place where he felt most comfortable on this earth.

He noticed that feeling as he left the airport terminal's glassed-in walk-way over the street, and hopped down the outdoor escalator to the rental car shuttles. The comfort of a primate on home ground—a familiarity in the slant of the light and the shape of the hills, but above all in the air itself, the way it felt on his skin, that combination of temperature, humidity, and salinity that together marked it as particularly San Diegan. It was like put-ting on familiar old clothes after spending a year in a tux.

He got in his rental car and drove out of the lot. North on the freeway, crowded but not impossibly so, people zipping along like starlings, follow-ing the two rules of flocking, *keep as far apart from the rest as possible,* and *change speeds as little as possible.* The best drivers in the world. Past Mission Bay and Mount Soledad on the left, into the region where every off-ramp had been a major feature of his life. Off at Gilman, up the tight canyon of apartments hanging over the freeway, past the one where he had once spent a night with a girl, ah, back in the days when such things had happened to him.

Then UCSD. Home base. Even after a year in the East Coast's great hardwood forest, there was something appealing about the campus's eucalyptus grove—something charming, even soothing. The trees had been planted as a railroad-tie farm, before it was discovered that the wood was unsuitable. Now they formed a kind of mathematically gridded space, within which the architectural mélange of UCSD's colleges lay scattered.

After an afternoon of departmental appointments, there was an hour and a half to go before his meeting with Derek. Parking at UCSD was a nightmare, but he had gotten a pass to a department slot from Rosario, and Torrey Pines was only a few hundred yards up the road, so he decided to walk. Then it occurred to him to take the climbers' route that he and some friends had devised when they were all living at Revelle; that would nicely occupy about the amount of time he had.

It involved walking down La Jolla Shores and turning onto La Jolla Farms Road and heading out onto the bluff of land owned by the university, a squarish plateau between two canyons running down to the beach, ending in a cliff over the sea. This land had never been built on, and as they had found ancient graves on it, graves dated to seven thousand years before the present, it was likely to stay empty. A superb prospect, and one of Frank's favorites places on Earth. In fact he had lived on it for a while, sleeping out there every night; he had had romantic encounters out there, oh my yes; and he had often dropped down the steep surfer's trail that descended to the beach right at Blacks Canyon.

When he got to the cliff's edge he found a sign announcing that the route was closed due to erosion of the cliff, and it was hard to argue with that, as the old trail was now a kind of gully down the edge of a sandstone buttress. But he still wanted to do it, and he strolled south along the cliff's edge, looking out at the Pacific and feeling the onshore wind blow through him. The view was just as mind-boggling as ever, despite the gray cloud layer; as often happened, the clouds seemed to accentuate the great distances to the horizon, the two plates of ocean and sky converging at such a very slight angle toward each other. California, the edge of history—a stupid idea, totally untrue in all senses of the word, except for this: it did appear to be the edge of something.

An awesome spot. And the tighter canyon on the south side of the empty bluff had an alternative trail down that Frank was willing to break the rules and take. No one but a few cronies of his had ever used this one, because the initial drop was a scarily exposed knife-edge of a buttress, the gritty sandstone eroding to steep gullies on both sides. The trick was to descend fast and boldly, and so Frank did that, skidding out as he hit the bottom of the inland gully, sliding onto his side and down; but against the other wall he stopped himself, and then was able to hop down uneventfully.

Down to the salt roar of the beach, the surf louder here because of the tall cliff backing the beach. He walked north down the strand, enjoying yet another familiar place. Blacks Beach, the UCSD surfers' home away from home.

The ascent to Torrey Pines Generique reversed the problems of the descent, in that here all the steepness was right down on the beach. A hanging gully dripped over a hard sill some forty feet up, and he had to free-climb the grit to the right of the green algal spill. After that it was just a scramble up the gully, to the clifftop near the hang glider port. At the top he discovered a sign that declared this climb too had been illegal.

Oh well. He had loved it. He felt refreshed, awake for the first time in weeks somehow. This was what it meant to be home. He could brush his hands through his slightly sweaty and seaspray-dampened hair, and walk in and see what might happen.

Onto the parklike grounds of Torrey Pines Generique, through the newly beefed-up security gates. The place was looking empty, he thought as he walked down the halls to Derek's office. They had definitely let a lot of people go.

Frank was ushered in by a secretary, and Derek got up from his broad desk to shake hands. His office looked the same as the last time Frank had visited: window view of the Pacific; framed copy of Derek's cover portrait on a *U.S. News & World Report*; skiing photos.

"So, what's new with the great bureaucrats of science?"

"They call themselves technocrats, actually."

"Oh I'm sure it's a big difference." Derek shook his head. "I never understood why you went out there. I suppose you made good use of your time."

"Yes."

"And now you're almost back."

"Yes. I'm almost done." Frank paused. "But like I said to you on the phone, I did see something interesting from someone who worked here."

"Right, I looked into it. We could still hire him full-time, I'm pretty sure. He's on soft money up at Caltech."

"Good. Because I thought it was a very interesting idea."

"So NSF funded it?"

"No, the panel wasn't as impressed as I was. And they might have been right—it was a bit undercooked. But the thing is, if it did work, you could test genes by computer simulation, and identify proteins you wanted. It would really speed the process."

Derek regarded him closely. "You know we don't really have funds for new people."

"Yeah I know. But this guy is a postdoc, right? And a mathematician. He was only asking NSF for some computer time really. You could hire him full-time for a starter salary, and put him on the case, and it would hardly cost you a thing. I mean, if you can't afford that . . . Anyway, it could be interesting."

"What do you mean, interesting?"

"I just told you. Hire him full-time, and get him to sign the usual contract concerning intellectual property rights and all. Really secure those."

"I get that, but interesting how?"

Frank sighed. "In the sense that it might be the way to solve your targeted delivery problem. If his methods work, and you get a patent on them, then the potential for licensing income might be really considerable."

Derek was silent. He knew that Frank knew the company was on life support. That being the case, Frank would not bother him with trifles, or even with big deals that needed capital and time. He had to be offering a fix.

"Why did he send this grant proposal to NSF?"

"Beats me. Maybe he was turned down by one of your guys here. Maybe his advisor told him to do it. But have your people working on the delivery problem take a look at his work. After you get him hired."

"Why don't you talk to them? Go talk to Leo Mulhouse about this."

"Well . . ." Frank thought it over. "Okay. I'll go see how things are going. You get this Pierzinski on board. We'll see what happens from there."

Derek nodded, still not happy. "You know, Frank, what we really need here is you. Things haven't been the same since you left. Maybe when you get back we could rehire you at whatever level UCSD will allow."

"I thought you just said you didn't have any money for hires."

"Well that's true, but for you we could work something out, right?"

"Maybe. But let's not talk about that now. I need to get out of NSF first, and see what my blind trust has done. I used to have some options here."

"You sure did. Hell, we could bury you in those, Frank."

"That would be nice."

Giving people options to buy stock cost a company nothing. They were feel-good gestures, unless everything went right with the company and the market; and with NASDAQ having been in the tank for so long, they were not often seen as real compensation anymore. More a kind of speculation. And in fact Frank expressing interest in them had cheered Derek up, as it was a sign of confidence in the future of the company.

Back outside, Frank sighed. Torrey Pines Generique was looking like a thin reed. But it was his reed, and anything might happen. Derek was good at keeping things afloat. But Sam Houston was dead weight. Derek needed Frank there as scientific advisor. Or rather consultant, given his UCSD position. And if they had Pierzinski under contract, things might work out. By the end of the year the whole situation might turn around. And if it all worked out, the potential was big. Even huge.

Frank wandered across the complex to Leo's lab. It was noticeably lively compared to the rest of the building—people bustling about, the smell of solvents in the air, machines whirring away. Where there's life there's hope. Or perhaps they were only like the band on the *Titanic,* playing on while the ship went down.

Frank went in and exchanged pleasantries with Leo and his people. He mentioned that Derek had sent him down to talk about their current situation, and Leo nodded noncommittally and gave him a rundown. Frank listened, thinking: Here is a scientist at work in a lab. He is in the optimal scientific space. He has a lab, he has a problem, he's fully absorbed and going full tilt. He should be happy. But he isn't happy. He has a tough problem he's trying to solve, but that's not it; people always have tough problems in the lab.

It was something else. Probably, that he was aware of the company's situation—of course, he had to be. Probably this was the source of his unease. The musicians on the *Titanic,* feeling the tilt in the deck. In which case there was a kind of heroism in the way they played on.

But for some reason Frank was also faintly annoyed. People plugging away in the same old ways, trying to do things according to the plan, even a flawed plan: normal science, in Kuhnian terms, as well as in the more ordinary sense. All so normal, so trusting that the system worked, when obviously the system was both rigged and broken. How could they persevere? How could they be so blinkered, so determined, so dense?

Frank slipped his content in. "Maybe if you had a way to test the genes in computer simulations, find your proteins in advance."

Leo looked puzzled. "You'd have to have a, what. A theory of how DNA codes its gene expression functions. At the least."

"Yes."

"That would be nice, but I'm not aware anyone has that."

"No, but if you did . . . Wasn't George working on something like that, or one of his temporary guys? Pierzinski?"

"Yeah that's right, Yann was trying some really interesting things. But he left."

"I think Derek is trying to bring him back."

"Good idea."

Then Marta walked into the lab. When she saw Frank she stopped, startled.

"Oh hi Marta."

"Hi Frank. I didn't know you were going to be coming by."

"Neither did I."

"Oh no? Well—" She hesitated, turned. The situation called for her to say something, he felt, something like "Good to see you," if she was going to leave so quickly. But she said only, "I'm late, I've got to get to work."

And then she was out the door.

Only later, when reviewing his actions, did Frank see that he had cut short the talk with Leo, and pretty obviously at that, in order to follow Marta. In the moment itself he simply found himself walking down the hall, catching up to her before he even realized what he was doing.

She turned and saw him. "What," she said sharply, looking at him as if to stop him in his tracks.

"Oh hi I was just wondering how you're doing, I haven't seen you for a while, I wondered. Are you up for, how about going out and having dinner somewhere and catching up?"

She surveyed him. "I don't think so. I don't think that would be a good idea. We might as well not even go there. What would be the point."

"I don't know, I'm interested to know how you're doing I guess is all."

"Yeah I know, I know what you mean. But sometimes there are things you're interested in that you can't really get to know anymore, you know?"

"Ah yeah."

He pursed his lips, looked at her. She looked good. She was both the strongest and the wildest woman he had ever met. Somehow things between them had gone wrong anyway.

Now he looked at her and understood what she was saying. He was never going to be able to know what her life was like these days. He was biased, she was biased; the scanty data would be inescapably flawed. Talking for a couple of hours would not make any difference. So it was pointless to try. Would only churn to the surface bad things from the past. Maybe in another ten years. Maybe never.

Marta must have seen something of this train of thought in his face, because with an impatient nod she turned and was gone.

A few days after Frank dropped by, Leo turned on his computer when he came in to the lab and saw there was an e-mail from Derek. He opened and read it, then the attachment that had come with it. When he was done he forwarded it to Brian and Marta. When Marta came in about an hour later she had already done some work on it.

"Hey Brian," she called from Leo's door, "come check this out. Derek has sent us a new paper from that Yann Pierzinski who was here. He was funny. It's a new version of the stuff he was working on when he was here. It was interesting."

Brian had come in while she was telling him this, and she pointed to parts of the diagram on Leo's screen as he caught up. "See what I mean?"

"Well, yeah. It would be great. If it worked . . . Maybe crunch them through this program over and over, until you see repeats, if you did . . . then test the ones with the ligands that fit best, and look strongest chemically."

"And Pierzinski is back to work on it with us!"

"Is he?"

"Yeah, he's coming back. Derek says we'll have him at our disposal."

"Cool."

Leo checked this in the company's directory. "Yep, here he is. Rehired just this week. Frank Vanderwal came by and mentioned this guy, he must have told Derek about it too. Well, Vanderwal should know, this is his field."

"It's my field too," Marta said sharply.

"Right, of course, I'm just saying Frank might have, you know. Well, let's ask Yann to look at what we've got. If it works . . ."

Brian said, "Sure. It's worth trying anyway. Pretty interesting." He googled Yann, and Leo leaned over his shoulder to look at the list.

"Derek obviously wants us to talk to him right away."

"He must have rehired him for us."

"I see that. So let's get him before he gets busy with something else. A lot of labs could use another biomathematician."

"True, but there aren't a lot of labs. I think we'll get him. Look, what do you think Derek means here, 'write up the possibilities right away'?"

"I suppose he wants to get started on using the idea to try to secure more funding."

"Shit. Yeah, that's probably right. Unbelievable. Okay, let's pass on that for now, damn it, and give Yann a call."

Their talk with Yann Pierzinski was indeed interesting. He breezed into the lab just a few days later, as friendly as ever, and happy to be back at Torrey Pines with a permanent job. He was going to be based in George's math group, he told them, but had already been told by Derek to expect to work a lot with Leo's lab; so he arrived curious, and ready to go.

Leo enjoyed seeing him again. Yann still had a tendency to become a speed-talker when excited, and he still canted his head to the side when thinking. His algorithm sets were works in progress, he said, and underdeveloped precisely in the gene grammars that Leo and Marta and Brian needed from him; but that was okay, Leo thought, because they could help him, and he was there to help them. They could collaborate, and Yann was a powerful thinker. Leo felt secure in his own lab abilities, devising and running experiments, but when it came to the curious mix of math, symbolic logic, and computer programming that biomathematicians dove into, he was way out of his depth. So Leo was happy to watch Yann sit down and plug his laptop into their desktop.

In the days that followed, they tried his algorithms on the genes of their "HDL factory" cells, Yann substituting different procedures in the last steps of his operations, then checking what they got in the computer simulations, and selecting some for their dish trials. Pretty soon they found one version of the operation that was consistently good at predicting proteins that matched well with their target cells—making keys for their locks, in effect. "That's what I've been hunting for the past year at least!" Yann said happily after one such success.

As they worked, Pierzinski told them some of how he had gotten to that point in his work, following aspects of his advisor's work at Caltech and the like. Marta and Brian asked him where he had hoped to take it all, in terms of applications. Yann shrugged; not much of anywhere, he told them.

"But Yann, don't you see what the applications of this could be?"

"I guess. I'm not really interested in pharmacology."

Leo and Brian and Marta stood there staring at him. Despite his earlier stint there, they didn't know him very well. He seemed normal enough in most ways, aware of the outside world and so on. To an extent.

Leo said, "Look, let's go get some lunch, let us take you out to lunch. I want to tell you more about what all this could help us with."

The lobbying firm of Branson & Ananda occupied offices off Pennsylvania Avenue, near the intersection of Indiana and C Streets, overlooking the Marketplace. Charlie's friend Sridar met them at the front door. First he took them in to meet old Branson himself, then led them into a meeting room dominated by a long table. Sridar got the Khembalis seated, then offered them coffee or tea; they all took tea. Charlie stood near the door, bobbing mildly about to keep Joe asleep on his back, ready to make a quick escape if he had to.

"So you've been a sovereign country since 1960?" Sridar was saying.

"The relationship with India is a little more . . . complicated than that. We have had sovereignty in the sense you suggest since about 1993." Drepung rehearsed the history of Khembalung, while Sridar took notes.

"So—fifteen feet above sea level at high tide," Sridar said at the end of this recital. "Listen, one thing I have to say at the start—we are not going to be able to promise you anything much in the way of results on the global warming side of things. That's been given up on by Congress—" He glanced at Charlie: "Sorry, Charlie. Maybe not so much given up on, as swept under the rug."

Charlie glowered despite himself. "Not by Senator Chase or anyone else who's really paying attention. And we've got a big bill coming up—"

"Yes, yes, of course," Sridar said, holding up a hand to stop him before he went into rant mode. "You're doing what you can. But quite a few members of Congress think of it as being too late to do anything."

"Better late than never!" Charlie insisted, almost waking Joe.

"We understand," Drepung said to Sridar, after a glance at Rudra. "We won't have any unrealistic expectations of you. We only hope to engage help that is experienced in the procedures used. We ourselves will be responsible for the content of our appeals to the reluctant bodies."

Sridar kept his face blank, but Charlie knew what he was thinking. Sridar said, "We do our best to give our clients all the benefits of our expertise. I'm just reminding you that we are not miracle workers."

"The miracles will be our department," Drepung said.

Charlie thought, these two jokers might get along fine.

Slowly they worked out what they would expect from each other, and Sridar wrote down the details of an agreement. The Khembalis were happy to have him write up what in essence was their request for proposal. Sridar remarked, "A clever way to make me write you a fair deal."

Later that day Sridar gave Charlie a call. Charlie was sitting on a bench in Dupont Circle, feeding Joe a bottle and watching two of the local chess hustlers practice on each other. They played too fast for Charlie to follow the game.

"Look, Charlie, this is a bit ingrown, since you put me in touch with these guys, but really it's your man that the lamas ought to be meeting. The Foreign Relations Committee is one of the main ones we'll work on, so it all begins with Chase. Can you set us up with a good chunk of the senator's quality time?"

"I can with some lead time," Charlie said, glancing at Phil's master calendar on his wrist screen. "How about next Thursday?"

"Perfect."

Here in the latter part of his third term, Senator Phil Chase had fully settled into Washington, and his seniority was such that he had become very powerful, and very busy. He had every hour from 6 A.M. to midnight scheduled in twenty-minute units. It was hard to understand how he could keep his easy demeanor and relaxed ways. It was partly that he did not sweat the details. He was a delegating senator, a hands-off senator, as many of the best of them were. Some senators tried to learn everything, and burned out; others knew almost nothing, and were in effect living campaign posters. Phil was somewhere in the middle. He used his staff well—as an exterior memory bank, as advice, as policy makers, even occasionally as a source of accumulated wisdom.

His longevity in office, and the strict code of succession that both parties obeyed, had landed him the chair of the Foreign Relations Committee, and a seat on Environment and Public Works. These were A-list committees, and the stakes were high. The Democrats had come out of the recent election with a one-vote advantage in the Senate, a two-vote disadvantage in the House, and the President was still a Republican. This was in the ongoing American tradition of electing as close to a perfect gridlock of power in Washington as possible, presumably in the hope that nothing further would happen and history would freeze forever. An impossible quest, like building a card house in a gale, but it made for tight politics and good theater.

In any case, Phil was now very busy, and heading toward reelection himself. His old chief of staff Wade Norton was on the road now, and though Phil valued Wade and kept him on staff as a telecommuting advisor, Roy and Andrea had taken over executive staff duties. Charlie did their environmental research, though he too was a part-timer, and mostly telecommuting.

When he did make it in, he found operations had a chaotic edge which he had long ago concluded was mostly engendered by Phil himself. Phil would seize the minutes he had between appointments and wander from room to room, looking to needle people. "We're surfing the big picture today!" he would exclaim, then start arguments for the hell of it. His staff loved it. Congressional staffers were by definition policy wonks; many had joined their high school debate clubs of their own free will, so talking shop with Phil was right up their alley. And his enthusiasm was infectious, his grin like a double shot of espresso. He had one of those smiles that invariably looked as if he was genuinely delighted. If it was directed at you, you felt a glow inside. In fact Charlie was convinced that it was Phil's smile that had gotten him elected the first time, and maybe every time. What made it so beautiful was that it wasn't faked. He didn't smile if he didn't feel like it. But he often felt like it. That was very revealing, and so Phil had his effect.

With Wade gone, Charlie was now his chief advisor on climate. Actually Charlie and Wade functioned as a sort of tag-team telecommuting advisor, both of them part-time, Charlie calling in every day, dropping by every week; Wade calling in every week, and dropping by every month. It worked because Phil didn't always need them for help when environmental issues came up. "You guys have educated me," he would tell them. "I can take this on my own. So don't worry, stay at the South Pole, stay in Bethesda. I'll let you know how it went."

That would have been fine with Charlie, if only Phil had always done what Charlie and Wade advised. But Phil had pressures from many directions, and he had his own opinions. So there were divergences. Like most congresspeople, he thought he knew better than his staff how to get things done; and because he got to vote and they didn't, in effect he was right.

On Thursday at 10 A.M., when the Khembalis had their twenty minutes with Phil, Charlie was very interested to see how it would go, but that morning he had to attend a Washington Press Club appearance by a scientist from the Heritage Foundation who was claiming rapidly rising temperatures would be good for agriculture. Assisting in the destruction of such people's pseudoarguments was important work, which Charlie was happy to do; but on this day he wanted to be there when Phil saw the Khembalis, so when the press conference was over and Charlie's quiver empty, he hustled back and arrived right at 10:20. He hurried up the stairs to Phil's offices on the third floor. At 10:23 A.M., Phil ushered the Khembalis out of his corner office, chatting with them cheerfully. "Yes, thanks, of course, I'd love to—talk to Evelyn about setting up a time."

The Khembalis looked pleased. Sridar looked impassive but faintly amused, as he often did.

Just as he was leaving, Phil spotted Charlie and stopped. "Charlie! Good to see you at last!"

Grinning hugely, he came back and shook his blushing staffer's hand. "So you laughed in the President's face!" He turned to the Khembalis: "This man burst out laughing in the President's face! I've always wanted to do that!"

The Khembalis nodded neutrally.

"So what did it feel like?" Phil asked Charlie. "And how did it go over?"

Charlie, still blushing, said, "Well, it felt involuntary, to tell the truth. Like a sneeze. Joe was really tickling me. And as far as I could tell, it went over okay. The President looked pleased. He was trying to make me laugh, so when I did, he laughed too."

"Yeah I bet, because at that point he had you."

"Well, yes. Anyway he laughed, and then Joe woke up and we had to get a bottle in him before the Secret Service guys did something rash."

Phil laughed and then shook his head, growing more serious. "Well, it's too bad, I guess. But what could you do. You were ambushed. He loves to do that. Hopefully it won't cost us. It might even help. But I'm late, I've got to go. You hang in there." And he put a hand to Charlie's arm, said good-bye again to the Khembalis, and hustled out the door.

The Khembalis gathered around Charlie, looking cheerful. "Where is Joe? How is it he is not with you?"

"I really couldn't bring him to this thing I was at, so my friend Asta from Gymboree is looking after him. Actually I have to get back to him soon," checking his watch. "But come on, tell me how it went."

They all followed Charlie into his cubicle by the stairwell, stuffing it with their maroon robes (they had dressed formally for Phil, Charlie noted) and their strong brown faces. They still looked pleased.

"Well?" Charlie said.

"It went very well," Drepung said, and nodded happily. "He asked us many questions about Khembalung. He visited Khembalung seven years ago, and met Padma and others at that time. He was very interested, very sympathetic. And best of all, he told us he would help us."

"He did? That's great! What did he say, exactly?"

Drepung squinted, remembering. "He said—'I'll see what I can do.'"

Sucandra and Padma nodded, confirming this.

"Those were his exact words?" Charlie asked.

"Yes. 'I'll see what I can do.'"

Charlie and Sridar exchanged a glance. Who was going to tell them?

Sridar said carefully, "Those were indeed his exact words," thus passing the ball to Charlie.

Charlie sighed.

"What's wrong?" Drepung asked.

"Well . . ." Charlie glanced at Sridar again.

"Tell them," Sridar said.

Charlie said, "What you have to understand is that no congressperson likes to say no."

"No?"

"No. They don't."

"They never say no," Sridar clarified.

"Never?"

"Never."

"They like to say yes," Charlie explained. "People come to them, asking for things—favors, votes—consideration of one kind or another. When they say yes, people go away happy. Everyone is happy."

"Votes," Sridar expanded. "They say yes and it means votes. Sometimes one yes can mean fifty thousand votes. So they just keep saying yes."

"That's true," Charlie admitted. "Some say yes no matter what they really mean. Others, like our Senator Chase, are more honest."

"Without, however, actually ever saying no," Sridar added.

"In effect they only answer the questions they can say yes to. The other questions they avoid in one way or another."

"Right," Drepung said. "But he said . . ."

"He said, 'I'll see what I can do.'"

Drepung frowned. "So that means no?"

"Well, you know, in circumstances where they can't get out of answering the question in some other way—"

"Yes!" Sridar interrupted. "It means no."

"Well . . ." Charlie tried to temporize.

"Come on, Charlie." Sridar shook his head. "You know it's true. It's true for all of them. *Yes* means maybe; *I'll see what I can do* means no. It means, not a chance. It means, I can't believe you're asking me this question, but since you are, this is how I will say no."

"He will not help us?" Drepung asked.

"He will if he sees a way that will work," Charlie declared. "I'll keep on him about it."

Drepung said, "You'll see what you can do."

"Yes—but I mean really."

Sridar smiled sardonically at Charlie's discomfiture. "And Phil's the most environmentally aware senator of all, isn't that right Charlie?"

"Well, yeah. That's definitely true."

The Khembalis pondered this. Drepung was now frowning.

"We too will see what we can do," he said.

CHAPTER 6

THE CAPITAL IN SCIENCE

Robot submarines cruise the depths, doing oceanography. Finally oceanographers have almost as much data as meteorologists. Among other things they monitor a deep layer of relatively warm water that flows from the Atlantic into the Arctic (ALTEX, the Atlantic Layer Tracking Experiment).

But they are not as good at it as the whales. White beluga whales, living their lives in the open ocean, have been fitted with sensors for recording temperature, salinity, and nitrate content, matched with a GPS record and a depth meter. Up and down in the blue world they sport, diving deep into the black realm below, coming back up for air, recording data all the while. Casper the Friendly Ghost, Whitey Ford, The Woman in White, Moby Dick, all the rest: they swim to their own desires, up and down endlessly within their immense territories, fast and supple, continuous and thorough, capable of great depths, pale flickers in the blackest blue, the bluest black. Then back up for air. Our cousins. White whales help us to know this world. The data they are collecting make it clear that the Atlantic's deep warm layer is attenuating. And so the Gulf Stream is slowing down.

The rest of Frank's stay in San Diego was a troubled time. The encounter with Marta had put him in a black mood that he could not shake.

He tried to look for a place to live when he returned in the fall, checking out some real estate pages in the paper, but it was discouraging. He saw that he would have to rent an apartment first, and take the time to look before trying to buy something. It was going to be hard, maybe impossible, to find a house he both liked and could afford. He had some financial problems. And it took a very considerable income to buy a house in north San Diego these days. He and Marta had bought a perfect couple's bungalow in Cardiff, but they had sold it when they split, adding greatly to the acrimony. Now the region was more expensive than a mere professor could afford. Extra income would be essential.

So he looked at some rentals in North County, and then in the afternoons he went to the empty office on campus, meeting with two postdocs who were still working for him in his absence. He also talked with the department chair about what classes he would teach in the fall. It was all very tiresome.

And worse than tiresome, when a letter appeared in his department mailbox from the UCSD Technology Transfer Office. Pulse quickening, he ripped it open and scanned it, then got on the phone.

"Hi Delphina, it's Frank Vanderwal here. I've just gotten a letter from your review committee, can you please tell me what this is about?"

"Oh hello, Dr. Vanderwal. Let me see . . . the oversight committee on faculty outside income wanted to ask you about some income you received from stock in Torrey Pines Generique. Anything over two thousand dollars a year has to be reported, and they didn't hear anything from you."

"I'm at NSF this year, all my stocks are in a blind trust. I don't know anything about it."

"Oh, that's right, isn't it. Maybe . . . just a second. Here it is. Maybe they knew that. I'm not sure. I'm looking at their memo here . . . ah. They've been informed you're going to be rejoining Torrey Pines when you get back, and—"

"Wait, what? How the hell could they hear that?"

"I don't know—"

"Because it isn't true! I've been talking to colleagues at Torrey Pines, but all that is private. So how could they possibly have heard that?"

"I said, I don't know." Delphina was getting tired of his indignation. No doubt her job put her at the wrong end of a lot of indignation.

He said, "Come on, Delphina. We went over all this when I helped start Torrey Pines, and I haven't forgotten. Faculty are allowed to spend up to twenty percent of work time on outside consulting. Whatever I make doing that is mine, it only has to be reported. So even if I did go back to Torrey Pines, what's wrong with that? I wouldn't be joining their board, and I wouldn't use more than twenty percent of my time!"

"That's good—"

"And most of it happens in my head anyway, so even if I did spend more time on it, how are you going to know? Are you going to read my mind?"

Delphina sighed. "Of course we can't read your mind. In the end it's an honor system. Obviously. We ask people what's going on when we see things in the financial reports, to remind them what the rules are."

"I don't appreciate the implications of that. Tell the oversight committee what the situation is on my stocks, and ask them to do their research properly before they bother people."

"All right. Sorry about that." She did not seem perturbed.

Frank went out for a walk around the campus. Usually this soothed him, but now he was too upset. Who had told the oversight committee that he was planning to rejoin Torrey Pines? And why? Would somebody at Torrey Pines have made a call? Only Derek knew for sure, and he wouldn't do it.

But others must have heard about it. Or could have deduced his intention after his visit. That had been only a few days before, but enough time had passed for someone to make a call. Sam Houston, maybe, wanting to stay head science advisor?

Or Marta?

Disturbed at the thought, at all these machinations, he found himself wishing he were back in D.C. That was shocking, because when he was in D.C. he was always desperate to return to San Diego, biding his time until his return, at which point his real life would recommence. But it was undeniable; here he was in San Diego, and he wanted to be in D.C. Something was seriously wrong.

Part of it must have been the fact that he was not really back in his San Diego life, but only previewing it. He didn't have a home, he was still on leave, his days were not quite full. That left him wandering a bit, as he was now. And that was unlike him.

Okay—what would he do with free time if he lived here?

He would go surfing.

Good idea. His possessions were stowed in a storage unit in Encinitas, so he drove there and got his surfing gear, then returned to the parking lot at Cardiff reef, at the south end of Cardiff-by-the-Sea. A few minutes' observation while he pulled on his long-john wetsuit (getting too small for him) revealed that an ebb tide and a south swell were combining for some good waves, breaking at the outermost reef. There was a little crowd of surfers and bodyboarders out there.

Happy at the sight, Frank walked into the water, which was very cool for midsummer, just as they all said. It never got as warm as it used to. But it felt so good now that he ran out and dove through a wave, whooping as he emerged. He sat in the water and pulled on his booties, velcroed the ankle strap of the board cord to him, took off paddling. The ocean tasted like home.

Cardiff reef was a very familiar break to him, and nothing had changed. He had often surfed here with Marta, but that had little to do with it. The waves were eternal, and Cardiff reef with its point break was like an old friend who always said the same things. He was home. This was what made San Diego his home—not the people or the jobs or the unaffordable houses, but this experience of being in the ocean, which for so many years of his youth had been the central experience of his life, everything else colorless by comparison, until he had discovered climbing.

As he paddled, caught waves, and rode the lefts in long ecstatic seconds, and then worked to get back outside, he wondered again about this strangely powerful feeling of salt water as home. There must be an evolutionary reason for such joy at being cast forward by a wave. Whatever; it was a lot of fun. And made him feel vastly better.

Then it was time to go. He took one last ride, and rather than kicking out when the fast part was over, rode the broken wave straight in toward the shore.

He lay in the shallows and let the hissing whitewater shove him around. Back and forth, ebb and flow. Grooming by ocean.

"Are you okay?"

He jerked his head up. It was Marta, on her way out.

"Oh, hi. Yeah I'm okay."

"What's this, stalking me now?"

"No," then realizing this might be a little bit true: "No!"

He stared at her, getting angry. She stared back.

"I'm just catching some waves," he said, mouth tight. "You've got no reason to say such a thing to me."

"No? Then why did you ask me out the other day?"

"A mistake, obviously. I thought it might do some good to talk."

"Last year, maybe. But you didn't want to then. You didn't want to so much that you ran off to NSF instead. Now it's too late. So just leave me alone, Frank."

"I am!"

"Leave me alone."

She turned and ran into the surf, diving onto her board and paddling hard. When she got out far enough she sat up on her board and balanced, looking outward.

Women in wetsuits looked funny, Frank thought as he watched her. Not just the obvious, but also the subtler differences in body morphology were accentuated. He could tell the difference from as far away as he could see people at all. Every surfer could.

What did that mean? That he was in thrall to a woman who despised him? That he had messed up the main relationship of his life and his best chance so far for reproductive success? That sexual dimorphism was a powerful driver in the urge to reproduction? That he was a slave to his sperm, and an idiot?

All of the above.

His good mood shattered, he hauled himself to his feet. He stripped off the booties and long john, toweled off at his rental car, drove back up to his storage unit, and dropped off his gear. Returned to his hotel room, showered, checked out, and drove down the coast highway to the airport, feeling like an exile, even here on his own home ground.

Something was deeply, deeply wrong.

He checked in the car, got on the plane to Dallas. Waiting in Dallas he watched America walk by. Who were these people who could live so placidly while the world fell into an acute global environmental crisis? Experts at denial. Experts at filtering their information. Many of those walking by went to church on Sundays, believed in God, voted Republican, spent their time shopping and watching TV. Obviously nice people. The world was doomed.

He settled in his next plane seat, feeling more and more disgusted and angry. NSF was part of it; they weren't doing a damn thing to help. He got out his laptop, turned it on, and called up a new file. He started to write.

Critique of NSF, first draft. Private to Diane Chang.

NSF was established to support basic scientific research, and it is generally given high marks for that. But its budget has never surpassed ten billion dollars a year, in an overall economy of some ten trillion. It is to be feared that as things stand, NSF is simply too small to have any real impact.

Meanwhile humanity is exceeding the planet's carrying capacity for our species, badly damaging the biosphere. Neoliberal economics cannot cope with this situation, and indeed, with its falsely exteriorized costs, was designed in part to disguise it. If the Earth were to suffer a catastrophic anthropogenic extinction event over the next twenty years, which it will, American business would continue to focus on its quarterly profit and loss. There is no economic mechanism for dealing with catastrophe. And yet government and the scientific community are not tackling this situation either, indeed both have consented to be run by neoliberal economics, an obvious pseudoscience. We might as well agree to be governed by astrologers. Everyone at NSF knows this is the situation, and yet no one does anything about it. They don't try to instigate the saving of the biosphere, they don't even call for certain kinds of mitigation projects. They just wait and see what comes in. It is a ridiculously passive position.

Why such passivity, you ask? Because NSF is chicken! It's a chicken with its smart little head stuck in the sand like an ostrich! It's a chicken ostrich (fix). It's afraid to take on Congress, it's afraid to take on business, it's afraid to take on the American people. Free market fundamentalists are dragging us back to some dismal feudal eternity and destroying everything in the process, all while we have the technological means to feed everyone, house everyone, clothe everyone, doctor everyone, educate everyone—the ability to end suffering and want as well as ecological collapse is right here at hand, and yet NSF continues to dole out its little grants, fiddling while Rome burns!!!

Well whatever nothing to be done about it, I'm sure you're thinking poor Frank Vanderwal has spent a year in the swamp and has gone crazy as a result, and that is true, but what I'm saying is still right, the world is in big trouble and NSF is one of the few organizations on Earth that could actually help get it out of trouble, and yet it's not. It should be charting worldwide scientific policy and forcing certain kinds of climate mitigation and biosphere management, insisting on them as emergency necessities, it should be working Congress like the fucking NRA does, to get the budget it deserves, which is a much bigger budget, as big as the Pentagon's, really those two budgets should

be reversed to get them to their proper level of funding, but none
of it is happening or will happen, and that is why I'm not coming
back and no one in his right mind would come back either

The plane had started to descend.

Well, it would need revision. Mixed metaphors; something was either a chicken or an ostrich, even if in fact it was both. But he could work on it. He now had a draft in hand, and he would revise it and then give it to Diane Chang, head of NSF, in the slim hope that it would wake her up.

The plane turned for its final descent into Ronald Reagan Airport. Soon he would be back in the wasteland of his current life. Back in the swamp.

Back in Leo's lab, they got busy running trials of Pierzinski's algorithm, while continuing the ongoing experiments in "rapid hydrodynamic insertion," as it was now called in the emerging literature. Many labs were working on the delivery problem and, crazy as it seemed, this was one of the more promising methods being investigated. A bad sign.

Thus they were so busy on both fronts that they didn't notice at first the results that one of Marta's collaborators was getting with Pierzinski's method. Marta had done her Ph.D. studying the microbiology of certain algae, and she was still coauthoring papers with a postdoc named Eleanor Dufours. Leo had met Eleanor, and then read her papers, and been impressed. Now Marta had introduced Eleanor to a version of Pierzinski's algorithm, and things were going well, Marta said. Leo thought his group might be able to learn some things from their work, so he set up a little brown-bag lunch for Eleanor to give a talk.

"What we've been looking into," Eleanor said that day in her quiet steady voice, very unlike Marta's, "is the algae in certain lichens. DNA histories are making it clear that some lichens are really ancient partnerships of algae and fungus, and we've been genetically altering the algae in one of the oldest, *Cornicularia cornuta*. It grows on trees, and works its way into the trees to a quite surprising degree. We think the lichen is helping the trees it colonizes by taking over the tree's hormone regulation and increasing the tree's ability to absorb lignins through the growing season."

She talked about the possibility of changing their metabolic rates. "Lately we've been trying these algorithms Marta brought over, trying to find algal symbionts that speed the lichen's ability to add lignin to the trees."

Engineering evolution, Leo thought. His lab was trying to do similar things, of course, but he seldom thought of it that way. He needed to get this outside view to defamiliarize what he did, to see better what was going on.

"Why speed up lignin banking?" Brian wanted to know. "I mean, what use would it be?"

"We've been thinking it might work as a carbon sink."

"How so?"

"Well, you know, people are talking about capturing and sequestering some of the carbon we've put into the atmosphere, in carbon sinks of one kind or other. But no method has looked really good yet. Stimulating plant growth has been one suggestion, but the problem is that most of the plants discussed have been very short-lived, and rotting plant life quickly releases its captured CO_2 back into the atmosphere. So unless you can arrange lots of very deep peat bogs, capturing CO_2 in small plants hasn't looked very effective."

Her listeners nodded.

"So, the thing is, living trees have had hundreds of millions of years of practice in not being eaten and outgassed by bugs. So one possibility would be to grow bigger trees. That turns out not to be so easy," and she sketched a ground and a tree growing out of it on the whiteboard, with a red marker so that it looked like something a five-year-old would draw. "Sorry. See, most trees are already as tall as they can get, because of physical constraints like soil qualities and wind speeds. So, you can make them thicker, or"—drawing more roots under the ground line—"you can make the roots thicker. But trying to do that directly involves genetic changes that harm the trees in other ways, and anyway is usually very slow."

"So it won't work," Brian said.

"Right," she said patiently, "but many trees host these lichen, and the lichen regulate lignin production in a way that might be bumped, so the tree would quite quickly capture carbon that would remain sequestered for as long as the tree lived.

"So, given all this, what we've been working on is a kind of altered tree lichen. The lichen's photosynthesis is accomplished by the algae in it, and we've been using this algorithm of Yann's to find genes that can be altered to accelerate that. And now we're getting the lichen to export the excess sugar into its host tree, down in the roots. It seems like we might be able to really accelerate the root growth and girth of the trees that these lichens grow on."

"Capturing like how much carbon?"

"Well, we've calculated different scenarios, with the altered lichen being introduced into forests of different sizes, all the way up to the whole world's temperate forest belt. That one has the amount of CO_2 that would be drawn down in the billions of tons."

"Wow."

"Yes. And pretty quickly, too."

"Watch out," Brian joked, "you don't want to be causing an ice age here."

"True. But that would be a problem that came later. And we know how to warm things up, after all. But at this point any carbon capture would be good. There are some really bad effects coming down the pike these days, as you know."

They all sat and stared at the mess of letters and lines and little tree drawings she had scribbled on the whiteboard.

Leo broke the silence. "Wow, Eleanor. That's very interesting."

"I know it doesn't help you with your delivery problem."

"No, but that's okay, that isn't what you do. This is still very interesting. It's a different problem is all, but that happens. This is great stuff. Have you shown this to the chancellor yet?"

"No." She looked surprised.

"You should. He loves stuff like this, and, you know, he's a working scientist himself. He still keeps his lab going even while he's doing all the chancellor stuff."

Now Eleanor was nodding. "I'll do that. He has been very supportive."

"Right. And look, I hope you and Marta keep collaborating. Maybe there's some aspect of hormone regulation you'll spot that we're not seeing."

"I doubt that, but thanks."

Soon after that, Leo got an e-mail from Derek, asking him to join a meeting with a representative of a venture capital group. This had happened a few times back when Torrey Pines was a hot new start-up, so Leo knew the drill, and was therefore extremely uncomfortable with the idea of doing it again—especially if it came to a discussion of "rapid hydrodynamic insertion." No way did Leo want to be supporting Derek's unfounded assertions to an outsider.

Derek assured him that he would handle any of this guy's "speculative questions"—exactly the sort of questions a venture capitalist would have to ask.

"And so I'll be there to . . ."

"You'll be there to answer any technical questions about the method."

Great.

Before the meeting Leo was shown a copy of the executive summary and offering memorandum Derek had sent to Biocal, a venture capital firm from which Derek had gotten an investment in the company's early years. This document was very upbeat about the possibilities of the hydrodynamic delivery method. On finishing it Leo's stomach had contracted to the size of a walnut.

The meeting was in Biocal's offices, located in an upscale building in downtown La Jolla, just off Prospect near the point. Their meeting room windows had a great view up the coast. Leo could almost spot their own building, on the cliff across La Jolla Cove.

Their host, Henry Bannet, was a trim man in his forties, relaxed and athletic-looking, friendly in the usual San Diego manner. His firm was a private partnership, doing strategic investing in biotechnologies. A billion-dollar fund, Derek had said. And they didn't expect any return on their investments for four to six years, sometimes longer. They could afford to work at the pace of medical progress itself. Their game was high-risk, high-return, long-range investment. This was not a kind of invest-ment that banks would make, nor anyone else in the lending world. The risks were too great, the returns too distant. Only venture capitalists would do it.

So naturally these guys' help was much in demand from small biotech companies. There were something like three hundred biotechs in the San Diego area alone, and many of them were hanging by the skin of their teeth, hoping for that first successful cash cow to keep them going or get them bought. Venture capitalists would therefore get to pick and choose what they wanted to invest in; and many of them were pursuing particular interests, or even passions. Naturally in these areas they were very well-informed, expert in combining scientific and financial analysis into what they called "doing due diligence." They spoke of being "value-added investors," of bringing much more than money to the table—expertise, networking, advice.

This guy Bannet looked to Leo to be one of the passionate ones. He was friendly but intent. A man at work. There was very little chance Derek was going to be able to impress him with smoke and mirrors.

"Thanks for seeing us," Derek said.

Bannet waved a hand. "Always interested to talk to you guys. I've been reading some of your papers, and I went to that symposium in L.A. last year. You're doing some great stuff."

"It's true, and now we're onto something really good, with real potential to revolutionize genetic engineering by getting tailored DNA into people who need it. It could be a method useful to a whole bunch of different therapies, which is one of the reasons we're so excited about it—and trying to ramp up our efforts to speed the process along. So I remembered how much you helped us during the start-up, and how well that's paid off for you, so I thought I'd bring by the current situation and see if you would be interested in doing a PIPE with us."

This sounded weird to Leo, like Indians offering a peace pipe, or college students passing around a bong, but Bannet didn't blink; a PIPE was one of their mechanisms for investment, as Leo quickly learned. "Private Investment in Public Equity." And for once it was a pretty good acronym, because it meant creating a pipeline for money to run directly from their cash-flush fund to Derek's penniless company.

But Bannet was a veteran of all this, alert to all the little strategic opacities that were built into Derek's typical talk to stockholders or potential investors. Something like sixty percent of biotech start-ups failed, so the danger of losing some or all of an investment to bankruptcy was very real. No way Derek could finesse him. They would have to come clean and hope he liked what he saw.

Derek finished leading Bannet through a series of financial spreadsheets on his laptop, unable to disguise their tale of woe. Bad profit and loss; layoffs; sale of some subsidiary contracts, even some patents, their crown jewels; empty coffers.

"We've had to focus on the things that we think are really the most important," Derek admitted. "It's made us more efficient, that's for sure. But it means there really isn't any fat anywhere, no resources we can put to the task, even though it's got such incredible potential. So, it seemed like it was time to ask for some outside funding help, with the idea that the financing now would be so crucial that the returns to the investor could and should be really significant."

"Uh-huh," Bannet said, though it wasn't clear what he was agreeing with. He made thoughtful clucking sounds as he scanned the spreadsheets, murmuring, "Um hmmm, um hmmm," in a sociable way, but now that he was thinking about the information in the spreadsheets, his face betrayed an almost burning intensity. This guy was definitely one of the passionate ones.

"Tell me about this algorithm," he said finally.

Derek looked to Leo, who said, "Well, the mathematician developing it is a recent hire at Torrey Pines, and he's been collaborating with our lab to test a set of operations he's developed, to see how well they can predict the proteins associated with any given gene, and as you can see," clicking his own laptop screen to the first of the project report slides, "it's been really good at predicting them in certain situations," pointing to them on the screen's first slide.

"How would this affect the targeted delivery system you're working on?"

"Well, right now it's helping us to find proteins with ligands that bind better to their receptor ligands in target organ cells. It's also helping us test for proteins that we can more successfully shove across cell walls, using the hydrodynamic methods we've been investigating for the past few months." He clicked ahead to the slide that displayed this work's results, trying to banish Brian's and Marta's names from his mind; he definitely did not want to call it the Popping Eyeball Method, the Exploding Mouse Method. "As you can see," pointing to the relevant results, "saturation has been good in certain conditions." This seemed a little weak, and so he added, "The algorithm is also proving to be very successful in guiding work we've been doing with botanists on campus, on algal designs."

"How does that connect with this?"

"Well, it's for plant engineering."

Bannet looked at Derek.

Derek said, "We at TPG plan to use it to pursue the improvement of targeted delivery. Clearly the method is robust, and people can use it in a wide variety of applications."

But there was no hiding it, really. Their best results so far were in an area that would not necessarily ever become useful to human medicine. And yet human medicine was what Torrey Pines Generique was organized to do.

"It looks really promising, eh?" Derek said. "It could be that it's an algorithm that is like a law of nature. The grammar of how genes express themselves. It could mean a whole suite of patents."

"Mm hmmm," Bannet said, looking down again at Derek's laptop, which was still at the financial page. Almost pathetic, really; except it must have been a fairly common story, so that Bannet would not necessarily be shocked or put off. He would simply be considering the investment on a risk-adjusted basis, which would take the present situation into account.

Finally he said, "It looks very interesting. Of course it's always a bit of a sketchy feeling, when you've gotten to the point of having all your eggs in one basket like this. But sometimes one is all you need. The truth is, I don't really know yet."

Derek nodded in reluctant agreement. "Well, you know. We believe very strongly in the importance of therapies for the most serious diseases, and so we concentrated on that, and now we kind of have to, you know, go on from there with our best ideas. That's why we've focused on the HDL upgrade. With this targeted delivery, it could be worth billions."

"And the HDL upgrade . . ."

"We haven't published those results yet. We're still looking into the patent situation."

Leo's stomach tightened, but he kept his face blank.

Bannet was even blanker; still friendly and sympathetic enough, but with that piercing eye. "Send me the rest of your business plan, and all the scientific publications that relate to this. All the data. I'll discuss it with some of my partners here. It seems like the kind of thing that I'd like to get my partners' inputs on. That's not unusual, it's just that it's bigger than what I usually do on my own. And some of my colleagues are into agropharmacy stuff."

"Sure," Derek said, handing over a glossy folder of material he had already prepared. "I understand. We can come back and talk to them too if you like, answer any questions."

"That's good, thanks." Bannet put the folder on the table. With a few more pleasantries and a round of hand-shaking, Derek and Leo were ushered out.

Leo found he had no idea whether the meeting had gone well or poorly.

CHAPTER 7

TIT FOR TAT

"Money is the mother's milk of politics," said Jesse Unruh long ago, but he might have been quoting something tapped in cuneiform on the tablets of Ur. Money is power; politics is the fight for power; politicians need money to stay in office; and so they all congeal together. Influence is the sour milk of politics.

Spending money on political campaigns is legal as part of the First Amendment's right to free speech, or so it has been asserted, most notably by the Roberts Supreme Court. So rich people are very loud speakers. This was something Phil Chase noticed every time he attended a fund-raiser, which happened on average twice a day. Some days his staff gave him a pass or failed to find suitable events, but other days were packed with half a dozen events, sequenced meticulously and carried out like commando operations. Cutting cash out of the heart of capital. Phil called it charm piracy, but only in conversation with his most trusted staffers. They laughed and told him to do his job.

Phil was one of the least wealthy senators, and had famously funded one of his earliest campaigns by asking supporters to send him all the change on their dressers and elsewhere in the house. "You'll be glad to get rid of it," he said. "Just be sure to pay the shipping costs too, or else I'll pay more in mail costs than I take in." Which was true; but mostly people paid for the postage, and he took in many tons of cash. Photos of him standing chest-deep in coins were popular.

Now it wasn't like that anymore. Breakfasts, lunches, dinners, cocktail par-

ties, mixers, seminars, meetings, soirées: each was important to the people there, so Phil had to gear up and perform, be there, be on. Luckily he enjoyed it. This was what made him good; he liked talking to people, he liked to perform. He thought if you gave him a chance, he could persuade you. Most people get over that, after experience teaches them otherwise, but Phil had the pigheadedness of his convictions.

Teachers' union, Chamber of Commerce, environmental NGO, liberal think tank, a pod of whales (he was friends with many big donors); this was just one day. The science of any given Wednesday. "So look," he would say, looking the donors in the eye, "anything you give the campaign will get well spent. You know my beliefs, and I'll never deviate from pursuing those beliefs, that's my promise." He thought it helped that he himself made the ask. His development people (i.e., his fund-raisers) weren't so sure, but he was the boss. And money kept coming in. Two fund-raisers a day, every day; thus seven hundred a year; thus 4,200 events in each term as senator. Money is speech; people like to talk; and loud people have things to say. Getting rich gave them lots of opinions. Phil was happy to let them speak through him.

Although sometimes, late at night, being driven back through the great dark capital, he would lean back in his seat and murmur, "Campaign finance reform. Roy, look into that again, will you?"

"Sure thing boss."

"What have we got tomorrow?"

"Breakfast with the Finance Reform Investment Group."

"Really? Breakfast?"

"Phil, you'll eat those guys for breakfast."

"True. But I hate the taste they leave in my mouth. Campaign finance reform, Roy. Write me up a bill about that. Pull out the file."

"Sure thing boss."

"Then who's for lunch?"

"You don't want to know."

Anna flew through the blur of a midweek day. Up and off, Metro to the office; pound the keys, the spreadsheet work eating up hours like minutes. Stop to pump, then to eat at her desk (it felt a little too weird to eat and pump at the same time), all the while data wrangling. Then a look at an e-mail from Drepung and Sucandra about their grant proposals.

Anna had helped them to write several proposals, and that had been fine, as they did all the real work, while she just added her expertise in grant writing, honed through some tens of thousands of grant evaluations. She definitely knew how to sequence the information, what to emphasize, what language to use, what supporting documents, what arguments. Every word and punctuation mark of a grant proposal she had a feel for, one way or the other. It had been a pleasure to apply that expertise to help the Khembalis.

Now she was pleased again to find that they had heard back from three of them, two positively. NSF had awarded them a starter grant in the "Tropical Oceans, Global Atmosphere" effort; and the INDOEX countries had agreed to include a big new monitoring facility on Khembalung. Altogether it meant funding streams for several years to come, tens of millions of dollars all told, with infrastructure built, and relationships with neighboring countries established.

"Very nice," Anna said, and cc'd the news to Charlie, sent congratulations to Drepung, and then got back to work on her spreadsheet.

After a while she remembered about some sheets she had printed up, and went around the corner to the Department of Unfortunate Statistics. She found Frank inside, shaking his head over the latest.

"Have you seen this one?" he said, gesturing with his nose at a taped-up printout of yet another spreadsheet.

"No, I don't think so."

"It's the latest Gini figures, do you know those?"

"No?"

"They're a measurement of income distribution in a population, so an index of the gap between rich and poor. Most industrialized democracies rate at between 25 and 35, that's where we were in the 1950s, see, but our numbers started to shoot up in the 1980s, and now we're worse than the worst third-world countries. Forty or greater is considered to be very inequitable, and we're at 52 and rising."

Anna looked briefly at the graph, interested in the statistical method. A Lorenz curve, plotting the distance away from perfect equality's straight line, which would tilt at forty-five degrees.

"Interesting . . . So this is for annual incomes?"

"That's right."

"So if it were for capital assets—"

"It would be worse." Frank shook his head, disgusted. He had come back from San Diego in a foul mood. No doubt anxious to finish and go home.

"Well," Anna said, "the Khembalis have gotten a couple of grants."

"Very nice, did you do it?"

"I just pointed them at things. They're turning out to be good at following through. And I helped Drepung rewrite their grant proposals. You know how it is, after doing this for a few years, you do know how to write a grant proposal."

"No lie. Nice job. Good to see someone doing something."

Anna returned to her desk, glancing after him. He was definitely edgy these days. He had always been that way, of course. Dissatisfied, cynical, sharp-tongued; it was hard not to contrast him to the Khembalis. Here he was, about to go home to one of the best departments in one of the best universities in one of the nicest cities in the world's richest country, and he was unhappy. Meanwhile the Khembalis were essentially multigenerational exiles, occupying a tidal sandbar in near poverty, and they were happy.

Or at least cheerful. She did not mean to downplay their situation, but these days she never saw that unhappy look that had so struck her the first time she had seen Drepung. No, they were cheerful, which was different than happy; a policy, rather than a feeling. But that only made it more admirable.

Well, everyone was different. She got back to the tedious grind of wrangling data. Then Drepung called, and they shared the pleasure of the good news about the grant proposals. They discussed the details, and then Drepung said, "We have you to thank for this, Anna. So thank you."

"You're welcome, but it wasn't really me, it's NSF."

"But you piloted us through the maze. We owe you big-time."

Anna laughed despite herself.

"What?"

"Nothing, it's just that you sound like Charlie. You sound like you've been watching sports on TV."

"I do like watching basketball."

"That's fine. Just don't start listening to rap, okay?"

"You know me, I like Bollywood. Anyway, you must let us thank you for this. We will have you to dinner."

"That would be nice."

"And maybe you can join us at the zoo when our tigers arrive. Recently a pair of Bengal tigers were rescued off Khembalung after a flood. The papers in India call them the Swimming Tigers, and they are coming for a stay at the National Zoo here, and we will have a small ceremony when they arrive."

"That would be great. The boys would love that. And also—" An idea had occurred to her.

"Yes?"

"Maybe also you could come upstairs and visit us here, and give one of our lunchtime lectures. That would be a great way to return a favor. We could learn more about your situation, and, you know, your approach to science, or to life or whatever. Something like that. Do you think Rudra would be interested?"

"I'm sure he would. It would be a great opportunity."

"Well not exactly, it's just a lunchtime series of talks that Aleesha runs, but I do think it would be interesting. We could use some of your attitude here, I think, and you could talk about these programs too."

"I'll talk to the rimpoche about it."

"Okay good. I'll put Aleesha in touch."

After that Anna worked on the stats again, until she saw the time and realized it was her day to visit Nick's class and help them with math hour. "Ah shit." Throw together a bag of work stuff, shut down, heft the shoulder bag of chilled milk bottles, and off she went. Down into the Metro, working as she sat, then standing on the crowded Red Line Shady Grove train; out and up and into a taxi, of all things, to get to Nick's school on time.

She arrived just a little late, dumped her stuff, and settled down to work with the kids. Nick was in third grade now, but had been put in an advanced math group. In general the class did things in math that Anna found surprising for their age. She liked working with them; there were twenty-eight kids in the class, and Mrs. Wilkins, their teacher, was grateful for the help.

Anna wandered from group to group, helping with multipart problems that involved multiplication, division, and rounding off. When she came to Nick's group she sat down on one of the tiny chairs next to him, and they elbowed each other playfully for room at the round low table. He loved it when she came to his class, which she tried to do on a semiregular basis.

"All right Nick quit that, show the gang here how you're going to solve this problem."

"Okay." He furrowed his brow in a way she recognized inside the muscles of her own forehead. "Thirty-nine divided by two, that's . . . nineteen and a half . . . round that up to twenty—"

"No, don't round off in the middle of the process."

"Mom, come on."

"Hey, you shouldn't."

"Mom, you're quibbling again!" Nick exclaimed.

The group cackled at this old joke.

"It's not quibbling," Anna insisted. "It's a very important distinction."

"What, the difference between nineteen and a half and twenty?"

"Yes," over their squeals of laughter, "because you should never round off in the middle of an operation, because then the things you do later will exaggerate the inaccuracy! It's an important principle!"

"Mrs. Quibler is a quibbler, Mrs. Quibler is a quibbler!"

Anna gave in and gave them The Eye, a squinting, one-eyed glare that she had worked up long ago when playing Lady Bracknell in high school. It never failed to crack them up. She growled, "That's Quibler with one *b*," melting them with laughter, as always, until Mrs. Wilkins came over to join the party and quiet it down.

After school Anna and Nick walked home together. It took about half an hour, and was one of the treasured rituals of their week—the only time they got to spend together, just the two of them. Past the big public pool, past the grocery store, then down their quiet street. It was hot, of course, but bearable in the shade. They talked about whatever came into their heads.

Then they entered the coolness of their house, and returned to the wilder world of Joe and Charlie. Charlie was bellowing as he cooked in the kitchen, an off-key, wordless aria. Joe was killing dinosaurs in the living room. As they entered he froze, considering how he was going to signify his displeasure at Anna's treasonous absence for the day. When younger this had been a genuine emotion; sometimes when he saw her come in the door he had simply burst into tears. Now it was calculated, and she was immune.

He smacked himself in the forehead with a Compsognathus, then collapsed to the rug face-first.

"Oh come on," Anna said. "Give me a break Joe." She started to unbutton her blouse. "You better be nice if you want to nurse."

Joe popped right up and ran over to give her a hug.

"Right," Anna said. "Blackmail will get you everywhere. Hi hon!" she yelled in at Charlie.

"Hi babe." Charlie came out to give her a kiss. For a second all her boys hung on her. Then Joe was latched on, and Charlie and Nick went into the kitchen. From there Charlie shouted out from time to time, but Anna couldn't yell back without making Joe mad enough to bite her, so she waited until he was done and then walked around the corner into the kitchen.

"How was your day?" Charlie said.

"I fixed a data error all day long."

"That's good dear."

She gave him a look. "I swore I wasn't going to do it," she said darkly, "but I just couldn't bring myself to ignore it."

"No, I'm sure you couldn't."

He kept a straight face, but she punched him on the arm anyway. "Smart-ass. Is there any beer in the fridge?"

"I think so."

She hunted for one. "There was some good news that came in, did you see that? I forwarded it. The Khembalis got a couple of grants."

"Really! That is good news." He was sniffing at a yellow curry bubbling in the frying pan.

"Something new?"

"Yeah, I'm trying something out of the paper."

"You're being careful?"

He grinned. "Yeah, no blackened redfish."

"Blackened redfish?" Nick repeated, alarmed.

"Don't worry, even I wouldn't try it on you."

"He wouldn't want you to catch fire."

"Hey, it was in the recipe. It was right out of the recipe!"

"So? A tablespoon each of black pepper, white pepper, cayenne, and chili powder?"

"How was I supposed to know?"

"What do you mean? You should have known what a tablespoon of pepper would taste like, and that was the least hot of them."

"I guess I didn't know it would all stick to the fish."

Nick was looking appalled. "I wouldn't eat that."

"You aren't kidding," Anna laughed. "One touch with your tongue and you would spontaneously combust."

"It was in a cookbook."

"Even going in the kitchen next day was enough to burn your eyes out."

Charlie was giggling at his folly, holding the stirring spoon down to Nick to gross him out, although now he had a very light touch with the spices. The curry would be fine. Anna left him to it and went out to play with Joe.

She sat down on the couch, relaxed. Joe began to pummel her knees with blocks, babbling energetically. At the same time Nick was telling her something about something. She had to interrupt him, almost, to tell him about the coming of the Swimming Tigers. He nodded and took off again with his account. She heaved a great sigh of relief, took a sip of the beer. Another day flown past like a dream.

Another heat wave struck, the worst so far. People had thought it was hot before, but now it was July, and one day the temperature in the metropolitan area climbed to 105 degrees, with the humidity over ninety percent. The combination had all the Indians in town waxing nostalgic about Uttar Pradesh just before the monsoon broke. "Oh yes just like this in Delhi, actually it would be a blessing if it were to be like this in Delhi, that would be an improvement over what they have now, they need the monsoon very badly."

The morning *Post* included an article informing Charlie that a chunk of the Ross Ice Shelf had broken off, a chunk more than half the size of France. The news was buried in the last pages of the international section. So many pieces of Antarctica had fallen off that it wasn't big news anymore.

It wasn't big news, but it was a big iceberg. Researchers joked about moving onto it and declaring it a new nation. It contained more fresh water than all the Great Lakes combined. And pouring down toward it, researchers said, was the rapid ice of the West Antarctic Ice Sheet, unimpeded now that the Ross Shelf in that region had embarked. This accelerated flow of ice had big implications. The West Antarctic Ice Sheet was much bigger than the Ross Ice Shelf, and if it broke up sea level might rise a few meters, quite quickly.

Charlie read on, amazed that he was learning this in the back pages of the *Post*. How fast could this happen? The researchers didn't appear to know. Charlie followed it up on the web, and watched one trio of researchers explain on camera that it could become an accelerating process, their words likewise accelerating a bit as if to illustrate how it would go. It might happen fast.

Charlie heard in their voices the kind of repressed delirium of scientific excitement that he had once or twice heard when listening to Anna talk about some extraordinary thing in statistics that he had not even been able to understand. This, however, he understood; they were saying that the possibility was very real that the whole mass of the West Antarctic Ice Sheet would break apart and float away, each giant piece of it then sinking more deeply into the water, thus displacing more water than it had when grounded in place—so much more that sea level worldwide could rise by an eventual total of up to seven meters. It depended on variables programmed into the models—on they went, the usual kind of scientist talk.

And yet the *Post* had it at the back of the international section! People were talking about it the same way they did any other disaster. There did not seem to be any way to register a distinction in response between one coming catastrophe and another. If it happened it happened. That seemed to be the way people were processing it. Of course the Khembalis would have to be extremely concerned. The whole League of Drowning Nations, for that matter. Really everyone. All of a sudden it coalesced into a clear vision, and what he saw frightened him. Twenty percent of humanity lived on coasts. He felt like he had one time driving in winter when he had taken a turn too fast and hit an icy patch he hadn't seen, and the car had detached and he found himself flying forward, free of friction or even gravity, as if sideslipping in reality itself. . . .

But it was time to go downtown. He was going to take Joe with him to the office. He pulled himself together, got out the stroller so they would spare each other their body heat. Life had to go on; what else could he do?

Out they ventured into the steambath of the capital. It really didn't feel that much different than an ordinary summer day; it was as if the sensation of heat hit an upper limit where it just blurred out. Joe was seat-belted into his stroller like a NASCAR driver, so that he would not launch himself out at inopportune moments. Naturally he did not like this, and he objected to the stroller because of it, but Charlie had decorated its front bar as an airplane cockpit dashboard, which placated Joe enough that he did not persist in his howls or attempts to escape.

They took the elevators in the Metro stations, and came up on the Mall to stroll over to Phil's office. A bad idea, as crossing the Mall was like being blanched in boiling air. Charlie, as always, experienced the climate deviation with a kind of grim "I told you so" satisfaction.

At Phil's they rolled around the rooms trying to find the best spots in the falls of chilled air pouring from the air-conditioning vents. Everyone was doing this, drifting around to find the coolest drafts, like a science museum exercise investigating the Coriolis force.

Charlie parked Joe out with Evelyn, who loved him, and went to work on Phil's revisions to the climate bill. It certainly seemed like a good time to introduce it. More money for carbon remediation, new fuel efficiency standards and the money to get Detroit through the transition to hydrogen, new fuels and power sources, carbon capture methods, carbon sink identification and formation, hydrocarbon-to-carbohydrate-to-hydrogen conversion funds and exchange credit programs, deep geothermal, tide power, wave power, money for basic research in climatology, money for the Extreme Global Research in Emergency Salvation Strategies project (EGRESS), money for the Global Disaster Information Network (GDIN), an escalating carbon tax—and so on and so forth. It was a grab bag of programs, many designed to look like pork to help the bill get the votes, but Charlie had done his best to give the whole thing organization, and a kind of coherent shape, as a narrative of the near future.

There were many in Phil's office who thought it was a mistake to try to pass an omnibus or comprehensive bill like this, rather than get the programs funded one by one, or in smaller related groupings. But the comprehensive had been Phil's chosen strategy, and Charlie agreed with it. He added language to make the revisions Phil wanted, pushing the envelope in each case. Now was the time to strike.

Joe was beginning to get rowdy with Evelyn, he could hear the unmistakable sound of dinosaurs hitting walls. All this language would get chopped up anyway; still, best get it armored against attack. Bill language as low-post moves to the basket, subtle, quick, unstoppable.

He rushed to a finish and took the revised bill in to Phil, with Joe leading the way in his stroller. They found the senator sitting with his back directly against an air-conditioning duct.

"Jeez Phil, don't you get too cold sitting there?"

"The trick is to set up before you're all sweaty." He glanced over Charlie's new revision, and they argued over some of the changes. At one point Phil looked at him: "Something bugging you today?" He glanced over at Joe. "Joe here seems to be grooving."

"It's not Joe that's getting to me, it's you. You and the rest of the Senate. Because the current situation requires a response that is more than business as usual. And that worries me, because you guys only do business as usual."

"Well . . ." Phil smiled. "We call that democracy, youth. It's a blessing when you think of it. Some give-and-take, and then some agreement on how to proceed. How can we do without that? If you have a better way of doing it, you tell me. But meanwhile, no more 'If I Were King' fantasies. There's no king and it's up to us. So help me get this final draft as tight as we can."

"Okay."

They worked together with the speed and efficiency of old teammates. Sometimes collaboration could be a pleasure, sometimes it really was a matter of only having to do half of it, and the two halves adding up to more than their parts.

Then Joe got restive, and nothing would keep him in his stroller but a quick departure and a tour of the street scene. "I'll finish," Phil said.

So, back out into the stupendous heat. Charlie was knocked out by it faster than Joe. The world melted around them. Charlie gumbied along, leaning on the stroller for support. Down an elevator into the Metro. Air-conditioning again, thank God. Crash into pink seat cushions. As they rode north, slumped and rocking slightly with their train, Charlie drowsily entertained Joe with some of the toys in the stroller, picking them up and fingering them one by one. "See, this turtle is NIH. Your Frankenstein monster is the FDA, look how poorly he's put together. This little mole, that's Mom's NSF. These two guys, they're like the guy on the Monopoly game, they must be the two parts of Congress, yeah, very Tammany Hall. Where the hell did you get those. Your Iron Giant is of course the Pentagon, and this yellow bulldozer is the U.S. Army Corp of Engineers. The magnifying glass is the GAO, and this, what is this, Barbie? That must be the OMB, those bimbos, or maybe this Pinocchio here. And your cowboy on a horse is the President of course, he's your friend, he's your friend."

They were both falling asleep. Joe batted the toy figures into a pile.

"Careful Joe. Ooh, there's your tiger. That's the press corps, that's a circus tiger, see its collar? Nobody's scared of it. Although sometimes it does get to eat somebody."

Phil took the climate bill back to the Foreign Relations Committee, and the process of marking it up began in earnest. To mark up was a very inadequate verb: "carving," "rendering," "hacking," "hatcheting," "stomping," any of these would have been more accurate, Charlie thought as he tracked the gradual deconstruction of the language of the bill, the result turned slowly into a kind of sausage of thought.

The bill lost parts as they duked it out. Winston fought every phrase of it, and he had to be given some concessions or nothing would proceed. No further increase in fuel efficiencies, no acknowledgment of any measurements like the ecological footprint. Phil gave on these because Winston was promising that he would get the House to agree to this version in conference, and the White House would back him too. And so entire methodologies of analysis were being declared off-limits, something that would drive Anna crazy. Another example of science and capital clashing, Charlie thought. Science was like Beaker from the Muppets, haplessly struggling with the round top-hatted guy from the Monopoly game. Right now Beaker was getting his butt kicked.

Two mornings later Charlie learned about it in the *Post*:

CLIMATE SUPERBILL SPLIT UP IN COMMITTEE

"Say what!" Charlie hadn't even heard of this possibility. He read paragraphs per eye-twitch while he told his phone to call Roy:

> *... proponents of the new bills claimed compromises would not damage effectiveness ... President made it clear he would veto the comprehensive bill ... promised to sign specific bills on a case-by-case basis ...*

"Ah shit. Shit. God damn it!"

"Charlie, that must be you."

"Roy what is this shit, when did this happen?"

"Last night. Didn't you hear?"

"No I didn't! How could Phil do this!"

"We counted votes, and the biggie wasn't going to get out of committee. And if it did, the House wasn't going to go for it. Winston couldn't deliver, or wouldn't. So Phil decided to support Ellington on Ellington's alternative fuels bill, and he put more of Ellington's stuff in the first several shorter bills."

"And Ellington agreed to vote for it on that basis."

"That's right."

"So Phil traded horses."

"The comprehensive was going to lose."

"You don't know that for sure! They had Speck with them and so they could have carried it on party lines! Who cares what kind of fuel we're burning if the world has melted! This was important, Roy!"

"It wasn't going to win," Roy said, enunciating each word. "We counted the votes and it lost by one. After that we went for what we could. You know Phil. He likes to get things done."

"As long as they're easy."

"You're still pissed off about this. You should go talk to Phil yourself, maybe it will impact what he does next time. I've got to get to a meeting."

"Okay maybe I'll do that."

And as it was another morning of Joe and Dad on the town, he was free to do so. He sat on the Metro, absorbing Joe's punches and thinking things over, and when he got the stroller out of the elevator on the third floor of the office he drove it straight for Phil, who today was sitting on a desk in the outer conference room, holding court as blithe and bald-faced as a monkey.

Charlie aimed the wadded *Post* like a stick at Phil, who saw him and winced theatrically. "Okay!" he said, palm held out to stop the assault. "Okay kick my ass! Kick my ass right here! But I tell you, they made me do it."

He was turning it into another office debate, so Charlie went for it full bore. "What do you mean? You caved, Phil. You gave away the store!"

Phil shook his head vehemently. "I got more than I gave. They're going to reduce carbon emissions anyway, we were never going to get more on that—"

"What do you mean!" Charlie shouted.

Andrea and some of the others came out of their rooms, and even Evelyn looked in, though mostly to say hi to Joe. It was a regular shtick: Charlie hammering Phil for his compromises, Phil admitting to all and baiting Charlie to ever greater outrage. Charlie, recognizing this, was still determined to make his point, even if it meant he had to play his usual part. Even if he didn't convince Phil, if Phil's group would bear down on him a little harder . . .

Charlie whacked Phil with the *Post*. "If you would have stuck to your guns we could have sequestered billions of tons of carbon!"

Phil made a face. "I would have stuck to my guns, Charlie, but then the rest of our wonderful party would have shot me in the foot with those guns. The House wasn't there either. This way we got what was possible. We got it out of committee, damn it, and that's not peanuts. We got out with the full roadless forest requirement and the Arctic refuge and the offshore drilling ban, all of those, and the President has promised to sign them already."

"They were always gonna give you those! You would have had to have died not to get those. Meanwhile you gave up on the really crucial stuff."

"Did not."

"Did too."

"Did not."

"Did too!"

Yes, this was the level of debate in the offices of one of the greatest senators in the land. It always came down to that between them.

But this time Charlie wasn't enjoying it like he usually did. "What *didn't* you give up," he said bitterly.

"Just the forests, streams, and oil of North America!"

Their little audience laughed. It was still a debating society to them. Phil licked his finger and chalked one up, then smiled at Charlie, a shot of the pure Chase grin, fetching and mischievous.

Charlie was unassuaged. "You'd better fund a bunch of submarines to enjoy all those things."

That too got a laugh. And Phil chalked one up for Charlie, still smiling.

Charlie pushed Joe's stroller out of the building, cursing bitterly. Joe heard his tone of voice and absorbed himself in the passing scene and his dinosaurs. Charlie pushed him along, sweating, feeling more and more discouraged. He knew he was taking it too seriously, he knew that Phil's house style was to treat it as a game, to keep taking shots and not worry too much. But still, he couldn't help it. He felt as if he had been kicked in the stomach.

This didn't happen very often. He usually managed to find some way to compensate in his mind for the various reversals of any political day. Bright side, silver lining, eventual revenge, whatever. Some fantasy in which it all came right. So when discouragement did hit him, it struck home with unaccustomed force. It became a global thing for which he had no defense; he couldn't see the forest for the trees, he couldn't see the good in anything. The black clouds had black linings. All bad! Bad bad bad bad bad bad bad.

He pushed into a Metro elevator, descended with Joe into the depths. They got on a car, came to the Bethesda stop. Charlie zombied them out of the Metro car. Bad, bad, bad. Sartrean nausea, induced by a sudden glimpse of reality; horrible that it should be so. That the true nature of reality should be so awful. The blanched air in the elevator was unbreathable. Gravity was too heavy.

Out of the elevator, onto Wisconsin. Bethesda was too dismal. A spew of office and apartment blocks, obviously organized (if that was the word) for the convenience of the cars roaring by. A ridiculous, inhuman autopia. It might as well have been Orange County.

He dragged down the sidewalk home. Walked in the front door. The screen door slapped to behind him with its characteristic whack.

From the kitchen: "Hi hon!"

"Hi Dad!"

It was Anna and Nick's day to come home together after school.

"Momma Momma Momma!"

"Hi Joe!"

Refuge. "Hi guys," Charlie said. "We need a rowboat. We'll keep it in the garage."

"Cool!"

Anna heard his tone of voice and came out of the kitchen with a whisk in hand, gave him a hug and a peck on the cheek.

"Hmm," he said, a kind of purr.

"What's wrong babe."

"Oh, everything."

"Poor hon."

He began to feel better. He released Joe from the stroller and they followed Anna into the kitchen. As Anna picked up Joe and held him on her hip while she continued to cook, Charlie began to shape the story of the day in his mind, to be able to tell her about it with all its drama intact.

After he had told the story, and fulminated for a bit, and opened and drunk a beer, Anna said, "What you need is some way to bypass the political process."

"Whoa babe. I'm not sure I want to know what you mean there."

"I don't know anyway."

"Revolution, right?"

"No way."

"A completely nonviolent and successful positive revolution?"

"Good idea."

Nick appeared in the doorway. "Hey Dad, want to play some baseball?"

"Sure. Good idea."

Nick seldom proposed this, it was usually Charlie's idea, and so when Nick did it he was trying to make Charlie feel better, which just by itself worked pretty well. So they left the coolness of the house and played in the steamy backyard, under the blind eyes of the banked apartment windows. Nick stood against the brick back of the house while Charlie pitched Wiffle balls at him, and he smacked them with a long plastic bat. Charlie tried to catch them if he could. They had about a dozen balls, and when they were scattered over the downsloping lawn, they recollected them on Charlie's mound and did it over again, or let Charlie take a turn at bat. The Wiffle balls were great; they shot off the bat with a very satisfying plastic whirr, and yet it was painless to get hit by one, as Charlie often did. Back and forth in the livid dusk, sweating and laughing, trying to get a Wiffle ball to go straight.

Charlie took off his shirt and sweated into the sweaty air. "Okay here comes the pitch. Sandy Koufax winds up, rainbow curve! Hey why didn't you swing?"

"That was a ball, Dad. It bounced before it got to me."

"Okay here I'll try again. Oh Jesus."

"Why do you say 'Jesus,' Dad?"

"It's a long story, ha. Okay here's another. Why didn't you swing?"

"It was a ball!"

"Not by much. Walks won't get you off de island mon."

"The strike zone is taped here to the house, Dad. Just throw one that would hit inside it and I'll swing."

"That was a bad idea. Okay, here you go. Ooh, very nice. Okay, here you go. Hey come on swing at those!"

"That one was behind me."

"Switch hitting is a valuable skill."

"Just throw strikes!"

"I'm trying. Okay here it comes, boom! Very nice! Home run, wow. Uh oh, it got stuck in the tree, see that?"

"We've got enough anyway."

"True, but look, I can get a foot into this branch . . . here, give me the bat for a second. Might as well get it while we remember where it is."

Charlie climbed a short distance up the tree, steadied himself, brushed leaves aside, reached in and embraced the trunk for balance, knocked the Wiffle ball down with Nick's bat.

"There you go!"

"Hey Dad, what's that vine growing up into the tree? Isn't that poison ivy?"

CHAPTER 8

A PARADIGM SHIFT

Let's rehearse what we know about who we are.

We are primates, very closely related to chimps and other great apes. Our ancestors speciated from the other apes about five million years ago, and evolved in parallel lines and overlapping subspecies, emerging most clearly as hominids about two million years ago.

East Africa in this period was getting drier and drier. The forest was giving away to grassland savannahs dotted with scattered groves of trees. We evolved to adapt to that landscape: the hairlessness, the upright posture, the sweat glands and other physical features. They all made us capable of running long distances in the open sun near the equator. We ran for a living and covered broad areas. We used to run game down by following it until it tired out, sometimes days later.

In that basically stable mode of living the generations passed, and during the many millennia that followed, the size of hominid brains evolved from about 300 cubic centimeters to about 1200 cubic centimeters. This is a strange fact, because everything else remained relatively stable. The implication is that the way we lived then was tremendously stimulating to the growth of the brain. Almost every aspect of hominid life has been proposed as the main driver of this growth, everything from the calculation of accurate rock throwing to the ability to dream, but certainly among the most important must have been language and social life. We talked, we got along; it's a difficult process, requiring lots of thought. Because reproduction is crucial to any defi-

nition of evolutionary success, getting along with the group and with the op-
posite sex is fundamentally adaptive, and so it must be a big driver of
increasing brain size. We grew so fast we can hardly fit through the birth
canal these days. All that growth from trying to understand other people, the
other sex, and look where we are.

Anna was pleased to see Frank back in the office, brusque and grouchy though he was. He made things more interesting. A rant against oversized pickup trucks would morph into an explanation of everything in terms of yes or no, or a discussion of the social intelligence of gibbons, or an algebra of the most efficient division of labor in the lab. It was impossible to predict what he would say next. Sentences would start reasonably and then go strange, or vice versa. Anna liked that.

He did, however, seem overly impressed by game theory. "What if the numbers don't correspond to real life?" she asked him. "What if you don't get five points for defecting when the other person doesn't, what if all those numbers are off, or even backwards? Then it's just another computer game, right?"

"Well—" Frank was taken aback. A rare sight. Immediately he was thinking it over. That was another thing Anna liked about him; he would really think about what she said.

Then Anna's phone rang and she picked up.

"Charlie! Oh dovelie, how are you?"

"Screaming agony."

"Oh babe. Did you take your pills?"

"I took them. They're not doing a thing. I'm starting to see things in the corners of my eyes, crawlies you know? I think the itches have gotten into my brain. I'm going nuts."

"Just hold on. It'll take a couple of days for the steroids to have an effect. Keep taking them. Is Joe giving you a break?"

"No. He wants to wrestle."

"Don't let him! I know the doctor said it wasn't transmissible, but—"

"Don't worry. Not a fucking chance of wrestling."

"You're not touching him?"

"And he's not touching me. He's getting pretty pissed off about it."

"You're putting on the plastic gloves to change him?"

"Yes yes yes yes, tortures of the damned, when I take them off the skin comes too, blood and yuck, and then I get *so* itchy."

"Poor babe. Just try not to do anything."

Then he had to chase Joe out of the kitchen. Anna hung up.

Frank looked at her. "Poison ivy?"

"Yep. He climbed into a tree that had it growing up its trunk. He didn't have his shirt on."

"Oh no."

"It got him pretty good. Nick recognized it, and so I took him to urgent care and the doctor put some stuff on him and put him on steroids even before the blistering began, but he's still pretty wiped out."

"Sorry to hear."

"Yeah, well, at least it's something superficial."

Then Frank's phone rang, and he went into his cubicle to answer. Anna couldn't help but hear his end of it, as they had already been talking—and then also, as the call went on, his voice got louder several times. At one point he said "You're kidding" four times in a row, each time sounding more incredulous. After that he only listened for a while, his fingers drumming on the tabletop next to his terminal.

Finally he said, "I don't know what happened, Derek. You're the one who's in the best position to know that. . . . Yeah that's right. They must have had their reasons. . . . Well you'll be okay whatever happens, you were vested right? . . . Everyone has options they don't exercise, don't think about that, think about the stock you did have. . . . Hey that's one of the winning endgames. Go under, go public, or get bought. Congratulations . . . Yeah it'll be fascinating to see, sure. Sure. Yeah, that is too bad. Okay yeah. Call me back with the whole story when I'm not at work here. Yeah bye."

He hung up. There was a long silence from his cubicle.

Finally he got up from his chair, squeak-squeak. Anna swiveled to look, and there he was, standing in her doorway, expecting her to turn.

He made a funny face. "That was Derek Gaspar, out in San Diego. His company Torrey Pines Generique has been bought."

"Oh really! That's the one you helped start?"

"Yeah."

"Well, congratulations then. Who bought it?"

"A bigger biotech called Small Delivery Systems, have you heard of it?"

"No."

"I hadn't either. It's not one of the big pharmaceuticals by any means, midsized from what Derek says. Mostly into agropharmacy, he says, but they approached him and made the offer. He doesn't know why."

"They must have said?"

"Well, no. At least he doesn't seem to be clear on why they did it."

"But it's still good, right? I thought this was what start-ups hope for."

"True . . ."

"You're not looking like someone who has just become a millionaire."

He quickly waved that away, "It's not that, I'm not involved like that. I was only a consultant, UCSD only lets you have a small involvement in outside firms, and I had to stop even that when I came here. Can't be working for the feds and someone else too, you know."

"Uh-huh."

"My investments are in a blind trust, so who knows. I didn't have much in Torrey Pines, and the trust may have gotten rid of it. I heard something that made me think they did. I would have if I were them."

"Oh well that's too bad then."

"Yeah yeah," frowning at her, "but that isn't the problem."

He stared out the window, across the atrium into all the other windows. There was a look on his face she had never seen before—chagrined—she couldn't quite read it. Distressed.

"What is then?"

Quietly he said, "I don't know." Then: "The system is messed up."

She said, "You should come to the brown-bag lecture tomorrow. Rudra Cakrin, the Khembali ambassador, is going to be talking about the Buddhist view of science. No, you should. You sound like them, at least sometimes."

He frowned as if this were a criticism.

"No, come on. You'll find it interesting, I'm sure."

"Okay. Maybe. If I finish a letter I'm working on."

He went back to his cubicle, sat down heavily. "God damn it," Anna heard him say.

Then he started to type. It was like the sound of thought itself, a rapid-fire plastic tipping and tapping, interrupted by hard whaps of his thumb against the space bar. His keyboard really took a pounding sometimes.

He was still typing like a madman when Anna saw her clock and rushed out the door to try to get home on time.

The next morning Frank drove in with his farewell letter in a manila envelope. He had decided to elaborate on it, make it into a fully substantiated, crushing indictment of NSF, which, if taken seriously, might inspire some changes. He was going to give it directly to Diane Chang, head of NSF. Private letter, one hard copy. That way she could read it, consider it in private, and decide whether she wanted to do something about it. Whatever she did, he would have taken his shot at trying to improve the place, and could go back to real science with a clean conscience. Leave in peace. Leave some of the anger in him behind. Hopefully.

He had heavily revised the draft he had written on the flight back from San Diego. Bulked up the arguments, made the criticisms more specific, made some concrete suggestions for improvements. It was still a pretty devastating indictment, but this time it was all in the tone of a scientific paper. No getting mad or getting eloquent. Neither chicken nor ostrich. Five pages single-spaced, even after he had cut it to the bone. Well, they needed a kick in the pants. This would certainly do that.

He read it through one more time, then sat there in his office chair, tapping the manila envelope against his leg, looking sightlessly out into the atrium. Wondering, among other things, what had happened to Torrey Pines Generique. Wondering if the hire of Yann Pierzinski had had anything to do with it.

Suddenly he heaved out of his chair, walked to the elevators with the manila envelope and its contents, took an elevator up to the twelfth floor. Walked around to Diane's office and nodded at Laveta, Diane's secretary. He put the envelope in Diane's in-box.

"She's gone for today," Laveta told him.

"That's all right. Let her know when she comes in tomorrow that it's there, will you? It's personal."

"All right."

Back to the sixth floor. He went to his chair and sat down. It was done.

He heard Anna in her office, typing away. He recalled that this was the day she wanted him to join her at the brown-bag lecture. She had apparently helped to arrange for the Khembali ambassador to give the talk. Frank had seen it listed on a sheet announcing the series, posted next to the elevators:

"Purpose of Science from the Buddhist Perspective."

It didn't sound promising to him. Esoteric at best, and perhaps much worse. That would not be unusual for these lunch talks, they were a mixed bag. People were burnt out on regular lectures, the last thing they wanted to do at lunch was listen to more of the same, so this series was deliberately geared toward entertainment. Frank remembered seeing titles like "Antarctica as Utopia," or "The Art of Body Imaging," or "Ways Global Warming Can Help Us." Apparently it was a case of the wackier the topic, the bigger the crowd.

This one would no doubt be well attended.

Anna's door opened; she was leaving for the lecture.

"Are you going to come?" she asked.

"Yeah, sure."

That pleased her. He accompanied her to the elevators, shaking his head at her, at himself. Up to the tenth floor, into the conference room. It held about two hundred people. When the Khembalis arrived, every seat was occupied.

Frank sat down near the back, pretending to work on his pad. Air-conditioned air fell on him like a blessing. People were sitting down in groups, talking about this and that. The Khembalis stood by the lectern. The old ambassador, Rudra Cakrin, wore his maroon robes, while the rest of the Khembali contingent were in off-white cotton pants and shirts, as if in India. Rudra Cakrin needed his mike lowered. His young assistant helped him, then adjusted his own. Translation; what a pain. Frank groaned soundlessly.

They tested the mikes, and the noise of talk dampened. The room was impressively full, Frank had to admit, wacky factor or not. These were people still interested enough in ideas to spend a lunch hour listening to a lecture on the philosophy of science. Surplus time and energy, given over to curiosity: a fundamental hominid behavioral trait. Also the basic trait that got people into science, surviving despite the mind-numbing regimes. Here he was himself, after all, and no one could be more burnt out than he was. Still following a tropism helplessly, like a sunflower turning to look at the sun.

The old monk cut quite a figure up at the lectern, incongruous at best. This might be an admirably curious audience, but it was also a skeptical gang of hardened old technocrats. A tough sell, one would think, for a wizened man in robes, now peering out at them as if from a distant century.

And yet there he stood, and here they sat. Something had brought them together, and it wasn't just the air-conditioning. They sat in their chairs, attentive, courteous, open to new ideas. Frank felt a small glimmer of pride. This is how it had all begun, back in those Royal Society meetings in London in the 1660s: polite listening to a lecture by some odd person who was necessarily an autodidact; polite questions; the matter considered reasonably by all in attendance. An agreement to look at things reasonably. This was the start of it.

The old man stared out with a benign gaze. He seemed to mirror their attention, to study them.

"Good morning!" he said, then made a gesture to indicate that he had exhausted his store of English, except for what followed: "Thank you."

His young assistant then said, "Rimpoche Rudra Cakrin, Khembalung's ambassador to the United States, thanks you for coming to listen to him."

A bit redundant that, but then the old man began to speak in his own language—Tibetan, Anna had said—a low, guttural sequence of sounds. Then he stopped, and the young man, Anna's friend Drepung, began to translate.

"The rimpoche says, Buddhism begins in personal experience. Observation of one's surroundings and one's reactions, and one's thoughts. There is a scientific . . . foundation to the process. He adds now, if I truly understand what you mean in the West when you say science. He says now, I hope you will tell me if I am wrong about it. But science seems to me to be about what happens that we can all agree on."

Now Rudra Cakrin interrupted to ask a question of Drepung, who nodded, then added: "What can be asserted. That if you were to look into it, you would come to agree with the assertion. And everyone else would as well."

A few people in the audience were nodding.

The old man spoke again.

Drepung said, "The things we can agree on are few, and general. And the closer to the time of the Buddha, the more general they are. Now, two thousand and five hundred years have passed, more or less, and we are in the age of the microscope, the telescope, and . . . the mathematical description of reality. These are realms we cannot experience directly with our senses. And yet we can still agree in what we say about these realms. Because they are linked in long chains of mathematical cause and effect, from what we can see."

Rudra Cakrin smiled briefly, spoke. It began to seem to Frank that Drepung's translated pronouncements were much longer than the old man's utterances. Could Tibetan be so compact?

"This network is a very great accomplishment," Drepung added.

Rudra Cakrin then sang in a low gravelly voice, like Louis Armstrong's, only an octave lower.

Drepung chanted in English:

> He who would understand the meaning of Buddha nature,
> Must watch for the season and the causal relations.
> Real life is the life of causes.

Rudra Cakrin followed this with some animated speech.

Drepung translated, "This brings up the concept of Buddha nature, rather than nature in itself. What is that difference? Buddha-nature is the appropriate . . . response to nature. The reply of the observing mind. Buddhist philosophy ultimately points to seeing reality as it is. And then . . ."

Rudra Cakrin spoke urgently.

"Then the response, the reply—the human moment—the things we say, and do, and think—that moment arrives. We come back to the realm of the expressible. The nature of reality—as we go deeper, language is left further behind. Even mathematics is no longer germane. But . . ."

The old man went on for quite some time, until Frank thought he saw Drepung make a gesture or expression with his eyelids, and instantly Rudra Cakrin stopped.

"But, when we come to what we should do, it returns to the simplest of words. Compassion. Right action. Helping others. It always stays that simple. Reduce suffering. There is something—reassuring in this. Greatest complexity of what is, greatest simplicity in what we should do. Much preferable to the reverse situation."

Rudra Cakrin spoke in a much calmer voice now.

"Here again," Drepung went on, "the two approaches overlap and are one. Science began as the hunt for food, comfort, health. We learned how things work in order to control them better. In order to reduce our suffering. The methods involved, observation and trial, in our tradition were refined in medical work. That went on for many ages. In the West, your doctors too did this, and in the process, became scientists. In Asia the Buddhist monks were the doctors, and they too worked on refining methods of observation and trial, to see if they could . . . reproduce their successes, when they had them."

Rudra Cakrin nodded, put a hand to Drepung's arm. He spoke briefly. Drepung said, "The two are now parallel studies. On the one hand, science has specialized, through mathematics and technology, on natural observations, finding out what is, and making new tools. On the other, Buddhism has specialized in human observations, to find out—how to become. Behave. What to do. How to go forward. Now, I say, they are like the two eyes in the head. Both necessary to create whole sight. Or rather . . . there is an old saying. Eyes that see, feet that walk. We could say that science is the eyes, Buddhism the feet."

Frank listened to all this with ever more irritation. Here was a man arguing for a system of thought that had not contributed a single new bit of knowledge to the world for the last 2,500 years, and he had the nerve to put it on an equal basis with science, which was now adding millions of new facts to its accumulated store of knowledge every day. What a farce!

And yet his irritation was filled with uneasiness as well. The young translator kept saying things that weirdly echoed things Frank had thought, or answered questions occurring to Frank at that very moment. Frank thought, for instance, Well, how would all this compute if remembering that we are primates recently off the savannah, foragers with brains that grew to adapt to that surrounding, would any of this make sense? And at that very moment, answering a question from the audience (they seem to have shifted into that mode without a formal announcement of it), Drepung said, still translating the old man:

"We are animals. Animals whose wisdom has extended so far as to tell us we are mortal creatures. We die. For thousands of years we have known this. Much of our mental energy is spent avoiding this knowledge. We do not like to think of it. Then again, we know that even the cosmos is mortal. Reality is mortal. All things change ceaselessly. Nothing remains the same in time. Nothing can be held on to. The question then becomes, what do we do with this knowledge? How do we live with it? How do we make sense of it?"

Well—indeed. Frank leaned forward, piqued, wondering what Drepung would tell them the old man had said next. That gravelly low voice, growling through its incomprehensible sounds—it was strange to think it was expressing such meanings. Frank suddenly wanted to know what he was saying.

"One of the scientific terms for compassion," Drepung said, looking around the ceiling as if for the word, ". . . you say, altruism. This is a question in your animal studies. Does true altruism exist, and is it a good adaptation? Does compassion work, in other words? You have done studies that suggest altruism is the best adaptive strategy, if seen from the group context. This then becomes a kind of . . . admonishment. To practice compassion to successfully evolve—this, coming from your science, which claims to be descriptive only! Only describing what has worked to make us what we are. But in Buddhism we have always said, if you want to help others, practice compassion; if you want to help yourself, practice compassion. Now science adds, if you want to help your species, practice compassion."

This got a laugh, and Frank also chuckled. He started to think about it in terms of prisoner's dilemma strategies; it was an invocation for everyone to make the "always generous" move, for maximum group return, maximum individual return. . . . Thus he missed what Drepung said next, absorbed in something more like a feeling than a thought: *If only I could believe in something, no doubt it would be a relief.* All his rationality, all his acid skepticism; suddenly it was hard not to feel that it was really just some kind of disorder.

And at that moment Rudra Cakrin looked right at him, him alone in all the audience, and Drepung said, "An excess of reason is itself a form of madness."

Frank sat back in his seat. What had the question been? Rerunning his short-term memory, he could not find it.

Now he was lost to the conversation again. His flesh was tingling, as if he were a bell that had been struck.

"The experience of enlightenment can be sudden."

He didn't hear that, not consciously.

"The scattered parts of consciousness occasionally assemble at once into a whole pattern."

He didn't hear that either, as he was lost in thought. All his certainties were trembling.

He thought: an excess of reason is itself a form of madness—it's the story of my life. And the old man knew!

He found himself standing. Everyone else was too. The thing must be over. People were filing out. They were massed in a group at the elevators. Someone said to Frank, "Well, what did you think?" clearly expecting some sharp put-down, something characteristically Frankish, and indeed his mouth was forming the words "Not much for twenty-five hundred years of concentrated study." But he said "Not" and stopped, shuddering at his own habits. He could be such an asshole.

The elevator doors opened and rescued him. He flowed in, rubbed his forearms as if to warm them from the conference room's awesome AC. He said to the inquiring eyes watching him, "Interesting."

There were nods, little smiles. Even that one word, often the highest expression of praise in the scientific tongue, was against type for him. He was making a fool of himself. His group expected him to conform to his persona. That was how group dynamics worked. Surprising people was an unusual thing, faintly unwelcome. Except was it? People certainly paid to be surprised; that was comedy; that was art. It could be proved by analysis. Right now he wasn't sure of anything.

". . . paying attention to the real world," someone was saying.

"A weak empiricism," said someone else.

"How do you mean?" the first person said.

The elevator door opened; Frank saw it was his floor. He got out and went to his office. He stood there in the doorway looking at all his stuff, scattered about for disposal or packing. Piles of books, periodicals, offprints. His exteriorized memory, the paper trail of his life. An excess of reason.

He sat there thinking.

Anna came in. "Hi Frank. How did you like the talk?"

"It was interesting."

She regarded him. "I thought so too. Listen, Charlie and I are having a party for the Khembalis tonight at our place, a little celebration. You should come if you want."

"Thanks," he said. "Maybe I will."

"Good. That would be nice. I've gotta go get ready for it."

"Okay. See you there maybe."

"Okay." With a last curious look, she left.

Sometimes certain images or phrases, ideas or sentences, tunes or snatches of tunes, stick in the head and repeat over and over. For some people this can be a problem, as they get stuck in such loops too often and too long. Most people skip into new ideas or new loops fairly frequently—others at an almost frightening rate of speed, the reverse of the stuck-in-a-loop problem.

Frank had always considered himself to be unstable in this regard, veering strongly either one way or the other. The shift from something like obsessive-compulsive to something like attention-deficit sometimes occurred so quickly that it seemed he might be exhibiting an entirely new kind of bipolarity.

No excess of reason there!

Or maybe that was the base cause of it all. An attempt to gain control. The old monk had looked him right in the eye. An excess of reason is itself a form of madness. Maybe in trying to be reasonable, he had been trying to stay on an even keel. Who could say?

He could see how this might be what Buddhists called a koan, a riddle without an answer, which if pondered long enough might cause the thinking mind to balk, and give up thinking. Give up thinking! That was crazy. And yet in that moment, perhaps the sensory world would come pouring in. Experience of the present, unmediated by language. Unspeakable by definition. Just felt or experienced in mentation of a different sort, languageless, or language-transcendent. Something other.

Frank hated that sort of mysticism. Or maybe he loved it; the experience of it, that is. Like anyone who has ever entered a moment of nonlinguistic absorption, he recalled it as a kind of blessing. Like in the old days, hanging there cleaning windows, singing, "What's my line, I'm happy cleaning windows." Climbing, surfing . . . you could think far faster than you could verbalize in your mind. No doubt one knew the world by way of a flurry of impressions and thoughts that were far faster than consciousness could track. Consciousness was just a small part of it.

He left the building, went out into the humid afternoon. The sight of the street somehow repelled him. He couldn't drive right now. Instead he walked through the car-dominated, slightly junky commercial district surrounding Ballston, spinning with thoughts and with something more. It seemed to him that he was learning things as he walked that he couldn't have said out loud at that moment, and yet they were real, they were felt; they were quite real.

An excess of reason. Well, but he had always tried to be reasonable. He had tried very hard. That attempt was his mode of being. It had seemed to help him. Dispassionate; sensible; calm; reasonable. A thinking machine. He had loved those stories when he was a boy. That was what a scientist was, and that was why he was a good scientist. That was the thing that had bothered him about Anna, that she was undeniably a good scientist but was a passionate scientist too, she threw herself into her work and her ideas, was completely engaged emotionally in her work. She cared which theory was true. That was all wrong, but she was so smart that it worked, for her anyway. If it did. But it wasn't science. To care that much was to introduce biases into the study. It wasn't a matter of emotions. You did science simply because it was the best adaptation strategy in the environment into which they had been born. Science was the gene trying to pass itself along more successfully. Also it was the best way to pass the hours, or to make a living. Everything else was so trivial and grasping. Social primates, trapped in a technocosmos of their own devise; science was definitely the only way to see the terrain well enough to know which way to strike forward, to make something new for all the rest. No passion needed to be added to that reasoned way forward.

And yet why did things live? What got them through it, really? What made them make all these efforts, when death lay in wait at the end for every one of them? This was what these Buddhists had dared to ask.

He was walking toward the Potomac now, along Fairfax Drive, a huge commercial street rumbling with traffic. Long lines of vehicles, with most of the occupants in them talking on phones. A strange sight when you looked at it!

Reason had never explained the existence of life. Life was a mystery; reason had tried and failed to explain it, and science could not start it from scratch in a lab. Little localized eddies of anti-entropy, briefly popping into being and then spinning out, with bits of them carried elsewhere in long invisible chains of code that spun up yet more eddies. A succession of pattern dust devils. A mystery, a kind of miracle—a miracle succeeding only where it found water, which gathered in droplets in the universe just as it did on a windowpane, and gave life sustenance. Water of life. A miracle.

He felt the sweat breaking out all over his skin. Tall trees, many species of trees and bushes; it could have been a botanical garden with a city laid into it, the plants a hundred shades of green. People walking by in small groups. Only runners were alone, and even they usually ran in pairs or larger groups. A social species, like bees or ants, with social rules that were invariant to the point of invisibility, people did not notice them. A species operating on pheromones, lucky in its adaptability, unstable in the environment. Knowledge of the existence of the future. A cosmic history read out of signs so subtle and mathematical that only the effort of a huge transtemporal group of powerful minds could ever have teased it out; but then those who came later could be given the whole story, with its unexplored edges there to take off into. This was the human project, this was science, this was what science was. This was what life was.

He stood there thrumming with thought, queasy, anxious, frightened. He was a confused man. Free-floating anxiety, he thought anxiously; except it had clear causes. People said that paradigm shifts only occurred when the old scientists died, that people individually did not have them, being too stubborn, too set in their ways, it was a more social process, a diachronic matter of successive generations.

Occasionally, however, it must be otherwise. Individual scientists, more open-minded or less certain than most, must have lived through one. Frank almost ran into a woman walking the other direction, almost said, "Sorry ma'am, I'm in the midst of a paradigm shift." He was disoriented. He saw that moving from one paradigm to the next was not like moving from one skyscraper to another, as in the diagrams he had once seen in a philosophy of science book. It was more like being inside a kaleidoscope, where he had gotten used to the pattern, and now the tube was twisting and he was falling and every aspect of what he saw was clicking to something different, click after click; colors, patterns, everything awash. Like dying and being reborn. Altruism, compassion, simple goddamned foolishness, loyalty to people who were not loyal to you, playing the sap for the defectors to take advantage of, competition, adaptation, displaced self-interest—or else something real, a real force in the world, a kind of physical constant, like gravity, or a basic attribute of life, like the drive to propagate one's DNA to subsequent generations. A reason for being. Something beyond DNA. A rage to live, an urge to goodness. Love. A green force, élan vital, that was a metaphysics, that was bad, but how else were you going to explain the data?

An excess of reason wasn't going to do it.

Genes, however, were very reasonable. They followed their directive, they reproduced. They were a living algorithm, creatures of four elements. Strings of binaries, codes of enormous length, codes that spoke bodies. It was a kind of reason that did that. Even a kind of monomania—an excess of reason, as the koan suggested. So that perhaps they were all mad, not just socially and individually, but genomically too. Molecular obsessive-compulsives. And then up from there, in stacked emergent insanities. Unless it was infused with some other quality that was not rational, some late emergent property like altruism, or compassion, or love—something that was not a code—then it was all for naught.

He felt sick. It could have just been the heat and humidity, the speed of his walking, something he ate, a bug that he had caught or that had bit him. It felt like all those, even though he suspected it was all starting in his mind, a kind of idea infection or moral fever. He needed to talk to someone.

But it had to be with someone he trusted. That made for a very short list. A very, very, very short list. In fact, my God, who exactly would be on that list, now that he came to think of it?

Anna. Anna Quibler, his colleague. The passionate scientist. A rock, in fact. A rock in the tide. Who could you trust after all? A good scientist. A scientist willing to take that best scientific attitude toward all of reality. Maybe that's what the old lama had been talking about. If too much reason was a form of madness, then perhaps passionate reason was what was called for. Passionate scientist, compassionate scientist, could analysis parse out which was which there? It could be a religion, some kind of humanism or biocentrism, philabios, philocosmos. Or simply Buddhism, if he had understood the old man correctly.

Suddenly he remembered that Anna and Charlie were hosting a party, and Anna had invited him. To help celebrate the day's lecture, ironically enough. The Khembalis would be there.

He walked, sweating, looking at street signs, figuring out where he was. Ah. Almost to Washington Boulevard. He could continue to the Clarendon Metro station. He did that, descended the Metro escalator into the ground. A weird action for a hominid to take—a religious experience. Following the shaman into the cave. We've never lost any of that.

He sat zoned until the change of lines at Metro Center. The interior there looked weirder than ever, like a shopping mall in hell. A Red Line Shady Grove train pulled in, and he got on and stood with the multitude. It was late in the day, he had wandered a long time. It was near the end of the rush hour.

The travelers at this hour were almost all professionally dressed. They were headed home, out to the prosperous parts of Northwest and Chevy Chase and Bethesda and Rockville and Gaithersburg. At each stop the train got emptier, until he could sit down on one of the garish orange seats.

Sitting there, he began to feel calmer. The coolness of the air, the sassy but soothing orange and pink, the people's faces, all contributed to this feeling. Even the driver of the train contributed, with a stop in each station that was as smooth as any Frank had ever felt, a beautiful touch on the big brakes that most drivers could not help but jerk to one degree or another. It was like a musical performance. The concrete caves changed their name-plates, otherwise each cave was almost the same.

Across from him sat a woman wearing a black skirt and white blouse. Hair short and curly, glasses, almost invisible touch of makeup. Bra strap showing at her collarbone. A professional of some sort, going home. Face intelligent and friendly-seeming, not pretty but attractive. Legs crossed, one running-shoed foot sticking into the aisle. Her skirt had ridden up her leg and Frank could see the side of one thigh, made slightly convex from her position and the mass of solid quadriceps muscles. No stockings, skin smooth, a few freckles. She looked strong.

Like Frank, she stood to get out at the Bethesda stop. Frank followed her out of the train. It was interesting the way dresses and skirts all were different, and framed or uniquely featured the bodies they covered. Height of bottom, width of hips, length and shape of legs, of back and shoulders, proportions of the whole, movement: the compounded variations were infinite, so that no two women looked the same to Frank. And he looked all the time.

This one was businesslike and moved fast. Her legs were longer than the usual proportion, which discrepancy drew the eye, as always. It was discrepancy from the norm that drew the eye. She looked like she was wearing high heels even though she wasn't. That was attractive, indeed women wore high heels to look like her. Another savannah judgment, no doubt—the ability to outrun predators as part of the potential for reproductive success. Whatever. She looked good. It was like a kind of balm, after what he had gone through. Back to basics.

Frank stood below her as they rose up the first escalator from trackside to the turnstiles, enjoying that view, which exaggerated the length of her legs and the size of her bottom. At that point he was hooked, and would therefore, as was his custom, follow her until their paths diverged, just to prolong the pleasure of watching her walk. This happened to him all the time, it was one of the habits one fell into, living in a city of such beautiful women.

Through the turnstiles, then, and along the tunnel toward the big escalator up and out. Then to his surprise she turned left, into the nook that held the station's elevators.

He followed her without thinking. He never took the Metro system's elevators, they were extremely slow. And yet there he was, standing beside her waiting for this one to arrive, feeling conspicuous but unable to do anything about it, except look up at the display lights over the elevator doors. Although he could just walk away.

The light lit. The doors opened on an empty car. Frank followed the woman in and turned and stared at the closing doors, feeling red-faced.

She pushed the street-level button, and with a slight lift they were off.

The elevator hummed and vibrated as they rose. It was hot and humid, and the little room smelled faintly of machine oil, sweat, plastics, perfume, and electricity.

Frank studiously observed the display over the doors. The woman did the same. She had the strap of her armbag hooked under her thumb. Her elbow was pressed into her blouse just over the waistline of her skirt. Her hair was so curly that it was almost frizzy, but not quite; brown, and cut short, so that it curled tight as a cap on her head. A little longer in a fringe at the back of her neck, where two lines of fine blond hairs curved down toward her deltoid muscles. Wide shoulders. A very impressive animal. Even in his peripheral vision he could see all this.

The elevator whined, then shuddered and stopped. Startled, Frank refocused on the control panel, which still showed them as going up.

"Shit," the woman muttered, and looked at her watch. She glanced at Frank.

"Looks like we're stuck," Frank said, pushing the UP button.

"Yeah. Damn it."

"Unbelievable," Frank agreed.

She grimaced. "What a day."

A moment or two passed. Frank hit the DOWN button: nothing. He gestured at the little black phone console set in the panel above the UP and DOWN buttons.

"I guess we're at the point this is here for."

"I think so."

Frank picked up the receiver, put it to his ear. The phone was ringing already, which was good, as it had no number pad. What would it have been like to pick up a phone and hear nothing?

But the ringing went on long enough to concern him.

Then it stopped, and a woman's voice said, "Hello?"

"Hi? Hey listen, we're in the elevator at the Bethesda Metro stop, and it's stuck."

"Okay. Bethesda did you say? Did you try pushing the CLOSE DOOR button then the UP button?"

"No." Frank pushed these buttons. "I am now, but . . . nothing. It feels pretty stuck."

"Try the DOWN button too, after the CLOSE DOOR."

"Okay." He tried it.

"Do you know how far up you are?"

"We must be near the top." He glanced at the woman, and she nodded.

"Any smoke?"

"No!"

"Okay. There's people on the way. Just sit tight and stay cool. Are you crowded in there?"

"No, there's just two of us."

"That's okay then. They said they'll be about half an hour to an hour, depending on traffic and the problem with the elevator. They'll call you on your phone there when they get there."

"Okay. Thanks."

"No problem. Pick up again if something changes. I'll be watching."

"I will. Thanks again."

The woman had already hung up. Frank did also.

They stood there.

"Well," Frank said, gesturing at the phone.

"I could hear," the woman said. She looked around at the floor. "I guess I'll sit down while we wait. My feet are tired."

"Good idea."

They sat down next to each other, backs to the back wall of the elevator.

"Tired feet?"

"Yeah. I went running today at lunch, and it was mostly on sidewalks."

"You're a runner?"

"No, not really. That's why my feet hurt. I ride with a cycling club, and we're doing a triathlon, so I'm trying to add some running and swimming. I could just do the cycling leg of a team, but I'm seeing if I can get ready to do the whole thing."

"What are the distances?"

"A mile swim, twenty-mile bike, ten-K run."

"Ouch."

"It's not so bad."

They sat in silence.

"So are you going to be late for something here?"

"No," Frank said. "Well, it depends, but it's just a kind of party."

"Too bad to miss that."

"Maybe. It's a work thing. There was a lunchtime lecture today, and now the organizer is having a thing for the speakers."

"What did they talk about?"

He smiled. "A Buddhist approach to science, actually. They were the Buddhists."

"And you were the scientists."

"Yes."

"That must have been interesting."

"Well, yes. It was. It's given me a lot to think about. More than I thought it would. I don't exactly know what to say to them tonight though."

"Hmm." She appeared to consider it. "Sometimes I think about cycling as a kind of meditation. Lots of times I kind of blank out, and when I come to a lot of miles have passed."

"That must be nice."

"Your science isn't psychology, is it?"

"Microbiology."

"Good. Sorry. Anyway, I like it, yeah. I don't think I could do it by trying for it, though. It just happens, usually late in a ride. Maybe it's low blood sugar. Not enough energy to think."

"Could be," Frank said. "Thinking does burn some sugars."

"There you go."

They sat there burning sugars.

"So what about you, are you going to be late for something?"

"I was going to go for a ride, actually. My legs would be less sore tomorrow if I did. But after this, who knows what I'll feel like . . . maybe I still will. If we get out of here pretty soon."

"We'll see about that."

"Yeah."

The trapped air was stifling. They sat there sweating. There was some quality to it, some combination of comfort and tension, their bodies simply breathing together, resting, almost touching, ever so slightly incandescent to each other . . . it was nice. Two animals resting side by side, one male one female. A lot of talk goes on below the radar. And indeed somehow it had come to pass that as they relaxed their legs had drifted outward, and met each other, so that now they were just very slightly touching, at the outsides of the knees, kind of resting against each other in a carefully natural way, her leg bare (her skirt had fallen down into her lap) and his covered by light cotton pants. Touching. Now the talk under the radar was filling Frank's whole bandwidth, and though he continued his part of the conversation, he could not have immediately said what they were talking about.

"So you must ride quite a lot?"

"Yeah, pretty much."

She was in a cycling club, she told him. "It's like any other club." Except this one went out on long bike rides. Weekends, smaller groups more often than that. She too was making talk. "Like a social club really. Like the Elks Club or something, only with bikes."

"Good for you."

"Yes, it's fun. A good workout."

"It makes you strong."

"Well, the legs anyway. It's good for legs."

"Yes," Frank agreed, and took the invitation to glance down at hers. She did as well, tucking her chin and looking as if inspecting something outside of herself. Her skirt had fallen so that the whole side of her left leg was exposed.

She said, "It bulks up the quads."

Frank intended to agree by saying "Uh-huh," but somehow the sound got interrupted, as if he had been tapped lightly on the solar plexus while making it, so that it came out "nnnnn," like a short hum or purr. A little moan of longing, in fact, at the sight of such long strong legs, all that smooth skin, the sweet curve of the under-thigh. Her knees stood distinctly higher than his.

He looked up to find her grinning at him. He hunched his shoulders and looked away just a touch, yes, guilty as charged, feeling the corners of his mouth tug up in the helpless smile of someone caught in the act. What could he say, she had great legs.

Now she was watching him with an interrogatory gaze, searching his face for something specific, it seemed, her eyes alight with mischief, amused. It was a look that had a whole person in it.

And she must have liked something about what she saw, because she leaned his way, into his shoulder, and then pressed further in and stretched her head toward his and kissed him.

"Mmm," he purred, kissing back. He shifted around the better to face her, his body moving without volition. She was shifting too. She pulled back briefly to look again in his eyes, then she smiled broadly and shifted into his arms. Their kiss grew more and more passionate, they were like teenagers making out. They flew off into that pocket universe of bliss. Time passed, Frank's thoughts scattered, he was absorbed in the feel of her mouth, her lips on his, her tongue, the awkwardness of their embrace. It was very hot. They were both literally dripping with sweat; their kisses tasted salty. Frank slid a hand under her skirt. She hummed and then shifted onto one knee and over onto him, straddling him. They kissed harder than ever.

The elevator phone rang.

She sat up. "Oops," she said, catching her breath. Her face was flushed and she looked gorgeous. She reached up and behind her and grabbed the receiver, staying solidly on him.

"Hello?" she said into the phone. Frank flexed under her and she put a hand to his chest to stop him.

"Oh yeah, we're here," she said. "You guys got here fast." She listened and quickly laughed: "No, I don't suppose you do hear that very often." She glanced down at Frank to share a complicit smile, and it was in that moment that Frank felt the strongest bond of all with her. They were a pair in the world, and no one else knew it but them.

"Yeah sure—we'll be here!"

She rolled off him as she hung up. "They say they've got it fixed and we're on our way up."

"Damn it."

"I know."

They stood. She brushed down her skirt. They felt a few jerks as the elevator started up again.

"Wow, look at us. We are just dripping."

"We would have been no matter what. It's hot in here."

"True." She reached up to straighten his hair and then they were kissing again, banging against the wall in a sudden blaze of passion, stronger than ever. Then she pushed him away, saying breathlessly, "Okay, no more, we're almost there. The door must be about to open."

"True."

Confirming the thought, the elevator began its characteristic slow-motion deceleration. Frank took a deep breath, blew it out, tried to pull himself together. He felt flushed, his skin was tingling. He looked at her. She was almost as tall as he was.

She laughed. "We are so busted."

The elevator stopped. The doors jerked open. They were still a foot below street level, but it was easy to step up and out.

Before them stood three men, two in workers' coveralls, one in a Metro uniform.

The one in the uniform held a clipboard. "Y'all okay?" he said to them.

"Yeah," "We're fine," they said together.

Everyone stood there for a second.

"Must have been hot in there," the uniformed one remarked.

The three black men stared at them curiously.

"It was," Frank said.

"But not much different than out here," his companion quickly added, and they all laughed. It was true; getting out had not made any marked change. It was like stepping from one sauna to another. Their rescuers were also sweating profusely. Yes—the open air of a Washington, D.C., evening was indistinguishable from the inside of an elevator stuck deep underground. This was their world: and so they laughed.

They were on the sidewalk flanking Wisconsin Avenue, next to the elevator box and the old post office. Passersby glanced at them. The foreman gave the woman his clipboard. "If you'd fill out and sign the report, please. Thanks. Looks like it was about half an hour from your call to when we pulled you."

"Pretty fast," the woman said, reading the text on her form before filling in some blanks and signing. "It didn't even seem that long." She looked at her watch. "All right, well—thanks very much." She faced Frank, extended a hand. "It was nice to meet you."

"Yes it was," Frank said, shaking her hand, struggling for words, struggling to think. In front of these witnesses nothing came to him, and she turned and walked south on Wisconsin. Frank felt constrained by the gazes of the three men; all would be revealed if he were to run after her and ask for her name, her phone number, and besides now the foreman was holding the clipboard out to him, and it occurred to him that he could read what she had written down there.

But it was a fresh form, and he looked up to see that down the street she was turning right, onto one of the smaller streets west of Wisconsin.

The foreman watched him impassively while the technicians went back to the elevator.

Frank gestured at the clipboard. "Can I get that woman's name, please?"

The man frowned, surprised, and shook his head. "Not allowed to," he said. "It's a law."

Frank felt his stomach sink. There had to be a physiological basis for that feeling, some loosening of the gut as fear prepared the body for fight-or-flight. Flight in this case. "But I need to get in touch with her again," he said.

The man stared at him, stone-faced. "Should have thought of that when you was stuck with her," he said, sensibly enough. He gestured in the direction she had gone. "You could probably still catch her."

Released by these words Frank took off, first walking fast, then, after he turned right on the street she had taken, running. He looked forward down the street for her black skirt, white blouse, short brown hair; there was no sign of her. He began sweating hard again, a kind of panic response. How far could she have gotten? What had she said she was late for? He couldn't remember—horribly, his mind seemed to have blurred on much that she had said before they started kissing. He needed to know all that now! It was like some memory experiment foisted on undergraduates, how much could you remember of the incidents right before a shock? Not much! The experiment had worked like a charm.

But then he found the memory, and realized that it was not blurred at all, that on the contrary it was intensely detailed, at least up until the point when their legs had touched, at which point he could still remember perfectly, but only the feel on the outside of his knee, not their words. He went back before that, rehearsed it, relived it—cyclist, triathlon, one mile, twenty mile, 10K. Good for the legs, oh my God was it. He had to find her!

There was no sign of her at all. By now he was on Woodson, running left and right, looking down all the little side streets and into shop windows, feeling more and more desperate. She wasn't anywhere to be seen. He had lost her.

It started to rain.

The doorbell rang. Anna went to it and opened it.

"Frank! Wow, you're soaked."

He must have been caught in the downpour that had begun about half an hour before, and was already finished. It was odd he hadn't taken shelter during the worst of it. He looked like he had dived into a swimming pool with all his clothes on.

"Don't worry," she said as he hesitated on the porch, dripping like a statue in a fountain. "Here, you need a towel for your face." She provided one from the vestibule's coat closet. "The rain really got you."

"Yeah."

She was somewhat surprised to see him. She had thought he was uninterested in the Khembalis, even slightly dismissive of them. And he had sat through the afternoon's lecture wearing one of his signature looks; he had a face able to express twenty minute gradations of displeasure, and the one at the lecture had been the one that said, "I'm keeping my eyes from rolling in my head only by the greatest of efforts." Not the most pleasant of expressions on anyone's face, and it had only gotten worse as the lecture went on, until eventually he had looked stunned and off in his own world.

On the other hand, he had gone to it. He had left in silence, obviously thinking something over. And now here he was.

So Anna was pleased. If the Khembalis could capture Frank's interest, they should be able to do it with any scientist. Frank was the hardest case she knew.

Now he seemed slightly disoriented by his drenching. He was shaking his head ruefully.

Anna said, "Do you want to change into one of Charlie's shirts?"

"No, I'll be all right. I'll steam dry." Then he lifted his arms and looked down. "Well—maybe a shirt I guess. Will his fit me?"

"Sure, you're only just a bit bigger than he is."

She went upstairs to get one, calling down, "The others should be here any minute. There was flooding on Wisconsin, apparently, and some problems with the Metro."

"I know about those, I got caught in one!"

"You're kidding! What happened?" She came down with one of Charlie's bigger T-shirts.

"The elevator I was in got stuck halfway up."

"Oh no! For how long?"

"About half an hour I guess."

"Jesus. That must have been spooky. Were you by yourself?"

"No, there was someone else, a woman. We got to talking, and so the time passed fast. It was interesting."

"That's nice."

"Yes. It was. Only I didn't get her name, and then when we got out they had forms for us to fill out and, and she took off while I was doing mine, so I never caught what hers was. And then the guy from the Metro wouldn't give it to me from her form, so now I'm kicking myself, because—well. I'd like to talk to her again."

Anna inspected him, startled by this story. He was looking past her abstractedly, perhaps remembering the incident. He noticed her gaze and grinned, and this startled her once again, because it was a real smile. Always before Frank's smile had been a skeptical thing, so ironic and knowing that only one side of his mouth tugged back. Now he was like a stroke victim who had recovered the use of the damaged side of his face.

It was a nice sight, and it had to have been because of this woman he had met. Anna felt a sudden surge of affection for him. They had worked together for quite some time, and that kind of collaboration can take two people into a realm of shared experience that is not like family or marriage but rather some other kind of bond that can be quite deep. A friendship formed in the world of thought. Maybe they were always that way. Anyway he looked happy, and she was happy to see it.

"This woman filled out a form, you say?"

"Yeah."

"So you can find out."

"They wouldn't let me look at it."

"No, but you'll be able to get to it somehow."

"You think so?"

Now she had his complete attention. "Sure. Get a reporter from the *Post* to help you, or an archival detective, or someone from the Metro. Or from Homeland Security for that matter. The fact you were in there with her, that might be the way to get it, I don't know. But as long as it's written down, something will work. That's informatics, right?"

"True." He smiled again, looking quite happy. Then he took Charlie's shirt from her and walked around toward the kitchen while changing into it. He took a towel from her and toweled off his head. "Thanks. Here, can I put this in your dryer? Down in the basement, right?" He stepped over the baby gate, went downstairs. "Thanks Anna," he called back up to her. "I feel better now." When he came back up, the sound of the dryer on behind him, he smiled again. "A lot better."

"You must have liked this woman!"

"I did. It's true, I did. I can't believe I didn't get her name!"

"You will. Want a beer?"

"You bet I do."

"In the door of the fridge. Oops, there's the door again, here come the rest."

Soon the Khembalis and many other friends and acquaintances from NSF filled the Quiblers' little living room, and the dining room flanking it, and the kitchen beyond the dining room. Anna rushed back and forth, carrying drinks and trays of food. She enjoyed this, and was doing it more than usual to keep Charlie from inflaming his poison ivy. As she hurried around she enjoyed seeing Joe playing with Drepung, and Nick discussing Antarctic dinosaurs with Curt from the office right above hers; he was one of the U.S. Antarctic Program managers. That NSF also ran one of the continents of the world was something she tended to forget, but Curt had come to the talk, and liked it. "These Buddhist guys would go over big in McMurdo," he told Nick. Meanwhile Charlie, skin devastated to a brown crust across wide regions of his neck and face, eyes brilliantly bloodshot with sleep deprivation and steroids, was absorbed in conversation with Sucandra. Then he noticed her running around and joined her in the kitchen to help. "I gave Frank one of your shirts," she told him.

"I saw. He said he got soaked."

"Yes. I think he was chasing around after a woman he met on the Metro."

"What?"

She laughed. "I think it's great. Go sit down, babe, don't move your poor torso, you'll make yourself itchy."

"I've transcended itchiness. I'm only itchy for you."

"Come on don't. Go sit down."

Only later in the evening did she see Frank again. He was sitting in the corner of the room, on the floor between the couch and the fireplace, quizzing Drepung about something or other. Drepung looked as if he was struggling to understand him. Anna was curious, and when she got a chance she sat down on the couch just above the two of them.

Frank nodded to her and then continued pressing a point, using one of his catchphrases: "But how does that work?"

"Well," Drepung said, "I know what Rudra Cakrin says in Tibetan, obviously. His import is clear to me. Then I have to think what I know of English. The two languages are different, but so much is the same for all of us."

"Deep grammar," Frank suggested.

"Yes, but also just nouns. Names for things, names for actions, even for meanings. Equivalencies of one degree or another. So, I try to express my understanding of what Rudra said, but in English."

"But how good is the correspondence?"

Drepung raised his eyebrows. "How can I know? I do the best I can."

"You would need some kind of exterior test."

Drepung nodded. "Have other Tibetan translators listen to the rimpoche, and then compare their English versions to mine. That would be very interesting."

"Yes it would. Good idea."

Drepung smiled at him. "Double-blind study, right?"

"Yes, I guess so."

"Elementary, my dear Watson," Drepung intoned, reaching out for a cracker with which to dip hummus. "But I expect you would get a certain, what, range. Maybe you would not uncover many surprises with your study. Maybe just that I personally am a bad translator. Although I must say, I have a tough job. When I don't understand the rimpoche, translating him gets harder."

"So you make it up!" Frank laughed. His spirits were still high, Anna saw. "That's what I've been saying all along." He settled back against the side of the couch next to her.

But Drepung shook his head. "Not making things up. Re-creation, maybe."

"Like DNA and phenotypes."

"I don't know."

"A kind of code."

"Well, but language is never just a code."

"No. More like gene expression."

"You must tell me."

"From an instruction sequence, like a gene, to what the instruction creates. Language to thought. Or to meaning, or comprehension. Whatever! To some kind of living thought."

Drepung grinned. "There are about fifty words in Tibetan that I would have to translate to the word *thinking*."

"Like Eskimos with snow, if it's true what they say about that."

"Yes. Like Eskimos have snow, we Tibetans have thoughts."

He laughed at the idea and Frank laughed too, shaken by that low giggle which was all he ever gave to laughter, but now emphatic and helpless with it, bubbling over with it. Anna could scarcely believe her eyes. He was as ebullient as if he were drunk, but he was still holding the same beer she had given him on his arrival. And she knew what he was high on anyway.

He pulled himself together, grew intent. "So today, when you said, 'An excess of reason is itself a form of madness,' what did your lama really say?"

"Just that. That's easy, that's an old proverb." He said the sentence in Tibetan. "One word means 'excess' or 'too much,' you know, like that, and *rig-gnas* is reason, or science. Then *zugs* is 'form,' and *zhe sdang* is 'madness,' a version of hatred, from an older word that was like angry. One of the *dug gsum,* the Three Poisons of the Mind."

"And the old man said that?"

"Yes. An old saying. Milarepa, I should think."

"Was he talking about science, though?"

"The whole lecture was on science."

"Yeah yeah. But I found that idea in particular pretty striking."

"A good thought is one you can act on."

"That's what mathematicians say."

"I'm sure."

"So, was the lama saying that NSF is crazy? Or that Western science is crazy? Because it is pretty damned reasonable. I'm mean, that's the point. That's the method in a nutshell."

"Well, I guess so. To that extent. We're all crazy in some way or other, right? He did not mean to be critical. Nothing alive is ever quite in balance. It might be he was suggesting that science is out of balance. Feet without eyes."

"I thought it was eyes without feet."

Drepung waggled his hand: either way. "You should ask him."

"But you'd be translating, so I might as well just ask you and cut out the middleman!"

"No," laughing, "I am the middleman, I assure you."

"But you can tell me what he would say," teasing him now. "Cut right to the chase!"

"But he surprises me a lot."

"Like when, give me an example."

"Well. One time last week, he was saying to me . . ."

But at that point Anna was called away to the front door, and she did not get to hear Drepung's example, but only Frank's distinctive laughter, burbling under the clatter of conversation.

By the time she ran into Frank again he was out in the kitchen with Charlie and Sucandra, washing glasses and cleaning up. Charlie could only stand there and talk. He and Frank were discussing Great Falls, both recommending it to Sucandra. "It's more like Tibet than any other place in town," Charlie said, and Frank giggled again, and more so when Anna exclaimed, "Oh come on love, they aren't the slightest bit the same!"

"No, yes! I mean they're more alike than anywhere else around here is like Tibet."

"What does that mean?" she demanded.

"Water! Nature!" Then: "Sky," Frank and Charlie both said at the same time.

Sucandra nodded. "I could use some sky. Maybe even a horizon." And then all the men were chuckling.

Anna went back out to the living room to see if anyone needed anything. She paused to watch Rudra Cakrin and Joe playing with blocks on the floor again. Joe was filled with happiness to have such company, stacking blocks and babbling. Rudra nodded and handed him more. They had been doing that off and on for much of the evening. It occurred to Anna that they were the only two people at the party who did not speak English.

She went back to the kitchen and took over Frank's spot at the sink, and sent Frank down to the basement to get his shirt out of the dryer. He came back up wearing it, and leaned against a counter talking.

Charlie saw Anna rest against the counter and got her a beer from the fridge. "Here snooks have a drink."

"Thanks dove."

Sucandra asked about the kitchen's wallpaper, which was an uncomfortably brilliant yellow, overlaid with large white birds caught in various moments of flight. When you actually looked at it it was rather bizarre. "I like it," Charlie said. "It wakes me up. A bit itchy, but basically fine."

Frank said he was going to go home. Anna walked him around the ground floor to the front door.

"You'll be able to catch one of the last trains," she said.

"Yeah I'll be okay."

"Thanks for coming, that was fun."

"Yes it was."

Again Anna saw that whole smile brighten his face.

"So what's she like?"

"Well—I don't know!"

They both laughed.

Anna said, "I guess you'll find out when you find her."

"Yeah," Frank said, and touched her arm briefly, as if to thank her for the thought. Then as he was walking down the sidewalk he looked over his shoulder and called, "I hope she's like you!"

Frank left Anna and Charlie's and walked through a warm drizzle back toward the Metro, thinking hard. When he came to the fateful elevator box he stood before it, trying to order his thoughts. It was impossible—especially there. He moved on reluctantly, as if leaving the place would put the experience irrevocably in the past. But it already was. Onward, past the hotel, to the stairs, down to the Metro entry level. He stepped onto the long down escalator and descended into the Earth, thinking.

He recalled Anna and Charlie, in their house with all those people. The way they stood by each other, leaned into each other. The way Anna put a hand on Charlie when she was near him—on this night, avoiding his poisoned patches. The way they shuffled their kids back and forth between them, without actually seeming to notice each other. Or their endlessly varying nicknames for each other, a habit Frank had noticed before, even though he would rather have not: not just the usual endearments like *hon, honey, dear, sweetheart,* or *babe,* but also more exotic ones that were saccharine or suggestive beyond belief—*snooks, snookybear, honeypie, lover, lovey, lovedove, sweetie-pie, angel man, goddessgirl, kitten,* it was unbelievable the inwardness of the monogamous bond, the unconscious twin-world narcissism of it—disgusting! And yet Frank craved that very thing, that easy, deep intimacy that one could take for granted, could lose oneself in. ISO LTR. Primate seeks partner for life. An urge seen in every human culture, and across many species too. It was not crazy of him to want it.

Therefore he was now in a quandary. He wanted to find the woman from the elevator. And Anna had given him the hope that it could be done. It might take some time, but as Anna had pointed out, everyone was in the data banks somewhere. In the Department of Homeland Security records, if nowhere else; but of course elsewhere too. Beg or break your way into Metro maintenance records, how hard could that be? There were people breaking into the genome!

But he wasn't going to be able to do it from San Diego. Or rather, maybe he could make the hunt from there—you could google someone from anywhere—but if he then succeeded in finding her, it wouldn't do him any good. It was a big continent. If he found her, if he wanted that to matter, he would need to be in D.C.

And what would he do if he found her?

He couldn't think about that now. About anything that might happen past the moment of locating her. That would be enough. After that, who knew what she might be like. She had after all jumped him (he shivered at the memory, still there in his flesh), jumped a total stranger in a stuck elevator after twenty minutes of conversation. There was no doubt in his mind that she had initiated the encounter; it simply wouldn't have occurred to him. Maybe that made him an innocent or a dimwit, but there it was. Maybe on the other hand she was some kind of sexual adventuress, the free papers might be right after all, and certainly everyone talked all the time about women being more sexually assertive, though he had seen little personally to confirm it. Though it had been true of Marta too, come to think of it.

Howsoever that might be, he had been there in the elevator, had shared all responsibility for what happened. And happily so—he was pleased at himself, amazed but glowing. He wanted to find her.

But after that—if he could do it—whatever might happen, if anything were to happen—he needed to be in D.C.

Fine. Here he was.

But he had just put his parting shot in Diane's in-box that very day, and tomorrow morning she would come in and read it. A letter that was, now that he thought of it, virulently critical, possibly even contemptuous—and how stupid was that, how impolitic, self-indulgent, irrational, maladaptive—what could he have been thinking? Well, somehow he had been angry. Something had made him bitter. He had done it to burn his bridges, so that when Diane had read it he would be toast at NSF.

Whereas without that letter, it would have been a relatively simple matter to re-up for another year. Anna had asked him to, and she had been speaking for Diane, Frank was sure. A year more, and after that he would know where things stood, at least.

A Metro train finally came rumbling windily into the station. Sitting in it as it jerked and rolled into the darkness toward the city, he mulled over in jagged quick images of memory and consideration all that had occurred recently, all crushed and scattered into a kind of kaleidoscope or mandala: Pierzinski's algorithm, the panel, Marta, Derek, the Khembalis' lecture; seeing Anna and Charlie, leaning side by side against a kitchen counter. He could make no sense of it really. The parts made sense, but he could not pull a theory out of it. Just a more general sense that the world was going smash.

And, in the context of that sort of world, did he want to go back to a single lab anyway? Could he bear to work on a single tiny chip of the giant mosaic of global problems? It was the way he had always worked before, and it might be the only way one could work, really; but might he not be better off deploying his efforts in a way that magnified them by using them in this small but potentially strong arm of the government, the National Science Foundation? Was that what his letter's furious critique of NSF had been all about—his frustration that it was doing so little of what it could? If I can't find a lever I won't be able to move the world, isn't that what Archimedes had declared?

In any case his letter was there in Diane's in-box. He had torched his bridge already. It was very stupid to forestall a possible course of action in such a manner. He was a fool. It was hard to admit, but he had to admit it. The evidence was clear.

But he could go to NSF now and take the letter back.

Security would be there, as always. But people went to work late or early, he could explain himself that way. Still, Diane's offices would be locked. Security might let him in to his own office, but the twelfth floor? No.

Perhaps he could get there as the first person who arrived on the twelfth floor next morning, and slip in and take it.

But on most mornings the first person to the twelfth floor, famously, was Diane Chang herself. People said she often got there at 4 A.M. So, well . . . He could be there when she arrived. Just tell her he needed to take back a letter he had put in her box. She might with reason ask to read it first, or she might hand it back, he couldn't say. But either way, she would know something was wrong with him. And something in him recoiled from that. He didn't want anyone to know any of this, he didn't want to look emotionally overwrought or indecisive, or as if he had something to hide. His few encounters with Diane had given him reason to believe she was not one to suffer fools gladly, and he hated to be thought of as one. It was bad enough having to admit it to himself.

And if he were going to continue at NSF, he wanted to be able to do things there. He needed Diane's respect. It would be so much better if he could take the letter back without her ever knowing he had left it.

Unbidden an old thought leapt to mind. He had often sat in his office cubicle, looking through the window into the central atrium, thinking about climbing the mobile hanging in there. There was a crux in the middle, shifting from one piece of it to another, a stretch of chain that looked to be hard if you were free-climbing it. And a fall would be fatal. But he could come down to it on a rappel from the skylight topping the atrium. He wouldn't even have to descend as far as the mobile. Diane's offices were on the twelfth floor, so it would be a short drop. A matter of using his climbing craft and gear, and his old skyscraper window skills. Come down through the skylight, do a pendulum traverse from above the mobile over to her windows, tip one out, slip in, snatch his letter out of the in-box, and climb back out, sealing the windows as he left. No security cameras pointed upward in the atrium, he had noticed during one of his climbing fantasies; there were no alarms on window framing; all would be well. And the top of the building was accessible by a maintenance ladder bolted permanently to the south wall. He had noticed that once while walking by, and had already worked it into various daydreams. Occupying his mind with images of physical action, biomathematics as a kind of climbing of the walls of reality. Or perhaps just compensating for the boredom of sitting in a chair all day.

Now it was a plan, fully formed and ready to execute. He did not try to pretend to himself that it was the most rational plan he had ever made, but he urgently needed to do something physical, right then and there. He was quivering with tension. The operation's set of physical maneuvers were all things he could do, and that being the case, all the other factors of his situation inclined him to do it. In fact he had to, if he was really going to take responsibility for his life at last, and cast it in the direction of his desire. Make possible whatever follow-up with the woman in the elevator he might later be able to accomplish.

It had to be done.

He got out at the Ballston station, still thinking hard. He walked to the NSF parking garage door by way of the south side of the building to confirm the exterior ladder's lower height. Bring a box to step on, that's all it would need. He walked to his car and drove west to his apartment over wet empty streets, not seeing a thing.

At the apartment he went to the closet and pawed through his climbing gear. Below it, as in an archeological dig, were the old tools of a window man's trade.

When it was all spread on the floor it looked like he had spent his whole life preparing to do this. For a moment, hefting his caulking gun, he hesitated at the sheer weirdness of what he was contemplating. For one thing the caulking gun was useless without caulk, and he had none. He would have to leave cut seals, and eventually someone would see them.

Then he remembered again the woman in the elevator. He felt her kisses still. Only a few hours had passed, though since then his mind had spun through what seemed like years. If he were to have any chance of seeing her again, he had to act. Cut seals didn't matter. He stuffed all the rest of the gear into his faded red nylon climber's backpack, which was shredded down one side from a rockfall in the Fourth Recess, long ago. He had done crazy things often back then.

He went to his car, threw the bag in, hummed over the dark streets back to Arlington, past the Ballston stop. He parked on a wet street well away from the NSF building. No one was about. There were eight million people in the immediate vicinity, but it was 2 A.M. and so there was not a person to be seen. Who could deny sociobiology at a moment like that! What a sign of their animal natures, completely diurnal in the technosurround of postmodern society, fast asleep in so many ways, and most certainly at night. Unavoidably fallen into a brain state still very poorly understood.

Frank felt a little exalted to witness such overwhelming evidence of their animal nature. A whole city of sleeping primates. Somehow it confirmed his feeling that he was doing the right thing. That he himself had woken up for the first time in many years.

On the south side of the NSF building it was the work of a moment to stand a plastic crate on its side and hop up to the lowest rung of the service ladder bolted to the concrete wall, and then quickly to pull himself up and ascend the twelve stories to the roof, using his leg muscles for all the propulsion. As he neared the top of the ladder it felt very high and exposed, and it occurred to him that if it were really true that an excess of reason was a form of madness, he seemed to be cured. Unless of course this truly was the most reasonable thing to do—as he felt it was.

Over the coping, onto the roof, land in a shallow rain puddle against the coping. In the center of a flat roof, the atrium skylight.

It was a muggy night, the low clouds orange with the city's glow. He pulled out his tools. The big central skylight was a low four-sided pyramid of triangular glass windowpanes. He went to the one nearest the ladder and cleaned the plate of glass, then affixed a big sucker to it.

Using his old X-Acto knife he cut the sun-damaged polyurethane caulking on the window's three sides. He pulled it away and found the window screws, and zipped them out with his old Grinder screwdriver. When the window was unscrewed he grabbed the handle on the sucker and yanked to free the window, then pulled back gently; out it came, balanced in the bottom frame stripping. He pulled it back until the glass was almost upright, then tied the sling-rope from the handle of the sucker to the lowest rung of the ladder. The open gap near the top of the atrium was more than big enough for him to fit through. Cool air wafted up from some very slight internal pressure.

He laid a towel over the frame, stepped into his climbing harness, and buckled it around his waist. He tied his ropes off on the top rung of the service ladder; that would be bombproof. Now it was just a matter of slipping through the gap and rappelling down the rope to the point where he would begin his pendulum.

He sat carefully on the angled edge of the frame. He could feel the beer from Anna's reception still sloshing in him, impeding his coordination very slightly, but this was climbing, he would be all right. He had done it in worse condition in his youth, fool that he had been. Although it was perhaps the wrong time to be critical of that version of himself.

Turning around and leaning back into the atrium, he tested the figure-eight device constricting the line—good friction—so he leaned farther back into the atrium, and immediately plummeted down into it. Desperately he twisted the rappelling device and felt the rope slow; it caught fast and he was bungeeing down on it when he crashed into something—a horrible surprise because it didn't seem that he had had time to fall to the ground, so he was confused for a split second—then he saw that he had struck the top piece of the mobile, and was now hanging over it, head downward, grasping it and the rope both with a desperate prehensile clinging.

And very happy to be there. The brief fall seemed to have affected him like a kind of electrocution. His skin burned everywhere. He tugged experimentally on his rope; it seemed fine, solidly tied to the roof ladder. Perhaps after putting the figure eight on the rope he had forgotten to take all the slack out of the system, he couldn't remember doing it. That would be forgetting a well-nigh instinctual action for any climber, but he couldn't honestly put it past himself on this night. His mind was full or perhaps overfull.

Carefully he reached into his waist bag. He got out two ascenders and carabinered their long loops to his harness, then connected them to the rope above him. Next he whipped the rope below him around his thigh, and had a look around. He would have to use the ascenders to pull himself back up to the proper pendulum point for Diane's window—

The whole mobile was twisting slightly. Frank grabbed it and tried to torque it until it stilled, afraid some security person would walk through the atrium and notice the motion. Suddenly the big space seemed much too well lit for comfort, even though it was only a dim greenish glow created by a few night-lights in the offices around him.

The mobile's top piece was a bar bent into a big circle, hanging by a chain from a point on its circumference, with two shorter bars extending out from it—one about thirty degrees off from the top, bending to make a staircase shape, the other across the circle and below, its two bends making a single stair riser down. The crescent bar hung about fifteen feet below the circle. In the dark they appeared to be different shades of gray, though Frank knew they were primary colors. For a second that made it all seem unreal.

Finally the whole contraption came still. Frank ran one ascender up his rope, put his weight on it. Every move had to be delicate, and for a time he was lost to everything else, deep in that climber's space of purely focused concentration.

He placed the other ascender even higher, and carefully shifted his weight to it, and off the first ascender. A very mechanical and straightforward process. He wanted to leave the mobile with no push on it at all.

But the second ascender slipped when he put his weight on it, and instinctively he grabbed the rope with his hand and burned his palm before the other ascender caught him. A totally unnecessary burn.

Now he really began to sweat. A bad ascender was bad news. This one was slipping very slightly and then catching. Looking at it, he thought that maybe it had been smacked in the fall onto the top of the mobile, breaking its housing. Ascender housings were often cast, and sometimes bubbles left in the casting caused weaknesses that broke when struck. It had happened to him before, and it was major adrenaline time. No one could climb a rope unaided for long.

But this one kept holding after its little slips, and fiddling with his fingertips he could see that shoving the cam back into place in the housing after he released it helped it to catch sooner. So with a kind of teeth-clenching patience, a holding-the-breath antigravitational effort, he could use the other one for the big pulls of the ascent, and then set the bad one by hand, to hold him (hopefully) while he moved the good one up above it again.

Eventually he got back up to the height he had wanted to descend to in the first place, and was finally ready to go. He was drenched in sweat and his right hand was burning. He tried to estimate how much time he had wasted, but could not. Somewhere between ten minutes and half an hour, he supposed. Ridiculous.

Swinging side to side was easy, and soon he was swaying back and forth, until he could reach out and place a medium sucker against Laveta's office window. He depressed it slightly as he swung in close, and it stuck first try.

Held thus against her window, he could pull a T-bar from his waist bag and reach over, just barely, and fit it into the window washer's channel next to the window. After that he was set, and could reach up and place a dashboard into the slot over the window, and rig a short rope he had brought to tie the sucker handle up to the dashboard, holding open Laveta's window.

All set. Deploy the X Acto, unscrew the frame, haul up the window toward the dashboard, almost to horizontal, keeping its top edge in the framing. Tie it off. Gap biggest at the bottom corner; slip under there and pull into the office, twisting as agilely as the gibbons at the National Zoo, then kneeling on the carpeted floor, huffing and puffing as quietly as possible.

Clip the line to a chair leg, just to be sure it didn't swing back out into the atrium and leave him stuck. Tiptoe across Laveta's office, over to Diane's in-box, where he had left his letter.

Not there.

A quick search of the desktop turned up nothing there either.

He couldn't think of any other high-probability places to look for it. The halls had surveillance cameras, and besides, where would he look? It was supposed to be here, Diane had been gone when he had left it in her in-box. Laveta had nodded, acknowledging receipt of same. Laveta?

Helplessly he searched the other surfaces and drawers in the office, but the letter was not there. There was nothing else he could do. He went back to the window, unclipped his line. He clipped his ascenders back onto it, making sure the good one was high, and that he had taken all the slack out before putting his weight on it. Faced with the tilted window and the open air, he banished all further consideration of the mystery of the absent letter, with a final thought of Laveta and the look he sometimes thought he saw in her eye; perhaps it was a purloined letter. On the other hand, Diane could have come back. But enough of that for now; it was time to focus. He needed to focus. The dreamlike quality of the descent had vanished, and now it was only a sweaty and poorly illuminated job, awkward, difficult, somewhat dangerous. Getting out, letting down the window, rescrewing the frame, leaving the cut seal to surprise some future window washer . . . Luckily, despite feeling stunned by the setback, the automatic pilot from hundreds of work hours came through. In the end it was an old expertise, a kid skill, something he could do no matter what.

Which was a good thing, because he wasn't actually focusing very well. On various levels his mind was racing. What could have happened? Who had his letter? Would he be able to find the woman from the elevator?

Thus only the next morning, when he came into the building in the ordinary way, did he look up self-consciously and notice that the mobile now hung at a ninety-degree angle to the position it had always held before. But no one seemed to notice.

CHAPTER 9

TRIGGER EVENT

Department of Homeland Security CONFIDENTIAL

Transcript NSF 3957396584

Phones 645d/922a

922a: Frank are you ready for this?

645d: I don't know Kenzo, you tell me.

922a: Casper the Friendly Ghost spent last week swimming over the sill between Iceland and Scotland, and she never got a salinity figure over 34.

645d: Wow. How deep did she go?

922a: Surface water, central water, the top of the deep water. And never over 34. 33.8 on the surface once she got into the Norwegian Sea.

645d: Wow. What about temperatures?

922a: 0.9 on the surface, 0.75 at three hundred meters. Warmer to the east, but not by much.

645d: Oh my God. So it's not going to sink.

922a: That's right.

645d: What's going to happen?

922a: I don't know. It could be the stall.

645d: Someone's got to do something about this.

922a: Good luck my friend! I personally think we're in for some fun. A thousand years of fun.

Anna was working with her door open, and once again she heard Frank's end of a phone conversation. Having eavesdropped once, it seemed to have become easier; and as before, there was a strain in Frank's voice that caught her attention. Not to mention louder sentences like:

"What? Why would they do that?"

Then silence, except for a squeak of his chair and a brief drumming of fingers.

"Uh-huh, yeah. Well, what can I say. It's too bad. It sucks, sure. . . . Yeah. But, you know. You'll be fine either way. It's your workforce that will be in trouble. . . . No no, I understand. You did your best. Nothing you can do after you sell. It wasn't your call, Derek. . . . Yeah I know. They'll find work somewhere else. It's not like there aren't other biotechs out there, it's the biotech capital of the world, right? . . . Yeah, sure. Let me know when you know. . . . Okay, I do too. Bye."

He hung up hard, cursed under his breath.

Anna looked out her door. "Something wrong?"

"Yeah."

She got up and went to her doorway. He was looking down at the floor, shaking his head disgustedly.

He raised his head and met her gaze. "Small Delivery Systems closed down Torrey Pines Generique and let almost everyone go."

"Really! Didn't they just buy them?"

"Yes. But they didn't want the people." He grimaced. "It was for something Torrey Pines had, like a patent. Or one of the people they kept. There were a few they invited to join the Small Delivery lab in Atlanta. Like that mathematician I told you about. The one who sent us a proposal, did I tell you about him?"

"One of the jackets that got turned down?"

"That's right."

"Your panel wasn't that impressed, as I recall."

"Yeah, that's right. But I'm not so sure—I don't think they were right." He grimaced, shrugged. "It was a mistake. Anyway, they'll get him to sign a contract that gives them the rights to his work, and then they'll have it to patent, or keep as a trade secret, or even bury if it interferes with some other product of theirs. Whatever their legal department thinks will make the most."

Anna watched him brood. Finally she said, "Oh well."

He gave her a look. "A guy like him belongs at NSF."

Anna lifted an eyebrow. She was well aware of Frank's ambivalent or even negative attitude toward NSF, which he had let slip often enough.

Frank understood her look and said, "The thing is, if you had him here then you could, you know, sic him on things. Sic him like a dog."

"I don't think we have a program that does that."

"Well you should, that's what I'm saying."

"You can add that to your talk to the Board this afternoon," Anna said. She considered it herself. A kind of human search engine, hunting math-based solutions . . .

Frank did not look amused. "I'll already be out there far enough as it is," he muttered. "I wish I knew why Diane asked me to give this talk anyway."

"To get your parting wisdom, right?"

"Yeah right." He looked at a pad of yellow legal-sized paper, scribbled over with notes.

Anna surveyed him, feeling again the slightly irritated fondness for him she had felt on the night of the party for the Khembalis. She would miss him when he was gone. "Want to go down and get a coffee?"

"Sure." He got up slowly, lost in thought, and reached out to close the program on his computer.

"Wow, what did you do to your hand?"

"Oh. Burned it in a little climbing fall. Grabbed the rope."

"My God Frank."

"I was belayed at the time, it was just a reflex thing."

"It looks painful."

"It is when I flex it." They left the offices and went to the elevators. "How is Charlie getting along with his poison ivy?"

"Still moaning and groaning. Most of the blisters are healing, but some of them keep breaking open. I think the worst part now is that it keeps waking him up at night. He hasn't slept much since it happened. Between that and Joe he's kind of going crazy."

In the Starbucks she said, "So are you ready for this talk to the Board?"

"No. Or, as much as I can be. Like I said, I don't really know why Diane wants me to do it."

"It must be because you're leaving. She wants to get your parting wisdom. She does that with some of the visiting people. It's a sign she's interested in your take on things."

"But how would she know what that is?"

"I don't know. Not from me. I would only say good things, of course, but she hasn't asked me."

He rubbed a finger gently up and down the burn on his palm.

"Tell me," he said, "have you ever heard of someone getting a report and, you know, just filing it away? Taking no action on it?"

"Happens all the time."

"Really?"

"Sure. With some things it's the best way to deal with them."

"Hmm."

They had made their way to the front of the line, and so paused for orders, and the rapid production of their coffees. Frank continued to look thoughtful. It reminded Anna of his manner when he had arrived at her party, soaking wet from rain, and she said, "Say, did you ever find that woman you were stuck in the elevator with?"

"No. I was going to tell you about that. I did what you suggested and contacted the Metro offices, and asked service and repair to get her name from the report. I said I needed to contact her for my insurance report."

"Oh really! And?"

"And the Metro person read it right off to me, no problem. Read me everything she wrote. But it turns out she wrote down the wrong stuff."

"What do you mean?"

They walked out of the Starbucks back into the building.

"It was a wrong address she put down. There's no residence there. And she wrote down her name as Jane Smith. I think she made everything up."

"That's strange! I guess they didn't check your IDs."

"No."

"I'd have thought they would."

"Maybe people just freed from stuck elevators are not in the mood to be handing over their IDs."

"No, I suppose not." An up elevator opened and they got in. They had it to themselves. "Like your friend, apparently."

"Yeah."

"I wonder why she would write down the wrong stuff though."

"Me too."

"What about what she told you—something about being in a cycling club, was it?"

"I've tried that. None of the cycling clubs in the area will give out membership lists. I cracked into one in Bethesda, but there wasn't any Jane Smith."

"Wow. You've really been looking into it."

"Yes."

"Maybe she's a spook. Hmm. Maybe you could go to all the cycling club meetings, just once. Or join one and ride with it, and look for her at meets, and show her picture around."

"What picture?"

"Get a portrait program to generate one."

"Good idea, although," sigh, "it wouldn't look like her."

"No, they never do."

"I'd have to get better at riding a bike."

"At least she wasn't into skydiving."

He laughed. "True. Well, I'll have to think about it. But thanks, Anna."

Later that afternoon they met again, on the way up to one of Diane's meetings with the NSF Science Board. They got out on the twelfth floor and walked around the hallways. The outer windows at the turns in the halls revealed that the day had darkened, low black clouds now tearing over themselves in their hurry to reach the Atlantic, sheeting down rain as they went.

In the big conference room Laveta and some others were repositioning a whiteboard and PowerPoint screen according to Diane's instructions. Frank and Anna were the first ones there.

"Come on in," Diane said. She busied herself with the screen and kept her back to Frank.

The rest of the crowd trickled in. NSF's Board of Directors was composed of twenty-four people, although usually there were a couple of vacant positions in the process of being filled. The directors were all powers in their parts of the scientific world, appointed by the President from lists provided by NSF and the National Academy of Science, and serving four-year terms.

Now they were looking wet and windblown, straggling into the room in ones and twos. Some of Anna's fellow division directors came in as well. Eventually fifteen or sixteen people were seated around the big table, including Sophie Harper, their congressional liaison. The light in the room flickered faintly as lightning made itself visible diffusely through the coursing rain on the room's exterior window. The gray world outside pulsed as if it were an aquarium.

Diane welcomed them and moved quickly through the agenda's introductory matter. After that she ran down a list of large projects that had been proposed or discussed in the previous year, getting the briefest of reports from Board members assigned to study the projects. They included climate mitigation proposals, many highly speculative, all extremely expensive. A carbon sink plan included reforestations that would also be useful for flood control; Anna made a note to tell the Khembalis about that one.

But nothing they discussed was going to work on the global situation, given the massive nature of the problem, and NSF's highly constricted budget and mission. Ten billion dollars; and even the $50 billion items on their list of projects only addressed small parts of the global problem.

At moments like these Anna could not help thinking of Charlie playing with Joe's dinosaurs, holding up a little pink mouselike thing, a first mammal, and exclaiming, "Hey it's NSF!"

He had meant it as a compliment to their skill at surviving in a big world, or to the way they represented the coming thing, but unfortunately the comparison was also true in terms of size. Scurrying about trying to survive in a world of dying dinosaurs—worse yet, trying to save the dinosaurs too—where was the mechanism? As Frank would say, How could that work?

She banished these thoughts and made her own quick report, about the infrastructure distribution programs that she had been studying. A lot of infrastructure had been dispersed in the last decade. Anna's concluding suggestion that the programs were a success and should be expanded was received with nods all around, as an obvious thing to do. But also expensive.

There was a pause as people thought this over.

Finally Diane looked at Frank. "Frank, are you ready?"

Frank stood to answer. He did not exhibit his usual ease. He walked over to the whiteboard, took up a red marker, fiddled with it. His face was flushed.

"All the programs described so far focus on gathering data, and the truth is we have enough data already. The world's climate has already changed. The Arctic Ocean ice pack breakup has flooded the surface of the North Atlantic with fresh water, and the most recent data indicate that that has stopped the surface water from sinking, and stalled the circulation of the big Atlantic current. That's been pretty conclusively identified as a major trigger event in Earth's climatic history. So, abrupt climate change has almost certainly already begun."

Frank stared at the whiteboard, lips pursed. "So. The question becomes, what do we do? Business as usual won't work. For you here, the effort should be toward finding ways that NSF can make a much broader impact than it has till now."

"Excuse me," one of the Board members said, sounding a bit peeved. He was a man in his sixties, with a gray Lincoln beard; Anna did not recognize him. "How is this any different from what we are always trying to do? I mean, we've talked about trying to do this at every Board meeting I've ever been to. We always ask ourselves, how can NSF get more bang for its buck?"

"Maybe so," said Frank. "But it hasn't worked."

Diane said, "What are you saying, Frank? What should we be doing that we haven't already tried?"

Frank cleared his throat. He and Diane stared at each other for a long moment, locked in some kind of undefined conflict.

Frank shrugged, went to the whiteboard, uncapped his red marker. "Let me make a list."

He wrote a 1 and circled it.

"One. We have to knit it all together." He wrote, "Synergies at NSF."

"I mean by this that you should be stimulating synergistic efforts that range across the disciplines to work on this problem. Then," he wrote and circled a 2, "you should be looking for immediately relevant applications coming out of the basic research funded by the foundation. These applications should be hunted for by people brought in specifically to do that. You should have a permanent in-house innovation and policy team."

Anna thought, That would be that mathematician he just lost.

She had never seen Frank so serious. His usual manner was gone, and with it the mask of cynicism and self-assurance that he habitually wore, the attitude that it was all a game he condescended to play even though everyone had already lost. Now he was serious, even angry it seemed. Angry at Diane somehow. He wouldn't look at her, or anywhere else but at his scrawled red words on the whiteboard.

"Third, you should commission work that you think needs to be done, rather than waiting for proposals and funding choices given to you by others. You can't afford to be so passive anymore. Fourth, you should assign up to fifty percent of NSF's budget every year to the biggest outstanding problem you can identify, in this case catastrophic climate change, and direct the scientific community to attack and solve it. Both public and private science, the whole culture. The effort could be organized like Germany's Max Planck Institutes, which are funded by the government to go after particular problems. There's about a dozen of those, and they exist while they're needed and get disbanded when they're not. It's a good model.

"Fifth, you should make more efforts to increase the power of science in policy decisions everywhere. Organize all the scientific bodies on Earth into one larger body, a kind of UN of scientific organizations, which then would work together on the important issues, and would collectively insist they be funded, for the sake of all the future generations of humanity."

He stopped, stared at the whiteboard. He shook his head. "All this may sound, what. Large-scaled. Or interfering. Antidemocratic, or elitist or something—something beyond what science is supposed to be."

The man who had objected before said, "We're in no position to stage a coup."

Frank shook him off. "Think of it in terms of Kuhnian paradigms. The paradigm model Kuhn outlined in *The Structure of Scientific Revolutions*."

The bearded man nodded, granting this.

"Kuhn postulated that in the usual state of affairs there is general agreement to a set of core beliefs that structure people's theories—that's a paradigm, and the work done within it he called 'normal science.' He was referring to a theoretical understanding of nature, but let's apply the model to science's social behavior. We do normal science. But as Kuhn pointed out, anomalies crop up. Undeniable events occur that we can't cope with inside the old paradigm. At first scientists just fit the anomalies in as best they can. Then when there are enough of them, the paradigm begins to fall apart. In trying to reconcile the irreconcilable, it becomes as weird as Ptolemy's astronomical system.

"That's where we are now. We have our universities, and the Foundation and all the rest, but the system is too complicated, and flying off in all directions. Not capable of coming to grips with the aberrant data."

Frank looked briefly at the man who had objected. "Eventually, a new paradigm is proposed that accounts for the anomalies. It comes to grips with them better. After a period of confusion and debate, people start using it to structure a new normal science."

The old man nodded. "You're suggesting we need a paradigm shift in how science interacts with society."

"Yes I am."

"But what is it? We're still in the period of confusion, as far as I can see."

"Yes. But if we don't have a clear sense of what the next paradigm should be, and I agree we don't, then it's our job now as scientists to force the issue and make it happen, by employing all our resources in an organized way. To get to the other side faster. The money and the institutional power that NSF has assembled ever since it began has to be used like a tool to build this. No more treating our grantees like clients whom we have to satisfy if we want to keep their business. No more going to Congress with hat in hand, begging for change and letting them call the shots as to where the money is spent."

"Whoa now," objected Sophie Harper. "They have the right to allocate federal funds, and they're very jealous of that right, believe you me."

"Sure they are. That's the source of their power. And they're the elected government, I'm not disputing any of that. But we can go to them and say, Look, the party's over. We need this list of projects funded or civilization will be hammered for decades to come. Tell them they can't give a trillion dollars a year to the military and leave the rescue and rebuilding of the world to chance and some kind of free market religion. It isn't working, and science is the only way out of the mess."

"You mean the scientific deployment of human effort in these causes," Diane said.

"Whatever," Frank snapped, then paused, blinking, as if recognizing what Diane had said. His face went even redder.

"I don't know," another Board member said. "We've been trying more outreach, more lobbying of Congress, all that. I'm not sure more of that will get the big change you're talking about."

Frank nodded. "I'm not sure they will either. They were the best I could think of, and more needs to be done there."

"In the end, NSF is a small agency," someone else said.

"That's true too. But think of it as an information cascade. If the whole of NSF was focused for a time on this project, then our impact would hopefully be multiplied. It would cascade from there. The math of cascades is fairly probabilistic. You push enough elements at once, and if they're the right elements, and the situation is at the angle of repose or past it, boom. Cascade. Paradigm shift. New focus on the big problems we're facing."

The people around the table were thinking it over.

Diane never took her eye off Frank. "I'm wondering if we are at such an obvious edge-of-the-cliff moment that people will listen to us if we try to start such a cascade."

"I don't know," Frank said. "I do think we're past the angle of repose. The Atlantic current has stalled. We're headed for a period of rapid climate change. That means problems that will make normal science impossible."

Diane smiled tautly. "You're suggesting we have to save the world so science can proceed?"

"Yes, if you want to put it that way. If you're lacking a better reason to do it."

Diane stared at him, offended. He met her gaze unapologetically.

Anna watched this standoff, on the edge of her seat. Something was going on between those two, and she had no idea what it was. To ease the suspense she wrote down on her handpad, "saving the world so science can proceed." The Frank Principle, as Charlie later dubbed it.

"Well," Diane said, breaking the frozen moment, "what do people think?"

A discussion followed. People threw out ideas: creating a kind of shadow replacement for Congress's Office of Technology Assessment; campaigning to make the President's scientific advisor a cabinet post; even drafting a new amendment to the Constitution that would elevate a body like the National Academy of Science to the level of a branch of government. Then also going international, funding a world body of scientific organizations to push everything that would create a sustainable civilization. These ideas and more were mooted, hesitantly at first, and then with more enthusiasm as the people there began to realize that they all had harbored various ideas of this kind, visions that were usually too big or strange to broach to other scientists. "Pretty wild notions," as one of them noted.

Frank had been listing them on the whiteboard. "The thing is," he said, "the way we have things organized now, scientists keep themselves out of political policy decisions in the same way that the military keeps itself out of civilian affairs. That comes out of World War Two, when science was part of the military. Scientists recused themselves from policy decisions, and a structure was formed that created civilian control of science, so to speak.

"But I say to hell with that! Science isn't like the military. It's the solution, not the problem. And so it has to insist on itself. That's what looks wild about these ideas, that scientists should take a stand and become a part of the political decision-making process. If it were the folks in the Pentagon saying that, I would agree there would be reason to worry, although they do it all the time. What I'm saying is that it's a perfectly legitimate move for us to make, even a necessary move, because we are not the military, we are already civilians, and we have the only methods in existence that are capable of dealing with these global environmental problems."

The group sat for a moment in silence, thinking that over. Monsoonlike rain coursed down the room's window, in an infinity of shifting delta patterns. Darker clouds rolled over, making the room dimmer still, submerging it until it was a cube of lit neon, hanging in aqueous grayness.

Anna's notepad was covered by squiggles and isolated words. So many problems were tangled together into the one big problem. So many of the suggested solutions were either partial or impractical, or both. No one could pretend they were finding any great strategies to pursue at this point. It looked as if Sophie Harper was about to throw her hands in the air, perhaps taking Frank's talk as a critique of her efforts to date, which Anna supposed was one way of looking at it, although not really Frank's point.

Now Diane made a motion as if to cut the discussion short. "Frank," she said, drawing his name out. "Fraannnnnk—you're the one who's brought this up, as if there is something we could do about it. So maybe you should be the one who heads up a committee tasked with figuring out what these things are. Sharpening up the list of things to try, in effect, and reporting back to this Board. You could proceed with the idea that your committee was building the way to the next paradigm."

Frank stood there, looking at all the red words he had scribbled so violently on the whiteboard. For a long moment he continued to look at it, his expression grim. Many in the room knew that he was due to go back to San Diego. Many did not. Either way Diane's offer probably struck them as another example of her managerial style, which was direct, public, and often had an element of confrontation or challenge in it. When people felt strongly about taking an action, she often said, You do it, then. Take the lead if you feel so strongly.

At last Frank turned and met her eye. "Yeah, sure," he said. "I'd be happy to do that. I'll give it my best shot."

Diane revealed only a momentary gleam of triumph. Once when Anna was young she had seen a chess master play an entire room of opponents, and there had been only one player he was having trouble with; at the moment he checkmated that person, he moved on with that same quick, satisfied look.

Now, in this room, Diane was already on to the next item on her agenda.

Afterward, the bioinformatics group sat in Anna and Frank's rooms on the sixth floor, sipping cold coffee and looking into the atrium.

Edgardo came in. "So," he said cheerily, "I take it the meeting was a total waste of time."

"No," Anna snapped.

Edgardo laughed. "Diane changed NSF top to bottom?"

"No."

They sat there. Edgardo went and poured himself some coffee.

Anna said to Frank, "It sounded like you were telling Diane you would stay another year."

"Yep."

Edgardo came back in, amazed. "Will wonders never cease! I hope you didn't give up your apartment yet!"

"I did."

"Oh no! Too bad!"

Frank flicked that away with his burned hand. "The guy who owns it is coming back anyway."

Anna regarded him. "So you really are changing your mind."

"Well . . ."

The lights went out, computers too. Power failure.

"Ah shit."

A blackout. No doubt a result of the storm.

Now the atrium was truly dark, all the offices lit only by the dim green glow of the emergency exit signs. EXIT. The shadow of the future.

Then the emergency generator came on, making an audible hum through the building. With a buzz and several computer pings, electricity returned.

Anna went down the hall to look north out the corner window. Arlington was dark to the rain-fuzzed horizon. Many emergency generators had already kicked in, and more did so as she watched, powering glows that in the dark rain looked like little campfires. The cloud over the Pentagon caught the light from below and gleamed blackly.

Frank came out and looked over her shoulder. "This is what it's going to be like all the time," he predicted gloomily. "We might as well get used to it."

Anna said, "How would that work?"

He smiled briefly. But it was a real smile, a tiny version of the one Anna had seen at her house. "Don't ask me." He stared out the window at the darkened city. The low thrum of rain was cut by the muffled sound of a siren below.

The Hyperniño, now in its forty-second month, had spun up another tropical system in the East Pacific, and now this big wet storm was barreling northeast toward California. It was the fourth in a series of pineapple express storms that had tracked along this course of the jet stream, which was holding in an exceptionally fast atmospheric river, headed directly at the north coast of San Diego County. Ten miles above the surface, winds flew at a hundred and seventy miles an hour, so the air underneath was yanked over the ground at around sixty miles an hour, all roiled, torn, downdrafted, and compressed, its rain squeezed out of it the moment it slammed into land. The sea cliffs of La Jolla, Blacks, Torrey Pines, Del Mar, Solana Beach, Cardiff-by-the-Sea, Encinitas, and Leucadia were all taking a beating, and in many places the sandstone, eaten by waves from below and saturated with rain from above, began to fall into the sea.

Leo and Roxanne Mulhouse had a front seat on all this, of course, because of their house's location on the cliff edge in Leucadia. Since he had been laid off, Leo had spent many an hour sitting before their west window, or even standing out on the porch in the elements, watching the storms come onshore. It was an astonishing thing to see that much weather crashing into a coastline. The clouds poured up over the southwest horizon and flew at him, and yet the cliffs and the houses held in place, making the compressed wind howl, boom, shriek.

This particular morning was the worst yet. Tree branches tossed violently; three eucalyptus trees had been knocked over on Neptune Avenue alone. And Leo had never seen the sea look like this before. All the way out to where rapidly approaching black squalls blocked the view of the horizon, the ocean was a giant sheet of raging surf. Millions of whitecaps rolled toward the land under flying spume and spray, the waves toppling again and again over infinitely wind-rippled gray water. The squalls flew by rapidly, or came straight on until they hit in black bursts against the house's west side. Brief patches and shards of sunlight lanced between these squalls, but failed to light the sea surface in their usual way; the water was too shredded. The gray shafts of light appeared to be eaten by spray.

Up and down Neptune Avenue, their cliff was wearing away. It happened irregularly, in sudden slumps of various sizes, some at the cliff top, some at the base, some in the middle.

The erosion was not a new thing. The cliffs of San Diego had been breaking off throughout the period of modern settlement, and presumably for all the centuries before that. But along the stretch of seaside cliff north and south of Moonlight Beach, the houses had been built close to the edge. Surveyors studying photos had seen little movement in the cliff's edge between 1928 and 1965, when the construction began. They had not known about the storm of October 12, 1889, when 7.58 inches of rain had fallen on Encinitas in eight hours, triggering a flood and bluff collapse so severe that A, B, and C Streets of the new town had disappeared into the sea. This was why the town's westernmost street was D Street, but they had not paused to ask about that. They also did not understand that grading the bluffs and adding drainage pipes that led out the cliff face destroyed natural drainage patterns that led inland. So the homes and apartment blocks had been built with their fine views, and then years of efforts had been made to stabilize the cliffs.

Now, among other problems, the cliffs were often unnaturally vertical as a result of all the shoring up they had been given. Concrete and steel barriers, ice-plant berms, wooden walls and log beams, plastic sheets and molding, crib walls, boulder walls, concrete abutments—all these efforts had been made in the same period when the beaches were no longer being replenished by sand washing out of the lagoons to the north, because all the lagoons had had their watersheds developed and their rivers made much less prone to flooding sand out to sea. So over time the beaches had disappeared, and these days waves struck directly at the bases of ever-steepening cliffs. The angle of repose was very far exceeded.

Now the ferocity of the Hyperniño was calling all that to account, overwhelming a century's work all at once. The day before, just south of the Mulhouses' property, a section of the cliff a hundred feet long and fifteen feet inland went, burying a concrete berm lying at the bottom of the cliff.

Two hours later a hemispheric arc forty feet deep had fallen into the surf just north of them, leaving a raw new gap between two apartment blocks—a gap that quickly turned into a gritty mudslide that slid down into the tormented water, staining it brown for hundreds of yards offshore. The usual current was southerly, but the storm was shoving the ocean as well as the air northward, so that the water offshore was chaotic with drifts, with discharge from suddenly raging river mouths, with backwash from the strikes of the big swells, and with the ever-present wind, slinging spray over all. It was so bad no one was even surfing.

As the dark morning wore on, many of the residents of Neptune Avenue went out to look at their stretch of the bluff. Various authorities were there as well, and interested spectators were filling the little cross streets that ran to the coast highway. Many residents had gone the previous evening to hear a team from the U.S. Army Corps of Engineers give a presentation at the town library, explaining their plan to stabilize the cliff at its most vulnerable points with impromptu riprap seawalls made of boulders dumped from above. This meant that in many places the already narrow beach would be buried, becoming a wall of boulders even at low tide—like the side of a jetty, or a stretch of some very rocky coastline. Some lamented this loss of the area's signature landscape feature, a beach that had been four hundred yards wide in the 1920s, and even now, the place that made San Diego what it was. There were people who felt the beach was worth more than the houses on the cliff edge. Let them go!

But the cliff-edge homeowners had argued that it was not necessarily true that the cliffside line of houses would be the last of the losses. Everyone now knew why the westernmost street in Encinitas was named D Street. The whole town stood on the edge of a sandstone cliff, when you got right down to it. If massive rapid erosion had happened before, it could happen again. One look at the raging surface of the Pacific was enough to convince people of this.

So that morning Leo found himself standing near the south end of Leucadia, his rain jacket and pants plastered to his windward side as he shoved a wheelbarrow over a wide plank path. Roxanne was inland at her sister's, so he was free to pitch in, and happy to have something to do. A county dump truck working with the Army Corps of Engineers was parked on Europa, and men running a small hoist were lifting granite boulders from the truck bed down into wheelbarrows. A lot of amateur help milled about. The county and Army people supervised the operations, lining up plankways and directing rocks to the various points on the cliff's edge where they were dumping them.

Hundreds of people had come out to watch the wheelbarrowed boulders bound down the cliff and crash into the sea. It was already the latest spectacle, a new extreme sport. Some of the bounding rocks caught really good air, or spun, or held still like knuckleballs, or splashed hugely. The surfers who were not helping (and there were only so many volunteers who could be put to use) cheered lustily at the most dramatic falls. Every surfer in the county was there, drawn like moths to flame, entranced, and on some level itching to go out; but it was not possible. The water was crazy everywhere, and when the big broken waves smashed into the bottom of the cliffs, surges of water shoved up, disintegrated into a white smash of foam and spray, hung suspended for a moment, then fell and muscled back out to sea, bulling into the incoming waves and creating thick tumultuous leaping backwash collisions, until all in the brown shallows was chaos and disorder, through which another surge crashed.

And all the while the wind howled over them, through them, against them. Even though the cliffs in this area were low compared to those at Torrey Pines, being about 80 feet tall rather than 350, that was still enough to block the terrific onshore flow and cause the wind to shoot up the cliffs and over them, so that a bit back from the edge it could be almost still, while right at the edge itself a blasting updraft was spiked by frequent gusts, like uppercuts from an invisible fist. Leo felt as if he could have leaned out over the edge and extended his arms and be held there at an angle—or even jump and float down. Young windsurfers would probably be trying that soon, or surfers with their wetsuits altered to make them something like flying squirrels. Not that they would want to be in the water now. The sheer height of the whitewater surges against the cliffside was hard to believe, truly startling. When they impacted the cliff, bursts of spray shot up into the wind and were whirled inland onto the houses and people.

Leo got his wheelbarrow to the end of the plank road, and let a gang of people grasp his handles with him and help him tilt the stone out at the right place. After that he got out of the way and stood watching other people work. Restricted access to some of the weakest parts of the cliff meant that this was going to take days. Right now the rocks simply disappeared into the waves. No visible result whatsoever. "It's like dropping rocks in the ocean," he said to no one. The noise of the wind was like jets warming up for takeoff, interrupted by frequent invisible whacks on the ear. He could talk to himself without fear of being overheard, and did. His eyes watered in the wind, but that same wind tore the tears away and cleared his vision again and again.

This was purely a physical reaction to the gale; he was basically very happy to be there. Happy to have the distraction of the storm. A public disaster, a natural event; it put everyone in the same boat, somehow. In a way it was even inspiring—not just the human response, but the storm itself. Wind as spirit. It felt uplifting. As if the wind had carried him off and out of his life.

Certainly it put things in a very different perspective. Losing a job—so what? How did that signify, really? The world was so vast and powerful. They were like fleas in it, their problems the tiniest of flea perturbations.

He returned to the dump truck and took another rock, and then focused on balancing it at the front end of the wheelbarrow, turning the wheelbarrow, keeping it moving over the flexing line of planks, shouldering into the blasts. Tipping a rock into the sea. Wonderful, really.

He was running the empty wheelbarrow back to the street when he saw Marta and Brian, getting out of Marta's truck at the end of the street. "Hey!" This was a nice surprise—they were not a couple, or even friends outside the lab, as far as Leo knew, and he had feared that with the lab shut down, he would never see either of them again.

"Marta!" he bellowed happily. "Bri-man!"

"LEO!"

They were glad to see him. They ran up and gave him a hug.

"How's it going?" "How's it going?"

The two of them were jacked up by the storm and the chance to do something. No doubt it had been a long couple of weeks for them too, no work to go to, nothing to do. Well, they would have been out in the surf, or otherwise active. But here they were now, and Leo was glad.

Quickly they all got into the flow of the work, trundling rocks out to the cliff. Once Leo found himself following Marta down the plank line, and he watched her bunched shoulders and soaking black curls with a sudden blaze of friendship and admiration. She was a surfer gal, slim hips, broad shoulders, raising her head to the wind and howling back at it. He was going to miss her. Brian too. It had been good of them to come by like this, but the nature of things was such that they would all find other work, and then they would drift apart. It never lasted with old work colleagues, the bond just wasn't strong enough. Work was always a matter of showing up and then enjoying the people who had been hired to work there too. Not only their banter, but also the way they did the work. They had been a good lab.

The Army guys were waving them back from the edge of the cliff. It had been a lawn and now it was all torn up, and there was a guy there crouching over a big metal box, USGS printed on his soaking windbreaker. Brian shouted in their ears: they had found a fracture in the sandstone parallel to the cliff's edge here, and apparently someone had felt the ground slump a little, and the USGS guy's instrumentation was indicating movement. It was going to go. Everyone dumped their rocks and hustled the empty wheelbarrows back to Neptune.

Just in time. With a short dull roar and whump that almost could have been the impact of a really big wave, the cliff edge slumped and disappeared. The crowd let out a shout that was audible above the wind. Now they could see through space to the gray sea hundreds of yards offshore. The new cliff edge was fifteen feet closer to them.

Very, very spooky. Leo and Brian and Marta drifted forward with the rest, to glimpse the dirty rage of water below. The break in the cliff extended about a hundred yards to the south, maybe fifty to the north. A modest loss in the overall scheme of things, but this was the way it was happening, one little break at a time, all up and down this stretch of coast. There was a whole series of faults parallel to the cliff, so that it was likely to flake off piece by piece as the waves gouged away support from below. That was how A, B, and C Streets had gone in a single night. It could happen all the way inland to the coast highway.

Amazing. Leo could only hope that Roxanne's mother's house had been built on one of the more solid sections of the bluff. It had always seemed that way when he descended the nearby staircase and checked it out; it stood over a kind of buttress of stone. But as he watched the ocean flail, and felt the wind strike them, there was no reason to think any section would hold. A whole neighborhood could go. And all up and down the coast people had built close to the edge, so it would be much the same in many other places.

No house had gone over in the slump they had just witnessed, but one at the southern end of it had lost part of its west wall and been torn open to the wind. Everyone stood around staring, pointing, shouting unheard in the roar of wind. Milling about, running hither and thither, trying to get a view.

There was nothing else to be done at this point. The end of their plank road was gone along with everything else. The Army and county guys were getting out sawhorses and rolls of orange plastic stripping; they were going to cordon off the street and shift the work efforts to safer platforms.

"Wow," Leo said to the storm, feeling the word ripped out of his mouth and flung to the east. "My Lord, what a wind." He shouted to Marta: "We were standing right out there!"

"Gone!" Marta shouted. "Gone like Torrey Pines Generique!"

Brian and Leo shouted agreement. Into the sea with the damned place!

They retreated to the lee of Marta's little Toyota pickup, sat on the curb behind its slight protection, and drank some espressos she had in the cab, already cold in paper cups with plastic tops.

"There'll be more work," Leo told them.

"That's for sure." But they meant boulder work. "I heard the coast highway is cut just south of Cardiff," Brian said. "Restaurant Row is totally gone. The overpass fell in and then the water started ripping both ways at the roadbed."

"Wow!"

"It's going to be a mess. I bet that will happen at the Torrey Pines river mouth too."

"All the big lagoons."

"Maybe, yeah."

They sipped their espressos.

"It's good to see you guys!" Leo said. "Thanks for coming by."

"Yeah."

"That's the worst part of this whole thing," Leo said.

"Yeah."

"Too bad they didn't hang on to us—they're putting all their eggs in one basket now."

Marta and Brian regarded Leo. He wondered which part of what he had just said they disagreed with. Now that they weren't working for him, he had no right to grill them about it. On the other hand, there was no reason to hold back either.

"What?" he exclaimed.

"I just got hired by Small Delivery Systems," Marta said, still almost shouting to be heard over the noise. She glanced at Leo uncomfortably. "Eleanor Dufours is working for them now, and she hired me. They want us to work on that algae stuff we've been doing."

"Oh I see! Well good! Good for you."

"Yeah, well. Atlanta!"

There was a whistle from the Army guys. A whole gang of people were trooping behind them down Neptune, south to another dump truck that had just arrived. There was more to be done.

Leo and Marta and Brian followed, went back to work. Some people left, others arrived. Lots of people were documenting events on their phones and cameras. As the day wore on, the volunteers were glad to take heavy-duty work gloves from the Army guys to protect their palms from further blistering.

About two that afternoon the three of them decided to call it quits. Their palms were trashed. Leo's thighs and lower back were getting shaky, and he was hungry. The cliff work would go on, and there would be no shortage of volunteers while the storm lasted. The need was evident, and besides it was fun to be out in the blast, doing something. Working made it seem practical to be out there, although many would have been out anyway, to watch the tumult.

The three of them stood on a point just north of Swami's, leaning into the storm and marveling at the spectacle. Marta was bouncing a little in place, stuffed with energy, totally fired up; she seemed both exhilarated and furious, and shouted at the biggest waves when they struck the stubborn little cliff at Pipes. "Look at that! Outside!" She was soaking wet, as they all were, the rain plastering her curls to her head, the wind plastering her shirt to her torso; she looked like the winner of some kind of extreme-sport wet T-shirt contest, her breasts and belly button and ribs and collarbones and abs all perfectly delineated under the thin wet cloth. She was a power, a San Diego surf goddess, and good for her that she had gotten hired by Small Delivery Systems. Again Leo felt a glow for this wild young colleague of his.

"This is so great!" he shouted. "I'd rather do this than work in the lab!"

Brian laughed. "They don't pay you for this, Leo."

"Ah hey. Fuck that. This is still better." And he howled at the storm.

Then Brian and Marta gave him hugs; they were taking off.

"Let's try to stay in touch you guys," Leo said sentimentally. "Let's really do it. Who knows, we may all end up working together again someday anyway."

"Good idea."

"I'll probably be available," Brian said.

Marta shrugged, looking away. "We either will be or we won't."

Then they were off. Leo waved at Marta's receding truck. A sudden pang—would he ever see them again? The reflection of the truck's taillights smeared in two red lines over the street's wet asphalt. Blinking right turn signal—then they were gone.

CHAPTER 10

BROADER IMPACTS

It takes no great skill to decode the world system today. A tiny percentage of the population is immensely wealthy, some are well-off, a lot are just getting by, a lot are suffering. We call it capitalism, but within it lies buried residual patterns of feudalism and older hierarchies, basic injustices framing the way we organize ourselves. Everybody lives in an imaginary relationship to this real situation; and that is our world. We walk with scales on our eyes, and only see what we think.

And all the while on a sidewalk over the abyss. There are islands of time when things seem stable. Nothing much happens but the rounds of the week. Later the islands break apart. When enough time has passed, no one now alive will still be here; everyone will be different. Then it will be the stories that will link the generations, history and DNA, long chains of the simplest bits—guanine, adenine, cytosine, thymine—love, hope, fear, selfishness—all recombining again and again, until a miracle happens

and the organism springs forth!

Charlie struggled to his feet and stood next to his bed, hands thrown out like a nineteenth-century boxer.

"What?" he shouted at the loud noise.

It was not an alarm. It was Joe in the room, wailing. He stared at his father amazed. "Ba."

"Jesus, Joe." The itchiness began to burn across Charlie's chest and arms. He had tossed and turned in misery most of the night, as he had every night since encountering the poison ivy. He had probably fallen asleep only an hour or two before. "What time is it? Joe, it's not even seven! Don't yell like that. All you have to do is tap me on the shoulder if I'm still asleep, and say, 'Good morning Dad, can you warm up a bottle for me?'"

Joe approached and tapped his leg, staring peacefully at him. "Mo da. Wa ba."

"Wow Joe. Really good! Say, I'll get you your bottle warmed up right away! Very good! Hey listen, have you pooped in your diaper yet? You might want to pull it down and sit on your own toilet in the bathroom like a big boy, poop like Nick, and then come on down to the kitchen and your bottle will be ready. Doesn't that sound good?"

"Ga da." Joe trundled off toward the bathroom.

Charlie, amazed, padded after Joe and descended the stairs as gently as he could, hoping not to stimulate his itches. In the kitchen the air was delightfully cool and silky. Nick was there reading a book. Without looking up he said, "I want to go down to the park and play."

"I thought you had homework to do."

"Well, sort of. But I want to play."

"Why don't you do your homework first and then play, that way when you play you'll be able to really enjoy it."

Nick cocked his head. "That's true. Okay, I'll go do my homework first." He slipped out, book under his arm.

"Oh, and take your shoes up to your room while you're on your way."

"Sure Dad."

Charlie stared in his reflection in the side of the stove hood. His eyes were round.

"Hmm," he said. He got Joe's bottle in its pot, stuck an earphone in his left ear. "Phone, give me Phil. . . . Hello, Phil, look I wanted to catch you while the thought was fresh, I was thinking that if we introduced the Chinese aerosols bill again, we could catch the whole air problem at a fulcrum and either start a process that would finish with the coal plants here on the East Coast, or else it would serve as a stalking horse, see what I mean?"

"Hmm, good idea Charlie, I'd forgotten that bill, but it was a good one. I'll give that a try. Call Roy and tell him to get it ready."

"Sure Phil, consider it done."

Charlie took the bottle out of the pot and dried it. Joe appeared in the door, naked, holding up his diaper for Charlie's inspection.

"Wow Joe, very good! You pooped in your toilet? Very good, here's your bottle all ready, what a perfect kind of Pavlovian reward."

Joe snatched the bottle from Charlie's hand and waddled off, a length of toilet paper trailing behind him, one end stuck between the halves of his butt.

Holy shit, Charlie thought. So to speak.

He called up Roy and told him Phil had authorized the reintroduction of the Chinese bill. Roy was incredulous. "What do you mean, we went down big-time on that, it was a joke then and it would be worse now!"

"Not so, it lost bad but that was good, we got lots of credit for it that we deployed elsewhere, and it'll happen the same way when we do it again because it's right, Roy, we have right on our side on this."

"Yes of course obviously but that's not the point—"

"Not the point? Have we gotten so jaded that being right is no longer relevant?"

"No of course not, but that's not the point either, it's like playing a chess game, each move is just a move in the larger game, you know?"

"Yes I do know because that's my analogy, but that's my point, this is a good move, this checks them, and they have to give up a queen to stop from being checkmated."

"You really think it's that much leverage? Why?"

"Because Winston has such ties to Chinese industry, and he can't defend that very well to his constituency, Christian realpolitik isn't a coherent philosophy and so it's a vulnerability he has don't you see?"

"Well yeah, of course. You said Phil okayed it already?"

"Yes he did."

"Okay, that's good enough for me."

Charlie got off and did a little dance in the kitchen, circling out into the living room, where Joe was sitting on the floor trying to get back into his diaper. Both adhesive tags had torn loose. "Good try Joe, here let me help you."

"Okay da." Joe held out the diaper.

"Hmm," Charlie said, suddenly suspicious.

He called up Anna and got her. "Hey snooks, how are you, yeah I'm just calling to say I love you and to suggest that we get tickets to fly to Jamaica, we'll find some kind of kid care and go down there just by ourselves, we'll rent a whole beach to ourselves and spend a week down there or maybe two, it would be good for us."

"True."

"It's really inexpensive down there now because of the unrest and all, so we'll have it to ourselves almost."

"True."

"So I'll just call up the travel agent and have them put it all on my business expenses card."

"Okay, go for it."

Then there was a kind of wet cracking sound, and Charlie woke up.

"Ah shit."

He knew just what had happened, because it had happened before. His dreaming mind had grown skeptical at something in a dream that was going too well or badly—in this case, his implausibly powerful persuasiveness—and so he had dreamed ever-more-unlikely scenarios, in a kind of test-to-destruction, until the dream had popped.

It was almost funny, this relationship to dreams. Except sometimes they crashed at the most inopportune moments. It was perverse to probe the limits of believability rather than just go with the flow, but that was the way Charlie's mind worked, apparently. Nothing he could do about it but groan and laugh, and try to train his sleeping mind into a more wish-fulfillment-tolerant response.

It turned out that in the waking world it was a work-at-home day for Anna, scheduled to give Charlie a kind of poison ivy vacation from Joe. Charlie was planning to take advantage of that to go down to the office by himself for once, and have a talk with Phil about what to do next. It was crucial to get Phil on line for a set of small bills that would save the best of the comprehensive.

He padded downstairs to find Anna cooking pancakes for the boys. Joe liked to use them as little frisbees. "Morning babe."

"Hi hon." He kissed her on the ear, inhaling the smell of her hair. "I just had the most amazing dream. I could talk anybody into anything."

"How exactly was that a dream?"

"Yeah right! Don't tease me, obviously I can't talk anybody into anything. No, this was definitely a dream. In fact I pushed it too far and killed it. I tried to talk you into going off with me to Jamaica, and you said yes."

She laughed merrily at the thought, and he laughed to see her laugh, and at the memory of the dream. And then it seemed like a gift instead of a mockery.

He scanned the kitchen computer screen for the news. Stormy Monday, it proclaimed. Big storms were swirling up out of the subtropics, and the freshly minted blue of the Arctic Ocean was dotted by a daisy chain of white patches, all falling south. Polar vortexes. The highest satellite photos, covering most of the Northern Hemisphere, reminded Charlie of how his skin had looked right after his outbreak of poison ivy. A huge white blister had covered Southern California the day before; another was headed their way from Canada, this one a real bruiser—big, wet, slightly warmer than usual, pouring down on them from Saskatchewan.

The media meteorologists were already in a lather of anticipation, not only over the Arctic blast but also a tropical storm now leaving the Bahamas.

"Not that impressive, this guy calls it! My God, everybody's a critic. Now people are reviewing the weather."

" 'Tasteful little cirrus clouds,' " Anna quoted from somewhere.

"Yeah. And I heard someone talking about 'an ostentatious thunderhead.' "

"It's the melodrama," Anna guessed. "Climate as bad art, as soap opera. Or some kind of reality show. Do you think you should stay home?"

"No it'll be okay. I'll just be at work."

"Okay." This made sense to Anna; it took a lot to keep her from going to work. "But be careful."

"I will. I'll be indoors."

Charlie went upstairs to get ready. A trip out without Joe! It was like a little adventure.

Although when he was out the door and walking up Wisconsin, he found he kind of missed his little puppetmaster. He stood at a corner, waiting for the light to change, and when a tall semi rumbled by he said aloud, "Oooh, big truck!" which caused the others waiting for the light to give him a look. Embarrassing. But it was truly hard to remember he was alone. His shoulders kept flexing at the unaccustomed lack of weight. The back of his neck felt the wind on it. It was somehow an awful realization: he would rather have had Joe along. "Jesus, Quibler, what are you coming to."

It was good, however, not to have the straps of the baby backpack cutting across his chest. Even without them the poison ivy damage was prickling at the touch of his shirt and the first sheen of sweat. Since the encounter with the tree he had slept so poorly, spending so much of every night awake in an agony of unscratchable itching, that he felt thoroughly and completely deranged. His doctor had prescribed powerful oral steroids, and given him a shot of them too, so maybe that was part of it. That or simply the itching itself. Putting on clothes was like a kind of skin-deep electrocution.

It had only taken a few days of that to reduce him to a gibbering semi-hallucinatory state. Now, over a week later, it was worse. His eyes were sandy; things had auras around them; noises made him jump. It was like the dregs of a crystal meth jag, he imagined, or the last hours of an acid trip. A sandpapered brain, spacy and raw, everything leaping into it through the portals of his senses.

He took the Metro to Dupont Circle, got off there just to take a walk without Joe. He stopped at Kramer's and got an espresso to go, then started around the circle to check the Dupont Second Story, but stopped when he realized he was doing exactly the things he would have done if he had had Joe with him.

He carried on southeastward instead, strolling down Connecticut toward the Mall. As he walked he admired a great spectacle of clouds overhead, vast towers of pearly white lobes blooming upward into a high pale sky.

He stopped at the wonderful map store on Eye Street, and for a while lost himself in the cloud shapes of other countries. Back outside the real clouds were growing in place rather than heaving in from the west or the southeast. Brilliant anvil heads were blossoming sixty thousand feet over-head, forming a hyper-Himalaya that looked as solid as marble.

He pulled out his phone and put it in his left ear. "Phone, call Roy."

After a second: "Roy Anastophoulus."

"Roy, it's Charlie. I'm coming on in."

"I'm not there."

"Ah come on!"

"I know. When was the last time I actually saw you?"

"I don't know."

"What are you going in for?"

"I need to talk to Phil. I had a dream this morning that I could convince anybody of anything, even Joe. I convinced Phil to reintroduce the Chinese aerosols bill, and then I got you to approve it."

"That poison ivy has driven you barking mad."

"Very true. It must be the steroids. I mean, the clouds today are like pulsing. They don't know which way to go."

"That's probably right, there's two low-pressure systems colliding here today, didn't you hear?"

"How could I not."

"They say it's going to rain really hard."

"Looks like I'll beat it to the office, though."

"Good. Hey listen, when Phil gets in, don't be too hard on him. He already feels bad enough."

"He does?"

"Well, no. Not really. I mean, when have you ever seen Phil feel bad about anything?"

"Never."

"Right. But, you know. He would feel bad about this if he went in for that kind of thing. And you have to remember, he's pretty canny at getting the most he can get from these bills. He sees the limits and then does what he can. It's not a zero-sum game to him. He really doesn't think of it as us-and-them."

"But it is us-and-them."

"True. But he takes the long view. Later some of the thems will be part of an us. And meanwhile, he finds some pretty good tricks. Breaking the superbill into parts might have been the way to go. We'll get back a lot of this stuff later."

"Maybe. We never tried the Chinese aerosols again."

"Not yet."

Charlie stopped listening to check the street he was crossing. When he started listening again Roy was saying, "So you dreamed you were Xenophon, eh?"

"How's that?"

"Xenophon. He wrote the *Anabasis,* which tells the story of how he and a bunch of Greek mercenaries got stuck and had to fight their way across Turkey to get home to Greece. They argue the whole time about what to do, and Xenophon wins every argument, and all his plans always work perfectly. I think of it as the first great political fantasy novel. So who else did you convince?"

"Well, I got Joe to potty-train himself, and then I convinced Anna to leave the kids at home and go with me on a vacation to Jamaica."

Roy laughed heartily. "Dreams are so funny."

"Yeah, but bold. So bold. Sometimes I wake up and wonder why I'm not as bold as that all the time. I mean, what have we got to lose?"

"Jamaica, baby. Hey, did you know that some of those hotels on the north shore there are catering to couples who like to have a lot of semi-public sex, out around the pools and the beaches?"

"Talk about fantasy novels."

"Yeah, but don't you think it'd be interesting?"

"You are sounding kind of, I don't want to say desperate here, but deprived maybe?"

"It's true, I am. It's been weeks."

"Oh poor guy. It's been weeks since I left my house."

Actually, for Roy a few weeks was quite a long time between amorous encounters. One of the not-so-hidden secrets of Washington, D.C., was that among the ambitious young single people who had gathered there to run the world, there was a whole lot of collegial sex going on. Now Roy said dolefully, "I guess I'll have to go dancing tonight."

"Oh poor you! I'll be at home, not scratching myself."

"You'll be fine. You've already got yours. Hey my food has come."

"So where are you anyway?"

"Bombay Club."

"Ah geez." This was a restaurant run by a pair of Indian-Americans, and was a favorite of staffers, lobbyists, and other political types.

"Tandoori salmon?" Charlie asked enviously.

"That's right. It looks and smells fantastic."

"Yesterday my lunch was Gerber's baby spinach."

"No. You don't really eat that stuff."

"Yeah sure. It's not so bad. It could use a little salt."

"Yuck!"

"Yeah, see what I do is I mix a little spinach and a little banana together?"

"Oh come on quit it!"

"Bye."

"Bye."

The light under the thunderheads had gone dim. Cloud bottoms were black, and splotches like dropped water balloons starred the sidewalk pavement. Charlie started hurrying, and got to Phil's office just ahead of a downpour.

He looked back out through the glass doors and watched the rain hammer down the length of the Mall. The skies had really opened. Raindrops remained large in the air, as if hail the size of baseballs had coalesced in the thunderheads and then somehow been melted back to rain again before reaching the ground.

Charlie watched the spectacle for a while, then went upstairs. There he found out from Evelyn that Phil's flight in had been delayed, and that he might be driving back from Richmond instead.

Charlie sighed. No conferring with Phil today.

He read reports instead, went down to clear his mailbox. Evelyn's office window faced south, with the Capitol looming to the left, and across the Mall the Air and Space Museum. In the rainy light the big buildings took on an eerie cast, like the cottages of giants.

Then it was past noon, and Charlie was hungry. The rain seemed to have eased a bit since its first impact, so he went out to get a sandwich at the Iranian deli on C Street, grabbing an umbrella at the door.

Outside it was raining steadily but lightly. The streets were deserted. Many intersections had flooded to the curbs, and in a few places well over the curbs, onto the sidewalks.

Inside the deli the grill was sizzling, but the place was almost empty. Two cooks and the cashier were standing under a TV that hung from a ceiling corner, watching the news. When they recognized Charlie they went back to looking at the TV. The characteristic smell of basmati rice enfolded him.

"Big storm coming," the cashier said. "Ready to order?"

"Yeah, thanks. I'll have the usual, pastrami sandwich on rye."

"Flood too," one of the cooks added.

"Oh yeah?" Charlie replied. "What, more than usual?"

The cashier nodded, still looking at the TV. "Two storms and high tide. Upstream, downstream, and middle."

"Oh my."

Charlie wondered what it would mean. He stood watching the TV with the rest of them. Satellite photos showed a huge sheet of white pouring across New York and Pennsylvania. Meanwhile the tropical storm was spinning past Bermuda. It looked like another perfect storm might be brewing. Not that it took a perfect storm these days to make the mid-Atlantic states seem like a literal name, geographically speaking. A far less than perfect storm could do it. The TV spoke of eleven-year tide cycles, of the strongest El Niño ever recorded. "It's a fourteen-thousand-square-mile watershed," the TV said.

"It's gonna get wet," Charlie observed.

The Iranians nodded silently. Five years earlier they would probably have been closing the deli, but this was the fourth perfect storm in the last three years, and like everyone else, they were getting jaded. It was Peter crying wolf at this point, even though the previous three storms had all been major disasters at the time, at least in some places. But never in D.C. Now people just made sure their supplies and equipment were okay and then went about their business, umbrella and phone in hand. Charlie was no different, he realized; here he was, getting a sandwich and going back to work. It seemed the best way to deal with it.

The Iranians finished his order, all the while watching the TV images: flooding fields, apparently in the upper Potomac watershed.

"Three meters," the cashier said as she gave him his change, but Charlie wasn't sure what she meant. The cook chopped Charlie's wrapped sandwich in half, put it in a bag. "First one is worst one."

Charlie took it and hurried back through the darkening streets. He passed an occasional lit window, occupied by people working at computer terminals, looking like figures in a Hopper painting.

Now it began to rain hard again, and the wind was roaring in the trees and hooting around the building corners. The curiously low-angle nature of D.C. made big patches of lowering clouds visible through the rain.

Charlie stopped at a street corner and looked around. His skin was on fire. Things looked too wet and underlit to be real; it looked like stage lighting for some moment of ominous portent. Once again he felt that he had crossed over into a space where the real world had taken on all the qualities of a dream, being just as glossy and surreal, just as stuffed to a dark sheen with ungraspable meaning. Sometimes just being outdoors in bad weather was all it took.

Back in the office he settled at his desk, and ate while looking over his list of things to do. The sandwich was good. The coffee from the office's coffee machine was bad. He wrote a memo for Phil, urging him to follow up on the elements of the bill that seemed to be dropping into cracks.

The sound of the rain made him think of the Khembalis and their low-lying island. What could they possibly do to help their watery home? Thinking about it he googled Khembalung, and when he saw there were over eight thousand references, googled "Khembalung + history." That got him only dozens, and he called up the first one that looked interesting, a site called "Shambhala Studies" from a .edu site.

The first paragraph left his mouth hanging open: *Khembalung, a shifting kingdom, previously Shambhala.* He skimmed down the screen, scrolling slowly:

> *when the warriors of Han invade central Tibet, Khembalung's turn will have arrived. A person will come from Drepung, a person named Sonam will come from the north, a person named Padma will come from the west*

"Holy shit—"

> *the first incarnation of Rudra was born as King of Olmolungring, in 16,017 B.C.*

then dishonesty and greed will prevail, an ideology of brutal ma-
terialism will spread all over the earth. The tyrant will come to
believe there is no place left to conquer, but the mists will lift and
reveal Shambhala. Outraged to find he does not rule all, the ty-
rant will attack, but at that point Rudra Cakrin will rise and lead
a mighty host against the invaders. After a big battle the evil will
be destroyed (see Plate 4).

"Holy God. What in the hell." Charlie read rapidly, face just inches from the screen, which was now also the dim room's lamp. Reappearance of the kingdom . . . reincarnation of its lamas . . .

Then a section describing the methods used for locating reincarnated lamas when they reappeared in a new life. The hairs on Charlie's forearms suddenly prickled, and a wave of itching rolled over his body. Toddlers spoke in tongues, or recognized personal items from the previous incarnation's belongings, or made or recognized certain mandala patterns—

His phone rang and he jumped a foot.

"Hello!"

"Charlie! Are you all right?"

"Hi babe, yeah, you just startled me."

"Sorry, oh good. I was worried, I heard on the news that downtown is flooding, the Mall is flooding."

"The what?"

"Are you at the office?"

"Yeah."

"Is anyone else there with you?"

"Sure."

"Are they just sitting there working?"

Charlie peered out of his carrel door to look. In fact his floor sounded empty. It sounded as if everyone was gathered down in Evelyn's office.

"I'll go check and call you back," he said to Anna.

"Okay call me when you find out what's happening!"

"I will. Thanks for tipping me. Hey before I go, did you know that Khembalung is a kind of reincarnation of Shambhala?"

"What do you mean?"

"Just what I said. Shambhala, the hidden magical city—"

"Yes I know—"

"—well it's a kind of movable feast, apparently. Whenever it's discovered, or the time is right, it moves on to a new spot. They recently found the ruins of the original one in Kashgar, did you know that?"

"No."

"Apparently they did. It was like finding Troy, or the Atlantis place on Santorini. But Shambhala didn't end in Kashgar, it moved. First to Tibet, then to a valley in east Nepal or west Bhutan, a valley called Khembalung. I suppose when the Chinese conquered Tibet the lamas had to move it down to the island."

"How do you know this?"

"I just read it online."

"Charlie that's very nice, but right now go find out what's going on down there in your office! I think you're in the area that may get flooded!"

"Okay, I will. But look," walking down the hall now, "did Drepung ever tell you how they figure out who their reincarnated lamas have been reborn as?"

"No. Go check on your office!"

"Okay I am, but look honey, I want you to talk to him about that. I'm remembering that first dinner, when the old man was playing games with Joe and his blocks, and Sucandra didn't like it."

"So?"

"So I just want to be sure that nothing's going on there! This is serious, honey, I'm serious. Those Tibetans looking for the new Panchen Lama, they got some poor little kid in terrible trouble with the Chinese a few years ago, and I don't want any part of something like that."

"What? I don't know what you're talking about Charlie, but let's talk about it later. Just find out what's going on there."

"Okay okay, but remember."

"I will!"

"Okay. Call you back in a second."

He went into Evelyn's office and saw people jammed around the south window, or in front of a TV set on a desk.

"Look at this," Andrea said to him, gesturing at the TV screen.

"Is that our door camera?" Charlie exclaimed, recognizing the view down Constitution. "That's our door camera!"

"That's right."

"My God!"

Charlie went to the window and stood on his tiptoes to see past people. The Mall was covered by water. The streets beyond were flooded. Constitution Avenue was floored by water that looked to be at least two feet deep, maybe deeper.

"Incredible isn't it."

"Look at that."

"Will you look at that!"

"Why didn't you guys call me?" Charlie cried, shocked by the view.

"Forgot you were here," someone said. "You're never here."

Andrea added, "It just came up in the last half hour. It happened all at once, it seemed like. I was watching." Her voice quivered. "It was like a hard downburst, and the raindrops didn't have anywhere to go, they were splashing into a big puddle everywhere, and then it was there, what you see."

Constitution looked like the Grand Canal in Venice. Beyond it the Mall was like a rain-beaten lake. Water sheeted equally over streets, sidewalks, and lawns. Charlie recalled the shock he had felt many years before, leaving the Venice train station and seeing water right there outside the door. A city floored with water. Here it was quite shallow, of course. But the front steps of all the buildings came down into an expanse of brown water, an expanse of water that was all at one level, as with any other lake or sea. Brown-blue, blue-brown, brown, gray, dirty white—drab urban tints all. The rain pocked it into an infinity of rings and bounding droplets, and gusts of wind tore cats' paws across it.

Charlie maneuvered closer to the window as people milled around. It seemed to him that the water in the distance was flowing gently toward them; for a moment it looked (and even felt) as if their building had cast anchor and was steaming westward. Charlie felt a lurch in his stomach, put his hand to the windowsill to keep his balance.

"Shit, I should get home," he said.

"How are you going to do that?"

"We've been advised to stay put," Evelyn said.

"You're kidding."

"No. I mean, take a look. It could be dangerous out there right now. That's nothing to mess with—look at that!" A little electric car floated or rather was dragged down the street, already tipped on its side. "You could get knocked off your feet."

"Jesus."

"Yeah."

Charlie wasn't quite convinced, but he didn't want to argue. The water was definitely a couple of feet deep, and the rain was shattering its surface. If nothing else, it was too weird to go out.

"How extensive is it?" he asked.

Evelyn switched to a local news channel, where a very cheerful woman was saying that a big tidal surge had been predicted, because the tides were at the height of an eleven-year cycle. She went on to say that this tide was cresting higher than it would have normally because Tropical Storm Sandy's surge was now pushing up Chesapeake Bay. The combined tidal and storm surges were moving up the Potomac toward Washington, losing height and momentum along the way, but meanwhile impeding the outflow of the river like a kind of moving dam. The Potomac, which had a watershed of "fourteen thousand square miles" as Charlie had heard in the Iranian deli—dammed. A watershed experiencing record-shattering rainfall. In the last four hours, ten inches of rain had fallen in parts of the watershed. Now all that water was pouring downstream and encountering the tidal bore, right in the metropolitan area. The four inches of rain that had fallen on Washington during the midday squall, while spectacular in itself, had only added to the larger problem, which was that there was nowhere for any of the water to go. All this the reporter explained with a happy smile.

Outside, the rain was falling no more violently than during many a summer shower. But it was coming down steadily, and striking water when it hit.

"Amazing," Andrea said.

"I hope this washes the International Monetary Fund away."

This remark opened the floodgates, so to speak, on a loud listing of all the buildings and agencies people most wanted to see wiped off the face of the earth. Someone shouted "the Capitol," but of course it was located on its eponymous hill, high ground that stayed high for a good distance to the east before dipping down to the Anacostia. The people up there probably wouldn't even get stranded, as the high ground ran both east and north without dipping to the level of the Mall.

But as for them: "We're here for a while."

"The trains will be stopped for sure."

"What about the Metro? Oh my God."

"I've gotta call home."

Several people said this at once, Charlie among them. People scattered to their desks and their phones. Charlie said, "Phone, get me Anna."

He got a quick reply: "All circuits are busy. Please try again." This was a recording he hadn't heard in many years, and it gave him a bad start. Of course it would happen at a moment like this, everyone would be trying to call someone, and towers and lines would be down. But what if it stayed like that for hours—or days? Or even longer? It was a sickening thought; he felt hot, and the itchiness blazed anew across his broken skin. He even felt dizzy, as if a limb were being threatened with immediate amputation—his sixth sense, in effect, which was his link to Anna. All of a sudden he understood how completely he took his state of permanent communication with her for granted. They talked a dozen times a day, and he relied on those talks to know what he was doing, sometimes literally.

Now he was cut off from her. Judging by the voices in the offices, no one's connection was working. They regathered; had anyone gotten an open line? No. Was there an emergency phone system they could tap into? No.

There was, however, e-mail. Everyone sat down at their keyboards, and for a while it was like an office of typists.

After that there was nothing to do but watch screens, or look out windows. They did that, milling about restlessly, saying the same things, trying the phones, typing, looking out the windows, or checking out channels and sites. The usual helicopter shots, and all other overhead views lower than satellite level, were impossible in the violence of the storm, but almost every channel had cobbled together or transferred direct images from various cameras around town, and one of the weather stations was flying drone camera balloons and blimps into the storm and showing whatever they got, mostly swirling gray clouds, but also astonishing shots of the surrounding countryside, now vast tree- and roof-studded lakes. One camera on top of the Washington Monument gave a splendid view of the extent of the flooding around the Mall, truly breathtaking. The Potomac had disappeared into the huge lake it was forming on the Mall, all the way up to the steps of the White House and the Capitol, both on little knolls, the Capitol's higher. The entirety of Southwest was floored by water, though its big buildings stood clear; the broad valley of the Anacostia looked like a reservoir. It seemed the entire city south of Pennsylvania Avenue was a lake marred by trees and building.

And not just there. Flooding had filled Rock Creek to the top of its deep but narrow ravine, and now water was spilling over at the sharp bends the gorge took while dropping through the city to its confluence with the Potomac. Cameras on the bridges at M Street caught the awesome sight of the creek roaring around its final turn west, upstream from M Street, and pouring over Francis Junior High School and straight south on 23rd Street into Foggy Bottom, where it joined the lake covering the Mall.

Then on to a different channel, a different camera. The Watergate building was indeed a curving water gate, like a remnant of a broken dam. The wave-tossed spate that indicated the Potomac looked as if it could knock the Watergate down. Likewise the Kennedy Center just south of it. The Lincoln Memorial, despite its pedestal mound, appeared to be flooded up to about Lincoln's feet. Across the Potomac the water was going to inundate the lower levels of Arlington National Cemetery. Reagan Airport was completely gone.

"Unbelievable."

Charlie went back to the view out their window. The water was still there. A voice on the TV said that ten million acre-feet of water was converging in the metropolitan area, and more rain was predicted.

Out the window Charlie saw that people were already taking to the streets around them in small watercraft, despite the wind and drizzle. Kayaks, a waterski boat, canoes, rowboats. Then as the evening wore on, and the dim light left the air below the black clouds, the rain returned with its earlier intensity. It poured down in a way that surely made it dangerous to be on the water. Most of the small craft had appeared to be occupied by men who it did not seem had any good reason to be out there. Out for a lark—thrillseekers, already!

"It looks like Venice," Andrea said, echoing Charlie's earlier thought. "I wonder what it would be like if it were like this all the time."

"Maybe we'll get to find out."

"How high above sea level are we here?"

No one knew, but Evelyn quickly clicked a topographical map to her screen. They jammed around her to look at it, or to get the address to bring it up on their own screens.

"Ten feet above sea level? Can that be true?"

"That's why they call it the Tidal Basin."

"But isn't the ocean what, fifty miles away? A hundred?"

"Ninety miles downstream to Chesapeake Bay," Evelyn said.

"I wonder if the Metro has flooded."

"How could it not?"

"True. I suppose it must have, at least in some places."

"And if in some places, wouldn't it spread?"

"There are higher and lower sections. Seems like the lower ones would for sure. And anywhere the entries are flooded."

"Well, yes."

"Wow. What a mess."

"Shit, I got here by Metro."

Charlie said, "Me too."

They thought about that for a while. Taxis weren't going to be running.

"I wonder how long it takes to walk home."

But then again, Rock Creek ran between the Mall and Bethesda.

Hours passed. Charlie checked his e-mail frequently, and finally there was a note from Anna: *we're fine here glad to hear you're set in the office, be sure*

to stay there until it's safe, let's talk as soon as the phones will get through, love
A and boys

Charlie took a deep breath, feeling greatly reassured. When the topo map had come up he had checked Bethesda first, and found that the border of the District and Maryland at Wisconsin Avenue was some two hundred and fifty feet above sea level. And Rock Creek ran well to the east. Little Falls Creek was closer, but far enough to the west not to be a concern, he hoped. Of course Wisconsin Avenue itself was probably a shallow stream of sorts now, running down into Georgetown—and wouldn't it be great if snobbish little Georgetown got some of this—but wouldn't you know it, it was on a rise overlooking the river, in the usual correlation of money and elevation. Higher than the Capitol by a good deal. It was always that way; poor people lived down in the flats, as witness Southeast near the Anacostia, now flooded completely.

It continued to rain. No calls got through. The people in Phil's office watched the TV, stretched out on couches, or even lay down to catch some sleep on chair cushions lined on the floor. Outside the wind abated, rose again, veered. Rain fell all the while. All the TV stations chattered on caffeinistically, talking to the emptied darkened rooms. It was strange to see how they were directly involved in an obviously historical moment, right in the middle of it in fact, and yet they too were watching it on TV.

Charlie could not sleep, but wandered the halls of the big building. He visited with the security team at the front doors, who had been using rolls of Department of Homeland Security gas-attack tape to try to waterproof the bottom halves of all the doors. Nevertheless the ground floor was getting soggy, and the basement even worse, though clearly the seal was fairly good, as the basement was by no means filled to the ceiling. Apparently over in the Smithsonian buildings, hundreds of people were moving things upstairs to save them from various flooding situations. Meanwhile in their building people mostly worked at their screens, though now some reported that they were having trouble getting online. If the internet went down, they would be completely out of touch. Actually if the internet itself went down, someone pointed out, civilization would be screwed. It was losing contact with the internet they were talking about here, which was bad enough.

Finally Charlie got itchy and tired enough to go back to Phil's office and lie down on a couch and try to sleep.

Gingerly he rested his fiery side on some couch cushions. "Owwwwww." The pain made him want to weep, and all of a sudden he wanted to be home so badly that he moaned. He needed to be with Anna and the boys; he was not himself when cut off from them. This was what it felt like to be in an emergency—scarcely able to believe it, but aware nevertheless that bad things could happen.

The itching tortured him. He thought it would keep him from getting to sleep, but he was so tired that after a period of hypnagogic tossing and turning, during which the memory of the flood kept recurring to him like a bad dream that he should have been relieved to find was not true, he drifted off.

Across the great river it was different. Frank was at NSF when the storm got bad. He had gotten authorization from Diane to convene a new committee; his acceptance of the assignment had triggered a wave of communications to formalize his return to NSF for another year; UCSD was fine with it. It was good for them to have people at NSF.

Now he was sitting at his screen, googling around, and for some reason he had brought up the website for Small Delivery Systems, just to look. While tapping through its pages he had come upon a list of publications by the company's scientists; this was often the best way to tell what a company was up to. And almost instantly his eye picked out one coauthored by Dr. P. L. Emory, CEO of the company, and Dr. F. Taolini.

Quickly he typed "consultants" into the search engine, and up came the company's page listing them. And there she was: Dr. Francesca Taolini, Massachusetts Institute of Technology, Center for Biocomputational Studies.

"Well I'll be damned."

He sat back, thinking it over. Taolini had liked Pierzinski's proposal; she had rated it very good, and argued in favor of funding it, persuasively enough that during the panel it had given him a little scare. She had seen its potential. Which meant . . .

Then Kenzo called up, raving about the storms and the flood, and Frank joined everyone else in the building in watching the TV news and the NOAA website, trying to get a sense of how serious things were. It became clear that things were serious indeed when one screen showed Rock Creek overflowing its banks and running down the streets toward Foggy Bottom. Then the screen shifted images to Foggy Bottom itself, where water was waist-deep everywhere; and then came images from the inundated-to-the-rooftops Southwest district, including the classically pillared War College Building at the confluence of the Potomac and the Anacostia, sticking out of the water like a temple of Atlantis. The Jefferson Memorial was much the same. Rain-lashed cameras all over the city transmitted more images, and Frank stared, amazed: the city was a lake.

The climate guys on the ninth floor were already posting topographical maps with the flood peaking at various heights. If the surge got to twenty feet above sea level at the confluence of the Potomac and the Anacostia, which Kenzo thought was a reasonable projection given the tidal bore and all, the new shore along this contour line would run roughly from the Capitol along Pennsylvania Avenue to where it crossed Rock Creek. The Capitol and White House would be spared, but everything south and west of them was doomed, and in fact under water already, as the videos confirmed. And upstream monitoring stations showed that the peak of the flood had not yet arrived.

"Everything has combined!" Kenzo exclaimed over the phone. "It's all coming together!" His usual curatorial tone had shifted to that of an impresario—the Master of Disaster—or even to an almost parental pride. He was as excited as Frank had ever heard him.

"Could this be a result of the Atlantic stall?" Frank asked.

"Oh no, very doubtful. This is separate I think, a collision of storms. Although the stall might bring more storms together like this."

"Jesus . . . Can you tell me what's going on here on the Virginia side?" There would be no way to cross the Potomac until the flooding was over. "Are people working anywhere around here?"

"They're sandbagging down at Arlington Cemetery," Kenzo said. "There's video of it on channel 44. They've got a call out for volunteers."

"Really!"

Frank took off. He took the stairs to the basement, to be sure he didn't get caught in an elevator, and drove his car up onto the street. It was awash in places, but only to a depth of a few inches. Possibly this would soon get worse; runoff wouldn't work when the river was flowing back up the drainpipes. But for now he was okay to drive to the river.

As he turned right and stopped for the light, he saw the Starbucks people out on the sidewalk, passing out bags of food and cups of coffee to the cars in front of him. Frank opened his window as one of them approached, and the employee passed in a bag of pastries, then handed him a paper cup of coffee.

"Thanks!" Frank shouted. "You guys should take over emergency services!"

"We already did. You get yourself out of here." She waved him on.

Frank drove east toward the river, laughing as he downed the pastry. Like everyone else still on the road, he plowed through the water at about five miles an hour. Fire trucks passed through at a faster clip, leaving big wakes.

As he crossed one intersection Frank spotted a trio of men ducking behind a building carrying something. Could there be looters? Would anyone really do that? How sad to think there were people so stuck in always-defect that they couldn't get out of it, even when a chance came for everything to change. What a waste of an opportunity!

Eventually he came to a roadblock and parked, following the directions of a man in an orange vest. Hard rain pounded down. In the distance he could see people passing sandbags along a line, just to the east of the U.S. Marines Corps War Memorial. He hustled over to join them.

From where he worked he could often see the Potomac, roiling down the Boundary Channel between the mainland and Columbia Island, piling up at the bridges, flooding the marinas, and rising toward the low-lying parts of Arlington National Cemetery. Hundreds or perhaps even thousands of people were working around him, carrying sandbags that looked like fifty-pound cement bags, and felt about that heavy. Big guys were lifting them off truck beds and passing them to people who passed them down the lines, or carried them over shoulders, to near or far sections of a sandbag wall under the Virginia end of Memorial Bridge, where firemen were directing construction.

The noise of the river and the rain together made it hard to hear. People shouted to each other, sharing instructions and news. The airport was drowned, old Alexandria flooded, the Anacostia valley filled for miles. The Mall a lake.

Frank nodded at anything said his way, not bothering to understand. He worked like a dervish. It was very satisfying. He felt deeply happy, and looking around he could see that everyone else was happy too. That's what happens, he thought, watching people carry limp sandbags like coolies out of an old Chinese painting. It takes something like this to free people to be always generous.

Late in the day he stood on their sandbag wall. It gave him a good view over the flood. The wind had died down, but the rain was falling almost as hard as ever. In some moments it seemed there was more water in the air than there was air.

His team had been given a break by a sudden end to the supply of sandbags. His back was stiff, and he stretched himself in circles, like the trees had been doing all day. The wind shifted frequently, and had included short hard blasts, vicious slaps like microbursting downdrafts. Now there was some kind of aerial truce.

Then the rain too relented. It became a very light drizzle, then a mist. Beyond the foamy water in the Boundary Channel he could see far across the Potomac proper, a swirling brown plate sheeted and lined with white foam. The Washington Monument was a dim obelisk on a water horizon. Lincoln Memorial and Kennedy Center were both islands in the stream. Black clouds formed a low ceiling above them, and between the two, water and cloud, he could feel the air being smashed this way and that. Despite the disorderly gusts he was still warm from his exertions; very wet, but warm, with only his hands and ears slightly nipped by the wind. He stood there flexing his spine, feeling the tired muscles of his lower back.

A powerboat growled slowly up the Boundary Channel below him. Frank watched it pass, wondering how shallow its draft was; it was twenty-five or maybe even thirty feet long, a sleek cabin cruiser. The illuminated cockpit shed its light on a person standing upright at the stern, looking like one of the weird sisters in the movie *Don't Look Now*.

This person glanced over at the sandbag levee, and Frank saw that it was the woman from the elevator in Bethesda. Shocked, he put his hands to his mouth and shouted, "HEY!" as loud as he could, emptying his lungs all at once.

No sign in the roar of the flood that she had heard him. Nor did she appear to see him waving. As the boat began to disappear around a bend in the channel, Frank spotted white lettering on its stern: GCX88A. Then it was out of sight.

Frank pulled his phone out of his windbreaker pocket, shoved it in his ear, then tapped the button for NSF's climate office. Luckily it was Kenzo who picked up. "Kenzo, it's Frank—listen, write down this sequence, it's very important, please? GCX88A, have you got that? Read it back. GCX88A. Great. Great. Wow. Okay, listen Kenzo, that's a boat's number, it was on the stern of a powerboat about twenty-six feet long. I need to know whose it is. Can you find that out for me? I'm out in the rain and can't see well enough to google it."

"I can try," Kenzo said. "Here, let me . . . well, it looks like the boat belongs to the marina on Roosevelt Island."

"That would make sense. Is there a phone number for it?"

"Let's see—that should be in the Coast Guard records. Wait, they're not open files. Hold a minute, please."

Kenzo loved little problems like this. Frank waited, trying not to hold his breath: another instinctive act. As he waited he tried also to etch the woman's face on his mind, thinking he might be able to get a portrait program to draw something like what he was remembering. She had looked serious and remote, like one of the Fates.

"Yeah, Frank, here it is. Do you want me to call it and pass you along?"

"Yes please, but write it down for me too, just in case."

"Okay, I'll pass you over and get off. I have to get back to it here."

"Thanks Kenzo, thanks a lot."

Frank listened, sticking a finger in his other ear. There was a pause, a ring. The ring had a rapid pulse and an insistent edge, as if it were designed to compete with the sounds of an inboard engine on a boat. Three rings, four, five; if an answering machine message came on, what would he say?

"Hello?"

It was her voice.

"Hello?" she said again.

He had to say something or she would hang up.

"Hi," he said. "Hi, this is me."

There was a static-filled silence.

"We were stuck in that elevator together in Bethesda."

"Oh my God."

Another silence. Frank let her assimilate it. He had no idea what to say. It seemed like the ball was in her court, and yet as the silence went on, a fear grew in him.

"Don't hang up," he said, surprising himself. "I just saw your boat go by, I'm here on the levee at the back of the Davis Highway. I called information and got your boat's number. I know you didn't want—I mean, I tried to find you afterward, but I couldn't, and I could tell that you didn't—that you didn't want to be found. So I figured I would leave it at that, I really did."

He could hear himself lying and added hastily, "I didn't want to, but I didn't see what else I could do. So when I saw you just now I called a friend who got me your boat's phone number. I mean how could I not, when I saw you like that."

"I know," she said.

He breathed in. He felt himself filling up, his back straightening. Something in the way she said *I know* brought it all back again. The way she had made it a bond between them.

After a time he said, "I wanted to find you again. I thought that our time in the elevator, I thought it was . . ." He couldn't think how to say it.

"I know."

His skin warmed. It was like a St. Elmo's fire running over him, he'd never felt anything like it.

"But—" she said, and he learned another new feeling: dread clutched him under the ribs. He waited as for a blow to fall.

The silence went on. An isolated freshet of rain pelted down, cleared, and then he could see across the wind-lashed Potomac again. A huge rushing watery world, awesome and dreamlike.

"Give me your number," her voice said in his ear.

"What?"

"Give me your phone number," she said again.

He gave her his number, then added, "My name is Frank Vanderwal."

"Frank Vanderwal," she said, then repeated the number.

"That's it."

"Now give me some time," she said. "I don't know how long." And the connection went dead.

The second day of the storm passed as a kind of suspended moment, everything continuing as it had the day before, everyone in the area living through it, enduring, waiting for conditions to change. The rain was not as torrential, but so much of it had fallen in the previous twenty-four hours that it was still sheeting off the land into the flooded areas, keeping them flooded. The clouds continued to crash together overhead, and the tides were still higher than normal, so that the whole piedmont region surrounding Chesapeake Bay was inundated. Except for immediate acts of a lifesaving nature, nothing could be done except to endure. All transport was drowned. Power losses left tens of thousands without electricity. Escapes from drowning took precedence even over journalism (almost), and although reporters from all over the world were converging on the capital to report on this most spectacular story—the capital of the hyperpower, drowned!—most of them could only get as close as the edges of the flood. Inside that boundary it was an ongoing state of emergency, and everyone was involved with rescues, relocations, and escapes of various kinds. The National Guard was out, all helicopters were enlisted into the effort; video and digital imagery was still incidental, which in itself meant ordinary law had been suspended. There was heavy pressure to bring things back to all-spectacle all-the-time. Part of the National Guard found itself posted on the roads outside the region, to keep people from flooding the area as the water had.

Very early on the second morning it became evident that while most areas had seen high water already, the flooding of Rock Creek had not yet crested. That night its headwaters had taken the brunt of one of the hardest downpours of the storm, and the already-saturated land could only shed this new rainfall into the streambed. The creek's drop to the Tidal Basin was precipitous in some places, and for most of its length the creek ran at the bottom of a narrow gorge carved into the higher ground of Northwest. There was nowhere to hold the excess flow.

All this meant big trouble for the National Zoo, which was located on a sort of peninsula created by three turns in Rock Creek. After the night's downpour, the staff of the zoo congregated in the offices to discuss the situation.

They had some visiting dignitaries on hand, who had been forced to spend the night there. Several members of the embassy of the nation of Khembalung had come to the zoo the morning before, as preparation for a ceremony welcoming two Bengal tigers brought there from their country. The storm had made it impossible for them to return to Virginia, and they had had to spend the night at the zoo, the tigers still in their individual cages.

Now they all watched together as one of the office's computers showed images of Rock Creek's gorge walls being torn away and washed downstream. Floating trees were catching in drifts against bridges over the creek, forming temporary impediments that forced water out into the flanking neighborhoods, until the bridges blew like failed dams, and powerful low walls of debris-laden water tore down the gorge harder than ever, ripping it away ever more brutally. The eastern edge of the zoo made it obvious how this endangered them; a light brown torrent was pouring around the zoo just a few feet below the grounds. That, plus the images on their computers, made it clear that the zoo was likely to be overwhelmed, and soon. It seemed likely it was going to turn into something like the reverse of Noah's flood, in that people would mostly survive, but two of every species drown.

The Khembali legation urged the National Park Service staffers to evacuate the zoo as quickly as possible. The time and vehicles necessary for a proper evacuation were completely lacking, of course, as the superintendent pointed out. But the Khembalis replied that by evacuation they meant opening all the cages and letting the animals escape. The zookeepers were skeptical, but the Khembalis turned out to be experts in flood response, well acquainted with the routines required in such situations. They quickly called up photos of the zookeepers of Prague, weeping by the bodies of their drowned elephants, to show what could happen if drastic measures were not taken soon enough. They then called up the Global Disaster Information Network, which had a complete protocol for this very scenario (threatened zoos), along with real-time satellite photos and flood data. It turned out that released animals typically did not roam far, seldom threatened humans (who were usually locked into buildings anyway), and were easy to recollect when the waters subsided. And incoming data showed Rock Creek was certain to rise further.

This prediction was easy to believe, given the roaring brown water bordering most of the zoo, almost topping the gorge. The animals certainly believed it, and were calling loudly for freedom. Pandas squeaked, monkeys screamed, the big cats roared, and every living creature, animal and human, was terrified by this cacophony. The din was terrific, beyond anything any jungle movie had dared. Panic was in the air.

Connecticut Avenue now resembled something like the old canal at Great Falls: a smooth, narrow run of water, paralleling a wild torrent. All the side streets were flooded as well. Nowhere was the water very high, however—usually under a foot—and so the superintendent, looking amazed to hear such sentences emerge from his mouth, said, "Okay let's let them out. Cages first, then the enclosures. Work from the gate down to the lower end of the park. Come on—there's a lot of locks to unlock."

In the dark rainy air, beside the roaring engorged creek, the staff and their visitors ventured out and began unlocking the animals. They drove them toward Connecticut Avenue when necessary, though most animals needed no urging, but bolted for the gates with a sure sense of the way to safety. Some, however, huddled in their enclosures or cages, and could not be coaxed out. There was no time to spare for any particular cage; if the animals refused to leave, the zookeepers moved on and hoped there would be time to return.

The tapirs and deer were easy. They kept the biggest aviaries closed, feeling they would not flood to their tops. Then the zebras, and after them the cheetahs, then the Australian creatures, kangaroos bounding away with great splashes. The pandas trundled out methodically in a group, as if they had planned this for years. Giraffes, hippos and rhinos, beavers and otters; after some consultation, and the coaxing of the biggest cats into the moving trucks still on hand, the pumas and smaller cats. Then bison, wolves, camels; the seals and sea lions; bears; the gibbons all in a troop, screaming with triumph; the single black jaguar slipping dangerously into the murk: the reptiles, the Amazonian creatures, already looking right at home; the prairie dog town, the drawbridge dropped to Monkey Island, causing another stampede of panicked primates; the gorillas and apes following more slowly. Now washes of brown water were spilling over the north end of the park and running swiftly down the zoo's paths, and the lower end of the zoo was submerged by the brown flow. Very few animals continued to stay in their enclosures, and even fewer headed by mistake toward the creek; the roar was simply too frightening, the message too clear. Every living thing's instincts were clear on where safety lay.

The water lapped higher again. It seemed to be rising in distinct surges. It had taken two full hours of frantic work to unlock all the doors, and as they were finishing, a roar louder than before overwhelmed them, and a dirty debris-filled surge poured over the whole park. Something upstream must have given way all at once. Any animals remaining in the lower section of the park were either swept away or drowned in place. Quickly the humans remaining drove the few big cats and polar bears they had herded into trucks out the entrance and onto Connecticut Avenue. Now all Northwest was the zoo.

The truck that contained the Swimming Tigers of Khembalung headed north on Connecticut, with the tigers in back and the Khembali delegation piled into its cab. They drove very slowly and cautiously through the empty, dark, watery streets. The looming clouds made it look like it was already evening.

As they drove, the Swimming Tigers banged around in back. They sounded scared and angry, perhaps feeling that all this had happened before. They did not seem to want to be in the back of the truck, and roared in a way that caused the humans in the cab to hunch forward unhappily. Then it sounded like the tigers were taking it out on each other; big bodies crashed into the walls, and the roars and growls grew angrier. There were hisses like boilers about to explode.

The Khembali passengers advised the driver and zookeeper. They nodded and continued north on Connecticut. Any big dip would make a road impassable, but Connecticut ran steadily uphill and northwest. Then Bradley Lane allowed the driver to get most of the way west to Wisconsin. When a dip stopped him, he retreated and worked his way farther north, following streets without dips, until they made it to Wisconsin Avenue, now something like a wide, smooth stream, flowing hard south, but at a depth of only six inches. They crept along against this flow until they could make an illegal left onto Woodson, and thus around the corner, into the driveway of a small house backed by a big apartment complex.

In the dark air the Khembalis got out, knocked on the kitchen door. A woman appeared, and after a brief conversation, disappeared.

Soon afterward, if anyone in the apartment complex had looked out of their window, they would have seen a curious sight: a group of men, some in maroon robes, others in National Park Service khakis, coaxing a tiger out of the back of a truck. It was wearing a collar to which three leashes were attached. When it was out the men quickly closed the truck door. The oldest man stood before the tiger, hand upraised. He took up one of the leashes, led the wet beast across the driveway to steps leading down to an open cellar door. Rain fell as the tiger stopped on the steps and looked around. The old man spoke urgently to it. From the house's kitchen window over them, two little faces stared out round-eyed. For a moment nothing seemed to move but the rain. Then the tiger ducked in the door.

Sometime during that second night the rain stopped, and though dawn of the third morning arrived sodden and gray, as the day progressed the clouds scattered, flying north at speed. By nine the sun blazed down onto the flooded city between big puffball clouds. The air was breezy and unsettled.

Charlie had again spent this second night in the office, and when he woke he looked out the window hoping that conditions would have eased enough for him to be able to attempt getting home. The phones were still down, although e-mails from Anna had kept him informed and reassured—at least until the previous evening's news about the arrival of the Khembalis, which had caused him some alarm, not just because of the tiger in the basement, but because of their interest in Joe. He had not expressed any of this in his e-mail replies, of course. But he most definitely wanted to get home.

Helicopters and blimps had already taken to the air in great numbers. Now all the TV channels in the world could reveal the extent of the flood from on high, and they did. Much of downtown Washington, D.C., remained awash. A giant shallow lake occupied precisely the most famous and public parts of the city; it looked like someone had decided to expand the Mall's reflecting pool beyond all reason. The rivers and streams that converged on this larger tidal basin were still in spate, which kept the new lake topped up. In the washed sunlight the flat expanse of water was the color of caffe latte, with foam.

Standing in the lake, of course, were hundreds of buildings-become-islands, and a few real islands, and even some freeway viaducts, now acting as bridges over the Anacostia valley. The Potomac continued to pour through the west edge of the lake, overspilling its banks both upstream and down whenever lowlands flanked it. Its surface was studded with floating junk which moved slower the farther downstream it got. Apparently the ebb tides had only begun to allow this vast bolus of water out to sea.

As the morning wore on, more and more boats appeared. The TV shots from the air made it look like some kind of regatta—the Mall as water festival, like something out of Ming China. Many people were out on makeshift craft that did not look seaworthy. Police boats on patrol were even beginning to ask people who were not doing rescue work to leave, one report said, though clearly they were not having much of an impact. The situation was still so new that the law had not yet fully returned. Motorboats zipped about, leaving beige wakes behind. Rowers rowed, paddlers paddled, kayakers kayaked; swimmers swam; some people were even out in the blue pedal boats that had once been confined to the Tidal Basin, pedaling around the Mall in majestic mini-steamboat style.

Although these images from the Mall dominated the media, some channels carried other news from around the region. Hospitals were filled. The two days of the storm had killed many people, no one knew how many; and there were many rescues as well. In the first part of the third morning, the TV helicopters often interrupted their overviews to pluck people from rooftops. Rescues by boat were occurring all through Southwest district and up the Anacostia basin. Reagan Airport remained drowned, and there was not a single passable bridge over the Potomac all the way upstream to Harpers Ferry. The Great Falls of the Potomac was no more than a huge turbulence in a nearly unbroken, gorge-topping flow. The President had evacuated to Camp David, and now he declared all of Virginia, Maryland, and Delaware a federal disaster area; the District of Columbia, in his words, "worse than that."

Charlie's phone chirped and he snatched it to him. "Anna?"

"Charlie! Where are you!"

"I'm still at the office! Are you home?"

"Oh good, yes! I'm here with the boys, we never left. We've got the Khembalis here with us too, you got my e-mails?"

"Yes, I wrote back."

"Oh that's right. They got caught at the zoo. I've been trying to get you on the phone this whole time!"

"Me you too, except when I fell asleep. I was so glad to get your e-mails."

"Yeah that was good. I'm so glad you're okay. This is crazy! Is your building completely flooded?"

"No no, not at all. Hardly at all. So how are the boys?"

"Oh they're fine. They're loving it. It's all I can do to keep them inside."

"Keep them inside!"

"Yes yes. So your building didn't flood? But isn't the Mall flooded?"

"Yes it is, no doubt about that, but not the building here, not too badly anyway. They're keeping the doors shut, and trying to seal them at the bottoms. It's not working great, but it isn't dangerous. It's just a matter of staying upstairs."

"Your generators are working?"

"Yes."

"I hear a lot of them are flooded."

"Yeah I can see how that would happen. No one was expecting this."

"No. Generators in basements, it's stupid I suppose."

"That's where ours is," Charlie remembered with a jolt.

"I know. But it's on that table, and it's working."

"What about food, how are we set there?" Charlie tried to imagine their cupboards.

"Well, we've got a bit. You know. It's not great. It will get to be a problem soon if we can't get more. I figure we might have a few weeks' worth in a pinch."

"Well, that should be enough. I mean, they'll have to get things going again by then."

"I suppose. We need water service too."

"Will the floodwaters drain away very fast?"

"I don't know, how should I know?"

"Well, I don't know—you're a scientist."

"Please."

They listened to each other breathe.

"I sure am glad to be talking to you," Charlie said. "I hated being out of touch like that."

"Me too."

"There are boats all around us now," Charlie said. "I'll try to get a ride home as soon as I can. Once I get ferried to land, I can walk home."

"Not necessarily. The Taft Bridge over Rock Creek is gone. You'd only be able to cross on the Mass. Ave. bridge, from what I can see on the news."

"Yeah, I saw Rock Creek flooding, that was amazing."

"I know. The zoo and everything. Drepung says most of the animals will be recovered, but I wonder about that." Anna would be nearly as upset by the deaths of the zoo's animals as she would be by people's. She made little distinction.

Charlie said, "I'll take Mass. Ave. then."

"Or maybe you can get them to drop you off west of Rock Creek, in Georgetown. Anyway, be careful. Don't do anything rash."

"I won't. I'll make sure to stay safe, and I'll call you regularly, at least I hope. That was awful being cut off."

"I know."

"Okay, well . . . I don't really want to hang up, but I guess I should. Let me talk to the boys first."

"Yeah good. Here talk to Joe, he's been pretty upset that you're not here, he keeps asking for you. Demanding you, actually—here," and then suddenly in his ear:

"Dadda?"

"Joe!"

"Da! Da!"

"Yeah Joe, it's Dad! Good to hear you, boy! I'm down at work, I'll be home soon buddy."

"Da! Da!" Then, in a kind of moan: "Wan daaaaaaaaaa."

"It's okay Joe," Charlie said, throat clenching. "I'll be home real soon. Don't you worry."

"Da!" Shrieking.

Anna got back on. "Sorry, he's throwing a fit. Here, Nick wants to talk too."

"Hey, Nick! Are you taking care of Mom and Joe?"

"Yeah, I was, but Joe is kind of upset right now."

"He'll get over it. So what's it been like up there?"

"Well you see, we got to burn those big candles? And I made a big tower out of the melted wax, it's really cool. And then Drepung and Rudra came and brought their tigers, they've got one in their truck and one in our basement!"

"That's nice, that's very cool. Be sure to keep the door to the basement closed by the way."

Nick laughed. "It's locked Dad. Mom has the key."

"Good. Did you get a lot of rain?"

"I think so. We can see that Wisconsin is kind of flooded, but there are still some cars going in it. Most of the big stuff we've only seen on the TV. Mom was really worried about you. When are you going to get home?"

"Soon as I can."

"Good."

"Yeah. Well, I guess you get a few days off school out of all this. Okay, give me your mom back. Hi babe."

"Listen, you stay put until some really safe way to get home comes."

"I will."

"We love you."

"I love you too. I'll be home soon as I can."

Then Joe began to wail again, and they hung up.

Charlie rejoined the others and told them his news. Others were getting through on their cell phones as well. Everyone was talking. Then there came yells from down the hall.

A police motor launch was at the second-floor windows, facing Constitution, ready to ferry people to dry ground. This one was going west, and, yes, would eventually dock in Georgetown, if people wanted off there. It was perfect for Charlie's hope to get west of Rock Creek and then walk home.

And so when his turn came he climbed out of a window, down into a big boat. A stanza from a Robert Frost poem he had memorized in high school came back to him suddenly:

> *It went many years, but at last came a knock,*
> *And I thought of the door with no lock to lock.*

The knock came again, my window was wide;
I climbed on the sill and descended outside.

He laughed as he moved forward in the boat to make room for other refugees. Strange what came back to the mind. How had that poem continued? Something something; he couldn't remember. It didn't matter. The relevant part had come to him, after waiting all these years. And now he was out the window and on his way.

The launch rumbled, glided away from the building, turned in a broad curve west, down Constitution Avenue. Then left, out onto the broad expanse of the Mall. They were boating on the Mall.

The National Gallery reminded him of the Taj Mahal—same water reflection, same gorgeous white stone. All the Smithsonian buildings looked amazing. No doubt they had been working inside them all night to get things above flood level. What a mess it was going to be.

Charlie steadied himself against the gunwale, feeling so stunned that it seemed he might lose his balance and fall. That was probably the boat's doing, but he was, in all truth, reeling. The TV images had been one thing, the actual reality another; he could scarcely believe his eyes. White clouds stood overhead in the blue sky, and the flat brown lake was gleaming in the sunlight, reflecting a blue glitter of sky, everything all glossy and compact—real as real, or even more so. None of his poison ivy visions had ever been as remotely real as this lake was now.

Their pilot maneuvered them farther south. They were going to pass the Washington Monument on its south side. They puttered slowly past it. It towered over them like an obelisk in the Nile's flood, making all the watercraft look correspondingly tiny.

The Smithsonian buildings appeared to be drowned to about ten feet. Upper halves of their big public doors emerged from the water like low boathouse doors. For some of the buildings that would be a catastrophe. Others had steps, or stood higher on their foundations. A mess any way you looked at it.

Their launch growled west at a walking pace. Trees flanking the western half of the Mall looked like water shrubs in the distance. The Vietnam Memorial would of course be submerged. The Lincoln Memorial stood on its own little pedestal hill, but it was right on the Potomac, and might be submerged to the height of all its steps; the statue of Lincoln might even be getting his feet wet. Charlie found it hard to tell, through the shortened trees, just how high the water was down there.

Boats of all kinds dotted the long brown lake, headed this way and that. The little blue paddle boats from the Tidal Basin were particularly festive, but all the kayaks and rowboats and inflatables added their dots of neon color, and the little sailboats tacking back and forth flashed their triangular sails. Brilliant sunlight filled the clouds and the blue sky. The festival mood was expressed even by what people wore—Charlie saw Hawaiian shirts, bathing suits, even Carnival masks. There were many more black faces than Charlie was used to seeing on the Mall. It looked as if something like Trinidad's Mardi Gras parade had been disrupted by a night of storms, but was reemerging triumphant in the new day. People were waving to each other, shouting things (the helicopters overhead were loud); standing in boats in unsafe postures, turning in precarious circles to shoot 360s with phones and cameras. It would only take a water-skier to complete the scene.

Charlie moved to the bow of the launch, and stood there soaking it all in. His mouth hung open like a dog's. The effort of getting out the window had reinflamed his chest and arms; now he stood there on fire, torching in the wind, drinking in the maritime vision. Their boat chugged west like a vaporetto on Venice's broad lagoon. He could not help but laugh.

"Maybe they should keep it this way," someone said.

A Navy river cruiser came growling over the Potomac toward them, throwing up a white bow wave on its upstream side. When it reached the Mall it slipped through a gap in the cherry trees, cut back on its engines, settled down in the water, continued east at a more sedate pace. It was going to pass pretty close by them, and Charlie felt their own launch slow down as well.

Then he spotted a familiar face among the people standing in the bow of the patrol boat. It was Phil Chase, waving to the boats he passed like the grand marshal of a parade, leaning over the front rail to shout greetings.

Like a lot of other people on the water that morning, he had the happy look of someone who had already lit out for the territory.

Charlie waved with both arms, leaning over the side of the launch. They were closing on each other. Charlie cupped his hands around his mouth and shouted as loud as he could.

"HEY PHIL! Phil Chase!"

Phil heard him, looked over, saw him.

"Hey Charlie!" He waved cheerily, then cupped his hands around his mouth too. "Good to see you! Is everyone at the office okay?"

"Yes!"

"Good! That's good!" Phil straightened up, gestured broadly at the flood. "Isn't this amazing?"

"Yes! It sure is!" Then the words burst out of Charlie: "So Phil! Are you going to do something about global warming now?"

Phil grinned his beautiful grin. "I'll see what I can do!"

PART TWO

FIFTY
DEGREES
BELOW

CHAPTER 11

PRIMATE IN FOREST

Nobody likes Washington, D.C. Even the people who love it don't like it. Climate atrocious, traffic worse: an ordinary midsized gridlocked American city, in which the plump white federal buildings make no difference. Or rather they bring all the politicians and tourists, the lobbyists and diplomats and refugees, all those people who come from somewhere else and thereafter spend their time clogging the streets and hogging the show, talking endlessly about the city on a hill while ignoring the actual city they are in. No—bastion of the world government, locked vault of the World Bank, fortress headquarters of the world police; no one can like that.

So naturally when the great flood washed over the city, the stated reactions were various, but the underlying subtext often was this: HA HA. For there were many people around the world who felt that justice had somehow been served.

Of course the usual things were said. Disaster area, emergency relief, immediate restoration, pride of the nation, etc. Indeed the President was firm in his insistence that it was everyone's patriotic duty to demonstrate a stalwart response to what he called "this act of climatic terrorism." "From now on," the President said, "we are at a state of war with nature. We will work until we have made this city even more like it was than before."

But ever since the Reagan era the Republican Party had been coming to Washington explicitly to destroy the federal government. They had talked about "starving the beast," but flooding would be fine. And how could the government continue to burden ordinary Americans when its center of operations was devastated? Obviously the flood was punishment for daring to tax income and pretending to be a secular nation. It reminded one of Sodom and Gomorrah, the prophecies specified in the Book of Revelation, etc.

Meanwhile those on the opposite end of the political spectrum likewise did not shed very many tears. As a blow to the heart of the galactic imperium it was a hard thing to regret. It might impede the ruling class for a while, might make them acknowledge that their economic system had changed the climate, and that this was only the first of many catastrophic consequences. If Washington was denied now that it was begging for help, that was only what it had always done to its victims. Nature bats last—poetic justice—reap what you sow—arrogant bastards—etc.

Thus the flood brought pleasure to both sides of the aisle. And in the days that followed Congress made it clear in their votes, if not in their words, that they were not going to appropriate anything like the amount of money it would take to clean up the mess. They said it had to be done; they ordered it done; but they did not fund it.

The city therefore had to pin its hopes on either the beggared District of Columbia, or the federal agencies specifically charged with disaster relief. Experts from these agencies tried to explain that the flood did not have a moral meaning, that it was merely a practical problem which had to be solved as a matter of public health and safety. The Potomac had ballooned into a temporary lake of about a thousand square miles; the lake had lasted only a week, but in that time inflicted great damage. Much of the city was trashed. Rock Creek had torn out its banks, the Mall was covered by mud; the Tidal Basin was now part of the river again, with the Jefferson Memorial standing in the shallows of the current. Many streets were blocked with debris; worse, in transport terms, many Metro tunnels had flooded, and would take months to repair. Alexandria was wrecked. Most of the region's bridges were knocked out or suspect. The power grid was uncertain, the sewage system likewise; epidemic disease was a distinct possibility.

Given all this, certain repairs simply had to be made, and many were the *calls for full restoration. But whether these calls were greeted with genuine agreement, Tartuffian assent, stony indifference, or gloating opposition, the result was the same: not enough money was appropriated to complete the job.*

Of course the nationally famous buildings were cleaned up, the Mall replanted with grass and new cherry trees, the Vietnam Memorial excavated, the Lincoln and Jefferson memorials recaptured from their island state. The Mall was for the most part restored. Elsewhere in the city, however . . .

It was not a good time to have to look for a place to live.

And yet this was just what Frank Vanderwal had to do. He had leased his apartment for the year during which he had planned to work for the National Science Foundation; then he had agreed to stay on for a second year. Now, a month after the flood, his apartment had to be turned over to its owner, a State Department person returning from Brazil. He had to find someplace else.

No doubt the decision to stay another year had been a really bad idea.

This thought weighed on him as he searched for a new apartment, and as a result he had not persevered as diligently as he ought to have. Very little was available in any case, and everything on offer was prohibitively expensive. Thousands of people had been drawn to D.C. by a flood that had also destroyed thousands of residences, and damaged thousands more beyond immediate reoccupation. It was a seller's market, and rents shot up accordingly.

Many of the places Frank had looked at were also physically repulsive in the extreme. That had damaged his will to hunt, no doubt about it. Now the day of reckoning had come. He had cleared out his stuff and cleaned up, the owner was due home that night, and Frank had nowhere to go.

It was a strange sensation. He sat at the kitchen counter in the dusk. The "Apartments for Rent" listing in that day's *Post* was less than a column long, and Frank had learned enough of its code by now to know that it held nothing for him. More interesting had been an article in the day's Metro section about Rock Creek Park. Officially closed due to severe damage, it was too large for the overextended National Park Service to be able to enforce the edict. As a result the park had become something of a no-man's-land, "a return to wilderness," as the article put it.

Frank surveyed the apartment. It held no more memories for him than a hotel would, as he had done nothing but sleep there. That was all he had needed from it, his life having been put on hold until his return to San

Diego. Now, well . . . it was like some kind of premature resuscitation, on a voyage between the stars. Time to wake up, time to leave the deep freeze and find out where he was.

Out on the Beltway he circled north and then east, past the elongated Mormon temple and the great overpass graffiti referencing it: SURRENDER DOROTHY! Off on Wisconsin, in toward the city. There was no particular reason for him to visit this part of town. The Quiblers lived over here, but that wasn't it.

He kept thinking: Homeless, homeless. You're homeless.

He came to the intersection at the Bethesda Metro stop, and suddenly it occurred to him why he might be there. Of course—this was where he had met the woman in the elevator. It made his heart pound just to remember it. Up there on the sidewalk to the right, beyond the red light—there stood the very elevator box they had emerged from. And then she had appeared to him again, on a boat in the Potomac during the great flood. He had called her boat and she had answered, had said she would call him. Had said *I know*.

The light turned green. She had not called and yet here he was, driving toward where they had met, as if he might see her. As if, if he had seen her, he would have a place to stay.

That was magical thinking at its most magical. And now he realized that in the past couple of weeks he had been looking for apartments in this area. So it was not just an isolated impulse, but a pattern of behavior.

Just past the intersection he turned into the Hyatt driveway. A valet approached and Frank said, "Do you know if there are any rooms available here?"

"Not if you don't got a reservation."

Frank drove back onto Wisconsin heading south, peering at the elevator kiosk as he passed it. She had given a fake name on the Metro forms they had filled out. She would not be there now.

Down Wisconsin, past the Quiblers' house a couple of blocks over to the right. That same night had been the party at their place. An excess of reason is itself a form of madness, the old ambassador had said to Frank. Frank was still pondering what that meant, and if it were true, how he might act on it.

But he couldn't visit Anna and her family now. Showing up unannounced, with no place to go—it would have been pitiful.

He drove on. Chevy Chase looked relatively untouched by the flood. He crossed to Connecticut Avenue, completely without a plan. Near the entrance to the National Zoo, damage from the flood suddenly became obvious, in the form of a mud-based slurry of trash and branches covering the sidewalks and staining the storefronts. Street repairs by night, in the usual way. Harsh spotlights lit the scene.

Impatiently Frank turned onto a side street. He found an empty parking spot on one of the residential streets east of Connecticut, parked in it.

He got out and walked back to the cleanup. It was still about 90 degrees out, and tropically humid. A strong smell of mud and rotting vegetation evoked the tropics, or Atlantis after the flood. Yes, he was feeling a bit apocalyptic. He was in the end time of something, there was no denying it. He wandered the streets toward Rock Creek Park, remembering the article in the *Post*. A return to wilderness.

At Broad Branch Road, Frank came to the park's boundary. There was no one visible in any direction. It was dark under the trees on the other side of the road; the yellow streetlights behind him illuminated nothing beyond the first wall of leaves. He crossed the street and walked into the forest.

The flood aftermath's vegetable stench was strong. Frank proceeded slowly over windrows of branches and trash, and an uneven deposition of mud. The root balls of toppled trees splayed up dimly, and snags caught at his feet. As his eyes adjusted he came to feel that everything was very slightly illuminated, mostly no doubt by the luminous cloud that chinked every gap in the black canopy.

He heard a rustle, then a voice, and slipped behind a large tree, heart pounding. Two voices were arguing, one of them drunk.

"Why you buy this shit?"

"Hey you never buy nothing. You need to give some, man."

The two passed by and continued east down the slope, their voices rasping through the trees. They sounded like the scruffy guys in fatigues who hung around Dupont Circle. Frank didn't want to deal with such people. He was annoyed; he wanted to be out in a pure wilderness, empty in the way his mountains out west were empty. Instead, harsh laughter nicotined through the trees like hatchet strokes. "Ha ha ha harrrrrr."

He slipped off in a different direction, through windrows of detritus. Branches clicked damply underfoot. It got steeper than he thought it would, and he stepped sideways to keep from slipping.

Then he heard another sound, quieter than the voices. A soft rustle and a creak, then a faint crack from the forest below and ahead. Something moving.

Frank froze. The hair on the back of his neck was standing up. Whatever it was, it sounded big. The article in the *Post* had mentioned that many of the animals from the National Zoo had not yet been recaptured. All of them had been let loose just before the zoo was inundated, to give them a chance of surviving. Some had drowned anyway; most had been recovered; but not all. Frank couldn't remember if any species in particular had been named. It was a big park of course. Possibly a jaguar had been mentioned.

He tried to melt into the tree he was leaning against.

Whatever it was below him snapped a branch just a few trees away. It sniffed; almost a snort. It was big, no doubt about it.

Frank could no longer hold his breath, but he found that if he let his mouth hang open, he could breathe without a sound. Most animals relied on scent anyway, and there was nothing he could do about his scent. This was a bad thought.

The creature had paused. It huffed. A musky odor wafting by was almost like the smell of the flood detritus. His heart tocked at the back of his throat.

A slow scrape, as of shoulder against bark. Another branch click. A distant car horn. The smell now resembled damp fur. Another crunch of leaf and twig, this time farther down the slope.

When he heard nothing more, and felt that he was alone again, he beat a retreat uphill and west, back to the streets of the city. It was frustrating, because now he was intrigued, and wanted to explore the park further. But he didn't want to end up one of those urban fools who ignored the reality of wild animals and then got chomped. Whatever that had been down there, it was big. Best to be prudent, and return another time.

After the gloom of the park, all Connecticut Avenue seemed as garishly lit as the work site down the street. The neighborhood resembled one of the Victorian districts of San Francisco. It was late now, the night finally cooling off. He could drive all night and never find a room.

He returned to his car. The Honda's passenger seat tilted back like a little recliner. The nearest streetlight was down at the corner.

He opened the passenger door, moved the seat all the way back, lowered it, slipped in, and sat down. He closed the door, lay back, stretched out. After a while he turned on his side and fell into an uneasy sleep.

For an hour or two. Then passing footsteps woke him. Anyone could see him if they looked. They might tap the window to see if he was okay. He would have to claim to be a visiting reporter, unable to find a room—very close to the truth, like all the best lies. Out here he was not bound to his real story.

He lay awake, uncomfortable in the seat, sure he would not fall back asleep; then he was lightly under, dreaming about the woman in the elevator. A part of his mind became aware that this was unusual, and he fought to stay submerged. He was speaking to her about something urgent. Her face was so clear, it had imprinted so vividly: passionate and amused in the elevator, grave and distant on the boat in the flood. He wasn't sure he liked what she was telling him. Just call me, he insisted. Give me that call and we can work it out.

Then the noise of a distant siren hauled him up, sweaty and unhappy. He lay there awhile longer, thinking about the woman. Once in high school he had made out with a girl in a little car like this one. He wanted the woman from the elevator. He wanted to find her. From the boat she had said she would call. I don't know how long, she had said. Maybe that meant long. He would just have to wait.

The sky was lightening. Now he definitely wouldn't be able to fall back asleep. With a groan he heaved himself up, got out of the car.

He stood on the sidewalk feeling wasted. The sky was a velvet gray, the air was cool. He walked east again, back into the park.

Dew polished the thick gray foliage. In the diffuse light the wet leaves looked like a forest of wax. Frank slowed down. He saw what looked like a trail, perhaps an animal trail. There were lots of deer in the park, the article had said. He could hear the sound of Rock Creek, a burbling that as he descended overwhelmed the city sounds and the perpetual grumble of trucking. The sky was lightening fast, and what had seemed to him cloud cover was revealed as a clear pale sky. Dim greens began to flush the grays.

It turned out that in this area, Rock Creek ran at the bottom of a fairly steep ravine, and the flood had torn the sidewalls away in places, as he saw when he came to a sudden drop-off. Below him, bare sandstone extruded roots like ripped wiring. He circled above the drop, dodging between low trees.

From a little clearing he could suddenly see downstream. The spate of water had torn the canyon clear. Everything that had been down there before—Beach Road, the small bridges and buildings, the ranger station, the picnic areas—all were gone, leaving a raw zone of bare sandstone, flat mud, thrashed grass, downed timber, and stubborn trees that were either clinging to life or dead in place. Many trees had been knocked over and yet held on by a few roots, forming living snags piled high with mud and trash. A larger snag downstream looked like a giant beaver dam, creating a dirt-brown pond.

The sky stood big and blue overhead, a tall dome that seemed to rise as the day lightened. Muddy Rock Creek burbled noisily down its course.

At the far edge of the pond a heron strode slowly, its knees bending backward. Long body, long legs, long neck, long head, long beak. A kind of dinosaur. And indeed nothing could have looked more pterodactylic. Sunlight blazed the tops of the trees across the ravine. Frank and the heron stood attentively, listening to unseen smaller birds whose wild twittering now filled the air. The heron's head cocked to one side. For a time everything was as still as bronze.

Then beyond the twittering came a different sound, fluid and clear, rising like a siren, like a hook in the flesh:

Oooooooooooooooooooop!

Gibbons at dawn. The gibbons were loose, still at large, free in the forest.

National Science Foundation, Arlington, Virginia, basement parking lot, 7 A.M. A primate sitting in his car, thinking things over. As one of the editors of *The Journal of Sociobiology,* Frank was always very aware of the origins of their species. Now he thought: Chimps sleep outdoors. Bonobos sleep outdoors.

Housing was ultimately an ergonomic problem. What did he really need? His belongings were here in his car, or upstairs in his office, or in boxes at UCSD, or in storage units in Encinitas, California. The fact that so much stuff was in storage showed how little it really mattered. By and large he was free of things. At age forty-three he no longer needed them. That felt a little strange, actually, but not necessarily bad. Did it feel good? It was hard to tell. It simply felt strange.

He got out of his car and took the elevator to the third floor, where there was a little exercise room, with a men's room off its entryway that included showers. In his shoulder bag he carried his laptop, his cell phone, his bathroom kit, and a change of clothes. Three shower stalls stood behind white curtains, near benches and lockers. Beyond extended the room with toilets, urinals, and a counter of sinks under a long mirror.

Frank knew the place, having showered and changed in it many times after lunchtime runs. Now he surveyed it with a new regard. It was as he remembered: an adequate bathroom, public but serviceable.

He undressed and got in one of the showers. A flood of hot water, almost industrial in quantity, washed away some of the stiffness of his uncomfortable night. Of course no one would want to be seen showering there every day. Not that anyone was watching, but some of the morning exercisers would eventually notice.

A membership in some nearby exercise club would provide an alternative bathroom.

What else did one need?

Somewhere to sleep, of course. The Honda would not suffice. If he had a van, though; and an exercise club membership; and this locker room, and his office upstairs, and the men's rooms up there . . . As for food, the city had a million restaurants.

What else?

Nothing he could think of. Many people more or less lived in this building, all the NSF hardcores who spent sixty or seventy hours a week here, ate their meals at their desks or in the neighborhood restaurants, only went home to sleep—and these were people with families, with kids, homes, pets, partners!

In a crowd like that it would be hard to stick out.

He got out of the shower, dried off (a stack of fresh white towels was there at hand), shaved, dressed.

He glanced in the mirror over the sink, feeling a bit shy. He didn't look at himself in mirrors anymore, never met his eye when shaving, stayed focused on the skin under the blade. He didn't know why. Maybe it was because he did not resemble his conception of himself, which was vaguely scientific and serious, even Darwinesque; and yet there in the glass was always the same old sun-fried jock.

This time he looked. To his surprise he saw that he looked normal—that was to say, the same as always. Normative. No one would be able to guess by his appearance that he was sleep-deprived, that he had been thinking some pretty abnormal thoughts, or, crucially, that he had spent the previous night in his car because he no longer had a home.

"Hmm," he told his reflection.

He took the elevator up to the tenth floor, still thinking it over. He stood in the doorway of his new office, evaluating the place by these new inhabitory criteria. It was a true room, rather than a carrel in a larger space, so it had a door he could close. It boasted one of the big inner windows looking into the building's central atrium, giving him a direct view of the mobile that filled the atrium's upper half.

This view was unfortunate, actually. He didn't want to look at that mobile, for not too long ago he had found himself hanging upside down from it in the middle of the night, working desperately to extricate himself from an ill-conceived and poorly executed break-and-enter job. It was an incident he would rather forget.

But there the mobile hung, at the new angle which Frank had given to it and which no one had noticed. Perhaps a reminder to—to what? To try not to do stupid things? To think things through before attempting them? But he always tried to do that, so the reminder was unnecessary. And drapes could be installed.

There was space for a couch against one wall, if he moved the bookcase. It would then be like a kind of living room, with the computer as entertainment center. There was an ordinary men's room around the corner, a coffee nook down the hall, the showers downstairs. All the necessities. As Sucandra had remarked once at the Quiblers', tasting spaghetti sauce with a wooden spoon: Aah—what now is lacking?

Same answer: Nothing.

It had to be admitted that he was contemplating this idea. This unsettled him pretty thoroughly. The idea was deranged, in the literal sense of being outside the range. Typically people did not choose to live without a home. No home to go home to; it was a little crazy.

But in some obscure way, that aspect pleased him too. It was not crazy in the way that breaking into the building through the skylight had been crazy, but it shared that act's commitment to an idea. And was it any crazier than handing well over half of your monthly take-home income to pay for seriously crappy lodging?

Nomadic existence. Life outdoors. So often he had thought about, read about, and written about the biological imperatives in human behavior—about their primate nature, and the evolutionary history that had led to humanity's paleolithic lifestyle, which was the suite of behaviors that had caused their brains to balloon as rapidly as they had; and about the residual power of all that in modern life. And all the while, through all that thinking, reading, and writing, he had been sitting at a desk. Living like every other professional worker in America, a brain in a bottle, working with his fingertips or his voice or simply his thoughts alone, distracted sometimes by daydreams about the brief bursts of weekend activity that would get him back into his body again.

That was what was crazy—living like that when he held the beliefs he did.

Now he was considering acting in accordance with his beliefs. Something else he had heard the Khembalis say at the Quiblers, this time Drepung: if you don't act on it, it wasn't a true feeling.

He wanted these to be true feelings. Everything had changed for him on that day he had gone to the Khembali ambassador's talk, and then run into the woman in the elevator, and afterward talked to Drepung at the Quiblers', and then, yes, broken into the NSF building and tried to recover his resignation. Everything had changed! Or so it had felt; so it felt still. But for it to be a true feeling, he had to act on it.

Meaning also, as part of all these new behaviors, that he had to meet with Diane Chang, and work with her on NSF's response to the climate situation.

This would be awkward. His letter of resignation, which Diane had never directly acknowledged receiving, was now an acute embarrassment to him. It had been an irrational attempt to burn his bridges, and by all rights he should now be back in San Diego with nothing but the stench of smoke behind him. Instead Diane appeared to have read the letter and then ignored it, or rather, considered how to use it to play him like a fish, and reel him back into NSF for another year of service. Which she had done very skillfully.

So now he found he had to stifle a certain amount of resentment as he went up to see her. He had to meet her secretary Laveta's steely eye without flinching; pretend, as the impassive black woman waved him in, that all was normal. No way to tell how much she knew of his situation, if anything.

Diane sat behind her desk, talking on the phone. She gestured for him to sit. Graceful hands. Short, Chinese-American, good-looking in a middle-aged way, businesslike but friendly. A subtly amused expression on her face when she listened to people, as if pleased to hear their news.

As now, with Frank. Although it could be amusement at his resignation letter, and the way she had jiu-jitsued him into staying at NSF. So hard to tell with Diane; and her manner, though friendly, did not invite personal conversation.

"You're in your new office?" she asked.

"My stuff is, anyway. It'll take a while to sort out."

"Sure. Like everything else these days! What a mess. I have Kenzo and some of his group coming this morning to tell us more about the Gulf Stream."

"Good."

Kenzo and a couple of his colleagues duly appeared. They exchanged hellos, got out laptops, and Kenzo started up his PowerPoint.

All the data, Kenzo explained, indicated a stall in what he called the "thermohaline circulation." At the north end of the Gulf Stream, where the water on the surface normally cooled and sank to the floor of the Atlantic before heading back south, a fresh layer on the surface had stalled the downwelling. With nowhere to go, the water in the current farther south had slowed to a halt.

Kenzo added that just such a stall had been identified as the primary cause of the Younger Dryas, a bitter little ice age that had begun about eleven thousand years ago, and lasted for a few thousand years. Its beginning had been almost unbelievably quick; the Greenland ice cores revealed it had happened in only three years. Three years, to shift from the global pattern called warm-wet to the pattern called cool-dry-windy. It was such a radical notion that it had forced climatologists to acknowledge that there must be nonlinear tipping points in the global climate, and thus introduce a new concept to climatology: abrupt climate change.

"What caused that stall?" Diane asked.

Kenzo clicked to an image of the Earth portraying the ice cap that had covered the Northern Hemisphere in the last ice age. The slow melting of this ice cap had created giant lakes resting on the remaining ice, and held in place by ice dams that were themselves melting. When the dams had given way, the fresh water had rushed down into the ocean, emptying volumes as large as the Great Lakes in a matter of weeks. Signs on the land showed this had happened down the St. Lawrence, the Hudson, and the Mississippi; out west, a lake covering most of Montana had drained down the course of the Columbia River several times, leaving an area in Washington called the scablands, where the floods had torn deep into the bedrock. Presumably the same thing had happened out east, but the scablands had been buried by the great eastern forest.

Frank, looking at the screen, thought of how Rock Creek had looked that morning. Theirs had been a very tiny flood relative to the ones Kenzo was describing, yet the watershed involved was devastated.

So, Kenzo continued, fresh water had dumped into the North Atlantic all at once, and blocked the thermohaline cycle. And nowadays the Arctic Ocean's winter sea ice had been breaking up into fleets of icebergs which sailed south on currents until they encountered the Gulf Stream, where they melted right in the Gulf Stream's downwelling areas. And the Greenland ice cap was melting faster than ever, and running into that same area.

"How much fresh water?" Diane asked.

Kenzo shrugged. "The Arctic is about ten million square kilometers. The sea ice these days is about five meters thick. Not all of that drifts into the Atlantic, of course. There was a paper that estimated that about twenty thousand cubic kilometers of fresh water had diluted the Arctic over the past thirty years, but it was plus or minus five thousand cubic kilometers."

They stared at the final slide. The implications tended to stall on the surface of the mind, Frank thought, like the water in the North Atlantic. The whole world, long used to the global climate mode called warm and wet, and now getting very much warmer because of anthropogenically released greenhouse gases, could paradoxically get thrust by all that into a global pattern that in the Northern Hemisphere could often be much colder. And the last time it happened, it had taken only three years. Hard to believe; but the Greenland ice core data were very clear, and the rest of the case equally persuasive—one might even say, in science's distinctive vocabulary of levels of certainty, compelling.

· · ·

When Kenzo and his team left, Diane said to Frank, "What do you think?"

"It looks serious. It may get people to take action."

"Except by now it may be too late."

"Yes."

They considered that in silence for a few silent moments, and then Diane said, "Let's talk about your second year here, how to get the most out of you."

That was a pretty blunt way to put it, given Diane's manipulations, but Frank was careful not to express any resentment. "Sure," he said. It had been documented that if you forced your face to take on pleasant expressions, your mood tended to follow. So, small smile of acceptance.

They worked their way down a list Diane had made of things NSF might do to deal with this abrupt climate change. As they did, Frank saw that Diane was well ahead of him in thinking about these things, which he found surprising, although of course it made sense; otherwise why would she have wanted him to stay? His letter would not have been what brought her the news of NSF's ineffectiveness.

She spoke very quickly. Slightly fog-minded, Frank struggled to keep up, looking at her more closely than ever before. Of course every face was inscrutable in the end. Diane's was dramatically planed, with cheekbones, forehead, and jaw all distinct and angled to each other. Formal; formidable. Asian dragon lady, yes. She drew the eye. She was about ten years Frank's senior, he gathered; a widow, he had heard; had been NSF head for a long time, Frank wasn't sure how long. Famous for her incredibly long days. They had called people like her workaholics before everyone got up to speed and the concept went away. Once Edgardo had said of her, she makes our Anna look like a slacker, and Frank had shuddered, because Anna was a maniac for work. Anything beyond that pretty much had to be insane. And this was who he was going to be working for.

Well, fine. He had not stayed in D.C. to fool around. He too wanted to work long hours. And now it was clear he would have Diane's ear and her support, therefore the cooperation of anyone he needed at NSF; things would thus get done.

He focused on her list:

* Coordinate already existing federal programs
* Establish new institutes and programs where necessary
* Work with Sophie Harper, NSF's congressional liaison, to educate all the relevant committees and staffs, and help craft legislation
* Work with the Intergovernmental Panel on Climate Change, the UN Environmental Program, and other international efforts
* Identify, evaluate, and rank all potential climate mitigations

This last item, to Frank, would create his real Things to Do list.

"We'll have to go to New York and talk to the UN," Diane said.

It would be interesting to watch her there. Asian martial arts were often about turning one's opponents' force against them. Certainly she had floored Frank that way. Maybe the rest of the world would follow.

But reviewing the list, he felt a surge of impatience. He tried to express this to Diane politely: he didn't want to spend his year starting studies. He wanted to find where small applications of money and effort could trigger large actions. He wanted to *do* things. Quickly he scribbled a new list:

* direct climate mitigation
* carbon sequestration (bio, physical)
* water cycle interventions
* clean renewable energy
* political action
* a new paradigm (permaculture)

Diane nodded. Her subtle amusement became a smile, perfectly scrutable. "You think big."

"It's a big situation. This Gulf Stream stall is only a proximate cause. The ultimate causes have to do with carbon burn, consumption levels, population, technology. We'll have to take all that on if we're going to actually do anything."

"There are other agencies working on these. Lots of this isn't our purview."

"Yes, but we are the National Science Foundation," emphasizing the words. "It isn't really clear what purview such an organization should have. Given the importance of science in this world, you could argue that it should be pretty much everything. But for sure it should be the place to coordinate the scientific effort. Beyond that, who knows? It's a new situation."

"True," she said, still smiling. "Well, okay! Let's go get some lunch and talk about it."

Frank tried to conceal his surprise. "Sure."

The hotel above the Ballston Metro offered a buffet lunch so fancy that it redefined the concept. The restaurant was cool and quiet. Diane appeared to know it well, and to have a corner table reserved. She filled a big plate with salad and some strips of seared flank steak, and took no bread. Iced tea without sugar. She was dressed in a businesslike skirt and heavy silk blouse, and Frank saw as he followed her that it was all perfectly tailored and fitted, and looked expensive. She moved gracefully, looked strong. Usually Frank was not attracted to short women, but when he was, it was a matter of proportion, and a kind of regal bearing. She wore flat shoes, and did not seem attentive to herself. Probably, judging by her food, thought of herself as overweight. But she looked good.

The irrepressible sociobiologist always inside Frank wondered if he was experiencing some bias here, given that she was a powerful alpha female, and his boss. Possibly all alpha females were physically impressive, possibly that was part of their alpha-ness. It was generally true of males.

They sat, ate, spoke of other things. Frank asked about her kids.

"Grown up and moved out. It's easier now." She spoke offhandedly.

"For a while it must have been busy."

"Oh yes."

"Where were you before NSF?"

"University of Washington. Biophysics. Then I got into administration there, then at triple-A S, then NIH. Now here." She shrugged, as if to admit that she might have gone down a wrong path somewhere. "What about you? What brought you to NSF?"

Well, I gambled with equity that wasn't entirely mine, lost it, went through a breakup, needed to get away. . . .

It wasn't a story he wanted to tell. Maybe no one's story could really be told. She had not mentioned her late husband, for instance. She would understand if he only spoke of his scientific reasons for coming to NSF: new work in bioalgorithms, need for a wider perspective to see what was out there, and so on.

She nodded, watching him with that amused expression, as if to say, I know this is only part of the story, but it's still interesting. He liked that. No wonder she had risen so high. Alpha females pursued different strategies than alpha males to achieve their goals; their alpha-ness derived from different social qualities.

"What about your living situation?" she asked. "Were you able to stay in the place you had?"

Startled, Frank said, "No. I was renting from a State Department guy who came back."

"So you managed to find another place?"

"Yes . . . For now I'm in a temporary place, and I've got some leads for a permanent one."

"That's good. It must be tough right now, with the flood."

"That's for sure. It's gotten very expensive."

"I bet. Let me know if we can help with that."

"Thanks, I will."

He wondered what she meant, but did not want to ask. "One thing I'm looking into is joining an exercise club around here, and Anna mentioned that you went to one?"

"Yes, I go to Optimodal."

"Do you like it?"

"Sure, it's okay. It's not too expensive, and it has all the usual stuff. And it's not just kids showing off. Most days I just get on a treadmill and go." She laughed. "Like a rat on a wheel."

Just like at work, Frank didn't say.

"Actually I've been trying more of the machines," she added. "It's fun."

Frank got the address from her, and they went back to the serving area for pie and ice cream (her portion small), and talked a bit more about work. She never even hinted at his resignation letter. That was strange enough to disturb his sense of being in a normal professional relationship. As if she were holding it over him.

Then, walking in the covered walkway above the street to the NSF building, she said, "Let's set up a regular meeting between us for every two weeks. I want to be kept up on what you're thinking."

Quickly he glanced down at her. She kept looking ahead.

"That's the best way to avoid any misunderstandings," she went on, still not looking at him. Then, as they reached the doors to their building, she said, "I want something to come of this."

"Me too," he assured her. "Believe me."

They approached the security desk. "So what will you do first?" she asked, as if something had been settled between them.

"To tell the truth, I think I'll go see about joining that health club."

She grinned. "Good idea. I'll see you there sometimes."

He nodded. "And, as far as my working committee, I'll start making calls. I'd like to get Edgardo on it, if you think that would be okay."

She laughed. "If you can talk him into it."

So. Frank returned to his office, collecting his thoughts. He sat at his new desk, looked out the window at the atrium mobile. Don't do stupid things!

He had spent the night in his car, then lunched with the director of the National Science Foundation, and no one was the wiser. He did feel a little spacy, but with appearances maintained, no one could tell. One retained a certain privacy.

Remembering a resolution he had made that morning, he picked up the phone and called the National Zoo.

"Hi, I'm calling to ask about zoo animals that might still be at large?"

"Sure, let me pass you to Nancy."

Nancy came on and said hi in a friendly voice, and Frank told her about hearing what seemed like a big animal, near the edge of the park at night. "Do you have a list of zoo animals still on the loose?"

"Sure, it's on our website. Do you want to join our group?"

"What do you mean?"

"There's a committee of the volunteer group, FONZ? Friends of the National Zoo. You can join that, it's called the Feral Observation Group."

"The FOG?"

"Yes. We're all in the FOG now, right?"

"Yes we are."

She gave him the website address, and he checked it out. It turned out to be a good one. Some fifteen hundred FONZies already. There was a page devoted to the Khembalis' swimming tigers, and on the FOG page, a list of the animals that had been spotted, and a list of animals missing and not yet seen. There was indeed a jaguar on this second list. The gibbons were on the spotted list: eight of them, all white-cheeked gibbons, along with three siamangs. Almost always in Rock Creek Park.

"Hmmm." Frank recalled the dawn cry, and pursued the creatures through their webpages. Gibbons and siamangs both hooted in a daily dawn chorus; siamangs were louder than gibbons, being larger. Could be heard six miles away, rather than the gibbons' one mile.

It looked like being in FOG might confer permission to go into Rock Creek Park; you couldn't observe animals in a place you were forbidden to enter. He called Nancy back. "Do FOG members get to go into Rock Creek Park?"

"Some do. We usually go in groups, but we have some individual permits."

"Cool. Tell me how I do that."

He left the building and walked down Wilson to the Optimodal Health Club. Diane had said it was within easy walking distance, and it was. That was good; and the place looked okay. Actually he had always preferred getting "exercise" by doing something challenging outdoors. Up until now he had felt that clubs like this were mostly just another way to monetize leisure time, charging for things people used to do outdoors for free. Silly as such.

But if you needed to rent a bathroom and shower, they were great.

So he did his best to remain expressionless (resulting in a visage unusually grim) while he gave the young woman at the desk a credit card and signed the forms. Full membership, no. Personal trainer, ready to take over his body but without incurring any legal liability, definitely not. He did pay extra for a permanent locker in which to store some of his stuff. Another bathroom kit there, another change of clothes; it would all come in useful.

He followed his guide around the rooms of the place, keeping his expressionless expression firmly in place. It was that or laugh out loud. By the time he was done the poor girl looked thoroughly unsettled.

Back at NSF he went into the basement to his Honda.

A great little car. But now it did not serve the purpose. He drove west on Wilson for a long time, until he came to the Honda/Ford/Lexus dealer where he had leased the car a year before. In this one aspect of the fiasco of remaining in D.C., his timing was good; he needed to re-up his car lease for another year, and the eager salesman handling him was happy to hear that this time he wanted to lease an Odyssey van. One of the best vans on the road, as the man told him while they walked out to view one. Also one of the smallest, Frank didn't say.

Dull silver, the most anonymous color around, like a cloak of invisibility. Rear seat removal, yes; therefore room in back for a single mattress, which he would have to purchase. Tinted windows all around the back, creating a high degree of privacy. It was almost as good as the VW van he had lived in for a couple of Yosemite summers, parked in Camp Four enjoying the stove and refrigerator and pop-top in his tiny motor home. Culturally the notion of small vehicle as home had crashed since then, having been based on a beat/hippie idea of frugality that had lost out to American excess.

But this Odyssey would do fine. Frank signed the forms. He saw that he might need to rent a post office box. But maybe his NSF address would do. He went back outside to take possession of his new bedroom.

His drove his new Odyssey directly to a storage place in Arlington, where he rented a unit. He liked the feel of the van; it drove like a car. In front of his storage unit he took out its backseats and put them in the oversized metal-and-concrete closet, along with most of the stuff that he had transferred from the old Honda. Possibly very little of it would ever come out again. Two quick stops later, and he had a single mattress which fit perfectly in the back of the van, as well as a set of sheets and pillows.

Then he drove to the Beltway, around in its jam to Wisconsin Avenue, down into the city. The newly ritualized pass by the elevator kiosk at Bethesda. Now he could have dropped in on the Quiblers without feeling pitiful, even though in most respects his circumstances had not changed since the night before. But now he had a plan. And a van. And this time he didn't want to stop. Over to Connecticut, down to the zoo, turn onto the same street he had the night before. He noted how the establishing of habits was part of the homing instinct.

Most streets in this neighborhood were permit parking by day and open parking by night, except for the one night a week they were cleaned. Once parked, the van became perfectly nondescript. Equidistant from two driveways; streetlight near but not too near. He would learn the full drill only by practicing it, but this street looked to be a good one.

Out and up Connecticut. Edward Hopper tableaux, end of the day. Like anywhere else in D.C., there were restaurants from all over the world. It wasn't just that one could get Ethiopian or Azeri, but that there would be choices: Hari food from southern Ethiopia, or Sudanese style from the north?

These days Frank was fondest of the Middle Eastern and Mediterranean cuisines, and this area of Northwest was rich in both, so that he had to think about which one he wanted, and whether to eat in or do takeout. He decided to do takeout. It was dinnertime but there was lots of light left; he could take a meal out into the park and enjoy the sunset. He walked Connecticut until he came on a Greek restaurant that would put dolmades and calamari in paper boxes, with a dill yogurt sauce in a tiny plastic container. Too bad about the ouzo and retsina, only sold in the restaurant; he liked those tastes. He ordered an ouzo to drink while waiting for his food, downing it before it even turned milky in its ice.

Back on the street. The taste of licorice enveloped him like a key signature, black and sweet. Steamy dusk of spring. Sweatslipping past two women; something in their sudden shared laughter set him to thinking about his woman from the elevator. Would she call? And if so, when? And what would she say, and what would he say? A lickerish mood, an anticipation of lust, like a wolf whistle in his mind. Vegetable smell of the flood. The two women passing him had been so beautiful. Washington was like that.

The food in his paper sack was making him hungry, so he turned east and walked into Rock Creek Park, following a bedraggled path that brought him to a pair of picnic tables, bunched at one end of a small, muddy lawn. A stone fireplace like a little charcoal oven anchored the ensemble. The brown grass was uncut. Birch and sycamore trees roofed the place. There had been lots of picnic areas in the park, but most had been located down near the creek, and thus washed away. This one was higher, in a little hollow next to Ross Drive. All of them, Frank recalled, used to be marked by big signs saying CLOSED AT DUSK. Nothing like that remained now. He sat at one of the tables.

He was about halfway through the calamari when several men tromped into the glade and sat at the other table or stood before the stone fireplace, bringing with them a heavy waft of stale sweat, smoke, and beer. Worn jackets, plastic bags: homeless guys.

Two of them pulled beer cans out of a paper grocery bag. A grizzled one in fatigues saluted Frank with a can. "Hey man."

Frank nodded politely. "Evening."

"Want a beer?"

"No thanks."

"What's a matter?"

Frank shrugged. "Sure, why not."

"Yar. There ya go."

Frank worked on his calamari and drank the offered Pabst Blue Ribbon, watching the men settle around him. His benefactor and two of the others were dressed in the khaki camouflage fatigues that signified Vietnam Vet Down On Luck (Your Fault, Give Money). Sure enough, a cardboard sign with a long story scrawled on it protruded from one of their bags.

Next to the three vets, a slight man with a dark red beard and ponytail sat on the table. The other three men were black, one of these a youth or even a boy. They sat down at Frank's table. The youngster unpacked a box that contained a chess set, chessboard, and timer. The man who had offered Frank a beer came over and sat down across from the youth as he set the board. The pieces were cheap plastic, the timer more expensive. The two started a game, the kid slapping the plunger on the timer down after pauses of about fifteen seconds, while the vet depressed his after a minute or more had passed, always declaring, "Ah fuck."

"Want to play next?" the boy asked Frank. "Bet you five dollars."

"I'm not good enough to play for money."

"Bet you that box of squid there."

"No way." Frank ate on while they continued. "You guys aren't playing for money," he observed.

"He already took all I got," the vet said. "Now I'm like pitching him batting practice. He's dancing on my body, the little fucker."

The boy shook his head. "You just ain't paying attention."

"You wore me out, Chessman. You're beating me when I'm down. You're a fucking menace. I'm setting up my sneak attack."

"Checkmate."

The other guys laughed.

Then three men ran into their little clearing. "Hi guys!" they shouted as they hustled to the far end of the site.

"What the hell?" Frank said.

The big vet guffawed. "It's the frisbee players!"

"They're always running," one of the other vets explained. He wore a VFW baseball cap, and his face was dissolute and whiskery. He shouted to the runners: "Hey who's winning!"

"The wind!" one of them replied.

"Evening, gentlemen," another said. "Happy Thursday."

"Is that what it is?"

"Hey who's *winning*? Who's *winning*?"

"The wind is winning. We're all winning."

"That's what you say! I got my money on you now! Don't you let me down now!"

The players faced a fairway of mostly open air to the north.

"What's your target?" Frank called.

The tallest of them had blue eyes, gold-red dreadlocks, mostly gathered under a bandana, and a scraggly red-gold beard. He was the one who had greeted the homeless guys first. Now he paused and said to Frank, "The trash can, down there by that light. Par four, little dogleg." He took a step and made his throw, a smooth uncoiling motion, and then the others threw and they were off.

"They run," the second vet explained.

"Running frisbee golf?"

"Yeah some people do it that way. Rolfing some people call it, running golf. Not these guys though! They just run without no name for it. They don't always use the regular targets either. There's some baskets out here, they're metal things with chains hanging from them. You got to hit the chains and the frisbees fall in a basket."

"Except they don't," the first vet scoffed.

"Yeah it's finicky. Like fucking golf, you know."

Down the path Frank could see the runners picking up their frisbees and stopping for only a moment before throwing again.

"How often do they come here?"

"A lot!"

"You can ask them, they'll be back in a while. They run the course forward and back."

They sat there, once or twice hearing the runners call out. Fifteen minutes later the men did indeed return, on the path they had left.

Frank said to the dreadlocked one, "Hey, can I follow you?"

"Well sure, but we do run it, as you see."

"Oh yeah that's fine, I'll keep up."

"Sure then. You want a frisbee to throw?"

"I'd probably lose it."

"Always possible out here, but try this one. I found it today."

"Okay."

Like any other climber, Frank had spent a fair amount of camp time toss-ing a frisbee back and forth. He much preferred it to hackysack, which he was no good at. Now he took the disk they gave him and followed them to their next tee, and threw it last, conservatively, as his main desire was to keep it going straight up the narrow fairway. His shot only went half as far as theirs, but he could see where it had crashed into the overgrown grass, so he considered it a success, and ran after the others. They were pretty fast, not sprinting but moving right along, at what Frank guessed was about a nine-minute-mile pace if they kept it up; and they slowed only briefly to pick up their frisbees and throw them again. It quickly became apparent that the slowing down, throwing, and starting up again cost more energy than run-ning straight through would have, and Frank had to focus on the work of it.

Some of the targets were trash cans, tree trunks, or big rocks, but most were metal baskets on metal poles, the poles standing chest high and sup-porting chains that hung from a ring at the top. Frank had never seen such a thing before. The frisbee had to hit the chains directly, so that its momen-tum was stopped and it fell in the basket. If it bounced out it was like a rim-mer in golf or basketball, and a put-in shot had to be added to one's score.

One of the players made a putt from about twenty yards away, and they all hooted. Frank saw no sign they were keeping score or competing. The dreadlocked player threw and his frisbee too hit the chains, but fell to the ground. "Shit." Off they ran to pick them up and start the next hole. Frank threw an easy approach shot, then tossed his frisbee in.

"What was par there?" he asked as he ran with them.

"Three. They're all threes but three, which is a two, and nine, which is a four."

"There's nine holes?"

"Yes, but we play the course backward too, so we have eighteen. Back-ward they're totally different."

"I see."

So they ran, stopped, stooped, threw, and took off again, chasing the shots like dogs. Frank got into his running rhythm, and realized their pace was more the equivalent of a ten- or eleven-minute mile. He could run with these guys, then. Throwing was another matter, they were amazingly strong and accurate; their shots had a miraculous quality, flying right to the baskets and often crashing into the chains from quite a distance.

"You guys are good!" he said at one tee.

"It's just practice," the dreadlocked one said. "We play a lot."

"It's our religion," one of the others said.

Then one of Frank's own approach shots clanged into the chains and dropped straight in, from about thirty yards out. The others hooted loudly.

On his next approach he focused on throwing at the basket, let go, watched it fly straight there and hit with a resounding clash of the chains. A miracle! A glow filled him, and he ran with an extra bounce in his step.

At the end of their round they stood steaming in the dusk, not far from the picnic area and the homeless guys. The players compared numbers, "twenty-eight," "thirty-three," which turned out to be how many strokes under par they were. Then high-fives and handshakes, and they began to move off in different directions.

"I want to do that again," Frank said to the dreadlocked guy.

"Anytime, you were keeping right with us. We're here most days around this time." He headed off in the direction of the homeless guys, and Frank accompanied him, thinking to return to his dinner site and clear away his trash.

The homeless guys were still there, nattering at each other like Laurel and Hardy: "I did not! *You* did." "I did not, *you* did." Something in the intonation revealed to Frank that these were the two voices he had heard the night before, passing him in the dark.

"Now you wanna play?" the chess player said when he saw Frank.

"Oh, I don't know."

He sat across from the boy, sweating, still feeling the glow of his miracle shot. Throwing on the run; no doubt it was a very old thing, a hunter thing. His whole brain and body had been working out there. Hunting, sure; and the finding and picking up of the frisbees in the dusk was like gathering. Hunting and gathering! And maybe these were not the same as hunting for explanations, or gathering data. Maybe only physical hunting and gathering would do.

The homeless guys droned on, bickering over their half-assed efforts to get a fire started in the stone fireplace. A piece of shit, as one called it.

"Who built that?" Frank asked.

"National Park. Yeah, look at it. Thing's got a *roof*."

"It looks like a smoker."

"They were idiots."

"It was the WPA, probly."

Frank said, "Isn't this place closed at dusk?"

"Yeah right."

"The whole fucking *park* is closed, man. Twenty-four seven."

"Closed for the duration."

"Closed until further notice."

"Five-dollar game?" the youngster said to Frank, rattling the box of pieces.

Frank sighed. "I don't want to bet. I'll play you for free." Frank waved at the first vet. "I'll be more batting practice for you, like him."

"Zeno ain't never just batting practice!"

The boy's frown was different. "Well, okay."

Frank hadn't played since a long-ago climbing expedition to the Cirque of the Unclimbables, a setting in which chess had always seemed as inconsequential as tiddly-winks. Now he quickly found that using the timer actually helped his game, by making him go with the flow of things, with the shape or pattern. In the literature they called this a "good-enough decision heuristic," although in this case it wasn't even close to good enough; he attacked on the left side, had both knights out and a great push going, and then suddenly it was all revealed as hollow, and he was looking at the wrong end of the endgame.

"Shit," he said, obscurely pleased.

"Told ya," Zeno scolded him.

The night was warm and full of spring smells, mixing with the mud stench. Frank was still hot from the frisbee run. Some distant gawking cries wafted up from the ravine, as if peacocks were on the loose. The guys at the next table were laughing hard. The third vet was sitting on the ground, trying to read a *Post* by laying it on the ground in front of the fitful fire. "You can only *see* the fire if you lie on the ground, or look right down the smoke hole. How stupid is that?" They rained curses on their miserable fire. Chessman finished boxing his pieces and took off.

Zeno said to Frank, "Why didn't you play him for money, man? Take him five blow jobs to make up for that."

"Whoah," Frank said, startled.

Zeno laughed, a harsh, ragged bray, mocking and aggressive, tobacco-raspy. "*HA ha ha.*" A kind of rebuke or slap. He had the handsome face of a movie villain, a sidekick to someone like Charles Bronson or Jack Palance. "Ha ha—what you think, man?"

Frank bagged his dinner boxes and stood. "What if I had beat him?"

"You ain't gonna beat him." With a twist of the mouth that added, Asshole.

"Next time," Frank promised, and took off.

Primate in forest. Warm and sweaty, full of food and beer, ouzo and endorphins. It was dark now, although the park was capped by the same noctilucent cloud it had worn the night before. This provided just enough light to see by. Tree trunks were obvious; Frank slipped through them as if dodging furniture in a dark house. He felt alert, relaxed. Exfoliating in the vegetable night, click of twigs under his feet. He swam through the park.

An orange flicker in the distance caused him to slow down, approach at an angle. He sidled closer like a spy or a hunter. It felt good. He got close enough to be sure it was a campfire, at the center of another brace of picnic tables. Here they had a normal fire ring to work with. Faces in the firelight: bearded, dirty, ruddy. Homeless guys like the ones behind him, or the ones on the street corners around the city. Mostly men, but there was one woman sitting by the fire knitting. She gave the scene a domestic look, like something out of Hogarth.

After a while Frank moved on, descending through trees. The gash of the torn ravine appeared below him, white in the darkness. The creek was a black ribbon cutting through it. Probably the moon was near full, somewhere above the clouds; there seemed to be more light than the city could account for.

A truck, rumbling in the distance. The sound of the creek burbling over stones. Distant laughter, a car starting; tinkle of broken glass; something like a dumpster lid slamming down. And always the hum of the city, a million noises blended together, like the light caught in the cloud. It was neither quiet, nor dark, nor empty. It was definitely not wilderness. It was city and forest simultaneously. It was hard to characterize how it felt.

Where would one sleep out here?

Immediately the question organized his walk. He had been wandering before, but now he was on the hunt again. He saw that many things were a hunt. It did not have to be a hunt to kill and eat animals.

He ranged up and away from the ravine. First in importance would be seclusion. A flat dry spot, tucked out of the way. There, for instance, a tree had been knocked over in the flood, its big tangle of roots raised to the sky, creating a partial cave under it—but too damp, too closed in.

Cobwebs caught his face and he wiped them away. He looked up into the network of black branches. Being up in a tree would solve so many problems. . . . That was a prehominid thought, perhaps caused merely by craning his neck back. No doubt there was an arboreal complex in the brain, crying, Go home, climb home!

He ranged uphill, mostly northward. A hilltop was another option. He checked out one of the knolls dividing Rock Creek's western tributaries. Nice in some ways, but as with root hollows, it was a place where other creatures might take refuge. A distant noise reminded him that this might include the zoo's jaguar.

He could always stay in his van, of course, but this felt somehow more real. He would need to make some daytime explorations, clearly. Scouting trips for the Feral Observation Group. We're all in the fog now, Nancy had said. He would spend some of his time hunting for animals. A kind of return to the paleolithic, right here in Washington, D.C. Repaleolithization: it sounded very scientific, like the engineers who spoke of amishization when they meant to simplify a design. Landscape restoration inside the brain. The pursuit of happiness; and the happiness was in the pursuit.

Frank smiled briefly. He realized he had been tense ever since leaving the rented apartment. Now he was more relaxed, watchful but relaxed, moving about easily. It was late, he was getting tired. Another branch across the face and he decided to call it a night.

He made his way west to Connecticut, hit it at Fessenden, walked south on the sidewalk blinking in the flood of light. It might as well have been Las Vegas or Miami to him now, everything blazing neon colors in the warm spring night. People were out. He strolled among them. The city too was a habitat, and as such a riot of sensation. He would have to think about how that fit in with the repaleolithization project, because cities were a big part of contemporary society, and people were obviously addicted to them. Frank was himself, at least to parts. The technological sublime made every-thing magical, as if they were tripping with the shaman—but all the time, which was too much. They had therefore lost touch with reality, gone mad as a collective.

And yet this street was reality too. He would have to think about all this.

When he came to his van no one was in sight, and he slipped inside and locked the doors. It was dark, quiet, comfortable. Very much like a room. A bit stuffy; he turned on the power, cracked the windows. He could start the engine and power the air conditioner for a while if he really needed to.

He set his wristwatch alarm for 4:30 A.M., afraid he might sleep through the dawn in such a room. Then he lay down on his mattress, and felt his body start to relax even further. Home sweet home! It made him laugh.

At 4:30 his alarm beeped. He squeezed it quiet and slipped on his running shoes and got out of the van before his sleepiness knocked him back down. Out into the dawn, the world of grays. This was how cats must see, all the grays so finely gradated. A different kind of seeing.

Into the forest again. The leafy venation of the forest air was a masterpiece of three-dimensionality, the precise spacing of everything suggesting some kind of vast sculpture. The human eye had an astonishing depth of field.

He stood over the tawny sandstone of the new ravine, hearing his breathing. It was barely cool. The sky was shifting from flat gray to pale blue.

"*Ooooooooooop!*"

He shivered deep in his flesh, like a horse.

The sound came from overhead, a rising "*ooooooooooo*" like the cooing of
a dove, or the call of a coyote. A voice, or a kind of siren—musical, unearthly, bizarre. Glissandos up and down. Voices, yes. Gibbons and/or siamangs. It sounded as if there were several of them. "*Oooop! Ooooooooooop!
Ooooooooooooop!*" Low to high, penetrating and pure. The hair on Frank's
neck stuck out.

He tried it himself. "Oooooooop!" he sang, softly. It seemed to fit in. He
could do a fair imitation of one part of their range. His voice wasn't as fluid,
or as clear in tone, and yet still it was somewhat the same. Close enough to
join in.

So he sang with them, and stepped ever so slowly between trees, trying
to catch a glimpse of them. They were feeding off each other's energy,
sounding more and more rambunctious. Wild animals! And they were celebrating the new day, there was no doubt about it. Maybe even celebrating
their freedom. To Frank it sounded like it. Certainly it was true for him—
the sound filled him, the morning filled him, spring and all, and he bellowed "Oooooooop oop oop!" voice cracking. He longed to sing higher; he
hooted as loudly as he could. The gibbons didn't care. It wasn't clear they
had even noticed him. He tried to imitate all the calls he was hearing, failed
at most of them. Up, down, crescendo, decrescendo, pianissimo, fortis-
simo. An intoxicating music. Had any composer ever heard this, ever used
this? What were people doing, thinking they knew what music was?

The chorus grew louder and more agitated as the sky lightened. When
sunlight pierced the forest they all went crazy together.

Then he saw three of them in the trees, sitting on high branches. He saw
their long arms and longer tails, their broad shoulders and skinny butts.
One swung away on arms as long as its body, landed on a branch by another, accepted a cuff and hooted some more. Again their raucous noise
buffeted Frank. When they finally quieted down, after an earsplitting climax, the green day was upon them.

Senator Phil Chase said, "You know, it's not a question of you being right and me being wrong."

"Of course not," Charlie Quibler replied.

Phil grinned. "We all knew that global warming was real."

"Yes, of course we did."

"No!" Joe Quibler murmured as he drowsed on Charlie's back.

Phil laughed to hear it. "You've got a lie detector there."

"Going off all the time, in this company."

"Ha ha. Looks like he's waking up."

Charlie glanced over his shoulder. "I better start walking."

"I'll join you. I can't stand any more of this anyway."

They were at the Vietnam Memorial, attending a ceremony to mark its reopening. Phil, a veteran who had served as an Army reporter in Saigon for a year, had said a few words; then the President had shown up, but only near the end, the feeling among his people being that this was one memorial better left buried in the mud. After that Phil was forgotten by the press on hand, which did not surprise him; but Charlie could tell by the slight tightness at the corner of his mouth that the calculated back of the hand to Vietnam had irritated him.

In any case they were free to leave. Normally Phil would have been whisked by car to his offices, but a cancellation had opened a half-hour slot in his schedule. "Let's go say hi to Abe," he muttered, and turned west. Offering this gift of time to Charlie; it was as close to an apology as Charlie would ever get.

An apology he possibly deserved, because Charlie's giant bill would have jump-started a real engagement with the climate change problem; but in the last phase of committee negotiations Phil had dismantled the bill to get a small part of it passed. He had promised Charlie he wouldn't, but he had, and without warning Charlie he was going to. "I am only doing the necessary," he said afterward in his fakey Indian accent. "I must first be doing the necessary."

Charlie still didn't believe it had been necessary. And it didn't help that since the flood Phil had been widely hailed as a prophet on climate. Phil had laughed at this little irony, had thanked Charlie, had ignored all Charlie's explicit and implied I-told-you-sos. Now he piled it on: "It's all really a compliment to you, Charles—to you and your unworkable brilliance."

"Yeah right," Charlie said. He was enjoying the situation too much to invent his side of their banter. Two old colleagues, out for a walk to the Lincoln Memorial; it was the rarest thing in town.

Landscaping equipment dotted the newly restored bank of the Potomac. The violent diesel huffing and puffing might have startled some sleeping children awake, but it served as a lullaby to Joe Quibler; the noise of trucks shifting gears on Wisconsin was his usual soporific, and he loved all big grinding sounds. So now he snoozed happily, head nestled into Charlie's neck.

This part of the Mall had been twenty feet under the rush of the Potomac during the flood, and being landfill to begin with, it had not put up very much resistance to the spate; much had been torn away, leaving the Lincoln Memorial an island in the stream. "Check it out," Charlie said to Phil, pointing up at the big white foursquare building. There was a dark horizontal line partway up it. "High-water mark. Twenty-three feet above normal."

Phil frowned at the sight. "The goddammed House is never going to appropriate enough to clean up this city."

Senators and their staffs often had an immense disdain for the House of Representatives. "True."

"It's too much like one of their Bible prophecies, what was that one?"

"Noah's flood? Revelation?"

"Maybe. Anyway they're loving it. No way they're going to allocate money to interfere with God's judgment. That would be worse than, than *what*—than *raising taxes*!"

Charlie said, "Joe'll wake up if you yell like that."

"Sorry. I'll calm down."

Joe rolled his head on Charlie's neck. "No," he said.

"Ha," Phil said, grinning. "Caught in another one."

Charlie could just glimpse the boy's red cheek and furrowed brow. He could feel Joe's agitation; clearly he was once more locked into one of his mighty dreams, which from his sleeping scowls and jerks appeared to be fierce struggles, filled with heartfelt *Nos*. Joe awakened from them with big sighs of relief, as if escaping to a quieter, lesser reality, a kind of vacation cosmos. It worried Charlie.

Phil noticed Joe's distress, patted his damp head. Step by broad step they ascended the memorial. To Phil this place was sacred ground. He loved Lincoln, had studied his life, often read in his collected works. "This is a good place," he said as he always did when here. "Solid. Foursquare. Like the Parthenon."

"Especially now, with all the scaffolding."

Phil looked in at the big statue, still stained to the knees, a sight that made him grimace. "You know, this city and the federal government are synonymous. They stand for each other, like when people call the administration 'the White House.' What is that, metonymy?"

"Metonymy or synecdoche, I can never remember which."

"No one can." Phil walked inside, stopped short at the sight of the stained inner walls. "Damn it. They are going to let this city sink back into the swamp it came out of."

"Synecdoche I think. Or the pathetic fallacy."

"Pathetic for sure, but how is it *patriotic*? How do they *sell that*?"

"Please Phil, you're gonna wake him up. They have it both ways, you know. They use code phrases that mean something different to the Christian right than to anyone else."

"Like 'the beast will be slain' or whatnot?"

"Yes, and sometimes even more subtle than that."

"Ha ha. Clerics, everywhere you look. Ours are as bad as the foreign ones. Make people hate their government at the same time you're scaring them with terrorists, what kind of program is that?" Phil drifted through the subdued crowd toward the left wall, into which was incised the Get-tysburg Address. The final lines were obscured by the flood's high-water mark, a sight which made him scowl. "They had better clean this up."

"Oh they will. He was a Republican, after all."

"Abraham Lincoln was no Republican."

"Hello?"

"The Republicans in Congress hated him like poison. The Copperheads did everything they could to sabotage him. They cheered when he was killed, because then they could claim him as a martyr and rip off the South in his name."

"Limited value in hitting them with that now."

"But it's still happening! I mean whatever happened to government of the people, by the people, and for the people not perishing from this earth?" Pointing at the marred lines on the wall.

"An idea that lost?" Charlie said, spurring him on.

"Democracy *can't* lose. It *has* to succeed."

" 'Democracy will never succeed, it takes up too many evenings.' "

"Ha. Who said that?"

"Oscar Wilde."

"Please. I mean, I see his point, but don't quote Oscar Wilde to me when I'm trying to think like Abraham Lincoln."

"Oscar Wilde may be more your level."

"Ha ha."

"Wilde was witty just like that."

"Ha ha *ha*."

Charlie gave up tweaking Phil in favor of contemplating the mud-stained statue of the sixteenth president. It was a great work: massive, brooding, uneasy. The big square-toed boots and obviously handmade broadcoat somehow evoked the whole world of the nineteenth-century frontier. This was the spirit that America had given to the world—its best gesture, its exemplary figure.

His oversized hands were dirty. The great bearded head looked sadly over them. The whole interior space of the building had a greatness about it—the uncanny statue, the high square ceiling, the monumental lettering of the two speeches on the side walls, the subdued people visiting it. Even the kids there were quiet. And yet there was a cheerfulness there, even an awe. It was as if church had turned real.

Perhaps it was this that woke Joe. He yawned, arched back in his seat, whacked Charlie on the head. "Down! Down!"

"Okay okay."

Charlie went back outside to let him down. Phil came along, and they sat on the top step and let Joe stretch his legs behind them.

A TV crew was working at the bottom of the steps, filming what looked to be a story on the memorial's reattachment to dry land. When the reporter spotted them, he came up to ask Phil if he would make a comment for the program.

"My pleasure," Phil said. The reporter waved his crew over, and soon Phil was standing before the camera in a spot where Lincoln loomed over his left shoulder. He launched into one of his characteristic improvs: "I'm sick of people putting Washington down," he said, waving a hand at the city. "What makes America special is our constitution, and the laws based on it—it's our *government* that makes America something to be proud of, and that government is based here. So I don't like to see people wrapping themselves in the flag while they trash the country they pretend to love. Abraham Lincoln would not stand for it—"

"Thanks, Senator! I'm sure we can use that. Some of it, anyway."

"I should hope so."

Then a shout of alarm came from inside the building, causing Charlie to shoot to his feet and spin around, looking for Joe—no luck. "Joe!" he cried, rushing inside.

Past the pillars he skidded to a halt, Phil and the TV crew hustling in behind him. Joe was sitting on Lincoln's knee, far above them, looking around curiously, seemingly unaware of the long drop to the marble floor.

"*Joe!*" Charlie tried to catch his attention without causing him to topple off. "Joe! Don't move! Joe! Stay there!"

How the hell did you get up there, he didn't add. Because Lincoln's marble chair was smooth and vertical on all sides; there was no way up it even for an adult. It almost seemed like someone had to have lifted him up there.

Of course he was an agile guy, a real monkey, very happy on the climbing structures at Gymboree. If there was a way, he had the will.

Charlie hustled around the statue, hoping to find Joe's route up and follow it himself. No such luck. "Joe! Stay there! Stay right there till we get you!"

A group was gathering at Lincoln's feet, ready to catch Joe if he fell off. He sat there looking down at them with an imperial serenity, completely at ease. The TV cameraman was filming everything.

The best Charlie could think to do was to request a boost from two willing young men, and clamber onto their shoulders as they stood on Lincoln's right boot and wrapped their arms around his calf. From there Charlie could reach up with his arms and almost reach Joe, although at that point it was a balancing act, and things were precarious. He had to talk Joe into toppling over into his hands, which of course took a while, as Joe was happy where he was. Eventually, however, he tipped forward and Charlie caught him, and let him down between his legs onto the two young men and a nest of hands, before falling back himself into the arms of the crowd.

The crowd cheered briefly, then gave them a little round of applause. Charlie thanked the two young men as he collected the squirming Joe from other strangers.

"Jesus, Joe! Why do you *do* these things?"

"Look!"

"Yeah yeah, look. But how the hell did you get up there?"

"Up!"

Charlie took some deep breaths, feeling sick to his stomach. If the TV station ran the story, which they probably would, and if Anna saw it, which she probably wouldn't, then he would be in big trouble. But what could you do? He had only taken his eye off him for a second!

Phil got back in front of the camera with them, heightening the chances it would make it to the news. "This is my young friend Joe Quibler and his father Charlie, a member of my staff. Good job, you guys. You know, citizens like Joe are the ones we have to think about when we consider what sort of world we're going to be passing along to them. That's what government is—it's making the world we give to our kids. People should think

about that before they put down Washington, D.C., and our country's government. Lincoln would not approve!"

Indeed, Lincoln stared down at the scene with a knowing and disen-
chanted air. He looked concerned about the fate of the republic, just as Phil
had implied.

The reporter asked Phil a few more questions, and then Phil indicated
he had to go. The TV crew quit, and the crowd that had stayed to watch
dissipated.

Phil phoned his office to get a car sent, and while they waited he shook
some hands. Charlie roamed the sanctum, Joe in his arms, looking for
routes up to Lincoln's lap. There were some disassembled scaffolds stacked
against the back wall of the chamber, next to an inner pillar; it was just
conceivable that Joe had monkeyed up those. Easier than doing a direttissima up Lincoln's calf, but still. It was hard to figure.

"God damn, Joe," Charlie muttered. "How do you do this stuff?"

Eventually he rejoined Phil, and they stood on the top steps of the memorial, holding Joe by the hand between them and swinging him out toward the reflecting pools, causing Joe to laugh helplessly.

Phil said, "You know, we're swinging him right over the spot Martin
Luther King stood on when he gave his 'I Have a Dream' speech. He is really touching all the bases today."

Charlie, still a little bit shaky with relief, laughed and said, "Phil, you
should run for president."

Phil grinned his beautiful grin. "You think so?"

"Yes. Believe me, I don't want to say it. It would mean endless hassle for
me, and I haven't got the time."

"You? What about me?" Phil was looking back up into the building.

"Endless hassle for you too, sure. But you already live that way, right? It
would just be more of the same."

"A lot more."

"But if you're going to run for high office at all, you might as well make
the biggest impact you can. Besides you're one of the only people in the
world who can beat the happy man."

"You think so?"

"I do. You're the World's Senator, right? And the world needs you, Phil. I mean, what are the rest of us going to do? We need help. It's more than just cleaning up the city here. It's the whole world needs help now."

"A godawful fate," Phil murmured, looking up at the somber and unencouraging Lincoln. A bad idea, Lincoln seemed to be saying. Serious business. Copperheads striking at heel, and head too. You put your life on the line. "I'll have to think about it."

CHAPTER 12

ABRUPT CLIMATE CHANGE

The ground is mud. There are a few sandstone rocks scattered here and there, and some river-rounded chunks of amber quartzite, but for the most part, mud. Hard to walk on, dismal to sit or lie on.

The canopy stands about a hundred feet overhead. In the summer it is a solid green ceiling, with only isolated shafts of sunlight slanting to the ground. The biggest trees shoot up without thinning, putting out their first major branches some forty feet overhead. There are no conifers. No needles on the ground, no pinecones. The annual drift of leaves disintegrates entirely, and that's the mud: centuries of leaf mulch.

The trees are either very big or very small, the small ones spindly, light-starved, doomed. It is hard to understand the forest's succession story. Only after Frank joined FOG did he learn that the succession was in fact messed up, its balance thrown off by the white-tailed deer, whose natural predators had all been eradicated. No more wolf or puma; and so all new trees were eaten by deer.

All the trees were third growth; the watershed had been clear-cut before the Civil War. During the war Fort DeRussy, at the high point of the park, had had a clear shot in all directions, and had once fired at Confederate scouts.

The park was developed in 1890 by Frederick Law Olmsted, and planned by his sons' firm. Now it was reverting to the great hardwood forest that had blanketed the eastern half of the continent for millions of years.

The forest floor was corrugated with small channels running down to Rock Creek, some as deep as thirty feet, but always mud troughs, with no stony creekbeds down their middles. Water didn't stay in them after a rain.

The forest appeared to be empty. The animals, both native and feral, stayed concealed.

There was trash all over. Plastic bottles were most common, then glass bottles, then boxes, shoes, plastic bag scraps . . . one plastic grocery bag hung from a branch like a prayer flag. There were many signs of the flood. The roads and picnic areas by the creek were now buried in mud or torn away. The gorge walls were scarred by landslides. Many trees had been uprooted, and some of these had been caught under the Boulder Bridge, forming a dam that retained a narrow lake upstream. The raw sandstone walls siding this lake were studded with boulders.

The higher roads and trails had survived. The Western Ridge Trail was intact. The nine numbered cross-trails now all ended abruptly at the new gorge. Before the flood there had been thirty little picnic areas in the park; now the higher ones were damaged, the lower ones gone. All had been paltry things, as far as Frank could determine in the aftermath—small clearings with picnic tables, fireplaces, a trash can. Site 21 was the worst in the park, two old tables in perpetual gloom, stuck at the bottom of a damp hollow that opened onto Ross Drive. With that road closed, it had gained some new privacy. Indeed in the mud under one table Frank found a used condom and a pair of women's pink underwear, Disney brand, picture of Ariel on waistband, tag saying Sunday.

East of site 21 the drop to the creek was steep. Big trees overhung the water. Boulders as big as cars stood in the stream. East of the ravine a steep wall of green loomed. If Beach Drive was not rebuilt, water would remain the loudest sound here, followed by insects. Some birds were audible. The squirrels had gray backs, and stomachs covered with fine coppery fur.

There were lots of deer, white-tailed in name and fact, big-eared, quick through the trees. It was a trick to move quietly through the forest after them, because small branches were everywhere underfoot, ready to snap in the mud. People were easier to track than deer. The windrows were the only good place to hide; the big tree trunks were broad enough to hide behind, but then you had to look around them to see, exposing yourself to view.

What would the forest look like in the autumn? What would it look like in winter? How many of the feral zoo animals could survive a winter out?

It turned out that Home Depot sold a pretty good treehouse kit. The heavy-duty hardware allowed one to collar several floor beams securely to trunk or major branches, and after that it was a simple matter of two-by-fours and plywood, cut to whatever dimensions one wanted. The rest of the kit consisted mostly of fripperies, the gingerbread fill making a Swiss Family allusion that caused Frank to smile, remembering his own childhood dreams: he had always wanted a treehouse. But these days he wanted it simple.

Getting that was complicated. For a while he left work as early as he could and drove to one edge of the park or another, testing routes and parking places. Then it was off into the park on foot, using a Potomac Appalachian Trail Club map to learn it. He hiked all the trails that had survived, but usually these were just jumping-off points for rambles in the forest and scrambles in the gorge.

At first he could not find a tree he liked. He had wanted an evergreen, preferably in a stand of other evergreens. But almost every tree in Rock Creek Park was deciduous. Beech, oak, sycamore, ash, poplar, maple—he couldn't even tell which was which. All of them had tall straight trunks, with first branches very high, and crowns of foliage above that. Their bark had different textures, however, and by that sign—bark corrugated in a vertical diamond pattern—he decided that the best trees were probably chestnut oaks.

There were many of these near site 21. One of them canted out and over-hung the creek. It looked as if its upper branches would have a nice view, but until he climbed it he wouldn't know.

While making his reconnaissances he often ran into the frisbee golfers, and when he did he usually joined them. In running the course they always passed site 21, and if the homeless guys were there, the second vet, whose name was Andy, would shout his abrasive welcome: "Who's *winning*? Who's *winning*?" The frisbee players usually stopped to chat for a moment. Spencer, the player with the dreadlocks, would ask what had happened lately, and sometimes get an earful in response. Then they were off again, Spencer in the lead, dreadlocks flying under bandana, Robin and Robert following at speed. Robin sounded like some kind of deist or animist, everything was alive to him, and after his throws he always shouted instructions to his frisbee or begged for help from the trees. Robert spoke more in the style of a sports announcer commenting on the play. Spencer emitted only shrieks and howls, some kind of shaman language; but he was the one who chatted with the homeless guys.

During one of these pass-bys Frank saw that Chessman was there, and under Zeno's baleful eye he offered to come back and play him for money. Chessman nodded, looking pleased.

So after the run Frank returned, toting a pizza in a box and a six-pack of Pabst. "Hey the doctor's here," Zeno said in his heavy joking tone. Frank ignored that, sat down and lost ten dollars to the boy, playing the best he could but confirming his impression that he was seriously outclassed. He said little, left as soon as it seemed okay.

The first time he climbed his candidate chestnut oak he had to use crampons, ice axe, and a telephone lineman's pole-climbing kit that he had from his window-washing days, dug out of the depths of his storage locker. Up the tree at dawn, kicking in like a telephone lineman, slinging up the strap and leaning back in his harness, up and up, through the scrawny understory and into the fork of the first two big branches. It was nice to be able to sink an ice axe in anywhere one liked; an awkward climb, nevertheless. It would be good to confirm a tree and install a ladder.

Up here he saw that one major branch curved out over the creek, then divided into two. That fork would provide a foundation, and somewhat block the view from below. He only needed a platform a bit bigger than his sleeping bag, something like a ledge bivouac on a wall climb. There was a grand view of the ravine wall opposite him, green to a height considerably higher than he was. Glimpses of the burbling creek downstream, but no view of the ground directly below. It looked good.

After that he parked and slept in the residential neighborhood to the west, and got up before dawn and hiked into the forest carrying lumber and climbing gear. This was pretty conspicuous, but at that time of day the gray neighborhood and park were completely deserted. It was only a ten-minute hike in any case, a drop through forest that would usually be empty even on a Sunday afternoon.

He only needed two dawn patrols to install a climbing ladder, wound on an electric winch that he reeled up and down using a garage-door remote he found at a hardware store. After that the two-by-sixes, the two-by-fours, and two three-by-five sheets of half-inch plywood could be hauled up using the ladder as a winch cable. Climb the ladder with the miscellaneous stuff, ice-axing into the trunk for balance, backpack full of hardware and tools.

Collar around trunk; beams on branches; plywood floor; low railing, gapped for the ladder. He maneuvered slowly around the trunk as he worked, slung in a self-belay from a piton nailed above him. Cirque du Soleil meets *Home Improvement*. Using woodscrews rather than nails reduced the sound of construction, while also making the thing stronger.

Every day an hour's work in the green horizontal light, and all too soon it was finished, and then furnished. A clear plastic tarp stapled and glued to the trunk overhead served as a see-through roof, tied out to branches on a slant to let the rain run off. The winch he screwed to the plywood just inside the opening in the rail. Duffel bag against the trunk holding rolled foam mattress, sleeping bag, pillow, lantern, gear.

Standing on the platform without his sling one morning, in the slanting light that told him it was time to drive to work, he saw that the thing was built. Too bad! He would have liked the project to have lasted longer.

Driving across town that morning, he thought, Now I have two bedrooms, in a modular home distributed throughout the city. One bedroom was mobile, the other in a tree. How cool was that? How perfectly rational and sane?

Over in Arlington he drove to NSF's basement parking lot, then walked over to Optimodal Health Club to shower.

Big, new, clean, blazingly well lit; it was a shocking contrast to the dawn forest, and he always changed at his locker feeling a bit stunned. Then it was off to the weight room.

His favorite there was a pull-down bar that gave his lats a workout they otherwise would not get. Low weight, high reps, the pull like something between swimming and climbing. A peaceful warm-up, on his knees as if praying.

Then over to the leg press. Here too he was a low-weight, high-rep kind of guy, although since joining the club it had occurred to him that precisely the advantage of a weight room over the outdoors was the chance to do strength work. So now he upped the weight, for a few hard pushes at the end of the set.

Up and down, back and forth, push and pull, all the while taking in the other people in the room: watching the women, to be precise. Lifting, running, rowing, whatever they did, Frank liked it. He had a thing for jock women that long predated his academic interest in sociobiology. Indeed it seemed likely that he had gotten into the latter to explain the former—because for as long as he could remember, women doing sports had been the ultimate stimulus to his attraction. He loved the way sports moves became female when women did them—more graceful, more like dance—and he loved the way the moves revealed the shapes of their bodies. Surely this was another very ancient primate pleasure.

At Optimodal this all remained true even though there was not a great deal of athleticism on display. Often it was a case of nonathletes trying to "get in shape," so that Frank was covertly observing women in various stages of cardiovascular distress. But that was fine too: sweaty pink faces, hard breathing; obviously this was sexy stuff. None of that bedroom silliness for Frank—lingerie, makeup, even dancing—all that was much too intentional and choreographed, even somehow confrontational. Lovelier by far were women unselfconsciously exerting themselves in some physical way.

"Oh hi Frank."

He jumped a foot.

"Hi Diane!"

She was sitting in a leg press seat, now grinning: "Sorry, I startled you."

"That's all right."

"So you did join."

"Yes, that's right. It's just like you said. Very nice. But don't let me interrupt you."

"No, I was done."

She took up a hand towel and wiped her brow. She looked different in gym clothes, of course. Short, rounded, muscular; hard to characterize, but she looked good. She drew the eye. Anyway, she drew Frank's eye.

She sat there, barefoot and sweaty. "Do you want to get on here?"

"Oh no, no hurry. I'm just kind of waking myself up to tell the truth."

"Okay."

She blew a strand of hair away from her mouth, kicked out against the weight ten times, slowing down in the last reps. She smelled faintly of sweat and soap. Presumably also pheromones, estrogens, and perfumes.

"You've got a lot on the stack there."

"Do I?" She peered at the weights. "Not so much."

"Two hundred pounds. Your legs are stronger than mine."

"I doubt that."

But it was true, at least on that machine. Diane pressed the two hundred ten more times; then Frank replaced her and keyed down the weights. Diane picked up a dumbbell and did some curls while he kicked in his traces. She had very nice biceps. Firm muscles under flushed wet skin. Absence of fur made all this so visible. On the savannah they would have been watching each other all the time, aware of each other as bodies.

He wondered if he could make an observation like that to Diane, and if he did, what she would say. She had surprised him often enough recently that he had become cautious about predicting her.

She was looking at the line of runners on treadmills, so Frank said, "Everyone's trying to get back to the savannah."

Diane smiled and nodded. "Easy to do."

"Is it?"

"If you know that's what you're trying for."

"Hmmm. Maybe so. But I don't think most people know."

"No. Hey, are you done there? Will you check me on the bench press? My right elbow kind of locks up sometimes."

So Frank held the handlebar outside her hand. A young woman, heavily tattooed on her arms, waited for the machine to free up.

Diane finished and Frank held out a hand to help her. She took it and hauled herself up, their grips tightening to hold. When she was up the young woman moved in to replace her, but Diane took up a towel and said, "Wait a second, let me wipe up the wet spot."

"Oh I hate the wet spot," the young woman said, and immediately threw a hand to her mouth, blushing vividly. Frank and Diane laughed, and seeing it the young woman did too, glowing with embarrassment. Diane gave the bench a final flourish and handed it over, saying, "If only it were always that easy!"

They laughed again and Frank and Diane moved to the next machine. Military press, leg curls; then Diane looked at her watch and said, "Oops, I gotta go," and Frank said "Me too," and without further ado they were off to their respective locker rooms. "See you over there." "Yeah, see you."

Into the men's room, the shower, ahhhh. Hot water must have been unusual in the hominid world. Hot springs, the Indian Ocean shallows. Then out on the street, the air still cool, feeling as benign as he had in a long time. And Diane emerged at the same time from the women's locker room, transformed into work mode, except wetter. They walked over to NSF together, talking about a meeting they were scheduled to attend later in the day. Frank arrived in his office at 8 A.M. as if it were any ordinary morning. He had to laugh.

The meeting featured a presentation by Kenzo and his team to Diane, Frank's committee, and some of the members of National Science Board, the group that oversaw the Foundation in board of directors style, if Frank understood it correctly. By the time Frank arrived, a large false-color map of the North Atlantic was already on the screen. On it the red flows marking the upper reaches of the Gulf Stream broke apart and curled like new ferns, one near Norway, one between Iceland and Scotland, one between Iceland and Greenland, and one extending up the long channel between Greenland and Labrador.

"This is how it used to look," Kenzo said. "Now here's the summer's data from the Argos buoy system."

They watched as the red tendrils shrank in on themselves until they nearly met, at about the latitude of southern Ireland. "That's where we're at now, in terms of temperature. Here's surface height." He clicked to another false-colored map that revealed what were in effect giant shallow whirl-pools, fifty kilometers wide but only a few centimeters deep.

"This is another before map. We think these downwelling sites were pretty stable for the last eight thousand years. Note that the Coriolis force would have the currents turning right, but the land and sea-bottom con-figurations make them turn left. So they aren't as robust as they might be. And see what we've got now—the downwelling has clearly shifted south."

"What happens to the water north of that now?" Diane asked.

"Well—we don't know yet. We've never seen this before. It's a freshwater cap, a kind of lens on the surface. In general, water in the ocean moves in kind of blobs of relative freshness or salinity, that mix only slowly. One team tracked the great salinity anomaly of 1968 to '82, that was a huge fresher blob that circled in the North Atlantic. It made one giant circuit, then sank on its second pass through the downwelling zone east of Green-land. Now with this freshwater cap, who knows? If it's resupplied from Greenland or the Arctic, it may stay."

Diane stared at the map. "So what do you think caused this cap?"

"It may be a kind of Heinrich event, in which icebergs float south. Hein-rich found these events by analyzing boulders that drop to the seafloor when icebergs melt. He theorized that any fresh water in the far North Atlantic—even rain—will interfere with downwelling. So now, we've got the Arctic sea ice breakup, plus Greenland is melting quicker than ever. Both are combining to freshen the North Atlantic. The strong implication is that we're in for a shift like the shift to the Younger Dryas."

"So." Diane looked at the board members in attendance. "We have compelling evidence for what is the best-identified trigger event for abrupt climate change. Happening again, now."

"Yes," Kenzo said. "A very clear case, as we'll see this winter."

"It will be bad?"

"Yes. Maybe not the full cold-dry-windy, but close enough. The jet stream is likely to wander more, sometimes shooting straight down from the Arctic, in what they call a polar vortex. It'll get cold and windy all over the Northern Hemisphere, but especially in the eastern half of North America, and all over Europe. You can bet on it."

"And so . . . the ramifications? In terms of telling Congress?"

Kenzo waved his hands in his impresario style. "You could reference that Pentagon report that said abrupt climate change would be a threat to national security, as they couldn't defend the nation from a starving world."

"Starving?"

"Well, there are no food reserves to speak of. I know the food production problem appears to be solved, but there were never any reserves built up. It's just assumed more could always be grown. But Europe pretty much grows its own food. That's six hundred and fifty million people. It's the Gulf Stream that allows that. The Gulf Stream moves about a petawatt northward, that's a million billion watts, or about a hundred times as much energy as humanity generates. Canada, at the same latitude as Europe, only grows enough to feed its thirty million people, plus about double that in grain. They could up it a little if they had to, but think of Europe with a climate suddenly like Canada's—how are they going to feed themselves? They'll have a four- or five-hundred-million-person shortfall."

"Hmm," Diane said. "That's what this Pentagon report said?"

"Yes. But it was an internal document, and its conclusions were inconvenient to the administration, so it was getting buried when someone on the team slipped it to *Fortune* magazine, and they published it. It made a little stir at the time, because it was the Pentagon, and the possibilities it outlined were so bad. People thought it might get the World Bank to change their investment pattern. The Bank's Extractive Industries Review Commission had recommended they cut off all investment in fossil fuels, and move that money into clean renewables. But in the end the Bank board voted to keep their investment pattern the same, which means ninety-four percent to fossil fuels and six percent to renewables. After that the Pentagon report experienced the usual fate."

"Forgotten."

"Yes."

"We don't remember our reports either," Edgardo said. "There are several NSF reports on this issue. I've got one here called 'Environmental Science and Engineering for the Twenty-First Century: The Role of the National Science Foundation.' It called for quadrupling the money NSF gave to its environmental programs, and suggested everyone else in government and industry do the same. Look at this table in it—forty-five percent of Earth's land surface transformed by humans—fifty percent of surface fresh water used—two-thirds of the marine fisheries fully exploited or depleted. Carbon dioxide in the atmosphere thirty percent higher than before the industrial revolution. A quarter of all bird species extinct." He looked up at them over his reading glasses. "All these figures are worse now."

Diane looked at the page Edgardo passed around, said, "Clearly ignorance has not been the problem. The problem is acting on what we know. Maybe people will be ready now. Better late than never."

"Unless it's too late," Edgardo suggested.

Diane had said the same thing to Frank in private, but now she said firmly, "Let's proceed on the assumption that it is never too late. I mean, here we are. So let's get Sophie in, and prepare something for the White House and the congressional committees. Some plans. Things we can do right now, concerning both the Gulf Stream and global warming more generally."

"We'll need to scare the shit out of them," Edgardo said.

"Yes. Well, the marks of the flood are still all over town."

"People are already fond of the flood," Edgardo said. "It was an adventure. It got people out of their ruts."

"Nevertheless," Diane said, with a grimace that was still somehow cheerful. Scaring politicians might be something she looked forward to.

. . .

Given all his work, Frank didn't usually get away as early as he would have liked. But the June days were long, and once in the park he could wander and look for animals. Just north of Military Road lay the site of Fort De-Russy, now low earthen bulwarks. One evening he saw movement inside the bulwarks: some kind of antelope, its neck stretched up as it pulled down a branch with its mouth to strip off leaves. Russet body, white stripes running diagonally up from white belly: an exotic for sure. A feral from the zoo, and his first nondescript!

It saw him, and yet continued to eat. Its jaw moved in a rolling, side-to-side mastication; the bottom jaw was the one that stayed still. It was alert to his movements, and yet not skittish. He wondered if escaped zoo animals were more trusting or less than the local natives. Something to ask Nancy.

Abruptly the creature shot away through the trees. It was big! Frank grinned, pulled out his FOG phone, and called it in. The cheap little cell phone was on something like a walkie-talkie or party line system, and Nancy or one of her assistants usually picked up right away. "Sorry, I don't really know what it was." He described it the best he could. Pretty lame, but what could he do? He needed to learn more. "Call Clark on phone twelve," Nancy suggested, "he's the ungulate guy." No need to GPS the sighting, being right in the old fort.

He hiked down the trail that ran from the fort to the creek, paralleling Military Road and then passing under its big bridge, which had survived but was still closed. It was nice and quiet in the ravine. Green light in the muggy late afternoon. He kept an eye out for animals, thinking about what might happen to them in the climate change Kenzo said was coming. All the discussion in the meeting had centered on the impacts to humans. That would be the usual way of most such discussions, but whole biomes would be altered, perhaps devastated. That was what they were saying, really, when they talked about the impact on humans: they would lose the support of the domesticated part of nature. Everything would go feral.

He walked south on a route that stayed on the rim of the damaged part of the gorge as much as possible. When he came to site 21 he found the homeless guys there as usual, sitting around looking kind of beat.

"Hey, Doc! Why aren't you throwing frisbee? They was just here."

"Were they? Maybe I'll catch them on their way back."

Frank regarded them; hanging around in the steamy sunset, smoking in their own fire, empties dented on the ground around them. Frank found he was thirsty, and hungry.

"Who'll eat pizza if I go get one?"

Everyone would. "Get some beer too!" Zeno said, with a hoarse laugh that falsely insinuated this was a joke.

Frank hiked out to Connecticut and bought thin-crusted pizzas from a little stand across from Chicago's. Back into the dusky forest, two boxes held like a waiter. Then pizza around the fire, with the guys making their usual desultory conversation. The vet always studying the *Post*'s federal news section did indeed appear well versed in the ways of the federal bureaucracy, and he definitely had a chip on his shoulder about it. "The left hand don't know what the right hand is doing," he muttered again. Frank had already observed that they always said the same things; but didn't everybody? He finished his slice and crouched down to tend their smoky fire. "Hey someone's got potatoes burning in here."

"Oh yeah, pull those out! You can have one if you want."

"Don't you know you can't cook no potato on no fire?"

"Sure you can! How you do think?"

Frank shook his head; the potato skins were charred at one end, green at the other. Back in the paleolithic there must have been guys hanging out somewhere beyond the cave, guys who had offended the alpha male or killed somebody by accident or otherwise fucked up—or just not been able to understand the rules—or failed to find a mate (like Frank)—and they must have hunkered around some outlier fire, eating lukewarm pizza and making crude chitchat that was always the same, laughing at their old jokes.

"I saw an antelope up in the old fort," he offered.

"I saw a tapir," the *Post* reader said promptly.

"Come on Fedpage, how you know it was a tapir."

"I saw that fucking *jaguar*, I swear."

Frank sighed. "If you report it to the zoo, they'll put you in their volunteer group. They'll give you a pass to be in the park."

"You think we need a pass?"

"We be the ones giving them a pass!"

"They'll give you a cell phone too." That surprised them.

Chessman slipped in, glancing at Frank, and Frank nodded unenthusiastically; he had been about to leave. And it was his turn to play black. Chessman set out the board between then and moved out his king's pawn.

Suddenly Zeno and Andy were arguing over ownership of the potatoes. It was a group that liked to argue. Zeno was among the worst of these; he would switch from friendly to belligerent within a sentence, and then back again. Abrupt climate change. The others were more consistent. Andy was consistently abrasive with his unfunny humor, but friendly. Fedpage was always shaking his head in disgust at something he was reading. The silent guy with the silky dark red beard was always subdued, but when he spoke always complained, often about the police. Another regular was older, with blond-gray hair, pockmarked face, not many teeth. Then there was Jory, an olive-skinned man with greasy black hair, who was if anything even more volatile than Zeno, but had no friendly mode, being consistently obnoxious and edgy. He would not look at Frank except in sidelong glances that radiated hostility.

Last among the regulars was Cutter, a cheery, bulky black guy, who usually arrived with a cut of meat to cook on the fire, always providing a pedigree for it in the form of a story of petty theft or salvage. Adventures in food acquisition. He often came with a couple of buddies, knew Chessman, and appeared to have a job with the city park service, judging by his shirts and his stories. He more than the others reminded Frank of his window-washing days, also the climbing crowd—a certain rowdy quality—life considered as one outdoor sport after the next. It seemed as if Cutter had somewhere else as his base; and he had also given Frank the idea of bringing by food.

Chessman suddenly blew in on the left flank and Frank resigned, shaking his head as he paid up. "Next time," he promised. The fire guttered out, and the food and beer were gone. The potatoes smoldered on a tabletop. The guys had slowed down in their talk. Redbeard slipped off into the night, and that made it okay for Frank to do so as well. Some of them made their departures into a big production, with explanations of where they were going and why, and when they would likely return again; others just walked off, as if to pee, and did not come back. Frank said, "Catch you guys," in order not to appear unfriendly, but only as he was leaving, so that it was not an opening to any inquiries.

Off north to his tree. Ladder called down, the motor humming like the sound of his brain in action.

The thing is, he thought as he waited, nobody knows you. No one can. Even if you spent almost the entirety of every day with someone, and there were pairs like that—even then, no. Everyone lived alone in the end, not just in their heads but even in their physical routines. Human contacts were parcellated, to use a term from brain science and systems theory; parcelled out. There were:

1. the people you lived with, if you did; that was about a hundred hours a week, half of them asleep;
2. the people you worked with, that was forty hours a week, give or take;
3. the people you played with, that would be some portion of the thirty or so hours left in a week.
4. then there were the strangers you spent time with in transport, or eating out or so on. This would be added to an already full calendar according to Frank's calculations so far, suggesting they were all living more hours a week than actually existed, which felt right. In any case, a normal life was split out into different groups that never met; and so no one knew you in your entirety, except you yourself.

One could, therefore:

1. pursue a project in paleolithic living,
2. change the weather,
3. attempt to restructure your profession, and
4. be happy,

all at once, although *not* simultaneously, but moving from one thing to another, among differing populations and behaving as if a different person in each situation. It could be done, because *there were no witnesses*. No one saw enough to witness your life and put it all together.

Through the lowest leaves of his tree appeared the aluminum-runged nylon rope ladder. One of his climbing friends had called this kind of ice-climbing ladder a "Miss Piggy," perhaps because the rungs resembled pig iron, perhaps because Miss Piggy had stood on just such a ladder for one of her arias in *Muppet Treasure Island*. Frank grabbed one of the rungs, tugged to make sure all was secure, and started to climb. The parcellated life. Fully optimodal. No reason not to enjoy it; and suddenly he realized that he *was* enjoying it. It was like being a versatile actor in a repertory theater, shifting constantly from role to role, and all together they made up his life.

Cheered by the thought, he ascended the upper portion of Miss Piggy, swaying as little as possible among the branches. Then through the gap, up and onto his plywood floor.

He hand-turned the crank on the ladder's spindle, to bring the ladder up after him without wasting battery power. Once it was secured, and the lubber's hole filled with a fitted piece of plywood, he could relax. He was home.

Against the trunk was his big duffel bag under a tarp, held in place by bungee cords. From the duffel he pulled the rolled-up foam mattress, as thick and long as a bed. Then pillows, mosquito net, sleeping bag, sheet. On these nights he slept under sheet and mosquito net, and only used the down bag near dawn.

Lie down, stretch out, feel the weariness of the day bathe him. Slight sway of the tree: yes, he was up in a treehouse.

This made him happy. His childhood fantasy had been the result of visits to the big treehouse at Disneyland. He had been eight years old when he first saw it, and it had bowled him over: the elaborate waterwheel-powered bamboo plumbing system, the bannistered stairs spiraling up the trunk, the big living room with its salvaged harmonium, catwalks to the separate bedrooms on their branches, open windows on all four sides . . .

His current aerie was a very modest version of that fantasy, of course. A ledge bivouac rather than the Swiss Family mansion, and indeed his old camping gear was well represented around him, augmented by some nifty car-camping extras, like the lantern and the foam mattress and the pillows from the apartment. Stuff scavenged from the wreckage of his life, as in any other Robinsonade.

The tree swayed and whooshed in the wind. He sat on his thick foam pad, his back holding it up against the trunk. Luxurious reading in bed. Around him laptop, cell phone, a little cooler; his backpack held a bathroom bag and a selection of clothing, all lit by a Coleman battery-powered lantern. In short, everything he needed. The lamp cast a pool of light onto the plywood. No one would see it. He was in his own space, and yet at the same time right in the middle of Washington, D.C. One of the ferals in the ever-encroaching forest. *"Oooop, oop oop ooooop!"* His tree swayed back and forth in the wind. He switched off his lamp and slept like a babe.

Except his cell phone rang, and he rolled over and answered it without fully waking. "Hello?"

"Frank Vanderwal?"

"Yes? What time is it?" And where am I?

"It's the middle of the night. Sorry, but this is when I can call." As he was recognizing her voice, she went on: "We met in that elevator that stuck."

Already he was sitting up. "Ah yeah of course! I'm glad you called."

"I said I would."

"I know."

"Can you meet?"

"Sure I can. When?"

"Now."

"Okay."

Frank checked his watch. It was three in the morning.

"That's when I can do it," she explained.

"That's fine. Where?"

"There's a little park, near where we first met. Two blocks south of there, a block east of Wisconsin. There's a statue in the middle of the park, with a bench under it. Would that be okay?"

"Sure. It'll take me, I don't know, half an hour to get there. Less, actually."

"Okay. I'll be there."

The connection went dead.

Again he had failed to get her name, he realized as he dressed and rolled his sleeping gear under the tarp. He brushed his teeth while putting on his shoes, wondering what it meant that she had called now. Then the ladder finished lowering and down he went, swaying hard and holding on as he banged into a branch. Not a good time to fall, oh no indeed.

Leaving the park the streetlights blazed in his eyes, caged in blue polygons or orange globes. It was like crossing an empty stage set. He drove over to Wisconsin and up it, turned right on Elm. There was the little park she had mentioned. He had not known it existed. It was dark except for one orange streetlight at its north end, near a row of tennis courts. He parked and got out.

Mid-park a small black statue of a female figure held up a black hoop. The streetlight and the city's noctilucent cloud illuminated everything faintly but distinctly. It reminded Frank of the light in the NSF building on the night of his abortive b-and-e, and he shook his head, not wanting to recall that folly; then he recalled that that was the night they had met, that he had broken into the NSF building specifically because he had decided to stay in D.C. and search for this woman.

And there she was, sitting on the park bench. It was 3:34 A.M. and there she sat, on a park bench in the dark. Something in the sight made him shiver.

She saw him coming and stood up, stepped around the bench. They stopped face-to-face. She was almost as tall as he was. Tentatively she reached out a hand, and he touched it with his. Their fingers intertwined. Slender long fingers. She freed her hand and gestured at the park bench, and they sat.

"Thanks for coming," she said.

"Oh hey. I'm so glad you called."

"I didn't know, but I thought . . ."

"Please. Always call. I wanted to see you again."

"Yes." She smiled a little, as if aware that *seeing* was not the full verb for what he meant. Again Frank shuddered: who was she, what was she doing?

"Tell me your name. Please."

". . . Caroline."

"Caroline what?"

"Let's not talk about that yet."

Now the ambient light was too dim; he wanted to see her better. She looked at him with a curious expression, as if puzzling how to proceed.

"What?" he said.

She pursed her lips.

"What?"

She said, "Tell me this. Why did you follow me into that elevator?"

Frank had not known she had noticed that. "Well! I . . . I liked the way you looked."

She nodded, looked away. "I thought so." A tiny smile, a sigh: "Look," she said, and stared down at her hands. She fiddled with the ring on her left ring finger.

"What?"

"You're being watched." She looked up, met his gaze. "Do you know that?"

"No! But what do you mean?"

"You're under surveillance."

Frank sat up straighter, shifted back and away from her. "By whom?"

She almost shrugged. "It's part of Homeland Security."

"What?"

"An agency that works with Homeland Security."

"And how do you know?"

"Because you were assigned to me."

Frank swallowed involuntarily. "When was this?"

"About a year ago. When you first came to NSF."

Frank sat back even further. She reached a hand toward him. He shivered; the night seemed suddenly chill. He couldn't quite come to grips with what she was saying. "Why?"

She reached farther, put her hand lightly on his knee. "Listen, it's not like what you're thinking."

"I don't know what I'm thinking!"

She smiled. The touch of her hand said more than anything words could convey, but right now it only added to Frank's confusion.

She saw this and said, "I monitor a lot of people. You were one of them. It's not really that big a deal. You're part of a crowd, really. People in certain emerging technologies. It's not direct surveillance. I mean no one is watching you or anything like that. It's a matter of tracking your records, mostly."

"That's all?"

"Well—no. E-mail, where you call, expenditures—that sort of thing. A lot of it's automated. Like with your credit rating. It's just a kind of monitoring, looking for patterns."

"Uh-huh," Frank said, feeling less disturbed, but also reviewing things he might have said on the phone, to Derek Gaspar for instance. "But look, why me?"

"I don't get told why. But I looked into it a little after we met, and my guess would be that you're an associational."

"Meaning?"

"That you have some kind of connection with a Yann Pierzinski."

"Ahhhhh?" Frank said, thinking furiously.

"That's what I think, anyway. You're one of a group that's being monitored together, and they all tend to have some kind of connection with him. He's the hub."

"It must be his algorithm."

"Maybe so. Really I don't know. I don't make the determinations of interest."

"Who does?"

"People above me. Some of them I know, and then others above those. The agency is pretty firewalled."

"It must be his algorithm. That's the main thing he's worked on ever since his doctoral work."

"Maybe so. The people I work for use an algorithm themselves, to identify people who should be tracked."

"Really? Do you know what kind?"

"No. I do know they're running a futures market. Do you know about those?"

Frank shook his head. "Like that Poindexter thing?"

"Yes, sort of. He had to resign, and really he should have, because that was stupid. But the idea of using futures markets itself has gone forward."

"So they're betting on future acts of terrorism?"

"No no. That was the stupid part, putting it like that. There's better ways to use those programs. They're just futures markets, when you design them right. They're like any other futures market. It's a powerful way to collate information. They outperform most of the other predictive methods we use."

"That's hard to believe."

"Is it?" She shrugged. "Well, the people I work for believe it. But the one they've set up is a bit different than the standard futures market. It's not open to anyone, and people aren't betting real money. It's like a virtual futures market, a simulation. There are these people at MIT who think they have it working well, and they've got some real-world results they can point to. They focus on people rather than events, so really it's a futures market on people instead of commodities. So Homeland Security and associated agencies like ours have gotten interested. We've got this program going, and you're part of it. It's a pilot program, but big, and I bet it's here to stay."

"Is it legal?"

"It's hard to say what's legal these days, don't you think? At least concerning surveillance. A determination of interest usually comes from the Justice Department, or is approved by it. It's classified, and we're a black program that no one will ever hear about. I think my bosses hope to keep using it without ever causing any fuss."

"So people are betting on who will do innovative work, or defect to China, or like that?"

"Yes. Like that. There are lots of different criteria."

"Jesus," Frank said, shaking his head in amazement. "But, I mean—who in the hell would bet on me?"

She laughed. "I would, right?"

Frank put his hand on top of hers and squeezed it.

"But actually," she said, turning her hand and twining her fingers with his, "I think most of the investors are various kinds of diagnostic programs."

Now it was Frank's turn to laugh. "So there are computer programs out there, betting I am going to become some kind of a security risk."

She nodded, smiling at the absurdity of it. Although Frank realized, with a little jolt of internal surprise, that if the whole project were centered around Pierzinski, then the programs might be getting it right. Frank himself had judged that Pierzinski's algorithm might allow them to read the proteome from the genome, thus giving them any number of new gene therapies, which if they could crack the delivery problem had the potential of curing many, many diseases. That would be a good in itself, and would also be worth billions, maybe even trillions. And Frank had without a doubt been involved with Yann's career, first on his doctoral committee, and then running the panel judging his proposal. He had impacted Yann's career in ways he hadn't even intended, by sabotaging his application, after which Yann had gone to Torrey Pines Generique and then Small Delivery Systems, where he was now.

Possibly the futures market had taken notice of all that.

Caroline was now looking more relaxed, perhaps relieved that he was not outraged or otherwise freaked out by her news. He tried to stay cool. What was done was done. He had tried to secure Pierzinski's work for a company he had ties to, yes; but he had failed. So despite his best (or worst) efforts, there was nothing now he needed to hide.

"You said MIT," he said, thinking things over. "Is Francesca Taolini involved with this?"

A surprised look, then: "Yes. She's another subject of interest. There's about a dozen of you. I was assigned to surveil most of the group."

"Did you . . . do you record what people say on the phone, or in rooms?"

"Sure. The technology has gotten really powerful, you have no idea. But it's only fully applied in some cases. Pierzinski's group—you guys are still under a less intrusive kind of thing."

"Good." Frank shook his head, like a dog shaking off water. His thoughts were skittering around in all directions. "So . . . you've been watching me for a year. But I haven't done anything."

"I know. But then . . ."

"Then what?"

"Then I saw you on that Metro car, and I recognized you. I couldn't believe it. I had only seen your photo, or maybe some video, but I knew it was you. And you looked upset. Very . . . intent on something."

"Yes," Frank said. "That's right."

"What happened? I mean, I checked it out later, but it seemed like you had just been at NSF that day."

"That's right. But I went to a lecture, like I told you."

"That's right, you did. Well, I didn't know that when I saw you in the Metro. And there you were, looking upset, and so—I thought you might be trailing me. I thought you had found out somehow, done some kind of back trace—that's another area I've been working on, mirror searching. I figured you had decided to confront me, to find out what was going on. It seemed possible, anyway. Although it was also possible it was just one of those freak things that happen in D.C. I mean, you do run into people here."

"But then I followed you." Frank laughed briefly.

"Right, you did, and I was standing there waiting for that elevator, thinking: What is this guy going to *do* to me?" She laughed nervously, remembering it.

"You didn't show it."

"No? I bet I did. You didn't know me. Anyway, then the elevator stuck—"

"You didn't stop it somehow?"

"Heck no, how would I do that? I'm not some kind of a . . ."

"James Bond? James Bondette?"

She laughed. "It is *not* like that. It's just surveillance. Anyway there we were, and we started talking, and it didn't take long for me to see that you didn't know who I was, that you didn't know about being monitored. It was just a coincidence."

"But you said you knew I had followed you."

"That's right. I mean, it seemed like you had. But since you didn't know what I was doing, then it had to be, I don't know . . ."

"Because I liked the way you looked."

She nodded.

"Well, it's true," Frank said. "Sue me."

She squeezed his hand. "It's okay. I mean, I liked that. I'm in kind of a bad . . . Well anyway, I liked it. And I already liked you, see? I wasn't monitoring you very closely, but closely enough so that I knew some things about you. I—I had to monitor some of your calls. And I thought you were funny."

"Yes?"

"Yes. You are funny. At least I think so. Anyway, I'm sorry. I've never really had to think about what I do, not like this, not in terms of a person I talk to. I mean—how horrible it must sound."

"You spy on people."

"Yes. It's true. But I've never thought it's done anyone any harm. It's a way of looking out for people. Anyway, in this particular case, it meant that I knew you already. I liked you already. And there you were, so, you know . . . it meant you liked me too." She smiled crookedly. "That was okay too. Guys don't usually follow me around."

"Yeah right."

"They don't."

"Uh-huhn. The man who knew too little, watched by the spy who knew even less."

She laughed, pulled her hand away, punched him lightly on the arm. He caught her hand in his, pulled her to him. She leaned into his chest and he kissed the top of the head, as if to say, I forgive you your job, I forgive the surveillance. He breathed in the scent of her hair. Then she looked up, and they kissed, very briefly; then she pulled away. The shock of it passed through him, waking him up and making him happy. He remembered how it had been in the elevator; this wasn't like that, but he could tell she remembered it too.

"Yes," she said thoughtfully. "Then we did that. You're a handsome man. And I had figured out why you had followed me, and I felt—oh, I don't know. I *liked* you."

"Yes," Frank said, still remembering the elevator. Feeling the kiss. His skin was glowing.

She laughed again, looking off at her memories. "I worried afterward that you would think I was some kind of a loose woman, jumping you like I did. But at the time I just went for it."

"Yes you did," Frank said.

They laughed, then kissed again.

When they stopped she smiled to herself, pushed her hair off her forehead. "My," she murmured.

Frank tried to track one of the many thoughts skittering back into his head. "You said you were in a kind of a bad?"

"Ah. Yes. I did."

The corners of her mouth tightened. She pulled back a bit. Suddenly Frank saw that she was unhappy; and this was so unlike the impression he had gained of her in the elevator that he was shocked. He saw he did not know her, of course he did not know her. He had been thinking that he did, but it wasn't so. She was a stranger.

"What?" he said.

"I'm married."

"Ahh."

"And, you know. It's bad."

"Uh oh." But that was good, he thought.

"I . . . don't really want to talk about it. Please. But there it is. That's where I'm at."

"Okay. But . . . you're out here."

"I'm staying with friends tonight. They live nearby. As far as anyone knows, I'm sleeping on their couch. I left a note in case they get up, saying

I couldn't sleep and went out for a run. But they won't get up. Or even if they do, they won't check on me."

"Does your husband do surveillance too?"

"Oh yeah. He's much further up than I am."

"I see."

Frank didn't know what to say. It was bad news. The worst news of the night, worse than the fact that he was under surveillance. On the other hand, there she was beside him, and they had kissed.

"Please." She put a hand to his mouth, and he kissed her fingertips. He tried to swallow all his questions.

But some of these questions represented a change of subject, a move to safer ground. "So—tell me what you mean exactly when you say surveillance? What do you do?"

"There are different levels. For you, it's almost all documentary. Credit cards, phone bills, e-mail, computer files."

"Whoah."

"Well, hey. Think about it. Physical location too, sometimes. Although mostly that's at the cell phone records level. That isn't very precise. I mean, I know you're staying over off of Connecticut somewhere, but you don't have an address listed right now. So, maybe staying with someone else. That kind of stuff is obvious. If they wanted to, they could chip you. And your new van has a transponder, it's GPS-able."

"Shit."

"Everyone's is. Like transponders in airplanes. It's just a question of getting the code and locking on."

"My Lord."

Frank thought it over. There was so much information out there. If someone had access to it, they could find out a tremendous amount. "Does NSF know this kind of stuff is going on with their people?"

"No. This is a black-black."

"And your husband, he does what?"

"He's at a higher level."

"Uh oh."

"Yeah. But look, I don't want to talk about that now. Some other time."

"When?"

"I don't know. Some other time."

"When we meet again?"

She smiled wanly. "Yes. When we meet again. Right now," lighting up her watch and peering at it, "shit. I have to get back. My friends will be getting up soon. They go to work early."

"Okay . . . You'll be okay?"

"Oh yeah. Sure."

"And you'll call me again?"

"Yes. I'll need to pick my times. I need to have a clear space, and be able to call you from a clean phone. There's some protocols we can establish. We'll talk about it. We'll set things up. But now I've gotta go."

"Okay."

A peck of a kiss and she was off into the night.

He drove his van back to the edge of Rock Creek Park, sat in the driver's seat thinking. There was still an hour before dawn. For about half an hour it rained. The sound on the van's roof was like a steel drum with only two notes, both hit all the time.

Caroline. Married but unhappy. She had called him, she had kissed him. She knew him, in some sense; which was to say, she had him under surveillance. Some kind of security program based on the virtual wagers of some MIT computers, for Christ's sake. Perhaps that was not as bad as it first sounded. A pro forma exercise. As compared to a bad marriage. Sneaking out at three in the morning. It was hard to know what to feel.

With the first grays of dawn the rain stopped, and he got out and walked into the park. Bird calls of various kinds: cheeps, trills; then a night thrush, its little melodies so outrageous that at first they seemed beyond music, they were to human music as dreams were to art—stranger, bolder, wilder. Birds singing in the forest at dawn, singing, *The rain has stopped! The day is here! I am here! I love you! I am singing!*

It was still pretty dark, and when he came to the gorge overlook he pulled a little infrared scope he had bought out of his pocket, and had a look downstream to the waterhole. Big red bodies, shimmering in the blackness; they looked like some of the bigger antelopes to Frank, maybe the elands. Those might bring the jaguar out. A South American predator attacking African prey, as if the Atlantic had collapsed back to this narrow ravine and they were all in Gondwanaland together. Far in the distance he could hear the siamangs' dawn chorus, he assumed; they sounded very far away. Suddenly something inside his chest ballooned like a throat pouch, puffed with happiness, and to himself (to Caroline) he whispered, "ooooooooop! ooooooooop!"

He listened to the siamangs, and sang under his breath with them, and fitted his digital camera to the night scope to take some IR photos of the drinking animals for FOG. In the growing light he could see them now without the scope. Black on gray. He wondered if the same siamang or gibbon made the first call every morning. He wondered if its companions were lying on branches in comfort, annoyed to be awakened; or if sleeping in the branches was uncomfortable, and all of them thus ready and waiting to get up and move with the day. Maybe this differed with animal, or circumstance—as with people—so that sometimes they snoozed through those last precious moments, before the noise become so raucously operatic that no one could sleep through it. Even at a distance it was a thrilling sound; and now it was the song of meeting Caroline, and he quit trying not to spook the big ungulents at the waterhole and howled. "OOOOOOOOP! OooooooooOOOOOOOOP OOP! OOP!"

He felt flooded. He had never felt like this before, it was some new emotion, intense and wild. No excess of reason for him, not anymore! What would the guru say about this? Did the old man ever feel like this? Was this love, then, and him encountering it for the first time, not ever knowing before what it was? It was true she was married. But there were worse entanglements. It didn't sound like it was going to last. He could be patient. He would wait out the situation. He would have to wait for another call, after all.

Then he saw one of the gibbons or siamangs, across the ravine and upstream, swinging through branches. A small black shape, like a big cat but with very long arms. The classic monkey shape. He caught sight of white cheeks and knew that it was one of the gibbons. White-cheeked gibbons. The whoops had sounded miles away, but they might have been closer all along. In the forest it was hard to judge.

There were more of them, following the first. They flew through the trees like crazy trapeze artists, improvising every swing. Brachiation: amazing. Frank photographed them too, hoping the shots might help the FOG people get an ID. Brachiating through the trees, no plan or destination, just free-forming it through the branches. He wished he could join them and fly like Tarzan, but watching them he knew just what an impossible fantasy that was. Hominids had come down out of the trees, they were no longer arboreal. Tarzan was wrong, and even his treehouse was a throwback.

Upstream the three eland looked up at the disturbance, then continued to drink their fill. Frank stood on the overlook, happily singing his rising glissando of animal joy, "oooooooooop!"

And speaking of animals, there was a party at the reopened National Zoo, scheduled for later that very morning.

The National Zoo, perched as it was on a promontory overlooking a bend in the Rock Creek gorge, had been hammered by the great flood. Lipping over from the north, the surge had scoured a lot of the zoo's fencing and landscaping away. Fortunately most of the buildings and enclosures were made of heavy concrete, and where their foundations had not been under-cut, they had survived. The national park system had been able to fund repairs internally, and given that most of the released animals had survived the flood, and been rounded up afterward rather easily (indeed some had returned to the zoo site as soon as the water subsided), reopening had oc-curred rather quickly. The Friends of the National Zoo, numbering over two thousand now, had pitched in with their labor and their collective memory of the park, and the reconstructed version now opening to the public looked very like the original, except for a certain rawness.

The tiger and lion enclosure, at the southern end of the park, was a cir-cular island divided into four quadrants, separated by a moat and a high outer wall from the human observers. On this special morning the enclo-sure was visited by the Khembali legation, on hand for their swimming ti-gers' welcoming ceremony, so ironically interrupted by the flood. The Quiblers were there too, of course; one of the tigers had spent two nights in their basement, and now they felt a certain familial interest.

Anna enjoyed watching Joe as he stood in his backpack on Charlie's back, happy to be up where he could see properly, whacking Charlie on the sides of the head and shouting, "Tiger? Tiger?"

"Yes, tiger," Charlie agreed, trying blindly to catch the little fists pum-meling him. "Our tigers! Swimming tigers!"

A dense crowd surrounded them, oohing together when the door to the tiger's inner sanctum opened and the big cats strode out, glorious in the sun.

"Tiger! Tiger!"

The crowd cheered. The tigers ignored the commotion. They padded around on the washed grass, sniffing things. One marked the big tree in their quadrant, protected from claws if not from pee by a new wooden cladding, and the crowd said, "Ah." Nick explained to the people around him that these were Bengal tigers that had been washed out to sea in a big flood of the Brahmaputra, not the Ganges; also that they had survived by swimming together for an unknown period of time, and that the Brahmaputra's name changed to the Tsangpo after a dramatic bend upstream. Anna asked if the Ganges too hadn't been flooding at least a little bit. Joe jumped up and down in his backpack, nearly toppling forward over Charlie's head. Charlie listened to Nick, as did Frank Vanderwal, standing behind them.

Rudra Chakrin gave a small speech, translated by Drepung, thanking the zoo and all its people, and then the Quiblers.

"Tiger tiger tiger!"

Frank grinned at Joe's excitement. "Ooooop!" he cried, imitating the gibbons, which excited Joe even more. It seemed to Anna that Frank was in an unusually good mood. Some of the FONZies came by and gave him a big round button that said FOG on it, and he took another one from them and pinned it to Nick's shirt. Nick asked the volunteers a barrage of questions about the zoo animals still on the loose, at the same time eagerly perusing the FOG brochure they gave him. "Have any animals have gotten as far as Bethesda?"

Frank replied for the FONZies, allowing them to move on in their rounds. "They're finding smaller ones all over. They seem to be radiating out the tributary streams from Rock Creek. You can check the website and get all the latest sightings, and track the radio signals from the ones that have been tagged. When you join FOG, you can call in GPS locations for any ferals that you see."

"Cool! Can we go and look for some?"

"I hope so," Frank said. "That would be fun." He looked over at Anna and she nodded, feeling pleased. "We could make an expedition of it."

"Is Rock Creek Park open yet?"

"It is if you're in the FOG."

"Is it safe?" Anna asked.

"Sure. I mean there are parts of the gorge where the new walls are still unstable, but we would stay away from those. There's an overlook where you can see the torn-up part, and a new pond where a lot of them drink."

"Cool!"

The larger of the swimming tigers slouched down to the moat and tested the water with his huge paw.

"Tiger tiger tiger!"

The tiger looked up. He eyed Joe, tilted back his massive head, roared briefly in what had to be the lowest frequencies audible to humans, or even lower. It was a sound mostly felt in the stomach.

"Ooooooh," Joe said. The crowd said the same.

Frank was grinning with what Anna now thought of as his true smile. "Now that's a vocalization," he said.

Rudra Chakrin spoke for a while in Tibetan, and Drepung then translated.

"The tiger is a sacred animal, of course. He stands for courage. When we are at home, his name is not to be said aloud; that would be bad luck. Instead he is called King of the Mountain, or the Big Insect."

"The Big Insect?" Nick was incredulous. "That'd just make him mad!"

Frank laughed. "Hey, I'm going to go see if I can set the gibbons off. Nick, do you want to join me?"

"To do what?"

"I want to try to get the gibbons to sing."

"Oh, no thanks. I think I'll stay here and keep watching the tigers."

"Sure. You'll be able to hear the gibbons from here, if they do it."

Eventually the tigers flopped down in the morning shade and stared into space. The zoo people made speeches as the crowd dispersed. Some pretty vigorous whooping from the direction of the gibbons' enclosure nevertheless did not sound quite like the creatures themselves. After a while Frank rejoined them, shaking his head. "There's only one couple that's been recovered. The rest are out in the park. I've seen them, it's neat," he told Nick. "You'll like it."

Drepung came over. "Would you join our party in the visitors' center?" he asked Frank.

"Sure, thanks. My pleasure."

They walked up the zoo paths to a building near the entry. Drepung led the Quiblers and Frank to a room in back, and Rudra Cakrin guided them to seats around a round table. He came over and shook Frank's hand: "Hello, Frank. Welcome. Please to meet you. Please to sit. Eat food, drink tea."

Frank looked startled. "So you *do* speak English!"

The old man smiled. "Yes, very good English. Drepung make me take lessons."

Drepung rolled his eyes and shook his head. Padma and Sucandra joined them as they passed out sample cups of Tibetan tea. The cross-eyed expression on Nick's face when he smelled his cup gave Drepung a good laugh. "You don't have to try it," he assured the boy.

"It's like each ingredient has gone bad in a completely different way," Frank commented after a taste.

"Bad to begin with," Drepung said.

"Good!" Rudra exclaimed. "Good stuff."

He hunched forward to slurp at his cup. He did not much resemble the commanding figure who had given the lecture at NSF, Anna thought, which perhaps explained why Frank was regarding him so curiously.

"So you've been taking English lessons?" Frank said. "Or maybe it's like Charlie said? That you spoke English all along, but didn't want to tell us?"

"Charlie say that?"

"I was just joking," Charlie said.

"Charlie very funny."

"Yes . . . so you are taking lessons?"

"I am scientist. Study English like a bug."

"A scientist!"

"I am always scientist."

"Me too. But I thought you said, at your lecture, that rationality wasn't enough. That an excess of reason was a form of madness."

Rudra consulted with Drepung, then said, "Science is more than reason. More stronger." He elbowed Drepung, who elaborated:

"Rudra Cakrin uses a word for science that is something like devotion. A kind of devotion, he says. A way to honor, or worship."

"Worship what, though?"

Drepung asked Rudra, got a reply. "Whatever you find," he said. "*Devotion* is a better word than *worship*, maybe."

Rudra shook his head, looking frustrated by the limited palette of the English language. "You *watch*," he said in his gravelly voice, fixing Frank with a glare. "*Look*. If you can. Seems like healing."

He appealed again to Drepung. A quick exchange in Tibetan, then he forged on. "Look and heal, yes. Make better. Make worse, make better. For example, take a *walk*. Look *in*. In, out, around, down, up. Up and down. Over and under. Ha ha ha."

Drepung said, "Yes, his English lessons are coming right along."

Sucandra and Padma laughed at this, and Rudra scowled a mock scowl.

"He seldom sticks with one instructor for long," Padma said.

"Goes through them like tissues," Sucandra amplified.

The old man said to Frank, "You come to our home, please?"

"Thank you, my pleasure. I hear it's very close to NSF."

Rudra shook his head, said something in Tibetan.

Drepung said, "By home, he means Khembalung. We are planning a short trip there, and the rimpoche thinks you should join us. He thinks it would be a big instruction for you."

"I'm sure it would," Frank said, looking startled. "And I'd like to see it. I appreciate him thinking of me. But I don't know how it could work. I'm afraid I don't have much time to spare these days."

Drepung nodded. "True for all. The trip is to be short for this very reason. That is what makes it possible for the Quibler family also to join us."

Again Frank looked surprised.

Drepung said, "Yes, they are all coming. We plan two days to fly there, four days on Khembalung, two days to get back. Eight days away. But a very interesting week, I assure you."

"Isn't this monsoon season there?"

The Khembalis nodded solemnly. "But no monsoon this year, and the two previous. Big drought. Another reason to see."

Frank nodded, looked at Anna and Charlie: "So you're really going?"

Anna said, "I thought it would be good for the boys. But I can't be away from work for long."

"Or else her head will explode," Charlie said, raising a hand to deflect Anna's elbow from his ribs. "Just joking! Anyway," addressing her, "you can work on the plane and I'll watch Joe. I'll watch him the whole way."

"Deal," Anna said swiftly.

"Charlie very funny," Rudra said again.

Frank said, "Well, I'll think it over. It sounds interesting. And I appreciate the invitation," nodding to Rudra.

Sucandra raised his glass. "To Khembalung!"

"No!" Joe cried.

CHAPTER 13

BACK TO KHEMBALUNG

One Saturday Charlie was out on his own, as Joe was at home with Anna, Nick out with Frank tracking animals. After running some errands he browsed for a bit in Second Story Books, when a woman approached him and said, "Excuse me, can you tell me where I can find William Blake?"

Surprised to be taken for an employee (they were all twenty-five and wore black), Charlie stared blankly at her.

"He's a poet," the woman explained.

So, not only taken for a Second Story clerk, but for the kind who did not know who William Blake was. "Poetry's back there," he finally got out, gesturing weakly toward the rear of the store.

The woman slipped past him, shaking her head.

Tiger tiger burning bright! Charlie didn't say. Don't forget to check the oversized art books for facsimiles of his engravings! he didn't exclaim. In fact he's a lot better artist than poet I think you'll find! Most of his poetry is trippy gibberish, I think you'll find! he didn't shout.

His cell phone rang and he snatched it out of his pocket. "William Blake was out of his mind!"

"Hello, Charlie?"

"Oh hi Phil. Hey do I look to you like a person who doesn't know who William Blake was?"

"I don't know, do you?"

"Shit. You know, great arias are lost to the world because we do not speak our minds. Most of our best lines we never say."

"I don't have that problem."

"No, I guess you don't. So what's up?"

"I'm following up on our conversation at the Lincoln Memorial."

"Oh yeah, good! Are you going to go for it?"

"I think I will, yeah."

"Great! You've checked with your money people?"

"Yes, that looks like it will be okay. There are an awful lot of people who want a change."

"That's for sure. But . . . do you really think you can win?"

"Yes, I think so. The feedback has been positive. But . . ."

"But what?"

Phil sighed. "I'm worried about what effect it might have on me. I mean— power corrupts, right?"

"Yes, but you're already powerful."

"So it's already happened, yes, thank you for that. But it's supposed to get worse, right? Power corrupts, and absolute power corrupts absolutely? Was it William Blake who said that?"

"It was Lord Acton."

"Oh yeah. But he left out the corollary. Power corrupts, absolute power corrupts absolutely, and a little bit of power corrupts a little bit."

"I suppose that must be so."

"And everyone has a little bit of power."

"Yes, I suppose."

"So we're all a little bit corrupt."

"Hmm—"

"Come on, how does that not parse? It does parse. Power corrupts, and we all have power, so we're all corrupt. A perfect syllogism, if I'm not mistaken. And in fact the only people we think of as not being corrupt are usually powerless. Prisoners of conscience, the feeble-minded, the elderly, saints, children—"

"My children have power."

"Yes, but are they perfectly pure and innocent?"

Charlie thought of Joe, faking huge distress when Anna came home from work. "No, they're a little corrupt."

"Well there you go."

"I guess you're right. And saints have power but aren't corrupt, which is why we call them saints. But where does that leave us? That in this world of universal corruption, you might as well be president?"

"Exactly! That's what I was thinking."

"So then it's okay."

"Yes. But the sad part is that the corruption doesn't just happen to the people with power. It spreads from them. I know this is true because I see it. Every day people come to me because I've got some power, and I watch them debase themselves or go silly in some way. I see them go corrupt right before my eyes. It's depressing. It's like having the Midas touch in reverse, where everything you touch turns to shit."

"The solution is to become saintlike. Do like Lincoln. He had power, but he kept his integrity."

"Lincoln could see how limited his power was. Events were out of his control."

"That's true for us too."

"Right. Good thought. I'll try not to worry. But, you know. I'm going to need you guys. I'll need friends who will tell me the truth."

"We'll be there. We'll call you on everything."

"Good. I appreciate that. Because it's kind of a bizarre thing to be contemplating."

"I'm sure it is. But you might as well go for it. In for a penny in for a pound. And we need you."

"You'll help me with the environmental issues?"

"As always. I mean, I've got to take care of Joe, as you know. But I can always talk on the phone. I'm on call any time—oh for God's sake here she comes again. Look Phil I'd better get out of here before that lady comes to tell me that Abraham Lincoln was a president."

"Tell her he was a saint."

"Make him your patron saint and you'll be fine bye!"

"That's bye, Mr. President."

Under surveillance.

After he had come down from the euphoria of seeing Caroline, talking to her, kissing her, planning to meet again—Frank was faced with the unsettling reality of her news. Some group in government had him under surveillance.

A creepy thought. Not that he had done anything he needed to hide—except that he had. He had tried to sink a young colleague's grant proposal, in order to secure that work in a private company he had relations with. And the first part of the plan had worked. Not that that was likely to be what they were surveilling him for—but on the other hand, maybe it was. The connection to Pierzinski was apparently why they were interested in him. Evidence of what he had tried to do—would there be any? Nothing he had done was in contradiction to NSF panel protocols. However, among other actions he was now remembering, he had made many calls to Derek Gaspar, CEO of Torrey Pines Generique. In some of these he had perhaps been indiscreet.

Well, nothing could be done about that now.

Frank stared at his office computer. It was connected to the internet, of course. It had virus protections, firewalls, encryption codes; but for all he knew, there were programs more powerful still, capable of finessing all that and probing directly into his files. At the very least, all his e-mail. And then phone conversations, sure. Credit rating, sure, bank records, all other financial activity—all now data for analysis by some kind of virtual futures market trading in newly emerging ideas, technologies, researchers. All speculated on, as with any other commodity. People as commodities—well, it wouldn't be the first time.

He went out to a local cybercafé and paid cash to get on one of the house machines. Seating himself before it with a triple espresso, he looked around to see what he could find.

Old sites told the story of the Policy Analysis Market proposal, which had blown up in the face of DARPA some time before. John Poindexter, of Iran-Contra fame, had set up a futures market in which participants could bet on potential events, including possibilities like terrorist attacks and assassinations. Within a week Poindexter had been forced to resign, and DARPA had cut off all funds not just for PAM, but for all research into markets as predictive tools. There were protests about this from parties convinced markets could be powerful predictors, distilling as they did the collective information and wisdom of many people, all putting their money where their mouths were. Different people brought different expertise to the table, it was claimed, and the aggregated information was thought to be better able to predict future performance of the given commodity than any individual or single group could.

This struck Frank as bullshit, but certainly the market fetishists would not give up on such a core idea just because of a single public relations gaffe. And indeed, Frank quickly came on news of a program called ARDA, Advanced Research and Development Activity, which had become home to both the Total Information Awareness program and the ideas future market. ARDA had been funded as part of the "National Foreign Intelligence Program," which was part of an intelligence agency that had not been publicly identified. "Evidence Extraction," "Link Discovery," "Novel Intelligence from Massive Data": all kinds of data-mining projects had disappeared down this particular rabbit hole.

Before it left public view, the idea futures market had already been fine-tuned to deal with first iteration problems. "Conditional bidding" allowed participants to nuance their wagers by making them conditional on intermediary events. And—this jumped out at Frank as he read—"market makers" were added to the system, meaning automated bidders that were always available to trade, so that the market would stay liquid even when there were few participants. The first market maker programs had lost tremendous amounts of money, so their programmers had refined them to a point where they were able to compete successfully with live traders.

Bingo. Frank's algorithmic investors.

The idea futures market concept had then gone black, along with ARDA itself. Wherever it was now, it undoubtedly included these programs that could trade in the futures of researchers and their ideas, predicting which would prosper by using the collective pooling of information envisioned in the Total Information Awareness concept, which had dreamed of collating all the information everywhere in the datasphere.

So: virtual markets, with virtual participants, creating virtual results, tracked by real people in real security agencies. All part of the newly secure environment as envisioned in the Homeland Security acts. That these people had chosen a Nazi title for their enterprise was presumably more a tribute to their ignorance and stupidity than to any evil intent. Nevertheless it was not reassuring.

Briefly Frank wondered if he could learn enough to do some reverse transcription, and use this system against itself. Cascading recombinants were part of the algorithm family that both Frank and Yann Pierzinski studied, and possibly formulations could be designed to help such a project.

Frank almost called Edgardo, because among other factors, Edgardo had come to NSF from DARPA. DARPA was like NSF, in that it staffed itself mostly with visiting scientists, although DARPA stints were usually four years rather than one or two. Edgardo, however, had lasted only a year. He had never said much about why, only once remarking that his attitude had not been appreciated. Certainly his views on this surveillance matter would be extremely interesting—

But of course Frank couldn't call him. His cell phone might be bugged; Edgardo's too. Suddenly he recalled the worker who had visited his new office to install a power strip. Could a power strip include a splitter that would direct all data flowing through it in two directions? And include a mike and so on?

Probably so. He would have to talk to Edgardo in person, and in a private venue. He needed to know more. He wanted to talk to everyone implicated in this, including Yann Pierzinski—which meant Marta too—which would be hard, terrible in fact, but Marta had moved to Atlanta with Yann, and they lived together there, so there would be no avoiding her. And then Francesca Taolini, who had arranged for Yann's hire by a company she consulted for, in the same way Frank had hoped to. Did she suspect that Frank had been after Yann? Did she know how powerful Yann's algorithm might be?

He googled her. Turned out, among many interesting things, that she was helping to chair a conference at MIT coming soon, on bioinformatics and the environment. Just the kind of event Frank might attend. NSF even had a group going to it already, he saw, to talk about the new federal institutes.

Meet with her first, then go to Atlanta to meet with Yann—would that make his stock in the virtual market rise, triggering more intense surveillance? An unpleasant thought; he grimaced.

He couldn't evade this surveillance. He had to continue to behave as if it weren't happening. Or rather, treat his actions as experiments in the sensitivity of the surveillance. Visit Taolini and Pierzinski, sure, and see if that gave his stock a bump. Though he would need Caroline to find out anything about that.

He e-mailed the NSF travel office and had them book him flights to Boston and back. A day trip ought to do it.

Some mornings he woke to the sound of rain ticking onto his roof and the leaves. Dawn light, muted and wet; he lay in his sleeping bag watching grays turn silver. His roof extended far beyond the edges of his plywood floor. When he had all the lines and bungee cords right, the clear plastic quivered tautly in the wind, shedding myriad deltas of water. Looking up at it, Frank lay there comfortably, dry except for that ambient damp that came with rain no matter what one did. Same with all camping, really. But mostly dry; and there he was, high in the forest in the rain, encased in the splashing of a million drips, and the wet whoosh of wind in the branches, remaining dry and warm watching it all. Yes, he was an arboreal primate, lying on his foam pad half in his sleeping bag, looking through a bead curtain of water falling from the edge of his roof. A silvery green morning.

Often he heard the other arboreal primates greeting the day. These days they seemed to be sleeping on the steep slope across the creek from him. The first cry of the morning would fill the gorge, low and liquid at first, a strange cross between siren and voice. It never failed to send a shiver down his spine. That was something hardwired. No doubt the hominid brain included a musical capacity that was not the same as its language capacity. These days people tended to use their musical brains only for listening, thus missing the somatic experience of making it. With that part gone, the full potential of the experience was lost. "Oooooop!" Singing, howling; it all felt so good. "Ooooh-oooooooooooo-da."

Something else to consider writing about. Music as primate precursor to language. He would add it to his list of possible papers, already scores if not hundreds of titles long. He would never get to them, but they ought to be written.

He descended to the ground without getting very wet. Onto the forest floor, not yet squishy, out to his van, around the Beltway, making the first calls of the day over his headset. Stop in at Optimodal, singing under his breath, "Optimodal, optimodal!" Into the weight room, where, it being 6 A.M., Diane was working on one of the leg machines. Familiar hellos, a bit of chat. Shower, change, walk over to NSF with Diane. Amazing how quickly people developed sets of habits. They could not do without them, Frank had concluded. Even his improvised life was full of them. It might be said that now he had an array of habits that he chose from, a kind of menu. Up to his office, check phone messages and e-mail, get coffee, start on the messages that needed action, and the making of a daily "Things to Do" list out of the standing one on the whiteboard. Bit of breakfast when his stomach reminded him it was being neglected.

One of his Things to Do was to attend another of Diane's meetings, this one attended by division heads, including Anna. Diane had been busy organizing her sense of the climate problem, structuring it in the broadest terms possible.

First, however, she had some good news to share: the appropriations committees in Congress had streamlined approval of two billion dollars for NSF to engage with climate issues as soon as possible. "They want us to take action, they said, but in a strictly scientific manner."

Edgardo snorted. "They want a silver bullet. Some kind of technical fix that will make the problem go away without any suffering on Wall Street."

"That doesn't matter," Diane said. "They're funding us, and we'll be making the determinations as to what might work."

She clicked to the first of her PowerPoint pages. "Okay. You can divide the problem into land, ocean, and atmosphere. On land, we have drought, loss of topsoil, desertification, and flooding. In the oceans, we have sea level rise, either slow because of general warming, or else fast, as a result of the West Antarctic ice sheet detaching. Probability of that one is very hard to calculate. Then also thermohaline circulation, in particular the North Atlantic stall. Also fisheries depletion, also coral reef loss. The oceans are more trouble than we're used to thinking. In the atmosphere, carbon dioxide buildup, also methane."

She clicked to the next slide. "Let's start with atmosphere, particularly the carbon dioxide. Now up to 450 parts per million, from 280 before the industrial revolution. Clearly, we need to slow down how much CO_2 we're putting into the atmosphere. What's putting carbon in the atmosphere? Mostly energy production and transport. So, we need cleaner cars and trucks and ships, and cleaner energy production. There's been a lot of work done on both fronts, but bottom line, the carbon and car industries are very big, and they work together to obstruct research and development of cleaner technologies. Partly because of their lobbying here in D.C., research into cleaner technologies is underfunded, even though some are ready to go, and could make a difference very rapidly.

"So. Given this situation, I think we have to identify the two or three most promising options in each big carbon area, and immediately support these options in a major way. Pilot projects, maybe competitions with prizes, certainly suggested tax structures and incentives to get private enterprise investing in it."

"Make carbon credits really expensive," Frank said.

"Make *gas* really expensive," Edgardo said.

"Yes. These are more purely economic or political fixes. We will run into political resistance on those."

"You'll run into political resistance on all these fronts."

"Yes. But we have to work for everything that looks like it will help."

Diane clicked to her next slide. "The system with the most potential is solar power, but that's already well understood. Less so is carbon capture and sequestering, and here we might help find ways to draw down some of the CO_2 already in the atmosphere. There are proven means to do this, but anything we could afford to build is too small. If anything's going to work, it almost certainly will have to use biological elements. The most obvious method here is to grow more plants. The other biological method suggested would involve some hypothetical engineered living system taking more carbon out of the atmosphere than it does now. This brings biotech into the game, and it could be crucial. It might create the possibility of drawdown working fast enough to help us."

For a while they discussed the logistics of initiating all the efforts Diane had sketched out so far, and then Anna took over the PowerPoint screen.

She said, "Another carbon sequestration, in effect, would be to *not* burn carbon that we would have using current practices. Meaning conservation. It could make a huge difference. Since the United States is the only country living at American consumption levels, if we consumed less, it would significantly reduce world levels."

She clicked to a slide titled CARBON VALUES. It consisted of a list of phrases:

* conservation, preservation (fuel efficiency, carbon taxes)
* voluntary simplicity
* stewardship, right action (religion)
* sustainability, permaculture
* leaving healthy support system for the subsequent generations

Edgardo was shaking his head. "This voluntary simplicity is not going to work. Not only are we fond of our comforts and toys, and lazy, but there is a hundred-billion-dollar-a-year industry fighting any such change, called advertising."

Anna said, "Maybe we could hire an advertising firm to design a series of voluntary simplicity ads, to be aired on certain cable channels."

Edgardo grinned. "Yes, I would enjoy to see that, but there is a ten-trillion-a-year economy that also wants more consumption. It's like we're working within the body of a cancerous tumor. It's hopeless, really. We will simply charge over the cliff like lemmings."

"Real lemmings don't run off cliffs," Anna quibbled. "People might change. People change all the time. It just depends on what they want."

She had been looking into this matter, which she jokingly called macro-bioinformatics: researching, refining, and even inventing various rubrics by which people could evaluate their consumption levels quantitatively, with the idea that if they saw exactly what they were wasting, they would cut back and save money. The best known of these rubrics, as she explained, were the various "ecological footprint" measurements. These had been originally designed for towns and countries, but Anna had worked out methods for households as well, and now she passed around a chart illustrating one method.

"The whole thing should be translated into money values at every step," Edgardo suggested. "Put it the way everyone in this culture can understand, the cost in dollars and cents. Forget the acreage stuff. People don't know what an acre is anymore, or what you can expect to extract from it."

"Education, good," Diane said. "That's already part of our task as defined. And it will help to get the kids into it."

Edgardo cackled. "Okay, maybe they will go for it, but also the economists should be trying to invent an honest accounting system that doesn't keep exteriorizing costs. When you exteriorize costs onto future generations you can make any damn thing profitable, but it isn't really true. I warn you, this will be one of the hardest things we might try. Economics is incorrigible. They call it the dismal science but actually it's the happy religion."

Frank tended to agree with Edgardo's skepticism about these kinds of social interventions; and his own interests lay in the category Diane labeled "Mitigation Projects." Now she took back the PowerPoint and clicked to a list which included several of the suggestions Frank had made to her earlier:

1. establish national institutes for the study of abrupt climate change and its mitigation, analogous to Germany's Max Planck Institutes;

2. establish grants and competitions designed to identify and fund mitigation work judged crucial by NSF;

3. review the already existing federal agencies to find potentially helpful projects, and coordinate them.

All good, but it was the next slide, "Remedial Action Now," that was most interesting to Frank. One of the obvious places to start here was the thermohaline circulation stall. Diane had gotten a complete report from Kenzo, and her tentative conclusion was that the great world current, though huge, could be sensitive to small perturbations—which meant it might respond to small interventions, if they could be directed well.

So, Diane concluded, this had to be investigated. How big a sea surface was critical to downwelling? How precisely could they pinpoint down-welling sites? How big a volume of water were they talking about? If they needed to make it saltier in order to force it to start sinking again, how much salt were they talking about? Could they start new downwellings where they used to happen?

Kenzo's eyes were round. He met Frank's gaze, waggled his eyebrows like Groucho. Pretty interesting stuff!

"We have to do something," Diane concluded, without glancing at Frank. He thought: She's been convinced. I was part of that. "The Gulf Stream is an obvious place to look at remediation, but there are lots of other ideas for direct intervention, and they need to be evaluated and prioritized accord-ing to various criteria—cost, effectiveness, speed, all that."

Edgardo grinned. "So—we are going to become global biosphere man-agers. We are going to terraform the Earth!"

"We already are," Diane replied. "The problem is we don't know how."

Sometimes in the afternoons, after talking for an hour with the UNEP officer to plan tidal energy capture, then speaking to people in an engineering consortium about cheap efficient photovoltaics, Frank would grow dizzy at the touch of the technological sublime, feeling that if they could enact all that they knew, it would go a long way toward averting catastrophe. It was hard to tell; so much was happening that any description of the situation had some truth in it, from "desperate crisis, extinction event totally ignored" to "minor problems robustly dealt with." It was necessary to forge on in ignorance of the totality. But in Frank's mind, science began to look like a pack on the move, big shadowy figures loping across the cave wall into the fray.

So he did his part, and then his watch alarm would go off, surprising him again, and it was off into the green end of the day, livid and perspiring. These summer days usually cooled off a little in the last hour before dark. The sun disappeared into the forest, and then, in the remaining hour of light, if Frank had managed to get over to Rock Creek Park, he would join the frisbee golfers, and run through the shadows throwing a disk and chasing it. Frank loved the steeplechase aspect of it, and the way it made him feel afterward. The things it taught him about himself: once he was running full tilt and a stride came down on a concealed hole with only his toes catching the far side, but by the time he was aware of that, his foot and leg had stiffened enough that he had already pushed off using only the toes. How had he done that? No warning, instant reaction—how had there been time? In a thousandth of a second his body had sensed the absence of ground, stiffened the appropriate muscles by the appropriate amount, and launched into an improvised solution, giving him about the same velocity as a normal stride.

Things like this happened all the time. So just how fast *was* the brain? It appeared to be almost inconceivably fast, and in those split seconds, extremely creative and decisive. Indeed, running steeplechase and watching what his body did, especially after unforeseen problems were solved, Frank had to conclude that he was the inadvertent jailer of a mute genius. His running foot would come down on nothing at all, he would fly forward in a tuck and roll, somersault back to his feet and run on as if he had practiced the move for years, only better—how could it be? Who did that?

Eleven million bits of data per second were taken in at the sensory endings of the nervous system, he read. In each second all these incoming data were scanned, categorized, judged for danger, prioritized, and reacted to, all continuously, second after second; and at the same time his unconscious brain did all that, in his conscious mentation he could be singing with the birds, or focusing on a throw, or thinking about what it meant to be under surveillance. Parallel processing in the parcellated mind, at speeds ranging from nearly instantaneous to months and years, if not decades.

So he played on, in a kind of ecstatic state. There was some quality to the game that seemed to transcend sports as he had known them; not even climbing resembled it. Surely it was closely analogous to the hominid hunting-and-gathering experience that was central to the emergence of humanity. As Frank ran the park with the guys, he sometimes thought about how it might have gone: I throw. I throw the rock. I throw the rock at the rabbit. I throw the rock at the rabbit in order to kill it. If I kill the rabbit I will eat it. I am hungry. If I throw well, I will not be hungry. A rock of fist size was thrown *just so* (the first scientist). It hit the rabbit in the leg but the rabbit ran away. When a rock hits a rabbit in the head it will usually stop. Hypothesis! Test it again!

The players collapsed at the end, sat around the final hole puffing.

"Forty-two minutes," Robert read from his watch. "Pretty good."

"We were made to do this," Frank said. "We evolved to do this."

The others merely nodded.

"*We* don't do it," Robin said. "The gods do it through us."

"Robin is pre-breakdown of the bicameral mind."

"Frisbee is Robin's religion."

"Well of course," Robin said.

"Oh come on," Spencer scolded, "it's bigger than that."

Frank laughed with the others.

"It is," Spencer insisted. "Bigger and older."

"Older than religion?" Frank asked.

"Older than *humanity*. Older than *Homo sapiens*."

Frank stared at Spencer, surprised by this chiming with his evolutionary musings. "How do you mean?"

Spencer grabbed his gold disk by its edge. "There's a prehistoric tool called the Acheulian hand axe. They were made for hundreds of thousands of years without any changes in design. Half a million years! That makes it a lot older than *Homo sapiens*. And the thing is, the archeologists named them hand axes without really knowing what they were. They don't actually look like they would make good hand axes."

"How so?" Frank said.

"They're sharpened all the way around, so where are you going to hold the thing? There isn't a good place to hold it if you hit things with it. So it couldn't have been a hand axe. And yet there are millions of them in Africa and Europe."

"Bifaces," Frank said, looking at his golf disk and remembering illustrations in articles he had read. "But they weren't round."

"No, but almost. And they're flat, that's the main thing. If you were to throw one, it would fly like a frisbee."

"You couldn't kill anything very big."

"You could kill small things. And this guy Calvin says you could spook bigger animals."

"Hobbes doesn't agree," Robert put in.

"No *really*!" Spencer cried, grinning. "This is a *real theory*, this is what archeologists are saying about these things. They call it the killer frisbee theory."

The others laughed.

"But it's *true*," Spencer insisted, whipping his dreads side to side. "It's *obviously* true. You can *feel* it when you throw."

"You can, Rasta man."

"*Everyone* can!" He appealed to Frank: "Am I right?"

"You are right," Frank said, still laughing at the idea. "I sort of remember that killer frisbee theory. I'm not sure it ever got very far."

"So? Scientists are not good at accepting new theories."

"Well, they like evidence before they do that."

"Some things are just too obvious! You can't be throwing out a theory just because people think frisbees are some kind of hippie thing."

"Which they are," Robert pointed out.

Frank said, "No. You're right." Still, he had to laugh; listening to Spencer was like seeing himself in a funhouse mirror, hearing one of his theories being parodied by an expert mimic. The wild glee in Spencer's blue eyes suggested there was some truth to this interpretation. Frank would have to be more careful in what he said to these guys.

But the facts of the situation remained, and could not be ignored. His unconscious mind, his deep mind, was at that very moment humming happily through all its parcellations. It was a total response. Deep inside lay an ancient ability to throw things at things, and that ability was waiting patiently for its moment of redeployment.

"That was good," he said as he got up to leave.

"Google Acheulian hand axes," Spencer said. "You'll see."

The next day Frank did that, and found it was pretty much as Spencer had said. Certain anthropologists had proposed that the rapid evolutionary growth of the human brain was caused by the calculations necessary for throwing things at a target; and a subset of these considered the bifaced hand axes to be their projectiles of choice, "killer frisbees," as one William Calvin indeed called them. Used to stampede animals at waterholes, he claimed, after which the hominids pounced on animals knocked over in the rush. The increase in predictive power needed to throw rocks accurately had led to the brain's growth.

Frank still had to laugh, despite his will to believe. As one of the editors of *The Journal of Sociobiology*, he had seen a lot of crazy theories explaining hominid evolution, and he recognized immediately that this was one to add to the list. But so what? It was as plausible as most of them, and given his recent experiences in the park, more convincing than many.

He stared at a website photo of a hand axe as he thought about his life in the park. He had written commentaries for the *Journal* suggesting that people would be healthier if they lived more like their paleolithic ancestors had. Not that they should starve themselves from time to time, or needed to kill all the meat they ate—just that incorporating more paleolithic behaviors might increase health and well-being. After all, a fairly well-identified set of behaviors, repeated for many generations, had changed their ancestors a great deal; had created the species *Homo sapiens*; had blown their brains up like balloons. Surely these were behaviors most likely to lead to well-being now. And to the extent they neglected these behaviors, and sat around inside boxes as if they were nothing but brains and fingertips, the unhealthier and unhappier they would be.

Frank clicked to a draft he had once made for this commentary, and found its list of all the paleolithic behaviors anthropologists had ever proposed as a stimulant to the great brain expansion. How many of these behaviors was he performing now?

* talking (he talked much of the day)
* walking upright (he hiked a lot in the park)
* running (he ran at lunch and with the frisbee guys)
* dancing (he seldom danced, but he did sometimes skip along the park trails while vocalizing)
* singing ("Ooooooooooop!")
* stalking animals (he tracked the ferals in the park for FOG)
* throwing things at things (he threw his frisbees at the baskets)
* looking at fire (he looked at the bros' awful fire)
* having sex (well, he was trying. And Caroline had kissed him)
* dealing with the opposite sex more generally (Caroline, Diane, Marta, Anna, Laveta, etc.)
* cooking and eating the paleolithic diet (research this; hard to cook these days, but not impossible)

* gathering plants to eat (he did not do that; must consider)
* killing animals for food (he did not want to do that, but frisbee
  golf was the surrogate)
* experiencing terror (he did not want to do that either)

It appeared by these criteria that he was living a pretty healthy life. The paleolithic pleasures, plus modern dental care; what could be nicer? Optimodal in the best possible sense.

He went back to the Acheulian hand axe link list, and checked out a commercial site called Montana Artifacts. It turned out that this site offered for sale an Acheulian axe found near Madrid, dated at between 200,000 and 400,000 years old. "Classic teardrop shaped of a fine textured gray quartzite. The surface has taken a smooth lustrous polish on the exposed faces. Superb specimen." One hundred and ninety-five dollars. With a few taps on his keyboard Frank bought it.

Primates in airplanes. Aack!

Flying now made Frank a little nervous. He gripped his seat arms, reminded himself of the realities of risk assessment, fell asleep. He woke when they started descending toward Logan. Landing on water, whoah—but no. The runway showed up in the nick of time, as always.

Then into Boston, a city Frank liked. Over to the conference at MIT.

Quickly Frank saw that getting an opportunity to talk in private with Dr. Taolini would be hard. She had helped organize the event, and was much in demand. The one time Frank saw her alone, in the hall before her presentation, she was talking on her phone.

But she saw him and waved him over, quickly ending her call. "Hello, Frank. I didn't know you were going to be here."

"I decided to come at the last minute."

"Good, good. You're going to tell us about these new institutes?"

"That's right. But I'd like to talk to you one-on-one about them, if you have the time. I know you're busy."

"Yes, but let's see . . ." checking her phone's calendar. "Can you meet me at the end of my talk?"

"Sure, I'm going to be there anyway."

"That's very nice."

Her talk was on algorithms for reading the genomes of methanogens. She spoke rapidly and emphatically, very used to the limelight: a star, even at MIT, which tended to be an all-star team. Stylish in a gray silk dress, black hair cut at shoulder length, framing a narrow face with distinct, even-chiseled features. Big brown eyes under thick black eyebrows, roving the audience between slides, conveying a powerful impression of intelligence and vivacity.

After her talk many people, mostly men, clustered around her with what seemed to Frank a more-than-scientific interest. Turning to answer a question she saw him and smiled. "I'll be just a minute." Tiny rush of pleasure at that; ha ha, I get to take the beauty away, ooooop!

Her voice was low and scratchy, indeed it would be nasal if it weren't so low. A kind of oboe or bassoon sound, very attractive. Some kind of accent, maybe Boston Italian, but so faint it was impossible for Frank to identify.

Then the others had been dealt with, and he was the only one left. He smiled awkwardly, feeling alert and on edge.

"Nice talk."

"Oh thanks. Shall we go outside? I could use some coffee."

"Sure, that would be nice."

They walked out into the bright sunlight on the Charles. Francesca suggested a kiosk on the other side of the Mass. Ave. bridge, and Frank followed her happily; Boston's river was full of light, open to the wind.

They talked about the dedicated institutes NSF was planning, and Francesca said she had done a postdoc at the Max Planck in Bremen and been impressed. Then they reached the kiosk, bought lattes and scones, walked back onto the bridge. Frank stopped to look at a women's eight, sculling underneath them like a big water bug. He would have liked to linger, but Francesca shivered.

"I get cold out here," she said. "It's like Byrd said—the coldest he ever got was on the bridges over the Charles."

"Byrd the polar explorer?"

"Yes. My husband did work on the Greenland ice cores, and he likes to read the polar classics. He told me Byrd said that, because I was always complaining about how cold I get."

"Well okay, back to land then."

"There's some benches in the sun just over there." She pointed.

They sat on a bench looking out at the river, eating their scones and talking. She was a beautiful woman. Frank had not fully noticed this during the panel meeting at NSF. Black tangled curls framing sharp Mediterranean features; neat in-tilting teeth; all of a piece, stylish and intelligent. If you were to play the game of choosing which movie star should play her, you'd have to go right to one of the ultimate Italian exotics, like Sophia Loren or Claudia Cardinale.

A joy even to watch her eat; and at this observation Frank could not help remembering a paper on human female sexual attractiveness which had argued that even facial beauty gave signs of reproductive prowess, symmetry revealing undamaged DNA, widely spaced eyes meaning good eyesight, and prominent cheekbones and a gracile jaw indicating "masticatory efficiency"—at which point in Frank's reading of the paper, Anna had looked in his door to see why he was laughing so hard.

"If you can chew your food well, it's sexy!" he had informed her, and handed her the article while he continued to chortle convulsively. Sociobiology could be so stupid! Anna too had laughed, her gorgeous mirth pealing through the halls.

Frank grinned again thinking of it, watching Francesca sip her latte. No doubt she masticated very efficiently. And had legs fast enough to escape predators, hips wide enough to give birth safely, mammary glands generous enough to feed infants, yes, sure, she had quite a figure, as far as one could tell under her dress—and of course one could tell pretty damn well. She would certainly have many successful offspring, and therefore was beautiful. All so much crap! No *reductio ad absurdum* was more absurd. There was something else going on here, something that did not have to do with adaptation.

"Yes, it's very busy," she was saying between mastications, in response to a question he didn't remember asking; she appeared to be unaware of his train of thought, but maybe not; he might be staring. "It works out—usually—but it feels so crazy. I don't know how, but"—swallow—"things just seem to get busier."

Frank nodded. "It's true," he said. "Even for me, and I'm not married."

She grinned. "But that can make you even busier, right?" Leaning into his shoulder slightly with hers, giving him a conspiratorial bump.

Startled, Frank had to agree. There were lots of ways to be busy, he said, and his days were very full. She sipped her latte, looking relaxed and somehow pleased. Not flirtatious, but expansive. She could do what she wanted; what man was going to object? She licked coffee from her upper lip, neat pink tongue like a cat's. For sure the symmetry-as-beauty hypothesis was wrong; Frank had a tendency to zero in on the asymmetries in other people's faces, and he had often noted how it was precisely the asymmetry that drew or hooked the eye, that tugged at it like a magnet. As now, seeing the way Francesca's sharp nose tilted very slightly to the left then back. Magnetic.

Of course he was envious of her too. Lab, tenure, home, partner, children: she had it all. And seemed relaxed and happy, despite her talk about the crazy pace. Fulfilled. As Frank's mom would have said, in one of her most annoying formulations, "she has it all put together, doesn't she?" At this point in his life Frank doubted that anybody on Earth "had it all put together" in the way his mom meant. But if anyone did, this woman might.

So: Frank chatted on happily, full of admiration, respect, envy, doubt, resentment, suspicion, and a lust that was perhaps transitory but nevertheless real. He had to mask that part. She would be used to seeing it in men, no doubt. Nonconscious regions of the mind were very sensitive to that.

He would also have to be very circumspect when it came to inquiring about her business affairs. This was one way of characterizing what he had come up to do, and as she was done with her scone, and no doubt would soon suggest returning to her duties, now was the time.

But it was a subject that scientists did not often discuss at academic meetings, as it was too much like prying into matters of personal income. How are you turning your scientific work into money? How much do you make? These questions weren't asked.

He tried a roundabout course. "Is the teaching load heavy here?"

It was.

"Do you have any administrative duties?"

She did.

"And you do some consulting too, I think you said?"

"Yes," she said, looking slightly surprised, as she had not said any such thing. "Just a little. It doesn't take much time. A company in London, another in Atlanta."

Frank nodded. "I used to do some of that in San Diego. The biotechs can use all the help they can get. Although they seem to have a hard time turning lab results into products. Like the stuff we evaluated on that panel last fall."

"Right, that was interesting."

This was likely to be mere politeness talking. But then she glanced at him, went on: "I saw one proposal there that I thought was a good one, that the panel ended up turning down."

"Yes?"

"Yes. By a Yann Pierzinski."

"Oh yes. I remember. That was a good one. I was the outside member of his doctoral committee at Caltech. He does really interesting work."

"Yes," she said. "But the panel didn't agree."

"No, I was surprised at that."

"Me too. So when Small Delivery told me they were looking for a bio-mathematician, I recommended him."

"Oh, is that what happened."

"Yes."

Her irises were a kind of mahogany color, speckled with lighter browns. Was this the face of what science could become, so vivacious and sophisticated?

"Well," he said carefully, "good for him. I liked his proposal too."

"You didn't seem to at the time."

"Well—I was on his doctoral committee. And I try not to be one of the evaluators in my panels anyway."

"No?"

"No. I just run the panel. I don't want to sway anyone."

"Then you must have to be careful which proposals you assign to Stuart Thornton," she said with a brief ironic smile.

"Oh I don't know!" he said defensively, startled. "Do you think so?"

"Hmm." She watched him.

"I guess I know what you mean. It was probably a mistake to invite him on the panel at all. But, you know." He waved a hand: people legitimately on the cutting edge deserved to be asked, no matter their personalities.

She frowned very slightly, as if she did not agree, or did not like him pretending she did not know what he had done.

Frank forged on. "Anyway it sounds like Yann ended up all right, thanks to you."

"Yes. Hopefully so." She sipped her latte. Her fingers were long, her fingernails polished with a clear gloss. A thin wedding band was the only jewelry she wore. Frank looked down, unwilling to meet her sharp gaze. Her shoes were open-toed, her toenails colored pink. Frank had always considered toenail polish to be a kind of intelligence test that its users had embarrassingly and publicly failed; but here was Dr. Taolini, tenured at MIT, a member of National Academy of Sciences, exposing pink toenails to the world. He would have to rethink some of his opinions.

"Still," he said tentatively, "even though Yann ended up all right, I'd like to get him into one of these new institutes."

"Maybe you can," she said. "Multiple appointments aren't that unusual anymore."

"In academia, anyway. Do you think his contract would allow for that kind of thing?"

She shrugged, made a little gesture of her own: how should I know?

He had learned what he was going to learn about her connection to Yann. Pressing further would look weird. She basked in the windy sun, would soon want to go back in to the conference.

He could ask her outright if she knew anything about the surveillance. He could share what he knew. It was another prisoner's dilemma: they both knew things the other could probably benefit from knowing, but it was a risk to bring them up; the other might defect. The safest thing was to defect preemptively. But Frank wanted to try the more generous strategies these days, and so he wanted to tell her: we're being watched by Homeland Security, in a surveillance clustered around Pierzinski. Did you know? Why do you think it's happening?

But then she could very justifiably ask, how do you know? And then he would be stuck. He could not say, because I've fallen in love with a spook who kissed me in an elevator, who told me all about it. That just wasn't something he wanted to say to this woman.

Although in another way he did. It would be great to be close enough to this person to confide in her. She might laugh, might lean into his shoulder again, to draw out more of the tale.

But in fact he wasn't that close to her. So he couldn't talk about it.

A different approach occurred to him. "I'm getting interested in finding algorithms or other rubrics for sorting through the various climate proposals we've gotten, to see if some are worth jumping on right now. Ways of checking not only the physical possibilities, which is the easy part in some senses, but also the economic and political viability of the plans."

"Yes?" she said, interested.

"I read about something I think came out of MIT, of course there's a million things coming out of MIT, but maybe you've heard of this one, a kind of ideas futures market? You gather a group of stakeholders, and sort the ideas by how much money people are willing to risk on them?"

"Yes, do you mean that simulation program for market makers?"

"Yes," Frank said. "I guess so."

She said, "I heard about it. To me it sounds like one of those situations where simulation misses the point. You might need real experts risking real money, to get the kind of feedback a futures market is supposed to give you."

"Yes, I wondered about that myself."

"So, I don't know. You should talk to Angelo Stavros."

"What department?" Frank said, getting out his phone to tap it in; then suddenly he recalled that his phone might be fully surveiled.

"Economics—but what is it?" She was watching him closely now, and he couldn't be sure if she knew more about the idea futures market or not.

"I was just thinking you're probably right. In the end it's going to take the usual analysis of the options, like we've always done before."

"Another panel, you mean."

"Yes," he laughed ruefully, "I suppose so."

Her smile was suddenly wicked, and over it her eyes blazed, they *italicized* her words: "Better not invite Thornton."

He walked the shore of the Charles, enjoying the wind ruffling the water.

So. Francesca Taolini appeared to have guessed what he had tried to do on that panel. Maybe putting Thornton on a panel was too blatant, like throwing a rock—thus drawing her attention, perhaps even sparking an extra interest in Pierzinski's proposal.

This realization was a shock, small but profound, like her bump of shoulder to shoulder. Balance thrown off. Presumably it would come back after a while. Meanwhile a shudder, an itch, an ache. In short, *desire*.

He found he was again a seer of beauty in women. On the river path in Boston this beauty was mostly expressed as youth and intelligence. That made sense; in this city there were sixty degree-giving institutions, some three hundred thousand college students; that meant a surplus of at least 150,000 more nubile young women than ordinary demographics would suggest. Maybe that was why men stayed in Boston when their college years were over, maybe that explained why they were so intellectually hyperactive, so frustrated, so alcoholic, such terrible drivers. It all seemed right to Frank. He was full of yearning, and the women on the river walk were all goddesses set loose in the sun. The image of Francesca Taolini even somehow made him angry; she had flirted with him casually, toyed with him. He wanted his Caroline to call him again, he wanted to kiss her and more. He *wanted* her.

Back in Rock Creek Park it was not like that. Frank hiked in to the picnic tables late that night, and Zeno saw him and bellowed, "Hey it's the Professor! Hey, wanna buy a fuck? She'll do it for five dollars!"

The guys jeered at this, while the woman sitting in their midst rolled her eyes and continued to knit. She'd heard it all before. Blond, square, stoical; Zeno and the rest were in fact pleased to have her there, they just showed it in stupid ways.

"No thank you," Frank said, and pulled a six-pack from a grocery bag to stop Zeno's foolery before it went any further.

The woman shook her head when offered a beer. "Day sixty-five," she said to Frank with a brief gap-toothed smile. "Day sixty-five, and here I am still hanging out with these bozos."

"Yarrr!" they cheered.

"Congratulations," Frank said.

"On what," Zeno quipped, "staying sober, or hanging with us?"

High humor in the park.

There were very few women to be seen out there, Frank thought as he sat at her table; those who did seemed sad drabs, just barely getting by. Homelessness was hard on anyone, but seemed to damage women more. They could not pretend it was some kind of adventure.

And yet the economy insisted on a minimum of 5.4 percent unemployment, to create the proper "wage pressure." Millions of people who wanted jobs went unhired and therefore couldn't afford a home, therefore suffered from "food insecurity," so that businesses could keep wages low. These people.

Unlike Frank. He was a dilettante here, dabbling, slumming. Choice made all the difference. He could have found a place to rent, he could have afforded a deposit and moved in. Instead he hung out tinkering with their crappy fire, then playing chess with Chessman, losing four games but making the last of them a real donnybrook. And when Chessman departed with his twenty, Frank got up and hiked into the night, made sure no one was following, went to his tree, called down Miss Piggy, and climbed up into his treehouse, there to lie down on the best bed in the world, and read by the light of his Coleman lantern, in the clatter of the wind in the leaves. Let the wind blow the world out of his hair. Rockabye baby, in the treetop. It was a relief to be there after the strangeness of the day.

Was curly hair adaptive? Tangled curls, black as a crow's wing?

He wanted her.

Damn it anyway. Sociobiology was a bad habit you could never get rid of. Once it invaded your thoughts it was hard to forget that humans beings were apes, with desires shaped by life on the savannah, so that every move in lab or boardroom became clearly a shove for food or sex, every verbal put-down from a male boss like the back of the hand from some hairy silverback, every flirt and dismissal from a woman like the head-turning-aside baboon, refusing acknowledgment, saying, You don't get to fuck me and if you try my sisters will beat you up; and every acquiescence was like the babs who accidentally had their pink butts stuck out when you went by, saying, I'm in estrus you can fuck me if you want, shouldering you companionably or staring off into space as if bored—

But the problem was, thinking of interactions with other people in this way was not actually *helpful*. For one thing it could often reduce him to speechlessness. Like at the gym for instance, my Lord if that was not the savannah he didn't know what was—and if that was the primal discourse, then he'd rather pass, thank you very much, and be a solitary. He was too inhibited to just lay it out there, and too honest to try to say it in euphemistic code. He was too self-conscious. He was too chicken. There was an awesome power in sex, he wanted it to go right. He wanted it to be part of a whole monogamy. He wanted love to be real. Science could go fuck itself!

Or: become useful. Become a help, for God's sake. It was the same in his personal life as it was for the world at large; if science wasn't helping then it was a sterile waste of time. It had to help or it was all for naught, and the world still nothing but a miserable fuckup. And him too.

The party traveling to Khembalung had grown to ten: the Quiblers and Frank, Drepung, Sucandra, Padma, and Rudra Cakrin, and the Khembali woman Qang, who ran the embassy's big house in Arlington.

Dulles to L.A. to Tokyo to Bangkok to Calcutta to Khembalung; for two days they lived in long vibrating rooms in the air, taking short breaks in big rooms on the ground. They ate meals, watched movies, went to the bathroom, and slept. In theory it should have been somewhat like a rainy weekend at home.

However, Charlie thought, a rainy weekend at the Quibler house could be a pain in the ass. It was not a good idea to confine Joe for that long. At home they would find ways for him to let off some steam. Here that was not an option.

They had flown business class, courtesy of the Khembalis, which gave them more room, though Anna could not help being concerned about the expense. Charlie told her not to worry about it, but she knew the Khembali budget and Charlie didn't. She never found it reassuring when someone who knew less about a situation than she did told her not to worry about it.

On the first plane Joe wanted to investigate every nook and cranny, and so Charlie followed him around, returning the smiles of those passengers who did in fact smile. When the food and drink carts filled the aisles he had to be lifted into his seat, struggling and proclaiming, "Airplane! Truck!" (The drink cart.) "People!" Eventually he ran out of gas and fell asleep curled in his seat next to Rudra Cakrin, who nodded off over him, occasionally holding Joe's wrist or ankle between two gnarled fingers. Anna sat on the other side of Joe, using up her laptop battery all in one go.

Hours later they floated down over the green fields of Japan, a startling sight if you were expecting nothing but Tokyoscapes. Then up a jetway, feeling slightly deranged; running around an airport acting as marshal to a

two-year-old minimum-security prisoner; then in another plane and rumbling into the air again. Nick kept on reading Carlyle's *History of the French
Revolution*. Charlie and Anna kept trading off the pursuit of their indefati-
gable toddler, Anna having given up making Charlie do it all, as they had
both known she would. Besides her laptop batteries were dead.

Bangkok's airport hotel, tall and white, stood over its big pool in intense
sunlight. Dazed wandering after Joe in the turquoise shallows, trying to
stay awake and unsunburnt, trying to keep Joe out of the deep end. The
water was too warm. Then back to a cool room, sleep, but then the alarm
oh my, middle of the night, ultragroggy, pack up and off to the airport
again to face its long lines, and get on what looked like the same plane.
Except on this one, orchids were pinned to the back of every seat. Joe ate
his before they could stop him. Anna went onto Charlie's laptop to see if it
could have been toxic. Apparently it could, but Joe showed no ill effects,
and Charlie ate a petal of his orchid too, in Anna's view merely compounding the problem with a very poorly designed follow-up experiment, though
he had intended it as reassurance.

In Calcutta they zombied through a reception at the Khembali legation,
dreaming on their feet, except for Joe, who slept on Charlie's back; then
they tumbled into beds, feeling the joy of horizontality; then the alarm
went off again. "Ah God." It was almost like being at home.

Back to the airport, off in a little sixteen-seater so loud that it made Joe
squeal with joy. Up and east, over the mind-boggling delta of the confluence of the Ganges and the Brahmaputra, the world's largest delta, also
most of Bangladesh. Green-brown islands in a brown-green sea: the delta
patterns ran south, and they flew down one channel until the islands spread
out more diffusely. Many were half-submerged, their drowned coastlines
visible in shallows. The water to the south shifted in distinct jumps from
brown-green to jade to sea blue.

One of the outermost islands, right on the border of the jade sea and the
blue, had a shoreline accentuated by a brown ring. As they descended, the
interior of this island differentiated into patterns of color, then into fields,
roads, rooftops. In the final approach they saw that the brown ring was a
dike, quite broad and fairly high. Suddenly it looked to Anna like the land

inside the dike was lower than the ocean around it. She hoped it was only an optical illusion.

Joe had mashed his face and hands against the window, looking down at the island and burbling: "Oh! My! Big truck! Big house!"

Frank, who had successfully slept through three-quarters of the flight, sat up on the other side of Joe, regarding him with a smile. "Oooooooop!" he gibboned, egging him on. Joe cackled to hear it. Then: touchdown.

They were greeted as they came off the plane by a large group of men, women, and children, all dressed in their finery, which meant ceremonial garb better suited to the roof of the world than the Bay of Bengal. On closer examination Anna saw that the fabrics wafting on the hot sea breeze were diaphanous cotton, silk, and nylon, though Tibetan in color and design. That was Khembalung in a nutshell.

Rudra Cakrin descended the plane first, with Drepung right behind him. A triumphant *blaaaaaaaaaaaaa* of brass long horns shattered the air so violently it seemed it might squeeze out rain. It was the brazen sound that had alerted Anna to the Khembalis in the first place, on their arrival in the NSF building. Everyone welcoming them bowed, and they looked down upon the black hair and colorful headgear of several hundred people. Joe's mouth hung open in a perfect O.

On the tarmac their hosts took the visitors in hand, leading them through the airport's little building, then into a van that drove them east on a broad, palm-lined boulevard of dusty white concrete. On each side extended flat fields, divided by rows of trees or shrubbery. Small buildings stood under drooping palm trees. Many of the plants looked desiccated, even brown.

"There has been drought for two years," one of their guides explained. "This is the third monsoon without rain, but we have hopes it will come soon. All Asia has been suffering from these two bad monsoons."

It made for a rather drab landscape. No plants they saw were native to the island, they were told. Everything was tended; even the ground itself had been imported, to raise the island a meter or two higher. Nick asked where the extra ground had come from, and they told him that a few surrounding islands had been dredged up and deposited here, also used to provide material for the dike. It had all been done under the direction of Dutch engineers some fifty years before. The dike was in sight through the trees wherever they went, raising the horizon a bit, so that it felt a little like driving around in a large roofless room, the sky like a white ceiling. The inner wall of the dike had been planted with flower beds that when in bloom would show the usual colors of the Tibetan palette—maroon and saffron, brown and bronze and red.

In a little town they got out of the van and crossed a broad pedestrian esplanade. The sea breeze poured over them, briny as seaweed: the smell of the Sundarbans, perhaps.

"Will we see more swimming tigers?" Nick inquired. He observed everything with interest, looking cool in his sunglasses. Joe had refused to wear his. He was taking in the scene so avidly he was in danger of giving himself whiplash. Anna was pleased to see this curiosity in the boys; America had not yet jaded them to the sheer difference of the rest of the world.

Their guides took them into their Government House. It was darker inside; by the time they had taken off sunglasses and adjusted to the relative gloom, they found Joe had run off ahead of them. The rough-hewn posts in each corner of the room were hung with demon masks, and they followed Joe to one of these collections. Each mask grimaced rotundly, almost exploding with fury, pain, repugnance. Stacked vertically they looked like the totem pole of a tribe of maniacs. Joe was embracing the bottom of the pole.

"Oooh! Oooh! Big—big—big—" His mouth hung open, his eyes bugged out; they could have molded a mask portraying astonishment from his face.

Frank laughed. "These are his kind of people."

"He probably thinks it's a stack of mirrors," Charlie said.

"Quit it," Anna said. "Be nice."

Charlie and Nick leaned their faces in to take photos of themselves on each side of Joe, eyes bugged, tongues thrust out and down. Hopefully they were not offending their hosts. But Anna saw that the guides were smiling.

"They're masks that hide your face but show your insides," Charlie said. "This is what we're all really like inside."

"No," Anna said.

"Oh come on. In your feelings? In your dreams?"

"I certainly hope not. Besides, where's the good feelings?"

She had been thinking of perhaps the curiosity mask, or the striving-for-accuracy mask, but Charlie gave her a Groucho wagging of the eyebrows and indicated with a look the paintings on the beams between wall and ceiling, which included any number of improbably entwined couples. Frank was frankly checking them out, nodding as if they confirmed some sociobiological insight only he could formulate, bonobo Buddhism or something like that. Anna snorted, pretty sure that the tantrically horny painters had to have been fantasizing certain elements of female flexibility, among other endowments. Maybe six arms made it easier to position oneself. Or perhaps there was no gravity in nirvana, which would also explain all the hemispherical tits. She wondered what Joe would make of those, being still a breast man of the first order. But for now he remained too fixated on the demon masks to notice them.

Then they were joined by scientists from the Khembalung Institute of Higher Learning. There were introductions all around, and Anna shook hands, pleased to see her correspondents at last, just as real and vivid as the demon masks. Frank joined them, and for a while they chatted about NSF and their various collaborations. Then Frank and Anna and Nick left Charlie and Joe, and followed their new hosts to the institute itself, where the new labs that NSF had helped fund were still under construction. Outside one of the rooms was a statue of the Buddha, standing with one hand raised before him palm outward, in a gesture like a traffic cop saying, "Stop."

"I've never seen him look like that," Anna said.

"This is, what say, the Adamantine Buddha," one of her pen pals told her. "The Buddha is represented in a number of different ways. He is not always meditating or laughing. When there is bad going on, the Buddha is as obliged to stop it as anyone. And since bad things happen fairly often, there has always been a figure to represent the Buddha's response."

Nick said, "He looks like a policeman."

Their guide nodded. "Police Inspector Sakyamuni. Who insists that we all must resist the three poisons of the mind: fear, greed, and anger."

"So true," Anna said. Frank was nodding also, lost in his thoughts.

"This aspect of Buddha-nature is also the one represented in the statues on the dike, of course."

"Can we go on it?" Frank and Nick asked together.

"Of course. We're very near it."

They finished their tour on a lawn surrounded on three sides by buildings, on the fourth, to the south, by the inner wall of the dike. The wall was a tilted lawn in this area, bisected by a set of broad stone steps leading to its top. Frank and Anna and Nick followed some of their guides up these steps; Charlie and Joe appeared below, and Joe began to run around on the grass.

On top they emerged into a stiff onshore wind. Out to sea lay a white fleet of tall clouds. A big statue of the Adamantine Buddha faced seaward, hand outstretched. From beside him they had a good view of both sea and land, and Anna felt herself lurch a little. "Wow," Nick said.

It was as it had appeared from the plane: the land inside the dike was slightly lower than the ocean surrounding it.

"Holland is like this in some places," Frank said to Anna as they followed Nick and the guides. "Have you ever seen their dikes?"

"No."

"Some of the polders there are clearly lower than the North Sea. You can walk the dikes, and it's the strangest sight."

"So it's true?" Anna asked, waving at Khembalung. "I mean—it looks like it must be."

One of their guides turned and said, "Unfortunately it is true. When land is drained here, it subsides. Dry land is heavier, and sinks, and then water wicks up into it. We have gone through cycle after cycle."

Anna shivered despite the hot wind. She felt faintly queasy and off-balance.

"Try looking only one way at a time."

Anna tried, setting her back to the island. Under a pastel blue sky, clouds flew in from the southwest. The sea bounced to the blue horizon, waves with whitecaps rolling in. Such a big world. Their guides pointed at the clouds, exclaiming that they looked like the beginning of the monsoon; perhaps the drought would end at last!

They walked along the dike, which was clearly old. A metal mesh at the waterline had rusted away, so that the boulders held in by the mesh were slumping, and in places had fallen. Their guides told them that dike maintenance was done with human labor, and the little machinery they had, but there were structural repairs needed that they could not afford, as they could see. Frank jumped onto the waist-high outer wall, setting a bad example for Nick, who immediately followed it.

Sucandra and Padma came up the broad stone staircase, and when they saw Frank and Nick they called, "Look to sea, the monsoon is coming!" They topped the wall and fell in with them. "We wanted to show you the mandala."

Back down on the dusty grass Charlie and Joe had been joined by Rudra, Drepung, and a group of Khembali youth who were creating a mandala on a giant wooden disk that lay on the lawn. "Let's join them," Sucandra suggested, and they walked down out of the wind. It certainly felt humid enough to rain.

The biggest sand mandalas took about a week to complete, they were told. Long brass funnels were held by the artists just an inch or so over the pattern, and when the funnels were rubbed with sticks, thin lines of colored sand fell from them. The colorists worked on their knees, scarcely breathing, rubbing the funnels rhythmically, gently, their faces down near the ground to watch the emerging line of sand; then with a quick tilt of the funnels they would stop the flow and sit back and turn to the others, often to crack a joke, or laugh.

When the design was completely colored in, there would be a ceremony to celebrate the various meanings it held, and then it would be carried to the long shallow reflecting pool in front of Government House, and tipped into the water.

"A real launch party," Charlie noted.

"It signifies the impermanence of all things."

To Anna that seemed like a waste of the art. She did not like the impermanence of all things, and felt there were already enough reminders of it. She liked to think that human efforts were cumulative, that something in every effort was preserved and added to the whole, scaffolding what came after. Perhaps in this case that would be the mandala's pattern, which would remain in their minds. Or maybe this art was a performance rather than an object. But what she wanted out of art was something that lasted.

Over on the other side of the mandala, Joe and Rudra were standing before a group of monks, and Rudra was chanting intently in his deep gravelly voice, a happy gleam in his eye. Those around him repeated the last word of every sentence, in a kind of shout or singing. Joe stamped his foot in time, crying, "No!" in unison with the rest of them. He hadn't even noticed Anna was there.

Then suddenly he took off directly toward the sand mandala, fists clenched and swinging like a miniature John Wayne. Anna cried out, "Joe!" but he did not hear her. The Khembalis actually made way for him, some of them with arms outstretched as if to create a better corridor. "Joe!" she cried again more sharply. "Joe! Stop!" He hesitated for a second, at the edge of the circle of brilliant color, then walked out onto it.

"JOE!"

No one moved. Joe stood peacefully at the center of the mandala, looking around.

Anna rushed down the steps to the edge of the circle. Joe's footprints had blurred some lines, and grains of colored sand were now out of place, scattered brilliantly in the wrong fields. Joe was looking very pleased with himself, surveying the pattern under his feet, a pattern made of colors almost precisely the same as the colors of his building blocks at home, only more vibrant. He spotted Rudra, and thrust an arm out to wave at him. "Ba!" he declared.

"Baaaa," Rudra replied, putting his hands together and bowing.

Joe's pose, which resembled that of the Adamantine Buddhas, gave him a kind of Napoleonic grandeur. Charlie, standing now beside Anna, shook his head. "Ya big old hambone," he muttered.

Joe dropped his arm, made a gesture at all the people watching him. A few drops of rain spattered down out of the low clouds bowling in from the sea, and the Khembalis oohed and aahed as they felt it and looked up.

Joe took off again, this time in the direction of the reflecting pool. Anna rushed around the circle of people to cut him off, but she was too late; he walked right into the shallows. "Joe!" she called out, to no effect. Joe turned and confronted the crowd that had followed him, standing knee-deep in the water. It was sprinkling steadily now, the rain warm on Anna's face, and all the Khembalis were smiling. Enough colored sand had stuck to Joe's feet that vermilion and yellow blooms now spread in the water around him.

"Rgyal ba," Rudra declared, and the crowded repeated it. Then: "Ce ba drin dran-pa!"

"What is he saying?" Anna asked Drepung, who now stood beside her, as if to support her if she fainted, or perhaps to stop her if she started in after Joe. Charlie stood on her other side.

"All hail," Drepung said. He looked older to Anna, his round face and little mouth finally at home. She had seen that he was a well-known and popular figure here.

Joe stood in the shallows regarding the crowd. He was happy. The Khembalis were indulging him, enjoying him. The warm rain fell on them like a balm. Suddenly Anna felt a shaft of happiness pierce her; her little tiger had seen that he was among friends, somehow, and at last he stood in the world content, relaxed, even serene. She had never seen him look like this. She had wanted so much for him to feel something like this.

Charlie, on the other hand, felt his stomach go tense at the sight of Joe in the pool. All his worries were being confirmed. He took a deep breath, thinking, Nothing has changed, you knew this already: they think he's one of their tulkus. That doesn't mean it's true.

He couldn't imagine what Anna was making of all this. He had tried to tell her about it during the flood in Washington, but she had not taken it in.

Standing beside each other, the two of them both felt the discrepancy in their reactions. And they sensed as well that their characteristic moods or responses were here reversed, Anna pleased by a Joe anomaly, Charlie worried.

Uneasily they glanced at each other, both thinking, This is backwards, what's going on?

"Big rain!" Joe exclaimed, looking up, and the crowd sighed appreciatively.

That night the visitors collapsed on the beds in their rooms, even Joe, and slept from the early evening through the night and well into the next morning. It had rained the whole time, and when they went back out after breakfast they found the island transformed; everything was drenched, with standing water everywhere. The Khembalis were happy to see it. Their visitors split into groups and took off in the rain as planned. Joe and Nick were taken to the school to see classes and playground games. Everywhere he went, Joe was indulged, including being left free to commune with every demon mask they passed. In the afternoon Nick left the group and joined Anna at the institute, where she talked with her contacts and the other scientists there. Charlie spent his time in Government House, talking to officials brought to him by Padma.

Frank was gone; they didn't know how he was spending his time, although once in passing Anna saw him in conversation with Sucandra and some of the local monks. Later she saw him on the dike, walking the berm path with Rudra Cakrin. Judging from his conversation at dinner, he had also spent time discussing agriculture out in the fields. But mostly he seemed to Anna as if he were a kind of religious pilgrim, eager for instruction and enlightenment. It was very unlike his manner back in Washington.

Next afternoon they visited the zoo, located in a big park at the northwest quadrant of the island. Many animals and birds of the Sundarbans were represented. The elephants had a large enclosure, but the largest enclosure of all was for the tigers. Most of these big cats had been swept to sea by one flood or another, then rescued by Khembali patrol boats. Now they lived in an enclosure thick with stands of elephant grass and saal trees, fronted by a big pond cut by a curving glass retaining wall, so that when they swam, they could be seen underwater. Their abrupt foursquare dives and subsequent splayed strokes turned feline grace unexpectedly aquatic, and underwater their fur streamed like seaweed. "Tiger! Tiger! Big big *tiger!*"

At the end of that wet day they sat in a hall and ate a meal anchored by curried rice. Nick was served a special order of plain rice, arranged by Drepung, but Joe was fine with the curry. Or so it seemed during the meal; but that night in their room he was fractious, and then, after a long nursing session, wide awake. Jet lag, perhaps. The rain was coming down hard, its drumming on the roof quite loud. Joe began to complain. Anna was asleep on her feet, but Charlie was out entirely, so she had to zombie on, hour after hour, mumbling replies to Joe's cheerful jabberwocking. She was on the verge of a collapse when a knock came at the door, and Frank looked in.

"I can't sleep, and I could hear you were up with Joe. I wondered if you wanted me to play with him for a while."

"Oh God bless you," she cried. "I was just about to melt." She fell on the couch and shut her sandy eyes. For a while her brain continued to turn, as her body dove into sleep and dragged her consciousness down with it.

"Nick sleeping. Da sleeping. Mama sleeping."

"That's right."

"Wanna play?"

"Sure. What you got here, trains? What about some airplanes, shouldn't you have some airplanes?"

"Got planes."

"Good. Let's fly, let's fly and fly."

"Fly!"

"Hey, those are your tigers! Well, that's okay. Flying tigers are just right for here. Swimming tigers too. Watch out, here he comes!"

"Tiger fly!"

Anna stitched the meandering border between sleep and dreams, in and out, up and down. Frank and Joe passed toys back and forth.

In the hour before dawn a hard knock battered their door, throwing Anna convulsively to her feet. She had been dreaming of the tigers' fluid swimming, up in the sky—

It was Drepung, looking agitated. "I'm sorry to disturb you, my friends, but a decision has been made that we must all evacuate the island."

This woke them all, even Charlie, who was usually so slow to rouse. Frank turned on all the lights, and they packed their bags while Drepung explained the situation.

"The monsoon has returned," he said. "This is a good thing, but unfortunately it has come at a time of especially high tides, and together with the storm surge, and the low air pressure, sea level is extremely high." He helped the comatose Nick into a shirt. "It's already higher on the dikes than is judged fully safe, higher than we have seen for many years, and some weaknesses in the dikes are being exposed. And now we have been informed that the monsoon or something else has caused breaking of some ice dams high in the drainage of the Brahmaputra." He looked at Charlie: "These big glacial lakes in the Himalaya are a result of global warming. The glaciers are melting fast, and now lots of glacial ice dams that create lakes behind them are giving way under these monsoon rains, adding greatly to the runoff. The Brahmaputra is already overflowing, and much of Bangladesh is faced with flooding. They called with the alarm from Dhaka just a short while ago." He checked his watch. "Just an hour ago, good. It goes fast. The surge of high water will arrive soon, and we are already at our limit. And as you have seen, the island is lower than the sea even at the best of times. This is the problem with using dikes for protection. If the dike fails, the result can be severe. So we must leave the island."

"How?" Anna exclaimed.

"Don't worry, we have ferries at the dock enough for all. Always docked here for this very purpose, because the danger is ever-present. We have used them before, when the rivers flood or there are high tides. Anything like that can flood us. The island is just too low, and unfortunately, getting lower."

"How much time do we have?" Anna said.

"Two or three hours. This is more than enough time for us. But we prefer that our guests leave by helicopter in a situation like this."

"How many people live here again?" Charlie asked as he threw their bathroom bags into his backpack.

"Twelve thousand."

"Wow."

"Yes. It is a big operation, but all will be well."

"What about the zoo animals?" Nick asked. By now their bags were packed, and Nick was dressed and looking wide awake.

"We have a boat for them too. It's a difficult procedure, but there is a team assigned to it. People with circus experience. They call it 'Noah Goes Fast.' How about you, are you ready?"

They were ready. Joe had watched all the action with a curious eye; now he said, "Da? Go?"

"That's right big guy. We're off on another trip."

Outside it was raining harder than ever, the cloud cover somewhat broken and flying north on a strong wind. They hustled into a van and joined a little traffic jam on the island's main road. All the crowded vans turned north toward the dock. Joe sat in Anna's lap looking out the window, saying, "Ba? Ba?" Nick was wide-eyed, but appeared too surprised by all the activity to formulate his usual barrage of questions. Their van joined the line going to the airport. Drepung leaned forward from his seat to show them the screen of his phone, which now displayed an image of the upper end of the Bay of Bengal and the lower delta of the Ganges and Brahmaputra. This satellite photo had rendered altimetry data in false color to show river and sea level departures from the norm, with the brilliant spectral band ranging from the cool blues and greens of normality to the angry yellows, oranges, and reds of high water. Now the right side of the delta ran red, the left side orange and then yellow. And the whole Bay of Bengal was light orange already.

Drepung put a fingertip to the screen, looking very serious. "See that little blue dot there? That's us. We are low. Orange all around us. That mean a couple meters higher than normal."

Charlie said, "That's not so bad, is it?"

"The dike is maxed out. They're saying now that they don't think it will be able to handle the flood surge." He leaned back to take a call on his phone. Then: "The helicopter is ready."

Their van arrived at the airport, circled the terminal, went directly out onto the wet tarmac near the helicopter landing site.

"Here in five minutes," Drepung said. Joe began to wail, and they let him down to run around. From time to time they looked at Drepung's phone and saw images of the delta, in real time but false color. "The Sundarbans," Drepung said, shaking his head at the array of blue dots. "They're meant to be amphibious."

Then a helicopter thwacked out of the dawn sky. "Good," Drepung said, and led them off the concrete pad, onto a flat field next to it. They watched the big helicopter drop through the clouds in a huge noise and wind of its own making, settling down on its pad like an oversized dragonfly. Joe howled at the sight. Charlie picked him up and felt the child clutch at him. They waited to be signaled over to the helo. Its blades continued to rotate, chopping the air loudly.

"Down!" Joe shouted in Charlie's ear. "Down! Down! Down! Down!"

"Let him down for a second," Anna said. "There's time, isn't there?"

Drepung was still at their side. "Yes, there's time."

Men in dark green uniforms were getting off the helicopter. Charlie put Joe down on the ground. Immediately Joe struck out for the helo, and Charlie followed, intent on stopping him. He saw that Joe's feet had sunk into what must have been very soft ground; water was quickly seeping into his prints. Charlie picked him up from behind, ignored his wails as he returned to the others. He looked back; Joe's watery prints caught little chips of the dawn light, looking like silver coins.

Then it was time to board. Joe insisted on walking himself, kicking furiously when held by either Charlie or Anna, shrieking "Down let down *let down*!" So they let him down, and held him hard by the hands and walked forward, Nick on the other side of Anna, all ducking instinctively under the high but drooping blades that guillotined the air so noisily.

In the helicopter it was a bit quieter. There were a few people already in the short rows of seats, and in the next half hour they were joined by others, about half of them Westerners, the rest perhaps Indians, including a bevy of wide-eyed schoolgirls. The Quiblers and Frank greeted each in turn, and the schoolgirls gathered to dote on Joe in their musical English. He hid his head from them, clung hard to Anna. Charlie looked out a little window beside them, set low so that right now he could see little more than the puddles on the concrete.

The noise of the engines got louder and up they lifted, tilting back and then forward, a strange sensation for anyone used to airplanes.

Out the lower window they caught a glimpse of the dike when they were just above its height, and there was the sea right there beyond it, lipping at the very top of the berm. The uncanny sight remained burned in their minds as the helo banked and they lost the view.

They made a rising turn over the island, and the view came back and went away, came back and went away. Joe leaned from Anna's arms to the window, trying to see better. Nick was looking out the same window from the seat behind. The sea was a dark brown, and on the island everything was soaked, gray-green fields lined with standing water—trees, rooftops, the plaza with the reflecting pool, all deep in shadow; then the ocean again, clearly as high as the dike. "There's where we were staying!" Nick called, pointing.

They banked in a gyre that cut through the bottom layers of the clouds. Dark, light, rain, clear, quickly from one state to the next. Rain skittered across the outside of the glass in sudden streaming deltas. They saw the ferries at the dock on the north side of the island, casting off. Drepung gave the Quiblers a thumbs-up. The helo continued its curve, and they saw other Sundarban islands, most now no more than shallow reefs. The channels between these were pale brown, flecked with dirty white.

They curved back over Khembalung and saw that the dike had been breached on its southwest curve, where it faced the battering of the storm surf. Brown water, heavily flecked with foam, poured whitely down onto the fields below the break, in its rush clearly ripping the gap in the dike wider. Soon Khembalung would look like all the other Sundarbans.

Now Joe crawled onto Charlie's lap and took a death grip on Charlie's neck, moaning or keening, it was hard to hear in all the racket, but somehow the sound of it cut through everything else. Charlie forced the hands on his neck to loosen their grip. "It's okay!" he said loudly to the boy. "It'll be okay! They're all okay! They're on the boats. Big boats! The *people* were *on* the *boats*! All the *people* were *on* the *boats*."

"Da, da, da," Joe moaned, or maybe it was "Na, da, na." He put a hand on the window.

"Oh my God," Charlie said.

Over Joe's head he could see again the gap where the ocean was pouring in; it was already much wider than before. It looked like the whole southwest curve would go. Already most of the interior fields were sheeted with water.

Ahead of them the pilot and copilot were shouting into their headsets. The helo tilted, spiraled higher. Clouds interrupted their view below. A loud buffeted ascent, then they caught sight of Khembalung again, from higher than before; through a break in the clouds it looked like a shallow green bowl, submerged in brown water until only an arc of the bowl's rim remained in air.

Charlie said, "Don't, Joe! I have to breathe."

"Ah gone! Ah gone!"

Abruptly the helicopter tilted away, and all they could see outside the window was cloud. The Sundarbans were gone, all their mangrove swamps drowned, all their tigers swimming. The helo flew off like a blown leaf. Joe buried his face in Charlie's chest and sobbed.

CHAPTER 14

IS THERE A
TECHNICAL SOLUTION?

No one thinks it will ever happen to them until suddenly they are in the thick of it, thoroughly surprised to be there.

A tornado in Halifax Nova Scotia; the third and catastrophic year of drought in Ireland; major floods on the Los Angeles River: these kinds of anomalies kept happening, at a rate of more than one a day around the world. Sooner or later almost everyone got caught up in some event, or lived in the midst of some protracted anomaly, for the weather events were both acute and chronic, a matter of hours or a matter of years.

Still it was hard to imagine it would ever happen to you.

At the poles the results were particularly profound, because of major and rapid changes in the ice. For reasons poorly understood, both polar regions were warming much faster than the rest of the planet. In the north the breakup of the Arctic Ocean's sea ice had led to the imminent extinction of many species, including the polar bear, and the stall of the Gulf Stream. In the south it had resulted in the rapid breakup of the giant ice shelves hugging the Antarctic coast, unblocking the big glaciers falling into the Ross Sea so that they became "ice rivers," moving so rapidly down their channels that they were destabilizing the West Antarctic Ice Sheet, the biggest variable in the whole picture: if this sheet came off its underwater perch on the seafloor, the world would suffer impacts greater by far than what had been witnessed already, most especially a rapid rise in sea level, up to as much as seven meters if the whole sheet came off.

Still it was hard to imagine it would ever happen to you.

There were further ramifications. The ocean bottom, where it drops from the continental shelves to the abyssal seafloor, is in many places a steep slope, and these slopes are coated by thick layers of mud that contain methane in the form of clathrates, a chemical form of freezing that cages molecules of the gas in a frozen matrix. As ocean temperatures rose, these chemical cages were being destabilized, and release of the methane could then cause underwater avalanches in which even more methane was released, rising through the water and rejoining the atmosphere, where it was a greenhouse gas much more powerful than carbon dioxide. Warmer atmosphere meant warmer ocean meant released methane meant warmer atmosphere meant—

It was a complex of cycles—geologic, oceanic, and atmospheric—all blending into each other and affecting the rest. The interactions were so complex, the feedbacks positive and negative so hard to gauge in advance, the unforeseen consequences so potentially vast, that no one could say what would happen next to the global climate. Modeling had been attempted to estimate the general rise in temperature, and actually the models had been refined to the point that there was some agreement as to the outside parameters of possible change, ranging from about a two- to an eleven-degree C rise—a big range, but that's how uncertain any estimates were at this point. And even if the estimates could have been tighter, global averages did not reveal much about local or ultimate effects, as people were now learning. There were nonlinear tipping points, and now some of these were beginning to reveal themselves. The stall of the Gulf Stream was expected to chill the winter temperatures in the Northern Hemisphere, especially on both sides of the Atlantic; further effects were much less certain. The recent two-year failure of the monsoon was not understood, nor its violent return. China's drought was ongoing, as was the longest-ever El Niño, called the Hyperniño. Desertification in the Sahel was moving south at an ever-increasing rate, and South America was suffering the worst floods in recorded history because of the rain brought by the El Niño. It had rained in the Atacama.

Wild weather everywhere, thus the most expensive insurance year ever, for the eighth year in a row. That was just a number, an amount of money distributed out through the financial systems of the world; but it was also a measure of catastrophe, death, suffering, fear, insecurity, and sheer massive inconvenience.

The problem they faced was that everything living depended on conditions staying within certain tight climatic parameters. The atmosphere was only so thick; as Frank put it once, talking to Anna and Kenzo, when you drive by Mount Shasta on U.S. Interstate 5, you can see the height of the livable part of the atmosphere right there before your eyes. No permanent human settlement on Earth was higher than Shasta's summit, at 14,200 feet, so the mountain served to show in a very visible form just how thick the breathable atmosphere was—and the mountain wasn't very tall at all, in comparison to the immense reach of the plateau the highway ran over. It was just a snowy hill! It was sobering, Frank said; after you saw the matter that way, looking at the mountain and sensing the size of the whole planet, you were changed. Ever afterward you would be aware of an invisible ceiling low overhead containing all the breathable air under it—the atmosphere thus no more than the thinnest wisp of a skin, like cellophane wrapped to the lithosphere. An equally thin layer of water had liquefied in the low basins of this lithosphere, and that was the life zone: cellophane wrapping a planet, a mere faint exhalation, wisping off into space. Frank would shake his head, remembering that vision driving over the shoulder of Shasta. At that moment the world had said to him, I AM.

Still, it was hard to imagine.

Frank's habits were his only home now, and so the trip to Khembalung and its aftermath made him feel a bit homeless all over again. What to do with the day: again this became a question he had to answer anew, hour by hour, and it was hard.

On the other hand, all the Khembali refugees flying into Washington helped him keep things in perspective. He was homeless by choice, they were not; he had his van, his tree, his office, his club—all the rooms of his house-equivalent, scattered around town; they had nothing. Their embassy's house in Arlington gave them temporary shelter, but everything there was in crisis mode, and would be for a long time.

And yet they were cheerful. Frank found this impressive, though he also wondered how long it would last. Doubly exiled, first from Tibet, then from their island; they joined the many other refugees who had come to Washington to plead their case, hoping to get back to their homes, then failing and never leaving, adding their children, cuisine, and holidays to the metro region's rich mix.

Because Khembalung was wrecked. There was some talk of draining the island and repairing the dike, but there was no ready source of electricity to drive the pumps, and no equipment available to rebuild the dike; though those problems could be dealt with, maybe, their freshwater supply appeared to have been compromised, and now the island was being thoroughly saturated by seawater.

Khembalung was simply too low. It had always been, and now, with sea level rising, the margin of safety had disappeared. No matter what they did, catastrophic floods were bound to inundate all the Sundarbans almost every year. Moon tides, storm surges, even the occasional tsunamis that were likely to become more frequent as methane clathrates triggered underwater landslides—all these would be flooding the coastal lowlands of the world more often.

So the expense and effort needed to pump out and rebuild Khembalung was likely to be wasted. And the Khembalis had other options, as there were Tibetan refugee colonies scattered around India. Also, some people at the D.C. embassy were now talking about buying land in the metro area, and settling there. Meanwhile, it could be said that the citizens of Khembalung had for their national territory one old Arlington house, and an office in the NSF building.

So it was a crowded house and office. Frank was amazed to see how crowded; he would drop by to say hi, and every time be struck anew at how many people could be crammed into a house without breaking anything but zoning codes. He carried boxes for them, then talked to Rudra in English, got the old man to teach him some Tibetan words. He was always happy to see them, and always happy to get out of there—to be able to drive over the Potomac to Rock Creek and the refuge of the forest.

The late summer days were still pretty long, and this was good, because Frank needed the light. He hiked into the park checking his FOG phone, getting the latest fixes and hoping he could locate the gibbons, who he had learned were a family, Bert and May and their kids, or the siamangs; but any ferals would do. In the last hour before sundown many of them made their way to the watering hole for a last drink for the night, and he often had good luck spotting them. Ostrich, tapir, spider monkey, eland, sitatunga, tamarind, red deer, brown bear; his list of personal sightings kept growing.

His Acheulian hand axe came in the mail at work, and he pulled it out of its bubble wrap and held it up to the light. Instantly it was his favorite rock. It had a lovely weight, and fitted his hand perfectly; it was the classic Acheulian oval, with a sharp tip at its smaller end. Chipped on both sides very expertly, so that it seemed as much a work of sculpture as a tool, a little Andy Goldsworthy sculpture; a petroglyph all by itself, speaking in its heft a whole world. Gray quartzite, slightly translucent, the chipped faces almost as smoothed by patination during their four hundred thousand years of exposure as the brown curve of the original core. It was beautiful.

He took it to the park and pulled it from his daypack to show to Spencer and Robin and Robert, and they spontaneously fell to their knees, crying out like the gibbons. "Ahh! Oh my God! Oh God, here it is." Robin sa-laamed to it, Spencer inspected every chip and curve, kissing it from time to time. "Look how perfect it is," he said.

"Look," Robin said when he held it, "it's shaped for a left-hander, see? It fits better when you hold it in your left hand." Robin was left-handed. "Do you think maybe *Homo erectus* were all left-handed, like polar bears? Did you know polar bears are all left-handed?"

"Only because you've told us a thousand times," Spencer said, taking it from him. "How old did you say?" he asked Frank.

"Four hundred thousand years."

"Unbelievable. But look, you know—I really hate to say this—but it doesn't look like it would fly like a frisbee."

"No, it doesn't."

"Also, that thing about how it wouldn't make a very good hand axe, be-cause it's sharpened all the way around? Actually it looks like you could hold it almost anywhere and still hit something. The edge isn't sharp enough to cut you."

"True."

"Have you tried throwing it yet?"

"No."

"Well heck, let's give it a try."

"Let's throw it at a rabbit!"

"Now come on."

"Hey we have to test this thing, how else are we going to do it? Throw it at one of those tapirs, it'll bounce right off them."

"No it won't."

"You kill it you eat it."

"Fine by me!"

They ran the course, and when they came to the meadow near picnic site 14, they stopped and Frank pulled out the axe, and they threw it at a tree (it left an impressive gash) and then at trash bottles set up on a log. Yes, you could break a bottle with it, if you could hit it; and it did tend to spin on its axis, though not necessarily horizontally; in fact it tended to rotate through a spiral as it flew forward.

"You could kill a rabbit if you hit it."

"True with an ordinary rock though."

"You could spook a big animal by the watering hole."

"True with an ordinary rock though."

"All right, okay."

"It'd work to skin an animal I guess."

"That's true," Frank said. "But they've tried that in South Africa, and they've found that they lose their edge really quick, like after one animal."

"That would explain why there are so many of them."

"Yeah, they think they knapped a new one pretty much anytime they needed to do something."

"Hmm, I don't know. This thing looks pretty perfect for a throwaway. It looks like someone's favorite tool."

"His Swiss Army knife."

"That's just patination. It's four hundred thousand years old, man. That's *old*. Older than art and religion, like you said."

"It *is* art and religion."

"A fossilized frisbee."

"A fossil killer frisbee."

"Except it doesn't look like that's what it was."

"Well, I'm sticking with it," Spencer said. "It's too good a theory to give up just because of some evidence."

"Yahhh!"

"And just anecdotal evidence at that! Means nothing!"

Frisbee golf in the last hour of light, running through the flickering shadow and light. Working up a sweat, making shots magnificent or stupid. Living entirely in his frisbee mind, nothing else intruding. The blessed no-time of meditation. Turning the moment into eternity.

His shelter was completely rainproofed now, and given the frequent summer showers, this made for a wonderfully satisfying situation: his little room, open-sided under its clear plastic canopy, was frequently walled by sheets of falling water, like a bead curtain perpetually falling. The rain pounded down with its plastic drumming noise, like the shower you hear in the morning when your partner gets up—a susurrus or patter, riding on the liquid roar of the forest and the clatter of the creek below. The air less humid than during those muggy days when the rain held off.

Often it rained just before dawn or just after. Charcoal turning gray in the dimness of a rainy day. Low clouds scudding overhead. Sometimes he would sleep again for another half hour. The night's sleep would be broken, no matter where he spent the night; something would bring him up, his heart racing for no reason, then the brain following: thinking about work, or Caroline, or Marta, the Khembalis, the homeless guys, the frisbee players, housing prices in north San Diego County—anything could spark it off, and then it was very difficult to fall back asleep. He would lie there, in his van or treehouse or very occasionally his office, aware that he needed more sleep, but unable to drop back in.

Rain at those times would be a blessing, as the sound tended to knock him out. And rain in the morning gave him time to lie there and think about projects, experiments, animals, papers, money, women. Time to remember that many men his age, maybe most men his age, slept with a woman every night of their lives, to the point where they hardly even noticed it, except in their partner's absence.

Better to think about work.

Or to look at the pattern leaves made against the sky, black against the velvet grays. Stiffly shift around, trying to wake up, until he was sitting on the edge of the platform, sleeping bag draped over him like a cape, feet swinging in air, to listen for the gibbons. Insomnia as a kind of a gift, then, from nature, or Gaia, or the animals and birds, or his unquiet unconscious. Of course one woke a little before dawn! How could you not? It was so beautiful. Sometimes he felt like he was sitting on the edge of some great thing that only he could see was about to happen. Some change like morning itself, but different.

Other days he woke and could only struggle to escape the knot his stomach had been tied into during the night. Then it took the gibbons to free him. If they were within earshot, and he heard them lift their voices, then all was immediately well within him, the knot untied. An aubade: all will be well, and all will be well, and all will be perfectly well. That was what they were singing, as translated by some nuns in medieval Europe. It was another gift. Sometimes he just listened, but usually he sang with them, if singing was the right word. He hooted, whooped, called; but really it was most like singing, even if the word he sang was always "ooooooooop," and every ooop was a glissando, sliding up or down. *Oooooooop! Oooooooop!*

If they sounded like they were nearby, he would descend from his tree and try to spot them. Light steps, looking down at the still-gray ground, seeking footfalls between the ubiquitous twigs, in the bare black mud. All the animals in the park were pretty skittish by now. At the least noise, someone in the gibbon gang would shout some kind of warning, often a loud "Aaack!" and then they would tarzan away with only a few muffled calls to indicate even what direction they had gone. Typically they moved fifty to a hundred yards before resettling, so if they spooked, Frank usually shifted his hunt to some other animal. You couldn't beat brachiation in a forest.

He would work his way down Rock Creek, headed for the waterhole overlook. FOG had put a salt lick on the edge of the new pool. He was careful in his final approach, because the overlook itself had been marked by big pawprints, feline in appearance but large, huge in fact—possibly sign of the missing jaguar, still unsighted, or at least unreported. Or maybe the prints were of one of the forest's smaller cats, the snow leopard or lynx, or the native bobcat. In any case, not a good animal to surprise. Sometimes he even approached the overlook clutching his hand axe, reassured by the heft of it.

Once there he could watch the animals below, drinking warily and taking licks of the salt lick. On this morning he saw two of the tiny tamarinds, a gazelle, an okapi, and the rhinoceros, all radio-tagged already. The day before he had seen a trio of red wolves bring down a young eland.

After the waterhole he explored, striking out to get mildly lost, in the process checking out the tributaries in Rock Creek's rippled watershed. Stealthy walking in the hope of spotting animals: again, as with the heft of the hand axe, or the swaying of his tree in the wind, it felt familiar to his body, as if he had often done it before. He felt used to things he had never done.

Slink of gray flashing over the creek.

In his memory he reconstructed the glimpse. Silvery fur; something like a fisher or minx. Bounding over the rocks in the creek, in a hurry.

Around a corner he came on the hapless tapirs, rooting in the mud. This forest floor did not have what they needed, and Frank had heard they were living off care packages provided by the zoo staff and FOG members. Some people argued that this meant they should be recaptured: only animals that could make their way in the forest on their own should be given permanent feral status. Many of the feral species were tropical or semitropical, and possibly the feral life for these creatures would have to come to an end, although it wasn't clear exactly how some of them could be recaptured.

Well, they would cross that bridge when they came to it. For now, GPS the tapirs, add them to his FOG phone's log. So far his list included forty-three nonnative species, from aardvarks to zebras. Then trudge out west to his van, to drive over the river to Optimodal. Often all this would happen and he would still get to the gym before seven.

After that, the day got more complicated. No meetings at eight, so a quick visit to the Optimodal weight room. If he ran into Diane, they worked out together. That was habitual, and it was getting a little complicated, actually. Not that it wasn't fun, because it was. Her hand on his arm: it was interesting. But friendly conversations and shared workouts with a woman at the gym suggested a certain kind of relationship, and when the woman in question was also one's boss—also single, or at least known to have been widowed several years before—there was no way to avoid certain little implications that seemed to follow, expressed by the ways in which they didn't meet each other's eye or discuss various matters, also little protocols and courtesies, steering clear of what might be more usual behaviors in the gym situation. He often began a workout feeling he was too preoccupied by other concerns to think about this matter; but quickly enough it was unavoidable. Diane's businesslike cheer and quick mind, her industry and amusement, her muscly middle-aged body flexing and pinking before him, sometimes under his care—it was impossible not to be affected by that. She looked good. He wanted Caroline to call him again.

To tell the truth, ever since his encounter with Francesca, all women looked good to him. In the Metro, at NSF, in the gym. Some mornings it was better just to shower and shave and get right over to work. Into his office, sit down with coffee, survey the huge list of Things to Do. Many of them were very interesting things, like:

1. Quantify the "estimated maximum takedown" for every carbon capture method suggested in the literature (for next Diane meeting)
2. Talk to Army Corps of Engineers
3. Formalize criteria for MacArthur-style awards to researchers
4. Talk to UCSD about assisting new institute in La Jolla

Pick one and dive in, and then it was a rapid flurry of meetings, phone calls, reading at furious speed, memos, reports, abstracts—God bless abstracts, if only everything were written as an abstract—what would be lost, after all?—then writing at the same furious speed, memos mostly, need to do this, need to do that. All the little steps needed if big things were ever going to get done.

Then another meeting with Diane and several members of the National Science Board. Potential partners were being identified in the scientific community, also supportive members of Congress, sympathetic committees. As Diane kept saying, they needed legislation, they needed funding. Meanwhile she was working with the Intergovernmental Panel on Climate Change, the International Council for Science, the World Conservation Union, the National Academy of Engineering, NASA and NOAA, the U.S. Global Change Research Program, the World Meteorological Organization, the World Resources Institute, the Pew Charitable Trust, the National Center for Atmospheric Research, the President's Committee of Advisors on Science and Technology, the Office of Science and Technology Policy, the Nature Conservancy, the Ecological Society of America, DIVERSITAS, which was the umbrella program to coordinate global research effort in the biodiversity sciences, and GLOBE, which stood for Global Learning and Observations to Benefit the Environment—

"And so on," she concluded, looking impassively at the PowerPoint slide listing these organizations. "There are many more. There is no shortage of organizations. Government agencies, UN, scientific societies, NGOs. Whether all these efforts can be coordinated and led to any useful action is another question. It's the question I want to discuss today, after we've gotten through the other items on the agenda. Because this is the real problem: we know, but we can't act."

The more Frank watched Diane in these meetings, the more he liked her. She got things done without making a fuss. She was not diverted, she kept to the important points. She didn't waste time. She worked with people and through people—as she did with Frank—and people worked like maniacs for her, thinking they were pursuing their own projects (and often they were), but enacting Diane's projects too; she was the one coordinating them, enabling them. Setting the pace and finding the money.

Now she came back to Frank's chief interest. "We have to consider potential interventions in the biosphere itself," shaking her head as if she couldn't believe what she was saying. "If there are ways to tip the global climate back out of this abrupt change, we should identify them and do them. Too much else will be hammered if we don't accomplish that. So, can it be done, and if so, how? Which interventions have the best chance, and which can we actually do?"

"It makes sense to work on the thing we've identified," Frank said.

Diane nodded. That meant the stalled downwelling of the thermohaline circulation, and she had already begun discussions with the UN and the IPCC broaching the possibility of overcoming the stall. "We'll get a report on that later. Right now, what about carbon capture methods?"

Frank went down the list he had compiled.

1. freezing carbon dioxide extracted from coal-fired power plants and other industrial sources, and depositing the dry ice on the

ocean floor near subduction zones or river deltas, where it would be buried,

2. injecting frozen CO_2 into emptied oil wells or underground aquifers,
3. fertilizing oceans with iron dust to grow phytoplankton and absorb CO_2, the tiny creatures then dying and falling to the ocean floor with their carbon,
4. gathering ag waste and converting it to ethanol for fuel,
5. growing biomass, both to burn in biofuels and to sequester carbon for the life of the plants (corn, poplar trees, etc.),
6. altering bacteria or other plant life to speed its carbon uptake, without releasing nitrous oxides that were more potent greenhouse gases than CO_2 itself.

This last point about nitrous oxide was vexing all plans to stimulate carbon drawdown by biological means. "It's the law of unintended consequences," as one ecologist had put it to Frank. Now Frank explained to Diane and the others: "Say your iron spurs the growth of marine bacteria, drawing down carbon, but the growth of some of those bacteria releases nitrous oxides. And NOs are a much worse greenhouse gas than CO_2. Also, a lot of the carbon in the ocean is fixed in dead diatom shells. Some marine bacteria feed on dead diatoms, and when they do, they free up that carbon, which had been fixed in carbonates that would have eventually become limestone. So is fertilizing the ocean with iron necessarily going to result in a net drawdown in greenhouse gases? No one can be sure."

"We need to be sure," Diane said.

"That's going to be hard in this area."

They discussed methods that had been proposed for direct climate alteration, including adding chemicals to jet fuel so that contrails would last longer and reflect more light back into space; seeding clouds; shooting dust or sulfur dioxide into the upper atmosphere in imitation of volcanoes; and flying various sunscreens to high altitude. Again, because of the complexity of the various feedback mechanisms, and the importance of water vapor both in blocking incoming light and holding in outgoing heat, it was hard to predict what the result of any given action would be. No one had a good sense of how clouds might change things.

"I don't think we're ready for anything like these projects!" Diane said. "We can't be sure what effects we'll get."

They were looking at a slide from a polar ecologist. Both poles were heating up fast, but especially the Arctic; and the slide informed them that one-seventh of all the carbon on Earth was cached in biotic material frozen in the Arctic permafrost, which was rapidly melting. Once the permafrost was liquefied, that carbon would reenter the atmosphere. "It could be another positive feedback, like the methane hydrates unfreezing on the continental shelves."

"Wouldn't the tundra just turn into peat bogs?" Frank asked.

"Peat bogs are anoxic. Permafrost isn't."

"Ah."

In a meeting the next day, a team from NOAA gave a presentation on potential schemes to intervene in the North Atlantic. It was a matter of sensitive dependencies, so there was chaos math involved. Frank was interested in the algorithms used in their modeling, but he saved that aspect for later; accuracy within orders of magnitude was probably good enough for now. How much water sank in the downwelling before the stall? What volume of water would have to sink to start it again? How much more saline would the sea have to be to sink through the fresh water now there? How much dry weight of salt would be needed to create that differential?

The NOAA people did their best with these questions. Frank and the others tried out various back-of-the-envelope calculations, and they talked over what it might take to bring that much salt to bear. It seemed within the industrial and shipping capacities of the advanced nations, at least theoretically—it was somewhat similar to the numbers involved in oil transport—although there were also questions concerning whether this would be a one-time application, or would have to be an annual thing to offset the Arctic sea ice that would presumably form every winter, break up every spring, and float south every summer.

"We can deal with that question later," Diane declared. "Meanwhile I want all the answers here as constrained as possible, so I can take a plan to Congress and the President. Anything that makes the point we are not helpless will be useful on other fronts. So this is as good a place to start as any."

Sometimes at lunch, Frank went out and ate with Anna and Drepung at the Food Factory. Drepung would come in with the latest news from the embassy, shaking his head as he ate. Every week it seemed clearer that they had lost Khembalung for good. Salvage plans had replaced restoration in his talk.

"Did you have any flood insurance?" Anna asked.

"No. I don't think anyone would underwrite it."

"So what will you do?"

Drepung shrugged. "Not sure yet."

"Ouch," Anna said.

"I do not mind it. It seems to be good for people. It wakes them up."

Frank nodded at this, but Anna only looked distressed. She said, "But you're making arrangements?"

"Yes, of course. Such freedom from habit cannot last, people would go mad." He glanced at Frank and laughed; Frank felt his face get hot. "We're talking with the Dalai Lama, of course, and the Indian government. Probably they would give us another island in the Sundarbans."

"But then it will only happen again," Frank pointed out.

"Yes, it seems likely."

"You need to get to higher ground."

"Yes."

"Back to the Himalayas," Anna suggested.

"We will see. For now, Washington, D.C."

"Go higher than that for God's sake!"

Sometimes Drepung would leave on errands and Frank and Anna would order another coffee and talk for a few minutes before taking the coffees back up to work. They shared their news in a desultory fashion. Anna's was usually about Charlie and the boys, Frank's about something he had done or seen. Anna laughed at the discrepancy: "Things are still happening to you."

Frank rolled his eyes at this. For a while they talked in a different way than usual, about how things felt; and they agreed that lives were not easily told. Frank speculated that many life stories consisted precisely in a search for a reiterated pattern, for habits. Thus, one's set of habits was somehow unsatisfactory, and you needed to change them, and were thereby thrown into a plot, which was the hunt for new habits, or even, but exceptionally, the story of the giving up of such a hunt in favor of sticking with what you have, or remaining chaotically in the existential moment (not adaptive if reproductive success were the goal, he noted under his breath). Thus Frank was living a plot while Anna was living a life, and when they talked about personal matters he had news while she had the "same old same old," which was understood by both to be the desired state, irritating and difficult though it might be to maintain.

Anna merely laughed at this.

One day the Things to Do list included a lunch meeting at a Crystal City restaurant with the four-star general who headed the U.S. Army Corps of Engineers, a friendly and unassuming man named Arthur Wracke, "pronounced *rack*," he said, "yes, as in rack and ruin." White-haired, brown-skinned, grizzled, a strangely pixie grin: unflappable. This, Frank saw, was what had gotten him his four stars. And along the way he had surely been in any number of political firestorms over major environmental interventions like the ones they were now contemplating at NSF.

When Frank wondered if any major climate mitigation was possible, physically or politically, Wracke waved a hand. "The Corps has always done things on a big scale. Huge scale. Sometimes with huge blunders. All with the best intentions of course. That's just the way things happen. We're still gung ho to try. Lots of things are reversible, in the long run. Hopefully this time around we'll be working with better science. But, you know, it's an iterative process. So, long story short, you get a project approved, and we're good to go. We've got the expertise. The Corps' esprit de corps is always high."

"What about budget?" Frank asked.

"What about it? We'll spend what we're given."

"Well, but is there any kind of, you know, discretionary fund you have?"

"We don't seek funding, usually," the general said.

"But could you?"

"Only in tandem with a request for action. Say you came to us with a request for action that would cost more than you have available. We could refer it up, and it would have to go to the Joint Chiefs of Staff to get supplementary funding. Do even the Chiefs have much discretionary funding?" He grinned. "Sure they do. But they got in trouble recently for what they were calling reprogrammed funding. Did not please certain congresspeople. Really, it all goes back to Congress. They control the purse strings. Even more than the President. So if *they* were to allocate funds, the Joint Chiefs would tell us to do it."

Frank nodded. "But if it was just the Pentagon . . ."

"We'd have to see. But we could make your case, and if the funding's there, we are good to go."

"Major climate mitigation."

"Oh heck yes. We like these kinds of challenges. Who wouldn't?"

Frank had to laugh. The world was their sandbox. Castles and moats, dams and bulwarks . . . they had drained and then rehydrated the Everglades, they kept New Orleans dry, most of the time; they had rerouted all the major rivers, irrigated the West, moved mountains. You could see all that right there on the general's happy face. Stewardship, sustainability—fine! Rack but not ruin! Working for the long haul just meant no end, ever, to their sandbox games.

"No deep ecologists in the U.S. Army Corps of Engineers, I guess."

"Ha ha." Wracke's eyes twinkled. "You give us a chance and we'll *become* deep ecologists. We'll go right down to the *mantle.*"

Driving back to the office, Frank considered the way some people enjoyed becoming the avatar of the institution they worked for, expressing their organization's personality like an actor in a role they love. Diane was somewhat like that herself, though as Edgardo had noted, she was pushing the NSF character into realms it had never entered before, so the vibe she had was not quite like Wracke's evocation of the Corps, which was supremely at ease, but rather that of a person in the midst of a great awakening, a coming into one's own. Diane as *Science Becoming Self-Aware.* Maybe even *Unbound.* Diane as Prometheus!

In the last hour of the workday Frank usually sat back in his office chair and glanced through jackets. Sometimes he couldn't stand that, and he scanned submissions to *The Journal of Sociobiology* instead. Maternal sentiment not innate, one paper said; this asserted because women in northern Taiwan, also European women in the medieval and early modern period, gave away their own children on a regular basis, for economic reasons. Maternal sentiment therefore perhaps a learned response. Frank had his doubts, and besides, all these conclusions were long since outlined in Hrdy, a source the paper's authors seemed unaware of. That ignorance, and the huge generalizations given the evidence, probably would doom this paper to rejection.

Abstract, conclusion; abstract, conclusion. Female brown capuchin monkeys throw things if they see other monkeys getting more than they got from an equivalent exchange. Aversion to inequity therefore probably very deep-rooted. Sense of fairness evolved early. Thus cooperative groups, long before hominids. Monkey ethics; interesting.

First primate found and identified, in China, 55 million years old. Named *Teilhardina,* very nice. One ounce; fit in the palm of your hand.

Groups of female baboons could coerce new male members of the troop into more peaceful behaviors. Females of the Japanese quail *Coturnix japonica* tended to choose the losers in male-male confrontations. Maybe that's why Caroline likes me, Frank thought, then grimaced at this traitorous self-judgment. It was postulated that for the female quails, choosing the loser reduced the risk of later injury, the males being rough during sex. Previously mated females more likely to choose losers than virgins were.

On he read, his face thrust forward into the laptop so eagerly that his nose almost touched the screen. There could not be another person on Earth who read these things with more intense interest than he did, for to him these were questions of immediate practice, influencing what he might do later that very day. To him every paper had the unwritten subtitle *How Should I Live Right Now?*

When his wristwatch alarm beeped the question always remained unanswered. Time to get up and invent the evening.

Run a round of frisbee, drop in on the bros, play chess with Chessman, visit the Quiblers, sit in Kramer's or Second Story to read, have an ouzo at Odysseus. For about a month he played chess with Chessman almost every night, becoming a regular mark, as Zeno put it, as Chessman was getting unbeatable. He played more than anyone else, he was a pro, and it might be that he was getting really good; Frank didn't play well enough to be sure. Paradoxically, the youth's style had become less aggressive. He waited for people to extend a little, then beat them. The games took more time, and maybe that was the point; it gave people hope, and thus might create more repeat customers.

In between games they sat by a kerosene lantern, nursing coffees or beers. Chessman read paperbacks under the lamp, books with titles like *One Hundred Best End Games*. Once it had been *The Immortal Games of Paul Morphy,* another time *The Genius of Paul Morphy.* Frank chatted with the others. It was yet another iteration of a conversation they had had many times, concerning the inadequacies of the National Park Service. All their various conversations were like performances of long-running plays, alternating in repertory. Laughs in the usual places. The bros laughed more than anyone Frank knew, but it was seldom happy laughter. They were shouting defiance. Vocalizations were as important to people as to gibbons. The daily hoot, *oooooooooop!*

So they sat there, telling stories. Awful things from Vietnam, a rare item in their repertory, but sometimes Zeno and Fedpage and Andy got a horrible urge to reminisce. More often they described recent scuffles, reenacted in full. The bros retained a choreographic memory of every fight they had ever been in. Then also, recent meals; ranger actions of any kind, important or trivial; the weather. Cutter would drop by almost every night, even though he clearly had somewhere else he could go. In that sense he was like Frank, and perhaps as a result he and Frank didn't talk much. The truth was that Frank spoke to few but Chessman and Zeno. Sometimes he would talk to Fedpage about items from the *Post*, or Andy would command that he join one of Andy's stock exchanges. Cutter always brought a six-pack or two, and they would fall to and divide the cans and drink until the drink was gone. This usually perked them up.

"Cutter is a tree surgeon," Zeno clarified to Frank, "our tree surgeon, currently unemployed."

"Not city parks?" Frank asked Cutter, gesturing at the patch on the shoulder of his shirt.

"Used to be."

"But you look like you're still doing it?"

"Oh I am, I am."

"Cutter is the keeper of the forest. He is the unsung savior of this fucking city."

"What else am I gonna do."

"So you cut on your own?"

"Yes I do."

"He steals gas outta cars to keep his chainsaw going, don't ya Cutter?"

"Someone's gotta do it. This town'd disappear like *that*."

"The forest it *wants* this city back, you know it does! *That's* who's winning."

"—two three years I swear. But city knows some of us'll keep at it, so they keep cutting staff."

"They cut more people than trees!"

Cutter laughed. "Yesterday Byron couldn't buckle his harness but in the last hole, you know he's so fat these days, and so it gave loose on him as he finished dropping a big branch, and he fell and popped out of the waist belt but his legs held, so he swung down and the chainsaw smacked him right here on top of his leg. So he's hanging there screaming like a fool, 'I cut my leg, I cut off my leg oh *God*!' But weren't no cut on his leg, just a bruise and a scrape. So we calling up to him, 'Byron you okay, ain't no cut on your leg, quit your wiggling, you gonna slip out your harness and crack your head like a egg.' But he was yelling so loud he never heard us, 'My leg, my leg, I've cut off my laaig! I can't *feel* it no more!' And we telling him, 'Open your eyes fool and look you're fine,' and he won't do it. 'I can't stand to see it!' His eyes all squished shut, 'No no *no*, I can't *do* it I can't stand to see it, I can't stand to *look* it's too horrible, I can *feel* it's gone, I can *feel* the blood *dripping*!'"

The bros loved this. "I can *feeeel* it!" It was obvious this was something they'd be saying for months to come, a new addition to their clutch of stock phrases.

"How'd you get him down?"

"We had to pinch his eyelids open and *make* him look."

Bursts of raucous laughter, shouted comments, a mocking reenactment of how it must have been. Another little climax of hilarity punctuating the day.

After that they sank slowly into sullen peacefulness or sullen squabbling, same as always. The various aches and complaints. Fedpage went back to his *Post,* the rest to the chessboard or the scraps on the grill topping the flue of the smoky fire. Dry leaves and wet branches, and again the meat was both black with smoke and undercooked. Prod the fire to keep it sputtering along. Out into the dark for a round of copious urination. Some slipped off to find another haunt; others slumped in their places, the evening's entertainment over.

Frank walked out into the night. Sound of the creek, the citysurround. Voices in the distance; there were people at site 20, as always, and also at 18, which was a surprise. As he closed on his tree it got quieter and so did he, making his final approach as quietly as possible, covered by the noise of the creek a short distance below. Under his tree he waited, listening carefully. Night goggles, survey the scene; nothing warm upstream or down. When he was convinced no one was nearby, he called down Miss Piggy and clambered up into the night, up into his aerie, like a mountaineer scaling a last overhang to a ledge camp.

He pulled through the gap in the rail and sat on the plywood. Cranking Miss Piggy up, it occurred to him that the rent he was saving these days might eventually enable him to afford a down payment on a house, when he finally returned to San Diego. A quick calculation indicated that to save enough, he would have to stay up here some five or six years.

Well—it could be worse. It was not such a bad prospect, really. Up in the night and the wind, swaying slightly north and south; how bad was that?

He lay down on his bed. In the mellow glow of his battery-powered Coleman lantern, he opened a paperback copy of Italo Calvino's *The Baron in the Trees*. He had seen the book in Second Story and bought it, thinking it might teach him something. But so far it had been short on logistical detail, and lacking also the explanatory power he was hoping for. The young baron had barged into the trees one day after a fight with his father, which was believable enough, but unilluminating. And his decision to stay up there the rest of his life, without ever coming down at all, was simply unreasonable. Cosimo could have done everything he had done and still come down from time to time. Not coming down made it more of a parable than a program. An allegory, perhaps, for staying in nature. Well, in that sense Cosimo was a hero, his story a good fable.

But Frank was content to be up here when he was, without wanting more. Around him the aging leaves clattered, and in the distance came the cry of a coyote, or maybe even a loon—in any case one of those crazies who would not shut up at night. Like certain of the bros. Every animal trait had its echo in some human quality. "Owwww," he howled quietly. "Owwww-www." The tree rocked him in its slight syncopation against the wind.

He wanted Caroline to call him. He was tired of waiting for her to call, why didn't she call? Surely she knew he was waiting. Even if she had trouble at home, even if she couldn't get away, surely she could call? Could she be in trouble? Could her husband (an awful phrase) have her under surveillance? Such tight surveillance that she couldn't get away to call? Could he have that same kind of surveillance trained on Frank, making it doubly hard for her to call? Was there some reason why she couldn't get loose like she had before? After all, she had both called and appeared in the Bethesda park. Perhaps it required a stay with her friends. Who were these friends she had stayed with? Whose boat had she been on during the flood? Had she been under surveillance then? Why didn't she . . . but maybe she couldn't—but why didn't she call?

He was getting sleepy. There were so many questions he couldn't answer, couldn't ask. So much he didn't know. There were so many times when he wanted to touch her again. Kiss her. Have his face in her hair. In her absence this specific desire was becoming a general desire, diffusing into the landscape itself. In D.C. that could be quite an experience; the women of Washington were gorgeous. All the exiled goddesses of Earth passed by on the street. Every woman metamorphosed into the movie star who would have played her on-screen; every woman became the avatar of her particular type, and yet remained completely herself. Why didn't she call?

Voices below. Frank hung like a spirit above them. No way people would see him in the dark, even infrared wouldn't work through the plywood and the branch-camouflaged insulation tacked to its underside; he had tested that to be sure.

The voices were discussing something, it sounded like plans. He surveiled until they moved off and were lost in the sound of the creek.

She didn't call because of surveillance. Frank had looked into this a little, what this might mean to be under surveillance in this day and age. But he had been using his computer at work to make the search, at first, and that began to seem like it might put out a flag of some kind. He had felt constrained, and started to do his research in the NSF library, a very different resource. Maybe he had already given himself away. Would they become suspicious (if they were watching), and conclude that he knew they were watching? And if so, would that increase or otherwise alter the watching?

Frank read and heard all kinds of things about modern surveillance, and whenever he asked Edgardo about it, when they would not be overheard, Edgardo would grin and nod and say, "That's right." He said, "That's right," to everything, until Frank said, "Are you saying you don't really know what's going on and neither does anyone else on Earth?"

"That's right."

It was an impossible situation. No amount of googling would clarify it, and indeed any very extensive hunt might catch someone's attention and make his situation worse. Better to lie low. Better to investigate by talking only to people who might know, who wouldn't tell anyone else, in places they wouldn't be overheard. Strange but true; the possibility of electronic surveillance was driving him back to the oldest technology of all, talking out in the open air.

He wondered if Yann knew he was under surveillance, or was the reason many of his acquaintances were also. He was going to have to talk to Yann.

He discussed with Diane his idea of head-hunting Pierzinski, and she liked it. Carbon sequestration was mostly a biological problem; the amount of carbon they wanted to shift was beyond any current industrial capacity. They needed to involve the bacterial world, if they could. Pierzinski had been working on an algorithm that might create a better ability to manipulate genomes, and apparently Yann and Eleanor and Marta were having their best successes at the bacterial level. So he should go to Atlanta and talk to Yann.

But talking to Yann meant he would have to see Marta. She and Yann lived together, so it seemed that if he flew down to meet with Yann, Marta would have to be part of it one way or another. That might be awful. The last time he had seen her had been terrible. However, too bad; he still had to do it. It would end up worse if he went down there and tried to see Yann while avoiding her. That would backfire for sure, although it might not be possible to make her any more angry with him than she already was, so maybe it didn't matter.

And a part of him wanted to see her again anyway. All these women he was thinking about—mainly Caroline, the thought of whom made his heart pulse, and also perhaps spread a certain feeling over thoughts of Diane and her clever calmness, or even Francesca—all these thoughts often led back to Marta, a woman he had lived with for years, someone he really knew and had had a relationship with, even if it had imploded. She would still be mad at him. But he had to see her.

.   .   .

From Atlanta's airport he took a shuttle to a hotel downtown. The area around Georgia Tech featured wide avenues running up and down low hills, between huge glossy skyscrapers, copper and blue and dragonfly green. The school's football stadium was below street level, reminding him of Khembalung.

After checking into the hotel Frank showered, then dressed with more care than usual. Uneasy glances in the mirror. Pierzinski had a little touch of Asperger's, not uncommon in mathematicians; over the phone he had agreed to Frank's request for a meeting with innocent delight, saying, "I'll bring Marta along, she'll love to see you."

Frank had recalled his last encounter with Marta in San Diego, and held his tongue. It was enough to make him wonder just how close Yann and Marta were. Maybe she was not in the habit of talking to Yann about her past. Frank hoped not.

Anyway, she would be there. Her connection to Yann still surprised Frank a little; Marta and Yann did not seem to him a likely couple; but then again what couple did?

Yann had suggested a restaurant nearby. Frank remained stuck in the bathroom. He really didn't want to go. He was afraid to go. He looked neon pink in the mirror, somewhat boiled by the shower. He looked like he was wearing a costume signifying "academic at lunch." Best give up on appearances. Marta knew what he looked like.

As did whoever was spying on him, and spying on Yann and Marta as well! A red-light situation: three of that market's commodities meeting.

He left the hotel and walked to the restaurant. It was a sultry night, a wet wind pouring like syrup through the streets. Marta had sent him directions in an e-mail that had no personal touches whatsoever. Not a good sign.

The restaurant turned out to be an old-fashioned saloon, thick with the smell of old cigar smoke and machine politics. Wooden beams crossed the ceiling in Tudor style, dividing the space into small rooms. Sports paraphernalia, TVs overhead. A perfect place to spy on someone. The walls of the entryway were covered with black-and-white photos of groups sitting at the biggest tables, men in vests. Campaign buttons surrounded the photos. It was hard for Frank to imagine Marta even entering such a place.

But she was there already, it turned out, seated in a booth at the back with Yann. "Hi Yann, hi Marta."

Yann rose and shook his hand; Marta didn't. After one charged look Frank avoided her gaze and sat down, trying not to cringe. He thought of Caroline, brought her deliberately to mind; the look in her eye; then by accident thought of Diane too. Francesca. Caroline's touch. He knew some powerful women: too many, one might say. He met Marta's eye again, held his ground. *Ooooop! Oooooop!*

They made small talk of the how-have-you-been variety, ordered drinks. It was early, and Frank and Marta declined food, while Yann ordered french fries. When they arrived Yann downed them like popcorn, bang bang bang.

Silence inevitably fell, Yann being so busy. "So what brings you here?" Marta said.

"Well, I'm doing another year at NSF."

Frank knew that Marta thought he had gone to NSF to escape her, back when they were breaking up. So this might be construed as saying he had had other reasons for going.

She wasn't buying it. "Why would you do that?"

"Well, I've gotten interested in things NSF can do that UCSD can't. National policy, and some big new programs. I was offered the chance to help with some of them, so I decided to give it a try."

"Uh-huh," Marta said. "So what are you doing?"

"Well, a number of things. But one of them is looking into trying to start up some institutes, like the Max Planck Institutes in Germany, that would focus on particular problems. And, you know, one of the obvious things to look at would be the stuff you guys were doing out in San Diego. You know, trying to do proteomics, with the idea that if we got that going properly, it might lead to some important advances. So I came down to see, well, you know—to see if you'd have any interest in joining something like that."

Well, if spies were listening in, then they knew all. Frank shuddered at the idea that he had ever tried to rig this game with his Thornton-in-the-panel.

Head-hunting, however, was standard practice.

"It's going fine here," Marta said curtly. "Small Delivery is part of Bizet."

One of the Big Pharms, as Edgardo put it. "We've got a budget bigger than anything NSF could offer."

This was not true, and Frank longed to say, *I've got two billion dollars to spend, does Bizet have two billion dollars?* He clamped his jaw shut; his jaw muscles would be bunching in a way she knew to notice. She knew him. He tried to relax. "Well . . . so, you're still working on the same stuff as in San Diego?"

The french fries were gone, and Yann nodded. "The algorithm is working best on plant genomes, so the algae work is getting really predictable."

Marta frowned. She didn't like Yann saying even this much.

Frank felt his stomach shrink. He and Marta had been together for four very intense years, and their breakup had been so terrible . . . the dread and remorse from that time were like a vise inside him still, ready to clamp anytime he thought about it. A lot of what had happened had been his fault. He had known that for most of the last year, but now it was all falling on him again. Anger vibed across the table at him in waves, and he couldn't meet her gaze.

Yann appeared oblivious to all this. It was kind of hard to believe. It was also hard to imagine these two together. Yann was describing some of the tweaking he had done to his algorithm, and Frank did his best to follow, and to ask the questions he had come down to ask. How did that work? How would that work? Would more research funds speed the work? It was important to concentrate. It was important to get a fix on how Yann's work was progressing. Frank still had ideas about where it could go, and he wanted to talk about that.

But it became clear Yann had changed emphasis during his time at Small Delivery. At first Frank didn't follow the significance of the change. "You're engineering lichen?" he asked, feeling that Marta's glare was making him stupid.

Marta answered for Yann. "It's not about human health anymore," she said sharply. "We're interested in engineering a tree lichen that will incorporate carbon into the host trees much faster than they do naturally."

Frank sat back. "So, a carbon sink thing?"

"Yes. A carbon sink thing."

Frank thought it over. "Why?" he said finally.

Yann said, "The problems with gene uptake in humans were getting too complicated, we just couldn't . . ."

"We couldn't make it work," Marta said flatly. "No one can. It may be the showstopper for the whole idea of gene therapy. They can't get altered genes into cells without infecting them with a virus, and a lot of times that's a really bad idea. That's what it comes down to."

"Well, but these nanobits look promising," Yann said enthusiastically. "We're making little bits of metal? They hold DNA on one side, and then when the metal bits embed in cell walls, the DNA leaves the nanobits and is taken up."

"In vivo?"

"No, in vitro, but they're about ready for phase ones."

"We," Marta corrected him.

"Yeah, but the other lab. And we're working on some Venter viruses too, you can build some pretty harmless viruses that alter the bacteria they jump into. The algorithms there are about the same as the lichen augmenters." Suddenly he looked at his watch. "Hey, I'm sorry Frank, but I have to go. I had a previous appointment I can't let down."

Abruptly he stood and extended a greasy hand to Frank, shook hands briefly, and with a quick wave to Marta was out the door.

Frank stared at the space Yann had vacated. What was Yann thinking, this was an appointment they had made, Frank had flown down for it! And now here he was alone with Marta. It was like the things that happened in his nightmares, and quickly fear began to fill him.

"Well," he said experimentally.

Marta continued to alternate between staring and glaring. Unbidden, and indeed squirting out with the sudden force characteristic of the return of the repressed, he recalled her on the beach at Cardiff Reef, shouting *leave me alone*.

"Look," he said abruptly, as if cutting her off in the middle of a rant, "I'm sorry."

"What?"

"I'm *sorry*."

"Hey. You don't *sound* sorry."

"I *am* sorry."

"Sorry for *what*?"

Frank pursed his lips, tried to achieve a level tone. It was a fair enough question after all.

"I'm sorry I borrowed money on the house without telling you about it. I owe you some money because of that."

"You owe me more than that."

Frank shrugged. "Maybe so. But I figure I owe you about $18,400 on the house deal." He was surprised how readily the figure came to mind. "I can at least pay you back the money. What you put into the place."

While they had been together, their financial arrangement had been informal; a mess, in fact. And so when they broke up, which had come as a surprise to Frank, the money situation had caused big trouble. It had not been entirely Frank's fault, or so he told himself. At the time they bought a house together in Cardiff, Marta had been in some sort of bankruptcy snarl with her soon-to-be ex-husband. She had married an ex-professor of hers, very foolishly it had seemed to Frank, and after the first year they had lived apart, but Marta had not bothered to get an official divorce until it became necessary. All this should have told Frank something, but it hadn't. Marta was therefore bogged in her ex's financial disasters, which had gone on for years—making her extra-intolerant of any funny business, as Frank only realized later, when his own affairs had gotten snarled in their turn. His had not been as bad as her ex's, but on the other hand, there were aspects that were maybe worse, as her ex had gotten into his trouble mostly after he and Marta had split up, whereas Frank had deliberately concealed from her a third mortgage on their house, which had been in his name only; a mortgage he had taken to give him money to invest in a biotech start-up coming out of UCSD. This start-up had sparked his interest but unfortunately no one else's, and soon the money from the third mortgage was gone, sucking all the equity they had accrued out of the place with it. So it was a really bad time for Marta to move out and demand that they sell the place and split the proceeds. He had had no time to put back the money, and when he confessed to her that there were no proceeds to split—that the money she had paid into the place, a matter of many thousands, was not there—she had freaked out. First she screamed at him, indeed threw a lamp at him; then she had refused to speak to him, or, later, to negotiate a payment schedule by which he could pay her back. At that point, it seemed to Frank, she actually wanted him to have ripped her off, the better to feel angry at him. Which no doubt helped her to avoid admitting to herself, or anyone else, that it was her wildness—specifically her sexual infidelities, always "a part of the deal" of being with her, as she claimed, but increasingly upsetting—that had caused him to demand a different basis to the relationship, which had then started the whole breakup in the first place. In other words, it had actually been all her fault, but with the money situation included, she didn't have to admit it.

He could only hope she knew this. She had to know it; and probably she felt some guilt or responsibility, which helped to make her so abrasive and hostile. She had cheated on him, and he had cheated her. Love and money. Ah well. The pointless wars of the heart.

"Why did you do it?" she burst out.

"Do what?"

"Why did you take out a third on *our house* without *telling me*? Why didn't you just *talk* about it? I would have been up for it."

Well, he owed her an explanation for this. "I don't know. I didn't think you would be up for it."

"Well either I would or I wouldn't, but since you lost it all, because it was a bad idea, maybe if I hadn't gone for it, it would have been for a good reason! I'm not *stupid* you know."

"I know."

"You *don't* know! You think I'm just a lab tech. You think I'm the surfer slut who kills the mice and makes the coffee—"

"I do not! No way!"

"Fucking right no way." She glowered viciously. She hated killing lab mice. "I've got my own lab here, and the stuff we're doing with Yann is really interesting. You'd be amazed."

"No I wouldn't."

"Yes you would! You have no idea."

"You're making a carbon sink organism. You told me. A way to sequester carbon quickly by biotechnical means."

"Yes."

"That's great. But you know," Frank said carefully, "much as we need a quick carbon capture these days, your customers are going to have to be governments. Corporations aren't going to pay for it, or be able get the permits. It's the U.S. government or the UN or something like that who will."

She glowered less viciously. "So?"

"So, you'll need to get government approvals, government funding—"

"It's no different than the drug stuff."

"Except for the customer. It won't be individuals, if I understand you right. It can't be. So it's not like drugs at all."

"Not that part. We know that."

"So, well, you know, you've got to have some government agencies on your side. DOE, EPA, OMB, Congress, the White House—they'll all have to be on board with it."

She waved all that away. "We're talking to the Russians."

This was news to Frank, and interesting, but he ignored it for the moment and said, "But if you had NSF behind you, you'd be set to get the rest of the U.S. government behind you too."

"What are you saying?"

"I'm saying I'm working on this stuff. I'm saying there's a committee at NSF that's working with two billion dollars in this year's budget alone."

There. He had said it.

She was determined not to be impressed. "So?"

"So, that's two billion dollars more than Small Delivery Systems has."

She cracked up despite herself. "You're head-hunting me. Or rather, you're head-hunting Yann."

"I am. You and Yann and Eleanor, and whoever else is working on this."

She stared at him.

"You and Yann could stay together," he heard himself saying. "Maybe the new institute could be put at UCSD, and you two could move back there."

She was frowning. "What do you mean?"

"Well, you know. You wouldn't end up with job offers in different places. That happens to couples all the time, you know it does. And you guys probably aren't done moving."

She laughed abruptly. "We're not a couple, either."

"What?"

"You are so stupid Frank."

"What do you mean?"

"Yann is gay. We're just friends. We share a house here. We share a lot more than you and I ever did. We talk instead of fight and fuck. It's very nice. He's a really good guy. But he has his boyfriends, and I have mine."

"Oh."

She laughed again, unamused. "You are such a . . ."

She couldn't think of a word that fit. Frank couldn't either. He waited, staring down at the battered wooden tabletop. He was such a—a what? A something. Really, there was no word that came to mind. A fool? A mess?

Was he any more of a mess than anyone else, though? Maybe so.

He shrugged. "Did you . . . know about Yann in San Diego?"

"Yeah sure. We were friends, we went out. It was nice not to have to think about guys. People left us alone, or went for Yann. He's a sweet guy, and this stuff in math—well, you know. He's a kind of genius. He's like Wittgenstein, or Turing."

"Hopefully happier than them."

"Were they unhappy?"

"I don't know. I seem to remember reading they were."

"Well, Yann seems pretty happy to me. He's really smart and really nice and he pays attention to my work." *Unlike you,* her expression said. "And he and Eleanor and I are getting good results."

"I'm glad. I really am! That's why I came down here. I wanted to tell you about this, this possibility, of federally funded work."

"Why not talk with the Small Delivery management?"

"I want the new institutes to be in full control of their scientific results. No private trade secrets or patents."

She thought that over. "What about with public universities?"

"Like UCSD and a federal lab, you mean?"

"Yeah."

"I think that would be okay. I wish there was more of it. And there will be. We're trying a bunch of things like that."

Marta nodded, interested despite herself.

"We've got the go-ahead," Frank said. "The go-ahead and the budget."

Now she was pursing her lips into a little bloodless bloom, her sign of serious thought. "San Diego."

"What?"

"You said UCSD."

"Yes, that's right. I'd have to recuse myself because of my position there, but it makes so much sense, Diane would run it through for me, I'm sure. Why? Do you want to move back there?"

"Fuck." She gave him another look. "What do you think?"

"I thought you liked it here."

"Oh for God's sake Frank. We're in Atlanta, Georgia."

"I know, I know. I thought it looked pretty nice, actually."

"My God. You've been out here too long."

"Probably so."

"It's warped your mind."

"That's very true."

Her stare grew suspicious, then calculating. "You can't possibly like Washington, D.C."

"Well, I don't know. I'm beginning to think it's okay."

"It's the East Coast, Frank! Jesus, you've lost your mind out here. It's a swamp! No beach, no ocean—"

"There's the Atlantic—"

"No *waves,* and it's hours to get to there, even if there were."

"I know."

"Frank," she said, looking at him with new interest. "You've gone crazy."

"A little bit, yeah."

"*That's* why you apologized to me."

"Well, I meant it. I should have said it before."

"That's true."

"So maybe I'm getting *less* crazy." He laughed at that idea, met her eye.

She shook her head. "I don't think so."

"Ah well."

She watched him, shrugged. "Time will tell."

Again Frank understood that he had lost a relationship with someone he could have gotten along with. But now, what had happened in the past had a kind of trajectory or inertia that could not be altered; the relationship was wrecked for good. He caught a quick glimpse of a different life, he and Marta still together in San Diego. But the bad things that had happened could never be undone, and that whole world of possibility was gone, popped like a soap bubble.

What if humanity's relationship to Earth was like that?

A nasty thought.

It occurred to him that he could warn Marta about the surveillance they were living under, Yann too. But as with Francesca, he found he wasn't ready for that—for what he would have to get into to tell her about it. I have this spook girlfriend, we're all under surveillance, we're part of an experiment where computer programs bet on us, and our stock may now be rising. No.

Instead he said, "So you would consider an offer to move your lab to a federal institute?"

"Maybe. I'll talk to Yann. But, you know, it might crimp any chance for big compensation for all this."

"Well, but it won't have much chance of happening at all if it stays in the private sector."

"That's what you say. I'll talk to Yann about it. And Eleanor. We'll come to a decision together."

Frank nodded, yeah yeah: point already taken, blade in to the hilt, no call to be twisting it.

Marta, eyeing him, relented. "Make it so it could get us back to San Diego. That might do it. I need to get back in the water."

Anna was convinced that Joe had caught something in Khembalung. He had been more than usually fractious on all the return flights, and worse as they went on, from the confused tears in the helicopter to the exhausted screams on the final L.A.-to-Dulles leg. What with that and their own exhaustion, and the shock of the flood overwhelming Khembalung, they had eventually reached the moment that sometimes happens in a bad trip, when everyone is thinking what a terrible idea it had been to go, and no one can think of anything to say, or even meet their fellow sufferers in the eye. Anna and Charlie had endured a few of these trips before, none quite so bad, but they both knew what the lack of eye contact meant and what the other one was thinking. Dispense with talk and do the necessary, in a kind of grim solidarity. Just get home.

But then, at home, Joe's dis-ease had continued, and to Anna he felt a little hot. She got out the thermometer, ignoring Charlie's heavy look, and biting her tongue to avoid yet another ridiculous argument on this topic of medical data gathering. Though he would not usually admit to it, Charlie suffered from a kind of magical thinking that believed that taking a temperature might invite an illness to appear which did not exist until it was measured. Anna suspected this came from the Christian Scientists in Charlie's family background, giving him a tendency to see illness as the taint of sin. This was, of course, crazy.

And Anna craved data, as usual. Taking a temperature was just a matter of getting more information. It always helped her to know things more precisely; the more she knew, the less her fears could imagine things worse than what she knew. So she took Joe's temperature without consulting Charlie, and found it registered 99.0.

"That's his *normal* temperature," Charlie pointed out.

"What do you mean?" Anna said.

"He always charts high."

"I don't remember that."

"Well it's true. It happens every time I take him in for a checkup. I don't think they've ever gotten a reading under 99 for him."

"Hmm." Anna let that go. She was pretty sure it wasn't true, but she certainly didn't want to get into an argument that could only be resolved by getting into medical records. She knew that Joe felt warmer now than he had before, in her arms and on the nipple. And his face was always flushed. "Maybe we should take him in to be checked anyway."

"I don't see why."

"Well, when is he scheduled for a checkup?"

"I don't know. It hasn't been that long since the last one."

Anna gave up on it, not wanting to seethe. She would wait and see how things went for a day or two more, then insist if necessary. Take him in herself if she had to.

After a fraught silence went on for quite a while, Charlie said, "Look, let's see how he goes. If it still seems like there's a problem I'll take him in next week."

"Okay, good."

So it went in the world of Charlie and Anna, a world of telepathic negotiations made out of silence and gesture; a world in which the sharp words were usually not spoken but felt in the air, or, if spoken in a sudden outburst of irritation, taken as one part of a mind reproving another, in the way one will easily snap at oneself for doing something foolish, knowing there is no one there to misunderstand or get upset.

But of course even an old matrimonial mindmeld is never total, and for his part, Charlie did not articulate, indeed hid in one of the far reaches of his mind, outside the reach of Anna's telepathy, his worries about what might be wrong with Joe. He knew that to Anna he seemed afraid of the idea of illness, ready always to ignore it or condemn it, and that to her this was inappropriate, craven, counterproductive. But first of all, mind-body studies of placebos and positive attitudes gave some support to the idea of not tolerating, or ritually opposing, the idea of illness; and second, if she knew what he was really worrying about, the whole Joe/Khembalung dynamic, she would have thought him naïve and credulous, even though she respected the Khembalis and knew (he hoped) that they took this kind of thing seriously. Better for her to think he was still just in his old curse-the-disease mode. So he kept his thoughts to himself.

Thus there was a dissonance that was palpable to both of them, an awareness that they were not as fully known to each other as they usually were. Which also would worry Anna; but Charlie judged this the lesser of two worries, and held his tongue. No way was he going to bring up the possibility of some kind of problem in Joe's spiritual life. What the hell was that, after all? And how would you measure it?

So at work Anna spent her time trying to concentrate, over a persistent underlying turmoil of worry about her younger son. Work was absorbing, and there was always more to do than time to do it. And so it provided its refuge.

But it was harder to dive in, harder to stay under the surface in the deep sea of bioinformatics. Even the content of the work reminded her, on some subliminal level, that health was a state of dynamic balance almost inconceivably complex, a matter of juggling a thousand balls while unicycling on a tightrope over the abyss—in a gale—at night—such that any life was an astonishing miracle, tenuous and brief. But enough of that kind of thinking! Bear down on the fact, on the moment and the problem of the moment!

Frequently she found herself unable to concentrate no matter her exhortations, and she would spend an hour or two digging around on the internet, to see if she could find anything useful for Diane and Frank. Old things that had worked but been forgotten; new things that hadn't yet been noticed or appreciated. This could be rather depressing, of course. The government sites devoted to climate change were often inadequate; conference proceedings on another page spoke of "climate change adaptation," ignoring the fact that "adaptation" had no meaning in regard to actual technologies, that the whole concept of "adaptation" to climate change was a replacement for "mitigation," and at this point completely hollow, a word only, a way of saying *Do nothing* or *Give up*. Whole conferences were devoted to that.

After discoveries like this she would move on and search elsewhere, on scientific sites that were more technically oriented. More and more it seemed to her that ordinary science was the only thing that worked in the world; so that even with abrupt climate change upon them, requiring an emergency response, dispersing science more rapidly was still not only the only thing she could do to help, but the only thing anyone could do.

Edgardo shook his head when she expressed this thought. "One tends to think only the method one knows will work."

"Yes I'm sure. But what if this time it's true?"

Once after one of these hunts, she went into one of Diane and Frank's meetings and said, "Let me tell you some history."

In her reading she had run across a description of a "Scientists for Johnson Campaign" in the presidential election of 1964. A group of prominent scientists, worried by Goldwater's nuclear bravado, had organized into what would later be called a political action committee, and taken out ads urging people to vote for Johnson. Dire warnings were made of what could happen if Goldwater won, and a vote for Johnson was portrayed as a vote for world peace, for the reality principle itself.

All of which had perhaps helped Johnson; but it backfired when Nixon won four years later, because he came into the White House convinced that all scientists hated him.

"But Nixon was paranoid, right?"

"Paranoid or clear-sighted."

"Both. He thought people hated him, and then he made it come true so he could feel clear-sighted."

"Maybe."

But for science this had been a bad thing. Nixon had first shut down the Office of Science and Technology, then demoted the remaining position of presidential science advisor out of the cabinet, exiling the office to the hinterlands. Then he had kicked NSF itself out of the White House, across the river to Arlington.

"It's like we're still in some feudal court," Frank observed, "where physical proximity to the king actually mattered."

"You're sounding like Edgardo."

"Yes, he said that today, actually."

In any case, science had been booted out of the policy arena, and never come back.

"Meaning?" Diane said.

"Meaning science isn't part of policy making anymore! It doesn't support candidates, and scientists never run for office themselves. They just ask for money and let it go at that."

"Science is a higher activity," Edgardo proclaimed. "What it does is so valuable that you have to give it a lot of money, no strings attached."

"Pretty clever."

"I think so."

"Too bad it doesn't work better though."

"Well, that's true. That's what we're working on."

Frank was shaking his head. "It seems to me that this story about Johnson and Nixon is just one more indication that science is generally thought of as being liberal politically."

No one wanted to think about this, Anna could tell.

"How so?" Diane asked.

"Well, you know. If the Republican Party has been hijacked by the religious right, or uses them, then the Democrats look like the party for secular people, including lots of scientists. It's like the debate over evolution all over again. Christianity versus science, now Republican versus Democrat."

This was a bad thought. Diane said, "We can't afford to get caught on one side of that."

Anna said, "But what if we *are* on one side? What if we've been put there by others?"

"Even so," Diane said. "Getting tagged as leaning Democrat could be really dangerous for science. We have to stay above that fray."

"But we may already be tagged. And we are trying to affect policy, right? Isn't that what this committee is about?"

"Yes. But we have to be jumping *on* the fray. Squashing it from above."

They laughed at this image. Edgardo said, "Beyond good and evil! Beyond Marx and Jesus! Prometheus unbound! Science über alles!"

Even Anna had to laugh. It was funny even though it wasn't; and less so the more she thought about it; and yet she laughed. As did the others.

Diane shook her head ruefully. "Oh well," she said. "Let's give it a try. Time for science in the capital."

Afterward the situation did not seem so funny. It did not help of course to come home to Joe's fever, after which nothing seemed funny. Charlie had already given in and taken him to the doctor, but they hadn't found anything.

It wasn't a matter of energy levels. Joe was as energetic as ever, if not more so. Hectic, irritable, ceaselessly in motion, complaining, interrupting . . . but had he ever been any different? This was what Charlie seemed to be implying, that Joe was perhaps just a little hotter now, more flushed and sweaty, but otherwise much the same feisty little guy.

But she wasn't buying it. Something was different. He was not himself.

Sometimes she worried so intensely that she could not talk to Charlie about it at all. What if she convinced him to join her in her worry, what good would that do him or any of them?

The best way to prevent worry was to be so busy by day that there was no time for it. Then, at night, to go to bed so exhausted that sleep hit like a wall falling on her, giving her several hours of oblivion. It was heavy and somehow unrestful sleep; she woke with the gears of her mind already engaged in something—memory, dream, work calculation—on it ran, unstoppable, thoroughly awake at 4:30 in the morning. Miserable.

And no matter where her night thoughts began, they always came back to Joe. When she remembered the situation her pulse would shoot up. Eventually she would get up, with a brief touch to the sleeping Charlie, and go stand in the shower for twenty minutes, trying to relax. What was worry, after all, but a kind of fear? It was fear for the future. And in fact the future was bound to bring its share of bad things, there was no avoiding that. So worry was really a hopeless enterprise, in that it could not do anything. It was an anticipation of grief, a nightmare of the future. A type of fear; and she was determined not to be afraid.

So she would steel herself and turn off the shower, and motor through her preparations for work, thinking about how to sequence the day's activities. But before she left she had to go up and nurse Joe, and so all her plans were overthrown by his hot little body lying cradled in her arms. His mouth was hot. The world was hotter, Joe was hotter, even Charlie was hotter. Everything seemed to have had more energy poured into it than it could handle. All but Anna, and her Nick. She put her sleeping wild man back in his crib and went to Nick's room and kissed her firstborn on his head, inhaling him gratefully, his cool curly hair—her soul mate in this chaos, her fellow stoic, her cool calculator—imperturbable, unflappable, amused by his hectic brother and everything else; amused where others would be enraged. Who could imagine a better older brother, or a better son, a kind of young twin to her. In a sudden blaze of maternal affection she held his shoulder, squeezed it as he slept; then clumped down the stairs and walked up Wisconsin to the reopened Metro, shaking her wet locks from side to side to feel their cool damp in the cool air.

Then meeting with Diane, wet-haired herself. Session with Alyssa on visiting program directors. Lunch at desk while reading papers to *The Journal of Biostatistics*. Calls one through six on her long list of calls to be made. Brief visit downstairs to the Khembali women in the embassy office, to see how they were doing with their resettlement issues. Then hellos to Sucandra and Padma, who were leading an English lesson; they enlisted her briefly to aid them, Anna feeling helpless across the great divide of languages. She resolved once again to learn Tibetan, tried to remember the words she heard them explaining. It was a habit of mind, this inhaling of information. Charlie would laugh at her.

Back to the office, glancing briefly at the Tibetan language cheat sheet. "The tide rises in six hours. The waves are hollow when the tide ebbs."

In the next meeting with Diane and Frank, Anna brought to the screen another web page she had found. This one was on FCCSET, the Federal Coordinating Council on Science, Engineering and Technology.

"What's this?" Frank said as he read over her shoulder. "Fuck set?"

"*No,* they pronounced it *Fix-it,*" laughing.

"Oh right, so very clever these acronyms. I like DICE, Dynamic Integrated Model of Climate and the Economy, where you just skip the *M.*"

"*Fix-it* was a program that looked at scientific problems and tried to identify already-existing federal programs that could match up with other programs, to work together on particular problems."

"So what killed it?"

"How do you know it got killed?"

Frank just looked at her.

"Well, it was a matter of money, I guess. Or control. The programs identified as worthy by Fix-it were automatically funded by the Office of Management and Budget. There was an OMB person sitting in on all the Fix-it meetings, and if the program was approved then it was funded."

"Now that's power!"

"Yes. But too much power, in the end. Because the top people in the agencies being identified didn't like getting funding like that. It took away from their control over the purse strings."

"Oh for Christ's sake. Is that really why it ended?"

"Apparently. I mean it didn't end, but it had that budgetary power taken away. So, I'm wondering if we could get Congress to bring it back."

"Worth a try," Diane judged.

Frank was still shaking his head. "Territoriality really does run deep. They might as well be peeing around the edges of their building."

"I guess."

"You don't sound convinced."

"I don't know. It's a theory. Anyway, I think we should try to reintroduce this program. You'd be able to get agencies all across the board coordinated. What if they were all doing parts of the same large project?"

Frank's eyebrows were arched. "Talk about a theory. This is Bob's Manhattan Project idea again."

"Well, the method is there," Anna claimed. "Potentially, anyway. What if you could get a proposal funded through all those agencies, using Fix-it as a coordinating committee?"

Diane liked the idea. "We need Congress to put it in place, obviously. I'll talk to Sophie."

After a moment's silence Frank said, "We could really use a president with that in his platform."

"Unlikely," Diane judged.

Frank scowled. "I don't see why. What century do people think they're living in?"

Anna and Diane shared a look, anticipating a rant, but Frank saw it and said, "Well, but why? Why why why? We should have a *scientist candidate* for president, some emeritus biggie who can talk, explaining what the scientific approach would be, and *why*. A candidate using ecological theory, systems theory, what-have-you, in-out throughputs, some actual economics . . ."

Diane was shaking her head. "Who exactly would that be?"

"I don't know, Richard Feynman?"

"Deceased."

"Stephen Hawking."

"British, and paralyzed. Besides, you know those emeritus guys. There isn't a single one of them who could go through the whole process without, I don't know . . ."

"Exploding?" Anna suggested.

"Yes."

"Make up a candidate," Anna said. "What science would do if it were in the White House."

"A phantom candidate," Frank said.

"Shadow candidate," Diane corrected. "Like in Europe."

"Or," Anna said, "just put the platform out there, with a virtual candidate. Dr. Science. See which party picks it up."

"Neither," Frank and Diane said together.

"We don't know that," Anna said. "And it would be safer than endorsing one party over the other, or starting some kind of scientific third party that would only hurt politicians who are on our side. Either way we could get pushed out of policy for years to come. Cast into the wilderness."

"We're already there," Frank pointed out.

"So what have we got to lose?"

"Well, that's true enough." Frank thought it over. "We could get hammered."

"Like we aren't already?"

"Hmmm."

"Maybe we have to take a stand. Maybe that's what it means to get involved in politics. You have to declare. You have to talk about what people should do."

They sat there, thinking things over. Edgardo walked in and they explained to him what they were thinking.

He laughed hard.

Frank kept scribbling. "Social Science Experiment in Politics."

"In *elective* politics," Anna insisted, frowning at Edgardo. "Then it's, what, SSEEP. Pronounced 'Seep.' Like we're *seeping* into policy."

"Seep!" Diane laughed. "We'll seep in like a bull in a china shop! Seep in and the whole shop will start screaming."

"Maybe so. But the china shop is going under. It needs a bull to, what, to pull the whole thing up to higher ground."

They laughed at this image.

"Well," Diane said, "we need to do everything we can. Sort all this out, Frank. Look into all of it."

Frank nodded. "Bold and persistent experimentation! I have a list here."

Diane waved a hand. "More later. I'm starving."

"Sure. You want to go get a bite?"

"Sure."

Anna quickly glanced down. They had just arranged a date, right in front of her eyes. And not the first one, from the sound of it.

She thought, What about Frank's woman from the elevator? Had he given up on her? That didn't seem like him. Anna was obscurely disappointed; she liked that story, that possibility. It had appealed to the romantic in her, which was buried but substantial. And as for Frank and Diane, well, she could not imagine what it meant. Surely she had misread the situation. Diane was nice, certainly; but even in the light of Anna's own puritanical work ethic, she was a bit much. What would she be like socially? It was hard to imagine.

And she herself would never know what Diane was like socially. She was a woman, and married; while Frank was a man, and unmarried; and Diane was now unmarried too, poor thing. And Frank had been plucked out from among the visiting program directors by Diane, to run her climate project committee.

"I've got to get home," she said, throwing her things together. Home to her boys, who would leap on her and say the same things, all deep in their own worlds, and the dinner only partly made. Although in the same flare of irritation she felt a deep relief and a desire to be there at once.

At home her boys did leap on her, as predictable as clockwork, and the house was warm with kitchen smells.

The flood had revolutionized their cooking habits, Charlie trying old recipes and new, based on whatever produce the grocery store had available. Tonight, Mexican. Joe commanded her attention, insisting on *Goodnight Moon* again, read in an up-tempo declamatory singsong very unsuited to the book's soporific nature, which worked like a charm on her no matter what, but not on him. He was fretful again, and sucked at her desperately, as if seeking a relief beyond food. She spoke in quiet tones to Nick, and he read as he replied, or didn't, mostly off in his own world. She tried not to worry about Joe, although his distemper had now lasted six weeks. Every test had been taken. Nothing had been discovered, except that slightly elevated temperature, which the record showed was real, if slight. Its periodicity reminded her of her own temperatures when she had kept records to find her time of ovulation every month.

The red face, the lack of ease. No matter how hard she tried she was still scared by these changes in him. She knew what he should be like. And she knew this had started after their trip to Khembalung. She watched him, and nursed him, and played with him—tried to feel him, there in his body—tried to think about work, while humming to him as he sucked. She crooned the book in Tibetan, "Don nom, zla-ba." Joe started slightly, hit her as he drowsed. Anna went back to the inviolable rhythms of the hypnotic little book; and she did everything she could to make herself stop worrying; but it never really went away. And so the days passed; and almost surreptitiously, while Charlie was doing other things, she took Joe's temperature, and charted it, then went on; and tried to think about work; but she would have given the Nobel Prize in Chemistry and the Gulf Stream itself for just a week of normal temperatures.

CHAPTER 15

AUTUMN IN NEW YORK

The most beautiful regatta in the history of the world convened that year on Midsummer Day, at the North Pole.

The sun hung at the same height in the sky all day long, blazing down on open water that appeared more black than blue. A few icebergs floated here and there, dolmens of jade or turquoise standing in the obsidian sea. Among them sailed or motored some three hundred boats and ships. Sails were of every cut and color, some prisming as they bent to the shifts of a mild southern breeze. All possible rigs and hulls were there: catamarans, schooners, yawls, ketches, trimarans; also square-riggers, from caravels to clipper ships to newfangled experiments not destined to prosper; also a quintet of huge Polynesian outriggers; also every manner of motor launch, rumbling unctuously through the sailboats; even a lot of single-person craft, including kayakers, and windsurfers in black drysuits.

The fleet jockeyed until their skippers linked up and formed a circle centered on the pole, rotating clockwise if seen from above. Everyone thus sailed west, following the two rules that birds use when flocking: change speed as little as possible, keep as far apart from everyone else as possible.

Senator Phil Chase smiled when the flocking rubric was explained to him. "That's the Senate for you," he said. "Maybe it's all you need to get by in life."

This was the fifth midsummer festival at the Pole. Every year since the Arctic Ocean had opened in summer, a larger and larger group of sea craft had sailed or motored north to party at the pole. By a happy coincidence, the

North Pole itself, as determined by GPS, was marked this year by a tall aqua-marine iceberg that had drifted over it. In the immediate vicinity of this newly identified "Pole Berg" idled many of the largest ships in the fleet. As always, the gathering had a Burning Man aspect, its excess and fireworks leading many to call it Drowning Man, or Freeze Your Butt Man.

This year, however, the party had been joined by the Inuit nation Nunavut and the Intergovernmental Panel on Climate Change, who had declared this "The Year of Global Environmental Awareness," and sent out hundreds of invitations, and provided many ships themselves, in the hope of gathering a floating community that would emphasize to all the world the undeniable changes already wrought by global warming. The organizers were willing to accept the risk of making the gathering look like a party, or even, God forbid, a celebration of global warming, in order to garner as much publicity as pos-sible. Of course a whole new ocean to sail on was no doubt a cool thing for sailors, but all the missing Arctic ice was floating down into the North Atlan-tic at that very moment, changing everything. IPCC wanted people to see with their own eyes that abrupt climate change was already upon them.

But of course there were many people there who did not regard the polar party in its official light, just as there were many in the world who did not worry overmuch about entering the Youngest Dryas. On the sail up to the festival, some of them had encountered an oil tanker making a dry run on a Great Circle route from Japan to Norway that passed near the pole: the Northwest Passage was open for business at last. Oil could be shipped directly from the North Sea to Japan, cutting the distance by two-thirds. Even if oil was passé now, Japan and the North Sea oil countries were nevertheless aw-fully pleased to be able to move it over the pole. They were not ashamed to admit that the world still needed oil, and that while it did, there would be reasons to appreciate certain manifestations of global warming. Shipyards in Glasgow, Norway, and Japan had been revitalized, and were now busy build-ing a new class of Arctic Sea tankers to follow this prototype, boldly going where no tanker had gone before.

Here at the pole on Midsummer Day, things looked fine. The world was beautiful, the fleet spectacular. In danger or not, human culture seemed to have risen to the occasion. Noon of summer solstice at the North Pole, a glorious armada forming a kind of sculpture garden. A new kind of harmonic convergence, Ommmmmmmm.

On one of the bigger craft, an aluminum-hulled jet-powered catamaran out of Bar Harbor, Maine, a large group of people congregated around Senator Phil Chase. Many of them were bundled in the thick red down jackets provided to guests by the National Science Foundation's Department of Polar Programs, because despite the black water and brilliant sun, the air temperature at the moment was 24 degrees Fahrenheit. People kept their hoods pulled forward, and their massed body warmth comforted them as they watched the group around Chase help him into a small rainbow-colored hot-air balloon, hanging over the top deck straining at its tether.

The World's Senator got in the basket, gave the signal; the balloon master fired the burners, and the balloon ascended into the clear air to the sound of cheers and sirens, Phil Chase waving to the fleet below, looking somewhat like the Wizard of Oz at the moment when the wizard floats away prematurely.

But Phil was on a line, and the line held. From a hundred feet above the crowd, Phil could be seen grinning his beautiful grin. "Here we are!" he announced over the fleet's combined radio and loudspeaker array; and of course millions more saw and heard him by satellite TV. A big buoy clanged the world to order as Phil raised a hand to still the ships' horns and fireworks.

"Folks," he said, "I've been working for the people of California for seventeen years, representing them in the United States Senate, and now I want to take what I've learned in those efforts, and in my travels around the world, and apply all that to serving the people of the United States, and all the world."

"President of the world?" Roy Anastopoulos said to Charlie, and began to laugh.

"Shh! Shh!" Charlie said to Roy. They were watching it on TVs in different parts of D.C., but talking on their phones as they watched.

"It's a crazy thing to want to do," Phil was conceding. "I'm the first to admit that, because I've seen what the job does to people. But in for a penny in for a pound, as they say, and we've reached a moment where somebody who can handle it needs to use the position to effect some good."

Roy was still giggling. "Be quiet!" Charlie said.

"—there is no alternative to global cooperation. We have to admit and celebrate our interdependence, and work in solidarity with every living thing. All God's creatures are living on this planet in one big complex organism, and we've got to act like that now. That's why I've chosen to announce my candidacy here at the North Pole. Everything meets up here, and everything has changed here. This beautiful ocean, free of ice for the first time in humanity's existence, is sign of a clear and present danger. Recall what it looked like here even five years ago. You can't help but admit that huge changes have already come.

"Now what do those changes mean? Nobody knows. Where will they lead? Nobody knows. This is what everyone has to remember; no one can tell what the future will bring. Anything can happen, anything at all. We stand at the start of a steep ski run. Black diamond for sure. I see the black diamonds twinkling everywhere down there. Down the slope of the coming decades we will ski. The moguls will be on us so fast we won't believe it. There'll be no time for lengthy studies that never do anything, that only hope business as usual will last for one more year, after which the profiteers will take off for their fortress mansions. That won't work, not even for them. You can get offshore, but you can't get off planet."

Cheers and horns and sirens echoed over the water. Phil waited for them to quiet back down, smiling happily and waving. Then he continued:

"It's one world now. The United States still has its historical role to fulfill, as the country of countries, the mixture and amalgam of all humanity, trying things out and seeing how they work. The United States is child of the world, you might say, and the world watches with the usual parental fascination and horror, anxiety and pride.

"So we have to grow up. If we were to turn into just another imperial bully and idiot, the story of history would be ruined, its best hope dashed. We have to give up the bad, give back the good. Franklin Roosevelt described what was needed from America very aptly, in a time just as dangerous as ours: he called for a course of 'bold and persistent experimentation.' That's what I plan to do *also. No more empire, no more head in the sand pretending things are okay. It's time to join the effort to invent a global civilization that we can hand off to all the children and say, 'This will work, keep it going, make it better.' That's permaculture, as some people call it, and really now we have no choice; it's either permaculture or catastrophe. Let's choose the good fight, and work so that our generation can hand to the next one this beautiful world.*

"That's the plan, folks. I intend to convince the Democratic Party to continue its historic work of helping to improve the lot of every man, woman, child, animal, and plant on this planet. That's the vision that has been behind all the party's successes so far, and moving away from those core values has been part of the problem and the failure of our time. Together we'll join humanity in making a world that is beautiful and just."

"We'll join humanity?" Roy said. "What is this, Democrats as aliens?" But Charlie could barely hear him over the ship horns and cheers. On the screen he could see they were beginning to reel Phil in like a big kite.

Living outdoors the seasons were huge. Talk about abrupt climate change—housebound people had no idea. Shorter days, cooler air, dimmer light slanting through the trees at a lower angle: you might as well be on a different planet.

It was one of the ironies of their time that global warming was about to freeze Europe and North America, particularly on the eastern seaboard. Kenzo predicted weeks of severe, record-shattering lows: "You're not going to believe it," he kept saying, although it was already beginning in Europe. "The winter high will park over Greenland and force the jet stream to polar vortex straight at us from Hudson Bay."

"I believe it," Frank replied. Although, in another irony, the weather at that moment was rather glorious. The days were warm, while the cold between 2 A.M. and sunrise was bracing. Only a few weeks past the worst of their Congolese summer, there was frost on the leaves at dawn.

For Frank these chill nights meant the deployment of his mountain gear, always a pleasure to him. He basked in that special warmth that hominids have enjoyed ever since they started wearing the furs of other animals. Clothes made the man, literally, therefore also one of the first instances of the technological sublime, which was to stay warm in the cold.

Waking up in his treehouse, Frank would wrap his sleeping bag around him like a cape and sit on the plywood edge, arms over the railing, swinging his heels in space, looking at the wall of trees across the gorge. The leaves were beginning to turn, invading the green canopy with splashes of yellow and orange and red. As a Californian Frank had seldom seen it, and had never imagined it properly. He had not understood that the colors would be all mixed together, forming a field of mixed color, like a box of Trix spilled over a lawn, spelling in its gorgeous alien alphabet the end of summer, the passing of time, the omnipresence of mortality. To all who took heed it was an awesome and melancholy sight.

He let down Miss Piggy, descended into this new world, walked absorbed in the new colors, the mushroomy smells, the clattering susurrus of leaves in the wind. The next hard frost would knock most of these leaves down, and then his jungle treehouse would be exposed to the gaze of those below. Lances of sunlight already reached many parts of the forest floor. The park was still officially closed, but Frank saw more and more people, not just the homeless but also ordinary citizens, the people who had used the park before the flood as a place to run or walk or bike or ride. Luckily the creekside roads and trails were irreparable, and few would venture past the giant beaver dam, which had started like a beaver dam and now really was one. You had to bushwhack to get around it. Still, the treehouse would be exposed for those who came up this far.

That was a problem for another day. Now Frank walked north on a deer's trail, observing how the changed colors of the leaves altered the sense of space in the forest, how there seemed to be an increase in sheer spaciousness. When he ran with the frisbee guys the leaves functioned as referent points, and he seemed to be engaging a new GPS system that locked him more than ever into the here-and-now. He saw just where he was, moment to moment, and ran without awareness of the ground, free to look about. Joy to be out on days so fresh and sunny, so dappled and yellow; immersion in the very image and symbol of change; very soon there would come an end to his tenuously established summer routines, he would have to find new ones. He could do that; he was even in a way looking forward to it. But what about the gibbons? They were subtropical creatures, as were many of the other ferals. In the zoo they would have been kept inside heated enclosures when temperatures dropped.

Native species, and zoo ferals from temperate or polar regions, would probably be all right. The white-tailed deer would mostly survive the winter, as always. But there were many feral species out there. Once when they were up in the thickets of the northwest corner of the park, coming back from the ninth hole, Spencer stopped in his tracks and everyone else froze instantly; this was one of the subgames they had invented, useful if they wanted not to spook animals.

"What in the fuck is that," Spencer whispered urgently to Frank.

Frank stared. It was a big ox, or a small bull, or . . .

It was huge. Massive, heraldic, thick-haunched, like something out of a vision; one of those sights so unbelievable that if you were dreaming it you would have woken up on the spot.

Frank got out his FOG phone, moving very slowly, and pushed the button for Nancy. How many times had he done this in the past weeks, moving the phone as slowly as he could, whispering, "Nancy—hi, it's Frank—can you tell me what I'm looking at?"

Pause, while Nancy looked at his phone's GPS position and checked it on her big board.

"Aha. You're looking at an aurochs."

"A what?"

"We're pretty sure it's an aurochs. North Europe, ice age—"

Suddenly it looked familiar to Frank.

"—some Polish researchers took frozen DNA from one and cloned them a few years ago. Birthed from cows. They had an enclosure in their southern forest with a herd in it. We don't know how these ones got here. Some kind of private dispersion, I think, like the guy who decided to transplant all the birds mentioned in Shakespeare to North America, and gave us starlings among other problems."

Frank took the phone from his ear, as Spencer's face was contorting grotesquely to convey the question WHAT WHAT WHAT.

"Aurochs," Frank whispered loudly.

Spencer's face shifted into his look for the Great Ah Ha of Comprehension, then to Delight. He looked at the beast, foursquare on the ridge, and in slow motion crumpled to his knees, hands clasping his frisbee before him in prayer. Robin and Robert held their frisbees before them as well, grinning as they always did. Robin stretched his hands palm out over his head.

Its proportions were strange, Frank saw, the rear legs and haunches big and rounded. A creature from the cave paintings, sprung live into their world.

Spencer stood back up. He held his frisbee out to the other guys, waggled his eyebrows, mimed a throw at the aurochs: make it a target? Eyes ablaze: never had Frank seen the shaman in Spencer so clearly.

Of course they had already discussed throwing at animals. It would be the greatest thing in the world to make targets of the ubiquitous deer, for instance. The stalk, the throw, the strike—exhilarating. Like catch-and-release fishing, only better. No one disputed this. The animals would not be hurt. It would be hunting without killing.

But really, as Spencer himself had argued when they discussed it, they were hunting without killing already. And sometimes, if they hit them, animals would get hurt. That was the whole point of the killer frisbee theory. If they wanted the animals to prosper in the park, which after all was not so big—if they wanted animals to inhabit the world with them, which also was not so big—then they oughtn't harass them by whacking them out of the blue with hard plastic disks. Best dharma practice was compassion for all sentient beings, thus using them for targets was contra-indicated. So they had refused the temptation.

Now Spencer's point seemed to be that this was a magical occasion, outside all everyday agreements. There stood an icon from the ice age—a living fossil, in effect, sprung to life from the cave paintings of Lascaux and Altamira—so that really they *had* to abandon their ordinary protocols to do justice to the beast, and enter the sacred space of the paleolithic mind. Make this magnificent creature their target as a sort of religious ritual, even a religious obligation one might say. All this Spencer conveyed by mime, making faces as contorted and clear as any demon mask.

"All at once," Frank whispered. The others nodded.

Frank aimed and threw with the rest of them, and four disks flashed through the forest. One hit a tree, another struck the aurochs on the flank, causing him to bolt up the ridge and away, out of sight before they were even done screaming. They high-fived each other and ran to collect their frisbees and play on.

Each blustery afternoon changed his life. That was autumn, that was how it should feel, the landscape suffused with the ache of everything fleeing by. A new world every heartbeat. He had to incorporate this feeling of perpetual change, make it an aspect of optimodality. Of course everything always changed! How beautiful that the landscape sang that truth so clearly!

More than ever he loved being in his treehouse. He would have to find a way to continue doing it as the winter came on, even in the midst of storms. John Muir had climbed trees during storms to get a better view of them, and Frank knew from his mountaineering days that storms were a beautiful time to be out, if one were properly geared. He could pitch his tent on the plywood floor, and his heaviest sleeping bag would keep him warm in anything. Would he bounce around like a sailor at the top of a mast? He wanted to find out. John Muir had found out.

He would not move indoors. He did not want to, and he would not have to. The paleolithics had lived through ice ages, faced cold and storms for thousands of years. A new theory postulated that populations islanded by abrupt climate change had been forced to invent cooperative behaviors in bad weather many times, ultimately changing the gene and bringing about the last stages of human evolution. Snowshoes, clothing as warm as Frank's, fire carriers. They had not only coped in the ice, but expanded their range.

Maybe they were going to have to do that again.

Clothing and shelter. At work Frank could see that civilized people did not think about these things. Most wore clothing suited to "room temperature" all the year round, thus sweltering in the summer and shivering in winter anytime they stepped out of their rooms—which however they rarely did. So they thought they were temperature tough guys, but really they were just indoors. They used their buildings as clothing, in effect, and heated or cooled these spaces to imitate what clothing did, no matter how crazy this was in energy terms. But they did it without thinking of it like that, without making that calculation. In the summer they wore blue jeans because of what people three generations before had seen in Marlboro ads. Blue jeans were the SUVs of pants, part of a fantasy outdoor life; Frank himself had long since changed to the Khembali ultralight cotton pants in summer, noting with admiration how the slight crinkle in the material kept most of the cloth off the skin.

Now as it got colder people still wore blue jeans, which were just as useless in cold as they were in heat. Frank meanwhile shifted piece by piece into his mountaineering gear. Some items needed cleaning, but were too delicate to run through a washing machine, so he had to find a dry cleaners on Connecticut, but then was pleasantly surprised to discover that they would take all his clothes; he had disliked going to the laundromat.

So, autumn weather, cool and windy: therefore, Patagonia's capilene shirts, their wicking material fuzzy against the skin; a down vest with a down hood ready to pull onto his head; nylon wind-jacket; Patagonia's capilene long underwear; wool pants; nylon windpants if windy. Thick Thurlo socks inside light Salomon hiking shoes. As an ensemble it actually looked pretty good, in an *Outside* magazine techno-geek way—a style which actually fit in pretty unobtrusively at NSF. Scientists signaled with their clothes just like anyone else, and their signal often proclaimed, "I am a scientist, I do things that Make Sense, so I Dress Sensibly," which could resemble Frank's mountaineering gear, as it meant recreational jackets with hoods, hiking boots, ski pants, wool shirts. So Frank could dress as a high-tech paleolithic and still look like any other NSF jock.

Work itself was becoming bogged down. The federal capital retained the psychic nature of the original swamp, and its function too, as all the toxins of the national life were dumped there to be broken down in its burbling pits. Trying to hack her way through this was getting Diane both results and resistance. She spent about fourteen hours a day, Frank reckoned, in meetings up on the eleventh floor at NSF and elsewhere in the area. Many of these meetings he only heard about, usually from Edgardo. Some agencies were interested in joining the cause, others resented the suggestion that things be done differently, considering it an attack on their turf. In general the farther removed from making policy, the more interested they were to help. But a fair number of agencies with regulatory power were fully turned by the industries they were supposed to regulate, and thus usually agents of the enemies of change; among these were the Department of Energy (nuclear and oil industry), the FDA (food and drug), the U.S. Forest Service and other parts of the Department of Agriculture (timber and ag), and the EPA (a curious mix, depending on division, but some of them bound to the pesticide industry and all under the thumb of the President). Republican administrations had regularly staffed these agencies with people chosen from the industries being regulated, and these people had then written regulations with the industries' profits in mind. Now these agencies were not just toothless but actively dangerous, no matter how good their people were at the technocrat level. They were turned at the top.

Thus it was that Diane had to work around and against several of these agencies. It was becoming clear that part of NSF's project had to include making efforts to get leadership of the captive agencies changed; and the turned agencies were now out to do the same to NSF. So, on top of everything else: war of the agencies. Edgardo went on a long paranoid aria, detailing just how bad it could be, all the ways Diane was going to have to be on guard. "I said to her I hope you have a very honest tax man, and she just laughed. 'Two can play at that game,' she said, 'and I'm cleaner than they are.' So off we go, off to the mattresses."

Frank sang, "Territoriality, ooooop! Does that mean we're screwed?"

"No, not necessarily. Diane will build alliances to get things done."

In Frank's meetings with her, Diane did not refer to this part of the struggle, preferring to discuss the technical aspects. The North Atlantic project was still being researched, and Diane still liked it very much, but she was concerned that they also pursue a vigorous hunt for some biologically based carbon capture method. Frank wondered if the legal and political problems inherent in releasing a genetically modified organism into the environment could ever be overcome; but he knew who to call about the technical aspects, of course.

He had been thinking of calling Marta and Yann again anyway. So, after a meeting with Diane, he steeled himself to the task. Thinking of the surveillance issue, he wondered if he should call them from a public phone, but realized both ends had to be unsurveilled for that to work. No, best to do this work in the open and let the chips fall where they may, the virtual spook stocks rise as they might. So he called them at their Small Delivery numbers, from his office.

"Hi Marta, it's Frank. I wanted to talk to you and Yann about the carbon capture work you described to me. Can you tell me how that study is coming along, I mean just in general terms?"

"It's going okay."

"So, you know—in the absence of long-term field studies, have you gotten any back-of-the-envelopes on how quickly it might work, or how much it might draw down?"

"We can only extrapolate from lab results."

"And what does that indicate, if anything?"

"It could be considerable."

"I see."

Marta said, "How's the San Diego project coming along?"

"Oh good, good. I mean, I'm recused from any direct action on that front, but I'm following the process, and people at UCSD and in the biotech community there are excited about it. So I think something will happen."

"And we'll have a place in it?"

"Yes, they're working on an offer. There's going to be a kind of MacArthur award committee disbursing money, awarded without applications."

"I see." Marta's voice was still skeptical, but Frank noted that she was not actively hostile either. "Well, I look forward to seeing how that goes."

"It would surely help you, if you're ever going to try to deploy anything like this lichen you've described."

"We've got an array of options," she said shortly, and would not elaborate. Maybe she too had a sense of the surveillance.

Next morning at NSF he found out from Edgardo that Diane had been in a fight with the President's science advisor, Dr. Zacharius Strengloft. Strengloft had suggested to her in a meeting with the Senate Natural Resources Committee that NSF should keep to its job of disbursing grant money. Diane had told him in no uncertain terms that NSF was run by her and the National Science Board and no one else. Senators and staff who had witnessed the confrontation would of course take differing meanings from it.

Soon after that Diane convened a full meeting of the National Science Board, NSF's board of directors. Clearly Diane wanted to make sure they were behind her for the coming battles. She made it a closed meeting, and when she came out of it Frank couldn't tell if she had gotten what she wanted or not. But later she told him they had been almost unanimous in their support for NSF trying to coordinate a national response, even an international response. Then he saw again the little smile that crossed her face sometimes when she had gotten her way in these struggles. She seemed unflustered, even content. She shook her head as she told Frank about it, put a hand to his arm, smiled her little smile. What a strange game they were caught in, she seemed to say. But no one was going to intimidate her. Frank certainly wouldn't want to be the one to try.

Meanwhile, to implement anything in the North Atlantic, they would have to coordinate plans with the UN, and really the whole world; get approvals, funding, the actual materials, whatever they might be. Eventually this need to liaise with international agencies impelled them to arrange a day's meetings at the UN. Diane asked Frank to join her for these, and he was happy to agree.

When hanging with the bros in the evenings, Frank sometimes became curious about their plans for the winter. The picnic tables and fireplace were not going to hack it as winter furniture. The fireplace was such a misbegotten thing that it was useless for heating, cooking, or fire-gazing. Perhaps that was the point. Surely the men of the CCC, or whoever had built the thing, had to have known better. Some of the other picnic sites had open fire rings, but the bros had chosen to hang here by the pizza oven.

One night Frank arrived to find they had tried to solve this problem by commandeering a steel trash barrel and starting a fire inside it, a fire that only just flickered over its rim. Possibly the entire barrel gave off some radiant heat, and the fire would not be visible from a distance, of course, if that was a concern. But it was a miserable excuse for a campfire.

"Hey Perfesser!" Zeno bellowed. "How's it hanging, man? We haven't seen you for a while."

The others chimed in with their habitual welcomes. "He's too *busy!*" "Those coeds *wanted* him."

They were all bulked up, thick with thrift shop sweaters and coats, and also, Frank was pleased to see, greasy down jackets. Old down jackets were probably cheap, being unfashionable; and there was nothing better in the cold.

"Hey," he said. "Super long time. What was it, yesterday?"

"Yarrr. Ha ha ha."

"I know you've done so much you want to tell me about."

"HA!!!" They crowed their approval of this jape. "We ain't done a fucking thing! Why should we?"

And yet it soon transpired that they had all experienced an extraordinary number of traumas since Frank last came around. They interrupted each other ceaselessly as they related them, making a mishmash that no one could have followed, but Frank knew from the start not to try. "Yeah *right*," was all he had to say from time to time. Again it struck him how well they recalled scrapes, scuffles, or fights; they could reenact every move in slow motion, and did so when telling their tale—it was part of the tale, maybe the most interesting part: "I twisted like this, and he missed over my *shoulder*, like this, and then I ducked," ducking and weaving against the absent but well-remembered opponent.

"We had to pull him right *off* the guy, yeah! I had to peel his fingers right off his *neck!* He was pounding his head right against the *concrete.*"

Finally they were done. Frank said, "Hey, your fire? It sucks."

A shout of agreement and dissent. Zeno said, "Whaddya mean, dude? It's perfect for shoving yer head in the can!"

"YARRR."

"That's the only way I'd see the actual fire," Frank countered. "Why don't you go where one of the good firepits are?"

They laughed at his naïveté. "That'd be too *good* for us!"

"Might make us a *fire* if we did that!"

One of them mimed a karate kick at the stone oven. "Piece of shit."

"You need fire," Frank said.

"We GOT a fire."

"Can't you knock the top of this thing off, or make a fire-ring next to it or something? Aren't there any demolition sites or construction sites around here where you could get some cinder blocks?"

"Don't be bringing the man down on us any more than he already is," Fedpage said.

"Whatever," Frank said. "You're gonna freeze your asses off."

"It's a half-assed fire."

"You have to put your hands right on the metal, it's ridiculous."

"No fucking way, it's warm from here!"

"Yeah right."

They settled in. The topic shifted to winter and winterizing in general, so Frank sat back and listened. No way were they going to respond to his words by jumping out into the night and putting together a decent fire ring. If that were their style they wouldn't have been out here in the first place.

A few of them discussed the prospects of sleeping at the Metro stops; the regulars for these spots had dispersed, so that good grates were going unclaimed. You could nest on a good site all day. But that risked a rousting by the cops. But if you didn't take the risk, you weren't likely to find a good spot.

Zeno declared he was going to build a hut and sleep right there by their site. Others agreed immediately that good shelters could be made. It all sounded hypothetical to Frank, he thought they were just covering for the fact that they didn't want to talk about where they really slept.

That made sense to Frank; he wasn't telling people where he slept either. The bros were under a different kind of surveillance than he was, more erratic but potentially much more immediate, with consequences much worse than Frank's (one hoped). They had police records, many of them extensive. Technically much of what they were doing was illegal, including being in Rock Creek Park at all. Luckily a lot of people were doing the same thing. It was the herd defense; predators would pick off the weak, but the bulk of the herd would be okay. The more the better, therefore, up to a point—a point they had not yet reached, even though many little squatter settlements and even what could be called shantytowns were now visible in flood-damaged parts of town, especially in the parks. Ultimately this might trigger some large-scale crackdown, and Rock Creek Park was high profile. But the gorge's new ravine walls were steep and unstable, impossible to patrol at night. To clear the gorge they would have to call out the National Guard—both of them, as Zeno always added. If they did that the bros could slip away and come back later.

Meanwhile, out of sight, out of mind. They were off the grid, they had slung their hooks, they had lit out for the territory. The firelight bounced on their worn faces, etching each knock and crease. Little more of them could be seen, making it seem a circle of disembodied masks, or a Rockwell Kent woodblock.

"There was this guy living on the streets in San Francisco who turned out was like totally rich, he was heir to a fortune but he just liked living outdoors."

"But he was a drunk too, right?"

"Fucking George Carlin is so funny."

"They said I was grade ten but they wouldn't give me dental."

Blah blah blah. Frank recalled a fire from his youth: two climber gals slightly buzzed had come bombing into Camp Four around midnight and hauled him away from a dying fire, insisting that he join them in a midnight swim in the Merced River, and who could say no to that. Though it was shocking cold water and pitch black to boot, more a good idea than a comfortable reality, swimming with two naked California women in the Yosemite night. But then when they got out and staggered back to the fire, near dead from hypothermia, it had been necessary to pile on wood until it was a leaping yellow blaze and dance before it to catch every pulse of lifesaving heat. Even at the time Frank had understood that he would never see anything more beautiful.

Now he sat with a bunch of red-faced homeless guys bundled in their greasy down jackets, around a fire hidden at the bottom of a trash can. The contrast with the night at Camp Four was so complete it made him laugh. Somehow it made the two nights part of the same thing.

"We should build a real fire," he said.

No one moved. Ashes rose on the smoke from the trash can. Frank reached in with a two-by-four and tried to stir it up enough to give them some flame over the rim. "If you have a fire but you can't see it," he said as he jabbed, "then you go out of your mind."

Fedpage snorted. "Central heating, right?"

"So everyone's crazy, yarr. Of course they are."

"*We* certainly are."

"Is that what did it hey?"

"Where there's smoke there's fire."

"When did someone first say that, a million years ago? Oooop!"

"Hey there monkey man, quit that now! You sound like Meg Ryan in that movie."

"Ha ha haaaa! That was so fucking funny."

"She was faking it! She was *faking it.*"

"I'll take it fake or not."

"As if you could tell!"

"—greatest human vocalization ever recorded."

"Yeah right, you obviously don't know your porn."

Things that would warm a body: laughter; reenacting fights; playing air guitar; playing with the fire; talking about sex; thinking about climber gals.

Knocking a stone oven apart would definitely warm the body. Frank got up. What he needed was a sledgehammer and a crowbar; what they had were some lengths of two-by-four and an old aluminum baseball bat.

One stone in the little opening at the top was loose in its cement. Frank moved to what looked like the right angle and smashed the stone with a two-by-four. The bros were pleased at the diversion, they guffawed and urged him on. He knocked the first stone down into the firepit, reached into the ashes and rolled it out. After that it was a matter of knocking stones off one at a time. He used the longest two-by-four and pounded away. The cement was old, and gradually the firepit came down.

Knee high it made a sensible firepit, with a gap in one side where the old doorway had been. He filled that gap with stones. There were enough left over to make another firepit if they wanted one. Or maybe bench supports, if they found some planks.

"Okay, let's move the trash can fire into the pit," he said.

"How you gonna pick it up? That can is red hot down there at the bottom, don't you pick that up!"

"You'll burn your fucking hands off man!"

"It's not red hot," Frank pointed out. "Let's a couple of us grab it around the top. Wear gloves and tilt it, and we'll lift the bottom with the studs here."

"Roll and burn your fucking leg off!"

"Yeah right!"

But Zeno was willing to do it, and so the rest gathered round. The ones who had gloves grasped the rim, lifted, and tilted. Frank and Andy wedged studs under the bottom from opposite sides and lifted it up. With a whoosh the whole fiery mass sparked into the new ring and blasted up into the night. Howls chased the uprush of smoke and sparks.

They sat around the cheery blaze, suddenly much more visible to each other.

"Now we need a pizza!"

"Who'll get a pizza?"

They all looked at Frank. "Ah shit," he said. "Where's Cutter."

"Get some beer too!" Zeno said, with the same fake laugh as before.

Kicking through piles of fallen leaves, the cold air struck him like a splash of water in the face. It felt good. He had to laugh: all his life he had traveled to mountains and polar regions to breathe air this bracing, and here it was, right in the middle of this ridiculous city. Maybe the seasons would become his terrain now, and the coming winter be like high altitude or high latitude. It could be good.

The afternoon before he and Diane were going to leave for New York, he played a game of frisbee golf with the frisbee guys. It was a perfect October day, Indian summer, and in the amber horizontal light of sunset they threw

across a stiff western breeze that brought a continuous rain of leaves spin-
nerdrifting down on them. Frank slung his disk through the forest's ticker-
tape parade, hooting with the rest, and was deep in the game when they ran
by the bros' clearing.

Spencer stopped so abruptly that Frank almost rammed into him, thinking, Aurochs, but then he saw half a dozen men wearing flak jackets, aiming big assault rifles at the astonished bros.

"Get down on the ground!" one of the men shouted. "Get down right
now! GET DOWN."

The bros dropped awkwardly, faces on the ground.

The frisbee players stayed frozen. One of the men turned and said to
them, "We'll be just a minute more here. Why don't you be on your way."

Frank and the frisbee guys nodded and took off down Ross, jogging
until they were around the corner, then stopping and looking back.

"What the fuck was that?"

"A bust."

"Yeah but who?"

"We'll find out on the way back."

They played on, distracted, missing shot after shot. On the way back
they hurried the pace, and came into site 21 huffing.

The guys were still there, sitting around—all but Jory.

"Hey guys what was that all about?" Spencer cried as they ran in. "That
looked horrible!"

"They rousted us," Zeno said.

Redbeard shook his head resentfully. "They made us lie down on the
ground like we were criminals."

"They didn't want any trouble," said Zeno. "They thought Jory might be
carrying."

Jory, the only one who had ever made Frank feel uncomfortable.

"They were ready to shoot us," Redbeard complained.

"Sure they were. They probably heard Jory was armed."

"So it was Jory they were after?" Spencer said. "What did he do?"

"Jory's the one who beat up on Ralph! Don't you know?"

"No."

"Yes you do, it was in the papers. Ralph got pounded by Jory and a guy, down at Eighteen."

"We had to pull him right *off* the guy, yeah! I had to peel his fingers right off his *neck*! He was pounding his head right against the *concrete*."

"Yeah, so Ralph was in the hospital after that, but then a couple weeks later Jory showed up again and started hanging out with us like nothing had happened."

"Jesus," Frank said. "Why didn't you go to the police and get rid of this guy?"

They shouted "YEAH RIGHT" at him in unison. Then, interrupting each other in their eagerness:

"What do you think *they're* going to do?"

"They'll call in and find my outstandings and get my parole officer—"

"Fuck that, they'll *beat* on you—"

"You could end up put away for fucking *years*."

Zeno's grin was sharklike. "Some things you just gotta live with, Doctor. The police are not there for us. Assholes come hang with us, that's just the way it is."

"Hard to believe," Frank said.

"Is it?"

On they ran, and after they had finished their game, Frank asked Spencer about it. "So they can't get help from the police if they need it?"

Spencer shook his head. "We can't either, for that matter. People without a legal place of residence are kind of outside the legal system. It's very property-based."

"Don't you guys have places to live?"

Spencer, Robin, and Robert laughed.

"We do have places to live," Spencer said, "but we don't pay for them."

"What do you do then?"

"We wander a bit. Just like you, right? We hunt and gather in the technosurround."

"A godly state," Robin said.

"Come to dinner and see," Spencer offered. "The fregans in Klingle Valley are having a potluck."

"I don't have anything to bring."

"Don't worry. There'll be enough. Maybe you can buy a bottle of wine on the way over."

On the walk through the park to Klingle Valley, one of the park tributaries of Rock Creek, Spencer and the others explained to Frank that they were ferals.

"You use that word?"

That was what they usually called their mode these days, yes; also squatters, scavengers, or fregans. There were ferals in every city. It was a kind of urban wilderness thing.

"Fregan, what's that?"

"It's like vegan, only they'll only eat food that they've gotten for free."

"Say what?"

"They eat out of dumpsters and such. Scavenge food going to waste."

"Whoah."

"Think about how many restaurants there are in D.C.," said Spencer. So many fine restaurants, so much wonderful food, and a certain percentage of it thrown away every night. Perfectly good fresh food. That was just the way the restaurant business operated. So, if you knew the routine at the dumpsters, and you resolved never to spend money on food, but always either to grow it or scavenge it—or kill it—then you were a fregan. They were going to a fregan potluck that very night. There would be lots of venison.

The house hosting the potluck was boarded up, having been badly damaged in a fire. They slipped in the back to find a party, a whole bunch of people, young and not so young, some tattooed and pierced, others tie-dyed and rastafied. There was a fire in the fireplace, but the flue wasn't drawing well; added to this smokiness was a funky mix of wet dog, patchouli, potluck food, and whatever was burning in a hookah in the corner: a mix of hash, cigars, and clove cigarettes, judging by the cloud Frank walked though.

The frisbee players were greeted warmly, and Spencer was acclaimed as some kind of local celebrity, a gypsy king. He introduced Frank very informally, and hustled him through to the food table—"always wisest to get it while you can"—and they feasted on a selection of Washington restauranteering's finest, slightly reconstituted for the occasion: steaks, quiche, salad, bread. Spencer ate like a wolf, and by the time they were done Frank was stuffed as well.

"See?" Spencer said as they sat on the floor watching the crowd flow by. "There are lots of empty buildings in this city. If you work as a team and spend your time taking care of business, then you can find shelter and food for free. Scavenge clothes or buy in thrift shops, talk with people or play frisbee for fun, walk wherever you go—you can step outside the money economy. Live off the excess, so you don't add to the waste. In fact you reduce waste. Do a little street theater down in the lawyer district for change, even do day labor or take a job. You don't actually need money, but a little bit helps."

"Wow," Frank said. "And about how many people are doing this?"

"Hard to tell. It's best to stay under the radar, because of just the sort of police issues you were asking the bros about. I think there's several hundred people at least in Northwest, maybe a thousand, who think of themselves as fregans or ferals. Obviously there are a lot more homeless people than that, but I'm talking about the people going at it like we are."

"Wow."

"It makes a huge difference how you think about what you're doing."

"That's very true."

A group in the corner started playing music: two guitars, mandolin, fiddle, wooden flute, a Bombay harmonium. Two young women came over to haul Spencer to his feet; a command performance, he was needed on percussion.

Frank said, "Thanks Spencer, I'm going to go soon."

"That's all right man, there'll be more of these. Frisbee tomorrow?"

"No, I've got to go to New York. I'll check in when I get back."

"See you then."

Frank and Diane took the train to New York. They sat facing each other over a table on the morning express from Union Station to Penn Station, rocking slightly as they worked on their laptops, stopping from time to time to sip their coffees and look out the window and talk. Sometimes this lasted half an hour, then they returned to work. It was companionable.

Out the windows flashed the backs of row houses, unkempt yards, old industrial buildings rusty and broken-windowed, all flying by click-click-click, sway sway click, gone. Over one of the great rivers, then by the gray Atlantic, mumbling its dirty whitecaps onshore.

Then descending underground, to go under the Hudson and enter Metropolis, just like Fritz Lang pictured it. Dark ancient brick walls, unmarked by any graffiti.

The train stopped in mid-tunnel.

"Did you ever live in New York?" Diane asked.

"No. I've hardly even visited."

"Wow."

"You lived here?"

"Yes, I went to Columbia."

"What for?"

"Med school."

"Really?"

"Yes, a long time ago."

"Did you practice medicine?"

"Sure. Five years, but then I got into research, and then administration, and that just kept going, I guess you'd say."

"I guess you would," peering at her screensaver, which cycled a succession of Asian American faces. "I mean, director of NSF—that's administration all right."

She sighed. "It's true. Things just kept happening."

She tapped a button and made the faces go away. Replacing them was her calendar, every hour and half hour filled. Under it was a spreadsheet of projects, a kind of Things to Do list, but with events categorized and broken down by background reading, pre-meetings, biographies of participants, and so on.

"You must have a system too," she noted, seeing him looking at it.

"Sure," Frank said. "A Things to Do list."

"That sounds healthier than this. So, are you enjoying yourself?"

"Well, I suppose I am."

She laughed. "More than last year anyway, I hope?"

He felt himself blushing. "Yeah, sure. It's more of a challenge, of course. But I asked for it." Wanting to avoid the topic of his lost letter, he said quickly, "I'll be a lot happier if the UN goes for one of these projects."

"Sure. But the work itself, in the building?"

"Yeah, sure. More variety."

"It still isn't research."

"I know. But I'm trying. Maybe it's a different kind. I don't know. I've never been too sure what we're up to at NSF."

"I know."

His face was fully hot now. He thought: Come on, don't be chicken here; if ever there was a chance to talk about this, it's here and now. Only a few short months before, Diane had taken Frank's angry critique of NSF and

1. pretended she had never seen it,
2. asked him to present its contents to the NSF Science Board, and
3. asked him publicly to stay at NSF another year and chair a committee

—thus, in front of his ostensible peer group, making him prove that he was not a blowhard, by taking on a difficult thankless job for the good of all.

And he had agreed to do it.

So he took a deep breath and said, "Why didn't you say anything when I gave you that letter?"

She pursed her lips. "I thought I did."

"Yes," he tried not to be irritated, "but you know what I mean."

She nodded. "It read to me like someone who was burnt out on doing jackets, and wanted to do something else. NSF itself didn't really seem to be what you were talking about, not to me."

"Well, maybe not entirely, but I did want to talk about it too."

"Sure. I thought you made some good points. I thought you might be interested in trying them out. So, here you are."

"So you let the other stuff go."

"It has to stay in your file, I can't change people's files. But there's no sense looking for trouble. I find letting trouble stay in a file often works pretty well. And in your case, it was all going to work out one way or another. Either you'd go back to San Diego, or you'd help us here. In that sense you did good to give it to me in person like you did, I mean just the hard copy."

"I tried to take it back," Frank confessed.

"You did? How?"

"I came back and looked for it. But Laveta had already given it to you."

"I see. I'm glad she did. I think it's worked out for the best."

Frank thought about it.

"Don't you?" she asked.

"Well, yes. I don't know. I guess I'm still finding out."

She smiled her little smile again, and he discovered he liked to see it. He liked to cause it.

The train moved again, and soon pulled into Penn Station. Up on the streets of Manhattan they walked through the immense slots created by the skyscrapers, across Midtown to the UN building, Frank goggling at the views with an ex–window washer's awe.

The day's work at the UN gave Frank the chance to see another side of Diane, perhaps a glimpse of her true métier, as some kind of international diplomat or technocrat. She knew all these people already, and in the meetings she got up from her seat from time to time to look over their shoulders at their screens, putting a hand to a shoulder while pointing and asking a question. They all had met many times, clearly; there was even a pause wherein the Secretary-General himself dropped by to say hi to her, thanking her lavishly for "all she was doing." Back in the discussions, she was always driving the issue, always pushing for action, occasionally joking about the fact that she was a representative of the United States and yet still promoting a vigorous array of environmental actions. She didn't overplay this, but her message seemed to be that although the United States historically had been a big part of the problem in global warming, that was about to change. As for the past, Diane and her allies had nothing to be ashamed of just because they had not prevailed politically. In one conversation she made the point that polls showed that a majority of American citizens wanted to protect the environment, and wanted their government to do something about climate change, so that it was not a matter of being outnumbered so much as denied, as part of a more general breakdown of democratic systems. Diane shrugged as she said this; no cause for outrage— the fight against greed was never going to end—meanwhile, she served as an ambassador for all the elements of American society who wanted to engage the problem. Now they might be moving into a position to prevail.

Mostly all this was implicit in her manner: cheerful, unapologetic, intent on the present, and on future results. She pushed relentlessly all day, typing memos into her pad and then without further ado moving on to the next matter, sometimes with a changed cast facing her, other times abruptly with the same people, with nothing more than an "Okay, what about this?"

Late in the day they met with representatives of the European carbon emissions trading group and futures market; there was a futures market in carbon credits, as there was for everything else, and Diane felt its calculations could be tweaked to make it more accurate and useful. The carbon treaty talks scheduled for the following year were almost certain to make emissions much more expensive, and this was the kind of prospect that often gave a huge push to a futures market, as people tried to buy while the commodity was still cheap. (Frank followed this discussion very closely, thinking about his own commodity status.) That kind of investment could generate a big fund in advance of the need for it in payouts, and that fund could be used to prime the pump for mitigation projects.

After that they met with delegations from China, then India, then the European Union and the African Union. Usually representatives from the Intergovernmental Panel on Climate Change were on hand, and the discussions had a hypothetical air; if Diane were the American president or a representative of his, they would have been more intent; as it was they knew they were dealing with a kind of shadow government figure, or with the amorphous scientific community out there beyond the government. Diane understood this and dealt with it tactfully; there were things NSF could do, and things it might do were the political climate to change.

After these meeting, it was the IPCC crowd itself who stayed on in the meeting rooms. The IPCC was one of the oldest and most influential global warming study groups; their list of suggested amelioration projects was huge, and they had already performed or commissioned preliminary studies of them, so that they had them sorted by cost, size, type, area, time needed, potential carbon drawdown, estimated time of sequestration, secondary effects, and many other determinants. Diane's and Frank's questions to them about an intervention in the North Atlantic broached new territory, however, and they were interested. The International Maritime Treaty was administered through the UN, so there were experts available to answer some of Diane's questions.

Then they were out of time, and it was dark outside, the windows reflecting them in the room. Workday over; Manhattan at cocktail hour.

"Dinner," Diane announced, looking down at the East River.

"Right," said Frank. He was hungry.

"Shall we try this place I know?"

They were on a date.

They were on a date in the big city, the world's great city, paradigmatic and incomparable. Manhattan always boggled Frank; he had spent very little time in it. Here the primate mind was stunned by the sheer verticality of the cliffs and canyons and towers. Add to those unnatural landforms the rivers of cars and taxis, and the omnipresence of people, hundreds in view at every moment, and the cumulative effect was staggering—literally so for Frank, as he had no inhibitions about spinning down the sidewalks, head swiveling like an owl's to see more. Diane had to grab his arm and pull him out of traffic when he tried to get a better view of the Chrysler Building.

Yes, there they were, arm in arm on the streets of Manhattan, laughing at Frank's hick amazement, his window washer's euphoria. West through Midtown, then up toward Central Park, where Diane knew a good restaurant. In the crowd at the next red light she slipped her arm out of his, which released him from an awkward position, in which his forearm had hung as if from an invisible sling to give her forearm something to rest on. These old postures. And yet the touch had coursed through him as he walked, like a light charge of electricity, or a new idea. *Ooooooooop.*

The restaurant proved to be run by Chinese or East Asians of some other kind, Frank didn't inquire because in every other respect the restaurant was pure Provençal. It was jammed into an archetypal Manhattan restaurant space, two stories of narrow rooms with a patio in the airshaft out back, a deep brick-walled enclosure filled by a hardy old tree.

Two faces in candlelight over a restaurant table: an old situation, and they both knew it. Although probably only Frank was also theorizing the event in terms of its million-year-old tradition. Two faces in the light of a fire, one male one female: eat, drink, man, woman. Big parts of the brain were no doubt ignited by the candlelight alone, not to mention the smells and tastes. A million years.

They talked about the day, the work in hand. Frank admitted to being impressed by the IPCC. "Still, I'd like to go faster. I think we need it."

"You think so?"

He told her about seeing Khembalung go under. Then his notions for dealing with the changing ocean, and for a really serious carbon drawdown.

Diane said, "So really you're talking about global cooling."

"Well, if we can warm it, maybe we can cool it too."

"But the warming took a lot. The whole world's economy, two hundred years."

"Well, but just by accident though. The economy wasn't dedicated to warming. It was just a byproduct."

"Making things cooler might be harder than warming."

"But if we actually direct part of the economy to that. Like as if paying for a war or something."

"Maybe." She thought about it, shook her head as if freeing herself from it.

Then they talked about their pasts, in brief disconnected anecdotes. She described her children, Frank his parents. This seemed odd, but then she described her parents too; quite like his in some ways, it sounded. Her mother had been born in China, and Diane could do a funny imitation of her primitive English, "You go in street car squish you like bug!" After that Frank could hear better the Chinese accent in Diane's own speech, which was perfectly grammatical and idiomatic, California Standard in fact, but with a lilt to it that he now understood better.

Then world events; problems in the Middle East; travels, New York; other meals in New York. They tried each other's dishes, refilled each other's wineglasses. They each drank half the bottle; then, over crème brûlée, sipped samples of cognac from a tray of ancient bottles offered for their inspection by the waiter.

Complex sensations, coursing through the brain. Some part of the parcellated mind watched all the parts come together. Nice to be so in the moment. Frank watched Diane's face and felt something like the glow he had felt when she took his arm on the street. She too was enjoying herself. Seeing that was part of the glow. Reciprocity: this kind of mutual enjoyment, he thought, only works if it *is* mutual. We live for this, we crave this. He felt a little vertiginous, as if climbing a hard pitch, or maybe the Chrysler Building up the street. Aware of a risk.

He saw again how beautiful her arms were. This was an Optimodal thing; not just biceps but the whole upper arm, amazingly thick front to back; unlike anyone else's arms. Gorgeous. It was different for everybody, what looked good to them. The argument that beauty corresponded to adaptive function was stupid. Deviance from the norm always drew the eye. Francesca Taolini had a crooked nose and various other asymmetries typical of narrow sharp-edged faces, and yet she was gorgeous; Diane had a blunt pentagonal face, perfectly symmetrical, and she too, while not as glamorous as Francesca, was still very attractive, one might even say charismatic. Yes, a true star that day at the UN. She drew the eye.

At a table near the door to the kitchen, another couple was having a similar sort of dinner, except they were much more demonstrative, more romantic; from time to time they even leaned together and kissed, in that New York way of pretending they were alone when they weren't. Frank thought they were showing off, and turned his head away; Diane saw them and his response too, and smiled her slight smile.

She leaned over and whispered, "They have wedding bands."

"Ah?"

"No way they are married to each other."

"Ahhh," Frank said.

She nodded, pleased by her deduction.

"The big city," Frank said awkwardly.

"It's true. I waited tables here for a while when I was going to school. I liked to guess the stories, like with these two, though this was easy. Usually it was harder. You only see an hour. But sometimes you can tell it's an important hour. People forget to eat, or they cry, or argue. You could see the story. The other girls thought I was crazy, but it was just to be doing something."

"Recreational anthropology."

She laughed. "Yes, or Nancy Drew. Passing the time."

Then they were done, the bill divided and paid. Out on the sidewalks she said, "Where are you staying?"

"The Metropolitan."

"Me too. Okay. We can walk through the park and see if the ice skating is going yet."

"It's certainly been cold enough for it."

As they walked into it, Central Park's similarity to Rock Creek Park struck Frank. Flat terrain instead of a ravine, but they were still in a piece of the great eastern hardwood forest. It was very familiar.

"I've been spending time around the National Zoo," Frank said impulsively. "It's kind of like this."

"What do you do there?"

"I've joined a group trying to keep track of the animals they haven't recaptured."

"That must be interesting."

"Yes, it is."

"And are you recapturing these animals?"

"Eventually I suppose they will. We're mostly watching them now. It would be hard to trap some of them. The gibbons are my favorite, and they can get away from people very easily, but they'll need some help with this cold."

"I like their singing."

"So do I!" Frank glanced down at her, suppressing several inane comments as they arose, in the end saying nothing. She walked beside him, relaxed and easy, her dark hair gleaming where it reflected a distant streetlight or park light, seeming unaware of his gaze.

"Ah look, it is going. How nice." She led him onto the bridge overlooking the northern bank of the ice rink. They leaned against it, watching New Yorkers expert and inexpert gliding over the illuminated white ice.

"Come on," Diane said, tugging his arm. "I haven't skated in years."

"Ah God," Frank said. "I'm terrible at it."

"I'll teach you."

She took his rental boots from him, demanded a stiffer and tighter pair from the help, then laced them up for him. "Nice and stiff, that's the secret. Now just stand straight and set a line. Glide forward. Shift quickly back and forth."

He tried it and it worked. Sort of. Anyway it went better than he remembered. He staggered around and tried not to fall or run into anybody. Diane glided past from time to time, undemonstrative but deft, throwing him off balance every time he caught sight of her. She skated with him, held him up, helped him up, then took off and skated by, red-cheeked and grinning.

"Okay," she said after a while. "I'm losing it here, my ankles are tired."

"Mine are broken."

Back into shoes, back walking on the ground—stumping along, it felt, after the skating. Frank felt a little tense, and they drew apart as they walked. Frank searched for something to talk about.

They walked more slowly, as if to prolong the evening, or stave off an awkward moment. Two single adults, out on a date in Manhattan, with empty rooms waiting in the same hotel; and no one on Earth knew where they were at that moment, except them. The theoretical possibilities were obvious.

But she was his boss, and about a decade older than him. Not that the age part mattered—though it did; it was the professional relationship that was the main thing, standing like the bottom half of a Dutch door between them. So much could go wrong. So much could be misinterpreted. They were going to be working together for the coming year, maybe more. And then there was Caroline too, the existence of whom had changed everything in his life; except not, it seemed, the content of this parcel of it.

The incorrigible scientist inside him was trying to analyze the situation. Every street they came to had a red light, and there was time to think, perhaps too much time. Alpha females often led their troop in all the fundamental ways, particularly matters of sexual access, meaning reproductive success. The alpha males (and really, in this situation Frank almost might be considered a beta male)—they were almost ceremonial in their powers. They got what they wanted, but did not control the troop.

Well, whatever; at this moment that wasn't really the point. He needed to know what to do. It was like being in high school. He had hated high school for this very reason.

Diane sighed. He glanced at her; she was smiling her little smile. "That was fun," she said. "I never take time like this anymore."

She was keeping a good distance between them.

"We'll have to do it in D.C.," Frank suggested. "Take a break."

"That would be nice. We might even have outdoor ice skating this winter, if the forecasts come true."

"Yes, that's right. Out on the Potomac for that matter."

Another block.

Frank said, "You do work long hours."

"No more than anyone else."

"I hear it's a lot more."

"Well, there's a lot to do. Anyway, it won't last much longer."

She pointed down a crossing street this time, rather than nudging him along. "Down that way. The hotel's at Fifty-first and Lex."

"Ah yeah. What do you mean, not much longer?"

"Well, my term is almost up."

"It's a term?"

"Yes, didn't you know?" She looked up at him, laughed at his expression. "Heading NSF is a presidential appointment, it lasts for six years. I have just over a year to go."

They stopped in front of their hotel.

"I didn't know that," Frank said stupidly.

"They must have told you when you did the orientation."

"Oh," said Frank. "I missed some of that."

"You blew it off."

"Well, yes, a little bit, not all of it . . ."

She watched him, seeming amused but guarded. He had suddenly learned she was not as powerful as he had thought. And power is attractive. On the other hand, this meant she was not going to be his boss indefinitely, which meant that particular strangeness would go away, leaving them unconstrained by work issues—by the past in any manifestation—free to examine whatever was between them. So, less powerful in the pure sense, but less constrained in her relation to him; and how did these factors affect his feelings?

She was watching his face to see!

He didn't know himself, so there was no way his face could show anything. But then that too must have been visible. And the unconscious mind—

He shivered at his own confusion, tried to smile. "So there's light at the end of your tunnel," he said.

"But I like the job."

"Ah. Yes. Well . . . that's too bad, then."

She shrugged. "I'll do something else."

"Dang."

She shrugged again. She was still watching him; interested in him. He wondered how much longer they could stand outside the hotel talking before it began to look strange.

"I want to hear more about this down in D.C.," he said. "What you're thinking of doing, and all."

"Okay."

"Good. Well, six o'clock train—shall we meet in the lobby and walk over to the station?"

"Sure." She nodded. "Five A.M. sharp."

They turned together into the hotel and walked to the elevator. Up it went, opened at the third floor:

"Good night."

"Good night."

"That was fun."

"Yes it was."

When Charlie cleaned house he worked in a burst of maniacal effort powered by very loud music, making the event into a kind of indoor extreme sport performed in a last-minute attempt to stave off utter shabbiness. The ancient insane and incontinent cats, the ineradicable musk that the swimming tiger had left in the basement (perhaps contributing to the cats' paranoia), Joe's depredations and accidents, Nick's absent-minded tendency to use the furniture as a napkin; all these left marks. Even the divinely slovenly Anna left marks, dropping her clothing wherever she happened to take it off, depositing books and papers and mail wherever she finished with them—all behaviors in stark contrast to the extreme order of her abstract thinking—these too had an impact. And Charlie himself was disorganized in both the abstract and the concrete; so that eventually their house's interior came to consist of narrow passageways through immense tottering middens of household detritus.

Charlie would therefore occasionally knock something over and block the way, notice the chaos, and freak out. He would leap into action, trying to rectify everything in a single morning. He had to begin by putting things away, to the extent possible, as all closets and drawers remained mysteriously full, despite all that was strewn at large. However, he at least got things off the floors, into stacks on tables and dressers near where they were supposed to go. Then he cleaned the bathrooms and the kitchen, scrubbing madly; then it was time for vacuuming.

All this was Charlie's version of the Zen meditation called "chop wood carry water," and he enjoyed it as such; but it had to be fueled by music or it was no good. Vacuum cleaning in particular needed music, fast intricate surging music that sounded good at high volume. The buzzsaw solos of Charlie Parker made an excellent vacuuming soundtrack, allowing Charlie to shout "Salt—PEEEEnuts!" over and over as he crashed about. Certain rock guitarists could of course push a vacuum as well; when Steve Howe was soloing the world practically vacuumed itself.

But the apotheosis of vacuum cleaning, Charlie had found over the years, was that part of Beethoven's late work that expressed the composer's sense of "the mad blind energy of the universe," which was just what vacuuming needed. These movements as defined by Beethoven's biographer Walter Sullivan, who had identified and named the mode, were those characterized by tunes repetitive and staccato, woven into fugues so that different lines perpetually overlapped in dense interference patterns, relentless, machinelike, interminable. Possibly only a deaf man could have composed such music. The famous second movement of the Ninth Symphony was a good example of this mode, but to Charlie the two very best examples were the finale of the Hammerklavier sonata, opus 106, and the Grosse Fugue, originally the finale of string quartet opus 130, later detached and designated opus 133. The finale of the Hammerklavier was so difficult to play that concert pianists often gave up performing it years ahead of their full retirement, while the Grosse Fugue had caused the first quartet that attempted it to beg Beethoven to write a replacement finale more within human capacities—a request which Beethoven had granted with a laugh, no doubt foreseeing that quartet players in the future would end up having to perform both finales, compounding their problem.

In any case, the cosmic inexorability of these two huge fugues made perfect music to propel a vacuum cleaner around the house. And long ago Charlie had discovered by accident that it worked even better to *play them both at once,* one on the stereo upstairs, the other downstairs, with the volumes on both stereos turned up to eleven.

Joe of course loved this unholy racket, real big truck music, and he insisted on lending a hand with the vacuuming itself, causing Charlie to dodge and leap about to avoid trampling him, and to catch the machine if it got loose and began to drag the undetachable toddler down some lane of open space toward furniture or walls. After a few such mishaps Joe would usually hand it back over and follow Charlie around, slinging dinosaurs into the vacuum's path to see if they would survive.

So, now a day came when Charlie was flying around the dining room, smashing chairs aside with the vacuum cleaner to make room under the table, lots of odd rattles and clunks under there as usual, glorying in the crisscross of the two monster fugues, the way they almost seemed to match each other, the piano rippling up and down within the massed chaos of the strings, everything wrong but right, insane but perfect—and then came that magic moment when both the hammering on the clavier and the grossness of the fugue quieted *at the same time,* as if Beethoven had somehow foreseen that the two pieces would be played together someday, or as if there was some underlying method in both, introducing a little eye to the storm before the exhilarating assault on all meaning and sense started to chomp away again—when Charlie looked around and saw that Joe was sitting on the floor of the living room, red-faced and openmouthed, bawling his eyes out, unheard in the cacophony.

Charlie killed the vacuum cleaner, rushed over to turn off Charles Rosen, then slid across the hardwood floor to snatch the boy up in his arms.

"Oh Joe! Joe! What's wrong, buddy? What's wrong?"

Joe stuck out his lower lip. "Loud."

"Oh God Joe I'm sorry. I'm sorry. But, you know—we're vacuuming! It's always loud when we vacuum the house."

"Too loud," Joe said, and whimpered pathetically.

Charlie hugged him, held him. "Sorry guy," he said. "I'm really sorry. I didn't know. This is the way we've always done it before."

And also, it seemed to him, in the past, if Joe had wanted something like the sound turned down, he would have let Charlie know by beating on his kneecap or launching a dinosaur at his head. Charlie was used to a very frank and open exchange of views with Joe, so that they would bicker with each other, sure, tussle, whack, yell—but cry? To have Joe Quibler whimpering in his arms pathetically, content to snuggle up against his chest . . . it was not right. And though it felt good to be able to comfort him, to rock him side to side in his arms, as he had many years before when trying to get Nick to fall asleep—humming gently the main theme of the Grosse Fugue until the Arditti Quartet finished with it upstairs, then continuing to hum it, until it became something like a lullaby for infant robots—it was still extremely disturbing. It just wasn't like Joe.

He sat down and for a long time hugged the child, communing. Then Joe looked up at the big front window, and his eyes grew round.

"Snow," he said.

"Yes, that's right, that's snow! Very good Joe! I didn't know you knew how to say that. It must be last winter since you saw snow, and you were just a baby then."

Joe conducted the snow with outstretched arms, looking rapt, or maybe just stunned. "Snow go down."

"It sure does. Wow, that's pretty heavy for a first storm. It looks like it's going to bury the house. I thought this was supposed to be global warming we were having."

"Berry house?"

"No not really, I was joking there. It might come up to the windows though, see? I don't think it will get any higher than that."

"No?"

"Oh, well, no reason really. It just never does. At least so far. And cold dry winters are supposed to be the thing now. The great paradox. I guess it's been kind of dry this fall. But now it's snowing. When it snows it snows." Charlie was used to babbling meaninglessly at Joe; they were privileged conversations, as between lawyer and client. It was actually a bit disconcerting to have Joe beginning to understand him.

Joe kept conducting the snow, his hands making evocative flutters downward.

Impulsively Charlie gave him another hug. The boy was hot as usual. Not by much, but Charlie could feel it. Anna was keeping a chart on him now, and she had established that he was hotter by day, just under a hundred, and a bit cooler at night, right over 98.6; average 98.9, she concluded after going through one of her statistical fits. It was a way of not thinking, Charlie thought. Quantification as coping. Charlie just felt the heat with his fingertips, as now. Joe shrugged him aside. He was more sensitive these days. Was that true? Well, there was this sudden aversion to Beethoven squared. But one of the weird things about living with a toddler was how fast they changed, and how hard it then became to remember what they had been like before the change, overwhelmed as that memory was by the present state, so vivid to the eye. Probably Joe *was* different, because of course, he had to be different. He was growing up. He was adding several million brain cells an hour, and several hundred experiences.

And occasionally he burst out with a newly angry version of his old vehemence, so it wasn't as if he were mellowing out. No one who knew him would put it that way. But before, he had been permanently and so to speak impersonally irritated, at the slowness of everything, perhaps; now when he got upset it appeared more deeply felt, and often directed at Charlie. It almost seemed as if he were *unhappy*. This had never been true before; Joe had been furious often, unhappy never. Even the thought of him unhappy cut Charlie to the quick. And fearful, needy, even affectionate . . . all these were strange things for Charlie to witness.

Now he watched Joe stare out the window at the falling snow: not writhing in his arms, not trying to throw anything, not bouncing around absorbed in solitary play, not babbling. Of course the snow was a startling sight, so fair enough. But Charlie was scared by the way Joe felt in his arms.

"Maybe we should go out there and play in the snow!"

"Okay."

"Come on, it'll be fun! We can dress warm and make a snowman. Throw snowballs."

"Okay Da."

Charlie sighed. No leap up, no marching to the door shouting GO GO GO with finger imperiously extended . . .

He got up and started to get them dressed. It was a long operation. It was eighteen degrees outside. Already he was thinking Fire in the fireplace, Thomas the Train on the carpet, snow drifting down outside the window. "We won't be able to stay out long."

The phone rang. "Oh, wait just a second here."

Joe's eyes bugged out in their old style. "Daaa! Wanna GO! GO!"

"Ha! I bet you do! Good for you! Just a second, ha ha. Hello?"

"Charlie it's Roy."

"Roy! How are you?"

"I'm fine you? Is this a good time?"

"No worse than usual."

"Still suffering the slings and arrows of outrageous children?"

"Yes. Joe and I are about to go outside in the snow, but I can talk to you out there. Let me get my earplug in."

"I won't keep you long, you guys just keep doing what you're doing. We've been talking about what Phil can say to counter the administration's attacks. Now that he's declared he's running, they're concerned, and they keep saying that he'll gut the economy in a futile attempt to reverse climate change."

"As opposed to letting it continue?"

"Yes. Adaptation opportunities are big in certain think tanks now. There are regions due to see more productive climates, they say."

"I'll bet they do. Let's use that as a slingshot to shoot things at them."

"But why shouldn't we just let private enterprise take care of it?"

"The free market is not good at disaster recovery. Catastrophe is not profitable."

"But they say it is."

"We'll have to point out that isn't true."

"Maybe that's why we keep losing."

"Think positive, Roy. Here, put your legs in first, it works better that way. It's warmer. No way are we going outside unless you agree to put that on. You're so funny!"

"Charlie, do you need to go?"

"No no. Hey, come on! No, not at all. Here we go. Now, what were we saying, that we're doomed to lose this election?"

"No, it's not that, I'm just trying to refine the message."

"Job creation! Helping people get through the bad weather by stimulating new industries."

"The time for a Works Progress Administration may have passed."

"Roy—"

"I'm just trying to see their next move!"

"You're bumming me out. I'm out in the beautiful white snow, whee!"

"Ooh! Ooh!"

"Okay Charlie. Call me back, I don't think my ear can handle you guys besporting yourselves like that."

"Right, think it over and I'll call you back hey Joe! Bye."

"Bye."

Charlie hustled after Joe, out into the street. Their street dead-ended right in front of their house, and there was a blanket of snow covering it. Joe kicked around in an ecstasy, his cheeks red, his eyes a brilliant blue. Charlie followed him calling, "Go! Ha! Take that!"

Snow drifted down on them. It was cold but almost windless. Beautiful, really. Maybe they could adapt to any climate.

Well, but that was thinking about individuals, the body in its clothing. The system more generally might not fare as well: food production, for instance.

As he danced in the snow, Charlie considered what could be said to the American public to convince them they needed to elect Phil Chase. Incumbents had an advantage, but the Republican Party had stood firm, so far, on a policy of denying that climate change had to be dealt with. Surely they could be held to account for that heedlessness?

Maybe, maybe not.

The snow lofted down. Looking up, it was strange to see so many tiny white missiles plunging down out of the gray cloud that covered the sky.

Individual flakes caught in Joe's hair. His mittens were too big; he looked displeased and shook his hands. Angrily he tried to pluck the mittens off, one hand then the other, but both hands were equally impeded.

"DAAAA!"

"No, Joe, wait, don't do that Joe, your hands will freeze. Cold! Cold!"

"Wanna! Wanna!" Joe flung his arms wildly around him, and off the mittens flew.

"Ah shit Joe. Come on. We'll have to go back inside if you do that."

"Wanna snow."

Happily Joe scooped up loose snow and smooshed it into snowballs to throw at his dad. Quickly his hands turned pink and wet, but he didn't seem to mind. Charlie helped him build a little snowman. Base, torso, head. The new snow cohered very nicely. Pinecones for snowman eyes. "Very cool."

Joe stood facing it. He put his red wet hands together. "Namaste," he said.

Charlie jerked upright. "What did you say?"

"No ma stay."

"Oh! You want to go back inside?"

"Owee." Holding out a red-and-white hand for Charlie's inspection.

"I bet! That looks cold! That's what I was telling you, about the mittens."

"Too big."

"Sorry. We'll look for some smaller ones."

Joe began kicking the snowman. Charlie watched him fondly. This was his Joe, kicking his creation to pieces. Like a sand mandala poured into the river. Huge gusto when wiping a slate clean. His snowsuit looked like it was covered with wet diamonds.

"Come on, let's go back inside. He's all gone now. People won't even know what we did. They'll think two big tigers have been out here wrestling."

"Coo Da."

Back inside they went to the kitchen and made hot chocolate. They took their cups out by the fire and put them on the coffee table, then wrestled casually, taking breaks to sip chocolate. Joe charged Charlie, slammed into him, then rolled away on the carpet, squealing happily; there was little he liked more, particularly when he knocked Charlie over. He growled like a dog, grunted like a martial artist, shrieked like a banshee; did not cry when he fell down.

Except this time he did. He bonked his head on the radiator and wailed. He just wasn't as tough these days. It took quite a bit of hot chocolate to make it okay. Then it was back to rolling, growling, shouting "Ha!" or "Gotcha," until they were content to lie there in a heap on the carpet. Charlie was exhausted; Joe faked exhaustion, to show what a mighty ordeal it had been to defeat the monster, then sat playing with his trains, shaking his head. "Po Da."

The fire crackled. Outside the snow fell. Looking up at it from the floor,

Charlie had the impression that it was aiming at him and just missing. Maybe this was just the way it was going to be now. Maybe that's the way it had always been. People had lived cocooned in oil for a few generations, but beyond that the world remained the same, waiting for them to re-emerge into it.

Joe was staring into the fire. He whimpered, as in the last gulp of a cry. Charlie leaned over and hugged him, held him; the boy felt hot again, slightly sweaty. He twisted a little, trying to get comfortable, and Charlie resisted an urge to squeeze him tightly; he put his nose into the boy's fine hair, breathed in the faint smell of infancy. All that was going away. Charlie was filled suddenly with a fearful joy, beautiful but frightening, like the snow outside. Snow inside him. They leaned against each other. They sighed one of their synchronized sighs, the same breath filling them, then leaving in a prolonged exhalation. Joe and Da by the fire.

CHAPTER 16

OPTIMODAL

Social Science Experiment in Elective Politics (SSEEP)

(notes by Edgardo Alfonso, for Diane Chang, also the Vanderwal committee and the National Science Board)

The experiment is designed to ask, if the scientific community were to propose a platform of political goals based on scientific principles, how would it be formulated, and what would the platform say?

In other words, what goals for improvement in society and government might follow logically from the aggregate of scientific findings and the application of the scientific method?

The platform could conceivably take the form of the "Contract with America" adopted by the Republican Party before the 1994 election (a kind of list of Things to Do):

"Contract with Humanity"
"Contract with Our Children"
"Contract with the Generations to Come"

commitment to inventing a sustainable culture

(Permaculture, first iteration
—what science is for)

Some kind of underlying macro-goal or foundational axiom set might have to be synthesized from the particulars of scientific practice and the composite standard model of physical reality expressed by the various disciplines.

1. One axiom or goal might be some form of the "Greatest good for the greatest number" rubric, without implying in any way that this "greatest good" could include or justify any planned or accepted structural or permanent disadvantaging of any minority of any size. As should be clear in the wording of the rubric, the greatest number is of course one hundred percent, including also the generations to come.

2. Even in the context of any religious or humanistic anthropocentrism, the life of our species depends on the rest of Earth's biosphere. Even the utilitarian view of nature as something distinct and subservient to humanity must grant the biosphere the status of a diffused expression and aspect of our bodies. Interdependence of all the components of biosphere (including humanity) is undeniable. An observable, confirmable fact (breathing).

   Given some version of these foundational axioms, the scientific community suggests these platform particulars for government:

(preliminary partial list, please add to it as you see fit)

"Contract with Our Children"

1. protection of the biosphere: sustainable uses; clean technologies; carbon balance; climate homeostasis.

2. protection of human welfare: universal housing, clothing, shelter, clean water, health care, education, legal rights for all.

3. *full employment: Current economy defines 5.4% unemploy-ment as optimum for desired "wage-pressure balance," treating labor (people) as a commodity and using a supply/demand pricing model. Five percent in USA = approx. fifteen million people. At the same time there is important work not being done.*

If government-created full employment reduced "wage pres-sure" (fear), forcing a rise in minimum wages from the private sector, this would help pull millions out of poverty, decrease their government dependence and social service costs, and in-ject and cycle their larger incomes back into the economy.

4. *Individual ownership of the majority of the surplus value of one's labor.*

People create by their work an economic value beyond what it costs to pay them and provide their means of production. This averages $66,000 per year for American workers, a sur-plus legally belonging to owners/shareholders.

American workers therefore receive between a tenth and a fourth of the actual value of their work. The rest goes to own-ers/shareholders.

A minimum share of 51% of the value of one's work should be returned to one as surplus value beyond salary, this value to be measured by objective and transparent accounting as de-fined by law.

3. *and 4. combined would tend to promote the greatest good for the greatest number, by distributing the wealth more equitably among those who have created it.*

5. *Reduction of military spending*

Match U.S. military expenditures to the average of other na-tions; this would halve the military budget, freeing over $400 billion a year.

More generally, all national militaries should be integrated in an international agreement upholding nonviolent conflict resolution.

Disproportionate size of U.S. military and arms industry a
waste of resources. Doubling since September 11, 2001, resem-
bles panic response or attempt at global hegemony. Results un-
dermine goals of the foundational axioms.

6. Population stabilization

Human population stabilized at some level to be determined
by carrying-capacity studies and foundational axioms. Best re-
sults here so far have resulted from increase in women's rights
and education, also a goal in itself, thus a powerful positive
feedback loop active within a single human generation.

Context/ultimate goal: Permaculture

A scientifically informed government should lead the way in the invention of
a culture which is sustainable perpetually. This is the only good bequest to the
generations to come. It is not adaptive to heavily damage the biosphere when
our own offspring and all the generations to follow will need it, like we do, in
order to survive. If reproductive success is defined as life's goal, as it is in evo-
lutionary theory, then stealing from descendants (kleptoparasitism) is mal-
adaptive.

Protection of the environment, therefore, along with restoration of
landscapes and biodiversity, should become one of the principal goals of the
economy. Government must lead the way in investigating potential climate-
altering strategies to mitigate current problems and eventually establish a
balance that can be maintained in perpetuity.

Process Notes: how to enact platform.

Broader outreach. Public discussion. Performance evaluation methodolo-
gies. Scientific organizations and universities as information transmitters.
Individuals in these organizations as catalysts in information cascade; also,
candidates for elections and appointments. Advocacy.

Study governing methods in other countries to suggest possible reforms to our system where currently function (democracy) is impaired. Some candidates for study:

> *Swiss presidential model (executive council)*
> *Australian ballot (preferential voting)*
> *transparency in government (freedom of information, watchdog groups); the rule of law*
> *mass action, grass roots, people power, democracy*

Diane and the Vanderwal committee sat around the table in the meeting room next to Diane's office. Some shook their heads as they read Edgardo's draft; others just gave up and held their heads in their hands.

"Okay," Diane said cheerfully. "Anyone want to add anything else?"

The first big windstorm tore the last leaves off the trees in a rush. When Frank got out of his van the wind cut into him, and he reached back for a windbreaker. The wind was loud in the branches, hooting and keening like the roar of jets. He ran to the park and stopped on the overlook. Leaves were tumbling down into the gorge, the stream was running with them; it looked like a million yellow paper boats had been launched and were now bouncing down the rapids together, covering the water entirely. Frank hooted loudly, "Ooooooop!" into the blanketing roar of the wind. Nothing would hear him. It was colder than it had yet been this year.

At his tree he called down Miss Piggy. He had to catch her on an inswing, and the climb was tough, up into piercing cold wind, swinging a little; then over the lip and onto the plywood. In his treehouse.

Only now it was like a crow's nest, swaying back and forth on the top of the mast. "Wow!" He sat down, belayed himself to the railing. Was it going to be possible to get used to this? He watched the wind toss the forest about. The canopy was a network of black branches and twigs bouncing vigorously in place, a few stubborn leaves flapping like prayer flags.

His own tree moved gently back and forth, back and forth. Rockabye baby. It seemed like it would be okay. He was liking it already. "Ooooop!"

He crawled over to his duffel, opened it, and pulled out his largest tent, a North Face South Col. It was very strong and stable, therefore quiet as tents went. It was meant for two people and a lot of gear.

He screwed ringbolt screws into the plywood, measuring carefully and staking down the tent as he went to make certain it was stretched out tautly.

He pulled the tent poles into their sleeves and posted them into their grommets, leaning into the windswept fabric of the tent until they were secure. He stepped in; it was really big for a two-person tent, expedition scale for sure, with room to stand right at the high point, sloping quickly down to the four corners. Cuben Fiber blue, and in the lantern's glow, the color of twilight. It smelled like the mountains.

He moved his duffel and the rest of his stuff inside. Zip the door shut, zooop! and he was in a Cuben Fiber–walled room. Like a kind of yurt. People had lived in yurts through entire ice ages. This one swayed, but that still seemed okay. It reminded him of waterbeds, back in the day. Rockabye baby!

He pulled out his sleeping bag, sat on his groundpad, draped the bag over his legs. Arranged his pillows. Everything was slightly blue, including his laptop screen. He regarded all of it with pleasure; this was the bedroom he loved most in the world, the only constant in all his years of wandering. Nothing lacking, everything at hand, the taut walls curving up aerodynamically.

He got comfortable and tapped around on the laptop. A little reading to help him to sleep. An article in *Nature*, linking paleoclimate and human evolution to severe fluctuations in climate, ice ages being repeated selectors for flexibility, innovation, and cooperation. Another altruism-as-adaptation argument, in other words. Frank wasn't sure it made the case that cooperation had been key. It was a group selection argument, and evolutionary theory was still struggling with the concept of group selection, as opposed to the solid case for kin selection, which one tended to see everywhere in nature. Living things would clearly sacrifice for their kin; whether they would for their group was less sure.

Still, it was interesting to think about. And it combined in a very interesting way with another article in *Nature* describing the latest in game theory studies of altruism. Prisoner's dilemma was part of it, of course. This *Nature* article described some new experiments. Researchers had first tried prisoner's dilemma using only always-defect and always-generous strategies—in essence, parasites and hosts. As predicted by previous results, the defectors took over the system; but the average fitness of the population then dropped.

A variant of the game was then introduced, called Snowdrift, in which players were supposedly stuck in cars in the snow, and could either get out and shovel, or not. The generous got points even if the other defected, because eventually their car would be clear. Here cooperators and defectors coexisted stably, in a mix determined by the details of the game rules.

The researchers then mapped the Snowdrift results onto a graph program, finding long tendrils of association between clusters of cooperators. When the tendrils were cut by rule changes, the clusters were destroyed by defectors. The implication was that islanding was dangerous, and that some rules allowed cooperation to prosper while others didn't. It was also interesting to consider what the analog of tendrils would be in real-world situations. Extending help to people from other groups, perhaps—as Anna had, for instance, when welcoming the Khembalis into her family's life after they appeared in the NSF building. This kind of generosity could be explained as group selection, but only if the definition of the group was enlarged, perhaps even by some leap of the imagination. Empathy. Someone in the *Journal* recently had suggested this was the story of human history so far, successive enlargement of the sense of the group.

The authors of this *Nature* article went on to tentatively suggest that generosity which held no advantage at all to the giver might be structurally sounder in the long run than generosity that brought some kind of return to the cooperator. The paper concluded with the reminder that at the beginning of life, RNA had had to cooperate with proteins and other molecules to band together and form cells. So clearly cooperation was a necessary component of evolution, and a strong adaptive strategy. The authors of the paper admitted that the reasons for the success of cooperation were not well understood. But certain proteins now ubiquitous in cells must have gotten there by being always generous.

Falling asleep in his tent, swaying gently, Frank thought: Now that is interesting . . . suggestive . . . something to be tried. I will be like that protein . . . or like Anna at work . . . I will be

always generous.

Winter came.

His treehouse was now visible from the ground, if one knew what to look for. But who was looking? And if anyone saw it, what could they do about it? Theoretically someone could lie in wait nearby, then arrest him or ambush him. But as he hiked in the park under the bare-limbed skeletal trees, over ground thick with rime-frosted and snowdrifted leaves, he could see sometimes half a mile in all directions, and in truth the park was nearly depopulate. He was much more likely to see deer than people. The only humans out in the area near his treehouse tended to be park staff or other FOG volunteers; and many of these were acquaintances by now. Even strangers did not represent a danger, during the day anyway. People out there in winter were often interested in being alone. You could tell when you spotted them whether this was true or not, in another of those unconscious calculations that the savannah brain was so good at. But mostly he just saw deer. He hiked the empty forest, looking for the aurochs and seeing only deer; although once he spotted what looked to him like an ibex, and Nancy ID'd as a chamois.

The other ferals he spotted were often suffering from the cold, and the sudden absence of leaves. So many were tropical or subtropical, and even if they could have withstood the cold, the disappearance of the leaves meant their food was gone. Seeing an eland snuffling in a pile of leaves packed into a windrow gave one a new respect for the native animals, who could survive such drastic changes in the environment. It was a tough biome, and the natives were tough customers. The coyotes were even getting kind of brash.

The zoo staff and FOG were now recapturing every endangered feral they could. The ones that remained elusive, or seemed to be doing okay, were aided by heated feeding stations. These were mostly simple two-walled shelters, L's with their open sides facing south. Frank helped build some, lifting panels and beams of playground plastic to be screwed into place. A few shelters were three-walled, and had trapdoors suspended over their open sides, so that the zoo staff could capture animals inside them. None of the FOG members liked it, but it beat a mass die-off.

So now there were parts of the park that seemed like an open-air unwalled zoo, with animals of many different species hanging out near the shelters and visiting when their kind of food was put out. It looked to Frank like these creatures felt they had returned to the zoo already, and were content to be there.

But not all the ferals came in from the cold. And some of the stubbornest animals were among those least capable of surviving. The gibbons and siamangs were only going to the shelters that did not have trapdoors, and leaving them as soon as they had eaten. The gibbons continued to brachiate through the leafless trees. The siamangs had been seen walking around on the ground, their long arms raised over their heads to keep them from dragging on the ground; it looked like they were trying to surrender and not succeeding, but if they saw people approaching they tarzanned away at high speed.

Both species were also now joining the ferals who were venturing out of the park into the residential neighborhoods nearby, finding sources of heat and food on their own; one siamang had been electrocuted while sleeping on a transformer, but now the rest didn't do that anymore. The gibbons Bert and May and their sons had been reported sleeping in a kid's backyard treehouse.

"If they obviously don't want to be recaptured," Frank said to Nancy, "then we should help them from the shelters, and let them stay feral." He knew most of the FOG membership felt the same.

Nancy said, "I'm afraid that if we don't bring them in, we'll lose them."

December days were too short. He tried to get in a short animal walk at dawn; then it was over to work, where things were hectic. Frank threw himself into his tasks, and the days passed in their usual rush; and then in the dusk, or in full dark, he hiked down into the park and climbed his hanging ladder.

Recline on his groundpad, then, in the open doorway of his tent. Only when it was windy did he retreat fully inside. As long as the air remained still, his heavy sleeping bag, which had kept him warm on climbs in Alaska and the Canadian Arctic, would do the same here. And the nights were too beautiful to miss. The highest branches spiked around him like a forest of giant thorns, the stars brilliant through their black calligraphy. He watched the stars, and read his laptop, or a paperback set under the lantern, until sleep came on him; then snuggled into the bag; slept well; woke serene, to the sight of the treetops bobbing and rustling on the dawn breeze. Lines of blackbirds flew out of town to look for food, under a flat sky of pewter and lead. Really the important thing was to be out in the world, to feel the wind and see the full spaciousness of being on a planet whirling through space. A feeling of beatitude; was that the right word? Sit up, click on the laptop, Google "beatitude"; then there on the screen:

> beatitude dips from on high down on us and we *see*. It is not in us so much as we are in it. If the air come to our lungs, we breathe and live; if not, we die. If the light come to our eyes, we see; else not. And if truth come to our mind we suddenly expand to its dimensions, as if we grew to worlds.

My Lord. Words of Ralph Waldo Emerson, from a website called Emersonfortheday.com. Frank read a little more: quite amazing stuff. He bookmarked the site, which apparently featured a new thought from the philosopher's writings every few days. Earlier samples read like some miraculously profound horoscope or fortune cookie. Reading them, Frank suddenly realized that the people who had lived before him in this immense hardwood forest had had epiphanies much like his. Emerson, the great Transcendentalist, had already sketched the route to a new kind of nature-worshipping religion. His journal entries in particular suited Frank's late night reading, for the feel they had of someone thinking on the page. This was a good person to know.

One night after he fell asleep skimming the site, his cell phone jolted him awake. "Hello?"

"Frank, it's Caroline."

"Oh good." He was already sitting up.

"Can you come see me, in the same place?"

"Yes. When will you be there?"

"Half an hour."

She was sitting on the same bench, under the bronze dancer. When she saw him approaching she stood, and they embraced. He felt her against him.

For a long time they breathed in and out, their bodies pressed together. A lot was conveyed, somehow. He could feel that she had been having a hard time—that she was lonely—that she needed him, in the same way he needed her.

They sat on the bench, holding hands.

"So," she said. "You've been traveling."

"Yes."

"Boston, Atlanta—Khembalung, even?"

"Yes, that's right."

"But—I mean—I told you this Pierzinski was probably the reason you were listed, right? And Francesca Taolini is on the list too?"

"Yes, you did." Frank shrugged. "I needed to talk to them. I couldn't do my job without talking to them. So I thought I'd go ahead, and see if you noticed any, I don't know—change in my status or whatever."

"Yes. I did."

"So, were we taped?"

"No. You mean beyond your phones? No. Not yet."

"Interesting."

She gazed at him curiously. "You know, this is serious. It's not a game."

"I know that. I'm not thinking of it as a game. More like an experiment."

"But you don't want to draw any more attention to yourself."

"I suppose not, but why? What could they do to me?"

"Oh I don't know. Every agency has its inspector general. You could suddenly find your travel expenses questioned. You could lose your job."

"Then I'd just go back to UCSD."

"I hope you don't do that."

He squeezed her hand. "Okay, but tell me more. Did my status change?"

"You went up a level."

"So my stock rose?"

"It did. But that's a different issue. Your stock rose, fine, but that means it hit an amount that triggered surveillance to go up. At that level, you'll have more intrusive methods applied. It's all set in the programs."

"But why, what for?"

"I'm sure it's something to do with Pierzinski, like you said last time.

Taolini was really googling him after your trip to Boston, him and you both."

"She was?"

"Yeah. She called up pretty much everything you've ever published. And lots of Pierzinski too. What did you two talk about?"

"She was on the panel I ran that reviewed Pierzinski's proposal."

"Yes, I know."

"So, we talked about the work he's doing, stuff like that."

"She looks like she's cute."

"Yes." He didn't know what to say. She laughed at him, squeezed his hand. Now that he was with her, he understood that the others were all just displacements of his real desire. "So my calls are being recorded?"

"Yes. I told you that last time."

"I guess you did. My cell phone?"

"Yes, but so far no one's actually checking them. They're just saved in your file. If you went up another level they'd get reviewed."

"And what about my FOG phone?"

"No. Isn't that just a walkie-talkie system?"

"Yeah."

"Those only work off one tower. I have to call your cell, but I don't like doing that anymore. I'm calling you from public phones, so someone would have to make a complete search of your file to find those calls, but they're there if they look hard enough. If someone knows my voice . . . Meanwhile, they can tell where you were when you got calls because of the towers involved."

"So you know where I am?"

"To an extent. Your van is tagged too. I can see you're spending time over near Rock Creek Park. Have you got a place over there?"

"Yes."

"You must be renting a room? There aren't any home arrangements showing. No water or electric or home phone or sewage."

"No."

"So you're renting a room?"

"Like that, yes."

She considered him. She squeezed his hand again. "I hope you trust me."

"Oh I do. It's just that I'm, I don't know. Embarrassed."

"Embarrassed?"

"Yes. Only not really." He met her gaze. "I live in a treehouse. I'm out in Rock Creek Park, living up in a little treehouse I built."

She laughed. Then she leaned in and gave him a peck on the cheek. "Good for you! Will you take me up to it sometime?"

"Oh yes," he said, warming. "I'd like that very much."

She was still leaning into him. They leaned wordlessly, feeling the pressure of arm against arm. Then they shifted, and suddenly were kissing.

It all came instantly back to him, he fell headlong into the space they had occupied in the elevator, as though the intervening months had vanished and they were back there again, passionately making out, deep in their bubble universe.

After some indeterminate time, they paused for breath. Such intensity could not be maintained; it had to lead somewhere else, either forward to orgasm or backward to talk. And since they were out on a park bench, since there were still so many questions pricking at other parts of his mind, he fell back toward talk. He wanted to know more—

But then she pulled him back to her to kiss again, and obviously that was a much better idea. Passion blew through him again, sexual passion, my God who could explain it? Who could even remember what it was like?

Again it went on for some time, he couldn't have said how long. The night was cold, her fingers were cool. The city rumbled around them. Distant siren. He liked the feel of her body under her clothes: ribby ribs, soft breasts. The iron solidity of her quads. She squeezed him, gasped and murmured a little, all through their kisses.

Again they came up for air.

"Oh my," she said. She shifted on the bench, conformed herself to him like a cat.

His questions slowly resurfaced. He looked down at her face, tucked against his shoulder.

"Are you staying with your friends again?"

"Yes." She looked at her watch. "Uh oh."

"What time is it?"

"Four."

"The witching hour."

"Yes."

"When do you have to be back?"

"Soon."

"And . . . look, is there some way I can call you? Is *your* phone tapped?"

"Maybe." She hesitated. "I don't want to use it for anything important."

"Ah." He thought about it. "There must be some protocols?"

She shook her head quickly. "It isn't like that in my department. Although sure, there are methods. We could use phone cards and public phones."

"We'd have to synchronize."

"Right, but that's part of the method."

"Fridays at nine kind of thing."

"Right. Let's do that. Let's find pay phones we think will work. There are still some left, like in Metro stations. We'll share numbers next time I call you, and after that we won't be putting anything on your phone. You might get bumped up again any time, the way things are going in the market. You guys are really impressing the investors." She looked at her watch. "Ah hell."

She twisted into him, kissed him again. "Hmmm," she said after a while. "I've gotta go. . . ."

"I understand. You'll call?"

"Yes. When I can. Get those pay phone numbers ready."

"I will."

One last kiss and she was off into the night.

Ooop oop!

Now Frank went fully optimodal. For a while he even experienced the "walking on air" phenomenon, surely a physiological effect caused by an incomplete integration of happiness into sense data. Life in his tree, in the winter forest, at the gym, at work, in restaurants, out in the hour of pale winter evening sun, running or throwing frisbees or stalking animals—every day parcellated but full, every night a forest adventure, always alive, always generous. Ooop!

How big the world became in a wind. Everything expanded, inside and out. Hike in the dreamlike black forest, huge and blustery. Evening sky over the black branches, violet in the east shading to aquamarine in the west, all luminous, a Maxfield Parrish sky, only now it was obvious that Parrish had never exaggerated at all, but only done his best to suggest a reality that was so much more vivid and intense than any art.

One evening he tromped into 21 not long after sunset and found only Zeno and Redbeard and Fedpage and a couple more. "Where is everybody?"

"Over on Connecticut."

"Seeking the heat, man."

"What about Chessman, where's he?"

Shrugs all around.

"Haven't seen him for a while."

"I bet he found a place to stay for the winter. He's smart."

"Come and go, Doctor Checkmate, come and go."

Frank couldn't read their attitude. He wondered if the chess hustlers at Dupont Circle might know where Chessman was, and resolved to visit and see. There was nothing more to be learned here.

Snow began to fall, small flakes ticking down. After the first heavy snowfall there had been little more; and it was usually this frozen frost, swirling on the wind. The bros noted it gloomily, wandered off. They had actually built the little shelters Zeno had proposed, Frank saw, in the dip they now called Sleepy Hollow, just to the west of the site. Some of them were already tucked into their low shelters, staring out red-eyed. Cardboard, trash bags, branches, sheets of plywood, drop cloths, two-by-fours, cinder blocks: under that, dirty nylon or even cotton sleeping bags, toeing into snowbanks. A sleeping bag needed a groundpad under it for it to work right.

Frank found himself annoyed. Living like rats when they didn't have to; it was incompetent. Even if it was all they could find to build with.

It was hard to judge what was happening with them. One time Frank was running with the frisbee guys, completely absorbed in it, when they came into 21 and there was a quartet of young black men, wearing multiple cotton hooded sweatshirts, hands deep in their pockets. Spencer pulled up sharply and turned to the tables. "Hey how's it going?"

"Oh good!" Zeno said sarcastically. "Real good! These brothers are wondering if we have any *drugs* to sell."

"*You* guys?" Spencer laughed, and Robert and Robin echoed him as they flanked him on both sides, their golf disks held before them like Oddjob's hat. Frank was just comprehending the situation when the young men joined the laughter, smiles flashing in the gloom, and headed down Ross without a farewell.

"Catch you guys," Spencer said as he moved on to the next tee.

"Yeah, catch you," Zeno growled. "Fucking drop by any time."

At work, a group from NOAA came over to discuss the Gulf Stream stall. They had done the calculations and modeling needed to say something quantitative about the idea of restarting the downwelling, and Diane had asked General Wracke and others to attend. The NOAA P.I. described the situation: before the Arctic icebergs had arrived, the surface in the downwelling regions had had a salinity of 31.0 psu (practical salinity units, roughly equivalent to grams of salt per kilogram of water). Now the surface salinity was 29.8. Following the P.I.'s red laser dot down the isopycnals on her graph, they could see just how much the salinity would have to be bumped to make the cap dense enough to sink.

The biggest downwelling region had been north of Iceland and east of Greenland, swirling down in giant whirlpools that were thirty or fifty kilometers wide, but only three or four centimeters deep. These whirlpools, visible only by satellite laser altimetry, were psychedelically obvious in their false color graphing. They were small areas compared to the total surface of the ocean, so the idea of restarting them did not seem immediately impossible; but as the P.I. pointed out, one could not restart the circulation merely by increasing density at the downwelling sites alone, separated from the Gulf Stream by hundreds of kilometers of stalled water. It would be necessary to draw the momentum of the Gulf Stream back up to the old sites first, by causing surface water to sink just north of the current new downwelling sites, then continue the process, in Pied Piper fashion, until they had drawn the Gulf Stream up behind them and could dump as much as needed in the old downwelling locations. This was the only method the NOAA team could think of, but it added greatly to the amount of water they had to sink—to "isopycnalate," as Edgardo called it.

Extensive modeling had led them to believe that in order to create the masses of sinking water necessary, they would have to alter its salinity about two psu, from 29.8 to 31.6—meaning the addition of about two grams of salt for every kilogram of water they had to alter. The necessary volume of water was less certain, depending as it did on assumptions plugged into the model, but the minimum they had gotten good results for was approximately five thousand cubic kilometers of water. So it would take them about ten billion kilograms of salt.

Five hundred million tons of salt.

Someone whistled.

"Just how much salt is that?" Frank asked.

Edgardo and General Wracke laughed. Diane smiled but said to the NOAA people, "Can you give us a sense of what that means in terms of volumes, availability, shipping capacities and so on?"

"Yes. We would have done it already, but we just finished the analysis this morning. But I have to say, before that, that we're still very uncertain about the wisdom of trying this at all. I mean we don't really know what it will do, and remembering the law of unintended consequences—"

"Please!" Edgardo said, raising a hand. "No more of this law of unintended consequences! There is no such law. You hear this said and then you look for the equation that expresses this law, or even the principle, and there is no equation or principle. There is just the observation that actions have unintended consequences, though sometimes they matter and other times not. It's like saying, 'Shit happens.' "

"Okay, maybe you're right. Although shit does happen."

"Just look into the practicalities of moving that quantity of salt," Diane said with her little smile. "It may be completely impossible, in which case no consequences will follow."

At night the trees of the forest were bare black statues, fractal and huge. There were points from which one could see down great lengths of the gorge. The snow was still rather thin on the ground, drifted into banks against the flood windrows and then iced over, leaving uneven layers of slimy black leaves underfoot. The resulting black-and-white patchwork made the topography of the park almost impossible to read, a kind of Rorschach space in which the tossing branches of the canopy were the best way to stay oriented to the ravine's forms. The wind hooted and roared like the air choir of the world, gibbons had nothing on the winter forest as far as vocalizations were concerned. Ooooooooooooooo!

Bouncing patterns, shifting whether he walked or didn't, and yet somehow the brain made the picture cohere. But sometimes it didn't, and briefly he would be in an abstract world, patterns shifting—ah, that was Military Road bridge—and then a sudden understanding of what he was seeing would snap back into place with its customary "YOU ARE HERE" function. It was remarkable just how much understanding one lost when the visual field went haywire—not just what one saw, but where one was, who one was; a glitch in which everything blanked for a moment, pure consciousness caught in a mystery—then bang, all the explanations falling back in at once, leaving only a faint memory of absence.

He was the paleolithic in the park. A recent article in *The Journal of Sociobiology* had reminded him of the ice man, who had died crossing a Tyrolean pass some five thousand years before. He had lain there frozen in a glacier until something, perhaps global warming, had caused him to emerge, in 1991. All his personal possessions had been preserved along with his body, giving archeologists a unique look at the technology of his time. Reading the inventory of his possessions, Frank had noticed how many correlations there were between his gear and the ice man's. Probably both kits were pretty much what people had carried in the cold for the last fifty thousand years.

The Alpine man had worn a coat made of sewn furs, its stitching very fine, the coat similar in design and effect to the down jacket Frank was wearing at that very moment. The Alpine man had worn a fanny pack like Frank's, filled with several small tools that added up to the equivalent of Frank's Swiss Army knife. The alpine man's unfinished copper-headed axe (a marvel) had no ready equivalent in Frank's equipment, though it resembled the ice axe he kept in his treehouse; and he had taken to carrying his Acheulian hand axe around with him, in his fanny pack or even sometimes in his hand, just for the pleasure of the heft of it. It might even do a little good, in terms of personal defense; there were some little gangs in the park that did not look good to Frank. Not to mention the jaguar.

The Alpine man had worn a backpack made of wood and leather, quite similar in design to Frank's nylon backpack; inside it were stuff sacks. A birch bark container had been designed to carry live embers, and there was also a little stone bowl in which to place flammable stuff to light by striking flints; all that was the equivalent of Frank's cigarette lighter. Frank also had a little Primus stove up in the treehouse, a primitive-looking steel thing that roared like a blowtorch and was almost as hot. How the Alpine man would have loved that! In effect Frank had a little bottle of fire he could light anywhere. The technological sublime indeed, when he had a little pot of coffee or soup on the boil.

The Alpine man had also carried a flat circular piece of white marble, holed through its middle. A loop of leather ran through the hole, and a number of smaller leather loops were tied around through the main loop: this "tassel," as the archeologists called it, looked to Frank like a sling of carabiners. It was the only possibly nonutilitarian piece on the man (though his skin had also displayed tattoos). The birch fungus in his fanny pack had perhaps been medicinal, like the aspirin in Frank's bathroom bag.

All down the list, familiar stuff. People still carried around stuff to do the same things. Frank's kit had a provenance of thousands of years. It was a beautiful thought, and made him happy. He was Alpine man!

And so when he hiked into site 21 and saw again the bros' ramshackle shelters, he said, "Come on guys. Let's try to at least get up to paleolithic code. I brought along a roll of ripstop nylon this time, check it out. First class army-navy surplus, it'll match your camo flak jacket color scheme."

"Yarrrr, fuck you!"

"Come on, I'm going to cut you all a tarp off the roll. Everyone in the park is under this stuff but you."

"How you know?"

"You Santa Claus?"

"He knows because he give it to them all is how."

"Yeah that's right. Just call me Johnny Appletent."

"Har har har! Perfesser Appletent!"

They cackled as he measured out rectangles of about ten by six, then cut them off with the scissors on his Swiss Army knife. He showed them how the nylon could be secured, in many cases right on top of their already existing shelters. "Dry means warm, bros, you know that." A well-set tarp was a complete home in itself, he told them. Sides down to the ground, suspend the middle on a line, high enough to sit up in at one end, don't worry about how low the rest of it was. The lower the warmer, except don't let it come down far enough to touch sleeping bags. Get plastic to put under the sleeping bags for God's sake. Groundpads too.

It was the kind of camp work that Frank enjoyed. He wandered around among them as they fiddled, evaluating their obstacles and the solutions they were concocting. They were inept, but winter camping was a learned skill. Maybe they had only stayed out in the summertime before, and in previous winters sought conventional shelter. Winter backpacking was a very technical matter—ultimately simple, but it took attention to detail, it was a meticulous thing if you wanted to stay comfortable. A technique. The

Alpine man would have been superb at it. And now they were all being carried up to the heights.

The bros lay there watching him or not, Andy calling "Watch out, will ya." Some lit cigarettes and blew plumes of smoke onto the new insides of their tarps, frosting them grayly.

"The first wind'll knock that down on you," Frank warned Andy. "Tie that far corner out to that tree."

"Yeah yeah."

"Here, I am going to save your lazy ass."

They all laughed at this.

"He's saving us now! Look out!"

"Preacher Pastor Perfesser."

"Yeah right!" Frank objected. "The Church of Dry Toes."

They liked this.

By the time all the tarps were set Frank's hands were white and red. He swung them around for a while, feeling them throb back to life, looking around at the scene. You could see another fire down toward the zoo.

He bid them good night. They mumbled things. Zeno said, "Nyah, get your ass outta here, quit bothering us with your crap, goddamn Peace Corps bleeding heart charity pervert think you know what you're doing out here fuck that shit, get outta here."

"You're welcome."

Another night, through the snowy forest under a full moon: a solid snowfall had come at last, and now a surreal whiteness blanketed everything, every bump and declivity defined by the snow's varied luminosity. Low noctilucent cloud, every black stroke of branch and twig distinct against it, snow whirling down, the flakes catching moonlight and sparking like bits of mica. The world all alive. "The great day in the man is the birth of perception" (Emersonfortheday, February 22).

Frank had taken his snowshoes and ski poles out of his storage unit, and now he cruised over drifts. No need to turn on his headlamp tonight; it was light you could read by.

He came on a black thing half-buried in snow. He stopped, fearing some child had died of exposure, thinking of Chessman. But when he knelt by the form he saw that it was a wombat. "Ah shit."

Two, actually. Mother and infant, dead. Frank called in the GPS location on his FOG phone, cursing sadly as he did. "God damn it. You poor guys."

It looked like Nancy was right. They needed to recover the warm-weather ferals. "Yeah," she confirmed when he called her next day, "a lot of them aren't making it. The shelters are helping, but we really have to bring them back in."

"I hope we can," Frank said.

At work Frank continued to hack away at his list of Things to Do, which nevertheless grew. Settling in after a session at Optimodal, he dealt with:

1. arranging small business exploratory grants for photovoltaic.
2. starting up the Max Planck equivalent in San Diego. This was proceeding nicely, and the Scripps Institution of Oceanography had pitched in to help. The Torrey Pines Generique facility was being reopened and a lot of hires made, by people aware of Yann, Marta and Eleanor.
3. consulting with the people dealing with the SSEEP melodrama, already a mess. The platform had been released, and many had weighed in on this idea of a "scientific political platform"— whether it was possible, whether it was a good idea, whether it was dangerous. Attacks in Congress and the press were common. Phil Chase had immediately embraced the platform as a scientifi-cally backed version of what he had been advocating all along.
4. investigating amorphous or glassy metals, in particular steel, made by scrambling the atomic structures of the metal with yt-trium, chromium, and boron, making the resulting "glassy steel" stronger, nonmagnetic, and less corrosive. All kinds of oceanproofed machinery could be made with this material.
5. talking to General Wracke about salt mining and transport ca-

pabilities. Wracke was upbeat; the quantities being discussed were not off the charts compared to other products. As he said, "There's a lot of salt in this world."

"Does it look like it would be expensive?" Frank asked.

"Depends what you call expensive. Billions for sure."

"Can you be more specific?"

"I'll get back to you on that."

"Thanks. Oh—different subject—does the Pentagon have an intelligence service of its own?"

Wracke laughed. "Is that a trick question?"

"No, how could it be?"

"You'll have to ask the CIA about that. But yes, sure. After the other intelligence agencies in this town let us down so bad, we almost had to have one, to get good data. We're the ones get killed by bad intel, you know. Why, is there some secret climate group you're having trouble with?"

"No no. I was just curious. Thanks. See you at the next meeting."

"I look forward to it. You guys are doing great."

In that same couple of weeks, along with everything else, Frank made an effort to locate Chessman. He centered the search on Dupont Circle, the city's outdoor chess epicenter. To ask there about a young black kid was to inquire about half the chess-playing population at least, and his motives also appeared to be questioned. So after a while, rather than ask, Frank simply watched, played and lost and walked, checking out the games, noting also the new little semi-winterized shelters popping up all over town.

Cleveland Park sported many of these camps, especially near buildings damaged by the flood. It seemed that the homeless population of Northwest must be in the thousands. Between Klingle Valley Park and Melvin Hazen Park, both small tributary ravines dropping into Rock Creek, there were many abandoned houses. If they had been burned out, squatters were likely to be occupying them.

This made for a very quiet neighborhood. No one wanted to attract the attention of the police. Lit windows Frank gave a wide berth, and so apparently did everyone else. Good avoidance protocols make good neighbors. Chessman might be tucked away in one of these hulks, but if so Frank wasn't going to find out by knocking on doors or looking in windows.

And he doubted the youth would be in any of them anyway. Chessman had had a healthy propensity for staying outdoors.

That being the case, where was he?

Then Frank ran into Cutter out on Connecticut, and two parcels in his mind connected. "Cutter, do you know what happened to Chessman?"

"No, I ain't seen him lately. Don't know what happened to him."

"Do you know anyone who might?"

"I don't know. Maybe Byron, he used to play chess with him. I'll ask."

"Thanks, I'd appreciate that. Do you know what his real name was?"

"No. Only thing I ever heard him called was Chessman."

In the park the forest now seemed wilderness, with most human signs snowed over. Distant firelight the only touch of humanity. Mirkwood or primeval forest, every tree Yggdrasil, Frank the Green Man. Encountering a structure was like stumbling on ruins. The Carter Barron Amphitheatre and the huge bridges south of the zoo looked like the work of Incans or Atlanteans.

Campfires in the park, unlike squatter houses, could be investigated. It was possible to approach them surreptitiously, to put them under surveillance, to see if any of the firelit faces were known to him. Stalking, pure and simple. Peering around trees, over flood snags, now flanked by snowdrifts. Rain had hardened the snow. Stepping through the crust made a distinct crunchy noise. One had to float on it, with one's weight on the back foot until the next step was pressed home. Time for one's tiger mind to come to the fore. Someone had reported seeing the jaguar again.

Once he came on a single old man shivering before a smoky little blaze, obviously sick, and he roused him and asked if the man could get himself to one of the homeless shelters on Connecticut, or the ER at the UDC hospital; stubbornly the old man turned away, not quite coherent, maybe drunk, but maybe sick. All Frank could do was call 911 and give GPS coordinates, and wait for an EMS team to hike in and take over. Even when healthy, living out here was a tenuous thing, but for a sick person it was miserable. The paramedics talked the man onto a stretcher and carried him out. The next night Frank passed by again, to see if he had returned and if he was okay. No one there, fire out.

And never a sign of Chessman. The longer it went on the less likely it seemed Frank would ever find him. The youth must have moved, either to a different part of the city or out of the area entirely.

One evening before climbing into his treehouse Frank hiked under the moon, in a stiff north wind that tossed the branches in a glorious skitter-skatter against the luminous gray sky. When he headed north the wind shoved his breath right into his lungs. How big the world became with moonlight on the snow.

Then he came over a rise and saw around site 21's fire shouting figures, fighting furiously. "Hey!" he cried, rushing down in a wild glissade. Something hit the fire and sparks exploded out of it; Frank saw someone swing something to hit one of the prone bros, and as Frank plunged through the last trees toward him, shouting and pulling the Acheulian hand axe from his fanny pack, the man looked up and Frank saw that it was the crazy guy who had chased him off Highway 66 in his pickup truck. Frank screamed and leaped forward feetfirst, kicking the man right above the knees. The man went down like a bowling pin and Frank jumped up over him with the hand axe ready to strike, then the man rolled to the side and Frank saw that he was not in fact the driver of the pickup, he had only looked like him. Then Frank was down.

He was on his knees and elbows and his hands were at his face, trying uselessly to catch the rush of blood from his nose. He didn't know what had hit him. Blood was shooting out both nostrils and he was also swallowing it as fast as he could so that he wouldn't choke on it. He felt nothing, but blood shot out in a black flood, he saw it pool on the ground under him. He heard voices but they sounded distant. Don't, he thought. Don't die.

Charlie was startled out of a dream in which he was protesting, "I can't do it," and so his first words into the phone were "I can't, what, what?"

"Charlie, this is Diane Chang."

Charlie saw the clock's red *4:30 a.m.* and said sharply, "What is it?"

"I just got a call from the UDC hospital. They told me that Frank Vanderwal was admitted to their ER about three hours ago with a head injury."

"Oh no, how bad is it? Is he all right?"

"Yes, but he has a concussion, and a broken nose, and he lost a lot of blood. Anyway, I'm going there now, I was just leaving for work anyway, but it'll take me a while to get to the hospital, and I realized it's near you and Anna and that you know Frank. You guys were the second number on his who-to-call form. So I thought you might be able to go over."

"Sure," Charlie said. "I can be there in fifteen minutes."

Anna was sitting up beside him, saying "What is it?"

"Frank Vanderwal's been injured. He'll be all right, but he's over at the UDC hospital. Diane thought—well here." He handed her the phone and got up to dress. When he was ready to go Anna was still on the phone with Diane. Charlie kissed the top of her head and left.

He drove fast through the nearly empty streets. In the ER reception the fluorescent lights hummed. The nurses were matter-of-fact, pacing themselves for the long haul. They treated Charlie casually; people came in like this all the time. Finally one of them led him down the concrete-floored hallway to a curtained-off enclosure on the right.

There lay Frank, pale, wired up, and IV'd. Two black eyes flanked a swollen red nose, and a bandage under his nose covered much of his upper lip.

"Hey Frank."

"Hey Charlie." He did not look surprised to see him. Behind his black eyes he did not look like anything could surprise him.

"They said your nose is broken and you've been concussed."

"Yes. I think that's right."

"What happened?"

"I tried to break up a fight."

"Jesus. Where was this?"

"Rock Creek Park."

"Wow. You were out there tracking the zoo animals?"

Frank frowned.

"Never mind, it doesn't matter."

"No, I was out there. Yes. I've been out there a lot lately. They've been trying to recapture the ferals, and they don't all have radio collars."

"So you were out there at night?"

"Yeah. A lot of animals are out then."

"I see. Wow. So what hit you?"

"I don't know."

"What's the last thing you remember?"

"Well, let's see . . . I saw a fight. I ran down to help. Some people I know were being attacked. Then something hit me."

"Never mind," Charlie said. Thinking seemed to pain Frank. "Don't worry about it. Obviously you got hit by something."

"Yes."

"Does your face hurt bad? It looks terrible."

"I can't feel it at all. Can't breathe through my nose. It bled for a long time. It's still bleeding a little inside."

"Wow." Charlie pulled a chair over and sat by the bed.

After a while a different nurse came by and checked the monitor. "How are you feeling?" she asked.

"Strange. Am I concussed?"

"Yes, like I told you."

"Anything else?"

"Broken nose. Maxillary bone, cracked in place. Some cuts and bruises. The doctor sewed you up a little inside your upper lip. When the anesthetic wears off it will probably hurt. Sorry. We put some blood back in you, and your blood pressure is looking, let's see . . . good. You took quite a whack there."

"Yes."

The nurse left. The two men sat under the fluorescent lights, among the blinking machinery. Charlie watched Frank's heartbeat on the monitor.

"So you've been going into Rock Creek Park at night?"

"Sometimes."

"Isn't that dangerous?"

Frank shrugged. "I didn't think so. A lot of the animals are nocturnal."

"Yes." Charlie didn't know what to say. He realized he didn't know Frank all that well; had met him only in party contexts really, except for the trip to Khembalung, but that had been a busy time. Anna liked Frank, always with an undercurrent of exasperation, but he amused her. And Nick really enjoyed doing the zoo thing with him.

Now he fell asleep. Charlie watched him breathe through his mouth. Strange to see such a self-contained person in such a vulnerable state.

Diane arrived, then Anna called as she was getting Nick up for school, wanting to know how Frank was. Frank woke up and Charlie handed his phone to him; now he looked slightly embarrassed. "Conked in the nose," he said to Anna as Diane pulled Charlie into the hall. "I don't remember much."

"Listen," Diane said, "Frank only had a driver's license and NSF card on him, and both had his address from last year. Do you know where he's living?"

Charlie shook his head.

Diane said, "He told me he had found a place over near you."

"Yes—he's been joining us for dinner sometimes, and I think he said he had a place over near Cleveland Park, I'm not sure." Frank seldom talked about himself, now that Charlie thought of it. He looked at Diane, shrugged; she frowned and led him back to Frank's bedside.

Frank handed Charlie his cell phone. Anna wanted to come over and give Frank a ride home when he was released.

Frank nodded when he heard this. "I'll have to get my van. She can drive me to it." He frowned.

"That's fine, we'll take care of that. But I wonder if you should drive."

"Oh sure. It's just a broken nose. I have to get my van."

Charlie and Diane exchanged a glance.

Charlie said hesitantly, "You know, we live near here, maybe we could help you get your van to our place, and you could rest up there until you felt well enough to drive home."

"It doesn't actually hurt." Frank thought it over. "Okay," he said at last. "Thanks. That would be good."

Frank was discharged that afternoon, by which time Anna had visited and gone on to work, and Charlie had returned with Joe. Before going to his car, Charlie checked at the desk. "I'm driving him. Did he give you an address?"

"4201 Wilson." The NSF building.

Charlie thought about that as he drove Frank back to their house. He said, "I can take you home instead if you want."

"No that's okay. I need to be taken back to my van so I can pick it up."

"There's no rush with that. You need some food in you."

"I guess," Frank said. "But I need to get my van before it gets towed. Tonight is the night that street has to be cleared for the street cleaners."

"I see." How come you know that, Charlie didn't say. "Okay, we'll get it first thing after dinner. It shouldn't be that late."

The other Quiblers welcomed Frank with great fanfare, marveling at his bulbous red nose and his colorful black eyes. Anna got takeout from the Iranian deli across the street, and after a while Drepung dropped by, having heard the news. He too marveled as he finished off the takeout. Frank had little appetite.

In the kitchen Charlie told Drepung about Frank's mystery housing. "Even Diane Chang doesn't know where he lives. I'm wondering now if he's living out of his van. He bought it right after he left his apartment in Virginia. And he knows which night of the week the street he's parked on gets cleaned."

"Hmmm," Drepung said. "No, I don't know what his situation is."

Out at the dining room table, Drepung said to Frank, "I know you are from San Diego, and I don't suppose you have family here. I was wondering if, while you are convalescing, you would move in with us at the embassy house."

"But you have all your refugees."

"Yes, but we have an extra bed in Rudra Cakrin's room. No one wants to take it. And he is studying English, as you know, so . . ."

"I thought he had a tutor."

"Yes, but now he needs a new one."

Frank cracked a little smile. "Fired another one, eh?"

"Yes, he is not a good student. But with you it will be different. And you once told me you had an interest in learning Tibetan, remember? So you could teach each other. It would help us. We can use help right now."

"Thanks. That's very kind of you." Frank looked down, nodded without expression. "I'll think about it." It seemed to Charlie that the concussion was still having its way with him. And no doubt a monster headache.

Drepung went to the kitchen to boil water for tea. "Not Tibetan tea, I promise! But a good herb tea for headache."

"Okay," Frank said. "Thanks. Although I don't really have a headache. I'm not sure why. I can't feel my nose at all."

CHAPTER 17

THE COLD SNAP

The weather got stranger and stranger. The new year's January saw:

High temperature in London for the week of Jan 10, −26 F. In Lisbon, a 60-degree drop in 7 minutes. Snow in San Diego, snow in Miami. New York Harbor froze over, trucks drove across. Reunion Island: 235 inches of rain in 10 days. In Montana, temperature dropped 100 degrees F in 24 hours, to −56 F. In South Dakota the temperature rose 60 degrees in 2 minutes. In Buffalo, New York, 30-foot snowdrifts blew in from frozen Lake Erie on 60 mph winds. Reindeer walked over fences from the zoo and went feral. On the Olympic Peninsula, a single downdraft knocked over 8 million board feet of trees.

In a North Sea storm similar to that of 1953, Holland suffered 400 dead and flooding up to 27 miles inland.

February was worse. That February saw:

A storm in New England with 112 mph winds. Waterloo, Iowa, had 16 days straight below 0 F. 7 inches snow in San Francisco. Great Lakes totally frozen over. Snow in L.A. stopped traffic. Ice in New Orleans blocked the Mississippi River. −66 F in Montana. 100 mph winds in Sydney Australia. Feb. 4, 180 tornadoes reported, 1,200 killed; named the "Enigma Outbreak."

A low-pressure system manifested the rapid intensification called "bombogenesis" and brought 77 inches of snow in 2 hours to central Maine. Reunion Island, 73 inches rain in a day. Winds 113 mph in Utah. Rhine floods caused $60 billion damage. An Alberta hailstorm killed 36,000 ducks.

A thunderstorm complex called a derecho struck Paris with hurricane force, causing $20 billion in damage. 150 mph wind in Oslo. Two Bengal tigers escaped a Madison, Wisconsin, zoo in a tornado. Thousands of fish fell in a storm on Yarmouth, England.

165 mph winds make a category 5 storm; there had been three in U.S. history; two struck Europe that February, in Scotland and Portugal.

Soon it would be Washington, D.C.'s turn.

During 1815's "year without summer," after the Tambora volcano exploded, average temperatures worldwide dropped 37 degrees F.

As soon as he felt he could make an adequate display of normality to the Quiblers, Frank thanked them for their hospitality and excused himself. They regarded him oddly, he thought, and he had to admit it was a bit of a stretch to claim nothing was wrong. Actually he felt quite bizarre.

But he didn't want to tell them that. And he didn't want to tell them that he had no place to go. So he stood in their doorway insisting he was fine. He could see Anna and Charlie glance at each other. But it was his business in the end. So Charlie drove him down to his van, and after a final burst of cheerful assurances he was left alone.

He found himself driving around Washington, D.C. It was like the night he lost his apartment; he drove aimlessly, and without deciding to, found himself on the streets west of Rock Creek Park.

His nose and the area behind it were numb as if shot with Novocain. He had to breathe through his mouth. The world tasted like blood. Things out the windshield were slightly distant, as if at the wrong end of a telescope.

He wasn't sure what to do. He could think of any number of options, but none of them seemed quite right. Go back to his tree? Drive to the NSF basement? Try to find a room? Return to the ER?

He had no feeling for which course to pursue. Like the area behind his nose, his sense of inclination was numb.

It occurred to him that he might have been hit hard enough to damage his thinking. He clutched the steering wheel as his pulse rose.

His heartbeat slowed to something more normal. Do anything. Just do anything. Do the easiest thing. Do the most adaptive thing.

He sat there until he got too cold. To stay warm on a night like this one he would have to either drive with the heater on, or walk vigorously, or lie in the sleeping bag in the back of the van, or climb his tree and get in the even heavier sleeping bag there. Well, he could do any of those, so . . .

More time had passed. Too cold to stay still any longer, he threw open the driver's door and climbed out.

Instant shock of frigid air. Reach back in and put on windpants, gaiters, ski gloves. Snowshoes and ski poles under one arm. Off into the night.

No one out on nights like this. At the park's edge he stepped into his snowshoes, tightened the straps. Crunch crunch over hard snow, then sinking in; he would have posted through if he had been in boots. So the snowshoes had been a good idea. Note to self: when in doubt, just do it. Try something and observe the results. Good-enough decision algorithm. Most often the first choice, made by the unconscious mind, would be best anyway. Tests had shown this.

Out and about, under the stars. The north wind was more obvious in the Rock Creek watershed, gusting down the big funnel and cracking frozen branches here and there. Snaps like gunshots amid the usual roar of the gale.

No one was out. No fires; no black figures in the distance against the snow; no animals. He poled over the snow as if he were the last man on Earth. Or left behind on some forest planet that everyone else had abandoned. Like a dream. When the dream becomes so strange that you know you're going to wake up, but then you discover that you're already awake—what then?

Then you know you're alive. You find yourself on the cold hill's side.

Back at site 21. He had come right back to the spot where he had gotten hurt, maybe it wasn't wise. He circled it from above for a while, checking to be certain it was empty. No one out. What if you had a world and then one night you came home to it and it was gone? This sometimes happened to people.

He clattered down to the picnic tables, sat on one, unbuckled his snowshoes. He looked around. Sleepy Hollow was empty, a very unappetizing snowy trench with black mud sidewalls, the sorry little shelters all knocked apart. Tables bare. Fire out. Ashes and charcoal all dusted with snow.

Strange to see.

So . . . He had run in from the direction of the zoo. Knocked one of the assailants down; funny how that skinny face and mustache had fooled him, taken him back to an earlier trauma, but only for a second. Facial recognition was another quick and powerful unconscious ability.

So. He had to have been about . . . about *here* when he was struck.

He stood on the spot. It did not seem to be true that the memory held nothing after such impacts; he actually recalled a lot of it. The moment of recognition; then something swinging in from his left. A quick blur. Baseball bat, branch, maybe a two-by-four . . . Ouch. He touched his numb nose in sympathy.

After that moment there were at least a few seconds he did not recall at all. He didn't recall the impact (although he did, in his nose, kind of; the feel of it) nor did he really recall falling to the ground. He must have gotten his hands out to catch himself; his left wrist was sore, and the first thing he remembered for sure was kneeling, and seeing his nose shoot out blood like a fountain. Trying to catch black blood in his hands; not stanch it, just catch it; finding it hard to believe just how much blood was pouring through his hands onto the ground, also down his throat at the back of his mouth. Swallowing convulsively. Then touching his nose, fearing to know what shape his fingers might find; finding it had no feeling, but that it seemed to be occupying much the same space as before. Peculiar to feel his own nose as if someone else's. It was the same now. His fingers told him the flesh was being manipulated, but his face didn't confirm it.

Very strange. And here he was. Back on the spot, some days later . . . let's see; must be . . . two days.

He crouched, looked around. He got on his hands and knees, in the same position he had been in while watching the blood fountain out of him. It was still seeping a little bit. Taste of blood. For a second during the prodigious flow he had wondered if he would bleed to death. And indeed there was a large black stain on the ground.

Now he twisted slowly this way and that, as if to prick more memories to life. He took off a glove and got his little keychain flashlight out of his pocket. He aimed the beam of light; frail as it was, it made the night seem darker.

There. Off to his right, up the slope of snow, half embedded. He leaped over with a shout, snatched it up and shook it at the wind. His hand axe.

He stared at it there in his hand. A perfect fit and heft. Superficially it looked like the other gray quartzite cobbles that littered Rock Creek. It was possible no one would ever have known it was different. But when he clutched it the shaping was obvious. Knapped biface. Frank whacked it into the nearest tree trunk, a solid blow. *Thunk thunk thunk thunk.* Quite a weapon.

He put it back in his jacket pocket, where it jostled nicely against his side.

He hiked through the trees under bouncing black branches, their flailing visible as patterns in the occlusion of stars. The north wind poured into him. Clatter and squeak of snowshoes. He slept in his van.

Inevitably, he had to explain what had happened to a lot of people. Diane of course had seen him at the hospital. "How are you feeling?" she asked when he went into Optimodal the next morning.

"I think a nerve must have been crushed."

She nodded. "I can see where the skin was split. Broken nose, right?"

"Yes. Maxillary bone. I just have to wait it out."

She touched his arm. "My boy broke his nose. The problem is the cartilage heals at new angles, so your breathing could be impaired."

"I hate having to breathe through my mouth when I have a cold."

"They can ream you out if you want. Anyway it could have been worse. If you had been hit a little higher, or lower—"

"Or to either side."

"True. You could have been killed. So, I guess your nose was like the air bag in a car."

"Ha ha. Don't make me laugh or I'll bleed on you." He held his upper lip between thumb and forefinger as he chuckled, squeezing it to keep from reopening the vertical cut. Everything had cracked vertically.

"Your poor lip. It sticks out almost as far as your nose. You look like the spies in 'Spy Vs. Spy.'"

"Don't make me laugh!"

She smiled up at him. "Okay I won't."

In his office about twenty minutes later, he smiled to think of her; he had to press his upper lip together.

His appreciation for Diane grew as he saw more of the responses he got to the injury. Oversolicitous, amused, uninterested, grossed out—they were bad in different ways. So Frank kept discussions limited. The frisbee guys were okay, and Frank told them a bit more about what had happened. There had been quite a few incidents like the fight Frank had joined, Spencer said: robbery, assaults, site stealing. For a while it had been really bad. Now, as the news of these attacks spread, and the cold got worse, the park had lost a lot of people, and the fights were fewer. But they hadn't ended, and the frisbee guys were now telling everybody to move around in packs.

Frank did not do this, but when he strapped on his snowshoes and went for walks, he kept away from the trails and did his best never to be seen.

Work was more problematic. When he sat down in his office, the list of Things to Do sometimes looked like a document in another language. He had to look up acronyms that suddenly seemed new and nonintuitive. OSTP? PITAC? Oh yeah. Office of Science and Technology Policy. Executive branch, a turned agency, an impediment to them. There were so many of those. PITAC: President's Information Technology Advisory Council. Another advisory body. Anna had a list of over two hundred of them, followed by a list of NGOs (nongovernmental organizations) just as long. All calling for some kind of action—from the sidelines. Unfunded. Anna had waved a whole sheaf of lists, not appalled or angry like Frank had been, more astonished than anything. "There's so much information out there. And so many organizations!"

"What does it all mean?" Frank had said. "Is it a form of paralysis, a way of pretending?"

Anna nodded. "We know, but we can't act."

The phrase, something Diane had once said, haunted him as he tried to get back to work. He knew what should come next for most of the items on his list of Things to Do, but there was no obvious mechanism for action in any case; nor any way to decide which to do first. Call the science and technology center coordinator's office, and see if the leasing of Torrey Pines Generique's empty facility was complete. Call Yann, and therefore Marta; put them in touch with the carbon drawdown team. Talk to Diane and General Wracke about the Gulf Stream. Check to see if photovoltaics clearly outperformed mirrors before dropping the mirror funding. Okay but which first?

He decided to talk to Diane. She could not only update him, but advise him on how to prioritize. Tell him what to do.

Again Diane was easier to talk to than anyone else. But after she told him what she had heard from Wracke and the Coast Guard, which seemed to indicate that assembling a transport fleet and loading it and sailing it to the Greenland Sea would be physically possible, she shifted to something else with a quick grimace. She appeared to be in the sights of NSF's new inspector general, appointed by the President. "I've got to meet with OMB and have it out," she said darkly. "Maybe call in the GAO for a cross-check to this guy."

"Is there any chance he'll . . ."

"No, I'm clean. If that's what you mean. They're looking at my son's affairs too. All the program directors; you too, I assume. We'll hope for the best. They can twist things that are real, and suddenly you're in trouble."

"Oh dear."

"It's all right. I can get some help. And the colder it gets this winter, the better for us. People are getting motivated. So, the colder the better!"

"Up to a point," Frank warned.

"True." She looked over his list. "Talk to your carbon drawdown people, we need to get them to commit to San Diego."

"Okay." That meant a call to Yann and Marta.

It was amazing how his pulse rose at the prospect. His lip throbbed with

each heartbeat. Every other item on his list seemed suddenly more pressing. Nevertheless, he took a deep breath and punched the number, wondering how much this would bump his stock in the futures market. If only
he could get some shares in himself, he could do things to raise their value,
and then sell! Maybe this was what was meant by the ownership society.
Maybe this was capitalism; you owned stock in yourself, and then by your
actions the price per share rose. Except you didn't own a majority share.
You might not own any shares, and have no way to buy in, as with the
spooks' virtual market. This could be common.

But maybe there were other markets.

Marta picked up, and Frank said in a rush, "Hi Marta it's Frank," then
asked her how it was going with the lichen project.

She said it was going pretty well. "Do you have a cold?"

"No."

They had engineered one of their tree lichens to export its sugar to the
tree faster than the original had. This lichen had always taken hormonal
control of its trees, and now it was moving sugar production from photosynthesis into the trees' lignin faster than before, which meant extra carbon added to the trees' trunks and roots. So far the alterations had been
simple, Marta said, and the trees would live for centuries, and had millions
of years' experience in not getting eaten by bacteria. The sequestration
would therefore last for the lifetime of the tree—not long on geological
scales, but Diane had declared early on that sequestration time was not to
be heavily weighted in judging the various proposals. Any port in a storm,
as she put it.

"That sounds great," Frank said. "Which trees do these lichen live on?"

The ones indigenous to the world-wrapping forest of the north sixties,
Marta said, meaning Europe, Siberia, Kamchatka, Alaska, and Canada.

"I see," Frank said.

"Yeah," Marta replied. "So what's up?"

"Well, I wanted to let you know that the new center is started in San
Diego. They're going to lease the old Torrey Pines Generique facility."

"You're kidding. Ha—you ought to hire Leo Mulhouse too. He'd get a
cell lab working better than anyone."

"That's a good idea, I'll pass that along. I liked him."

Frank described the input from UCSD, Scripps, Salk, the San Diego biotech council. Then he told her about NSF's new unsolicited grants program. "The possibility is definitely there for grants without external review."

He couldn't say any more; indeed, even saying this much might be dangerous: surveillance, recorded phone line, conflict of interest, hostile inspector general . . . shit. He had to leave the rest unsaid, but the implications seemed pretty damned obvious. And head-hunting was still legal, he assumed.

"Yeah it sounds good," Marta said sullenly, clearly in no mood to be grateful, or to hope. "So what?"

Frank had to let it go. He didn't say, A government will have to give permission to release a genetically modified organism designed to alter the atmosphere. He didn't say, I've arranged things so that you and Yann can go back to San Diego and work on your projects with more funding. She could figure it out, and no doubt already had, which was what was making her grumpy. She didn't like anything that might impede her being mad at him.

He stifled a sigh and got off as best he could.

One windless night he snowshoed out and saw that some fires were back. Sparks in the darkness. People out and about. Perhaps it was the stillness.

Under the luminous cloud the snow was brilliant white. The forest looked like the park of some enormous estate, everything groomed perfectly for a demanding squire. Far to the north a movement in the trees suggested to him the aurochs, or something else very big. The jaguar wouldn't be that big.

The bros were back home, he was happy to see, several of them sitting at the picnic tables, a few standing by a good fire in the ring.

"Hey Perfesser! Perfesser Nosebleed! How ya doing, man?"

They did not gather around him, but for a moment he was the center of attention. "I'm okay," he said.

"Good for you!"

"You look terrible!"

"Now's when you should pop him on the nose if you were ever gonna!"

Frank said, "Oh come on!"

Zeno laughed at this: "That scared ya huh? Don't want a pop eh?"

"I don't have to ask who's winning now!" Andy cried. "The other guy's winning!"

Frank said, "Don't make me laugh or I'll bleed on you."

This pleased them very much. They went on ragging him. He threw a branch on the fire and sat down next to the woman, who nodded her approval as she counted stitches.

"You did good," she told him.

"What do you mean?"

"The bozos here say you came blasting in like the cavalry."

"So who were those guys?" Frank asked the group.

"Who knows?"

"Fucking little motherfuckers."

"It's one of them Georgia Avenue gangs, man, those guys live off the streets like us, or worse."

"But the guys beating on you were white," Frank pointed out.

The fire crackled as they considered this.

"It's getting kind of dangerous out here," Frank said.

"It always was, Nosebleed."

"Just got to keep out of the way," the woman murmured as she began needling again, bringing the work up close to her eyes.

"How you doing?" Frank asked her as the others returned to their riffs.

"Day hundred and forty-two," she said with a decisive nod.

"Congratulations, that's great. Are you keeping warm?"

"Hell no." She guffawed. "How would I do that?"

"Did you get one of my tarps?"

"No, what's that?"

"I'll bring them out again. Just a tarp, like a tent fly, you know."

"Oh." She was dismissive; possibly she had a place to sleep. "How'd you do up at the hospital?"

"What? Oh fine, fine."

She nodded. "They've got a good ER."

"Did you—I mean, I don't remember going there."

"I'm not surprised."

Frank was. He could recall the blow, the moments immediately afterward. It hadn't occurred to him that the next thing he recalled after that was sitting in the ER waiting room, bleeding into paper towels waiting to be seen. "How'd I get up there?"

"We walked you up. You were okay, just bleeding a lot."

"I don't remember that part."

"Concussion, I'm sure. You got hammered."

"Did you see what hit me?"

"No, I was tucked down in a layby during the fight. Zeno and Andy found you afterward and we took you on up. You don't remember?"

"No."

"That's concussion for you."

One day at NSF he worked on the photovoltaics. Department of Energy was squawking that this was their bailiwick. Then his alarm went off and he went down and sat in his van.

He couldn't figure out what to do next.

He could taste blood at the back of his throat.

What did that mean? Was something not healing right, some ruptured blood vessel still leaking? Was there pressure on his brain?

Blood was leaking, that was for sure. But of course there must still be swelling inside; he still had a fat lip, after all, and why should swelling inside go away any faster? His black eyes were still visible, though they were turning purple and brown. Who knew? And what now?

He could go to the doctor's. He could visit the Quiblers, or the Khembalis. He could go to his treehouse. He could go back up to work. He could go out to dinner. He could sleep right there in the NSF basement, in the back of his van.

His sense of indecision hadn't been this strong for a while. He was pretty sure of that. Recalling the past week, it seemed to him that it had been getting better. Now worse. Again the stab of an elevated heart rate galvanized him. Maybe this was what they meant by the word *terror*.

He felt chilled. And in fact it was freezing in his van. Should he put on his down jacket, or—but stop. He grabbed the down jacket and wrestled his way into it, muttering, "Do the obvious things, Vanderwal, just do the first fucking thing that pops into your head. Worry about it later. Leap before you look."

Indecision. Before his accident he had been much more decisive. Wait, was that right? No. That could not be quite true. Maybe it was before he came to Washington that he had been sure of himself. But had he been? Had he ever been?

For a second he wasn't sure of anything. He thought back over the years, reviewing his actions, and wondered suddenly if he had ever been quite sane. He had made any number of bad decisions, especially in the past few years, but also long before that. All his life, but getting worse, as in a progressive disease. Why would he have risked Marta's part of their equity without asking her? Why would he ever have gotten involved with Marta in the first place? How could he have thought it was okay to sabotage Pierzinski's grant proposal? What had he been thinking, how had he justified it?

He hadn't. He hadn't thought about it; one might even say that he had managed to avoid thinking about it. It was a kind of mental skill, a negative capability. Agile in avoiding the basic questions. He had considered himself a rational, and, yes, a good person, and ignored all signs to the contrary. He had made up internal excuses, apparently. All at the unconscious level, in a world of internal divisions. A parcellated mind indeed. But brain functions *were* parcellated, and often unconscious. Then they got correlated at higher levels—that was consciousness, that was choice. Maybe that higher system could be damaged even when most of the parts were okay.

He twisted the rearview mirror around, stared at himself in it. For a while there in his youth he would stare into his eyes in a mirror and feel that he was meeting some Other. After returning from a climb where a falling rock had missed him by a foot—those kinds of moments.

But after Marta left he had stopped looking at himself in the mirror.

Now he saw a frightened person. Well, he had seen that before. It was not so very unfamiliar. He had never been so sure of himself when he was young. When had certainty arrived? Was it not a kind of hardening of the imagination, a dulling? Had he fallen asleep as the years passed?

Nothing now was clear. A worried stranger looked at him, the kind of face you saw glancing up at the clock in a train station. What had he been feeling these last several months before his accident? Hadn't he been better in that time? Had he not, from the moment Rudra Chakrin spoke to him, tried to change his life?

Surely he had. He had made decisions. He had wanted his treehouse. And he had wanted Caroline. These sprang to mind. He had his desires. They might not be entirely conventional, but they were strong.

Maybe it was a little convoluted to be relieved by the notion that having been a fuckup all his life, there did not have to be a theory of brain trauma to explain his current problems. To reassure himself that he was uninjured and merely congenitally deformed, so that was okay. Maybe it would be better to be injured.

He fell asleep at the wheel, thinking, I'll go back to the treehouse. Or out to San Diego. Or out to Great Falls. Or call the Khembalis . . .

The next morning he did not have to decide what to do, as the conference room next to Diane's office filled with European insurance executives, come to discuss the situation. They politely ignored Frank's face as Diane made the introductions. They were from the four biggest re-insurance companies, Munich Re, Swiss Re, GE Insurance Solutions, and General Re. Two CEOs were there, also Chief Risk Officers, Heads for Sustainability Management, and some men called "nat cat" guys, experts in natural catastrophes, and in the mathematical modeling used to develop scenarios and assign risk values.

"We four handle well over half of the total premium volume in re-insurance," the Swiss Re CEO told Diane and the rest. "Ours is a specialized function, and so we are going to need help. Already we are stretched to the limit, and this winter is going very badly in Europe, as you know. The destruction is really severe. Food shortages will come very quickly if winters become like this regularly. We are having to raise premiums immediately, just to make this first round of payouts. Re-insurance is just one part of a distributed load, but in a situation like this, essentially unprecedented, re-insurance is caught at the end of the stick. This may be the last payout that re-insurance can afford to pay. After that the system will be overwhelmed, and it will be bailout by governments."

So naturally they were interested in mitigation possibilities, and they had heard that the most advanced work in the United States was being done here at NSF. Diane agreed this was so, and told them about the North Atlantic project they were evaluating. It turned out they had been discussing the same idea among themselves; all over Europe people hoped it might be possible to "restart the Gulf Stream," because otherwise European food security was in danger.

They brought up the PowerPoint and ran through isopycnal tables, each curve on the graph suggestive of the slide of cold salty water to the seafloor.

The bad winter they were now experiencing might help restart the oceanic circulation, one nat cat expert pointed out. The Arctic sea ice might bulk to a thickness that wouldn't break up and drift south in the spring. In the fall surface temperatures would drop, and if they had a fleet loaded with salt, ready to go . . .

Everyone agreed they were onto something. Diane explained that the UN approved the plan; the remaining problems were likely to be financial and logistical, and perhaps political within the United States.

But maybe the United States was not a make-or-break participant, the Europeans suggested. Neither Diane nor Frank had entertained that notion before, but now they exchanged the blank glance that had replaced raised eyebrows between them to express discreet surprise. "We insure each other," one of them said. "We keep a kind of emergency fund available."

"This idea is not actually very expensive, compared to some."

Wow, Frank said to Diane with another blank look.

He was reading in his sleeping bag when his cell phone rang and he snatched it up.

"Frank, it's Caroline."

"Oh good."

"Are you all right?"

"I'm all right. I broke my nose, it's all stuffed up."

"Oh no, what happened?"

"I'll tell you about it when we meet."

"Okay good. Can you meet?"

"Of course. I have two black eyes."

"That's okay. Listen, can we meet at your place in Rock Creek Park?"

He swallowed. "Are you sure?"

"Yes."

"Do they—is it known where it is?"

"Yes. But I think I can help with that."

"Oh, well. Sure. I wanted to show it to you anyway."

"Tell me where to meet you."

He descended and crossed the park. His heart was beating hard, his lip throbbing. Everything seemed transparent at the edges, the branches tossing overhead. At the corner of Broad Branch and Grant he stood in a shadow, listening to the city and the roar of the wind, watching the luminous cloud pour overhead. He shivered convulsively, started to hop and dance in place.

She turned the corner and he stepped out into the light of a streetlamp. She saw him and quickly crossed the street, banged into him with a hug, started to kiss him but drew back. "Oh my God sorry! Your poor face."

"It doesn't feel that bad."

"Let's go to your place," she said.

"Sure." He turned and led her into the park. Under the trees he took her by the hand and followed the cross trail.

"Wow, you're really in here."

"Yes. So now your surveillance knows I'm here? How did that happen?"

She tugged at his hand. "You know your stuff is chipped, right?"

"No, what's that?"

"Microchips."

He stopped, and she stood beside him, squeezing his hand, holding his arm with her other hand. This was how the gibbons often touched.

"You know how everything now is sold with an electronic chip in it? They're really small, but they bounce a microwave back to a reader, with their ID and location. Businesses use them for inventory."

"How do they know what stuff is mine?"

"Because you bought most of it with credit cards. It's easy." She sounded exasperated; she wanted him up to speed on this stuff.

"So they always know where I am?"

"If you're within the range of a beam. Which you are most places."

"Shit."

She squeezed his arm. "But not out here."

Frank started walking again. For a second he did not remember where they were, and he had to stop and think before he could go on.

"No one will be able to track us up in my tree?"

"No. The usual chips don't have much range. Someone would have to be out here with a scanner nearby."

"Is my stock still rising?"

"Yes."

"But why?"

"Not sure. Whatever you're up to at NSF, I guess."

He looked over his shoulder. "Maybe it was meeting you that did it."

"Ha ha." He could tell by her hand that she wasn't amused by this.

"But we'll be okay now," he repeated.

"Yes. Well, in terms of being tracked tonight. But if someone came out here it might be different. I brought a reader wand with me, and I think we can clean you out. Maybe even move all the chips somewhere else, so it will look like you've moved. I don't know. I've never dechipped anyone before."

Frank thought about this as they crossed Ross and made the final drop to the edge of the gorge. Under his tree he took out his remote and called down Miss Piggy. He looked at the remote.

"I bought this with a credit card," he said.

"Radio Shack?"

"Jesus."

She laughed. "I just guessed that. But it's in your records, I'm sure."

"Shit."

Miss Piggy hummed down out of the night, looking like the ladder you climb to get into the flying saucer. Frank showed her where to grab, where to step. "You go first and I'll hold it steady."

Up she went, quick and lithe, a black mass in the stars overhead. When she was off he climbed swiftly, pulled through the entry hole.

"This is so cool!"

"Ah. Thanks." He sat down beside her. "I'm glad you like it."

"I love it. We used to have a treehouse in our backyard."

"Really! Where was this?"

"Outside Boston. My dad built it in an old tree, I don't know what kind, but it was wider than it was tall. We had several platforms, and a big staircase running down to the ground."

"Nice."

"This is smaller," she noted, and pulled closer to him. They sat side by side, cold hands entwined on top of her legs. The wind was tossing the tree gently north and south. "It's like a nest."

"Yes. We can get out of the wind if we need to," indicating the tent.

"I like it out here, if it doesn't get too cold."

"Let's use it as a wind-block, then."

They shifted into the lee of the tent, bumping against each other as the tree swayed.

"It's like being on a train."

"Or a ship."

"Yes, I suppose so."

They huddled together. Frank felt too strange to kiss; he was distracted, and it was hard to get used to the presence of someone else in his tree-house. "Um—do you think you could show me what you mean about the chips?"

She dug in her jacket pocket, took out a short metal wand, like the devices used by airport security. "Do you have some light?"

"Sure," he said, and clicked on the Coleman lamp. The lit circle on the plywood floor gleamed under them, ruining their night vision. The wind hooted and moaned.

She had him bring his belongings to her one by one. Sometimes she would get a beep as she passed the wand over them, and these she put to one side. Clock, lightweight sleeping bag, some of the clothes, even the little stove.

"Damn," he said.

"Yeah. That's the way it is. You're not as bad as some. A lot of your gear must be pretty old."

"Definitely."

"That's the way to do it. If you want to get out from under surveillance, you have to go back in time."

"You mean only use old stuff?"

"That's right. But really, you don't want to get entirely clear. That would trigger interest you don't want. But there are levels and levels. You could make it so that nothing on you tells where you are at any given moment. That might not even be noticed. The program would use the stuff you have, like your phone. It would assume you are where your phone is."

She had finished with his things. Now she leaned away from him, sweeping the foot of the platform methodically, right to left, coming back to them by a foot or so per sweep, then past them and to the wide part at his head, and around the corner. Then inside the tent. It was a small platform, but she was being thorough. "I don't think it's known that you're up in a tree. Before you told me, I thought you were just camped out in the woods, on the ground. I wonder if anyone's come out to ground-check you."

She waved the wand over him, and it beeped.

"Shit," she said.

She moved him. It wasn't where he was sitting. It was him.

"Maybe my clothes?"

She grinned. "We'll have to check. Get into the tent."

They brought the Coleman lamp inside with them, zipped down the tent door. Frank turned on his little battery heater, and they watched its element turn orange and begin radiating. The wind was still noisy, and they could feel the tree swaying, but quickly the warm air cocooned them.

She helped him unbutton his shirt, pull it off. The air was still cool. She ran the wand over him. It beeped when she held it over the middle of his back.

"Interesting. That's the same spot it was on me."

"You were chipped too?"

"That's right."

"By who?"

She didn't answer. "Here, turn your back to the lamp. Have you got an extra flashlight? Yes? Good. Here, let me." She inspected him. He could feel her fingers on his back, poking and then squeezing. "Aha. There it is."

"You sure it isn't just a blackhead?"

"Actually it looks more like a tick, you know how when you pull off a tick and part of it breaks in you?"

"Yuck. You're grooming me."

"That's right. Then it'll be your turn to groom me." She kissed the nape of his neck. "Hold steady now. I brought some tweezers."

"How did you get yours out?"

"I had a hell of a time. I had to use a barbeque tong. Like a back scratcher. I watched in the mirror and gouged it out."

"Back stabber."

"Yes. I backstabbed myself, but I'll never do it to you. Except now."

"Don't make me laugh or I'll bleed on you."

"You're going to bleed anyway." She poked gently at his back.

"How the hell did they get it in me?"

"Don't know. When you hurt your nose did you go to a hospital?"

"Yes. I was there for a few hours."

"Maybe that was when. Okay, here it is. Hold steady."

Then a quick cut. Frank held himself immobile. Now she was wiping off his back with her fingers, and kissing his spine at the base of his neck. She ripped open a little square Band-Aid and applied it to the spot.

"You thought of everything," he said.

"I hope so."

"What about you?"

"What do you mean?"

He picked up the wand.

"Oh that. I think I'm okay."

But he ran it over her anyway, and it beeped over her back.

Her mouth tightened to a hard line. "Shit."

"It wasn't there before?"

"No." She ripped off her jacket, took the wand, and ran it over it. No beep. She pulled her shirt off over her head; shocking lovely freckled white skin, spine deep in a furrow of muscles, ribs, shoulder blades, the curve of her right breast in its bra cup as she faced away from him. He ran the wand over her back, listened for the beep, watched for the green light. Like finding the stud in a wall; but nothing. He ran it over her crumpled shirt and it beeped. "Aha."

"Okay," she said, spreading the shirt out and inspecting it. "That's good. Here. It'll just be a few millimeters long." She ran the wand over the shirt, inspected the part under the beep. "In a seam. Here." She cut with keychain scissors, held up a tiny black cylinder, like a tiny bike pump valve stopper.

"Maybe there's another one in your bra," Frank suggested, and she laughed and leaned forward to kiss him; and then they were hugging hard, kissing lightly, she only brushing her lips against his, murmuring, "Oh, oh, it must hurt, I'm going to hurt you," and him replying, "It's all right, it's all right, kiss me."

They got off the rest of their clothes, then onto his groundpad, under his unzipped sleeping bags. Warm and cozy and yet still bobbing on the wind, and finally completing the dive they had launched in their stuck elevator, so many months before; they fell in, and were both seized up in it together. This was Frank's overriding impression, to the extent he had any thoughts at all; the togetherness of it. She kissed him gingerly, squeezed him hard, as sure with her caresses as she had been with her little surgery. Frank began to bleed again down the back of his throat; he tasted blood and was afraid she could too.

"I'm going to bleed on you I'm afraid."

"Here—let's turn over."

She straightened her left leg under his right, and they rolled to that side together as if they had done it a thousand times, then crabbed back onto the mattress pad. Frank swallowed blood, held her as she moved on him. Off they went again.

Afterward she lay beside him, her head on his chest. He could feel that she could hear his heartbeat. He ran his fingers through the tight curls of her hair. "Wow."

"I know."

"I needed that."

"Me too." She shifted her head to look at him. "How long has it been?"

Frank calculated. Marta, the last time . . . quite some time before she moved out. Some of those last times had been very strange: sex as hatred, sex as despair. Usually he managed not to know that a nearly eidetic memory of those encounters had been seared into him, but now he glimpsed them, quickly shoved them away again in his mind. "About a year and a half? Jesus."

"It's been four years for me."

"What?"

"That's right." She made a face. "I told you. We don't get along."

"But . . ."

"I know. That's just the way it is. He has other interests."

"Someone else, you mean?"

"I don't know."

"But that chip in your shirt?"

"That was him."

"So—he keeps tabs on you?"

"Yes."

"But why?"

She shrugged. "Just to do it. I don't know really. He started working with another agency, and it seems to have gotten worse since then. He's always been kind of obsessive. It's a control thing."

"So this new job is with another security agency?"

"Oh yes. I think it's linked to Homeland Security. Maybe a black-black inside it."

"So, these chips. Will he know you've been here?"

"No, he would have to be following me. The chips ping back a radio signal, but the range isn't very big. It's getting bigger though, and they've been installing transmitters that will give comprehensive coverage in the capital area. But it hasn't been activated yet. I think you still need to be nearby to get a bounce from a chip. Not that he wouldn't do that too. But he's out of town."

Frank didn't know what to say.

Long silence. They let it go. There they were, after all, just the two of them. Rocking back and forth. She laid her head on his chest. Back and forth, back and forth.

"This feels so good. It's like being in a cradle."

"Yes," Frank said. "You can tell which direction the wind is coming from. Tonight it's from the north, behind our head. When the tree swings toward our feet there's a little pause at the end, while the wind holds it there. Then it springs back with an extra little push, like it's been released. Whereas behind our heads we're going into the wind, so it slows sooner and makes the turnaround quicker, with no extra acceleration from the release. See, feel that?"

"No." She giggled.

"Feel it again. Downwind, upwind, downwind, upwind. They're different."

"Hmm. So they are. Like a little hitch."

"Yes."

"It's like clocks going tick tock. Supposedly there's hardly any difference between the two sounds."

"True." Frank felt a deep breath fill him, lifting her head. "I'm so glad you don't think I'm crazy."

"Me? I'm in no position to think anyone else is crazy. I am fully out there myself."

"Maybe we all are now."

"Maybe so."

They lay there, swaying back and forth. Please time stop now. The wind strummed the forest; they could hear individual gusts sweep across the watershed. Creaking branches, the occasional snap and crash, all within a huge airy whoosh, keening and hooting, filling everything with its continuo.

They talked quietly about treehouses. She told him all about the one in her backyard, her nights out, her tea parties, her cats, a neighborhood raccoon, a possum. "I thought it was a big rat. It scared me to death."

Frank told her about his love for the Swiss Family treehouse at Disneyland. "I had a plan to hide when the park closed. Tom Sawyer Island was divided by a fence, with a maintenance area north of the public part. I was sure I could swing around the fence and hide, but then I would be stuck on the island. I decided in the summer that would be okay, I could swim over to Frontierland and sneak through New Orleans to the tree. Clothes on my head, towel, the whole bit. I practiced swimming without my arms."

She laughed. "Why didn't you do it?"

"I couldn't think of what to tell my parents. I didn't want them to worry."

"Good boy."

"Well, I would have gotten in such trouble."

"True."

Later she said, "Do you think we could open the tent and look at the stars? Would we get blasted by wind?"

"Somewhat. We can move halfway out and zip down the tent door. I do that a lot."

"Okay let's try it."

He zipped open the tent. The cold poured in on them, and they bundled into the sleeping bag. Frank zipped it up until only their faces emerged from the hood of the bag. Set properly on the groundpad they started to warm up against each other. They kissed as much as Frank's face could handle, which was not much. When they started to make love they fell into it more languorously. They moved with the sway of the tree in the wind, a slow back and forth, like being on a train or a truly huge waterbed. But this was too perfect and they started to laugh, they had to break rhythm with the tree and they did.

Afterward he said, "What should I do about these chips?"

"I'll leave you this wand. You can get completely clear, and they might not have this spot GPS'd. Could you move to another tree?"

"I guess so." Frank realized he had grown fond of his tree, even though there were ten thousand just like it.

"That way, if you kept it a clean site, they wouldn't know where you were. When you were away from your van, anyway."

"I'd have to leave a lot of stuff in the van."

"They would think you were living in it. You'd have to wand yourself when you came up here, and see if you'd picked anything up. If you wanted to be serious about it, you'd get rid of the van and cell phone, and only use public stuff, and buy everything with cash. We call it devolving."

Frank laughed. "I've been trying to do that."

"I can see that. But you'd have to do it here too."

He nodded. He put his face into the hair on the top of her head. Tight curls, a kind of lemon and eucalyptus shampoo; he felt her body on his, and another jolt of desire ran through him. She was helping him. She was strong, bold, interested. She liked him, she wanted him. After four years she would probably want anybody, but now it was him.

"What about you?" he said.

She shrugged.

"So does your, does he know that you know he's spying on you?"

"He must." Her grimace as underlit by Frank's floor lamp gave her the look of one of the Khembali demon masks: fear, despair, anger. Seeing it Frank felt a wave of deep dislike for her husband pour through him. He wanted to get rid of him. Remove him like a chip. Protect her, make her happy—

"—but we don't talk about it," she was saying.

"That sounds bad."

"It is bad. I need to get out of there. But there are some complications having to do with his new job. Some things I need to do first." She fell silent, and her body, though still on top of his, was not melted into him as before. This was another new sensation, her otherness, naked and on top of him. He shivered and pulled the down bag up higher on them.

"So you got your pay phone numbers."

"Yes." He had remembered despite the injury.

"And when will we talk?"

"Nine P.M. every Friday?"

"Sure. And if we have to miss for some reason, the next week for sure. And if we miss again, I'll call your cell phone."

"Okay," he said. "Good."

Her warmth coursed into him. Up in the tree they hugged each other. This moment of the storm.

Leap before you look.

Now winter arrived in earnest. A series of brutal storms fell on the city, like the ones that had struck London only drier. Kenzo said there hadn't been a winter like this since the Younger Dryas. It was worse than the Little Ice Age, average temperatures down thirty degrees.

Frank spent as much time as he could out in these storms. He loved being in them. He loved the way he felt after the night with Caroline. The walking-on-air sensation returned, obviously a specific body awareness in response to certain emotional states, giving birth to the cliché. Lightness of being.

Then also the intense winter was like moving into ever higher altitudes or latitudes. He was in the wilderness and he was in love, and the combination was a kind of ecstatic state, a new realm of joy—

> the joy which will not let me sit in my chair, which brings me bolt upright to my feet, and sends me striding around my room, like a tiger in his cage—and I cannot have composure and concentration enough even to set down in English words the thought which thrills me, what if I never write a book or a line?—for a moment, the eyes of my eyes were opened.

Emersonfortheday indeed! A man who knew how joy could loft you. No wonder they named schools after him! You could learn a lot just by reading him alone. *The eyes of my eyes were opened.*

He snowshoed the park regularly, but also began to range more broadly in the city, taking long walks to each side of the park. This was where the homeless guys were finding refuge, and where the fregans and ferals made their homes. Frank decided that whenever he did not know what to do, he was going to go out and visit as many of the bros and the other homeless of Northwest as he could, and make sure their gear kit was up to the ferocity of the elements. Even if he found total strangers huddled on the Metro vents and in the other little heat sinks of the city, he talked to them too; and if they were at all responsive he got them under another layer of nylon, at the very least. Most had some down or wool on them, but a surprising number were still shivering under cotton, cardboard, plastic, foam rubber, newspaper. Frank could only shake his head. Don't wear cotton! he would insist to perfect strangers. Some of them even recognized him as Johnny Appletent.

He started visiting thrift and sporting goods stores, buying overlooked or sale items, particularly synthetic clothes, and cheap but effective down bags. Once he bought a whole rack of capilene long underwear and matching long-sleeved shirts. These were really nice, similar to the inner layers he wore himself, and the next time he was out in the park and saw some of the bros in Sleepy Hollow, their shelters more knockabout than ever, he threw a top-bottom pair knotted together in to each one of them. "Here, wear this against your skin. Nothing but this stuff against your skin. *No cotton!* Throw all that cotton crap away. You're going to freeze in that cotton shit."

"It's fucking cold."

"Yeah it's cold. Get this gear on and stay out of the wind when it blows."

"No shit."

Andy said, "It's not the cold, it's the wind." *The wee-und.*

"Yeah yeah yeah. That's right."

"That's what everybody says."

Frank snorted. "That's for sure."

It was the new truism, and already Frank was sick of it. Just as in summer people said, "It's not the heat, it's the humidity," until you wanted to scream, in the winter they said, "It's not the cold, it's the wind." So tedious to hear over and over! But Andy's default mode was repetition of the obvious.

Certainly it was true. On windless nights Frank snowshoed through the forest completely removed from the cold; his exertion warmed him, and his heat was trapped in his layers of clothing, under jacket and windpants. The only problem was not to break a sweat. He might as well have been in a spacesuit.

But in a wind everything changed. How big the world became, yes, but how cold too! His outer layer was as windproofed as you could get, but the wind still rattled through it and sucked every move he made. On the very worst nights, if he wanted to walk into the wind he had to turn his back to it and crab backward to keep his face from frostbite. During the days he had taken to wearing sunglasses with a nosepiece, because with his nose numb all the time, he couldn't be sure if it was getting frostbitten or not. More than once it had been white in the mirror when he got back in his van. The nosepiece helped with that, although it gave him a medieval look, like a burgher out of Brueghel. At the end of a walk icicles of snot would hang from it, but his nose stayed unfrozen.

Fine for his poor nose, but then he discovered there were other protrusions that also needed extra protection; he finished one long tramp on a windy Saturday afternoon, stopped in the forest to pee, and discovered to his dismay that his penis was as numb as his nose! Numb with cold, meaning, oh my, yes; it was thawing out in his hand, as painful a needling effect as he had ever felt, a burning *agony* lasting minutes. He cried and his nose ran and it all froze on his face: an unusual demonstration of the density of nerve endings in that area, as in that illustration of the body in which parts were sized in proportion to how many nerves they had, making a nightmare figure with giant mouth, hands, and genitalia.

The frisbee guys already knew all about this problem. Penile frostbite was a serious concern, and extra precautions simply had to be taken; at the least, a sock or glove jammed into one's shorts, but also windproof nylon shorts, longer jackets, all that kind of thing.

"What you need is a rabbit fur jock strap. You could make a fortune selling those."

So Frank never again forgot to pay attention to this matter, and not just for himself. A couple of weeks later, when he clattered into Sleepy Hollow:

"Hey, Nosebleed!"

"Hello gentlemen. How are your penises?"

"Yarrrr!" Wild cackles, laughter: "Now the truth comes out! Now we know what he's here for!"

"You wish. Are you managing to stay unfrostbitten?"

"NO."

Various grumbles and moans.

"Look, there's a shelter open over by UDC, it's a closed high school gym and some classrooms, it's pretty nice."

"We know. Fuck you."

"Mr. Nose. Mr. Nosey Noser."

"Mr. Nosey Nose That Knows It All."

"Yeah well it beats freezing to death."

"Yarrr, fuck off. We have our ways."

"It is our fate to stay out here, but we will survive."

"I hope so."

Friday came and he went out to eat at a Mexican restaurant on Wisconsin near the Metro. He could tell already this would become his Friday night routine. It was an unpretentious little place where Frank could sit at the bar reading his laptop. Go to Emersonfortheday.com, search "fate":

> Mountains are great poets, and one glance at this cliff undoes a great deal of prose. All life, all society begins to get illuminated and transparent, and we generalize boldly and well. Space is felt as a great thing. There is some pinch and narrowness to us, and we laugh and leap to see forest and sea, which yet are but lanes and crevices to the great Space in which the world swims like a cockboat in the sea.

So true. But that turned out to be from the essay "Fate," not about fate per se. Try again, word search in texts:

> The right use of Fate is to bring up our conduct to the loftiness of nature. A man ought to compare advantageously with a river, an oak, or a mountain. He shall have not less the flow, the expansion, and the resistance of these.

Oh my yes. So well put. What a perceptive and eloquent worshipper of nature old Waldo was. And why not. New England had heroic weather, often casting its prosaic forest right up to the heights of the Himalaya.

But it was almost nine. He hopped up and paid his bill, using cash, which he did now as often as he could.

The pay phone he had chosen was in the Bethesda Metro complex itself, down by the bus stop. There were several ancient phones in a row, neglected and unnecessary, and he went to the one on the end and pulled out a phone card, ran it through the slot, dialed her number.

No answer. He let it ring a long time, then hung up.

He stood by the phone, thinking things over. Was this bad? She had said it might not work every week. He had no idea what her daily routine was. How did that work, with a husband you hadn't slept with for four years?

When the phone rang he jumped a foot and snatched it up. "Hello?"

"Hi Frank it's Caroline. Did you call before?"

"Yes."

"Sorry, this is as early as I could do it. I was hoping you'd still be there."

"Sure. We should have a kind of window anyway."

"True."

"So . . . how's it going?"

"Oh, crazy. All over the place."

"Everything's okay?"

"Yes."

Gingerly they reestablished the intimacy they had inhabited the week before. It was hard over the phone, but that voice in his ear brought back a lot of it, and he took chances: How are things going at home? I thought of you. . . . Then she was telling him about her relationship, a bit, and the link between them was there again, that sense of closeness she could establish with a look or a touch, or, now, with her voice, clear and low. The distance between her and her husband had existed for years, she said; maybe since the beginning. They had met at work, he was older; he had been one of her bosses, now in a different agency, "blacker than black." They had not had any huge fights, ever, but for some years now he had not been home much, or showed any interest in her sexually ("Incredible," Frank said). But before they had met he had worked for a while in Afghanistan, so who knew where he was at.

This gave Frank a chill. "How did you two hook up?"

"I don't know. My sister says I like to fix messed-up guys not that I mean you!" she added in a rush.

Frank only laughed. "That's all right. Maybe your sister was right. I am certainly messed up, but you *are* fixing me."

"And you me, believe me."

But then, she went on, she had discovered by accident that he had chipped her, why she did not know; and a cold war, silent and strange, had begun.

Frank shivered at the thought of this. They talked about other things, then. Their workouts, the weather: "I thought about you the other night when it got windy."

"Me you too."

Their windy night, oh my—

"I want to see you again," she said urgently.

"When can we?" His voice cracked, he was just as urgent.

"I don't know. I'll look for a chance. Maybe next week?"

"Okay, next week then. Which one of us should call, by the way?"

"I'll call you. I'll start with this same number."

"Okay good."

He walked back to his van, passing their elevator box on Wisconsin, then their little park. His Caroline places. This would be a new addition to his set of habits, he could tell; and all the rest would be transformed by it. He had gone feral, he had gone optimodal, he had become the Alpine man; and on Friday evenings he would talk to his Caroline on the phone, and that would lift and carry everything else, including the next time they met. Oh God he was in love.

But faster than Frank could follow, winter went from the sublime to the ridiculous, and then to the catastrophic. He was enjoying it right up to the moment it started killing people.

That night, for instance, it was cold but not terribly so; its bite was invigorating. It made so much difference *how* you were experiencing it—not just what you wore, but how you felt about it. If you thought of it as an Emersonian transcendental expedition, ascending further in psychic altitude or latitude the colder it got, then it was just now getting really interesting—they were up to like the Canadian Arctic or the High Sierra, and that was beautiful. A destination devoutly to be wished.

But then temperatures plummeted even further, a drop that took them to the equivalent of Antarctica or the Himalayas, both very dangerous places to be.

This drop was like a cold snap in a cold front; it arrived at midnight, and by 2 A.M. he could not get warm even in his sleeping bag—a rare experience for him, and frightening as such. He fired up the space heater and cooked the air in the tent for a while, and that helped. But the heat sucked out of the tent the moment he killed the heater, and after a couple of burns he decided he had to go for a walk, maybe even a drive, to soak in some of his van's warmth.

Climbing down Miss Piggy was a nasty surprise. He started to swing in the wind, and then his hands got too cold to hold on to the rungs properly, so that he had to hook his elbows over and hang on for dear life, waiting for the wind to calm, but it didn't. He had to descend one rung at a time, setting his freezing feet as securely as possible and then reaching down for another elbow hook.

Finally he dropped onto the snow. He pushed the remote, but the ladder did not swing up into the night. Battery too cold.

Really very cold. You could only survive exposure to this kind of cold with the appropriate gear. Even ensconced in his spacesuit, Frank was struggling to stay warm. This was a temperature so low that it was equivalent to being in the death zones of Everest, or on the Antarctic plateau.

And yet people were still out there in cotton, in blue jeans or black leather jackets, for God's sake. Newspaper insulation for the most hapless. And the animals, all but the polar ones—if they weren't in one of the shelters, they would be dying. The wind cut into him in a way he had felt only a few times before, most of those in the Yukon's Cirque of the Unclimbables. For it to happen in this semitropical city was bizarre, and an immediate emergency. And indeed it sounded like people were calling 911. He could hear sirens from every direction.

He could take care of himself, of course. Ceaseless motion was the key. But even hiking hard, he got cold. He had forgotten what a furious assault cold made on you; he had to bury his face in the windward side of his hood, and had no idea how his nose was faring. For a while he even got lost. Narrow as it was, the park that night was too wide to safely cross.

He headed uphill, hoping it was west but knowing he would emerge from the park eventually if he kept going in a single direction. He kicked up the sides of snowdrifts, noticing again what a huge difference his snowshoes made. It would have been horrible to post up a slope of snow like that. And yet he was one of the few people in the city using snowshoes. Only the FOG people used them, as far as he had seen.

He came out on Broad Branch Road, almost exactly where he had hoped to be. God bless the unconscious mind.

He was very happy to hear his van start when he turned the key. After revving the engine, he drove off with the heater on high. The van rocked on the gusts. The few other vehicles on the streets were weaving like drunks. SUVs finally looked at home, as if they had all moved to Fairbanks.

After driving for a while he warmed up. The day arrived on a broad red sky. He snowshoed back out into the park, went first to 21 to check on the bros.

"Hey, Noseman! You should have a fucking barrel of brandy under your chin."

"I'm amazed you guys are alive. How did you do it?"

"The fire." Zeno gestured at it, pale in its giant mound of ashes. "We sat right next to it all night long."

"We kept it real big, we had to keep running out for more branches, shit. It was so fucking cold. I stood like six inches from this mother bonfire and even so my backside was freezing. One side of me was frying and the other was freezing."

"It was cold all right. Do you have enough firewood, or what are you burning?"

"We have all the flood wood."

"Isn't it green still?"

"Fuck yeah, but we've got a can of gas, and Cutter keeps siphoning cars to fill it up. Car gas burns like a motherfucker, it *explodes* in that fire, you've got to be really careful."

"Okay, well don't burn yourself up. There's that shelter up at UDC—"

"Yeah yeah gowan! Gowan witcha! Go help some of them poor fools out there who probably need it."

This was a valid point, and so Frank snowshoed back out into the city.

In Starbucks they said at dawn it had been fifty below zero Fahrenheit. Almost a hundred degrees below the average daytime temperature for the day—now that was climate change. Sirens were still howling all over the city.

Frank called Diane. She was already at work, of course, but only because she had spent the night there. Forget about coming in, she told him. "No one should even try. I mean, can you believe this?"

"I believe it," said Frank.

All the mid-Atlantic states had already been declared a disaster area, Diane said. Federal employees and everyone else were being told to stay home, everyone but emergency personnel. Lines were down and areas with power outages were in crisis mode. Water mains had frozen and burst, so there were fires going unfought, and meanwhile, no doubt thousands were in danger of freezing to death in their own homes. Six A.M. and already it was a huge emergency.

"Okay Diane, I'll stay in touch today and I'll keep my phone on."

"What are you going to do?"

"I'm going to see how I can help at the zoo, I think. There are still a lot of feral animals out there."

"You be careful! It's dangerous when it's this cold."

"Yeah I will. I've got polar gear, I'll be okay."

So Frank was free to do what he wanted to. "Ooooop!"

All the streets in Northwest were very close to empty. No more blue jeans and windbreakers; the only ones out and about were dressed as if for a day of very cold skiing. These greeted Frank with the cheeriness of people who have survived a rapture and inherited the world. They were mostly men at first, out to see if they could help, out for the hell of it; then there were quite a few women too, more and more as the day wore on, often in bright ski colors. Esprit de corps was high. People waved as they passed, stopped to talk. All agreed that anybody out without good gear would quickly go hypothermic, while on the other hand, good gear and constant exertion meant one could thrive. It was a stunning experience of the technological sublime, an obvious natural religion. Space was indeed felt as a great thing. And some of the coffee shops were still open, so Frank ducked in them from time to time, like everyone else, for a break from the penetrating chill. Heated caves, there to take shelter in any time it got to be too much—as long as the area had electricity, of course. Areas without power would probably need evacuation.

"I'm from Ohio," one man said to Frank outside a Starbucks. "This is nothing!"

"Well, it's pretty cold," Frank said.

"True! But it's not windy. Thank God for that. Because it's not the cold . . ."

Having toured Connecticut Avenue, Frank began a comprehensive hunt through Rock Creek Park, venturing down every side trail. He was relieved to find that the park was basically empty. Deer were tucked into their brakes and hollows; he wondered whether these would be enough. They might be, as snow was a tremendous insulator and windguard. These deer had gone through winters before, and if some now died, the truth was, they could use some culling. It was the feral exotics he really worried about.

Then he found three people, still huddled together in a wood-and-cardboard shelter, down by site 9. At first he thought they were dead; then they stirred. He called 911 and waited, getting colder and colder as he tried unsuccessfully to rouse them, until some firemen got there. He helped them get the three up to the road and the truck, two on stretchers; the one who had been in the middle had done a bit better.

He went back to look for more. Rock Creek itself was frozen to its bottom, of course. The whole park was quiet, the city unusually quiet too, except for the ongoing wail of sirens. The firemen had said that with demand for juice so high, power might go everywhere. The grid masters had initiated preemptive brownouts to keep from blowing the system. Fire trucks were the only vehicles that would still start reliably, because they were kept in heated garages. Battery heaters were crucial at temperatures like these, but of course no one had them.

"My van started this morning," Frank had told the firemen.

"You get one start, usually, but don't be sure it'll happen again. It's fifty below!"

"I know."

Lucky no wind! they said.

Now Frank checked the hot boxes left out for the ferals. If there was a loss of power to these the result would be devastating. Every box was crowded with a menagerie of miserable animals, like little shipwrecked bits of Noah's Ark, every creature subdued and huddled into itself. The gibbons hung from the corners of the roof near the heating elements, their little faces frowning like Stan Laurel after a reversal.

Frank called in to Nancy to report. Zoo staff were doing what they could to collect creatures, but the holdouts were skittish and determined to escape capture; if the zoo folks tried for them now, they stood a good chance of driving them away and thus killing them. Best to let them take to the shelters, and hope it would be enough.

"Is the power to their heaters on generator standby?"

"No. Cross your fingers. The substation on Military Road knows we're a priority."

He continued with his survey. The low sun turned everything blinding silver. By now the temperature had risen to about twenty below, which in combination with the midday sunlight made a huge difference in how it felt to walk around. It came back to his body memory how major distinctions could be made between cold and supercold, so that eventually ten below became comfortable, because thirty below was so miserable; ten above became shirtsleeve weather, while fifty below was always the verge of death.

Power went out west of Connecticut, and Frank went over and helped for a while with a crew going door-to-door to make sure people were all right, occasionally carrying hypothermics out to fire trucks and ambulances. Eventually his hands got too cold and he had to retreat into a UDC coffee shop and drink coffee with the other adventurers sardined into the place. Painful buzz of fingers regaining feeling. Then the coffee shop had to stop serving, as its pipes had frozen and water supplies on hand were all used up. They stayed open just to provide shelter. Damage to pipes alone was sure to cost millions, someone said, and take weeks or months to fix. People didn't think about these kinds of things until they happened, and then it was like discovering yet another Achilles' heel, because it had ruptured.

The sounds of sirens seemed to be converging on them. Frank went out and looked around, saw black smoke rising in a thick plume over the neighborhood between Connecticut and the park, just south of where his van was parked. He hustled over there, slapping his tingling hands together as he walked.

It looked as though squatters might have accidentally set an abandoned house on fire. Already the blaze was out of hand, several houses burning, a whole knot of trees roaring in pale flames. The radiant heat beat on Frank's face. When the fire trucks arrived they found that the water had frozen in the fire hydrants. They had to work on that instead of on the fire. A helicopter chattered in and dropped its load of chemicals, to no great effect as far as Frank could tell. It had to be dangerous to fly helicopters in this kind of cold; they did it in Antarctica, but those helos were specially prepped. No doubt the Antarctic guys at NSF were extremely busy right now, helping in any way they could. Corps of Engineers likewise. It was essential they keep the power on. If there was any kind of general power outage, many people would die.

Talking to some of the firemen around the hydrant, Frank learned that there were already a couple dozen fires in the metro area. All emergency response people were out working, and the National Guard had been called up. Everyone else was being urged to stay home. Nevertheless the number of people walking the streets increased as the day wore on, all bundled and ski-masked in otherwise empty streets. It looked as if bank robbers had pulled off a major revolution.

A fire started in Georgetown, which then lost power. Frank drove down there, as his van kept starting, and he served as a taxi for a couple of hours, shuttling people from frigid houses and apartments to Georgetown University, where generators were keeping most of the buildings warm. George Washington University Hospital was also working on generators, and for a while it was clear that taxiing people was the best thing Frank could do to help; but then the streets began to jam up with traffic, amazingly—it was still twenty below, and yet stop-and-go had returned to Foggy Bottom. So he parked in Georgetown and joined a group of volunteers going door-to-door in the area without power, making sure everyone was out who wanted to be out.

The residential streets of Georgetown were a surprise to Frank. He had never been in this part of town, and it was like being transported to some quaint and comfortable old quarter of a northern European town. Colorful, neat, handmade, human scale—the streets were like what Main Street in Disneyland had always hoped to suggest, or like the village in a snow-filled paperweight.

The sky overhead was unlike that in any paperweight, dark with smoke that streamed in fat bands all across the sky. A huge population lived hidden in the forest around the city, and nearly every single fireplace must have had a blaze in it; a certain percentage of these must have gone wrong and burned down their houses, adding their greater smokes to the chimney fires, so that now the sky was streaked with black. Flakes of ash drifted down, lighter than snowflakes. Frank's nose kept him from smelling the smoke, but he could taste it as grit on his tongue. He wondered if he would ever be able to smell again.

A fire truck wailed down Wisconsin, and the firemen in it jumped out and carried a pump and hose line down to the Potomac. It took some awkward work with chainsaws to break through the ice, now a big white sheet from bank to bank. A crowd gathered to watch and cheer, their breath frosting over them in a small cloud. Sputter and roar of a big Honda generator, downshift as the pump motor engaged, a moment of suspense while nothing happened; then the flattened hose bulked like a snake swallowing a mouse, and water shot out of the big nozzle held by two firemen, who quickly secured it to a stand and aimed the white flow at the leading edge of their blaze. The crowd cheered again. Spray flying upward from the jet of water had time to freeze in the air and flock the nearby rooftops. A tall black man grinned at Frank: "They froze that fire."

Late in the day Frank returned to the Potomac to walk out on the river ice. Scores of people had had the same idea. It had been the same in London two weeks before, when all over the world people had seen images of the festival the Londoners had spontaneously thrown, celebrating the freeze in Elizabethan style. Now on the Potomac people were mostly standing around or skiing, or playing football or soccer, or ad hoc versions of curling. One or two wore ice skates and glided through the crowd, but most were slipping around in boots or their ordinary shoes. A hot dog cartman was busy selling out his entire stock. The ice on the river was mostly white, but here and there it was as clear as glass, with black water visible below. It was freaky at first to walk on these clear sections, but even big groups leaping into the air did not cause a shudder in the ice, which looked from the occasional hole chopped in it to be about two feet thick.

When sunset slanted redly across the Potomac, the scene struck Frank like another vision out of Brueghel, one of the Flemish winter canal scenes, except most of this city's people were black. Out here you could finally see that, in a way Northwest and Arlington never quite revealed. It was like Carnavale on ice, the celebrants improvising clothing warm enough to keep them out there, which then became costumes. A giant steel drum band added to the Caribbean flavor. Snowfights and slip-and-slides, break dancing and curling that was more like bowling; touch football, tackle football, it all was happening out there between Virginia and the District on this sudden new terrain. In the fading light the whole world took on a smoky red cast, the river ice both white and red, and the contrast between the snow and the dark faces diminished to the point where Frank could see people properly. It seemed to him a beautiful populace, every race and ethnicity on Earth there—the black faces vivid and handsome, cheerful to the point of euphoria—the white folk flushed as red as the snow, dressed like L.L.Bean models or gypsies or Russians—all partying together on the frozen Potomac, until with the coming of dark it got too cold to stay out any longer.

Fires burned all night and the next day, but temperatures never dropped lower than ten below. Some in the coffee shops next morning thought the smoke was creating a smudge pot effect, the ultimate urban heat island; but even out in the country temperatures had not dropped as low as the night before. The low had been a freak, and even the *Post* the next morning had a headline like a tabloid: FIFTY DEGREES BELOW.

In the days that followed it remained well below zero, keeping the city in crisis mode. First the great flood, now the great freeze, with widespread fires as well—what next? "There's an excellent chance of drought next summer," Kenzo cackled when Frank talked to him on the phone. "We could hit for the cycle. And it's going to get windy tomorrow."

NSF stayed closed. Frank called Diane every morning, and once when he lamented the lost work time she said, "Don't worry about that, I'm working Congress every day, I take them out until they are frostbit, and every one of them will vote for what we ask next time. It couldn't be better."

So Frank would wish her good luck, then spend the day hiking in the park and doing FOG work. Repair a hot box, resupply food, help lift out a tranquilized camel, always keeping an eye out for Chessman or the bros. Down to Dupont Circle, up to Adams Morgan, crossing the frozen creekbed marveling at the stream's white arabesques, the frolic architecture of ice and snow.

On the third night of the cold snap he ran into the bros, hunkered in a concrete embayment behind a Dupont Metro station grating. They had walled off the indentation from the sidewalk with refrigerator boxes, and added a roof of flattened boxes as well. The interior was even frosting up like an old refrigerator.

"Come on you guys," Frank said. "You should get to one of the shelters, the wind is supposed to hit soon. This is serious."

"It's always been serious, Bleeder."

"Hey who's winning! Where's that barrel of brandy?"

"The UDC gym is open as a shelter."

"Fuck that."

"This is warmer here."

"Yeah yeah. Whatever."

He went up into the UDC shelter himself, and spent an hour or two walking down the rows of cots, handing out paper cups of hot chocolate. The homeless or the heatless, it was hard to tell the difference in here. He ran across the knitting woman, sitting on her cot knitting away, and greeted her with pleasure. He sat and they talked for a while.

"Why won't the guys come in?"

"They're stubborn. What about you, have you come in?"

"Well, no. But I don't need to."

She smiled her gap-toothed smile. "You're all the same."

"Hey what about Chessman? Do you know what happened to him?"

"I don't. He just stopped showing up. It don't mean nothing. He probably moved."

"I hope."

She knitted on imperturbably. She had knitted herself pale yellow gloves that left her fingertips free, poking out of the fabric like tree roots. "He lived over in Northeast somewhere. His people may have moved."

"You don't think something bad happened to him?"

She shook her head, counting under her breath. "I don't think so. I've been living out for twelve years. Hardly anything bad ever happens. It's not so much dangerous as it is unhealthy."

"I suppose so. Don't you want a place?"

"Sure. But, you know. Wherever you are is a place."

"If you see Chessman will you tell me?"

"Sure I will. I was gonna do that anyway. I'm curious myself."

Frank wandered up Connecticut, looking into coffee shops and cafés. He was not reassured by the woman's words. He started calling people whose whereabouts he did know. The Quiblers were fine, Charlie and Anna working from home, school canceled, fire in the fireplace. Anna noted that hoarding had begun at the grocery stores, and that this was a breakdown in social trust that could be very debilitating to normal supply logistics. It was starting to happen at gas stations too, lines forming, people freezing as they waited, all on their cell phones out stamping their feet. Frank promised to drop by the Quiblers and say hi. Same with the Khembalis, who again offered him a place to stay, despite the crowd. He promised to drop by.

He gave Spencer a call, and the shaman picked up after the first ring. "Hello?"

"Hey why no frisbee, what the hell?"

Spencer laughed appreciatively. "We tried, believe me! But when the disks hit a tree they shattered! We broke a whole bunch Monday, although we did establish the low temperature record, of course. Maybe we should try again."

"That would be fun. Where you guys staying, are you warm?"

"Oh yeah, we're squatting around like always. There's a place on McKinley just off Nebraska that's got good insulation and a big fireplace, you should join us, have a meal."

"Still doing the fregan thing?"

"Sure, it works even better now, the dumpsters are like big freezers."

"Maybe I'll just look for you in the park."

"Ha ha, you chicken. We'll give you a call next time we go out."

Then it was back on the street.

The cold snap went on so long it somehow stabilized. Search and rescue got turned over to the professionals, and Frank didn't quite know what to do. He could go back in the park, he could drive into the office and do some work, he could go to Optimodal and take a hot shower . . . he stopped himself from thinking about plans. Stay in the moment. There was a lot to do still in Northwest.

Just as he thought that, he saw Cutter, out in the street working on a tree that had split and fallen across three of the street's four lanes. Frank joined him and offered help that Cutter gladly accepted. As they worked Cutter said that a column of water had evidently filled a crack in the trunk, then frozen and split the tree apart. Frank picked up cut branches and carried them to the pile they had established on the sidewalk. Cutter thanked him without taking an eye off his work. "You seen the park guys?" he asked Frank.

"Yeah I ran into them, they seem to be okay."

Cutter shook his head. "They ought to get a place."

"No lie. You've got a lot of new work like this, I take it?"

"Oh Lordy! We should cut down every tree in this city. They all gonna fall on something they not s'pose to."

"I'm sure. Will this cold kill them?"

"Not necessarily. Not except they split open like this."

"So how do you choose which ones to work on?"

"I drive till I see one in the street."

"Ha. Is it okay if I help you some more?"

"Course it is."

It was good work, absorbing and warm. Dodge around the trees and the cars, never stop moving, get the wood off the street. The chainsaw was loud. It took four people to lift the biggest sections of trunks over into the gutters.

Frank stayed with them through the rest of that afternoon. After a while he felt comfortable enough to say, "You guys shouldn't wear cotton against the skin, it's the worst possible stuff for cold."

"What, are you a vapor barrier man? I hate that shit."

They were all black. They lived over in Northeast, but had worked mostly Northwest when they had worked for city Parks. One of them went on about being from Africa and not capable of handling this kind of cold.

"We're all from Africa," Frank said.

"Very true but your people obviously left there before mine did. Your people look to have gone directly to the North Pole."

"I do like the cold," Frank admitted.

"Like to die in it, myself."

That night Frank slept in his van, and took a dawn walk to rejoin Cutter's crew. Deer nibbled among the snowdrifts; the rest of the animals stuck near the hot boxes. The gibbons looked increasingly unhappy, but Nancy said attempts to capture them had only caused them to swing away through the trees, hooting angrily. The zoologists were thinking of trying to dart them with tranquilizers.

Temperatures remained below zero, but a full load of traffic returned to the streets, and there were a great number of trees and branches to be cleared. The tree crew put out orange plastic stripping to keep crowds away from their work, especially when things were falling. Frank carried wood. No way did he want to go up in a tree and end up like poor Byron, hollering "My leg my leg . . ." So, chop wood, carry water, sure; also chop water, carry wood.

When they broke for lunch he left them and walked down to the UDC shelter, then the Dupont Metro vent, then back up to the zoo, where many people from FOG and FONZ were working. In the zoo enclosures they were supplementing the regular heating system with battery-powered space heaters. The zoo animals looked miserable anyway, and quite a few had died.

It was such a busy week that Frank almost forgot when Friday rolled around, until that morning, when it became all he thought about. He ate Friday evening at the Rio Grande, then stood stamping his feet and blowing into his gloved hands at his pay phone in Bethesda.

But no call; and when it was ten after nine, he called Caroline's number, and let it ring and ring, with never an answer.

What did that mean?

He would find out next Friday, at best. So it seemed. Suddenly their system looked very inadequate. He wanted to talk to her!

Nothing to be done. He tried one last time, listened to the ring. No answer. He had to do something else. He could go to work, or he could . . . no. Just leap. Deflated or not, indecisive or not.

Walking back to his van, he called Diane on his cell phone, as he had every day of the cold snap. She always answered, and her cheery voice held no huge aura of meaning or possibility. She thought it had been a very good week for their cause. "Everybody knows now that the problem is real. This isn't like the flood; this could happen three or four times every winter. Abrupt climate change is real, no one can deny it, and it's a big problem. Things are a mess! So, come on in as soon as they call off the shutdown. There are things we can do."

"Oh I will," Frank promised.

But the cold snap went on. The jet stream was running straight south from Hudson Bay. The wind strengthened and added to every problem—fire, frostbite, downed trees, downed power lines. It began to seem like street work and polar emergency services were all Frank had ever done. Get up in the frigid van and drive to get warm. Hike out to the treehouse, climb the trunk to pull Miss Piggy up a ways and tack her there on a piton; then downclimb the tree, most awkwardly. Scrounge like a real homeless person for cold-weather clothing he could give away. His own gear at fullest deployment was more than adequate: an old knit hat, a windbreaker shell with a hood, a windstopped fleece jacket, very warm; capilene long underwear and long-sleeved shirt, InSport briefs that had a windstop panel in front, which would also hold a mitten to give his privates extra protection, until the rabbit fur arrived; then some bike shorts with the padding ripped out, some fleece knickerbockers, and then pants which covered the feet and went up to the waist, though they should have gone higher. Then his Salomon walking boots and Thorlo synthetic socks, seamless and perfect; he even started putting one of them down the front of his pants, instead of a mitten. Very rabbit furlike. And low-topped gaiters to keep the snow out of his boots, stylish, like black spats. Over all that, on windy days, a jacket that went down to the thighs, and covered the hands and stuck out far beyond the face; a baseball hat to keep snow off the face, help with sun in eyes. Ski gloves, snowshoes, ski poles.

Equipped like that, Frank was probably the best-dressed man in the city. He was the Alpine man, come back to life! And his goal, Johnny Appletent-like, was to get everybody else living outdoors into gear that was at least adequate. Or into shelters at night if the cold was too much. It was no easy task, because it called not only for acquisition of gear that was disappearing fast from all the thrift shops (though people didn't recognize wool, apparently), but the money to fund it. He used a grant from the zoo's feral fund, considering that with that name it was not even a case of reprogrammed funds. But the distribution of the gear could be tricky. No one liked gratitude, but many people were cold enough to take what he gave them. Cotton and cardboard were no longer hacking it. The stubborn ones were likely to die. The newspapers reported that a few hundred already had. Frank could scarcely believe some of the stories in the *Post* about the dumb things people had done and were still doing. They could be six inches from safety and not recognize it. It was as John Muir had said of the Donner Party; a perfectly fine winter base camp, botched by ineptitude. But they didn't know. It was a technique, and if you didn't have it you died. It wasn't rocket science, but it was mandatory.

Frank had to be careful not to get careless himself. He stayed out all day every day, and part of him was beginning to think he had it wired, so that he spent longer sessions out. Sometimes he discovered he was so ravenous or thirsty that he was going to keel over; he blew into the coffee shops shivering hard, only to discover white patches on his chin, and fiendishly pinpricking fingers and ears. God knew what was happening to his poor nose. Emergency infusions of hot chocolate, blowing across the top and burning his mouth to gulp some down, burning his esophagus, feeling his insides burning while his extremities fizzed with cold. Hot chocolate was the perfect start on a return to proper heat and energy.

One night he found the bros back in the park, around a very hospitable bonfire. Just outside the light the body of a deer lay partly skinned, steaks hacked out of its flank.

"—so fucking cold it made me stupid."

"Like that's what did it."

"—I couldn't even talk for a couple days. Like my tongue was froze. Then I could talk, but I only knew like ten words."

"That happened to me," Fedpage put in. "I started talking in old English, and then German. You know, 'Esh var *kalt*.' The Germans really know how to say it. And then just grunts and moans for a while. For esh var kallllt."

"You're funny Fedpage. You were wasted in Vietnam."

"I was indeed wasted in Vietnam."

Fluctuating radiant pulses of heat washed over their faces.

Frank sat by the fire and watched it. "So you guys really were in Vietnam."

"Of course."

"You must be pretty old then."

"We are pretty old then! Fuck you. How the fuck old are you?"

"Forty-three."

"What a kid."

"We're twice as old as that, kid. No wonder your nose bleeds."

"In point of fact I'm sixty-five," said Fedpage.

"Boomer scum."

"Yeah, he went to the University of Vietnam."

"So what was it like?"

"It was fucked! What do you think?"

"At least it wasn't cold," Zeno said dourly. "It might have been fucked but at least you didn't freeze your dick off."

"I told you to put a sock down there."

"Put a sock on it! Good idea!"

Fedpage, solemn, calculating: "I would need one of them knee socks."

General mirth. Discussion of burning sensations during penile thawing. Listing of exceptional cases of genital trauma. Frank watched Zeno brood. Zeno noticed and snapped, "It was fucked, man."

"It was everything," Fedpage said.

"True. It was every kind of thing. There were some guys over there who joined up specifically to kill people. Some people were like that. But most of them weren't, and for them it was hell. They didn't know what hit them. We just did what we were told and tried to stay alive."

"Which we did."

"But we were lucky! It was sheer dumb luck. When we were in Da Nang we could just as easily been overrun."

"What happened there?" Frank said.

"We got caught by the Tet Offensive—"

"He don't know about any of that. We were cut off, okay? We were surrounded in a town and we got hammered. They killed a lot of us and they would have killed all of us but except for the Air Force made some passes. Bombed the shit out of them."

"Dropped us food too."

"That's right, we were going to starve as well as get massacred. It was a race to see which. Incompetent bastards."

"We shared the last food, remember that?"

"Of course. A spoonful each. Didn't do us a bit of good."

"It was a team thing. You should have seen Zeno the time we heloed down into a minefield and the medic wouldn't get out to help some wounded. Zeno just jumped out and ran right across that minefield. He led those brothers back just like there weren't no mines out there. Even after one went off and DX'd a guy who didn't follow right in his footsteps."

"You did that?" Frank said.

"Yeah well," Zeno said. He looked away, shrugged. "That was my Zeno's paradox moment, right? I mean if you're always only halfway there, then you can't ever step on no mine."

Frank laughed.

"It was great," Fedpage insisted.

"No it wasn't," Zeno said. "It was just what it was. Then you get back to the States and it's all like some bad movie. Some stupid fucking sitcom. That's America man. It's all such bullshit. People act like they're such big deals, they act like all their rules are real when really they're just bullshit so they can keep you down and take everything for themselves."

"True," Fedpage said.

"Ha. Well, here we are. Looks like the fire is about halfway down. Who's going to go get more wood for this fire, I ain't gonna do it."

"So did you ever go up to the shelter?"

"Sure."

The hard wind finally struck as forecast, and it got bad again for a couple of days, as bad as in the beginning. "It ain't the cold, it's the—"

"Shut the fuck up!"

Frozen branches snapped and fell all over town, on people, cars, power lines, rooftops. Frank went out every day and helped Cutter and his crew. Then one day, when he was clearing a fallen tree from a downed power line, a branch swung his way and thwacked him on the face.

"Oh sorry I couldn't get that! Hey Frank! Hey are you okay?"

"I'm okay," Frank said, hands at his face. He still couldn't feel his nose. He tasted blood at the back of his throat, swallowed. It was nothing new. It happened from time to time. It even tasted like old blood, leftover from the original injury. He shook it off, kept on carrying wood.

The next morning, however, he got out of his van and walked up and down Connecticut, and he couldn't decide what to do. Time for a leap before you look, therefore; do whatever came to hand. But where to start?

He never started. He walked up Connecticut to Chevy Chase Circle, then back down to the zoo. How big the world became when it tasted like blood.

He stopped at a stoplight to think it over. He could help at the zoo, or he could help Cutter, or he could look for Chessman, or he could help at the shelter, or he could go to work, or he could go for a run, or a hike, or a climb. Or he could read a book. His current reading was *The Long Winter* by Laura Ingalls Wilder, a real beauty, the story of a small Dakota town surviving the extreme winter of 1880. The town had lost all contact with the rest of humanity, cut off by huge snowpacks from October to May. Talk about island refugia! He had gotten to the part where they were almost starving.

So he could read. He could sit in a coffee shop and read his book, and no one would have any reason to object. Or he could work out at the club. Or . . .

He was still standing aimlessly, miserably, when his cell phone rang.

It was Nick Quibler. School had been canceled for the day, and he was wondering if Frank was available to go on a FOG hunt.

"I sure am," Frank croaked. "Thanks for thinking of it."

When Charlie got home from the grocery store, where all the shelves had been largely empty, Anna and Joe were out, but Nick was there playing his pad.

"Hey Nick, how was your FOG trip with Frank?"

"Oh. Well, it wasn't a big accident."

"Uh oh." This phrase was a family joke, recalling a time when a much younger Nick had tried to delay telling his parents about something bad he had caused to happen at preschool. But this time Nick wasn't smiling. Curiously focused on his pad, in fact. "What do you mean it wasn't a big accident?"

"Well, you know. No *people* got hurt."

"That's good, but what did happen?"

"Well. You know. It wasn't so good for one of the gibbons."

"Uh oh, how so?"

"One died."

"Oh no! How did it happen?" Hand to Nick's shoulder; Nick stayed focused on the game. "What happened, bud?"

"Well you see, it's too cold for them now."

"I bet! That's true for a lot of the animals, right?"

"Right. And so they have these heated shelters out in the park, and all the animals are using them now, but some of the animals are hard to catch even when they do use them. The gibbons and siamangs are like that, they sit on the roofs and run away if you try to get close, and some of them have died. They found two of them frozen. So they decided they better try to capture the ones still out there, before they died too."

"That makes sense."

"Yeah, but they're really hard to get near. They swing through the trees? It's really cool. So you have to kind of hunt them if you want to, you know."

"Uh oh."

"Yeah. You have to shoot them with a tranquilizer dart."

"Oh yeah. I used to see that on *Wild Kingdom*."

"They do it on Animal Planet all the time."

"Do they. That's good to know. That's continuity. But I remember one time when I was a kid, this hippo got out of Lion Country Safari, and they shot it with too much."

"No, not that."

"What then?"

"Well, they're always up in the trees. And Frank is the only one who can get very close to them."

"Ha. Our Frank is something."

"Yeah, he can sound just like them. And he can walk without making any noise. It's really cool."

"How the heck does he do that?"

"He looks where he's going! I mean he walks along and his face is pointed right down at the ground most of the time."

"Ah yeah. And so?"

"So we were up by Military Road and we got a call that someone had spotted a gibbon pair near the Nature Center going down toward the creek, so we went down the creekbed, you can walk right on the ice, and we got in those rocks down by the creek?"

"Which?"

"The Nook and Cranny rocks, you can see through the cranny upstream, so we laid in wait for a while and . . ." Nick went silent.

"What do you do when you're lying in wait?"

"We just stand there real quiet. You be careful about how you breathe, it's pretty cool."

"Ah yeah. And so then?"

"So then three gibbons came past us, and they weren't up very high and Frank had the gun balanced on the Nook and was ready for them. He shot one right in the butt, but then some people yelled."

"Other FOG people?"

"No, just we didn't know who, and the gibbons took off and Frank took off running after them."

"Didn't you too?"

"Yeah I did, but he was fast. I couldn't keep up. So but neither could he, not with the gibbons, they just fly along, but the one he shot fell. From way up there."

"Oh no."

"Yeah."

"Oh no. So Frank couldn't . . ."

"No. He tried but he couldn't keep up. He wasn't there to catch it."

"So it died?"

"Yeah. Frank picked it up. He checked it out."

"He was hoping it was still alive."

"Yeah. But it wasn't. It got killed by the fall. I mean it looked okay, but it was . . . loose. It wasn't there."

"Oh no. How awful. What did Frank do?"

"He was kind of upset. He sat down with it and cried."

"Ah yeah." Charlie squeezed his son's shoulder. "Where is he now?"

"No one knows. He ran off."

The bare branches overhead were like black lightning bolts striking up out of the Earth into the clouds. Like decision maps, first choose this, then that. He was cold, cold in his head somehow. All his thoughts congealed. Maybe if he weren't injured. Maybe next winter. Maybe if it wasn't a long winter. Maybe they all had to find their cave. *Fur es war kalt.*

Wind ripped through the branches with a sound like tearing cloth. A big sound. Under it the city hummed almost inaudibly. Snow cracked as he stepped on it. There was no way to walk quietly now. The branches overhead were like black fireworks, flailing the sky. He moved under them toward the gorge, shifting his weight one pound at a time.

Eventually he came to one of the heated shelters. Little square hut, its open side facing south. All its interior surfaces emanated heat, like a big toaster oven left open. A bad thought, given the way toaster ovens worked.

Inside, and scattered around the opening, they stood or sat or lay. Rabbits, raccoons, deer, elands, tapirs, even foxes, even a bobcat. Two ibexes. None meeting the eye of any other; all pretending they were each alone, or with only their own kind. As when trapped on an island created in a flood, it was a case of stay there or die. So, truce. Time out.

Very slowly he approached. He kept his head down, his eyes to the side. He sidled. He crabbed. Shoulders hunched lower and lower. He turned his back to them entirely as he closed on them, and sat down in the lee of the shelter, about fifteen feet out from it, in a little hollow floored with snow. He shifted back toward them to get off the snow, onto a decomposed black log. Fairly dry, fairly comfortable. The heat from the shelter was palpable, it rushed over him intermittently on the wind, like a stream. He rested his head on his chest, arms around his knees. A long time passed; he wasn't sleepy, but long intervals passed during which no thoughts came to him. A gust of chill air roused him, and he shifted so he could see more of the shelter out of the corner of his eye. At the very edge of his peripheral vision lay what could have been the jaguar.

The animals were not happy. They all stared at him, wary, affronted. He was messing up a good situation. The lion had lain down with the lamb, but the man was not welcome. He wanted to reassure them, to explain to them that he meant no harm, that he was one of them. But there were no words.

Much later there was a crack, a branch breaking. In a sudden flurry many animals slipped away.

He looked up. It was Drepung, and Charlie Quibler. They approached him, crouched by his side. "Come with us, Frank," Drepung said.

CHAPTER 18

ALWAYS GENEROUS

The scientific literature on the effects of damage to the prefrontal cortex was vast. Its existence bespoke a variety and quantity of human suffering that was horrible to contemplate, but never mind; it was rehearsed here in the course of attempting to reduce that suffering. Among the cases discussed were traumas so much worse than what Frank had suffered that he felt chastened, abashed, lucky, frightened. He wasn't even sure his brain had been injured. He wasn't sure it wasn't just a broken nose and the taste of blood at the back of his throat. Not much compared to an iron spike through the skull.

Nevertheless it was his injury, and how he felt about it was now also part of the symptomology, because emotions were generated or coordinated or felt in the prefrontal cortex, and so the precise kind of emotional change experienced was an indication of what trauma might have occurred. The dysfunction could be very precise and limited: some subjects were rendered incapable of compassion or embarrassment but could still feel happiness or fear, others felt no dismay or even laughed at crippling disabilities they were quite aware of, and so on. Trauma victims thus became in effect experiments, testing what happened if you removed parts of a very complex system.

Frank clicked and read apprehensively, reminding himself that knowledge was power. "Fear and Anxiety: possible roles of the amygdala and bed nucleus of the stria terminalis." "Impaired recognition of emotion in facial expressions following bilateral damage to the human amygdala." The amygdala was behind the nose, a little distance in. A famous case of short-term amnesia *had been nicked in the amygdala when a fencing foil went in through his nose.*

"Emotion: an evolutionary byproduct of the neural regulation of the autonomic nervous system." The sociobiological view, for once of less interest to Frank. He would come back to that later. "Reciprocal limbic-cortical functioning and decision-making: converging PET findings in lack of affect and indecision." "Neuroanatomical correlates of happiness, sadness, and decisiveness." Both studies of the emotion/decision connection. "Subgenual prefrontal cortex abnormalities in mood disorders." Study of a case who was unusually wild and incompetent in life decisions, unlike anyone else in her family, and then they remembered that when she was an infant a car had run over her head.

"From the nose to the brain." Oh my. There were synapses that ran from one end of the head to the other. They went from the nose to everywhere. Scent of course, also memory, also behaviors associated with pleasure. These tapped into dopamine that was made available in the nucleus accumbens in the basal forebrain, behind the back of the mouth. The availability depended on a long biochemical sequence functioning well at every point.

The right frontal cortices were more associated with negative emotions than the left; the right somatosensory cortices were active in integrating body management, which might be why it was the apparent seat of empathy. Blocking oxytocin in a female prairie vole did not interfere with its sex drive, but with the attachment to its partner that would usually correlate to sex. Suppressing vasopressin had the same effect on male voles, who would normally be faithful for life, voles being monogamous. You needed both the insula and the anterior cingulate working well to be able to experience joy. Fluency of ideation increased with joy, decreased with sorrow. The brain was often flooded with endogenous opioid peptides such as endomorphins, enkephalin, dynorphin, endorphins—all painkillers. You needed those. Brain systems that made ethical decisions were probably not dedicated to ethics exclusively, but rather also to biological regulation, memory, decision-making, and creativity. In other words, to everything. You needed joy to function well. In fact, it appeared that competent or successful decision-making depended on full capa-

bility in all the emotions; and these in turn depended on a healthy prefrontal cortex.

It looked to Frank like all the new research was adding up to a new model or paradigm in which emotion and feeling were finally understood to be indispensable in the process of proper reasoning. Decision-making in particular was a reasoning process in which the outcomes of various possible solutions were judged in terms of how they might feel. Without that, the ability to decide well was crippled. This was news: the Greek and Enlightenment definition of reason as a process that needed to ignore emotions had been wrong. Descartes and most of Western philosophy since the Greeks had been wrong. It was the feel of a potential action one looked for. Reason required emotion.

Judging from the evolutionary history of the brain, it seemed clear that feelings had entered the picture in prehuman species, as part of social behaviors. Sympathy, attachment, embarrassment, pride, submission, censure and recompense, disgust (at cheaters), altruism, compassion: these were social feelings, and arrived early on, before language. And they were perhaps more important than conscious thought, as overall cognitive strategy was formed by unconscious mentation in regions such as the ventromedial frontal lobe (right behind the nose). Life was feeling one's way toward a goal, which goal ultimately equated to achieving and maintaining certain feelings.

So an excess of reason was indeed a form of madness! Just as Rudra Cakrin had said. It was something the Buddhist tradition had discovered early on, by way of introspection and analysis alone. Which was impressive, but Frank found himself comforted to have the assertion backed by scientific research and a neurological explanation. It was a chance to come at the problem in a fresh way, with new data. Buddhist thinkers, and those in Western philosophical tradition who used introspection and logic alone to postulate "how the mind works," had been mulling over the same data for thousands of years, and now seemed caught up in preconceptions, distinctions, and semantic hairsplitting of all kinds. Also, introspection never gave them the means to investigate unconscious thought; and unconscious thought was proving to be crucial. Even consciousness, standing there in the mirror to be looked at (maybe)—even what could be introspected or deduced was so extremely com-

plex that you could not think your way through it. It needed a group effort, working on the physical action inside the brain. It needed science.

And now science was using new tools to move beyond its first achievements in taxonomy and basic function; it was getting into analysis of evidence collected from living minds, from brains both healthy and damaged. It was a huge effort, involving many labs and scientists, and was still involved in the process of paradigm construction. Some academic philosophers cast scorn on the simplicity of these researchers' early models, but to Frank it was better than continuing to elaborate theories generated by the evidence of introspection alone. Obviously there was still far to go, but until you took the first steps you would never be on the way.

It was noticeable that the Dalai Lama always welcomed the new results from brain science. It would help Buddhists to refine their own beliefs, he said; it was the obvious thing to do. And it was true that many academic philosophers interested in consciousness also welcomed the new findings.

Welcomed or not, the papers from the new body of work were accumulating. And so Frank lay there in bed, reading them on his laptop, unable to figure out what he felt, or what he should do next, or if he had a physical problem at all. Damasio, a leader in this new research: "The system is so complex and multilayered that it operates with some degree of freedom." Oh yes, he was free, no doubt—but was he damaged? What did he feel? What was this feeling, like oceans of clouds in his chest? And what should he do next?

The Khembali house in Arlington was just as crowded as Frank had thought it would be, maybe even more so. It was a big house, perhaps built to be a boardinghouse from the start, with a ground floor of big public rooms and three floors of bedrooms above, many of them off long central hallways, and an extensive basement. But as a good percentage of the Khembali populace was housed in these rooms, all of them were overflowing.

Clearly it would be best if he continued to live out of his van. But his Khembali friends were adamant in their invitation. Sucandra said, "Please, Frank. Stay with Rudra Cakrin in his room. No one else will do it, and yet he needs someone. And he likes you."

"Doesn't he like everybody?"

Sucandra and Padma regarded each other.

"Rudra was the oracle," Padma told Frank.

"So?"

Sucandra said, "It seems one old Bön spirit that used to visit him comes back from time to time."

"Also," Padma added, "he seems to feel we have lost Tibet. Or failed to recover it. He doesn't think he will see it again in this life. It makes him . . ."

"Irritable."

"Angry."

"Perhaps a little mad."

"He does not blame you for any of this, however."

"To him you represent another chance for Tibet."

"No, he just likes you. He knows the situation with Tibet is hopeless, at least for some time to come."

An exile. Frank had never been an exile in the formal sense, and never would be; but living on the East Coast had given him a profound sense of not being at home. Bioregional displacement, one might call it, and for a long time he had hated this place. Only in the last year had the forest begun to teach him how it could be loved. And if the great eastern hardwood forest had repelled him, how much more might it repel a man from the tree-less roof of the world? A man who knew he could never go home?

So Frank felt he understood that part of Rudra's moodiness. The visiting demon, however . . . Well, these were religious people. They weren't the only religious people Frank knew. It should resemble talking to Baptists, and he had done that. It was just another worldview in which the cosmos was filled with invisible agents. He could always focus on the shared pain of displacement. Besides, Sucandra and Padma were asking for his help.

So that night Drepung took him in to see Rudra Cakrin, in a tiny room off the stair landing before the flight to the attic, a space that might once have been a closet. There was only room for a single bed and a slot between it and the wall.

Rudra was sitting up in bed. He had been ill, and looked much older than Frank had ever seen him. "Please to see you," he said, peering up at him as they shook hands. "You are my new English teacher, Drepung say. You teach me English, I teach you Tibetan."

"That would be good," Frank said.

"Very good. My English better than your Tibetan." He smiled, his face folding into its map of laugh wrinkles. "I don't know how we fit two beds in here."

"I can unroll a groundpad down here," Frank suggested. "Take it up by day."

"Good idea. You don't mind sleep on floor?"

"I've been sleeping in a tree."

Startled, Rudra refocused on Frank. Again the strange intensity of his gaze; he looked right into you. And who else had Frank told about his tree-house? No one but Caroline.

"Good idea!" Rudra said. "One thing—I cannot be, what say—guru for you."

"That's okay, I already have a guru. He teaches me frisbee."

"Good idea."

Afterward Frank said to Drepung, "He seems fine to me."

"So you will share a room with him?"

"Whatever you like. I'm your guest. You decide."

"Thank you. I think it will be good for both of you."

There was no denying that Frank felt deeply uneasy about moving indoors, as if he were breaking a promise to someone. A kind of guilt, but more importantly, a profound physical unease, a tightness in the chest, a numbness in the head. But it was more all-encompassing than that.

On waking in the mornings he would get up from his groundpad in Rudra's room, roll it up, stick it under Rudra's bed, and go downstairs and out the door, almost sick to his stomach with anxiety. Shivering in the driver's seat of his van, he would wake up the rest of the way, then drive over to Optimodal, getting there just as they unlocked the doors. Diane was often already there waiting, slapping her mittened hands together. She always had a cheery smile to greet him. He found her consistency impressive. Sometimes his smile in response must have looked wan indeed. And in fact she sometimes put a hand to his arm and asked if he were all right. He always nodded. Yes; all right. Not good not bad. Not anything he could define. Nose still stuffed up, yes, but otherwise okay. Ready to go.

And in they would go, for a workout that was now semiautonomous; they had got past feeling they needed to team up to be friendly, and merely did their own things in such an order that they were often in the same room, and could sometimes talk, or help out with weights or holding ankles. Then it was off to the showers and the daily blessing of hot water running over him. Presumably on the other side of the wall Diane was doing the same under a shower of her own. By now Frank could visualize pretty well what Diane would look like. She would look good. Probably this didn't matter. It only made him worry about Caroline and what might have happened to her.

But he worked every day with Diane, and he couldn't help but admire how skillful she was, and determined. They were entering the final stage of arrangements for their North Atlantic intervention, and Diane devoted a good part of every day talking to the people running parts of it. The International Maritime Organization was in charge of shipping; UNEP was making arrangements for salt; the big four re-insurance companies were providing or raising the funding. Wracke and the Corps were providing engineering.

There were some 3,500 oil tankers in operation around the world, they had learned, and about thirty percent of those were still the older single-hulled kind that were legally required to be replaced. Five hundred Very Large Crude Carriers were identified by the IMO as being past due for retirement, and as this meant either the breaker's yard or legal complications, the shipowners were being very accommodating about letting them be used to move salt. These old single-hulled VLCCs had an average capacity of ten million tons, small compared to the Ultra Large Crude Carriers now replacing them, but taken altogether, enough to do the job.

So shipping capacity was not proving to be the choke point of the operation. Nor was coming up with enough salt. Five hundred million metric tons was about two years of total world production, but this was more a matter of demand than supply; the salt industry in the Caribbean alone had years of salt dried in the pans ready to go, and the hardrock mines of New Brunswick and the rest of Canada also had a huge inventory.

Thus the plan was physically possible, and the harsh winter meant it was now welcomed with cries of hope and anticipation, rather than the raised eyebrows and shaking heads that had met it the previous summer. Indeed the futures market in salt had already jumped, Frank was interested to learn; prices had shot up five hundred percent. Fortunately enough futures had been bought by Swiss Re to bypass this inflation. The full complement of salt would be ready later that year, at about the same time the fleet of tankers was ready to be filled. The project was on course for a rendezvous of the fleet that fall; the unlikely-sounding idea, first broached in Diane's office, was going to happen, at a total cost of what looked to be about a hundred billion dollars. Swiss Re reported the fund-raising was on schedule, and anticipated no problems.

"That's how desperate this winter has made people," Edgardo observed.

"I told you the cold snap was a good thing," Diane replied.

Frank found it interesting, but beyond that felt little. It was hard to connect all the activity to the brainstorming of last summer, when it had been only one of many ideas, and not the most likely at that. Now it had the look of something obvious and inevitable, what Edgardo called a silver bullet solution; a grand exercise in planetary engineering that was exciting worldwide attention, funding, and controversy.

Very interesting, sure; but now it was out of their hands, and Frank's daily work centered on other things. The Carbon Capture Campaign legislation was about to be introduced in the House, and Frank was involved with the graphs and tables evaluating options. And the SSEEP project was still generating huge amounts of trouble for NSF, as many accused them of illegally entering into presidential politics, and in a most crassly unfashionable Old Left way at that. Diane occasionally thought she would get fired over it. The heat came from all directions, even the Phil Chase campaign, which now appeared to regard the SSEEP platform as some kind of third-party competition. Judging by the results so far, it had possibly been a bad idea to suggest a scientific approach to political problems, but on most days Frank was still glad they had tried it. Something had to be done. Although choosing which something remained a problem. One morning, walking from Optimodal to work, Diane said to him, "So what are you going to work on this morning?"

And Frank, distracted, said, "I don't know. I could meet with Kenzo, or talk to George in Engineering, or call Yann. Or I could work on the Stirling calculations, or check into those flexible mirrors. Or call up the photovoltaics group. Or I could call Wracke, or the people at NASA to see if their heavy-duty booster is going to be ready this decade. Or there are these glassy metals I could—"

The light changed and they crossed Wilson. Diane, laughing at him, said, "You sound like I feel." But she didn't know how he felt; because he truly didn't know what to do. But then going into the building, the way she looked up at him, he saw that she knew that.

In the evenings Frank returned to the Khembali house. He learned that it had an "entertaining kitchen," occupying the back half of the house's ground floor. It had been big to begin with, and was now equipped as if for a restaurant and bakery. Its exquisite heat always enveloped a dozen women and half a dozen men, shouting over the steamy clangor in Tibetan, and also in guttural English.

Early on Drepung introduced Frank to two men and three women who seemed to run the kitchen.

"So good to have you," one said.

"Welcome to Khembalung," said another.

"Can I help?" Frank asked.

"Yes. The bread will soon be ready to take out, and there are many potatoes to peel for dinner."

"How many do you feed per meal?" Frank asked later, surveying the bustle as he scraped the skin off a potato.

"Hundred. First hundred eat here, the rest have to eat out. Or leftovers. Makes people timely."

"Wow."

Sucandra came by when he was finished, and led him out to show him the back yard, now a frozen garden patch. "Best to join garden duty now," Sucandra suggested. "It will be very nice in the spring."

Frank nodded, inspecting the trees in the yard. Possibly one at the back could support a platform. Something to bring up later, obviously.

Sucandra and Padma's room was a half flight below Frank and Rudra's. This meant Frank had someone to talk to even when Rudra was asleep or Drepung was gone. Sometimes one of them came up to translate something Rudra wanted to say but couldn't. Mostly the two new roommates were left to hash it out. In practice this meant a few exchanges a day, combining with a formal lesson in the last hour before the old man fell asleep. Rudra would nod out over *Richard Scarry's Best Word Book Ever,* muttering in his gravelly low voice, "chalk, pencil sharpener, milk, cookies, paper clip, thumbtacks, lost clothing drawer," chuckling as his finger tapped on the latest appearance of the pig man with the windblown hat. He would tell Frank the Tibetan words for these items, sometimes, but the main focus of their sessions was on English; Frank could learn Tibetan or not, Rudra did not care, he even appeared to scoff at the idea. "What's the use?" he would growl. "Tibet gone, ha." Many odd things appeared to strike him funny, and he laughed with an abrupt low "Ha," as if laughter were a surprise attack against invisible demons.

Frank was content to lie there on his groundpad, listening to the old man read and working on his laptop.

"Pumpkin, ghost—what say?" This was something the Khembalis often said as a kind of "um" or "er" as they searched for the right word, so Frank had to be prompted to treat it as a real question.

"Oh sorry. That's a witch on a broom, but he's made the witch an owl."

"Ghost festival?"

"Yes, I suppose so."

"That is very danger." Tibetan was made of syllable roots that stayed the same in different word forms, and Frank noticed that a lot of the Khembalis used English nouns the same way, letting them do the work of verbs and modifiers: "You will learn to meditation." "He became enlightenment."

As they drifted off to sleep the two of them would hold strange conversations, involving both languages and a lot of confusion. Companionship without comprehension; it was just the kind of company that suited Frank. It reminded him of the bros in the park. In fact he told Rudra about his acquaintances in the park, and the winter they had had.

"Wandering tramps are often spirits in disguise."

"I'm sure."

The whole situation in the household was proving more congenial than Frank had expected it to be. Not knowing the language excused him from many conversations, but there were always people around, faces gradually known, amazing faces, but few of them named or spoken to. That too was somewhat like being in the park with the bros. But it was warmer; and easier. He didn't have to decide where to be so often, where to go. What to do next—it was as simple as that. He didn't have to decide what to do every hour or so. That was hard even without damage to the prefrontal cortex.

One decision remained easy; on Friday after work, he drove over to Bethesda and ate at Rio Grande, and then at quarter to nine he was standing before his telephone at the Metro bus stop. He waited through nine, and at 9:05 called Caroline's number. No answer.

What could have happened? What should he do? What might keep her from calling? Deep uneasiness was almost indistinguishable from fear.

He was walking sightlessly down Wisconsin toward his van, deep in his uneasiness, when his cell phone rang. He snatched it out of his pocket, while at the same time seeing that he was standing right before the elevator box that he and Caroline had emerged from last year. His heart leaped—"Hello?"

"Frank it's me."

"Oh good. What's happening?"

"—really sorry, I couldn't get there last week and I thought I'd be able to make it this week but I couldn't. I can't talk long I just slipped out."

"Is something wrong?"

"Well yeah, but look I need to just set up another call here and get off. He's suddenly asking me to do things on Fridays and I don't know if it means anything, but can you be there at that number next Monday at nine?"

"Sure but hey listen, can you make a call to the Khembali embassy house in Arlington? They're not under his surveillance are they?"

"I don't think so. Who are they?"

"Embassy of Khembalung, in Arlington. I'm staying there now and so you can call me there whenever. In the evenings I'll likely be around."

"Okay I'll look for a chance and call soon. I'm so sorry about this. He's changed jobs again and it's getting really complicated."

"That's okay I'm just glad to hear from you!"

"Yeah I bet, I mean I would be too. I'll call real soon okay?"

"Okay."

"Love you bye.

"Bye."

It was amazing how much better he felt. Lack of affect was clearly not his problem; on the contrary, he had to avoid being overwhelmed by feelings.

Giddy with relief, happy, worried, pleased, in love, frightened: but what did all those feelings combined add up to? This was what the studies never seemed to discuss, that you could feel so many different things at the same time. He felt *Caroline*. The uncanny presence of their elevator box, standing there before him throughout their conversation, had given him a palpable sense of her, an instant connection from the moment she spoke. Some quality in her voice drew his affections out. He wanted her to be happy. He wanted to be with her.

Leap before you look, stop trying to decide, just act on the spur of the moment. On Saturday he went over to Rock Creek, first to move most of his stuff from his treehouse to his van, then to play a round with Spencer and Robert and Robin. The frisbees still tended to shatter if they hit a tree straight on, but other than that the frisbee guys seemed fine with the hard winter. Spencer said it was the same with all the fregans. They were Ice Age people.

And the bros were back by their fire, stubbornly enduring the cold. The pile of ashes in their fireplace was huge, and the area beyond Sleepy Hollow where the deer carcasses lay was beginning to look like a real shambles. Fedpage handed Frank a paper plate with a scorched venison steak when he sat down.

"Thanks."

"You're welcome. It's a little bloody, but—"

"Blood for the hemophiliac! Just what he needs!"

"Uh-huh. Hey, Fedpage, how many spy agencies are there?"

"Sixteen."

"Jesus."

"That's how many they admit to. Actually there's more. It's like those Russian nested dolls, with blacks and superblacks inside."

"Spy versus spy."

"That's right. They fight like dogs. They guard their turf by getting blacker." This statement made Cutter laugh. "Nobody even knows everything that's out there. Not the President nor anyone else."

"How can that happen?"

"There's no enemy, that's why. They pretend there's terrorists, but that's just to scare people. Actually they like terrorists. That's why they went into Iraq, they got oil and terrorists out of it, it was a two-for-one. Much smarter than Vietnam. Because it's all about funding. The spooks' job is to keep their funding."

"Shit," Frank said. He prodded his steak, which suddenly tasted off. "I think you guys need to kill another deer maybe."

"Ha ain't nothing wrong with that deer! It's Fedpage making you sick!"

Some afternoons Frank walked around Arlington. He had never spent much time there, and this was an odd time to get acquainted with it, its big streets were so wintry. Broad avenues ran for miles westward, tall buildings erupting out of the forest in every kind of mediocre urban conglomeration. He could walk to the Khembali house from NSF in half an hour, so some days he did that, hiked through the snow with cars belching past like steam-powered vehicles.

At night after dinner he went up to his room and read on his mattress, chatting with Rudra every half hour or so. Otherwise he drifted around on the internet, looking at things that came when he googled Khembalung. What he read often caused him to shake his head.

before the great guru Milarepa left Tibet for the Glorious Copper-Colored Mountain, he made a tour of Tibet, among other tasks finding hidden valleys, or beyuls

"Guru Rudra, what is a beyul?"

"Hidden valley."

"Like Khembalung?"

"Yes."

"But you were on an island?"

"Hidden valley moves from time to time. This what Rikdzin Godem say. He was guru who knew about hidden valleys. From Tsang, fourteen century. He talk about the Eight Great Hidden Valleys, but Khembalung seems to be only one ever visible. A refuge in the kaliyuga, fourth of the four ages. Iron age of degradation and despair."

"Is that what we're in?"

"Can't you tell?"

"Ha ha. What else did he say about them?"

"He say many things. He described how to get in. When it would be good to enter, what would be the omens. What say, the power places in Khembalung. The magic."

"Oh my. And what was that?"

"Like Khembalung as you saw it. A place for good. A buddhafield."

"Buddhafield?"

"A space where Buddhism is working."

"I see."

"Compassion increase, wisdom."

"And Khembalung was like that."

"Yes."

"And where was it, before your island?"

"At head of Arun valley. Phumchu, we call it in Tibetan. And over Tsibri La, into Tibet. That was the trouble."

"China?"

"Yes."

"Why is China so much trouble, do you think?"

"China is big. Like America."

"Ah. So you left there."

"Yes. South gate in a cave, downvalley to Darjeeling."

"Does anyone go through that hidden valley anymore?"

"They go through without seeing. Too busy!" A gravelly chuckle. "Buddhafield not always visible. In this case, Dorje Phakmo, the Adamantine Sow, lies along that valley."

"A pig?"

"Subtle body, hard to find."

Another time, because of that:

"So animals are kind of magical too?"

"Of course. Obvious when you see them, right?"

"True," Frank said. He told Rudra about his activities with FOG, including the arrival in Rock Creek park of the aurochs.

"Very good!" Rudra exclaimed. "I liked them."

"Uh-huhn. What about tigers?"

"Oh, I like them too. Very good animal. Scary, but good. They have scary masks, but really they are friendly helpers. At power places they are tame."

"Tame?"

"Tame. Friendly, helpful, courteous."

"Kind, obedient, cheerful, brave, clean, and reverent?"

"Yes. All those."

"Hmm."

Another time, Frank read a passage on his screen and said, "Rudra, are you *the* Rudra Cakrin, the one people write about?"

"No."

"You're not? There's more than one?"

"Yes. He is very old."

"Sixteen thousand years before the birth of Christ, it says here."

"Yes, very old. I am not that old." Gurgle. "Almost, but not."

"So are you some kind of bodhisattva?"

"No no. Not so good as that, no."

"But you are a lama, or what say, a tulku or what have you?"

"What have you, I guess. I am a voice."

"A voice?"

"You know. Vehicle for voice. Spirits seem to speak through me."

"Like in those ceremonies, you get taken over and say things?"

"Yes."

"That looks like it must hurt."

"Yes, it seems so. I don't remember what happens then. But afterward I often seem to be sore."

"Does it still happen?"

"Sometimes."

"Are you scheduled for a ceremony anytime soon?"

"No. You know—retired."

"Retired?"

"Is that not word? What say, get old, give up work?"

"Yes, that's retirement. I just didn't know that your kind of job allowed for retirement."

"Of course. Very hard job."

"I imagine so."

Frank googled "oracle, Tibetan Buddhist," and read randomly for a while. It was pretty alarming stuff. What always got him was how elaborated everything was in Tibetan Buddhism; it was not a simple thing, like he imagined American Protestant churches being, with their simple creeds, some vague tripartite divisions, and a relatively straightforward story about God's single visit to Earth. Instead, a vastly articulated system of gods and spirits, with complicated histories and interactions, and ongoing appearances in this world. The oracles when possessed would grow taller, lift enormously heavy costumes, cause medallions on their chest to bounce outward under the force of their elevated heartbeat. If certain powerful spirits entered the oracle, he had less than five minutes to live. Blood would gush from nose and mouth, bodies go completely rigid.

Maybe this was all a matter of adrenaline and endorphins. Maybe this was what the body was capable of when the mind was convinced of something. Oxytocined by the cosmic spirit. But in any case they were quite serious about it; to them it was real. "The system is so complex and multilayered that it operates with some degree of freedom." The mind, ordering the incoming data one way or another: different realities resulted. And what if they were evaluated on the basis of how they made one feel? On that basis there was certainly no justification to condescend to these people, no matter what strange things they said. They were in far better control of their feelings than Frank was, and often they seemed filled with joy.

Through all of March the winter stayed as cold and windy as ever. Twelve days in a row set record lows, and on March 23 it was twenty below at noon. Frank worried that any trees that had survived the worst of the winter would have their blooms killed in the frigid spring, and then where would they be? What would the East Coast be like if its great hardwood forest died? Would whole biomes collapse as a result, would agriculture itself be substantially destroyed? How would Europe feed itself? What might happen to Asia's already shaky food security? It seemed to him sometimes that a winter this severe might change things for good.

In this context the campaign for the presidential election looked more trivial than ever. Phil Chase wrapped up the Democratic nomination, the President's team upped the firepower of their attacks on him; the SSEEP virtual candidate caused trouble for everybody. Frank couldn't be bothered, and it seemed there were others like him out there. The long winter came first in the news and in people's thoughts.

In April the increasing length of the days became impossible to miss. Spring was here, snow or not. By the first of May there was so much more light that there simply had to be more heat; and then one day without warning it hit eighty degrees, and everything sweltered. The world steamed, thawed branches drooped, thawed pipes leaked, wires shorted, mold grew. Mosquitoes came back, and everyone began to wonder if the hard winter had really been that bad after all.

When Frank visited Rock Creek he found Cutter on Connecticut again, using his old orange cones and orange tape to clear space around a tree canted at a forty-five-degree angle.

"How's it going?"

"Pretty good! Spring has sprung!"

"Did the trees live?"

"Most of them yeah. Lot of dead branches. It'll make for a busy summer. I swear the forest gonna take over this city."

"I bet. Can I join you sometime?"

"Sure you can. Do you own a chainsaw?"

"No, can't say I do."

"That's all right. There's other help you can do."

"I can always drag wood away."

"Exactly."

"So where do you take the wood?"

"Oh all kinds of places. I take it to a friend and we cut it for firewood."

"And that's okay?"

"Oh sure. There's an awful lot of trees need trimming. Lot of it being done by freelancers. The city need help, and the wood can be the pay."

"It sounds like it works pretty well."

"Well . . ." Cutter laughed.

"Hey, did you ever find out anything more about Chessman?"

"No, not really. I asked Byron but he didn't know. He said he thought maybe he moved. There was a chess tournament up in New York he said Chessman talked about."

"About playing in it?"

"I don't know."

"Did Byron know his name?"

"He said he thought his name was Clifford."

All the branches sprouted with tiny buds of a vivid light green, a color Frank had never seen before, which glowed on cloudy days, and sparked in his peripheral vision like fireflies. Green buds on a wet black bough, life coming back to the forest. It could not have been more beautiful. No moment in a Mediterranean climate could ever match this moment of impossible green.

He started going over to the park again, while at the same time he felt less anxious about living at the embassy house.

And yet he never returned to feeling himself. His face was still numb, inside his nose and right below it, and behind it. When he was shaving he saw that the numb part of his upper lip looked inert, and thus to himself he seemed deformed. He could not smile properly. He didn't know how he felt about that. He supposed that the effect for others was slight, and that if noticed at all people did not talk about it, out of politeness.

The bros did not worry about that kind of thing. "Hey Jimmy! Jimmy Durante! How's it hanging, did your dick survive its frostbite? Did your nose heal straight? Can you breathe through it anymore?"

"No."

"HA ha ha. Hey mouthbreather! I knew you wouldn't be able to, the first time I saw it."

"So who were those guys anyway?" Frank asked again.

"Who the fuck knows? We never saw them again."

"Lucky for you."

"No lie."

"You guys could use a phone. Whip it out and 911 in situations like that."

"Yeah right!"

"So that being the case, I brought you all application cards so you can get into FOG, the zoo group."

"No way."

"They tell me the park is going to be regulated this summer, so you'll need to be a member to be able to stay in the park."

"You think the cops will act any different just because we got some card?"

"Yes, I do. Plus, they give you a cell phone if you're a member. It's a little party line, but it works."

"Oh good I always wanted a little party line!"

"Shut up and fill out the form here. Come on, you can put down any name you want. And it can't possibly break any parole agreements. No one's gonna throw you in jail for joining the Friends of the National Zoo."

"Ha ha! Who you saying is on parole?"

"Yeah who you saying is on parole? At least we got *noses*."

"Ha ha. Just fill out the form."

Coming up to their little closet, Frank heard someone in there talking to Rudra, and came up to the door curious to see who it was, as the old man seemed somewhat neglected in the house. But no one else was in there. Rudra started at the sight of Frank, stared up at him with an addled look, as if he had forgotten who Frank was.

"Sorry," Frank said. "I didn't mean to startle you."

"I am happy you did."

"Talking to yourself, were you?"

"Don't think so."

"I thought I heard somebody."

"Interesting. Sometimes I, what say . . . I sing to myself. One kind of Tibetan singing makes two sounds from one voice. Head note? Overtone?" He opened his mouth and emitted a bass note lower than Frank would have expected from such a slight body; and at the same time there was a scratchy harmonic floating in the room.

"Very nice," Frank said. "Like Louis Armstrong."

Rudra nodded. "Very fine singer." He opened his mouth again, sang deeply, "The odds, were a hundred to one against us," like Louis played at two-thirds normal speed.

"That's right, very good! So you like him?"

"Very fine singer. Head tone very strong."

"Interesting." Frank unrolled his groundpad, laid himself out.

"Go to park?"

"Yes."

"Find your friends?"

"Some of them." Frank began to describe them and the situation out there—the bros, the fregans, his own project. He lay down on his back and left the laptop off, and talked about the paleolithic, and how the brain had evolved to feel good because of certain stimuli caused by behaviors performed repeatedly in the two-million-year run-up to humanity; and how they should be able to feel good now by living a life that conformed as closely to those early behaviors as possible. Which was what he had been trying to do, in his life out in the park.

"Good idea!" Rudra said. "Original mind. This is Buddhism also."

"Yes? Well, I guess I'm not surprised. It seemed to me that you were talking about something like that when you spoke at NSF last year."

Rudra didn't appear to remember this talk, which had been such a shattering experience for Frank—a real paradigm buster, as Edgardo would say. Frank did not press the matter, feeling shy at admitting to the old man what a profound effect he had created, with what had apparently been an offhand comment. Instead he described to Rudra the ways in which he felt that prisoner's dilemma modeled ethics in a scientific way, how the games were scored and the strategies judged, and how, at the start of the winter, he had come to the tentative conclusion that it was best to pursue the strategy called always generous.

"Good idea," Rudra said. "But what are these *points*? Why play for *points*?"

"That's what Anna said too. You know—I don't know."

. . .

Frank was still pondering this when Sucandra and Padma clomped up the stairs to see how the old man was doing. "Cookies," Sucandra said, holding out a plate. "Fresh out of the oven."

He and Padma sat on the floor in the doorway, and the four of them ate sugar cookies like kids at a sleepover.

"These are good," Frank said. "I've been getting so hungry this winter."

"Oh yes," Sucandra said. "One gets much hungrier in the cold."

"And much colder when you're hungry," Padma added.

"Yes," Sucandra said. "We learned that both ways, didn't we?"

"Yes."

Frank looked at them. "The Chinese?"

"Yes," Sucandra said. "In their prison."

"How long?"

"Ten years."

Frank shook his head, trying to imagine this and failing. "How much did you get to eat?"

"A bowl of rice a day."

"Did people starve?" Frank said, looking at the remaining cookies on the plate.

"Yes," Sucandra said. "Died from hunger, died from cold."

Padma nodded. "Others survived, but lost their wits."

"Maybe we all did."

"Yes, no doubt."

"But I know who you mean. We had this old monk, you see, who was shitting some kind of tapeworm. Long red thing, segmented. Like millipede without legs. We knew this because he cleaned them up when it happened, and brought them to the group to offer to the rest of us as food."

"He claimed a Bön spirit was inside his body, making food for us."

Frank said, "So what did you do?"

"We chopped the worms up very fine and added them to the rice."

"No doubt it added some protein to our diet."

"Not much, it was more a gesture."

"But anything helped at that point."

"It's true. I kind of got to looking forward to it."

They grinned at each other, looked shyly at Frank.

"It helped us feel together. People need to be part of a group."

"And to help the old monk. He would get very distraught."

"But then he died."

"Yes, that's right. But then the rice seemed to be missing something!"

One morning, spring and all, like some May day they had assumed would never come again, Charlie drove out to Great Falls and met Frank and Drepung. Frank was going to teach them the basics of rock climbing.

Anna did not approve, but Frank assured her he would make it safe, and her risk assessment realism impelled her to concede it was probably all right. Charlie, disappointed that he had lost this best excuse to back out, now walked the short trail to the gorge, carrying a backpack of Frank's gear and a few tight loops of nylon rope. They came to a spot on the gorge cliff which Frank declared was the top of a good teaching route.

He uncoiled one length of rope and tied it off around the trunk of the tree. He pointed down the cliff. "See the flat spot down at the bottom? We can walk down to it, like on stairs, over here. Then you can climb the wall. It'll be like a climbing wall in a gym." They stood on the rim looking down at the river's white roil and rumble. "There's almost every kind of hold here," Frank continued. "Conveniently identified by chalk marks. I'll have you top-belayed the whole time, so even if you slip, you'll only bounce in place. The rope flexes, so you won't get cut in two. I'll have you jump off on purpose to see what it feels like."

Charlie and Drepung exchanged a glance. Apparently neither would die today as the result of being a bad student, something both had often been in their pasts. That established, they became happier and put on their harnesses cheerfully, indeed prone to sudden bursts of muffled hilarity. It was pretty lame, and Frank shook his head. Then they studied Frank's knots, and learned the simple but effective belaying systems used by climbers. Frank was very clear and businesslike in his explanations, and patient with their fumbling and misunderstanding. He had done this before.

When he seemed to feel they had absorbed the necessary minimum, he retied all their knots himself, then ran Charlie's rope through a carabiner tied to their tree and wrapped it around his waist. Charlie then carefully descended the staircase analog that ran down to a floor just above the river. Standing at the bottom Charlie turned to look up at Frank.

"Okay," Frank said, pulling the rope between them taut. "On belay."

"On belay," Charlie repeated. Then he started climbing, focusing on the wall and seeing it hold by hold. The chalk marks did indeed help. Monkey up the chalky knobs and nicks. He heard Frank's suggestions as if from a distance. Don't look down. Don't try to pull yourself up by the arms. Use your legs as much as possible. Keep three points attached at all times. Never lunge.

His toe slipped and he fell. *Boing,* fend off wall; bounce gently; he was okay. Relocate holds, get back to climbing. Was that all? Why, it wasn't anywhere near as bad as he had thought it would be! With such a system in place, there wasn't the slightest danger!

The way Frank failed to agree with this served to refocus Charlie's attention on the wall.

Some of what Charlie was doing resembled the scrambling he had done on backpacking trips in the Sierra. The motions were the same, but here they happened on a surface drastically more vertical than any he and his backpacking friends would have attempted. Indeed if he had ever wandered onto such a face during a scramble in the Sierra, he would have been paralyzed with fear.

But being top-roped really did remove most of the fear, and with it gone, there was room to notice other feelings. The action felt like a kind of acrobatics, unrehearsed and in slow motion. Charlie became absorbed in it for a long time, slowing down as the holds seemed scarcer, until his fingers began to hurt. For a while nothing existed except for the rock face and his search for holds. Once or twice Frank spoke, but mostly watched. The tug of his belay, while reassuring, did not actually pull Charlie up; and now he began to struggle, with only a final awkward lunge getting him up to the rim.

Very absorbing stuff! And now a surge of I'M STILL ALIVE was flowing through him. He saw how people might get hooked.

Then it was Drepung's turn. Charlie sat with his feet swinging over the edge, watching happily. From above Drepung looked bulky, and his expression as he searched the rock face was uncomfortable. Charlie had years of scrambling experience; Drepung did not. After hauling himself up the first few holds he looked down once, and after that he seemed a bit glued to the rock. He muttered something about a traditional Tibetan fear of falling, but Frank would have none of it. "That's a tradition everywhere, I assure you. Just focus on where you're at, and feel the belay. Jump off if you want to see how it'll feel."

"It seems I will get to find out soon enough."

He was slow, but he kept trying. His moves were pretty sure when they happened. His small mouth pursed in a perfect little O of concentration. In a few minutes he made it and hauled himself beside Charlie, uttering a happy "Ha."

Frank had them do it again, trying other routes on the face; then they belayed each other, nervously, with Frank standing beside the belayer making sure all was well. Lastly he had them rappel down, in a simple but scary operation like the old Batman, but for real. They practiced until their hands got too tired and sore to hold on to anything.

After that (it had taken a couple of hours) Frank changed his belay to another tree on the cliff top. "It looks like Juliet's Balcony and Romeo's Ladder survived the flood. I'm going to do one of those, or Gorky Park." He dropped away, leaving Charlie and Drepung sitting happily on the cliff's edge, kicking their heels against the rock and taking in the view. To their left the rearranged falls roared down its drops, every step along the way boiling whitely. Below them Frank was climbing slowly.

Suddenly Charlie leaped up shouting, "Where's Joe! Where's Joe!"

"Not here," Drepung reminded him. "With Anna today, remember?"

"Oh yeah." Charlie sank back down. "Sorry. I forgot."

"That's okay. I take it you are used to watching him."

"Yes."

Charlie sat back down, shaking his head. Slowly Frank ascended toward them. As he looked up for his next hold his face reminded Charlie of Buster Keaton; he had that same wary and slightly baffled look, ready for anything—unflappable, although *not* imperturbable, as his eyes revealed just as clearly as Keaton's that in fact he was perturbed most of the time.

Charlie had always had a lot of sympathy for Buster Keaton. Life as a string of astonishing crises; it seemed right to him. He said, "Drepung?"

"Yes?"

Charlie inspected his torn hand. Drepung held his own hand next to it; both were chewed up by the day's action.

"Speaking of Joe."

"Yes?"

Charlie heaved a sigh, feeling the worry that had built up in him. "I don't want him to be any kind of special person for you guys."

"What?"

"I don't want him to be a reincarnated soul."

". . . Buddhism says we are all such."

"I don't want him to be any kind of reincarnated lama. Not a tulku, or a bodhisattva, or whatever else you call it. Not someone your people would have any religious interest in at all."

Drepung inspected his palm. The skin was about the same color as Charlie's, maybe more opaque. Let that stand for us, Charlie thought. He couldn't tell what Drepung was thinking. Except he did seem at a loss.

This tended to confirm Charlie's suspicions. He said, "You know what happened to that new Panchen Lama."

"Yes . . ."

"So you know what I mean. They picked a little boy, and the Chinese took him and he has never been seen again."

Drepung nodded, looking upset. "That was bad."

"Tell me. Tell me what happened."

Drepung grimaced. "The Panchen Lama is the reincarnation of the Buddha Amitabha. He is the second most important spiritual leader in Tibetan Buddhism. His relationship with the Dalai Lama has always been complicated. The two were often at odds, but they also help to choose each other's successors. Then in the last couple of centuries the Panchen Lama has often been associated with Chinese interests, so it got even more complicated."

"Sure," Charlie said.

"So, when the tenth Panchen Lama died, in 1989, the identification of his next reincarnation was obviously a problem. Who would make the determination? The Chinese government told the Panchen Lama's monastery, Tashilhunpo, to find the new reincarnation. So, that was proper, but they also made it clear they would have final approval of the choice."

"Of course."

"So Chadrel Rimpoche, the head of Tashilhunpo, contacted the Dalai Lama in secret, to get his help, as was proper in the tradition. His group had already identified several children in north Tibet as possibilities. So the Dalai Lama performed divinations to discover which of them was the new Panchen Lama. He found that it was a boy living near Tashilhunpo. The signs were clear. But now the question was, how were they going to get that candidate approved by the Chinese, while also hiding the involvement of the Dalai Lama."

"Couldn't Chadrel Rimpoche just tell the Chinese that's who it was?"

"Well, but the Chinese had introduced a system of their own. It involved a thing called the Golden Urn. The three top names are put into this urn, and the name drawn from the urn is the correct one."

"What?" Charlie cried. "They draw the name out of a hat?"

"Out of an urn. Yes."

"But that's crazy! I mean presumably if there is a reincarnated lama in one of these kids, he is who he is! You can't be drawing a name from a hat."

"One would suppose. But the Chinese have never been averse to harming Tibetan traditions, as you know. Anyway, in this case the Dalai Lama's divination found a boy in a region under Chinese control, so it seemed as if chances for Chinese approval were fairly good. But there was concern that the Chinese would use the urn to deliberately choose someone other than the one Chadrel Rimpoche recommended."

"Sure. And so?"

"And so, the Dalai Lama decided to announce the identity of the boy, thinking that the Chinese would then be pressured to conform to Tibetan wishes, but be satisfied that it was a boy living under their control."

"Oh no," Charlie said. "I'm surprised anyone could have thought that, knowing the Chinese."

Drepung sighed. "It was a gamble. The Dalai Lama must have felt that it was the best chance they had."

"But it didn't work."

"No."

"So what happened to the boy?"

"He and his parents were taken into custody. Chadrel Rimpoche also."

"Where are they now?"

"No one knows."

"Now see? I don't want Joe to be any part of that sort of thing!"

Drepung sighed. Finally he said, "The Panchen Lama is a special case, very highly politicized, because of the Chinese. Many returned lamas are identified without any such problems."

"I don't care! You can't be sure whether it will get complicated or not."

"No Chinese are involved in this."

"I don't care!"

Drepung hunched forward, as if to say, What can I do, I can't do anything.

"Look," Charlie said. "It's upsetting Anna. She doesn't believe in anything you can't see or quantify, you know that. It upsets her even to try. If there's this kind of stuff about Joe, it will freak her out. She's trying not to think about it right now, and even that is freaking her out. She's not good at not thinking about things. She thinks about things."

"I'm sorry."

"You should be. I mean, think of it this way. If she hadn't befriended you guys like she did when you first came here, then you would never even have known Joe existed. So in effect you are punishing Anna for her kindness to you."

Drepung pursed his lips unhappily. He looked like he had while climbing.

"Besides," Charlie pressed, "the whole idea that your kid is somehow not just, you know, your kid—that he's someone else somehow—that in itself is upsetting. Offensive, one might even say. I mean he is a reincarnation already, of me and Anna."

"And your ancestors."

"Right, true. But anyone else, no."

"Hmmm."

"You see what I mean? How it feels?"

"Yes." Drepung nodded, rocking his whole body. "Yes, I do."

They sat there, looking down at the river. A lone kayaker was working her way upstream against the white flow. Below them Frank, who was standing by the shore again, was staring at her.

Charlie gestured down at Frank. "He seems interested."

"Indeed he does."

They watched Frank watch her.

"So," Charlie persevered, "maybe you could talk to Rudra Cakrin about this. See if there is some kind of, I don't know, exorcism he can do. Just some kind of I don't know what. A re-individuation ceremony. To clear him out, and, well—leave him alone. Are there such ceremonies?"

"Well . . . in a manner of speaking, yes. I suppose."

"So will you talk to Rudra about doing it? Maybe just without much fanfare, so Anna doesn't know about it?"

Drepung was frowning. "If she doesn't know, then . . ."

"Then it would be for me. Yes. For me and Joe. It would get to Anna by way of us. Why, does it have to be public?"

"No no. It's not that."

"What—you don't want to talk to Rudra about it?"

"Well . . . Rudra would not actually be the one to decide about such a matter."

"No?" Charlie was surprised. "Who then? Someone back in Khembalung, or Tibet?"

Drepung shook his head.

"Well who then?"

Drepung lifted his hand as if to inspect it again. He pointed the bloodied thumb at himself. Looked at Charlie.

Charlie shifted to get a better look at him. "What, you?"

Drepung nodded with his body again.

Charlie laughed shortly. All of a sudden many things were becoming clear. "Why you rascal you!" He gave the young man a light shove. "You guys have been running a scam on us the whole time."

"No no. Not a scam."

"So what is Rudra then, some kind of servant, some old retainer you're doing a prince-and-pauper switch with?"

"No, not at all. He is a tulku too. But not so, that is to say, in the Khembali order there are also relationships between tulkus, like the ones between the Dalai Lama and the Panchen Lama."

"So you're the boss, you're saying."

Drepung winced. "I am the one the others regard as, you know. Leader."

"Spiritual leader? Political leader?"

Drepung wiggled a hand.

"What about Padma and Sucandra?"

"They are in effect like regents, or they were. Like my brothers now, advisors. They tell me so much."

"I see. And so you stay behind the scenes here."

"Or in front of the scenes. The greeter."

"Both in front and behind."

"Yes."

"Very clever. It's just what I thought all along."

"Really?"

"No. I thought Rudra spoke English."

Drepung nodded. "His English is not so bad. He has been studying. Though he does not like to admit it."

"But listen, Drepung—you do these kinds of switches and cover stories because you know it's a little dangerous out there, right? Because of the Chinese?"

Drepung pursed his lips. "Well . . ."

"And think about it like this—*you* know what it means to suddenly be called someone else! You must!"

At this Drepung blinked. "Yes. It's true. My mother was never really reconciled. She would put my hand on her and say, 'You came from here.'"

"What do they think now?"

"They are no longer in those bodies."

"Ah." He seemed young to have lost both parents. But who knows what they had lived through. Charlie said, "But you know what I'm talking about."

"Yes."

For a long time they sat in the misty rumble of the Great Falls, looking down at Frank, who had now unclipped from his rope and was walking over the jumbled rocks by the water, attempting, it appeared, to keep the kayaker in sight as she approached the foot of the falls proper.

Charlie pressed on. "Will you do something about this then?"

Drepung rocked again. Charlie was beginning to wonder if it signaled assent or not. "I'll see what I can do."

"Now don't you be giving me that!"

"What? Oh! Oh, no, no—I meant it for real!"

They both laughed, thinking about Phil Chase and his *I'll see what I can dos.* "They all say it," Charlie complained.

"Well, they *are* seeing what they can do. You must give them that."

"I don't give them that. They're seeing what they *can't* do."

Drepung waggled a hand. He too had had to put people off, Charlie saw. They leaned out to try to spot Frank.

As they peered down, Charlie found that he felt better. Talking with someone else about it had eased his sense of isolation. He wasn't used to having something he couldn't talk to Anna about.

And the news that Drepung was the true power in Khembali affairs, once he got over it, was actually quite reassuring. Rudra Cakrin was, when all was said and done, a strange old man. It was far better to have someone he knew and trusted in charge of this business.

"I'll talk to Rudra Cakrin about it," Drepung said.

"I thought you said he was a front man."

"No no. A . . . a colleague. I need to consult with him, for sure. For one thing he would probably conduct the ceremony. He is the oracle. That means he will know which ceremonies. There are some precedents. Certain accidents, mistakes rectified . . . there are some things I can look into."

Charlie nodded. "Good. Remember Anna welcoming you to NSF."

"Yes." Drepung grimaced. "Actually, the oracle told us to go there."

"Come on, what, he said, 'Move to 4201 Wilson Boulevard'?"

"Not exactly."

"No I guess not! Well, whatever. Just remember how Anna feels. It's probably very much like your mom felt."

Charlie was surprised to hear himself going for the jugular like that. Then he thought of Joe clutching at him, frightened and pitiful, and his mouth clenched. He wanted all this business cleared away. The fever would then also leave.

They watched the river roil by. White patches on black water.

"Look—it looks like Frank is trying to catch that kayaker's attention."

"It sure does."

The woman was now resting, paddle flat across the kayak in front of her, gliding downstream. Frank was hurrying downstream to stay abreast of her, stumbling once or twice on the rocky bank, hands to his mouth to cup shouts out to her. He started waving his arms up and down. He came to a flatter patch and ran to get ahead of her. He semaphored with his arms, megaphoned with his hands, jumped up and down.

"He must know that person?"

"Or something. But she must be hearing him, don't you think?"

"It seems like it. Seeing him too, for that matter. She must not want to be interrupted."

"I guess."

It was hard to see how she couldn't be noticing him, which meant she must be ignoring him. She floated on, and he continued to chase her, scrambling over boulders now, shouting still.

She never turned her head. A big boulder blocked Frank's way and he slipped, went to his knees, held out his arms; but now she was past him, and did not look back.

Finally his arms fell. Head bowed, shoulders slumped: the very figure of a man whose hopes have been dashed.

Charlie and Drepung looked at each other.

"Do you think that Frank is seeming kind of . . ."

"Yes."

CHAPTER 19

LEAP BEFORE YOU LOOK

Frank dropped by the Quiblers' on a Saturday morning to pick up Nick and go to the zoo. He got there early and stood in the living room while they finished their breakfast. Charlie, Anna, and Nick were all reading as they ate, and so Joe stared at the back of his cereal box with a look of fierce determination, as if trying to crack the code of this staring business by sheer force of will. Seeing it Frank's heart went out to him, and he circled the table and crouched by him to chat.

At the zoo Frank and Nick first attended a workshop devoted to learning how to knap rocks into blades and arrowheads. Frank had noticed this on the FONZ website and of course had been very interested, and Nick was up for anything. So they sat on the ground with a young ranger who reminded Frank of Robin. This man wandered around, crouching to show each cluster how to hit the cores with the breaker stones so that they would flake properly. With every good knap he yelled, "Yeah!" or "Good one!"

It was the same process used to make Frank's Acheulian hand axe, although their modern results were less shapely, and of course the newly cracked stone looked raw compared to the patina that burnished the old axe's broken surfaces. No matter—it was a joy to try, as satisfying as looking into a fire. It was one of those things you knew how to do the first time you tried it.

Frank was happily knapping away a protrusion on the end of a core, enjoying the clacks and chinks and the smell of sparks and rock dust in sunlight, when he and Nick both smashed their hands at the same time. Nick's chin trembled and Frank growled as he clutched his throbbing thumb. "Oh man. My nail is going to be purple, dang it! What about yours?"

"Forefinger," Nick said. "Middle knuckle."

The ranger came over grinning. "That, gentlemen, is what we call the granite kiss. Anyone in need of a Band-Aid?"

Frank and Nick declined.

After they were done they went over to look at the gibbons and siamangs.

All the feral primates had either died or been returned to the zoo. This morning Bert and May and their surviving kids were out in the triangular gibbon enclosure. They only let out one family at a time. Frank and Nick joined the small crowd at the railing to observe. The people around them were mostly young parents with toddlers. "Mon-key! Mon-key!"

Bert and May were relaxing in the sun as they had so many times before, on a small platform just outside the tunnel to their inside room. Nothing in the sight of them suggested that they had spent much of the previous year running wild in Rock Creek Park. May was grooming Bert's back, intent, absorbed, dexterous. Bert seemed zoned out. Never did they meet the gaze of their human observers. Bert shifted to get the back of his head under her fingers, and she immediately obliged, parting his hair and closely inspecting his scalp. Then something caused him to give her a light slap, and she caught his hand and tugged at it. She let go and climbed the fence to intercept one of their kids, and suddenly those two were playing tag. When they passed Bert he cuffed at them, so they turned around and gang-tackled him. When he had disentangled himself from the fray he swung up the fence to the south corner of the enclosure, where it was possible to reach through and pull leaves from a tree. He munched a leaf, fended off one of the passing kids with an expert backhand.

It seemed to Frank that they were restless. It wasn't obvious; at first glance they appeared languid, melting into their positions even when hanging from the fence. So they looked mellow. But after a while it became evident that every ten minutes they were doing something else. Racing around the fence, eating, grooming, rocking; they never did anything for more than a few minutes.

Now the younger son raced around the top of the fence, then cast himself into space in a seemingly suicidal leap, but crashed into the canvas loop that crossed the cage just above the ground, hitting it with both arms and thus breaking his fall sufficiently to avoid broken bones. Clearly it was a leap he had made many times before, after which he always ran over to hit his dad.

Wrestling on the grass. Did Bert remember wrestling his elder son on that same spot? Did the younger son remember his brother? Their faces, even while tussling, were thoughtful and grave. They looked like animals who had seen a lot. This may have just been an accident of physiognomy.

Some teenagers came by and hooted inexpertly, hoping to set the animals off. "They only do that at dawn," Nick reminded Frank; despite that, they joined the youths' effort. The gibbons did not. The teenagers looked a bit surprised at Frank's expertise. Oooooooooooop! Oop oop ooooop!

Now Bert and May rested on their porch. Bert looked at the empty food basket, one long-fingered thumbless hand idly grooming May's stomach. She lay flat on her back, looking bored. From time to time she batted Bert's hand. It looked like the stereotypical dynamic: male groping female who can't be bothered. But when May got up she suddenly bent and shoved her butt at Bert's face. He looked for a second, leaned in and licked her; pulled back; smacked his lips like a wine taster. No doubt he could tell exactly where she was in her cycle.

The humans above watched without comment. After a while Nick suggested checking out the tigers, and Frank agreed.

Walking down the path to the big cat island, the image of May grooming Bert stuck in Frank's mind. White-cheeked gibbons were monogamous. Several primate species were. Bert and May had been a couple for over twenty years, more than half their lives. Bert was thirty-six, May thirty-two.

When a human couple first met, they presented a facade of themselves to the other, a performance of the part of themselves they thought made the best impression. If both fell in love, they entered a space of mutual regard, affection, lust; it swept them off their feet, yes, so that they walked on air, yes.

But if the couple then moved in together, they quickly saw more than just the performance that up to that point was all they knew. At this point they either both stayed in love, or one did while one didn't, or they both fell out of love. Because reciprocity was so integral to the feeling, mostly one could say *that they either stayed in love or they fell out of it. In fact, Frank wondered, could it even be called love if it were one-sided, or was that just some kind of need, or a fear of being alone, so that the one "still in love" had actually fallen out of love also, into denial of one sort or another? Frank had done that himself. No, true love was reciprocal; one-way love, if it existed at all, was some other emotion, like saintliness or generosity or devotion or goodness or pity or ostentation or virtue or need or fear. Reciprocal love was different from those. So when you fell in love with someone else's presentation it was a huge risk, because it was a matter of chance whether on getting to know one another you both would stay in love with the larger, more various characters who emerged from behind the masks.*

Bert and May were past that problem.

The swimming tigers were flaked out in their enclosure, lying like any other cats in the sun. Tigers were not monogamous. They were in effect solitaries, who went their own ways and crossed paths only to mate. Moms kicked out their cubs after a couple of years, and all went off on their own.

These two, however, had been thrown together, as if by fate. Swept out to sea in the same flood, rescued by the same ship, kept in the same enclosure. Now the male rested his big head on the female's back. He licked her fur from time to time, then plopped his chin on her spine again.

Maybe there was a different way of coming to love. Spend a lot of time with a fellow traveler; get to know them across a large range of behaviors; then have that knowledge ripen into love.

The swimming tigers looked content. At peace. No primate ever looked that peaceful. Nick and Frank went to get snow cones. Frank always got lime; Nick got a mix of root beer, cherry, and banana.

The Khembali house stayed busy. It jumped with a sense of crammed life that to Frank felt surreal. Sometimes it was very obvious that a whole town had moved into a single house. Sometimes as he sat in a corner of the big kitchen, peeling potatoes or drying dishes, he would look at all the industrious faces, cheerful or harried as they might be, and think: This is almost entertaining. Other times the tumult would get to him and his train of thought would leave the room and return to the forest in his mind. It was dark in that particular parcellation, the sound of the wind in the trees always there. The leaves and the stars and the creek were peaceful company.

"People are so crazy," he would say to Rudra Cakrin.

"Ha ha."

Some nights he stayed late at work, working on his list or talking on the phone to a contact of Diane's in Moscow, a Dmitri. Late night in D.C. was midday in Moscow, and Frank could call to discuss the Russians' carbon capture plans. Dmitri's English was excellent. He claimed that no decisions had been made about interventions of any kind.

After these conversations Frank sometimes just slept there on his office couch, as he had planned to back at the beginning. It was comfortable enough, but now Frank found he missed his conversations with Rudra Cakrin. No other part of the day held as many surprises. Even talking to Diane or Dmitri wasn't as surprising, and the two D's were pretty surprising. Sometimes Frank found himself jealous; Diane and Dmitri were old friends, and Frank could hear her voice take on the quality it had when one great power was speaking to another. Dmitri had carte blanche to experiment with one-sixth of the land surface of the Earth. That was power; there were bound to be surprises there.

Even so, Rudra was more surprising. One night Frank was lying on his groundpad in the light of his laptop, trying to tell Rudra again about the impact the old man's lecture at NSF had had on him. He asked about the particular sentence that had acted on him like a sort of catalyst—"An excess of reason is itself a form of madness"—but Rudra only snorted.

"Milarepa say that, because his guru beat him all the time, and always for a reason. So Milarepa never think much of reason. But why should you? Hardly anyone ever use reason."

"I guess not." Frank described what had happened to him after hearing the phrase, venturing that Zen koans or paradigm busters caused actual physical changes in the brain, leading to new parcellations that reorganized both conscious and unconscious thought. "Then on the way to the Quiblers I got stuck with a woman in an elevator, I'll tell you about that some other time. . . ."

"Dakini!" Rudra said, eyes gleaming.

"Maybe," Frank said, googling the word—some kind of female Tantric spirit—"anyway meeting her convinced me I had to stay in D.C. another year, and yet I had already put a bad resignation letter in Diane's in-box. So I decided I had to get it back, and the only way to do it was to break into the building through the skylight and go into her office through the window."

"Good idea," Rudra said. For the first time it occurred to Frank that when Rudra said this he might not always mean it. An ironic oracle: another surprise.

Another time Rudra knocked his water glass over and said, "Karmapa!"

"Karmapa, what's that, what say, three jewels?"

"Yes. Name of founder of Karma Kagyu sect."

"So, like saying Christ or something."

"Yes."

"You Buddhists are pretty mellow with the curses, I guess that makes sense. It's all like 'Heavens to Betsy'!"

Rudra grinned. "Gyakpa zo!"

"What's that one?"

"Eat shit."

"Whoah, okay then! Pretty good."

"What about you, what you say?"

"Oh, we say eat shit also, although it's pretty harsh. Then, like 'God damn you' or whatever . . ."

"Means maker of universe? Condemn to hellworld?"

"Yeah, I guess that's right."

"Pretty harsh!"

"Yes," laughing, "and that's one of the mild ones."

Another night, shockingly warm, the house stuffy and murmurous, creaking under the weight of its load, Frank complained, "Couldn't we move out to the garden shed or something?"

"Garden shed?" Rudra said, holding up his hands to make a box.

"Yes, the little building out back. Maybe we could move out there."

"I like that."

Frank was surprised again. "It would be cold."

"Cold," Rudra said scornfully. "No *cold*."

"Well. Maybe not for you. Or else you haven't been outside lately at night. It was as cold as I've ever felt it, back in February."

"Cold," Rudra said, dismissing the idea. "Test for oracle, see if Dorje truly visits, one spends night naked by river with many wet sheets. Wear sheets through the night, see how many one can dry."

"Your body heat would dry out a wet sheet?"

"Seven in one night."

"Okay, well, let's ask about the shed then. I need to move outdoors."

"Good idea."

Frank added that to his list of Things to Do, and when the house mother got time to look at the shed with him, she was quick to approve. She wanted their closet, to house two elderly nuns who had just arrived.

The shed was dilapidated in the extreme. It stood in the back corner of the lot under a big tree, and the leaf fall had destroyed the shingles. Frank swept off some of the mulch and tarped over the roof, with a promise to it to make proper repairs in the summer. Inside its one room they moved two old single beds, a bridge table with a lamp, two chairs, and a space heater.

Immediately Frank felt better.

"Nice to lose things," Rudra commented.

Frank quoted Emersonfortheday: " 'One is rich in proportion to the things one doesn't need.' "

"We seem to be getting very rich."

The Khembalis' vegetable garden lay outside their door. It was obses-sively tended, even in winter, and now that spring was here the black soil was dotted everywhere by new greens. By day the garden was filled with elderly Khembalis weeding and gossiping. Frank joined Rudra and this group for a couple of hours on Sunday mornings, puttering about in the usual gardening way. Rudra spoke to the others in quick Tibetan, not try-ing to keep Frank in the conversation. Frank was still trying to learn, but the language's origins were not Indo-European, and it seemed to Frank very alien. To compound his difficulties, Khembali was an eastern dialect of Tibetan. It made for slow going. It was embarrassing that Anna was still better at it.

The lengthening days got fuller. Optimodal, then work; run at lunch when he could get away, then back to work; in the evenings over to the park for a frisbee run, passing the bros and catching a brief burst of their rambunc-tious assholery; then to a restaurant, often an impulse stop; then back to the house, to help where he could, usually the final cleanup in the kitchen. By the time he went out to the shed and Rudra, he was almost asleep.

Rudra was usually sitting up in bed. Sometimes he seemed to be day-dreaming. He seemed attentive to the quality of Frank's silences. Some-times he watched Frank without actually listening to him. Frank found that unnerving—although sometimes, when he quit talking and sat on his bed, reading or tapping away at his laptop, he became aware of a feeling that seemed in the room rather than in himself, of peacefulness and calm. It emanated from the old man. Rudra would watch him, or space out; per-haps emit a few bass notes, with their head tones buzzing in a harmonic fifth. Meditation, Rudra said once when asked. What might meditation be said to be doing? Could one disengage the active train of consciousness, leaving only awareness? Without falling asleep? And what then was the mind doing? Was the deep thinking in the unconscious continuing to cog-itate in its own hidden way, or did it too calm down? Was there someone there, below the radar, walking the halls of the parcellated mind?

God he hoped so. It was either that or else he was zoning through his days in a haze of indecision. It could be that too.

He was almost asleep one night when his cell phone beeped, and he roused to answer it, knowing it was her.

"Frank it's me."

"Hi." His heart was pounding. The sound of her voice had the effect of cardiac paddles slapped to his chest: it was frightening to feel so much.

"Can you meet?"

"Yeah sure."

"I know you're in Arlington. The Lincoln Memorial, in an hour?"

"Sure."

"Not on the front steps. Around the back, between it and the river."

"Isn't that still fenced off?"

"South of that, then. South of the bridge then, on the new levee path."

"Okay."

"Okay see you."

Rudra turned out to have been sitting up in the gloom. Now he was looking at Frank as if he'd understood every word, as why not; it had not been a complicated conversation.

Frank said, "I'm going out."

"Yes."

"I'll be back later."

"Back later." Then, as Frank was leaving: "Good luck!"

The banks of the Potomac between the Watergate and the Tidal Basin had been rebuilt with a broad levee just in from the river, topped by a path running under a double row of cherry trees. The Corps of Engineers had displayed their usual bravura style, and the new cherry trees were enormous. Under them at night Frank felt dwarfed, and the entire scene took on a kind of pharaonic monumentalism, as if he had been transported to the banks of the Nile.

He stopped to look over the water to Theodore Roosevelt Island, where during the great flood he had seen Caroline in a boat, motoring upstream. That vision stood like a watermark in his mind. He had never remembered to ask her what she had been doing that afternoon. She had stood alone at the wheel, looking straight ahead: sometimes life became so dreamlike, everything felt heraldic or archetypal, etched since the beginning of time, so that one could only perform actions that already existed. Ah God, these meetings with Caroline made him feel so strange, so alive and somehow more-than-alive. He would have to ask Rudra about the nature of that feeling, if he could find some way to convey it. See if there was a Buddhist mental realm it corresponded to.

There under the new trees stood the Korean War Memorial. Caroline emerged from these trees, saw him and waved. She hurried up the next set of broad shallow steps, and there under the cherry trees they embraced. She hugged him hard. Her body felt tense, and out here in the open he felt apprehensive himself. "Let's go back to my van," he suggested. "It's too open here."

"No," she said, "your van chip is on active record now."

"So they know I'm here?"

"It's being recorded. There's comprehensive coverage in D.C. now. So they know where you drive. But they don't know I'm here."

"Are you sure?"

"Yes. As sure as I can be." She shivered.

He held her by the arm. "You're not chipped?"

"No. I don't think so. Neither of us is."

She took a wand from her pocket, checked them both. No clicks. They walked under the cherry trees, dark overhead against the city's night cloud. There were a few solitaries out, mostly runners, then another couple, possibly trysting like Frank and Caroline.

"How can you stand it?" Frank said.

"How does anybody stand it? We're all chipped."

"But most people, no one wants to trace them."

"I don't know if that's true. The banks want to know. That means most people." She shrugged; just the way things were. Best not to want privacy.

But now, under the cherry trees, they were alone. No cars, no chips, phones left in their cars. They were off the net. No one else in the world knew where they were at that moment. It was somewhat like being in their little bubble universe of passion. A walking version of that union. Frank felt her upper arm press against his, felt the flushing in his skin, the quickened pulse. It must be love, he thought. Even with Marta it had never been like this. Or was it perhaps just the element of danger that enveloped Caroline?

They sat on one of the benches overlooking the Tidal Basin. For a while they kissed. The feeling that poured through Frank then had less to do with their caresses, ravishing as they were, than with the sense of sharing a feeling; the opening up to one another, the vulnerability of giving and receiving. Very possibly, Frank thought in one of their hard silent hugs, their histories had caused them both to want more than anything else this feeling of commitment. After all the bad things that had happened, to be with someone, to let down one's guard, to inhabit a shared space . . . Them against the world. Or outside the world. Maybe she was like him in this: that she wanted a partner. He could not be certain. But it felt like it.

She curled against him. Frank warmed to her manner, her physical grace, her affection. It was different with her, it just was.

But she wasn't free. Her situation was compromised, even scary. She was breaking promises both personal and professional. That in itself didn't bother Frank as perhaps it should have, because she was doing it for him. Especially since she also made him feel that somehow he deserved it, that she liked him for real reasons. That she was right to do what she was doing, because of the way he was to her. Reciprocity, hard to believe: but there she was.

The world seeped back. A distant streetlight winked on the breeze.

"You're staying with those friends again?"

She nodded into his shoulder. Her body felt like she was falling asleep. He found this very moving; he could not remember the last time a woman had fallen asleep in his arms. He thought, Maybe this is what it would be like. You would only ever know by doing it.

"Hey gal. What if one of your friends wakes up in the night?"

"I told you. I left a note on the couch, saying that I couldn't sleep and went for a run."

"Ah." It was interesting to think of friends who would believe that.

"But I should start back in a while."

"Damn."

She sighed. "We need to talk."

"Good."

"Tell me—do you think elections matter?"

"What? Well, sure. I mean, what do you mean?"

"I mean, do you think they really matter?"

"Hmmm," Frank said.

"Because I'm not sure they do. I think they're just a kind of theater, you know, designed to distract people from how things are really decided."

"You sound like some of my colleagues at work."

"I'm being very scientific, I'm sure." Her smile was brief and perfunctory. "You know this futures market I'm supervising?"

"Sure. What, are they betting on the election now?"

"Of course, but you can do that anywhere. What my group is betting on has more to do with side effects of the election. Only now it's more like causes."

"What do you mean?"

"There are people who can influence the results."

"How do you mean?"

"Like, a group involved with voting machine technology."

"Uh oh. You mean like tweaking them somehow?"

"Exactly."

"So your futures market is now going bullish on certain people involved with voting technology?"

"That's right. And not only that, but those people include my husband and his colleagues."

"He's not doing what you're doing?"

"Not anymore. He's moved again, and his new job is part of this stuff. This group may even be the originators of it."

"A government agency working on fixing elections? How can that be?"

"That's the way it's evolved. The voting system is vulnerable to tampering, so there are agencies trying to figure out every way it can happen, so they can counter them. They pass that up the chain, and then one of the more politicized agencies takes that information and puts it in the right hands at the right time. And there you have it."

"You sound like it's happened already before?"

"Hard to say. Maybe so."

"Jesus. So how does it work, do you know?"

"Not the technical details. I know they target certain counties in swing states. They use various statistical models and decision-tree algorithms to pick which ones, and how much to intervene."

"I'd like to see this algorithm."

"Yes, I thought you might." She reached into her purse, pulled out a thumb drive. She handed it to him. "This is it."

"Whoah," Frank said, staring at it. "What should I do with it?"

"I thought you might have some friends who could put it to use."

"Shit. I don't know."

She watched him take it in.

"Do you think it matters?" she asked again.

"What, who wins the election, or whether there's cheating?"

"Both. Either."

"Well. I should think election fraud is always bad."

"I suppose."

"How could it not be?"

"I don't know. It may have been mostly cheating for a while now. Or theater at best. Distracting people from where the decisions are really made."

"But something like this would be more than theater."

"So you think it does matter?"

"Well . . . yeah." Frank was a little shocked that she would even wonder about it. "It's the law. I mean, the rule of law."

"I suppose so." She shrugged. "I mean, here I am giving this to you, so I must think so too. So, well—can you help fix it?"

He squeezed the little thumb drive. "Fix the fix?"

"Yes."

"I'd like to, sure. I don't know if I can."

"It'd be a matter of programming. Reprogramming."

"Sounds good. I can't do it. But I do have a friend at NSF who does encryption, now that I think of it, and he worked at DARPA. He's a mathematician, he might be able to help. Does your futures market list him? Edgardo Alfonso?"

"I don't know. I'll look."

"What about anyone else at NSF?"

"Yeah sure. Lots of NSF people. Diane Chang's stock is pretty high right now, for that matter."

"Is that right?"

"Yes." She watched him think it over.

Finally he shrugged. "Maybe saving the world is profitable."

"Or unprofitable."

"Hmmmmm. Listen, if you could get me a list of everyone listed in my market, that would be great. If Edgardo isn't on the list, all the better."

"I'll check. He would be discreet?"

"Yes. He's a friend, I trust him. And to tell the truth, he would greatly enjoy hearing about this."

She laughed briefly. "He likes bad news?"

"Very much."

"He must be a happy guy these days."

"Yes."

"Okay. But don't tell too many people about this. Please."

"No. But the ones I do may want to get into this program."

"Sure, I know. I've been thinking about that. It'll be hard to do without anyone knowing it's been done." She scowled. "In fact I can't think of a good way. *I* might have to do it. You know. At home."

"Listen, Caroline," he said, spooked by the look on her face. "I hope you aren't taking any chances here!"

She frowned. "What do you think this is? I told you, he's strange."

"Shit." He hugged her hard.

After a while she shrugged in his grasp. "Let's just do this and see what we see. I'm as clean as I can be. I don't think he has any idea what I've been up to. I've made it look like I'm chipped twenty-four/seven and that I'm not doing anything. I can only really get away at night, when he expects me to be sleeping. I leave the whole kit in the bed and then I can do what I need to. But if I dropped the kit, it would show something was wrong. So, you know. So far so good."

"No one suspects you of anything?"

"Not of anything more than marital alienation. There are some friends who know about that. But it's been going on for years. No. No one suspects."

"Even if they're in the business of having that kind of idea?"

"No. They think they know it all. They think I'm just . . . But it's gone so far past what they can know. Don't you understand? The technical capacity has expanded so fast, no one's really grasped the full potential of it yet."

"Maybe they have. You seem to have."

"But no one's listening to me."

"But there could be others like you."

"True. That may be happening too. There are superblacks now that are essentially flying free. But hopefully we won't run into one."

"Into a different one, you mean." If her husband thought his secrets were entirely safe from an estranged wife who did nothing more than sullenly perform her midlevel tech job, then maybe they could investigate without tripping any alarms. He didn't really know; counterintelligence was dark stuff, a secret field.

They sat side by side, uneasy. Around them the city pulsed and whirred in its dreams. Such a diurnal species; here they were, surrounded by five million people, but all of them conked like zombies, leaving them in the night alone.

She nudged into his shoulder. "I should go."

"Okay."

They kissed briefly. Frank felt a wave of desire, then fear. "You'll call?"

"I'll call. I'll call your Khembali embassy."

"Okay good. Don't be too long."

"I won't. I never have been."

"That's true."

They got up and hugged. He watched her walk off. When he couldn't see her anymore he walked back up the levee path. A runner passed going the other way, wearing orange reflective gloves. After that Frank was alone in the vast riverine landscape. The view up the Mall toward the Capitol was as of some stupendous temple's formal garden. The smell of Caroline's hair was still in his nostrils, preternaturally clear and distinct. He was afraid for her.

Frank drove back to NSF and slept in his van, or tried to. Upstairs early the next morning, feeling stunned and unhappy, he looked at the thumb drive Caroline had given him. Clearly he had to do something with it. He was afraid to put it in his computer. Who knew what it would trigger or wreak or connect to.

He could put it in a public computer. He could turn off his laptop's transmitter permanently. He could buy a cheap laptop and never airport it at all. He could . . .

He went for a run with Edgardo. When they got to the narrow path that ran alongside Highway 66, he said, "Edgardo, do you think the election matters?"

"What, the presidential election?"

"Yes."

Edgardo laughed, prancing for a few strides to express his joy fully. "Frank, you amaze me! What a good question!"

"But you know what I mean."

"No, not at all. Do you mean, will it make a difference which of these candidates takes office? Or do you mean elections in general are a farce?"

"Both."

"Oh, well. I think Chase would do better than the President on climate."

"Yes."

"But elections in general? Maybe they don't matter. But still let's say they are good. Good soap opera, at least, but also they are symbols, and symbolic action is still action. We need the illusion they give us, that we understand things and have some control. I mean, in Argentina, when elections went away, you really noticed how different things felt. As if the law had gone. Which it had. No, elections are good. It's voters who are bad."

Frank said, "That's interesting. I mean—if *you* think they matter, then I find that reassuring."

"You must be very easily reassured."

"Maybe I am. I wouldn't have thought so."

"You're lucky if you are. But—why do you need reassurance?"

"I've got a thumb drive back in my office that I'd like to show you. But I'm afraid it might be dangerous."

"Dangerous to the election?"

"Yes. Exactly."

"Oh ho." Edgardo ran on a few strides. "May I ask who gave it to you?"

"A friend in another agency."

"Aha! Frank, I am surprised at you. But this town is so full of spooks, I guess you can't avoid them. The first rule when you meet one is to run away, however." Edgardo considered it. "Well, I could put it in a laptop I have."

"You wouldn't mind?"

"That's what it's for."

"Do you still have contacts with people at DARPA?"

"Sort of." He shook his head. "That might not be where I would go to get help anyway. You could never be sure if they weren't the source of your problem in the first place. Do you know what the drive has on it?"

Frank told him what Caroline had said about the plan to fix the election. As he spoke he felt the oddity of the information coming out of his mouth, and Edgardo glanced at him, but mostly ran on nodding.

"Does this sound familiar?" Frank asked. "You're not looking shocked."

"No, of course not. It's been a real possibility for some time now. Assuming that it hasn't already happened."

"Aren't there any safeguards? Ways of checking for accuracy, or making a proper recount if they need to?"

"There are. But neither is foolproof, of course."

"How can that be?"

"That's just the way the technology works. That's the system Congress has chosen to use. Convenient, eh?"

"So you think there could be interventions?"

"Sure. I've heard of programs that sort races as they're being tallied, and tag ones that are close but outside the margin of error, so there won't be automatic recounts to gum up the works. Then they enact a tweak that reverses just enough ballots to change the result, but again by more than the margin of error."

"Could you counter one of these, if you saw it in advance? Some kind of reverse transcription that would neutralize the tweak?"

"Me?"

"Or people you know."

"Let me look at what you have. If it looks like it might be what you think, then I'll pass it along to some friends of mine."

"Thanks, Edgardo."

"But here we come to the bike path, let's change the subject. Give me what you've got, and I'll see what I can do. But give it to me at the Food Factory, at three, and let's not talk about this in the building."

"No," Frank said, interested to see that Edgardo appeared to assume that the building was compromised. So the surveillance was real. Of course Caroline had said it was. But it was interesting to hear it from a different source.

Back at work, checking the clock frequently, Frank saw in an e-mail from Diane that Yann Pierzinski was high on the list for the Grants for Exploratory Research program. He smiled, then frowned. The new institute would be in the Torrey Pines Generique facility; Leo Mulhouse had even been hired to run a lab; it all added up to good news. Which of course he ought to share with Marta.

For a while he found more pressing things to do, but it kept coming to mind, and he found he wanted to tell her anyway, to hear her reaction— how she would manage to downplay it. So that afternoon, after running down to Food Factory and giving Edgardo the drive, Frank called Small

Delivery Systems and asked for Marta. After a minute she got on, and Frank said hi.

She greeted him coolly, and he hacked his way through the preliminaries until her lack of cooperation forced him to the point. "I got it arranged like you asked. There's to be a new federal climate center housed in Torrey Pine Generique's old facility. And your team is listed for a big Grant for Exploratory Research. So now you can go back to San Diego."

"I can go wherever I want," she said. "I don't need your permission or your help."

"No, that isn't what I meant."

"Uh-huh. Don't be trying to buy me off, Frank."

"I'm not. I mean, I owe you that money, but you wouldn't take it. Anyway this is a good thing. Yann and you get one of the grants, and this will be one of the best research labs anywhere for what you guys are up to."

"We already have a lab."

"Small Delivery is too small to deliver."

"Not so. We've just gotten a contract from the Russian government. We're licensing the genome for our altered tree lichen to them, and we'll be helping them to manufacture and distribute it in Siberia this fall."

"But—wow. Have you had any field trials for this lichen?"

"This is the field trial."

"What? How big an area?"

"Lichen propagate by wind dispersion."

"That's what I thought! Have the Russians talked to us or the UN?"

"The President believes it's an internal matter."

"But the wind blows from Russia to Alaska."

"No doubt."

"And so to Canada."

"Sure. The spruce forest wraps the whole world," Marta agreed. "Our lichen could eventually spread through that whole latitude."

"And what's the estimated maximum CO_2 takedown from that?"

"Eleanor thinks maybe a hundred parts per million."

"Holy shit!"

"I know, it's a lot. But we can always put carbon back into the atmosphere if we need to. This drawdown at max would only take us most of the way back to before the industrial revolution anyway, so the models we run show it will be a good thing, even if it draws down more."

"I don't know how you can say that!"

"That's what our models show."

"Any idea how fast the propagation will go?"

"It kind of depends on how we distribute it in the first place."

"Jesus, Marta. So the Russians are just *doing* this?"

"Yes. The President thinks it's too important to risk sharing the decision with the rest of the world. Democracy could hang up their best chance of a rescue, he apparently said. They now think that global warming is more of a disaster for them than for anyone else. So they're bummed."

"Everyone's bummed," Frank said.

"Yeah but Russia is actually doing something about it. So quit trying to buy me off, Frank. We're going to be doing fine on our own. We've got some performance components in our contract that look good."

Villas are cheap in Crimea, Frank didn't say.

"The new center hired Leo Mulhouse to run a lab," he said instead.

"That's good." She didn't want to give him any credit. No matter what you do you'll still be an asshole, her silence said. "He's good. See you Frank."

He called Diane and had to leave a message, but at the end of the day she called back. He told her what Marta had said, and she was just as surprised as he had been. Part of him was pleased by this; it meant she had been deceived by Dmitri. Not that she sounded like a woman betrayed. "Things are getting interesting, aren't they?"

Meanwhile science itself proceeded as usual, which is to say, very slowly.

Anna Quibler liked it that way. Take a problem, break it down into parts (analyze), quantify whatever parts you could, see if what you learned suggested anything about causes and effects; then see if this suggested anything about tangible things to do. She did not believe in revolution of any kind, and only trusted the mass application of the scientific method to get any real-world results. "One step at a time," she would say to her team, or Nick's math group at school, or the National Science Board; and she hoped that as long as chaos did not erupt worldwide, one step at a time would eventually get them to some tolerable state.

Of course there were all the hysterical operatics of "history" to distract people from this method and its incremental successes. The wars and politicians, the police state regimes and terrorist insurgencies, the gross injustices and cruelties, the unnecessarily ongoing plagues and famines—in short, all the mass violence and rank intimidation that characterized most of what filled the history books; all that was real enough, indeed all too real, undeniable—and yet it was not the whole story. It was not really history, if you wished to include everything important that had happened to humans through time. Because along with all the violence, underneath the radar, inside the nightmare, there was always the ongoing irregular pulse of good work, often, since the seventeenth century, created or supported by science. Ongoing increases in health and longevity, for larger percentages of the population: that could be called progress. If they could hold on to that, and get everyone to that bettered state, it would *be* progress.

Anna was thus a progressive in that limited sense, of evolution not revolution. And for her, science was progress—its mode of production, if she understood that term. Science was both the method of analysis and the design for action.

The action itself—that was politics, and thus a descent back into the Bad Zone of history, with all its struggles and ultimately its wars. But those could be defined as resistance to the plan, its attempted replacement by a violent counterplan. If ever violence was justified, as necessary to put a good plan into action, the secondary results usually were so bad that the justification was proved untrue, the plan itself betrayed by the negative effects of its violent implementation. No; progress had to be made peaceably and collectively. It did not arrive violently. It had to be accomplished by positive actions. Positive ends required positive means, and never otherwise.

Except, was this true? Sometimes her disgust with the selfishness of the administration she was working for grew so intense that she would have been very happy to see the population rise up and storm the White House, tear it down, and hand the furniture to the overstuffed fools who had already wrecked the rest of the government. Violent anger if not violent action.

Given these feelings, one obvious opportunity for constructive action had been getting scientists involved in the presidential campaign. Whether or not the SSEEP idea was a good one was very hard to judge, but in for a penny in for a pound, and she had figured that as an experiment it would give some results, one way or another. Unless it didn't because of a poor design, with any real results lost in the noise of everything else. The social sciences, she thought, must have a terrible time designing experiments that yielded anything confirmable.

So, ambiguous results, at best; but meanwhile it was still worth trying.

Her actual involvement with the election campaign was at third or fourth remove, which was just the way she liked it, and probably the only way that it remained legal. In the end, she could certainly talk to Charlie about things Phil Chase could do as a candidate, if he wanted to, that might help him win.

This was partly the scientist's usual disconnect from politics, which was itself partly a realism about doing what one could. In any case she preferred spending that kind of time working on specific things. She had already gotten Charlie to convince Phil to introduce a bill that would revive FCCSET in an even stronger form, as part of a "Climatic Planned Response," or CPR.

Now she was finding the fossil remnants of various foreign aid programs that had been focused on science infrastructural proliferation, as she called it. Some of these were inactive for lack of funding; others had been discontinued.

"Let's fund them ourselves when we can't find anyone else," she suggested to Diane. "Let's get a group together to start rating these projects."

"And Frank would say we should start issuing requests for proposals."

NSF was now disbursing money at an unprecedented rate. The ten billion a year they had only recently achieved looked like pump-priming compared to what they were now passing out. Though Congress still would not fully fund the repair of the District of Columbia, the right people on the right committees had been scared enough by the bad winter to start funding whatever efforts seemed most likely to keep their own districts from harm. NSF had a supplement this year of twenty billion, and if they could find good ways to spend other federal money, Congress now tended to back them.

"This winter caused them to see the light," Edgardo said.

Anna maintained that the economy could always have paid for public work like this—that it was not even a particularly large share of the total economy—but they had lived in a war economy for so long that they had forgotten how much humans produced.

"Interesting," Edgardo said, looking intently at her. She very seldom talked about politics. "I wonder if we blew the fossil fuels on wars, and lost the chance to use that one-time surplus to construct a utopian scientific society. So now we are doomed to struggle in extreme danger for some birth-defected smaller version of just-good-enoughness."

"One step at a time," Anna insisted. "By the year 2500 it should all look the same."

She liked the way she could make Edgardo laugh. It was easy, in a way; you only had to say out loud the most horrible thing you could imagine and he would shout with laughter. And she had to admit there was something bracing about his attitude. He bubbled away like a fountain of acids, everything from vinegar to hydrochloric, and it made you laugh. Once you had said the worst, a certain sting was removed; the secret fear of it, perhaps, the superstition that if you said it aloud you made it more likely to come to pass, as with Charlie and disease. Maybe the reverse was true, and nothing you said out loud could thereafter come true, because of the Pauli exclusion principle or something like it. So now she exchanged dire prophecies with Edgardo freely, to defuse them and to make him laugh.

You needed a theory of black comedy to get through these days anyway, because there was little of any other kind around. Anna worked every minute until her alarm went off and it was time to go home. Then she took the Metro home, thankful that it was running again, using that time stubbornly to continue processing jackets, as she used to before the Foundation had gone into crisis mode. Continuing the real work. At home she found Charlie had been once again sucked into helping Phil Chase's campaign, an inevitable process now that it was coming down to the wire, so that he had barely managed to watch Joe while talking on the phone, and had not remembered to go to the store. So off she went, driving so she could stock up on more groceries than could be carried, boggled once again by the destitute look of their grocery store, the best one in the area but sovietized like all the rest of them by the epidemic of hoarding that had plagued her fellow citizens ever since the cold snap, if not the flood. Hoarding represented a loss of faith in the system's ability to supply the necessities. While there might have been some rational basis to it in the beginning, what it now meant was huge sections of shelves were empty, particularly of those products that would be needed in an emergency: toilet paper, bottled water, flour, rice, canned goods. People were storing these in their houses rather than letting them be stored in the store. She was still waiting for the time when every house maxed out, so that when the stores got things they would not fly out the door.

It also looked like certain fresh foods were permanently in shorter supply than they had been before the long winter. This was a different problem entirely.

So she had to hunt for whatever could be used, buy a few meals' worth of ingredients, some fast stuff, and hurry home to find Charlie still on the phone, vociferating, while also placating Joe about Anna's absence. He had gotten water on to boil, so they were that far along. But Nick had spaced on homework, and Joe was whining, and Charlie was engrossed in trying to get his boss elected president, after which things would supposedly calm back down. Aaack!

Oh well; time to heft Joe onto her hip and see if he would help make a salad, while consulting with Nick on math. It would all be okay by the year 2500.

Not for the first time, it struck her that things were calmer and more relaxing at work than they were at home. Or rather, that wherever she was, it always seemed like it was calmer at the other place. Was that normal?

Back at work, where the supposed calm was again not actually noticeable as such, climate amelioration projects were still taking up the bulk of their efforts. Carbon capture and sequestration, cleaner energy sources, cleaner transport: each area by itself was massive and complex, and correlating them was more than they could do. Although Frank had established a model modeling group.

Meanwhile they continued the work on their own fronts. Bioinformatics was still expanding at tremendous speed, although here as elsewhere they were running into the same problem they had encountered with the climate: they knew things, but they couldn't act on them. Getting genetically modified DNA into living humans was still proving to be an enormous obstacle.

On the climate front, the North Atlantic project was entrained and happening, therefore out of their hands. Everywhere else they were running into the difficulty Edgardo had named Fat Dog Syndrome; the dog was too fat for the tail to wag it, no matter how excited the tail got. They tried to quantify this impression by using cascade math to model ways for distributing money that would perturb other sources of it, finding capital at "high angles of repose" in venture capital, pension funds, investment banks, the stock markets, futures markets. Indeed, if they could get the markets to invest, they would be tapping into the economy's surplus, redirecting it to purposes actually useful. But whether these efforts were useful in the real world was an open question.

"Big profits in global cooling," Edgardo said sardonically, meaning the opposite, she supposed.

"Perturbation." Anna liked the sound of the word and the concept. "It's a network, and we perturb it in ways that stimulate harmonics." She thought the math describing this systems behavior was more interesting than cascade theories, which always went back to chaos. Her urge to orderliness made her interested in chaos theory, but the math itself was not as appealing to her as the stuff on harmonics in a network, which tended to describe stabilities rather than breakdowns. Just neater somehow.

"Like a cat's cradle," Diane said once.

"I wish," Anna said. "If only we could just stick in some fingers and lift it out into something entirely new! And simpler. Release a few complications—that used to be a cool move in cat's cradle when I was a girl. . . ."

But the truth was, the interlocking networks of human institutions were woven into such a tight mesh that it was hard to get any wave functions or simplifications going. They were tied down like Gulliver by all their rules and regulations. Only the violence of the original perturbations—the flood, the freeze—got them any flex. More than that they would have to create themselves.

So their work went on, under the radar for the most part, unreported in the news. The only exceptions were the most large-scale weather projects. For these public scrutiny was intense, reactions all over the map. But people were ready to try things. The traffic jams and empty stores and brownouts were getting to them in ways that news reports of distant storms had not.

Phil Chase was noticing that on the campaign trail. "People are fed up with the disruptions," he said. "Listen to what they're telling us. Too many hassles when things break down. Try anything you can think of, they're saying, to get levels of service and convenience back to what they used to be." In his speeches he started to say something FDR had said back in the 1930s: "The solution is to be found in a program of bold and persistent experimentation."

As a scientist Anna had to like that. They were designing, funding, and executing experiments. Compiling a hypothetical candidate's most scientifically defensible positions was just one experiment among all the rest. Maybe it would work, maybe it wouldn't, but they would learn something either way. She even began to see what she thought might be ripples caused by her perturbations, cascading through the global scientific network of institutions. Tugging on the cat's cradle, bouncing on the trampoline.

In the presidential campaign, when Phil was asked about the "Virtual Scientist Candidate," he would smile his glorious smile. "In Europe a candidate like that is called a shadow candidate. I take the people inventing this candidate to be our allies, because if you judge the effect of your vote by rational scientific criteria, then you will never throw it away on a splinter party that doesn't have a chance in our winner-take-all system. You vote for the potential winner most likely to express something like your views, and at this moment I'm that man. So the science guy is *my* shadow."

And his numbers rose. It seemed to Anna that it was going to be a really close election; so close she could hardly stand to contemplate it.

Edgardo agreed. "People like it that way. Seesaw back and forth, try to get it perfectly level for election day. Confound the polls by sitting inside the margins of error. That way the day itself will bring a surprise. A bit of drama, just for its own sake. Policy has nothing to do with it, life and death have nothing to do with it. People just like a good race. They like their little surprises."

"They may get a big surprise this time," Anna said.

"They don't like big surprises. Only little surprises will do."

On it went. The summer passed, and one day the Department of Energy was on their side—it was actually unnerving—as they were in hot pursuit of what looked like a really powerful photovoltaic panel. Anna went on to her other work, feeling pleased. Perturbation of the network! Cat's cradle, slip and pull! When she went home she would be able to sit there and listen to Charlie's talk about the campaign without getting as anxious and irritated as before—knowing, as she watched the news sprawl across the screen like a giant reality show they could not escape, that always underneath it the great work rolled on.

Anna's great work, however, was a linear process, and it existed in a world with important nonlinear components. One morning at home with Joe, Charlie got a call from Roy Anastopoulos. "Roy!"

"Charlie are you sitting down?"

"I am not sitting down, I *never* sit down, but nothing you can tell me will need me sitting down!"

"That's what you think! Charlie I've got Wade Norton on the other line and I'm going to patch him in. Wade? Can you still hear me?"

A second or two, and then Charlie heard Wade, speaking from Antarctica: "I can still hear you. Hi Charlie, how are you?"

"I'm fine, Wade," resisting the urge to speak louder so that Wade could still hear him down there at the bottom of the world. "What's happening?"

"I'm on a flight over the Ross Sea, and I'm looking at a big tabular berg that's just come off from the coastline. Really really really big. It'll be on the news soon, but I wanted to call you guys and tell you. The West Antarctic Ice Sheet has started to come off big-time."

"Oh my God. You're looking at a piece of it already off?"

"Yes. It's about a hundred miles long, the pilot says."

"My God. So sea level has already gone up a foot?"

"You got it Charlie! I was trying to tell Roy."

"That's why I told you to sit down," Roy put in.

"I had better sit down," Charlie admitted, feeling a little wobble, as for instance the axis of the Earth. "Any guesses down there as to how fast the rest will come off?"

"No. They don't know. Faster than they expected. Some of them are running a pool, and the bets range from a decade to a century. Apparently the goo underneath the ice is like toothpaste. It lets the ice slide, and the tides tug at it, and there's an active volcano down there too."

"Shit."

"So we're talking sea level rise?" Roy asked, trying to get confirmation.

"Yes!" Wade said. "Hey boys I've got to go, I just wanted to let someone know. I'll talk to you more soon."

He got off and Charlie then explained the situation to Roy. Giant ice sheet, warming, cracking—sliding off its underwater perch—displacing more water than it had when perched, floating away in chunks. If the whole ice sheet came off, sea level would go up seven meters. A quarter of the world's population would be affected, meaning perhaps a hundred trillion dollars in human and natural capital at risk. Conservatively. Possibly much more. In fact, impossible to quantify in money terms. It was not a fungible event.

Roy said, "Okay, I get it. Sounds like it will help Phil in the campaign."

"Roy, please. Not funny."

"I'm not being funny!" Although he was laughing like a loon. "I'm talking about the problem! If Phil doesn't win, what do you think will happen?"

"Okay okay. Shit. My God." Everything Anna and her colleagues had been doing to restart the Gulf Stream was as nothing to this news. Changing currents, maybe—but *sea level*? "The stakes just keep getting higher."

"Yes. That's why they call it climate change."

"What do you mean?"

"I mean they're trying to pretend it's only about climate! When really it's about everything—it's *everything change*."

CHAPTER 20

PRIMAVERA PORTEÑO

Kenzo had run the numbers and found that most seasonal weather manifestations varied about eight percent, year to year—temperature, precipitation, wind speed, and so on. Now all that was over. They had passed the point of criticality, they had tipped over the tipping point, in the same way a kid running up a seesaw will get past the axis and somewhere beyond and above it tip the whole thing and plummet down the falling board. They were in the next mode, and coming into the second winter of abrupt climate change.

The President announced on the campaign trail that he had inherited this problem from his Democratic predecessors, and only free markets and a strong national defense could battle this new threat, which he called climatic terrorism. "I'm proud to say that on my watch the National Science Foundation has initiated a great counterterrorist operation in the North Atlantic, which will soon restore the Gulf Stream and show how American know-how is a match for anything."

This played well, like most things the President did. He got a great deal of credit for taking on the weather in such a forceful and market-based manner, bypassing the scientists and liberals and striking a blow for freedom and the salt industry. Anna, watching the TV, hissed like a teakettle; Charlie threw Joe's dinosaurs at the radiator. The President's numbers went up. Only Diane was calm. She said, "Don't worry. It only means we're winning."

And Phil Chase blew through the President's claims with a laugh. "The salt fleet is an international project, coordinated through the UN. The part of it we're paying for comes from an appropriation Congress made because of a bill I wrote. The President tried to kill the project. Come on! You all know which candidate will work to protect the environment, and it's me, me and my party. Let's turn it into a big party. We can make things better for our kids, and that'll be our fun. That's the way it's always been until now, so you can't let the fear and greed guys scare you till you cut and run. This new climate is an opportunity. We needed to change, and now we will, because we have to."

This played well too, much to the pundits' private surprise (in public they always knew everything). Now Phil was polling neck-and-neck with the President, doing particularly well among the boomers and their children the echo boomers, the two biggest demographic groups.

The President's team continued to transpose what was working for Chase into the President's campaign. They began to proclaim the bad weather to be an economic opportunity of the first order. New businesses, even entire new industries, were there for the making! The bad weather was obviously another economic opportunity for market-driven reforms.

However, since he had been elected with the help of big oil and everything transnationally corporate, and had done more than any previous president to strip-mine the nation and use it as a dumping ground, he was not as convincing as Phil. It was getting hard to believe his assertion that the invisible hand of the market would solve everything, because, as Phil memorably put it, the invisible hand never picks up the check.

So the campaign wallowed in its falsity and tedium, and as the summer passed it became ever tighter, just as all the media, hopeful for customers, wished. There was enough bad weather to keep Phil in the chase, as he put it.

So his campaign was doing well, and he kept it up with events all over the world, including a return to the North Pole a year after announcing his candidacy. It was a bit of a throwback to his old World's Senator mode, but his team could only follow his lead. "I have to run on my record, there's no other way to do it. I am what I am." He started saying that too. "I am what I am."

"And that's all what I am," Roy always sang when he said it, "I'm Popeye the sailor man! Toot toot!"

Charlie had to admit that since the climate problem was global, campaigning everywhere made a sort of sense. Meanwhile the President remained reso-

lutely nationalistic; it was always America this and freedom that, no matter how transnational and unfree the content of his positions. Patriotism as xenophobia was part of his appeal to his base, and it worked for them. But Phil's people had a different idea.

One unexpected problem was that the "Scientific Virtual Candidate" was polling well, despite the fact that the candidate was nonexistent and would not appear on any ballots. Most of those potential votes came from Phil's natural constituency, and so it was accomplishing the usual third-party disaster of undercutting precisely the major party most closely allied to its views.

Phil looked to Charlie on this. "Charlie, you have to talk to your wife and her colleagues at NSF. I don't want to be accidentally Nadered by those good people. Tell them whatever they want, I'm their best chance."

"I don't want to depress them that much," Charlie deadpanned, which got a good Phil chuckle, rueful but pleased. His fear that running for President was going to lose him all real human contact (the unconscious goal of many a previous president) was so far proving unfounded. "Thanks for that thrust of rapierlike wit," he said. "There aren't enough people saying bad things about me these days. You are indeed a brother, and we are a real foxhole fraternity, shelled daily as we are by Fox. But don't forget to talk to NSF." As far as Charlie could tell he was still enjoying himself enormously.

And Charlie did ask Anna and Frank what the plans were for the candidate experiment. They both shrugged and said the genie was out of the bottle. At NSF they talked to the SSEEP team, who were of course already aware of the historical precedents and the negative ramifications of any partial real-world success of their campaign. Until preferential voting was introduced, third parties could only wreck their own side.

Frank got back to Charlie. "They're on it."

"How so, meaning what?"

"They're waiting for their moment."

"Ahhhhh."

This moment came in late September, when a hurricane veered north at the last minute and hammered New Jersey, New York, Long Island, and Connecticut, and to a lesser extent the rest of New England. These were blue states already, but with big SSEEP numbers as well, so that after the first week of emergencies had passed, and the flooding subsided, a SSEEP conference was held in which representatives of 167 scientific organizations debated what to do in as measured and scientific a manner as they could manage—which in the event meant a perfect storm of statistics, chaos theory, sociology, econometrics, mass psychology, ecology, cascade mathematics, poll theory, historiography, and climate modeling. At the end of which a statement was crafted, approved, and released, informing the public that the "Scientific Virtual Candidate" was withdrawing from all campaigns, and suggesting that any voters who had planned to vote for it consider voting for Phil Chase, as being an "electable first approximation of the scientific candidate," and "best real current choice." Support for preferential or instant runoff voting method was also strongly recommended, as giving future scientific candidates the chance actually to win representation proportional to the votes they got, improving democracy if judged by representational metrics.

This announcement was denounced by the President's team as prearranged collusion and a gross sullying of the purity of science by an inappropriate and unscientific descent into partisan politics. The scientific candidate immediately issued a detailed reply to these charges in the form of all its calculations, and a description of the methods used to reach its conclusions, including point-by-point comparisons of the various planks of all the platforms, indicating that at this point Phil was closer to science than the President.

"You think?" Roy Anastopoulos said to Charlie over the phone. "I mean, duh. I hope this helps us, but isn't it just another of those scientific studies that make a huge effort to prove the sky is blue? Of course Phil is more scientific! He's running against a man aligned with rapture enthusiasts, people who are getting ready to take off and fly to heaven!"

"Calm down Roy, this is a good thing. This is connect-the-dots."

In public Phil welcomed the new endorsement, and he welcomed the voters attending to it, promising to do his best to adopt the planks of the scientific platform into his own. "Try me and see," Phil said. "Given the situation, it makes sense. The President isn't going to do anything. He and his oil-and-guns crowd will just try to find an island somewhere to skip to when they're done raiding the world. They'll leave us in the wreckage and build themselves bubble fortresses, that's been their sick plan all along. Building a good world for our kids is our plan, and it's scientific as can be, but only if you understand science as an ethical system and not just a method for seeing the world. What this political endorsement underlines is that science contains in it a plan for dealing with the world we find ourselves in, a plan which aims to reduce human suffering and increase the quality of life on Earth for everyone. In other words, science is a kind of politics already, and I'm proud to be endorsed by the scientific community, because its goals match the values of justice and fairness that we all were taught are the most important part of social life and government. So welcome aboard, and I appreciate the help, because there's a lot to do!"

Thus ended the most active part of the first Social Science Experiment in Elective Politics. There would be much analysis, and the follow-up studies would suggest new experiments the next time around. The committee was there in place at the National Academy of Sciences, and it would have looked bad at that point if anyone inside or outside the Academy had tried to shut it down.

Diane, under stupendous heat from Republicans in Congress for appearing to have used a federal agency to support a political candidate, went to the hearings and shrugged. "We'll study it," she said.

"Would you fund an experiment like that again?" yelled Senator Winston.

"It would depend on its peer review," she said. "If it was given a good ranking by a peer-review panel, then yes."

The debate roared on. The National Science Foundation had jumped into politics and the culture wars. Its age of innocence was over at last.

Frank and Rudra Cakrin continued to spend the last hour of their nights out in their shed, talking. They talked about food, the events of the day, the garden, and the nature of reality. Most of their talk was in English, where Rudra continued to improve. Sometimes he gave Frank a Tibetan lesson.

Rudra liked to be outside. His health seemed to Frank poor, or else he was frail with age. On their trips out together Frank gave him an arm at the curbs, and once he even pushed him in a wheelchair that was stored inside the house underneath the stairwell. A few times they went for a drive in Frank's van.

One day they drove out to see their future home. The Khembalis had finalized the purchase of some land in Maryland they had located, a property upstream on the Potomac, badly damaged in the great flood. A farmhouse on the high point of the acreage had been inundated to the ceiling of the first floor. Padma and Sucandra had decided the building could be repaired, and the land itself was worth the price.

So Frank drove out the George Washington Parkway, Rudra peering from the passenger seat with a lively eye, talking in Tibetan. Frank tried to identify what words he could, but it didn't add up to much—*malam,* highway, *sgan,* hill; *sdon-po,* tree. It occurred to him that maybe this was what conversation always was, two people talking to themselves in different languages, mostly to clarify themselves to themselves. Or else just filling the silence, singing *ooop ooop.*

He tried to resist this theory, so Edgardoesque, by asking specific questions. "How old are you?"

"Eighty-one."

"Where were you born?"

"Near Drepung."

"Do you remember any of your past lives?"

"I remember many lives."

"Lives before this life?"

Rudra looked out the window. "Yes."

"Not interrupted by any deaths?"

"Many deaths."

"Yes, but I mean, your own deaths?"

Rudra shrugged. "This does not seem to be the body I used to inhabit."

Out on the farm, Rudra insisted on trudging up to the land's high point, a low ridge at the eastern edge of the property, just past the ruined farmhouse.

They looked around. "So you'll make this your new Khembalung."

"Same Khembalung," Rudra said. "Khembalung is not a *place*." He waved his arm at the scene. "A name for a way." He wiggled his hand forward like a fish, as if indicating passage through time.

"A moveable feast," Frank suggested.

"Yes. Milarepa said this, that Khembalung moves from age to age. He said it will go north. Not until now have we seen what he meant. But here it is."

"But Washington isn't very far north of your old Khembalung."

"From Khembalung you go north, keep going over top of world and down the other side. Here you are!"

Frank laughed. "So now this is Khembalung?"

Rudra nodded. He said something in Tibetan.

"What's that?"

"The first Khembalung was recently found, north of Kunlun Mountains. Ruins located, under mountain in Takla Makan."

"They found the original? How old was the site?"

"Very old."

"Yes, but did they say a date by chance?"

Rudra frowned. "Eighth century in your calendar?"

"Wow. I bet you'd like to go see that."

Rudra shook his head. "Stones."

"I see. You like this better."

"Sure. More lively. Live living."

"That's true. So, a great circle route, and Shambala comes to us."

"Good way to put it."

Slowly they walked down to the riverbank, a broad swath of mud curving around the ridge and then away to the southeast. The curve, Frank thought, might be another reason the land had been for sale. The natural snake-slither of riverine erosion would perhaps eat this mud bank, and then the devastated grass above it. Possibly a well-placed wall could stabilize the bank at certain critical points. "I'll have to ask General Wracke out for your homecoming party," Frank said as he observed it. "He'll have suggestions for a wall."

"More dikes, good idea."

On their way back to the van they passed a stand of trees, and Frank parked Rudra under one to take a quick survey of the grove. Two sycamores, a truly giant oak; a stand of pines.

"This looks really good," he said as he came back to Rudra. "Those are good trees, you could build in several of them."

"Like your treehouse."

"Yes, but right here. Bigger, and lower."

"Good idea."

All systems were go for the salt fleet now converging in the ocean west of Ireland. In the meantime the news shifted south, where the West Antarctic Ice Sheet continued to detach, in small but frequent icebergs at its new margin. The big fragment was adrift in the Antarctic Ocean, a tabular berg as big as Germany and thicker than any ice shelf had ever been, so that it had in fact raised sea level by several inches. Tuvalu was being evacuated; further ramifications of this event were too large to be grasped. Through October it remained just one more bit of bad news among the rest. Sea level rise, oh my; but what could anyone do?

Frank sat in a room at NSF with Kenzo and Edgardo, looking at data from NOAA. He had some ideas about sea level, in fact. But now the topic of the hour switched back to the Gulf Stream. Data coming back from the RUVs, collared whales, ships, and buoys were encouraging. Conditions were ripe; everything was shaping up well for their intervention. The fleet of single-hulled VLCC tankers had been loaded at the many salt pans and ports around the Caribbean and New Brunswick that had been called upon, and they were almost all at the rendezvous point. The fleet was now headed north, and the photos were hard to believe, the sheer number of ships making it look like Photoshopping for sure.

Then the dumping of the salt began, and the photos got even stranger. It was scheduled to last two weeks, and halfway through it, three days before the presidential election, Frank got a call from Diane.

"Hey, do you want to go out and see the salting in person?"

"You bet!"

"There's an empty seat you can have, but you'll have to get ready fast."

"I'm ready now."

"Good for you. Meet me at Dulles at nine."

Ooooop! A voyage to the Atlantic, to see the salt fleet with Diane!

Their trip to Manhattan came to mind; and since then they had spent a million hours together, both at work and in the gym. So when they sat down that night in adjoining seats on Icelandic Air's plane, and Diane put her head on his shoulder and fell asleep even before it took off, it felt very natural, like all the rest of their interactions.

They came down on Reykjavik just before dawn. The surface of the sea lay around the black bulk of Iceland like a vast sheet of silver. By then Diane was awake; back in D.C. this was her usual waking hour, unearthly though that seemed to Frank, who had just gotten tired enough to lean his head on hers. These little intimacies were shaken off when seatbacks returned to their upright position. Diane leaned across Frank to look out the window; Frank leaned back to let her see. Then they were landing, and into the airport. Neither of them had checked luggage, and they weren't there long before it was time to join a group of passengers trammed out to a big helicopter. On board, earplugs in, they rose slowly and then chuntered north over empty blue ocean.

Soon after that, passengers with a view were able to distinguish the tankers themselves, long and narrow, like Mississippi River barges but immensely bigger. The fleet was moving in a rough convoy formation, and as they flew north and slowly descended, there came a moment when the tankers dotted the ocean's surface for as far as they could see in all directions. Lower still and they looked like black syringes in rows on a blue table, ready to give their "long injections of pure oil," as Gary Snyder had put it back in 1955.

The helicopter landed on a landing pad at the back end of a tanker called the *Hugo Chavez,* an Ultra Large Crude Carrier with a gigantic bridge next to the pad. From this height the ships around them looked longer than ever, all plowing broad white wakes into a swell from the north that seemed miniature in proportion to the ships, but it became clear from the windcaps and spray that the salt armada was in fact crashing through a stiff wind, almost a gale. Looking in the direction of the sun the scene turned black-and-white, like one of those characteristically windblown chiaroscuro moments in *Victory at Sea.*

When they got out of the helo the wind blasted through their clothes and chased them upstairs to the bridge. There a crowd of visitors larger than the crew had a fine view over a broad expanse of ocean, crowded with immense ships.

Looking away from the sun the sea was like cobalt. From its bridge the *Hugo Chavez* looked like an aircraft carrier with the landing deck removed. The quarterdeck that held the bridge at its top was tall, but only a tiny part of the craft; the forecastle looked like it was a mile away. The intervening distance was interrupted by a skeletal rig that resembled a loading crane, but also reminded Frank of the giant irrigation sprayers one saw in California's Central Valley. The salt in the hold was being vacuumed into this device, then cast out in powerful white jets, a couple hundred meters to both sides. The hardrock salt had been milled into sizes ranging from table salt grains to bowling balls. In the holds it looked like dirty white gravel and sand. In the air it looked almost like dirty water or slush, arching out and splashing in a satisfyingly broad swath. Between the salt fall and the ship's wakes, and the whitecaps, the blue of the ocean was infinitely mottled by white. Looking west it turned to silver on pewter and lead.

Diane watched the scene with her nose almost on the glass. She smiled at Frank. "You can smell the salt."

"The ocean always smells like this."

"It seems like more today."

"Maybe so." She had grown up in San Francisco, he remembered. "It must smell like home." She nodded happily.

They followed their hosts up a metal staircase to a higher deck of the bridge, a room with windows on all sides. It was this room that made the *Hugo Chavez* the designated visitor or party ship, and now the big glass-walled room was crowded with dignitaries and officials. Here they could best view the long ships around them. Each one cast two long, curving jets out to the sides from its bow, like the spouts of right whales. Every element was repeated so symmetrically that it seemed they had fallen into an Escher print.

The tankers flanking theirs seemed nearer than they really were because of their great size. They were completely steady in the long swells. The air around the ships was filled with a white haze. Diane pointed out that the diesel exhaust stayed in the air while the salt mist did not. "They look so dirty. I wonder if we couldn't go back to sails, just let everything go slower. Let's look into that."

They moved from one set of big windows to the next, taking in the views.

"It's like the San Joaquin Valley," Frank said. "There are these huge irrigation rigs that roll around spraying stuff."

Diane nodded. "I wonder if this will work."

"Me too. If it doesn't . . ."

"I know. It would be hard to talk people into trying anything else."

Around the bridge they walked. Everyone else was doing the same, in a circulation like any other party. Blue sky, blue sea, the horizon ticked by tiny wavelets; and then the fleet, each ship haloed by a wind-tossed cloud of white mist. Frank and Diane caught each other by the shoulder to point things out, just as they would have in Optimodal. A bird; a fin in the distance.

Then another group arrived in the room, and soon they were escorted to Diane: the Secretary-General of the UN; Denmark's environmental minister, who was the head of their Green Party and a friend of Diane's from earlier times; lastly the prime minister of Great Britain, who had done a kind of Winston Churchill during their hard winter, and who now shook Diane's hand and said, "So this is the face that launched a thousand ships," looking very pleased with himself. Diane was distracted by all the introductions. People chatted as they circled the room, and after a while Diane and Frank stood in a big circle listening to people, their upper arms just barely touching as they stood side by side.

After another hour of this, during which nothing varied outside except a shift west in the angle of the sun, it was declared time to go; one didn't want the helicopters to get too far from Reykjavik, and there were other visitors waiting in Iceland for their turns to visit; and the truth was, they had seen what there was to see. The ship's crew therefore halted the *Hugo Chavez*'s prodigious launching of salt, and they braved the chilly blast downstairs and got back in their helo. Up it soared, higher and higher. Again the astonishing sight of a thousand tankers on the huge burnished plate spreading below them, instantly grasped as unprecedented: the first major act of planetary engineering ever attempted, and by God it looked like it.

But then the helo pilot ascended higher and higher, higher and higher, until they could see a much bigger stretch of ocean, water extending as far as the eye could see, for hundreds of miles in all directions—and all of it blank, except for their now tiny column of ships, looking like a line of toys. And then ants. In a world so vast, could anything humans do make a difference?

Diane thought so. "We should celebrate," she said, smiling her little smile. "Do you want to go out to dinner when we get back?"

"Sure. That would be great."

Election day saw winter return to Washington in force. It was icy everywhere, in places black ice, so that even though everything seemed to have congealed to a state of slow motion, cars still suddenly took flight like hockey pucks, gliding majestically over the roads and looking stately until they hit something. Sirens Dopplered hither and yon, defining the space of the city that was otherwise invisible in its trees. Again there were scheduled brownouts, and the wood smoke of a million fireplace fires rose with the diesel smoke of a million generators, their gray and brown strands weaving in the northwest wind.

The polls were open, however, and the voters who still voted in person lined up all bundled in their winter best—a best that was much better than it had been the year before. The story of the day became the story of the impact of the cold on the physical vote, and which party's faithful would brave it most successfully, and which would benefit most from this clear harbinger of another long winter. The first exit polls showed a tight race, and as no one believed in exit polls anymore anyway, anything was possible. It felt like Christmas.

And in fact it was the Buddhist holiday celebrating Dorje Totrengtsel. To celebrate it, and perform a dedication ceremony for their new home in the country, the Khembalis had scheduled a big party.

It took well over an hour for the Quiblers to drive out to the farm, Charlie at the wheel of their Volvo station wagon inching along, Anna in the back with the boys. Joe declaimed a long monologue on the snowy view, and his displeasure that they were not stopping to investigate it: "Look! Stop! Look! Stop the car!"

When they got to the farm they found Frank was just arriving himself. They parked next to his van and walked around the farmhouse.

Drepung and Rudra were out back on the snowy lawn, steam pouring from their mouths and noses. They were kicking patterns of frosty green out of the thick flock of new snow on the grass. At the center of this improvised mandala stood a blocky shapeless snowman with a demon mask hung on its head, grinning maniacally into the wind. Before it lay a lower block of snow, like the altar stone at Stonehenge. On the flattish top of this mass, some of Joe's building blocks were stacked, in two towers. Two red then green, two red then yellow.

The two men waved cheerily when they saw the Quiblers. They pointed at their handiwork, and watched with pleasure as Joe in his thick snowsuit and boots trundled ahead of the rest to investigate. They lifted him between them the better to see the two towers his blocks now made. He kicked reflexively at the stacks, and Rudra and Drepung laughed and swung him back and forth, each holding with both hands one of the toddler's mittened fists. When he kicked over one of them, they put him down with many congratulations. "Ooooh! Karmapa!"

Frank went inside to check on lunch, and came back out carrying two paper cups of a hot mulled cider that he reported had no yak butter in it. He gave one to Anna. Charlie sniffed the steam pouring off it and went in to get one of his own. He spent a while in there talking to Sridar, his old lobbying partner who had taken on the Khembalis as a client, and was now representing them to Congress, with some success and a great deal of amusement. They exchanged the usual sentiments on the election taking place, shaking their heads in the attempt to pretend they did not hope very much.

When Charlie went back outside, he felt again how frigid the day was. Anna huddled against him, nearly shivering despite her bulky coat. The Khembalis and Joe did not seem to mind. Now they were walking around the snow figure in a little march, chanting nonsense together, a string of syllables followed by a big "HA," repeated again and again. Joe stomped into the snow as deeply as Drepung, his eyes ablaze under his hood, his cheeks bright red.

"He's getting too hot in his suit," Charlie said.

"Well, he can't take it off."

"I guess not."

"They're having fun," Frank observed. "Joe must be heavy the way he sinks into that snow."

"Yeah," Charlie said. "He's like made out of lead."

Frank saw Nick standing off to one side and called, "Hey Nick, do you want to go down to the river and see if there are any beavers or anything?"

"Sure!" They took off down the lawn, talking animals.

Now Rudra stood still, facing Joe. Joe stopped to peer up at him, looking surprised that their march had halted. "Ho," he said.

Rudra leaned down and gently rubbed a handful of snow in Joe's face. Joe spluttered and then shook his head like a dog.

"Hey what is he doing?" Anna demanded.

"He's helping him," Charlie said, holding her arm.

"What do you mean helping? That doesn't help him!"

"It doesn't hurt. It's part of their little ceremony."

"Well it's not okay!"

"Leave them alone," Charlie said. "Joe doesn't mind it, see?"

"But what are they doing?"

"It's just a little ceremony they have."

"But why?"

"Well, you know. Maybe he's just trying to lower his temperature."

"Oh come on!"

"Come on yourself. Just let them do it. Joe is loving it, and they think they're helping."

Anna glowered. "They're only going to give him a cold."

"You know perfectly well being cold has nothing to do with catching a cold. What an old wives' tale."

"Old wives' tales usually contained real observations, smart guy. And turns out when you get cold your immune system is suppressed, so if there happens to be a virus around you're more likely to catch it."

"But he's not getting too cold. Leave them alone. They're having fun."

Except then Joe howled a quick protest. Rudra and Drepung looked startled; then Drepung turned Joe by the shoulder, so that he was facing the snowman. Seeing the mask again Joe quietened. He tilted his head, scowled hideously at the snowman: no mere piece of wood was going to outscowl him.

Straightening up beside him, Rudra pointed at the demon mask, then up at the low clouds purling overhead. Suddenly he twisted and as it were corkscrewed upward, thrusting himself up and back until he looked straight up at the sky. He shouted, "Dei tugs-la ydon ysol! Ton pa, gye ba! Ton pa, gye ba!"

Shocked, Joe looked up at Rudra so quickly that he plumped onto his butt. Rudra leaned over him and shouted "Gye ba!" with a sudden ferocity. Joe scrambled away, then jumped up to trundle down the slope of the lawn as fast as he could.

"Joe!" Anna cried, and with a quick spasm she was away and running through the snow. "Joe! Joe!"

Joe, still running for the river, did not appear to hear her. Then he tripped and fell in a perfect face plant, sprawling down the snow slope and leaving behind a long snow angel. Anna reached him and slipped herself trying to stop. Down she went too; then Drepung joined them and helped them both up, saying, "Sorry, sorry, sorry."

Rudra stayed up by the snowman, swaying and jerking. He staggered to the snowman, pulled off its demon mask, threw it at his feet, and stomped on it. "HA! TON PA! HA! GYE BA! HAAAAAA!"

Hearing this Joe wailed, beating at the snow and then at Anna's outstretched arms. Drepung ventured to touch him once lightly on the shoulder. Joe buried his head in Anna's embrace. Rudra, now sitting on the ground next to the flattened mask, watched them; he waved at Joe when Joe looked over Anna's shoulder. Joe blinked big tears down his cheeks, shuddering as he calmed. For a long time Joe and Rudra stared blankly at each other.

Charlie walked over to help the old man to his feet. Both Rudra and Drepung seemed satisfied now, relaxed and ready to move on to other things. Seeing it, Charlie felt a certain calmness fill him too. He and Rudra went down and flanked Joe and Anna, took Joe's mittened and snow-caked little hands, squeezed them. Joe looked around at the farmhouse and the tent filling with guests, the expanse of snow falling down to the river. Charlie clapped Drepung on the shoulder, held it briefly.

"What?" Anna demanded.

"Nothing. Nothing. Let's go in and see what they have to eat, shall we?"

Late that afternoon, when the Khembalis' party was breaking up, and they had heard all about the trip out to see the salt fleet, the Quiblers asked Frank if he wanted to come over for dinner and watch the election returns.

"Thanks," he said, "but I'm going to go to dinner with Diane."

"Oh I see."

"Maybe I can drop by afterward, see the late returns."

"Sure, whatever."

Frank went to his van, drove carefully back to the Khembali house in Arlington. Out in the cold garden shed he changed clothes, trying to think what would look nice. He was going out to dinner with his boss, who would not be his boss for much longer, so that different hypothetical possibilities might then open. It was interesting, no matter how uneasy he felt whenever he thought of Caroline.

Then one of the kitchen girls called out to the shed from the house door: phone call. He went inside, picked up the house's phone. "Hello?"

"Frank is that you?"

"Yes—Caroline?"

"Yes."

"Is everything okay?"

"No, everything is not okay. I need to see you, now."

"Well, but I've got something, I'm really sorry—"

"Frank *please*! I think he found out I gave you that stuff. So I've only got a little time. I've got to initiate Plan B or else. I need your help."

"You're leaving him?"

"Yes! That's what I'm telling you. I've left already. That's done. But I need help getting away and—you're the only one I trust." Her voice twisted at the end, and suddenly Frank understood that she was afraid. He had never heard that in her before, and had not recognized it.

Frank clutched the phone hard. "Where are you?"

"I'm in Chevy Chase. I'll meet you at your tree."

"Okay. It'll take me half an hour. Maybe longer with the ice."

"Okay good. Good. Thanks. I love you Frank." She hung up.

Frank groaned. He stared at the embassy's phone in his hand. "Shit," he said. That someone as bold and competent as her should be afraid . . . "I love you too," he whispered.

His stomach had shrunk to the size of a baseball. What would this husband of hers do? He picked up the house phone and called Diane.

Maybe she too was bugged. She was doing the same kind of thing as Frank, wasn't she?

"Hello, Diane? It's Frank. Listen I'm really sorry about this, but something has come up here and I just have to help out, it's a kind of emergency. So I need to, I mean can we take a rain check, and do our dinner tomorrow or whenever you can?"

Very short pause. "Sure, of course. No problem."

"Thanks, I'm really sorry about this. See there's this," but he hadn't thought anything up, a stupid mistake, and he was going to say "something at the embassy" when she heard the pause and cut him off:

"No it's fine, don't worry. We'll do it another time."

"Thanks Diane. I appreciate it. How about tomorrow then?"

"Um, no—tomorrow won't work, my daughter is coming in. Here—oh, wait. I don't see my calendar. Tell you what, let's just say soon."

"Okay, soon. Thanks. Sorry."

"No problem."

End of call. He put the receiver down, stood there.

"Ah fuck."

He drove over to Van Ness, parked in one of his old spots on Brandywine, walked east into the forest. Slowly he approached his tree, coming to it on the remains of Ross Drive. He saw no one. But then there she was, stepping out from behind a thick oak. He went to her and they hugged hard.

She pulled back and looked at him. Even in the dark he could see that her nose was red, her eyes red-rimmed.

She sniffed, shook her head. "Sorry. It's been a very bad day." She handed him another thumb drive. "Here. This is more of their shit. It's a new super-black, outside Homeland Security."

Frank took the drive, put it in his jacket pocket. "What happened?"

"We had a fight. I mean that used to happen a lot, but this time it was—I don't know. Bad. Scary. I'm sick of feeling this way. Really, being around him—it's bad for me. I know better. I can't stand it anymore."

"He didn't find something out?"

"He didn't say anything directly, but I think he did, yes. I don't know. If he found out about me taking the election program . . ." She shuddered, thinking about it. Then: "It might explain some things. I mean he chipped me again, since I last saw you. New kinds that he thought I didn't know about. They hop on you. When I found them I left them in until today, but I took them out, and then I used his code to get what I could about this new superblack onto a thumb drive. I don't know how much it'll tell anyone. Then I left."

"Are you sure you found all the chips on you?"

"Yes. The bastard. He is so . . . He spies and spies and spies."

"So, I mean, can you be sure you found everything he's doing?"

"Yes, I ran all the diagnostics, and I saw what he had on me. Now I'm out of there. He'll never see me again."

The bitter twist to her mouth was one Frank had not seen before, but it was familiar in his own muscles from certain moments of his own breakup with Marta. The wars of the heart, so bitter and pointless.

"Where will you go?" he said.

"I have a Plan B. It's got an ID all set up, a place, even a job. It's not too far away, but far enough I won't run into him."

"I'll be able to see you?"

"Once I get settled. That's why I set it up this way. If I were on my own I'd go, oh I don't know. Tibet or something. The end of the Earth."

Frank shook his head. "I want you closer than that."

"I know."

They hugged harder. In the darkness of the park it was almost quiet: the sound of the creek, the hum of the city. Two against the world. Frank felt her body, her heat, the pulse in her neck. The scent of her hair filled him.

Don't disappear, he thought. Stay where I can find you. Stay where I can be with you.

Frank felt her shudder. It was cold again, not as cold as in the depths of last winter, but well below freezing. The creek rang with the tinkling bell-like sound it took on when all its eddies were frozen over. Caroline's body was quivering under his hands, shivering with cold, or tension, or both. He held her, tried to calm her with his hands. But he too was shivering.

Downstream on the path he saw a brief movement. Black into black. Involuntarily he pulled her to him and around to the other side of the oak.

"What?"

"Look," he said very quietly, "are you sure you aren't still chipped some-how?"

"I don't think so, why?"

"Because I think there's someone watching us."

"Oh my God."

"Don't try to look. Here, I've got the scanner you gave me." He thought it over, one scenario then another. "Would he have other people helping him?"

"Not for this," she said. "I don't think so anyway. Not unless he figured out that I copied the vote program."

"Shit. Let's check you right here, okay?"

"Sure."

He pulled the wand from his pocket, so much like an airport security device. Bar codes in the body. He ran it over her. When he had it against the top of her back it beeped.

"*Shit*," she exclaimed under her breath. She whipped off her jacket, laid it on the ground, ran the wand over it. It beeped again. "God *damn* it."

"At least it isn't in your skin."

"Yeah well."

"You checked before you left your place?"

"Yes I did, and there wasn't anything. I wonder if there's something about me leaving the house. A tick, they call these. Set to jump when motion sensors go off. Something stuck to the door lintel or someplace. God *damn* him."

Frank was trying to see over her shoulder, down the path where he had seen movement. Feeling grim, he pulled out his FOG phone and called Zeno's.

It rang twice. "How does this thing work? Hey, Joe's Bar and Grill! Who the fuck are you?"

"Zeno it's Frank."

"Who?"

"*Frank*. Professor Nosebleed."

"Oh hey, Nosey! What's happening man? Did you spot the jaguar?"

It sounded like he'd downed a couple of beers. "Worse than that," Frank said, thinking hard. "Look Zeno, I've got a problem and I'm wondering if you could give me a hand."

"What you got in mind?"

"The thing is, it might be kind of dangerous. I don't want to get you into it without telling you that."

"What kind of danger?"

"I've got a jacket here that people are using to tail me with. People I really need to get away from. What I want to do is have them follow the jacket away from me, while I clear out of here."

"Where are ya?"

"I'm in the park. Are you at your usual spot?"

"Where else."

"What I was hoping is that I could run by you guys, like I'm playing frisbee golf, and hand off the jacket to you and keep on running. Then if one of you would hustle the jacket out to Connecticut, and leave it in the laundromat next to Delhi Dhaba, I could turn the tables on these people, pick them up when they follow the jacket, and then tail them back to where they came from."

"Shit, Noseman, it sounds like you must be some kind of a spook after all! So you been out here hiding among us, is that it?"

"Sort of, sure."

"Harrrrrr. I knew it musta been something."

"So are you up for it? While you've got the jacket you'll have to move fast, but I don't think they'll do anything to you, especially out on Connecticut. It's more a surveillance kind of thing."

"Ah fuck that." Zeno brayed his harsh bray. "It won't be no worse than the cops. Parole officers stick that shit right into your *skin*."

"That's right. Okay, thanks. We'll come through in about ten minutes."

"We? Who's this *we*?"

"Another spook. You know how it is."

"A lady spook? You got a lady in distress there maybe?"

Sometimes it was alarming how quick Zeno guessed things. "Are the rest of the bros there with you?"

"Of course."

"Good. Maybe they can add to the confusion. When we pass through and hand off the jacket, have them—"

"We'll beat the shit out of them!"

"No no no." Frank felt a chill. "They could be armed. You don't want to fuck with that. Maybe just go off in two or three groups. Give you some cover, create some confusion."

"Yeah sure. We'll deal."

"Okay, thanks. See you soon. We'll come in from the creek side and just pass right on through."

Frank pushed the END button. He looked at the chip wand. "Could this wand be chipped itself?"

"I don't know. I guess so."

"We'll leave it here. You said in the elevator you were training for a tri-athlon, right?"

"Yes?"

"Is your husband a runner?"

"What? No."

"Okay." He took her by the arm and led her off the path, up into the trees. "Let's run. We'll go past my park friends and give them your jacket, then take off on the ridge trail north. He won't be able to keep up with us, and after a while he won't know where you are."

"Okay."

Off they ran, Caroline fast on Frank's heels. He ran up Ross to site 22, then turned up the trail that ran to the Nature Center, hurrying the pace so that they would gain some time. Behind him he heard the faint crackle of the pursuit.

They crossed the frisbee golf course, and then Frank really pushed it. At a certain point her husband wouldn't be able to keep up. Once you were winded the will counted for nothing. As animals he and Caroline were stronger, and out here they were animals. Down the narrow fairway of hole five, leading her between the trees to the left so they wouldn't be seen. Running almost as hard as he could in the dark, Caroline right behind.

Then he was in site 21 and the bros were all standing around, wide-eyed and agog at the sight of them. Even in the midst of his adrenaline rush Frank saw that he would never hear the end of this.

He gestured to Caroline, helped her out of her jacket.

"Hi guys." He met Zeno's eye. Now more than ever Zeno looked impressive, like Lee Marvin in his moment of truth.

"Thanks," Frank said, tossing the jacket at him in their usual aggro style.

"Where do you want me to go again?"

"Delhi Dhaba. Drop the jacket in the laundromat next door and get the fuck out of there."

"Sure."

"The rest of you wait a second and then wander off. Stick together though."

"Yeah man."

"We'll beat the fuck out of them."

"Just keep moving. Thanks boys."

And with that Frank took Caroline by the hand and they were off again.

Running down the hole-seven fairway he pulled off his down jacket, then passed it back to her. "Here, put this on."

"No I'm okay."

"No you're not, you were shivering already."

"What about you?"

"We run the course out here in T-shirts all the time. I'm used to it. Besides you've got to keep on going after this, right? Whereas I can go home."

"Are you sure this isn't chipped too?"

"Yes. I've owned it for twenty years, and no one else has been anywhere near it."

"Okay, thanks."

She pulled it on as they jogged, and then they started running full speed.

"You okay?" Frank said over his shoulder.

"Yeah fine. You?"

"I'm good," Frank said. And he was; his spirits were rising as he got on the ridge path and led her north on it. Frozen mud underfoot, frigid air rushing past him; there was no way anyone on foot, without chips to aid them, could track them for long when they were moving like this.

He passed hole eight and turned up cross trail 7, and soon they were out onto Brandywine, and rising to Connecticut.

Just short of the avenue, where there was still some darkness to huddle in, he stopped her, held her. As they hugged he felt for the Acheulian hand axe, there in his jacket pocket against her side.

"What is that?" she asked.

"My lucky charm."

"Pretty heavy for a lucky charm."

"Yeah, it's a rock. I like rocks."

They stood there, arms around each other, poorly lit by a distant street-light. Her face twisted with distress; why couldn't it be simple? her look seemed to say. Why couldn't they just be here?

But it wasn't simple.

"The Van Ness Metro is just down there," Frank said, pointing south on Connecticut.

"Thanks."

"Where will you go?"

"I've got a place set up." Then: "Listen, I heard what you said to those guys, but don't you stick around and mess with him," she said, waving to the east. "He's dangerous. Really. And we don't want him to know you had anything to do with this."

"I know," Frank said. They hugged again. Briefly they kissed. He liked the feel of her in his jacket.

"Here," she said, "you should take your jacket back. I'm going to get in the Metro, and then I'll be in my little underground railroad, and I won't need it."

"You're sure?"

"Yes."

"Okay." He took the jacket from her, put it on, put the hand axe back in its pocket. "Where will you go?"

"I'll contact you as soon as I can," she said. "We'll set up a system."

"But—"

"I'll let you know! Just let me go—I have to go!"

"Okay!" Frank said, frustrated.

Then she was off. Watching her turn the corner and disappear he felt a sudden stab of fear. God *damn* this guy, he thought.

He walked north to Delhi Dhaba and passed it, glanced into the laundromat next door. It was almost empty, only a couple of young women folding clothes together at the tables. Caroline's black ski jacket was already there, hanging from the door of a dryer. No sight of Zeno or any of the rest of the bros. Frank walked down to the corner and stood at the bus stop, then sat on the bench in its little shelter, consciously working to slow his breathing and pulse.

Ten minutes passed. Then three men in black leather jackets approached the laundromat, hands in their pockets. One, a tall, heavyset blond man, appeared to be checking a very heavy watch. He looked at the other men, gestured inside the laundromat. One turned and settled at the door, looking up and down Connecticut. The others went in. Frank sat there looking across the street away from them. The man guarding the door registered him along with the three others waiting at the bus stop, then he turned his attention to the various people walking up and down the sidewalks.

The two men reappeared in the doorway, the blond man holding Caroline's jacket. That was him, then. Frank's teeth clenched. The three men conferred. They all surveyed the street, and the blond man appeared to check his watch again. He looked up, toward Frank; said something to the others. They began to walk down the sidewalk toward him.

Shocked at this turn of events, Frank got up and hustled around the corner of Davenport. As soon as the buildings at the corner blocked their view of him he bolted, running hard east toward the park. Looking back once, he saw that they were there on Davenport, also running; chasing him down. The blond man ran with his right hand in his jacket pocket.

Frank turned on Linnaean, running harder. East again on Brandywine, a real burst of speed, unsustainable, but he wanted to get into the trees again as soon as he could. As he pounded along, gasping, he thought about the man spotting him by way of his wrist device, and decided that his down jacket must be compromised now too. Caroline had worn it, she had been chipped with a tick, these ticks were probably not used alone but in little swarms; she could have had some in her hair, who knew, but if one or more had fallen or migrated from her hair onto his jacket, he would be chipped himself. That had to be it.

Or maybe he had just been chipped all along.

He flew down the slope to site 21, found it still empty, the neglected fire still flickering. Off with his jacket, off with his shirt. The frigid air hit him and he growled. He took the hand axe out of the jacket and put it into his pants pocket.

He ran up into the mass of trees west of the site, stopped and rubbed his hands over his neck, gently and then roughly; felt nothing. He ran his hands through his hair again, leaning forward and down, pulling at his locks and shaking his head like a wet dog. Tearing at his scalp. Best he could do. Now he had to move again, just in case; he circled around the site and ducked behind one of the big flood windrows, crouched and got a view of the picnic table, between two branches.

He heard them before he saw them, all three men crashing down Ross into the site. They stopped when they saw his jacket and shirt, turned quickly and looked around them, surveying their surroundings like a team that had done it before. Frank felt the tousled hair rise on the back of his neck. His teeth were clenched.

The blond man's hair caught a gleam of firelight. He picked up the jacket, hefted it. Then the shirt. Now came the test. Was there still a tick on Frank? The three men turned in circles, looking outward, and as they did the blond man checked his wrist. Frank stayed frozen in place, waiting for a sign. The blond man's chest rose and fell, rose and fell. He was winded. Frank tried to imagine his thoughts, then fell squeamishly away. He didn't want to know what went on in a mind like that. Plots, counterplots, chipping people— spying on his own wife—out here in Rock Creek Park in the middle of the night, chasing people down. It was ugly.

Frank felt the frozen air as if he were clothed in an invisible shirt made of his own heat. Outside that, it was obviously cold, but inside his shell he seemed okay, at least for now. When he moved he pushed through the shell into the chill.

Up on Ross came the sound of people walking, then Zeno's nicotine voice. Frank shifted down, pulled his phone from his pocket, and punched the REPEAT CALL function.

"Hey Blood, wassup?"

"Zeno they're back at your picnic table," Frank whispered. "They've got guns."

"Oh ho."

"Don't go down there."

"Don't you worry. Do you need help?"

"No."

"We'll deploy anyway. Ha—too bad you can't call the jaguar out on these guys, eh?"

"Yeah," Frank said, and thought to add that he was going to be the jaguar tonight; but Zeno wasn't listening. Frank could hear over the phone that he was telling the bros the situation. In the open air their noise had abruptly died away.

Then: "Hey fuck that!" Andy exclaimed, carrying both over the phone and through the air.

On the phone Frank heard Zeno say, "Fucking A, Blood, here comes the cavalry—"

Then the forest filled with howls, the crash of people through the forest— and from down near the creek, BANG BANG BANG!

The men at the picnic tables had dropped out of sight. But their conference was brief; after about five seconds they burst to their feet and ran away, south on Ross. Shrieks and howls followed them through the darkness.

Frank took off after them. Howling marked where the bros were in their pursuit, and thunks and crashes made it clear rocks were being thrown.

Frank darted from tree to windrow to tree, keeping above and abreast of the running men. When they came down the slope to Glover, two of them turned left, while the blond man turned right. Frank followed him, worrying briefly that the two others would come back and jump on the tail of any pursuit. Hopefully Zeno and the bros had already laid off. Nothing to be done about that now. He needed to concentrate on following the blond man.

Stalking prey at night, in the forest. How big the world got when you could taste blood. The frigid air cut through the radiance of his body heat, it drove into him, but it was only part of the chase, part of what made him utterly on point. All the hours he had spent out in this park filled him, he knew where he was and what he needed to do. It all came down to pursuit.

The trees lining Glover were thick, the ground covered with branches, leaves, patches of new snow. He had trailed feral animals here. A human would be both more aware and more oblivious. The blond man was striding rapidly up the road, stopping from time to time to look back. He appeared to be holding a pistol in his right hand. Frank froze when he looked around, then darted from tree to tree, moving only when the man's back was to him. Stay parallel to him but always behind his peripheral vision; be ready to freeze, stop when his head turned; it was like a game, feet lightly thrusting forward, feeling their way to silent landings, over and over, on and on; freezing to check the quarry from behind a trunk, one eye out, as in all the hide-and-seek games of childhood, but now performed with total concentration. On the hunt, yes, huge areas opening inside him—he could see in the dark, he could gazelle through the forest over downed branches without a sound, freeze faster than a head could whip around, all with a fierce cold focus. When the man whipped his head around Frank found himself as still as a statue before the blond head had moved even an inch, before Frank himself knew it had moved; yet he could barely see it in the dark, just a gleam reflecting distant streetlights through the trees.

At Grant Road the man turned west. He walked out on the street, to Davenport and west toward Connecticut. Now they were under streetlights again, and very few people were out at this hour—none visible at this moment. Frank had to drop back, move across people's front lawns. The man continued to whip his head around to look back from time to time. Frank lagged as far as he could while still keeping him in sight, but still, if he could see the man, the man could see him. His van was one block over, on Brandywine; he could drop down to it on Thirtieth, unlock by remote as he approached, snatch out a sweater and windbreaker, put them on as he walked, then continue out to Connecticut and hope to relocate the man. The man was out of sight for the moment, so Frank crossed the street and took off in a dash, tearing around the corner and ripping open his van door, getting the clothes on as he took off again west on Brandywine.

He slowed as he approached Connecticut. And there was the blond man, hurrying past him down the big avenue, glowering.

Frank fell in behind him. They were approaching the Van Ness/UDC Metro station. At the top of the escalator the man glanced one last time over his shoulder, a sneer twisting his face, the petulant sneer of a man who always got what he wanted—

Frank snatched the hand axe from his pocket and threw it as hard as he could. The stone spun through the air on a line and flashed past the man's head so close to his left ear that the man lurched reflexively to the right, disappearing abruptly from view as the stone whacked into the concrete wall backing the escalator hole.

Frank ran to it, slowed, looked down into the big oval tunnel, caught sight of the blond man running down the last risers into the station below. Frank circled the opening, picked up his hand axe lying on the sidewalk. It looked the same, maybe a new chip on one edge. There was a deep gash in the concrete wall. He felt it with a finger, found his hand was trembling.

Back to the escalator, down behind a pair of students, pass them on the left. Windbreaker hood over his head? No. Nothing unusual. But it was cold. He pulled the hood over his head, put his hands in the windbreaker's pockets, axe cradled in the right hand. His hands were cold, ears too. Nose running.

Down into the station, buy ticket, through the turnstiles. Look over the metal rail, assuming that the blond man would be going toward Shady Grove: yes. There he was, blond hair gleaming in the dim light of the station.

Frank grabbed a free paper from a trash can, descended to trackside, sat on one of the concrete benches pretending to read. The blond man stood by the track. The lights in the floor flashed on and off. In the dim warmth they felt the first blast of wind from the coming train.

Frank got on the car ahead of the one the man entered. He was pretty sure the man would get off at Bethesda, as Caroline had that first time. So when they rolled into Bethesda he got off a little before the man did, walked to the up escalator ahead of him, took it up without looking back. Through the turnstiles, up the last long escalator, standing to the right as so many people did.

Near the top the blond man brushed by him on the left, already talking on his cell phone. "We'll find her," he said as he passed. "I know she did it."

Frank stayed on his big riser, teeth clenched. He followed the man across the bus level of the station to the last escalator, up that. Then south on Wisconsin, just the way Caroline had gone that first time, including a right turn on a side street. The man was still talking on his phone, not looking around. Barking an order, laughing once. An ugly sound. Frank tried to relax his jaw, he was going to break a tooth. He was hot inside his windbreaker, breaking a sweat. A few blocks west of Wisconsin the man put his phone in his pocket and soon after that turned up the broad stairs of a small apartment building on Hagar. He entered the building without looking back.

Frank waited for a few minutes, looking at the building. He didn't want it to be over. Suddenly he saw what to do. He went up the steps to the apartment door, jabbed every little black doorbell on the panel to the left of the door, then hustled across the street and stood under a streetlight casting a cone of orange light on the sidewalk and part of the street. He stood under one edge of the light, pulling the hood of his windbreaker far forward. His face was sure to be in shadow: a black absence, like a hit man. He thrust the pointed end of the hand axe forward in the windbreaker pocket until it pushed at the cloth.

The curtain in the window on the top floor twitched. His quarry was looking down at him. Frank tilted his head up just enough to show that he was returning the gaze. He held the pose for a few seconds, long enough to make his point. *The hunter hunted.* Hunted by a murderous watcher, always there to haunt one's dreams. Then he stepped back and out of the cone of light, into dark shadows and away.

After that Frank walked back out to Wisconsin.

He started to shiver in his thin sweater and windbreaker. Up to the Metro.

He felt stunned. Some of what he had done in the heat of the moment now shocked him, and he reeled a bit as he remembered, growing more and more appalled—throwing the hand axe at him? What had he been thinking? He could have killed the guy! Good, good riddance, that would have taught him—except not! It would have been terrible. The police would have hunted for Caroline. They would have been hunting for him too, without knowing they were; but Caroline when she heard about it would have known who did it, and no matter what, it would have been terrible. Crazy. Leap before you look, okay, but what if your leaps were crazy? He didn't even want to be out there! He had broken a date with Diane to do this shit!

Back up Wisconsin again. He didn't know what to do. He wondered if he would ever see Caroline again. Maybe she had used him to help her get away, the same way he had used the bros to help him. Well sure. That was what had happened, in effect. And he had offered to do it. But still . . .

Down into the Metro, nervous waiting, down to Van Ness, out of the Metro. Back in his van Frank changed clothes again. Despite the cold his shirt was soaked with sweat. Pull on his capilene undershirt, thick sweater; in the van's mirror he could see that once again he looked fairly normal. Incredible.

He sat in the driver's seat. He didn't know what to do. His hands were still shaking. He felt sick.

Eventually the cold drove him to start the engine. Then, driving north on Connecticut, he thought of going to the Quiblers. He could sit there and drink a beer and watch the fucking election results. No one would care if he didn't say anything. Warm up. Play chess or Scrabble with Nick and watch the TV.

He got in the left-turn lane at Bradley. Waiting for the light he remembered the bros and pulled out his FOG phone, hit RESEND.

"Hey Nosey."

"Zeno are you guys okay?"

"Yeah sure. Are you?"

"I'm okay. Hey listen, my clothes I left there at the tables are chipped with some kind of microwave transmitter."

"We figured as much. So you got parole officers too, eh?"

"I guess so."

"Ha. We'll DX your stuff. But what was with that gal, eh? Don't you know not to mess with parole officers?"

"Yeah yeah. What about you, what was that shooting, who did that? I didn't think you guys were carrying."

"Yeah right." Zeno snorted. "We kill those deer with our teeth."

"Well, there is that."

"Shit's dangerous out here. I can't hardly keep Andy from popping people in situations like that. Everyone's a gook when he gets excited."

"Well, it did put those guys on the run."

"Sure. Better than getting hit in the face with a two-by-four."

"Yeah, true. So—thanks for the help."

"That's okay. But don't do shit like that to us no more. We get enough excitement as it is."

"Yeah okay."

Charlie answered the doorbell and was happy to see Frank. "Hey Frank, good to see you, come on in! The Khembalis came over on their way home too, and the early returns are looking good pretty good."

"My fingers are crossed," Frank said, but as he took off his windbreaker he looked unhopeful. Inside the entryway he stopped as he saw people sitting in the living room by the fire. He went over and greeted Drepung and Sucandra and Padma, done with their own party, and then Charlie introduced him to Sridar. Again it seemed to Charlie that Frank was unusually subdued. No doubt many of his big programs at NSF were riding on the election results.

Charlie went out to the kitchen to get drinks, and circulating as he did in the next hour, he only occasionally noticed Frank, talking or playing with Joe, or watching the TV. Results were coming in more quickly now. The voting in every state was tight, the results as predicted: the red states went to the president, the blue states to Phil Chase. The exceptions tended to balance out, and it became clear that this time it was going to come down to the western states. Chase had a decent chance of winning the whole West Coast, and if some of the late-reporting states went his way, the election too. It was all hanging in the balance.

Charlie sat above Nick on the couch, watching the colored maps on the TV, talking sometimes on the phone with Roy. Joe was sitting on the floor, putting together the wooden train tracks and babbling to himself. Charlie watched him very curiously, not sure what he was seeing yet. Anna had taken Joe's temperature when they got home, curious at the effect of the snow, Charlie assumed. It had been 98.2; she had shaken her head, said nothing.

Charlie felt a bit drained, perhaps of the feeling of oppression that had been weighing on him for a long time, lifted now and leaving a lightness that felt also a bit empty perhaps. He didn't know what he felt. He saw that Drepung too was keeping an eye on Joe; and on him.

Frank sat on the couch across from them, chewing a toothpick and looking tense. The evening wore on. Eventually the Khembalis said their goodbyes and left. "I'll be home in a bit," Frank said to them.

When they were gone, Frank glanced at Charlie. "Mind if I stay and see it out?"

"Not at all. As long as it doesn't go on for three months."

"Ha. It is looking close."

"I think California will put us over the top."

"Maybe so."

They watched on. Eastern states, central states, mountain states. Joe fell asleep on the floor; Nick read a book, lying sleepily on the couch. Charlie went to the bathroom, came back downstairs. "Any more states?"

Anna and Frank shook their heads. Things appeared to be hung up out west. Frank sat hunched over, eating his toothpick fragment by fragment. Anna sighed, went out to the kitchen to clean up. She did not like to hope for things, Charlie knew, because she feared the disappointment if her hopes were dashed. You should hope anyway, Charlie had told her more than once. We have to hope.

Hopes are just wishes we doubt will come true, she always replied. She preferred waiting, then dealing with whatever happened. Work on the moment.

But of course it was impossible not to hope, no matter what one resolved. Now she clattered dishes nervously in the kitchen, hoping despite herself. Therefore irritated.

"I wonder what's up," Charlie said.

"Hnn."

Frank was never a big talker, but tonight the cat seemed to have got his tongue. Charlie always tried to fill silences made by other people, it was a bad habit but he was helpless to stop it, as he never noticed it was happening until afterward. "Okay, here's what's going to happen," he said now. "All the West is going to go for the President except California and Oregon, but that'll be enough for Phil to win."

"Maybe."

They watched the numbers on the screens get bigger. The minutes dragged by. Anna came back in and sat by Charlie, began falling asleep. Even before the boys had arrived nothing had been able to keep her awake past her bedtime, and now she had ten years of sleep deprivation to catch up on.

Then Charlie clicked away from a commercial to find that NBC was declaring California had gone for Phil Chase, which gave him 275 electoral votes and made him the winner. They got to their feet, cheering. Anna woke up confused: "What? What? Can it be? Can it be real?" She made them click around and confirm it on the other channels, and they all confirmed it. "Oh my God," she cried, and started to weep with joy. Charlie and Frank toasted with beer, got Nick a soda to toast with them. Joe woke up and climbed into Anna's lap; she channel-surfed, being suddenly eager to soak in all the information that she could. "How did this *happen*?" There were claims of irregularities in Oregon voting machines, apparently, where the margin of victory was especially tight. But Oregon, like California, had voting machine safeguards in place, and the officials there were confident the result would be validated.

Charlie gave Roy a call, and in the middle of the first ring Roy came on singing, "Ding dong, the witch is dead, the witch is dead, the witch is dead, ding dong, the wicked witch is dead!"

"Jesus Roy I could be a Republican staffer calling to congratulate you—"

"And I wouldn't give a damn! The wicked witch is *dead*! And our boss is *president*!"

"Yes, we're in for it now."

"Yes we are! You're going to have to come back to work, Chucker! No more Mr. Mom for you!"

"I don't know about that," Charlie said, glancing over at Joe, who was burbling happily at Anna as she leaned forward to hear the TV better. A traitorous thought sprang into his mind: That isn't my Joe.

"—get yourself down to the convention center and celebrate! Bring the whole family!"

"I don't know," Charlie said to Phil, then to Anna and Frank: "Should we go down to the headquarters and celebrate?"

"No," Anna and Frank said together.

"Maybe I'll go down there later," Charlie told Roy.

"Later, later, what's with later? This is the moment!"

"True. But it's a party that will last awhile."

"All night my friend. I wouldn't mind seeing you in the flesh, we need to confer big-time now! Everyone is going to get a new job, you realize that."

"Yes," Charlie said. "Advisor to the president."

"Friend of the president! We're his friends, Charlie."

"Us and twenty thousand other people."

"Yes but no, we're in the goddamned *White House*."

"I guess we are. Jesus. Well, Phil will be great. If anyone can stay human in that job, he can."

"Oh sure, sure. He'll be human, he'll be all too human."

"He'll be more than human."

"That's right! So get your ass down here and party!"

"Maybe I will."

Charlie let him get back to it. The house suddenly seemed quiet. Joe was still playing cheerfully on the couch next to Anna. She got up, smiling now, and started to clean up. Frank got up to help her.

"This should help all your projects big-time," Charlie said to him. "Phil is really into them."

"That's good. We'll need it."

"He'll probably appoint Diane Chang to a second term at NSF."

"Huhn," Frank said, looking over at him. "Really?"

"Yeah, I think so. I've heard that discussed. He likes what she's been doing, of course. How could you not?"

"I hadn't thought of that." Frank picked up a plate, looking distracted.

They finished cleaning up. "I guess I'll be off," Frank said. "Thanks for having me over."

The drive back to Khembali House took a long time. Frank chose to drive down Wisconsin and cross the Potomac on the Key Bridge, the shortest route physically, but it was a mistake; the streets were packed with people, literally packed, so that cars had to inch along, nudging their way forward through a mass of celebrating humanity. The District of Columbia had voted nine to one for Democratic candidates for many years, and now a good proportion of the ninety percent were in the streets partying, and cars be damned. A sudden Carnavale had burst onto Wisconsin. It had the feel of that day in the cold snap when everyone had gone out on the frozen Potomac. The city, surprised by joy.

Frank watched through the windows of his van, feeling detached. No doubt it was good news—indeed very good news—but he could not feel it. He was still too disturbed by what had happened with Caroline and her husband.

Inching forward, he gave Edgardo a call.

When Edgardo picked up, Frank's ear was blasted by the sound of one of Astor Piazzolla's wild tangos, the bandoneon leading the charge with such scrunching dissonances that Frank's phone screeched. "LET ME TURN IT DOWN" he heard as he held the phone at arm's length.

"Sure."

"Okay I'm back! Who is it?"

"It's Frank."

"Ah, Frank! How are you!"

"I'm okay. So, what happened?"

Edgardo laughed. "Didn't you hear? Phil Chase won!"

Behind his voice the tango kept charging along, and the shifting static in the phone led Frank to think that Edgardo might be dancing around his apartment.

"I know that, but how?"

"We will certainly be talking about how this happened for a long time,

Frank, and I'm sure it will keep us entertained for many runs to come. But I predict right now that no one will ever be able to say exactly why this election came out the way it did." He laughed again, seemingly at the way he could use such idiotic pundit clichés to convey exactly what he meant: *not now.* Of course. And maybe never. "Meanwhile just enjoy yourself, Frank. Celebrate."

In the background the tango band twirled on. Frank pushed END on his phone; he could tell Edgardo about the new thumb drive later. Best not to use phones anymore, as Edgardo had reminded him. He shook his head: his leap-before-you-look strategy was not able to notice all the potential consequences of an act. It was not working. He was simply confused.

He dropped into Georgetown. It was even more crowded than upper Wisconsin had been, but soon he would cross to Arlington, and presumably over there it wouldn't be like this. Frank was pretty sure Arlington wouldn't be celebrating at all. That would be all right with Frank.

Then just before the Key Bridge, traffic came to a complete halt. Downstream to the left he could see fireworks, shooting up off the levee next to the Lincoln Memorial, bursting over their own reflections in the black Potomac. All the celebrants crowding the street and sidewalk were cheering, many jumping up and down. Drivers of cars in front of Frank were giving up and getting out to stretch their legs, or join the party. Some of them climbed onto their cars.

Frank got out too, smacked by the cold into a new awareness of the night and the crowd. Every boom of the fireworks brought another cheer, and all the skyward-tipped faces shone with the succession of mineral colors splashing over them. Frank was seized by the arms by two young women, pulled into their dance as they sang, "Happy Days Are Here Again," kicking out in time before him. To keep step he started kicking as well, adding gibbon hoots to the general din. So what if sea level was rapidly rising, so what if there were lichen out there sucking carbon out of the sky—so what if the whole world had just seized the tiger by the tail! They were under a new dispensation, they were entering a new age! Oooooooooooop!

Then traffic was moving again, and Frank had to smooch his dancers and dash to his van. Into its warmth and over the bridge, creeping forward slowly, the fireworks still showering sparks into the river.

. . .

Over in Arlington it was entirely different: dark, empty, a little bit spooky. Street trees bounced and flailed on the wind. Snow blanketed the big open spaces downtown. Wilson Boulevard was deserted, just as he had thought it might be. There were two countries bound together now, and one of them was not celebrating. A cold and windy night to be sure. Hard to sustain being out on such a night, if one were not in Carnavale mode. Where would the knitting woman be tonight, for instance? And where was Chessman? Where would the bros sleep on this night? Did it matter to any of them that Phil Chase had won the election? In a system that demanded five percent unemployment, so that fifteen million people were going hungry, without jobs or homes, and an ice age coming on—did any election matter?

By the time Frank drove up to the curb outside Khembali House it was well after midnight, and he was exhausted. All was dark, the wind hooting around the eaves. The house had a presence in the night—big, solid, and he had to say, comforting. It was not his home, but it did feel like a place he could come to. Inside it were people he trusted.

Through the gate and around the back. Thank God they did not go in for those great Tibetan mastiffs that terrorized Himalayan villages. All was peaceful in the snowed-over autumn garden. Little scraps of prayer-flag flapped on a string in the breeze.

The light was on in their shed. He turned the doorknob gently and urged the door open with its most silent twist.

Rudra was sitting up in bed reading. "It's okay," he said. "No need to be quiet."

"Thanks."

Inside it was nice and warm. Frank was still shivering, though it was not visible on the surface. He sat down on his bed, cold hands between his legs and tucked under his thighs. Like sitting on two lumps of snow.

His main cell phone was on his bedside table, blinking. He pulled a hand out and tapped it to check. Message from Diane. Called; would call back. He stared at it.

"You also got call tonight on phone in house."

"What? I did?"

"Yes."

"Did they leave a message?"

"Qang say, a woman call, very late. Said, tell Frank she is okay. She will call again."

"Oh. Okay."

Frank sat there. He didn't know what to think. He could think this, he could think that. Could, could, could, could, could. Diane had called. Caroline had called.

"Windy."

"Sure is."

"Good night?"

"I guess so."

"You are not happy at election result?"

"Yeah, sure. It's great. If it holds."

"Good for Khembalung, I think."

"Yes, probably so. Good for everyone." Except for fifteen million of us, he didn't say.

"And your voyage, out to the fleet? Went well?"

"Oh, yeah, sure. Yeah, it was very interesting. We seeded the ocean. Poured five hundred million tons of salt in it."

"You put salt in ocean?"

"That's right."

Rudra grinned. Once again the thousand wrinkles in his face reconfigured into their particular map of delight. How often he must have smiled—

"I know I know!" Frank interrupted. "Good idea!"

Rudra laughed his helpless deep belly laugh. "Salt to ocean! Oh, very good idea!"

"Well, it was. We may have saved the world with that salt. Saved it from more winters like the last one, and this one too."

"Good."

Rudra considered it. "And yet you do not seem happy, my friend."

"No. Well." A deep, deep breath. ". . . I don't know. I'm cold. I'm afraid we're in for another bad winter, whether the salt works or not. I don't think any of the feral animals left will make it if that happens."

"You put out shelters?"

"Yes." An image: "I was in one of those myself, when Drepung found me and brought me here."

"You told me that."

"It was filled with all kinds of different animals, all in there together."

"That must have looked strange."

"Yes. And they saw me, too. I sat right down by them. But they didn't like it. They didn't like me being there."

Rudra shook his head regretfully. "No. The animals don't love us any-more."

"Well. You can see why."

"Yes."

They sat there, staring at the orange glow of the space heater.

Rudra said, "If winter is all that is troubling you, then you are okay, I think."

"Ah well. I don't know."

The taste of blood. Frank gestured at his cell phone, put his cold hand back under his thigh, rocked forward and back, forward and back. Warm up, warm up. Don't bleed inside. "There's too many . . . different things going on at once. I go from thing to thing, you know? Hour to hour. I see people, I do different things with them, and I'm not . . . I don't feel like the same person with these different people. I don't know what I'm doing. *I don't know what to do.* If anyone were watching they'd think I had some kind of mental disorder. Because I don't make any sense."

"But no one is watching."

"Except what if they are?"

Rudra shook his head. "No one can see inside you. So no matter what they see, they don't know. Everyone only judges themself."

"That's not good!" Frank said. "I need someone more generous than that!"

"Ha ha. You are funny."

"I'm serious!"

"A good thing to know, then. You are the judge. A place to start."

Frank shuddered, rubbed his face. Cold hands, cold face; and dead behind the nose. "I don't see how I can. I'm so different in these different situations. It's like living multiple lives. I mean I just act the parts. People believe me. But I don't know what I feel. I don't know what I mean."

"Of course. This is always true. To some you are like this, to others like that. Sometimes a spirit comes down. Voices take over inside you. People take away what they see, they think that is all there is. And sometimes you want to fool them in just that way. But want to or not, you fool them. And they fool you! And on it goes—everyone in their own life, everyone fooling all the others—No! It is easy to live multiple lives! What is hard is to be a whole person."

PART THREE

SIXTY DAYS AND COUNTING

CHAPTER 21

A NEW REALITY

"I believe the twenty-first century can become the most
important century of human history. I think a new reality is
emerging. Whether this view is realistic or not, there is no
harm in making an effort."
    —*The Dalai Lama, November 15, 2005, Washington, D.C.*

Why do you do what you do?

  I guess because we still kind of believe that the world can be saved.

  We? The people where you work?

  *Yes. Not all of them. But most. Scientists are like that. I mean, we're seeing
evidence that we seem to be starting a mass extinction event.*

  What's that?

  *A time when lots of species are killed off by some change in the environ-
ment. Like when that meteor struck and killed off the dinosaurs.*

  So people hit Earth like meteor.

  *Yes. It's getting to be that way for a lot of the big mammals especially. We're
in the last moments already for a lot of them.*

  No more tigers.

  *That's right. No more lots of things. So . . . most of the scientists I know
seem to think we ought to limit the extinctions. Just to keep the lab working.*

  The Frank Principle.

  (Laughs.) I guess. Some people at work call it that. Who told you that?

Drepung. Saving world so science can proceed. The Frank Principle.

Right. It's like Buddhism, right? Might as well make a better world.

Yes. So, your National Science Foundation—very Buddhist!

Ha ha. I don't know if I'd go that far. NSF is mostly pragmatic. They have a job to do and a budget to do it with. A rather small budget.

But a big name! National—Science—Foundation. Foundation means base, right? Base of house?

Yes. It is a big name. But I don't think they regard themselves as particularly big. Nor particularly Buddhist. Compassion and right action are not their prime motivation.

Compassion! So what! Does it matter why, if we do good things?

I don't know. Does it?

Maybe not!

Maybe not.

By the time Phil Chase was elected president, the world's climate was already far along on the way to irrevocable change. There were already 500 parts per million of carbon dioxide in the atmosphere, and another hundred would be there soon if civilization continued to burn its fossil carbon. Just as Franklin Delano Roosevelt was elected in the midst of a crisis that worsened before it got better, they were entangled in a moment of history when climate change, the destruction of the natural world, and widespread human misery were combining in a toxic and combustible mix. The new president had to contemplate drastic action while at the same time being constrained by any number of factors, not least the huge public debt created deliberately by the administration preceding his.

It did not help that the weather that winter careened wildly from one extreme to another, but was mainly almost as cold as the previous record-breaking year. Chase joked about it everywhere he went: "It's ten below zero, aren't you glad you elected me? Just think what it would have been like if you hadn't!" He would end speeches with a line from the poet Percy Bysshe Shelley:

"O, Wind, if Winter comes, can Spring be far behind?"

"Maybe it can," Kenzo pointed out with a grin.

In any case it was a fluky winter, and the American people were in an uncertain state of mind. Chase addressed this: "The only thing we have to *fear,*" he would intone, "is abrupt climate change!" He would laugh, and some people would laugh with him, understanding that there was indeed something to fear, but that they could do something about it.

His transition team worked with an urgency that resembled desperation. Sea level was rising; global temperatures were on the whole rising; there was no time to lose. Chase's good humor and casual style were therefore welcomed, when they were not reviled—much as it had been with FDR in the previous century. He would say, "We got ourselves into this mess and we can get out of it. The problems create an opportunity to remake our relationship to nature, and create a new dispensation. So—happy days are here again! Because we're making history, we are *seizing* the planet's history, I say, and turning it to the good."

Some scoffed; some took heart; some waited.

As far as Frank Vanderwal was concerned, there was something reassuring about the world being so messed up. It made his own life look like part of a trend, and a small part at that. Perhaps so small as to be manageable.

Although it didn't feel that way. There were reasons to be very concerned, even afraid. Caroline had disappeared on election night, chased by her husband and other armed agents of some superblack intelligence agency. She had stolen her husband's plan to steal the election, and Frank had passed it to Edgardo, to what effect he did not know. To help Caroline, Frank had had to break a date with Diane, his boss and a woman he loved—although what that meant, given the passionate affair he was carrying on with Caroline, he did not know. There was a lot he didn't know; and he could still taste blood at the back of his throat, months after his nose had been broken. He could not think for long about anything. He was living a life that he called parcellated, but others might call crazy. He could have been back home in San Diego by now, and instead he was a temporary guest of the embassy of the drowned nation of Khembalung. But hey, everyone had problems! Why should he be any different?

Although brain damage would be a little more than different. Brain damage meant something like—mental illness. It was a hard phrase to articulate when thinking about oneself. But it was possible his injury had exacerbated a lifelong tendency to make poor decisions. It was hard to tell. He thought all his recent decisions had been correct, at least in the moment he made them. Should he not therefore have faith that he was following a valid line of thought? He wasn't sure!

Thus there were days when he welcomed the world's bad news, so much larger and wilder than his own. And he saw that other people were doing the same.

. . .

At the National Science Foundation, Frank and many others were trying to deal with the climate problem. To do so, they had to keep trying to understand:

1. the ambiguous results of their Atlantic salting operation;
2. the equally ambiguous proliferation of a genetically modified "fast tree lichen" that had been released by the Russians in Siberia;
3. the ongoing detachment of the West Antarctic Ice Sheet, and the resulting rapid rise of sea level;
4. the ongoing introduction of about nine billion tons of carbon dioxide into the atmosphere every year, ultimate source of many other problems;
5. the ensuing uptake of some four billion tons of carbon into the oceans;
6. the rise of the human population by about 100 million people a year;
7. and lastly, the cumulative impacts of all these events, gnarled together in feedback loops of all kinds.

It was a formidable list, and Frank worked hard to keep his focus on it.

But he was beginning to see that his personal problems—especially Caroline's disappearance, and the election-tampering scheme she was tangled in—were not going to be things he could ignore by focusing on the big picture. They pressed on his mind.

She had called the Khembali embassy on election night, and left a message saying that she was okay. Earlier, in Rock Creek Park, she had told him she would be in touch as soon as she could.

He was therefore waiting for that contact, he told himself. But it had not come. And Caroline's ex, who had also been her boss, had been following her that night. The ex knew that Caroline knew he was following her, and that night he had also seen that Caroline had received help in escaping from him. So now this man might still be looking for her, and might also be looking for that help she had gotten, as another way of hunting for her.

Or so it seemed. Frank couldn't be sure. He sat at his desk at NSF, staring at his computer screen, trying to think it through. He could not seem to do it. Whether it was the difficulty of the problem, or the inadequacy of his mentation, he could not be sure; but he could not do it.

So he went to see Edgardo. He entered his colleague's office and said, "Can we talk about the election result? What happened that night, and what might follow?"

"Ah! Well, that will take some time to discuss. And we were going to run today anyway. Let's talk about it while en route."

Frank took the point: no sensitive discussions in their offices. Surveillance all too possible.

In the locker room they changed into running clothes, then Edgardo took from his locker a security wand that resembled those used in airports, and had been used by Caroline. Frank was startled to see it, but nodded silently and allowed Edgardo to run it over him. Then he did the same for Edgardo.

They appeared to be clean of devices.

As they ran the streets, Frank said, "Have you had that thing for long?"

"Too long, my friend." Edgardo veered side to side as he ran, warming up in his usual extravagant manner. "But I haven't had to get it out for a while."

"Don't you worry that having it there looks odd?"

"No one notices things in the locker room."

"Are our offices bugged?"

"Yes. Yours, anyway. But coverage is very spotty, just by the nature of things. The various agencies that do this have different interests and abilities, and very few even attempt total surveillance. And then only for crucial cases. Most of it is what you might call statistical in nature, covering parts of the datasphere. You can slip out of such surveillance."

"What about these so-called total information awareness systems?"

"Mostly they mean electronic data. Then also you might be chipped in various ways, which would give your GPS location, and perhaps record what you say. Followed, filmed—sure, all that's possible, but it's expensive. But now we're clear. So tell me what's up."

"Well—like I said. About the election results, and that program I gave you. From my friend. What happened?"

Edgardo grinned under his mustache. "We foxed that program. You could say that we unstole the vote in Oregon, right in the middle of the theft."

"We did?"

"Yes. The program was a stochastic tilt engine, which had been installed in some of Oregon and Washington's voting machines. My friends figured that out and managed to write a disabler, and get it introduced at the very last minute, so there wasn't time for the people who had installed the tilter to react to our change. From the sounds of it, a very neat operation."

Frank felt a glow spread through him as he tried to comprehend it. Not only the election, derigged and made honest—not only Phil Chase elected by a cleaned-up popular and electoral vote—but his Caroline had proved true. She had risked herself and come through for the country; for the world, really.

So maybe she would come through for him too.

This train of thought led him to a new flood of fear for her.

Edgardo saw at least some of this, for he said, "So your friend is for real."

"Yes."

"It could get tricky for her," Edgardo suggested. "If the tweakers try to find the leakers. As we used to say at DARPA."

"Yeah," Frank said, his pulse rate rising at the thought.

"You've sent a warning?"

"I would if I could."

"Ah!" Edgardo was nodding. "Gone away, has she?"

"Yes," Frank said; and then it was all pouring out of him. He told Edgardo the story of how they had met, and what had followed. This was something he had never managed to do with anyone, and now it felt as if his silence had been a dam that had failed and let forth a flood.

It took a few miles to tell. The meeting in the stuck elevator, the sighting of her on the Potomac during the flood, the brief phone call—her subsequent call—their meetings, their—affair.

And then, her revealing the surveillance program she was part of, and after that how she had had to run away on election night, and how he had helped her to evade her husband and his companions, who were now certainly connected with the attempted election theft.

Edgardo bobbed along next to him as he told the tale, nodding at each new bit of information, lips pursed tightly, head tilted to the side. It was like confessing to a giant praying mantis.

"So," he said at last. "Now you're out of touch with her?"

"That's right. She said she'd call me, but she hasn't."

"But she will have to be careful, since her husband knows about you."

"Yes. But—will he be able to identify who I am, do you think?"

"I think that's very possible, if he has access to her files."

"She worked for him."

"So. And he knows someone helped her that night."

"More than one person, actually, because of the guys in the park."

"Yes. That might help muddy the waters. But still, say he goes through her records to find out who she has been in contact with—will he find you?"

"I was one of the people she had under surveillance."

"But there will be a lot of those. Anything more?"

Frank tried to remember. "I don't know," he confessed. "I thought we were being careful, but . . ."

"Did she call you on your phone?"

"Yes, a few times. But only from pay phones."

"But she might have been chipped at the time."

"She tried to be careful about that."

"Yes, but it didn't always work, isn't that what you said?"

"Right. But—I don't think she ever said my name."

"Well—if you were ever both chipped at the same time, he would be able to see when you got together. And if he sourced all your cell phone calls, some would come from pay phones, and he might be able to cross-GPS those with her."

"Are pay phones GPS'd?"

Edgardo nodded. "They stay in one spot, which you can then GPS."

"Oh. Yeah."

Edgardo cackled at Frank as they ran. "There's lots of ways to find people! There's your acquaintances in the park, for instance. If he went out there and asked around, with a photo of you, he might be able to confirm."

"I'm just Professor Nosebleed to them."

"Yes, but the correlations." After a silence had stretched out a quarter mile, Edgardo said, "You perhaps ought to take some kind of preemptive action."

"What do you mean?"

"Well. You followed him to their apartment, right?"

"Yes."

"Not your wisest move of that night, by the way."

Frank didn't want to explain that his capacity for decision-making had likely been injured, and perhaps not good to begin with.

"—but now we can probably use that information to find out his cover identity."

"I don't know the address."

"You need to get it. Also the names on the doorbell plate, if any. But the apartment number for sure."

"Okay, I'll go back."

"Good. Be discreet. With that information, my friends could help you. Given what's happened, they might make it a high priority."

"And who do your friends work for?"

"Well. They're scattered around. It's a kind of internal check group."

"And you trust them on this kind of stuff?"

"Oh yes." The reptilian look in Edgardo's eye gave Frank a shiver.

In the days that followed, Frank passed his hours feeling baffled, and, under everything else, afraid. He would wake in the mornings, take stock, remember where he was: in the Khembali embassy house's garden shed, with Rudra snoring up on the bed and Frank on his foam mattress on the floor.

The daylight slanting through their one window would usually rouse him. He would listen to Rudra, call up on his laptop Emersonfortheday. com:

> We cannot trifle with this reality, this cropping-out in our planted gardens of the core of the world. No picture of life can have any veracity that does not admit the odious facts. A man's power is hooped in by a necessity which, by many experiments, he touches on every side until he learns its arc.

Maybe Emerson too had been hit on the head. Frank wanted to look into that. And he needed to look into Thoreau, too. Recently the keepers of the site had been posting lots of Henry David Thoreau, Emerson's young friend and occasional handyman. Amazing that two such minds had lived at the same time, in the same town—even for a while the same house. Thoreau, Frank was finding in these morning reads, was the great philosopher of the forest at the edge of town, and as such very useful to Frank—often more so than the old man himself.

Today's Thoreau was from his journal:

> I never feel that I am inspired unless my body is also. It too spurns a tame and commonplace life. They are fatally mistaken who think, while they strive with their minds, that they may suffer their bodies to stagnate in luxury or sloth. A man thinks as well through his legs and arms as his brain. We exaggerate the importance and exclusiveness of the headquarters. Do you sup-

pose they were a race of consumptives and dyspeptics who invented Grecian mythology and poetry? The poet's words are, "You would almost say the body thought!" I quite say it. I trust we have a good body then.

Except Thoreau *had* been a consumptive, active though he was in his life as a surveyor and wandering botanist. This passage had been written only two years before he died of tuberculosis, so he must have known by then that his lungs were compromised, and his trust in having a good body misplaced. For lack of a simple antibiotic, Thoreau had lost thirty or forty years. Still he had lived the day, and paid ferocious attention to it, as a very respectable early scientist.

And so off! Up Frank would leap, thinking about what the New England pair had said, and slipping out the door in a frame of mind to see the world and act in it.

No matter how early it was, he always found some of the old Khembalis already out in the garden they had planted in the backyard, mumbling to themselves as they weeded. Frank might stop to say hi to Qang if she was out there, or dip his head in the door to tell her whether he would be home for dinner that night; that was hardly ever, but she liked it that he let her know.

Then off to Optimodal on foot, blinking in the morning light, Wilson Avenue all rumbly and stinky with cars. Into the gym for a quick workout to get his brain as fully awake as it got these days. There was something wrong in there, a fog in certain areas. It was easiest to do the same thing every day, reducing the decisions he had to make. Habitual action was a ritual that could be regarded as a kind of worship of the day. And it was so much easier.

Sometimes Diane was there, a creature of habit also, and uneasily he would say hi, and uneasily she would say hi back. They were still supposed to be rescheduling that dinner, but she had said she would get back to him about it, and he was therefore waiting for her to bring it up, and she wasn't. This was adding daily to his anxiety. Who knew what anything meant really.

. . .

Back in his office Frank would sit at his desk, staring at his list of Things to Do, in a vain attempt to take his mind off Caroline. Ordinarily the list would be enough to distract anyone. Its length and difficulty made it all by itself a kind of blow to the head. It induced an awe so great that it resembled apathy. They had done so much and yet there was so much left to do. And as more disasters blasted into the world, their Things to Do list would lengthen. It would never shorten. They were like the Dutch boy sticking his fingers into the failing dike. What had happened to Khembalung was going to happen everywhere.

But there would still be land above sea level. There would still be things to do. One had to try.

Caroline had spoken of her Plan B as if she had confidence in it. She must have had a place to go, a bank account, that sort of thing.

Frank checked out the figures from the oceanography group. The oceans covered about seventy percent of the globe. About two hundred million square kilometers, therefore, and in the wake of the first really big chunks of the West Antarctic Ice Sheet floating away, sea level had risen about twenty centimeters. The oceanographers had been measuring sea level rise a millimeter at a time, so they were blown away, and spoke of this rise as of a Noah's flood. Kenzo was bursting with amazement and pride.

Back-of-the-envelope calculation: 0.2 meters times the 200 million square kilometers, was that 40,000 cubic kilometers? A lot of water. Measurements from the last few years had Antarctica losing 150 cubic kilometers a year, with 30–50 more coming off Greenland. So about two hundred years' worth had come off in one year. No wonder they were freaking out. The difference no doubt lay in the fact that the melt before had been actual melting, whereas now what was happening was a matter of icebergs breaking off their perch and sliding down into the ocean. Obviously it made a big difference in how fast it could happen.

Frank brought the figures in with him to the meeting of Diane's strategic group scheduled for that afternoon, and listened to the others make their presentations. They were interesting talks, if daunting. They took his mind off Caroline, one had to say that. At least most of the time.

At the end of the talks, Diane described her sense of the situation. For her, there was a lot that was good news. First, Phil Chase was certain to be more supportive of NSF than his predecessor was, and to have more belief in science in general. Second, the salting of the North Atlantic appeared to be having the effect they had hoped for: the Gulf Stream was now running at nearly its previous strength, following its earlier path in a manner that indicated the renewed pattern was fairly robust.

Diane moved on to the West Antarctic Ice Sheet situation. One of Kenzo's oceanographer colleagues gave them a presentation showing with maps and satellite photos the tabular superbergs that had detached and floated away.

Diane said, "I'd like some really good three-D graphics on this, to show the new president and Congress, and the public too."

"All very well," Edgardo said, "but what can we do about it, aside from telling people it's coming?"

Not much; or nothing. Even if they somehow managed to lower the level of atmospheric carbon dioxide, and therefore the air temperatures, the already rising ocean temperatures would be slow to follow. There was a continuity effect.

So they couldn't stop the WAIS from detaching.

They couldn't lower the rising sea level that resulted.

And they couldn't deacidify the ocean.

This last was a particularly troubling problem. The ocean had become measurably more acid, going from 8.2 to 8.1 on the pH scale, which was a logarithmic scale, so that the 0.1 shift meant thirty times more hydrogen atoms in the water. Certain species of phytoplankton would have their thin calcium shells eaten away. A number of species would go extinct, and these very species constituted a big fraction of the bottom of the ocean's food chain.

But deacidifying the ocean was not an option. A Royal Society paper had calculated that if they mined and crushed exposed limestone and marble in the British Isles, "features such as the White Cliffs of Dover would be rapidly consumed," because it would take sixty square kilometers of limestone mined a hundred meters deep, every year, just to hold the status quo. All at a huge carbon cost for the excavations, of course, exacerbating the very problem they were trying to solve. But this was just a thought experiment anyway. It wouldn't work; it was an unmitigatable problem.

And that afternoon, as they went down Diane's list together, they saw that almost all the changes they were seeing were not susceptible to mitigation. Their big success of the fall, the restarting of the thermohaline cycle, had been an anomaly in that sense. The Gulf Stream had rested so closely to a tipping point that humans had, by an application at the largest industrial scale they commanded, managed to tip that balance—at least temporarily. Perhaps they had even escaped the Youngest Dryas. So now, in one of those quick leaps that humans were prone to make (although science was not), people were talking about the climate problem as if it were something that they could geo-engineer their way out of, or even had solved already!

It wasn't true. Most of the problems were so big they had too much momentum for people to marshal any way to slow them, much less reverse them.

So, at the end of this meeting, Edgardo shook his head. "This is grim! There is not much we can do! We would need much more energy than we command right now. And it would have to be clean energy at that."

Diane agreed. "Clean power is our only way out. That means solar power, I'd say. Maybe wind, although it would take an awful lot of pylons. Maybe nuclear, just one last generation to tide us over. Maybe ocean power too, if we could properly tap into currents or tides or waves. To me—when I look at factors like technical readiness and manufacturing capability, I'd say our best chance lies in solar. A kind of Manhattan Project devoted to solar power."

She raised a finger: "And when I say Manhattan Project, I don't mean the kind of silver bullet that people seem to mean when they say Manhattan Project. I mean the part of the Manhattan Project that entrained twenty percent of America's industrial capacity to make the bomb material. That's the kind of commitment we need now. Because if we had good solar power—"

She made one of her characteristic gestures, one that Frank had become very fond of: an opening of the palm, turned up and held out to the world. "We might be able to stabilize the climate. Let's organize the case, and take it to Phil Chase, and get him prepped for when he takes office."

After the meeting, Frank couldn't focus. Caroline had not called for yet another day. No telling where she was or what she was doing.

That night he wandered up Connecticut Avenue to the big bridge over Rock Creek, guarded by its four Disneyesque lion statues, then continued to the clutch of restaurants on the far side of the bridge, and chose one of the Indian ones. Ate a meal thinking about the names on the wine list. Vineyards in Bangalore, why was this surprising? Read his laptop over milk tea.

When it was late enough, he headed northwest, toward Bethesda. Night in the city, sound of distant sirens. For the first time in the day he felt awake. It was a long hike.

On Wisconsin he came into the realm of Persian rug shops, slowed down. It was still too early. Into a bar, afraid to drink, afraid to think. A whisky for courage. Out again, west into the tangle of streets backing Wisconsin. The Metro stop had been a fountain of money pouring up out of the earth, overwhelming whatever had been here before. Some of the old houses that still remained suggested an urban space of the 1930s, almost like the streets of Georgetown. This was the Quiblers' neighborhood, but he didn't want to intrude, nor was he in the mood to be sociable. Too late for that, but not early enough for his task. He was in the neighborhood of Caroline and her ex-husband. He circled. Finally it was late enough: midnight. His pulse was beginning to pound a little in his neck, and he wished he hadn't had that whisky. The streets were not entirely empty; that wouldn't happen until more like two. But that was okay. Up the steps of the apartment building that Caroline's ex had gone into. He shone his penlight on the address list under its glass, took a photo of it with his phone. Quite a few of the little slots were blank. He photoed the street address above the door as well, then turned and walked away from the streetlight he had stood under on that fateful night—his own fate, Caroline's, the nation's, maybe the world's—who knew? Probably it only felt that way. His heart was beating hard. Fight or flight, sure; but what if one could neither fight nor flee?

He turned a corner and ran.

Back in his office. Late in the day. He had given Edgardo his information from Bethesda. Soon he would have to decide again what to do after work.

Unable to face that, he continued to work. If only he could work all the time, he would never have to decide anything.

He typed up his notes from Diane's last two meetings, looked them over. It had come to this: they had fucked up the world so badly that only the rapid invention and deployment of some kind of clean power would be enough to extricate them from the mess. If it could be done at all.

That meant solar, as Diane had concluded. Wind was too diffuse, waves and currents too hard to extract energy from. Fusion was like the mirage on a desert road, always the same distance away. Ordinary nuclear—well, that was a possibility, as Diane had pointed out. It was dangerous and created waste for the ages, but it might be done. Some kinds of cost-benefit analysis might favor it.

But it was hard to imagine making it really safe. To do so they would have to become like the French (gasp!), who got ninety percent of their power from nuclear plants, all built to the same stringent standards. Not the likeliest scenario for the rest of the world, but not physically impossible. The U.S. Navy had run a safe nuclear program ever since the 1950s. Frank wrote on his notepad: *Is French nuclear power safe? Is U.S. Navy nuclear safe? What does safe mean? Can you recycle spent fuel and guard the bomb-level plutonium that would finally reduce out of it?* All that would have to be investigated. A method could not be taken off the table just because it created poisons that would last fifty thousand years.

On the other hand, solar was coming along fast enough to encourage Frank to hope for more. There were problems, but ultimately the fundamental point remained: in every moment an incredible amount of energy rained down from the sun onto the Earth. That was what oil was, after all; a small portion of the sun's energy, captured by photosynthesis over millions of years—all those plants, fixing carbon and then dying, then getting condensed into a sludge and buried. Millions of years of sunlight caught. Every tank of gas burned about a hundred acres of what had been a forest's carbon. This was a very impressive condensate! It made sense that matching it with the real-time energy input from any other system would be difficult.

But sunlight itself rained down perpetually. About seventy percent of the photosynthesis that took place on Earth was already entrained to human uses, but photosynthesis only caught a small fraction of the total amount of solar energy striking the planet each day. Those totals, day after day, soon dwarfed even what had been trapped in the Triassic fossil carbon. Every couple of months the whole Triassic's capture was surpassed. So the potential was there.

This was true in so many areas. The potential was there, but time was required to realize the potential, and now it was beginning to seem like they did not have much time. Speed was crucial. This was the reason Diane and others were still contemplating nuclear.

It would be good if they needed less energy, but this was an entirely different problem, dragging in many other issues—technology, consumption, lifestyles, values, habits—also the sheer number of humans on the planet. Perhaps ten billion was too many. It was possible that three billion was too many. Their eight billion could be a kind of oil bubble.

Edgardo was not calling, neither was Caroline calling.

Desperate for ways to occupy his mind—though of course he did not think of it that way, in order not to break the spell—Frank began to look into estimates of the Earth's maximum human carrying capacity. This turned out (usefully enough for the real purpose of distracting himself) to be an incredibly vexed topic, argued over for centuries already, with no clear answers found. There were estimates for the Earth's human carrying capacity ranging from one hundred million to twelve trillion. Quite a spread! Although here the outliers were clearly the result of heavily ideological analyses; the high estimate appeared to be translating the sunlight hitting Earth directly into calories, with no other factors included; the low estimate appeared not to like human beings, even to regard them as some kind of parasite.

The majority of serious opinions came in between two billion and thirty billion. This was satisfyingly tighter than the seven magnitudes separating the outlier estimates, but for practical purposes still a big variance, especially considering how important the real number was. If the carrying capacity of the planet was two billion, they had badly overshot and were in serious trouble. If on the other hand thirty billion was correct, they had some wiggle room.

But there were hardly any scientific or governmental organizations even looking at this issue. Zero Population Growth was one of the smallest advocacy groups in Washington, which was saying a lot; Negative Population Growth (a bad name, it seemed to Frank) turned out to be a mom-and-pop operation run out of a garage, and now defunct. It was bizarre.

He read one paper, written as if by a Martian, that suggested if humanity cared to share the planet with the other species, especially the mammals—and could they really survive without them?—then they should restrict their population to something like two billion, occupying only a networked fraction of the landscape. Leaving the rest of the animals in possession of a larger networked fraction. It was a pretty persuasive paper.

As another occupier of his thoughts (though now hunger was going to drive him out into the world), he looked into theories of long-term strategic policy, thinking this might give him some tools for thinking through these things. It was another area that seemed on the face of it to be important, yet was under-studied as far as Frank could tell. Most theorists in the field, he found, had agreed that the goal or method of long-term strategic thinking ought to be "robustness," which mean that you had to find things to do that would almost certainly do some good, no matter which particular future came to pass. Nice work if you could get it! Although some of the theorists actually had developed rubrics to evaluate the robustness of proposed policies. That could be useful. But when it came to generating the policies, things got more vague.

Just do the obvious things, Vanderwal. Do the necessary.

Diane was already acting in the manner suggested by most long-term strategy theorizing, because in any scenario conceivable, copious amounts of clean solar energy would almost certainly be a good thing. It was a *robust plan.*

So, solar power. Southern California Edison had built a 500-megawatt solar plant, full size relative to conventional types. That meant practical experience with real-world, commercial technology. Also manufacturing ability ready to be deployed. All good news when contemplating the need for speed.

Banishing the thought (recurrent about every hour) that they should have been doing this a long time ago, Frank called SCE and asked a long string of questions of the CPM (the Cognizant Program Manager, a useful acronym that only NSF appeared to use). This turned out to be a man who was more than happy to talk—who would have talked all day, maybe all night. With difficulty Frank got him to stop. Lots of enthusiasm there.

Well, more grist for the mill. Over the past year Frank had been giving alternative energy about a quarter of his working time, and now he saw he was going to have to bump that up. Everything from now on would be jacked to emergency levels. Not a comfortable feeling, but there was no avoiding it. It was like an existential condition, as if he had become Alice's White Rabbit: I'm late! I'm late! I'm late! And most of the time he managed to obscure from his conscious train of thought the true source of his anxiety.

One day when he was deep in work's oblivion, Diane appeared in his doorway, startling him. He was pleased, then nervous; they had not yet found a new balance. When Caroline had called Frank with her emergency situation, Frank had canceled with Diane before thinking of any plausible non-other-woman-related excuse, and so had given no explanation at all—which opacity was suspicious, and probably more impolite than the cancellation per se. Opacity was seldom conducive to rapport.

"Hi, Diane," he said now, aping normality. "What's happening?"

She looked at him curiously. "I just got a call from Phil Chase."

"Wow, what did he want?"

"He asked me if I would be his science advisor."

Frank found he was standing. He reached out and shook Diane's hand, then hugged her. "Now that is news we *have* to celebrate," he declared, seizing the bull by the horns. "I'm so sorry about that other night, I still owe you dinner! Can I take you out tonight?"

"Sure," she said easily, as if there had been no problem. She was so cool; maybe there never had been a problem. "Meet you at"—she checked her watch—"at six, okay? Now I'm going to go call my kids."

But then she stopped on her way out, and again looked at him oddly. "You must have had something to do with this," she said suddenly.

"Me? I don't think so! What do you mean?"

"Talking to Charlie Quibler?"

"Oh, no. I mean, I've talked to Charlie about some of our stuff—"

"And he's Chase's environment guy."

"Well yes, but you know, Charlie's just part of a large staff, and he's been staying at home with Joe, so he hasn't been a major factor with Chase for some time. Mostly just a voice on the phone, and he says he doesn't get listened to. He says he's like Jiminy Cricket to Pinocchio, when Pinocchio's nose was at its longest."

Diane laughed. "Yeah sure. Let's meet over at Optimodal, shall we? Let's say seven instead of six. I want to run some of this off."

Now that was something he could understand. "Sure. See you there."

Frank sat in his chair feeling his chest puffed out: another cliché revealed to be an accurate account of emotion's effects on the body. Everyone was the same. It occurred to him that maybe Charlie *had* had something to do with it, after all. Someone must have advised Chase whom to choose for this post, and as far as Frank knew, Chase and Diane had never met. So— that was interesting.

Frank went over to the Optimodal Health Club just after six, waved to Diane on the elliptical in the next room, and stomped up the StairMaster about a thousand vertical feet. After that he showered and dressed, getting into one of his "nicer" shirts, and met Diane out in the lobby. She too had changed into something nice, and for a second Frank considered the possibility that she lived out of her office and Optimodal, just as he had contemplated doing before building his treehouse. What evidence did he or anyone else have to disprove it? When they arrived in the morning she was there, when they left at night she was there. There were couches in her big office, and she went to Optimodal every morning of the week, as far as he knew. . . .

But then again, she certainly had a home somewhere. Everyone did, except for him. And the bros in the park. And the fregans and ferals proliferating in the metropolis. And indeed some twenty or thirty million people in America, he had read. Even so, one thought of everyone as having a home.

Enough—it was time to focus on the moment and their date. It had to be called that. Their second date, in fact, the first one having occurred by accident in New York. And now they were in a Lebanese restaurant in Georgetown that Diane had recently discovered.

And it was very nice. Now they could celebrate not only the Atlantic salting operation, but its success; and also Diane's invitation to become the new presidential science advisor.

She was pleased with this, Frank could see. "Tell me about it," he said when they were settled in. "Is it a good position? I mean, what does the science advisor do?" Did it have any power, in other words?

"It all depends on the president," Diane said. "I've been looking into it, and it appears the position began as Nixon's way of spanking the science community for publicly backing Johnson over Goldwater. He abolished his science advisory committee and established this position. So it became a single advisor he could appoint without approval, and then stick on the shelf. Which is where they have usually stayed."

That didn't sound good. "But?"

"Well, in theory, if a president were listening, it could get interesting. There could be more coordination of the sciences in federal efforts. We've seen that at NSF. Ideally it would be a cabinet post."

"The science czar."

"Yes." She was wrinkling her nose. "Except that would create huge amounts of trouble, because really, most of the federal agencies are already supposed to be run scientifically, or have the sciences as part of their operation. So if someone tried to start a Department of Science, it would poach on any number of other agencies, and none of them would stand for it. They would gang up on such an advisor and kill him, like they did the so-called intelligence czar."

This gave Frank a chill. "Yeah, I guess that's right."

"So, now, maybe I could act like a kind of personal advisor. You know. If we presented a menu of really robust options, and Chase chose some of them to enact, it would be the President who would be advocating for scientific solutions."

"Which he might want to do, given the situation."

"Yes. Although Washington has a way of bogging people down."

"The swamp."

"Yes, the swamp. But if the swamp freezes over"—they laughed—"then maybe we can ice-skate over the obstacles!"

Frank nodded. "Speaking of which, we were supposed to be going to try ice skating down here, when the river froze over."

"That's right, we were. I think the Georgetown Rowing Club is going to rent skates, we can go check it out. They're going to put out floodlights and boundary lines and everything."

"Good for them! Let's go take a look after dinner."

And so they finished the meal cheerfully, moving from one great Levantine dish to the next. And by the time they were done they had split a bottle of a dry white wine. They walked down to the Potomac arm in arm, as they had in Manhattan so very briefly. They walked the Georgetown waterfront.

Then they came to the mouth of Rock Creek, a tiny little thing. Following it upstream in his mind, Frank came to the park and his treehouse, standing right over a bend in this same creek—and thus it occurred to him to think, Here you are fooling around with another woman, while your Caroline is in trouble God knows where. What would she think if she saw you?

Which was a hard thought to recover from; and Diane saw that his mood had changed. Quickly he suggested they warm up over drinks.

They retired to a bar overlooking the river and ordered Irish coffees. Frank warmed up again, his sudden stab of dread dispelled by Diane's calmness, by the aura of reality she had. It was reassuring to be around her; precisely the opposite of the feeling he had when—

But he stayed in the moment. He agreed with Diane's comment that Irish coffee provided the perfect compound of stimulant and relaxant, sugar and fat, hydration and warmth. "It must have been invented by scientists," she said.

Frank said, "It's what they always used to serve at the Salk Institute after their seminars. They've got a patio deck overlooking the Pacific, and everyone would go out with Irish coffees and watch the sunset."

"Nice."

Later, as Frank walked her back up through Georgetown to her car, she said, "I was wondering if you'd be interested in joining my staff. It would be an extension of the work you've been doing at NSF. I mean, I know you're planning to go back to San Diego, but until then, you know . . . I could use your help."

Frank had stopped walking. Diane turned and glanced up at him, shyly it seemed, and then looked down M Street. The stretch they could see looked like the Platonic form of a midwestern main street, totally unlike the rest of D.C.

"Sure," Frank heard himself say. He realized that in some sense he *had* to accept her offer. He had no choice; he was only in D.C. now because of her previous invitation to work on the climate problem. And they were friends, they were colleagues; they were . . . something. "I'll have to check back home, make sure it will be okay with UCSD. But I think it could be really interesting."

"Oh good. Good. I was hoping you'd say yes."

The next morning at work, his doorway darkened, and he swung his chair around, expecting to see Diane—

"Oh! Edgardo!"

"Hi, Frank. Hey, are you up for getting a bite at the Food Factory?" Waggling his eyebrows Groucho-istically.

"Sure," Frank said, trying to sound natural.

On the way to the Food Factory, Edgardo surreptitiously ran a wand over Frank, and gave it to Frank, who did the same for him. Then they went in and stood at a bar, noisily eating chips and salsa.

"What is it?"

"A friend of mine has tracked down your friend and her husband."

"Aha! And?"

"They work for a unit of a black agency called Advanced Research and Development Agency Prime. The man's name is Edward Cooper, and hers is Caroline Churchland. They ran a big data mining effort."

"She didn't work *for* him?"

"No. My friend says it was more like the other way around. She headed the program, but he was brought in to help. He came from Homeland Security, and before that CIA, where he was on the Afghanistan detail. My friend says the program got a lot more serious when he arrived."

"Serious?"

"Some surveillance issues. My friend didn't know what that meant. And then this attempt on the election that she tipped us to."

"But *he* worked for *her*?"

"Yes."

"And when did they get married?"

"About two years before he joined her project."

"And he worked for her."

"Yes. Also, my friend thinks he probably knows where she's gone."

"What!"

"That's what he said. On the night she disappeared, there was a call from a pay phone she had used before, to the Khembali embassy. That was to you?"

"She left a message," Frank said, more and more worried. "But so?"

"So then there was another call from that phone, to a number in Maine. My friend found the address for that number, and it's your friend's college roommate. And that roommate has a vacation home on an island up there. And the power has just been turned on for that vacation home. So he thinks that's where she's gone. And, as I'm sure you can understand, if he can track her that well at his remove, then her husband is likely to be even faster at it."

"Shit." Frank's feet were suddenly cold. Another thing that happened to everyone.

"Shit indeed. Possibly you should warn her. If she thinks she's hidden . . ."

"Sure," Frank said, thinking furiously. "But another thing—if her ex could find her, couldn't he find me too?"

"Maybe so."

They regarded each other.

"We have to neutralize this guy somehow," Frank said.

Edgardo shook his head. "Do not say that, my friend."

"Why not?"

"Neutralize?" He dragged out the word, his expression suddenly black. "Eliminate? Remove? Equalize? Disable? DX? Disappear? Liquidate?"

Shocked, Frank said, "I don't mean any of those! I just meant neutralize. As in, unable to affect us. Made neutral to us."

"Hard to do," Edgardo said. "I mean, get a restraining order? You don't want to go there. It doesn't work even if you can get them."

"Well?"

"You may just have to live with it."

"*Live* with it? With *what*?"

Edgardo shrugged. "Hard to say right now."

"I can't *live with it* if he's trying to harm her, and there's a good chance of him finding her."

"I know."

"I'll have to go find her first."

Edgardo nodded, looking at him with an evaluative expression. "Yes."

At the Quiblers' house in Bethesda this unsettled winter, things were busier than ever. This was mainly because of Phil Chase's election, which of course had galvanized his staff, turning them into part of a larger transition team.

A presidential transition was a major thing, and there were famous cases of failed transitions which put a spur to their rears. It was important to make a good start, to craft the kind of "first hundred days" that had energized the administration of Roosevelt in 1933, setting the model for followers to emulate. Critical appointments had to be made, bold new programs turned into law.

Phil was well aware of this challenge, and determined to meet it. "We'll call it the First Sixty Days," he told his staff. "Because there's no time to lose!" He had not slowed down since the election. Ignoring the claim of irregularities in the Oregon vote—claims which had become standard ever since the tainted elections at the beginning of the century—and secure in the knowledge that the American public did not like to think about troubling news on this front no matter who won, Phil was free to forge ahead from dawn till midnight, and often long past it. He was lucky he was one of those people who only needed a few hours of sleep a day to get by.

Not so Charlie, who was jolted out of sleep far too often by calls from Roy Anastopoulos, now Phil's new chief of staff, asking him to come down to the office and pitch in.

"Roy, I can't," Charlie would say. "I've got Joe here, Anna's off to work already, and we've got Gymboree."

"Gymboree? Am I hearing this? Charlie which is more important to the fate of the republic, advising the President or going to Gymboree?"

"False choice," Charlie would snap. "Although Gymboree is far more important if we want Joe to sleep well at night, which we do. You're talking to me now, right? How would this change if I were down there in person?"

"Yeah yeah yeah yeah, hey Chucker I gotta go now, but listen you *have* to come in from the cold, this is no time to be babysitting, we've got the fate of the world in the balance and we need you here taking one of these *crucial jobs* that no one else can fill as well as you. Joe is around two, right? So you can put him in the daycare here at the White House, or anywhere else in the greater metropolitan region for that matter, but you *have to be here* or else you will have *missed the boat.* Phil isn't going to stand for someone phoning in, not when the world is sinking and freezing and drowning and burning up and everything else!"

"Roy. Stop. I am talking to you like once an hour, maybe more. I couldn't talk to you more if we were handcuffed together."

"Yeah it's nice it's sweet it's one of the treasured parts of my day, but *it's a face business,* you know that, and I haven't *seen* you in months, and Phil hasn't either, and I'm afraid it's getting to be a case of *not seen not heard.*"

"Are you establishing a climate task force?"

"Yes."

"Are you going to ask Diane Chang to be the science advisor?"

"Yes. He already did."

"And you're proposing the legislative package to the Congress?" This was Charlie's big omnibus bill, brought back from death by dismemberment.

"Yes."

"So how exactly am I being cut out? That's every single thing I've ever suggested to you!"

"But Charlie, I'm looking *forward* to how you *will be cut out.* You've gotta put Joe in daycare and come in from the cold."

"But I don't want to."

"I gotta go you get a grip and get down here bye."

He sounded truly annoyed. But Charlie could speak his mind with Roy, and he wasn't going to let the election change that. And when he woke up in the morning, and considered that he could either go down to the Mall and talk policy with policy wonks all day, and get home late every night, or he could spend that day with Joe wandering the parks and bookstores of Bethesda, calling in to Phil's office from time to time to have those same policy talks in mercifully truncated form, he knew very well which day he preferred. It was an easy call, a no-brainer. He liked spending time with Joe. With all its problems and crises, he enjoyed it more than anything he had ever done. And Joe was growing up fast, and Charlie could see that what he enjoyed most in their life together was only going to last until preschool, if then. It went by fast!

Indeed, in the last week or so it had seemed that Joe was changing so fast that Charlie's desire to spend time with him was becoming as much a result of worry as desire for pleasure. Because it seemed he was dealing with a different kid. But Charlie suppressed this feeling, and tried to pretend to himself that it was only for positive reasons that he wanted to stay home.

Only occasionally, and for short periods, could he think honestly about this. Nothing about the matter was obvious, even when he did try to think about it. Because ever since their trip to Khembalung, Joe had been different—feverish, hectic, and irritable in a way that was unlike his earlier irritability, which had seemed to Charlie a kind of cosmic energy, a force chafing at its restraints. After Khembalung it had turned peevish, even pained.

All this had coincided with what Charlie regarded as excessive interest in Joe on the part of the Khembalis, and Charlie had gotten Drepung to admit that the Khembalis thought Joe was one of their great lamas, reincarnated in Joe's body. That's how it happened, to their way of thinking.

After that news, and also at Charlie's insistence, they had performed a kind of exorcism ritual designed to drive any reincarnated soul out of Joe, leaving the original inhabitant, which was the only one Charlie wanted in there. But now he was beginning to wonder if that ritual had been a good idea. Maybe, he was beginning to think, his original Joe had been the personality that the Khembalis had driven out.

Not that Joe was all that different. His fever was gone, and it was true he was more relaxed. But to Charlie, he was different in ways Charlie found hard to characterize. Chiefly, the boy was now too content with things as they were. Joe had never been like that, not since the very moment of his birth, which from all appearances had angered him greatly. Charlie could still remember seeing his little red face, just out of Anna, pissed off and yelling.

But none of that now. No tantrums, no imperious commands. He was calm, he was biddable; he was even inclined to *take naps*. It just wasn't Joe.

Given these new impressions, Charlie was not at all inclined to put Joe in a new situation, thus confusing the issue even further. He wanted to hang out with him, see what he was doing and feeling; he wanted to *study* him. This was what parental love came down to, apparently, especially with a toddler, a human being in one of the most transient and astonishing of all life stages. Someone coming to consciousness!

But the world was no respecter of Charlie's feelings. Later that morning his cell phone rang again, and this time it was Phil Chase himself.

"Charlie, how are you?"

"I'm fine, Phil, how are you? Are you getting any rest?"

"Yeah sure. I'm on my postelectoral vacation, things are very relaxed."

"Right. That's not what Roy tells me. How's the transition coming?"

"It's coming fine, as I understand it. I thought that was your bailiwick."

Charlie laughed with a sinking feeling. Already he felt the change in Phil's status weighing on him, making the conversation somewhat surreal. He had worked for Phil for a long time, but always while Phil had been a senator; Charlie had long since gotten used to the considerable and yet highly constrained power that a senator wielded. It had become normalized, indeed had become kind of a running joke between them, in that Charlie often had reminded Phil just how completely circumscribed his power was.

Now that just wasn't going to work. The President of the United States might be many things, but unpowerful was not among them. Many administrations preceding Phil's had worked very hard to expand the powers of the executive branch beyond what the constitutional framers had intended, and the result was an apparatus of power that if properly understood and utilized could, to an extent, rule the world. Bizarre but true: the President of the United States could rule the world, both by direct fiat and by setting the agenda that everyone else had to follow or be damned. World ruler. Not really, of course, but it was as close as one could get. And how exactly did you joke about that?

"Your clothes are still visible?" Charlie inquired, oppressed by these thoughts.

"To me they are. But look," passing on a full riposte—although Phil could no doubt see the comedy of omnipotence as well as the comedy of constraint—"I wanted to talk to you about your position in the administration. Roy says you're being a little balky, but obviously we need you."

"I'm here already. I can talk twelve hours a day, if you like."

"Well, but a lot of these jobs require more than that. They're in-person jobs, as you know."

"What do you mean, like which ones?"

"Well, like for instance head of the EPA."

"WHAT?" Charlie shouted. He reeled, literally, in that he staggered slightly to the side, then listed back to catch himself. "Don't you be scaring me, Phil! I hope you're not thinking of making appointments as stupid as that! Jesus, you know perfectly well I'm not qualified for that job! You need a first-rate scientist for that one, a major researcher with some policy and administrative experience, we've talked about this already! Every agency needs to feel appreciated to keep esprit de corps at the highest levels, you know that! You aren't making a bunch of stupid political appointments, are you?"

Phil was cracking up. "See? That's why we need you down here!"

Charlie sucked down some air. "Oh. Ha ha. Very funny. Jesus H. Christ in a bucket, don't be scaring me like that, Phil."

"I was serious, Charlie. You'd be fine heading the EPA. We need someone there with a global vision of the world's environmental problems. And we'll find someone like that. But that wouldn't be the best use for you, I agree."

"Good." Charlie felt as if a bullet had just whizzed by his head. He was quivering as he said, very firmly, "Let's just keep things like they are with me."

"No, that's not what I mean, either. Listen, can you come down here and at least talk it over with me? Fit that into your schedule?"

Well, shit. How could he say no? This was his boss, also the President of the United States. But if he had to talk to him in person about it . . . He sighed. "Yeah, yeah, of course. Your wish is my demand."

"Bring Joe if you can, I'd enjoy seeing him. We can take him out for a spin on the Tidal Basin."

"Yeah yeah." What else could he say?

The problem was that *Yeah yeah* was pretty much the only thing you could say, when replying to the President of the United States making a polite request of you. Perhaps there had been some presidents who had established a limit there, by asking for impossible things and then seeing what happened; power could quickly bring out the latent sadism in the powerful; but if a sane and clever president wanted only ever to get yeses in response to his questions, he could certainly frame them to make that happen. That was just the way it was.

Certainly it was hard to say no to a president-elect inviting you and your toddler to paddle around the Tidal Basin in one of the shiny blue pedal boats docked on the east side of the pond.

And once on the water, it indeed proved very hard to say no to Phil. Joe was wedged between them, life-jacketed and strapped down by Secret Service agents in ways that even Anna would have accepted as safe. He was looking about blissfully; he had even been fully compliant and agreeable about getting into the life jacket and being tied down by the seat belts. It had made Charlie seasick to watch it. Now it felt like Phil was doing most of the pumping on the boat's foot pedals. He was also steering.

Phil was always in a good mood on the water, rapping away about nothing, looking down at Joe, then over the water at the Jefferson Memorial, the most graceful but least emotional of the city's memorials; beaming at the day, sublimely unaware of the people on the shore path who had noticed him and were exclaiming into their phones or taking pictures with them. The Secret Service people had taken roost on the paddle boat dock, and there were an unusual number of men in suits walking the shore among the tourists and joggers.

"Where I need you in the room," Phil said out of the blue, "is when we gather a climate change task force. I'll be out of my depth in that crowd, and there'll be all kinds of plans put forth. That's where I'll want your impressions, both real-time and afterward, to help me cross-check what I think. It won't do to have me describe these things to you after the fact. There isn't time for that, and besides I might miss the most important thing."

"Yeah, well—"

"None of that! This task force will set the agenda for a lot of what we do. It'll be my strategy group, Charlie, and I'm saying I need you in it. Now, I've looked into the daycare facilities for children at the White House. They're adequate, and we can get to work making them even better. Joe will be my target audience. You'd like to play all day with a bunch of kids, wouldn't you Joe?"

"Yeah Phil," Joe said, happy to be included in the conversation.

"We'll set up whatever system works best for you, what do you think of that?"

"I like that," Joe said.

Charlie started to mutter something about the Chinese women who buried their infants up to the neck in riverbank mud every day to leave them to go to work in the rice paddies, but Phil overrode him.

"Gymboree in the basement, if that's what it takes! Laser tag, paintball wars—you name it! You'd like paintball wars, wouldn't you Joe?"

"Big truck," Joe observed, pointing at Independence Avenue.

"Sure, we could have big trucks too. We could have a monster truck pull right on the White House lawn."

"Monster *truck*." Joe smiled at the phrase.

Charlie sighed. It really seemed to him that Joe should be shouting *big truck right now,* or trying to escape, or crawling around among the pedals underfoot, or leaping overboard to go for a swim. Instead he was listening peacefully to Phil's banter, with an expression that said he understood just as much as he wanted to, and approved of it in full.

Ah well. Everyone changed. And in fact, that had been the whole point of the ceremony Charlie had asked the Khembalis to conduct! Charlie had requested it—had insisted on it, in fact! But without, he now realized, fully imagining the consequences.

Phil said, "So you'll do it?"

"I don't know."

"You more or less have to, right? I mean, you're the one who first suggested that I run, when we were over at Lincoln."

"Everyone was telling you that."

"No they weren't. Besides, you were first."

"No, you were. I just thought it would work."

"And you were right, right?"

"Apparently so."

"So you owe me. You got me into this mess."

Phil smiled, waved at some tourists as he made a broad champing turn back toward the other side of the basin. Charlie sighed. If he agreed, he would not see Joe anywhere near as much as he was used to—an idea he hated. On the other hand, if he didn't see him as much, he wouldn't notice so often how much Joe had changed. And he hated that change.

So much to dislike! Unhappily he said, "I'll have to talk to Anna about it. But I think she'll go for it. She's pretty pro-work. So. Shit. I'll give it a try. I'll give it a few months, and see how it goes. By that time your task force should be on its way, and I can see where things stand, and go emeritus if I need to."

"Good." Phil pedaled furiously, almost throwing Charlie's knees up into his chin. He said, "Look, Joe, all the people are waving at you!"

Joe waved back. "Hi people!" he shouted. "Big truck, right there! Look! I like that big truck. That's a good truck."

And so: change. The inexorable emergence of difference in time. Becoming. One of the fundamental mysteries.

Charlie hated it. He liked being; he hated becoming. This was, he thought, an indicator of how happy he had been with the way things were. Mr. Mom: he had loved it. Just this last May he had been walking down Leland Street and had passed Djina, one of the Gymboree moms he knew, biking the other way, and he had called out to her, "Happy Mother's Day!" and she had called back, "Same to you!" and he had felt a glow in him that had lasted an hour. Someone had understood.

Of course the pure mom routine of the 1950s was an Ozzie and Harriet nightmare, a crazy-making program so effective that the surprise was that there were any moms at all in that generation who had stayed sane. Most of them had gone nuts in one way or another, because in its purest form that life was too tied down to the crucial but mindless daily chores of child-rearing and house maintenance—"uncompensated labor," as the economists put it, but in a larger sense than what they meant with their idiot bean counting. Coming in the fifties, hard on the heels of World War Two's shattering of all norms, its huge chaotic space of dislocation and freedom for young women, it must have felt like a return to prison after a big long breakout.

But that wasn't the life Charlie had been leading. Along with the child care and the shopping and the housework had been his "real" work as a senatorial aide, which, even though it had been no more than a few phone conversations a day, had bolstered the "unreal" work of Mr. Momhood in a curious dual action. Eventually which work was "real" had become a moot point; the upshot was that he felt fulfilled, the lucky and accidental recipient of a full life. Maybe even overfull! But that was what happened when Freud's short list of the important things in life—work and love—were all in play.

He had had it all. And so change be damned! Charlie wanted to live on in this life forever. Or if not forever, then as long as the stars. And he feared change, as being the probable degradation of a situation that couldn't be bettered.

But here it was anyway, and there was no avoiding it. All the repetitions in the pattern were superficial; the moment was always new. It had to be lived, and then the next moment embraced as well. This was what the Khembalis were always saying; it was a Buddhist basic. And now Charlie had to try to believe it.

· · ·

So, the day came when he got up, and Anna left for work, then Nick for school; then it was Joe and Da's time, the whole day spread before them like a big green park. But on this day, Charlie prepped them both to leave, while talking up the change in the routine. "Big day, Joe! We're off to school and work, to the White House! They have a great daycare center there, it'll be like Gymboree!"

Joe looked up. "Gymboree?"

"Yes, *like* Gymboree, but not exactly." Charlie's mood plummeted as he thought of the differences—not one hour but five, or six, or eight, or twelve—and not parents and children together, but the child alone in a crowd of strangers. And he had never even liked Gymboree!

More and more depressed, he strapped Joe into his stroller and pushed him to the Metro. The tunnel walls were still discolored or even wet in places, and Joe checked everything out as on any other trip. This was one of their routines.

Phil himself was not in the White House yet, but the arrangements had been made for Joe to join the daycare there, after which Charlie would leave and walk over to the Senate offices. Up and out of the Metro, into warm air, under low windy clouds.

Charlie had gotten out at Smithsonian, and the Mall was almost empty, only a few runners in sight. He pushed Joe along faster and faster, feeling more and more desolate—unreasonably so, almost to the point of despair—especially as Joe continued to babble on happily, no doubt expecting something like their usual picnic and play session on the Mall. Hours that no matter how tedious they had seemed at the time, were now revealed as precious islands in eternity, as paradises lost. And it was impossible to convey to Joe that today was going to be different. "Joe, I'm going to *drop you off* at the daycare center here at the White House. You're going to get to play with the other kids and the teachers and you have to do what the teachers say for a *long time*."

"Cool Dad. Play!"

"Yeah that's right. Maybe you'll love it."

It was at least possible. Vivid in Charlie's mind was Anna's story about taking Nick to daycare for the first time, and seeing Nick's expression of stoic resignation, which had pierced her so. Charlie had seen the look himself, taking Nick in those first few times. But Joe was no stoic, and would never resign himself to anything. Charlie was anticipating something more like chaos and disorder, perhaps even mayhem, Joe moving from protest to tirade to rampage. But who knew? The way Joe was acting these days, anything was possible. He might love it. He could be gregarious, and he liked crowds and parties. It was really more a matter of liking them too much.

In any case, in they went. Security check, and then inside and down the hall to the daycare center, a well-appointed and very clean place. Lots of little kids running around among toys and play structures, train sets and bookshelves and Legos and all. Joe's eyes grew round. "Hey Dad! Big Gymboree!"

"That's right, like Gymboree. Except I'm going to go, Joe. I'm going to go and leave you here."

Charlie's voice broke as he said this, and he had to look up and away. The daycare woman would surely think he was crazy, but the tears were rolling down his cheeks anyway.

"Bye Dad!" And off Joe ran without a backward glance.

CHAPTER 22

CUT TO THE CHASE

"And if you think this is utopian, please think also why it is such."

—*Brecht*

Phil Chase was a man with a past. He was one of Congress's Vietnam vets, and that was a pretty rambunctious crowd. They had license to be a little crazy, and not all of them took it, but it was there if they wanted it.

Phil wanted it. He had always played that card to the hilt. Unconventional, unpredictable, devil-may-care. And for well over a decade his particular shtick had been to be the World's Senator, phoning in his work or jetting into D.C. at the last minute to make votes. All this had been laid before the people of California explicitly, with the invitation to vote him out if they did not like it. But they did. Like a lot of California politicians who had jumped onto the national stage, his support at home was strong. Now that he was president his numbers had polarized more than ever, in the usual way of American politics, everyone hooked on the soap opera of cheering for or against celebrities.

So a checkered past was a huge advantage in creating a spectacle. In his particular version of the clichéd list, Phil had been a reporter for the Los Angeles Times, *a surfboard wax manufacturer, a VA social worker, a college lecturer in history, a sandal maker, and apprentice to a stonemason. From that job he had run for Congress from Marin County, and won the seat as an outsider Democrat. This was a difficult thing to do. The Democratic Party hated outsiders to win office at the first try; they wanted everyone to start at the bottom and work their way up until thoroughly brainwashed and obliged. Worse yet, Phil had then jumped into a senatorial race and ridden the state's solid Democratic majority into the Senate, even though the party was still offended and not behind him.*

Soon after that, his wife of twenty-three years, his high school sweetheart, who had served in Vietnam as a nurse to be closer to him after he was drafted, died in a car crash. It was then that Phil started his globetrotting. Because he kept his distance from D.C. through those years, no one in the capital knew much about his personal life. What they knew was what he gave them. From his account it was all travel, golf, and meetings with foreign politicians, often in Asia.

In his frequent returns to California, he was much the same. For a while he pursued his "Ongoing Work Education," Project OWE, because he owed it to his constituents to learn what their lives were like. His staff pronounced it Project Ow, however, because of the injuries he incurred while taking on various jobs around the state for a month or three, working at them while continuing to function as senator in D.C., which irritated his colleagues no end. In that phase, he had worked as a grocery store bagger, construction worker, real estate agent, plumber (or plumber's helper as he joked), barrio textile seamstress, sewage maintenance worker, trash collector, stockbroker, and a celebrated stint as a panhandler in San Francisco, during which time he had slept at undisclosed locations in Golden Gate Park and elsewhere around the city, and asked for spare change for his political fund—part of his "spare change" effort, in which he had also asked California citizens to send in all the coins accumulating on their dressers, a startlingly successful plan that had weighed tons and netted him millions, entirely funding his second run for senator, which he did on the cheap and mostly over the internet.

He had also walked from San Francisco to Los Angeles, climbed the Seven Summits (voting on the clean air bill from the top of Mount Everest), swum from Catalina Island to the Southern California mainland, and across Chesapeake Bay, and hiked the Appalachian Trail from end to end. ("Very boring," was his judgment. "Next time the PCT.")

All these activities were extraneous to his work in the Senate, and time-consuming, and for his first two terms he was considered within the Beltway to be a celebrity freak, a party trick of a politician and a lightweight in the real world of power (i.e., money) no matter how far he could walk or swim. But even in that period his legislation had been interesting in concept (his contribution) and solidly written (his staff's contribution), and cleverly pursued and promoted, with much more of it being enacted into law than was usual. This was not noted by the press, always on the lookout for bad news and ephemera, but by his third term it had begun to become evident to insiders that he had been playing the inside game all along, and only pretending to be an outsider, so that his committee appointments were strong, and his alliances within the Democratic Party apparatus finally strong, and across the aisle with moderate Republicans and fellow Vietnam vets, even stronger. He also had done a good job making his enemies, taking on flamboyantly bad senators like Winston and Reynolds and Hoof-in-mouth, whose subsequent falls from grace on corruption charges or simply failed policies had then retroactively confirmed his early judgments that these people were not just dunderheads but also dangerous to the republic.

So when the time came, everything he had done for twenty years and more turned out to have been as it were designed to prepare him not only for his successful run for the presidency, but for his subsequent occupancy as well, a crucial point which many previous presidents had obviously forgot. The world travel, the global network of allies and friends, the OWE program, the legislation he had introduced and gotten passed, his committee work—all fit a pattern, as if he had had the plan from the start.

Which he totally denied; and his staff believed him. They thought in their gossip among themselves that they had seen him come to his decision to run just a year before the campaign (at about the same time, Charlie thought, that he had met with the Khembali leaders). Whether he had harbored thoughts all along, no one really knew. No one could read his mind, and he had no close associates. Widowed; kids grown; friends kept private: to Washington he seemed as lonely and impenetrable as Reagan, or FDR, or Lincoln— all friendly and charming people, but distant in some fundamental way.

In any case he was in, and ready and willing to use the office as strong presidents do—not only as the executive branch of government, whipping on Congress to get things done, but also as a bully pulpit from which to address the world. His high positive/high negative polling continued, but outside the United States his positives were higher than any American president's since Kennedy. And interest was very high. All waited through the few weeks left until his inauguration; there was a feeling of stillness, as if the pendulum swinging them all together helplessly had reached a height, and paused in space, just before falling the other way. People began to think that something might really happen.

It seemed to Frank that with Phil Chase coming into office, it might be very interesting to be presidential science advisor, or even an advisor to that advisor. But there were aspects of the new job that were disturbing as well. It was going to mean increasing the distance between himself and the doing of science proper, and therefore move him further away from what he was good at. That was what it meant to be moving into administration.

His intrusion on the Khembalis was another problem. Rudra's failing health was a problem. His own injury, and the uncertain mentation that had resulted (if it had), was a very central problem—perhaps *the* problem. Leaving NSF, meaning Anna and the rest of his acquaintances (except for Edgardo and Kenzo, who were also joining Diane's team), that too was a problem.

Problems required solutions, and solutions required decisions. And he couldn't decide. So the days were proving difficult.

Because above and beyond all the rest of his problems, there was the immediate one: he had to—*had to*—warn Caroline that she was findable. He had to warn her! Not that he was sure where she was. She might be on that island in Maine, but unless he went and looked he couldn't know. But if he went, he could not do anything that might expose her (and him too) to her husband. His van was chipped with a GPS transponder—Caroline was the one who had told him about it—so it could be under surveillance, and tracked wherever it went. He could easily imagine a program that would flag any time his van left the metropolitan area. This was a serious disadvantage, because his van was his shelter of last resort, his only mobile bedroom, and all in all, the most versatile room in the disassembled and modular home that he had cast through the fabric of the city.

"Can I dechip my van?" he asked Edgardo next day on their run, after wanding them both again. "For certain? And, you know, as if by accident?"

"I should think so," Edgardo replied. "It might be something you would need some help with. Let me look into it."

"Okay, but I want to go soon."

"To Maine?"

"Yes."

"Okay, I'll do my best. The person I want to talk to is not exactly on call. I have to meet in a context like this one."

But that night, as Frank was settling down in the garden shed with Rudra, Qang came out to tell him there was a man to see him. Frank's pulse jumped—

But it was Edgardo, and a short man, who said "hello" and after that spoke only to Edgardo, in Spanish. "Umberto here is another porteño," Edgardo said. "He helps me with matters such as this."

Umberto rolled his eyes dramatically. He took Frank's keys and went at the van, pulling up the carpet from the floor, running various diagnostics through a laptop, complaining to Edgardo all the while. Eventually he opened the hood and unbolted a small box from the crowded left engine wall. When he was done he gave the box to Frank and walked off into the dark, still berating Edgardo.

"Thanks!" Frank called after him. Then to Edgardo: "Could I see how he did that, so I can put it back in?" He peered at the engine wall, then the bolts in his hand, then the holes the bolts had come out of. It looked like a wrench kit would do it. "Okay, but where do I put it now?"

"You must leave it right here where it would be, so that it seems your van is parked here. Then replace it when you return."

"Out here on the street?"

"Isn't there a driveway to this house?"

"Yeah, I can leave it there I guess. Buried in this gravel here."

"There you go."

"And other than that, I'm clean?"

"That's what Umberto said. Speaking only of the van, of course."

"Yeah. I've got the wand for my stuff. But is that enough? The van won't look weird to toll gates for not having the box, or anything like that?"

"No. Not every vehicle has these things yet. So far, the total information society is not total. When it is you won't be able to do stuff like this. You'll never be able to get off the grid, and if you did it would look so strange it would be worse than being on the grid. Everything will have to be re-thought."

"Jesus." Frank grimaced. "Well, by then I won't be involved in this kind of stuff. Listen, I think I'm going to take off now and get a few hours of driving in. It'll take me all of tomorrow to get there as it is."

"That's true. Good luck my friend. Remember—no cell phone calls, no ATMs, no credit cards. Do you have enough cash with you?"

"I hope so," feeling the thickness of his wallet.

"You shouldn't stay away too long anyway."

"No. I guess I'm okay, then. Thanks for the help."

"Good luck. Don't call."

Grumpily Frank got in his van and drove north on 95. Transponders embedded in every vehicle's windshields . . . except would that really happen? Was this total information project perhaps crazy enough to fail, ultimately? Or—could it be stopped? Could they go to Phil Chase and lay out the whole story, and get him to root out Caroline's ex and his whole operation? Or were the spy agencies so imbricated into the government (and the military) that they were beyond presidential control, or even presidential knowledge? Or inquiry?

If it weren't for his going-off-grid status, he would have called up Edgardo to ask his opinion on this. As it was he could only worry, and drive.

Somewhere in New Jersey it occurred to him that as he was on the road north, he must therefore have decided to go. He had decided something! And without even trying. Maybe decisions now had to occur without him really noticing them happening, or wondering how. It was so hard to say. In this case, he had no choice; he *had* to warn her. So it had been more of a life override than a decision. Maybe one went through life doing the things one had to do, hooped by necessity, with decisions reserved for options, and therefore not really a major factor in one's life. A bad thought or a good one? He couldn't tell.

A bad thought, he decided in the end. A bad thought in a long night of bad thoughts. Long past midnight he followed the taillights ahead of him, and the traffic slowly thinned and became mostly trucks. Across New Jersey, over the Hudson, otherwise tunneling on endlessly through the forest. Even the trucks were gone. Finally he felt in danger of falling asleep at the wheel, got off, and found a side road parking lot, empty and dark, where he felt comfortable parking and locking the doors and crawling into the back to catch a few hours' sleep.

Dawn's light woke him and he drove on, north through New England, fueled by the worst 7-Eleven coffee ever, coffee so bad it was good, in terms of waking him up. Surely someone had poured battery acid in it. There was too much time to think. If Caroline was the boss, and her ex worked for her, then . . . 95 kept on coming, an endless slot through endless forest. Finally he came to Bangor, Maine, and turned right, driving over hills and across small rivers, then through the standard array of franchises in Ellsworth. During the night he had driven back into full winter; a blanket of dirty snow covered everything. He passed a shut-down tourist zone, the motels, lobster shacks, and antique stores all looking miserable under their load of ice and snow.

Then he crossed the bridge that spanned the tidal race to Mount Desert Island. By then the round gray tops of the island's little range of peaks had appeared several times. They were bare rock mountaintops, shaved into graceful curves by the immense force of the ice age's ice cap. Frank had googled the island on a cybercafé's rented computer, and the information had surprised him. It turned out this little island was where the American wilderness movement had begun, in the form of the painter Frederic Church, who had come here in the 1840s to paint. In getting around the island, Church had invented what he called "rusticating," by which he meant wandering on mountainsides just for the fun of it, and sometimes camping on them. He also had taken offense at the logging on the island, and worked to get it forbidden. All this at the same time Emerson and Thoreau were writing. Something had been in the air. Eventually all that led to the national park system, and Mount Desert Island had been the third one, the first east of the Mississippi, and the only one created by citizens donating their own land. Acadia National Park now took up about two-thirds of the island.

Nervously Frank drove through Somesville, at the head of Somes Sound. This turned out to be a scattering of white houses on the sides of the road. He looked for something like a village commercial center but did not see one.

Now he was getting quite nervous. Just the idea of seeing her. He didn't know how to approach her. In his uncertainty he drove past the right turn that headed to her friend's place, and continued on to a town called Southwest Harbor. He wanted to eat something, also to think things over.

In the only café still open he ordered lunch. He didn't want to catch Caroline unawares; that could be a bad shock. On the other hand there didn't seem any other way to do it. Sitting in the café drinking espresso (heavenly after the battery acid), he ate his sandwich and tried to think. They were the same thoughts he had been thinking the whole drive. He would have to surprise her—then immediately explain why, the possible danger she was in—so that she did not jump to the conclusion that he was stalking her. They could talk; he could see what she wanted to do, perhaps even help her to move somewhere else, if that's what she wanted. Although in that case . . .

Well, but he had run through all these thoughts a thousand times during the drive. All the scenarios led to a point beyond which it was hard to imagine. He had to go to work on Monday. Or he should. And so . . .

He finished his lunch and walked around a little. Southwest Harbor ringed a small bay surrounded by forested hills, and filled with working boats and docks. It was quiet, empty; picturesque, but in a good way. A working harbor.

He would have to risk dropping in on her. The wand said he was clean. Edgardo's friend had said his van was clean. He had driven all night, he was five miles away from her. Surely the decision had already been made!

So he got in his van, and drove back up the road to the Somesville fire station, where he took a left and followed a winding road through bare trees. Past an iced-over pond on the right, then another one on the left, this one a lake that was narrow and long, extending south for miles, a white flatness at the bottom of a classic U-shaped glacial slot. Soon after that, a turn on a gravel road.

He drove slower than ever, under a dense network of overarching branches. Houses to the left were fronting the long frozen lake. Caroline's friend's place was on the right, where the map suggested it would overlook a second arm of the lake.

Her friend's house had no number in its driveway, but by the numbers before and after it, he deduced that it had to be the one. He turned around in a driveway, idled back up the road.

The place had a short gravel curve of driveway, with no cars in it. At the end of the driveway stood a house, while to the right was a detached garage. Both were dark green with white trim. Ah; the house number was on the garage.

He didn't want to drive into the driveway. On the other hand it must look odd, him idling on the road, looking in. He drove farther, back in the direction of the paved road. Then he parked at a wide spot, cursing under his breath. He got out and walked quickly up the driveway to the house in question.

He stopped between the house and the garage, under a big bare-limbed tree. No one was visible through the kitchen window. He was afraid to knock on the kitchen door. He stepped around the side of the house, looking in the windows running down that side. Inside was a big room, beyond it a sunporch facing the lake. The lake was down a slope from the house. There was a narrow path down, flanked by stone-walled terraces filled with snow and black weeds. Down at the bottom of the path was a little white dock and boathouse.

The door of the boathouse swung open from inside.

"Caroline?" Frank called down.

Silence. Then: "Frank?"

She peeked around the edge of the little boathouse, looking up for him with just the startled unhappy expression he had feared he would cause.

Then she almost ran up the path. "Frank, what is it?" she exclaimed as she hurried up. "What are you doing here?"

He found he was already halfway down the path. They met between two blueberry bushes, him with a hand up as if in warning, but she crashed through that and embraced him—held him—hugged him. They clung to each other.

Frank had not allowed himself to think of this part (but he had anyway): what it meant to hold her. How much he had wanted to see her.

She pushed back from him, looking past him up to the house. "Why are you here? What's going on? How did you find me?"

"I needed to warn you about that," Frank said. "My friend at NSF, the one who helped me with the election stuff you gave us? He has a friend who was looking into your ex and what he's doing now, because they want to follow up on the election. So then this guy said that he knew where you probably had gone."

"Oh shit." Her hand flew to her mouth. Another body response common to all. She peered around him again up the driveway.

"So, I wanted to see if he was right," Frank continued, "and I wanted to warn you if he was. And I wanted to see you anyway."

"Yes." They held hands, then hugged again. Squeezed hard. Frank felt the fear and isolation in her.

"So." He pulled back and looked at her. "Maybe you should move."

"Yeah. I guess so. Possibly. But—well, first tell me everything you can. Especially about how this person found me. Here, come on up. Let's get inside." She led him by the hand, back up the garden path to the house.

She entered it by way of the sunporch door. The sunporch was separated from the living room by diamond-paned windows above a wainscoting. An old vacation home, Frank saw: handmade, scrupulously clean, old furniture, paintings on every wall that appeared to be the work of a single enthusiast.

Caroline gestured. "I first visited Mary here when we were six."

"Wow."

"But we haven't been in touch for years, and Ed never knew about her. In fact, I can't imagine how your friend's friend tracked down the association."

"He said you called an old roommate, and this was her place."

She frowned. "That's true."

"So, that's how he tracked this place down. And if he could do it, so could your ex, presumably. And besides," he added sharply, surprising them both, "why did you tell me that he was your boss?"

Silence as she stared at him. He explained: "My friend's friend said you were actually your husband's boss. So I wanted to know."

She glanced away, mouth tight for just an instant.

"Come on," she said, and led him through the living room to the kitchen.

There she opened the refrigerator and got out a pitcher of iced tea. "Have a seat," she said, indicating the kitchen table.

"Maybe I should move my van into the driveway," Frank remembered. "I didn't want to shock you by driving in, and I left it out on the road."

"That was nice. Yeah, go move it in. At least for now."

He did so, his mind racing. It was definitely foolish of her to remain exposed like this. Probably they should be leaving immediately.

He reentered the kitchen to find her sitting at the table, looking down at the lake. His Caroline. He sat down across from her.

She looked at him across the table. "I was not Ed's boss," she said. "When I first came to the office, I was part of his team. I was working for him. But when the futures market was established I was put in charge of it, and I reported to people outside our office. Ed kept doing his surveillance, and his group used what we were documenting, when it helped them. That's the way it was when you and I met. Then he moved over to Homeland Security."

She took a sip of iced tea, met his eye again. "I never lied to you, Frank. I never have and I never will. I've had enough of that kind of thing. More than you'll ever know. I can't stand it anymore."

"Good," Frank said, feeling awkward. "But tell me—I mean, this is another thing I've wondered about, that I've never remembered to ask you—what were you doing on that boat during the big flood, on the Potomac?"

Surprised, she said, "That's Ed's boat. I was going up to get him off Roosevelt Island."

"That was quite a time to be out on the river."

"Yes, it was. But he was helping people at the marina to get their boats down to below Alexandria, and on one of the trips he stayed behind while I went back to ferry another group. So it was kind of back and forth."

"Ah." Frank put a hand onto the table, reaching toward her. "I'm sorry," he said. "I didn't know what to think. We never have had much time. Whenever we've gotten together, there's been more to say than time to say it."

She smiled. "Too busy." And she put her hand on his.

He turned his palm up, and they intertwined fingers, squeezed hands. This was a whole different category of questions and answers. Do you still love me? Yes, I still love you. Do you still want me? Yes, I still want you. All that he had felt before, during that hard hug on the garden path, was confirmed.

Frank took a deep breath. A flow of calmness spread from his held hand up his arm and then through the rest of him. Most of him.

"It's true," he said. "We've never had enough time. But now we do, so—tell me more. Tell me everything."

"Okay. But you too."

"Sure."

But then they sat there; it seemed artificial just to begin their life histories. They let their hands do the talking for a while instead. They drank tea. She talked a little about coming to this place when she was a girl. Then about being a jock, as she put it—how Frank loved that—and how that had gotten her into various kinds of trouble. "Maybe it was a matter of liking the wrong kind of guy. Guys who are jocks are not always nice. There's a certain percentage of assholes, and I could never tell in time." Reading detective stories when she was a girl. Nancy Drew and Sue Grafton and Sara Paretsky, all of them leading her down a path toward intelligence, first at the CIA ("I wish I had never left"), then to a promotion over to Homeland Security. That was where she had met Ed. The way at first he had seemed so calm, so capable, and in just the areas she was then getting interested in. The intriguing parts of spook work. The way it let her be outdoors, or at least out and about—at first. Like a kind of sport. "Ah yeah," Frank put in, thinking of the fun of tracking animals. "I did jobs like that too, sometimes. I wanted that too."

Then the way things had changed, and gone wrong, in both work and marriage. How bad it had gotten. Here she grew vague and seemed to suppress some agitation or grimness. She kept looking out the window, as did Frank. A car passed and they both were too distracted by it to go on.

"Anyway, then you and I got stuck in the elevator," she resumed. She stopped, thinking about that perhaps; shook her head, looked out the kitchen window at the driveway again. "Let's get out of here," she said abruptly. "I don't like . . . Why don't we go for a drive in your van. I can show you some of the island, and get some time to think. I can't think here now. It's giving me the creeps that you're here, I mean in the sense of . . . And we can put your van someplace, if I decide to stay. Just in case. I have my car parked at the other end of the lake. I've been sailing down to it when I want to drive somewhere."

"Sailing?"

"Iceboating."

"Ah. Okay," Frank said. They got up. "But—do you think we even ought to come back here?"

She frowned. He could see she was getting upset. His arrival had messed up what she had thought was a good thing. "I'm not sure," she said uneasily. "I don't think Ed will ever be able to find that one call I made to Mary."

"But—if he's searching for something? For an old connection?"

"Yes, I know." She gave him an odd look. "I don't know. Let's get going. I can think about it better when I get away from here."

He saw that it was as he had feared; his arrival was bad news. He wondered uneasily if she had planned ever to contact him again.

They got in Frank's van, and he drove back toward Somesville, then around the head of the sound, then east through more forests, past more lakes.

Eventually she had him park at a feature called Bubble Rock, which turned out to be a big glacial erratic, perched improbably on the side of a granite hill. Frank looked at the rocky slopes rising to both sides of the road, amazed; he had never seen granite on the East Coast before. It was as if a little patch of the Sierra Nevada had been detached and cast into the Atlantic. The granite was slightly pinker than in the Sierra, but otherwise much the same.

"Let's go up the Goat Trail," she said. "You'll like it, and I need it."

She crossed the road and stood facing the steep granite slope. "This is Pemetic Mountain," she said. "And somewhere here is the start of the Goat Trail." She walked back and forth, scanning the steep rock wall looming over them. The pink granite was blackened with lichen. "Mary's father was really into the old trails on the island," Caroline said. "Aha." She pointed at a rusted iron rod protruding from a big slab of rock, about head high. She climbed past it. "This was the first trail, he said. More of a marked route than a trail. It's not on the maps anymore. See, there's the next trail duck." Pointing above.

"Ah yeah." Frank followed, watching her. This was his Caroline. She climbed with a sure touch. They had never done anything normal together before, in the light of day. She had talked about cycling, going for runs. This slope was easy but steep, and in places icy. A jock. Suddenly he felt the Caroline surge that had been in him all along, banked and waiting.

The rock reared up into a wall of broken battlements thirty or forty feet high, one atop the next. Caroline led the way up through breaks in these walls, following a route marked by small stacks of flat rocks. In one of these breaks a crack was filled with big flat stones set in a rough but obvious staircase; this was as much of a trail as Frank had yet seen. "Mary's father wouldn't even step on those stones," Caroline said, and laughed. "He said it would be like stepping on a painting or something. A work of art. We used to laugh at him so much."

"I should think the guy who made the trail would like it to be used."

"That's what we used to say."

As they ascended they saw three or four more little staircases, always making a hard section easier. After an hour or so the slope laid back in a graceful curve, and they were on the rounded top of the hill. Pemetic Mountain, said a wooden sign on a post stuck into a giant pile of stones. 1,247 feet.

The top was an extensive flat ridge, running south toward the ocean. Its knobby bare rock was interspersed with low bushes and sandy patches. Lichen of several different colors spotted the bedrock and the big erratics left by the ice. It resembled any such knob in the Sierra, but the air had a distinct salt tang, and off to the south lay the vast blue plate of the ocean. Amazing. Forested islands dotted the water offshore; wisps of fog lay farther out to sea. To the immediate right and left rose other mountaintops, all rounded to the same whaleback shape.

"Beautiful!" Frank said. "Mountains and ocean both. I can't believe it."

Caroline gave him a hug. "I was hoping you would like it."

"Oh yes. I didn't know the East Coast had a place like this!"

"There's nowhere else like it."

They hugged for so long it threatened to become something else; then they separated and wandered the peak plateau for a while. It was cold in the wind, and Caroline suggested they return. "There's a real trail down the northeast side, the Ravine Trail. It goes down a little cut in the granite."

They headed off the northeast shoulder of the hill, and were quickly down into scrubby trees. They hiked down a good trail, and Frank followed the graceful figure of his lover or girlfriend or he didn't know what, descending before him like a tree goddess. Some kind of happiness or joy or desire began to seep under his worry. Surely it had been a good idea to come here. He had had to do it; he couldn't have not done it.

They hiked down giant granite stones set in a rough staircase, and Frank said, "This trail is amazing."

"I don't think there's anything like them anywhere else," Caroline said. "Even here it was only a brief fad. But a fad in granite never goes away."

Frank laughed. "It looks like something the Incas might have done."

"It does, doesn't it?" She glanced back up the snowy stone steps.

"I can see why you would want to stay here," Frank said cautiously.

"Yes. I love it."

"But . . ."

"I think I'm okay here," she said.

Frank shrugged. "You don't want to leave."

"It's true," she said. "I like it here. And I *feel* hidden."

"But now you know better. Someone looked for you and found you."

"I guess," she muttered.

They came to the road, walked back to his van. She had him drive along the shore of what she called Jordan Pond. "Some of my first memories are from here," she said, looking out the window. "We came almost every summer. I always loved it. Then Mary's parents got divorced and we stopped coming."

"Ah."

"So, she and I started college and roomed together that first year. But to tell the truth, I hadn't thought of her for years. But when I was thinking about how to really get away, if I ever wanted to, I remembered this place. I never talked to Ed about Mary, and I just made the one call to her."

"What did you say?"

"I gave her the gist of the situation. She was willing to let me stay."

"That's good. Unless . . . I don't know. I mean, you tell me how dangerous these guys are. Some shots were fired that night in the park, after you left. My friends were the ones who started it, but your ex and his friends definitely shot back."

Now she looked appalled. "I didn't know."

"Yeah. I also . . . I threw a rock at your ex," he added lamely.

"You what?"

"I threw my hand axe at him. I saw a look on his face I didn't like, and I just—did it."

She squeezed his shoulder. Her face had the grim expression it took on whenever she was thinking about her ex. "I know that look," she said. "I hate it too." Then: "I'm sorry I got you into this."

"No, please. Anyway, I missed him. Luckily. But he saw the rock go by his head. He took off running down the Metro stairs. So he definitely knows something is up." Frank didn't mention going by their apartment afterward and ringing the doorbell; he was already embarrassed enough. "What I'm worried about is if he starts looking, and happens to replicate what my friend's friend did."

"I know." She sighed. "I guess I'm hoping he's not that intent on me anymore. I have him chipped, and he's always at his office, moving from room to room. I've got him covered with a spot cam on our apartment, things like that, and he seems to be in his ordinary routine."

"But he could do that while sending his team here to check things out."

She sighed. "I hate to leave here when there might not be a reason to."

Frank said nothing; his presence was proof there was a reason. Thus it had indeed been a bad thing. The transitive law definitely applied to emotions.

She directed him through some turns, and then they were driving around the head of Somes Sound again, back toward her place. As he slowed through Somesville, he said, "Where should we put my van?"

She ran her hands through her short curls, thinking it over. "Let's put it down by my car. I'm parked at the south end of Long Pond. First drop me off at the house, then drive down there, and I'll sail down on the iceboat and get you."

So he turned at the firehouse, drove to her place and dropped her off, feeling nervous as he did so. Then he followed her instructions, back toward Southwest Harbor, then west through the forest again, on a winding small road. He only had a rough sense of where he was, but then he was driving down an incline, and the smooth white surface of Long Pond appeared through the trees. The southern end of its long arm was walled on both sides by steep granite slopes, six or seven hundred feet high: a pure glacial U, floored by a lake.

He parked in the little parking lot by the pump house and got out. The wind from the north slammed him in the face. Far up the lake he saw a tiny sail appear as if out of the rock wall to the left. It looked like a big windsurfing sail. Faster than he would have thought possible it grew larger, and the iceboat swept up to the shore, Caroline at the tiller, turning it in a neat curlicue to lose speed and drift backward to shore.

"Amazing," Frank said. He stepped in and sat next to her. The iceboat was a wooden triangular thing, obviously handmade, more like a soapbox derby car than a boat. Three heavy struts extended from the cockpit, one ahead and two sideways and back. It was odd looking, but Caroline was obviously familiar with it. Her face was flushed with the wind, and she looked pleased in a way Frank had never seen before. She pulled the sail taut and twisted the tiller, which set the angles of the big metal skates out at the ends of the rear struts, and with a clatter they gained speed and were off in a chorus of scraping.

The iceboat did not heel in the wind, and when gusts struck it merely squeaked and slid along even faster, the skates making a loud clattery hiss. When a really strong gust hit, the craft rocketed forward with a palpable jolt. Frank's eyes watered heavily in the wind. He ducked when Caroline told him to, their heads together as the boom swung over them during a tack. To get up the lake they would have to tack often; the craft couldn't point far up into the wind.

As they worked their way north, Caroline explained that Mary's grandfather had built the iceboat. "He built everything there, even some of the furniture. He dug out the cellar, built the chimney, the terraces, the dock, the rowboats. . . ." Caroline had met this grandfather only once, when very young.

"This last month I've been feeling like he's still around the place, like a ghost, but in the best kind of way. The first night I got here the electricity wasn't on and there was no sound at all. I began to hear myself breathing. I could even hear my heart beat. And then there was a loon on the lake. It was so beautiful. And I thought of Mary's grandfather building everything, and it seemed like he was there. Not a voice, just part of the house. It was comforting."

"Good for him," Frank said. He liked the sound of such a moment, also that she had noticed and felt it. It occurred to him again how little he knew her. She was watching the ice ahead of the boat, holding the boom line and the tiller, making small adjustments as if performing a kind of dance with the wind. And there they were skittering across the frozen surface of the lake, the ice blazing under a low tarnished sun that smeared through long bars of cloud, the wind flying through him as if the gusts were stabs of feeling for her. He had thought she would be like this, but they had spent so little time together he could not be sure. But now he was seeing it. His Caroline, real in the sunlight and the wind. A gust of wind was a surge of feeling.

She brought the iceboat around again and continued that smooth curve into a channel that began the other arm of the lake. Here the north wind was somewhat blocked by the peninsula separating the two arms of the lake, and the ice boat slid along with less speed and noise. Then another curve, and they were headed into the wind again, on the short arm of the lake's Y shape, running toward a little island she called Rum Island, a round bump of snow and trees.

As they were about to pass Rum Island, something beeped in Caroline's jacket pocket. "Shit!" she said, and snatched out a small device, like a hand-held GPS. She steered with a knee while she held it up to her face to see it in the sunlight. She cursed again. "Someone's at camp."

She swerved, keeping Rum Island between the iceboat and Mary's place. As they approached the island she turned into the wind and let loose the sail, so that they skidded into a tiny cove and onto a tiny gravel beach. They stepped over the side onto icy gravel, tied the boat to a tree, made their way to the island's other side. The trees on the island hooted and creaked like the Sierras in a storm, a million pine needles whooshing their great chorale. It was strange to see the lake surface perfectly still and white under such a hard blow.

Across that white expanse, the green house and its little white boathouse were the size of postage stamps. Caroline had had binoculars in the boat, however, and through them the house's lake side was quite distinct; and through its big windows there was movement.

"Someone inside."

"Yes."

They crouched behind a big schist erratic. Caroline took the binoculars back from him and balanced them on the rock, then bent over and looked through them for a long time. "It looks like Andy and George," she said in a low voice, as if they might overhear. "Uh oh—get down," and she pulled him down behind the boulder. "There's a couple more up by the house, with some kind of scope. Can those IR glasses you use to spot animals see heat this far away?"

"Yes," Frank said. He had often used IR when tracking the ferals in Rock Creek. He took the binoculars back from her and looked around the side of the boulder near the ground, with only one lens exposed.

There they were—looking out toward the island—then hustling down the garden path and onto the ice itself, their long dark overcoats flapping in the wind. "Jesus," he said, "they're coming over here to check! They've seen us."

"Damn," she said. "Let's go, then."

They ran back over the little island to the iceboat. A hard kick from Caroline to its hull and it was off the gravel. Push it around, get in and take off, waiting helplessly for the craft to gain speed, which it did with an icy scratching that grew louder as they slid away from the island and skidded south.

Skating downwind did not feel as fast as tacking across it had, but soon they rounded the end of the peninsula between the two arms of the lake, and Caroline steered the craft in another broad curve, and it picked up speed and shot across the ice, into the gap leading to the longer stretch of the lake. Looking back, Frank got a last glimpse of the men crossing the lake. One of them held a phone to his ear. Then the peninsula blocked the view.

"The ones still at the house will drive around the lake," Frank said. "Do you think they can get to the southern end of the lake before we do?"

"Depends on the wind," Caroline said. "Also they might stop at Pond's End for a second, to see if we're coming up to that end."

"It wouldn't make sense for us to do that."

"Unless we had parked there. But they'll only stop a second, because they'll be able to see us. You can see all the way down the lake."

"So then?"

"I think we can beat them. If the wind holds, I'm sure we can."

The craft emerged from the channel onto the long stretch of the lake, where the wind was even stronger. Looking through the binoculars as best he could given the boat's chatter, Frank saw a dark van stop at the far end of the pond, then after a few moments drive on.

He had made the same drive himself a couple of hours before, and it seemed to him it had taken about fifteen minutes, maybe twenty, to get to the south end of the pond by way of the small roads through the woods. But he hadn't been hurrying. At full speed it might take only half that.

But now the iceboat had the full force of the north wind funneling between the granite cliffs, and the gusts felt stronger than ever, even though they were running downwind. The boat only touched the ice with the edges of its metal runners. Caroline's attention was fixed on the sail, her body hunched at the tiller and line. Frank didn't disturb her, but only sat on the gunwale opposite to the sail, as she had told him to do. The stretch of the lake they had to sail looked a couple of miles long. In a sailboat they would have been in trouble. On the ice, however, they zipped along as if in a catamaran's dream, almost frictionless despite the loud noise of what friction was left. Frank guessed they were going about twenty-five miles an hour, maybe thirty; it was hard to tell. Fast enough. The dwarf trees on the granite slopes to each side whistled, the sun was almost blocked by the western cliff. Caroline spared a moment to give Frank a look, and it seemed she was going to speak, then shook her head and simply gestured at the surrounding scene, her mouth tight. It was magnificent; but they were on the run.

"Them showing up so soon suggests I tipped them off somehow," he said.

"Yes." She was looking at the sail.

"I'm sorry. I thought I needed to warn you."

Her mouth stayed tight. She said nothing.

The minutes dragged, but Frank's watch showed that only eight had passed when they came to the south end of the lake. Caroline pulled the tiller and boom line and brought them into the beach next to the pump house, executing a bravura late turn that hooked so hard Frank was afraid the iceboat might be knocked on its side. Certainly a windsurfer or catamaran would have gone down like a bowling pin. But there was nothing for the iceboat to do but groan and scrape and spin, screeching to a stop, then drifting back onto the beach.

"Hurry," Caroline said, and jumped out and ran up to Frank's van.

Frank followed. "What about the boat?"

She grimaced. "We have to leave it!" Then, when they were in his van: "I'll call Mary when I can get a clean line and tell her where it is. I'd hate for Harold's boat to be lost because of this *shit*." Her voice was suddenly vicious.

Then she was all business, giving Frank directions; they got out to a paved road and turned right, and Frank accelerated as fast as he dared on the road, which was often in shadow, and seemed a good candidate for black ice. When they came to a T-stop she had him turn right. "My car's right there, the black Honda. I'm going to take off."

"Where?"

"I've got a place in mind. I've got to hurry, I don't want them to catch me at the bridge. You should get off the island too. Go back home."

"Okay," Frank said. He could feel himself entering one of his indecision fugues, and was grateful she had such a strong sense of what they should do. "Look, I'm sorry about this. I thought I had to warn you."

"I know. It's not your fault. None of this is your fault. It was good of you to try to help. I know why you did it." And she leaned over and gave him a quick peck of a kiss before she got out.

"I'm pretty sure my van is clean," Frank said. "And my stuff too."

"They may have you under other kinds of surveillance. Satellite cameras, or people just tailing you."

"Satellite cameras? Is that possible?"

"Of course." Annoyed that he could be so ignorant.

Frank shrugged, thinking it over. He would have to ask Edgardo. Right now he was glad she was giving him directions.

She came around the van and leaned in. Frank could see she was angry.

"You'll be able to come back here someday," he said.

"I hope so."

"You know," he said, "instead of holing up somewhere, you could stay with people who would keep you hidden."

"Like Anne Frank?"

Startled, Frank said, "Well, I guess so."

She shook her head. "I couldn't stand it. And I wouldn't want to put anyone else to the trouble."

"Well, but what about me? I'm staying with the Khembalis in almost that way already. They're very helpful, and their place is packed."

Again she shook her head. "I've got a Plan C, and it's down in that area. Once I get into that I can contact you again."

"If we can figure out a clean system."

"Yes. I'll work on that. We can always set up a dead drop."

"My friends from the park live all over the city—"

"I've got a plan!" she said sharply.

"Okay." He swallowed, tasted blood at the back of his throat.

"What?" she said.

"Nothing," he said automatically.

"Something!" she said, and reached in to touch the side of his head. "Tell me what you just thought. Tell me, I've got to go, but I don't like that look!"

He told her about it as briefly as he could. Taste of blood. Inability to make decisions. Maybe it was sounding like he was making excuses for coming up to warn her. She was frowning. When he was done, she shook her head.

"Frank? Go see a doctor."

"I know."

"Don't say that! I want you to promise me. Make the appointment, and then go see the doctor."

"Okay. I will."

"All right, now I've got to go. I think they've got you chipped somehow. Be careful and go right back home. I'll be in touch."

"How?"

She grimaced. "Just go!"

A phrase which haunted him as he made the long drive south. Back to home; back to work; back to Diane. Just go!

He could not seem to come to grips with what had happened. The island was like a dream it was so vivid and surreal, but detached from any obvious meaning. Heavily symbolic of something that could nevertheless not be decoded. They had hugged so hard, and yet had never really kissed; they had climbed together, they had iceboated on a wild wind, and yet in the end she had been angry, perhaps with him, and holding back from saying things, or so it had seemed. He wasn't sure.

Mile after mile winged by, minute after minute; on and on they went, by the tens, then the hundreds. And as night fell, and his world reduced to a pattern of white and red lights, with glowing green signs and their white lettering, his feel for his location on the globe became entirely theoretical to him, and everything grew stranger and stranger. Some kind of fugue state, the same thoughts over and over. Obsession without compulsion. Headlights in the rearview mirror; who could tell if they were from the same vehicle or not?

It became hard to believe there was anything outside the lit strip of the highway. Once Kenzo had shown him a USGS map of the United States that had displayed the human population as raised areas, and on that map the 95 corridor had been like an immense Himalaya from Atlanta to Boston, rising from both ends to the Everest that was New York. And yet driving right down the spine of this great density of his species, he could see nothing but the walls of trees lining both sides of the endless slot. He might as well have been driving south though Siberia, or over the face of some empty forest planet, tracking some great circle route that was only going to bring him back around the world to where he had started. The forest hid so much.

Despite the reestablished Gulf Stream, a strong cold front rode the jet stream south from Hudson Bay and arrived just in time to strike the inauguration. When the day dawned, temperatures in the capital region hovered around zero degrees Fahrenheit, with clear sunny skies and a north wind averaging fifteen miles an hour. Everyone out of doors had to bundle up, so it was a slow process at all the security checkpoints. The audience settled onto the cold aluminum risers set on the east side of the Capitol, and Phil Chase and his entourage stepped onto the dais, tucked discreetly behind protective glass. The cold air and Phil's happy, relaxed demeanor reminded Charlie of films of the Kennedy inauguration. His boy was huddled against him, heavy as a rock, dragging him down but keeping him warm. "Dad, let's go to the zoo! Wanna go to the zoo!"

"Okay, Joe, but after this, okay? This is history!"

"His story?"

Phil stood looking out at the crowd after the oath of office was administered by the Chief Justice, a man about ten years younger than he was. With a wave of his gloved hand he smiled his beautiful smile.

"Fellow Americans," he said, pacing his speech to the reverb of the loudspeakers, "you have entrusted me with the job of president during a difficult time. The crisis we face now, of abrupt climate change and crippling damage to the biosphere, is a very dangerous one, to be sure. But we are not at war with anyone, and in fact we face a challenge that all humanity has to meet together. On this podium, Franklin Roosevelt said, 'This generation has a rendezvous with destiny.' Now it's true again. We are the generation that has to deal with the profound destruction that will be caused by the global warming already set in motion. The potential disruption of the natural order is so great that scientists warn of a mass extinction event. Losses on that scale would endanger all humanity, and so we cannot fail to address the threat. The lives of our children, and all their descendants, depend on us doing so.

"So, like FDR and his generation, we have to face the great challenge of our time. We have to use our government to organize a total social response to the problem. That took courage then, and we will need courage now. In the years since we used our government to help get us out of the Great Depression, it has sometimes been fashionable to belittle the American government as some kind of foreign burden laid on us. That attitude is nothing more than an attack on American history, deliberately designed to shift power away from the American people. I want us to remember how Abraham Lincoln said it: 'that government of the people, by the people, and for the people shall not perish from this Earth.' This is the crucial concept of American democracy—that government expresses what the majority of us would like to do as a society. It's us. We do it to us and for us. I believe this reminder is so important that I intend to add the defining phrase 'of the people, by the people, and for the people' every time I use the word 'government,' and I intend to do all I can to make that phrase be a true description.

"So, this winter, with your approval and support, I intend to instruct the executive branch of government of the people, by the people, and for the people, to initiate a series of federal actions designed to meet the problem of global climate change head-on. We will deal with it working together with the rest of the world. It's a global project, so we will help the developing world to develop using clean technology, so that all the good of development will not be drowned in its bad side effects—often literally drowned. In our own country, meanwhile, we will do all it takes to shift to clean technologies as quickly as possible."

Phil paused to survey the crowd. "My, it's cold out here today! You can feel right now, right down to the bone, that what I am saying is true. We need to change the way we do things. And it's not just a technological problem, having to do with our machinery alone. The devastation of the biosphere is also a result of there being too many human beings for the planet to support over the long haul. If the population continues to increase as it has in the past, all progress we might make will be overwhelmed.

"But what is very striking to observe is that everywhere on this Earth where good standards of justice prevail, the rate of human reproduction is at about the replacement rate; while wherever justice is denied to some portion of the population, especially to women and children, the rate of reproduction either balloons to unsustainably rapid growth rates, or crashes outright. Now you can argue all you want about why this correlation exists, but the correlation itself is striking and undeniable. So this is one of those situations where what we do for good in one area, helps us again in another. It is a positive feedback loop with the most profound implications. Consider: for the sake of climate stabilization, there must be population stabilization; and for there to be population stabilization, *justice must prevail.* Every person on the planet must live with the full array of human rights that all nations have already ascribed to when signing the UN Charter. When we achieve that, at that point, and at that point only, we will begin create a sustainable civilization.

"To help that to happen, I intend to make sure that the United States joins the global justice project *fully, unequivocally,* and *without any double standards.* This means abiding by all the clauses of the UN Charter and the Geneva Conventions, which after all we have already signed. It means supporting UN peacekeeping forces, and supporting the general concept of the United Nations as the body that resolves international conflicts. It means supporting the World Health Organization, and women's education, and women's rights everywhere, even in cultures where men's tyranny is claimed as some sort of tradition. All these commitments on our part will be crucial if we are serious about building a sustainable world. There are three legs to this effort, folks: technology, environment, and social justice. None of the three can be neglected.

"So, some of what we do may look a little unconventional at first. And it may look more than a little threatening to those few who have been trying to buy our government of the people, by the people, and for the people, and use it to line their own pockets while the world goes smash. But you know what? Those people need to change too. They're out in the cold the same as the rest of us. So we will proceed, and hope those opposed come to see the good in it.

"Ultimately we will be exploring all peaceful means to initiate positive change, in order to hand on to the generations to come a world that is as beautiful and bountiful as the one we were born into. We are only the temporary stewards of a mighty trust, which includes the lives of all the future generations to come. We are responsible to our children and theirs. What we do now will reveal much about our character and our values. We have to rise to the occasion, and I think we will. I am going to throw myself into the effort wholeheartedly and with a feeling of high excitement, as if beginning a long journey over stormy seas."

"Good," Charlie said into his phone. "He's still saying the right stuff."

"Heck yeah," Roy replied in his ear. "But you know the old saying: an ounce of law is worth a pound of rhetoric." Roy himself had made up this old saying, and trotted it out as often as possible. He was somewhere on the opposite side of the viewing stands from Charlie and Joe, but with all the hats and mufflers and ski masks, Charlie could not spot him. Roy continued, "We'll see if we can wag the dog or not. Things bog down in this town."

"I think the dog will wag us," Charlie said. "I think we are the dog. We're the dog of the people, by the people, and for the people."

"We'll see. Everything depends on how the start goes."

As chief of staff, Roy had already worked so hard on the transition that Charlie feared he had lost sight of the big picture. Charlie said, "A good start would help, but whatever happens, we have to persevere. Right, Joe?"

"Go Phil! Hey, Dad? It's cold."

The transition team had concocted a "First Sixty Days," in effect a gigantic list of Things to Do. Many federal agencies had been deliberately disabled by previous administrations, and required a complete retooling to be able to function. In others, change at the top would rally the efforts of a permanent staff of professional technocrats. Each agency had to be evaluated, and the amount of attention given to them adjusted accordingly.

For Charlie this meant working full-time, as agreed with Phil. Everyone else was going full speed, and he felt an obligation to match them. Up before sunrise, therefore, groggy in the cold dark of winter. Get Joe up, or at least transferred sleeping into his stroller. Quick walk with Anna to the Bethesda Metro, companionable, as if they were still in bed together, or sharing a dream; Charlie could almost fall back asleep on such a walk. Then down into the Earth, to slump in a bright vinyl seat and snooze against Anna to Metro Center, where she changed trains while the boys went up to the sidewalk, to have a last brisk walk together to the White House, Joe often awake and babbling. There pass through security, down to the daycare center, where Joe bounced impatiently in his stroller until he could clamber off and plow into the fun. He was always one of the first kids there and one of the last to leave, and that was saying a lot. But he did not remark on this or seem to mind. He was still nice to the other kids. Indeed the teachers all told Charlie how well he got along with the other kids.

Charlie found these reports depressing. He remembered Gymboree, indeed had been traumatized by certain incidents at Gymboree. But now, as everyone pointed out, Joe was calm to the point of detachment. Serene. In his own space. In the daycare he looked somewhat like he would have during a quiet moment on the floor of their living room; perhaps a bit more wary. It worried Charlie more than he could say. Anna would not understand the nature of his concern, and beyond that, there was no one else with whom to share this feeling that Joe had changed and was not himself. That wasn't something you could say.

Sometimes he brought it up with Anna obliquely, as a question, and she agreed that Joe was different than he had been before his fever, but she seemed to regard it as normal for childhood, and mostly a function of learning to talk. Her theory was that as Joe learned to talk he got less frustrated, that his earlier tempestuousness had been frustration at not being able to communicate what he was thinking.

But this theory presupposed that the earlier Joe had been inarticulate and in possession of thoughts he had wanted to communicate but couldn't, which did not match Charlie's experience. In his opinion Joe had always communicated exactly whatever he was feeling or thinking. Even before he had any language his thoughts had been perfectly explicit, though not linguistic. They had been precise feelings and Joe had expressed them precisely, and with operatic virtuosity.

But now it was different. To Charlie, radically different. Anna didn't see that, and it would upset her if Charlie could persuade her to see it, so he didn't try. He wasn't even sure what it was he would be trying to convey. He didn't *really* believe that the real Joe had gone away as a result of the Khembalis' ceremony for him. When Charlie had made the request, his rather vague notion had been that such a ceremony would dispel the Khembalis' interest in Joe, their belief that he harbored the spirit of one of their reincarnated lamas. Altering the Khembalis' attitude toward Joe would then change Joe himself, but in minor ways—ways that Charlie now found he had not fully imagined, for how exactly had he thought that Joe was "not himself," beyond being feverish, and maybe a bit subdued, a bit cautious and fearful? Had that really been the result of the Khembalis' regard? And if their regard changed, why exactly would Joe go back to the way he was before—feisty, bold, full of himself?

Perhaps he wouldn't. It hadn't worked out that way, and now Charlie's ideas seemed flawed to him. Now he had to try to figure out just exactly what it was he had wanted, what he thought had happened in the ceremony, and what he thought was happening now.

It was a hard thing to get at, made harder by the intensity of his new schedule. He only saw Joe for a couple hours a day, during their commutes, and their time in the Metro cars often had both of them asleep on the ride in, and tired and distracted on the way home. Charlie would sit Joe beside him, or on his lap, and they would talk, and Joe was pretty similar to his old self, babbling at things outside the window or in his stroller, or referring to events earlier in his day, telling semicoherent stories. It was hard to be sure what he was talking about most of the time, although toys and teachers and the other kids clearly formed the basis of most of his conversation.

But then they would walk home and enter life with Anna and Nick, and often that was the last they would have to do with each other until bedtime. So—who knew? It was not like the old days, with the vast stretches of hours, weeks, seasons, extending before and behind them in a perpetual association not unlike the lives of conjoined twins. Charlie now saw only fragmentary evidence. It was hard to be sure of anything.

Nevertheless. He saw what he saw. Joe was not the same. And so trapped at the back of his mind (but always there) was the fear that he had somehow misunderstood and asked for the wrong thing for his son—then gotten it.

As the winter deepened it became more expensive to warm the entire house. Anna programmed the house's thermostat to choreograph their evenings, so that they congregated in the kitchen and living room in the early evenings, then followed the heat upstairs in the hour before sleep. It worked fairly well, reinforcing what they would have done anyway. But one exceptionally cold night in early February the power went out, and everything was suddenly different.

Anna had a supply of flashlights and candles in a cabinet in the dining room, and quickly she banged her way to them and got some candles lit in every room. She turned on a battery-powered radio, and Nick twiddled the dial trying to find some news. While Charlie was building up the fire in the fireplace, they listened to a crackly voice say that a cold front like one from the winter before had dropped temperatures by sixty degrees in twenty minutes, causing a surge in demand or a malfunction at some point in the grid, thus crashing the system.

"I'm glad we got home," Anna said. "We could have been in the Metro."

They could hear sirens beginning to oscillate. The streets clotted with cars, as they could see out on Wisconsin, just visible from their front window. When Charlie stepped outside to get more firewood from their screened-in porch, he smelled the smell of a power outage, unexpectedly familiar from the winter before: exhaust of burned generator fuel, smoke of green firewood.

Inside the boys clamored for marshmallows, and Anna found a bag of them at the back of a kitchen cabinet. Anna passed on trying one, to Joe's amazement, and went to the kitchen to whip up a late salad, keeping the refrigerator door open for as short a time as possible, wondering how quickly an unopened refrigerator would lose its chill. She resolved to buy a couple of thermometers to find out. The information might come in useful.

Back in the living room, Charlie had finished lighting all the candles in the house, a profligacy that created a fine glow. Carrying one upstairs, Anna watched the shadows shift and flicker with her steps, and wondered if they would be warm enough up there that night; the bedrooms felt colder than the inside of the refrigerator. She wondered briefly if a refrigerator would work to keep things from freezing in a subzero house.

"We should maybe sleep on the couches down here," she said when she was back downstairs. "Do we have enough firewood to keep a fire all night?"

"I think so," Charlie said. "If the wood will burn."

Last winter all the cured firewood had been bought and burned, and this year green wood was almost all that was available; it burned very poorly, as Charlie was now finding out. He threw in a paraffin-and-sawdust log and used his massive wrought-iron fire tongs to lift the heavy real logs over the fake one, to dry them out and keep things going.

"Remind me to buy dry wood next time."

Anna took her bowl back into the kitchen. Water was still running, but it wouldn't for long. She filled her pots, and a couple of five-gallon plastic jugs they had in the basement. These too would freeze eventually, unless she put them near the fire. They needed a better blackout routine, she saw. She took the jugs out to the living room and saw the boys settling in on the couches. This must be how it had been, she thought, for generations on end; everyone huddling together at night for warmth. Probably she would have to work from home the next day, though her laptop battery was depleted. She wished laptop batteries lasted longer.

"Remind me to check the freezer in the morning. I want to see if things have started to thaw."

"If you open it, it will lose its cool."

"Unless the kitchen is colder still. I've been wondering about that."

"Maybe we should just leave the freezer door open then."

They laughed at this, but Anna still felt uneasy.

They built a city on the coffee table using Joe's blocks, then read by candlelight. Charlie and Nick hauled an old double mattress that they called the Tigers' Bed up from the basement, and they laid it right before the fire, where Joe used it as a trampoline which could easily slingshot him right into the blaze.

When everything was arranged, Charlie read aloud some pages from *The Once and Future King,* about what it was like to be a goose migrating over the Norwegian Sea—a passage that entranced Anna and the boys. Finally they put out the candles and fell asleep—

Only to awaken together, surprised and disoriented, when the power came back on. It was 2 A.M., and beyond the reach of the smoldering fire the house was very cold, but fully lit, and buzzing with the sounds of its various machines. Anna and Charlie got up to turn the lights off. The boys were already asleep again by the time they got back downstairs.

The next day things were back to normal, more or less, though the air was still smoky. Everyone wanted to tell stories about where they had been when the power went off, and what had happened to them.

"It was actually kind of nice," Charlie said the next night at dinner.

Anna agreed uneasily. "It wouldn't be if the power were still off now."

CHAPTER 23

GOING FERAL

Again foul weather shall not change my mind,
But in the shade I will believe what in the sun
I loved.

—*Thoreau*

Against the pressure of one's fear must be held the power of cognition.

Examination of the relevant literature, however, revealed that there were cognitive illusions that were as strong as optical illusions. This was an instructive analogy, because many optical illusions fooled one no matter how fully one understood the illusion and tried to compensate for it. Spin a disk with certain black-and-white patterns, and colors appear undeniably. There were cognitive errors just like that. Calculating probabilities, various statistical effects; cognitive scientists had devised several tests of these mental skills, and even working with statisticians as their subjects, they found everyone prone to certain cognitive errors, which they had given names like anchoring, ease of representation, the law of small number, the fallacy of near certainty, asymmetric similarity, trust in analogy, neglect of base rates, and so on.

One test that had caught even Frank, despite his vigilance, was the three-box game. Three boxes were presented all closed, with one ten-dollar bill hidden in one of them; the experimenter knew which. Subject chooses a box, at that point left closed. Experimenter then opens one of the other two boxes, always an empty one. Subject then offered a chance to either stick with his first choice, or switch to the other closed box. Which should he do?

Frank decided it didn't matter; fifty-fifty either way.

But each box at the start had a one-third chance of being the one. When subject chooses one, the other two then have two-thirds of a chance of being right. After experimenter opens one of those two boxes, and it's empty, those two boxes still have two-thirds of a chance, which is now concentrated in the remaining unchosen box; while the subject's original choice still has its original one-third chance. So one should always change one's choice to the unopened box one hadn't chosen! Odds are two-thirds to one-third that the other box will be the right one.

Well, shit. Put it that way and it was undeniable, even though it still seemed wrong, indeed painfully counterintuitive. When Anna got the answer right the moment Frank described the test to her, he still felt that only proved Anna's Spocklike quality of mind; he laughed at her, but the problem's solution still felt deeply wrong. But this was the point: human cognition (which might leave Anna slightly to one side) had all kinds of blind spots like this. One scientist had concluded by saying, We're so bad at seeing reality, we simulate in our actions what we wish had already happened.

People acted, in short, by projecting their desires.

Well—but of course. Wasn't that the point?

But clearly it could lead to error. The question was, could one's desires be defined in such a way as to suggest actions that were truly going to help make the desires come to pass, in a future still truly possible?

And could that be done if there was a numb spot behind one's nose—a pressure on one's thoughts—a suspension of one's ability to decide anything?

Then also, could it be that these cognitive errors existed for society as a whole, just as they did for individuals? Could they map a way forward despite the inherent errors? Some spoke of "cognitive mapping" when they discussed taking social action: one mapped the immense unknowable civilization, or reality itself, not by knowing all of it, but by marking routes through it. So that they were not the map or the radar system, but the pilot.

At that point it became clear even mapping was an analogy. As such Anna would not think much of it, nor the cognitive scientists; "trust in analogy" was one of their identified errors. But everyone needed a set of procedures to nav-

igate their days: the science of that particular Wednesday (Emerson). Using flawed equipment (the brain, civilization) one tried to optimize results. Some kind of robustness in the totality of the flawed instruments and procedures.

Something from Aldo Leopold: What's good is what's good for the land.

Something from Rudra Cakrin (although he said it was from the Dalai Lama, or the Buddha himself): Try to do good for other people. Your happiness lies there.

Try it and see. Make the experiment and analyze it. Try again. Act on your desires.

But what do you really want?

And can you really decide?

One day when Frank woke up in the garden shed with Rudra, it took him quite a while to remember where he was, also who—long enough that when he sat up he was actively relieved to be Frank Vanderwal, or anybody.

Then he had trouble figuring out which pants to put on, something he had never considered before in his life. Then he realized he did not want to go to work, although he had to. Was this unusual? He wasn't sure.

As he munched on a PowerBar and waited for his bedside coffee machine to provide, he clicked on his laptop, and after the portentous chord announced the beginning of his cyberday, he went to Emersonfortheday. com.

"Hey, Rudra, are you awake?"

"Always."

"Listen to this. It's Emerson, talking about my parcellated mind theory:

> 'It is the largest part of a man that is not inventoried. He has many enumerable parts: he is social, professional, political, sectarian, literary, and is this or that set and corporation. But after the most exhausting census has been made, there remains as much more which no tongue can tell. And this remainder is that which interests. Far the best part of every mind is not that which he knows, but that which hovers in gleams, suggestions, tantalizing, unpossessed, before him. This dancing chorus of thoughts and hopes is the quarry of his future, is his possibility.'"

"Maybe," Rudra said. "But whole sight is good too. Being one."

"But isn't it interesting he talks about it in those terms?"

"It is common knowledge. Anyone knows that."

"I guess. I think Emerson knows a lot of things I don't know."

Emerson was also a man who had spent time in the forest. Frank liked to read the signs of this: "The man who rambles in the woods seems to be the first man that ever entered a grove, his sensations and his world are so novel and strange." That was right; Frank knew that feeling. Hikes in the winter forest, so surreal—Emerson knew about them. He had seen the woods at twilight. "Never was a more brilliant show of colored landscape than yesterday afternoon; incredibly excellent topaz and ruby at four o'clock; cold and shabby at six." The quick strangeness of the world, how it came on you all of a sudden: now, for Frank, this feeling started on waking. Coming up blank, the primal man, the first ever to wake. Strange indeed, not to know who or what you were.

Often these days he felt he should be moving back out into the park, living in his treehouse. That would mean leaving the Khembalis, which was bad. On the other hand, in some ways it would be a relief. He had been living with them for almost a year now, hard to believe, but it was true, and they were so crowded. They could use all the extra space they could get. Besides, it felt like time to get back outdoors and into the wind. Spring was coming, spring and all.

But there was Rudra to consider. As his roommate, Frank was part of his care. He was old, frail, sleeping a lot. Frank was his companion and friend, English teacher and Tibetan student. Moving out would disrupt all that.

He read on for a while, then realized he was hungry, and that in poking around and thinking about Emerson and Thoreau, and cognitive blind spots, he had been reading for over an hour. Rudra had gotten up and slipped out. "Aack!" Time to get up! Seize the day!

Up and out then. Another day. Best get more to eat. But from where?

He couldn't decide.

A minute or two later, angrily, and before even actually getting up, he grabbed his phone and made the call. He called his doctor's office, and found that, regarding a question like this, the doctor couldn't see him for a week.

That was fine with Frank. He had made the decision and made the call. Caroline would have no reason to reproach him, and he could go on. Not that something didn't have to be done. It was getting ridiculous. It was a—an obstacle. A disability. An injury, not just to his brain, but *to his thinking*.

.   .   .

That afternoon, his worry about Caroline being so sharp, he made arrangements to go out on a run with Edgardo. It was an afternoon so cold that no one but Kenzo would have gone out with them, and he was away at a conference, so after they cleared themselves with the wands (which Frank now questioned as fully reliable indicators), off they went.

The two of them ran side by side through the streets of Arlington, bundled up in nearly Arctic running gear, their heavy wool caps rolled up just far enough to expose their ears' bottom halves, which allowed sound into the eardrums so they could hear each other without shouting or completely freezing their ears. Very soon they would be moving with Diane over to the Old Executive Offices, right next door to the White House; this would be one of their last runs on this route. But it was such a lame route that neither would miss it.

Frank explained what had happened in Maine, in short rhythmic phrases synchronized with his stride. It was such a relief to be able to tell somebody about it. Almost a physical relief. One *vented,* as they said.

"So how the heck did they follow me?" he demanded at the end of his tale. "I thought your friend said I was clean."

"He thought you were," Edgardo said. "And it isn't certain you weren't. The timing of their arrival could have been a coincidence."

Frank shook his head.

"It could have," Edgardo insisted. "In fact you might have saved her, think of it that way!"

This startled Frank, as he had not thought of it. "But not likely," he said.

"Well, there may be other ways you are chipped, or they may have followed you physically. But the question now is, where has she gone."

"She said she has a Plan C that no one can trace. And she said it would get her down to this area. That she'd get in touch with me. I don't know how that will work. Anyway now I'm wondering if we can, you know, root these guys out. Maybe sic the President on them."

"Well," Edgardo said, elongating the word for about a hundred yards.

"These kinds of black operations are designed to be insulated, you know. To keep those above from having responsibility for them."

"But surely if there was a problem, if you really tried to hunt things down from above? Following the money, for instance?"

"Maybe. Black budgets are everywhere. Have you asked Charlie?"

"No."

"Maybe you should, if you feel comfortable. Phil Chase has a million things on his plate. It might take someone like Charlie to get his attention."

Frank nodded. "Well, whatever happens, we need to stop those guys."

"We?"

"I mean, they need to be stopped. And no one else is doing it. And, I don't know—maybe you and your friends from your DARPA days, or wherever, might be able to make a start. You've already made the start, I mean, and could carry it forward from there."

"Well," Edgardo said. "I don't know. I shouldn't speak to that."

Frank focused on the run. They were down to the river path now, and he could see the Potomac was frozen over again, looking like a discolored white sheet that had been pulled over the river's surface and then tacked down roughly at the banks. The sight reminded him of Long Pond and the shocking sight of those men striding across the ice toward them; his pulse jumped, but his hands and feet got colder. The tip of his nose, numb at the best of times, was more numb than usual. He squeezed and tugged it to get some feeling and blood flow.

"Nose still numb?"

"Yes."

Edgardo broke into the song "Comfortably Numb": "I—I, have become, comfortably numb," then scat-singing the famous guitar solo, "Da daaaa, da da da da da-da-daaaaaa," exaggerating Gilmour's bent notes. "Okay! Okay, okay, is there anybody *in there*? Just knock if you can *feel me*." Abruptly he broke off. "I will go talk to my friend whom you met. He's into this stuff and he has an interest. His group is still looking at the election problem, for sure."

"Do you think I could meet him again? To explore some strategies?" And ask a bunch of questions, he didn't say.

"Maybe. Let me talk to him. It may be pointless to meet. It depends. I'll check. Meanwhile you should try your other options."

"I don't know that I have any."

"Are you still having trouble making decisions?"

"Yes."

"Go see your doctor, then."

"I did! I mean, I've got an appointment. The time has almost come."

Edgardo laughed.

"Please," Frank said. "I'm trying. I made the call."

But in fact, when the time came for his doctor's appointment, he went in unhappily. Surely, he thought obstinately, deciding to go to the doctor meant he was well enough to decide things!

So he felt ridiculous as he described the problem to the doctor, a young guy who was looking rather dubious. Frank felt his complaint was vague at best, as he very seldom tasted blood at the back of his throat anymore. But he could not complain merely of feeling indecisive, so he emphasized the tasting a little more than the most recent data would truly support, which made him feel even more foolish. He hated visiting the doctor at any time, so why was he here just to exaggerate an occasional symptom? Maybe his decision-making capability was damaged after all! Which meant it was good to have come in. And yet here he was making things up. Although he was only trying to physicalize the problem, he told himself. To describe real symptoms.

In any case, the doctor offered no opinion, but only gave him a referral to an ear, nose, and throat guy. It was the same one Frank had seen immediately after his accident. Frank steeled himself, called again (two decisions?), and found that here the next appointment available was a month away. Happily he wrote down the date and forgot about it.

Or would have; except now he was cast back into the daily reality of struggling to figure out what to do. Hoping every morning that Emerson or Thoreau would tell him. So he didn't really forget about the appointment, but it was scheduled, and he didn't have to go for a long time, so he could be happy. Happy until the next faint taste of old blood slid down the back of his throat, like the bitterness of fear itself, and he would check and see the day getting nearer.

Once he noticed the date when talking with Anna, because she said something about not making it through the winter in terms of several necessary commodities that people had taken to hoarding. She was now studying choice rubrics in variable information states to try to understand hoarding better.

"It's called 'always defect,'" Frank insisted.

"Okay, but then look at what that *leads to*."

"All right."

Clearly Anna was incensed at how unreasonable people were being. To her it was a matter of being logical. "Why don't they just do the math?"

A rhetorical question, Frank judged. Though he wished he could answer it, rhetorically or not, in a way that did not depress him. His investigations into cognition studies were not exactly encouraging. Logic was to cognition as geometry was to landscape.

After this conversation, Frank recalled her saying "end of the winter" as if that were near, and he checked his desk calendar—the date circled for his ENT appointment was circled there, and not too far away.

So he went to the doctor when the day came. Ear, nose, and throat—but what about *brain*? He read *Walden* in the waiting room, was ushered into an examination room to wait and read some more, then five minutes of questions and inspections, and the diagnosis was made: he needed to see another specialist. A neurologist, in fact, who would have to take a look at some scans, possibly CT, PET, SPECT, MRI; the brain guy would make the calls. The ENT guy would give him a referral, he said, and Frank would have to see where they could fit him in. Scans; the reading and analysis of the brain guy; then perhaps a reexamination by the ENT. How long would it all take? Try it and see. They hurried scheduling a bit when the questions were about the brain, but only so much; there were a lot of other people out there with equally serious problems, or worse ones.

So, Frank thought as he went back to work in his office. You could buy DVD players for thirty dollars and flat-screen TVs for a hundred, to experience vicariously the lives that your work and wages did not give you the time and money to live (that T-shirt seen on Connecticut Avenue, "Medieval Peasants Worked Less Than You Do")—everything was cheap, overproduced—except you lived in a permanent shortage of doctors, artificially maintained. But there was nothing for it but to think about other things, when he could; and when not, to bide his time and try to work, like everyone else. But clearly the system itself had some cognitive errors.

It had been every kind of winter, warmer, drier, stormier, colder. Bad for agriculture, good for conversation. A cold front swept south and knocked them back into full winter lockdown, the river frozen, the city frozen, every Metro vent steaming frost, such that the city looked like it had been built on a giant hot spring. When the sun came out everything glittered.

For Frank this was another ascent into what he thought of as high latitude or altitude, because weather *was* landscape, in that however the land lay underfoot, it was weather that gave you a sense of where you were. If it was below zero, then you were in the Arctic. You found yourself on the cold hill's side, and recalled in the body that the brain had ballooned in the depths of the ice ages. No wonder the mind lit up like a fuse in such air!

And so Frank got out his snowshoes and gaiters and ski poles, and drove over to Rock Creek Park and went out for hikes, just as he had the winter before. And though this year there was not that sense of discovery, it was certainly just as cold. Wind barreling down the great ravine, the icy gorge looking from its rim as blasted by the great flood as the day the waters had receded.

The park was emptier this year, however. Or maybe it was just that there was no one at site 21. But many other sites were empty too. Maybe people had finally found shelter. In theory one could sleep out in temperatures like this, if one had the right gear and the right expertise, but it took time and energy to accomplish, and would still have been dangerous; it would have to be one's main activity. No doubt some people were doing it, but most had found refuge in the coffee shops by day, and the shelters and feral houses by night. As Frank himself had, when taken in by the Khembalis.

Leaving, in these most frigid days, the animals. He saw the aurochs once; and a Canada lynx (I call it the Concord lynx, Thoreau said), as still as a statue of itself; and four or five foxes in their winter white. Also a moose, a porcupine, a coyote, and scads of deer; also rabbits. These last two were the obvious food for what predators there were. Most of the exotic ferals were gone, either recaptured or dead. Although once he spotted what he thought was a snow leopard. And people said the jaguar was still at large.

As were the frisbee guys. One Saturday Frank heard them before he saw them—hoots over a rise to the north—Spencer's distinctive yowl, which meant a long putt had hit its mark. Cheered, Frank moved toward the sound, snowshoes sinking deep in the drifts, and suddenly there they were, running on little plastic snowshoes, without poles, and throwing red, pink, and orange frisbees, which blazed through the air like beacons from another universe.

"Hi guys!" Frank called.

"Frank!" they cried. "Come on!"

"You bet," Frank said. He left his poles and daypack under a tree at site 18, and borrowed one of Robert's disks.

Off they went. Quickly it became clear to Frank that when the snow was as hard as it was, running on snowshoes was about as efficient as walking on them. One tended to leap out of each step before the snowshoe had sunk all the way in, thus floating a bit higher than otherwise.

Then he threw a drive straight into a tree trunk, and broke the disk in half. Robert just laughed, and Spencer tossed him a spare. The guys did not overvalue any individual disk. They were like golf balls, made to be lost.

Work as hard as they did, and you would sweat—just barely—after which, when you stopped, your sweat would chill you. As soon as they were done, therefore, Frank found out when they thought they would play again, then bid farewell and hustled away, back to his daypack and poles. A steady hike then, to warm back up; little glissades, tricky traverses, yeoman ups; quickly he was warm again and feeling strong, and somehow full, the joy of the frisbee buzzing through the rest of the day. The joy of the hunt and the cold.

He walked by his tree, looked up at it longingly. He wanted to move back to it. But he wanted to stay with Rudra too. And Caroline's ex might be keeping watch out here. The thought made him stop and look around. No one in sight. He would have to wand his tree to see if any bugs were there. The floorboards of the treehouse were visible if you knew where to look, but as Frank did know, it was hard for him to judge how obvious they were.

The following Monday he arranged a run with Edgardo again. The need to speak securely was going to drive them to new levels of fitness.

"So did you ever hear anything back from your friend?" he said.

"Yes. A little. I was going to tell you."

"What?"

"He said, the problem with taking the top-down approach is the operation might be legally secret, so that the President might have trouble finding it."

"You're kidding."

"No. He said that most presidents want it that way, so they aren't breaking the law by knowing, if the operation chooses to do something illegal for the higher good. So, Chase might have to order a powerful group under his direct command to seek out a thing like this."

"Jesus. Are there any such powerful groups?"

"Oh sure. He would have his choice of three or four. But this presumes that you could get him interested. A president has a lot on his plate. He has a staff to filter what comes in, so there are levels. So, these people we're interested in know that, and they trust he would never go after something this little."

"Something as little as stolen presidential elections?"

"Well, maybe, but how much would he want to know, when he just won?"

They paced on while Frank tried to digest this.

"So did your friend have any other ideas?"

"Yes. He said it might be possible to get these people in trouble with an agency less black than them. Some kind of turf battle or the like."

"Ahhh . . ."

Quickly Frank began to see possibilities. While at NSF, Diane had fought other agencies all the time, usually David-and-Goliath-type actions, as most of NSF's natural rivals in the federal bureaucracy were far bigger than it. And size mattered in the feds, as elsewhere, because it meant money. This little gang of security thugs Frank had tangled with were surely treading on some other more legitimate agency's turf. Possibly they had even started in some agency and gone Rambo without the knowledge of their superiors.

"That's a good idea. Did he have any specific suggestions?"

"He did, and he was going to work up some more. It turns out he has reasons to dislike these guys beyond the destruction-of-democracy stuff."

"Oh good."

"Yes. It is best never to rely on people standing on principle."

"So true," Frank said grimly.

This set off Edgardo's raucous laugh and his little running prance of cynical delight. "Ah yes, you are learning! You are beginning to see! My friend said he will give me a menu of options soon."

"I hope it's real soon. Because *my* friend's out there enacting her Plan C, and I'm worried. I mean she's a data analyst, when you get right down to it. She isn't any kind of field spook. What if her Plan C is as bad as her Plan B?"

"That would be bad. But my friend has been looking into that. I asked him to and he did, and he can't find her. She seems to be really hidden this time."

"That's good. But her ex might know more than your friend."

"Yes. Well, I'll see my friend as soon as I can. I have to follow our protocol though, unless it's an emergency. We only usually talk once a week."

"I understand," Frank said, then wondered if he did.

With Chase now in office the new administration's activity level became manic. Among many more noted relocations, Diane and all the rest of the science advisor's team moved into their new offices in the Old Executive Offices, just to the west of the White House and within the White House security barrier.

So Frank gave up his office at NSF, which had served as living room and office in his parcellated house. As he moved out he felt a bit stunned, even dismayed. He had to admit that the habits that had made that modular house were now demolished. He followed Diane to their new building, wondering if he had made the right decision to go with her. Of course his real home now was the Khembali embassy's garden shed. He was not really homeless. Maybe it was bad not to have rented a place somewhere.

Then Diane convened a week's worth of meetings with all the agencies and departments she wanted to deal with, and during that week he saw that being inside the White House compound was going to be good, and that he needed to be there for Diane. She needed the help; there were scores of agencies that had to be gathered into the effort they had in mind, and even after the long winter, not all of their managers were convinced they needed to change. "They're being actively passive-aggressive," Diane said with a wry grin.

"Such trivial crap they're freaking about," Frank complained. He was amazed it didn't bother her more. "EPA trying to keep USGS from interpreting pesticide levels they're finding, because interpretation is EPA's job? Energy and Navy fighting over who gets to do nuclear?"

She waved it away. "Turf battles matter in Washington. We're going to have to get things done using these people, and we'll have to be scrupulous in keeping their boundaries. There's no time to change the bureaucracy, we've got bigger fish to fry. So I plan to keep these folks happy."

It made sense when she put it that way, and after that he understood better her manner with the technocrats. She was always conciliatory, asking questions, even laying out her ideas as questions.

"Not that that's what I always do," Diane said, when Frank once made this observation to her. She looked ashamed.

"What do you mean?" Frank asked quickly.

"Well, I had a bad meeting with the deputy secretary of energy. He's a holdover, and he was negative about alternative energy. So I got him fired."

"You did?"

"I guess so. I sent a note over to the President describing the problem I was having, and the next thing I knew he was out."

"Do people know that's how it happened?"

"I think so."

"Well—good!"

She laughed ruefully. "I've had that thought myself. But it's strange."

"Get used to it. We probably need a whole bunch of people fired."

"Yes, but I never had the power to do it."

To change the subject to something more comfortable for her, Frank said, "I'm having some luck getting the military interested. They're the eight-hundred-pound gorilla, and if they were to come down on our side, as being critical to national defense, these other agencies would either get on board or die."

"Maybe," Diane said. "But what *they* are you talking about?"

"People I know, like General Wracke. Also some of the chief scientists. They're not in the decision-making loop, but they're easier to convince about the science. I show them their own Marshall Report, which rates climate change as more of a threat than terrorism. It seems to help."

"Can you make a copy of that for distribution?"

"Yes. It would also make sense to reach out to all the scientists in government, and ask them to get behind the National Academy statement on the climate for starters, then help us to work on the agencies they're involved with."

"Sure. But there's upper management who will be against us no matter what, because that's why they were appointed in the first place."

"There's where your firing one of them may have an effect." Frank grinned and Diane made a face.

"So maybe it's time to talk to Energy," she said. "If they're scared they'll lose funding, that's the moment to strike."

"Which means we should be talking to OMB too?"

"Yes. We definitely need OMB on our side. That should be possible, if Chase has appointed the right people there."

"And then the appropriations committees."

"The best chance there is to talk to their staffs, and win some seats in the midterms. For these first two years, it'll be uphill when it comes to Congress."

"At least he's got the Senate."

"Yes, but really you need both."

Frank saw it anew: hundreds of parts to the federal government, each part holding a piece of the jigsaw puzzle, jockeying to determine what kind of picture they all made. War of the agencies, the Hobbesian struggle of all against all. It needed to be changed to some kind of dance.

In his truncated time off it was hard to get hours in with Nick, and Nick was often busy with other people in FOG, including a youth group, as well as with all his other activities at school and home. They still held to a meeting at the zoo every third Saturday morning, more or less, starting with an hour at the tiger enclosure, taking notes and photos, then doing a cold-certification course, or walking up to the beaver pond to see what they might see. But that time quickly passed, and then Nick was off. Frank missed their longer days out together, because Nick was a funny kid.

He missed his time with Anna too. Nietzsche had declared friendship between men and women impossible, but Nietzsche had written very many stupid things, had terrible relationships with women, and then gone insane. Surely on the savannah there would have been all sorts of friendships between the sexes. Indeed on the savannah things might have been a little more flexible at the margins. Certainly he missed his time with her. At work in particular, he missed her very much. Focusing on his list of Things to Do, about twice a day he would have gone to ask her a question about something. But not anymore.

The swap-out to clean power was clearly still the crux, for him and for everyone, and it was going to be very expensive. But not as expensive as not changing, as Diane kept saying to the re-insurance companies. Say it cost a trillion dollars to install clean energy generators and change out the transport fleet. Weigh that against the financial benefit to civilization of "biosphere services," now valued at $175 trillion a year. Didn't that pencil out? It seemed like it would have to. If it didn't, then maybe there was something wrong with their accounting system. Electricity now cost about six cents a kilowatt-hour, and they spoke of clean energy costing up to ten—then said it couldn't be done? For financial reasons? "It wouldn't take much of an added carbon price to make clean energy pencil out immediately," Frank said to Diane over the phone. "Companies like Southern California Edison must be begging for that, they'll make a killing when that happens, they're so far ahead."

"True."

"I wonder what would happen if the re-insurance companies refused to insure oil companies?"

"Good idea." She sighed. "If only we could sic the re-insurance companies on the World Bank and the IMF."

"Maybe we can. Phil Chase is president now."

"So maybe we can! Hey, it's two already—have you had lunch?"

In his office, Frank smiled. "No, you wanna?"

"Yes. Give me five minutes."

"Meet you at the elevator."

So they had lunch, and among other things talked over their move to the White House. Diane said, "My guess is Chase is still trying to work out what's possible. He's talked quite a line, but now push has come to shove, and it's a big machine he's got to put in gear. I got a whole string of questions from him about the technical agencies, and just today I got an e-mail asking me to submit a thorough analysis of all the particulars of the New Deal—what he called the scientific aspects of the New Deal. I have no idea what he means."

Nevertheless, she had looked into it. There had been five New Deals, she said. Each had been a distinct project, with different goals and results. She listed them with a pen on the back of a napkin:

1. Hundred Days, 1933
2. Social Security, 1935
3. Keynesian stimulation, 1938 (this, she explained, had been enacted partly to restart things, partly to restore what the Supreme Court had blocked)
4. the defense buildup of 1940–41, and
5. the GI Bill of Rights of 1944.

"Number five was entirely FDR's idea, by the way. Nothing has ever done more for ordinary Americans, the analysis said. It made the postwar middle class, and the baby boom."

"Encouraging," Frank said, studying the list.

"Very. Granted, this all took twelve years, but still. It doesn't even count the international stuff, like prepping for the war, or winning it. Or the UN!"

"Impressive," Frank said. "Let's hope Chase can do as well."

Here Diane looked doubtful. "One thing seems pretty clear already," she confessed. "He's too busy with other stuff for me to be able to talk to him much in person. I mean, I've barely met him yet."

"*That's* not good." Frank was surprised to hear this.

"Well, he's pretty good at replying to his texts. And his people get back to me when I send along questions or requests."

"Maybe I should ask Charlie for help on this."

"That would be good."

It seemed to Frank, watching her, that she had forgotten his abrupt cancellation of their post–North Atlantic date. Or—since no one ever really forgot things like that—to have let it go. Forgiven, if not forgotten—all he could expect, of course. Maybe it had only been a little weird. In any case a relief, after his experiences with Marta, who neither forgot nor forgave.

Which reminded him that he had to talk to Marta sometime soon about Small Delivery Systems' Russian experiment. Damn.

As always, the thought of having to communicate with his ex-partner filled Frank with a combination of dread and perverse anticipation, which came in part from trying to guess how it would go wrong this time. For it would go wrong. He and Marta had always had a stormy relationship, and Frank had come to suspect that all Marta's intimate relationships were stormy. Certainly her relations with her ex-husband had been inflamed, one of the reasons she and Frank too had come to a nasty end. Marta had needed to keep her name off the paperwork on the house she and Frank had bought together, to keep it clear of the bankruptcy morass created by Marta's always soon-to-be ex. This had created the possibility for Frank alone to sign a third mortgage, taking their equity and losing it in a surefire biotech that had bombed.

A very bad idea, one of a string of bad decisions Frank had made in those years, many clustered around Marta. So it was perverse, a kind of nostalgia for bad times, that made Frank somewhat look forward to talking to her. In any case he had to call her, because she was his contact with the Russian lichen project, and he needed to know how that was going. Given the ongoing opacity of Russian government and science, a reliable or semi-reliable informant was crucial. So the call had to be made. Or rather, the visit. Because he wanted to see the new facility too. NSF had rented the building once occupied by Torrey Pines Generique, and offered contracts to an array of people, including Yann and Marta. The new head of the institute had called a conference to discuss proposals for new action, and Yann and Marta were on the program. Frank called the travel office to have them book a flight for him.

For the Quiblers, the winter's blackouts developed routines, with the inconveniences balanced by seldom-indulged pleasures: fire in the fireplace, candles, blankets, blocks, books. Anna had taken up knitting again, so when the power went out, she helped get things settled and then got under a comforter and clicked away. Charlie read aloud to them. He and Anna discussed whether they should buy satellite phones, so they could stay in contact if caught out when the next one hit. The blackouts were getting more frequent; it was widely debated whether they were caused by overdemand, mechanical failure, sabotage, computer viruses, corporate rigging, or the cold, but no one could deny they were becoming regular occurrences.

On this particular dark evening, after Anna had gone to the appropriate drawer and cabinets and got out their blackout gear, there came a knock at their door, very unusual. So much so that Nick said, "Frank must be here!"

And so he was.

He stamped in looking freeze-dried, put the back of his hand to their cheeks and had them shrieking. "Is it okay?" he asked Charlie uncertainly.

"Oh sure, sure, what do you mean?"

"I don't know."

It seemed to Charlie almost as if Frank's thinking had been chilled on the hike over; his words were slow, his manner distracted. He had been out snowshoeing in Rock Creek Park, he said, checking on his homeless friends, and had decided afterward to drop by.

"Good for you. Have some tea with us."

"Thanks."

Nick and Joe were delighted. Frank brought a new element to the power-free evening with his hint of mystery and strangeness. "Tiger man!" Joe exclaimed. Nick talked with him about animals, while Joe plucked the appropriate plastic animals out of his big box as they spoke, lining them up in a parade on the floor for their inspection. "Tiger tiger tiger!" he said, pleasing Charlie; lately he had been showing a preference for zebras and hippos.

Frank and Nick agreed there were very few ferals still free, all Arctic or mountain species. The other exotics had come in from the cold, or died.

Here Charlie noticed Nick smoothly change the subject before the gibbons might come to anyone's mind: "What about your friends?"

The human ferals, Frank said, were still pretty easy to find. "My own group is kind of scattered. But I think there'll be more and more people like them as time goes on. Housing is just too expensive."

Later, when the boys were asleep, Frank hunkered down by the fire, holding his hands to it and staring into the flames.

"Charlie," he said hesitantly, "has anyone on Chase's staff been looking into the election, the talk of irregularities?"

"No one I know of."

"I'm surprised."

"Well, it's kind of a Satchel Paige moment."

"What does that mean?" Anna said.

"Don't look back—something might be gaining on you."

Frank nodded. "But what if something *is* gaining on you?"

"I think that was Satchel's point. But what do you mean?"

"What if there was a group that tried to steal the election, but failed?"

Charlie was surprised. "Then good."

"But what if they're still out there?"

"I'm sure they are. It's a spooky world."

Frank glanced quickly at Charlie, then nodded, the corners of his mouth tight. "A spooky world indeed."

"You mean spooks," Anna clarified.

Frank nodded, eyes still on the fire. "There's seventeen intelligence agencies in the federal government now. And some of them are not fully under anyone's control."

"How do you mean?"

"You know. Black agencies, so black they've disappeared."

"Disappeared?" Charlie said.

"No oversight. No connections. I don't think even the President knows about them. I don't think anyone knows about them, except the people in them."

"But how would they get funding?"

Anna laughed at that, but Frank frowned. "I suppose from a slush fund. Surely there's money sloshing around? Especially in intelligence?"

Charlie nodded. "A hundred billion a year. And black program money is black too. I've heard of that."

"Well . . ." Frank paused. "They are a danger to the republic."

"Whoah." Charlie had never heard Frank say anything like that.

Frank shrugged. "Sorry, but it's true. If we mean to be a constitutional government, then we're going to have to root out some of these groups. Because they are a danger to democracy and open government as we're used to thinking of it. They're trying to move all the important stuff into the shadows."

"And so . . ."

"So I'm wondering if you could direct Chase's attention to them. Make him aware of them, and urge him to root them out."

"Do you think he could?"

"I should hope so!" Frank looked disturbed at the question. "I mean, if he followed the money, made his secretaries and agency heads account for all of it—maybe sicced the OMB on all the black money to find out who was using it, and for what . . . couldn't you?"

"I'm not sure," Charlie admitted. "Maybe."

"The Pentagon can't account for its outlays," Anna pointed out grimly, knitting like one of the women under the guillotine, *click click click*! "They have a percentage gone missing every year that is bigger than NSF's entire budget."

"Gone missing?"

"Unaccounted for. Unaccountable. I call that gone missing." Anna's disapproval was like dry ice, smoking with cold.

"But if it were done by a competent team," Frank persisted, "without any turned people on it, and presidential backing to look into everything?"

Charlie still was dubious, but said, "In theory that would work."

"But?"

"Well, the government, you know. It's big. It has lots of nooks and crannies. Like what you're talking about—black programs that have been firewalled so many times, there are blacks within blacks, superblacks, superblack-blacks. With black accounts and dedicated political contributions, so that the money is socked away in Switzerland, or Wal-Mart . . ."

"Jesus. There are government programs with that kind of funding?"

Charlie shrugged. "Maybe."

Frank was staring at him, startled, perhaps even frightened. "In that case we could be in big trouble."

Anna was shaking her head. "A complete audit would find even that. It would include all accounts of every federal employee or unit, and also what they're doing with every hour of their work time. It's a simple spreadsheet."

"But it could be faked so easily," Charlie objected.

"Well, you have to have some way to check the data."

"But there are hundreds of thousands of employees."

"I guess you'd have to use a statistically valid sampling method."

"But that's the kind of method that programs can hide in!"

"Hmm." Now Anna was frowning too. She was also sending curious glances Frank's way. This was a pretty un-Franklike inquiry, in both content and style. "Maybe you'd have to be completely comprehensive with the intelligence and security agencies. Account for everything."

Charlie said, "So, that being the case, they probably aren't there. They're probably in Commerce or the Treasury. Which all by itself is huge."

Frank said, "So maybe it isn't possible."

Charlie and Anna did not reply; each was thinking it over.

Frank sighed. "Maybe if we found a specific problem, and told whoever could best stop it? Wouldn't that *be* the President?"

Charlie said, "I should think the President would always be strongest at that kind of thing. But there are a lot of demands on his time."

"Everyone keeps saying that. But this could be important. Even crucial."

"Then I hope it would get attended to. Maybe there's a unit designed to do it. In the Secret Service or something."

Frank nodded. "Maybe you could talk to him, then. When you think it's a good time. Because I know where to start the hunt."

Charlie and Anna glanced at each other, saw that neither knew what he was talking about.

"What do you mean?" Charlie said.

"I've run across some stuff," Frank said, adjusting a log in the fire.

Then the power flickered and hummed back on, and after a while Frank made his excuses and took off, still looking distant and thoughtful.

"What was that all about?" Charlie said.

"I don't know," Anna replied. "But I'm wondering if he found that woman in the elevator."

Anna had been pleased when Diane asked her to join the presidential science advisor's staff, but it didn't take long for her to decide against accepting.

She knew she was right to do so, but explaining why to Diane and Frank had been a little tricky. She couldn't just come out and say, "I prefer doing things to advising people to do things," or, "I like science more than politics." It wouldn't have been polite, and besides, she wasn't sure that was the real reason anyway. So all she could do was claim an abiding interest in her work at NSF, which was true. It was always best when your lies were true.

"But you're the one who's been finding all these good programs," Frank said. "You'd be perfect to help this project. You could maybe come on loan."

This confirmed Anna's suspicion that it was Frank's idea to invite her over to the White House. Very nice of him, she liked that very much—but she said, "I can keep doing that from here, and still run my division too."

Frank frowned, almost said something, stopped. Anna could not guess what it might have been. Some personal appeal? He looked a bit flushed. But maybe he was abashed at the thought of how little time he now had to give to his work on algorithms, his actual field. With this move he had shifted entirely to policy—to administration. To politics, in a word.

Of course maybe their circumstances called for a shift from science to policy, as an emergency measure. Also an application of science *to* policy, which she knew was what Frank had intended. Anna knew it was very common among scientists to be science snobs, and hold that no work in the world was as worthy as scientific research. Anna did not want to fall prey to that error, even though she felt it pretty strongly herself, or at least felt that she was better at science than at any of the mushier stuff. Correcting for that bias adequately was one part of her confused feelings about all this. She made lists of the arguments pro and con, attempting to quantify and thus clarify her feelings. The balance was close.

In the end she held to her refusal, and to her job at NSF. And as she sat in the Metro on the way home, she thought somewhat grimly that it was too bad that Charlie hadn't stuck to his guns too, and refused his new job offer like she had. Because here she was going home early again, to pick up Nick from school and take him to his piano lessons.

Of course Charlie's situation had been different, a case of "come back or lose your job." Still—if he had held—how much easier life would have been for her. Not that she ever shirked any work at all, but it would have been easier for the boys too. Not so much Nick, but Joe. She was intensely worried about Joe going into the White House daycare center. Was he ready for that? Would it make him even stranger—stranger and more difficult—than he already was? Or would it normalize him? Was he perhaps autistic? Or just fractious? And why was he fractious? And what would be the effect on him (and on the other children) of confining him in a single room or group or situation for an entire day? Even Charlie, with all his energy and flexibility, had not been able to keep up with Joe's demand for the new. She was afraid that in a daycare Joe and everyone around him would go mad.

Not that she put it exactly that way to herself. In her conscious mind she focused on incremental changes, specific worries, without moving on to larger vaguer concepts. This was one of many differences between her and Charlie, many of which were revealed when they both worked at home. This was a bad system for other reasons, because it meant Joe was around too, scheming for attention while she attempted to work; but sometimes it just had to be done, as when the Metro was down. And there she would be, at the computer, staring at a spreadsheet, entering data on pesticides in stream water as part of a project to measure their effects on amphibians, endless lists of chemical and product names collated from a wide range of studies, so that quantities had to be reformatted and analyzed, meaning a whole flurry of highly specific technical e-mails from colleagues to be dealt with, math or chemistry or statistical methodology, working in the parts-per-billion range—

And at the same time Charlie would be audible from the floor below, trying to amuse Joe while holding a simultaneous headphone conversation with his friend Roy, shouting out things like, "Roy these are not IDIOTS you're dealing with here, you can't just LIE to them! WHAT? Okay well maybe you can lie to THEM, but make it a smart lie. Put it at the level of myth, these are like Punch and Judy figures, and your people want to be doing the punching! Sledgehammer them in the forehead with this stuff! JOE! STOP THAT!"

Sledgehammer them in the forehead? Anna couldn't bear to listen.

But now this was Charlie's work, full-time and more—meaning, as in the old days, evenings too. Of course Anna spent a lot of evenings working, but for Charlie it was something he had not done since Joe had arrived. Endless phone conversations, how much help could these be? Of course there was the new administration's First Sixty Days to execute, accounting for much of this rush, but Anna doubted that much would come of that. How could it? The system was slower than that. You could only do things at the speed they could be done.

So, whereas before she had most often come home to find the house in an uproar, Charlie cooking operatically while Joe banged pots and Nick read under the lamp at his corner of the couch, with the dinner soon to be on the table, now she often got home to find Nick sitting there like an owl, reading in the dark, and no one else home at all—and her heart would go out to him, all alone at 7 P.M., age twelve—

"You'll go blind," she would say.

"Mom," he would object happily.

—and she would kiss his head and turn on his light and barge around turning on other lights before going out to the kitchen to rustle something up before she starved—and sometimes there would be nothing in the fridge or the cupboards that she could cook or eat, and grumpily she would throw on her daypack and tell Nick to answer the phone, if she did not need him along to carry extra bags, and would walk down the street to the Giant grocery store, still grumpy at first but then enjoying the walk—

And then at the grocery story there would be no meat on the shelves, and few fresh veggies, fewer fruits. She would have to forget about her list and troll the aisles for something palatable, amazed once again at the sight of so many empty shelves—she had thought like everyone else that it would be a temporary thing—then getting angry at people for their selfish hoarding instincts. It had spread far beyond toilet paper and bottled water, to almost every shelf in the store, but particularly to all the foods she most liked to eat.

All this stuff distracted her as she worked, but it also caused her to think about the situation. She had chosen to stay at NSF because she felt that she could do more there, and that NSF still had a crucial part to play. It was a small agency but it was central, at the heart of all their solutions. So she continued to do her work, and when she could she kept working on the FCCSET program, which Diane was going to try to get Chase to reinstate. Coordinating all the federal agencies into an overarching project architecture had huge potential.

In searching for other programs like that, she talked to Alyssa to Diane and Edgardo, to Drepung and Sucandra. Sucandra she found particularly interesting. He was the one who had been her Cognizant Program Manager, so to speak, at the Khembalung Institute for Higher Learning; and he had been the single most disconcerting person she had ever talked to about the underlying purposes of science, being a doctor himself, but of Tibetan medicine; also a kind of Buddhist teacher to her, as well as her Tibetan tutor, which she liked the best, as being most straightforward of their interactions. In that context she mentioned to him once her attempt to balance her scientific work with something larger, something at the policy level.

Sucandra said to her: "Look to China."

CHAPTER 24

THE
TECHNOLOGICAL SUBLIME

A formalized "shortage economics" Anna had run across had been pioneered by one János Kornai, a Hungarian economist who had lived in the Soviet-controlled era. Anna found certain insights of his useful, particularly those having to do with hoarding.

One day when she was visiting with Frank and Edgardo after a meeting in the Old Executive Offices, she showed Kornai's book to them. Edgardo happily pored over the relevant pages, chuckling at the graphs and charts. "Wait, I want to scan this page." He was still the happiest purveyor of bad news, and indeed had recently confessed that he was the one who had started the Department of Unfortunate Statistics, no surprise to his two friends.

"See?" Anna said, pointing to the top of one diagram. "It's a decision tree, designed to map what a consumer does when faced with shortages."

"A shopping algorithm," Frank said with a short laugh.

"Have we made these choices?" Edgardo asked.

"You tell me. Shortages start because of excess demand, a disequilibrium which leads to a seller's market, creating what Kornai calls suction."

"As in, this situation sucks," Edgardo said.

"Maybe. So the shelves empty, because people buy when they can. Then queuing starts, either as a physical line or a waiting list."

"I like this term 'investment tension,'" Edgardo said, reading ahead on the page. "When there aren't enough machines to make what people want. But that's surely not what we have now."

"Are you sure?" Frank said. *"What if there's a shortage of energy?"*

"It should be the same," Anna said. *"So, in a 'shortage economy' you get shortages that are general, frequent, intensive, or chronic. The twentieth-century socialisms had all these. Although Kornai points out that in capitalism you have chronic shortages in health care and housing. And now we have intensive shortages too, during the blackouts. No matter what the product or service is, you get consumers who have a 'notional demand,' which is what they would buy if they could, and then 'completely adjusted demand,' which is what they really intend to buy knowing all the constraints. Between those you have 'partially adjusted demand,' where the consumer is ignorant of what's possible, or in denial, and still not completely adjusted. So the move from notional demand to completely adjusted demand is marked by failure, frustration, dire rumors, forced choices, and so on down his list. Finally the adjustment is complete, and the buyer has abandoned certain intentions, and might even forget them. Kornai compares that moment to workers in capitalism who stop looking for work, and so aren't counted as unemployed."*

Frank read aloud, *"'A curious state of equilibrium can arise,'"* and laughed. *"So you just give up on your desires! It's almost Buddhist."*

"I don't know." Anna frowned. *"'Forced adjustment equilibrium'? That doesn't sound to me like what the Khembalis are talking about."*

"Although they are making a forced adjustment," Frank mused. *"And would probably agree we are forced to adjust to reality, if we want equilibrium."*

"Listen to this," Edgardo said, and read: *"'The less certain the prospect of obtaining goods, the more intensively buyers have to hoard.' Oh dear, oh my; here we are in a partially adjusted demand, but we don't have monetary overhang, or even a black market, to take care of some of our excess demand."*

"So, not much adjustment at all," Frank noted.

"I've seen examples of all these behaviors already at the grocery store," Anna said. *"The frustrating thing is that we have adequate production but still have excessive demand, because people don't trust that there will be enough."*

"Maybe thinking globally, they are right," Edgardo pointed out.

"But see here," Anna went on, *"how he says that socialism is a seller's mar-*

ket, while capitalism is a buyer's market? What I've been wondering is, why shouldn't capitalism want to be a seller's market too? I mean, it seems like sellers would want it, and since sellers control most of the capital, wouldn't capital want a seller's market if they could get it? So that, if there were some real shortages, real at first, or temporarily real, wouldn't they seize on those, and try to keep the sense that shortages are out there, maybe create a few more, so that the whole system tipped from a buyer's to a seller's market, even when production was actually adequate if people trusted it? Wouldn't profits go up?"

"Prices would go up," Edgardo said. "That's inflation. Then again, inflation always hurts the big guys less than the little guys, because they have enough to do better at differential accumulation. And it's differential accumulation that counts. As long as you're doing better than the system at large, you're fine."

"Still," Frank said. "The occasional false shortage, Anna is saying. Or just stimulating a fear. Pretending we're at war, all that. To keep us anxious."

"To keep us hoarding!" Anna insisted.

Edgardo laughed. "Sure! Like health care and housing!"

Frank said, "So we've got all the toys and none of the necessities."

"It's backwards, isn't it," Anna said.

"It's insane," Frank said.

Edgardo was grinning. "I told you, we're stupid! We're going to have a tough time getting out of this mess, we are so stupid!"

Again Frank flew out to San Diego. Descending the escalator from the airport's glassed-in pedestrian walkway, he marveled that everything was the same. The only sign of winter was a certain brazen quality to the light, so that the sea was a slate color, and the cliffs of Point Loma a glowing apricot. His heart's home, a gorgeous Mediterranean Pacific.

He had not bothered to make hotel reservations. Rent a van and that was that—no way was Mr. Optimodal, Son of Alpine Man, going to pay hundreds of dollars a night for the dubious pleasure of being trapped indoors at sunset! The light at dusk over the Pacific was too superb to miss. And the Mediterranean climate meant every night was good for sleeping out, the salt-and-eucalyptus air the atmosphere of his home planet.

During the day he dropped by his storage locker in Encinitas and got some gear, and that night he parked the van on La Jolla Farms Road and walked out onto the bluff between Scripps and Blacks canyons. This plateau, owned by UCSD, had been left empty, a rare thing. In fact it might be the only one left. And its sea cliff was the tallest in all of Southern California, towering 350 feet directly over the water. A freak of both nature and history, in short, and one of Frank's favorite places.

As he walked out to the edge of the cliff, it occurred to him that on the night he had lost his apartment and gone into Rock Creek Park, he had been expecting something like this: instant urban wilderness, empty and overlooking the world. To bang into the bros in the claustrophobic forest had been a shock.

At the cliff's edge were small scallops in the sandstone like little hidden rooms. He had slept in them when a student, camping out for the fun of it. The scallop farthest south had been his regular spot. Twenty-five years since the last time he had spent the night there. He wondered what that kid would think to see him here now.

He slept fitfully, and in the gray wet dawn hiked up to his rented van and dropped off his sleeping bag and groundpad, then continued on to campus and the huge new gym called RIMAC. His faculty card got him in, and he showered and shaved, then walked to Revelle College for a catch-up session at the department. A good effort now would save him all kinds of punitive work when he finally made it back.

After that he bought an outdoor breakfast at the espresso stand overlooking the women's softball diamond, and watched the team warm up as he ate. Oh my. How he loved American jock women. These threw the ball like people who fully understood the simple joy of throwing something at something. The softballs were like intrusions from some more Euclidean universe, rocks as Ideas of Order. When the gals threw them the pure white spheres did not illustrate gravity or the wind, as frisbees did, but rather a point drawing a line. Whack! Whack! God that shortstop had an arm. Frank supposed it was perverted of him to be sitting there regarding women's softball as some kind of erotic dance, but oh well, he couldn't help it; it was a very sexy thing.

After that he walked down La Jolla Shores Road to the Visualization Center at Scripps. This was a room located at the top of a wooden tower six stories tall. Two or three of the bottom floors were occupied by a single computer, a superpowerful behemoth like something out of a 1950s movie. The top room was the visualizing room, holding a 3-D wraparound theater. Two young women in shorts, graduate students of the professor who had invited Frank to drop by, greeted him and tapped up their show, placing Frank in the central viewing spot and giving him 3-D glasses. When the room went dark the screen disappeared and Frank found himself standing on the rumpled black floor of the Atlantic. He was just south of the sill that ran like a range of hills between Iceland and Scotland, they told him, looking north into the flow at the two-thousand-meter depth. Small temperature differences were portrayed in transparent false colors, so that he stood in flowing banners of red, orange, yellow, green, blue, and indigo. The main flow was about chest high on Frank. Like standing in a lava lamp, one of the techs suggested, although Frank had been thinking he was flying in a rainbow that had gone through a shredder. The pace of the flow was speeded up, the techs told him, but it was still a stately waving of flat bands of red and orange, ribboning south through the blues and blue-greens, then rolling smoothly over a blue and purple layer and down, as if passing over a weir.

"That was five years ago," one of the grad students said. "Watch now, this is last year this time—"

The flow got thinner, slower, thinner. A yellow sheet, roiling under a green blanket in a midnight blue room. Then the yellow thinned to nothing. Green and blue pulsed gently back and forth, like kelp swinging in a swell.

"Wow," Frank said. "The stall."

"That's right," the woman at the computer said. "But now watch."

The image lightened; tendrils of yellow appeared, then orange; then ribbons of red appeared and coalesced in a broad band. "It's about ninety percent what they first measured."

"Wow," Frank said. "Everyone should see this. I mean, it's so spacey."

"Well, we can make DVDs, but it's never the same as, you know, what you have here. Standing right in the middle of it."

"No. Definitely not." For a time he stood and luxuriated in the wash of colors running past and through him. It was like a slo-mo screening of the hyperspace travel at the end of *2001: A Space Odyssey*. The underside of the Gulf Stream was flowing through his head.

Then it was less than a mile's walk back up the road (though he was the only person walking it), and he was north of the university, at the old Torrey Pines Generique facility, now the NSF Regional Research Center in Climate and Earth Sciences, RRCCES, which of course they were pronouncing "recess."

The reception room was much the same. The labs themselves were still under construction. His first meeting was with Yann Pierzinski. Frank had always liked Yann, and that was easier than ever now that he knew Yann and Marta were just friends and not a couple. His earlier notion that they were a couple had not really made sense to him, not that any couple made sense, but his new understanding of Yann, as Marta's housemate and some kind of gay genius, like Leonardo or Turing, did make sense, maybe only because Yann was odd. Creative people *were* different—unless of course they weren't. But Yann was.

Now they discussed the new institute, an intriguing array of scientists being asked to collaborate, ranging from the most theoretical of theorists to the most empirical of experimentalists. As one of the only first-rank mathematicians working on gene expression, and one with actual field experience in designing and releasing an engineered organism into the wild, Yann was going to be a central figure, leading the application of modern biotech to climate mitigation.

Yann's specialty was Frank's too, and as Frank had been on Yann's doctoral committee, and had employed him for a while, he knew what Yann was up to. But in the past two years Yann had been hard at work, and was now far off into new developments, to the point where he was certainly one the field's current leaders, and as such, getting a little hard to understand. It took some explaining to bring Frank up to speed, and speed was the operative word; Yann had a tendency to revert to a childhood speech defect called speed-talking, which emerged whenever he got excited or lost his sense of himself. So it was a very rapid and tumbling tutorial that Yann now gave him, and Frank struggled just to follow him.

It was fun, indeed a huge pleasure, to follow him at all. And interesting too, in what might follow from his work in real-world applications. They might be able to call a particular protein out of the vasty deep of a particular gene, Frank suggested; and it would come when they called.

"Yes," Yann agreed, "I guess maybe. I hadn't thought about it that way." This kind of obliviousness had always been characteristic of him. "But maybe. You'd have to try some trials. Take the palindromic codons and repeat them, see if they make the same choice if that's the only codon you have."

Frank made a note of it. It sounded like some good lab work would be needed. "You've got Leo Mulhouse back here, right?"

Yann brightened. "Yeah, we do."

"Why don't we go ask him what he thinks?"

. . .

So they went to see Leo, which was also a kind of flashback for Frank, in that it was like the last time he had seen him. Same people, same building— had all that stuff out in D.C. really happened? Or was it here he was dreaming, of a world in which promising human health projects were properly funded?

But after a while he saw it wasn't the same Leo. As with the lab, Leo looked the same but had changed inside. He was less optimistic, more guarded. Almost certainly he had gone through a very stressed job hunt, in a tight market. That could change you all right.

Now Leo looked at Yann's protein diagrams, and nodded uncertainly. "So, you're saying repeat the codons and see if that forces the expression?"

Frank intervened. "Also, maybe focus on this group here, because if it works like Yann thinks, then you should get palindromes of that too. . . ."

"Yeah, that would be a nice result." The prospect of such a clear experiment brought back an echo of Leo's old enthusiasm. "That would be clean," he said. "If that would work . . . I mean, there would still be the insertion problem, but, you know, NIH is really interested in solving that. . . ."

Getting any engineered genes into living humans had proven to be the stopper for gene therapy. Literally hundreds of potential therapies, or even outright cures, remained only ideas because of this stumbling block. It vexed the entire field; it was the reason venture capital had mostly gone away, in search of quicker and more certain returns. If insertion wasn't solved, it could mean that gene therapy would never be achieved at all.

To Frank's surprise, it was Yann who now said, "There's some cool new stuff about insertion at Johns Hopkins. They've been working on metallic nanorods. The rods are a couple hundred nanometers long, half nickel and half gold. You attach your altered DNA to the nickel side, and some transferrin protein to the gold, and when they touch cell walls they bind to receptors, and cross into vesicles, and those migrate inside the cell. Then the DNA detaches and goes into the nucleus, and there it is. Your altered gene is delivered."

"Really?" Leo said. He and his Torrey Pines Generique lab had looked at a lot of options on this front, and none had worked. "What about the metals?"

"They just stay in the cell. They're too small to matter. And the nickel is magnetic, so they're using magnets to direct the nanorods where they want."

"Wow. That would be cool."

Leo was very interested; he seemed to be suggesting in his manner that insertion was the last problem facing them. If that were true, Frank thought . . . for a while he was lost in the possibilities.

Leo sometimes stopped and looked around at all the new machinery as if he were in the dream of a boy on Christmas—everything he ever wanted, enough to make him suspicious and afraid he might wake up. Cautious enthusiasm, if there could be such a thing. Frank felt a pang of envy: the tangible work that a scientist could do in a lab was a very different thing from the amorphous work that was consuming him in D.C. Was he even doing science at all, compared to these guys? Had he not somehow fallen off the wagon? And once you fell off, the wagon rolled on; frequently in this discussion he could barely follow what they were saying!

Then Marta walked in the room and he couldn't have followed them even if they had been reciting their ABCs. That was the effect she had on him.

And she knew it, and did all she could to press home the effect. "Oh hi, Frank," she said with a microsecond pause discernable only to him, after which she merrily joined the other two, pushing the outside of the discussion envelope, where Frank was certain to be most uncomprehending.

Irritating, yes. But then again this was stuff he wanted to know. So he worked on focusing on what Yann was saying. It was Yann who would be leading the way, and emphasizing this truth with his attentiveness was the best way Frank had of getting back at Marta, anyway.

So they jostled each other like kids sticking elbows into ribs, as Yann invented the proteomic calculus right before their eyes, and Leo described some of the experiments they might run to refine their manipulations. A very complicated and heady hour. RRCCES was off to a good start, Frank concluded at the end of it, despite his sore ribs. Combine this place with UCSD and the rest of the San Diego biotech complex, not to mention the rest of the world, and the result could be extraordinary, a newly powerful biotech which they would then have to aim somehow.

Which was where the work at the White House would come in. There had to be some place where people actually discussed what to do with the advances science continually made. Somewhere there had to be a way to prioritize that didn't have to do with immediate profit for investors. If it took ten years of unprofitable research to lift them into really robust health care, leading to long healthy lives, shouldn't there be some place in their huge economy to fund that?

Yes.

Which was why he did not have to feel superfluous, or that he was wasting his time or fooling around. As Marta was implying with all her digs.

But then she said, offhandedly, as if trying to be rude, "We're going to go out to dinner to celebrate getting the lab back. Do you want to join us?"

Surprised, Frank said, "Yeah, sure."

Ah God—those two words committed him to an awkward evening, nowhere near as serene as eating tacos on the edge of Blacks Cliffs would have been. Decisions—why be so fast with them? Why be so wrong? Now he would be pricked and elbowed by Marta's every glance and word, all night long.

And yet nevertheless he was glad to be with them, slave as he was to *Homo sapiens'* tendency to sociability. And also, to tell the truth, he was feeling under some kind of new dispensation with Marta: not that she had forgiven him, because she never would, but that she had at least become less angry.

As him with her.

Mixed feelings, mixed drinks, mixed signals. They ate in Del Mar, at one of the restaurants near the train station, on the beach. The restaurant's patio and its main room were both flooded with sunset, the light both direct and reflective, bouncing off the ocean and ceilings and walls and mirrors until the room was as hyperilluminated as a stage set, everyone in it as vivid and distinct as a movie star; air filled with the clangor of voices and cutlery punctuating the low roar of surf; air thick with salt mist, the glorious tang of Frank's home ground. Perhaps only Frank came from a place that allowed him to see how gorgeous all this was.

Then again, now that he thought of it, Marta and Yann were just returning from a year in Atlanta, a year that could have been permanent. And they too looked a little heady with the scene.

And there was an extra charge in this restaurant, perhaps—some kind of poignant undercurrent to the celebrating, as if they were drinking champagne on a sinking liner. Because for this row of restaurants it was the end time. This beach was going to go under, along with every other beach in the world. And what would happen to the beach cultures of the world when the beaches were gone? They too would go. A way of life was going to vanish.

Places like this first. Even now, high tides had waves running into the patio wall, a waist-high thing with a stairway cut through it to get to the beach. Frank nursed his margarita and listened to the others talk, and felt Marta's elbow both metaphorically and sometimes literally in his ribs. He could feel her heat, and was aware of her kinetically, just as he had been years before when they had first started going out, meeting in situations just like this, drinks after work, and she the wild woman of the lab, expert at the bench or out in the waves, and passionate.

After dinner they went out for a walk on the beach. Del Mar's was almost the only beach in North County left with enough sand for a walk. Surfers, shrieking kids in bathing suits, sand castle engineers, runners, couples and groups on parade. Frank had played all these parts in his time. All there together in the horizontal light. His heart and mind were filled with the light.

They came to the mouth of the Del Mar River and turned back. Marta walked beside Frank. Leo and Yann were chattering before them. They fell behind a little bit farther.

"Happy to be back?" Frank ventured.

"Oh God yes. You have *no idea*," and all of a sudden she collared him and gave him a quick rough hug, intended to hurt. He knew her so well that he could interpret this irritated gratitude precisely. He knew also that she had

had a couple of margaritas and was feeling the effects. Although just to be back in San Diego was doubtless the biggest part of her mood, the boisterous high spirits he remembered so well. She had been a very physical person.

"I can guess," Frank said.

"Of course," she said, gesturing at the sea grumbling to their right. "So—what are you doing, Frank? Why are you still there and not back here?"

"Well . . ." How much to tell? His decision gears crunched to a halt with a palpable shudder. "I'm interested in the work. I moved over to the presidential science advisor's office."

"I heard about that. What will you do there?"

"Oh, you know. Be an advisor to the advisor."

"Diane Chang?"

"That's right."

"She seems to be doing some good stuff."

"Yes, I think so."

"Well, that's good. . . ." But still: "I bet you wish you could do that from here." Gesturing again at the sea. "Don't you have to get back to UCSD soon?"

"Eventually, sure. But the department is happy to have me out there."

"Sure, I can see that."

She considered it as they walked along behind the other two. "But—but what about the rest of it? What about *girls*, Frank, have you got a *girl-friend*?"

Oh God. Stumped. No idea what to reveal or how. And he had only a second before she would know something was up—

"Ah ha!" she cried, and crashed her shoulder into him, like she used to—just like Francesca Taolini had in Boston, so familiar and intimate, but in this case real, in that Marta really did know him. "You *do* have one! Come on, tell me!"

"Well yes, kind of."

"*Kind of*. Yes? And? Who is it?"

She had not the slightest idea that it might be Diane Chang, despite him having said he was following her to the White House. But of course—

people didn't think that way. And it was not something Frank had told anyone about, except maybe Rudra. It was not even really true.

But what then could he say? I have two sort-of girlfriends? My boss, whom I work for and who is older than I am and whom I have never kissed or said anything even slightly romantic to, but love very much, then also a spook who has disappeared, gone undercover, a jock gal who likes the outdoors (like you) and with whom I have had some cosmic outdoor sex (like we used to have), but who is now off-radar and incommunicado, I have no idea where? Whom I'm scared for and am desperate to see?

Oh, and along with that I'm also still freaked out by my instant attraction to an MIT star who thinks I am a professional cheater, and yes I still find you all too attractive, and remember all too well the passionate sex we used to have when we were together, and wish you weren't so angry at me, and indeed can see and feel right now that you're maybe finally giving up on that, and aren't as angry as you were in Atlanta. . . .

He too had had a couple of margaritas in the restaurant.

"Well? Come on, Frank! Tell me."

"Well, it isn't really anything quite like that."

"Like *what*! What do you *mean*?"

"I've been busy."

She laughed. "You mean you're too busy to call them back afterward? That's what *too busy* means to me."

"Hey."

She crowed her laugh, and Yann and Leo looked over their shoulders to see what was going on. "It's all right," Marta called, "Frank is just telling me how he neglects his girlfriend!"

"Am not," Frank explained to them. Yann and Leo saw this was not their conversation and turned back to their own.

"I bet you do though," she went on, chortling. "You did me."

"I did not."

"You did too."

"Did not."

"Did too."

Frank shrugged. Here they were again.

"You wouldn't even go dancing with me."

"But I don't know how to dance," he said. "And we still went anyway, all the time." Except when you wanted to go by yourself to meet new guys and maybe disappear with them for the night.

"Yeah right. So come on, who is it? And why are you so busy anyway? What do you do besides work?"

"I run, I climb, I play frisbee golf, I go for walks—"

"Go for *walks*?"

"—snowshoeing, tracking animals—"

"Tracking *animals*?" She had gotten to the snorting phase of her laughter.

"Yes. We follow the animals that escaped from the National Zoo, and do feral rescue and the like. It's interesting."

She snorted again. She was thinking like the Californian she was: there were no such things as *animals*.

"I go ice skating, I'm going to start kayaking again when the river thaws. I stay busy, believe me."

"When the river *thaws*. But come on, you're never too busy for *company*."

"I guess."

"So. Okay."

She saw that he wasn't going to say anything to her about it. She elbowed him again, and let it pass. She caught them up to the others.

The sun was almost down now, and the ocean had taken on the rich glassy sheen that it often did at that hour, the waves greenly translucent.

"Have you been out surfing yet?" he asked.

"Yeah, sure. What about you?"

"Not on this trip."

They came back to their restaurant, went through to the parking lot, stood in a knot to say good-byes.

"Yann and I are going to go dancing," Marta said to Frank. "Do you want to come along?"

"Too busy," Frank said promptly, and grinned as she cried out and punched him on the arm.

"Oh come on, you're out here visiting! You don't have any work at all."

"Okay," he said. Dancing, after all, was on his paleolithic list of Things to Do. "What is it, some kind of rave again? Do I have to blast my mind with ecstasy to get with the beat?"

"*Rave*. That isn't even a word anymore. It's a band at the Belly Up."

"A rave band," Yann confirmed.

Frank nodded. "Of course." That was Marta's thing.

"Come on," Marta said. "It only means you'll know how to do it. No swing or tango. Just bop and groove. You could use it, if you're so busy there."

"Okay," he said.

Leo had already driven off. He was outside Marta's sphere of influence.

So he followed Yann and Marta up the coast highway to Solana Beach, and turned inland to the Belly Up, a big old Quonset hut by the train tracks that had hosted concerts and dances for decades now.

This night's act appeared to be catering to the gay and lesbian crowd, or maybe that was just what the Belly Up audience always looked like these days. Although the band was a mostly butch all-girl acid reggae thing, with perhaps a score of people on the little stage, and a few hundred bopping on the dance floor. So he could join Yann and Marta both on the dance floor, and start dancing (that curious moment when the rules of movement changed, when one *began* to dance) and then it was *bop rave bop rave bop*, in the heavy beat and the flashing lights, easy to lose one's mind in, which was always good, that dionysiac release into shamanic transcendence, except when it involved losing his sense of all that had gone on between him and Marta (Yann was somewhere nearby) and also his sense of just how dangerous it would be to regard her only as a sexy woman dancing with him, seemingly oblivious to him but always right there and deep in the rhythm, and occasionally giving him a light bang with hip or shoulder. (In the old days these bumps would have come from pubic bone as well.) He had always loved the way she moved. But they had a history together, he struggled to remember. A really bad history. And he was already overcommitted and overentangled in this realm, it would be crazy and worse to have anything more to do with Marta in that way. He had gotten her back to San Diego as a way to make up for taking their money out of their house without telling her, and that was that—they were even! No more entanglements needed or wanted!

Although he did want her. Damn those softball players anyway.

"Here eat this," she shouted in his ear, and showed him a pill between her forefinger and thumb. Ecstasy, no doubt, as in the old days.

"No!"

"Yes!"

The paleolithics had gotten stupendously stoned, he recalled, in the midst of their dionysiac raves. Some of their petroglyphs made this perfectly clear, depicting people flying out of their own heads as birds and flames. He remembered the feeling of well-being this particular drug used to give him when he danced on it, and let her shove the pill in between his teeth. Nipped her fingers as she did. Leap before you look.

He danced with his back to her, and felt her butt bumping his as he looked at the other dancers. Quite a radical scene for good old San Diego, which Frank still thought of as a sun-and-sports monoculture, a vanilla Beach Boys throwback of a place, hopelessly out of it in cultural terms. Maybe one had to stay out in the water all the time for that to be true anymore. Although in fact the surf culture was also crazed. Certainly it was true that in the Belly Up of the beast, in the cacophonous sweaty strobed space of the rave, there were plenty of alternative lifestyles being enacted right before his very eyes. Most provocatively in fact. Some very serious kissing and other acts, dance as simulated standing sex—heck, actual standing sex, if you were at all loose with the definition. A very bad context in which to keep only pure thoughts about his bouncing surfer-scientist ex, who always had been a party gal, and who was now looking like someone who did not remember very well the bad parts of their past together.

Maybe there was such a thing as being too forgiven.

Random thoughts began to bounce to their own rave in his head. Oh dear he was feeling the buzz. Could one get away with just one night of sex without consequences? Go out to Blacks Cliffs, for instance, and then later

pretend it was just an aberration or had not happened at all? Marta had
certainly done that before. It was pretty much a modus vivendi for her. But
practical problems—she had rented a house with Yann again, Yann would
know: bad. He didn't have a hotel room to go to, and didn't want Marta to
know that—bad. So—no place to go, even though the cliffs would have
been so nice, a trysting place of spectacular memory. In fact he had gone
out there with two or three different women through his undergraduate
years, among them some of the nicest women he had ever met. It had been
so nice, it would be so nice, it was all jostling in his head, Caroline, Diane,
the dance, two young beauties groping each other in the crush of bouncing
bodies, oh my, it was having an effect on him—an unusually vivid effect.
Not since a well-remembered dance in a bar on the Colorado River during
spring break had he gotten an erection while on a dance floor dancing. It
was not the effect ecstasy usually had on him. He really must be feeling it,
Marta and her vibe, and her butt. And, yes, her pubic bone.

Maybe that was the cause of the erection. He turned to her again, and
naturally now when she bumped against him she hit him and felt it, and
grinned.

They had to shout in each other's ears to be able to hear each other
within the surround-sound of the crunchingly loud bass.

"I guess you liked the tab!"

"I don't remember ecstasy doing this!"

She laughed. "They mix in Viagra now!" she shouted in his ear.

"Oh shit!"

"Yann's friends make them, they're great!"

"What the fuck, Marta!"

"Yeah well?"

"No way! You're kidding me!"

Angry, even fearful, he stopped dancing and stared at her bopping in
front of him. "I don't like it! It's making me feel sick!"

"You'll get used to it!"

"No! No! I'm gonna go, I'll see you later!"

"Okay go then!"

She looked surprised, but not horribly displeased. Amused at him.

Maybe it really was just the new dance drug. Maybe it was revenge. Or an experiment. Or that there would still be a lot of potential partners there for her, for dancing or anything else, so it didn't matter what he did. Who knew San Diego could be so depraved? People were totally making out right in front of his eyes. There were so many doing it they had a kind of privacy in numbers.

"See you then!" Marta said in his ear, and gave him a swift sweaty hug and a kiss, already looking around for Yann or whomever. Happy, he thought—maybe even happy at becoming free from her anger at him—or happy at her last little tweak of revenge. Happy to see him go! Maybe all the prurient thoughts about the two of them together had been his only, and not hers. And the pill just the new dance pill.

He pondered this as he walked through the dark gravel parking lot to his rented van, cooled swiftly by his sweat and the salty night air, his erection like a rock in his pants. She didn't care!

The erection was not a comfortable feeling, not a natural feeling, not a sexual feeling. Normally Frank was as happy as the next guy to have an erection, meaning very happy, but this was ridiculous. He was drugged by drugs, it had no connection to his feelings—he might as well be at the doctor's, undergoing some horrible diagnostic! People were so stupid. Talk about technology replacing the natural pleasures, this really took the cake!

He cursed Marta viciously as he drove. Marine layer gusting in, lit by the city from underneath, then out over the sea darker, lit only by moonlight from above. Marta angry at him; would he miss that when it was gone? A particular feeling was a particular relationship. Then again, now he was angry at her. There was something pressing on his brain, even more than the usual; a headache was coming on, the likes of which he had never felt before. A migraine, perhaps, simultaneously with a drug-induced hard-on that hurt. It was like priapism—maybe it was priapism! The side effect warnings on the TV ads mentioned this, and it was said to be a serious danger. Terrible permanent damage could result. Shit—he was going to have to go find an ER somewhere and confess all. Tell the truth, that he hadn't known he was taking it, and get laughed at as a liar.

He cursed again, drove up the long hill of Torrey Pines, past their new facility and UCSD. Park on La Jolla Farms Road and walk out onto the bluff in the dark, his stuff in a daypack.

He had spent some sexy nights out here, he thought as he throbbed. Oh well. Now he just wanted to be free of it. Just embrace the cliff and make love to Mother Earth. But it hurt and his head pounded and he was afraid. It felt as if an orgasm would blow out every little sac, or shoot his spine right out of him while his head exploded. Horror movie images—damn Marta anyway. What a horrible drug thus to ruin one of the best feelings of all. Some guys must be so desperate. But of course. Create performance anxiety and then sell a cure for it. Everyone desperate for love, so now you could buy love, of course, but it hurt. Would he have to give up and go to the ER and explain—have to feel the needles stuck in there to drain him, or whatever they did?

Abruptly he got up and downclimbed over the lip of his little scallop, out onto the cliff. Now he was hanging there in space, and could slip and die at any moment. Not a good move really. Fear, real fear, stuck him like a stab in the ribs, and his blood rushed everywhere in him, hot and fast. Suddenly the sandstone was as if lit from within. His left foot was on a gritty hold, and slipping slightly. He grasped a shrub that had sent a branch over the lip, wondered if it would hold his weight. It was terrible climbing rock, gritty and weak, and suddenly he was angry as well as afraid. Sound of the surf cracking below—350 feet below. Hanging by a shrub on Blacks Cliff. He set his feet and pulled smoothly back up onto his scallop, a desperately graceful little move.

And the blood had indeed evacuated his poor penis. Detumescence, a new pleasure, never before experienced as such. Blessed relief. Even his head felt a little better. And he had worked his will over a powerful drug, and over Marta too. Hopefully he had survived undamaged. Little sacs, all overfull; he was going to be sore, he could tell. It felt like last winter's brush with penile frostbite.

Scared back to normality. Not a smart move. The margaritas might be implicated in that one. Leap before you look, sure—but not really.

He took a deep breath, feeling foolish in multiple ways. Well, no one else knew the full extent of his folly. And he was back in his cliff edge scallop.

He could sit on his sleeping bag, breathe deeply, shake his head shuddering, like someone casting off a nightmare.

So much for Marta. She could not have cured him of his momentary lust for her any more effectively than if she had given him its exact antidote. Homeopathic poison; just her style. He recalled the last time he had taken mescaline, back in the days he had slept out here, throwing up and thinking it was stupid to poison oneself to get high. But that was what life with Marta had been. He liked her in some ways, he liked her energy and her wit, but there had always been so much he didn't like about her. And any excess of her good qualities quickly also became obnoxious.

He wanted his Caroline. Somewhere out east she too was alone, and thinking of him. He knew it was true at least some of the time. How he wanted to *talk* to her! Cell phone to cell phone—surely they could both get one on some account unknown to her ex? He needed to talk to her!

Like he could always talk to Diane.

Slowly the susurrus of surf calmed him, and then, as his body relaxed, it helped make him sleepy. For a long time he just sat there. In D.C. it was 3 A.M. Diane and Caroline, his own personal D.C. He was jet-lagged. San Diego, or really this campus, these very cliffs—this beautiful place . . . this was his home. The ocean made him happy. The ground here was good. Just to be here, to feel the air, to feel the thump of the breaking waves, to hear their perpetual grumble and hiss, grumble and hiss, crack grumble and hiss . . . To breathe it. Salt air fuzzy in the moonlight. The brilliant galaxy of light that was La Jolla, outlining its point. Ah, if only he knew what to do.

Phil Chase called his blog "Cut to the Chase." He wrote his entries late at night before falling asleep, and hit SEND without even a spell check, so that his staff got some horrible jolts with their morning coffee, even though Phil had clearly stated at the top of the home page that these were his private musings only, blogged to put the electorate in touch with his thinking as a citizen, and no reflection of formal policies. No impact on anything—just like any other blog.

CUT TO THE CHASE

Today's Post:

We Americans don't want to be ignorant about our relationship to the world. If we're five percent of the world's population and burning a quarter of the carbon burned every year, we need to know that. It's not a trivial thing and we can't just deny it. It's a kind of obesity.

There are different kinds of denial. One is sticking your head in the sand. You manage not to know anything. Like that public service ad where there's a bunch of ostriches down on a big beach, and all the big ones have their heads in the sand, and some of the little ones do too, but a lot of the little ones are running around, and they see a giant wave is coming in and they start yelling down the holes to the big ones, *There's a wave coming!* and one of the big ones pulls his head out and says *Don't worry, just stick your head in like this,* and the little ones look at each other and figure that if that's what their parents are doing it must be okay, so they stick their heads in the sand too. A sad moment.

But there are other kinds of denial that are worse. There's a response that says I'll never admit I'm wrong, and if it comes to a choice between admitting I'm wrong or destroying the whole world, then destroy it. That's the *Götterdämmerung*, in which the doomed gods decide to tear down the world rather than admit defeat. The god-damning of the world. Let's not do that. It wouldn't be the American way. We're supposed to be the hope of the world.

Back in D.C. it was still so cold that the idea he could have been surfing the day before struck Frank as impossible. Crossing the continent in March was like changing planets. It was a bigger world than they thought.

It was so many planets at once. The Hyperniño had left California, following the Pacific Ocean's warm water to the west, which signaled the onset of a La Niña, predicted to be devastating to Southeast Asia. Now all of California was in a major drought. The East Coast, meanwhile, was still in cold storage, making snow that had the consistency of Styrofoam.

At the embassy, the younger Khembalis were tropical creatures, and walked around blue-lipped; those of Rudra's generation never seemed to notice the cold at all. They left their arms bare in frigid temperatures.

Rudra often was reading in bed when Frank came in, or looking at picture books. Then one day Qang brought him a laptop, and he chuckled as he tapped away at it, looking at photo collections of various sorts, including pornography. Other times Frank found him humming, or asleep with a book on his chest. When he was up and about, he was slower than ever. When Frank and he went for walks, they always got out the wheelchair, as if this was how they had always done it.

Frank said, "Listen to this: 'If he had the earth for his pasture and the sea for his pond, he would be a pauper still. He only is rich who owns the day. There is no king, rich man, fairy or demon who possesses such power as that.'"

Rudra said, "Emerson?"

"Right." They had begun a game in which Rudra tried to guess which of the two New Englanders Frank was reading from. He did very well at it. Not that it was very hard.

"Good man. Means, go for a walk?"

It was too much like a dog begging to go out. "Sure."

And so out they would go, Rudra bundled in down jacket and blankets against the cold, Frank in a suitable selection from his cold-weather gear.

They had a route now that took them north to the Potomac at the mouth of Windy Run, which was often free of ice, and thus a waterhole frequented by deer, foxes, beaver, and muskrats. They looked for these regulars, and any unusual visiting animals, and then the wind would force them to turn their backs and head downstream for a bit, on a rough old asphalt sidewalk, after which they could angle up 24th Street, and thus back to the house. The walk took about an hour, and sometimes they would stop by the river for an hour. Once as they turned to go Frank saw a flash, and had the impression it might have been an antelope. It would have been the first time in Virginia he had seen an exotic, and as such worthy of calling in to Nancy. But he wasn't sure, so he let it go.

The quiet neighborhood between the Rock Creek Park and Connecticut Avenue was looking more withdrawn than ever. It had always been empty-seeming compared to most of D.C., but now three or four houses had burned and not been rebuilt, and others were still boarded up from the time of the great flood. At night these dark houses gave the whole area an eerie cast.

Some of the dark houses gleamed at the cracks or smoked from the chimneys, and if after a hike in the dusk Frank was hungry, or wanted company, he would call up Spencer and see if he was in any of these places. Once when Spencer answered they found he was inside the very house Frank was looking at.

In Frank went, uncertain at first. But he was a familiar face, so without further ado he helped to hold a big pot over the fire, ate broiled steak, and ended up banging on the bottom of an empty trash can while Spencer percussed his chair and sang. Robert and Robin showed up, ate, sang duets to Robert on guitar, then pressed Spencer and Frank to go out and play a round of night golf.

It was full moon that night, and once they got going, Frank saw that they didn't need to see to play their course. They had played it so many times that they knew every possible shot, so that when they threw they could feel in their bodies where the frisbee was going to land, could run to that spot and nine times out of ten pick it up. Although on that night they did lose one of Robert's, and spent a few minutes looking for it before Spencer cried, as he always did in this situation, "LO AND BEHOLD," and they were off again.

Socks and shoes got wet with melted snow. No snowshoes tonight, and so he leaped through drifts and abandoned his feet to their soggy fate. On a climbing expedition it would have meant disaster. But in the city it was okay. There was even a certain pleasure in throwing caution to the wind and crashing through great piles of snow, which ranged from powder to concrete in consistency.

Then in the middle of one leap he hooked a foot and crashed down onto a deer layby, panicking the creatures, who scrambled under him. Frank tried to leap away too, slipped and fell back on a doe; for a second he felt under him the warm quivering flank of the animal, like a woman trying to shrug off a fur coat. His shout of surprise seemed to catapult them both out of the hole in different directions, and the guys laughed at him. But as he ran on he could still feel in his body that sudden intimacy, that kinetic jolt: a collision with a woman of another species!

Power outages were particularly hard on the few feral exotics still out. The heated shelters in Rock Creek Park were operating again, and they all had generators for long blackouts, but the generators made noise and belched out noxious exhaust, and none of the animals liked them, even the humans. On the other hand, the deep cold of these early spring nights could kill, so many animals hunkered down in the shelters when the worst cold hit; but they were not happy. It would have been better simply to be enclosed, Frank sometimes felt; or rather it was much the same thing, as they were chained to the shelters by the cold. So many different animals together—it was so beautiful and unnatural, it never failed to strike Frank.

Such gatherings gave the zoo's zoologists a chance to do all kinds of things with the ferals, so the FOG volunteers who were cold-certified were welcomed to join them. With Frank's help, Nick was now the youngest cold-certified member of FOG, which seemed to please him in his quiet way. Certainly Frank was pleased—though he also tried to be there whenever Nick was out on FOG business in extreme cold, to make sure nothing went wrong. Hard cold was dangerous, as everyone had learned by now. The tabloids were rife with stories of people freezing while waiting for a light to change, or on their front doorsteps trying to find the right key, or even in their beds at night when an electric blanket failed. There were also many Darwin Award winners, feeding the tabloids' insatiable hunger for stupid disaster. Frank wondered if a time would come when people got so much disaster in their own lives they would no longer need to vampire onto others' disasters. It hadn't happened yet.

Frank and Nick got back in the pattern in which Frank dropped by on Saturday mornings and off they would go, sipping from travel cups of coffee and hot chocolate Anna had provided. They started at the shelter at Fort DeRussy. On this morning they spotted a tapir that was on the zoo's wanted list.

They called it in and waited uneasily for the zoo staff to arrive with the dart guns and nets and slings. They had a bad history together on this front, and could not help remembering the gibbon that had fallen to its death after Frank hit it with a tranq dart. Neither mentioned this, but they spoke little until the staffers arrived and the tapir was shot by one of them. At that the nearby deer bolted, and the humans approached. A big RFID chip was inserted under the tapir's thick skin. The animal's vital signs seemed good. Then they decided to take it in anyway. Too many tapirs had died. Nick and Frank helped hoist the animal onto a gurney big enough for all of them to get a hand on. They carried the unconscious beast like its pallbearers. From a distant ridge, the aurochs looked down on the procession.

After that the two of them hiked down the streambed to the zoo. Rock Creek was frozen solid. Often the ice was whipped into a frothy meringue. The raw walls of the flood-ripped gorge were in a freeze-thaw cycle that left frozen spills of yellow mud splayed over the ribbon of creek ice.

Up and into the zoo parking lot. The zoo itself was just waking up in the magnesium light of morning, steam frost rising from nostrils and exhaust vents. There were more animals than people. Compared to Rock Creek it was crowded, however, and a good place to relax in the sun, and down another hot chocolate.

The tigers were just out, lying under one of their powerful space heaters. They wouldn't leave it until the sun struck them, so it was better now to visit the snow leopards, who loved this sort of weather, and indeed were creatures who could go feral in this biome and climate. There were people in FOG advocating their release, along with that of some other winterized predators, as a way of getting a handle on the city's deer infestation. But others at the zoo objected on grounds of human and pet safety, and it didn't look like it would happen anytime soon. The zoo got enough grief already for its support of the feral idea; advocating the freeing of predators would make things crazy.

After lunch they would hitch a ride from a staffer back up to Frank's van, or snowshoe back to it. If the day got over the freezing mark, the forest would become a dripping rainbow world, tiny spots of color prisming everywhere.

Then back to the Quiblers, where Nick would have homework, or tennis with Charlie. On some days Frank would stay for lunch. Then Charlie would see him off: "So—what are you going to do now?"

"Well, I don't know. I could . . ."

Long pause as he thought it over.

"Not good enough, Frank. Let's hear you choose."

"Okay then! I'm going to help the Khembalis move stuff out to their farm!" Right off the top of his head. "So there."

"That's more like it. When are you going to see the doctor again?"

Glumly: "Monday."

"That's good. You need to find out what you've got going on there."

"Yes." Unenthusiastically.

"Let us know what you find out, and if there's anything we can do to help. Like if you have to have your sinuses roto-rootered, or your nose broken again."

"I will."

It still felt strange to Frank to have his health issues known to the Quiblers. But he had been trying to pursue a course of open exchange of (some) information with Anna, and apparently whatever she learned, Charlie would too, and even Nick to an extent. Frank hadn't known it would be like that, but did not want to complain, or even to change. He was getting used to it. And it was good Charlie had asked, because otherwise he might not have been able to figure out what to do. The pressure there was becoming like a kind of wall inside him.

So: off to Khembali House, to fill his van with a load of stuff. The construction of their new compound in Maryland was coming along. Enough Khembalis had gotten licensed in the trades that they could do the work legally on their own. The whole operation ran like some big family or baseball team, everyone pitching in and getting things done, the labor therefore outside the money economy. It was impressive what could be done that way.

Frank still had his eye on the big knot of trees that stood on the high point of the farm. They were mostly chestnut oaks, like his treehouse tree but much bigger, forming a canopy together that covered most of an acre. It seemed to him that the interlaced inner branches formed a perfect framework for a full Swiss Family extravaganza, and Padma and Sucandra liked the idea. So there was that to be planned. Spring was about to spring, and there were materials and helpers on hand. No time like the present! Leap before you look! But maybe peek first.

All the various scans that Frank's doctors had ordered had been taken, at an increasing pace, as they seemed to find things calling for some speed. Now it was time to meet with the brain guy.

This was an M.D. who did neurology, also brain and face surgery. So just in ordinary terms a very imposing figure, and in paleolithic terms, a shaman healer of the rarest kind, being one who actually accomplished cures. Awesome: scarier than any witch doctor. Whenever the technological sublime was obvious, the fear in sublimity came to the fore.

The doctor's office was ordinary enough, and him too. He was about Frank's age, balding, scrubbed very clean, ultra-close-shaven, hands perfectly manicured. "Have a seat," he said, gesturing at the chair across his desk.

When Frank was seated, he described what he had found in Frank's head. "That's a subdural hematoma," he said, pointing to a light spot in an array of spots that roughly made the shape of a brain section—Frank's brain. The CT scan and the MRI both showed this hematoma, the doctor went on, and pretty clearly it was a result of the trauma Frank had suffered. "Lots of blood vessels were broken. Most were outside the dura. That's the sac that holds your brain. But there are veins called bridging veins, between the dura and the surface of the brain. Some of them broke, and appear to be leaking blood."

"But when I taste it?"

"That must be encapsulated blood in scar tissue outside the dura, here." He pointed at the MRI. "Your immune system is trying to chip away at that over time, and sometimes when you swing your head hard, or raise your pulse, there might be leaking from that encapsulation into the sinus, and then down the back of your throat. That's what you're tasting. But the subdural hematoma is inside the dura, here. It may be putting a bit of pressure on your frontal cortex, on the right side. Have you been noticing any differences in what you think or feel?"

"Well, yes," Frank said, thankful and fearful all at once. "That's really what brought me in. I can't make decisions."

"Ah. That's interesting. How bad is it?"

"It varies. Sometimes any decision seems really hard, even trivial ones. Occasionally they seem impossible. Other times it's no big deal."

"Any depression about that? Are you depressed?"

"No. I mean, I have a lot going on right now. But I often feel pretty great. But—confused. And concerned. Worried about being indecisive. And—afraid I'll do something—I don't know. Stupid, or—dangerous. Wrong, or dangerous. I don't trust my judgment." And I have reasons not to!

"Uh-huh," the doctor was writing all this down on Frank's chart. Oh great. Confessing to his health insurance. Not a good idea. Perhaps a bad decision right here and now, in this room. A sample of what he was capable of.

"Any changes in your sense of taste?"

"No. I can't say I've noticed any."

"And when you taste that blood taste, does it correlate with periods of decisiveness or indecisiveness?"

"I don't know. That's an interesting thought, though."

"You should keep a symptom calendar. Dedicate a calendar to just that, put it by your bed and rate your day for decisiveness. From one to ten is the typical scale. Then also, mark any unusual tastes or other phenomena— dizziness, headaches, strange thoughts or moods. Moods can be typified and scaled too."

Frank was beginning to like this guy. Now he would become his own experiment, an experiment in consciousness. He would observe his own thoughts, in a quantified meditation. Rudra would get a kick out of that; Frank could hear his deep laugh already. "Good idea," he said to the doctor, hearing the way Rudra would say it. "I'll try it. Oh, I've forgotten to mention this—I still can't feel anything right under my nose. It's numb. It feels like a nerve is gone."

"Oh yeah? Well—" Looking at the scans. "Maybe something off the nine nerve. The glossopharyngeal nerve is near the encapsulation."

"Will I get that feeling back?"

"You either will or you won't," the doctor said. All of them said that; it must be the standard line on nerve damage, like the line about the President having so much on his plate. People liked to say the same things.

"And the hematoma?"

"Well, it's been a while since your injury, so it's probably pretty stable. It's hypodense. We could follow it with serial scans, and it could resolve itself."

"And if it doesn't?"

"We could drain it. It's not a big operation, because of the location. I can go in through the nose. It looks like it would be straightforward," checking out the images again. "Of course, there's always some risk with neurosurgery. We'd have to go into that in detail, if you wanted to move forward with it."

"Sure. But do you think I should?"

He shrugged. "It's up to you. The cognitive problems you're reporting are fairly common for pressure on that part of the brain. It seems that some components of decision-making are located in those sulci. They have to do with the emotional components of risk assessment and the like."

"I've read some of the literature," Frank said.

"Oh yes? Well, then, you know what can happen. There are some unusual cases. It can be debilitating, as you know. Some cases of bad decision-making, accompanied by little or no affect. But your hematoma is not so big. It would be straightforward to drain it, and get rid of that encapsulated clot too."

"And would I then experience changes in my thinking?"

"It's possible. Usually that's the point, so patients like it, or are relieved. Others get agitated by the perception of difference."

"Does it go away, or do they get used to it?"

"Well, either, or both. Or neither. I don't really know about that part of it. We focus on draining the hematoma and removing that pressure."

It will or it won't. "So if I'm not in too much distress, maybe I ought not to mess with it?" Frank said. He did not want to be looking forward to brain surgery; even clearing out his sinuses sounded pretty dire to him.

The doctor smiled ever so slightly, understanding him perfectly. "You certainly don't want to take it lightly. However, there is a mass of blood in there, and often the first sign of it getting bigger is a change in thinking or feeling, or a bad headache. Some people don't want to risk that. And problems in decision-making can be pretty debilitating. So, some people preempt any problems and choose to have the surgery."

Frank said, "This is just the kind of decision I can't make anymore!"

The doctor laughed briefly, but his look was sympathetic. "It would be a hard call no matter what. Why don't you give it a set period of time and see how you feel about it? Make some lists of pros and cons, mark on your symptoms calendar how you feel about it for ten days running, stuff like that. See if one course of action is consistently supported over time."

Frank sighed. Possibly he could construct an algorithm that would make the decision for him. Some kind of aid. Because it was a decision that he could not avoid; it was his call. And doing nothing was a decision too. But possibly the wrong one. So he had to decide, he had to consciously decide. Possibly it was the most important decision he had to make right now.

"Okay," he said. "I'll try that."

Back at work, Frank tried to concentrate. He simply couldn't do it. Or he concentrated, but it was on the word *hematoma*. *Chronic subdural hematoma.* Pressure on the brain. He thought, I can concentrate just fine, I can do it for hours at a time. I just can't *decide*.

He closed his eyes, poked at his Things to Do list with a pen. That was what it had come to. Ah. It was time to talk to one of the big pools of accumulated capital: the re-insurance companies, with total assets in the ten-trillion-dollar range. Already an appointment; he hadn't had to make a decision. Check calendar before going through such torture. If he could keep his calendar full, there would be no need to decide anything. Or to wonder where Caroline was and why she hadn't contacted him yet.

The re-insurance companies had underwritten most of the previous year's North Atlantic salt fleet, so they were already aware of the huge costs of such projects, but also were the world's experts in the even bigger costs of ignoring oncoming problems. Ultimately they had been the ones who had paid for the recovery from the long winter, and they had their cost/benefit algorithms.

Diane had invited representatives of the four big re-insurance companies to meet with her task force. About twenty people filled the conference room in the Old Executive Offices, including Anna, over for the day from NSF.

After Diane welcomed them, she got to the point in her usual style, and invited Kenzo to share what was known about the global situation. Kenzo waved at his PowerPoint slides like a pops orchestra conductor. Then one of the re-insurance nat cat (natural catastrophe) guys from Swiss Re gave a talk which made it clear that in insurance terms, sea level rise was the worst impact of all. A quarter of humanity lived on coastlines. About a fifth of the total human infrastructure was at risk, he said, if sea level rose even two meters; and this was the current best guess as to what would happen in the coming decade. If the breakup of the West Antarctic Ice Sheet continued and went all the way, they were facing a rise of seven meters.

It was something you could be aware of without quite comprehending. They sat around the table pondering it.

Frank seized his pen, squeezed it as if it were his recalcitrant brain. "I've been looking at some numbers," he said haltingly. "Postulating, for the sake of argument, that we develop really significant clean energy generation, then, observe, the amount of water displaced by the detached Antarctic ice so far is on the order of forty thousand cubic kilometers. Now, there are a number of dry basins in the Sahara Desert and all across Central Asia, and in the basin and range country of North America. Also in southern Africa. In effect, the current position of the continents and the trade wind patterns have desiccated all land surfaces around the thirtieth latitudes north and south, and in the south that doesn't mean much, but in the north it means a huge land area dried out. All those basins together have a theoretical capacity of about sixty thousand cubic kilometers."

He looked up from his laptop briefly, and it was as he had expected; they were looking at him like he was stark raving mad. He shrugged and forged on:

"So you could pump a lot of the excess seawater into these empty basins in the thirties, and perhaps stabilize the ocean's sea level."

"Holy moly," Kenzo said in the silence after it was clear Frank was done. "You'd alter the climate in those regions tremendously if you did that."

"No doubt," Frank said. "But, you know, since the climate is going haywire anyway, it's kind of like, so what? Would we even be able to distinguish these impacts from all the rest?"

Kenzo laughed.

"Well," Frank said defensively, "I thought I'd at least run the numbers."

"It would take a lot of power to pump that much water," Anna said.

"I have *no idea* what kind of climate alterations you would get," Kenzo said happily.

Frank said, "Did the Salton Sea change anything downwind of it?"

"Well, but we're talking like a thousand Salton Seas here," Kenzo said. He was still bug-eyed at the idea; he had never even imagined curating such a change, and he was looking at Frank as if to say, Why didn't you mention this before? "It would be a real test of our modeling programs," he said, looking even happier. Almost giddy: "It might change everything!"

"And yet," Frank said. "People might judge it preferable to displacing a quarter of the world's population. Remember what happened to New Orleans when it flooded. We couldn't afford to have ten thousand of those, could we?"

"If you had the unlimited power you're talking about," Anna said suddenly, "why couldn't you just pump the equivalent of the displaced water back up onto the Antarctic polar plateau? Let it freeze back up there?"

Again the room was silent.

"Now there's an idea," Diane said. She was smiling. "But Frank, where are these dry basins again?"

Frank brought that slide back up. The basins, if all of them were entirely filled, could take about twenty percent of the predicted rise in sea level if the whole WAIS came off. It would take about thirty terawatts to move the water. The cost in carbon for that much energy would be ten gigatons, not good, but only a fraction of the overall carbon budget at this point. Clean energy would be better, of course. What the effect on local ecologies would be was, as Kenzo had said, impossible to calculate.

"Those are some very dry countries," Diane said after perusing Frank's map. "Dry and poor. I can imagine, if they were offered compensation to take the water and make new lakes, some of them might decide to roll the dice and take the environmental risk, because net effects might end up being positive. It might make opportunities for them that aren't there now. There's not much going on in the Takla Makan these days, that I know of."

The Swiss Re executive returned to Anna's comment, suggesting that the system might be able to go through proof of concept in Antarctica. Antarctic operations would incur extra costs, to keep pumps and pipelines heated; on the other hand, environmental impacts would be minimal, and population relocation not an issue. Maybe they could even relocate the excess ocean water entirely on the Antarctic polar cap. That would mean shifting water that floated away from the West Antarctic Ice Sheet up to the top of the East Antarctic Ice Sheet.

"Of course if we're going to talk about stupendous amounts of new free energy," Anna pointed out, "you could do all sorts of things. You could desalinate the seawater at the pumps or at their outlets, and make them freshwater lakes in the thirties, so you wouldn't have Salton Sea problems. You'd have reservoirs of drinking and irrigation water, you could replenish groundwater, build with salt bricks, and so on."

Diane nodded. "True."

"But we don't have stupendous new sources of clean energy," Anna said.

Good photovoltaics existed, Frank reminded her doggedly. Also good Stirling engines, good wind power, and promising ocean energy systems.

That was all very well, Diane agreed. But there remained the capital investment problem, and the other transitional costs associated with changing over to any of these clean renewables. Who was going to pay for it?

It was the trillion-dollar question.

Here the re-insurance people took center stage. They had paid for the salting of the North Atlantic by using their reserves, then upping their premiums. Their reserves were huge, as they had to be to meet obligations to the many insurance companies paying them for re-insurance. But swapping out the power generation system was two magnitudes larger a problem, more or less, than the salt fleet had been, and it was impossible to front that kind of money—almost impossible to imagine collecting it.

"It's only four years of the American military budget," Frank pointed out.

People shrugged, as if to say, But still—that was a lot.

"It will take legislation," Diane said. "Private investment can't do it."

General agreement, although the re-insurance guys looked unhappy. "It would be good if it made sense in market terms," the Swiss Re executive said.

This led them to a discussion of macroeconomics, or maybe it was political economy; and in that concept space, they kept coming back to the idea of major public works. No matter what kind of economic ideology you brought to the table, the world they were in was resolutely Keynesian, meaning a mixed economy in which government and business existed in an uneasy interaction. Public works projects were sometimes crucial to the process, especially in emergencies, but that meant legislating economic activity, and so they needed to have the political understanding and support it would take to do that. If they had it, they could legislate investment, and then in effect print the money to pay for it. That was standard Keynesian practice, used by governments ever since the third New Deal of 1938, as Diane told them now. It could be handed to Chase as a kind of program, a mission architecture. A list of Things to Do.

After that, they heard a report from the Russian environmental office. The altered tree lichens they had distributed in Siberia were surviving the winter like any ordinary lichen. Dispersal had been widespread, uptake on trees rapid. The only problem the Russian could see was that it was possible that the lichen would become too successful. What they were seeing now led them to think they might have overdispersed. Since most of what they had dispersed had survived, by next summer the Siberian forest near the site would reap whatever the winds and Russians had sown. In the lab it was proving to grow more like algal blooms encased in mushrooms than like ordinary lichens. "Fast lichen, we call it," the Russian said. "We didn't think was possible, but we see it happening."

All that was very interesting, but when Frank got back in his office, he found that his computer wouldn't turn on. And when the techs arrived to check it out, they isolated the machine quickly, then carried the whole thing out. "That's one bad virus," one of them said. "Very dangerous."

"So was I hacked in particular?" Frank asked.

"Yes."

Charlie's daytime outings with Joe had to happen on weekends now. Even though they were past the First Sixty Days, and had gotten a pretty good run out of them, they were trying to keep the momentum going, and things kept popping up to derail their plans, sometimes intentional problems created by the opposition, sometimes neutral matters created by the sheer size of the system. Roy was pushing so hard that sometimes he even almost lost his cool. Charlie had never seen that, and would have thought it impossible, at least on the professional level. Calmness at speed was his signature style, as with certain surfing stars. And even now he persisted with that style, or tried to; but the workload was so huge it was hard. They were far past the time when he and Charlie were able to chat about things like they used to. Now their phone conversations went something like:

"Charlie it's Roy have you met with IPCC?"

"No, we're both scheduled to meet with the World Bank on Friday."

"Can you meet them and the Bank team at six today instead?"

"I was going to go home at five."

"Six then?"

"Well if you think—"

"Good okay bye."

"Bye"—said to the empty connection.

Charlie stared at his phone and cursed. He cursed Roy, Phil, the World Bank, the Republican Party, and the universe. Because it was nobody's fault.

He hit the phone button for the daycare.

He was going to have to carve time for an in-person talk with Roy, a talk about what he could and couldn't do. That would be an unusual meeting. Even though Charlie was now at the White House fifty hours a week, he still never saw Roy in person; Roy was always somewhere else. They spoke on the phone even when one of them was in the West Wing and the other in the Old Executive Offices, less than a hundred yards away. For a second Charlie couldn't even remember what Roy looked like.

So; call to arrange for "extended stay" for Joe, a development his teachers were used to. This meeting took precedence, because they needed the World Bank executing Phil's program; in the war of the agencies, now very intense, the World Bank and the International Monetary Fund were among the most mulish of their passive-aggressive opponents. Phil had the power to hire and fire the upper echelons in both agencies, which was good leverage, but it would be better to do something less drastic, to keep the midlevels from shattering. A meeting with both them and the Intergovernmental Panel on Climate Change, a UN organization, might be a good venue for exerting some pressure. The IPCC had spent many years advocating action on the climate front, and all that time they had been flatly ignored by the World Bank. If there was now a face-off, a great reckoning in a little room, then it could get interesting. Charlie hoped so, because whether it was useful or not, Joe was going to have to get by for the extra hours.

But the meeting was a disappointment. The two groups came from such different worldviews that it was only an illusion they were speaking the same language; for the most part they used different vocabularies, and when by chance they used the same words, they meant different things by them. They were aware at some level of this underlying conflict, but could not address it; and so everyone was tense, with old grievances unsayable and yet fully present.

The World Bank guys said something about nothing getting cheaper than oil for the next fifty years, ignoring what the IPCC guys had just finished saying about the devastating effects of fifty more years of burning oil. They had not heard that, apparently. They believed everything was fungible with everything else, and defended having invested ninety-four percent of the World Bank's energy investments in oil exploration as necessary, given the world's dependence on oil—apparently unaware of the circular aspect of their argument. And, being economists, they were still exteriorizing costs without even noticing it or acknowledging such exteriorization had been conclusively demonstrated to falsify standard accounting of profit and loss. Everything fungible: it was as if the world were not real, as if the physical world, reported on by scientists and witnessed by all, could be ignored, and because their fictitious numbers therefore added up, no one could complain.

Charlie gritted his teeth as he listened and took notes. It was science versus capitalism, yet again. The IPCC guys spoke for science and said the obvious things, pointing out the physical constraints of the planet, the carbon load now in the atmosphere altering everything, and the resultant need for heavy investment in clean technology by all concerned, including the World Bank, as one of the great drivers of globalization. But they had said it before to no avail, and now it was happening again. The World Bank guys talked about rates of return and the burden on investors, and the unacceptable doubling of the price of a kilowatt-hour. Everyone there had said all these things before, with the same lack of communication and absence of concrete results.

Charlie thought of Joe, over at the daycare. He had never stayed there long enough even to see what they did all day long. Guilt stuck him like a sliver under the fingernail. In a crowd of strangers, fourteen hours a day. The Bank guy was going on about differential costs, "and that's why it's going to be oil for the next twenty, thirty, maybe even fifty years," he concluded. "None of the alternatives are competitive."

Charlie's pencil tip snapped. "Competitive for *what*?" he demanded.

He had not spoken until that point, and now the edge in his voice stopped the discussion. Everyone stared at him. He stared back at the World Bank guys.

"Damage from carbon dioxide emission costs about fifty dollars a ton, but in your model no one pays it. The carbon that British Petroleum burns per year, by sale and operation, runs up a damage bill of fifty billion dollars. BP reported a profit of twenty billion, so actually it's thirty billion in the red, every year. Shell reported a profit of twenty-three billion, but if you added the damage cost it would be eight billion in the red. These companies should be bankrupt. You support their exteriorizing of costs, so your accounting is bullshit. You're helping to bring on the biggest catastrophe in human history. If the oil companies burn the thousand gigatons of carbon that you are describing as inevitable because of your financial shell games, then two-thirds of the species on the planet will be endangered, including humans. But you keep talking about fiscal discipline and competitive edges in profit differentials. It's the stupidest head-in-the-sand response possible."

The World Bank guys flinched at this. "Well," one of them said, "we don't see it that way."

Charlie said, "That's the trouble. You see it the way the banking industry sees it, and they make money by manipulating money no matter what happens in the real world. You've spent a trillion dollars of American taxpayers' money over the lifetime of the Bank, and there's nothing to show for it. You go into poor countries and force them to sell their assets to foreign investors and to switch from subsistence agriculture to cash crops, then when the prices of those crops collapse you call this nicely competitive on the world market. The local populations starve and you then insist on austerity measures even though your actions have shattered their economy. You order them to cut their social services so they can pay off their debts to you and to your private associates, and you devalue their real assets and then buy them on the cheap and sell them elsewhere for more. The assets of that country have been strip-mined and now belong to international finance. That's your idea of development. You were intended to be the Marshall Plan, and instead you're carpetbaggers."

One of the World Bank guys muttered, "But tell us what you really think," while putting his papers in his briefcase. His companion snickered, and this gave him courage to continue: "I'm not gonna stay and listen to this," he said.

"That's fine," Charlie said. "You can leave now and get a head start on looking for a new job."

The man blinked hostilely at him. But he did not otherwise move.

Charlie stared back at him for a while, working to collect himself. He lowered his voice and spoke as calmly as he could manage. He outlined the basics of the administration's new mission architecture, including the role that the World Bank was now to play; but he couldn't handle going into detail with people who were furious at him, and in truth had never been listening. It was time for what Frank called limited discussion. So Charlie wrapped it up, then gave them a few copies of the mission architecture outline, thick books that had been bound just that week. "Your part of the plan is here. Take it back and talk it over with your people, and come to us with your plan to enact it. We look forward to hearing your ideas. I've got you scheduled for a meeting on the sixth of next month, and I'll expect your report then." Although, since we will be decapitating your organization, it won't be you guys doing the reporting, he didn't add.

And he gathered his papers and left the room.

Well, shit. What a waste of everyone's time.

He had been sweating, and now out on the street he chilled. His hands were shaking. He had lost it. It was amazing how angry he had gotten. Phil had told him to go kick ass, but it did no good to yell at people like that. It had been unprofessional; out of control; counterproductive. Only senators got to rave like that. Staffers, no.

Well, what was done was done. Now it was time to pick up Joe and go home. Anna wouldn't believe what he had done. In fact, he realized, he would not be able to tell her about it; she would be too appalled. She would say, "Oh Charlie," and he would be ashamed of himself.

But at least it was time to get Joe. At this point Joe had been at daycare for twelve hours. "God *damn* it," Charlie said viciously, all of a sudden as angry as he had been in the meeting, and glad he had shouted. Years of repressed anger at the fatuous destructiveness of the World Bank and the system they worked for had been unleashed all at once; the wonder was he had been as polite as he had. The anger still boiled in him uselessly, caustic to his own poor gut.

Joe, however, seemed unconcerned by his long day. "Hi Dad!" he said brightly from the blocks corner, where he had the undivided attention of a young woman. "We're playing chess!"

"Wow," Charlie said, startled; but by the girl's sweet grin, and the chess pieces strewn about the board and the floor, he saw that it was Joe's version of chess, and the mayhem had been severe. "That's really good, Joe! But now I'm here and it's time, so can we help clean up and go?"

"Okay Dad."

On the Metro ride home, Joe seemed tired but happy. "We had Cheerios for snack."

"Oh good, you like Cheerios. Are you still hungry?"

"No, I'm good. Are you hungry, Dad?"

"Well, yes, a little bit."

"Wanna cracker?" And he produced a worn fragment of a Wheat Thin from his pants pocket, dusted with lint.

"Thanks, Joe, that's nice. Sure, I'll take it." He took the cracker and ate it. "Beggars can't be choosers."

"Beggars?"

"People who don't have anything. People who ask you for money."

"Money?"

"You know, money. The stuff people pay with, when they buy things."

"Buy things?"

"Come on Joe. Please. It's hard to explain what money is. Dollars. Quarters. Beggars are people who don't have much money and they don't have much of a way to get money. All they've got is the World Bank ripping their hearts out and eating their lives. So, the saying means, when you're like a beggar, you can't be too picky about choosing things when they're offered to you."

"What about Han? Is she too picky?"

"Well, I don't know. Who's Han?"

"Han is the morning teacher. She doesn't like bagels."

"I see! Well, that sounds too picky to me."

"Right," Joe said. "You get what you get."

"That's true," Charlie said.

"You *get* what you *get* and you *don't* throw a *fit*!" Joe declared, and beamed. Obviously this was a saying often repeated. A mantra of sorts.

"That's very true," Charlie said. "Although to tell the truth, I did just throw a fit."

"Oh well." Joe was observing the people getting on at the UDC stop, and

Charlie looked up too. Students and workers, going home late. "These things happen," Joe said. He sat leaning against Charlie, his body relaxed, murmuring something to the tiny plastic soldier grasped in his fist, looking at the people.

Then they were at the Bethesda stop, and up the long escalator to the street, and walking down Wisconsin together with the cars roaring by.

"Dad, let's go in and get a cookie! Cookie!"

It was that block's Starbucks, one of Joe's favorite places.

"Oh Joe, we've got to get home, Mom and Nick are waiting to see us."

"Sure Dad. Whatever you say Dad."

"Please, Joe! Don't say that!"

"Okay Dad."

Charlie shook his head as they walked on, his throat tight. He clutched Joe's hand and let Joe swing their arms up and down.

CHAPTER 25

UNDECIDED

Pleasure is a brain mechanism. It's a product of natural selection, so it must be adaptive. Sexual attraction is an index of likely sexual pleasure.

Frank stopped in his reading. Was that true?

The introduction to this book claimed the collected sociobiological papers in it studied female sexual attractiveness exclusively, because there were more data about it. Yeah right. Also, female sexual attractiveness was easier to see and describe and quantify, as it had more to do with physical qualities than with abstract attributes such as status or prowess or sense of humor. Yeah right! What about the fact that the authors of the articles were all male? Would Hrdy agree with any of these justifications? Or would she laugh outright?

Evolutionary psychology studies the adaptations made to solve the information-processing problems our ancestors faced over the last couple million years. The problems? Find food; select habitat; stay safe; choose a mate. Obviously these are diverse problems in different domains. No general-purpose brain mechanism to solve all problems, just as no general-purpose organ to solve all physiological problems. Food choice different from mate choice, for instance.

Was this true? Was not consciousness itself precisely the general-purpose brain mechanism this guy claimed did not exist? Maybe it was like blood, circulating among the organs. Or the whole person as a gestalt decision maker.

Anyway, mate choice; in this study, males choosing females (again). Sexual attraction had something to do with it. (Was this true?) Potential mates vary in mate value. Mate value can be defined as how much the mate increases reproductive success of the male making the choice. (Was this true?) Reproductive success potential can be determined by a number of variables. Information about some of these variables was available in specific observable characteristics of female bodies. Men were therefore always watching very closely. (This was true.)

Reproductive variables: age, hormonal status, fecundity, birth history.

A nubile female was one having begun ovulation, but never yet pregnant. Primitive population menarche average start, 12.4 years; first births at 16.8 years; peak fertility between 20 and 24 years; last births at around 40 years. In the early environment in which they evolved, women almost always were married by nubility (how could this be known?). The biological fathers of women's children were likely to be their husbands. Women started reproducing shortly after nubility, one child every three or four years, each child nursed intensively for a few years, which suppressed further conception.

A male who married a nubile female had the maximum opportunity to father her offspring during her most fecund years, and would monopolize those years from their start, thus (presumably) never investing in other men's children.

If mate selection had been for the short term only, maximal fecundity would be preferred to nubility, because chance of pregnancy was better. So sexual attraction to nubility rather than to maximal fecundity indicates it was more a wife detector than a short-term, one-time mother detector.

Was this true?

In the early environment, female reproductive time lasted about 26 years, from 16 to 42, but this included average of 6 years of pregnancy, and 18 years of lactation. Thus females were pregnant or nursing for 24 of the relevant 26 years, or 92 percent of reproductive life. So, between average first-birth age (17) and last-conception age (39), average woman was nonpregnant and nonlactating for 2 years; thus 26 ovulations total. Say 3 days of fecundity per cycle; thus females were capable of conceiving on only 78 of 8,030 days, or one percent of the time. Thus only about one in a hundred random copulations could potentially result in conception.

Did this make sense? It seemed to Frank that several parts of an algorithm had been crunched into one calculation, distorting all the findings. Numbers for numbers' sake; continuing specific operations after an averaging was one sign, "random copulation" another, because there was no such thing; but that was the only way they could get the figure to be as low as one percent.

In any case, following the argument, a nubile woman before first pregnancy was more fecund than a fully fecund woman in her early twenties, if one were considering her lifetime potential. And so nubility cues were fertility cues, as males considered their whole futures as fathers. (But did they?) Thus natural selection assigned maximum sexual attractiveness to nubility cues. And this attraction to nubility rather than fecundity indicated monogamous tendencies in males; male wants long-term cohabitation, with its certainty about parentage for as many offspring as possible.

And what were nubility cues? Skin texture, muscle tone, stretch marks, breast shape, facial configuration, and waist-to-hip ratio. All these indexed female age and parity. Female sexual attractiveness varied inversely with WHR, which was lowest at nubility; higher when both younger and older. Etc. Even the face was a reliable physical indicator. (Frank laughed.) Selection showed a preference for average features. This was asserted because students in a test were asked to choose a preferred composite; the "beautiful composite," as created by both male and female subjects, had a shorter bottom half of the face than average, typical of a twelve-year-old girl; full lips in vertical dimension, but smaller mouth than average. Higher cheekbones than average, larger eyes relative to face size; thinner jaw; shorter distances between nose and mouth, and between mouth and chin. High cheekbones and relatively short lower face and gracile jaw indicated youth, low testosterone/estrogen ratio, and nullipara. Bilateral symmetry was preferred. Deviation in hard tissue reduced sexual attractiveness more than the same amount of deviation in say nose form, which could have resulted from minor mishap indicating little about design quality. Ah, Francesca Taolini's beautiful crooked nose, explained at last!

As was "masticatory efficiency." This was the one that had gotten Frank and Anna laughing so hard, that day when Frank had found this study. Sexy chewing.

In the early environment, total body fat and health were probably correlated, so fat, what little could be accumulated, was good. Now that was reversed, and thinner meant both younger and healthier. Two possible readings, therefore, EE and modern. Which might explain why all women looked good to Frank, each in her own way. He was adaptable, he was optimodal, he was the paleolithic postmodern!

Were women evaluating men as mates in the same way? Yes; but not exactly. A woman knew her children were biologically hers. Mate choice thus could focus on different criteria than in effect capturing all of a mate's fecundity. Here is where the sociobiologist Hrdy had led the way, by examining and theorizing female choice.

Patriarchy could thus be seen as a group attempt by men to be more sure of parentage, by controlling access. Men becoming jailers, men going beyond monogamy to an imprisoning polygamy, as an extension of the original adaptive logic—but an extension that was an obvious reductio ad absurdum, ending in the seraglio. Patriarchy did not eliminate male competition for mates; on the contrary, because of the reductio ad absurdum, male competition became more necessary than ever. And the more force available, the more intense the competition. Thus patriarchy as a solution to the parentage problem led to hatred, war, misogyny, harems, male control of reproductive rights, including anti-abortion laws (those photos of a dozen fat men grinning as they signed a law), and, ultimately, taken all in all, patriarchy led directly to the general very nonadaptive insanity that they lived in now.

Was that true? Did sociobiology show how and why they had gone crazy as a species? Could they, using that knowledge, work backward to sanity? Had there ever been sanity? Could they create sanity for the first time, by understanding all the insanities that had come before? By looking at adaptation and its accidental byproducts, its peacock exaggerations past the point of true function?

And could Frank figure out what he should do about his own mating issues? It brought on a kind of nausea to be so undecided!

Most of the Khembalis still in the D.C. area were moving out to their farm in Maryland. The compound was nearly finished, and although a thin layer of hard snow still lay on the ground, spring was springing, and they were beginning to clear the area they wanted to cultivate with crops. They rented a giant rototiller, and a little tractor of their own was on its way. Sucandra was excited. "I always wanted to be a farmer," he said. "I dreamed about it for years, when we were in prison. Now it looks just like it did in my dream."

"When the ground thaws," Frank suggested.

"Spring is coming. It's almost the equinox."

"But growing season starts late here, doesn't it?"

"Not compared to Tibet."

"Ah."

Sucandra said, "Will you move out here, and build your treehouse?"

"I don't know. I need to talk it over with Rudra."

"He says he wants to. Qang wonders if he should stay closer to hospital."

"Ah. What's wrong with him, do they know?"

Sucandra shrugged. "Old. Worn out."

"I suppose."

"He will not stay much longer in that body."

Frank was startled. "Has he got something, you know—progressive?"

Sucandra smiled. "Life is progressive."

"Yes." But he's only eighty-one, Frank didn't say. That might be far beyond the average lifespan for Tibetans. He felt a kind of tightness in him.

"I don't know what I'll do," he said at last. "I mean, I'll stay where he is. So—maybe now I'll work on the treehouse, and stay in Arlington with him."

"That would be fine, of course. Thank you for thinking of it that way."

Disturbed, Frank went up the hill to the copse of trees at the high point.

He walked around in the grove, trying to concentrate. They were beautiful trees, big, old, intertwined into a canopy shading the hilltop. If only they lived as long as trees. He went back to his van and got his climbing gear. It was sunny but cold, a stiff west wind blowing. He knew that up in the branches it would be colder still. He wasn't really in the mood to climb a tree, and you needed to be in the mood. It was more dangerous than most rock-climbing.

But here he was. Time to amp up and ramp up, as they used to say when window washing—often before smoking huge reefers and downing extra-tall cups of 7-Eleven coffee, admittedly—but the point still held. One needed to get psyched and pay attention. Crampons, lineman's harness, strap around, kick in, deep breath. Up, up, up!

Eyes streaming in the cold wind. Blink repeatedly to clear vision. Through the heavy low branches, up to the level under the canopy, where big branches from different trees intertwined. In the wind he could see the independent motion of all the branches. Hard to imagine, offhand, what that might mean in terms of a treehouse. If an extensive treehouse rested on branches from more than one tree, wouldn't it vibrate or bounce at cross-purposes, rather than sway all of a piece, as his little Rock Creek tree-house did? An interference pattern might be like living in a perpetual earthquake. What was needed was a big central room, perhaps, set firmly on one big trunk in the middle, with the other rooms set independently on branches of their own—yes, much like in the Swiss Family treehouse at Disneyland. He had heard it was the Tarzan treehouse now, but he wasn't willing to accept that. Anyway the design was sound. He saw the potential branches, made a first sketch while hanging there. It could be good.

And yet he wasn't looking forward to it.

Then he saw that the smallest branches around him were studded with tiny green buds. They were the particular light vivid green that Frank had never seen in his life until the previous spring, out in Rock Creek Park: deciduous bud green. The color of spring. Ah yes: could spring ever be far behind? The so-called blocked moments, the times of stasis, were never really still at all. Change was constant. Best then to focus on the new green buds, bursting out everywhere.

Thoreau said the same, the next morning. Frank read it aloud: "March fans it, April christens it, and May puts on its jacket and trousers. It never grows up, but is ever springing, bud following close upon leaf, and when winter comes it is not annihilated, but creeps on mole-like under the snow, showing its face occasionally by fuming springs and watercourses."

Rudra nodded. "Henry say, 'The flower opens, and lo! another year.'"

Thoughts of spring came to Frank often after that, partly because of the green now all over town, and partly because Chase kept referring to his First Sixty Days as a new spring. It struck Frank again when he went with Diane and Edgardo over to the White House to witness the dedication of the new solar projects. Phil had ordered that photovoltaic panels be put back in place, as Carter had done it in his time, to power the White House. When there was some debate as to which system should be installed, he had instructed them to put in three or four different systems, to make a kind of test.

The purple-blue of the photovoltaic panels was like another kind of spring color, popping out in the snowy flower beds. Phil made a little speech, after which he was to be driven to Norfolk Naval Station; he had already had the Secret Service swap out his transport fleet, so now instead of a line of black SUVs pulling through the security gate, it was a line of black bulletproof Priuses. These looked so small they resembled the miniature cars that Shriners drove in parades. Chase laughed hardest of all, jumping out and directing the traffic so that the little cars made a circle around him. As he waved good-bye to the crowd, Frank noticed that he still wore a wedding band.

The White House demonstration project was only a tiny part of the solar power push; it was also that volatile time that came early in any new technology, when decisions about many of the basic structures and methods emerged from a general confusion. The small scale of this test was not going to be fair to Stirling engines in competition with photovoltaic. PV panels could be scaled to any size, which made them best for home use, while the external heat engine required mirrors big enough to heat the heating element fully. It was a system meant for power plants. So the test here was only a PR thing. Still, not a bad idea. To see the systems creating electricity, even on cloudy days, was suddenly to understand that they had the means for the world's deliverance already at hand.

That shifted the debate from technology to finance. Chase began advocating home installation tax credits so big that the cost of a system would equal about three years of electricity bills. A subsidy like that would make a huge difference. The cost to the federal budget would be about a third the cost of the last war. The main problem would be supplying enough silicon.

One of the workmen scaling the southwest corner of the White House was having trouble, even though belayed from the roof. Frank shook his head, thinking: I could do better than that. Cutter and his friends could do better.

Later that spring, when the time came to move to Maryland, Frank drove Rudra out there in his van. Everything they had had in the garden shed barely covered the floor of the van's rear. This was pleasing, but leaving their garden shed was not. As Frank closed and locked the door for the last time, he felt a pang of nostalgia. Another life gone. Some feelings were like vague clouds passing through one, others were as specific as the prick of acupuncture needles.

As they drove up the George Washington Parkway he still felt uneasy about leaving, and he thought maybe Rudra did too. Rudra had left the shed without a look back, but now he was staring silently out at the Potomac. Very hard to tell what he might be thinking. Which was true of everyone of course.

The farm was bristling with people. They had built the treehouse in the hilltop grove, using Frank's design but building in a very heavy *dzong* or hill fortress style, each room so varnished and painted with the traditional Tibetan colors that they perched in the branches like giant toy chests—rather wonderful, but not at all like the airy structures of the Disneyland masterpiece Frank had been conceptualizing.

The design, however, had held. There was a grand central room, like a cottage that the biggest tree had grown through and uplifted thirty feet. This circular room had an open balcony or patio all the way around it, and from this round patio several railed staircases and catwalks led over branches or across open space, out and up to smaller rooms, about a dozen of them.

Sucandra arrived and pointed out one of the lowest and outermost of the hanging rooms, on the river side: this was to be Frank and Rudra's room. The roommates nodded solemnly at this news; it would do. It definitely would do.

Late that day, having moved in, they looked back into the grove from their doorway and saw all the other rooms, their windows lit like lanterns in the dusk. On the inside their room was small. Even so their belongings looked rather meager, stacked in cardboard boxes in one corner. Sucandra and Padma and Qang all stood in the doorway, looking concerned. They had not believed Rudra's assurances that the broad circular staircase and the narrow catwalk out the low branch would present no problems to him. Frank didn't know whether to believe him either, but so far the old man had ascended and descended with only the help of the railing and some sulfurous muttering. And if problems arose, there was a kind of giant dumbwaiter or open lift next to the trunk, that could carry him up and down. Even now they were using it to bring up their furniture—two single beds, a table and chairs, two small chests. Once all that was moved in the room looked more normal.

So. Here they were. Rudra sat before the window, looking down at the river. He had his laptop on the table, and he seemed content. "Very nice outlook," he said, pointing out. "Nice to have such a view."

"Yes," Frank said, thinking of his treehouse in Rock Creek. Rudra would have enjoyed it. It might be possible to lash the old man to Miss Piggy and then haul him up using the winch. He couldn't weigh more than a hundred pounds.

But here they were. And in fact the view was much more extensive than Rock Creek's had been. The sweep of the Potomac was now a glassy silver-green, with bronze highlights under the far bank. The expansion of space over the river, and the big open band of sky over it, struck Frank with a kind of physical relief, a long ahhhhhhh. This was what you never got in the forest, this kind of open spaciousness. No wonder the forest people had loved their rivers—not just great roads for them, but the place of the sky and the stars!

In the days that followed, Frank woke at dawn to look out at this prospect, and saw at different times on the river highlights of yellow or rose or pink, and once it was a clean sheet of gold. A mist would often be rolling over the glass, wisping up on puffs of wind. On windy mornings waves would push upstream like a tide. Sometimes the wind was enough to create whitecaps, and their room would bounce and sway in a way very unlike his old treehouse. There he had been on a vertical trunk, here a horizontal branch; it made a big difference.

In their new room Rudra did not talk as much as before. He slept a lot. But sometimes he would be sitting up in bed, humming or reading when Frank came home, or looking at his laptop screen, and then they would chat as before.

"Nice day?"

"Yes."

"More salt in ocean?"

"Precisely. What about you?"

"Oh, very nice. Sun on water flicker nicely. And some tantric websites."

"It's like you're back in Shambala then."

"No *like*. This *is* Shambala."

"So it follows you around? It's a kind of, what, a phase space, or a magnetic field around you, or something like that?"

"Buddhafield, I think you mean. No, Shambala is not like that. The Buddhafield is always there, yes. But that can be wherever you make it. Shambala is a particular place. The hidden valley. But the valley moves. We performed the ceremony that asked if it should be here. The spirits said yes."

"Were you the, the what do you call it?"

"The voice? Oracle? No. I'm not strong enough anymore. Retired, like I told you. But Qang did well. Guru Rimpoche came to her and spoke. Khembalung is drowned for good, he said. Shambala is now right here."

"Wow," Frank said. As if on cue, when he looked out their window he saw the light of the rising moon, squiggling over the river in big liquid S's.

. . .

Another time Frank was out on the river with Drepung and Charlie. They had kayaked out from the boathouse at the mouth of Rock Creek. Rock Creek where it debouched into the Potomac was a very undistinguished little channel, still raw from the great flood, all sand and sandstone and mangled trees.

On this day there was practically no downstream flow in the great river, and they were able to paddle straight across to Roosevelt Island and poke into the many little overhangs there, to look up the slope of the island park through forest. Deer after deer; it was disturbing to Frank to see what a population boom there was among them, a kind of epidemic. The native predators that were now returning, and the occasional exotic feral (the jaguar?), were nowhere near numerous enough to cull them. Big rabbits, as everyone called them. One had to remember they were wild creatures, big mammals, therefore to be loved. That vivid embrace with the doe. It was an old mistake not to value the common wildlife. They did that with people and look at the result.

So: deer; the occasional porcupine; foxes; once a bobcat; and birds. They were almost back to the old depopulate forest from the time before the flood. Frank found this depressing. He grew almost to hate the sight of the deer, as they were in some sense the cohort of humans, part of humanity's own overpopulation surge. Then again, having them around beat a forest entirely empty; and from time to time he would catch a glimpse of something *other*. Brindled fur, striped flank, flash of color like a golden tamarind monkey; these and other brief signs of hidden life appeared. Because of the road bridges, Roosevelt Island was not really an island after all, but a sort of big wilderness peninsula. In that sense Teddy Roosevelt had the greatest D.C. monument of them all.

But on this day, as they were paddling back from the upstream tip of the island to the boathouse, Frank felt cold water gushing over his feet, thighs, and butt, all at once—catastrophic leak! "Hey!" he shouted, and then he had to hurry to wiggle out of the kayak's skirt and into the river. It really was coming in fast. Nothing for it but to start swimming, Charlie and Drepung there by his side, full of concern, and close enough that Frank was able to hold on to Charlie's stern end with one hand, and grasp the sunken bow of his kayak in the other, and kick to keep his position as the link between the two as Charlie dug in and paddled them back across the river to their dock. Cold but not frigid. Suddenly swimming! As if in San Diego. But the river water tasted silty.

Back on the dock they hauled Frank's kayak up and turned it over to drain it and inspect the bottom. Up near the very front, the hull had split along the midline, gaping wide enough to let in the water that had sunk it. "Factory defect," Frank said with quick disapproval. "Look, it split a seam. It must have been a bad melt job. I'll have to give the kayak company some grief about it."

"I should say so!" Charlie exclaimed. "Are you okay?"

"Sure. I'm just wet. I'll go get a change of clothes from my car." And Frank rolled the kayak back over, noting that neither Charlie nor Drepung seemed aware that this kayak, like most, was a single cast piece of plastic, with no seam on the keel to delaminate. They took his explanation at face value.

Which was a relief to him, as it would have been hard to find a way to explain why someone would want to melt a flaw into his kayak that would crack under the pressure of his paddling. He was having a hard time with that himself.

He opened his van and got out a change of clothes, looking around at the interior of the van curiously, feeling more and more worried—worried and angry both. Someone trying to harass him—to intimidate him—but why? What reaction did they want to induce from him, if any? And how could he counter them without falling into that particular reaction?

Caroline's ex—that face, sneering as he descended into the Metro. And Frank had thrown the hand axe at him. Suddenly the feeling came over Frank, in a wave, that he would throw it again if he had the chance. He wanted the chance. He realized he was furious and trying not to feel that. Also scared—mainly for Caroline, but for himself too. Who knew what this asshole would do?

.   .   .

He changed clothes in his van, made the short drive up Rock Creek Parkway to the zoo, parked off Broad Branch, and walked through the green trees out to Connecticut Avenue and the Delhi Dhaba. He found himself inside, seated at a corner table looking at a menu, and realized he had not decided a single move since leaving the boathouse. It had been automatic pilot; but now he had a menu to choose from, and he couldn't. Decision trees. The automatic pilot was gone. Something hot and angry; just order the curry like always. Indigestion before he had even started eating. Off again through the early evening. The days were getting longer. Twilight at the overlook, the salt lick at the bottom of the ravine. Big bodies in infrared. Most were deer, but also Ethiopian antelope; ibex; hedgehog. Rock Creek was still the epicenter of the feral population.

Back in his van he found the engine wouldn't start. Startled, he cursed, jumped out, looked under the hood.

The battery cables had been cut.

He tried to collect his thoughts. He looked up and down the dark streets. The van had been parked more or less at random, and locked. No way to get the hood up without getting inside the van; no way of getting into the van without a key. Well, dealers had master keys. Presumably spooks did too.

This must mean that Edward Cooper knew who he was. Knew that he was Caroline's helper, and no doubt presumed to be more, as he had thrown his hand axe at his head, etc. Cooper had him chipped, or at least his van.

The hair on the back of Frank's neck prickled. His feet were cold. He looked around casually as he called AAA on his FOG phone and waited for a tow. When the guy in the tow truck took a look under the hood, he said, "Ha." He took out his toolbox, installed a replacement cable. Frank thanked him, signed, got in the driver's seat; the engine coughed and started. Back out to the Khembalis' farm. He didn't know what else to do.

That night as he turned the matter over in his mind, he began to get both angrier and more frightened. If they had found him, did that mean they had found Caroline too? And if so what would they do? Where would they stop? What was their point?

And *where was Caroline*?

He had to talk to Edgardo again.

So he did, out on their lunch run the next day. They ran down the Mall toward the Lincoln Memorial. It was a good running route, almost like a track: two miles from the Capitol to the Lincoln Memorial, on grass or decomposed granite all the way. There were other runners in the White House compound, and sometimes they went out with some OMB guys, but Edgardo and Frank now usually ran by themselves. It gave them the chance to talk.

They had run a chip wand over each other before taking off, and after they got going Frank described what was happening.

"My computer crash could have been them too. Maybe they were erasing signs that they had broken into my system."

"Maybe." Edgardo was shaking his head back and forth like Stevie Wonder, his lips pursed unhappily. "I agree, if they are the ones vandalizing your stuff, then they must have found out you're the one who helped. But I'm wondering how they did that, if they did."

"And if they've managed to relocate Caroline as well."

"That doesn't follow," Edgardo pointed out. "You're not trying to hide, and she is."

"I know. I'm just wondering. I'm worried. Because I don't know how they found me."

They pounded on a few paces thinking about it.

"Do you have no way of getting in contact with her?"

"No."

"You need that. That should be a normal part of the repertory. Next time she contacts you, tell her you need a dead drop, or a dedicated phone."

"I said that up on Mount Desert Island, believe me."

"She was reluctant?"

"I guess. She said she would get in touch. But that was four months ago."

"Hmm."

More running. Frank had begun to sweat.

Edgardo said, "I wonder. You said she said she is surveilling her ex. So if you can use that surveillance, tap into it to get a message to her . . ."

"Like pin a message to his door, and hope she'll see it and read it on camera before he gets home?"

"Well, something like that. You could show up at his doorstep, hold up a sign, then off you go. Your gal can stop her video, if she's got one there, and read what you've said."

"I have to be sure not to lead him to her though." A few more strides. Frank snorted unhappily. "It's too complicated, this stuff. I hate it. I just want to be able to call her."

"You need a dead drop. They're easy to set up."

"Yeah, but I need to find her first."

"Yeah yeah. You need to change vans too, if that's really how they followed you north. My friend still doesn't believe that."

"Yeah well they just found it again. I should get rid of it."

"Wait till you need to be clear, then buy an old one for cash. But for now let's just run. That's all the going round in circles we need right now."

"Okay. Sorry. Thanks."

"No problem. We will figure something out and prevail. The world and your love life deserve no less."

"Shit."

"Did you schedule a time for that nasal surgery yet?"

"No! Let's just run!"

The feeling of helplessness and indecision grew in him until he couldn't sleep at night. You have to decide to sleep a night through. In one of the long cold insomniac hours, listening unhappily to Rudra's uneven snore, he realized he had to do something about finding Caroline, no matter how futile it might be, just to give himself some small release from the anxiety of the situation. So the next night, after Rudra fell asleep, he drove to Bethesda, and at 3 A.M. parked and walked quickly to the apartment building that Caroline and her ex had lived in. If Caroline had the place under surveillance then she would presumably have some kind of motion sensor on a camera. If she saw Frank in that doorway, she would know that he wanted her to contact him. Caroline's ex might also have a security camera on the building, but it had to be tried.

He walked up to the steps, looked out at the buildings across the street, said "call me," feeling awkward. Then off again into the night. Lots of people came to that door, there was no guarantee she would see him, but it was the best he could do. He couldn't decide whether it was adequate or not. When he tried to figure out what to do he felt dizzy and sick to his stomach.

He went to work the next day wondering if she would see him. Wondering where she was and what she was thinking. Wondering how she could stay away from him so long. He wouldn't have done it to her.

At work they were still settling into the Old Executive Offices. Diane and the others were obviously pleased to be there. It still amazed Frank that physical proximity mattered in questions of power. It was as clear a sign of their primate nature as any he could think of, as it made no sense given current technology. But Nixon had kicked his science advisor out of these offices, so Phil Chase's order to return to the fourth floor of this old monstrosity, and take up one whole wing, was a sign. And there was even a practical sense in which it was useful, in that once inside the security barrier of the White House compound, they were free to walk next door any time they wanted, to consult in person with the President's various staffers, or even with the man himself.

Their building was officially named after Eisenhower, but in practice always referred to by its older name, the Old Executive Offices. It was spectacularly ugly on the outside, disfigured by many pairs of nonfunctional pillars, some rising from ground level to the third floor, others filling embrasures on the upper stories, and all blackened as if by one of London's coal smogs.

Inside it was merely a very old musty office, retrofitted for modern conveniences a few too many years before, and otherwise about as dim as the outside of the hulk might suggest. For those coming over from the light-filled NSF tower in Arlington it was a real step down, but all they really needed were rooms with electrical outlets and high-speed internet, and these they had. And it had to be admitted that it was interesting to look out one's window across a little gap to the business side of the White House. A sign that Phil Chase understood the importance of science.

So, at least, Diane seemed to take it. She had commandeered one of the offices with a window facing the White House, and set her desk in such a way that she saw it when she looked up. She still did not actually see Phil Chase much, but he texted her on a regular basis, and Charlie and other staffers were always dropping by.

Her main conference room was across the hall from her office, and as soon as it was outfitted she convened the climate group. Frank took notes doggedly, trying to stay focused. It looked like the Arctic ice would not break up this summer, which would set a base for an even thicker layer next winter. This meant that the northern extension of the Gulf Stream would probably stay salty for the next few seasons, which meant the Gulf Stream's heat would again be transferred north, and this in turn would bring heat back to the Arctic. To Frank it was beginning to look like a lose-lose situation, where no matter what they did things were likely to degrade. It was a war of feedback loops, and very difficult to model. Kenzo pointed to the graphs on his last slide and simply shrugged. "I don't know," he said. "Nobody knows. There are too many factors in play now. Cloud action itself is enough to confound the models. The one thing I can say for sure is we need to reduce carbon emissions as fast as possible. We're in damage control mode at best, until we get to clean energy and transport. The seawater pH change alone is a huge problem, because if the ocean food chain collapses . . ."

"Can that danger be quantified?" Diane asked.

"Sure, they're trying. What's clear is that if the plankton and the coral reefs both die, the oceans could go catastrophic. A major mass extinction, and there's no recovering from that. Not in less than several million years."

Unlike his pronouncements on the weather, Kenzo exhibited none of his usual happy ringmaster air. This stuff could not be interpreted as too interesting scientifically to be lamented; it was simply bad, even dire. To see Kenzo actually being serious startled Frank, even frightened him. Kenzo Hayakawa, unhappily making a dire warning? Could there be a worse sign?

And yet there were things to try. Springtime reports from Siberia indicated that the Russians' altered lichen was still growing faster than predicted. "Like pond scum," one of the Russians reported. This was very unlike ordinary lichen, and seemed to confirm the idea that the bioengineered version was behaving more like algae or fungus than the symbiosis of the two, which is what lichen was. That was interesting, perhaps ominous; Kenzo thought it could cause a major carbon drawdown from the atmosphere if it continued. "Unless it kills the whole Siberian forest, and then who knows? Maybe instead of gray goo, we die by green goo, eh?"

"Please, Kenzo."

"Hey I'm not joking. It's a bummer they let that stuff loose, that's all."

After the meeting Diane came by Frank's new office, which had no living room feel whatsoever—in fact it looked like he had been condemned to clerk in some bureaucratic hell, right next to Bob Cratchit or Bartleby the Scrivener. Even Diane noticed this, to the point of saying, "It's a pretty weird old facility."

"Yes. I don't think I'll ever like it like I did NSF."

"No. Want to go out and hunt for a new coffee place?"

"Sure." Frank got his windbreaker from its hook and they left the building and then the compound. Just south of the White House was the Ellipse, and then the Washington Monument, towering over the scene like an enormous sundial on a English lawn. The buildings around the White House included the Treasury, the World Bank, and any number of other massive white piles, filling the blocks so that every street seemed walled. It was very bad in human terms; even Arlington was better.

But there were many coffee shops and delis tucked into ground-floor spaces, and so the two of them hiked in an oblong pattern, looking at the possibilities and chatting. Nothing looked appealing, and finally Diane suggested one of the tourist kiosks out on the Mall. They were already east of the White House, and when they came out on the great open expanse into low sun they could see much of official Washington, with the Capitol and the Washington Monument towering over everything else. That was the dominant impression Frank had of downtown at this point; the feel of it was determined principally by the height limit, which held all buildings to a maximum of twelve stories, well under the height of the Washington Monument. The downtown was therefore as if sheared off by a knife at that height, an unusual sight in a modern city, giving it a nineteenth-century look, as for instance Paris after Haussmann. This odd invisible ceiling gave D.C. whatever human feel it had.

Diane nodded as he tried to express these mixed feeling. She pointed out the lion statues surrounding Ulysses S. Grant: "See, they're Disney lions!"

"Like the ones on the Connecticut Avenue bridge."

"I wonder which came first, Disney or these guys?"

"These must have, right?"

"I don't know. Disney lions have looked the same at least since *Dumbo*."

"Maybe Disney came here and saw these."

Within a week they had a new regular walk together. One afternoon as they drank their coffee, Diane suggested they return to work by way of a pass through the National Gallery annex, and there they found a Frederic Church exhibit. "Hey!" Frank said, remembering his intense time on Mount Desert Island, which he now saw through the eyes of the painter who had invented rusticating. His paintings were superb. He had put a photorealist technique in the service of a Transcendentalist eye; the result was the visionary, sacred landscape of Emerson and Thoreau, right there on the walls of the National Gallery. "My God," Frank said more than once. This was also the time of Darwin and Humboldt, and the wall-sized *Heart of the Andes,* fifteen feet high and twenty wide, stood there illustrating all of natural selection at once.

"It's like the IMAX movie of its time," Diane said.

In the next room they saw Church grow older and go hallucinogenic. They were the best landscape paintings Frank had ever seen. A giant close-up of the water leaping off the lip of Niagara Falls; the Parthenon at sunset; waves striking the Maine coast. Frank goggled so much that Diane laughed at him, but he could not restrain himself. How was it he had never been exposed to this art? What was American education anyway, that they could all grow up and not be steeped in Emerson and Thoreau, Audubon and Church? It was like inheriting billions and then forgetting you had it, only worse, because the kind of poverty involved was so much more profound.

Finally Diane put her hand to his arm and directed him out of the gallery and back toward their new office. Back into the blackened old building, if not arm in arm, than shoulder to shoulder.

Their next meeting had to do with the latest news from Antarctica. Researchers were trying to determine how much of the West Antarctic Ice Sheet might come off, and how fast. They had found that several big ice streams, which ran like immense glaciers through more stationary parts of the ice sheet, had accelerated beyond even the accelerations documented in previous decades. Correlated with this, all Antarctic temperatures, of air, water, and ice, had gone up, and this was causing meltwater on the surface of the ice sheet to pour down holes and cracks, where it refroze, expanded, and split the ice around it. When this "water wedging" reached all the way through the ice sheet, the water flowed down unimpeded and pooled underneath the ice, thus lubricating its slide into the sea.

So the ice streams were moving faster because there was more under-ice meltwater flowing downstream and carrying the ice overhead with it. This explained why the ice streams were now acting more like slow stupendous rivers than glaciers as usually observed.

Diane interrupted the two glaciologists making the report before they got too deep into the mysteries of their calling. "So what kind of sea level rise are we looking at?" she asked. "How much, and when?"

The glaciologists and the NOAA people looked around at each other, then made a kind of collective shrug. "It's difficult to say," one finally ventured. "It depends so much on stuff we don't know."

"Give me parameters then, and your best bets."

"Well, I don't know, I'm definitely getting out of my comfort zone here, but I'd say as much as half of the West Antarctic Ice Sheet could detach in the next several years. Here, and here," red-lighting the map, "are under-ice ranges connecting the Peninsular Range and the Transantarctics, and those create catchment basins which will probably anchor a good bit of these regions," making big red circles. Having made his uncertainty disclaimer, he was now carving up the map like a geography teacher. Diane ignored this discrepancy, as did everyone else; it was understood that he was now guessing, his red circles not data but rather him thinking aloud.

"So—that implies what, a couple-few meters of sea level rise?"

"Yes. A couple."

"So, okay. That's pretty bad. Time scales, again?"

"Hard to say? Maybe—if these rates hold—thirty years? Fifty?"

"Okay. Well . . ." Diane looked around the room. "Any thoughts?"

"We can't afford a sea level rise that high."

"What do you mean? It's not like we can stop it."

They turned with renewed interest to Frank's suggestion of flooding the world's desertified lake basins. An informal NSF study had suggested that big salt lakes would indeed cause clouds to form and precipitation to fall downwind, so some watersheds would receive more water. Local weather patterns would change with this rise in humidity, but as they were changing anyway, specific changes might be hard to distinguish from background. Ultimate effects impossible to predict. Frank noted how many studies were coming to that conclusion. It was like nerve damage, or brain surgery.

They all looked at each other. Maybe, someone suggested, if that's what it takes to save the seacoasts from flooding, the global community could compensate the new lakes' host nations for whatever environmental damage was assessed. Possibly a seawater market could be established along with a carbon market; possibly they could be linked. Surely the most prosperous quarter of humanity could find ways to compensate the people, often poor, who would be negatively impacted by the creation of these seawater reservoirs.

Frank said, "I've tried some back-of-the-envelope numbers, estimating the capital worth of the major port cities and other coastal infrastructure, and gotten figures like two quadrillion dollars."

General Wracke, an active member of Diane's advisory group, put his hands together reverently. "That's a lot of construction," he said.

"Yes. On the other hand, for comparison purposes, the infrastructural value of property in the superdry basins of Africa, Asia, and the American basin and range comes to well under ten billion dollars, unless you throw in Salt Lake City, which by the way has a legal limit in Utah state law as to how high the Great Salt Lake is allowed to rise, not much higher than it is now. I don't know why they did that. Anyway, in global terms, financially or even demographically, there's almost nothing in those basins. Statistically insignificant populations to displace, plus the possibility of building new settlements by new water. Local weather deranged, but it is already. So . . ."

The general nodded and asked about pumping water back up onto the East Antarctic Ice Sheet, which was very high and stable. Another part of the NSF report was devoted to this question. The pumped seawater would freeze and then sit unconformably as a kind of salty ice cap on the fresh ice cap. Every cubic kilometer of seawater placed up there would reduce sea level by that same amount, without the radical changes implied by creating new salt seas all across the thirties north and south. Could only pump half of the year if using solar power to move the water uphill.

The energy requirements needed to enact the lift and transfer remained a stumbling block; they would have to build many powerful clean energy systems.

But they had to do that anyway, as several of them pointed out. The easy oil would soon be gone, and burning the oil and coal that was left would cook the world. In fact they would have to leave some 2,500 gigatons of fossil carbon in the ground, as what the report called "stranded assets." Estimated worth in current markets, $1,600 trillion. Estimated cost to civilization, Frank's $2 quadrillion. Estimated cost to the biosphere, the sixth great mass extinction event in Earth's history. Clean energy therefore seemed to pencil out. So if they had it, and some combination of sunlight, wind, wave, tide, currents, nuclear, and geothermal power were harnessed to create civilization's energy, it would not only replace the burning of fossil fuels, which was imperative anyway, but possibly provide the power to save the current sea level as well.

But where's the money going to come from to do it? someone asked.

"The military budgets of the world equal about two trillion dollars a year," Frank noted, "half of that coming from the United States. Maybe we can't afford that anymore. Maybe that money could be reallocated. And we do need a really big manufacturing capacity here, which is what the military-industrial complex already is. Same with the carbon industry, for that matter. What if those complexes were redirected to these projects? How long would it take for them to reconfigure and do the job?"

Dream on, someone muttered.

Others thought it over, or punched numbers into their phones, testing possibilities. Of course redirecting the military and fossil fuel subsidies of the world was unrealistic. But it was worth bringing up, Frank judged, to suggest the size of the world's industrial capacity. What could be done if humanity were not trapped in its own institutions? " 'To wrest Freedom from the grasp of Necessity,' " Frank said. "Who said that?"

Again people were beginning to look at him strangely. Dream on, oh desperate dreamer, their looks said. But it wasn't just him who was desperate.

"You're beginning to sound like the Khembalis," Anna said. But it was clear she liked that, she was pleased by that. And if Anna approved, Frank felt he must in some sense be on the right track.

By the time they were done with that meeting it was late, the wind barreling through the empty streets of the federal district.

"What about dinner?" Diane said to Frank when they had a moment in private, and Frank nodded. She said, "I still don't know any restaurants around here, but we can look."

"Let's see what we find."

And off they went, on another date in the nation's capital.

It was a fun date. They found a Greek restaurant, and sat across a little table and talked over the meeting and the day and everything else. Frank drank a glass of retsina, a glass of ouzo, and a cup of Greek coffee, all while wolfing down dolmades, sliced octopus legs in oil, and moussaka. He laughed a lot. Looking across the table at Diane's round face, so vivacious and intelligent, so charismatic and powerful, he thought: I love this woman.

He could not think about the feeling. He shied away from the thought and just felt it. Everything else at the moment was unreal, or at least nonpresent. He focused on the present in the way Rudra was always encouraging him to do. The advantages of such a focus were evident in a certain calmness that spread through him, a feeling that might have been happiness. Or maybe it was the food, the alcohol, the caffeine. The tastes and looks and sounds. Her face. Were those the elements of happiness? A smile, a glance, Emerson had said, what ample borrowers of eternity they are!

Afterward they walked back to the compound, and Frank walked her to her car in the underground parking lot.

"Good night, that was nice."

"Yes it was." She looked up and Frank leaned over, their lips met in a perfect little kiss, and off he went.

He drove to the Khembali farm with his heart all aflutter. He didn't know what he thought. Rudra was asleep and he was glad, and then sorry. He tried to sleep and could not sleep. Finally he sat up and turned on his laptop.

Thoreau was a solitary. He fell in love with his brother's girlfriend, and proposed to her after his brother had proposed to her and been turned down. Henry too was turned down. There were rumors the girl's father did not think the Thoreaus were good enough for her. But if she had insisted . . .

Anyway Henry became a solitary. "There was a match found for me at last. I fell in love with a shrub oak."

That night the website had something from his journal:

> I spend a considerable portion of my time observing the habits
> of the wild animals, my brute neighbors. By their various move-
> ments and migrations they fetch the year about to me. Very sig-
> nificant are the flight of the geese and the migration of suckers,
> etc., etc. But when I consider that the nobler animals have been
> exterminated here,—the cougar, panther, lynx, wolverine, wolf,
> bear, moose, deer, the beaver, the turkey, etc., etc.,—I cannot
> but feel as if I lived in a tamed, and, as it were, emasculated
> country. Would not the motions of those larger and wilder ani-
> mals have been more significant still? Is it not a maimed and
> imperfect nature that I am conversant with? As if I were to study
> a tribe of Indians that had lost all its warriors. When I think
> what were the various sounds and notes, the migrations and
> works, and changes of fur and plumage which ushered in the
> spring and marked the other seasons of the year, I am reminded
> that this my life in nature, this particular round of natural phe-
> nomena which I call a year, is lamentably incomplete. I list to a
> concert in which so many parts are wanting. The whole civilized
> country is to some extent turned into a city, and I am that citi-
> zen whom I pity. All the great trees and beasts, fishes and fowl
> are gone.

From his journal, March 23, 1856. He had been thirty-eight years old. What would he think now, after another century and a half of destruction and loss? Maybe he would not have been surprised. He had seen it already started. Frank groaned.

"What wrong?"

"Oh, nothing. Sorry I woke you."

"I was not sleeping. I don't sleep much."

"You sounded like you were sleeping."

"No."

"Maybe you were dreaming."

"No. What wrong?"

"I was thinking about all the animals that are in trouble. In danger of extinction. Thoreau was writing about the predators being wiped out."

"Ah well. You still see animals in park?"

"Yes, but mostly just deer now."

"Ah well."

Rudra fell back asleep. After a while Frank drifted into uneasy dreams. Then he was awake again and thinking about Diane. He wasn't going to fall asleep; it was four. He got up and made his way out of the treehouse and across the farm to his van. Back into the city, down Connecticut from the already-crowded Beltway. Left on Brandywine, park on Linnean, get out and cross Broad Branch, and thus out into Rock Creek Park.

He hiked around the rim of the new gorge, and saw nothing but a single deer. He hiked up to Fort DeRussy, back down on the eastern wild way, and saw nothing but a trio of deer, standing upslope like wary statues. He decided as he watched them that he would be the predator—that he would scare these creatures, and at the same time test his ability, and see how long he could keep them in sight, not as a stalker, but a predator in pursuit. He set the timer on his wristwatch to zero, clicked it, and took off after them, up the open forest floor with its black soil underfoot, sprinting hard. They bolted over the nearest ridge, he flew up to it—no deer to be seen! Empty forest! But where had they—he stopped his watch. 4.82 seconds. He barked a laugh and stood there for a while, panting.

When he started walking again he headed toward site 21, to see if the guys were there, and check in with his treehouse.

Except from a distance he saw that something was wrong with it. He ran to it, trying to understand the gap in the air. When he got there he saw it had been cut down.

He inspected the trunk. Cut by a chainsaw, a smallish one it seemed by the sweep of the cut marks. The tree had fallen across Rock Creek; you could have used the trunk as a bridge over the stream. Maybe someone had needed a bridge. But no. You could cross the creek almost anywhere.

The treehouse itself was part of the wreckage on the far bank. At some point last year he had removed all of his gear except for the winch.

He crossed the creek on boulders, took a look; the winch was gone. Only the plywood sheets and two-by-fours were left, horribly askew, with some of the plywood loose on the ground.

He sat down next to these fragments. They were just sticks. He was never going to have lived in this treehouse again. So it didn't matter. Still he felt as if stabbed in the heart.

Edward Cooper had probably done this, or had it done. Of course it might have been total strangers, looking to scavenge whatever the treehouse might have held, like for instance the winch. Surely this Cooper would have left the winch as part of his revenge, as mockery. But maybe not. He didn't really know. There seemed to be a pattern—computer, kayak, van. His stuff and his life. It looked like deliberate action.

He didn't know what to do.

One Saturday the Quiblers got to a project they had been planning for some time, which was the installation of garden beds in the backyard. No more suburban lawn wasting their land!

And indeed it was a great pleasure to Charlie to cut big rectangles of turf out of the backyard and wheelbarrow these out to the street for disposal by the composting trucks. He was sick of mowing that yard. There was some old lumber stacked at the back of the garage, and now he and Nick laid lengths of it down in the remaining lawn to serve as borders. Then they transferred many wheelbarrow loads of expensive amended soil from the pile in the driveway where the dump trunk had left it, around the house to the rectangles, dodging Joe at many points along the way. The resulting raised beds were loamy and black and looked highly productive and artificial.

Nick and Anna were now working the soil in, and planting their first vegetables. It was full spring now, middle of May, steamy and green, and so they planted the usual summer vegetables: tomatoes, zucchini, strawberries, peppers, pumpkins, melons, basil, eggplant, cilantro, cucumbers.

Nick stood looking down at a broccoli plant, small and delicate between his feet. "So where will the broccoli come out?" he asked Charlie.

Charlie stared at the plant. It looked like an ornamental. "I don't know," he confessed, feeling a little jolt of fear. They didn't know anything.

Nick rolled his eyes. "Well, if we're lucky they won't show up at all."

"Come on now. Broccoli is good for you."

One of their agreements was that they would plant vegetables that Nick and Joe liked to eat, which was a severe constraint, but one they had agreed to, because it was not exclusive; they were planting for Anna and Charlie too. But for the boys it was down to potatoes, an entire bed of them, and carrots. Joe would eat some other vegetables, but Nick would not, and so he was put in charge of the carrot bed. These were to be planted from seed, and apparently the soil had to be specially amended. Sandy soil was best,

and white cloth laid over the soil during germination was recommended—by Drepung, who was serving as their consultant on this project.

"Although it shouldn't be me," he kept saying, "I don't know anything
about gardening really, it's all Qang at our place, you should have her over
to do things like plant carrot seed. That one is tricky. She would do a fire
puja."

Still, he helped them to get it planted, on his hands and knees digging,
and showing worms to Joe. After the planting it was mostly a matter of
watering and weeding. Also removing snails and slugs. Joe carried these
carefully to the back of their lot, where they could start life over in the
weeds bordering the lawn.

"Don't overwater," Charlie advised Nick as he sprayed water from a hose.
"You have to be precise in how much you water them. I estimate this much,
if you want to be accurate," waving the spray back and forth.

"Do you mean accurate or precise?" Anna asked from the new flower
bed.

"No quibbling allowed."

"I'm not quibbling! It's an important distinction."

"What do you mean? *Accurate* and *precise* mean precisely the same
thing!"

"They do not."

"What do you mean," Charlie was giggling at her now, "how so?"

"Accuracy," she said, "means how close an estimate is to the true value.
So if you estimate something is five percent and it turns out to be eight
percent, then you weren't very accurate."

"This is statistics."

"Yes. And precision refers to how broad your estimate is. Like, if you
estimate something is between five and eight percent, then you aren't being
very precise, but if you say between 4.9 and 5.1 percent, then it's more precise."

"I see," Charlie said, nodding solemnly.

"Quit it! It's a very important distinction!"

"Of course it is. I wasn't laughing at that."

"At what then?"

"At you!"

"But why?"

"Oh, no reason."

"It is a real distinction," Nick pointed out to Charlie.

"Oh of course, of course!"

This then became one of the recurrent motifs of the Quiblers on patrol, a distinction applicable, once you agreed it existed, to an amazing number of situations. Precise or accurate? Well, let's think about it.

On the way to the garden store to get more stakes and other supplies, Charlie said, "I wonder how many cubic feet of compost we need if we want to cover all four of the beds, let's see, they're six by twelve, say a foot deep in compost, make it simple . . ."

"Mom can tell you."

"No that's all right, I'm working on it—"

"Two hundred and eighty-eight cubic feet," Anna said, while driving.

"I told you she could."

"It isn't fair," Charlie said, still looking at his fingers. "She uses all these tricks from when she was in math club."

"Come on," Anna objected.

Nick was helpless with laughter. "Yeah right—she uses all these clever fiendish tricks—like *multiplication*," and they laughed all the way to the store.

Unfortunately their new spring quickly became the hottest and driest on record in the Potomac watershed, and soon, it having been a dry winter also, the region had to resort to water rationing. Between that and the mosquitoes, everyone began to reminisce with affection about the long winter, and wonder if it had been such a good idea to restart the Gulf Stream, since cold winters were so much preferable to drought. Crops were dying, the rivers falling low, streams drying out, fish populations dying; it was bad. A bit of snow and cold would have been easy in comparison. You could always throw on more clothes when it got cold, but in this heat!

But of course they didn't have a choice.

The Quiblers did what they could to micro-irrigate their crops, and they had enough water for such a small garden; but many of the plants died anyway. "We're only going to have about a fifty percent survival rate, if that!"

"Is that being accurate or being precise?"

"I hope neither!"

Anna was going to websites like safeclimate.net or fightglobalwarming.com and seeing how they rated when she entered their household statistics on a carbon burn chart. She was interested in the different methods the sites were using. Some accepted general descriptions as answers, others wanted the figures from your heating and electric bill, from your car's odometer, and its real miles per gallon. Your actual air travel miles, with charts of distances between major flying destinations there to make the calculation. "The air travel is killer," Anna muttered. "I thought it was a really energy-efficient way to travel, but not really."

Giving her numbers to play with was like giving catnip to the cats, and Charlie watched her affectionately, but with a little bit of worry, as she speed-typed around on a spreadsheet she had adapted from the chart. Despite their garden's contribution to their food supply, which she estimated at less than two percent of their caloric intake, and the flex schedule for power that they had signed up for with their power provider, still they were burning about seventy-five tons of carbon a year. Equivalent to eight football fields of Brazilian rain forest, the site said. Per year.

"You just can't get a good number in a suburban home with a car and all," she said annoyed. "And if you fly at all."

"It's true." Charlie stared over her shoulder at her spreadsheet. "I don't see what else we can do here either, given the infrastructure."

"I know. But I wish there was a way. Nick! Turn that light off, please!"

"Mom, you're the one who told me to turn it on."

"That's when you were using it. Now you're not."

"Mom."

CHAPTER 26

SACRED SPACE

Being Argentinean, he was angry. Not that all Argentineans were angry but many were, and rightfully so, after the dirty war and its dirty resolution—a general amnesty for everybody for everything, even the foulest crimes. In other words repression of the past and of even the idea of justice, and of course the return of the repressed is guaranteed, and always a nightmare.

So Edgardo Alfonso had left Argentina behind, like so many other children of the desaparacedos, *unable to live among the torturers and murderers who were free to walk the streets and ride the trams, who stared at Edgardo over their newspapers which held on their backsides the articles Edgardo had written identifying and denouncing them. He had had to leave to remain sane.*

So of course he was at the Kennedy Center to see an evening of Argentinean tango, Bocca's troupe on Bocca's farewell tour, where the maestro would dance with a ladder and handstand his way to heaven one last time, to Piazzolla's "Soledad." Edgardo cared nothing for dance per se, and despised tango the dance the way certain Scottish acquaintances winced at the sound of bagpipes; but Edgardo was a Piazzollista, and so he had to go. It was not often one got a chance to hear Astor Piazzolla's music played live, and of course it would never be the same with Astor gone, but the proof of the strength of his composing was in how these new bands backing the dance troupes would play their accompaniments to the dancers, tangos for the most part made of the utterly clichéd waltzes, two-steps, ballads, and church music that had been cobbled together to make old-style tango, and then they would start a piece by

Astor and the whole universe would suddenly become bigger—deeper, darker, more tragic. A single phrase on the bandoneon and all of Buenos Aires would appear in the mind at once. The feeling was as accurate as if music possessed a kind of acupuncture that could strike particular nerves of the memory, evoking everything.

The audience at the Kennedy Center was full of Latin Americans, and they watched the dancers closely. Bocca was a good choreographer and the dances were insistent on being interesting—men with men, women with women, little fights, melodramas, clever sex—but all the while the band was hidden behind a black curtain, and Edgardo began to get angry yet again, this time that someone would conceal performers for so long. Their absence bit him and he began to hate the dancers, he wanted to boo them off the stage, he even wondered for a second if the music had been prerecorded and this tour being done on the cheap.

Finally however they pulled back the curtain, and there was the band: bandoneon, violin, piano, bass, electric guitar. Edgardo already knew they were a very tight group, playing good versions of the Piazzolla songs, faithful to the originals, and intense. Tight band, incandescent music—it was strange now to observe how young they were, strange but wonderful: music at last, the ultimate point of the evening. Huge relief.

They had been revealed in order to play "Adios Nonino," Piazzolla's good-bye to his dead father, his most famous song out of the hundreds in his catalog, and even if not the best, or rather not Edgardo's favorite, which was "Mumuki," still it was the one with the most personal history. Edgardo's father had been disappeared. God knew what had happened to him, Edgardo resisted thinking about this as being part of the poison, part of the torture echoing down through the years, one of the many reasons torture was the worst evil of all, and, when the state used and condoned it, the death of a nation's sense of itself. This was why Edgardo had had to leave, also because his mother still met every Thursday afternoon in the Plaza de Mayo in Buenos Aires with all the other mothers and wives of the desaparacedos, all wearing white scarves symbolic of their lost children's diapers, to remind Argentina and the world (and in Buenos Aires these two were the same) of the crimes that still needed to be remembered, and the criminals who still must face justice. It was more than Edgardo could face on a weekly basis. Now even in his nice apartment east of Dupont Circle he had to keep the blinds shut on Sunday mornings so as not to see the dressed-up kindly Americans, mostly black, walking down the street to their church, so as not to start again the train of thought that would lead him to memories and the anger. Especially now that the Americans too had become torturers.

He had to look away or it would kill him. His health was poor. He had to run at least fifty miles a week to keep himself from dying of anger. If he didn't he couldn't sleep and quickly his blood pressure ballooned dangerously high. You could run a lot of anger out of you. For the rest, you needed Piazzolla.

His own father had taken him to see Piazzolla at the Teatro Odeón, in 1973, shortly before being disappeared. Piazzolla had recently disbanded his great quintet and gone to Europe with Amelita, gone through the melodramas of that relationship and its breakup and a succession of bands trying to find a Europop sound, trying electronica and string quartets and getting angrier and angrier at the results (though they were pretty good, Edgardo felt), so that when he came back to Buenos Aires for the summer of '73–'74 and regathered the old quintet (with the madman Tarantino sitting in on piano) he was not the same confident composer devoted to destroying tango and rebuilding it from the ground up for the sake of his modernist ambitions, but a darker and more baffled man, an exile back home again but determined to forge on no matter what. But now more willing to admit the tango in him, willing to admit his genius was Argentinean as well as transcendental. He could now submit to tango, fuse with it. And his audience was much changed as well, they no longer took Piazzolla for granted or thought he was a crazy egotist. With the quintet dispersed they had finally understood they had been hearing something new in the world, not just a genius but a great soul, and of course at that point, now that they had understood it, it was gone.

But then it had come back. Maybe only for one night, everyone thought it was only for one night, everyone knew all of a sudden that life itself was a fragile and evanescent thing and no band lasted long, and so the atmosphere in the theater had been absolutely electric, the audience's attentiveness quivering and hallucinatory, the fierce applause like thanks in a church, as if finally you could do the right thing in a church and clap and cheer and whistle to show your appreciation of God's incredible work. At the end of the show they had leaped to their feet and gone mad with joy and regret, and looking around him young Edgardo had understood that adults were still as full of feeling as he was, that they did not "grow up" in any important respect, and that he would never lose the huge feelings surging in him. An awesome sight, never to be forgotten. Perhaps it was his first real memory.

Now, here, on this night in Washington, D.C., the capital of everything and of nothing, the dancers were dancing on the stage and the young band at the back was charging lustily through one of Piazzolla's angriest and happiest tunes, the furiously fast "Michelangelo 70." Beautiful. Astor had understood how to deal with the tragedy of Buenos Aires better than anyone, and Edgardo had never ceased to apply his lesson: you had to attack sadness and depression head on in a fury, you had to dance through it in a state of utmost energy, and then it would lead you out the other side to some kind of balance, even to that high humor that the racing tumble of bandoneon notes so often expressed, that joy that ought to be basic but in this world had to be achieved or as it were dragged out of some future better time: life ought to be joy, some-day it would be joy, therefore on this night we celebrate that joy in anticipa-tion, and so capture an echo of it, a ricochet from the future. That this was the best they could do in this supposedly advanced age of the world was funny. And there weren't that many things that were both real and funny, so there you had to hang your hat, on how funny it was that they could be as gods in a world more beautiful and just than humanity could now imagine, and yet instead were torturers on a planet where half the people lived in extreme im-miseration while the other half killed in fear of being thrust into that immis-eration, and were always willing to look the other way, to avoid seeing the genocide and speciescide and biospherecide they were committing, all unnec-essarily, out of fear and greed. Hilarious! One had to laugh!

During intermission the beautifully dressed people filled the halls outside and gulped down little plastic flutes of wine as fast as they could. The sound of three thousand voices all talking at once in a big enclosed space was per-haps the most beautiful music of all. That was always true, but on this night there was a lot of Spanish being spoken, so it was even more true than usual. A bouncing glossolalia. This was how the apostles had sounded when the tongues of fire had descended on them, all trying to express directly in scat singing the epiphany of the world's glory. One of Piazzolla's bandoneon lines even seemed to bounce through the talk. No doubt one appeal of that thin nasal tone was how human it sounded, like the voice of a lover with a cold.

And all the faces. Edgardo was on the balcony with his elbows resting on the railing, looking down at the crowd below, all the hair so perfect, the raven blaze of glossy black tresses, the colorful clothes, the strong faces so full of the character of Latin America. This was what they looked like, they had nothing to be ashamed of in this world, indeed where could you find handsomer faces.

His friend Umberto stood down there near the door, holding two wine flutes. When he looked up and met Edgardo's eye, Edgardo raised his chin. Umberto jerked his head a fraction, indicating a meeting; Edgardo nodded once.

During the final song of the evening Edgardo closed his eyes and listened to the band rip through "Primavera Porteño," one of the greatest of all the maestro's compositions, bobbing and tapping his feet, uncaring of the people around him, let them think what they like, the whole audience should be on its feet at this moment! Which they were during the long ovation afterward, a nice thing to be part of, a Latin thing, lots of shouting and whistling, at least for an audience at the Kennedy Center. There was even a group above him to the right shouting, "As-tor—As-tor—As-tor!" which Edgardo joined with the utmost happiness, bellowing the name up at the group of enthusiasts and waving in appreciation. He had never gotten the chance to chant Astor's name in a cheer before, and it felt good in his mouth. He wondered if they did that in Buenos Aires now, or if it only happened in Europe, or here—Astor the perpetual exile, even in death.

Show over. All the people mingling as they made their exit. Outside it was still stifling. More Spanish in the gorgeous choir of the languages. Edgardo walked aimlessly in the crowd, then stopped briefly below the strange statue located on the lawn there, which appeared to portray a dying Quixote shooting a last arrow over his shoulder, roughly in the direction of the Saudi Arabian embassy. And there was Umberto approaching him, lighting a cigarette and coughing, and together they walked to the railing overlooking the river.

They leaned on the rail and watched obsidian sheets of water glide past.

They conversed in Spanish:

"So?"

"We're still looking into ways of isolating these guys."

"Is she still helping?"

"Yes, she's the decoy while we try to cut these guys out. She's playing the shell game with them."

"And you think Cooper is the leader?"

"Not sure about that. He may have a stovepipe that goes pretty high. That's one of the things we're still trying to determine."

"But he's part of ARDA?"

"Yes."

"And where did they relocate that most exciting program?"

"In a group suspended between Homeland and NSA. ARDA Prime."

Edgardo laughed. He danced a little tango step while singing the bitter wild riff at the start of "Primavera Porteño." "They are so fucking stupid, my friend! Could it get any more byzantine?"

"That's the point. It's a work of art."

"It's a fucking shambles. They must be scared out of their wits, granting they ever had any wits, which I don't. I mean if they get caught . . ."

"It will be hard to catch them outright. I think the best we can do is cut them out. But if they see that coming, they will fight."

"I'm sure. Is all of ARDA in on it?"

"No, I don't think so."

"That's good. I know some of those guys from my time at DARPA. I liked them. Some of them, anyway."

"I know. I'm sure the ones you liked are all innocent of this."

"Right." Edgardo laughed. "Fuck them. What should I tell Frank?"

"Tell him to hang in there."

"Do you think it would be okay to tip him that his girlfriend is still involved in a root canal?"

"I don't know." Umberto sucked on his cigarette, blew out a long plume of white smoke. "Not if you think he'll do anything different."

All Frank could think about now was how he could get in touch with Caroline. Apparently showing up in her surveillance of her ex had not worked; there was no way of telling why. Surely she had motion sensors to flag appearances. And so . . . Something must be wrong.

He could go to Mount Desert Island. He thought there was a good chance that Edgardo was right about her staying there. It was a big island, and she had obviously loved it; her idea of hiding out was tied to that place. If she kept a distance from Mary's place, somewhere else on the island, her ex would assume she had bolted elsewhere, and she would be able to lie low.

But in that case, how would Frank find her?

What would she have to have? What would she not stop doing? Shopping for food? Getting espressos? Bicycling?

He wasn't really sure; he didn't know her well enough to say. She had said there was great mountain biking to be had on the gravel carriage roads on the island, where no one would see you except other bikers. Did that mean he should go up and rent a mountain bike and ride around this network, or hang out at the backwoods intersections of these gravel roads, and wait for her to pass by? No. It took a long time to drive up there and back. If you couldn't fly you had to drive. And there was so much going on in D.C., and around the world; he needed to go to San Diego again, he needed to visit London, and to see that site in Siberia.

On the other hand, his tree had been cut down, his battery cables cut, his kayak wrecked, his computer destroyed. He had to deal with it somehow. It was in his face and in his thoughts. He had to do something.

Instead, he sat in the garden at the farm and weeded. He woke up at dawn to find Rudra at the window, looking out at the river. Quicksilver slick under mist streamers. Trees on the far bank looking like ghosts.

He helped Rudra with his morning English lessons. Rudra was now working from a primer prepared under the tutelage of the Dalai Lama, used to teach the Tibetan-speaking children their English:

"'There are good anchors to reality and bad anchors to reality. Try to avoid the bad ones.' Ha!" Rudra snorted. "Thanks for such wisdom, oh High Holiness! Look, he even calls them the Four Bad D's. It's like the Chinese, they are always Four Thises and Six Thats."

"The Eight Noble Truths?" Frank said.

"Bah. That's Chinese Buddhism."

"Interesting. And what exactly are the Four Bad D's?"

"Debt, depression, disease, death."

"Whoah. Those are four bad D's, all right. Are there four good D's? Are there four good, I don't know, anchors to reality?"

"Children, health, work, love."

"Man you are a sociobiologist. Could you add habits, maybe?"

"No. Number very important. Only room for four."

Frank laughed. "But it's such a good anchor. It's what allows you to love your life. You love your habits the way you love your home. As a kind of gravity that includes other emotions. Even hate."

Rudra shrugged. "I am an exile."

"Me too."

Rudra looked at him. "You can move back to your home?"

"Yes."

"Then you are not an exile. You are just not at home."

"I guess that's right."

"Why would you not move home if you could?"

"Work?" Frank said.

But it was a good question.

That night, as they were falling asleep in the ever so slightly rocking dark of their suspended room, the wind rustling the leaves of the grove, Frank came back to the morning's conversation.

"I've been thinking about good correlations. We need a numbered list of those. My good correlation is the one between living as close to a prehistoric life as you can, and being happy, and becoming more healthy, and reducing your consumption and therefore your impact on the planet. That's a very good correlation. Then Phil Chase had another one at his inaugural. He talked about how social justice and women's rights correlates with a steady-state replacement rate for the population, which would mean the end of rapid population growth, and thus reduce our load on the planet. That's another very good correlation. So, I'm thinking of calling them the Two Good Correlations."

"Two is not enough."

"What?"

"Two is not a big enough number for this kind of thing. There is never the Two This or the Two That. You need at least three, maybe more."

"But I only know two."

"You must think of some more."

"Okay, sure." Frank was falling asleep. "You have to help me though. The question will be, what's the third good correlation?"

"That's easy."

"What do you mean, what is it?"

"You think about it."

For some reason no one was hanging out at site 21 these days. Maybe the heat and the mosquitoes. Back at the farm Frank yanked weeds. He cut the grass of the lawn with a hand scythe, swinging it like a golf club, viciously driving shot after shot out to some distant green. At night in the dining room he ate at the end of a table, reading, bathed in a sea of Tibetan voices. Sometimes he would talk to Padma or Sucandra, then go to bed and read his laptop for a while. He missed the bros and their rowdy assholery. It occurred to him one night in the dining hall that not only was bad company better than no company, there were times when bad company was better than good company. But it was a different life now.

At work, project ideas were being screened by Diane's team, and some were getting placed into the mission architecture. There were very few weak points or question marks in this architecture! They could swap out power and transport in less than ten years!

But even if they were to stop burning carbon entirely, which was only a theoretical possibility for the sake of calculation, global temperatures would continue to rise for many years. The continuity effect, they called it, and it was a nasty problem to contemplate. It was an open question whether temperatures even in the best-case scenario might rise high enough to cross thresholds to create further positive feedbacks that would cause temperatures to rise even more. Models were not at all precise on this subject.

They continued to discuss the sea level problem, and Frank said, "China appears to like the idea. They say they've already done similar things, at Three Gorges of course, but also at four more dams like Three Gorges. Those are mostly for hydroelectric and flood control, but they're also seeing climate effects downwind. So they feel they've got experience with the process, and say they would be willing to do more of it. And the biggest basins on Earth are all theirs."

"But, saltwater lakes?"

"Any lake helps cloud formation, and those clouds hydrate the deserts downwind by precipitating out, and the rain is fresh water."

"Still, it's hard to imagine them sacrificing that much land."

"True. But clearly there's going to be something like carbon credits here, some kind of seawater credits, given to countries for taking up seawater. Maybe it will be combined with carbon trading, so that taking up seawater earns carbon credits. Or earns funding for desalination plants on the basin's new shorelines. Or whatever. Some kind of compensation."

Diane said, "I suppose we could arrange a treaty with them."

Later they worked on the Antarctic aspect of the plan. The dry basins of the world didn't have enough capacity to keep sea level in place anyway, so they needed to push the Antarctic idea too. If that ended up working, then in theory the East Antarctic Ice Sheet would be able to handle all possible excess, and the dry basins up north would only be filled if the net effects of doing so looked good to the host country.

"Sounds good. But it's a lot of water."

. . .

That night Frank walked out of the security gate on 17th Street, at the south end of the Old Executive Offices, and across the street there was a woman standing as if waiting for the light to change. His heart pounded in his chest like a child trying to escape. He stared—was it really her?

She nodded, jerked her head sideways: *follow me*. She walked up to G Street and Frank did too, on the other side of the street. His pulse was flying. An amazing physical response—well, but she had been out of touch and now there she was, her face so vivid, so distinctly hers, leaping out of reality into his mind. Oh my, oh my. Maybe she had seen him in her surveillance camera, or heard his mental call. So often telepathy seemed real. Or maybe she had been discovered and forced to go on the run again. In need of his help. It could be anything.

A red light stopped him. She had stopped too, and was not crossing with the green to him. Apparently they were to walk in parallel for a while, west on G Street. It was a long light. If you felt each second fully, a lifetime would become an infinity. Maybe that was the point of being in love, or the reward. Oh my. He could feel the knock of his heart in the back of his nose. He followed her down G Street, past the Watergate complex, across the parkway, through the boating center parking lot, down into the trees at the mouth of Rock Creek, where finally they could converge, could crash into each other's arms and hug each other hard, hard, hard. Ah God, his partner in exile, his fellow refugee from reality, here at last, as real as a rock in his hands.

"What's up?" he said, his voice rough, out of his control. Only now did he feel just how scared he had been for her. "I've been scared!" he complained. "Look, I *have* to have a way to get in touch with you. We *have* to have a drop box or something. I can't stand it when we don't. I can't stand it anymore!"

She pulled back, surprised at his vehemence. "Sorry. I've been working out my routines, figuring out what I can do and what I can't. They're still after me, and I wasn't sure I could stay off their radar. I didn't want to get you caught up in anything."

"I already *am* caught up in it. I am fully caught up in it!"

"Okay, okay. I know. But I had to make sure we were both clear. And usually you're not. They know about the Khembalung embassy house, and their place in Maryland too."

"I'm sure they do. What about now? Am I clear?"

She took a wand out of her pocket, ran it over him. "Right now you are. It happens most often right when you leave work. The chips are mostly in stuff you leave at your other places. But I had to see you. I *needed* to see you."

"Well good." Then he saw on her face how she felt, and his spirits ballooned: at this first flash of reciprocation, the feeling blazed up in him again. Love was like a laser beam bouncing between two mirrors. She smiled at the look on his face, then they embraced and started to kiss, and Frank was swept away in a great wave of passion, like a wave catching him up in the ocean. Off they went in it, but it was more than passion, something bigger and more coherent, a feeling *for her,* his Caroline—an overwhelming feeling. "Oh my," he said.

She laughed, trembling in his arms. They hugged again, harder than ever. He was in love and she was in love and they were in love with each other. Kissing was a kind of orgasm of the feelings. He was breathing heavily, and she was too—heart pounding, blood pulsing. Frank ran a hand through her hair, feeling the tight curl, the thick springiness of it. She tilted her head back into the palm of his hand, giving herself to him.

They were in a dark knot of trees. They sat on the previous year's mat of leaves, burrowed into them as they kissed. A lot of time was lost then, it rushed past or did not happen. Her muscles were hard and her soft spots were soft. She murmured, she hummed, she moved without volition against him.

After a while she laughed again, shook her head as if to clear it. "Let's go somewhere and talk," she said. "We're not that well hidden here."

"True." In fact the Rock Creek Parkway, above them through the trees, was busy with cars, and in the other direction they could see a few of the lights of the Georgetown riverfront, blinking through branches.

When they were standing again she took his face in both hands and squeezed it. "I *need* you, Frank."

"I knee woo too," he said, lips squeezed vertically.

She laughed and let his face go. "Come on, let's go get a drink," she said. "I've got to tell you some stuff."

They walked up to the footbridge over Rock Creek, then along the promenade fronting the Potomac. Down into a sunken concrete plaza, set between office buildings, there was a row of tables outside a bar. They floated down the steps hand in hand and sat at one of them.

After they ordered (she a Bloody Mary, he white wine), she pressed a forefinger into the top of his thigh. "Look—another reason I had to see you— I'm pretty sure that Ed is on to who you are. I think he's tracking you."

"He's been doing more than that," Frank said. "That's why I wanted to find you. I've been getting harassed these last few weeks." He told her all that had happened, watching her mouth tighten at the corners as he described each incident. By the time he was done her mouth was turned down like an eagle's.

"That's him all right," she said bitterly. "That's him all over."

Frank nodded. "I was pretty sure."

He had never seen her look so grim. It was frightening, in more ways than one. You would not want her angry at you.

They sat there for a few moments. Their drinks arrived and they sipped.

"And so . . . ?" Frank said.

After another pause, she said slowly, "I guess I think you've got to disappear, like I did. Come with me and disappear for a bit. My Plan C is working. I'm in the area here, and I have a solid cover, with a bank account and apartment lease and car. I don't think he can find any of it. At this point I'm the one surveilling him, and I can see that he's still looking, but he's lost my trail."

"But he's tracking the people you were surveilling," Frank supposed.

"I think that's right."

"And so, he's figured out I must be the one who helped you get away?"

"Well—judging by what he's doing to you, I think he might still not be quite sure about it. He may be kind of testing you, to see if you'll jump. To see if you react like you know it's him. And if you did, then he'd know for sure. Also, you might then lead him to me."

"So—but that means if I disappear, then he'll be sure I'm the one. Because I'll have jumped, like he was looking for."

"Yes. But he must be pretty sure anyway. And then he won't be able to find you. Which is good, because I'm just—I'm afraid what he might do."

Frank was too, but he did not want to admit it. "Well, but I can't—"

"I've got an ID all ready for you. It's got a good legend and a deep cover. It's just as solid as mine."

"But I can't leave," Frank objected. "I mean, I have my job to do. I can't leave that right now." And your fucking ex can't make me, he didn't say.

She frowned, hesitated. Maybe her ex was worse than Frank had thought. Although what did that mean? Surely he wouldn't—wouldn't—

She shook her head, as if to clear it. "If there was someone at your work that you could explain the situation to, that you trusted? Maybe you could set up a system and send your work in to them, and like that."

"A lot of it is done in meetings now. I don't think that would work."

"But . . ." She scowled. "I don't like him knowing where you are!"

"I know. But, you know." Frank felt confused, balked—caught. And now he was sliding down into his zone of confusion, beginning to blank out at the end of trains of thought. "I have to keep doing my job," he heard himself say. "Maybe I could just make a strong effort to keep off the radar when I'm away from work. You know—show up for work out of the blue, be there in the office, in a high-security environment. Then disappear out of the office at the end of the day, and he won't be able to find where. Maybe I could do that."

"Maybe. That's a lot of exposure to get away from every day."

"I know, but—I have to."

She was shaking her head unhappily—

"It's okay," he said. "I can do it. I mean it. The White House compound is a secure environment. So when I'm where they know I work, I'll have security. When I don't have security, they won't know where I am. I'd rather do it that way than stop everything I'm doing!"

"Well that's what I had to do!"

"Yes, but you had to, because of the election and everything." Because you were married to him, he didn't say.

She was eagle-mouthed again. "But you're in on that too, okay? Thanks to me. I'm sorry about that, but it's true, and you can't just ignore it. That would be like I was being, when you showed up and I didn't want to leave camp." She sipped at her drink, thinking things over. At last she shook her head unhappily. "I'm afraid of what he might do."

"Well, but to you too," Frank said. "Maybe you should go back up to Mount Desert Island. I was thinking if you stayed away from your friend's place, it would be a good place to hide."

She shook her head more vehemently. "I can't do that."

"Why not?"

"I've got stuff I've gotta do here." She glanced at him, hesitated, took another drink. She frowned, thinking again. Their knees were pressed together, and their hands had found each other on their own and were clutched together, as if to protest any plan their owners might make that would separate them.

"I really think you should come with me," she said. "Get off the grid."

Frank struggled for thought.

"I can't," he said at last.

She grimaced. She seemed to be getting irritated with him, the pressure of her hand's grip almost painful.

Worse yet, she let go of him. She was somehow becoming estranged, withdrawing from him. Even angry at him. An invitation to be with her, all the time—"Listen," Frank said anxiously, "don't be mad at me. Tell me how we're going to keep in touch now. We *have* to have a way. I have to."

"Okay, yeah, sure."

But she was upset by his refusal to go with her, and distracted. "We can always do a dead drop," she said as she continued to frown over other things. "It's simple. Pick a hidden spot where we leave notes, and only check the spot when you're positive you're clean, say once a week."

"Twice a week."

"If I can." Her mouth was still pursed unhappily. She shook her head. "It's better to have a regular time, and keep to that schedule."

"Okay, once a week. And where?"

"*I* don't know." She seemed to be getting more and more frustrated.

"How about where we were making out, back there in the trees?" Frank suggested, trying to press past her mood. "Can you find that spot again?"

She gave him a very sharp look, it reminded him of Marta. Women as being weak at geography—he hadn't meant that. Although it was true there were some who were clueless.

"Of course," she said. "Down there by the mouth of the creek. But—it should be a place where we can tuck notes, and be sure we can find them."

"We can go back out there and bury a plastic bag under leaves."

She nodded unenthusiastically. She was still distracted.

"Are you sure you don't want to go back up to Mount Desert Island?"

"Of course I do!" she snapped. "But I can't, okay? I've got stuff I've got to do around here."

"What? Maybe I can help."

"You can't help! Especially not if you stay exposed in your job and all!"

"But I have to do that."

"Well. There you are then."

He nodded, hesitantly. He didn't understand, and wasn't sure how to proceed. "Shall we go back out there and pick a spot?"

"No. There's a pair of roots there with a hole between them. I felt it under me, it was under my head. You can put something in that gap, and I'll find it. I need to get going." She checked her watch, looked around, stood abruptly; her metal chair screeched over the concrete.

"Caroline—"

"*Be careful,*" she said, leaning down to stare him right in the face. She brought her hand up between their faces to point a finger at his nose, and he saw it was quivering. "I mean it. You're going to have to be really careful. I can see why you want to keep going to work, but this is no game we're caught in."

"I know that! But we're stuck with it. Don't be mad at me. *Please.* There's just things we both still have to do."

"I know." Her mouth was still a tight line, but now at least she was looking him in the eye. "Okay. Let's do the dead drop, every week. I'll check on Saturdays, you check Wednesdays."

"Okay. I'll leave something there for this Saturday, and you get it and leave something for Wednesday."

"Okay. But if I can't, check the next week. But I'll try." And with a peck to the top of his head she was off into the dark of Georgetown.

Frank sat there, feeling stunned. A little drunk. He didn't know what to think. He was confused, and for a moment overwhelmed, feeling the indecision fall hard on him. When you feel love, elation, worry, fear, and puzzlement, all at once, and all at equally full volume, they seemed to cancel each other out, creating a vacuum, or rather a plenum. He felt Carolined.

"Fuck," he said half-aloud. It had been that way from the moment they met, only now it was intensified, fully present in his mind, felt in his body. Abruptly he finished his drink and took off into the dark. Over the creek's footbridge, back to the spot where they had kissed.

One of the trees on the river side of their impromptu layby had the two big roots she had referred to, growing out in a fork and then plunging down into the rich loamy earth and reuniting, leaving a leaf-filled pocket. He tore one of the clear plastic credit card holders out of his wallet, took a receipt from his pocket, and wrote on the back:

I LOVE YOU I'LL LOOK EVERY WEDNESDAY WRITE ME

Then he put it in the sleeve and buried it under leaves and hoped she would find it, hoped she would use the drop and write him. It seemed like she would. They had kissed so passionately, right here on this very spot, only an hour or so before. Why now this edge of discord between them?

Well, that seemed pretty clear: her desire for him to disappear with her. Obviously she felt it was important, that he might even be in danger if he didn't join her. But he couldn't join her.

That feeling was in itself interesting, now that he thought of it. Was that a sign of decisiveness, or just being balky? Had he had any choice? Maybe one would never go into hiding unless there were no other choice. This was probably one cause of Caroline's irritation; she had to hide, while he didn't. Although maybe he did and just didn't know it.

Big sigh. He didn't know. For a second he lost his train of thought and didn't know anything. What had just happened? He looked down on the bed of leaves they had lain on. Caroline! he cried in his mind, and groaned aloud.

He was sitting with Rudra at the little table under their window, both of them looking at laptops and tapping away, the room slightly swaying on a wind from the west. After the heat of the day, the cool fragrance coming off the river was a balm. Moonlight squiggled on the black sweep of the water. Frank was reading Thoreau and at one point he laughed and read aloud to Rudra:

> "We hug the earth—how rarely we mount! Methinks we might elevate ourselves a little more. We might climb a tree, at least. I found my account in climbing a tree once. It was a tall white pine, on the top of a hill; and though I got well pitched, I was well paid for it, for I discovered new mountains on the horizon which I had never seen before—so much more of the earth and the heavens. I might have walked about the foot of the tree for three score years and ten, and yet I certainly should never have seen them."

Rudra nodded. "Henry likes the same things you do," he observed.
"It's true."
"A treehouse is a good idea," Rudra said, looking out at the dark river.
"It is, isn't it?"
Frank read on for a while, then: "Listen to this, he might as well be here:

> "'I live so much in my habitual thoughts that I forget there is any outside to the globe, and am surprised when I behold it as now— yonder hills and river in the moonlight, the monsters. Yet it is salutary to deal with the surface of things. What are these rivers and hills, these hieroglyphics which my eyes behold? There is something invigorating in this air, which I am peculiarly sensible is a real wind, blowing from over the surface of a planet. I

look out at my eyes, I come to my window, and I feel and breathe the fresh air. It is a fact equally glorious with the most inward experience. Why have we ever slandered the outward?'"

"What say, speak bad?" Rudra asked. "About this?" He waved at their view. "Maybe that is your third good correlation. The outer and the inner."

"I want something more specific."

"Maybe he means we should stop reading, and look at the river."

"Ah yes. True."

And they did.

But the next night, when Frank drove into the farm's parking lot after work, late, and got out of his van and headed for the treehouse, Qang came out of the big farmhouse and hurried over to intercept him.

"Frank, sorry—can you come in here, please?"

"Sure, what's up?"

"Rimpoche Rudra Cakrin has died."

"*What?*"

"Rudra died this day, after you left."

"Oh no. Oh no."

"Yes. I am afraid so." She held his arm, watched him closely.

"Where is he? I mean—"

"We have his body in the prayer room."

"Oh no."

The enormity of it began to hit him. "Oh, no," he said again helplessly.

"Please," she said. "Be calm. Rudra must not be disturbed now."

"What?" So he had misheard—

"This is an important time for his spirit. We here must be quiet, and let him focus on his work in the bardo. What say—help him on his way, by saying the proper prayers."

Frank felt himself lose his balance a little bit. Gone weak at the knees— yet another physiological reaction shared by all. Shock of bad news, knees went weak. "Oh no," he said. She was so calm about it, standing there talking about helping Rudra through the first hours of the afterlife—suddenly he realized he was living with aliens. They didn't even look human.

He went over and sat down on the front steps of the house. Everything still scrubbed, new paint, Tibetan colors. Qang was saying something.

After a while it was Drepung sitting beside him. Briefly he put an arm around Frank's shoulders and squeezed, then they just sat there side by side. Minutes passed; ten minutes, maybe fifteen.

"He was a friend," Frank explained. "He was my friend."

"Yes. He was my teacher."

"When—when did you meet him?"

"I was ten."

Drepung explained some of Rudra's role in Khembalung, some of his personal history. Frank glanced up once and saw that tears had rolled down Drepung's broad cheeks as he spoke, even though his voice and manner were calm. This was a comfort to Frank.

"Tell me what happens now," he said when Drepung was silent.

Drepung then explained their funeral customs. "We will say the first prayers for a day and a half. Then later there will be other ceremonies, at the proper intervals. Rudra was an important guru, so there will be quite a few. The big one will be after forty days, and then one last one at forty-nine days."

Eventually they got up and clomped up the central stairs of the tree-house, winding around the trunk. Then down the catwalk to their room.

Others had already been there. Presumably this was where Rudra had died. The sight of the empty and sheetless bed cast another wave of grief through Frank. He sat down in the chair by the window, looked down at the river. He thought that if they had not left their garden shed, Rudra would not have died.

Well, that made no sense. But Frank saw immediately that he could not continue to stay there. It would make him too sad. Then again (remembering his conversation with Caroline) moving out would help his evasion of Cooper anyway. He was free to go and do the necessary things.

. . .

In the days that followed, Frank moved his stuff out of the Khembali tree-house back into his van, now the last remaining room of his modular house, compromised though it might be. He usually parked it in the farm's parking lot, just to be near Drepung and Sucandra and Padma; he found that comforting, and he did not want them to think that he had abandoned them or gone crazy or anything. "You need the room," he kept saying about the treehouse. "I like it better now to be in my van." They accepted that and put four people in the room.

As the days passed they went through one or the other of the various stages of Rudra's passage through the bardo—Frank lost track of the details, but he tried to remember the last funeral's date, said to be the most important one for those who wished to honor the memory of that particular incarnation.

He was at a loss for what to do when not at work. The Old Executive Offices were nowhere near as comfortable to spend time in as the NSF building. It was not possible to sleep there, for instance, without security dropping by. Meanwhile his van was probably GPS'd, and would be one of the ways Edward Cooper was tracking him. He needed it for a bedroom and to get to the Khembalis, and yet he wanted to be able to leave the grid when he left work.

He didn't know. Show up to work, work, disappear, then show up again the next day. This was important, given the things that were happening.

If he got Edgardo's help to take all the transponders out of his van?

That would alert Cooper that Frank knew the chips were there and had removed them. It was better the way it was, perhaps, so that he could find them and remove them when he really had to, then travel off-grid. That was what Edgardo had meant.

He didn't know what to do. He couldn't figure it out, and he had no place to stay. What to do, how to live. Always a question, but never more so than now. He could do this, he could do that.

Do the duty of the day. (Emerson.)

.   .   .

The easiest thing was to work as long as possible. It was a kind of default mode, and he needed that now. He needed work and he needed a home; he needed things simple, and essentially decision-free. The fewer decisions the better. His incapacity was stronger than ever. He needed a job that filled all the waking hours, and he had that. But now Optimodal was not optimal, and he didn't want to go to the farm, and his treehouse was gone. His modular home had washed away in the flood of events. All he had left was his van, and it was chipped.

Out of habit he went back out to site 21. Summer was fully upon them, and all the leaves were green. But the site was empty these days, and Sleepy Hollow had been dismantled. He sat there at the table wondering what to do.

Spencer and Robin and Robert came charging in, and Frank leaped up. "Thank God," he said, hugging them; they always did that, but this time it mattered.

They ran the course in an ecstasy, as usual, but for Frank there was an extra element, of release and forgetfulness. Just to run, just to throw, crashing through the greenery everywhere around them. They ran in a swirl of becoming. Everyone died sometime; but it was life that mattered.

Afterward Frank sat down with Spencer near the chuckling creek, brown and foamy. "I'm wondering if I could join your fregans," he said.

"Well, sure," Spencer said, looking surprised. "But I thought you lived with the Khembalis?"

"Yes. But my friend there died, and I—I need to get away. There are some issues. I'm under a weird kind of surveillance, and I want to get away from that. So, I'm wondering if you would mind, maybe—I don't know. Introducing me to some people or whatever. Like those times we went to a dinner."

"Sure," Spencer said. "That happens every night. No problem at all."

"Thanks."

"So you're doing something classified then?"

"I don't know."

Spencer laughed. "Well, it doesn't matter. Life outdoors is a value in itself. You'll like it, you'll see."

So he went with Spencer, on foot, to the house of choice for that evening—a boarded-up monster, not a residential house but a half-block apartment complex that had been wrecked in the flood and never renovated. There were a lot of these, and the ferals and fregans now had maps and lists, locks and keys and codes and phones. Every few nights they moved to a new place, within a larger community that was also moving around. Spencer started calling Frank on his FOG phone to let him know where they would be that night, and Frank started leaving work at more or less the normal time, using a wand Edgardo gave him to see that he was clear, then meeting Spencer in the park, running a frisbee round, then walking somewhere in Northwest to the rendezvous of the night. Once or twice Frank joined the dumpster-diving teams, and was interested to learn that most restaurant dumpsters were now locked shut. But this was to satisfy insurance company liability concerns more than to keep people from the food, because for every dumpster they visited they had either the key or the combination, provided by kitchen workers who were either sympathetic or were living the life themselves. And so they would go into the workspaces behind the city's finest, and set a lookout, and then unlock the dumpster and remove the useful food, which often was set carefully in one corner.

It wasn't even that smelly an operation, Frank learned (although sometimes it was). They would hustle off with backpacks full of half-frozen steaks or big bags of lettuce, or potatoes, really almost all the raw materials of the wonderful meals the restaurants made, and by the time they got to the house for the night, its kitchen would be powered by a generator in the backyard, or the fireplace would be ablaze with a big fire, and cooks would be working on a meal that would feed thirty or forty people.

Frank floated through all this like a jellyfish. He let the tide of humanity shove him along. This way or that. Billow on the current. He was grunioning in the shallows of the city.

Then it came time for the last of Rudra's major funerals. Frank was surprised to see the date on his watch. Well, that was interesting. Forty-nine days had passed and he hadn't quite noticed. Now it was the day.

He didn't know what to do.

He didn't want to go. He didn't want to admit Rudra was dead, he didn't want to feel those feelings again. He didn't want to think that Rudra was alive but in some horrible netherworld, where he was having to negotiate all kinds of terrors in order to get to the start of some putative next life. It was absurd. He didn't want any of it to be real.

He sat there at his desk in his office, paralyzed by indecision. He *could not decide.*

A call came on his FOG phone.

It was Nick Quibler. "Frank, are you okay? Did you forget that it's the day for Rudra's funeral?"

Nick did not sound accusatory, or worried, or anything. Nick was good at not sounding emotional. Teenage flatness of affect.

"Oh yeah," he said to the boy, trying to sound normal. "I did forget. Thanks for calling. I'll be right over. But don't let them delay anything."

"I don't think they could even if they wanted to," Nick said. "It's a pretty strict schedule, as far as I can tell." He had taken an interest in the supposed sequence of events Rudra had been experiencing during these days in the bardo, reading the *Tibetan Book of the Dead* and telling Frank too many of the details. Suddenly it all seemed to Frank like a cruel hoax, a giant fiction meant to comfort the bereaved. People who died were dead and gone. Their soul had been in their brains and their brains decomposed and the electrical activity was gone. And then they were gone too, except to the extent they were in other people's minds.

Well, fair enough. He was going to the funeral now. He had decided. Or Nick had decided.

Suddenly he understood that he had been sitting there about to miss it. He was so incapacitated that he had almost missed his friend's funeral. Would have missed it, if not for a call from another friend. Before leaving he grabbed up the phone and called up the neurologist's office. "I have a referral from Dr. Mandelaris for elective surgery," he explained. "I'd like to schedule that now please. I've decided to do it."

Every summer Charlie flew back to California to spend a week in the Sierra Nevada, backpacking with a group of old friends. This year Charlie had invited Frank to join the group, thinking it might be good R&R after his brain surgery. Charlie was a little surprised when Frank accepted, which he did without explanation. Frank's usual reticence had recently scaled new heights.

Anna was glad to hear he was going. Since Rudra's death, he had seemed to her lonely. This was news to Charlie, although anyone could see that the death of Rudra Cakrin had shaken him. When he showed up for the forty-nine-day ceremony, quite late—most of the gazillion prayers over—he had been obviously distressed. He had arrived in time for the part where everyone there took bites out of little cakes they had been given, then turned the remaining pieces back in, to help sustain Rudra's spirit—a beautiful idea—but Frank had eaten his piece entirely, having failed to understand. It was always a shock to see someone whom one regarded as unemotional suddenly become distraught.

Then soon after that Frank had had the surgery to correct problems behind his nose. "No big deal," he said, but Anna just shook her head at that.

"It's right next to his brain," she told Charlie.

They all visited him in the hospital, and he said he was fine, that it had gone well. And yes, he would like to join the backpacking trip. It would be good to get away. Would he be okay to go to high altitude? He said he would be.

After that everyone got busy with day camp and swim lessons for Nick, the White House for Charlie and Joe, NSF for Anna; and they did not see Frank again for a couple weeks, until suddenly the time for the Sierra trip was upon them.

Charlie's California friends were fine with the idea of an added member, which they had done before, and they were looking forward to meeting him.

"He's kind of quiet," Charlie warned them.

. . .

This annual trek had been problematized for Charlie ever since Nick's birth, him being the stay-at-home parent, and Joe's arrival had made things more than twice as bad. But now they had coverage for both boys several hours a day, which meant Anna could continue to work almost full-time. This was crucial; the loss of even a couple of hours of work a day caused her brow to furrow vertically and her mouth to set in a this-is-not-good expression.

Charlie knew the look well, but tried not to see it as the departure time approached. "This will be good for Frank," he would say.

"It'll be good for you too," Anna would reply; or not reply at all.

Actually she would have been completely fine with him going, Charlie thought, if she did not still have residual worries about Joe. When Charlie realized this by hearing her make some non sequitur that skipped to the subject, he was surprised; he had thought he was the only one still worrying about Joe. He had assumed Anna would have had her mind put fully at ease by the disappearance of the fever. That had always been the focus of her concern, as opposed to the matters of mood and behavior which had been bothering Charlie.

Now, however, as the time for the mountain trip got closer and closer, he could see on Anna's face all her expressions of worry, visible in quick flashes when they discussed things, or when she was tired. Charlie could read a great deal on Anna's face. He didn't know if this was just the ordinary result of long familiarity or if she was particularly expressive, but certainly her worried looks were very nuanced, and, he had to say, beautiful. Perhaps it was just because they were so legible to him. You could see that life *meant something* when looking at her; her thoughts flickered over her face like flames over burning coals, as if one were watching some dreamily fine silent-screen actress. To read her was to love her. She might be, as Charlie thought she was, slightly crazy about work, but even that was part of what he loved, another manifestation of how much she cared. One could not care more and remain sane. Mostly sane.

But Anna had never admitted, or even apparently seen, the Khembali connection to the various changes in Joe. To her there was no such thing as a metaphysical illness, because there was no such thing as metaphysics. And there was no such thing as psychosomatic illness in a three-year-old, because a toddler was not old enough to have problems, as his Gymboree friend Cecelia had put it.

So it had to be a fever. Or so she must have been subconsciously reasoning. Charlie wondered what would happen if Anna were the one on hand when Joe went into one of his little trances, or said "Namaste" to a snowman. He wondered if she knew Joe's daytime behavior well enough to notice the myriad tiny shifts that had occurred in him since the election day party at the Khembalis.

Well, of course she did; but whether she would admit some of these changes were connected to the Khembalis was another matter.

Maybe it was better that she couldn't be convinced. Charlie himself did not want to think there was anything real to this line of thought. It was one of his own forms of worry, perhaps—trying to find some explanation other than undiagnosed disease, or mental problem. Even if the alternative explanation might in some ways be worse. Because it disturbed him, even occasionally freaked him out. He could only think about it glancingly, in brief bursts, and then quickly jump to something else. It was too weird to be true.

But there were more things in heaven and earth, etc.; and without question there were very intelligent people in his life who believed in this stuff, and acted on those beliefs. That in itself made it real, or something with real effects. If Anna had the Khembalis over for dinner while Charlie was gone, maybe she would see this. Even if the only "real" part of it was that the Khembalis believed something was going on, that was enough, potentially, to make for trouble.

In any case, the trouble would not come to a head while he was out in the Sierras. He would only be gone a week, and Joe had been much the same, week to week, all that winter and spring and through the summer so far.

So Charlie made his preparations for the trip without talking to Anna about Joe, and without meeting her eye when she was tired.

It was harder with Joe himself: "When you going Dad?" he would shout on occasion. "How long? What you gonna do? Hiking? Can I go?" And then when Charlie explained that he couldn't, he would shrug. "Oh my." And make a little face. "See you when you back Dad."

It was heartbreaking.

On the morning of Charlie's departure, Joe patted him on the arm. "Bye Da. Be *careful*," saying it just like Charlie always said it, as a half-exasperated reminder, just as Charlie's father had always said it to him, as if the default plan were to do something reckless, so that one had to be reminded.

Anna clutched him to her. "Be careful. Have fun."

"I will. I love you."

Charlie and Frank flew from Dulles to Ontario together, making a plane change in Dallas. Frank had had his operation eighteen days before. "So what was it like?" Charlie asked him.

"Oh, you know. They put you out."

"For how long?"

"A few hours I think."

"And after that?"

"Felt fine."

Although, Charlie saw, he seemed to have less to say than before. So on the second leg of the trip, with Frank sitting beside him looking out the window of the plane, Charlie fell asleep.

It was too bad about the operation. Charlie was in an agony of apprehension about it, but as Joe lay there on the hospital bed he looked up at his father and tried to reassure him. "It be all right Da." They had attached wires to his skull, connecting him to a bulky machine by the bed, but most of his hair was still unshaved, and under the mesh cap his expression was resolute. He squeezed Charlie's hand, then let go and clenched his fists by his sides, preparing himself, mouth pursed. The doctor on the far side of the bed nodded; time for delivery of the treatment. Joe saw this, and to give himself courage began to sing one of his wordless marching tunes, "Da, da da da, da!" The doctor flicked a switch on the machine and instantaneously Joe sizzled to a small black crisp on the bed.

Charlie jerked upright with a gasp.

"You okay?" Frank said.

Charlie shuddered, fought to dispel the image, clutching the seat arms.

"Bad dream," he got out. He hauled himself up in his seat and took some deep breaths. "Just a little nightmare. I'm fine."

But the image stuck with him, like the taste of poison. Very obvious symbolism, of course, in the crass way dreams sometimes had—image of a fear he had in him, expressed visually, sure—but so brutal, so ugly! He felt betrayed by his own mind. He could hardly believe himself capable of imagining such a thing. Where did such monsters come from?

He recalled a friend who had once mentioned he was taking St. John's wort in order to combat nightmares. At the time Charlie had thought it a bit silly; the moment you woke up from dreams you knew they were not real, so how bad could a nightmare be? Now he knew, and finally he felt for his old friend Gene.

So when his old college roommates Dave and Vince picked them up at the Ontario airport and they drove north in Dave's van, Charlie and Frank were both a bit subdued. They sat in the middle seats of the van and let Dave and Vince do most of the talking up front. These two were more than willing to fill the hours of the drive with tales of the previous year's work in criminal defense and urology. Occasionally Vince would turn around in the passenger seat and demand some words from Charlie, and Charlie would reply, working to shake off the trauma of the dream and get into the good mood he knew he should be experiencing. They were off to the mountains—the southern end of the Sierra Nevada was appearing ahead to their left, the weird desert ranges were off to their right. They were entering Owens Valley, one of the greatest mountain valleys on the planet! It was typically one of the high points of their trips, but this time he wasn't quite into it.

In Independence they met the van bringing down the two northern members of their group, Jeff and Troy, and they all wandered the little grocery store there, buying forgotten necessities or delicacies, happy at the sudden reunion of all these companions from their shared youth—a reunion with their own youthful selves, it seemed. Even Charlie felt that, and slowly managed to push the horrible dream away from his conscious awareness and his mood.

Frank meanwhile was an easy presence, cruising the tight aisles of the rustic store peering at things, comfortable with all their talk of gear and food and trailhead firewood. Charlie was pleased to see that although he was still quiet, a tiny little smile was creasing his features as he looked at displays of beef jerky and cigarette lighters and postcards. He looked relaxed. He knew this place.

Out in the parking lot, the mountains to east and west hemmed in the evening sky, and told them they were already in the Sierras—or in the space the Sierras defined, which very much included Owens Valley. To the east, the dry White Mountains were dusty orange in the sunset; to the west, the huge escarpment of the Sierra loomed over them like a stupendous serrated wall. Together the two ranges created a sense of the valley as a great roofless room.

The room could have been an exhibit in a museum, illustrating what California had looked like a century before. Around that time Los Angeles had stolen the valley's water, as described in the movie *Chinatown* and elsewhere. Ironically, this had done the place a favor of sorts, by forestalling subsequent development and letting it be a more natural place.

They drove the two cars out to the trailhead. The great escarpment fell directly from the crest of the Sierra to the floor of Owens Valley, the whole plunge of ten thousand feet right there before them—one of the biggest escarpments on the face of the planet. It formed a very complex wall, with major undulations, twists and turns, peaks and dips, buttress ridges, and gigantic outlier masses. Every low point in the crest made for a potential pass into the backcountry, and many not-so-low points had also been used as cross-country passes. One of the games that Charlie's group of friends had made over the years was to try to cross the crest in as many places as they could. This year they were going in over Taboose Pass, "before we get too old for it," as they said to Frank.

Taboose was one of what Troy had named the Four Bad Passes (Frank smiled to hear this). They were bad because their trailheads were all on the floor of Owens Valley, and thus about five thousand feet above sea level, while the passes on the crest, usually about ten miles away from the trailheads, were all well over eleven thousand feet high. Thus six thousand vertical feet, usually hiked on the first day, when their packs were heaviest. They had once ascended Sawmill Pass, and once come down Shepherd's Pass; only Baxter and Taboose remained, and this year they were going to do Taboose, said to be the hardest of them all.

They drove to a little car campground by Taboose Creek and found it empty, which increased their good cheer. The creek itself was almost completely dry—a bad sign, as it drained one of the larger east-side canyons. There was no snow at all to be seen up on the crest, nor over on the White Mountains.

"They'll have to rename them the Brown Mountains," Troy said. He was full of news of the drought afflicting California for the last few years. Troy went into the Sierras a lot, and had seen the damage himself. "You won't believe it," he told Charlie ominously.

They partied through the sunset around a picnic table crowded with gear and beer and munchies. One of the range's characteristic lenticular clouds formed like a spaceship over the crest and turned pale orange and pink as the evening lengthened. Taboose Pass itself was visible above them, a huge U in the crest. Clearly the early native peoples would have had no problem identifying it as a pass over the range, and Troy told them of what he had read about the archeological finds in the area of the pass while Vince barbequed filet mignon and red bell peppers on a thick old iron grate.

Frank prodded the grate curiously. "I guess these things are the same everywhere," he said. "In Rock Creek they're like this."

They ate dinner, drank, caught up on the year, reminisced about previous trips. Charlie was pleased to see Vince ask Frank some questions about his work, which Frank answered briefly if politely. When they were done eating he walked up the creekside on his own, looking around as he went. Charlie relaxed in the presence of his old friends. Vince regaled them with ever-stranger tales of the L.A. legal system, and they laughed and threw a frisbee around, half-blind in the dusk. Frank came out of the darkness to join them for that. He turned out to be very accurate with a frisbee.

Then as it got late they slipped into their sleeping bags, promising they would make an early start—even, given the severity of the ascent facing them, an actual early start, as opposed to their legendary early start, meaning noon.

So they woke to alarms before dawn, and packed in a hurry while eating breakfast, then drove up a gravel road to a tiny trailhead parking lot, hacked into the last possible spot before the escarpment made its abrupt jump off the valley floor.

They rose quickly, and could see better and better just how steep the escarpment was. Polished granite overhead marked where the glacier had run down the ravine. The ice had carved a trough in hard orange granite.

After about an hour the trail ran beside the dry creekbed. Now the stupendous battlements of the side walls of the ravine rose vertically to each side, constricting their view of anything except the sky above and a shrinking wedge of valley floor behind them and below. None of the escarpment canyons they had been in before matched this one for chiseled immensity and steepness.

Troy often talked as he hiked, muttering mostly to himself, so that Charlie behind him only heard every other phrase—something about the Sierras having a lighter glaciation than the Alps, so the tops of the plutons had been left intact, not gotten etched away by ice until there were only horns and deep valleys. The Alps' high basins had been ground away, and thus (Troy concluded triumphantly) one had the explanation for the infinite superiority of the Sierra Nevada for backpacking purposes.

Something like that. Troy was their mountain man, their navigator, gear innovator, geologist, and all-around Sierra guru. He spent a lot of hiking time alone, and although happy to have his friends along, still had a tendency to hold long dialogues with himself, as he must have done when on his solo trips. His overarching thesis was that if backpacking were your criterion of judgment, the Sierra Nevada of California was an unequaled paradise, and essentially heaven on Earth. All mountain ranges were beautiful, of course, but backpacking as an activity had been invented in the Sierra by John Muir and his friends, so it worked there better than anywhere else. Name any other range and Troy would snap out the reason it would not serve as well as the Sierra, if backpacking was what you wanted. This was a game he and Charlie played from time to time.

"Alps."

"Rain, too steep, no basins, dangerous. Too many people."

"But they're beautiful right?"

"Very beautiful."

"Colorado Rockies."

"Too big, no lakes, too dry, boring."

"Canadian Rockies."

"Grizzly bears, rain, forest, too big. Not enough granite. Pretty though."

"Andes."

"Tea hut system, need guides, no lakes. I'd like to do that though."

"Himalayas."

"Too big, tea hut system. I'd like to go back though."

"Pamirs."

"Terrorists."

"Appalachians."

"Mosquitoes, people, forest, no lakes. Boring."

"Transantarctics."

"Too cold, too expensive. I'd like to see them though."

"Carpathians?"

"Too many vampires!"

And so on. Only the Sierras had all the qualities Troy deemed necessary.

No argument from Charlie—although he noticed it looked today about as dry as the desert ranges to the east. It seemed they were in the rain shadow of the range even here. The Nevada ranges must have been completely baked.

All day they hiked up the great gorge. It twisted and then broadened a little, but otherwise changed little as they rose. Orange rock leaped at the dark blue sky, and the battlements seemed to vibrate in place as Charlie paused to look at them—the effect of his heart pounding in his chest. Trudge trudge trudge. It was a strange feeling, Charlie thought, to know that for the next hour you were going to be doing nothing but walking— and after that hour, you would take a break and then walk some more. Hour following hour, all day long. It was so different from the days at home that it took some getting used to. It was a different state of consciousness; only the experience of his previous backpacking trips allowed Charlie to slip back into it so readily. Mountain time: slow down. Pay attention to the rock. Look around. Slide back into the long ruminative rhythms of thought that plodded along at their own pedestrian pace, interrupted by examination of the granite, or the details of the trail as it crossed the meager stream, which to everyone's relief was making occasional excursions from beneath boulderfields. Or a brief exchange with one of the other guys, as they came in and out of a switchback, and thus came close enough to each other to talk. In general they hiked spread up and down the trail.

So the day passed. Sometimes it would seem to Charlie like a good allegory for life itself. You just keep hiking uphill.

Frank hiked sometimes ahead, sometimes behind. He seemed lost in his thoughts, or the view, never particularly aware of the others. Nor did he seem to notice the work of the hike. He drifted up, mouth hanging open as he looked at the ravine's great orange sidewalls.

In the late afternoon they trudged up the final stony rubble of the headwall, and into the pass—or onto it, as it was just as huge as the view from below had suggested: a deep broad U in the crest of the range, two thousand feet lower than the peaks marking each side of the U. These peaks were over a mile apart; and the depression of the pass was also nearly a mile from east to west, extremely unusual for a Sierra pass; most dropped away immediately on both sides, sometimes very steeply. Not so here, where a number of little black-rimmed ponds dotted an uneven granite flat.

"It's so big!"

"It looks like the Himalayas," Frank remarked as he walked by.

Troy had dropped his pack and wandered off to the south rise of the pass, checking out the little snow ponds tucked among the rocks. Now he whooped and called them all over to him. They stood up and rubber-legged to him.

He pointed triumphantly at a low ring of stacked granite blocks, set on a flat tuck of decomposed granite next to one of the ponds. "Check it out guys. I ran into the national park archeologist last summer, and he told me about this. It's the foundation of a Native American summer shelter. They built some kind of wicker house on this base. They've dated them as old as five thousand years up here, but the archeologist said he thought they might be twice as old as that."

"How can you tell it's not just some campers from last year?" Vince demanded in his courtroom voice. This was an old game, and Troy immediately snapped back, "Obsidian flakes in the Sierra all come from knapping arrowheads. Rates of hydration can be used to date when the flaking was done. Standard methodology, accepted by all! And—" He reached down and plucked something from the decomposed granite at Vince's feet, held it aloft triumphantly: "Obsidian flake! Proof positive! Case closed!"

"Not until you get this dated," Vince muttered, checking the ground out. "There could have been an arrowhead-making class up here just last week."

"Ha ha ha. That's how you get criminals back on the streets of L.A., but it won't work here. There's obsidian everywhere you look."

And in fact there was. They were all finding it; exclaiming, shouting, crawling on hands and knees, faces inches from the granite. "Don't take any of it!" Troy warned them, just as Jeff began to fill a baggie with them. "It screws up their counts. It doesn't matter that there are thousands of pieces here. This is an archeological site on federal land. You are grotesquely breaking the law there Jeffrey. Citizen's arrest! Vincent, you're a witness to this!"

"Awesome," Charlie said.

Troy abandoned the game, nodded, sat down on the rock. "It really gives you a sense of them. The guy said they probably spent all summer up here. They did it for hundred of years, maybe thousands. The people from the west brought up food and seashells, and the people from the east, salt and obsidian. It really helps you to see they were just like us."

Frank was on his hands and knees to get his face down to the level of the low rock foundation, his nose inches from the granite, nodding as he listened to Troy. "It's beautiful drywall," he commented. "You can tell by the lichen that it's been here a long time. It's like a Goldsworthy. This is a sacred place."

Finally they went back to their packs, put them back on their backs, and staggered down into a high little basin west of the pass. The day's hump up the great wall had taken it out of them. When they found a flat area with enough sandy patches to serve as a camp, they sat next to their backpacks and pulled out their warm clothes and their food bags and the rest of their gear, and had just enough energy and daylight left to get water from the nearest pond, then cook and eat their meals. They groaned stiffly as they stood to make their final arrangements, and congratulated each other on the good climb. They were in their bags and on the way to sleep before the sky had gone fully dark.

Before exhaustion knocked him out, Charlie looked over and saw Frank sitting up in his sleeping bag, looking at the electric blue band of sky over the black peaks to the west. He seemed untired by their ascent, or the sudden rise to altitude; absorbed by the immense spaces around them. Wrapped in thought. Charlie hoped his nose was doing all right. The stars were popping out overhead, swiftly surpassing in number and brilliance any starscapes they ever saw at home. The Milky Way was like a moraine of stars. Sound of distant water clucking through a meadow, the wind in the pines; black spiky horizons all around, the smooth airy gap of the pass behind. It was a blessing to feel so tired in such a place. They had made the effort it took to regather, and here they were again, in a place so sublime no one could truly remember what it was like when they were away, so that every return had a sense of surprise, as if reentering a miracle. Every time it felt this way. It was the California that could never be taken away.

Except it could.

Charlie had, of course, read about the ongoing drought that had afflicted California for the last few years, and he was also familiar with the climate models which suggested that the Sierra would be one of those places most affected by the global rise in temperature. California's wet months had been November through April, with the rest of the year as dry as any desert. A classic Mediterranean climate. In the past, however, precipitation had fallen on the Sierra as snow; this had created a thick winter snowpack, which then took most of the summer to melt. That meant that the reservoirs in the foothills got fed a stream of melting snow at a rate that could then be dispersed out to the cities and farms. In effect the Sierra snowpack itself had been the ultimate reservoir, far bigger than what the artificial ones behind dams in the foothills could hold. Now, with global temperatures higher, more of the winter precipitation came down as rain. The annual reservoir of snow was smaller, even in good years; and in droughts it hardly formed at all.

California was in an uproar about this. New dams were being built, and the movement to remove the Hetch Hetchy dam had been defeated, despite the fact that the next reservoir down the Tuolumne had the capacity to hold all Hetch Hetchy's water. State officials were also begging Oregon and Washington to allow a pipeline to be built to convey water south from the Columbia River. The Columbia dumped a huge amount into the Pacific, one hundred times that of the maximum flow of the Colorado River, and all of it *unused*. But naturally the citizens of Oregon and Washington had refused to agree to the pipeline, happy to stick it to California. Only the possibility that many Californians would then move north, bringing their obese equities with them, was causing any of them to reconsider. But as clear cost-benefit analysis was not the national strong suit, the battle would go on for the foreseeable future.

In any case, no matter what political and hydrological adjustments were made in the lowlands, the High Sierra meadows were dying.

This was a shock to witness. It had changed in the three years since Charlie had last been up. He hiked down the trail on their second morning with a sinking feeling in his stomach. They were walking down the side of a big glacial gorge to the John Muir Trail. When they reached it, they headed north on it for a short distance, going gently uphill. As they hiked, it became obvious that the high basin meadows were much too dry for early August. They were desiccated. Ponds were often pans of cracked dirt. Grass was brown. Plants were dead: trees, bushes, ground cover, grasses. Even mosses. There were no marmots to be seen, and few birds. Only the lichen seemed okay—although as Vince pointed out, it was hard to tell. "If lichen dies does it lose its color?" No one knew.

After a few discouraging miles they turned left and followed a dry creek uphill to the northwest, aiming at the Vennacher Needle—"One of those famous blunt-tipped needles," as Vince pointed out. Up and up, over broken granite much whiter than the orange stuff east of Taboose Pass. There was no easy way into Lakes Basin, their destination; they were hiking up to one of these entry points now, a pass called Vennacher Col.

The eastern approach to the col got steeper as they approached it, until they were grabbing the boulders to help pull themselves up. And the other side was said to be steeper! But the destination was a basin very remote, empty of trails and people, and dotted with lakes—many lakes—lakes so big, Charlie saw with relief as he pulled into the airy pass, that they had survived the drought. They glittered like patches of cobalt silk in the white granite below.

Very far below: for the western side of Vennacher Col was a very steep glacial headwall. In short, a cliff. The first five hundred vertical feet of their drop lay right under their toes, an airy nothing.

Troy had warned them about this. The Sierra guidebooks all rated this side of the pass class 3. In climbing terms, it was the crux of the week. Normally they avoided anything harder than class 2, and now they were remembering why.

"Troy?" Vince said. "Why are we here?"

"We are here to suffer," Troy intoned.

"It was your idea to do this; what the fuck?"

"I came up this way with these guys once. It's not as bad as it looks."

"You think you came up it," Charlie reminded him. "It was twenty years ago and you don't remember exactly what you did."

"It had to be here."

"Is this class two?" Vince demanded.

"This side has a little class three section that you see here."

"You're calling this cliff little?"

"It's mostly a class-two cliff."

"But don't you rate terrain by the highest level of difficulty?"

"Yes."

"So this is a class-three pass."

"Technically, yes."

"Technically? You mean in some other sense, this cliff is not a cliff?"

"That's right."

The distinction between class 2 and class 3, Charlie maintained, lay precisely in what they were witnessing now: on class 2, one used one's hands for balance, but the terrain was not very steep, so that if one fell one could not do more than crack an ankle, at most. So the scrambling was fun. Whereas class 3 indicated terrain steep enough that although one could still scramble up and down it fairly easily, a fall on it would be dangerous—perhaps fatally dangerous—making the scramble nerve-racking, even in places a little terrifying. The classic description in the Roper guidebook said it was "like ascending a steep narrow old staircase on the outside of a tower, without banisters." But it could be much worse than that. So the distinction between classes 2 and 3 was fuzzy in regard to rock, but very precise emotionally, marking the border between fun and fear.

The five old friends wandered back and forth anxiously on the giant rocks of the pass, peering down at the problem and talking it over. Frank sat off to the side, looking around at the view.

No one was happy at the prospect of getting down the wall. It was very exposed. Charlie wanted to be happy with it, but he wasn't. Maybe Troy could downclimb it, and presumably Frank, being a climber. But the rest of them, no.

Charlie looked around to see what Frank might say. Finally he spotted him, sitting on the flat top of one of the pass rocks, looking out to the west. It seemed clear he didn't care one way or the other what they did. As a climber he existed in a different universe, in which class 3 was the stuff you ran down on after climbing the real thing. Real climbing *started* with class 5, and even then it only got to what climbers would call serious at 5.8 or

5.9, or 5.10 or 5.11. Looking at the boulder stack again, Charlie wondered
what 5.11 would look like—or feel like to be on! Never had he felt less inclined to take up rock climbing. But Frank didn't look like he was thinking
about the descent at all. He sat on his block looking down at Lakes Basin,
biting off pieces of an energy bar. Charlie was impressed by his tact, if that's
what it was. Because they were in a bit of a quandary, and Charlie was
pretty sure that Frank could have led them into the slot, or down some
other route, if he had wanted to. But it wasn't his trip; he was a guest, and
so kept his counsel. Or maybe he was just spacing out, even to the point of
being unaware there was any problem facing the rest of them. He sat staring at the view, chewing ruminatively, body relaxed. A man at peace. Charlie wandered up the narrow spine of the pass to his side.

"Nice, eh?"

"Oh, my, yes," Frank said. "Just gorgeous. What a beautiful basin."

"It really is."

"It's strange to think how few people will ever see this," Frank said. He
had not volunteered even this much since they had met at Dulles, so Charlie crouched by his side to listen. "Maybe only a few hundred people in the
history of the world have ever seen it. And if you don't see it, you can't really imagine it. So it's almost like it doesn't exist for most people. So really
this basin is a secret. A hidden valley you have to search for. And even then
you might never find it."

"I guess so," Charlie said. "We're lucky."

"So lucky."

"How's your head feel up here?"

"Oh good. Good, sure. Interesting!"

"No postop bleeding, or psychosis or anything?"

"No. Not as far as I can tell."

Charlie laughed. "That's as good as."

He stood and walked to where the others were discussing options.

"What about straight down from the lowest point here?" Vince demanded.

Charlie objected, "That won't work—look at the drop." He still wanted to
try the boulder stack.

"But around that buttress down there, maybe," Dave pointed out. "Something's sure to go around it."

"Why do you say that?"

"I don't know. Because it always goes in the Sierra."

"Except when it doesn't!"

"I'm going to try it," Jeff declared, and took off before anyone had time to point out that since he was by far the most reckless among them, his ability to descend a route said very little about it as far as the rest of them were concerned.

Ten minutes later, however, he was a good portion of the way down the cliff, considerably off to the left as they looked down, where the steepness of the rock angled outward, and looked quite comfy compared to where they were.

He yelled back up at them, "Piece of cake! Piece of cake!"

"Yeah right!" they all yelled.

But there he was, and he had done it so fast that they had to try it. They found some very narrow ledges hidden under the buttress, trending down and left, and by holding on to the broken wall next to their heads, and making their way carefully along the ledges and down from ledge to ledge, they all quickly followed Jeff to the less steep bulge in the cliff, and from there each took a different route to a horrible jumble of rocks in a flat trough at the bottom.

"Wow!" Charlie said as they regathered on a big rock among the rest, next to a little bowl of caked black dust that had once been a pool of water. "That was class two! I was wrong. It wasn't so bad! Wasn't that class two?" he asked Troy.

"It probably was," Troy said.

"So you guys just discovered a class-two route on a wall that all the guidebooks call class three!"

"How could that happen?" Vince wondered. "Why us?"

"We were desperate," Troy said, looking back up. From below the cliff looked even steeper than it had from above.

"That's probably actually it," Charlie said. "The class ratings up here have mostly been made by climbers, and when they came up to this pass they probably saw the big slot in the face, and ran right up it without a second thought. The fact it was class three meant nothing to them, so they never noticed there was a much trickier class-two line off to the side, because they didn't need it."

Frank nodded. "Could be."

"We'll have to write to the authors of the guidebooks and see if we can get them to relist Vennacher Col as class two! We'll call it the Jeffrey Direttissima."

"Very cool. You do that."

"Actually," Vince pointed out, "it was my refusal to go down the slot that caused Jeff to take the new route, and I'm the one that spotted it first, so I think it should be called the Salami Direttissima. That has a better ring to it anyway."

That night, in a wonderful campsite next to the biggest of the Lakes Basin's lakes (none had names), their dinner party was extra cheery. They had crossed a hard pass—an impossible pass—and were now in the lap of beauty, lying around on groundpads dressed like pashas in colorful silken clothing, drinking an extra dram or two of their carefully hoarded liquor supplies, watching the sun burnish the landscape: water copper, granite bronze, sky cobalt. On the northern wall of the basin a single tongue of cloud lapped up the slope like some sinuous creature, slowly turning pink.

After dinner the Maxfield Parrish blues of the twilight gave way to the stars, and then the Milky Way. The lake beside them stilled to a starry black mirror. Quickly the cold began to press on the little envelopes of warmth their clothes created, and they slid into their sleeping bags.

Voices by starlight. But it's stupid. It's just your genes making one last desperate scream when they can feel you falling apart. They want you to have more kids to up their chance of being immortal, they don't give a shit about you or your actual happiness.

If you're just fooling around, if you don't mean to leave your wife and go with that person, then it's like masturbating in someone else's body.

Yuck! Jesus, yuck!

Hoots of horrified hilarity, echoing off the cliffs across the lake. That's so gross I'll never again be able to think about having an affair!

So I cured you. So now you're old. Your genes have given up.

My genes will never give up.

The little stove pellet burned out. The hikers went quiet and were soon asleep, under the great slow wheel of the stars.

The next day they were to explore the Lakes Basin. It was a beautiful day, the heart of the trip, just as it was the heart of the pluton, and that pluton the heart of the Sierra itself. No trails, no people, no views out of the range. They would be walking in the heart of the world.

On such days some kind of freedom descended on them. Mornings were cold and clear, spent lazing around their sleeping bags and breakfast coffee. They chatted casually, discussed the quality of their night's sleep. They asked Charlie about what it was like to work for the President. "He's a good guy," he told them. "He's not a normal guy, but he's a good one. He's still real. He has the gift of a happy temperament. He sees the funny side of things." Frank listened to this closely, head cocked to one side.

Once they got packed up and started, they wandered apart, or in duos, catching up on the year's news, on the wives and kids, the work and play, the world at large. Stopping frequently to marvel at the landscapes that constantly shifted in perspective around them. It was very dry, a lot of the fellfields and meadows were brown, but the lakes were still there and their borders were green as of old. The distant ridges; the towering thunderheads in the afternoon; the height of the sky itself; the thin cold air; the pace of the seconds, tocking at the back of the throat; all combined to create a sense of spaciousness unlike any they ever felt anywhere else. It was another world.

But this world kept intruding.

Their plan was to exit the basin by way of Cartridge Pass, which was south of Vennacher Col, on the same border ridge of the pluton. This pass had been the original route for the Muir Trail; the trail over it had been abandoned in 1934, after the replacement trail over Mather Pass was completed. Now the old trail was no longer on the maps, and Troy said the guidebooks described it as being gone. But he didn't believe it, and in yet another of his archeological quests, he wanted to see if they could relocate it.

Vince said, "So this is another cross-country pass."

"Maybe."

Once again they were on the hunt. They hiked slowly uphill, separating again into their own spaces. Then on southeast slope of the headwall their shouts rang out once more. Right where one would have hiked if one were simply following the path of least resistance up the slope, a trail appeared. As they hiked up it became more and more evident, until it began to switchback up a broad talus gully that ran up between solid granite buttresses. Here it became as obvious as a Roman road, because its bed was made of decomposed granite that had been washed into a surface and then in effect cemented there by years of rain, without any summer boots ever breaking it up. It looked like the nearly concretized paths that landscapers created with decomposed granite in the world below. People had only hiked it for some thirty or forty years—unless the Native Americans had used this pass too, and it was another obvious one, so maybe they had—in which case people had hiked it for five or ten thousand years. In any case a great trail, with the archeological component adding to the sheer physical grandeur of it.

"There are lost trails like this on an island in Maine," Frank remarked to no one in particular. He was looking around with what Charlie now thought of as his habitual hiking expression. It seemed he walked in a rapture.

The pass itself gave them long views in all directions—north back into the basin, south over the giant gap of the Muro Blanco. Peaks in all directions. After a leisurely lunch in the sun, they put on their packs and started down into the Muro Blanco. The lost trail held, thinning through high meadows, growing fainter as they descended, but always still there.

But here the grass was brown. This was a south-facing slope, and it almost looked like late autumn. Not quite, for autumn in the Sierra was marked by intense fall colors in the ground cover, including a neon scarlet on slopes backlit by the sun. Now that ground cover was simply brown. It was dead. Except for fringes of green around drying ponds, or algal mats on the exposed pond bottoms, every plant on this south-facing slope had died. It was as burnt as any range in Nevada. One of the loveliest landscapes on the planet, dead before their eyes.

They hiked at their different paces, each alone on the rocky rumpled landscape. Bench to bench, fellfield to fellfield, each in his own private world.

Charlie fell behind the rest, stumbling from time to time in his distress, careless of his feet as his gaze wandered from one little ecodisaster to the next. He loved these high meadows with all his heart, and the fellfields between them too. Each had been so perfect, like works of art, as if hundreds of meticulous bonsai gardeners had spent centuries arranging each watercourse and pad of moss. Every blade of grass deployed, every rock in its proper place. It had never occurred to Charlie that any of it could ever go away. And yet here it was, dead.

Desolation filled him. It pressed inside him, slowing him down, buffeting him from inside, making him stumble. Not the Sierra. Not the Sierra. If everything living that he loved in this Alpine world died, then it would not be the Sierra. Suddenly he thought of Joe and a giant stab of fear pierced him like a sword, he sank back and sat down on the nearest rock, felled by the feeling. Never doubt our emotions rule us; and no matter what we do, or say, or resolve, a single feeling can knock us down like a sword to the heart. A dead meadow—image of a black crisp on a bed—Charlie groaned and put his face to his knees.

He tried to pull himself back into the world. Behind him Frank was still wandering, lonely as a cloud, deep in his own space; but soon he would catch up.

Charlie took a deep breath, pulled himself together. Several more deep breaths. No one would ever know how shaken he had been by his thoughts. So much of life is a private experience.

Frank stood over him, looked at him with his head cocked. "You okay?"

"I'm okay. You?"

"I'm okay." He gestured around them. "Quite the drought."

"That's for sure!" Charlie shook his head violently from side to side. "It makes me sad—it makes me afraid! I mean—it looks so bad. It looks like it could be gone for good!"

Frank shrugged. "There's been droughts up here before. They've found dead tree stumps that had time to grow pretty big, a couple hundred feet down in Lake Tahoe. That had to be a long drought. Seems like it dries out up here sometimes."

"Yes. But—you know. What if it lasts a hundred years? What if it lasts a thousand years?"

"Well, sure. That would be bad. But we're doing so much to the weather. And it's pretty chaotic anyway. Hopefully it will be all right."

Charlie shrugged. This was thin comfort.

Again Frank regarded him. "Aside from that, you're okay?"

"Yeah, sure." It was so unlike Frank to ask, especially on this trip, that Charlie felt an urge to continue: "I'm worried about Joe. Nothing in particular. It's just hard to imagine, sometimes, how he is going to get by in this world."

"Your Joe? He'll get by fine. You don't have to worry about him."

Frank stood over Charlie, hands folded on the tops of his walking poles, looking out at the sweep of the Muro Blanco, the great canyon walled by long cliffs of white granite. At ease; distracted. Or so it seemed. As he wandered away he said over his shoulder, "Your kids will be fine."

CHAPTER 27

EMERSON FOR THE DAY

There are days which are the carnival of the year. The angels assume flesh, and repeatedly become visible. The imagination of the gods is excited and rushes on every side into forms.

—*Emerson*

Wake up Sunday morning. In the van, outside a fregan potluck house in Foggy Bottom. Put on clothes, "scientist nice," meaning shirt with collar. Walk to the Optimodal that Diane found near the White House. Shower and shave, then east on G Street. Find a deli open for lunch; most of them closed. Eat lunch and then continue east to the MCI Center, where the Wizards play basketball.

A building like all the others in the area, filling a whole block. This one has glass doors by the dozen, poster-holders between the doors, advertising events. Lines of people outside. Many Asians; many of them in Asian attire.

Wait in line, then give an attendant a Ticketron ticket. Inside, wander the hallway looking at the tunnel entries, checking section numbers. Hallway lined with food stalls and souvenir stands and restrooms, as in any sports arena. Beer, wine, hot dogs, pretzels, nachos. Like a basketball game, or a rock concert. Strange to see when attending a talk by the Dalai Lama.

Plan to meet the Quiblers at their seats, a good thing; impossible to tell if one has circled ninety degrees. Which way north? No way to tell.

After 270 degrees, perhaps, come to proper number and show ticket to usher, get ushered to seat. Great seats if it were basketball, in the middle just above floor, which is now occupied by rows of chairs, slowly filling with peo-

ple. Stage at the end of the floor where one basket would be. Empty seats; presumably the Quiblers'. An hour and a half before start. Don't want to be late for the Dalai Lama! Arena at this point nearly empty. And big. A big oval of seats, rising to a great height on all sides. Was that glassed row what they called luxury boxes? Maybe the Dalai Lama is not a sellout.

But he is. Arena fills. Quiblers show up around half an hour before the start. Shake hands with Charlie and the boys, give Anna a hug. She too dressed up, as if giving a talk at a conference. Looks nice. All the women there look nice.

Sit and chat about the crowd and the venue and the event, the boys looking around with the same curious expression one can feel in one's own face. Watching people. Mesmerized by the sight of so many people, pouring in tunnels from the concourse and taking their seats. Charlie says capacity twenty thousand, but with the section behind the stage cordoned off, thirteen thousand. Thirteen thousand human beings, all races and ethnicities seemingly represented. All gathered to hear one man speak. This is Washington, D.C. Capital of the world.

A big screen behind the stage. They test a video system that shows, greatly magnified on the screen, the image of an armchair on the stage, which makes the actual chair suddenly look tiny. There are two armchairs and a coffee table, all on a carpet. Small tree in pot behind. Bouquets of flowers.

People appear onstage, causing a groundswell of voices, then applause. An American woman welcomes the crowd now packing the arena, no unoccupied seats to be seen. A Democratic congresswoman introduces the Dalai Lama, at great length and with little eloquence. Then a pause; the hall goes silent.

"What?" Joe asks, looking around bug-eyed.

A cluster of people in maroon robes walk up the steps onto the stage, and sudden applause bursts out. Everyone stands. Joe stands on his chair, then climbs into Charlie's arms. His head is then just higher than Charlie's. Now it can be seen how their faces look alike.

Dalai Lama onstage. A big swell of applause. He wears the kind of robe that leaves his arms bare. He holds his hands together, bows slightly in various directions, smiling graciously. All this is repeated hugely on the screen.

The face familiar from photographs. An ordinary Tibetan monk, as he always says himself.

On the stage with him appears a shorter Tibetan man in a Western three-piece suit. This man sits in the armchair on the right and watches as twenty or thirty more people ascend the stairs onto the stage. They are all dressed in colorful national or ethnic clothes, Asian in look. Lots of white, splashes of color.

They array themselves in a line facing the Dalai Lama, and the American woman who first welcomed them returns to the lectern to explain to the audience that these are representatives of all the Buddhist communities in Asia who regard the Dalai Lama as their spiritual leader. More applause.

Each representative approaches the Dalai Lama in turn, holding a white scarf. With a bow the Dalai Lama takes the scarves, bows again, often touching foreheads with the person who has approached, then puts the scarves around their necks. After a verbal exchange not broadcast to the crowd, the representatives move to one side.

Some are clearly almost overwhelmed by this interaction. They crab toward him, or walk bent in a bow. But the Dalai Lama greets all with a grin and a greeting, and when they leave him they are straightened up and more relaxed.

The last dignitary to approach is Drepung, in flowing white robes. It takes checking on the big screen to be sure of this. Yes, their Drepung. Joe is jerking up and down in Charlie's arms, pointing. Nick too is pointing.

The effect of the two images, one little and three-dimensional, one huge and two-dimensional, creates a kind of hyperreality, a five-dimensional vertigo. On the screen, one can see that under his white ceremonial robes Drepung is still wearing his running shoes, now more enormous than ever. He bounces toward the Dalai Lama with a huge grin on his face, the Dalai Lama matching it watt for watt; they seem to know each other. The Dalai Lama bows as Drepung approaches, Drepung bows, they keep eye contact all the while. They meet and touch foreheads, Drepung bowing lower to make this contact, even though the Dalai Lama is not a small man. The crowd cheers. Many Asians around them are weeping. Drepung hands the Dalai Lama the white scarf he is carrying, and the Dalai Lama touches it to his forehead and puts it around Drepung's neck, Drepung bowing low to receive it. When that's done they speak for a bit in Tibetan, laughing at something. The Dalai Lama asks a question, Drepung cocks his head to the side, nods, makes some jest; laughing, the Dalai Lama turns and takes a white scarf from one of his aides standing behind, then gives it to Drepung. Drepung touches it to his forehead, then extends it over the Dalai Lama's bowed head and places it around his neck, to huge cheers. The Dalai Lama laughs and vamps for a second, to audience laughter, then gestures Drepung off the stage as if shooing away a fly.

The white-scarved group also leaves the stage. The Dalai Lama sits down in the armchair to the left. He puts on a radio microphone that works well, as everyone finds out when he says in a deep voice, "Hello." Amplification in the arena is clearer than one would have thought possible.

The crowd says hello back. The Dalai Lama kicks off his sandals, leaves them on the carpet, and tucks his feet up under his legs, in either a meditation pose or just a comfortable position. Bare arms make it seem he could be cold, but no doubt he is used to it and does not notice. It's hot outside anyway.

He begins to speak, but in Tibetan. Around his amplified words is silence. The airy whoosh of the building's ventilation system becomes audible: surreal, the visible presence of thirteen thousand people but no crowd noise at all. All quiet, all listening intently to a man speaking a language they don't know.

Low sonorous Tibetan, unlike the sound of Chinese, or the other East Asian languages. Yes, he sounds like Rudra Cakrin. Then he pauses, and the man in the other armchair speaks in English. Ah, the translator. Presumably he is summarizing what the Dalai Lama just said. Voices booming out of the giant black scoreboard console hanging over center court.

The translator finishes translating what was apparently an entirely conventional welcome, and the Dalai Lama starts again in Tibetan. This is going to be a long affair. Then all of a sudden the Dalai Lama switches to English. "I hope we can talk about all this in the rest of our time together. How to live in this world. How to achieve peace and balance."

His English is perfectly clear. He jokes about his inability in it, and from time to time he dives back into Tibetan, apparently to be sure of being accu-

rate about important things. Possibly even here his attempt in English would be more interesting than the translator's more expert locutions. In any case, back and forth between languages they bounce, both getting some laughs.

The Dalai Lama talks about the situation they find themselves in, "a difficult moment in history," as he calls it, acknowledging this truth with a shrug. Reality is not easy; as a Tibetan, this has been evident all his life; and yet all the more reason not to despair, or even to lose one's peace of mind. One has to focus on what one can do oneself, and then do that, he says. He says, "We are visitors on this planet. We are here for ninety or one hundred years at the very most. During that period, we must try to do something good, something useful, with our lives. Try to be at peace with yourself, and help others share that peace. If you contribute to other people's happiness, you will find the true goal, the true meaning of life."

He sounds so much like Rudra Cakrin. Suddenly it's hard to believe that such an idiosyncratic mind as Rudra Cakrin's can be gone. Many of the people here presumably do not believe it. The man speaking is agreed to be the fourteenth reincarnation of a particular mind. Although in an interview published that morning in the Post, the Dalai Lama was asked when he had first recalled his previous lives, and he replied, "I have never had that experience," and then added, "I am an ordinary human being." He did not even make any particular claim to special knowledge, or expertise in anything metaphysical.

Now he says, "What happens beyond our senses we cannot know. All we can see indicates that everything is transitory."

This is not the kind of thing a religious leader is expected to say—admissions of ignorance, jokes about translation error. The whole situation feels nonreligious, more like a fireside chat than the Sermon on the Mount. Maybe the Sermon on the Mount would have felt like that too.

"Knowledge is important, but much more important is the use toward which it is put. This depends on the heart and mind of the one who uses it."

It's the argument for always generous. Even if you only manage to love your own DNA, it exists in a diffuse extension through the biosphere. All the eukaryotes share the basic genes; all life is one. If you love yourself, or just want to survive—or maybe those are the same thing—then the love has to diffuse out into everything, just to be accurate.

To love accurately. The Dalai Lama says something about mindful consumption. We eat the world the way we breathe it. Thanks must be given, devotion must be given. One must pay attention, to do what is right for life.

These are all the things a sociobiologist would recommend, if he could talk about what ought to be as well as what is. Buddhism as the Dalai Lama's science; science as the scientist's Buddhism. Again, as when Rudra Cakrin gave his lecture at NSF, it all becomes clear.

Time passes in a flow of ideas. A couple of hours, in fact; no concessions to any supposedly short attention spans. And the crowd is silent and attentive. The time has gone fast somehow, and now the Dalai Lama is winding things up by answering questions submitted by e-mail, read by his translator from a printout.

"Last question, Rebecca Sampson, fifth grade: Why does China want Tibet so bad?"

Nervous titter from the crowd.

The Dalai Lama tilts his head to the side. "Tibet is very beautiful," he says, in a way that makes everyone laugh. A certain tension dissipates. "Tibet has a lot of forests. Animals, minerals—not so many vegetables." Another surprised laugh, rustling unamplified through the arena like wind in the trees.

"Most of all, Tibet has room. China is a big country, but it has a lot of people. Too many people for them on their own land, over the long term. And Tibet is at the roof of Asia. When you are in Tibet, no one can attack you from above! So, there are these strategic reasons. But most of them, when examined, are not very important. And I see signs that the Chinese are beginning to realize that. There are ways of accommodating everybody's desires, and so I see some progress on this matter. They are willing to talk now. It will all come in time."

Soon after that they are done. Everyone is standing and clapping. A moment of union. Thirteen thousand human beings, all thankful at once.

Say good-bye to the Quiblers. Wander with the crowd, disoriented, uncaring; it doesn't matter where you leave the building. Just get outside.

Outside. Westward on H Street. Quickly separate from the crowd that together has witnessed such a remarkable event. Back among the strangers of the city; no more union. Over to G Street and west, past the White House with its fence, past the ugly Old Executive Offices, don't turn in there to work. Just look. Think about the place from the outside. From the Dalai Lama's point of view. Why had the Dalai Lama given Drepung a scarf to bless and then put around his own neck? He hadn't done that with anyone else. Must ask Drepung. Some kind of power.

What was it the Dalai Lama said about compassion?

The words are gone, the feeling remains. Did he really use the word oxytocin, *did he really say "positron emission topography," laughing with the translator as he mangled the phrase? What just happened?*

One can always just walk away. The Dalai Lama had said that for sure. Things you don't like, things you think are wrong, you can always just walk away. You will be happier. Love and compassion are necessities, not luxuries. Without them humanity cannot survive. But compassion is not just a feeling. To make it true compassion, you have to act.

Homeless nights in the city. Slip out the security gate at sunset and off the grid, into the interstices, following the older system of paths and alleys and rail beds that web the urban forest like animal trails. Join the ferals in the wind.

Frank worked from dawn until sunset on weekdays. The rest of the time he wandered the streets and the parks and the cafés. He turned in his van to the Honda place in Arlington, then paid cash to one of the fregans for a VW van with a burnt-out engine, and got Spencer to sign the papers to take ownership of it. He slept in it while he and Spencer and Robin and Robert worked at replacing its engine. It turned out Robin and Robert had VW experience, and they did not mind sitting around in a driveway after a run, fingering over a pile of parts. Apparently this was a recognized form of post-frisbee entertainment.

"The VW engine is the last piece of technology humans could actually understand. You look under the hood of a new car, it's like whoah."

"I lived in one of these for three years."

"I lost my virginity in one of these."

General laughter. Spencer sang, "I would fight for hippie chicks, I would die for hippie chicks!"

"See if you can get the fan belt slipped over that there now."

> Emerson: "The one thing which we seek with insatiable desire is to forget ourselves, to be surprised out of our propriety, to lose our memory and to do something without knowing how or why; in short to draw a new circle. The way of life is wonderful; it is by abandonment. A man never rises so high as when he knows not whither he is going."

If that were true, then all should be well. He should be very high indeed. Decision was a feeling. In the morning he woke up in the back of the

VW van, and saw his Acheulian hand axe up there on the dashboard, and his whole life and identity leaped to him, as solid as that chunk of quartzite. Awake at dawn: now was the time to eat a little breakfast bar, read a little Emerson. So he did. No pressure inside, impeding his progress through time; he flowed with perfect equanimity. "To hazard the contradiction—freedom is necessary. If you please to plant yourself on the side of Fate, and say, Fate is all; then we say, a part of Fate is the freedom of man. Forever wells up the impulse of choosing and acting."

And so it did. With a sure hand he opened the door on the day.

He got rid of his cell phone. He stopped using credit cards or checks; he got cash from the ATM in the office, and he did all his e-mail there. He kept his FOG phone, but did not use it. He left the system of signs.

Most of his waking hours he worked at the Old Executive Offices. While the VW van was still being repaired, when he had an hour he took the Metro out to Ballston to see Drepung and some of the other Khembalis at their office in the NSF building. Sometimes he walked from there out to the embassy house in Arlington. Once he looked in the garden shed.

When they got the VW van running (it sounded like Laurel and Hardy's black truck) he added visits to the farm, to see the gang and help out in the garden. He never stayed long.

At the office he started working with a team from the OMB on funding proposals. They had done some macrocalculations for strategic planning purposes, and it turned out they could swap out the electricity generating infrastructure for about three hundred billion dollars—an astonishing bargain, as one OMB guy put it. Stabilizing sea level might cost more, because the amount of water involved was simply staggering. Sustainable ag, on the other hand, was only expensive in terms of labor. If it wasn't going to be fossil fueled, it was going to be much more labor intensive. They needed more farmers, they needed intensive management grass range ranchers. In other words they needed more cowboys, incredible though that seemed. It was suggestive, when one thought of the federal lands in the American West, and public employment possibilities. The emptying high plains—

they could repopulate a region where too few people meant the end of town after town. Landscape restoration—habitat—buffalo biome—wolves and bears. Grizzly bears. Cost, about fifty billion dollars. These are such bargains! the OMB guy kept exclaiming. It doesn't take that much to prime the pump! Who knew?

A little before sunset, unless something was absolutely pressing, Frank would take off into the streets. Check for tails, sprint at a few strategic moments down little cross-streets, to test those behind him; no one could follow him without him seeing them. Sometimes he then took the Metro up to the zoo; sometimes he walked all the way. It was only two miles, about thirty minutes' hiking. When traffic was bad the drive wouldn't be much faster. The city felt larger than it was because in cars there were so many delays; and when walking, the distances took a bit long. At a running pace you saw how compact it was.

Run off the map and into the forest. *In good health, the air is a cordial of incredible virtue. Crossing a bare common, in snow puddles, at twilight, under a clouded sky, without having in my thoughts any occurrence of special good fortune, I have enjoyed a perfect exhilaration. I am glad to the brink of fear.*

That was it exactly: glad to the brink of fear. It filled you up. The wind in your face. Those Concord guys! That America's first great thinkers had been raving nature mystics was not accident, but inevitable. The land had spoken through them. They had lived outdoors in the great stony forest of New England, with its Himalayan weather. The blue of the sky, the abyss of fear behind things. A day out on the river, skinny-dipping with Ellery Channing.

One evening as he hiked past site 21 he saw that the old gang was back, looking as if they had never been away.

"Zeno, Fedpage, Andy, Cutter!"

"Hey there! Doctor Blood! Where you been?"

"How are you guys, where *you* been?"

"We haven't been anywhere," Zeno declared.

"What!" Frank cried. "You haven't been here!"

Cutter waved a hand at two of his city park friends, sitting at the table with him. "Out and about, you know."

Andy yelled, "What do you mean where you been? Where *you* been?"

"I've been staying with some friends," Frank said.

"Yeah well—us too," Zeno growled.

"Any sight of Chessman?"

"No." And stupid of you to ask.

"Are you still doing stuff with FOG?"

"With FOG! Are you kidding?"

They told him about it all together, Zeno prevailing in the end: "—and Fedpage is still pissed off at them!"

"He sure has bad luck with that federal government."

"You mean they have bad luck with him! He's a Jonah!"

"I am not a Jonah! I'm just the only one who looks up my rights in the personnel policies and then sticks up for them."

"You need to be more ignorant," Zeno instructed.

"I do! I've *got* to stop reading this shit, but I can't." He was reading the *Post* as he said this, so the others laughed at him.

Actually, it transpired, he was still doing some work with FOG, despite his beef with them; he was helping Nancy to organize chipping expeditions to tag more animals. To no one's surprise, the bros had liked being given little dart guns, which shot chipped darts the size of BBs. And they liked the hunts when they went out in beater lines to shoot all the unchipped animals they could find.

"The problem," Zeno told Frank, "is that half the animals are already chipped, and we aren't supposed to plunk them twice, but it's so tempting once you've got one in your sights."

"So you shoot anyway?"

"No, we start shooting each other!" Triumphant laughter at this. "It's like those paintball wars. Andy must have ten chips in him by now."

"That's only cause he shot so many people first!"

"Now there are surveillance screens in this city where he is like twelve people in one spot."

"He's a jury!"

"So don't you be trying to send us on no more secret spy missions," Andy told Frank. "We're all lit up like Christmas trees."

"Protective coloration," Frank suggested. "I should pass through you guys every night."

"Don't," Zeno warned. "We take this opportunity to say no to Doctor No."

"Yeah well, sorry about that guys. But it was a long time ago, and lately whenever I came out here, you guys weren't around."

"We've been around," Zeno said.

A silence stretched, and Frank sat on his old bench. "Why are you pissed off at FOG?" he asked Fedpage. "How did you get bogarted by the evil Big Brother that is Friends of the National Zoo?"

"The Department of Parkland Security, you mean? Look, all I was saying was that we were doing regular national park work on a volunteer basis, and that made us subject to federal liability, which means we *have* to sign their stipulated waivers or else it's the NPS that would be left liable for any accidents, whereas with the waivers it would fall on Interior's general personnel funds, which is where you would want it if you wanted any timely compensation! But what do I know?"

Zeno said, "So get on that, Blood. We want that fixed."

"Okay. Well hey guys, I was just passing through on my way to meet the frisbee guys, I'm going to go join them. But it's good to see you. I'll drop on by again. I'm doing some sunset counts for FOG, and dawn patrols too, so I'll be around. Are folks hanging here much now?"

No replies, as usual. The bros were never much on discussing plans.

"Well, I'll see you if I see you," Frank said.

"*I'll* join you for a FOG walk," Fedpage said darkly. "You need to hear the whole story about them."

That day's sunset was now gilding the autumn forest's dull yellows and browns. Leaves covered the surrounding hillsides to ankle depth everywhere they could see. Cutter gestured at the view with the can of beer in his hand: "Ain't it pretty? All these leaves, and nobody's gonna have to leaf-blow them away."

Fedpage did join him on a dawn patrol one morning. The two of them wandered slowly up the ravine, peering through the trees, pinging animals they saw with their FOG RFID readers. Fedpage talked under his breath most of the time. Perhaps obsessive-compulsive, with huge systems in his mind which made better sense to him than he could convey to other people. He was not unlike Anna in this intense regard for systems, but did not have Anna's ability to assign them their proper importance, to prioritize and see a path through a pattern, which was what made Anna so good at NSF. Without that component, or even radically lacking in it, Fedpage was living on the street and crying in his beer, always going on about lost battles over semi-hallucinated bureaucratic trivia. An excess of reason a form of madness, indeed.

You needed it all working, or things got strange. Indecisiveness was a kind of vertigo in time, a loss of balance in one's sense of movement into the future. When you weren't actually in the state, it was hard to remember it. "Forever wells up the impulse of choosing." So it seemed when all was well.

He and Fedpage came on an old man, comatose in his layby—blue-skinned, clearly in distress. The two of them kneeled over him, trying to determine if he was still alive, calling Nancy and 911 both, then wondering whether they should try to carry him out to Broad Branch Road, or wait where they were and be the ping for the rescue team. Fedpage babbled angrily about poor response time averages while Frank sat there wishing he knew more about medical matters, resolving (yet again) to at least take a CPR course.

He said this and Fedpage snorted. "Like Bill Murray in *Groundhog Day.*"

Bill Murray, trying to help a stricken homeless guy. Yet another truth from that movie so full of them; if you really wanted to help other people, you would have to devote years of your life to learning how.

He tried to express this to Fedpage, just to pass the time congealing around them. Fedpage nodded as he listened to the stricken man's stertorous breathing. "Maybe it's just sleep apnea we got here. What a great fucking movie. Me and Zeno were arguing about how many years that day had to go on for Bill Murray. I said it couldn't be less than ten years, because of the piano lessons and the med school and the, you know," and he was off on a long list of all of the character's accomplishments and how many hours it would have taken to learn these skills, and how much time he had had for them in any given version of the repeated day. "Also, though, when you think about it, if Bill Murray can do different things every day, and get a different response from the people around him, just how exactly is that different from any ordinary day? It ain't any different, that's what! Other people don't remember what you did the day before, they don't give a shit, they've got their own day to deal with! So in essence we're all living our own Groundhog Day, right? Every day is always just the same fucking day."

"You should be a Buddhist," Frank said. "You kind of are."

"Yeah *right*. I don't go in for that hippie shit."

"It's not hippie shit."

"Yeah it is. How you know."

"I talk to them is how I know. I *lived* with them."

"That proves my point. I mean you don't just *live* with people, do you."

All while the old man cradled between them gasped, or did not gasp. Eventually the rescue guys arrived, and under a blistering critique from Fedpage got him out to their ambulance. There Fedpage tried to grill them on the paperwork required of all involved, but the meds waved him away and drove off.

Talking to Fedpage was like talking to Rudra Cakrin. Frank knew some strange people. Some of these people had problems.

None more so, for instance, than the blond woman from the park. Frank saw her again, one evening at site 21 when some of them were there, and he said "Hi," and sat down next to her to ask how she was doing.

"Oh—day eighteen," she said, with a wry look.

Frank said, "Well. Eighteen's better than none."

"That's true."

"But, you know, after all this time, I still don't think we've ever been introduced. I'm Frank Vanderwal." He stuck out a hand, which she took and shook daintily, with her fingertips.

"Deirdre. Nice to meetcha, ha ha."

"Yeah, the bros aren't much on introductions. Hey Deirdre, any sign of Chessman?"

"No, I ain't seen him. I'm sure he's moved."

And on from there. She was happy to talk. Lots happened when you were homeless. It was starting to get cold again. She was staying at the UDC shelter. The whole gang had spent most of the summer there, or over at the camp in Klingle Park. Lots of people were going feral in Northwest—it made it safer in some ways, more dangerous in others. It could be fun; it could be too fun.

"Have you looked into that house on Linnean?" Frank asked.

"Yeah, I think I know the one you mean. Bunch of kids. They don't want old drunk ladies there."

"Oh I don't know. They seemed friendly to me. All kinds of people. I think you'd be fine with them."

"I don't know. They drink a lot."

"Who doesn't?" Frank said, which made her laugh. "Well, maybe one of those church outreach groups," he added, "if that's what you're looking for. There wouldn't be any drinking there."

"Okay okay, maybe I better check out those kids after all!"

The next morning, Emerson:

"Yesterday night, at fifteen minutes after eight, my little Waldo ended his life."

Only son. Scarlet fever. Six years old.

Frank wandered the streets of the city. Strange to feel so bad for a man long dead. Reading all the ecstatic sentences one could conclude Emerson had been some kind of space cadet, soaring through some untroubled space cadet life. But it wasn't so. "To be out of the war, out of debt, out of the drought, out of the blues, out of the dentist's hands, out of the second thoughts, mortifications, and remorses that inflict such twinges and shooting pains—out of the next winter, and the high prices, and company below your ambition ...." This was the world they all lived in. He had loved a world where death could strike down anyone at any time. A young wife—a treasured friend—even his own boy. A boy like Nick or Joe. And it was still like that now. The odds had been improved, but nothing was certain. Surgeons had drained a blood clot on his brain. Without science he would have died, or been one of those mysterious people who always fucked up, who could not conduct their lives. All from a pop on the nose.

Whereas now, on the other hand, he was wandering the streets of Washington, D.C., a homeless person working at the White House with burntout Vietnam vets for friends, and a spook girlfriend he did not know how to find. Miracles of modern medicine! Well, not all of that was his fault. Some kind of fate. Followed step by step it had all made sense. It was just a situation. It could be dealt with. It could be surfed. All his people were alive, after all—except Rudra Cakrin—and there he did what he could to keep the old man alive in his thoughts. Rudra would have said this, Rudra would have thought that. Good idea!

Up 19th Street to Dupont and then Connecticut, into his neighborhood of restaurants, bookstores, the laundromat by UDC. Certain neighborhoods became one's own, while the great bulk of the city remained no more than terrain to be traversed. Only a few city dwellers had London taxi driver knowledge of their city. He followed his routes in the great metropolis.

He seldom went to the Optimodal that Diane had found; it was one of his known places when not at work, and thus to be avoided. It meant he didn't see Diane then, which was too bad, but they still did their lunch walks on most days. She was getting frustrated at the many ways things could bog down.

He went to the drop spot under the tree again, and found undisturbed the last note he had left for Caroline. He crumpled it up, left another one.

HI ARE YOU OKAY? WRITE ME

He left it and walked away.

The following week, only that note was there.

He stood there in the knot of trees. Autumn forest, brassy in the afternoon light. Where was she, what was she doing? Even without a clot on the brain one could feel baffled. Right here they had lain kissing. Two creatures huddled together. Something was keeping her from making the drop.

The Air Intelligence Agency. Army Intelligence and Security Command. Central Intelligence Agency. National Clandestine Service. Coast Guard Intelligence. Defense Intelligence Agency. Office of Intelligence, Department of Energy (really?). Bureau of Intelligence and Research, Department of State. Office of Intelligence Support, Department of the Treasury. National Security Division, Federal Bureau of Investigation. Information Analysis and Infrastructure Protection Directorate. Marine Corps Intelligence Activity. National Geospatial-Intelligence Agency. National Intelligence Council. National Reconnaissance Office. National Security Agency. Office of Naval Intelligence. United States Secret Service.

The Covert Action Staff. The Department of Homeland Security, Office of Intelligence and Analysis. The Directorate of Operations. Drug Enforcement Administration. Office of National Security Intelligence.

The United States Intelligence Community (a cooperative federation).

Out his run with Edgardo the next day, he said, "Are there really as many intelligence agencies as they say there are?"

"No." Pause for a beat. "There are more."

"Shit." Slowly, haltingly, Frank told him about the situation with Caroline and the dead drop. "She said she would use it. So I'm worried."

They ran on in silence from the Washington Monument to the Capitol, and then back to the Washington Monument again; an unprecedented span of silence in Frank's experience of running with Edgardo. He waited curiously.

Finally Edgardo said, "You should consider that maybe she is out of town. That she is involved in the effort to deal with these guys, and has to stay away."

"Ah."

It was like taking a pressure off the brain.

Thoreau said, "I rejoice that there are owls. Let them do the idiotic and maniacal hooting for men. It is a sound admirably suited to swamps and twilight woods which no day illustrates, suggesting a vast and undeveloped nature which men have not recognized. They represent the stark twilight and unsatisfied thoughts which all have."

Ooooooooop! And the gibbon chorus at dawn? It represented joy. It was saying *I'm alive*. Bert still started it every morning he was out in the enclosure at dawn. May too was an enthusiast. Sleeping in his VW van on Linnean, he could start each day joining the zoo chorus. It was the best way to start the day.

"While the man that killed my lynx (and many others) thinks it came out of a menagerie, and the naturalists call it the Canada lynx, and at the White Mountains they call it the Siberian lynx—in each case forgetting, or ignoring, that it belongs here—I call it the Concord lynx."

There were no lynxes in Massachusetts now.

But the Rock Creek hominid persisted. Ooooop! One could follow Rock Creek from the Potomac all the way up to the zoo, with a few little detours. North of that came the beaver pond, and then site 21. Back out to Connecticut, to an early dinner, pay with cash, big tip, so easy; off again into the park.

There he ran into Spencer and Robert and Robin, as planned; hugs all around. They were an affectionate group. Sling the friz, running and hooting through the dim yellow world, working up a sweat. The flight of startled deer, their eponymous white tails. Stand around afterward, feeling the blood bump.

The autumn colors in Rock Creek were not like those in New England, they were more muted, more various—not Norman Rockwell, but Cézanne—or, as Diane suggested when Frank put it that way to her, Vuillard.

Vuillard? he asked.

She took him on a lunch break back to the Mellon room at the National Gallery. Eating hot dogs sitting on the steps, and then going in to examine the subtle little mud-toned canvases of Vuillard. Wandering side by side, arms bumping, heads together. Was that tan or umber or what. Imagine his palette at the end of the day. Like something the cat threw up.

She too was affectionate. She took his arm to propel him along. "So how does your head feel today?" she would ask.

"About the same as yesterday."

She squeezed his arm. "I don't ask *every* day. Still feeling better?"

"I am. You know, Yann's doing some amazing things out there in San Diego." It probably sounded like a change of subject, but it wasn't.

"Yeah, like what?"

"Well, I think they've worked out how to get their DNA modifications into human bodies. The insertion problem may have been solved, and if that happens, all kinds of things might follow. Gene therapies, you know."

"Wow. Nice to think that something's going right."

"Indeed."

"It would be ironic to think that just as we were inventing real health care we burned the planet down instead."

He laughed.

"Don't laugh or I'll bleed on you," she said dourly. She too had lost someone young, he remembered suddenly; her husband had died of cancer in what must have been his forties or fifties. "So," she persisted, "have you got the feeling in your nose back?"

"No."

"Maybe they'll learn to regrow nerves."

"I think they may. There are some angles converging on that one."

"Cool." She sighed.

"I've gotta get back," Frank said. "I've got a call in with Anna, to talk about coordinating all her Fix-it agencies, you should drop in on that."

"Okay I will." As they started back: "I'm glad you're feeling better."

. . .

Mostly he left the VW van in a driveway behind a feral potluck house on Linnean. If he drove it at all, mostly out to the farm, he checked it thoroughly first. Dry-cleaning, Edgardo called it. It always proved free of all chips, tags, and transponders. Easy to believe when you looked at it: VW vans as a class were getting kind of old and skanky. But what a fine house. And sitting in the curved vinyl seat at night, reading his laptop on the curved little table, Thoreau seemed to second the thought:

> In those days when how to get my living honestly, with freedom left for my proper pursuits, was a question which vexed me even more than it does now, I used to see a large box by the railroad, six feet long by three wide, in which the workmen locked up their tools at night; and it suggested to me that every man who was hard pushed might get him such a one for a dollar, and, having bored a few auger holes in it, to admit the air at least, get into it when it rained and at night, and shut the lid and hook it, and so have freedom in his mind, and in his soul be free. This did not seem the worst alternative, nor by any means a despicable resource. I should not be in so bad a box as many a man is in now.

Thoreau had understood. Put such a box in a tree, and you had your treehouse. Put the box in a book and you had *Walden*. Put the box on wheels and you had your VW van. Frank printed the passage out and stuck it on the wall the next time he was at the fregan potluck. They too had found the key. He ate with them about three nights a week, all over Northwest, in house after house. There were feral subcultures: there was a farmer's market wing, and a hunter's crowd, and dumpster purists, and many other ways of going feral in the city.

At work Frank was making wonderful strides with the guy from OMB who was administering the Fix-it program that Anna had rediscovered. His name was Henry, and he worked with Roy and Andrea and the rest of the

White House brain trust. Right now, he and Frank were teaming up on the clean energy part of the mission architecture. The Navy had made an agreement with the Navaho nation to build and run a prototype nuclear power plant that would reuse fuel rods and were overengineered for safety. Meanwhile Southern California Edison had agreed to build a dozen more Stirling heat engine solar power generators, for themselves and other energy companies around the American West, and a dozen more for federal plants that were going to be built on BLM land, using a federal grant program. SCE had also won the contract to build the first generation of fully clean coal plants, which would capture both the particulates and the carbon dioxide and other greenhouse gases on firing, so that all they would be releasing from the pipe was steam. The first plants were to be built in Oklahoma, and the CO_2 collected in the process was to be injected into nearby depleted oil wells. Oil wells nearby that were still working would look to see if they got any uptick in pressure differentials, making for a complete systems test.

"Sweet," the OMB's Henry commented. He was about thirty, it seemed to Frank, utterly fresh and determined. He was unfazed by the past, even unaware of it. The defeats and obstructions, the nightmarish beginning to the century, so balked and stupidified; none of that meant a thing to him. And Washington had hundreds of these kids ready to rip. The world was full of them. He said, "That's a good big subunit of the whole mission architecture, up and running."

"True," Frank said. "I think the question now is how quick we can ramp."

"I wonder how much investment capital is out there. Or whether trained labor will be the real shortage."

"I guess we'll find out."

"That's a good thought." And young Henry grinned.

Evening in the park, and Frank buzzed Spencer and joined him and Robin and Robert at a new fregan house. East, into a neighborhood he had never been in before, in which burned or boarded-up buildings stood mutely between renovated towers guarded by private security people. An awkward mix it seemed, and yet once inside the boarded-up shell of a brownstone, it proved to be as sheltered from the public life of the city as any other place. Home was where the food was.

Same crowd as always, a mix of young and old. Neo-hippie and post-punk, making some new thing that Frank couldn't name with a media label. The fregan way. Mix of races, ethnicities, modes of operation. A potluck indeed. It was like this every night in so many different places around Northwest. What was happening in Washington, D.C.? What was happening anywhere else, everywhere else? No one could be sure. The media was a concocted product, reporting only a small fraction of the culture. What would people do for a sense of the zeitgeist when the culture had fractalized and parcellated and the media become not a mirror, but one artifact among many? Had it ever been any different? Was this somehow new? If people walked away from the old mass culture of mass consumption, and everybody did something homegrown, what would that be like?

"How many fregan houses are there altogether, do you suppose?" Frank asked Spencer as they sat on the floor over their plates.

Spencer shrugged. "Lots I guess."

"How do you choose which to go to?"

"Friends spread the word. I generally know by five, or Robert."

"Not Robin?"

"Robin usually just goes where we go. You know Robin. He barely knows what city we're in."

"Which *planet* is this?" Robin asked from behind them.

"See? He doesn't want to be distracted with irrelevancies. Anyway, you can always call me."

"I only have my FOG phone now," Frank said. "And even that I'm trying not to use too much. I want to stay off the grid when I'm not at work."

"I know," Spencer said as he chewed, glancing at Frank speculatively. He swallowed. "I should tell you, no one can guarantee this group doesn't have informants in it. You know. It's loose at the edges, and law enforcement is kind of nervous about the feral concept. I've heard there are people taking money from the FBI to make some bucks, and they tell them all sorts of things."

"Of course." Frank looked around. No one looked like an informant.

Spencer went back to wolfing down his meal. There was a big crowd tonight and there wasn't going to be quite enough food. At the start of every potluck they had all started to say a little thanksgiving. In most houses, they all said together, "Enough is as good as a feast," sometimes repeating it three or four times. Maybe that was the third great correlation, enough and happiness. Or maybe it was science and Buddhism. Or compassion and action. No, these were too general. It was still out there. Or maybe there were more than three. The Five Great Correlations. The Nine Great Correlations.

One day Spencer called Frank on his FOG phone. "Hey Frank, did you check out your Emerson for the day?"

Frank had everyone reading it now. "No," he said.

"Then here, listen to it. 'I remember well the foreign scholar who made a week of my youth happy by his visit. "The savages in the islands," he said, "delight to play with the surf, coming in on the top of the rollers, then swimming out again, and repeat the delicious maneuver for hours." Well, human life is made up of such transits.'

"—Did you hear that, Frank?"

"Yes."

"Ralph Waldo Emerson, saying that *life is like surfing*? Is that great or *what*?"

"Yes, that's pretty great. That's our man."

"Who was this guy? Do you think somebody's making these quotes up?"

"No, I think Emerson made them up."

"It's so perfect! He's like your Dalai Lama."

"That's very true."

"The Waldo Lama. He's like the great shaman of the forest!"

"It's true, he is. Although even more so his buddy Thoreau, when it comes to the actual forest."

"Yeah that's right. Your treehouse guru. The man in the box. They are *teaching you*, baby!"

"You're teaching me."

"Yes I am. Well okay then, bro, just wanted to make sure you didn't miss that one. Surf your way up here and we'll tee off at around five."

"Okay, I'll try to be there."

In all the wandering, work was his anchor. These days he focused mostly on the problems cropping up as they tried to convince all the relevant agencies to act on their part of the mission architecture. He also worked on obtaining UN and national approvals for the seawater relocations. Holland was taking the lead here, also England, and really most countries wanted sea level stabilization, so the will was there, but problems were endless. The war of the agencies had gone international.

The technical issues in powering such a massive relocation of seawater were becoming more obvious. They mostly involved matters of scale or sheer number. Floating platforms like giant rafts could be anchored next to a coastline, and they could move about, they did not have to have a fixed location. Pumps were straightforward, although they had never wanted pumps so large and powerful before. Pipelines could be adapted from the oil and gas industry, although it would be good to have much bigger pipes, if they could power them. Power remained the biggest concern, but if the rafts held an array of solar panels big enough, then they could be autonomous units, floating wherever they wanted them to go. Pipelines had to be run to the playas they wanted to fill. China and Morocco and Mauritania had been the first to agree to run prototype systems.

Down in Antarctica, they could set them anywhere around the big eastern half of the continent, and run heated pipelines up to the polar plateau, where several depressions would serve as catchment basins. Cold made things more complicated down there technologically, but politically it was infinitely easier. SCAR, the Scientific Committee on Antarctic Research, had approved the idea of the project, and they were as close to a government as Antarctica had. In some senses NSF was the true government of Antarctica, and the relevant people at NSF were good to go. They saw the need. Saving the world so science could proceed: the Frank Principle was standard operating procedure at NSF. It went without saying. Which was a relief to Frank. He didn't really like the sound of the Frank Principle. He wanted to be the one who coined the Nine Great Correlations.

After another long day at work, about a week later, Diane asked whether he wanted to get something to eat, and he said of course.

At dinner in a restaurant on Vermont Avenue she talked about the tendency for innovation to bog in groups of more than a few people, which she called reversion to the norm. Frank laughed at that, thinking it would be a good joke to share with Edgardo. He ate his dinner and watched her talking. From time to time he nodded, asked questions.

Phil Chase was too busy to give much time to their issues, and he was having trouble getting legislation and funding from Congress for his initiatives. Access to him was controlled by Roy Anastopoulos and Andrea Palmer, and while they said Chase remained interested in climate and science, he was still going to trust Diane and the agencies to do their jobs, while he focused on his, which ranged all across the board; his time was precious. Not easy to get a piece of it, or even to contact him properly. Get on with it, his staffers seemed to be saying.

Diane wasn't pleased with their priorities. She asked Frank if he would mind asking Charlie to ask Roy to ask Chase about certain things more directly; she laughed as she said this. Frank smiled and nodded. He would talk to Charlie. He thought word could get passed along. Maybe in Washington, D.C., he suggested, six degrees of separation was not the maximum separating any two people, but the minimum. Diane laughed again. Frank watched her laugh, and oceans of clouds filled his chest.

Anna Quibler had been researching the situation in China, and she found it troubling. Their State Environmental Protection Administration had several Environmental Protection Bureaus, and environmental laws were on the books. There were even some nongovernmental organizations working to keep the crowded country's landscape clean. But the government in Beijing had given power for economic development to local governments, and these were evaluated by Beijing for their economic growth only, so laws were ignored, and there was no body that had a good handle on the total situation. That sounded familiar, but in China things were amplified and accelerated. Now an NGO called Han Hai Sha (Boundless Ocean of Sand) was sending reports to a division of the Chinese Academy of Sciences that collated information from all Chinese environmental studies. For a country of that size, there weren't very many of these studies, but the upshot was clear: China was a terrible mess. Rapid economic growth had been the ruling principle in Beijing for decades now, with a billion people occupying about as much land as Brazil or the United States. The list of environmental problems the Chinese scientists had gathered was already large, but Anna's contact said that big areas in the west were going unstudied and unreported. Strip mining, coal power generation, deforestation, urbanization of river valleys, cement production and steel manufacturing, new dams, use of dangerous pesticides: all these factors were combining downstream, in the eastern half of the country, in the big river valleys and on the coasts, and in the many megacities quickly paving over their best farmland. Many Chinese scientists saw signs of a disaster unfolding.

Cumulative impacts, Anna sighed, the most complex and vexing subject in biostatistics; and the Chinese problem was macrobiostatistics, or meta-analysis. Anna's correspondent Fengzhen called what he saw coming "a general system crash," meaning ecology, agriculture, and society all together. He spoke of indicator species already extinct, dead zones in rivers and offshore, poisoned soils, and other signs that this general crash might be starting. It was a theory he was working on. He compared the Chinese situation to the coral reefs, which had died in about a five years' span just a decade earlier. All coral reefs died, he wrote in an e-mail. All China could likewise die.

Anna read this and swallowed hard. She wrote back asking if he and his colleagues could identify the worst two or three impacts they were seeing, with their causes and possible mitigations, and she clicked SEND with a sinking feeling. NSF had an international program in which U.S. scientists teamed with foreign scientists, and the infrastructure was given to the foreign teams afterward. A good idea; but it didn't look like it was going to be adequate for dealing with this one!

Early one Saturday morning, Charlie met Frank and Drepung on the Potomac, at the little dock by the boathouse at the mouth of Rock Creek, and they put their rented kayaks in the water just after dawn, the sun like an orange floating on the water. They stroked upstream on the Maryland side, looking into the trees to see if there were any animals out. Then across the copper sheen to the Virginia side, to check out a strange concrete outfall there. "That's where I used to bring Rudra Cakrin," Frank said, pointing at the little overlook at Windy Run.

Then he stroked ahead, smooth and splashless. He was not much more talkative here than in the Sierras, mostly looking around, paddling silently.

On this morning, his habits suited Charlie's purposes. Charlie slowed in Frank's wake, and soon he and Drepung were a good distance behind.

"Drepung?"

"Yes, Charlie?"

"I wanted to ask you something about Joe."

"Yes?"

"Well . . . I'm wondering how you would characterize what's going on in him now, after the . . . ceremony that you and Rudra conducted last year."

Drepung's brow furrowed. "I'm not sure what you mean."

"Well—some, I don't know—some sort of spirit was expelled?"

"In a manner of speaking."

"Well," Charlie said. He took a deep breath. "I want it to come back."

"What do you mean?"

"I want my Joe back. I want whoever he was before the ceremony. That's the real Joe. I've come to realize that. I was wrong to ask you to do anything to him. Whatever he was before, that was him. Do you see what I mean?"

"I'm not sure. Are you saying that he's changed?"

"Yes! Of course that's what I'm saying! Because he has changed! And I didn't realize . . . I didn't know that it took all of him, even the parts that, that I don't know, to make him what he is. I was being selfish, I guess, just because he was so much work. I rationalized that it wasn't him and that it was making him unhappy, but it *was* him, and he wasn't unhappy at all. It's now that he seems unhappy, actually. Or maybe just not himself. I mean he's easier than before, but he doesn't seem to be as interested in things. He doesn't have the same spark. I mean . . . what was it that you drove out of him, anyway?"

Drepung stared at him for a few strokes of the paddle. Slowly he said, "People say that certain Bön spirits latch on to a person's intrinsic nature, and are hard to dislodge with Buddhist ceremonies. The whole history of Buddhism coming to Tibet is one fight after another, to drive the Bön spirits out of the land and people, so that the nonviolence of Buddhism could take the upper hand. It was hard, and there were many contradictions involved, as usual if you try too hard to fight against violent feelings. That itself can quickly become another violence. Some of the early lamas had lots of anger themselves. So the struggle never really ended, I guess you would say."

"Meaning there are still Bön spirits inhabiting you people?"

"Well, not everyone."

"But some?"

"Yes. Rudra was often pestered. He could not get rid of one of them. And he had invited them into him so many times when serving as the oracle, it made him susceptible. Anyway this one would not leave him. This was one of the reasons he was so irritable in his old age."

"I never thought he was that bad." Charlie sighed. "So where is that Bön spirit now, eh? Is Rudra's soul still having to deal with it in the bardo?"

"Possibly so. We cannot tell from here."

"He'll get reborn at some point, presumably."

"At some point."

"But so . . . Are there ceremonies to call spirits into you?"

"Sure. That's what the oracle does, every time there is a visitation."

"Aha. So listen, could you then *call back* the spirit that you exorcised from Joe? Could you explain it was a mistake, and invite him back?"

Drepung paddled on for a while. The silence lingered. Ahead of them Frank was now drifting into the shallows behind a snag.

"Drepung?"

"Yes, Charlie. I'll see what I can do."

"Drepung! Don't give me that one again!"

"No, I mean it. In this case, I think I know what you mean. And I have the right figure in mind. The one that was in Joe. A very energetic spirit."

"Yeah, exactly."

"And I know the right ceremony too."

"Oh good. Good. Well—let me know what I can do, then?"

"I will. I'll have to talk to Sucandra about it, but he will help us. I will tell you when we have made the arrangements, and divined the right time for it."

"The right time for what?" Frank asked, as they had caught up to him, or at least were within earshot. On the water that was often hard to determine.

"The right time to put Joe Quibler in touch with his spirit."

"Aha! It's always the right time for that, right?"

"To everything its proper moment."

"Sure. Look—there's one of the tapirs from the zoo, see it?"

"No?"

"It's the same color as the leaves."

"Ah yeah. So how are the feral animals doing generally?"

"It depends on their natural range. Some species have been spotted seven hundred miles from the zoo, and up to thirty latitude lines out of their natural range. Anna's helping Nick and his group to make a habitat corridor map, networking all the remaining wildernesses together. It's a GIS thing."

"So if we want it, we can have the animals back."

"Yeah. It would be cool if the President would back the initiatives coming out of the animal rights community."

Charlie laughed. "He's got a lot on his plate. I don't know if he's got time for that one right now. It's a hard thing to get his attention these days."

For Frank this was a new issue, but Charlie had been dealing with it for years, since long before Phil had become president. It simply was not easy to get any time with someone so powerful. Now Charlie could see that Frank and Diane were also running into that problem. Even though Diane was the presidential science advisor, she still did not often see him. He was booked by the minute. No matter how sympathetic Andrea and Roy were to the scientists, there was very little presidential time available. On they had to go, flying in formation; and the days ripped away as in the calendar shots of old movies.

But then one afternoon, after Frank had given Charlie a call to beg for some intercession on the nuclear regulations issue, and Charlie had passed the word along in a call to Roy, he got a call back from that so-busy man.

It was right before dinnertime. "The boss is ready to call it a day, but he wants to talk to your people about this regulation relief. So he's proposed one of his little expeditions over to the Tidal Basin. We take some takeout to the blue pedal boats, and have a picnic on the water."

"Oh good," Charlie said. "I'll call Frank and we'll meet you down there."

"Not me, I've got stuff to do. Andrea will be going though."

Charlie called Frank and described the plan.

"Good idea," Frank said.

The President would be driven over by his Secret Service detail, and as normal hours of operation for the tourist concession there were done for the day, it would be easy to take over the dock and the tidal pool, and unobtrusively secure the perimeter. The National Park Service was fine with it; indeed this was already a little presidential tradition, and from their perspective, a good thing.

The time being what it was, Charlie decided to take Joe along. He went down to daycare and found him occupied in some game or other with a girl his age, but he was happy to join the expedition and drive across the Mall.

After they parked on 15th Street and got out and walked down to the pedal boat dock, where Phil and Andrea and some of the Secret Service guys were already standing, Charlie followed Joe a short way up the basin's shore path, agreeing that some rocks to throw in the water would be just the thing.

Looking north at the Mall Charlie saw Diane, Frank, Kenzo, and Edgardo walking down 17th Street. They were a good-looking group, Charlie thought. Edgardo was gesturing in the midst of some comic soliloquy, making the rest laugh. Frank and Diane walked a bit behind, in step, heads together. As they crossed Independence Avenue at the light, Diane slipped her arm under Frank's, and as they reached the curb he helped her up with what almost looked like a little squeeze. They were laughing. A couple, out on a balmy evening.

They came down to the Tidal Basin on the pedestrian path, and Charlie and Joe joined them on the way to the dock. Some national park rangers were untying a clutch of the blue pedal boats. The little round lake was empty, the round-topped Jefferson Memorial reflected upside down in it. The late light burnished things. On the dock Charlie saw in the rangers that look of contained excitement that surrounded the presidency at all times. This would make for a story later, people's faces said. Another Phil Chase moment to add to all the rest.

Phil was expert in ignoring all that, crying out hellos to rangers he had seen before, making it clear he was a regular. His security people were forming a scarcely visible human barrier, intercepting tourists approaching to rubberneck. Joe rushed to the boats lined up against the dock, attempting to get in the first one, but Charlie caught him just in time by the arm. "Wait a second, big guy, you have to have a life jacket on. You know that, you're so funny," feeling pleased to see this flash of the old enthusiasm.

"Hey Joe!" Phil exclaimed. "Good to see you buddy, come on, let's be the first ones out! I think I see Pedal Boat One right here in front," stepping down into it.

He reached out for Joe, which meant that Charlie was going to have to join him, and so Charlie took a kid's life preserver from the ranger offering it and tried to get one of Joe's arms through it. A quick wrestling match, similar to the ones honed by long practice during baby backpack insertions, got him started, but then Charlie looked up to see that Frank had taken Diane by the upper arm and slipped through the group to the edge of the dock. "Here," Frank said, ushering Diane into Phil's boat and looking strangely intent. "I've got to be the one who goes out with Joe, I promised him that when I last took out Nick, so I need to go out with Joe and Charlie. So here, Diane, you go with the President this time, you guys need to talk anyway." She looked surprised.

"Good idea!" Phil said, reaching out to help her step into the boat. He smiled his famous smile. "Let's get a head start on them."

"Okay," Diane said as she sat down. Frank turned away from them to greet Joe and lead Charlie to another boat.

Phil and Diane pedaled away from the dock. Charlie and Frank got in the next one, held in place by rangers with boathooks, and they took Joe and strapped him in between them. By the time they were ready to go some time had passed; Phil and Diane were already mid-pond, chomping away like a little steamboat across the coppery water. Frank waved to them, but they did not see; they were laughing at something, their attention already otherwise engaged.

CHAPTER 28

TERRAFORMING EARTH

PC: *Morning Charlie. Have some coffee. Joe, do you want coffee?*

JQ: *Sure Phil.*

CQ: *How about hot chocolate.*

PC: *Oh yeah, that's what I'm having. Since we've got rain on our dawn patrol. Although rain has gotten a lot more interesting than it used to be, eh?*

CQ: *Droughts will do that.*

PC: *Yes. But now is the winter of our wet content. Here you go, Joe. Here you go, Charlie. These south windows are big, aren't they. I like looking at rain out the window. Here Joe, you can put those right here on the carpet. Good.*

(pause. slurping.)

PC: *So, Charlie, I've been thinking that we can't afford to bog down like we kind of are. We have to go fast, so maybe we can't afford to fight capitalism anymore. They've rigged the numbers and rewritten the laws.*

CQ: *So, let me guess, now you want to make saving the world a capitalist project? Make it some kind of canny investment opportunity?*

PC: *This is why you are one of my trusted advisors, Charlie. You can guess what I'm thinking right after I say it.*

JQ: *Ha Dad.*

CQ: *Ha yourself.*

PC: *So yes, that's what you do. Without conceding that private ownership of the public trust is right, but only conceding it has bought up so much of the next thirty years. Heck it supposedly owns the world in perpetuity. We'll change that later. Right now we have to harness it to our cause, and use it to solve our problem. If we can do that, then the capitalism we end up with won't be the same one we began with anyway. The rescue operation is so much larger than anything else we've ever done that it will change everything.*

CQ: Or so you hope!

PC: It's what I'm going to try. I think we are more or less forced to try it that way. I don't see any alternative. If we don't get infrastructure and transport swapped out as fast as possible, the world is cooked. It's like our First Sixty Days never ended, but only keep rolling over. It's like sixty days and counting all the time. So we have to look to what we have. And right now we have capitalism. So we have to use it.

CQ: I don't see how.

PC: Well, capitalism has a lot of capital. And a lot of it they keep liquid and available for investment. It runs into trillions. And they want to invest it. At the same time there's an overproduction problem. If they make more than they can sell of things, they're screwed. So all capital is on the hunt for a good investment, some thing or service that isn't already overproduced. Looking to maximize profit, which is the goal that all business executives are legally bound to pursue, or they can be fired and sued by their board of directors.

CQ: Yeah, but crisis recovery isn't profitable, so what's your point?

PC: My point is there's an immense amount of capital looking to invest! Because capital accumulation really works, at least at first, but it works so well it stops growing so fast, and without maximum growth you can't get maximum profit. So you need to find new markets. And so, this has been what has been going on for the last few hundred years, capital moving from product to product but also from place to place, and what we've got now as a result is uneven development. Some places were developed centuries ago, and some of those have since been abandoned, as in the rust belts. Some places are newly developed and cranking, others are being developed and are in transition. And then there are places that have never been developed, even if their resources were extracted, and they're pretty much still in the Middle Ages. And this is what globalization has been so far—capital moving on to new zones of maximized return. When that declines, they look around to see where they might alight next, and then they take off for there.

CQ: The World Bank, in other words. That's what I told them. I lost my mind. I took off my shoe and beat on their table.

PC: That's right, that meeting was reported to me, and I wish I had been there to see it. First you laugh in the President's face, and then you scream at the World Bank in a fury. That was probably backward, but never mind. I'm glad you did it. I think the decapitation is going rather well over there. Their midlevel was stuffed with idealistic young people who went there to change it from within, and now they're getting the chance.

CQ: I hope you don't tape these conversations.

PC: Why not? It makes it a lot easier to put them in my blog.

CQ: Come on, Phil. Do you want me to talk or not?

PC: You can be the judge of that, but right now I am enjoying laying out for us the latest from geographic economics. Capital finds a likely place to develop next, and off it goes, see? Place to place. The people left behind either adjust to being on their own, or fall into a recession, or fall into a full-on rust belt collapse. Whatever happens to them, global investment capital will never again be interested. That's the point at which you begin to see people theorizing bioregionalism, as they figure out what the local region can provide on its own. They're making a virtue out of necessity, because they've been developed and are no longer the best profit. And somewhere else the process has started all over.

CQ: So soon the whole planet will be developed and modernized and we'll all be happy! Except for that fact that it would take eight Earths to support every human living at those levels of consumption! So we're screwed!

JQ: Dad.

PC: No, that's right. That's what we're seeing. The climate change and environmental collapse are us hitting the limits. We're overshooting the carrying capacity of the planet, or the consumption level, or what have you.

CQ: Yes.

PC: And yet capitalism continues to vampire its way around the globe, determined to remain unaware of the problem it's creating. Individuals in the system notice, but the system itself doesn't notice. And some people are fighting to keep the system from noticing, God knows why. It's a living I guess. So the system cries: It's not me! As if it could be anything else, given that human beings are doing it, but that's what the system claims anyway, It's not me, I'm the cure! and on it goes, and soon we're left with a devastated world.

CQ: I'm wondering where you'll take this. It's not sounding that good.

PC: Well, think about both parts of what I've been saying. The biosphere is endangered and therefore so are humans. Meanwhile capitalism needs investment opportunities. So saving the biosphere IS the next investment opportunity! It's massive, it's hungry for growth, people want it. People need it.

CQ: People don't care.

PC: No, people care. People want it. And capital always likes a desire it can make into a market. Heck it will make up desires if it needs to, so real ones are welcome. So it's a perfect fit of problem and solution.

CQ: Phil please, don't be perverse. You're saying the problem is the solution, it's double talk. If it were true, why isn't it happening already?

PC: It isn't the easy money yet. Capital always picks the low-hanging fruit first, as having the best rate of return. Maximum profit is usually found in the path of least resistance. And right now there are still lots of hungry undeveloped places, and we haven't yet run out of fossil carbon to burn. You know the reasons—it would be a bit more expensive at the start, so the profit margin is low, and since only the next quarter matters, it doesn't get done.

CQ: Right, and so?

PC: So that's where government of the people, by the people, and for the people comes into the picture! And we in the United States have the biggest and richest and most powerful government in the world! It's a great accomplishment for democracy, often unnoticed—we the people have got a whole lot of the world's capital. We're so big we can PRINT MONEY! So we have the power to pay for things. So we can aim capitalism in any direction we want, by setting its rules, and by leading the way with our own capital into new areas, thus creating the newest region of maximum profit. So the upshot is, if we can get Congress to commit federal capital first, and also to erect certain little strategic barriers to impede the natural flow of capital to the path of least resistance but maximum destruction, then we might be able to change the whole watershed.

CQ: How many metaphors are you going to mix into this stew?

PC: They are all part of a heroic simile, obviously, having to do with land-scape and gravity. A very heroic simile, if I may say so.

JQ: Heroic!

PC: That's right Joe. You are a good kid. You are a patriotic American tod-dler. So Charlie, can you write me some speeches putting this into inspiring and politically correct terminology?

CQ: Why do you have to be politically correct anymore? You're the president!

PC: So I am. More coffee? More hot chocolate?

One day an e-mail came from Leo Mulhouse in San Diego, forwarding a review paper about nonviral insertion. The new RRCCES lab had gotten really good results in introducing an altered DNA sequence into mice using nanorods. It looked like the long-awaited targeted delivery system was at hand.

Frank stared at the paper. There were a bunch of reasons piling up to go out to San Diego again. Actually there were several places he wanted to visit in person. Taken together they implied more travel than he had time for; he didn't know exactly what to do, and so went nowhere, and the problem got worse. It wasn't quite like his indecision fugue state; it was just a problem. But it was Diane who suggested that he string all the trips together in a quick jaunt around the world, dropping in on Beijing, the Takla Makan, Siberia, and England. He could start with San Diego, and the White House travel office could package it so it would only take him ten days or so. So he agreed, and then the day of his departure was upon him, and he had to dig out his passport and get his visas and other documents from the travel office, and put together a travel bag and jump on the White House shuttle out to Dulles.

As soon into his flight as he could turn on his laptop, he checked out a video from Wade Norton. The little movie even had a soundtrack, a hokey wind and bird-cry combination, even though the sea looked calm and there were no birds in sight. The black rock of the coastline was filigreed with frozen white spume, a ragged border separating white ice and blue water. Summer again in Antarctica. The shot must have been taken from a helicopter, hovering in place.

Then Wade's voice came over the fake sound: "See, there in the middle of the shot? That's one of the coastal installations."

Finally Frank saw something other than coastline: a line of metallic blue squares. Photovoltaic blue. "What you see covers about a football field. The sun is up twenty-four/seven right now. Ah, there's the prototype pump, down there in the water." More metallic blue: in this case, thin lines, running from the ocean's edge up over the black rocks, past field of solar panels on the nearby ice, and then on up the Leverett Glacier toward the polar cap.

"Heated pumps and heated pipelines. It's the latest oil tech, ironically. And it's looking good, but now we need a lot more of it. And a lot more shipping. The pipes are huge. They're as big as they could make them and still get them on ships. Apparently it helps the thermal situation to have them big. So they're taking in like a million gallons an hour, and moving it at about ten miles an hour up the glacier. The pipeline runs parallel to the polar overland route, that way they have the crevasses already dealt with. I rode with Bill for a few days on the route, it's really cool. So there's your proof of concept. They've mapped all the declivities in the polar ice, and the oil companies are manufacturing the pumps and pipes. They're loving this plan, as you can imagine. The only real choke points in the process now are speed of manufacture and shipping and installation. They haven't got enough people who know how to do the installing. You need some thousands of these systems to get the water back up onto the polar plateau."

Here Frank got curious enough to get on the plane's phone and call Wade directly. He had no idea what time it was in Antarctica, he didn't even know how they told time down there, but he figured Wade must turn his phone off when he didn't want to get calls.

But Wade picked up, and their connection was good, with what sounded like about a second in transmission delay.

"Wade, it's Frank Vanderwal, and I'm looking at that e-mail you sent with the video of the prototype pumping system."

"Oh yeah, isn't that neat? I heloed out there day before yesterday."

"Yeah," Frank said. "But tell me, does anyone down there have any idea how frozen seawater is going to behave on the polar cap?"

"Oh sure. It's kind of a mess. You know, when water freezes the ice is fresh and the salt gets extruded, so there are layers of salt above and below and inside the new ice, so it's kind of slushy or semi-frozen. So the pour from the pumps spreads really flat on the polar cap, which is good, because then it doesn't pile up in big domes. After that the salt kind of clumps and rises together, and gets pushed onto the surface, so what you end up with is a mostly solid freshwater ice layer, with a crust of salt on top of it, like a little devil's golf course type feature. Then the wind will blow that salt down the polar cap and disperse it as a dust. So, back into the ocean again! Pretty neat, eh?"

"Interesting," Frank said.

"Yeah. If we build enough of these, it really will be kind of a feat. I mean the West Antarctic Ice Sheet is definitely falling into the ocean. No one can stop that now. But we might be able to pump the water back onto east Antarctica."

"What about the desert basins in the north thirties?" Frank said. "A lot of those are being turned into salt lakes. It'll be like a bunch of giant Salton Seas."

"Is that bad?"

"I don't know, what do you think about that?"

"More water? Probably good for people, right? I mean, it wouldn't be good for arid desert biomes. But maybe we have enough of those. And desertification is becoming a big problem in some regions. If you were to create some major lakes in the western Sahara, it might slow down the desertification of the Sahel. I think that's what the ecologists are talking about now. They're loving this stuff. I think they love it that the world is falling apart, it makes the earth sciences all the rage. They're like atomic scientists in World War Two."

"I suppose they are. But on the other hand . . ."

"Yeah, I know. Better if we didn't have to do all this stuff. Since we do, though, it's good we've got some options."

"I hope this doesn't give people the feeling that we can just silver-bullet all the problems and go on like we were before."

"No. Well, we can think about crossing that bridge if we get to it."

"True."

"Have to hope the bridge is still there at that point."

"True."

"So you're flying where?"

"I'm on my way around the world."

"Oh cool. When are you going to meet with Phil about these pumps?"

"Diane will do it."

"Okay good. Say hi to him, or have her say hi to him. It's been a lot harder to get him on the phone since he got elected."

"I bet."

"I keep telling him to come down here, and he always says he will."

"I'm sure he wants to."

"Yeah he would love it."

"So Wade, are you still seeing that woman down there?"

"It's complicated. Are you still seeing that woman in D.C.?"

"It's complicated."

Satellite hiss, as they both were cast into thoughts of their own—then short and unhumorous laughs from both of them, and they signed off.

In San Diego, Frank rented a van and drove up to RRCCES on North Torrey Pines Road.

The new labs were up and running, crowded and busy. A functioning lab was a beautiful thing to behold. A bit of a Fabergé egg; fragile, rococo, needing nurturance and protection. A bubble in a waterfall. Science in action. In these they changed the world. And now—

Yann came in. "You have to go to Russia."

"I am."

"Oh! Good. The Siberian forest is amazing. It's so big even the Soviets couldn't cut it down. We flew from Chelyabinsk to Omsk and it went on and on."

"And your lichen?"

"It's way east of where we spread it. The uptake has been amazing. It's almost scary."

"Almost?"

Yann laughed defensively. "Yeah, well, given the problems I see you guys are having shifting away from carbon, a little carbon drawdown overshoot might not be such a bad thing, right?"

Frank shook his head. "Who knows? It's a pretty big experiment."

"Yeah it is. Well, you know, it'll be like any other experimental series, in that sense. We'll see what we get from this one and then try another one."

"The stakes are kind of high."

"Yeah true. Good planets are hard to find." Yann shrugged. "Maybe the stakes have always been high, you know? Maybe we just didn't know it before. Now we know it, and so maybe we'll do things a little more—"

"More carefully? Like putting in suicide genes or negative feedback constraints? Or any kind of environmental safeguards?"

Yann shrugged, embarrassed. "Yeah sure."

He changed the subject, with a look heavenward as if to indicate that what the Russians had done was beyond his control. "But look here, I've been working on those gene expression algorithms, and I've seen a wrinkle in the palindrome calculation. I want you to take a look at it and see what you think."

"Sure," Frank said.

They went into Yann's office, a cubicle just like any other, except that the window's view was of the Pacific Ocean from three hundred feet up. Yann brought up one colored pattern after another, until it looked like the London tube map replicated several times around a vertical axis. He squished that image into the top of his screen and then under it began writing equations. It was like working through a cipher set in which the solution to each step cast a wave of probabilities that then had to be explored, and then again like that through iterations within sets, with decision-tree choices to determine the steps that properly followed. Algorithms, in short; or in long. They dug in, Yann speed-talking all the while, free associating as well as running a quick tutorial for Frank, Frank squinting, frowning, asking questions. Yann was now the leader of the pack, no doubt about it. It was like watching Richard Feynman chalkboarding quantum chromodynamics for the first time. A new understanding of some aspect of the world. They were in the heart of science, the basic activity, the equations both matched against reality and examined for their own internal logic as math.

"I have to pee," Yann announced mid-equation, and they broke for the day. Suddenly it was dinnertime.

"That was good," Frank said. "Jeez, Yann. Do you know what you're saying here?"

"Well, I think so. But you tell me. I only learn what this stuff might mean when you tell me. You and Leo."

"Because it depends on what he can do."

"Right. Although he's not the insertion guy, as he's always saying."

"Which is what we need now."

"Well, that's more Marta and Eleanor. They're doing their thing, and they're hooked into a whole network of people doing that."

"So those nanorods are working?"

"Yeah. They'll tell us about it if we go up to Paradigms for drinks. The gang usually meets there around this time on Friday. But first let's go talk to Leo, and then we can tell him to join us too."

"Good idea."

Leo was in his office reading online. "Oh hi guys, hi Frank. Out here again I see."

"Yes, I'm doing some other stuff too, but I wanted to check in and see how things are coming along."

"Things are coming along fine." Leo had the paws-dug-in look of a dog with a bone. Still looking at his screen as he spoke with them. "Eleanor and Marta are putting the triple nanorods through all kinds of trials."

"So it's nanotechnology at last."

"Yeah, that's right. Although I've never seen how nanotechnology isn't just what we used to call chemistry. But anyway here I am using it."

"So the nanorods are moving your DNA into mice?"

"Yes, the uptake is really good, and the rods don't do anything but cross over and give up their DNA, so they're looking like very good insertion agents."

"Wow."

Yann described to Leo some of his new work on the algorithm.

"Combine the two advances," Frank murmured. "And . . ."

"Oh yeah," Leo said, smiling hungrily. "Very complementary. It could mean—" And he waved a hand expressively. Everything.

"Let's go get that drink," Yann said.

Marta was looking good, although Frank was utterly inoculated by the poisoning incident. She had been out in the water that day, and it was a truism among surfers that salt water curled hair attractively. Bad hair became good hair, good hair became ravishing. People paid fortunes to get that very look. And of course the sunburn and bleaching, the flush in the skin. "Hi, Frank," she said and pecked him hard on the cheek, like taking a bite out of him. "How's it going out in the nation's capital?"

He glowered at her. "It's going well, thanks." Ms. Poisoner.

"Right." She laughed at his expression and they went into the bar.

Eleanor joined them; she too was looking good. Frank ordered a frozen margarita, a drink he never drank more than a mile away from the California coastline. They all decided to join him and it became a pitcher, then two. Frank told them about developments in D.C., and they told him what they had been hearing from Russia, also the lab news, and the latest from North County. Leo took the lead here, being utterly exposed by events; he and his wife lived right on the cliffs in Leucadia, and were embroiled in the legal battle between the neighborhood and the city of Encinitas as to what should be done. All the cliffside houses in Leucadia had been condemned, or at least legally abandoned by the city, and it was uncertain what was going on, given all the lawsuits, but for sure it was making for huge insurance and liability problems, and the involvement of the California Coastal Commission and the state legislature. A lot of Leucadia depended on the outcome.

"It sounds awful."

"Yeah, well. It's still a great place to live. When I'm lying there in bed and I hear the surf, or when the hang-gliders come by our porch, or we see the green flash, or the dolphins bodysurfing—well, you know. It makes the legal stuff seems small. I figure we've already seen the worst we're likely to see."

"So you're not trying to sell?"

"Oh hell no. That would be an even bigger problem. No, we're there for good. Or until the house falls in the water. I just don't think it will."

"Are other people there trying to sell?"

"Sure, but that's part of the problem, because of what the city's done. Some people are still managing to do it, but I think both parties have to sign all kinds of waivers. Those that do manage to sell are getting hardly anything. They're almost all for sale by owner. Agents don't want to mess with it."

"But you think it will be okay."

"Well, physically okay. If there's another really big storm, we'll see. But I think our part of the street is on a kind of hard rib in the sandstone, to tell you the truth. We're a little bit higher. It's like a little point."

"Sounds lucky."

Marta was looking at him, so Frank said, "How is your lichen doing?"

She crowed. "It's going great! Get ready for an ice age!"

"Uh oh."

But she was not to be subdued, especially not after the second pitcher arrived. The lichen was in the forest east of Chelyabinsk, with coverage estimates of thousands of hectares, and millions of trees, each tree potentially drawing down several hundred kilograms of carbon more than it would have. "Do the math!"

"You might need methane to keep things warm enough," Leo joked.

"Unless the trees die," Frank said, but under his breath so that no one noticed. Yann was looking a little uncomfortable as it was. He knew Frank thought the experiment had been irresponsible.

"It's getting so wild," Eleanor said.

Leo's wife Roxanne joined them, and they ate dinner at the beach restaurant by the train station. A convivial affair. Wonderful to see how results in the lab could cheer a group of scientists. Afterward Leo and Roxanne went home, and Frank nodded to Marta and Yann's invitation to join them and Eleanor again at the Belly Up. "Sure."

Off to the Belly Up. Into the giant Quonset, loud and hot. Dance dance dance. Don't take any pills from Marta. Eleanor was a good dancer, and she and Marta bopped together as a team. She had an arm tattoo which Frank saw clearly for the first time: a Medusa head with its serpentine hair and glare, and a circle of script around it; above it read *Nolo mi tangere,* below, *Don't Fuck With Me.* Yann disappeared, Eleanor and Marta danced near Frank, occasionally turning to him for a brief pas-de-trois, hip-bumping, tummy-bumping, chest-bumping, oh yes. Easy to do when you had eaten the antidote!

Then off into the night. A pattern already. The habit was formed with the second iteration. Frank drove to his storage locker and then out to the coast highway and south to Blacks, remembering the wild ride with the horrible hard-on. So much for Marta. He laid out his bed out on the cliff in his old nook. He sat there slowly falling asleep. Maybe the third good correlation was the simultaneous development of the proteomics algorithm with the targeted insertion delivery. It was the best night's sleep he had had in months.

His flight out the next day left in the afternoon, so the next morning he gave Leo a call. "Hey Leo, when Derek was on the hunt right before Torrey Pines got sold, did you ever go out and do the dog-and-pony with him?"

"Yeah I did, a few times."

"Did you ever meet anyone interesting in that process?"

"Well, let me think. . . . That was a pretty crazy time." After a pause he said, "There was a guy we met near the end, a venture capitalist named Henry Bannet. He had an office in La Jolla. He asked some good questions. He knew what he was talking about, and he was, I don't know. Intense."

"Do you remember the name of his firm?"

"No, but I can google him."

"True. But I can do that too."

Frank thanked him and got off, then googled Henry Bannet. The one on the website for a firm called Biocal seemed right. A couple more taps and the receptionist at Biocal was answering the phone. She put him through, and no more than fifteen seconds after starting his hunt, he was talking to the man.

Frank explained who he was and why he was calling, and Bannet agreed to look into the matter, and meet with him next time he was in town.

After that Frank put his bathing suit and fins in his daypack and walked down to La Jolla Farms Road, and then down the old road to Blacks Beach.

Being under its giant sandstone cliff gave Blacks a particular feel. Change into bathing suit, out into the swell, "Ooooop! Ooooop!" Fins tugged on and out he swam, tasting the old salt taste as he went. Mother Ocean, cool and salty. The swell was small and from the south. There weren't any well-defined breaks at Blacks, but shifting sandbars about a hundred yards off-shore broke up the incoming waves, especially when the swell was from the south. Presumably the great cliff itself provided the sand for the sandbars, as it did for the beach, which was much wider than most of North County's beaches these days.

Outside it was classic Blacks. Swells reared up suddenly, hollowed slowly, broke with sharp clean reports. Long slow lefts, short fast rights. Frank swam and rode, swam and rode, swam and rode. It was like knowing how to ride a bicycle. What had Emerson said about surfing? All human life was like this. If only! Emerson had a certain optimism in him, no doubt about it; he was buoyant, he tended to soar. Life was not surfing, but Emerson was a surfer.

On the beach a young couple had just arrived. The guy had on long flowing white pants and a long-sleeved white shirt, also a wide-brimmed white hat, and a long yellow scarf or burnoose wrapped high around his neck. He even had on white gloves. Some issues with sun, it appeared, and what Frank could see of his face was albino pink. His companion was twirling around him in ecstatic circles, swinging her long black hair around and pulling off her clothes—shirt over her head and thrown at him, pants pulled off and handed to him. She danced around him naked, arms extended, then dashed out into the surf.

Well, that was Blacks Beach for you. Frank stroked out and caught another wave, singing Spencer's song about the VW van: I would fight for hippie chicks, I would die for hippie chicks. Inshore the woman dove into the broken waves while her companion stood knee deep, watching her. An odd couple—

But weren't they all!

After that, Asia. First a flight to Seattle, then a long shot to Beijing. Frank slept as much as he could, then got some views of the Aleutians, followed by a pass over the snowy volcano-studded ranges of Kamchatka.

The Beijing meeting, called Carbon Expo Asia, was both a trade show and a conference on carbon emissions markets, sponsored by the International Emissions Trading Association. Carbon was a commodity with a futures market, like Frank himself. With Phil Chase in office the value of carbon emissions had soared. Now, however, futures traders were beginning to wonder if carbon might become so sharply capped, or the burning of it become so old-tech, that emissions would radically decrease and their futures would lose all value in a market collapse. So there were countervailing pressures coming to bear on the daily price and its prognosis, as in any futures market.

All these pressures were on display for Frank to witness. Naturally, Chinese traders were prominent, and the Chinese government appeared to be calling the shots. They were trying to bump the present price up, by holding China's potential coal burning over everyone else's head, as a kind of giant environmental terrorist threat. By threatening to burn their coal they hoped to create all kinds of concessions, and essentially get their next generation of power plants paid for by the rest of the global community. Or so went the threat. The Chinese bureaucrats wandered the halls looking fat and dangerous, as if explosives were strapped to their waists, implying that if their requirements were not met they would explode their carbon and cook the world.

The United States meanwhile still had the second-biggest carbon burn ongoing, and from time to time could threaten to claim that it was proving harder to cut back than they had thought. So all the big players had their cards, and in a way it was a case of mutual assured destruction all over again. Everyone had to agree on the need to act, or it wouldn't work for any of them. So everyone was dealing, the Americans as much as anyone. It was like a giant game of chicken. And in a game of chicken, everyone thought the Chinese would win. They were bloody-minded hardball players, and only a hundred guys there had to hold their nerve, rather than three hundred million; that was a seven magnitude difference, and should have guaranteed China could hold firm the longest. If you believed the theory that the fewer were stronger in will than the many. It might be possible to imagine that three hundred million would simply steamroll any hundred people anywhere.

It was an interesting test of America's true strength. Did the bulk of the world's capital still reside in the United States? Yes. Did the U.S.'s military strength matter in this world of energy technology? Maybe. Was it a case of dominance without hegemony, as some were describing it, so that in the absence of a war, America was nothing but yet another decrepit empire, falling by history's wayside? Hard to say. If America stopped burning twenty-five percent of the total carbon burned every year, would this make the country geopolitically stronger or weaker? Probably stronger, but who knew? One would have to measure many disparate factors that were not usually calculated together. It was a geopolitical mess to rival the end of World War Two and the negotiations establishing the UN.

Then the meeting was over, with lots of trading done, but little accomplished toward a global treaty. That was becoming the usual way of these meetings, the American rep told Frank wearily at the end. Once you were making what could be called progress (meaning inventing another way to make money, it seemed to Frank), no one was inclined to push for anything more.

Frank then caught a Chinese flight down to the Takla Makan desert, in far western China, and landed at Khotan, an oasis town on the southern edge of the Tarim Basin. There he was loaded with some Hungarian civil engineers into a minibus and driven north, to the shores of the new salt sea. Throughout the drive they saw plumes of dust, as if from a volcanic explosion, rising in the sky ahead of them. As they approached, the yellow wall of rising dust became more transparent, and finally was revealed to be the work of a line of gigantic bulldozers, heaving a dike into place on an otherwise empty desert floor. It looked like the Great Wall was being reproduced at a magnitude larger scale.

Frank got out at a settlement of tents, yurts, mobile homes, and cinder block structures, all next to an ancient dusty tumbledown of brown brick walls. He was greeted there by a Chinese-American archeologist named Eric Chung, with whom he had exchanged e-mails.

Chung took him by jeep around the old site. The actual dig occupied only a little corner of it. The ruins covered about a thousand acres, Chung told him, and so far they had excavated ten.

Everything in sight, from horizon to horizon, was a shade of brown: the Kunlun Mountains rising to the south, the plains, the bricks of the ruin, and in a slightly lighter shade, the newly exposed bricks of the dig.

"So this was Shambala?" Frank said.

"That's right."

"In what sense, exactly?"

"That was what the Tibetans called it while it existed. That arroyo and wash you see down the slope was a tributary of the Tarim River, and it ran all year round, because the climate was wetter and the snowpack on the Kunluns was thicker, and there were glaciers. They're saying that flooding the Tarim basin may mean this river would run again, which is one of the reasons we have to get the dig at the lower points done fast. Anyway, it was a very advanced city, the center of the kingdom of Khocho. Powerful and prominent in that time. It was located on a precursor of the Silk Road, and was a very rich culture. The Bön people in Tibet considered it to be the land of milk and honey, and when the Buddhist monasteries took over up there on the plateau, they developed a legend that this was a magical city. Guru Rimpoche then said it was a magic city that could move from place to place, and that started their Shambala motif. It reminds me of the Atlantis myth."

"What do you mean?" Frank asked.

"Well, Plato wrote a thousand years after the explosion at Thera, but he still described certain aspects of the Minoan colony pretty well. The circular shape of the island, the building types, and so on. In this case here, the time lag is about the same, and Shambala was always described in the literature as being square, with the corners at the four cardinal points, and surrounded by water. What we're finding here are irrigation ditches that leave the riverbed upstream from the site, and circle it and rejoin the river downstream. And the city is platted in a square oriented north-south-east-west. So it fits the pattern, it has the name, it's the right period. So, that's the sense in which we call it Shambala. It's really it."

"Wow. So it's like finding Troy, or the Minoan place on Santorini."

"Yes, exactly. A very exciting find. And the Chinese so far are being pretty good about it. That big dike is being built to keep the site out of the water. And it looks like they're hoping to create a new tourist destination. We're already seeing some Shangri-la hotels and travel companies springing up out here."

"Amazing," Frank said. "How old is it, did you say?"

"Eighth century."

"And was it founded by a Rudra Cakrin?"

"Yes, that's right. Very good."

"But I read that he founded the city in sixteen thousand B.C.?"

"Yes," Chung said, laughing, "the stories do say that, but it's the same with Plato saying Atlantis was ten thousand years old and a hundred miles across. These stories appear to get their figures exaggerated by about a factor of ten, then it levels off and holds."

"Interesting." They walked past a cleared area. "This was a temple site?"

"Yes, we think so."

Frank took from his daypack a matchbox-sized container of Rudra's ashes that Qang had given him. He opened it and cast the fine gray ash into the wind. The little cloud puffed and drifted away onto the ground.

"Back where you began," Frank said, "and where it all might begin again. Thank you teacher, thank you friend. We didn't have much time together, but it was enough. And enough is as good as a feast."

An Aeroflot flight then, during which he caught sight of the Aral Sea, which apparently was already twice as big as before its rehydration had begun, thus almost back to the size it had been before people began diverting its inflow a century before. All kinds of landscape restoration experiments were being conducted by the Kazakhs and Uzbekis around the new shoreline, which they had set legally in advance and which now was almost achieved. From the air the shoreline appeared as a ring of green, then brown, around a lake that was light brown near the shoreline, shading to olive, then a murky dark green, then blue. It looked like a big vernal pool.

Later the plane landed and woke Frank. He got off and was greeted by an American and Russian from Marta and Yann's previous company, Small Delivery Systems. It was cold, and there was dirty snow on the ground. Winter in Siberia! Although in fact it was not that cold, and seemed rather dry and brown.

They drove off in a caravan of four long gray vans, something like Soviet Land Rovers, it seemed, creaky like the plane, but warm and stuffy. They progressed over a road that was not paved but did have a fresh pea gravel spread over it, and a coating of frost. The vehicles had to keep a certain distance from each other to avoid having their windshields quickly pitted and starred.

Not far from the airport the road led them into a forest of scrubby pines. It looked like Interstate 95 in Maine, except that the road was narrower, and unpaved, and the trees therefore grayed by the dust thrown up by passing traffic. They were somewhere near Chelyabinsk 56, someone said. You don't want to go there, a Russian added. One of Stalin's biggest messes. Somewhere southeast of the Urals, Frank saw on a phone map.

Their little caravan stopped in a gravel parking lot next to a row of cabins. They got out, and locals led them to a broad path into the woods. Quickly Frank saw that the roadside dust and frost had obscured the fact that all the trees in this forest had another coating: not dust, but lichen.

It was Small Delivery Systems' lichen. Frank saw now why Marta had been not exactly boasting, nor abashed, nor exuberant, nor defensive, but some strange mixture of all these. The lichen was obviously doing well, to the point where a balance had clearly been lost; lichen plated everything: trunk, branches, twigs—everything but the pine needles themselves. Such a thorough cloaking looked harmful. A shaft of sunlight cut through the clouds and hit some trees nearby, and their cladding of lichen made them gleam like bronze.

The Small Delivery people on-site were sanguine about this. They did not think there would be a problem. They said the trees were not in danger. They said that even if some trees died, it would only be a bit of negative feedback to counter the carbon drawdown. If a certain percentage took on lignin so fast they split their trunks, or had roots rupture underground, then that would slow any further runaway growth of lichen. Things would then eventually reach a balance.

Frank wasn't so sure. He did not think this was ecologically or physiologically sound. Possibly the lichen could go on living on dead trees; certainly it could spread at the borders of the infestation to new trees. But these were not the people to talk to about this possibility.

The new lichen started out khaki, it appeared, and then caked itself with a layer that was the dull bronze that eventually dominated. As with the crustose lichen of the High Sierra that you saw everywhere on granite, it was quite beautiful. The little bubbles of its surface texture had an insectile sheen. That was the fungus. Frank recalled a passage in Thoreau: "The simplest and most lumpish fungus has a peculiar interest to us, because it is so obviously organic and related to ourselves; matter not dormant, but inspired, a life akin to my own. It is a successful poem in its kind."

Which was true; but to see it take over the life it was usually symbiotic with was not good. It looked like the parts of Georgia where kudzu had overgrown everything.

"Creepy," Frank remarked, scraping at an individual bubble.

"It is kind of, isn't it?"

"How do the roots look?"

"Come see for yourself." They took him to an area where the soil had been removed from beneath some sample trees. Here they saw both before and after roots, as some trees had been girdled and killed and their roots exposed later, to give them baseline data. Near them some living trees, or trees in the process of being killed by the exposure of their roots, were standing in holes balanced on their lowest net of fine roots, leaving most of the root balls exposed. The root balls were still shallow, in the way of evergreens, but the lichen-infested trees had roots that were markedly thicker than the uninfested trees.

"We started by treating an area of about a thousand square kilometers, and now it's about five thousand."

"About the size of Delaware, in other words."

Meaning some tens of million trees had been affected, and thus tens of millions of tons of carbon had been drawn down. Say a hundred million tons for the sake of thinking—that was about one percent of what they had put into the atmosphere in the year since the lichen was released.

Of course if it killed the forest, a lot of that carbon would then be eaten by microbes and respired to the atmosphere, some of it quickly, some over years, some over decades. This, Frank's hosts assured him, given the situation they were in, was a risk worth taking. It was neither a perfect nor a completely safe solution, but then again, none of them was.

Interesting to hear this reckless stuff coming from the Russians and the Small Delivery Systems people about equally, Frank thought. Who had persuaded whom was probably irrelevant; now it was a true folie à deux.

He had stood a thousand feet tall, it had seemed, on the floor of the Atlantic; now it looked like he had been miniaturized, and was threading his way through the mold in a petri dish. "Really creepy," he declared.

Certainly time to declare limited discussion. It was impossible to tease out the ramifications of all this, they depended so heavily on what happened to the various symbioses feeding each other, eating each other. There would need to be some kind of Kenzo modeling session, in which the whole range of possibilities got mapped, then the probabilities of each assessed. Feedback on feedback. It was probably incalculable, something they could only find out by watching what happened in real time. Like history itself. History in the making, right out there in the middle of Siberia.

Then it was on to London, by way of Moscow, which he did not see at all. In his London hotel after the flights, he was jet-lagged into some insomniac limbo, and couldn't sleep. He checked his e-mail and then the internet. His browser's home page news had a little item about Phil Chase and Diane opening a National Academy of Sciences meeting together. He smiled ruefully, clicked to Emerson, where a search using the word *traveling* brought up this:

> Traveling is a fool's paradise. Our first journeys discover to us the indifference of places. At home I dream that at Naples, at Rome, I can be intoxicated with beauty and lose my sadness. I pack my trunk, embrace my friends, embark on the sea and at last wake up in Naples, and there beside me is the stern fact, the sad self, unrelenting, identical, that I fled from. I seek the Vatican and the palaces. I affect to be intoxicated with sights and suggestions, but I am not intoxicated. My giant goes with me wherever I go.

From "Self-Reliance." Frank laughed, then showered and went to bed, and in the midst of his giant's buzzing, the luxury of lying down took him away.

The conference he was attending was in Greenwich, near the Observatory, so that they could inspect in person the Thames River Barrier. Witness the nature of the beast. The barrier was up permanently these days, forming a strangely attractive dam, composed of modular parts in a curve like a longbow. Ribbed arcs. They only came down to the level of the surface of the river, which still ran out underneath them, so they only blocked any water higher than that from flooding up the stream. One could therefore walk to its end on the north bank of the river, up onto a platform, and see that the seaward side of the river was a plane of water distinctly higher than the plane of water on the London side, upstream. It was weird, and reminded Frank of the view from the dike surrounding Khembalung, right before the monsoon had drowned the island.

Now he walked in a state of profound jet lag: sandy-eyed, mouth hung open in sleepy amazement, prone to sudden jolts of emotion. It was not particularly cold out, but the wind was raw; that was what kept him awake. When the group went back inside and took up the work on the sea level issues, he fell asleep, unfortunately missing most of a talk he had really wanted to see, on satellite-based laser altimetry measurements. An entire fleet of satellites and university and government departments had taken on the task of measuring sea level worldwide. Right before Frank fell asleep, the speaker said something about sea level rise slowing down lately, meaning their first pumping efforts might be having an effect, because other measurements showed the polar melting was continuing apace, in a feedback loop many considered unstoppable. This was fascinating, but Frank fell asleep anyway.

When he woke up he was chagrined, but realized he could see the paper online. The general upshot of the talk seemed to have been that they could only really stem the rise by drawing down enough CO_2 to get the atmosphere back to around 250 parts per million, levels last seen in the Little Ice Age from 1200 to 1400 A.D. People were murmuring about the nerviness of the speaker's suggestion that they try for an ice age, but as was pointed out, they could always burn some carbon to warm things if they got too cold. This was another reason to bank some of the oil that remained unburned.

"I can tell you right now my wife's going to want you to set the thermostat higher," someone prefaced his question, to general guffaws. They all seemed much more confident of humanity's terraforming abilities than seemed warranted. It was a research crowd rather than a policy crowd, and so included a lot of graduate students and younger professors. The more weathered faces in the room were looking around and catching each other's eye, then raising eyebrows.

His plane landed at JFK, and after that Frank had scheduled in a layover of several hours before his commuter pop down to D.C. The plan had puzzled the woman in the White House travel office, but he had only said, "I have some business in New York that day."

First he called Wade Norton. "Could we hold a conference in Mc-Murdo?"

"I don't know! I mean, NSF would probably hate it, but maybe not. It might be good publicity. Good for the budget."

"Okay. I'll check with Diane about it. I think it would help light a fire under people."

"Okay. Hey, how's it going with her?"

"Good. She and Phil seem good for each other."

"Ah yeah, that's nice. Phil needed someone."

"Diane too. So hey, how's it going with Val?"

"Ah, well. Good when I see her. I'll see her again in about a month."

"Whoah. So, is she off with . . . ?"

"Yes, I think she's with X, for part of that time, anyway. She's with some kind of polar cap sailing village."

"What did you say?"

"Tents on big sleds, like catamarans. They put up sails when the wind is right and move around."

"Like iceboats?"

"Yes, like that I guess, but they're like big rafts, and there's a bunch of them, moving around together. A sailing village."

"Wow, that sounds interesting."

"Yeah, they're like Huck Finn on the ice cap."

"So—but it's going well when you do see her."

"Oh yeah. Sure. I can't wait."

"And the, the other guy?"

"I like X. We get along well. I mean, we're friends. We don't talk about Val, that's understood. But other than that we're like any other friends. We understand each other. We don't talk about it, but we understand."

"Interesting!" Frank said, frowning. "It's—kind of hard to imagine."

"I don't even try. That's part of how it works."

"I see." Though he didn't.

"You know how it is," Wade said. "When you're in love, you take what you can get."

"Ahhh."

Then he got in a taxi and gave the driver the address of a YMCA in Brooklyn. He sat back in the backseat and watched the city flow by. It went on and on. Frank felt dumbstruck with jet lag, but as the taxi driver pulled up next to yet another block-long five-story building, he was also curiously tense.

The chess tournament was taking place in a gym that had room for only one basketball court and a single riser of stands. Stale old locker smell. There was a pretty good crowd in the stands.

Frank climbed the metal stairs to the top riser and sat down behind a couple of guys wearing Yankees caps. For some reason he didn't want to be seen. He only wanted to see.

Down there at one of the tables, Chessman was playing a girl. Frank shuddered with surprise, startled by the sight even though he had been (mostly) expecting it. Clifford Archer, the tournament website had said, under-sixteen level, etc. It had seemed like it had to be him.

And there he was. He looked a bit older and taller, and was wearing a checked shirt with a collar. Frank felt himself grinning; the youth held the same hunched position over this game that he had had at the picnic tables.

Maybe he had moved up here with family, as Deirdre had guessed. Or was doing it on his own somehow, following his chess destiny.

Every game in progress was represented as a schematic on a screen set up at the far end of the room, and after Frank identified Chessman's game he could follow its progress move by move. In his jet-lagged state and his low level of expertise he found it hard to judge how the game was going; they were in an odd configuration, somewhere in the midgame, Chessman playing black and seeming to be pushed to the edges a bit more than was usual for him, or safe.

Frank studied the game, trying to get what Chessman was up to. It reminded him sharply of the long winter, when he had first met the bros and built his treehouse. He hadn't cared then what happened in the games. Now he was rooting for Chessman, but in ignorance. The two players had both lost about the same number and strength of pieces.

Then the girl took one of Chessman's bishops, but it was a sacrifice (Frank hadn't seen it) and after that Chessman's trap was revealed. He had her in a pincer movement of sorts, although she had a lot of pieces in the middle.

The men sitting on the riser just below him were murmuring about this, it seemed. Frank leaned forward and said in a low voice, with a gesture:

"Is that young man doing well?"

They both nodded, without looking back at him. One muttered from the side of his mouth, "He's very patient."

The other one nodded. "He plays black even when he's playing white. He's like good at waiting. He's going to win this one, and she's a junior master."

And though Frank couldn't see it, the Yankee fan was right. Chessman made a move, hit his timer, and leaned back. The girl scowled and resigned, shook hands with Clifford, smiling crookedly, and went to rejoin her coach for a postmortem.

Chessman stood. No one joined him, and he was not looking around.

He walked over to the officials' table, and some of the people standing there congratulated him. Frank stood, walked down the stairs to the floor of the gym, crossed the court, and approached the officials' table.

He paused when he saw the youth in conversation with someone there, talking chess, it was clear. Chessman was animated, even cheerful. There was a look on his face that Frank had never seen before. Frank stopped in his tracks. He hesitated, watching, thinking it over. Finally he turned and left the gym.

The next day Frank ran with Edgardo, and told him about his trip, then said to him, "You know, I've been remembering what you said about Caroline, but I'm getting scared. And it occurred to me that maybe your friends might be in some sort of contact with her, if what you said happened to be the case, and if so, that they might be able to tell her that I really, really want to see her. I need to see her, if it's at all possible. Because I'm scared."

"Yes, yes yes yes yes," Edgardo said, as if pooh-poohing the idea. Then he made no other response, and after a while changed the subject to the difficulties that Chase was having with Congress.

The following Wednesday after dinner, Frank went to the mouth of Rock Creek to check the dead drop, and there was a new note.

OUR FIRST SPOT MIDNIGHT LOVE C

In just a couple of hours, if she meant tonight! Thank God he had checked! Thank God and thank Edgardo. Frank ran to his VW van and drove north on Wisconsin at speed, in a state of high excitement. In Bethesda he took a right and parked in a dark spot near the little park where they had first met. He walked to the bench under the little statue of the girl holding up the hoop. The empty cipher, there in the dark; and suddenly there she was, standing before him.

They banged together and hugged. "Where have you been?" Frank demanded roughly, face in her hair. "I've been so scared."

She shook her head for him to be silent, ran a wand over him. "I heard," she said at last, hugging him again. "I've had to be away. But I've been in contact with your friend's friends, and they told me you were concerned."

"Ah. Good old Edgardo."

"Yes. But you need to understand, I have to stay clear of any possibility of them finding me. And a lot of the time you've been chipped."

"I'm trying to stay completely clean when I'm not at work! I got rid of my van and got a new one, an old one I mean, and it's clean too."

"Did you come here in it?"

"Yes."

"Let's go check it out."

He led her to it, holding her hand. At the van she said, "Ah, cute," and checked it with her wand and another device from her fanny pack. "It's all clear." And then they kissed, and then they were climbing inside the van, kissing their way to the little mattress up in the back.

Once again everything else fell away, and he was lost in the little world they made together, completely inside the wave. There was no sexier space than the little overhead mattress of a VW van. And something about it, some quality—the presence of ordinary sheets and pillows, the fact that she had come out of hiding to reassure him, their complete nakedness, which had never before been true—the comfort and warmth of this little nook— even the fact that Diane was with Phil now, and Frank entirely committed, no confusion, mind clear, all there, all one, undamaged and whole—the look in her eye—all these things made it the sweetest time yet, the most passionate. The calmest and deepest and most in love.

Afterward she fell asleep in his arms. For an hour or two he lay there holding her, breathing with her. Then she stirred and roused herself. "Wow, that was nice. I needed that."

"Me too."

"I should go," she said. She rolled over onto him, pushed his numb nose with a finger. "I'm going to be out of touch again. I've still got some things I've got to do. Your Edgardo's friends are looking like they will turn out to be a help when the time comes, so look to word from him."

"Okay, I will."

"There'll come a time pretty soon when we should be able to act on this. Meanwhile you have to be patient."

"Okay, I will."

She rolled off him, rooted around for her clothes. In the dark he watched her move. She hooked her feet through her underwear and lay on her back and lifted up her butt to pull them up and on, a nifty maneuver that made him ache with lust. He tugged at the underwear as if to pull it back down but she batted his hand away, and continued to dress as if dressing in tents or VW vans or other spaces with low headroom was a skill she had had occasion to hone somewhere. It was sexy. Then they were kissing again, but she was distracted. And then with a final kiss and promise, she was off.

One afternoon at work, just before she left, Anna Quibler got an e-mail from her Chinese contact Fengzhen. It was a long one, and she made a quick decision to read it on her laptop on the Metro ride home.

As she read, she wished she had stayed in the office so she could make an instant reply. Although the truth was there was nothing immediate she could say; Fengzhen had made it clear that his letter spoke for a group in the Chinese Academy of Sciences that wasn't able to get word out officially, as their work had been declared sensitive by the government and was now fully classified, not to say eliminated. The group wanted Anna and the NSF to know that the ongoing drought in western China had started what they called an ecological chain reaction at the headwaters of the Yangtze and the Yellow Rivers; the "general systems crash" that Fengzhen had mentioned in his last e-mail was very close to beginning. All the indicator species in the affected areas were extinct, and dead zones were extending down the upper reaches of several watersheds. Fengzhen mentioned maps, but the e-mail had not had any attachments. He referenced her previous question, and said that as far as the group could tell, clean coal plants and a greatly reduced pesticide load, and a cleaned and reengineered waterway system, were three things that must be done immediately. But as he had said before, it was a matter of cumulative impacts, and everything was implicated. The coming spring might not come. His study group, he went on, wanted to go beyond the diagnostic level and make an appeal for help. Could the U.S. National Science Foundation offer any aid, or any suggestions, in this emergency?

"Shit," Anna said, and shut down her laptop.

In Bethesda, she made sure Nick was okay and then walked on to the grocery store to see if there were any vegetables left, thinking furiously. In the grocery store's parking lot she called Diane Chang's number at work. No answer. Then her cell phone number. No answer there either. Maybe she was hanging with the President. Anna left a message: "Diane, this is Anna Quibler. I need to talk to you at your soonest convenience about reports I'm getting from a contact in the Chinese Academy of Sciences concerning environmental problems they're seeing there. I think we need to make some kind of response to this, so let's talk about it as soon as we can, thanks, bye."

She had just gotten home from the grocery store with the fixings for goulash (paprika was good at masking the taste of slightly elderly veggies), and was boiling water and badgering Nick to get to his homework, when Charlie and Joe burst in the door shouting, and at the same moment the power went out.

"Ah shit!"

"Mom!"

"I mean shoot, of course. Dang it!"

"Karmapa!"

"Heavens to Betsy. I can't make dinner without power!"

"And I can't do my homework," Nick said cheerfully.

"Yes you can."

"I can't, the assignment is online!"

"You've got a syllabus page in your notebook."

"Yeah but tonight was added on, it's only online."

"You can do the next thing on the syllabus."

"Ah Mom!"

"Don't 'Ah Mom' me! I'm trying to find the candles here, Charlie can you help get them out?"

"Sure. Wow, these feel funny."

"I hope they aren't all—yep, they are. Melted like the Wicked Witch of the West. Dang it. Why—"

"Did you find matches there too?"

Charlie shuffled into the dark kitchen and gave her a hug from the side. Joe suddenly limpeted onto her legs, moaning, "Momma Momma Momma."

"Hi guys," she said resignedly. "Help get some candles lit. Some of these should work. Come on you guys, we're in the dark here."

They got some misshapen candles lit and placed them in the living room and the kitchen, and on the dining room table in between. Anna cooked spaghetti on their Coleman stove, heating a jar of sauce, and Charlie got a fire going in the fireplace. They settled in to eat. Nick ran down the batteries in his reader, then read by the light of two candles. Charlie typed on his laptop and Anna did the same; the laptop screens were like directional lanterns. They ate frozen yogurt and ice cream before it melted. It was quiet outside, compared to the normal city hum. It had been a while since the last blackout, and it was comforting to fall into the routine. Sirens in the distance. The clouds out the window were dark—no moon, apparently, and no city light bouncing off the clouds. "Should we turn on the radio?"

"No."

They would wait on the generator too. Crank it if they had to.

After a while they got out Apples to Apples and played a few rounds. Joe joined them in the game while continuing to draw with Anna on a big sheet of poster paper they had spread on the floor. He had recently taken to drawing in a big way, mostly sketching stick figures of various creatures, often red creatures with a kind of Precambrian look, flying over stick forests of blue or green. Now he continued to draw while insisting on being part of the game, so that they dealt him a hand, and Anna helped him to read what his cards said, whispering in his ear to his evident delight. The game—junior level, for Joe's sake—dealt people hands of cards on which were printed various nouns, and then an adjective card was turned up by the player whose turn it was, and the rest provided nouns facedown, and that player shuffled them and read them aloud, modified by the common adjective, and picked which combination he or she liked the best. The adjective now was SLIMY; the nouns read aloud by Nick were SLIMY ANTS, SLIMY MARSHMALLOWS, and SLIMY PIPPI LONGSTOCKING. You picked nouns tailored to that particular judge, or else just gave up and tried to be funny. It was a good game, and although Joe was somewhat out of his depth and would not admit it, his choice of nouns often had a Dada quality that seemed inspired, and he won about as frequently as any of them.

On this night he was into it. He got a hand he didn't like for some reason, and threw the cards down and said, "These are bad! I poop on these cards!"

"Joe."

"I gotta win!"

"It doesn't matter who wins," Charlie said as always.

"Why do we keep the adjectives we win then?" Nick would always ask.

"We do that because they describe us so well when we read them aloud at the end," Charlie would always respond. This was his addition to the game, as for instance, at the end of this one: "I'm noisy, soft, happy, strange, slimy, and old!" he read. "Pretty accurate, as usual."

Nick said, "I'm weird, wonderful, useful, skinny, slippery, and sloppy."

Anna was good, hard, spooky, sharp, and important. Ever since she had won the cards for dirty and fat she had been unenthusiastic about Charlie's addition to the game. Joe was great, short, smooth, fancy, jolly, strong, creepy, and loud. As usual, he had won the most.

"What does it mean when an illiterate person wins a game that's written down?" Charlie wondered.

"Be nice," Anna said.

After that they sat and watched the fire. The rumble of other people's generators sounded almost like traffic on Wisconsin. The chill air outside the front door smelled of two-stroke engines and fires in fireplaces. The smell of last winter, and the winter before; the smell of winter.

Inside they huddled by the fire. It had been well below freezing for the last week, probably the cause of the blackout, and it was going to be very cold upstairs, with the wind rattling the windows. And in the morning the fire would be out. After some discussion they decided to sleep in the living room again. The couches would do fine for Nick and Joe, and Anna and Charlie hauled the tigers' mattress up the stairs from the cellar. All this was a ritual now; sometimes they did it without the excuse of a blackout.

Faces ruddy in the flickering firelight. It reminded Charlie of camping out, although they never got to have fires in the Sierra anymore. Anna read *Goodnight Moon* to Joe yet one more time (at times like this he demanded old favorites), while Nick and Charlie read books silently to themselves. This put all four of them out pretty quickly.

The next morning they saw that a little snow had fallen. They were just settling in for the day, Charlie planning to roast some green firewood over the flames of drier wood, when the power came back on with its character-istic click and hum. It had been eleven hours. On the news they found out that electricity for essential services had been provided to Baltimore by the nuclear aircraft carrier USS *Theodore Roosevelt* and that this had helped the power company get back online faster.

The day was already disarranged, so Charlie took Nick to school, then returned home, where he and Anna and Joe tried to settle in. None of them seemed to be enjoying this situation, Anna and Charlie trying to work in quick shifts while the other occupied Joe, who was curious to know why he wasn't at daycare; and after a couple hours' struggle, Charlie suggested he take Joe out for a walk while Anna continued to work.

"Good idea," Anna said. Then her phone rang, and she picked up. "Oh hi Diane, thanks for getting back to me. Yeah too bad about the blackout, I know what you mean. But look, I'm glad you called, because the situation in China is getting really serious, did you check out the e-mail I forwarded to you? Yeah, I know. Definitely bad news. But look, there's something I saw on the news that gave me an idea. Did you hear about the nuclear air-craft carrier patching into the system in Baltimore and powering up parts of the city for a while? Yeah. Well I was wondering if that might be a way we could help the Chinese. Yeah I know. But even so, it might give them just enough of a bootstrap. I know."

Charlie interrupted to say he and Joe were going out, and she waved and continued talking to Diane.

Outside it was a crisp, clear day. According to the little backpacking ther-mometer hanging from the bottom of the baby backpack (Anna's idea, more data) the temperature outside was very near zero. It would have been perfect conditions for the baby backpack, because with Joe on his back they would keep each other warm. But Joe refused to get in it. "I wanna walk," he said. "I'm too big for that now, Dad."

This was not literally true. "But we could keep each other warm," he said.

"No."

"Okay then."

It occurred to Charlie that it had been quite a while since Joe had been willing to get in the thing and take a ride. And it was looking a little small. Possibly Joe had gotten into it for the last time, and its final usage had passed without Charlie noticing. With a pang Charlie put it into the depths of the vestibule closet. How he had loved carrying Nick and then Joe around. He had done a lot of backpacking in his life, but no load had ever felt as good to him as his boys. Instead of weighing him down they had lifted him up. Now that was over.

Oh well. You can't stop time. They set out together on a walk through the hilly neighborhoods east of Wisconsin Avenue.

On a bright chill Saturday morning not long after that, Charlie once again joined Drepung and Frank on the Potomac, this time at a put-in just downstream from Great Falls, on the Maryland side.

Mornings on the river were filled with a blue glassy light. The deciduous trees were bare, the evergreens dusted with snow.

Frank generally paddled ahead of the other two, silent as he so often was, absorbed in the scene. Charlie and Drepung followed at a distance, talking.

"Did Frank tell you he visited the original Shambala?" Drepung asked.

"No, what do you mean?"

Drepung explained.

"It seems a funny place for Shambala to have begun," Charlie said. "Out there in the middle of nowhere."

"But in the eighth century it was somewhere, and, well, howsoever it came about, that's where it was."

"But eventually it ended up in Khembalung."

"Yes. That is simply the Sherpa word for Shambala. It came into use when the city was in a hidden valley east of Everest."

"But then the Chinese came."

"Yes. Then the inhabitants moved to the island."

"Now under the Bay of Bengal."

"Yes."

"And so what becomes of Khembalung now?"

Drepung smiled and waggled his paddles. "Always here and now, right? Or at the farm in Maryland, in any case."

"If you say so. And what about this original site?"

"Frank said it will be close to the shore of a new lake, but they are going to build a dike that will keep it dry."

"Another dike?"

Drepung laughed. "Yes, it does sound a bit too familiar, but I've looked at the maps and heard the plans, and it sounds as if the dike will be rather huge, and more than enough to serve the purpose."

"Why are the Chinese doing this?"

"I think they see it as a tourist attraction. They are going to excavate the ancient city and clean it up, and call it Shangri-la, and hope that tourists will come to see it. Then also, maybe go boating or swimming when the sea is filled."

"Amazing."

"Yes, isn't it? But a good thing too. Shambala is the Buddhist utopia. So, the more this idea is in the world, the more people will think about why they are not living in such a place. It stands for a different way of life."

"Yes."

"Also, in the political sense, it seems to me that it's a little bit of a Chinese concession to the Dalai Lama. It's part of their campaign to reconcile."

Charlie was surprised. "Do you think there is such a campaign?"

"Yes, I think they want it. Even if only to serve their own purposes."

"I'm surprised to hear you say that. Are you sure?"

Drepung nodded. "There are informal talks with the Chinese."

For a while they paddled hard to catch up with Frank, who was crossing to the Virginia side to look into the gap between Arlington and Theodore Roosevelt Island. Charlie watched Drepung paddle, looking smooth and effortless.

"Drepung? Can you tell me what's going on with Joe and all?"

"Oh yes. I meant to tell you. Sucandra says that he and Qang can serve as the voice of Milarepa. Qang has done a divination to locate the spirit we exiled from Joe, and she says it is ready to come back. It was not happy to be expelled."

Charlie laughed at that; it sounded like Joe. What if his spirit came back even angrier than before? But he forged on: "Qang . . . ?"

"Yes, she is the servant of Tara, and has taken on much of the work of Rudra Cakrin, now that he is gone on."

"And so—do you know when this can happen?"

"Yes." Drepung glanced over at him. "The ceremony that marks the Maryland farm as the current manifestation of Shambala is next Saturday."

"Oh yeah, we got your invitation. I thought it said a housewarming."

"Same thing. So, if you could come early, we could have this private ceremony. Then the afternoon could be devoted to celebrating all these things."

"Okay," Charlie said, swallowing hard. "Let's do it."

"You are sure?"

"Yes. I want Joe back. The original Joe."

"Of course. Original mind! We all want that." Drepung smiled cheerfully and called, "Hey Frank!" And dug his paddle tips in.

So that Saturday the Quiblers dressed up again, which was unusual enough to put them in a fun mood, as if preparing for a costume party, or even Halloween: the boys and Charlie in shirts with collars, Anna in a dress: amazing!

Charlie drove them out the Canal Road to the Khembali farm, concocting the need for some meeting with Drepung to get them out there early. It was not far from the truth, and Anna did not question it.

So they arrived around ten, to find the compound decorated with swatches of cloth dyed in vivid Tibetan hues, draped over the buildings and hanging from tall poles to form a big awning or tent on the lawn sloping down to the riverside.

Joe said, "Momma! Dad! It's a color house! It's a sky fort! Look!" He took off in the direction of the tent.

"Good!" Charlie said. "Be careful!"

"Will you go with him and watch?" Anna asked. "I want to see what Sucandra and Qang did with the kitchen remodel."

"Sure, although I think I see those two down in the tent right now. But I'll tell them that you're checking it out and they'll be on up I'm sure."

"Thanks."

Off she went inside. Charlie stood by Nick, who was looking at the party preparations, still ongoing. Nick said, "I wish Frank still lived here."

"Me too. But I'm sure he'll be here soon."

"Do you think I can go up in the treehouse anyway?"

"Sure. No one will mind. Go check it out. Don't fall out."

"Dad, please."

"Well. Be careful."

Off went Nick. It was all working out very well.

Charlie walked down to the big suspended awning, his heart pounding.

Joe was standing in the middle of a circle of elderly Khembalis, looking around curiously. Sucandra was the youngest one there; Qang was chanting, her voice lower than most men's. Joe nodded as if keeping time to her chant. White smoke billowed out of giant censers and bowls set around a low candle-covered table, on which stood a big statue of the Adamantine Buddha, the stern one with his hand outstretched like a traffic cop.

The candle flames danced on some breeze that Charlie could not feel. An old man on the opposite side of the circle from Qang shouted something. Joe, however, did not seem to notice the shout. He was staring at Qang and the others around her with the same absorption he displayed when watching one of his favorite truck videos. He raised a hand, and seemed to conduct Qang in her singing. She stared fiercely at him, cross-eyed and looking a bit mad. Charlie wondered if she was possessed by the spirit in question.

Finally she took some saffron powder from a bowl held before her by the man on her right, and held it out for Joe's inspection. He put his finger in it, regarded the tip of his finger, sniffed it. Qang barked something and he looked up at her, held his hand out toward her. She nodded formally, theatrically, and took up a bowl of flower petals from the woman on the other side of her. She held the bowl out to Joe, and he took a fistful of pink flower petals, staining them saffron with his finger. The circle of elderly Khembalis joined the chanting, and began shuffling in a clump-footed dance around Joe, punctuating their chant with rhythmic short exclamations, somewhat like the "HAs!" that Rudra had shouted in Joe's face the previous year. Some of them smacked their hand cymbals together, then held the vibrating little disks over their heads. Joe began a little two-step, hands clasped behind his back, reminding Charlie of the dance of the munchkins welcoming Dorothy to Oz. Then as the chanting rose to a peak, Qang stepped forward and put her hand on Joe's head. He stilled under it. The woman beside Qang put the rest of the flower petals on the back of

Qang's hand, and Qang flicked them into the air when she moved her hand away.

Joe sat down on his butt as if his hamstrings had been cut. Charlie rushed to his side, cutting through the dancers.

"Joe! Joe, are you okay?"

Joe looked up at him. His eyes were round, they bugged out like the eyes of the demon masks up at the farmhouse. Wordlessly he struggled to his feet, ignoring Charlie's outstretched hand offering help. He took a swipe at Charlie:

"No, Da! Do it MY SELF. Wanna GO OUT! Wanna GO!"

"Okay!" Charlie exclaimed. Instantly he worried that Anna would be concerned by this linguistic regression. But it happened sometimes to young kids, and surely it wouldn't last long. "Hey there, Joe. Good to see you buddy. Let's go outside and play."

He glanced up at Qang, who nodded briefly at him before she returned her gaze to Joe. She seemed herself again.

"Daaaaaaaaaaaaaaaaa! Come! ON!"

"Okay sure! Let's go! Let's see if we can find Nick up in the treehouse, shall we? Treehouse? What say?"

"Treehouse? Good!" And his face scrunched into a climber's scowl before he marched out the tent door, like Popeye on a mission.

"Okay!" Charlie looked at Qang. "I better catch up. Hey Joe! Wait a second!"

When Anna came out from the Khembali farmhouse, where she had been conferring with Padma about the reestablishment of the Khembali Institute of Higher Learning, and the possibility of transferring the Khembali/NSF collaborative funds to studying Chesapeake Bay rather than the Bay of Bengal, she found all three of her boys up in the treehouse, running from one room to the next on the network of catwalks. One of the catwalks was as flexible as a bouncy bridge, and the three of them were busy finding the sweet spot that would cast Joe the highest when Charlie and Nick jumped. Anna could have told them from many previous ground observations that there would be two sweet spots, one each about halfway between the mid-point and the ends, but they seemed to have to rediscover that fact every time.

Charlie had gone exuberant, as he often did in these situations. He was getting to be more Joe's age than Joe himself. Although it would have been hard to tell at that moment, given Joe's helpless giggling, and his shrieks of delight at every sprung launching. He had always loved weightlessness. Even in his first weeks, when colic had so often left him wretched, if she had tossed him lightly up and then gently supported him on the way down, never quite releasing her hold on his body and head, he would goggle and go still, then rapt. At the time she had postulated that the weightlessness reminded him of being in the womb, before the outer world had inflicted colic and all its other trials on him. Now, watching him fly, she thought maybe it was still true.

Charlie, on the other hand, just liked playing. Anything would do. In the absence of anything else he would pitch pennies against a wall, or flick playing cards into a pan set across the floor. Wrestle with the boys, especially Joe. Make paper airplanes out of the newspaper. Throw rocks, preferably into water. They all liked that. Very likely during some part of this day she would find them down on the banks of the Potomac, grubbing for pebbles to throw in the stream.

CHAPTER 29

THE DOMINOES FALL

You must not only aim aright,
But draw the bow with all your might.
                    —*Thoreau*

Tuberculosis progressed in Thoreau until it was clear he was dying. He was forty-four, and just beginning to become a well-known writer. In the bold if morbid style of the time, people dropped by to visit him on his deathbed. It became a kind of tourist destination for the New England intelligentsia. Stories were told to illustrate his flinty character. God knows what he thought of these visits. He played his part. A few weeks before he died, a family friend asked him "how he stood affected toward Christ." Thoreau answered, as reported later in The Christian Examiner, *that "a snowstorm was more to him than Christ."*

His aunt Louisa asked him if he had made his peace with God, and he replied, "I did not know we had ever quarreled."

Parker Pillsbury, an abolitionist and family friend, dropped by near the end and said to him, "You seem so near the brink of the dark river, that I almost wonder how the opposite shore may appear to you."

Thoreau said, "One world at a time."

Then he died, and for Emerson it was yet another in the series of catastrophic premature deaths that had struck his loved ones. Wife, child, friend. In read-

ing Emerson's eulogy for Thoreau, Frank could sense the intense care the old man had taken to give a fair and full portrait. "In reading Henry Thoreau's journal, I am very sensible of the vigor of his constitution. That oaken strength which I noted whenever he walked, or worked, or surveyed wood-lots, Henry shows in his literary task. He has muscles, and ventures on and performs feats which I am forced to decline. In reading him, I find the same thought, the same spirit that is in me, but he takes a step beyond, and illustrates by excellent images that which I should have conveyed in a sleepy generality. 'Tis as if I went into a gymnasium, and saw youths leap, climb, and swing with a force unapproachable—though their feats are only continuations of my initial grapplings and jumps."

Emerson went on, "He knew the country like a fox or a bird, and passed through it as freely by paths of his own. His power of observation seemed to indicate additional senses. He saw as with microscope, heard as with ear trumpet, and his memory was a photographic register of all he saw and heard. He thought that, if waked up from a trance, in this swamp, he could tell by the plants what time of year it was within two days.

"To him there was no such things as size. The pond was a small ocean; the Atlantic, a large Walden Pond. He referred every minute fact to cosmical laws."

In short, a scientist.

But Emerson's grief also had an edge to it, a kind of anger at fate which spilled over into frustration even with Thoreau himself:

"I cannot help counting it a fault in him that he had no ambition. Wanting this, instead of engineering for all America, he was the captain of a huckleberry-party."

Whoah. That was pretty harsh, especially in a eulogy. And Frank saw reason to believe that this was not the first time Emerson had used the phrase—and that the first time it had been said right to Thoreau's face. They had argued a lot, and about things they both thought mattered, like how to live in a nation where slavery was legal. And in Thoreau's journal, whenever he was grumbling about the terrible inadequacies of friendship, it was pretty clear that he was usually complaining about Emerson. This was particularly true whenever he wrote about The Friend. It made sense, given the way they were;

Emerson had a huge range of acquaintances and spread himself thin, while Thoreau had what Frank thought would now be called social anxieties, so that he relied heavily on a few people close to him. It would not have been easy for any friend to live up to his standards. Emerson said, "I think the severity of his ideal interfered to deprive him of a healthy sufficiency of human society."

In any case they clashed, two strong thinkers with their own ideas, and so they saw less of each other, and Emerson disapproved of Thoreau's withdrawal, and his endless botanizing.

Only in the privacy of his journal did Thoreau make his rebuttal to Emerson's waspish accusation; this was why Frank thought Emerson had made it directly—perhaps even shouted it: he imagined the two men out in Emerson's yard, Thoreau having dropped by without warning, withdrawn and contrary, headed into the woods, and the lonely old gabster hurt by this, and frustrated to see the potential great voice of the age go missing in the swamps—"You could be engineering all America, and yet off you go to be captain of a huckleberry party!"

Thoreau wrote: "To such a pass our civilization and division of labor has come, that A, a professional huckleberry-picker, has hired B's field; C, a professed cook, is superintending the cooking of a pudding made of the berries; while Professor D, for which the pudding is intended, sits in his library writing a book. That book, which should be the ultimate fruit of the huckleberry field, will be worthless. There will be none of the spirit of the huckleberry in it. The reading of it will be a weariness to the flesh. I believe in a different kind of division of labor, and that Professor D should divide himself between the library and the huckleberry-field."

Four days later, still nursing this riposte, he wrote:

"We dwellers in the huckleberry pastures are slow to adopt the notions of large towns and cities and may perchance be nicknamed huckleberry people."

In the end, despite these spats, the two men were friends. They both knew that a twist of fate had thrown them into the same time and place, and they both treasured the contact. Thoreau wrote of his employer, teacher, mentor, friend:

"Emerson has special talents unequalled. The divine in man has had no

more easy, methodically distinct expression. His personal influence upon young persons greater than any man's. In his world every man would be a poet, Love would reign, Beauty would take place, Man and Nature would harmonize."

Interesting how even here Thoreau alluded to that source of conflict between them, the question of how to make an impact on the time. Meanwhile, Emerson thought Thoreau had disappeared into the woods and failed to live up to his promise; he could not foresee how widely Thoreau would eventually be read. It took many decades before Thoreau's journals were published, and only then was his full accomplishment revealed, a very rare thing: the transcription of a mind onto the page, so that it was as if the reader became telepathic and could hear someone else thinking at last; and what thoughts! Of how to be an American, and how to see the land and the animals, and how to live up to the new world and become native to this place. His Walden was a kind of glorious distillate of the journal, and this book grew and grew in the American consciousness, became a living monument and a challenge to each generation in turn. Could America live up to Walden? Could America live up to Emerson? It was still an open question! And every day a new answer came. Frank, reading them in awe, having found the true sociobiology at last, a reading of the species that could be put to use, looked around him at all the ferals he lived among, at the polyglot conclave of all the peoples in the city; and he watched the animals coming back to the forest, and thought about how it could be; and he saw that it could happen: that they might learn how to live on this world properly, and all become huckleberry people at last.

Emerson, meanwhile, lived on. He carried the burden of grief and love, and his tribute to his young friend ended with the love and not the reproach, as it should be. "The scale on which his studies proceeded was so large as to require longevity, and we were the less prepared for his sudden disappearance. The country knows not yet, not in the least part, how great a son it has lost. It seems an injury that he should leave in the midst of his broken task which none else can finish. But wherever there is knowledge, wherever there is virtue, wherever there is beauty, he will find a home."

. . .

Frank tried to make one of those homes. He read Emerson and Thoreau. He forwarded the link to Emersonfortheday.com in all his e-mails, and posted printouts of various passages for the ferals to enjoy at the potlucks, and read passages aloud to people; and eventually a lot of his friends were also reading the site. Diane was a big fan, and she had gotten Phil Chase interested as well.

Phil's hunt for America's past, and an exemplary figure to give him inspiration and hope, was still focused on FDR, for obvious reasons; but he was capable of appreciating the New England pair as well, especially when Diane shoved a passage in front of his face at breakfast. It became a part of their morning routine. One day he laughed, beating her to the punch: "By God he was a radical! Here it is 1846, and he's talking about what comes after they defeat slavery. Listen to this:

"'Every reform is only a mask under cover of which a more terrible reform, which dares not yet name itself, advances. Slavery and anti-slavery is the question of property and no property, rent and anti-rent; and anti-slavery dare not yet say that every man must do his own work. Yet that is at last the upshot.'"

"Amazing," Diane said. "And now we're here."

Phil nodded as he sipped his coffee. "You gotta love it."

Diane looked at him over the tops of her glasses. A middle-aged couple at breakfast, reading their laptops. "You've got to do it," she corrected.

Phil grinned. "We're trying, dear. We're doing our best."

Diane nodded absently, back to reading; she was, like Emerson, already focused on the next set of problems.

As Phil himself also focused, every day, day after day; his waking life was scheduled by the quarter hour. And some things got done; and despite all the chaos and disorder in America and the world, in the violent weather swings both climatic and political, the Chase administration was trying everything it could think to try, attempting that "course of bold and persistent experimentation" that FDR had called for in his time; and as a result, they were actually making some real progress. Phil Chase was fighting the good fight. And so naturally someone shot him.

It was a "lone assassin," as they say, and luckily one of the deranged ones, so that he fired wildly from a crowd and only got Phil once in the neck before bystanders dragged him to the ground. Phil was carried back into his car and rushed to Bethesda Naval Hospital, his people working on him all the way, and they got him into intensive care alive. After that the doctors and nurses went at him. The news outside the ICU was uncertain, and rumors flew.

By then it was around eight in the evening. Phil had been on his way to the Washington Hilton for the annual White House Correspondents' Dinner, at which Phil had been expected to shine. After the shooting many attendees stayed, standing around in quiet groups, waiting grimly to hear the news.

All the Quiblers were at home. When Roy called they were having dinner. Charlie jumped over to switch on the TV, and then they were confronted with the usual images, repeated over and over like a nightmare you could never escape: reporters outside the hospital, administration spokespeople, including Andrea looking pinched and white-faced and speaking as calmly as she could. And, of course, jostled and bouncing images of the shooting itself, caught mostly in the immediate aftermath, looking like something from an art film or reality TV.

Charlie and Anna sat on the couch before the TV holding hands, Anna squeezing so hard that Charlie had to squeeze back to protect his bones. Nick sat with his face right before the screen, big-eyed and solemn; Joe didn't understand what the fuss was about, and so began to get angry. Very soon he would begin to demand his proper spot in the limelight. Anna started to cry, bolted up, and went to the kitchen, cursing viciously under her breath. She had never shown any great regard for Phil Chase or for politicians in general, but now she was crying in the kitchen, banging the teapot onto the stove as if crushing something vile.

"He's not dead yet," Nick called out to the kitchen. His chin was trembling; Anna's despair was infecting him.

Charlie clung to hope. That was what he had at that moment. Anna, he knew, hated to hope. It was in her a desperate and furious emotion, a last gesture.

Now she stormed past them to the door, yanked her coat from the closet. "God damn this country," she cried. "I can't stand it. I'm going for a walk."

"Take your phone!" Charlie cried as the door slammed behind her.

The Quibler boys stared at each other.

"It's all right," Charlie said, swallowing hard. "She'll be right back. She just needed to get away from—from all that," waving at the screen.

Already all the channels were deep into the tabloid mode that was the only thing American media knew anymore. Phil's struggle for life was now that beat that came right before the commercials, that moment when they were left hanging, on the edge of their seats, until the show returned and the story was resolved one way or the other. It was all perfectly familiar, rehearsed a million times. Charlie watched it sick with fear, but also increasingly with disgust, feeling that all those TV shows somehow brought things like this into being, life imitating art, yes, but always only the worst art, the stupid art that coated the world like shit.

For him, as for all the older viewers, there were other reasons than TV to feel this sick familiarity: the big assassinations of the sixties, 9/11, the attempt on Ford, the attempt on Reagan. It happened all the time. It was a part of America. In reaction to it they would all mouth the same platitudes they had said before. The lone assassin would turn out to be a nonentity, and no one would point out that the constant spew of hatred against Phil in the right-wing media had spurred on such madmen, just as no one had said it about the Oklahoma City bomber, when for lack of anything else the hatred had been directed at the federal government. Their culture was a petri dish in which hatred and murder were bred on purpose by people who intended to make money from them. And so it had happened again, and yet the people who had filled the madman's addled mind with ideas, and filled his hand with the gun, and even now were sneering in their commentaries that Chase had brought it on himself, daring so much, flouting so much, the only surprise being that it hadn't happened sooner—these people would never acknowledge or even fully understand their complicity.

These dismal thoughts ricocheted around Charlie's mind as he quivered with the shock of the news, and of Anna's sudden revulsion and exit. He was trembling, curled over his stomach. He sat beside Nick, swept Joe up into his arms, then let him struggle free. But for once Joe didn't go too far away, and Nick leaned into his other side, crouched in his enfolding arm. They watched the reporters breathlessly reporting what they had already reported, waiting right there on camera for more news. Charlie turned down the sound and tried to call Roy, but Roy's phone was busy. Probably he was deluged with calls. The fact that he had called Charlie first was a reflex, a reach for an anchor. Roy needed Charlie to know what he knew. But by now he was no doubt overwhelmed. Nothing to do but wait. "Come on, Phil," Charlie muttered. But it didn't feel good to say that. "The longer it goes on," he said to Nick, "the better the chances are that he'll be all right. They can do amazing things in intensive care these days."

Nick nodded, round-eyed. Phrases splintered in Charlie's mind as he watched his boys and tried to think. He wanted to curse, mindlessly and repetitively, but for the boys' sake he didn't. Joe knew he was upset, and so occupied himself in the way he usually did when that happened, getting absorbed in his blocks and dinosaurs. Nick was leaning against him as if to shore him up. Charlie felt a surge of love for them, then fear. What would become of them in such a fucked-up world?

"What's so wrong?" Joe asked, looking at Charlie curiously.

"Someone tried to hurt Phil."

"A guy shot him," Nick said.

Joe's eyes went round. "Well," he said, looking back and forth at their faces. "At least he didn't shoot the whole world."

"That's true," Nick said.

"You get what you get," Joe reminded them.

Anna barged back in the door. "Sorry guys, I just had to get away."

"That's okay," they all told her.

"Any news?" she asked fearfully.

"No."

"He's still alive," Nick pointed out. Then: "We should call Frank. Do you think he's heard?"

"I don't know. It depends where he is. Word will have spread fast."

"I can call his FOG phone."

"Sure, give it a try."

Anna came over and plumped down heavily on the couch. "What, you have the sound off?"

"I couldn't stand it."

She nodded, the corners of her mouth locked tight. She put her arm around his shoulders. "You poor guy. He's your friend."

"I think he's going to be all right," Charlie declared.

"I hope so."

But Charlie knew what that meant. Hope is a wish that we doubt will come true, she had once said to him, on a rare occasion when she had been willing to discuss it; she had been quoting some philosopher she had read in a class, Spinoza or Schopenhauer, Charlie couldn't remember, and wasn't about to ask now. He found it a chilling definition. There was more to hope than that. For him it was a rather common emotion, indeed a kind of default mode or state of being; he was always hoping for something. Hoping for the best. There was something important in that, some principle that was more than just a wish that you doubted would come true: it was an essential component of dealing with life. The tug of the future. The reason you tried. You had to hope for things, didn't you? Life hoped to live and then tried to live. "He's going to be all right," Charlie insisted, as if contradicting someone, and got up to go to the kitchen, his throat suddenly clenching. "If he was going to die he would have already," he shouted into the living room. "Once they get someone into intensive care they hardly ever die."

This was not true, and he knew it. On TV it was true; in real life, not. He slung the refrigerator door open and looked in it for a while before realizing there was nothing in there he wanted. He had not eaten dinner but his appetite was gone. "God damn it," he muttered, shutting the door and going to the window. In the wall of the apartment wrapping the back of their house, almost every window flickered with the blue light of people watching their TVs. Everyone caught in the same drama. "Fuck. Fuck. Fuck." He went back out and joined the family.

Phil survived. It turned out as Charlie had hoped, which was mere luck, because it could have turned out the other way; hopes are often dashed. But once they got him into intensive care, they gave him transfusions and sewed up the damage, which luckily was not as bad as it could have been— stabilized him and got him through the crisis hours, and after that he was "resting comfortably," although from what Roy told Charlie, in a call at five the next morning, neither of them even thinking yet of sleep, still deep in the horrible hours, it was not comfortable at all. The bullet had ticked the edge of his Kevlar vest and then run up through his neck, tearing through flesh but missing the carotid, the jugular, the spine, and the vocal cords. A lucky shot. But he was in considerable pain, Roy said, despite the sedation. The Vice President was nominally in charge, but obviously Roy and Andrea and the rest of the staff were doing a lot of the work.

By the time Charlie got to see Phil, over a week later, they had moved him back to the White House. When Charlie's time came, he found Phil sitting up in a hospital-style bed located in the Oval Office, with a mass of paperwork strewn on his lap and a phone headset on his head. It seemed possible he was trying deliberately to look like FDR, headset mouthpiece resembling in its cocked angle FDR's cigarette holder, but maybe it was just a coincidence.

"It's good to see you," Charlie said, shaking his hand gingerly.

"Good to see you too Charlie. Can you believe this?"

"Not really."

"It's been surreal, I'll tell you."

"How much of it do you remember?"

"All of it! They had to knock me out to operate on me. I hate that."

"Me too."

Phil regarded him. It seemed to Charlie that for a second Phil was remembering who Charlie was. Well, fair enough; he had gone on a long journey.

Now he said, "It always seems like there's a chance you won't wake up."

"I know," Charlie said. "Believe me. But you woke up."

"Yes."

There was a tightness to Phil's mouth which looked new to Charlie, and reminded him of Anna. Also his face was pale. His hair was as clean as usual; nurses must be washing it for him.

"Enough of that." Phil sat up farther. "Have you had any ideas about how we can use this to really take over Congress at the midterm elections?"

Charlie laughed. "Isn't it a bit early for that?"

"No."

"I guess. Well, how about handgun regulation? You could call for it with this Congress, then use their lack of response to beat on them."

"We would need poll numbers. As I recall it's not a winning issue."

Charlie laughed at Phil's bravura, his everything-is-politics pose; he knew Phil believed in that style. Then again, Phil was looking serious. It occurred to Charlie that he was looking at a different person.

"I'm not so sure," Charlie said. "The NRA wants us to think that, but I can't believe most Americans are in favor of handguns, can you?"

Phil gave him a look. "Actually I can."

"Point taken," Charlie conceded, "but still. I wonder about it. I don't believe it. It doesn't match with what I see."

"People want to know they can defend themselves."

"The defense doesn't come from *guns*. It comes from the rule of law. Most people know that."

Phil gave him the over-the-glasses look. "You have a lot of faith in the American electorate, Charlie."

"Well, so do you."

"That's true." Phil nodded and then winced. He took off the phone headset with his right arm, keeping his head as still as possible. He sighed. "It's good to remind me. All this has left me a bit shaken."

"Jesus, I'll bet."

"All he had to do was shoot a little higher and I would have been a goner.

He was only about thirty feet from me. I saw something out of the corner of my eye and looked over. That's probably what saved me. I can still see him. He didn't look that crazy."

"He was, though. He's spent some time in institutions, they say, and a lot more living at his mom's, listening to talk radio."

"Ah yeah. So, like the guy who shot Reagan."

"That's right."

"At the same place too. It's like a goddam rerun. 'Hi honey, I forgot to duck!' "

"He also said to his surgeons, 'I hope none of you are Democrats.' "

Phil laughed so hard he had to rein himself in. "That poor guy didn't know whether he was in a movie or not. It was all a movie to him."

"That's true."

"At least he thought he was playing the good guy. He was a cloth-head, but he thought he was doing good."

"A fitting epitaph."

Phil looked around the office. "I've been thinking that JFK was really unlucky. A lot of these people are so crazy they're incompetent, but his guy was an expert marksman. Amazingly expert, when you think about it. Long shot, moving target—I've been thinking that maybe the conspiracy folks are right about that one. That it was too good a shot to be real."

It was a gruesome topic. But natural enough for Phil to be interested in it right now. Indeed, he went methodically down through the list: Lincoln had been shot point-blank, Garfield and McKinley likewise; and Reagan too; while the woman who took a potshot at Ford could hardly even be said to have tried. "And a guy shot at FDR too, did you know that? He missed Roosevelt, and Roosevelt got a good night's sleep that night and never mentioned the matter again. But the mayor of Chicago was hit and later on he died."

"Like John Connally in reverse."

"Yeah." Phil shook his head. "FDR was a strange man. I mean, I love him and honor him, but he's not like Lincoln. Lincoln you can understand. You can read him like a book. It's not that he wasn't complex, because he was, but complex in a way you can see and think about. FDR is just mysterious.

After he got polio he put on a mask. He played a part as much as Reagan. They even called him the Sphinx, and he loved that." He paused, thinking it over. "I'm going to be like that," he said suddenly, glancing at Charlie.

"Hard to believe," Charlie said.

Phil smiled the ghost of his famous smile, and Charlie wondered if they would ever see the full version again.

Then there was a knock on the door, and Diane Chang came in.

"Hi honey," Phil said, "I forgot to duck!" And there was the full smile.

"Please," Diane said severely. "Quit it." She explained to Charlie: "He says that every time I come in." To Phil: "So stop. How do you feel?"

"Better, now that you're here."

"Are you still doing Reagan or are you just happy to see me."

The men laughed, and again Phil winced. "I need my meds," he said. "President on drugs!"

"Rush Limbaugh is outraged about it."

They laughed again, but Phil really did seem to be hurting.

"I should let you go," Charlie said.

Phil nodded. "Okay. But look, Charlie."

Now he had a look Charlie had never seen before. Some kind of contained anger—it made sense. But Phil had always been so mellow. Hyperactive but mellow. Seemingly mellow. But maybe before the shooting was when Phil had worn the mask, Charlie thought suddenly; maybe now they were seeing more of him rather than less; seeing the real him at last.

"I want to put this to use," Phil said. "We've gotten a good start on the climate problem, but there are other problems just as bad. So I want to push the process, and I'm willing to try all kinds of things to make it happen."

"Okay," Charlie said. "I'll think about things to try." By God I will!

He watched Phil squeeze Diane's hand. Test the limits, make an experiment in politics, in history itself. Just how far would Phil go? And how far could he get?

Everyone was a little shaken in those first few days after Phil got shot, although as it became clear he would recover, people tended to return from out of that nightmare, that briefly glimpsed bad alternative history, without any lingering sense that things could now be different—because they weren't, and it was too hard to imagine what things would be like without Phil Chase. So it was just something that had almost happened, and on they went.

But not everyone. To Frank's surprise, one of those who seemed to have been shaken the most was Edgardo. In the immediate aftermath his saturnine face had been set in a murderous expression all the time, and the first time they went out for a run afterward, with Kenzo and a couple of guys from the OMB they had met in the White House men's locker room, he had run around the Mall twice without saying anything at all, a thing of such rarity that Kenzo and Frank looked at each other, uneasy, even a little frightened.

"What's up Edgardo?" Kenzo finally said. "Cat got your tongue?"

"You people are idiots. You are always killing your best leaders. You might as well be some banana republic in Latin America! You're just as bad as all the juntas you set up down there, I suppose it has to be that way. The good ones you kill and the bad ones you give all your money and kiss their ass."

"Geez. Remember, the guy only wounded him. And it was a crazy guy."

"It always is. They are easy to find here. Pick anyone."

"Well, gee. Maybe we should change the subject. Have you thought of a new bestseller to write?"

For a long time Edgardo had entertained them on their runs with accounts of the nonfiction books he would write for the bestseller list, popularizing recent findings in the sciences. "Come on," Kenzo encouraged him, "what was that last one? *Why We Fuck Up*?"

"That would be too long to write," Edgardo said. "That is all of Wikipedia, at the least."

The OMB guys floated back within earshot. "Edgardo, are you talking politics again?"

"Am I talking politics? What kind of a redundancy is that, when are any of us not talking politics? When you talk, you're talking politics."

"I didn't know that. I don't think of it that way."

"It makes no difference what you think. It's all politics. You people in this country don't even know how good you've had it, to be able to just talk politics, rather than shoot it. So you do these kinds of things and don't even notice how dangerous it is. Someday you will unleash the furies of *la violencia* down on your idiot heads, and only then will you know what you have lost."

Phil started sending to Congress new volleys of legislation, all kinds of bills that pressured members of Congress either to vote for his programs or be exposed as obstacles, which would then initiate high-profile midterm election campaigns to remove them. This was already getting a lot of bills passed, and by the midterms it might become possible to build a solid majority and then accelerate even further. So: judicial appointments, executive actions, all were intensified, and coordinated into a single larger campaign by Roy and the brain trust. Fuel efficiency standards of eighty miles a gallon. A doubling of the gas tax, a "true cost" tax for carbon, end of all carbon-mining and carbon-burning subsidies. A return to progressive tax rates, including progressive taxes on capital assets, not just incomes; this set off shrieks from the oligarchy like nothing else. An end to all corporate loopholes and offshoring of profits. Heavy financial support for the World Health Organization. AIDS and malaria eradication funds. Environmental rules forced onto the World Trade Organization's agreements and treaties. Gun control legislation to give the NRA nightmares.

All this made it clear that Chase's team was using the tactic called flooding, which had been used to such effect by the criminals who had hijacked the presidency at the start of the century. It was like a flurry in boxing, the hits coming three or four a week, or even per day, so that under the onslaught the opposition could not react—not to individual slaps nor to the general deluge. Right-wing pundits were wondering if Chase had arranged to get shot to gain this advantage: why had the gunman used a .22, where was the evidence he had actually been shot, could they stick a minicam down the hole? No? Wasn't that suspicious, that he wouldn't allow that?

But this was weak, and in Congress the hammering went on. Roy said to Charlie, "The media is to legislation as professional wrestling is to Olympic wrestling. The real power moves are hard to see. We've got them on the run, so what's your latest?" The need for a constant stream of good initiatives was getting such that Roy was now hectoring the brain trust to think faster.

"This is just the start," Phil would say at the end of his press conferences, especially to any question that implied he had become more radical. "All this had to be done. No one denies that, except for special interests with a greedy financial stake in things staying the same. We the people intend to overturn those destructive tendencies, so grab this tiger by the tail and hold on tight!"

A few Saturdays later, the three kayakers went out on the Potomac, again putting in just downstream from Great Falls.

The overflow channels on the Maryland side had been so torn by cavitation in the great flood that things had changed there, and one new channel dropped down a series of flat sections in a very regular way. A few adjustments with concrete and dynamite had made it even more regular, so that kayakers could paddle up it one level at a time, catching a rest on the flats before the next push. Naturally it was called the Fish Ladder. "Some people make it all the way up, and then ride the big drops back down."

"Some people," Charlie said, looking over at Drepung and rolling his eyes. "Don't you do that, Frank?"

"I don't," Frank said. "I can't get to the top. It's hard. I've gotten around two-thirds of the way up it, so far."

They rounded the bend leading into Mather Gorge, and the falls came in sight. The air was filled with an immediate low roar, and with clouds of mist. The surface of the river hissed with breaking bubbles.

The lowest rung of the Fish Ladder by itself turned out to be more than Charlie and Drepung wanted to attempt, but Frank went at the bottom drop full speed, hit the white flow and fought up to the first flat, then waved at them to give it a try. They did, but found themselves stalling and sliding backward down the white water, struggling to stay upright.

Frank rode back down the drop and paddled over to them.

"You have to accelerate up the drop," he explained.

"By just paddling faster?" asked Drepung.

"Yes, very fast and sharp. You have to dig hard."

"Okay. But if it catches you and throws you back, do you try to go backward, or turn sideways on the way down?"

"I turn sideways, for sure."

Drepung and Charlie gave the lowest flume a few more tries, learning to turn as they stalled, which was in itself quite a trick; and near the end of an hour they both made it up to the first level patch of water, there to hoot loudly against the roar, turn, gulp, and take the fast slide back down to the foamy sheet of fizzing brown water. Yow! While they were doing this, Frank ascended six of the ten rungs of the chute, then turned and bounced down drop by drop, rejoining them red-faced and sweating.

After that they floated back downstream toward their put-in, looking over at the Virginia side to spot climbers on the dark walls of Mather Gorge. Frank got interested in a woman climbing solo on Juliet's Balcony, and led them over to watch her climb for a while. Charlie and Drepung reminisced about their climbing lesson on this wall as if it had been an expedition to Everest.

While paddling back across the river, Frank said, "Drepung, I've got a question I've been meaning to ask—that day at the MCI Center, what was that with you putting a scarf around the Dalai Lama's neck, before he gave his talk?"

"Yeah, what was that about?" Charlie chimed in.

Drepung paddled on for a while.

"Well, you know," he said at last, looking away from the other two, so that he was squinting into the sunlight squiggling over the river. "Everyone needs someone to bless them, even the Dalai Lama. And Khembalung is a very important place in Tibetan Buddhism."

Frank and Charlie gave each other a look. "We knew that, but like just how important?" Charlie asked.

"Well, it is one of the power spots, for sure. Like the Potala, in Lhasa."

"So the Potala has the Dalai Lama, and Khembalung has you?"

"Yes. That's right."

"And the Panchen Lama?" Charlie asked. "What's his power spot?"

"Beijing," Frank said.

Charlie laughed. "It was somewhere down in Amda, right?"

Drepung said, "No, not always."

Charlie said, "But he's the one who was said to be on somewhat equal terms with the Dalai Lama, right? You told me that—that the two of them represented the two main sects, and helped to pick each other when they were finding new ones. Kind of a back-and-forth thing."

"Yes," Drepung said.

"So, but there's a third one? I mean is that what you're saying?"

"No. There are only the two of us."

And Drepung looked over at them.

Charlie and Frank stared back at him, mouths hanging open. They glanced at each other to confirm they were both getting the same message.

Charlie said, "*You're* the Panchen Lama? That's what you're saying?"

"Yes."

"But—but . . ."

"I thought the new Panchen Lama was kidnapped by the Chinese," Frank said.

"Yes."

"But what are you saying!" Charlie cried. "You escaped?"

"I was rescued."

Frank and Charlie paddled themselves into positions on either side of Drepung's kayak, both facing him from close quarters. They laid their paddles over the kayaks to make themselves into a loose raft, and as they slowly drifted downstream together, Drepung told them his story.

"Do you remember what I told you, Charlie, about the death of the Panchen Lama in 1986?"

Charlie nodded, and Drepung quickly recapped for Frank:

"The last Panchen Lama was a collaborator with the Chinese for most of his life. He lived in Beijing and was a part of Mao's government, and he approved the conquest of Tibet. But this meant that the Tibetan people lost their feeling for him. While to the Chinese he was always just a tool. Eventually, their treatment of Tibet became so harsh that the Panchen Lama also protested, privately and then publicly, and so he spent his last years under house arrest.

"So, when he died, the world heard of it, and the Chinese told the monastery at Tashilhunpo to locate the new Panchen Lama, which they did. But the abbot there secretly contacted the Dalai Lama, to get his help with the final identification. At that point the Dalai Lama publicly identified one of the children, living near Tashilhunpo, thinking that because this boy lived under Chinese control, the Chinese would accept the designation. That way the Panchen Lama, although under Chinese control, would continue to be chosen in part by the Dalai Lama, as had always been true."

"And that was you," Charlie said.

"Yes. That was me. But the Chinese were not happy at this situation, and I was taken away by them. Another boy was designated the true Panchen Lama."

Drepung shook his head at this, then went on: "Both of us lived in custody, and were raised in secret. No one knew where we were kept."

"You weren't with the other boy?"

"No. I was with my parents, though. We all lived in a big house together, with a garden. But then when I was eight, my parents were taken away. I never saw them again. I was brought up by Chinese teachers. It was lonely. It's a hard time to remember. But then, when I was ten, one night I was awakened from sleep by some men in gas masks. One had his hand over my mouth as they woke me, to be sure I would not cry out. They looked like insects, but one spoke to me in Tibetan, and told me they were there to rescue me. That was Sucandra."

"Sucandra!"

"Yes. Padma also was there, and some other men you have seen at the embassy house. Most of them had been prisoners of the Chinese at earlier times, so they knew the Chinese routines, and helped plan the rescue."

"But how did they find you in the first place?" Frank said.

"Tibet has had spies in Beijing for a long time. There is a military element in Tibet, people who keep a low profile because of the Dalai Lama's insistence on nonviolence. Not everyone agrees with him on that. So there were people who started the hunt for me right after I was taken by the Chinese, and eventually they found an informant and discovered where I was being held."

"And then they did some kind of a . . . ?"

"Yes. There are still Tibetan men who have experience in entering China to perform military operations, and they were happy to have another opportunity. There are some who say the Dalai Lama's ban on violence only allows the world to forget us. They want to fight, and they think it would bring more attention to our cause. So the chance to do something was precious. When these men told me about my rescue, which they did many times, they were very pleased with themselves. Apparently they spied on the place to learn the routines, and rented a house nearby, and dug a tunnel into our compound. On the night of my rescue they came up from below and filled the air of the house with a gas, so when they rescued me they looked like insects because of their masks, but they spoke Tibetan, which I had not heard since my parents were taken away. So I trusted them. Really I understood right away what was happening, and I wanted to escape. I put on a mask and led them out of there! They had to slow me down!"

He chuckled briefly, but with the same grim expression as before. Anna had spoken from the very start of a look she had seen on Drepung's face that pierced her, but Charlie had not seen it. Now he did.

"So," he said, "you're the Panchen Lama. Holy shit."

"Yes."

"So that's why you've been laying low in the embassy and all. Office boy or receptionist or whatnot."

"Yes, that's right. And indeed you must not tell anyone."

"Oh no, we won't."

"So your real name is . . ."

"Gedhun Choekyi Nyima."

"And Drepung?"

"Drepung is the name of one of the big monasteries in Tibet. It is not actually a person's name. But I like it."

They drifted downriver for a while.

"So let me get this straight!" Charlie said. "Everything you guys told us when you came here was wrong! You, the office boy, are actually the head man. Your supposed head man turned out to have been a minor servant, like a press secretary. And your monk regents are some kind of a gay couple."

"Well, that's about right," Drepung said. "Although I don't think of Padma and Sucandra as a gay couple."

Frank said, "I don't mean to stereotype anyone, but I lived in the room next to them for a few months, and, you know, they are definitely what have you. Companions."

"Yes, of course. They shared a prison cell for ten years. They are very close. But ..." Drepung shrugged. He was thinking about other things. Again the tightened mouth, with its undercurrent of pain and anger. Of course it would be there—how could it not? Once Drepung had said to Charlie that his parents were no longer living; presumably, then, he had reason to believe that the Chinese had killed them. Perhaps his rescuers had discovered this for sure. Charlie didn't want to ask about it.

"What about the other Panchen Lama?" he said. "The boy that the Chinese selected?"

Drepung shrugged. "We are not sure he is still alive. Our informants have not been able to find him in the way they found me. So he is missing. Someone said, if he is alive, they will bring him up stupid."

Charlie shook his head. It was ugly stuff. Not that it didn't fit right in with centuries of bitter Chinese-Tibetan fighting, ranging from propaganda attacks to full-on war—and now, for the previous half century, a kind of slow-motion genocide, as Tibetans were overwhelmed in their own land by millions of Han colonials. The amazing thing was that the Tibetan response had been as nonviolent as it had been. But the means really were the ends for these guys. Charlie supposed it was because of the Dalai Lama, or their Buddhist culture, if that wasn't saying the same thing. They had a belief system that allowed them to agree with the Dalai Lama that going the route of violence would mean losing even if they won. They would get there on their own terms, if they could. And so Drepung had been snatched out of captivity with a kind of Israeli or *Mission: Impossible* deftness, and now here he was, out in the world. Taking the stage in front of thirteen thousand people with the Dalai Lama himself. How many there had known what they were seeing?

"But Drepung, don't the Chinese know who you are?"

"Yes. It is pretty clear they do."

"But you're not in danger?"

"I don't think so. They've known for a while now. I am a topic in the ongoing negotiations with the Chinese leadership. It's a new leadership, and they are looking for a solution. The Dalai Lama is talking to them, and I've been involved too. And now Phil Chase has been told of my identity, and certain assurances have been given. I have a kind of diplomatic immunity."

"I see. And so—what now? Now that the Dalai Lama has been here, and Phil has endorsed his cause?"

"We go on from that. Part of the Chinese government is angry now, at us and at Phil Chase. Another part would like the problem to be over. So it is an unstable moment. Negotiations continue."

"Wow, Drepung."

Frank said, "Is it okay if we keep calling you that?"

"No, you must call me Your High Holiness." Drepung grinned at them, slapped a paddle to spray them. Charlie saw that he was happy to be alive, happy to be free. There were problems, there were dangers, but here he was, out on the Potomac. They spread back out and paddled in to shore.

CUT TO THE CHASE

My blog for the day, your Phil Chase speaking:

I've been remembering the fear I had. It's made me think about how a lot of people have to live with a lot of fear, every day. Not acute fear maybe, but chronic, and big. Of course we all live with fear, you can't avoid it. But still, to be afraid for your kids. To be afraid of getting sick. That fear itself makes you sick. To be afraid of losing your home, of going hungry. Those are fears we could remove. It seems to me now that government of the people, by the people, and for the people should be about removing all the fears that we can. There will be some fears we can't remove, but we can do better at removing the fear of destitution, and our fear for our kids and the world they'll inherit.

Guaranteed health insurance is part of that. We've been working on that for some time now, but it remains to be finished. Make sure everyone has it—all the healthiest countries do it that way.

Another thing we could do would be to institute full employment. Government of the people, by the people, and for the people could offer jobs to everyone who wants one. It would be like the Works Progress Administration during the Depression, only more wide-ranging. Because there's an awful lot of work that needs doing, and we've got the people to do it. We could do it.

One interesting aspect of full employment as an idea is how it reveals the fear that lies at the heart of our current system. They call it "wage pressure" but really they mean "fear of not having a job." In effect, capitalism keeps wage earners so scared that they will take any job they can get, at any wages, even below a living wage, because that's so much better than nothing. And so all wage earners and most salary earners are kept under the thumb of capital owners, and have no leverage to better their deal in the system.

But if government of the people, by the people, and for the people were offering all citizens employment at a real living wage, then private business would have to match that or they wouldn't be able to get any labor. Supply and demand, baby—and so the bids for labor would get competitive, as they say. That all by itself would raise the income and living standards for about seventy percent of our population, faster than any other single move I could think of. A huge help to the middle class, meaning everyone.

Of course it's a global labor market, and so we would need other countries to enact similar programs, but we could work on that. We could take the lead and exert America's usual heavyweight influence. We could put the arm on countries not in compliance, by keeping our investment capital out of places trying to undercut us. Globalization is well enough established that the tools are there to leverage the whole system, and we own the capital that constitutes the leverage. You could leverage the system toward justice just as easy as toward extraction and exploitation. In fact it would be easier, because people would like it and support it. I think it's worth a try. I'm going to go to Congress to discuss it and see what we can do.

Previous post:

People have been asking me what it's like to get shot. It's pretty much as you'd expect. It's bad. It's not so much the pain, which is too big to feel, you go into shock immediately, at least I did—I've hurt more than that just stubbing my toe. It's the fear. I knew I'd been shot and figured I was dying. I thought when I lost consciousness that would be it. I knew it was in my neck. So that was scary. I figured it was over. And then I felt myself losing consciousness. I thought, *Bye, Diane, I wish I had met you sooner! Bye, world, I wish I were staying longer!* I think that must be what it's going to be like when it really does happen. When you're alive, you want to live.

So, but they saved me. I got lucky. The doctors told me it happens more often than you might think. Bullets are going so fast, they zip through and they're gone. They tell me George Orwell got shot in the neck and lived. I always liked *Animal Farm*. The end of that book, when you couldn't tell the pigs from the men—I always thought that ending was not about the pigs, but about the men from the other farms. That would be us. People you couldn't tell from pigs. Although pigs are nicer, on the whole. Orwell still has a lot to say to us.

Frank spent Sunday afternoon with Nick and the FOG people, manning a blind north of Fort DeRussy. It overlooked an animal trail, and sightings of big mammals were common: bear, wolf, coyote, lynx, aurochs, fox, tapir, armadillo, and lastly the one that had brought them there on this day, reported a few days back, but as a questionable: jaguar? Yes, there were still some sightings of the big cat. So they were there to see if they too could spot it.

It didn't happen. There was much talk of how the jaguar could have survived the winters, whether it had inhabited one of the caves in the ravine wall and eaten deer, or had found a hole in an abandoned building and gone dumpster diving like the rest of the city's ferals. All kinds of speculation was bandied about, but no sighting.

Nick was getting a ride home with his friend Max, so Frank walked south, down the ravine toward the zoo. And there it was, crouching on the overlook, staring down at the now-empty salt lick. Frank froze as smoothly as he could.

It was black, but its short fur had a sheen of brown. Its body was long and sleek, its head squarish, big in proportion to the body. Gulp. Frank slipped his hand in his pocket, grasped the hand axe, and pulled it out, his fingers automatically turning it until it nestled in its best throwing position. Only then did he begin to back up, one slow step at a time. He was downwind of it. One of the cat's ears twitched in his direction; he froze again. He needed some other animal to wander by and provide a distraction. Certainly the jaguar must have become extremely skittish in the time since the flood. Frank had assumed it was just a story. But here it lay in the dusk of the evening. Frank's blood was rushing through him in a hot flood, a total adrenal awareness. You could see well in the dark if you had to.

After a tiptoed retreat gained him a few more yards, Frank turned and ran as fleet as a deer. He had never run so hard in his life, and yet it was effortless.

He came out on Broad Branch and jogged to Connecticut. Everything was pulsing in his vision. He made a call to Nancy and gave her the news.

"Oh my God," she said. For a few seconds neither of them could speak. Finally she said, "Well, I'll mark it. Congratulations."

"Yeah," he said. "Thanks." His skin was everywhere wet with sweat.

"Was it beautiful?"

"Oh yes. Yes. And—scary. I ran like a rabbit!"

"I bet you did. Well, you're lucky. I'll tell the others."

After that he walked up and down Connecticut for a while, exulting in the memory of the sighting, reliving it, fixing it. Big cat in the dusk, in his park. What a privilege! What a world!

Eventually he found he was hungry. A Spanish restaurant on T Street had proven excellent in the past, and so Frank went to it and sat at one of its porch tables, next to the rail, looking at the passersby on the sidewalk. He was reading his laptop when suddenly Caroline's ex sat down across from him. Edward Cooper, there in the flesh, big and glowering.

Frank, startled, recovered and glared at him. "What?" he said sharply.

The man stared back at him. "You know what," he said. His voice was a rich baritone, like a radio DJ. "I want to talk to Caroline."

"I don't know what you mean," Frank said.

The blond man made a sour face. Aggrieved; tired of being patient. "Don't," he said. "I know who you are, and you know who I am."

Frank saved, shut down, closed the lid of his laptop. This was strange; possibly dangerous; although the encounter with the jaguar put that in perspective, because it didn't feel as dangerous as that. "Then why would I tell you anything about anybody?"

He could feel his pulse jumping in his neck and wrists, feel he was red-faced. He put his laptop in his pack on the floor, sat back. Without planning to, he reached in his jacket pocket and grasped the hand axe, turned it over in his hand until he had it in its proper grip. Hefted it. He met the man's gaze.

Cooper continued to stare him in the eye. He crossed his arms over his chest, leaned back in his chair. "Maybe you don't understand. If you don't tell me how to get in touch with her, then I'll have to find her using ways she won't want me to use."

"I don't know what you mean."

"But she will."

Frank studied him. It was rare to see someone display aggravation for an extended period of time. The world did not live up to this man's standards, that was clear in the set of his mouth, of his whole face. He was sure he was right. Right to be aggrieved. It was a little bit of a shock to see that Caroline had married a man who could not be fully intelligent.

"What do you want?" Frank said.

Cooper gestured that aside. "What makes you think you can barge into a situation like this and know what's going on?" he asked. "Why do you even think you know what's going on here?"

"You're making it clear," Frank said.

The man waved that away too. "I know she's fed you a line about us. That's what she does. Do you really think you're the first one she's done this kind of thing to?"

"What kind of thing?"

"Wrapped you around her little finger! Used you to get what she wants! Only this time she's gotten in over her head. She's broken the National Security Act, her loyalty oath, her contract, federal election law—it's quite a list. She could get thirty years with that list. If she doesn't turn herself in, if she's caught, it's likely to happen."

Frank said, "I can see why she would stay away from you."

"Look. Tampering with a federal election is a serious crime."

"Yes it is."

The man smiled, as if Frank had given something away. "You could be charged as an accessory, you know. That's a felony too. We have her computers, and they're full of the evidence we need to convict. She's the only one who had the program that turned the vote in Oregon."

Frank shrugged. Talk talk talk.

"What, you don't care? You don't care that you're involved in a felony?"

"Why should I believe you?"

"Because I don't have any reason to lie to you. Unlike her. What I don't understand is why you'd keep covering for her. She's lied to you all along. She's using you."

Frank stared at him. He was squeezing the hand axe hard, and now he started tapping it lightly against his thigh.

Finally he said, "Just by the way you're babbling I can tell you're completely full of shit."

The man's cheeks reddened. Frank pressed on: "If I knew a woman like that, I wouldn't cheat on her, or spy on her, or try to get her arrested for things that I myself did."

"She's got you hoodwinked, I see."

This was pointless; and yet Frank wasn't sure how to get away. Possibly the man was armed. But there they were in a public restaurant, out on the sidewalk. Surely he could not be contemplating anything too drastic.

"Why are you bothering me?" Frank said. "What's she to you? Do you know her? Do you know anything about her? Do you love her?"

Cooper was taken aback by this, and his face reddened further. Thin-skinned people, Frank thought, were so often thin-skinned. "Give me a break," he muttered.

"No, I mean it," Frank insisted. "Do you love her? Do you? Because I love her."

"For Christ's sake," the man said, affronted. "That's the way she always does it. She could charm the eyes off a snake. You're just her latest mark. But the fact remains, she's in big trouble."

"*You're* in big trouble," Frank said, and stood. He was still squeezing the hand axe in his jacket pocket. Whatever happened, he was at least ready.

Cooper shifted in his chair. "What the fuck," he complained, feeling the threat. "Sit down, we're not done here."

Frank leaned over and picked up his daypack. "You're done," he said.

Frank's waiter approached. "Hi," he said to Cooper, "can I get you anything?"

"No." Caroline's ex stood abruptly, lurching a little toward Frank as he did. "Actually, you can get me away from this guy," and he gestured contemptuously at Frank and walked out of the restaurant.

Frank sat back down. "A glass of the house red, please."

But that was only bravado. He was distracted, even from time to time afraid. His appetite was gone. Before the waiter returned for his food order he downed the glass, put a twenty under it, and left the restaurant. After checking out the street in both directions, he headed back into the park.

He was not chipped, as far as he could tell by the wand Edgardo had given him. He did not see anyone tailing him. He had not let any of the White House security people see which direction he went after he left the compound and crossed the street. He had not used his FOG phone. He had not eaten with the fregans for a while. Still, Cooper had known where he was. Well, he had used the FOG phone to call Nancy. First time in a long time. Could that have been enough?

The next day he called Edgardo, and they made a run date for lunch. From the 17th Street security gate they ran south, past the Ellipse and out onto the Mall. Once there they headed toward the Lincoln Memorial.

Edgardo took a wand from his fanny pack and ran it over Frank, and then Frank ran it over him. "All clear. What's up."

Frank told him what had happened.

Edgardo ran for a time silently. "So you don't know how he located you."

"Not unless it was my FOG phone. But he showed up about fifteen minutes after I used it. Seems like he already must have had me tagged."

Edgardo puffed as he ran for a while. "That's bad," he said.

"Also, even though I've seen her twice, I still don't have a way to get hold of her. She's only used the dead drop that once." For which, thank you forever.

Edgardo nodded. "Like I said. She's got to be somewhere else."

They ran on for a long time. Past the Vietnam Memorial, past Lincoln; turn left at the Korean War Memorial, east toward the Washington Monument.

Finally Edgardo said, "I think this might mean we can't wait any longer. Also this may be a good opportunity. If he is trying to force you to act, which it looks like he is, then if you do something that looks rash, he'll think you're reacting to his pressure, and he'll believe it even if you do something that isn't very smart. So that may make it a good time. He'll think it's his trap working and won't see ours. So . . . I want to get you together with my friend Umberto again. He's working with your friend, and I want him to tell you about that. She's out of town, as I suggested."

"Okay, sure. I'd like to talk to him."

Edgardo pulled his phone out of his fanny pack and squeezed one button. A quick exchange in Spanish, followed by "Okay, see you there." He put the phone away and said, "Let's cross and go back. He'll meet us down by the Kennedy Center."

So when they passed the Vietnam Memorial this time, they continued west until they reached the Potomac, then ran on the riverside walk. As they approached one of the little bartizans obtruding from the new river wall, they came on Umberto in a black suit, putting a big ID tag away in his inner pocket. Frank wondered if he had just come out of the State Department, which was just behind them.

In any case he walked with Frank and Edgardo until they could stop at a section of railing they had to themselves, within the shadow and rumble of the Roosevelt Bridge. Umberto wanded them, and Edgardo wanded Umberto, and then they spoke in Spanish, and then Umberto turned to Frank.

"Your friend Caroline has been away from here, working on the problem of the election tampering from a distance. We have reason to worry for her safety, and recently we've worried that the people we're dealing with might also have had something to do with the attempt on the President's life. So now we have contacted another unit that can help to deal with problems like this."

"Which one?" Frank asked. That list of intelligence agencies . . .

"They're an executive task force, a part of the Secret Service working with the GAO."

"The GAO?"

"It's a unit of theirs that works on the black programs."

"You're getting your help from the GAO?"

"Yes, but we are stovepiped to the President. He is overseeing all this work very closely."

"Good. So what's happening with Caroline?"

"Lots. As you may or may not know, she was in charge of a program that linked to the unit we are worrying about, the so-called ARDA Prime. Then she came to us, or we found each other, when she got the election tampering to you, and through you and Edgardo, to us."

"So you've been working with her since then?"

"Yes. But we haven't had much more contact with her than you have, from what Edgardo tells me. She's been very concerned to be sure she is working with people she can trust, and understandably so, given what's happened. So we've had to do things her way, to show her she can trust us. She's been doing work on her own that she's gotten to us, some data mining and even physical surveillance of the problem people, so we can make the case against them stick. Now we feel we are ready to do a root canal on these guys, and this confrontation you experienced may give us an opening by which to draw them out."

"Good," Frank said.

Umberto glanced at Edgardo, then said, "The problem is, they've gone inactive since the assassination attempt. I think that attack wasn't their idea, but it scared them. Now they are very quiet. But still a threat, obviously. So, we know who they are, but they've been clever about distancing themselves from their activities, and they aren't doing anything now that we can stick them with. So, we think your friend is dealing with this problem, from her angle. She doesn't have anything to use, and she wants to stay away from her husband."

Umberto stopped, looked at Frank as if it were Frank's turn to speak.

Frank said, "He came right up to me in a restaurant, and asked me where she was."

"So Edgardo said."

"And, well, she's not leaving anything at our dead drop."

"Yes. But I can get a message to her."

Frank nodded briefly. It was irritating that she was contacting them but not him; that he needed a black wing of the GAO to contact his girlfriend for him. And that she was part of that world. "And say what?" he asked.

"We were thinking that, since this group wants to find her, that might be the way to pull them out of their quiet mode."

"Make her the bait in a trap, you mean?"

"Yes. Both of you, actually. We would plan something with the two of you, because you are under their surveillance, while they seem to have lost her. So you would be the realistic way that they found her. We would arrange a thing in which it looked like you were contacting her, trying to keep it secret, but accidentally revealing to her husband where you two plan to meet. Then if they respond, and try to kidnap her, or both of you—"

"Or kill us?"

"Well, we would hope it would not start with that, because they would not want to risk such a serious thing, or really to draw any attention to her until they have her. We think they want to frame her for the election tampering so they don't have that hanging over them. So in effect they want to arrest her and turn her in. So, we would have people in place, such that they would be apprehended the moment they showed up to grab you two. Your exposure would be minimal."

"Can't you just arrest them and charge them with what they've done? Election tampering, illegal surveillance?"

Umberto hesitated. "Their surveillance may be legal," he said finally. "And as for the election tampering, the truth is, it seems as though they have succeeded pretty thoroughly in framing your friend. As far as we can prove, it all came from her office and her computer."

"But she's the one who gave it to you!"

"We know that, and that's why we're going with her. But the evidence we actually have implicates her and not them. And ARDA Prime is a real group, working legitimately under the NSA umbrella. So we have to have something else."

Frank tried to remember if Caroline had mentioned taking the vote tilting program out of her own computer or not.

Disturbed, he said, "Edgardo? If I'm going to go along with something like this, I have to be sure it's going to work." He remembered the SWAT team they had run into in the park, busting the bros with overwhelming force. "That it's being done by professionals."

Edgardo nodded. "They can brief you, and you can judge for yourself.

And she'll judge it too. She'll be in on the plan. It's not like you will be deciding for her."

"I should hope not."

"We would also study the situation very closely, until we understand better how they have been tracking you, so we can deal with that and put it to use."

"Good."

"Stay late tonight at work," Umberto said. "I'll call around nine to get you a confirmation."

"Confirmation?"

"Yes. I can't guarantee it for tonight, but I'll try. Just stay late. So we can get you the assurances you require."

"Okay."

"Let's get back to the office," Edgardo suggested. "This has been a long run."

On the way back, after a long silence, Frank said, "Edgardo, what's this about it all coming from her computers?"

"That's what they're finding."

"Could her husband have set her up like that?"

"Yes, I think so."

"But, on the other hand, *could* she have done the whole thing herself? Written the tampering program, I mean, and then leaked that to us so we would counteract it, and thus tip the election to Chase?"

Edgardo glanced at him, surprised perhaps that such a scenario would occur to him. "I don't know. Is she a programmer?"

"I don't think so."

"Well, then. That would be a very tricky program to write."

"But all the tampering comes from her computer."

"Yes, but it could have been done elsewhere and then downloaded into her computer, so that this is all we can see now. Part of a frame job. I think her husband set her up from the start."

So Frank went back to his office, and tried to think about work, but couldn't. Diane came by with news that the Netherlands had teamed with the four big re-insurance companies to fund a massive expansion of the Antarctic pumping project, with SCAR's blessing. The new consortium was also willing to team with any country that wanted to create saltwater lakes to take on some of the ocean excess, providing financing, equipment, and diking expertise.

Frank found it hard to concentrate on what Diane was saying. He nodded, but Diane stared at him with her head cocked to the side, and said suddenly, "Why don't we go out and get lunch. You look like you could use a break."

"Okay," Frank said.

When they were in one of the loud little lunch delis on G Street he found he could focus better on Diane, and even on their work. They talked about Kenzo's attempt to judge the effect of the new lakes, and Diane said, "Sometimes it feels so strange to me, these big landscape engineering projects. I mean, every one of these lakes is going to be an environmental problem for as long as it exists. We're taking steps now that commit humanity to like a thousand years of planetary homeostasis."

"We already took those steps," Frank said. "Now we're just trying to keep from falling."

"We probably shouldn't have taken the steps in the first place."

"No one knew."

"I guess that's right. Well, I'll talk with Phil about this Nevada business. Nevada could turn into quite a different place if we proceeded with all the proposals. It could be like Minnesota, if it weren't for all the atomic bomb sites."

"A radioactive Minnesota. Somehow I don't think so. Does the state government like the idea?"

"Of course not. That's why I need to talk to Phil. It's mostly federal land, so the Nevadans are not the only ones who get to decide, to say the least."

"I see," Frank said. And then: "You and Phil are doing well?"

"Oh yes." Now she was looking at her food. She glanced up at him: "We're thinking that we'll get married."

"Holy moly!" Frank had jerked upright. "That's doing well, all right!" She smiled. "Yes."

Frank said, "I thought you two would get along."

"Yes."

She did not show any awareness that his opinion had had any bearing on the matter. Frank looked aside, took another bite of his sandwich.

"We have a fair bit in common," Diane said. "Anyway, we've been sneaking around a little, because of the media, you know. It probably would be possible to keep doing it that way, but, you know—if we get caught then they will make a big deal, and there's no reason for it. We're both old, our kids are grown up. It shouldn't be that a big deal."

"Being first lady?" Frank said. "Not a big deal?"

"Well, it doesn't have to be. I'll keep on being the science advisor, and no one pays any attention to them."

"Not before! Now with this it will be a big deal. They'll accuse you of what-do-you-call-it."

"Maybe. But maybe that would be good. Whatever works, right? So we'll see."

"Well—whatever!" Frank put his hand on hers, squeezed it. "That's not what matters, anyway! Congratulations! I'm happy for you."

"Thanks. I think it will be okay. I hope so."

"Oh sure. Heck, the main thing is to be happy. The other stuff will take care of itself."

She laughed. "That's what I say. I hope so. And I am happy."

"Good."

She gave him a searching look. "What about you, Frank?"

"I'm working on it." Frank smiled briefly, changed the subject back to the salt lakes and the work at hand.

Diane followed the change of subject willingly. "I've been talking with Anna and her Chinese contacts, things are bad there, and we're working up a plan together that we may have to put into action really soon, because the problem is going from chronic to acute, they say. Could be we'll have to do something dramatic pretty soon . . ."

And they continued to share shop talk.

Then Frank went back to work, and stayed late. And around eleven, as he was falling asleep at his desk, there was a knock at his door, and it was Umberto and Phil Chase himself, and a tall black man Frank had never seen before, whom they introduced: Richard Wallace, Government Accountability Office.

They sat down and discussed the situation for most of an hour. Chase let the others do most of the talking; he seemed tired, and looked like he was in a bit of pain. His neck was still bandaged in front. Not once did he smile or crack one of the jokes that Charlie had said were constant with him.

"We need to clean this up," he said to Frank in concluding the meeting. "Our intelligence agencies are a total mess right now, and that's dangerous. Some of them are going to have to be sorted out confidentially, that's just the nature of the beast. These are my guys for improving that situation, they report directly to me, so I'd appreciate it if you'd do what you can to help them. It won't be tonight, but soon."

"I'll help," Frank promised. They shook hands as they left, and Chase gave him a somber look and a nod. Clearly he also had no idea that Frank might have played any part in him getting together with Diane. There was something satisfying in that. All these spooks, and right in their midst Frank had pulled off the best trick of all. Matchmaker matchmaker! In every gain a loss; in every loss a gain (Emerson).

One afternoon when Charlie went down to the White House's daycare center to pick up Joe, the whole staff of the place came over to meet with him.

"Uh oh," Charlie said as he saw them converging. Joe was meanwhile looking studiously out the glass doors into the playground.

Charlie said, "What's he done now?"

What a pleasure to say that!

But he knew that the part of him that was pleased was not to be revealed at that moment. So he was probably showing a certain defensiveness, but that would be natural; and in truth his feelings were mixed.

The young woman in charge that day, an assistant to the director, listed Joe's infractions in a calm, no-nonsense tone: knocking down a three-year-old girl; throwing toys; throwing food; roaring through naptime; cursing.

"Cursing?" Charlie said. "What do you mean?"

A young black woman had the grace to smile. "When we were trying to get him to quiet down he kept saying, 'You suck.'"

"Except some of us heard it differently," the assistant director added.

"Wow," Charlie said. "I don't know where he would have heard that. His brother doesn't use that kind of language."

"Uh-huh. Well anyway, that was not the main problem."

"Of course."

"The thing is," the young woman said, "we've got twenty-five kids in here that we have to give a good experience. Their parents all expect that they'll be safe and comfortable while they're here with us."

"Of course."

The quartet of young women all looked at him.

"I'll see what I can do," Charlie promised.

Then Joe crashed into him and wrapped himself around his right leg. "Da! Da! Da! Da!"

"Hi Joe. I'm hearing that you weren't very nice today."

Joe stuck out his lower lip. "Don't like this place."

"Joe, be polite."

"DON'T LIKE THIS PLACE!"

Charlie looked at the women beseechingly. "He seems kind of tired. I don't think he slept very well last night."

"He seems changed to me," one of the other women observed. "He used to be a lot more relaxed here."

"I don't know if I'd ever describe Joe as being what you'd call relaxed," Charlie said.

But it was no time for quibbling. In fact it was time for limited discussion, time to extricate the Quiblers on hand from the scene of the crime ASAP. Charlie went into diplomatic mode and made their exit, apologizing and promising it would go better. Agreeing to a meeting time for a strategy session, as the assistant director called it.

On the Metro home Charlie sat with Joe trapped between him and the window of the car. Joe stood on his seat and held the bar on the back of the seat before him, rocking forward and back, and sideways when the train turned, into Charlie or the window. "Watch out, Da! Watch out!"

"I'm watching out, monkey. Hey, watch out yourself. Sorry," this to the man in the seat ahead. "Joe, quit that. Be careful."

Charlie was both happy and unhappy. This was the Joe that he knew and loved, back full force. Underneath everything else, Charlie felt a profound sense of relief and love. His Joe was back. The important thing was to be gung ho, to tear into life. Charlie loved to see that. He wanted to learn from that, he wanted to be more like that himself.

But it was also a problem. It had to be dealt with. And in the long run, thinking ahead, this Joe, his beloved wild man, was going to have to learn to get along. If he didn't, it would be bad for him. Over time people had their edges and rough spots smoothed and rounded off by their interactions with each other, until they were like stream boulders in the Sierra, all rounded by years of banging together. At two years old, at three, you saw people's real characters; then life started the rounding process. Days of sitting in classes—following instructions—Charlie plunged into a despair as he saw it all at once: what they did to kids so that they would get by. Education as behavioral conditioning. A brainwashing that they called socialization. Like something done to tame wild horses. Put the hobbles on until they learn to walk with them; get the bit in the mouth so they'll go the direction you want. They called it breaking horses. Suddenly it all seemed horrible. The original Joe was better than that.

"You know, Joe," Charlie said uncertainly, "you're going to have to chill out there at daycare. People don't like it when you knock them over."

"No?"

"No."

"I knock you over, ha."

"Yes, but we're family. We can wrestle because we know we're doing it. There's a time and a place for it. But with the other kids at daycare, you know—no. They don't know how tough you are."

"Rough and tough!"

"That's right. But some kids don't like that. And no one likes to be surprised by that kind of stuff. Remember when you punched me in the stomach and I wasn't expecting it?"

"Da go owee, big owee."

"That's right. It can hurt people when you do that. You have to only do that with me, or with Nick if he feels like it."

"Not Momma?"

"Well, if you can get her to. I don't know though. It might not be a good habit, or . . . I don't know. I don't think so. You can ask her and see. But you have to ask. You have to ask everybody about that kind of stuff. Because usually roughhousing is just for dads. That's the thing about dads, you can beat on them. That's what they're for."

"When we get home?"

"Yeah, sure. When we get home." Charlie smiled ruefully at his younger son. "You get what you get, remember?"

"You get what you get and you don't throw a fit!"

"That's right. So don't throw any fits. We'll make it work, right Joe?"

Joe patted him on the shoulder solicitously. "Good Da."

· · ·

But this was only one of many such occurrences. Charlie began to dread the trip down to the daycare center to pick Joe up; what would he have perpetrated this time? Fitting a Play-Doh hat to a sleeping girl; climbing the fence and setting off the security alarm; plugging the sink with Play-Doh and climbing in the little "bath" that resulted . . . he was very creative with Play-Doh, as the sympathetic young teacher named Desiree noted, trying to reduce the tension in one of these postmortem sessions.

But reducing the tension was getting harder to do. The woman in charge asked Charlie to take Joe in to their staff doctor for an evaluation, and that led to an evaluation by a child psychiatrist, which led to a sequence of unilluminating tests; which led, finally, to a suggestion that they consider trying one of the very successful ameliorating drug therapy regimes, among them the paradoxical-sounding but clinically proven Ritalin.

"No," Charlie said, politely but firmly. "He's three years old. A lot of people are like this at three. I was probably like this at three. It isn't appropriate."

"Okay," the doctors and daycare people said, their faces expressionless.

Charlie was afraid to hear what Anna thought about it. Being a scientist, she might be in favor of it.

But it turned out that being a scientist, she was deeply suspicious that the suggested treatment had been studied rigorously enough. The fact that they didn't know the mechanism by which these stimulants calmed certain kids made her almost contemptuous; Charlie had never seen her so disdainful of other scientific work. No drug therapies, she said. My Lord. Not when they don't even have a mechanism. The flash-freeze of her disrespect.

"Look," Charlie said to the daycare director once, "I like the way he is."

"Then maybe you should be the one taking care of him," she said. Which he thought was pretty bold, but she met his eye; she had her center to consider. And she had seen what she had seen.

"Maybe I should."

On the Metro ride home, Charlie watched Joe as the boy stared out the window. "Joe, do you like daycare?"

"Sure, Da."

"Do you like it as much as going to the park?"

"Let's go to the park!"

"When we get home."

The three kayakers were out at Great Falls again, testing themselves against the Fish Ladder. Charlie and Drepung were getting better at it; they could rush up three or four drops before they tired and turned and rode the drops back down. Frank was getting almost all the way to the top.

When they were done, and just riding the current downstream to their put-in, they discussed the latest in the ongoing negotiations between the Dalai Lama and the Chinese government. Drepung was excited about the possibilities.

As they closed onshore, Frank said, "So, Drepung, do you believe in the reincarnation stuff?"

"What do you mean?"

"Do you think you are the reincarnation of all the Panchen Lamas?"

Even as Frank was saying it, Charlie saw a bit of physical resemblance between the youth and photos he had seen of the previous Panchen Lama. It was a look in the eye, similar to the look on Drepung's face when Frank had given them climbing lessons. A wary, worried look—even a repressed fear. Of course it made sense. The Chinese government considered itself to be the master of the Panchen Lama.

"So you're part of the negotiations with the Chinese?" Charlie said.

"Yes."

"But could you get, you know, remanded to them?"

"No, that won't happen. The people and the Dalai Lama are behind me."

"Shouldn't you be announcing who you are, as a safeguard?"

"That's one of the bargaining chips still out there, of course."

"You wouldn't want to be too late with that!"

"No."

Charlie thought it over. "My Lord. What a world this is."

"Yes."

"So," Frank persisted, "have you ever had memories of previous incarnations?"

"No."

Frank nodded. "That's what the Dalai Lama said too, in the paper. He said he was an ordinary human being."

"I am even more ordinary, as you know."

"So why should you continue to believe you're the reincarnation of some previous person?"

"We are all such. You know—one's parents."

"Yes, but you're talking about something else. Some wandering spirit, moving from body to body."

"We all have those too."

"But identifiable, from life to life?"

Drepung paused, then said, "I myself think it is a heuristic device only."

Charlie laughed. "A teaching device? A metaphor?"

"That's what I think."

Charlie pondered that in the context of what had been happening to Joe.

"And what does it teach us?" Frank asked.

"Well, that you really do go through incarnations, in effect. That in any life your body changes, and where you live changes—the people in your life, your work, your habits. All that changes so much that in effect you pass through several incarnations in any one biological span. And what I think is, if you consider it that way, it helps you not to have too much attachment. You go from life to life. Each day is a new thing."

"That's good," Frank said. "I like that. The science of this particular Wednesday."

Charlie was still thinking about Joe.

A few weeks later, by dint of some major begging, Charlie got Roy to give him ten minutes of Phil's morning time. Dawn patrol, as it turned out, because it was not only the best time to fit something in, as Phil himself remarked, it was also the traditional time for him and Charlie to meet. On this occasion, however, a Sunday morning.

Charlie showed up at the White House having slept very little the night before. Phil met him in a car at the security gates, and they were driven down Constitution and past the front of the Lincoln Memorial. "Let's walk from here," Phil suggested. "I need the exercise."

So they got out and were followed by Phil's Secret Service team through the Korean War Memorial. It was a foggy morning, so early that the sun was not yet up. The pewter statues hiked uphill through the mist, forever frozen in their awful moment of dread. The top of the memorial was backed by a retaining wall on which was carved the message FREEDOM IS NOT FREE.

Phil stood staring at it. Charlie left him to his thoughts and walked over to the apex of the statues. *We here honor our sons and daughters who answered the call to defend a country they did not know and a people they never met.*

Phil rejoined him. "Doesn't it seem like these memorials are getting better and better? This place is a heartbreaker."

"They found a really good sculptor."

"Let's walk down and see FDR. He always cheers me up."

"Me too."

It took several minutes to walk from the Korean to the Franklin Delano Roosevelt Memorial, skirting the north bank of the Tidal Basin and heading for the knot of trees around it. On first arrival it looked unprepossessing; one felt that FDR had been shortchanged compared to the rest. It was a kind of walled park, open to the sky, the walls made of rough-hewn red granite. Little pools and waterfalls were visible farther ahead, but it was all very unobtrusive, like a kid's playground in some suburban midwestern park.

But then they came to the first statue of the man—in bronze, almost life-sized, sitting on a strange little wheelchair, staring forward blindly through round bronze spectacles. He looked so human, Charlie thought, compared to the monumental gravity of the statue of Lincoln in the Lincoln Memorial. This, the statue said, had been another ordinary human being. Behind the statue on a smoothed strip of granite were words from Eleanor Roosevelt that underscored this impression:

> Franklin's illness gave him strength and courage he had not had before. He had to think out the fundamentals of living and learn

the greatest of all lessons—infinite patience and never-ending persistence.

"Yes," Phil murmured as he scanned the words. "To think out the fundamentals of living. He was forty when the polio hit him, did you know that? He had had a full life as a normal person, I mean, unimpeded. He had to adapt."

"Yes," Charlie said, and thought of what Drepung had said on the river. "It was a new incarnation for him."

"And then he got so much done. There were five separate New Deals, did you know that?"

"Yes, you've told me about that."

"Five sets of major reforms. Diane has done a complete analysis of each."

"He had huge majorities in Congress," Charlie pointed out.

"Yeah, but still. That doesn't guarantee anything. You still have to think of things to try. People have had big majorities in Congress and totally blown it."

"That's true."

"What would he do now?" Phil asked. "I find myself wondering that. He was pretty creative. The fourth and the fifth New Deals were mainly his ideas."

"That's what you've said."

Phil was standing before the statue now, leaning a bit forward so that he could stare right into the stoical, blind-seeming face. The current president, looking for guidance from Franklin Delano Roosevelt; what a photo op! And yet here were only Charlie and the Secret Service guys to witness it, as well as a runner who passed through with a startled expression, but did not stop. No real witness but Charlie; and Charlie was about to jump ship.

He was feeling too guilty to let the walk go on any further without reference to this. So as they moved to the next room of the open gallery he tried to change the subject to his own situation, but Phil was absorbed in the Depression statues, which Charlie found less compelling despite their inherent pathos: Americans standing in a bread line, a man sitting listening to a fireside chat on a radio. "I see a nation one-third ill-fed, ill-housed, ill-clothed."

"It's almost like the problem is the reverse now," Phil observed. "I see a nation one-third too fat, too clothed, too McMansioned, while the third that is ill-fed and ill-housed still exists."

"And they're all in debt, either way."

"Right, but what do you do about that? How do you talk about it?"

"Maybe just like you are now. These days, Phil, I think you get to say what you want. Like on your damn blog."

"You think?"

"Yes. But look—Phil. I asked for some time today so I could talk to you about my job. I want to quit."

"What?" Phil stared at him. "Did you say quit?"

"Well, not quit exactly. What I want is to go back to working at home."

As Phil continued to stare at him, he tried to explain. "I want to take care of Joe again. He's having some problems getting along at the daycare center. It's not their fault, but it just isn't working. I think it would be better if we stayed home until he gets to kindergarten. It would be better for him, and the truth is I think it would be better for me, too. I like spending time with him, and I seem to do better with him than most people. And it won't last long, you know? I already saw it with Nick. It just flashes right by. A couple of years from now everything will be different, and I'll feel better about leaving him all day."

"These are critical years," Phil pointed out.

"I know. But maybe they all are."

In the memorial they were moving from the Depression to the Second World War, as if to illustrate this thought. In this open room there was a different statue of FDR, bigger and in the old style, draped in the dramatic sweep of a naval cape, free of glasses and looking off heroically into the distance.

"I don't want to stop working for you," Charlie said, "not at all, but the thing is, most of what I'm doing I could do over the phone, like I did before. I thought I was doing okay then, and you've got all the technical advice you could ever want, so all I'm doing is political advice."

"That's important," Phil said. "We've got to get these changes enacted."

"Sure, but I can do that over the phone. I'll work online, and I'll work nights after Anna gets home."

"Maybe," Phil said. He was not pleased, Charlie could tell. He approached the big second statue, which included, off to one side, a statue of the Roosevelts' dog, a Scottie. Phil scolded it: "And your little dog too!"

The bronze had gone green on this version of FDR, everywhere except for the forefinger of the hand stretched out toward viewers. So many people had touched it that it was polished until it looked golden.

Phil touched it too, then Charlie.

"The magic touch," Phil said. "How touching. You know, every person that touches this finger still believes in government and justice. It's a religious feeling. Do you think any Republicans touch it?"

"I don't think they even come here," Charlie said, suddenly gloomy. He recalled reading that FDR had been pretty ruthless with aides who no longer served his purposes. They had disappeared from the administration, and from history, as if falling through trapdoors. "We're two countries now I guess."

"But that won't work," Phil said, holding on to the statue's gleaming finger. "May the spirit of FDR bring us together," he pretended to pray, "or at least provide me with a solid working majority."

"Ha ha." Again Charlie marveled at the photo ops being missed. "You should bring the press corps down here with you and talk about this. Why is *this* not the great moment in American history? You should say it is—up until now, anyway. Give people a tour of FDRness, and a look into what you admire about Roosevelt. Remember the time we were at the Lincoln Memorial with Joe, and that TV crew was there? It could be like that. For that matter you could do Lincoln again. Do them both. Take people around all the memorials, and talk about what matters to you in each of them. Give people some history lessons, and some insights into your own thinking about where we are now. Keep calling these years we're in another rendezvous with destiny. Call for a new New Deal. These are the times that try men's souls, and so forth."

"I don't think there are any monuments to Thomas Paine in this town,"

Phil said, smiling at the thought.

"Maybe there should be. Maybe you can arrange for that."

"In my copious spare time."

Phil slapped hands with FDR and moved on. They went into the final room of the gallery, where an amazingly lifelike statue of Eleanor Roosevelt stared out from an alcove embossed with the emblem of the United Nations.

"The UN was his idea, not hers," Phil objected. "She worked for it after it was established, but he had the idea for it even before the war. World peace, the rule of law, and the end to all the empires. It was amazing how hard he tweaked Churchill and de Gaulle on that. He wouldn't lift a finger to help them keep their empires after the war. They thought he was just being a lightweight, but he was serious. He just didn't want to come off as all holier-than-thou about it. Like his wife here used to."

"But he was holier-than-thou, compared to Churchill and de Gaulle."

"No, de Gaulle was the holy one in that crowd. Roosevelt was an operator. And everyone was holier than Churchill."

"This is what you should be saying. So—what do you say?"

"About becoming a memorial tour guide?"

"No, about whether I can do my job from home again."

"Well, Charlie, I think you're doing good work. We need to get to sustainability as fast as we can, as you know. There's a lot riding on it. But, heck. If your kid needs you, then you've got to do it."

"I think he does. Him and me both."

"Well, there you are."

"I can still do the daily phone thing with Roy, and come in with Joe like I used to. And we'll get a majority at the midterms, and you'll get re-elected—"

"You think so?"

"I'm sure of it. And by then Joe will be in kindergarten, and this phase will have passed. I'll be anxious to get back to work then, so I don't want you to drop me, you know? That's what FDR did to his aides."

"I'm not as tough as he was."

"I don't know about that. But I'll want to come back."

"We'll see," Phil said. "You never know what will happen."

"True."

Charlie felt disappointed, even worried; what would he do for work, if he couldn't work on Phil's staff? He had been doing it for twelve years now.

But he wanted to stay with Joe. Actually, he wanted it all. But no one got to have it all. He was lucky he had as much as he had. He would have to keep working hard to stay innovative from home, over the phone. It could be done; he had done it before.

Phil gestured to his guys, following them at a not-so-discreet distance, and a car came to pick them up less than a minute later. Back to the White House; back to work; back to the world; back home. Phil was silent on the drive and appeared to be thinking of other things, and Charlie didn't know what he felt.

One strangely balmy winter day Frank got the word from Edgardo during their run: time to act. They had everything staked out and rehearsed, and today was the day. Good. But between lunch and dinner the thunderheads grew, and big news arrived from China: there had been some kind of crisis declared, and ordinary law and all normal activities there were suspended. The American nuclear submarine fleet had turned up en masse in Chinese harbors, along with several aircraft carriers; but this was by Chinese invitation, and the fleet had immediately plugged into the Chinese electrical grid and taken over generating electricity for essential services in certain areas. The rest of the country's grid had been shut down. And Phil Chase had landed in Beijing, apparently to consult with the Chinese leadership. The Secretary-General of the UN and representatives from other countries had also flown in. From the sounds of it, the Chinese appeared to be attempting a kind of near-instantaneous transformation of their infrastructure—the "Great Leap Forward at Last," as one of the news strips at the bottom of the TV screens put it—but only to escape falling into a bottomless pit of ecological collapse. And so the attention of the world was transfixed.

All that was very interesting, and maybe good, maybe bad, maybe irrelevant, in terms of its potential impact on their own operation. But there was no mechanism for bailing on it that Frank knew of; no one called him; and all he could do was grit his teeth and wait for the time to arrive.

Finally the hour came. He was in his office, his door was closed. He knew just how his FOG phone was bugged, and by whom. Time to play his part. He picked up the FOG phone, dialed the number he had been given.

Caroline picked up.

"Hey," Frank said.

"Oh hey! What's up? Why are you—"

"I've got to see you, I've got the proof you wanted. Meet me down where we met before, by the river, about nine."

"Okay," she said, and hung up.

He stood. Took the Kevlar vest from his desktop and put it on. Kevlar: bulletproof. This was what Phil Chase had to deal with all the time. The feeling of being a potential target. For Phil, the feeling of having been shot, and then going out there again.

He left the White House compound, aware of just which one of the security guys at the gate had been tacking a new kind of chip on him. It had taken them a while to figure that out. The guard hadn't been there all the time, but he had been there a lot, and they had made sure he was going to be there now: thin face, impassive look, didn't quite meet the eye. Do it again, asshole. This time they needed it done.

Once out on the sidewalk he put the earbuds of his iPod look-alike in his ears. "Did he do it?"

"Yes," he heard in his right ear. The voice sounded a little odd; this was an encrypted line, and in transit was flying up and down the radio band in a pattern of its own, only to be reconstituted in Frank's little iPod thing.

He walked west on G Street to the Watergate, then across the Rock Creek Parkway, through the boat club parking lot, where his VW van was parked; then past the van, over the little bridge crossing the creek, and onto the Georgetown waterfront. It was about eight thirty.

Then that part of the city lost power. "Shit," Frank said. The entire waterfront of Georgetown was now dark, and people were calling out and wandering in the sudden gloom.

"This is bad," he said.

Voice in his right ear: "Proceed for now. She says she can make the rendezvous, and they're gathering for that."

Frank went down to the water's edge and watched cars' headlights on the Virginia side of the river. George Washington Parkway right on the water, Arlington streets above it. Generators were bringing light back here and there across the city, on both sides of the river.

In this partial light Caroline appeared, looking flushed and intent. They met and hugged, then spoke like amateur actors, their voices extra expressive, at times almost cutting each other off in their eagerness to say their lines. They rolled their eyes at each other, tried to pace themselves better. Two bad actors in the dark. He could see she was wearing another Kevlar vest under her blouse, and thought that her ex might be able to see it too. He handed her a little keychain flash drive; this was their supposed crucial information, the MacGuffin in their little plot.

Awkwardly he put his arm around her shoulder, and they rested at the river rail for a moment, itching at the unfelt transference of the new type of surveillance tick that had been lofted onto him by the security guard—a thing of plastic and quartz, pinging at a frequency their wands didn't cover. A chip programmed to jump on contact and then stay put, apparently; the GAO team had been confident it would shift from Frank to Caroline when they were close enough for it to sense her body heat. A nano-event neither of them could feel except in the rigidity of their muscles as they braced for it, and in a kind of itch on the inside of the skull.

Together they hiked back over the little bridge, and stopped by Frank's van. They embraced and drew apart, looking helplessly at each other, just barely visible to each other in the dark, and even that only by the light of car headlights on the Rock Creek Parkway. This was a dark part of town even when the power was on. Frank let go of her hand and watched her walk away.

Now she was walking in a crowd of Umberto and Wallace's people, special ops agents disguised as tourists, which explained their daypacks and camera gear, their iPod earbuds, their aimless gawking and walking. It was a very professional team, far more expert than an ordinary SWAT team. Frank knew this and yet still he found himself stiff with dread.

He hopped up in his van's driver's seat, preparing to be carjacked or shot; the presence of Umberto's guys quietly sitting in the back of the van was little comfort, considering what a good sniper could do. And the blackout was a factor they had not planned on, so it was really dark out there; and blackouts always induced a little chaos. Caroline was walking over toward the Watergate and then the Kennedy Center. The special ops teams were following her or already out there ahead of her, waiting for Cooper's group to make its move. They were sure these people had overheard the first call from Frank, because they knew Frank had been followed since then. Because they had flooded the area, and indeed constituted almost everyone in the area, they were confident they would spot any people approaching her with intent, well before these people got near her. At that point they would close in and forestall any such approach with overwhelming force. That anyway was the plan.

Frank's part in the charade designed to get Cooper's group to act had him passing along vital information, indeed proof of a crime. So now he was done, and he sat there uncomforted by his guards in back, expecting to be shot or blown up. But in fact the van and the parking lot and the surrounding area were fully secured, and now one of his guards was wanding him with a much bigger device than any he had seen before. There was still a nanochip there on the back of his jacket, much smaller than a tick, though they called it that. In the dark they would never be able to find it in the fabric of the jacket.

"I'm going to leave it here and follow her," Frank said.

His guards frowned.

"Is there anyone following me?" Frank asked.

"No," the one in back said. "It looks like they're just going for her."

"I'm going over there," Frank said, and snatched the hand axe out of his jacket pocket and jumped back out into the dusk.

"Stay out of the way!" one of the guards exclaimed to him. The other was saying something over his comms. Frank hustled off, hoping they would not pursue him and tackle him. He had no illusions that he could elude them if they wanted to stop him. For now it seemed that they were willing to let him go. Maybe it was even better bait for their trap.

He was still hearing the team's comms in his right earbud. A voice reported that her tick was now taking pings. The location of the pinger was not yet ID'd. Frank knew that this kind of little tick had to be pinged from within a range of a couple hundred yards, so he began to run, dashing across the Rock Creek parkway during a too-small gap in the traffic, headlights coming at him, car horn Dopplering its displeasure at him, then he was racing across black grass on the roadside to Virginia Avenue, so much darker than usual. Passing headlights had destroyed his night vision without illuminating much outside the roadway. A different voice in his earbud complained that there was very dense ping traffic in the area, which was making it difficult to identify point sources; possibly some of these were decoys, a deliberate interference pattern. Frank felt a stab of fear on hearing this, and ran harder still. Decoys? Had Caroline's ex seen this ambush coming, and taken steps to foil it?

It was hard to tell who in the earbud was saying what. A police car with its siren screaming zoomed through the momentarily stilled traffic. Some of the buildings with generators were lighting up. Frank said, "Can you patch me into her wire?"

"Yeah," said a voice in his ear; sounded like the main guard in his van. There was a click, and then he could hear her whisper: "I'm going past the Watergate. I'm not sure what to do. It's pretty well lit here."

"Stick to the plan," someone said.

"I just saw them," she said. "I'm going to step into this espresso shop on the southeast side of the Watergate, they've got a generator going."

"Okay. Stay cool now. They won't want any fuss."

Someone else said, "We have visual."

"On her or the tail?"

"Both!"

Frank ran as hard as he could around the northeastern curve of the Watergate complex, hand axe in his right hand ready to throw. It seemed possible that a man hit by Tasers might spasm so violently as to pull a trigger, or before he was struck down might shoot Caroline in the head—shoot the moment he saw he was pursued—

He rounded the easternmost curve of the Watergate and saw that Caroline was being escorted out the espresso shop door by two men, one on each side of her, both holding her by the arm. Their backs were to him, and Frank froze as he would have in the woods, then walked at a normal pace after them. Cooper was on her right, looking down at her, saying something to her, though his jaw was set. Frank hefted the hand axe, grasped it in a throwing grip. "Come on guys," he whispered.

Then Cooper stopped, looked around, and began to pull something from his jacket pocket. Figures leaped out of the dark as Frank threw his stone. It was a perfect throw, but in the time it took for it to flash through the night to its target Cooper had been tackled from three directions and flattened to the ground; the stone flew over the mass of struggling men and hit one of the SWAT guys beyond them square in his flak-jacketed chest. The man's rifle jerked up and pointed right at Frank. For a moment everything froze; Frank's hands were up over his head, and he could feel his eyes bugging out like the guy in the Goya painting about to get shot.

No one shot him. Three or four rifles were trained on him. The man on the other side of Caroline was under as many assailants as Cooper, and Caroline had jumped away from them and was now surrounded by four men in flak jackets with rifles at the ready, pointed outward from her. Fifty yards down the street a brief scrum erupted, and several rifles got redirected that way. Off to the side another sudden group coalesced out of the dark, men holding guns trained on a pair of other men. All the struggling took place in a furious silence, except for a single heavy shout: *"Freeze!"* And indeed soon after that everything went still.

Caroline looked around at the scene, eyes wide, and saw Frank. He circled the crowd of flak-jacketed men trussing up Cooper and his partner as they lay prone on the sidewalk, giving them a wide berth, and went to her. Briefly they clasped hands, squeezed hard. She was white-faced, her gaze fixed on her trussed and prone ex as if on a beast that might still break free and leap at her.

Umberto appeared before them, rotund in his flak jacket. "Into the Watergate," he said. "We have one of the condos there, and they've got their generator going."

Near the end of their debriefing, with Cooper and his crew long since taken away, and Umberto and the other men there absorbed in the progress of other parts of the root canal, Frank and Caroline realized they were no longer needed. Umberto noticed them standing there and waved them away. The operation was going well, he indicated. There would be no one left free to bother them.

As they were leaving, the man Frank had hit in the chest with his hand axe gave it back to him, frowning heavily as he thumped it into Frank's palm. "You could hurt somebody," he said. "Maybe leave it on your mantelpiece."

"On my dashboard," Frank promised.

They found themselves alone, standing outside what had been the Watergate's old hotel lobby entrance. The blackout still darkened much of the city, although generators now lit many buildings. Sirens in the distance sawed at the night.

"So you threw your rock at him again," Caroline said.

"Yes. I would have got him if they hadn't taken him down."

"You could have wrecked everything."

"I know, but we'd gone off the plan. I didn't want him to shoot you before they got him, or get Tasered and spaz out and shoot you by accident. I just did it."

"I know. But that guy was right. You should put it away."

"I'll put it in my glove compartment," Frank said. "It'll be like my home defense system."

"Good."

Frank said, "You know, your ex kept saying that you tweaked the election all by yourself."

She stared at him. "I'm sure he did! That's how he tried to set it up, too. But I've got the evidence of how he framed me, along with everything else. And now these guys have it too."

"Well good. But why didn't you tell me from the start that you were working with these guys?" Frank gestured in the direction of the mouth of Rock Creek. "You could have told me back in the summer."

"It's best never to say any more than necessary in situations like that. I was trying to keep you out of it."

"I was already in it! You should have told me!"

"I didn't think it would help! So quit about that! It's been tough. It's been over a *year* since I had to go under, do you realize that?"

"Yes of course I do! It feels like it's been about ten!"

Frank put up a hand. Clearly it was time for limited discussion. Gingerly he reached for her, palm out. Her hand reached out and met his, and their fingers intertwined. For a while their fingers did the talking. "Okay," he said, "I'm sorry. I don't mean to complain. I've been scared."

"Me too."

They walked down the Watergate driveway under its awning to Virginia Avenue. They could see cars' lights crossing the Key Bridge. Their cold hands were continuing their own quick conversation. For a long time they just stood on the sidewalk there, looking around.

"Do you think it's really over?" she asked in a low voice.

"I think maybe so."

She took a deep breath, shuddered as she let it out. "I can't even tell anymore. The group he was part of was pretty extensive. I don't know if I'm going to feel comfortable, just—you know. Coming back out into the open."

"Maybe you don't have to. They'll help you set up something new, like in witness protection. I asked them about it."

"Yeah me too."

"I want to show you San Diego."

She looked hard at him, eyes searching his face, trying to read something. Their hands were still squeezed hard together. Things were not normal between them, he saw. Perhaps she was still angry at him for asking about the election stuff. For wanting to know what was going on. "Okay," she said. "Show me."

CHAPTER 30

YOU GET WHAT YOU GET

But our Icarian thoughts returned to ground
And we went to heaven the long way round.
—Thoreau

CUT TO THE CHASE

Today's post:

I think for a long time we forgot what was possible. Our way of life damaged our ability to imagine anything different. Maybe we are rarely good at imagining things could be different. Maybe that's what we mean when we talk about the Enlightenment. For a while there we understood that the ultimate source of power is the imagination.

Listen to this: "Through new uses of corporations, banks and securities, new machinery of industry, of labor and capital—all undreamed of by the Fathers—the whole structure of modern life was impressed into the service of economic royalists. It was natural and perhaps human that the privileged princes of these new economic dynasties, thirsting for power, reached out for control of government itself. They created a new despotism and wrapped it in the robes of legal sanction. In its service new mercenaries sought to regiment the people, their labor and their property. And as a result the average man once more confronts the problem that faced the Minute Man. For too many of us life was no longer free; liberty no longer real; men could no longer follow the pursuit of happiness. Against economic tyranny such as this, the American citizen could appeal only to the organized power of the Government."

That was Franklin Roosevelt, talking as president in 1936. Is that radical enough for you? Is it beautiful enough? In the same speech he said, "There is a mysterious cycle in human events. To some generations much is given. Of other generations much is expected. This generation of Americans has a rendezvous with destiny." And by God they met that destiny. They did what they could in their time.

But then we forgot. We went back to imagining that things could only be as they are. We lived into a strange new feudalism, following ways that were unjust and destructive and yet were presented as the only possible reality. We said "people are like that," or "human nature will never change" or "we are all guilty of original sin," or "the free market is reality itself." And we went along with those old ideas, and made them the law of the land. The entire world became legally bound to accept this feudal injustice. It was global and so it looked like it was universal. The future itself was bought, in the form of debts, mortgages, contracts—all spelled out by law and enforced by police and armies. Alternatives were unthinkable. Even to say things could be otherwise would get you immediately branded as unrealistic, foolish, naïve, insane, utopian.

But that was all delusion. Every few years things change completely, even though we can't quite remember how it happened or what it means. Change is real and it's unavoidable. And we can organize our affairs any way we please. We are free to act. It's a fearsome thing, this freedom, so much so that people talk about a "flight from freedom"—that we fly into cages and hide, because our freedom is so profound that it's a kind of abyss. To actually choose in each moment how to live is too scary to endure.

So we lived like sleepwalkers. But the world is not asleep, and outside our dream things continued to change. Trying to shape that change is a good thing to do. Some pretend that making a plan is instant communism and the devil's work, but it isn't so. We always have a plan. Neoliberal economics is a plan—it plans to give over all decisions to the blind hand of the market. But the blind hand never picks up the check. And, you know—it's blind. To deal with the global environmental crisis we now face without making any more plan than to trust the market would be like saying, We have to solve this problem so first let's put out our eyes. Why? Why not use our eyes? Why not use our brain?

Because we're going to have to imagine our way out of this one.

That's why we made the recent deal with China. It's one of the greatest win-win treaties of all time. Consider that we had a massive trade deficit running with China, and they had bought a lot of our debt as well. And because of their population and their manufacturing capabilities, and their low wages, which of course depressed wages for every other worker in the world, there wasn't an obvious way out of that huge imbalance. They had us. We were getting whipped in the market by a command-and-control political structure that could inflict austerity measures on its own people, allowing them to win that particular competition. So a dictatorship was doing better at the market than democracies were. I leave it as an exercise for my readers to hash out what that might mean in political science terms, but in the real world it was a big problem!

And yet at the same time this so-called success of the Chinese was achieved partly by treating their people and landscape like disposables, and that simply isn't true. So those false economies were backlashing on them in bigger and bigger ways, creating terrible physical problems, worse problems than ours, really, because we've been cleaning up our land and air and water for decades now, as part of the smart governance of the people, by the people, and for the people, so that our troubles are mostly on paper. But the Chinese have trashed China itself, and had entered a major ecological crash. Maybe global warming and the giant drought it caused in East Asia was the final push, but certainly their own poisonous habits had pooled up on them, and the cumulative impacts were going to kill entire regions and endanger the lives of one-sixth of humanity.

That wouldn't have been good for any of us. I know there are people saying that the worse things go for the Chinese, the better off we are, but it doesn't work that way. The carbon they put in the air was going everywhere on Earth, even if China took the brunt of it. And in any case they were desperate enough to be in need of our aid, and to ask us for it—so we were obliged to help, just *as fellow human beings. The fact that it gave us bargaining leverage with them that we hadn't had before was just the silver lining on a big black cloud.*

Ultimately, everyone on Earth had an interest in helping the Chinese escape an acute extinction event. We needed to help, and the situation was so urgent that ordinary procedures weren't going to do it. So I talked to President Hu (and yes, he was on first) and our teams hammered out a deal in record time, which the Senate immediately approved 71 to 29, because it was that good a deal.

So then, at the invitation of the Chinese government, we docked sixty ships of our nuclear fleet in Chinese ports, and provided them with well over five hundred megawatts for essential services. They shut down the dirtiest coal plants in the affected areas, and replaced them with new clean plants, in less than two weeks. We also helped to pay for these plants. We also gave China all the scientific help we could, everything our environmental science community has learned. Our Army Corps of Engineers and the Department of Agriculture went there to consult, and we're also sending over security experts to help keep track of expenditures, so that we don't have any of the contract corruption that occurred under some lax previous administrations. My recent reorganization of our nation's intelligence services (see my earlier post on the cleaning up of that swamp) has created some redundancies that give us the personnel to fulfill some of these new cooperative security responsibilities, both in Beijing and on-site in the drought-affected areas. We were pleased to send one entire group to the Takla Makan.

So we're doing a lot for them, and they're doing a lot for us, and everyone is benefiting. What are they doing for us? They've agreed to cut their carbon emissions so steeply that they will be challenging the rest of the Asia Pacific Six, which is us, Australia, Japan, South Korea, and India, to match them, and they are committed to investing heavily in clean renewables in the other five countries in the group. As part of that effort they will be building zero-emission power plants for us in the United States, on federal land, to be run by the Department of Energy. Clean renewable power will quickly become part of the public trust. A public utility district, very large.

The Chinese have also negotiated a successful compromise with the Dalai Lama, so that Tibet will take its rightful place among the semiautonomous ethnic regions that are important features of both China and the United States, here in the form of our Native American reservations. The Chinese leadership has embraced diversity, and the world rejoices at the Tibetan settlement. I particularly appreciate the extension of civil liberties and personal security to all Chinese religious groups, including all Buddhist monks and nuns and their leaders. That's all been very good accommodation of everyone's interests.

I'll add more on that later, but now Diane says it's time for bed. Thanks to everyone for their best wishes, by the way!

Phil's response to respondent 3,581,332:

I know people have been saying I have put the pedal to the metal ever since I got shot, and you know what? It's true. So sue me! (But don't.) I know people also say I've gotten to be like Paul Revere—you know, a little light in the belfry—but that is not true. I am more sane now than I have ever been.

So, thanks in advance.

Phil's response to respondent 4,520,334:

What I do is mix soy sauce and a dry white wine about half and half, and then add a big dash of tarragon vinegar, and a teaspoon of brown sugar, a tablespoon of olive oil, and about a teaspoon each of ginger and mustard powder, and a dash of garlic powder. Mix that up and the longer you marinate things in it the better, but just dipping it in will do too, if you're in a hurry. Best on veggies, chicken, and flank steak. Sear the meat and then cook at a lower heat.

Cookbook to follow, when I get more time.

Frank and Caroline flew together out to San Diego.

There was an awkwardness between them now that Frank didn't understand. It was as if, now that they were free to do what they wanted, they didn't know what it was. It reminded Frank in a rather frightening way of his old inability to decide—of how that had felt. They had no habits. They sat side by side, and long silences grew.

Before they left, Frank had dropped by the office. He had walked into Edgardo's office and given the Argentinean a big hug, his cheek crushed against the tall man's skinny chest. "Thanks Edgardo."

Edgardo had smiled his wry smile. "You are welcome, my friend. It was my pleasure, believe me."

They had then discussed the situation, as conveyed by Umberto. It sounded like things would be okay. Phil was untangling the intelligence community, though that would take some doing. Frank then explained his plan, and Edgardo had raised a finger to add something. She might not want to talk much about this last year of hers, he had warned. She may never want to. A lot of us are like that. I don't know if she is, but if so, be ready for it. It may always, always be a case of limited discussion.

Frank had nodded, thinking it over.

Besides, Edgardo had continued, look: even if she did fix the election single-handedly, and then framed her ex to make it look like he framed her, what's anyone to do about that now? What good would it do to expose that?

Frank's uneasy shrug had sparked Edgardo's most delighted and cynical laugh. It echoed in his mind all the way across the country.

In San Diego, Frank drove their rental car up to La Jolla. First to the top of Mount Soledad, to show her the area from on high; then down to UCSD, where he walked her through the eucalyptus groves in their ranks and files and diagonals. Up the great promenade between the big pretty buildings, up the curving path on the east side of the library, an inlaid piece of sculpture made to resemble a snake's back. An inscription from Milton carved into the snake's head made it clear just which snake it was. A library as the forbidden Tree of the Knowledge of Good and Evil: very apt.

Caroline smiled when she saw it, and kissed Frank on the cheek. "Want an apple?" That was the best sign he had gotten from her all day, and his spirits expanded a bit.

"You like this place?"

"Yes. Any library that has Lucifer and the Cat in the Hat outside it is my kind of place."

Then west across Torrey Pines, onto the bluff overlooking the Pacific. He pointed out his bedroom nook, and watched her look out at the view. San Clemente Island was visible on the horizon, seventy miles out to sea. He could see that she liked this place too. Then they returned to the streets, and up Torrey Pines to the new institute.

Into Leo's lab. Leo regarded Caroline with interest as Frank introduced them.

"Leo, this is my friend,—"

"Carrie Barr," Caroline said, and put out her hand.

"Hi," Leo said, taking it. "Leo Mulhouse. Good to meet you."

After a bit of chat about their trip out:

"Are the insertions still going well?" Frank asked.

"They're good," Leo said. "Results are really good right now."

Frank explained to Caroline some of what they were doing, and tried to answer her questions with the right amount of technical detail, never an easy thing to judge. She looked different to Frank now, as if she had instantly become a Californian now that she was here. Maybe it was that he had so seldom seen her in the sun. It was hard to believe how little time they had actually spent together. He didn't know how much biology she knew, or whether she was interested in it.

After that, Frank had a meeting on campus. "Do you want to join me for it, or do you want to have a look around?"

"I'll have a look around."

"Okay. Let's meet back at Leo's lab in an hour, okay?"

"Fine." Off she went.

Frank walked over to the coffee kiosk in the eucalyptus grove at the center of campus, where he had arranged to meet with Henry Bannet of Biocal. They shook hands, and in short order were looking at a PowerPoint show that Frank had cobbled together for him. As Frank spoke, he added stuff Leo had just told him a few minutes before. Bannet proved to be much as Leo had said: pleasant, professionally friendly, all in the usual way—but he had a quickness of eye that seemed to indicate some kind of impatience. Once or twice he interrupted Frank's explanations with questions about Yann and Eleanor's methods. He knew a lot. This guy, Frank thought, wanted gene therapy to work.

"Have you talked to your tech transfer office about this?" Bannet asked.

"It's Eleanor Dufours who is the P.I.," Frank said. "She'll be the one leading the way with any start-up."

"Okay," Bannet said, looking at bit surprised. "We can discuss that later."

By the time Frank got back to Leo's lab, Caroline was already there, and so were Marta and Eleanor, with Marta looking most intrigued.

"Frank!" Marta said. "I didn't know you were going to be out here again so soon."

"Yes, I am. Hi, Eleanor. Have you guys met my friend—"

"Yes," Caroline said. "Leo introduced us." Then for a second everyone was saying something at once.

After a brief laugh, they fell silent. "Well!" Marta said. She had a gleam in her eye that Frank had seen before. "What a lucky coincidence! We were just going to grab Leo for dinner in Del Mar, to celebrate the latest results—did he tell you about those? Why don't you two join us?"

Frank said, "Oh, well—"

"Sure," Caroline said, "that sounds great."

So there they were at their usual beach restaurant in Del Mar, talking away. Given the results in the lab, they had a lot to be cheerful about. Caroline was seated on one side of Frank, Marta on the other. This made him very uneasy, but there was nothing he could do. And besides he too had cheerful news, in the form of his meeting with Henry Bannet.

"So does that mean you're moving back?" Marta said to Frank when the others were all talking among themselves.

"Yes, I think so."

"You've been out there a long time—what has it been, three years?"

"I guess so," Frank said. "It feels like more." One of Drepung's reincarnations, for sure.

After dinner Marta invited them to come along with them to the Belly Up, and again Caroline agreed before Frank could beg off. So there they were, in the crush of dancers on the floor of the Belly Up, Frank dancing with three women, watching Marta and Caroline shouting over the music into each other's ears and then laughing heartily, before excusing themselves and going off to the ladies' room. Frank watched this appalled. He had never even imagined Marta and Caroline meeting, much less becoming friendly. Now he was surprised to see that they looked somewhat alike, or were in some deeper way similar. And really, now that he thought of it, it was a little gratifying that Marta liked Caroline—a kind of approval of his judgment, or of his D.C. life. Part of a more general amnesty. But it also felt like trouble, in some obscure way Frank could not pin down. At the very least it probably meant he was going to get laughed at a lot. Well, nothing to be done about that. There were worse fates.

Frank had made reservations for the night at a motel in Encinitas, but for some reason he was nervous about that; and besides, he wanted to take Caroline up to Leucadia. He wasn't going to be able to sleep until he did.

So he explained as they left the Belly Up, and she nodded, and he drove north on the coast highway.

"So?" Frank said. "How are you liking it?"

"It's beautiful," she said. "And I like your friends. But, you know—I'm not sure what I would do out here."

"Well—anything you want, right? I mean, you're going to have to do something somewhere, right? You aren't going back into intelligence . . . ?"

But maybe she thought she was. Maybe that was it.

She didn't say anything, so he dropped it, more uncertain than ever.

He turned left off the coast highway in Leucadia, drove to Neptune. He parked a little down from Leo's house. As they walked up the street, gaps to their left revealed the enormous expanse of the Pacific, vast and gray under the marine layer, which was patterned by moonlight. Like something out of a dream. He had her here with him at last. Breaking waves cracked and grumbled underfoot, and the usual faint haze of mist salted the air.

He stopped in the street in front of one of the cliffside houses. The cliff here had given way in the big storms of a few years ago, and even the streetside wall of this particular house was cracked. It appeared that one corner of its outer foundation overhung the new face of the cliff. There was a FOR SALE BY OWNER sign stuck in the Bermuda grass of a narrow front lawn.

Frank said, "I followed up on something Leo said, and checked the USGS study of this part of the coast, and he's right—this is a little buttress here, a little bit of a point, see? We're a touch higher, and the iceplant doesn't grow as well on the cliff, and there was this erosion, but the point itself is strong. I think this will be the last erosion here for a while. And there are things you can do to shore up the bluff. And, you know, if worse came to worst, we could tear down this house entirely and build nearer the street. Something small and neat."

"Like in this tree?" Caroline said, gesturing at the big eucalyptus tilting over them.

Frank grinned. "Well, incorporating it maybe. We'd have to save it somehow."

She smiled briefly, nodded. "My treehouse man."

She walked out to the edge of the cliff, looked down curiously. Anywhere else on Earth this would be a major sea cliff; here it was a little lower than average for North County, at about seventy feet. Everywhere sea cliffs were eroding at one rate or another.

"There's a staircase down to the beach, just past Leo and Roxanne's,"

Frank told her, pointing to the south. "There's a bike lane on the coast high-way that runs from here all the way down to UCSD. I think it's about twelve miles. You could get a job down there on campus, or nearby, and we could bike down there to work. Take the coast cruiser when we need to. We could make it work."

"Well good," Caroline said, staring at him in the moonlight. "Because I'm pregnant."

Frank dreamed that Charlie came to him at the end of a day's work and said, "Phil wants to see Rock Creek," and off they went in a parade of black Priuses.

In the park it was as snowy as in the depths of the long winter, and they crunched on snowshoes through air like dry ice. At site 21 the bros had a bonfire going, and Frank introduced the bundled-up Phil as an old friend and the bros did not notice him, they were focused on the bonfire and their talk—all except Fedpage, who looked up from the *Post* he was feeding to the fire. He studied Phil for a second and his eyebrows shot up. "Whoah!" he said, and knocked his glasses up his nose to have a better look. "What's this, some kind of Prince Hal thing?" He jerked his head to the side to re-direct Zeno's attention to the visitor. "Oh, hey," Zeno said as he saw who it was. Frank was afraid he would go all blustery and false like he so often did with Frank himself, but Phil slipped through all that and soon they were adding fuel to the fire while talking about Vietnam, and Zeno was fine. Frank felt a glow of pleasure at that. But otherwise it was cold, unless you sat too close to the fire, and the hour grew late, and on and on the Viet vets reminisced; Frank shared a glance with the Secret Service man sitting be-side him, a black man he had never seen before (and on waking he would remember this man's face so clearly, it was utterly distinct, a face he had never seen before—where did the faces in dreams come from, who were they?) and their shared glance told them that they both knew the President liked this kind of scene, that he was a bullshitter at heart, so they were going to be there all night, talking Vietnam.

But then Spencer and Robin and Robert came roaring through and Frank leaped up to join their night golf. They were going long, they said. It was too beautiful not to. They were shooting new holes all the way down Rock Creek and past the Watergate, curving one shot into the Lincoln Me-morial to smack Abe's left knee, then across to the Korean vets, where one of the doomed statues had his hand out as if to make a catch; then on to the

Tidal Basin, threading the cherry trees lining the west bank, so that it took finesse as well as brute distance to do well; and then out to the FDR memorial, where the final hole was declared to be the gold forefinger of Roosevelt's second statue. Frank threw his Frisbee and realized as it curved away that its flight was so perfect that it would hit the finger right on the tip, and so he woke up.

They got back to D.C. just in time for another party at the Khembali farm. It was a Saturday on which Frank had a zoo morning scheduled with Nick, so he showed up at the Quiblers' house at around ten.

"How was San Diego?" they asked him. They knew that he was planning to move back there.

"It was good." He smiled what Anna called his real smile. "I found out that my girlfriend is pregnant."

"Pregnant?" Anna cried—

"Girlfriend?" Charlie exclaimed.

The two of them looked at each other and laughed at their nicely timed response, also their mutual ignorance.

Then Anna snapped her fingers and pointed at him. "It's that woman you met in the elevator."

"Well yes, that's right."

"Ha! I knew it! Well!" She gave him a hug. "I guess you're glad now that you went to that brown-bag talk at NSF!"

"And came to your party afterward. Yes, that was quite a day. You did a good thing to set that up." Frank shook his head as he remembered it. "Everything changed on that day."

Anna clapped her hands a little. "Frank that is *good* news, so when do we get to meet her?"

"She's coming to the party this afternoon, so we'll meet her out there. She couldn't make it to the zoo, though, she had to do some stuff."

"Okay, good then. Off we go."

They walked up to the Bethesda Metro, trained down to the zoo. In through the front gates—an entry Frank and Nick rarely used—past the pandas, then down toward the tigers, Joe racing ahead in perpetual danger of catching a toe and launching himself into a horrible face-plant. "Joe, slow down!" Charlie cried uselessly as he took off in pursuit.

Frank walked between Nick and Anna, all three looking for the golden tamarind monkeys and other little ferals squirreling around freely in the trees. By the time they had dropped in to see which gibbons were out, and continued down to the tiger enclosure, Joe was up on Charlie's shoulders, dangerously canted over the moat.

Their swimming tigers were basking in the sun. The male was draped against the tree like a tiger rug, his mouth hanging open. The female lay en couchant, long and sleek, staring sphinxlike into emptiness.

For a long time no one moved. Other people drifted by.

"I saw the jaguar," Frank told them. "It was casual at the time, or, I don't mean casual—I was totally scared and ran away as soon as I could—but I didn't fully get it, how great it was to see it, until a few days later."

"Wow," Nick said. "Did you get a GPS?"

"It was at the overlook."

"No."

"Yes."

"Wow."

After awhile longer they went to get snow cones, even though it was just before lunch. Frank got lime; Nick got a mix of root beer, cherry, and banana.

Then Frank took off to go pick up his girlfriend, and the Quiblers went back to the house before continuing out to the farm.

The Khembalis' party was a big one, combining as it did several celebrations, not just the Shambala relocation, but also the Buddhist plumblossom festival, which now would always mark the auspicious day when the Dalai Lama and the Chinese government had agreed on his return to Tibet. The treaty had been signed there in Washington, at the White House, just the day before. And now also it was Frank's going-away party, and even a sort of shower; and last but not least, Phil and Diane were going to drop by for a bit. Their presence added to the crowd, as well as making the party into a kind of wedding reception, because the first couple had made their actual nuptials a completely private affair a few days before. Parts of the punditocracy were squawking that this fait accompli was an unholy alliance of science and politics, but Phil had only laughed at this and agreed, adding, "What are you gonna do?"

So when they arrived, there was the usual stir. But as soon as they had accepted a toast from all they insisted that the party refocus on the Khembalis, and the return of the Dalai Lama to Tibet, which meant the return to the Tibetan people of some kind of autonomy or, as Phil reminded them briefly, semiautonomy. "No person or institution or nation is ever more than semiautonomous anyway," Phil said in his remarks, "so it's very good, a welcome development that truly dwarfs any personal cause for celebration we might have. Although the personal causes in this case are all quite glorious."

To which everyone said, "Hear hear."

Frank and Caroline wandered the compound together, running into people Frank knew and chatting with them over cups of champagne and unidentifiable hors d'oeuvres. Padma led them through every room in the much-articulated treehouse, and Caroline laughed to see Frank's face as he contemplated the new upper reaches of the system. He took her out the old limb to show her where he and Rudra had lived, and then he was given a tour of the farm's current crops, and the orchard of apple saplings, just recently planted, while Caroline was taken in hand by Qang to meet some of the other Khembali women.

When Frank rejoined them, Caroline was still deep in conversation with Qang, who was answering her questions with a smile.

"Yes," Qang was saying, "that is probably what they have always stood for. We call them demons, but of course one could also say that they are simply bad ideas."

"So sometimes, when you do those ceremonies to drive out demons, you could say that in a sense you're holding a ceremony to drive out bad ideas?"

"Yes, of course. That is just what an exorcism of demons is, to us."

"I like that," Caroline said, looking over at Frank. "It makes it kind of explicit, and yet—religious. And it—you say it works?"

"Yes, very often it does. Of course, sometimes you need to do it more than once. We had to exorcise Frank's friend Charlie twice, for instance, to drive out some bad ideas that had taken root in him. But I believe it worked in the end."

She turned to Frank to include him in the conversation.

"It sounds like something I could use," Frank said.

"Oh, no. I think you have never been infected by any bad ideas!"

Qang's merry look reminded him of Rudra, and he laughed. "I'm not so sure of that!"

Qang said, "You are only infected by good ideas, and you wrestle with them very capably. That's what Padma says."

"I don't know about that."

"It sounds right to me," Caroline said, slipping an arm under Frank's. "I, on the other hand, could use a thoroughgoing exorcism. In fact I'd like to order up a full-on reincarnation, or not exactly, but you know. A new life."

"You can do that," Qang said, smiling at her. "We all do that. And especially when you have a child."

"I suppose so."

Sucandra joined them. "So, Frank," he said, "now you go back to your old home."

"Yes, that's right. Although it will be different now."

"Of course. The two of you together—very nice. And you will work for the institute you helped to start out there?"

"I'll work with them, but my job will be back at the university. I've been on a leave of absence, so I have to go back."

"But your research will connect to that of the institute?"

"Exactly. Some of my colleagues there are exploring some new possibilities. There's an old student of mine who is doing remarkable things. First came genomics, and now he's helping to invent what you could call proteomics. It looks like they'll be starting up a small company of their own. In fact, I've been talking to Drepung about the idea of you guys investing in this company. If Khembalung has any kind of investment portfolio, you might want to talk with them. Because if things pan out for them the way I think they might, there'll be some very important medical treatments to come out of it."

"Good, good," Sucandra said, and Qang nodded too. "Qang here heads that committee."

"Yes," Qang said, "I will talk to them. If we can make investments that help health, it's a good thing. But Sucandra is our doctor, so he will have to take a look too."

Sucandra nodded. "What about you, will you be investing in this new company?"

Frank laughed. "I might if I had anything to invest. Right now all I have is my salary. Which is fine. But we're buying a house, so there won't be much extra. But that's okay. If it works there'll be enough for everybody."

"A nice thought."

Then Drepung joined them. He was wearing his Wizards basketball shirt and his enormous Reeboks, and the cord to his iPod was entangled in his turquoise and coral necklaces.

"What about you, Drepung?" Frank asked. "Will you be moving back to Tibet?"

"Oh no, I don't think so!" Drepung grinned. "Only room for one big lama in Lhasa! Besides, I like it here. And I am obliged to stay in any case. It's part of the deal with the Chinese, more or less. And besides, this is Khembalung now! And not just the farm, but really the whole D.C. area. So I have work to do here as an ambassador."

"Good," Frank said. "They can use you."

"Thank you, I will give it a good try. What about you, Frank? Won't you miss this place when you go back to San Diego?"

"Yes, I will. But I need to get back. And people always visit D.C. All kinds of reasons bring you back."

"So true."

"Maybe I'll see you out there too."

"I hope so. I'll try to visit."

Neither man was under any illusion as to how frequently this was likely to happen. Friendships divided by continents grew more distant, there was no avoiding that.

. . .

Frank looked around at the crowd. He knew a lot of the people there. If he had stuck to his plan and stayed just a year, and lived that year like a ghost, he would have passed through and gone home without regrets. No one would even have been aware of his passing. But it had not happened that way. It all came down to the people you ran into.

This was accentuated when the Quiblers arrived. Charlie pretended to be cheery about Frank's departure, but he also shook his head painfully—"I don't know who'll get us out on the river now."

Anna was simply sad. "We'll miss you," she said, and gave him a hug. "The boys will miss you."

Nick was noncommittal. He looked off to the side. He spoke of the latest developments in their feral research program, steadfastly focused on the details of a new spreadsheet Anna had helped him set up, on which he could record all their sightings by species, and not only keep an inventory, but enter range parameters, to gauge which species might be able to go truly feral. There was also a GIS program that let you identify or design habitat corridors. It was very interesting.

Frank nodded and made some suggestions. "We'll keep in touch by e-mail," he said at one point when he saw Nick looking away. "Then hey—maybe when you go off to college, you can come to UCSD. It's a really fun school."

"Oh yeah," Nick said, brightening. "Good idea."

Anna was startled at this suggestion, and Charlie actually winced. Neither was used to the idea of Nick growing up. But there he stood, almost as tall as Anna, and four or five inches taller than when Frank had met him. He was changing by the day, almost by the hour.

The Quiblers wandered the party. Nick and Anna talked about the swimming tigers with Sucandra as they all stood under the treehouse, looking up to watch Charlie chase Joe around the various catwalks.

"It's gotten so big."

"Yes, people like to live up there. People like to work on it too."

"It would be cool," Nick said.

Sucandra nodded. "You all should consider moving out here with us," he said to them. "We would be so happy to have you here with us. You are already Khembalis, as far as we are concerned. And I think you would like it. A community like this is a kind of extended family. And of course group living is very thrifty," he added with a smile at Anna. "Energy consumption would be only a fraction of that used by an ordinary suburban house. Carbon burn very low."

"That's true," Anna said.

"Hey MOMMA!" Joe shouted down at her from the highest catwalk.

"Hi monkey," she called up. "Did you lose Dad?"

"Yeah, I did!"

"Oh my," Anna muttered.

Actually Charlie was not far below Joe, although on a different catwalk; he had gotten lost at an intersection. He retraced his last steps, and turned a corner—and there was Roy Anastopoulos.

"Roy!"

"Charlie!"

They gave each other a hug.

"It's good to see you!" Charlie said. "I didn't know you were going to be here."

"No, well, when we heard about Phil and Diane coming out to get a marriage blessing from the Dalai Lama, we asked if we could tag along and join in."

"So—you mean—you and Andrea?"

Roy nodded. "Yes. We got married yesterday at the courthouse." Andrea appeared, and showed him their shiny new wedding bands. "Now we're here for the blessing."

"Wonderful!" Charlie said. "Wait till Anna hears!"

He yelled down to the ground: "Hey Anna!" Then: "Just a second, I have to catch up to Joe. In fact, if you could take this catwalk across to over there, and wait? Maybe you can help me cut him off at the pass."

"Sure."

Back on the ground Anna was indeed delighted with their news. They gathered with the rest of the guests on the lawn in front of the main house, and cheered the appearance of the Dalai Lama, entering the big tent with Drepung, and followed by Phil and Diane, then Roy and Andrea. A troop of Khembalis in their best Tibetan finery performed a brief dance, accompanied by the drums, horns, and swirls of incense that reminded Anna of the first time she had seen the Khembalis, performing a similar ceremony in the NSF building.

The Dalai Lama, cheerfully sublime as always, led Phil and Diane through a brief set of Buddhist wedding vows, then did the same for Roy and Andrea. While they were still up there, Drepung gestured to Frank and Caroline to come up to the front, and they came out of the crowd to applause. Diane gave Frank a quick high-five.

Drepung was the one who led Frank and Caroline through their vows, ending with a blessing on them:

> This couple has come together at last.
> There is a presence that gives the gifts.
> The spirit of Tara has saved us from demons.
> You are the wind. We're dust blown into shapes.
> You are the spirit. We're intertwining hands.
> You are the clarity. We're this language that tries to say it.
> You are joy. We're all the different kinds of laughing.
> When the ocean surges, don't let me just hear it.
> Let it splash inside my chest!

Then he and the Dalai Lama stood side by side, and reached out together to join the hands of the three couples. For a moment everything was still; then with a blast on the long Tibetan horns, the party began in earnest.

"Here," Nick said as the Quiblers prepared to leave, and he shoved an envelope into Frank's hand. "FOG made a going-away card out of your phone log. Almost everybody signed it. Jason was out of town."

"Thanks," Frank said. Most of those people he had never met in person; they had been voices over the phone, or names on the sighting board. "Tell them I'll miss them. Tell them I'll try to get something like this started in San Diego."

"Will there be any animals to see out there?"

"No, not really. You're lucky with what you have here. Out there it's down to birds and rabbits, I'm afraid. Maybe I'll have to arrange a breakout at the San Diego Zoo."

Joe, nearly asleep on Charlie's shoulder, heard the word *zoo* and rolled his head to the side.

"Tiger," he murmured, and pounded Charlie's chest with a single solid tap.

Charlie put his chin on the round blond head. "You're my tiger," he said. Joe drifted back off.

When the Quiblers got home they changed out of their party clothes and went out in the yard to work on the garden. At four their doorbell rang, and Frank's friend Cutter appeared at their door, a burly man with big scarred hands and a friendly smile. Behind him his crew were already unloading gear from their truck. The PV panels had arrived at last. Joe ran around the house to investigate, and he and Charlie watched fascinated as the ladders were assembled and scaled. The nimble climbers disappeared onto the roof and then dropped ropes beside the ladder, to help stabilize their climb and also to haul things up. The struts and wiring had been installed weeks ago, but there was a waiting list for the solar panels themselves. Now they were hooking them to a hoist line. Soon what Charlie and Joe could see of the south side of the roof was covered with gear. It was going to be a grid of four photovoltaic panels, capable of generating all the house's electricity when the sun was shining, and of putting some power into batteries for the nights. Whenever more electricity was generated by the panels than they used in the house, the excess would be fed back into the grid, and they would be paid for it by the public utility district that had recently replaced the private company as their power provider. This was going to give them a big drop in their carbon burn numbers, and Anna and Nick were very pleased at that.

With a wave to Joe, Cutter and his team took off.

The photovoltaics were indeed very good for their carbon burn score, and their garden helped a little; but still they were scoring pretty high, and Anna was getting frustrated. "You just can't do it in a suburban home, when you own a car and a phone and all the stuff."

"We're doing better," Charlie reminded her.

"Yeah, but we're hitting limits." Anna stared at her spreadsheet. "I don't see what else we can do here, either, given the infrastructure and all. I wonder if we should take up the Khembalis' offer and move in with them."

Charlie rolled his eyes. "It seems to me they're crowded enough."

"Well, some of them have gone back to India. They say there's room."

"I don't know. Would you want to do that?"

"I don't know. In a way I think it would be nice."

Charlie did not reply. He knew that Anna was concerned about their carbon burn. The numbers had hooked her in their usual way. For the sake of an elegant result she would contemplate almost anything. And to be fair, Charlie recalled now how involved she had been with the Khembalis from the very start—inviting them over, becoming friends with Sucandra and Qang, helping their Institute of Higher Learning—learning Tibetan for the fun of it.

"Let's talk to the boys about it," he temporized.

"Sure. And maybe check it out the next time we're out there for dinner. See what it might really entail."

"If we can. We might not be able to tell in a visit."

"Well, of course."

"And, you know," he reminded her, "we're doing better here than most people who live in a single-family house."

"True. But maybe that isn't good enough anymore."

After that Charlie wandered around the house, feeling strange. It was almost sunset outside, and inside the house it was getting dark. The others were out in the kitchen, clattering about as they got dinner started.

Charlie stood in the living room looking around. Something about it caught his eye. A quality of the evening light. It looked like a place that had been lived in long ago. There was a tangle of trucks on the carpet, but otherwise things were cleaned up. It looked spare. Perhaps Frank's comment about Nick going to UCSD had put him in an odd frame of mind. Of course all these things would happen. But the years after Nick's birth had been so intense; and since Joe's arrival, even more so. It had filled his mind. It had crowded everything else out; it had seemed the only reality. He could have said, Once there was an island in time, just off Wisconsin Avenue: a mother, a father, two boys, two cats; and it seemed like it would last forever. But then . . .

That was all it took, just *then* and *then* and another *then*. Enough thens and then the island was gone. Someday other people would live in this house. It was an odd thought to have. Charlie sat on the couch, looked around at the room as if it might vanish. One day he would break this couch under him into splinters so it would fit in the trash cans to be hauled away. Island after island went under, and the little Khembalung moved somewhere else.

The phone rang.

"Charlie, can you get that please? I've gotta—Joe! No Joe, we'll get that— oh—oh, okay. Okay! Charlie, never mind! Joe's got it!"

Frank went down to the Potomac for one last trip out before they left.

It was a hot spring day, the world green and steaming. Charlie couldn't make it; Drepung couldn't make it. Caroline was driving down from the farm later with a picnic lunch; she too was busy, and said she would get to Great Falls before he was finished. She planned to sit on the bluff overlooking the downstream end of Mather Gorge, near the put-in, while he paddled up the Fish Ladder.

An hour later, while taking a rest from his salmon leaps up the Ladder, he looked up at the bluff but did not see her.

When he looked back at the falls, the woman kayaker he had seen twice before was already three steps up the Ladder and ascending like a kingfisher or a water ouzel. As before, the sight of her leaped into his vision, it was like being nudged by the side of the world: broad shoulders, big lats, a thick braid of black hair bouncing on her neck—for an instant, a profile—maybe that was it—or the way she moved. Beautiful. He took off after her, he didn't know why; he intended nothing by it, he knew his Caroline would soon be there; it was just curiosity that put him in pursuit, some itch to see, some urge to follow.

Hard paddle into the first white drop, punching into the flow to get enough acceleration to slide up onto the flat spot above. Do it again. Do it again. Each flat spot had a slightly different length, leading to a different speed of water at the infall. The drops got harder, though in truth they were almost as even as stairs—but not quite—and near the top, the ones that were just a bit taller took a terrific effort to ascend.

But he made it to the top. His lungs were burning and his arms were on fire. He had never managed it before and here he was, on the big sweep of the upper Potomac.

But there she was, rounding a bend upstream, still paddling hard. Frank set off in pursuit, confident that now he had ascended the ladder there were no impediments to catching her. He took off at a racing pace.

But so had she. When he rounded the first bend she was already at the next one; and when he rounded that, his arms in a hot lactic scream, she was even farther ahead, in the long straight section that came there. And yet it wouldn't be that long before she made it to the next bend; and she was still paddling hard. Frank pushed one last time, breathing hard now, sweating until his eyes stung, trying to ignore the lactic acid in the muscles of his arms and chest, until the time came that they felt like blocks of wood. His kayak was slowing down.

When he rounded the bend at the end of the straight, she was disappearing ahead. Gone. He had to give up.

He stopped and sucked down air, sweating, wiping sweat off his eyebrows with the backs of his hands. Cramps flickered through his muscles. He let the kayak drift downstream on the current. He had given it his all. Chasing beauty upstream until he couldn't anymore. A very fast goddess. Oh well.

Now there was the Great Falls of the Potomac to attend to. Very few took the biggest drops in a kayak; they could be fatal. Only the best professionals would even think of it. Everyone else ran the various alternatives, not just the Fish Ladder but other parts of the complex of falls on the Maryland side, more or less difficult.

He took the drop called the Ping Pong, struggling with the big bounces in the midsection, his arms burning again, almost too tired to perform the absolutely necessary course corrections, but too tired to risk an overturn either. He had to stay upright, he was panting as he worked, and would not be able to hold his breath for long. He had to stay upright!

He got through the drops. In the hissing white flow of recollecting water at the bottom of the falls he floated thankfully, spent. He had just enough strength left to paddle to the Virginia shore. On the bluff overhead, Caroline was watching him.

He grabbed the put-in boulder on the shore, wearily hauled himself in. Undid his apron and struggled to follow his paddle up onto the rocky jumble at the bottom of the bluff. Stiff and sore. Sweat poured out from his head. He stumbled back into the shallows and sat down in the river, then lay back and let the water pour over him. Ahhh, cool water. Just what he needed. Up again, spluttering and gasping. Cooler already.

He hiked up the steep little cleft in the bluff. Sat beside Caroline with a squish. Dripped river water. He was still sweating.

Caroline regarded him. "So," she said. "You came back."

"What do you mean?" Frank said. "I never left."

"I guess that's true."

They sat there, looking down at the river. Below them a pair of kayakers were putting in; one paddled backward upstream. A wind threw a quick cat's paw across the surface of the river, and on the opposite shore the wall of green trees bobbed and flailed. In the sky to the north a cloud was rearing high into the sky, its white lobes aquiver with the promise of storms to come.

"I love you."

ACKNOWLEDGMENTS

Thanks for help on Part One to: Guy Guthridge, Grant Heidrich, Charles Hess, Tim Higham, Dick Ill, Chris McKay, Oliver Morton, Lisa Nowell, Ann Russell, Mark Schwartz, Jim Shea, Sharon Strauss, and Buck Tilley.

On Part Two, thanks to: Jürgen Atzgerstorfer, Terry Baier, Willa Baker, Guy Guthridge, George Hazelrigg, Charles Hess, Tim Higham, Neil Koehler, Rachel Park, Ann Russell, Tom St. Germain, Michael Schlesinger, Mark Schwartz, Jim Shea, Gary Snyder, Mark Thiemens, Buck Tilley, and Paul J. Werbos.

On Part Three, thanks to: Charles N. Brown, Joy Chamberlain, Rita Colwell, William Fox, Doug Fratz, Anne Groell, Jennifer Holland, Jane Johnson, Mark Lewis, Rich Lynch, Lisa Nowell, Michael Schlesinger, Jim Shea, Darko Suvin, Ralph Vicinanza, Paul J. Werbos, and Donald Wesling.

For this version, a special thanks to Jane Johnson and Anne Groell.

ABOUT THE AUTHOR

KIM STANLEY ROBINSON is a winner of the Hugo, Nebula, and Locus awards. He is the author of more than twenty books, including the bestselling Mars trilogy and the critically acclaimed *Forty Signs of Rain, Fifty Degrees Below, Sixty Days and Counting, The Years of Rice and Salt,* and *Galileo's Dream*. In 2008 he was named one of *Time* magazine's "Heroes of the Environment." He serves on the board of the Sierra Nevada Research Institute. He lives in Davis, California.